LETTERS IS "A LANDMARK!"*

"A prodigous and quite remarkable achievement."

—*The Washington Post*

"NEVER MIND McDONALD'S. JOHN BARTH'S NEW TWO-AND-A-HALF POUNDER COMES WITH EVERYTHING....FASCINATING!"

—*United Press International*

"Don't deprive yourself of this succulent feast."

—*Cleveland Plain Dealer*

"A TESTAMENT TO BARTH'S TREMENDOUS TALENT AND WIT...A TREASURE FOR THOSE WHO DELIGHT IN BARTH'S DAZZLING AND UNPARALLELED INGENUITY."

—*Publishers Weekly*

"Formidable fun...an epic of games and *contre-temps*."

—*Village Voice*

"THE MOST AMBITIOUS WORK YET FROM THIS IMMENSELY TALENTED CREATIVE ARTIST WHO IS IN OUR OPINION THE MOST IMAGINATIVE MAKER OF FICTION IN AMERICA TODAY....A MAJOR WORK OF ART AND A MODERN MASTERPIECE."

—*Dallas Morning News*

Books by John Barth

THE FLOATING OPERA

THE END OF THE ROAD

THE SOT-WEED FACTOR

GILES GOAT-BOY

LOST IN THE FUNHOUSE

CHIMERA

LETTERS

```
A    NOLD TIMEE PISTO LARY NOV      E L
B    Y        S      E     V    E N     F I
C    T        I      T     I    O U     S
D    RO       L      L     S&   DRE     A M
E    R        S      E     A    C H     I O
F    W        H      I     C    H I     M A
G INE SHIM    S      E     LFAC T U      A L
```

a novel
JOHN BARTH

FAWCETT COLUMBINE

NEW YORK

A Fawcett Columbine Book
Published by Ballantine Books

Copyright © 1979 by John Barth

All rights reserved. Published in the United States by Ballantine Books, a
division of Random House, Inc., New York, and in Canada by Random
House of Canada, Limited, Toronto, Canada.

ISBN 0-449-90090-8

Designed by Helen Barrow
This edition published by arrangement with G. P. Putnam's Sons

Manufactured in the United States of America

First Fawcett Columbine Edition: April 1982
First Ballantine Books Edition: August 1982

10 9 8 7 6 5 4 3 2

for Shelly

L E T T E R S

1

MARCH 1969						
S	1	**A**	15	22	29	
F		**B**	14	21	28	
T		**C**	13	20	27	
W		**D**	12	19	26	
T		**E**	11	18	25	
F		**F**	10	17	24	31
S		**G I N E**			30	

Lady Amherst
Todd Andrews
Jacob Horner
A. B. Cook
Jerome Bray
Ambrose Mensch
The Author

A: *Lady Amherst to the Author*. *Inviting him to accept an honorary doctorate of letters from Marshyhope State University. An account of the history of that institution.*

Office of the Provost
Faculty of Letters
Marshyhope State University
Redmans Neck, Maryland 21612

8 March 1969

Mr John Barth, Esq., Author

Dear sir:

At the end of the current semester, Marshyhope State University will complete the seventh academic year since its founding in 1962 as Tidewater Technical College. In that brief time we have grown from a private vocational-training school with an initial enrollment of thirteen students, through annexation as a four-year college in the state university system, to our present status (effective a month hence, at the beginning of the next fiscal year) as a full-fledged university centre with a projected population of 50,000 by 1976.

To mark this new elevation, at our June commencement ceremonies we shall exercise for the first time one of its perquisites, the awarding of honorary degrees. Specifically, we shall confer one honorary doctorate in each of Law, Letters, and Science. It is my privilege, on behalf of the faculty, (Acting) President Schott, and the board of regents of the state university, to invite you to be with us 10 A.M. Saturday, 21 June 1969, in order that we may confer upon you the degree of Doctor of Letters, *Honoris Causa*. Sincerely hopeful that you will honour us by accepting the highest distinction that Marshyhope can confer, and looking forward to a favourable reply, I am,

Yours sincerely,

Germaine G. Pitt (Amherst)
Acting Provost

GGP(A)/ss

P.S.: A red-letter day on my personal calendar, this—the first in too long, dear Mr B., but never mind *that!*—and do forgive both this presumptuous postscriptum and my penmanship; some things I cannot entrust to my "good right hand" of a secretary (a hand dependent, I

3

have reason to suspect, more from the arm of our esteemed acting president than from my arm, on which she'd like nothing better, if I have your American slang aright, than to "put the finger") and so must pen as it were with my left, quite as I've been obliged by Fate and History—my own, England's, Western Culture's—to swallow pride and

But see how in the initial sentence (*my* initial sentence) I transgress my vow not to go on about myself, like those dotty women "of a certain age" who burden the patience of novelists and doctors—their circumstantial ramblings all reducible, I daresay, to one cry: "Help! Love me! I grow old!" Already you cluck your tongue, dear Mr-B.-whom-I-do-not-know (if indeed you've read me even so far): life is too short, you say, to suffer fools and frustrates, especially of the prolix variety. Yet it is you, sir, who, all innocent, provoke this stammering postscript: for nothing else than the report of your impatience with just this sort of letters conceived my vow to make known my business to you *tout de suite,* and nothing other than that vow effected so to speak its own miscarriage. So perverse, so helpless the human heart!

And yet bear on, I pray. I am. . .what I am (rather, what I find to my own dismay I am become; I was not always so. . .): old schoolmarm rendered fatuous by loneliness, indignified by stillborn dreams, I prate like a "coed" on her first "date"—and this to a man not merely my junior, but. . . No matter.

I *will* be brief! I *will* be frank! Mr B.: but for the opening paragraphs of your recentest, which lies before me, I know your writings only at second hand, a lacuna in my own life story which the present happy circumstance gives occasion for me to amend. Take no offence at this remissness: for one thing, I came to your country, as did your novels to mine, not very long since, and neither visitor sojourns heart-on-sleeve. A late good friend of mine (himself a Nobel laureate in literature) once declared to me, when I asked him why he would not read his contemporaries—

But Germaine, Germaine, this is not germane! as my ancestor and namesake Mme de Staël must often have cried to herself. I can do no better than to rebegin with one of her own (or was it Pascal's?) charming openers: "Forgive me this too long letter; I had not time to write a short." And you yourself—so I infer from the heft of your *oeuvre,* stacked here upon my "early American" writing desk, to which, straight upon the close of this postscript, I will address me, commencing with your earliest and never ceasing till I shall have overtaken as it were the present point of your pen—you yourself are not, of contemporary authors, the most sparing. . .

To business! *Cher Monsieur* (is it French or German-Swiss, your name? From the lieutenant who led against the Bastille in *Great-great-great-great-great-grand-mère's* day, or the late theologian of our own? Either way, sir, we are half-countrymen, for all you came to light in Maryland's Dorset and I in England's: may this hors d'oeuvre keep your appetite for the entrée whilst I make short work of soup and salad!). . .

4

Salad of laurels, sir! Sibyl-greens, Daphne's death-leaves, honorific if worn lightly, fatal if swallowed! I seriously pray you will take it, this "highest honour that Marshyhope can bestow"; I pray you will not take it seriously! O this sink, this slough, this Eastern Shore of Maryland, this marshy County Dorchester—whence, to be sure, *you* sprang, mallow from the marsh, as *inter faeces* etc. we are born all. Do please forgive— whom? How should you have heard of me, who have not read you and yet nominated you for the M.U. Litt.D.? I have exposed myself already; then let me introduce me: Germaine Pitt I, née Gordon, Lady Amherst, late of that *other* Dorset (I mean Hardy's) and sweeter Cambridge, now "Distinguished Visiting Lecturer in English" (to my ear, the *only* resident speaker of that tongue) and Acting (!) Provost of Make-Believe University's Factory of Letters, as another late friend of mine might have put it: a university not so much pretentious as pretending, a toadstool blown overnight from this ordurous swamp to broadcast doctorates like spores, before the stationer can amend our letterhead!

I shall not tire you with the procession of misfortunes which, since the end of the Second War, has fetched me from the ancestral seats of the Gordons and the Amhersts—where three hundred years ago is reckoned as but the day before yesterday, and the 17th-Century Earls of Dorset are gossipped of as if still living—to this misnamed shire (try to explain, to your stout "down-countian," that *-chester‹castra* = camp, and that thus *Dorchester,* etymologically as well as by historical prece- dent, ought to name the seat rather than the county! As well try to teach Miss Sneak my secretary why *Mr* and *Dr* need no stops after), which sets about the celebration this July of its tercentenary as if 1669 were classical antiquity. Nor shall I with my passage from the friendship— more than friendship!—of several of the greatest novelists of our century, to the supervisal of their desecration in Modern Novel 101–102: a decline the sadder for its parallelling that of the genre itself; perhaps (God forfend) of Literature as a whole; perhaps even (the prospect blears in the eyes of these. . .yes. . .colonials!) of the precious Word. These adversities I bear with what courage I can draw from the example of my favourite forebear, who, harassed by Napoleon, abused by her lovers, ill-served by friends who owed their fortunes to her good offices, nevertheless maintained to the end that animation, generosity of spirit, and brilliance of wit which make her letters my solace and inspiration. But in the matter of the honorary doctorate and my— blind—insistence upon your nomination therefor, I shall speak to you with a candour which, between a Master of Arts and their lifelong Mistress, I must trust not to miscarry; for I cannot imagine your regarding a distinction so wretched on the face of it otherwise than with amused contempt, and yet upon your decision to accept or decline ride matters of some (and, it may be, more than local) consequence.

Briefly, briefly. The tiny history of "Redneck Tech" has been a seven-year battle between the most conservative elements in the state— principally local, for, as you know, Mason and Dixon's line may be said to run north and south in Maryland, up Chesapeake Bay, and the Eastern Shore is more Southern than Virginia—and the most "liberal" (mainly not native, as the natives do not fail to remark), who in higher latitudes would be adjudged cautious moderates at best. The original college was endowed by a local philanthropist, now deceased: an excellent gentleman whose fortune, marvellous to tell, derived from *pickles*. . .and whose politics were so Tory that, going quite crackers in his final years, the dear fellow fancied himself to be, not Napoleon, but *George III*, still fighting the American Revolution as his "saner" neighbours still refight your Civil War. His Majesty's board of trustees was composed exclusively of his relatives, friends, and business associates—several of whom, however, were of more progressive tendencies, and sufficiently influential in this Border State to have some effect on the affairs of the institution even after it joined the state university complex. Indeed, it was they who pressed most vigorously, against much opposition, to bring the college under state administration in the first place, hoping thereby to rescue it from parochial reaction; and the president of the college during these first stages of its history was a man of respectable academic credentials and reasonably liberal opinions, their appointee: the historian Joseph Morgan.

To console the Tories, however, one John Schott—formerly head of a nearby teachers college and a locally famous right-winger—was appointed provost of the Faculty of Letters and vice-president of (what now was awkwardly denominated) Marshyhope State University College. A power struggle ensued at once, for Dr Schott is as politically ambitious as he is ideologically conservative, and had readily accepted what might seem a less prestigious post because he foresaw, correctly, that MSUC was destined for gigantic expansion, and he sensed, again correctly, opportunity in the local resentment against its "liberal" administration.

In the years thereafter, every forward-looking proposal of President Morgan's, from extending visitation privileges in the residence halls to defending a professor's right to lecture upon the history of revolution, was opposed not only by conservative faculty and directors of the Tidewater Foundation (as the original college's board of trustees renamed itself) but by the regional press, state legislators, and county officials, all of whom cited Schott in support of their position. The wonder is that Morgan survived for even a few semesters in the face of such harassment, especially when his critics found their Sweet Singer in the person of one A. B. Cook VI, self-styled Laureate of Maryland, of whom alas more later—I daresay you know of that formidable charlatan and his mind-abrading doggerel, *e.g.*:

> Fight, Marylanders, nail and tooth,
> For John Schott and his Tow'r of Truth, etc.

Which same tower, presently under construction, was the gentle Morgan's undoing. He had—aided by the reasonabler T.F. trustees,

6

more enlightened state legislators, and that saving remnant of civilised folk tied by family history and personal sentiment to the shire of their birth—managed after all to weather storms of criticism and effect some modest improvements in the quality of instruction at Marshyhope. Moreover, despite grave misgivings about academic gigantism, Morgan believed that the only hope for real education in such surroundings was to make the college the largest institutional and economic entity in the area, and so had led the successful negotiation to make Marshyhope a university centre: not a replica of the state university's vast campus on the mainland, but a smaller, well-funded research centre for outstanding undergraduate and postgraduate students from throughout the university system: academically rigorous, but loosely structured and cross-disciplinary. So evident were the economic blessings of this coup to nearly everyone in the area, Morgan's critics were reduced to grumbling about the radical effects that an influx of some seven thousand "outsiders" was bound to have on the Dorset Way of Life— and Schott & Co. were obliged to seek fresh ground for their attack.

They found it in the Tower of Truth. If the old isolation of Dorchester was to be sacrificed any road on the altar of economic progress (so their argument ran), why stop at seven thousand students—a kind of academic elite at that, more than likely long-haired radicals from Baltimore or even farther north? Why not open the doors to *all* our tidewater sons and daughters, up to the number of, say, seven times seven thousand? Fill in sevenfold more marshy acreage; make seven times over the fortunes of wetland realtors and building contractors; septuple the jobs available to Dorchester's labour force; build on Redmans Neck a veritable City of Learning, more populous (and prosperous) by far than any of the peninsula's actual municipalities! And from its centre let there rise, as a symbol (and advertisement) of the whole, Marshyhope's beacon to the world: a great white tower, the Tower of Truth! By day the university's main library, perhaps, and (certainly) the seat of its administration, let it be by night floodlit and visible from clear across the Chesapeake—from (in Schott's own pregnant phrase) "Annapolis at least, maybe even Washington!"

In vain Morgan's protests that seven thousand dedicated students, housed in tasteful, low-profile buildings on the seven hundred acres of farmland already annexed by MSUC, represented the maximum reasonable burden on the ecology and sociology of the county, and the optimal balance of economic benefits and academic manageability; that Schott's "Tower of Truth," like the projected diploma mill it represented, would violate the natural terrain; that the drainage of so much marsh would be an ecological disaster, the influx of so huge a population not a stimulus to the Dorset Way of Life but a cataclysmic shock; that both skyscrapers and ivory towers were obsolete ideals; that even if they weren't, no sane contractor would attempt such a structure on the spongy ground of a fresh-filled fen, et cetera. In veritable transports of bad faith, the Schott/Cook party rhapsodised that Homo

7

sapiens himself—especially in his rational, civilised, university-founding aspect—was the very embodiment of "antinaturalness": towering erect instead of creeping on all fours, opposing reason to brute instinct, aspiring ever to what was deemed beyond his grasp, raising from the swamp primordial great cities, lofty cathedrals, towers of learning. How were the fenny origins invoked of Rome! How *learning* was rhymed with *yearning*, *Tow'r of Truth* with *Flow'r of Youth!* How was excoriated, in editorial and Rotary Club speech, "the Morgan theory" (which he never held) that the university should be a little model of the actual world rather than a lofty counterexample: lighthouse to the future, ivory tower to the present, castle keep of the past!

Cook's rhetoric, all this, sweetly resounding in our Chambers of Commerce, where too there were whispered libels against the luckless Morgan: that his late wife had died a dozen years past in circumstances never satisfactorily explained, which however had led to Morgan's "resignation" from his first teaching post, at Wicomico Teachers College; that his absence from the academic scene between that dismissal (by Schott himself, as ill chance would have it, who damningly refused to comment on the matter, declaring only that "every man deserves a second chance") and his surprise appointment by Harrison Mack II as first president of Tidewater Tech was not unrelated to that dark affair. By 1967, when Morgan acquiesced to the Tower of Truth in hopes of saving his plan for a manageable, high-quality research centre, the damage to his reputation had been done, by locker-room couplets of unacknowledged but unmistakable authorship:

> Here is the late Mrs Morgan interred,
> Whose *ménage à trois* is reduced by one-third.
> Her husband and lover survive her, both fired:
> *Requiescat in pacem* the child they both sired, etc.

In July of last year he resigned, ostensibly to return to teaching and research, and in fact is a visiting professor of American History this year at the college in Massachusetts named after my late husband's famous ancestor—or was until his disappearance some weeks ago. John Schott became acting president—and what a vulgar act is his!—and yours truly, who has no taste for administrative service even under decent chiefs like Morgan, but could not bear to see MSUC's governance altogether in Boeotian hands, was prevailed upon to act as provost of the Faculty of Letters.

How came Schott to choose me, you ask, who am through these hopeless marshes but (I hope) the briefest of sojourners? Surely because he rightly distrusts all his ordinary faculty, and wrongly supposes that, visitor and woman to boot, I can be counted upon passively to abet his accession to the actual presidency of MSU—from which base (read "tow'r," and weep for Marshyhope, for Maryland!) he

8

will turn his calculating eyes to Annapolis, "maybe even Washington"! Yet he does me honour by enough distrusting my gullibility after all to leave behind as mine his faithful secretary-at-least: Miss Shirley Stickles, sharp of eye and pencil if not of mind, to escape whose surveillance I am brought to penning by hand this sorry history of your nomination.

Whereto, patient Mr B., we are come! For scarce had I aired against my tenancy the provostial chamber (can you name another university president who smokes cigars?) when there was conveyed to me, via his minatory and becorseted *derrière-garde,* my predecessor's expectation, not only that I would appoint at once a nominating committee for the proposed Litt.D. (that is, a third member, myself being already on the committee *ex officio* and Schott having appointed, by some dim prerogative, a second: one Harry Carter, former psychologist, present nonentity and academic vice-president, Schott's creature), but that, after a show of nomination weighing, we would present to the board of regents as our candidate the "Maryland Laureate" himself, Mr Andrew Cook!

Schott's strategy is clear: to achieve some "national visibility," as they say, with his eyesore of a Tower; a degree of leverage (in *honoris causa*!) in the state legislature with his honorary doctorates (the LL.D., of course, will go to the governor, or the local congressman); and the applause of the regional right with his laurelling of the hardy rhymer of "marsh mallow" and "beach swallow"—a man one could indeed simply laugh at, were there no sinister side to his right-winged wrongheadedness and his rape of Mother English.

Counterstrategy I had none; nor motive, at first, beyond mere literary principle. Unacquainted with your work (and that of most of your countrymen), my first candidates were writers most honoured already in my own heart: Mrs Lessing perhaps, even Miss Murdoch; or the Anthonys Powell or Burgess. To the argument (advanced at once by Dr Carter) that none of these has connexion with MSUC, I replied that "connexions" should have no connexion with honours. Yet I acceded to the gentler suasion of my friend, colleague, and committee appointee Mr Ambrose Mensch (whom I believe you know?): Marshyhope being not even a national, far less an international, institution, it were presumptuous of us to think to honour as it were beyond our means (literally so, in the matter of transatlantic air fares). He then suggested such Americans as one Mr Styron, who has roots in Virginia, and a Mr Updike, formerly of Pennsylvania. But I replied, cordially, that once the criterion of mere merit was put by, to honour a writer for springing from a neighbouring state made no more sense than to do so for his springing from a neighbouring shire, or civilisation. Indeed, the principle of "appropriateness," on which we now agreed if on little else, was really Carter's "connexion" in more palatable guise: as we were in fact a college of the state university and so far specifically regional, perhaps we could after all do honour without presumption only to a

9

writer, scholar, or journalist with connexion to the Old Line State, preferably to the Eastern Shore thereof?

On these friendly deliberations between Mr Mensch and myself, Dr Carter merely smiled, prepared in any case to vote negatively on all nominations except A. B. Cook's, which he had put before us in the opening minutes of our opening session. I should add that, there being in the bylaws of the college and of the faculty as yet no provision for the nomination of candidates for honorary degrees, our procedure was *ad hoc* as our committee; but I was given to understand, by Sticklish insinuation, that if our nomination were not unanimous and soon forthcoming, Schott would empower his academic vice-president to form a new committee; further, that if our choice proved displeasing to the administration, the Faculty of Letters could expect no budgetary blessings next fiscal. Schott himself, with more than customary tact, merely declared to me his satisfaction, at this point in our discussions, that we had decided to honour a native son. . .

"*I.e.*, the Fair-Land Muse himself," Mr Mensch dryly supposed on hearing this news (the epithet from Cook's own rhyme for Maryland, in its local two-syllable pronunciation). I then conveyed to him, and do now to you, in both instances begging leave not to reveal my source, that I had good reason to believe that beneath his boorish, even ludicrous, public posturing, Andrew Burlingame Cook VI (his full denomination!) is a dark political power, in "Mair'land" and beyond: not a kingmaker, but a maker and unmaker of kingmakers: a man behind the men behind the scenes, with whose support it was, alas, not unimaginable after all that John Schott might one day cross the Bay to "Annapolis, maybe even Washington." To thwart Cook's nomination, then, and haply thereby to provoke his displeasure with our acting president, might be to strike a blow, at least a tap, for decent government!

I speak lightly, sir (as did Germaine de Staël even in well-founded fear of her life), but the matter is not without gravity. This Cook is a menace to more than the art of poetry, and any diminution of his public "cover," even by denying him an honour he doubtless has his reasons for desiring, is a move in the public weal.

And I now believe, what I would not have done a fortnight past, that with your help—*i.e.*, your "aye"—he may be denied. "Of course," Mr Mensch remarked to me one evening, "there's always my old friend B. . . ." I asked (excuse me) whom that name might name, and was told: not only that you were born and raised hereabouts, made good your escape, and from a fit northern distance set your first novels in this area, but that my friend himself—*our* friend—was at that moment under contract to write a screenplay of your newest book, to be filmed on location in the county. How would your name strike Carter, Schott, and company? It just might work, good Ambrose thought, clearly now warming to his inspiration and wondering aloud why he hadn't hit on it before—especially since, though he'd not corresponded with you for years, he was immersed in your fiction; is indeed on leave from teaching this semester to draft that screenplay.

In sum, it came (and comes) to this: John Schott's appointment to the presidency of MSU is quietly opposed, in our opinion, by moderate elements on the board of regents and the Tidewater Foundation, and it can be imagined that, among the more knowledgeable of these elements, this opposition extends to the trumpeting false laureate as well. Their support comes from the radical right and, perversely, the radical left (that minority of two or three bent on destroying universities altogether as perpetuators of bourgeois values). A dark-horse nominee of the right colouration might just slip between this Scylla and this Charybdis.

Very casually we tried your name on Harry Carter, and were pleased to observe in his reaction more suspicious curiosity than actual opposition. This curiosity, moreover, turned into guarded interest when Ambrose pointed out (as if the thought had just occurred to him) that the "tie-in" at our June commencement of the filming of your book and the county's Tercentennial (itself to involve some sort of feature on "Dorchester in Art and Literature") would no doubt occasion publicity for Marshyhope U. and the Tower of Truth. He, Ambrose—he added with the straightest of faces—might even be able to work into the film itself some footage of the ceremonies, and the Tower. . .

This was last week. Our meeting ended with a sort of vote: two–nothing in favour of your nomination, Dr Carter abstaining. To my surprise, the acting president's reaction, relayed through both Dr Carter and Miss Stickles, is cautious nondisapproval, and today I am authorised to make the invitation.

You are, then, sir, by way of being a compromise candidate, who will, I hope, so far from feeling therein compromised, come to the aid of your friend, your native county, and its "largest single economic [and *only* cultural] entity" by accepting this curious invitation. Moreover, by accepting it promptly, before the opposition (some degree of which is to be expected) has time to rally. That Schott even tentatively permits this letter implies that A. B. Cook VI has been sounded out and, for whatever mysterious reasons, chooses not to exercise his veto out of hand. But Ambrose informs me, grimly, that there is a "Dr Schott" in some novel of yours, too closely resembling ours for coincidence, and not flatteringly drawn: should he get wind of this fact (Can it be true? Too delicious!) before your acceptance has been made public. . .

Au revoir, then, friend of my friend! I hold your first novel in my hand, eager to embark upon it; in your own hand you may hold some measure of our future here (think what salubrious effect a few well-chosen public jibes at the "Tow'r of Truth" and its tidewater laureate might have, televised live from Redmans Neck on Commencement Day!). Do therefore respond at your earliest to this passing odd epistle, whose tail like the spermatozoon's far outmeasures its body, the better to accomplish its single urgent end, and—like Molly Bloom at the close

11

of *her* great soliloquy (whose author was, yes, a friend of your friend's friend)—say to us *yes*, to the Litt.D. *yes*, to MSU *yes*, and *yes* Dorchester, *yes* Tidewater, Maryland *yes yes yes!*

Yours,
GGP(A)

B: *Todd Andrews to his father.* The death and funeral of Harrison Mack, Jr.

Dorset Hotel
High Street
Cambridge, Maryland 21613

March 7, 1969

Mr. Thomas T. Andrews, Dec'd
Plot # 1, Municipal Cemetery
Cambridge, Maryland 21613

Dear Father:

Brrr! Old fellow in the cellarage, what gripes you? Every night since Tuesday's full moon you've crawled about (in your Sunday best) under the stage of my drifting dreams. . .like me some 30 years ago under the stage of Captain Adams's showboat, trying unsuccessfully to turn myself off. Last night I left a particularly good dream to investigate the noise (in the dream it was a certain August afternoon 37 years past; I and the century were 32 and off weekending with my friends the Macks in their Todds Point summer cottage; Harrison Mack, alive and happily uncrowned, had gone for ice; I was napping; so was the century; Jane Mack—26 again and naked!—was just about to slip in from the kitchen and take me by the sweetest surprise of my life. . .), and there *you* swung, Father mine, blackfaced and belted 'round the neck as in February 1930, not a smudge on you. No returning to my Floating Theatre then! And tonight, *soixante-neuf* once more with this kinky crone of a century, here in my old hotel room— that's not a March draft I feel on my hackles; those clunks and clanks aren't sclerosis of the heat pipes or Captain Adams retuning his calliope: it's *you*, old mole! Come to join the party? Come to watch through the keyhole while your old son (older than his dad now!) tries to get it up for Grandma Mack?

We fetch one body to the boneyard; a hearseful of ghosts hitches home with us.

Very well, groundhog: I'm late with the letter for your 39th deathday, and better the dead father should hear from the son than vice versa. February 2, it happens, was the day we buried Harrison Mack, His Majesty having died by his own design (but not by his own hand) four days earlier, to no one's surprise. Harrison's "identification"

12

with George III, as his doctors called it, had gone beyond even my description in last February's letter. Everyone at Tidewater Farms went about in Regency getup—except Harrison himself, for the reason I've mentioned before (which will make the contest over *his* estate even livelier than the fight over his father's): that the more *accurate* his madness became, so to speak, the more he fancied himself, not George III sane, but George III *mad;* a George III, moreover, who in *his* madness believed himself to be Harrison Mack sane. Thus in the end he pretended to think everyone in the house crazy for wearing 1815 costume—and managed his business affairs with more clarity and good sense than at any time since the onset of his "madness" in the latter 1950's.

Jane spared herself (no way she could've known it was his final year) by going off to England in pursuit of chimeras of her own. Who can blame her? In her absence, Lady Amherst (Germaine Pitt, from the college) took charge of the household, luckily for Harrison. Drawing on her acquaintance with British history and manners—and the admirable tolerance of the English for eccentricity, especially among the gentry— she directed the masquerade with skill, even with good taste. She herself took the role of "Lady Elizabeth Pembroke," the king's early friend and focus of his senile dreams, the love of his life: they gave his biography a happy ending by coming back to each other's arms "in his latter years," as they put it, since they could not agree what year it was. In "Lady Liza's" pretended view, Harrison being 73, 1968 was 1812 at the latest, and he had at least eight more years to live. To this, George III would reply that "Harrison Mack" was but a figment of his mad imagination, whose age had no bearing on his own; that inasmuch as he dated his irrevocable madness from the death of his daughter and his retirement from the throne (*i.e.*, his disowning of Jeannine Mack after her first divorce, his retirement from Mack Enterprises, and his moving to Redmans Neck—all in 1960), "1968" was actually 1819: he would be 81 on June 4 and would die next January 29. Lady Amherst would point out that if events were to determine dates rather than vice versa, he had even longer than eight years to live, for the Regency had yet to be established. Did he really believe that his son was running Mack Enterprises and the Tidewater Foundation?

Thus she explained Harrison's old quarrel with Drew Mack, not with any ill will toward the boy (she's a decent sort, Lady A.; even Jane still admires her; no malice in her that I can see toward anyone but Schott & Co., who deserve it), but to keep Harrison from reasoning himself into your country before his time. In the same vein, with a kind of dark understanding between them that I can only half follow myself (and half is too much by half on this subject), she'd remind him that the Revolution itself was still some years to come: 1968 could well be 1768, and himself in the prime of his career! But Harrison would answer with a rueful smile that he was not so easily gulled, even by those dear to him: she knew as well as he that the "revolution to come" would be not

13

the First but the Second, and that its direction was neither in his hands, who had lost America in 1776, nor in his "self-styled son's," who had nearly lost Canada in 1812, but in hands more powerful and adroit than either's.

With uneasy glances at me—how many of these history lessons, so tender and so serious, yet so lunatic, I audited!—Lady A. could rejoin only that Harrison was forsaking fact for speculation: if he put off dying until the commencement of that "Second Revolution," he had at least a hundred fifty years to live.

"Not years, dear Liza," the king would say—or "Germaine" if he was calling himself "Harrison" at the moment. "You and Todd will bury me next Groundhog's Day."

And we did. I daresay it took some enterprise in the inner sanctums of Harrison Mack's incorporated psyche to bring about his first stroke in mid-January and hold off the second till the month's end. The first fetched Jane home from her adventures and left her husband blind ("Why not 1813 and seven years to go?" I asked Lady A., having checked the history books on G. III's blindness. But she declared, in tears, he was another king now, old broken Lear, and she no longer "Elizabeth Pembroke" but a superannuate Cordelia). The second stroke killed him. On your deathday—which Harrison still remembered as the cause of my endless *Inquiry,* my presence in this hotel, my old *Floating Opera* story, these epistles to the dead-letter file in the Cambridge P.O., the whole bearing of my life—we put him under in their family plot at Tidewater Farms.

It's a plot of which "Farmer George" (so G. III and H.M. II liked to call themselves) is the sole identified tenant: long before there was a Maryland it had been an Algonquin burial ground; from George I the First to George III the Second, that aboriginal fertilizer had nourished crop after crop for English and American planters: tobacco, cotton, corn, tomatoes. Harrison acquired it (and the rest of Redmans Neck) from old Colonel Morton in 1955, when Mack Enterprises picked up Morton's Marvelous Tomatoes. The burial ground he reclaimed for its original crop; the other 1,999 acres he put into soybeans, stables, mansion-houses, the Mack Enterprises Research and Development Facility, the Tidewater Foundation, and Tidewater Technical College.

This reclamation, or recycling, was more or less the theme of my eulogy, which I delivered at Jane's request. Harrison—*my* Harrison, back when Jane was *our* Jane (Spanish Civil War days, Roosevelt days, sweet days of last night's dream, that Depressioned you to death and brought me to life!)—Harrison would've got a kick out of it. My text was the motto of Marshyhope State University College: *Praeteritas futuras fecundant,* which the *Undergraduate Bulletin* approximates as "The future is enriched by the past." As befits a good agribusiness school, Tidewater Tech (on which we first bestowed the motto) used to misrender it "The past is the seedbed of the future." But we knew what we meant,

14

Harrison and I: not *fecundant* even in the sense of "fertilizes," but *stercorant:* The past manures the future.

I'd proposed it as the Mack family motto in 1935—Floating Theatre days!—when we learned that Harrison's father, in his last years, had caused his poop to be preserved in pickle jars. In '37, when we used those jars (I mean the gardener's *misuse* of them as fertilizer for Mrs. Mack's zinnias) to win Harrison the family estate, I proposed it again, in English, to Jane—but the Macks had tired by then of our *ménage à trois* and were beginning to lose their sense of humor. Imagine my surprise, as they say, in 1957 or thereabouts (Eisenhower days! Middle middle age!), when they and I resumed our acquaintance and I learned (a) that Mack Pickles, now known as Mack Enterprises, was diversifying into soya-oil plastics, chemical fertilizers, artificial preservatives, and frozen-food plants; (b) that Jane herself was more and more the guiding force of the company; and (c) that as Harrison willingly gave way to her and to his new eccentricities, his old sense of humor began to return, and *Praeteritas futuras stercorant* (soberly given by their P.R. people as "The future grows out of the past") was the corporation motto! Above it, on letterhead, label, and billboard, an elderly gentleman in muttonchop whiskers, pince-nez spectacles, and Edwardian greatcoat, standing in a newly furrowed field amid a horse-drawn plow, a three-masted ship, and a single-stacked factory, shook hands across the generations with a horn-rimmed, crew-cut, gratefully grinning young man (not *futuras* after all, but the *praesentis* of the 1950's) waist-deep in soybeans, diesel tractors, propellor-engined airliners, and half a dozen smoking stacks.

Even in his next-to-last year, when Jane vetoed the effluent-purifiers and electrostatic precipitators urged upon Mack Enterprises by the new environmentalists, Harrison was capable of sighing slyly, "The past craps up the future." And so my eulogy turned Ecclesiastes into a prophet of industrial recycling and rebirth control, as who should say to scrap metal, "Out of Buicks art thou come; to Buicks thou shalt return"; or compare my friend's body in the Indian graveyard to those fish (I worked in the resurrected Christ somewhere along here) that Squanto taught the Pilgrim fathers to plant with their corn.

Praeteritas futuras fecundant: The king is dead; long live the king!

Lady Amherst, a better Latinist than I, detected the irony, but took it as it was intended and without offense. Her new friend Ambrose Mensch was all grins; but people regard him as an oddball anyhow. The widow was moved, not indecorously, and thanked me afterward, with no detectable irony of her own, for "a lovely tribute to the Harrison we both loved so." The rest of the company either took my words at face value or paid them no attention. Drew Mack was there, stony-faced, with his handsome wife, Yvonne, both in dark dashikis for the occasion. His sister—now Jeannine Patterson Mack Singer Bernstein Golden, by my count; "Bea Golden" on last summer's programs of *The Original*

15

Floating Theatre II—was supported in her grief and gin (so the recipe smelt to me, flavored with latakia and too much of something by Givenchy) by the remarkable "Reggie Prinz": his Jewish Afro more formidable than Yvonne Mack's *Afro* Afro, his wire-rimmed eyeglasses harking back to Old Man Praeteritas in the picture, his hands (despite himself, I trust) framing hypothetical cinema-shots of ourselves, the house, the grave, nearby Marshyhope Creek and College. Of him, no doubt, more later. Who else? The ubiquitous but elusive Laureate of Maryland, A. B. Cook, read off a poem for the occasion, the closing alexandrines of which—

> This marshy Indian Plot where sleeping Mack's interr'd
> Shall grow the royal Tow'r his Dreams on us conferr'd—

brought stifled groans from Lady A. and young Mensch and pursed the lips of Cook's even more elusive son, introduced to me later as Henry Burlingame VII. John Schott, however, was moved to single-handed applause, as it were, and triumphant red-faced glare. As for Jerome Bray, the final graveside guest—a madder chap in my estimation than poor Harrison at his dottiest, and whose presence there no one could account for—his face was impassive as a visitor's from another country, or planet.

How comes A. B. Cook VI, you ask, to have a son named Henry Burlingame VII? So did I, of the ever-smiling laureate himself, at the reception after the funeral, and was answered by Lord Tennyson paraphrased:

> If you knew *that* flower's crannies,
> You would know what God and man is.

Overhearing which, Lady Amherst commented with just-audible asperity, "We'd know of more than one marshy plot too, I daresay." Schott harrumphed; Cook bowed to his critic; Ambrose Mensch, at her side, wondered as if innocently whether "royal dreams" was in good eulogistic taste, considering. "Not to mention the play on *interred*," Lady A. added coolly. At the time I thought she referred merely and cleverly to the *stercorant* business in my tribute.

To all such jibes the Maryland Laureate was deaf. His son (who, one now discovered, spoke English with a heavy *Québécois* accent) politely asked Lady A. to explain the pun; Mensch volunteered for that duty and led the lad aside, out of earshot of Jane, who was listening with strained but ever cool expression to Schott's hearty condolences while, as it seemed to me, trying to catch my attention. "Bea Golden" was in smoky conversation and transaction with the bartender, while managing simultaneously to keep an eye on her current lover and, if I'm not mistaken, on Ambrose Mensch as well, whom she'd greeted earlier with a string of *Dahlings* effusive even for her. Drew and Yvonne Mack consulted each other; Mr. Bray, himself. Reggie framed us all in his imaginary camera.

Of Jeannine Mack's paternity, Father of mine, I'm still in doubt, 35 years after the fact. If she's Harrison's daughter, she's a throwback to some pickle farmer earlier than her grandsire. What *I* see in her, alas for "Bea Golden," is our own progenitors, yours and mine: the drawling, cracker Andrewses from down-county. Misfortunate child, her redneck genes never at home in those blue-blood boarding schools and hunt clubs! For all her *mahvelouses,* put her in any pahty and it's the help she'll be most at home with: the barkeep, the waiters and musicians. No question she'd've flourished as a down-home Andrews, drinking beer and making out at fifteen and sixteen in the back seats of Chevrolets; left to herself she'd 've been impregnated at seventeen by some local doctor's boy during the Choptank Yacht Regatta and settled down happily somewhere in the county to raise a family; by now their kids would be off to college; they themselves would be tired of weekend adulteries with the local country-clubbers; they'd be buckled down comfortably for a boozy but respectable middle age, he in waterfront real estate and Annapolis politics, she on the school board and tercentennial committee. As is, she's staler at 35 than her mother at 63. The very obverse of her brother, Jeannine has, I am confident, never in her incoherent life voluntarily read a newspaper, much less a book, or been moved by a work of art or a bit of history, reflected on life beyond her own botch of it, felt compassion for the oppressed, or loved a fellow human being. I'm told she's divorcing again, and feels the charmless Prinz to be her great chance. . .

Ach, liebe Tochter, mein Herz schmerz!

Drew Mack, on the other hand, is altogether his father's son, the more so with every fresh rebellion. How could Harrison ever have wondered? Underneath the beard and jeans and dashiki, Drew's as sleek and ample as a prize Angus; the same steak-fed, Princeton-radical Harrison whom I first met in Baltimore in '25, beaten up by Mack Senior's strikebreakers for teaching the "Internationale" to his fellow pickle-pickets. Drew it was who revealed to me, without himself realizing it, the *real* sense of that pun Lady Amherst saw and groaned at. To his mother's visible distress, and my surprise, when I made to leave for Cambridge at the end of the funeral festivities, he and Yvonne insisted on driving me (I'd come out with young Mensch); we'd no sooner squeezed into his discreetly battered Volvo wagon than he announced—

But I'm ahead of myself, and behind on my sleep. Still to describe is the *ménage* back at Tidewater Farms—Jane and Germaine (the latter scarcely yet moved out from the royal chambers, the former scarcely moved back in) outladying each other at one moment across the funeral baked meats, embracing tearfully the next; Ambrose and Reggie deep in cinematographic argument in the library; "Bea Golden" passed out somewhere upstairs; a raw snow just beginning to come down on Redmans Neck from a sky too leaden to alarm any groundhog with his own shadow. . .

But the quick must rest, if the dead will not. I'll finish Calliope's music another night, now I've got the keys tuned: introduce you to the other haunts who've dropped in on me lately, *hic et ubique,* and bring you up to date: 52nd anniversary, so I see on my calendar, of my enlistment against the kaiser in 1917.

Back to your hole, old pioner; wane with the Worm Moon! Leave me to deal with the ghosts of the living: that's work enough for your *Liebes*

Todd

C: *Jacob Horner to Jacob Horner. His life since* The End of the Road. *The remarkable reappearance, at the Remobilization Farm, of Joseph Morgan, with an ultimatum.*

11 P.M. 3/6/69

TO: Jacob Horner, Remobilization Farm, Fort Erie, Ontario, Canada
FROM: Jacob Horner, Remobilization Farm, Fort Erie, Ontario, Canada

Cyrano de Bergerac, Elizabeth Barrett Browning, Ring Lardner, Michelangelo: happy birthday. The Alamo has fallen to Santa Anna; its garrison is massacred. FDR has closed the banks. Franco's cruiser *Baleares* has been sunk off Cartagena. Napoleon's back from Elba: we approach Day One of the Hundred Days.

In a sense, you Remain Jacob Horner. It was on the advice of the Doctor that in 1953 you Left the Teaching Profession; for a time you'd Been A Teacher of Prescriptive Grammar at the Wicomico State Teachers College in Maryland, now the Wicomico campus of Marshyhope State University.

The Doctor had brought you to a certain point in your Original Schedule of Therapies (this was October 27, 1953: anniversary of Madison's Annexation Proclamation concerning West Florida and of Wally Simpson's divorce, birthday of Captain Cook, Paganini, Theodore Roosevelt, Dylan Thomas, Catherine of Valois), and, as you'd Exceeded his prescriptions by perhaps Impregnating your Only Friend's Wife, Arranging an illegal abortion which Mrs. Morgan did not survive, and Impersonating several bona fide human beings in the process, he said to you: "Jacob Horner, you mustn't Work any longer. You will have to Sit Idle for a time."

You Shaved, Dressed, Packed your Bags, and Called a taxi to fetch you to the terminal, where you were to Join the Doctor's other patients for the bus ride north. While you Waited for the cab, you Rocked in your Chair and Smoked a cigarette, your Last. You were Without

Weather. A few minutes later the cabby blew his horn; you Picked Up your Two Suitcases and Went Out, Leaving your bust of Laocoön where it stood, on the mantelpiece. Your Car, too, since you Saw no further use for it, you Left where it was, at the curb, and Climbed into the taxi.

Interminable, that journey, up the Susquehanna and Juniata, into the cold, dilapidated Alleghenies. You Wintered near the Cornplanter Indian Reservation in northwestern Pennsylvania. In the spring, having learned from his Indian clients that the house he'd rented, together with the village and surrounding countryside, would be under water following the government's completion of nearby Kinzua Dam, the Doctor reestablished the Farm somewhat closer to the state line, which eventually he crossed to a pleasant site above Lily Dale, New York, Spiritualist Capital of America. There you Remained for a decade before Moving to the present establishment in Canada, at the opposite end of the Peace Bridge from Buffalo.

In the evening of October 25, 1954—100th anniversary of the charge of the Light Brigade at Balaklava, 1651st of the beheading of the twin saints Crispin and Crispian, 142nd of Commodore Decatur's defeat of H.M.S. *Macedonia* off the Azores, 1st of Renée Morgan's death by aspiration of regurgitated sauerkraut under anesthesia during abortion—the Doctor's new Seneca Indian assistant performed upon you at your Suggestion a bilateral vasectomy to render you sterile: a doctored male. In the evening of October 4, 1955, two years before *Sputnik,* happy birthday Frederic Remington, as an exercise in Scriptotherapy you Began an account of your Immobility, Remobilization, and Relapse, entitled *What I Did Until the Doctor Came.* By means that you have not yet Discovered (your Manuscript was lost, with certain of the Doctor's files, in the move from Pennsylvania to New York), this account became the basis of a slight novel called *The End of the Road* (1958), which ten years later inspired a film, same title, as false to the novel as was the novel to your Account and your Account to the actual Horner-Morgan-Morgan triangle as it might have been observed from either other vertex.

Not long after first publication of that book, its narrative mainspring, coiled like the Chambered Nautilus or Lippes Loop, was rendered quaint as *Clarissa Harlowe*'s by the development, legalization, and general use of oral contraceptive pills, together with the liberalization of U.S. abortion laws. Rennie Morgan, however, and her unborn child, perhaps legitimate, remained dead.

Of the subsequent history of Joseph Morgan you Had No Inkling; of your Own there was none, virtually, in the fifteen years between 1954 and this evening. South Vietnamese Premier Ky walked out of the Paris peace conference to protest "the bombardment of his nation's cities by North Vietnamese artillery"; U.S. Astronaut Schweickart took a space walk from the orbiting Apollo-9 vehicle; at the State University of New York at Buffalo a protest "teach-in" against U.S. involvement in

19

Southeast Asia continued, but most classes went on as usual. You had Prepared your almanac card for the day and were Rocking in your Chair on the porch of the Remobilization Farm after dinner, along with Pocahontas, Monsieur Casteene, Bibi, and other of the patients, Regarding the foul rush of Lake Erie from under the ice toward Niagara, when Tombo X, the Doctor's Chief Medical Assistant (and son) announced the arrival of a new patient: middleaged mothafuckin paleface hippie look like Tim Leary after a bad trip, two mothafuckin honky cats with him, go tell um get they paleface asses back to the U.S.M.F.A. As the Doctor's Administrative Assistant, you Went to the Reception Room, accompanied by M. Casteene.

Tressed and beaded, buckskinned, sere, Joe Morgan regarded you with manic calm.

"You're going to Rewrite History, Horner," he declared: the same clear, still voice that had terminated your Last Conversation with him, in 1953. "You're going to *Change the Past*. You're going to Bring Rennie Back to Life."

As before, you Could Not Reply. Gracious, ubiquitous Monsieur Casteene, frowning Tombo X, and the two impassive young men— Morgan's *sons*, dear God!—led him off toward the Progress and Advice Room for his preadmission interview, and you Returned here to the porch to Write this letter.

Tomorrow, Luther Burbank Day, Madame de Staël will flee Paris to Coppet, her Swiss estate, before Napoleon's advance. Franco will bomb Barcelona, killing 1,000. The Germans, in violation of the Locarno Pact, will occupy the Rhineland, and U.S. troops will cross the Rhine at Remagen Bridge. Jacob Horner, you Like to Imagine, will Step into the poisoned river and Sweep beneath the flaking bridge; past the poisonous plants of Ford and the intakes of the sources of their power; down the cold rapids by Goat Island; over the crumbling, tumbling American Falls at last.

Good riddance.

D: *A. B. Cook IV to his unborn child.* The origins of the Castines, Cookes, and Burlingames.

At Castines Hundred
Niagara, Upper Canada

. 5 March 1812

Dearest Henry or Henrietta Burlingame V,

Dreary, frozen weather the fortnight past; half a foot of new wet snow, the wind off Lake Ontario shaking the house. Then this morning, ere dawn, a cracking thunderstorm, 1st of the year, after which the skies clear'd, the wind turn'd southerly, from off Lake Erie, &

20

wondrous warm. By dawn 'twas spring; by noon, summer! And so all day your mother & I stroll'd and play'd along the heights by Queenstown, hearing the ice crack like artillery & watching the snow go out in miniature Niagaras. A magical day; I do not wonder you flail'd about in Andrée's belly, a-fidget to be out & on with it in such weather, till we had to sit on a rock, under the guns of Fort Niagara across the way, and sing you back to sleep in midafternoon.

Evening & chill again now, the autumn of this one-day year. 'Tis your sweet mother I've sung to sleep, with a Tarratine lullaby learnt from another Andrée Castine, ancestor of us all. No more playing 'twixt the featherbeds for us till after you're born—hasten the day! She sleeps. You too, I trust: by simple love engender'd 'mid plots & counterplots enough to spin the head. The old house is still, but the fire burns on; I feel my lifetime pulsing out like blood from an artery. Day before yesterday 'twas 1800: I was fresh from France with the Revolution under my belt, and Father (perhaps) was ushering in the century by running for vice-president of the U. States under the name of Aaron Burr, denying even to me he was the 4th Henry Burlingame. Where did the dozen years go? Now I am 36, racing pell-mell to the grave; *ma petite cousine* your mother is a full-blown woman of 23. Bonaparte's bleeding Europe white; the Hawks in Washington see their chance to snatch the Canadas & the Floridas; by summer we shall be at such a war as to disunite the States of America. Cities will burn & thousands die ere you're wean'd, my precious—and this in no small part your great-grandfather's doing, & your grandfather's. Aye, and your father's as well, God forgive us! Yet I have never been more happy, more alive & more at peace, nay nor more in love than at this parlous hour.

Little woman or man to be: what blood runs in your veins! Blood of Castines, Cookes, & Burlingames whose histories, more intricate than History, are interlaced as capillaries. 'Tis a tale I knew but partially till this fortnight, when, perforce sequester'd here for a time with Andrée's parents whilst the world looks in vain for the impostor "Comte de Crillon," I have had both leisure & opportunity to search thro certain documents of our family. Nay, more, your mother & I have studied them with amazement, & have espied in them a Pattern, so we believe, that bids to change the course of our lives. It is to fix this pattern for ourselves that I mean to draw it out now for you, in the hope it may spare you half a lifetime of misdirected effort. For we firmly believe, Andrée & I, that ours has been a line of brilliant failures, and that while it may be too late for ourselves to do more than cancel out, in the latter half of our lives, our misguided accomplishments in the earlier, *you* may be the 1st true winner in the history of the house.

'Tis the house of Burlingame & Cook I speak of: the English side of the family, by contrast to which the French, or Castine, side has been a very model of consistency. The Barons Castine still inhabit St. Castine in Gascony, as they have for centuries: the American branch of the family descends from the 1st adventurous baron of the line, a young

André Castine who came to Canada toward the end of the 17th Century. He took to wife a Tarratine Indian whom tradition declares to have been the daughter of "Chief Madocawando," and from whom we Cooks & Burlingames inherit one half of the Indian blood that has served so many of us so well.

This "Monsieur Casteene," as he was known to the English colonials, became a much-fear'd figure in the provinces of New York & New England in the 1690's; even as far south as Maryland it was thot that he & the "Naked Salvages of the North" might sweep down & drive the English back into the sea. Amongst the children of André Castine & Madocawanda (a gifted woman who added French & English to her Indian dialects, & so master'd European manners that she quite charm'd the skeptical Gascoignes upon her one visit to St. Castine) was a daughter, Andrée, who married Andrew Cooke III and grandmother'd both the present Andrée & myself.

All subsequent male Castines have follow'd the peaceful example of their Gascon forebears and contented themselves with hunting, farming, timbering, & the breeding of handsome 1st cousins for the Cookes & Burlingames to wed. These *belles cousines* share their husbands' penchant for political intrigue: a penchant that so marks our line, its genealogy, on the Burlingame side especially, is as tangled as the plots we've been embroil'd in.

To deal 1st with the simpler Cooks (or Cookes, as we then spelt it): Of the 1st Andrew Cooke we know nothing, save that he & someone begot Andrew II, of the Parish of St. Giles in the Fields, London. Andrew II was a tobacco factor in the Maryland plantations, who in the middle 17th Century acquired from Lord Baltimore patent to "Malden on the Chesapeake," now call'd Cooke's Point. Upon his wife Anne Bowyer he got twins, Anna & Ebenezer, of whom more anon. Upon his mistress from the neighboring point—a well-born French girl, disown'd by her father, Le Comte Cécile Édouard, for an earlier *amour*—he got a natural daughter, Henrietta, who bore her mother's later married name of Russecks. Now, since *my* mother, Nancy Russecks Burlingame, was descended from this same Henrietta, 'twas but a partial pretence when I took the name Comte de Crillon for my recentest adventure: you spring from a Huguenot count on one side & a Gascon baron on the other, not to mention Tarratine royalty from Madocawanda Castine and Ahatchwhoop royalty from the Burlingames, whom I've yet to get to!

Thus Andrew II. His son Ebenezer Cooke is of no great interest to us, despite his claim to have been Poet Laureate of Maryland. He seems to have lost the family estate thro bumbling innocence, & to have regain'd it in some fashion by marrying a prostitute. An unsuccessful tradesman gull'd of his goods, he could make no more of his misfortunes than a comical poem, *The Sot-Weed Factor*. No better in the bed than at the writing desk, he got but one child, which died a-borning and fetch't its mother off into the bargain—and that ends the tale of your only artist ancestor.

But not your only artful! For with Anna Cooke, Eben's twin, we come to the Protean Burlingames, whose operations have been at once so multifarious & so covert, that while 'tis certain they have alter'd & re-alter'd the course of history, 'tis devilish difficult to say just how, or whether their intrigues & counter-intrigues do not cancel one another across the generations. For a tree which, left to itself, would grow straight, if pull'd equally this way & that will grow. . .straight!

The 1st Henry Burlingame (a fair copy of whose *Privie Journall* I found last week among the family papers) was one of that company of gentlemen who came to make their fortunes in Virginia with the 1st plantation in 1607, and, disaffected by the hardships of pioneering, made trouble for Captain John Smith—whose *Secret Historie of the Voiage up the Bay of Chesapeake* we also possess. The two documents together tell this story: In 1608, thinking to divert the mutinous gentlemen, Smith led them on a voyage of exploration from Jamestown to the head of Chesapeake Bay, to find whether it might prove the long-sought Northwest Passage to the Pacific. After a scurrilous adventure amongst the Accomack Indians of the Eastern Shore (detail'd in Smith's history), Burlingame became a kind of leader of the anti-Smith faction, to whom he threaten'd to tell "the true story of Pocahontas" if Smith did not leave off harassing him & return the party to Jamestown. For it was Burlingame's opinion (set forth persuasively in the *Privie Journall*) that Smith was a mere swaggering opportunist & self-aggrandizer, out for glory at anyone's cost. But Smith's own account (I mean the *Secret Historie*) is also persuasive. I conceive him to have been at once an able & daring leader & a thoro rogue; our ancestor to have been both a great complainer by temperament & a man much justified in his complaints.

In any event, so aggravated grew the dispute that shortly afterwards—the party having put ashore in the Maryland marshes & been taken captive by Ahatchwhoop Indians—Smith turn'd a tribal custom into a stratagem for ransoming himself & the rest of his company at Burlingame's expence. It was the wont of the Ahatchwhoops, upon the death of their king, to choose his successor by a contest of gluttony, he acceding to the throne who could outgorge his competitors. Such was the principle, which must have produced some odd administrators had it not in fact been modified to permit an able but temperate candidate to enter the lists by proxy, sharing the privileges of office (including the queen's favors) with his corpulent champion, but retaining the authority himself. Smith duped Burlingame (a man of great appetite, & half-starved) into taking the field on behalf of one Wepenter, a politico of modest stomach who must otherwise lose to his gluttonous rival for the kingdom and the hand of lusty Princess Pokatawertussan. Thinking it a mere eating contest with a night of love its prize, our forebear set to with a will & narrowly bested his fat opponent Attonceaumoughhowgh ("Arrow-Target"), who died on the spot of overeating. Grateful Wepenter takes the throne, & in the morning sets Smith's party free. But when Burlingame makes to join them (having been too ill all night of indigestion to claim his trophy), he is fetcht back in triumph by the Ahatchwhoops, their captive & co-king!

There end both the *Privie Journall* & the *Secret Historie*. Not till nearly a century later (in 1694) does anyone learn the subsequent fate of our progenitors. Old Andrew II, it seems, in 1676 engaged as tutor for the twins Ebenezer & Anna Cooke a young Cantabridgean of many parts, named Henry Burlingame III: a master of all the arts & sciences (& an array of secular skills as well, from opium smuggling to sedition) who however had no idea who his parents were or whence came his name & numeral. His researches into this subject had directed all his life, led him deep into the politics of colonial America, involved him in a dozen disguises (for which he had the original gift pass'd down to the rest of us) & as many conspiracies—chiefly Leisler's Rebellion in New York & John Coode's in Maryland. It also brot him in touch with "Monsieur Casteene," as a secret agent either for the French against the British or vice-versa—the 1st of what will be a grand series of such uncertainties!—and with conspiracies of runaway Negro slaves & beleaguer'd Indians to drive their white oppressors from the continent.

But it was his hapless pupil Ebenezer, by this time (the 1690's), done with school & in midst of his own misadventures, who stumbl'd by chance on what his tutor had subverted governments to find. Driven by a storm upon Bloodsworth Island in the lower Chesapeake, the secret base of those disaffected Indians & escaped slaves, Cooke & his companions are taken prisoner by the old Tayac Chicamec, Chief of the Ahatchwhoops, whom he discovers to be (and he owes his life to the discovery—the tale is too involv'd to repeat) none other than the son of Henry Burlingame I & Pokatawertussan: in short, Henry Burlingame II, the missing link between John Smith's scapegoat & the twins' formidable tutor! In Chicamec's possession is the portion of Smith's *Secret Historie* describing Burlingame's abandonment, and Chicamec repeats his father's vow to exterminate the "English Devils"—a resolve pass'd down thro Chicamec to his sons.

Now, as Chicamec himself was a halfbreed & his queen as well (the daughter of an errant Jesuit priest & an Ahatchwhoop maiden), their three sons were born in a variety of shades. The 1st, Mattasinemarough, was a pure-blood Indian. The 2nd, Cohunkowprets, a halfbreed like his parents. The 3rd, white-skinn'd and therefore doom'd, was named (nay, *label'd,* in red ochre on his chest) *Henry Burlingame III,* & set adrift in a canoe on the ebb tide down the Chesapeake—whence he was rescued by a passing English vessel, adopted by its captain, and fetch back to England to begin his quest.

There is too much more to the story for this letter—enough to make a novelsworth of letters, Richardson-fashion! Indeed, I see now I must write you at least thrice more, one letter for each generation from this Burlingame III to yourself, if I am to introduce you properly to your sires & show forth that aforementioned pattern, which at this point is as yet unmanifest. But of this H.B. III, your great-great-grandfather, four things more need saying, all connected, ere I close.

1st, his brother's name, Cohunkowprets, means "bill-o'-the-goose" in the Algonkin dialect of the Ahatchwhoops, and Chicamec's middle son was thus denominated because, like his brothers & his grandfather (but not his father), he was born so underendow'd in the way of private parts as to move his mother to exclaim on 1st sight of him (in effect & in Algonkin), "A goose hath peckt him peckerless!" This characteristic—like a tendency to plural births—afflicts us Burlingames in alternate generations. More accurately, since the time of H.B. III, when our line began to exchange the surnames *Cooke* & *Burlingame* in succeeding generations, it has afflicted all the Burlingames: you yourself, we expect, should you emerge a Henry, will be but a few centimeters' membership from Henriettahood in this particular. Yet do not despair, for as my existence attests (& that of Andrew Cooke III, my grandfather, & of Chicamec as well, my grandfather's grandfather), the Burlingames have found ways to overcome their deficiency. We shall pass along to you, when you reach young manhood, the "Secret of the Magic Eggplant," which, I now learn, we took originally from the *Privie Journall*.

Indeed (here is my 2nd point), as a man born short of the average stature may outdo taller men in feats of manliness, so Henry Burlingames III & IV (the latter my father) were men of uncommon sexuality. H.B. III, who concerns us here, was by his own denomination a "cosmophilist," who not only lusted after both his charges, Anna & Ebenezer Cooke, but claim'd to have had carnal connection as well with sundry sorts of barnyard animals, plants, inanimate objects, the very earth itself—long before his discovery of John Smith's eggplant recipe made it possible for him to beget a child.

Thirdly, from this "cosmophilism," or erotical love of the world, must have stem'd H.B. III's endless interests: his passion for everything from astronomy, music, politics, rope-splicing, & chess, to the practice of medicine, law, & nautical piracy, for example; in particular for what he call'd "the game of governments," and my father "the practice of history." He successfully impersonated, at various times, both Lord Baltimore & Baltimore's arch-enemy John Coode; perhaps "Monsieur Casteene" as well. At 1st, one gathers, the motive for his intrigues, at least their occasion, was his research into his parentage: the *Secret Historie* & *Privie Journall* were involved in Coode's conspiracies against Baltimore, and thus involved anyone who sought them. Later, when Ebenezer Cooke had brot to light his tutor's lineage, Governor Nicholson of Maryland prevail'd upon Burlingame to forestall—if possible, to subvert—that "Bloodsworth Island Conspiracy" of Indians & Negroes. Burlingame accepted the task with relish; but the Cooke twins apparently fear'd that his fascination with his newfound brothers might win out over his loyalty to white civilization. According to my grandfather, who wrote of these things some decades later, they wonder'd whether Burlingame, once on Bloodsworth, would work to

25

divide the jealous factions of ex-slaves & Indians from several tribes, or to unite them, ally them with Casteene's "Naked Indians of the North," & return America to its aboriginal inhabitants.

What follow'd historically is known: there were no concerted risings of Negroes & Indians, only isolated massacres of white settlements such as Albany & Schenectady. Bloodsworth Island by 1700 was uninhabited marsh, as it is today. But it is not known whether this failure of the Conspiracy represents failure or success on the part of H.B. III. The man was 40 when he left Cooke's Point for Bloodsworth Island early in 1695 (Ebenezer having regain'd his estate & been reunited with his sister & his former tutor). In April of the same year, as he had pledg'd, Burlingame reappear'd at Malden, in Ahatchwhoop dress, to wed Anna—who, however, for reasons unknown, postponed the marriage until the fall, when Burlingame's assignment from Governor Nicholson should be completed. Her fiancé yielded to her wish & return'd to the island—never to be heard from again.

But they must have spent that final night in each other's arms, "supping ere the priest said grace," as Ebenezer puts it in his poem, with some assistance from the Eggplant Secret: for Anna found herself with child immediately thereafter, and in January 1696 (1695 in the old style) she was deliver'd of a son—your great-grandfather, of whom I shall write in my next letter. Enough to say now (my 4th & last matter for this night) that to cover the scandal—Ebenezer's own harlot bride having died in childbirth two months previously—he & Anna gave out that he Ebenezer was the child's father & she its aunt, and *Andrew Cooke III* was so named & raised.

Everyone at Malden & the neighboring plantations, by this same Andrew's account, knew the story to be false, and unkindly assumed, from the twins' general closeness, that he was not only a bastard but the child of incest as well. This suspicion was not without effect on the young man's life.

But that is matter for another evening: sufficient here to record that it is with Andrew III that the Cooks & Burlingames begin alternating surnames thro the line of their 1st-born sons, Andrew Cooke III's being named Henry Burlingame IV, and Burlingame IV's Andrew Cooke IV. *I.e.*, myself, who at my dear wife's suggestion have dropt the *e* from *Cooke* as superfluous, and the male-primogenitural restriction as an affront to the splendid women of the Castines. Yourself therefore will be *Burlingame V*, whether Henry or Henrietta. With that name will be bequeatht to you a grand objective, & a formidable bloodline to aid your attaining it.

Of these—& of that Pattern, the inspiration of this letter which has fail'd to get to it—more to come, when I shall complete the chronicle of these III's and IV's. 'Tis far past midnight now; the wind has dropt, the fire burnt down; 'tis cold. From the neighboring farm a late dog barks; pretty Andrée stirs, stir'd in turn perhaps by you. 1812, 1812! I shall hold you both close now till you've quieted, without knowing who restored your peace. May we together, some sweeter year to come, do as much for History!

Till when, & forever, I am,

Your loving father,
Andrew Cook IV

E: ***Jerome Bray to Todd Andrews.*** *Requesting counsel in an action of plagiarism against the Author. His bibliography and biography. Enclosures to the Author, to George III, and to Todd Andrews.*

Jerome Bonaparte Bray
General Delivery
Lily Dale, N.Y. 14752

March 4, 1969

Mr. Todd Andrews
Executive Director, Tidewater Foundation
c/o Andrews, Bishop, & Andrews, Attorneys
Court Lane
Cambridge, Md. 21613

Dear Mr. Andrews:

Every ointment has a chink. Agreeable as it was to meet last month the executive director of the Tidewater Foundation—benefactor of our LILYVAC project and thus midwife as it were to the 2nd Revolution—we regret that our meeting was occasioned by the funeral of His Royal Highness Harrison Mack II: the most powerful, the most trustworthy, and the most RESET If we seemed to you (or to the widowed queen or the royal mistress) distracted, even "tranced" that afternoon, we plead our bereavement (but *Le roi est mort; vive le roi!*) and the season. Even now our winter rest period is not ended; we can scarcely hold pen to page for drowsiness; we must count on another to RESET Yet we cannot leave this topic without presuming to warn you against Ambrose M., that person who chauffeured you to Mr. Mack's funeral and is so bent on ingratiating himself in our circle. Never mind his attentions to Lady A. and to Miss Bea Golden, whose beautiful name he is not worthy to pronounce: our information is that A.M. is the tool and creature of the Defendant hereinafter named: we say no more.

R. Prinz, too, must be dealt with. But that is another matter.

Enclosed (with its own enclosures) is a letter we are posting today to Buffalo, N.Y. It is our intention to bring an action for plagiarism against the addressee. Since, in your capacities as director of and counsel to the Tidewater Foundation, you are the only attorney with whom we have connection, it is our wish to retain you as our counsel in

27

this suit. Unless, indeed, you agree with us that the Foundation itself should bring the action in our behalf.

Our principal complaint, set forth in the attached, is the Defendant's perversion (into his "novel" *Giles Goat-Boy,* 1966) of our *Revised New Syllabus* of the Grand Tutor Harold Bray. But that is merely the latest and chiefest of his crimes against us, which extend the length of our bibliography. To wit:

a. *The Shoals of Love, or, Drifting and Dreaming,* by "J. A. Beille" (Backwater, Md.: Wetlands Press, 1957): a novel in the format of a showboat minstrel show (But none of our books is mere fiction. See our letter to you of July 4, 1967, enclosed). Its ostensible subject is the star-crossed lovers Ebenezer and Florence, end-man and -woman of a blackface minstrel troupe aboard a drifting theater in the Chesapeake estuaries, whose love is thwarted by the heroine's father, Mr. Interlocutor. Ebenezer is driven to the brink of humanism until Florence discovers a way to communicate with him not only despite but *through* her father, as a cunning wrestler turns his adversary's strength to his RESET By means of *double-entendres* in the minstrel-show routine (echoing of course the great *double-entendre* of the "novel" itself) the lovers conduct their pathetic intercourse. The story climaxes with Flo's ingenious re-choreography of the "breakdown" dance, which itself climaxes the nightly show, into an elaborate kinetic code, not unlike the worker-dance "language" that inspires her: its message is that Eb must sink the Floating Theatre that very night and fly with Flo to some hive of refuge. Whether or not Eb gets the message is heartbreakingly left for the reader to wonder—as the Author, no less heartbroken, wonders whether his lost parents are getting his message through the pseudofictive text. See Enclosure #3.

b. *The W sp,* by "Jean Blanque" (Wetlands Press, 1959): the terse companion piece to *Shoals.* Its anonymous hero, a handsome young entomologist from a small agricultural college in Maryland, doing field work on Batesian mimicry in the Dorchester marshes, comes to realize that, as if "bitten by the love-bog," he esteems the objects of his researches above his human partners; that his human roles have been as it were mere protective camouflage. As autumn passes, he withdraws into a tent of his own making in the saltmarsh, where the "novel" leaves him in a dormancy from which, perhaps, he wakes ½-tranced come spring and takes flight with his 1,000,000 brothers. Dream? Hallucination? Transfiguration? The question is tantalizingly unresolved, while the reader her/himself takes wing on the heart-constricting beauty of the closing passage, a description of the mating flight.

c. *Backwater Ballads,* by "Jay Bray" (Wetlands Press, 1961), our *magnum opus:* a cycle of 360 tales set in the Backwater National Wildlife Refuge, our birthplace, at all periods of its history (*i.e.,* 1600–1960: 1 tale for each year, each degree of the cycle, and each day of the ideal year, of which our actual calendars are but the corrupt approximation). The tales are told from the viewpoint of celestial Aedes Sollicitans, a freshmarsh native with total recall of all her earlier hatches, who each year bites 1 visitor in the Refuge and acquires, with her victim's blood, an awareness of his/her history. The 1st is the Tayac Kekataughtassapooekskunoughmass, or "90 Fish," King of the Ahatchwhoop Indians. The 9th is Captain John Smith of Virginia; the 10th Henry Burlingame I, my own foster father's great-great-great-great-great-great-grandfather. The 360th (and the 1st to give himself to her unreservedly) is the Author, whom in return she gratefully "infects" with her narrative accumulation.

Compare these with the Defendant's impostures. And having compared (and subdued the indignation that must follow your comparison!), let us arrange a meeting, either in your office or here in Lily Dale—where in your other capacity you can satisfy yourself with the progress of LILYVAC II on the NOVEL project—prepare our briefs, file our suit, and, companions-in-arms such as the world has never RESET He shall pay.

Were we not so sleep-ridden, we could not close without a word on the success of our fall work period; the 1st phase of the 3rd year (V) of the 5-year NOVEL plan (see Enclosure #2). But we must rest, rest for the prodigious labors of the coming spring, when in any case Ms. Bernstein will submit to the Foundation our full and confidential ½-annual report. Then let us together RESET JBB 3 encl.

(ENCL. 1)

Jerome Bonaparte Bray
General Delivery
Lily Dale, N.Y. 14752

March 4, 1969

"J.B.," "Author"
Dept. English, Annex B
SUNY/Buffalo
Buffalo, N.Y. 14214

"Dear" "sir":

Enclosed (so that you cannot pretend not to know us) are printouts of letters from us to His late Majesty George III of Maryland and to Mr. Todd Andrews of the Tidewater Foundation—who also acts as our attorney, and from whom, in that latter capacity, you will presently be hearing.

We know very well that August 5 of this year will be the 3rd anniversary of 1st publication of "your" "novel" *G.G.B.* and that therefore on that date the statute of limitations will run on actions against you connected with that "work." 5 months hence! But it is your time, not the statute, that runs out. Only the press of other business

29

(and our absolute need for rest at this season) has kept us from bringing you sooner to account. But our eye has been upon you as yours has been upon the calendar.

Nearly 7 years have passed since the *true* Giles delivered to our trust the *Revised New Syllabus* of his ascended father Harold Bray, Grand Tutor of the universal University. *4 years ago tonight* we roused from the profoundest torpor of our life to read that Tutor-given text, and to commence the great work of expunging from it the corruptions and perversions of the Antitutor and false Giles, your Goat-Boy. Like you, he believed he had triumphed over Truth, not knowing that his nemesis but awaited the proper hour to sting!

With tonight's Worm Moon (which by summer will become a Conqueror indeed) that hour is come. We ourselves must return for a time yet into rest; indeed we can scarcely hold pen to paper for drowsiness; must count on another to post this ultimatum. But justice now is hatched and stirring: when you next hear from us (a month hence, if you have not by then made the reparations our attorney will demand) we shall be fully awake and at work on our grand project. Do not imagine that because your thefts are of gn_t-like inconsequence by comparison with our Revolutionary NOVEL, they will go unpunished. For as our noble forebear, while conquering Europe and administering the Empire, could attend with equal firmness to such details as correcting our namesake's American marriage, so we, while supervising the Novel Revolution, will not fail to attend also to your exposure and ruin.

B.

cc. T. Andrews
2 encl.

(ENCL. 2)

Enclosure #1

On board the Gadf_y III, *Lake Chautauqua, New York, 14 July 1966*
To His Majesty George III of England
Tidewater Farms, Redmans Neck, Maryland 21612

Your Royal Highness,

On 22 June 1815, in order to establish a new and sounder base of empire, we abdicated the throne of France and withdrew to the port of Rochefort, where 2 of our frigates—new, fast, well-manned and -gunned—lay ready to run Your Majesty's blockade of the harbor and carry us to America. Captain Ponée of the Méduse *planned to engage on the night of 10 July the principal English vessel, H.M.S.* Bellerophon, *a 74-gunner but old and slow, against which he estimated the* Méduse *could hold out for 2 hours while her sister ship, with our party aboard, outran the lesser blockading craft. The plan was audacious but certain of success. Reluctant, however, to sacrifice the* Méduse, *we resolved instead like a cunning wrestler to turn our adversary's strength to our advantage: to reach our goal by means of, rather than despite, Your Majesty's navy; and so we addressed to your son the Prince Regent the following:*

Isle of Aix, 12 July 1815

In view of the factions that divide my country and of the enmity of the greatest powers in Europe I have brought my political career to a close and am going like Themistocles to seat myself on the hearthstone of the British people. I put myself under the protection of English Law and request that protection of Your Royal Highness, as the most powerful, the most trustworthy, and the most generous of my enemies.

Having sent our aide-de-camp before us with this message and instructions to request from the Prince Regent passports to America, on Bastille Day we put ourself and our entourage in the hands of Commander Maitland aboard Bellerophon *and left France. Alas, Your Majesty's own betrayal and confinement on the mischievous charge of insanity should have taught us that our confidence in your son and his ministers was ill placed, more especially as it is with the Muse of the Past that we have ever gone to school for present direction. When therefore we learned from Admiral Sir George Cockburn that our destination was to be, not London and Baltimore, but St. Helena, like a derelict student we applied in vain to our old schoolmistress for vindication:*

On board Bellerophon, *at sea*

. . .I appeal to History. History will say that an enemy who waged war for 20 years against the English people came of his own free will, in his misfortune, to seek asylum under her laws. What more striking proof could he give of his esteem and his trust? But what reply was made in England to such magnanimity? There was a pretense of extending a hospitable hand to that enemy, and when he had yielded himself up in good faith, he was sacrificed.

Our maroonment on that desolated rock, under the boorish Cockburn and his more boorish successors, we need not describe to 1 so long and even more ignobly gaoled. We, at least, had the consolation that our exile was both temporary and as it were voluntary: we needed no Perseus to save us; we could have escaped at any time, and waited 7 years only because that period was needed for us to exploit to best advantage our martyrdom, complete the development of that stage of our political philosophy set down in the Memorial of St. Helena, *and execute convincingly the fiction of our death in 1821; also for our brother Joseph in Point Breeze, New Jersey, our officers at Champ d'Asile in the Gulf of Mexico, and our agents in Philadelphia, Baltimore, Barataria, Bloodsworth Island, and Rio de Janeiro to complete the groundwork for our American operations.*

By means which we will not here disclose (but which must bear some correspondence to those by which Your Majesty effected his own escape from Windsor), we departed St. Helena in 1822 for my American headquarters—1st in a house not far from your own in the Maryland marshes, ultimately in western New York—an area to which our attention had been directed during our 1st Consulship by Mme de Staël (who owned 23,000 acres of St. Lawrence County) in the days before that woman, like Anteia or the wife of Potiphar, turned against

31

us. Here, for the last century and ½, we have directed our operatives in the slow elaboration of our grand strategy, 1st conceived aboard **Bellerophon,** whereof the time has now arrived to commence the execution: a project beside which Jena, Austerlitz, Ulm, Marengo, the 18th Brumaire, even the original Revolution, are as our ancient 18-pounders to an H-bomb, or our old field glass to the Mt. Palomar reflector: we mean the New, the 2nd Revolution, an utterly Novel Revolution!

"There will be no innovations in my time," Your Majesty declared to Chancellor Eldon. But the truly revolutionary nature of our project, as examination of the "Bellerophonic" prospectus (en route to you under separate cover) will show, is that, as the 1st genuinely scientific model of the genre, it will of necessity contain nothing original whatever, but be the quintessence, the absolute type, as it were the Platonic Form expressed.

The plan is audacious but certain of RESET Nothing now is wanting for immediate implementation of its 1st phase save sufficient funding for construction of a more versatile computer facility at our Lily Dale base, and while such funding is available to us from several sources, the voice of History directs us to Your Royal Highness, as the most powerful, the most trustworthy, and the most generous of RESET Adversaries, we shook the world; as allies, who could withstand us? What might we not accomplish?

In 1789 Your Majesty "recovered" from the strait-waistcoat of your 1st "madness," put to rout those intriguing with your son to establish his regency, and until your 2nd and "final" betrayal by those same intriguers in 1811, enjoyed an unparalleled popularity with your subjects—as did we between Elba and St. Helena. Then let us together, from our 2nd Exiles, make a 2nd Return, as more glorious than our 1st as is its coming, to a world impatient to be transfigured, has been longer. To the once-King of the Seas, the once-Monarch of the Shore once again extends his hand. Only grasp it and, companions-in-arms such as this planet has not seen, we shall be Emperors of the world.

N.

(ENCL. 3)

Enclosure #2

July 4, 1967

TO: *Mr. Todd Andrews, Executive Director, Tidewater Foundation, Marshyhope State University College, Redmans Neck, Md. 21612*

FROM: *Jerome B. Bray, General Delivery, Lily Dale, N.Y. 14752*

RE: *Reapplication for Renewal of Tidewater Foundation Grant for Reconstruction of Lily Dale Computer Facility for Reimplementation of NOVEL Revolutionary Project*

Sir:

Inasmuch as concepts, including the concepts Fiction and Necessity, are

32

more or less necessary fictions, fiction is more or less necessary. Butterf_ies *exist in our imaginations, along with* Existence, Imagination, *and the rest. Archimedeses, we lever reality by conceiving ourselves apart from its other things, them from one another, the whole from unreality. Thus Art is as natural an artifice as Nature; the truth of fiction is that Fact is fantasy; the made-up story is a model of the world.*

Yet the empire of the novel, vaster once than those combined of France and England, is shrunk now to a Luxembourg, a San Marino! Its popular base usurped, fiction has become a pleasure for special tastes, like poetry, archery, churchgoing. What is wanted to restore its ancient dominion is nothing less than a revolution; indeed, the Revolution is waiting in the wings, the 2nd Revolution, *and will not stay for the Bicentennial of the 1st, than which it bids to be as more glorious as its coming, to a world impatient to be* RESET Now of *"science fiction" there is a surfeit; of* scientific *fiction, none. Attempts to classify "scientifically" the themes of existing fiction (e.g. Professor Thompson's* Motif Index of Folk Literature) *or even its dramatical morphology (e.g. the admirable reduction, by Professors Propp and Rosenberg, of the "Swan-Geese" folktale to the formula*

$$\gamma\beta\delta ABC \uparrow \left\{ \frac{[DE \; Neg \; F \; Neg]^3}{DEF} \right\} \; GHIK \downarrow Pr[DEF]^3 Rs$$

—*these are steps in the right direction, but halting as a baby's, primitive as Ben Franklin and his kite—and made by* scholars, *to the end merely of understanding for its own sake! They are like the ponderings of historians upon the Napoleonic Wars; whereas our own textual analyses (beginning with the grand* Concordance of the Revised New Syllabus *from which the Revolutionary* NOVEL *Project grew) are like the Emperor's own examinations of military history—to the end, not merely of understanding, but of mastering and perfecting it, in order, like a cunning wrestler, to* RESET We were born on August 15, 1933, in the Backwater Wildlife Refuge on the Eastern Shore of Maryland, and raised by 1 of the staff rangers in the absence of our true parents, who for reasons of state were obliged to keep their whereabouts hidden and were never able to communicate with their only child except by coded messages which not even Ranger Burlingame was privy to. These messages trace our descent "originally" from the abortive marriage in 1803 of our namesake the Emperor's brother Jérôme and Elizabeth Patterson of Baltimore; more immediately from their grandson Charles Joseph Bonaparte and the Tuscarora Indian Princess Kyuhaha Bray, Charles's wife in the eyes of God and the Iroquois though not in the white man's record books during his tenure as Indian Commissioner in 1902 under President Theodore Roosevelt. There being at present no bona fide Bonapartes more closely related than ourself to the late Emperor, we have in fact some just pretension to the throne of France—which it is not our concern to press here, but which we do not doubt was instrumental in eliciting support for our original Tidewater Foundation grant from Mr. Harrison Mack, as the most powerful, the most trustworthy, and the most RESET Under various assumed names, for our own protection, and in circumstances as strait as our ancestor's on*

St. Helena, we completed our higher education in sundry night schools and supported ourself by teaching technical and business-letter writing, 1st in the Agricultural Extension Division of the state university, later at Wicomico Teachers College, most recently in Fredonia, New York. We shall not describe here the conspiracies of anti-Bonapartists and counterrevolutionaries which drove us from academic pillar to post: they did all in their power, vainly, to mock and frustrate our literary career, knowing that our writings were never the fictions they represented themselves as being, but ciphered replies to those parental communications which have sustained us through every ordeal.

Of the fictions qua *fictions you will have heard, all published by the* Wetlands Press *under various* noms de plume: The Shoals of Love, *by "J. A. Beille" (a name meant to echo* Beyle, *the French Bonapartist a.k.a.* Stendhal); The Wa_p, *by "Jean Blanque"; and* Backwater Ballads, *by "Jay Bray." The use of our Indian ancestor's surname in that last* nom de plume *was a coded challenge to our enemies; it elicited an altogether unexpected result, which changed our life. By the time* Ballads *appeared in print (to go unnoticed, like its predecessors, by the anti-Bonapartist literary establishment, but not by those for whom its private message was intended), we were at work on another "novel," to be called* The Seeker, *whose hero reposes in a sort of hibernation in a certain tower, impatient to be RESET For reasons we did not ourself understand at the time, our work on this fiction had come to a standstill: then in September 1962 we were vouchsafed our 1st bodily visitation by an emissary of our parents—though we did not recognize him as such until some years later. This episode is recounted in the "Cover-Letter to the Editors and Publisher" of the "novel"* Giles Goat-Boy *(1966): an account accurate enough in its particulars, since the text was lifted outright from our* Revised New Syllabus; *yet wholly perverted, since its "author" is either the leader or the tool of the anti-Bonapartists who have done all in their power, vainly, to RESET O stop New ¶*

Harold Bray, *not the impostor Giles Goat-Boy, was Grand Tutor of the universal University! Persecuted and driven thence by agents of the Antitutor, he was revealed to us that night by his emissary as our ancestor on that campus beyond, as truly as the Bonapartes are our ancestors in this world. The coincidence of his surname and that of our Tuscarora grandmother is no coincidence!*

Apprehensive of yet another plot against us, we were at 1st skeptical of this visitation and hesitant to read the manuscript entrusted to us by our visitant. In the year 1963/64, at the age of 30, we found ourself plunged into deepest torpor, not only during our normal rest period, but during our spring and fall work periods as well. Not recognizing that condition as the prelude to a grander pitch and stage of action, we sought help in nearby Lily Dale: 1st among the spiritualists who swarm there (and whose messages from our parents were transparently false); then among the activators of the famous Remobilization Farm, which had yet to be harried from the country by enemies not unconnected to our own.

The multitudinous and ingenious therapies of the Doctor's staff restored us to the path of destiny (rather, revealed to us we had never left it) and prompted us to read The Revised New Syllabus, *which did the rest. To the Farm we owe* the pleasure of remeeting a former teacher (Mr. Jacob Horner, instructor in prescriptive grammar during our student nights at Wicomico Teachers College, now administrative assistant of the Farm, whom it will be our pleasure to engage as syntactical analyst in the NOVEL project when the 5-Year Plan is implemented) and the establishing of 2 invaluable associations: with M. Casteene, like ourself descended from French and Indian nobility, and eager to coordinate his historical enterprises and our own; and with H.R.H. Harrison Mack's Tidewater Foundation, which we discovered (from M. Casteene) to be among the enlightened philanthropies on which the Remobilization Farm depends for support—and to which we turned in turn when we were ourself remobilized in 1965.

We straightway resigned our post at Fredonia (students the country over were by this time becoming impossible to teach in any case) and established ourself at Lily Dale to begin our Concordance to the R.N.S., supporting ourself as best we could by raising goats for fudge and slaughter and piloting the excursion boat Gadfl_ III (named for my lost father; never mind) on nearby Chautauqua Lake. In 1966, as your files will show, on the advice of M. Casteene we applied to Mr. Mack and were awarded a modest grant by the Tidewater Foundation for construction of a preliminary computer facility to aid in the Concordance— whose implications we ourself scarcely realized to be as revolutionary as intuited by M. Casteene and Mr. Mack's son, Drew.

That same year (we mean 1966/67) we suffered 1 grave setback and reaped 2 unexpected windfalls. The setback was publication on August 5 of the spurious G.G.B., our manuscript edition of R.N.S. having been pirated from Wetlands Press by a carefully placed anti-Bonapartist eager to ingratiate himself with the New York trade publishers. We had counted on royalties from that work to set us free of the goats and Gadf_y... But no matter: He or she shall pay for her/his piracy, as shall in time the 1 who took our initials with our text and published the Syllabus not even as a ciphered message in the guise of fiction, much less as plain and passèd truth, but as mere entertainment!

Had the blow fallen a year or 2 earlier, during our vulnerable period, we might have succumbed. But we were supported in our adversity by the foundation grant, by the ready progress of the Concordance program, and by the 2 windfalls aforementioned. The 1st (too personal to detail in this letter) was our meeting of and subsequent association with Ms. Merope Bernstein, a brilliant student of political economy, entomology, and computer science at Brandeis U., who, dissatisfied as we with the academic establishment, had dropped out in her final semester to do fieldwork in militant ecology. We met at an anti-DDT pray-in-and-spray-out on the grounds of the old Chautauqua Institution on the evening of August 15, 1966, our 31st birthday and the most beautiful evening of our life. We can say no more.

The 2nd windfall was the unexpected turn taken by our researches this past spring, when we completed the Concordance program and reviewed the initial computer printouts. You will recall that even in our 1st application we intimated (and could have no more than intimated, so tentative were our own speculations at that time) that the Concordance was to be "novel," even "revolutionary": the "Bellerophonic Prospectus" which we submitted to the foundation through Mr.

Mack merely suggested that the circuitry of our proposed LILYVAC should be capable of mimicking prose styles on the basis of analyzed samples, and even of composing hypothetical works by any author on any subject. In our fall 1966 programming, stung by the spurious Giles, we made provisions for experiments in this line, thinking that publication of such canards as an End of the Road Continued or a Sot-Weed Redivivus or a Son of Giles might expose, confound, and neutralize our enemies; might even force reparations to aid our great work and set us free of the goats and RESET So successful was our circuitry and program design (despite the modest, even primitive, facility that is LILYVAC I), the 1st printouts, we are happy to report, transcended these petty possibilities.

We say transcended, rather than exceeded, because like a gift from the Grand Tutor, what LILYVAC gave us was not exactly what we had petitioned for, its superior "eyes" having espied in our data what ours had not. It did indeed produce a few pages of mimicry, in the format of letters written by our enemies and others; it even synopsized, as if in farewell to our Concordance project, a scripture to be called Revised New Revised New Syllabus. But the burden of its message to us was, not to abandon these enterprises, but to incorporate them into the grander project herewith set forth, to be code-named NOVEL.

The details are too sensitive to entrust to the ordinary post; we shall confide them to the foundation through Mr. Drew Mack on a "need-to-know" basis. But bear in mind that we are not an homme de lettres; that The Shoals of Love, The Was_, and Backwater Ballads were not mere novels, but documents disguised in novel format for the purpose of publicly broadcasting private messages to our parents—who, we now have reason to believe, have not been deaf to those cunning, painful ciphers, and may be replying to us in kind through LILYVAC.

Bear in mind also and therefore that any description of our revolutionized project is perforce cryptic and multireferential; when we say NOVEL, for example, we refer at once to at least 5 things: (a) (what we take to be) a document in the guise of an extended fiction of a revolutionary character; (b) a 5-year plan for the composition of that document; (c) a 5-year plan for effecting, in part by means of that document, certain novel and revolutionary changes in the world; (d) the title of a (also known as RN) and the code name of b and c; and (e) the code name for this Novel Revolution itself and the 5 several years of its implementation, which Ms. Bernstein and we have abstracted from LILYVAC's printout instructions as follows:

1. 1966/67 (Year N [already completed in essence, without our knowing the true significance of our labors]): Programming of LILYVAC I to mimic prose styles on the basis of analyzed specimens. Composition of hypothetical fictions. Neutralization of leading anti-Bonapartists and exaction of reparations for plagiarism [these last have yet to be achieved]. Poisoned entrails.

2. 1967/68 (Year O): Programming of LILYVAC II [i.e., the modifications and extensions of LILYVAC I to be made this fall with Tidewater Foundation funds, contingent on renewal of our grant] with data for The Complete and Final Fiction: e.g. analyses of all extant fiction, its motifs, structures,

strategies, etc. Production of an abstract model of the perfect narrative, refined from such crudities as are now available, e.g. the "Swan-Geese" formula cited earlier. Toad that under cold stone days and nights has 31 sweltered venom sleeping got.

3. 1968/69 (Year V): 1st trial printouts of RN and analysis of same. Fillet of a fenny snake.
4. 1969/70 (Year E): Completion of analysis. Eye of newt. Reprogramming of LILYVAC II (or construction of LILYVAC III) for composition of Final Fiction RN.
5. 1970/71 (Year L): Final print-out of NOVEL (i.e., RN). Revelation of true identity. Rout of impostors and pretenders. Assumption of throne of France. Restoration of "Harrison Mack II" to throne of England. Destruction of all existing stocks of insecticides and prohibition of their manufacture forever. Toe of frog. Reunion with parents. Commencement of New Golden Age.

We have explained already that LILYVAC found it unnecessary actually to compose the hypothetical fictions, having adumbrated their possibility and demonstrated the capacity. Nor can it be said that the creature who appended his name to the false Giles has been neutralized: we have not got all the birds out of LILYVAC I, and its capacity, while exceeding what could have been expected of so modest a facility, falls short of our requirements for years O through L—a discrepancy which we look to the Tidewater Foundation to rectify. But he shall pay.

Moreover and finally, our spring work period was abbreviated by an almost successful attempt on the part of our enemies to assassinate us in late May of this year. In the guise of Chautauqua County officials and with the pretext of "fogging the woods around Lily Dale against lake-flies," they laid a cloud of poison gas about the car in which Ms. Bernstein and we had parked, en route from our afternoon's work, in order to review our draft of this very letter. Thanks to her quick action in rolling up the windows and taking the wheel, and the admirable traction of our loyal VW on marshy woodland lanes, we made good our escape. Ms. Bernstein, we are relieved to report, suffered no more than a few tears and sneezes; we on the other hand were gassed to unconsciousness for 24 hours, suffered delirium, nausea, poisoned entrails, and muscular spasms for the following week, and still experience occasional twitches and a sustained low-grade nervous disorder. They shall pay.

But we survived! (The innocent lake-blanks, alas, did not.) And, come August 15 and the commencement of our fall work period, we shall proceed with the implementation of Year O, for which nothing is wanted save sufficient funding for the redesign of LILYVAC I. And while such funding is available to us from several sources, the voice of History directs us to RESET Complimentary Close

JBB

F: *Ambrose Mensch to Yours Truly (and Lady Amherst)*. *A de-cla-ra-ti-on and an ex-hor-ta-ti-on. With several postscripts.*

The Lighthouse, Mensch's Castle
Erdmann's Cornlot
Dorset, Maryland

March 3, 1969

FROM: Ambrose Mensch, Whom It Concerned
TO: Yours Truly (cc. Germaine Pitt)
RE: Your blank and anonymous letter to me of May 12, 1940

Dear Sir or Madam:
Fill in the blank: AMBROSE LOVES _____.

A.

P.S. (to G.P.): Dear Distinguished Visiting Lecturer in English and Acting Provost of the Faculty of Letters of Marshyhope State University College Germaine Gordon Pitt Lady Amherst: I love you! And I shall in your pursuit surely make an ass of

P.P.S.: Sixth love of my life, admirable GGPLA: here are the first five "Words of Five Syllables" in the old *New England Primer:*

> Ad-mi-ra-ti-on
> Be-ne-fi-ci-al
> Con-so-la-ti-on
> De-cla-ra-ti-on
> Ex-hor-ta-ti-on

They correspond, sort of, to this affair's predecessors; also to the Story Thus Far (thus far unknown to you) of our relation, whereof we are come to Stage D already and shall by this letter be fetched E-ward.

In my student days, Lady, when science had still not purged itself of 19th-Century pathos, the first principle of embryology was that Ontogeny Recapitulates Phylogeny: that the evolutionary history of the individual rehearses the ditto of his race. Law too lovely to be true! Which therefore I here take as first rule of my next fiction: its plot shall be the hero's recapitulation, at the midpoint of his life, of his Story Thus Far, the exposition and complications of its first half, to the end of directing his course through the climax and dénouement of its second. My hero Perseus (or whoever), like a good navigator, will decide where to go by determining where he is by reviewing where he's been. And inasmuch as my life here in the Lighthouse is itself a species of fiction, it follows that law of reenactment. On May 12, 1940, when I was ten, I found a note in a bottle along the Choptank River shore just downstream from where I write this: half a sheet of coarse ruled stuff, torn from a tablet and folded thrice; on a top line was penned in deep red ink TO WHOM IT MAY CONCERN; on the next-to-bottom, YOURS TRULY. The lines between were blank—a blank I've been trying now for 29 years to fill! All my fictions, all my facts, Germaine, are replies to that *carte blanche;* this, like them, I'll bottle and post into the broad Choptank, to run with the tide past cape and cove, black can, red nun, out of the river and the Bay, down to the oceans of the world. My Perseus story (if I write it) will echo its predecessors as middle-aged Perseus rehearses his prior achievements, before adding to their number; the house I live in is built from the stones of my family's history, our past fiascos reconfigured. (And Marshyhope's up-going Tower of Truth, worse luck for it, is rising on footers of those same false stones.) No wonder, then, dear G, if to my eyes these ABC's from the *N.E.P.* spell *Q.E.D.* E.g.:

1. *Ad-mi-ra-ti-on.* When first I beheld you in the halls of Marshyhope last fall, an English tea rose among our native cattails and marsh lilies, et cetera. In fact, admirable lady, as a sometime scholar I had admired already your editions of Mme de Staël's letters and your articles on her connection with Gibbon, Byron, Constant, Napoleon, Jefferson, Rousseau, Schlegel, & Co.; also your delicate commentary on Héloïse's letters to Peter Abelard; also your discreet recollections of H. G. Wells, James Joyce, Hermann Hesse, Aldous Huxley, Evelyn Waugh, and Thomas Mann. *Oeuvre*wise, milady, we were well met ere we met!

Even if, as I quite imagine, my own obscure, tentative, maverick "writings" (I mean the works of "Arthur Morton King") have yet to swim into your ken. What must you make, Fair Embodiment of the Great Tradition, of my keyless codes, my chain-letter narratives with missing links, my edible anecdotes, my action-fictions, my *récits concrets,* my tapes and slides and assemblages and *histoires trouvées?* No matter: yours not to admire, but to be admired! I know a little of your history; I admire it. I know a bit more of your struggle with our horse's ass of an acting president, John

who does not even caricature very well. . .; I admire it. I know what I hear of your kindness to poor old Harrison Mack in his last year or so. . .; ditto, perhaps most of all.

2. *Be-ne-fi-ci-al* it has been to my somewhat battered spirit to work with you on the ad hoc nominating committee for the MSUC Litt.D. My

curriculum vitae, as you must know from your provostial files, has been on the margins of the academic as well as of the literary establishment; I've used the campuses, and been by them used, only in times of material or spiritual want: a chronic but intermittent and seldom intense condition. Enough for this postpostscript to say that Affair E had ended, painfully, last summer: as sore a business as Aeneas's jilting Dido, but not, I trust, so fatal. Imagine an Aeneas who has ceased to love the queen, yet who for various reasons does not cut his anchor cables and run for Rome, but stays on in Carthage, in the very palace! Too distracted to compose (I was anyhow done with avant-garde contraptions, was looking for a way back to aboriginal narrative, a route to the roots), I lost myself with relief in the easier gratifications of teaching, reading, committee work, and the search for a project to reorient me with my muse: to bridge the aforementioned gap between Whence and Whither.

Thus lost, what I found instead was a muse to reorient me with my projects—a role you were serenely unaware of playing. That you had personally known, even been on more or less intimate terms with, several old masters of modernist fiction as well as their traditionalist counterparts, made you for me Literature Incarnate, or The Story Thus Far, whose next turning I'd aspired to have a hand in. That you were. . .a few years my senior (who have been 40 since I was 20, and shall continue to be till 60) aroused me the more: for so is Literature! Your casualest remarks I read as portents and fetched to the Lighthouse to examine for their augury. "Did you know," you asked me once over post-committee coffee in the Faculty Club, "that James Joyce was terribly interested in the cinema, and had a hand in opening the first movie-house in Dublin? But of course, as his eyesight failed. . ." And you added, "Curious that Jorge Borges, our other great sightless modernist, has always been attracted to the cinema too; I believe he's even done filmscripts, hasn't he?" Yet you had no idea that I was at that moment wrestling with the old rivalry between page and screen, making notes for an unfilmable filmscript, and being tempted by Reg Prinz's invitation to do a screenplay of a certain old friend's new book! What's more, one of the principals of that book itself (at least in my screenplay notes) is a woman much resembling yourself, who has a tempestuous affair with a brash American some calendar years her junior and some light-years her social inferior! If our connection was not plotted in heaven, dear Germaine, it's because our Author lives elsewhere. May you too find it *be-ne-fi-ci-al!*

3. As I hope you found my attempt at *con-so-la-ti-on* last month at Harrison Mack's funeral, when, it seemed to me, our relationship escalated to a third stage. For one thing, I *touched* you—even embraced you for the first time, under pretext of consoling a bereft colleague. You were startled! But for all you knew, such unwonted familiarity might be customary among Americans: another manifestation of our aggressive informality, like my suddenly addressing you as "Germaine"

40

instead of "Lady Amherst" or (à la Schott) "Mrs. Pitt." Yet it's an English proverb, not an American, that the time to pay court to a widow is en route home from the funeral. If you were not quite rewidowed by Mack's death (not having been quite his wife), I wasn't quite paying court yet, either, when I seized the opportunity of your uncertain new standing at Tidewater Farms to console you diplomatically out to dinner and back to your pre-Mack lodgings.

There—by confiding to your new friend-in-need that you had no convenient way to remove from the Mack residence a number of gifts from His Late Majesty which ought not to be inventoried with his estate, and by permitting me to oblige you by fetching them at once in my car, and by confiding further thereupon (at my request and discreetly) some details of the George III/Lady Pembroke masquerade you'd carried off so admirably to old Mack's benefit—you gave me grounds to confide to *you* my own more-or-less bereft and therefore eligible status as a divorcé with custody of a handicapped daughter.

For which afflictions of fortune you duly consoled me in your turn. Whence we moved to consoling each other, with your good Dry Sack, for the limitations of life in the academic and geographical backwaters of my Maryland; and you complimented my speech with having but a very inconspicuous American accent, and no Eastern Shore brogue at all; and I complimented you on your graceful acceptance of your fallen lot—but was by this time lost in admiration of your yet-youthful great gray eyes, your less gray hair, your excellent skin (especially for a Briton, Ma'am) and dentition, your sturdy breasts and waist and hips—which, together with your okay legs, put me strickenly in mind of Never Mind Whom, fifth love of my life, that Dido aforementioned (but *her* thighs tended to Italian amplitude, yours to a Kentish, downs-trekking, partridge-potting muscularity).

Consoled and consoling to my cups by midnight, having exploited your reluctance to be rude, but acceding at last to your reminder that Monday was a workday for the living, I went home to my Lighthouse imagining how it would be to divest an acting provost and genuine English gentlewoman of her tweeds. Would her underthings give off heather, saddle leather? Her voice—of all her admirables the admirablest, the very pitch and timbre of *La Belle Lettre sans Merci*—what does it say, how sound, in carnal transport? Et cetera—my interest mounting, so to speak, in the month between then and now. I contemplate as always my camera obscura (of which, as of the Lighthouse and Mensch's Castle, more anon); but instead of the river, the town, the vanished seawall which begins our family saga, I see you.

4. *De-cla-ra-ti-on:* AMBROSE LOVES <u>LADY AMHERST</u>.

5. *Ex-hor-ta-ti-on:* Dear dignified Germaine: let us be lovers! Come play Danaë in this cracked tower! Muse of Austen, Dickens, Fielding, Richardson, and the rest: reclaim your prodigal! Speak love to me, Mother Tongue! O Britannia, your lost colony is reconquered!

P.P.P.S.: The sixth word, Ma'am, is *for-ni-ca-ti-on.*

41

P.P.P.P.S.: The seventh, *ge-ne-ra-ti-on!*

P.P.P.P.P.S.: The eighth and ninth—but seven will suffice. We have come to that sixth, Sixth Sweetheart: I declare a state of loving war upon your heart as upon a tower, which I will take by storm or siege unless, as I exhort, you yield in the great tradition of British triumphs and defeats: without a fuss. In letters to come (i.e., to go, bottled and corked, to Yours Truly on future tides) I shall fill in some earlier blanks. Till when I declare myself, exhortingly, my A.,

Your
A

G: *The Author to the Reader.* LETTERS *is "now" begun.*

"March 2, 1969"

Dear Reader, and
    Gentles all: *LETTERS* is now begun, its correspondents introduced and their stories commencing to entwine. Like those films whose credits appear after the action has started, it will now pause.
    If "now" were the date above, I should be writing this from Buffalo, New York, on a partly sunny Sunday mild for that area in that season, when Lake Erie is still frozen and the winter's heaviest snowfall yet ahead. On the 61st day of the 70th year of the 20th century of the Christian calendar, the human world and its American neighborhood, having survived, in the main, the shocks of "1968" and its predecessors, stood such-a-way: Clay Shaw was acquitted on a charge of involvement in the assassination of President John Kennedy, Sirhan Sirhan was pleading in vain to be executed for assassinating Senator Robert Kennedy, and James Earl Ray was about to be convicted of assassinating the Reverend Martin Luther King, Jr. Ex-President Dwight Eisenhower was weakening toward death after abdominal surgery in February; ex-President Lyndon Johnson, brought down by the Viet Nam War, had retired to Texas; his newly inaugurated successor, Richard M. Nixon, was in Paris conferring with French President de Gaulle and considering the Pentagon's new antiballistic missile program. The North Vietnamese were pressing a successful offensive toward Saigon while the Paris peace conference—finally begun in January after the long dispute over seating arrangements—entered Week Six of its four-year history. Everywhere university students were rioting: the Red Guard was winding up Mao's Cultural Revolution in China; the University of Rome was closed; martial law had been imposed here and there in Spain, tear gas and bayonets in Berkeley and Madison; in Prague students were burning themselves alive to protest Soviet occupation of their country. Hostility between the Russians and the Chinese was on the verge of open warfare at the border of Sinkiang Province; along

42

Israel's borders with Egypt, Syria, and Jordan, things once again had crossed that verge. The U.S.S. *Pueblo* inquiry, souvenir of one war ago, was still in progress. The Apollo-9 spacecraft was counting down for launch toward its moon-orbiting mission, the French-British *Concorde* for the first supersonic transport flight, both to be accomplished on the following day. Ribonuclease, the "key to life," had just been synthesized for the first time in a chemical laboratory; in another, also for the first time, a human egg was successfully fertilized outside the human body. The economy of the United States was inflating at a slightly higher annual rate than the 4.7% of 1968, which had been the highest in seventeen years; the divorce rate was the highest since 1945. Having affirmed the legality of student protest "within limits," our Supreme Court was deciding on the other hand to permit much broader use of electronic surveillance devices by law-enforcement agencies. Every fourth day of the year, on the average, an airliner had been hijacked: fifteen so far. Before the month expired, so would Mr. Eisenhower; and before the year, Senator Everett Dirksen, Levi Eshkol, Ho Chi Minh, and Mary Jo Kopechne, with difficult consequences for Senator Edward Kennedy. Tom Mboya would be assassinated in Nairobi, Sharon Tate and her friends massacred in California, large numbers of Southeast Asians in Southeast Asia. Sirhan Sirhan would be sentenced to death, James Earl Ray to 99 years' imprisonment; Charles Manson and Family would be arrested and charged with the Tate killings, but the Green Beret murder trials would be dropped when the C.I.A. forbade its implicated agents to testify. Abe Fortas would resign from the U.S. Supreme Court and be replaced by Warren Burger, whose court (in opposition to President Nixon) would order immediate desegregation of Southern schools and soften the penalties for possession of marijuana; the U.S. Court of Appeals would reverse the 1968 conviction of Dr. Benjamin Spock and his alleged coconspirators; and Judge Julius Hoffman would begin the trial of the Chicago Seven for inciting riot at the 1968 Democratic National Convention. The Russian-Chinese border fighting would be "resolved" by talks between Aleksei Kosygin and Chou En-lai, and Chairman Mao would declare the Cultural Revolution accomplished. While the Paris peace talks reached an impasse, the cost to the United States of the Viet Nam War would reach 100 billion dollars, fresh U.S. atrocities would be reported, the draft lottery would begin, the first contingent of American troops would be withdrawn from South Viet Nam, the Defense Department would deny, untruthfully, the presence and activity of U.S. forces in Laos, the student riots, strikes, and building seizures would spread to every major campus in the nation, and a quarter-million demonstrators, the largest such crowd in the 193 years of the Republic, would march in Washington on the occasion of the "Moratorium." U.S. forces in Spain would practice putting down a hypothetical anti-Franco uprising; U Thant would declare the Mideast to be in a state of war; the British Army would take over the policing of Northern Ireland after a resurgence of warfare between Catholics and Protestants; China would explode thermonuclear test weapons in the atmosphere; the U.S. and Russia would reply with underground thermonuclear explosions of their own, in the Aleutians and Siberia, and begin arms-limitation conferences in Helsinki. President Ayub would resign in Pakistan, Georges Pompidou would succeed Charles de Gaulle in France, Golda Meir the late Levi Eshkol in Israel, and a military junta the deposed president of Bolivia. Nixon would lift the ban on arms sales to Peru (and meet with President Thieu on Midway, and exercise his broader "bugging" rights against political dissenters, and postpone the fall desegregation deadline for Southern schools, and close the Job Corps camps, and visit South Viet Nam, and greet the returning Apollo-11 astronauts aboard the U.S.S. *Hornet)*. Those latter, and their successors in Apollo-12, would have left the first human footprints on the moon and fetched home a number of its rocks to prove it, despite which evidence a great many Americans would half-believe the whole exploit to have been faked by their government and the television networks; the Mariner spacecrafts 6 and 7 would photograph canalless, lifeless Mars; Russia's Venus 5 and 6 would reach their namesake planet and reveal it also to be devoid of life. The New York State legislature would defeat a liberalized abortion bill. Complete eyes would join hearts and kidneys on the growing list of successfully transplanted human parts. The Department of Health, Education, and Welfare would recommend an absolute ban on the use of DDT. Unemployment, inflation, prime-interest, and first-class-postage rates would rise in the United States, the stock market plunge; 900 heroin deaths, mostly of young people, would be reported in New York City; the Netherlands would temporarily shut off public water when U.S. nerve gas accidentally poisoned the Rhine. Dorchester County, Maryland, would celebrate its Tercentenary; fire would melt a wax museum at Niagara Falls, and the American Falls itself would be turned off for engineering surveys. At least six more airliners would be hijacked; Thor Heyerdahl in *Ra I* would embark upon the Atlantic, along with tropical storms Anna, Blanche, Carol, Debbie, Eve, Francelia, Gerda, *et al.;* in East Pakistan a child would be swallowed by a python; the National Committee on Violence would describe the 1960's as one of the most violent decades in United States history, but the French wine-growers association would declare '69 a vintage year.

But every letter has two times, that of its writing and that of its reading, which may be so separated, even when the post office does its job, that very little of what obtained when the writer wrote will still when the reader reads. And to the units of epistolary fictions yet a third time is added: the actual date of composition, which will not likely correspond to the letterhead date, a function more of plot or form than of history. It is *not* March 2, 1969: when I began this letter it was October 30, 1973: an inclement Tuesday morning in Baltimore, Maryland. The Viet Nam War was "over"; its peacemakers were honored with the Nobel Prize; the latest Arab-Israeli war, likewise "over," had preempted our attention, even more so the "energy crisis" it occasioned, and the Watergate scandals and presidential-impeachment moves—from which neither of those other crises perfectly diverted us. The campuses were quiet; the peacetime draft had ended; détente had been declared with Russia and proposed with China—unthinkable in 1969!—but the American defense budget was more enormous than ever. In Northern Ireland the terrorism continued; the generals had taken over in Greece and Chile, and Juan Perón was back in Argentina; Sirhan Sirhan and James Earl Ray were still in jail, joined by Charles Manson and Lieutenant Calley of the My Lai massacre. The Apollo space program was finished; there would not likely be another human being on the moon in this century. We were anticipating the arrival of the newly discovered comet Kohoutek, which promised to be the most spectacular sight in the sky for many decades. Meanwhile the U.S. Supreme Court had struck down all antiabortion laws but retreated from its liberal position on pornography, and the *re*trials of the Chicago Seven had begun. The prime interest rate was up to 10%, the Dow-Jones Industrial Average, after a bad year, up to 980, first-class postage up to eight cents an ounce. Airport security measures had virtually eliminated skyjacking except by Palestinian terrorists; the "fuel shortage," in turn, was occasioning the elimination of many airline flights. Plans for the 1976 U.S. Bicentennial were floundering.

Now it's not 10/30/73 any longer, either. In the time between my first setting down "March 2, 1969" and now, "now" has become January 1974. Nixon won't go away; neither will the "energy crisis" or inflation-plus-recession or the dreadfulnesses of nations and their ongoing history. The other astronomical flop, Kohoutek, will, to return in 75,000 years, as may we all. By the time I reach *Yours Truly*. . .

The plan of *LETTERS* calls for a second Letter to the Reader at the end of the manuscript, by when what I've "now" recorded will seem already as remote as "March 2, 1969." By the time *LETTERS* is in print, ditto for what shall be recorded in that final letter. And—to come at last to the last of a letter's times—by the time *your* eyes, Reader, review these epistolary fictive *a*'s-to-*z*'s, the "United States of America" may be setting about its Tri- or Quadricentennial, or be still floundering through its Bi-, or be a mere memory (may it have become again, in that case, like the first half of one's life, at least a pleasant memory). Its citizens and the planet's, not excepting yourself and me, may all be mainly just a few years older. Or perhaps you're yet to have been conceived, and by the "now" your eyes read *now*, every person now alive upon the earth will be no longer, most certainly not excepting

Yours truly,

I: *The Author to Whom It May Concern.* *Three concentric dreams of waking.*

3/9/69: I woke half tranced, understanding where I was but not at once who, or why I was there, or for how long I'd slept. By the sun—and my watch, when I thought to check it—it was yet midsummer midafternoon, a few hours into Cancer, hotter and hazier than when I'd dozed off. The slack tide had turned, was just commencing its second flow; but the marsh was still in full siesta, breathless. Two turkey buzzards circled high over a stand of loblolly pines across the creek from those in whose steaming shade I lay. The only other sign of life, besides the silent files of spartina grass, was the hum of millions upon millions of insects—assassin flies, arthropods, bees above all, and beetles, dragonflies, mosquitoes—going about their business, which, in the case of one *Aedes sollicitans,* involved drawing blood from the back of my right hand until I killed her.

The movement woke me further: I recognized that before consulting my wristwatch I'd felt for a pocketwatch—a silver Breguet with "barleycorn" engine-turning on the case, steel moon hands, and a white enameled face with the seconds dial offset at the VII, the maker's name engraved in secret cursive under the XII, and my father's monogram, *HB,* similarly scribed before the appropriate Roman numeral IV—a watch which I did not possess, had never possessed, which could not with that monogram be my father's, which did not so far as I know exist! Reached for it (in the watch pocket of the vest I didn't wear, didn't own) with more reflexive a motion than then turned my left wrist. I'd perspired in my sleep, whereinto I'd fallen (whence such locutions in—what year was it?) in midst. . .in midst of revisiting the Maryland marshes at the midpoint of my life; perspired the more now, more awake, at feeling one foot still in distant time or dreams.

I knew "myself," come briefly down under Mason and Dixon's to visit certain cattailed, blue-crabbed, oystered haunts of—aye, there was the rub: I had been going to say "my youth," but what that term referred to, like dim stars and ghost crabs, I could not resolve when I looked straight at it. And when I looked away—at a periwinkle, say, self-encapsulated on a nearby reed—from my mind's eye-corner I could just perceive, not one, but several "youths," all leading—but by different paths, in different ages!—to this point of high ground between two creeklets where I lay, stiff as if I'd slept for twenty decades or centuries instead of minutes. There was the neutral, sleep-wrapped, most familiar youth, neither happy nor unhappy, begun in Gemini 1930, raised up in sunny ignorance through Great Depression, Second War, and small-town Southern public schools. I knew *that* chap, all right: dreamer of sub-sea-level dreams from the shores of high transmontane lakes; his was the history most contiguous with the hour I'd waked to.

But beside it, like a still-sleeping leg that its wakened twin can recognize, was another history, a prior youth, to whom that pocket-watch and vest and a brave biography belonged. They shared one name's initial: bee-beta-beth, the Kabbalist's letter of Creation, whence derived, like life itself from the marsh primordial, both the alphabet and the universe it described by its recombinations. Beyond that, and their confluence in the onstreaming Now, they had little in common, for this youth's youth was all bravura, intrigue and derring-do, sophistication and disguise. Coeval of the nation in whose founding his father had played a certain role, he had grown up between its two wars of independence, come to disbelieve in both father and fatherland, striven to disunite the but slightly united states—and then (a lurid memory here of bomb burst, rocket glare: not the clearest of illuminations) at the midpoint of his wayward life had seen a different pattern in the past, changed heart again, retreated from fatherland to Mother Marsh in vast perplexity to sort things out, dozed off for a moment in the resinous shade. . .

Then what was this third, faint-bumbling B, most shadowy of all, but obscured more by mythic leagues of time than by self-effacement or disguise? And not *retreated* to the midday marsh, but fallen into it as though from heaven, become a blind, lame, vatic figure afloat on the tepid tide, reciting a suspect version of his history, dozing off in midexposition. . .?

I woke half tranced, understanding where I was but not at once why I was there. Then the dream came clear. It's Sunday afternoon, March 9, '69, 157th anniversary of President Madison's disclosure of the notorious "Henry Letters" to Congress in 1811, cool and cloudy in Buffalo, New York. I have breakfasted early, read through the Sunday *Times*, taken a restless midafternoon nap—and dreamed once again of waking in the Maryland marshes.

No doubt the dream, above recorded, had been prompted by a recent invitation to visit that state in June for my maiden honorary degree. Its content was clear: my ancient wish to write the comic epic that Ebenezer Cooke, 17th-Century Laureate of Maryland, put aside to write his *Sot-Weed Factor*, and which I myself put aside for the novel *LETTERS: a Marylandiad*. Its hero would live the first half of his life in the first three dozen years of the republic (say, 1776–1812) and the second half in its "last" (say, 1940–1976), with a 128-year nap between, during which—unlike Rip Winkle's case—the country ages but the sleeper doesn't. Enjoying the celebrated midlife crisis, he wanders alone at midday (make it 21 June 1812 or thereabouts) into the marshes, "devouring his own soul," etc., dozes off, and wakes as it seems to him a very short while later. Begin perhaps with his waking, half tranced, with that odd sense of an additional past, a double history, one contiguous to "now" and one Revolutionary.

But in this latest dream there was a third. . .

47

Relate: Greece is to Rome as Rome is to the U.S.: *translatio studii,* "westward the course of empire," "manifest destiny." Joel Barlow, Philip Freneau. *Iliad: Aeneid::Aeneid:Marylandiad,* the second an imitation of the first, the third a parody of the second.

Back to *LETTERS:* notes on Ambrose Mensch's story about Perseus, Andromęda, Medusa.

Work in: "2nd Revolution" (1812 War called Second War of Independence). Eben Cooke's *Sot-Weed Redivivus* (1730). Roman economy slave-based, like early U.S.; Romans "invented" satire (also, especially under Augustus, bureaucracy, civil service, the mercantile middle class, and red tape). Ebenezer Cooke an "Augustan" poet. Rome built on *marshes* between those seven hills. Crank explanation of Empire's fall: anopheles mosquito from those marshes. Sleeping sickness. Cooke in *Sot-Weed Redivivus* advises Marylanders to drain marshes. Philip Freneau traces Indians from Carthaginians; ditto Cooke in *The Sot-Weed Factor* (1698).

Marshes: associated with both decay and fertility, female genitalia (cf. Freudians on Medusa), death and rebirth, miasma (pestilence, ague, rheumatism, sinusitis), evil, damnation, stagnation (e.g. Styx, Avernus; also Ezekiel 47:11). Behemoth sleeps in cover of reeds (Job 40:11). Marsh ibis sacred to Thoth, inventor of writing. Reed pens and styli; papyri. East Anglia fenlands associated with eccentricity, independent-spiritedness, fertility, dialects, odd customs. "The Marsh King" (Alfred the Great, 848?–900). 12th-Century Chinese story-cycle *Shui-liu Chuan:* "Men of the Marshes." Maryland is "Border State": tidewater marsh also, between land and sea. Irish bog-peat: not only sphagnum but shrub *Andromeda.*

Back to Perseus.

Great sleepers, arranged alphabetically: Arthur, Barbarossa, Brunhilde, Charlemagne, Francis Drake, Endymion, Epimenides, Finnegan, Herla, Honi the Circle Drawer, John the Divine, Peter Klaus, Lazarus, Mahdi, Merlin, Odin, Ogier the Dane, Oisin, old Rip (fell asleep just before Revolution, woke after), Roderick the Goth, Sebastian of Portugal, the Seven Ephesians, Siegfried, Sleeping Beauty, Tannhäuser, William Tell, Thomas of Erceldoune, Wang Chih.

Postscript 3/9/74: I wake half tranced, understanding where I am and then, aha, why I'm here: in Baltimore, whereto I'd not contemplated moving at all in 1969. Once again the fiction has been not autobiographic but mildly prophetic. In 1960, in the draft of a story about Ambrose Mensch, I placed a nonexistent point of land on the south bank of Choptank River just downstream from the bridge at Cambridge, Maryland; in 1962 the Corps of Engineers redredged the ship channel, dumped the spoil where the old East Cambridge seawall was, and *voilà!* Having decided in 1968 that the "Author" character in *LETTERS* would be offered an honorary doctorate of letters from a Maryland university, I receive in 1969 just such an invitation in the mail. And presuming in 1969 to imagine, in notes for Jerome Bonaparte Bray's story *Bellerophoniad*, a "hero" (Bellerophon, slayer of the Chimera) who falls from mythic irreality into the present-day Maryland marshes—I find myself back in the Old Line State.

Just as Eben Cooke put aside his *Marylandiad* to write *The Sot-Weed Factor*—and the "editor" of *Giles Goat-Boy* put aside his novel *The Seeker* to edit *The Revised New Syllabus,* and J. Bray's LILYVAC computer put aside its *Concordance* to propose the revolutionary novel *NOTES*—so I put aside, in 1968, in Buffalo, a *Marylandiad* of my own in favor of the novel *LETTERS,* whereof Mensch's *Perseid* and Bray's *Bellerophoniad* were to be tales-within-the-tale. Then, in '69, '70, and '71, I put by *LETTERS* in pursuit of a new chimera called *Chimera:* serial novellas about Perseus, Bellerophon, and Scheherazade's younger sister. Now (having put by Buffalo for Baltimore) it's back to *LETTERS,* to history, to "realism". . .and to the revisitation of a certain marsh where once I wandered, dozed, dreamed.

But though I have returned to Maryland, I shall not to Cooke's *Marylandiad*. One must take care what one dreams. And there are projects whose fit fate is preemption: works meant ever to be put aside for works more pressing; dreams whose true and only dénouement is the dreamer's waking in the middle, half tranced, understanding where he is but not at once why he's there.

LETTERS: an old time epistolary novel by seven fictitious drolls & dreamers, each of which imagines himself actual. They will write always in this order: Lady Amherst, Todd Andrews, Jacob Horner, A. B. Cook, Jerome Bray, Ambrose Mensch, the Author. Their letters will total 88 (this is the eighth), divided unequally into seven sections according to a certain scheme: see Ambrose Mensch's model, postscript to Letter 86 (Part S, p. 769). Their several narratives will become one; like waves of a rising tide, the plot will surge forward, recede, surge farther forward, recede less far, et cetera to its climax and dénouement.

On with the story.

49

N: *The Author to Lady Amherst. Politely declining her invitation.*

Department of English, Annex B
State University of New York at Buffalo
Buffalo, New York 14214

March 16, 1969

Prof. Germaine G. Pitt (Amherst)
Acting Provost, Faculty of Letters
Marshyhope State University
Redmans Neck, Maryland 21612

Dear Professor Pitt (Amherst?):

Not many invitations could please me more, ordinarily, than yours of March 8. Much obliged, indeed.

By coincidence, however, I accepted in February a similar invitation from the main campus of the State University at College Park (it seems to be my year down there), and I feel that two degrees in the same June from the same Border State would border upon redundancy. So I decline, with thanks, and trust that the ominous matters you allude to in your remarkable postscript can be forestalled in some other wise.

Why not award the thing to our mutual acquaintance Ambrose Mensch? He's an honorable, deserving oddball and a bona fide avant-gardist, whose "career" I've followed with interest and sympathy. A true "doctor of letters" (in the Johns Hopkins Medical School sense), he is a tinkerer, an experimenter, a slightly astigmatic visionary, perhaps even a revolutionizer of cures—and patient Literature, as your letter acknowledges, if not terminal, is not as young as she used to be either.

Cordially,

P.S.: "I have made this longer only because I did not have the leisure to make it shorter": Pascal, *Letters provinciales,* XVI. Perhaps Mme de Staël was paraphrasing Pascal?
P.P.S.: Do the French not customarily serve the salad *after* the entrée?

E: *The Author to Lady Amherst. A counterinvitation.*

Department of English, Annex B
State University of New York at Buffalo
Buffalo, New York 14214

March 23, 1969

Prof. Germaine G. Pitt (Amherst)
Acting Provost, Faculty of Letters
Marshyhope State University
Redmans Neck, Maryland 21612

Dear Professor Pitt (Amherst):

Ever since your letter of March 8, I have been bemused by two coincidences (if that is the word) embodied in it, of a more vertiginous order than the simple coincidence of the College Park invitation, which I had already accepted, and yours from Marshyhope, which I felt obliged therefore to decline in my letter to you of last Sunday.

The first coincidence is that, some months before the *earlier* invitation—last year, in fact, when I began making notes toward a new novel—I had envisioned just such an invitation to one of its principal characters. Indeed, an early note for the project (undated, but from mid-1968) reads as follows:

> A man (A——?) is writing letters to a woman (Z——?). A is "a little past the middle of the road," but feels that "the story of his life is just beginning," *in medias res.* Z is (*a*) Nymph, (*b*) Bride, and (*c*) Crone; also Muse: i.e., *Belles Lettres.* A is a "Doctor of Letters" (honorary Litt.D.): degree awarded for "contribution to life of literature." Others allege he's hastening its demise; would even charge him with malpractice. Etc.

Then arrived in the post the College Park invitation in February and yours in March. I was spooked more by the second than the first, since it came not only from another Maryland university, but from— well, consider this other notebook entry, under the heading "Plot A: Lady ____ & the Litt.D.":

> A (British?) belletrist "of a certain age," she has been the Great Good Friend of sundry distinguished authors, perhaps even the original of certain of their heroines and the inspiration of their novels. Sometimes intimates that *she* invented their best conceptions, her famous lovers merely transcribing as it were her conceits, fleshing out her ideas—and not always faithfully (i.e., "doctoring" her letters to them). Etc.

This circa September 1968. Then, two weeks ago, your letter, with its extraordinary postscript. . .

Hence my bemusement. For autobiographical "fiction" I have only disdain; but what's involved here strikes me less as autobiography than as a muddling of the distinction between Art and Life, a boundary as

51

historically notorious as Mason and Dixon's line. That life sometimes imitates art is a mere Oscar Wilde-ish curiosity; that it should set about to do so in such unseemly haste that between notes and novel (not to mention between the drafted and the printed page) what had been fiction becomes idle fact, invention history—disconcerting! Especially to a fictionist who, like yours truly, had long since turned his professional back on literary realism in favor of the fabulous irreal, and only in this latest enterprise had projected, not without misgiving, a détente with the realistic tradition. It is as if Reality, a mistress too long ignored, must now settle scores with her errant lover.

So, my dear Lady Amherst: this letter—my second to you, ninth in the old *New England Primer*—is an *In-vi-ta-ti-on* which, whether or not you see fit to accept it, I pray you will entertain as considerately as I hope I entertained yours of the 8th instant: Will you consent to be A Character in My Novel? That is, may I—in the manner of novelists back in the heroic period of the genre—make use of my imagination of you (and whatever information about yourself it may suit your discretion to provide in response to certain questions I have in mind to ask you) to "flesh out" that character aforenoted? Just as you, from *my* side of this funhouse mirror, seem to have plagiarized my imagination in your actual life story. . .

The request is irregular. For me it is unprecedented—though for all I know it may be routine to an erstwhile friend of Wells, Joyce, Huxley. What I'd like to know is more about your history; your connection with those eminent folk; that "fall" you allude to in your postscript, from such connection to your present circumstances at MSUC; even (as a "lifelong mistress of the arts" you will surely understand) more delicate matters. If I'm going to break another lance with Realism, I mean to go the whole way.

I am tempted to make your acquaintance directly, prevailing upon our mutual friend to do the honors; I'd meant to pay a visit to Dorchester anyhow in June, from College Park. But I recall and understand Henry James's disinclination to hear *too much* of an anecdote the heart of which he recognized as a potential story. Moreover, in keeping with my (still vague) notion of the project, I should prefer that our connection be not only strictly verbal, but epistolary. Cf. James's notebook exclamation: "The correspondences! The correspondences!"

Here's what I can tell you of that project. For as long as I can remember I've been enamored of the old tale-cycles, especially of the frame-tale sort: *The Ocean of Story, The Thousand and One Nights,* the *Pent-, Hept-,* and *Decameron*s. With the help of a research assistant I recently reviewed the corpus of frame-tale literature to see what I could learn from it, and started making notes toward a frame-tale novel. By 1968 I'd decided to use documents instead of told stories: texts-within-texts instead of tales-within-tales. Rereading the early English novelists, I was impressed with their characteristic awareness that they're *writing*

—that their fictions exist in the form, not of sounds in the ear, but of signs on the page, imitative not of life "directly," but of its documents— and I considered marrying one venerable narrative tradition to another: the frame-tale and the "documentary" novel. By this time last year I had in mind "an open (love) letter to Whom It May Concern, from Yours Truly." By April, as grist for what final mill I was still by no means certain, I had half a workbookful of specific formal notes and "incidental felicities": e.g., "Bit #46," from Canto XVIII of Dante's *Paradiso:* the choirs of the blessed, like sailors in formation on an aircraft-carrier deck or bandsmen at halftime in an American football match, spell out with themselves on the billboard of Heaven DILIGITE IUSTITIAM QUI IUDICATIS TERRAM ("Love justice, [ye] who judge [on] earth"); or #47, an old English hornbook riddle in the Kabbalistic tradition of the Holy Unspeakable Name of God: "AEIOU His Great Name doth Spell;/Here it is known, but is not known in Hell."

I could go on, and won't. "The correspondences!" I was ready to begin. All I lacked were—well, characters, theme, plot, action, diction, scene, and format; in short, a story, a way to tell it, and a voice to tell it in!

Now I have a story, at least in rough prospectus, precipitated by this pair of queer coincidences. Or if not a story in Henry James's sense, at least a narrative method in Scheherazade's.

But it is unwise to speak much of plans still tentative. Will you be my "Lady A," my heroine, my creation?

And permit *me* the honor of being, as in better-lettered times gone by, your faithful

Author

2

1969	S	**N**	**O**	**L**	**D**		*Lady Amherst*
	F	**Y**	11	18	25		*Todd Andrews*
	T	**T**	10	17	24		*Jacob Horner*
	W	**R**	**O**	16	23	30	*A. B. Cook*
	T	**R**	8	15	22	29	*Jerome Bray*
APRIL	M	**W**	7	14	21	28	*Ambrose Mensch*
	S	**S**	**H**	**I**	**M**	27	*The Author*

N: *Lady Amherst to the Author. Rejecting his counterinvitation.*

Office of the Provost
Faculty of Letters
Marshyhope State University
Redmans Neck, Maryland 21612

5 April 1969

Mr John Barth, Esq.
Dept of English, Annex B
SUNY/Buffalo

Dear Mr B.:
    No!
    I am *not* Literature! I am *not* the Great Tradition! I am *not* the
aging Muse of the Realistic Novel! I am not

                                Yours,
                                Germaine G. Pitt (Amherst)
                                Acting Provost
GGP(A)/ss

O: *Lady Amherst to the Author. Reconsidering.*

Office of the Provost
Faculty of Letters
Marshyhope State University
Redmans Neck, Maryland 21612

12 April 1969

Dear Mr B.:
    On the 22nd of this month I shall turn. . .forty-five. Germaine de
Staël, at that age, had borne four children—one by her husband, two by
her lover Narbonne, one by her lover Benjamin Constant—and was
about to conceive her fifth and last, by a coarse young fellow half her
age, whom her son Auguste (almost his coeval) called Caliban. The
child, imbecilic last fruit of middle-aged passion, fatigue, and opium,
would be named Giles, attributed to fictitious parents (Theodore Giles
of Boston and Harriette, née Preston), and regarded jokingly by the
household as a native American. . . But Germaine herself much
admired Americans; spoke of them on her deathbed as *"l'avant-garde du
genre humain, l'avenir du monde";* was in correspondence with Thomas

Jefferson and Gouverneur Morris about moving to her property in Leroysville, New York, to escape Napoleon—and herself nicknamed her idiot child by her peasant lover *Petit Nous:* "Little Us". . .

We British are great stoics; we French, famously unsentimental. But I cannot reflect on these things dry-eyed. I have no children (and no novels, and no estates), but my years have been hardly less vicissitudinous than my namesake's; more so than anyone supposes; more so than I myself can believe. In our place and time a woman my age may expect, for better or worse, three or four decades yet to live; in this country especially, she may look and dress half her age, play tennis daily, dance all night, take lovers and the Pill. . .

Today, sir, I am very tired; those decades to come weigh me down like a heavy sentence. Today I could wish to be a middle-aged widow of the lower class in a Mediterranean village: already wrinkled, fallen-breasted, gone in the teeth, dressed in black, supernumerary, waiting to die.

Well.

Your letter to me of 16 March, declining our honorary degree, was cordial, if disappointing and problematical (the matter is far from resolved). Your follow-up letter of the 23rd was similarly cordial but, at least as I then regarded it, impertinent; hence my peremptory no of Saturday last. My reasons were several, over and above the vexing problem of thwarting John Schott and A. B. Cook; but I was in no humour just then to set them forth. I shall do so now.

In latter March (as promised in my initial letter), I read your *Floating Opera* novel, having been introduced earlier by Ambrose Mensch to the alleged original of your character Todd Andrews. I enjoyed the story—the first novel of an ambitious young man—but I felt a familiar uneasiness about the fictive life of real people and the factual life of "fictional" characters—familiar because, as I'm sure I have intimated, I've "been there before." I could not look forward to being there again: yet again more or less artfully misportrayed for purposes not my own, however commendable; yet again "immortalised" like the victims of Medusa or the candid cameraman: picking their noses, scratching their backsides. Too, there was to be considered the fallen state of Literature, in particular of the Novel, most especially of trade fiction publishing in your country, as I learn about it from Ambrose Mensch. No, no, it was an impertinence, your suggestion that I offer my life for your literary inspection, as women used to offer their handbags for Isaac Babel's!

A life, at that, lately turned 'round such sharp, improbable corners (even in the little space between my first letter and your reply) that I can scarcely recognise it any longer as my own, far less understand or rationally approve it. For Mme de Staël—I think for history generally— April truly *is* the cruellest month, as my old friend and fellow cat-lover once wrote: the tumultuous month when Cain slew Abel, when Jesus (and Dante) descended into Hell; when Shakespeare and Cervantes and

Abraham Lincoln and Martin Luther King, Jr. (and Germaine de Staël's beloved father) all died; when the *Titanic* sank and the American Revolution began and Napoleon abdicated and the crew of the H.M.S. *Bounty* mutinied and all the black slaves in New York rebelled; when both ill-starred Germaines (and *"Petit Nous"*) were born; and when, in 1794, that other, better Germaine wrote despairingly from Coppet to her lover Narbonne in England: "Apparently, everything I believed I meant to you was a dream, and only my letters are real. . . ."

I am distraught, as even my penmanship attests. You found disconcerting, you say, certain "spooky" coincidences between my first letter to you and your notes toward a new novel. *I* find disconcerting, even alarming, some half-prophetic correspondences between your reply and the course of my current life: so much so that I am led (yet another manifestation of *early* middle-aged foolishness, no doubt) seriously to reconsider your proposal, or proposition. I have much to tell, no one to tell it to. . .

But you must swear to me, by the Muse we both honour, that you are not nor have lately been in communication with Ambrose Mensch, as he has sworn to me he is not with you. Can you, sir, will you so swear? To

Yours sincerely,
Germaine Pitt
24 L Street
Dorset Heights, Maryland 21612

L: *Lady Amherst to the Author.* Confessing her latest love affair and the excesses of its current stage.

24 L Street
Dorset Heights, Maryland 21612

19 April 1969

My dear B.,

L Street and its companions—five long vowelled avenues crosshatched through sand and weeds by a score of short consonantal streets—comprise what is euphemistically called, by its "developers," the residential "development" of a large corn and tomato field belonging to Mack Enterprises, Inc. Lying athwart an ever shallower winding creek midway between Cambridge and Redmans Neck, at the vertiginous "Heights" of five to seven feet above mean low water, it consists presently of the low-rise brick apartment house at 24 L—tenanted by new MSUC faculty, married graduate students, and (as of a few weeks ago) myself—and three prefabricated "model homes," unoccupied. The rest is scrub pine, weedy drainage ditches, wooden temporary street signs, and advertising brochures. Mrs Jane Mack, whose backward brainchild Dorset Heights is, confidently expects the burgeoning of

Marshyhope U., and the consequent demand for low-cost housing in its proximity, to turn this paper *polis* into a town half the size of Cambridge by 1976 and to swell her already distended fortune: the capital for its next phase of construction she has borrowed against her expectation of a settlement in her favour, rather than her children's, of her late husband's disputed estate.

Jane and I have, you see, since Harrison Mack's death, become— rather, rebecome—friends: more or less, and *faute de mieux*, and warily at that. The woman is civilised. She is uncommonly handsome for her sixty-some years; could almost pass for my coeval. She is very consciously in that line of shrewd *Baltimoriennes* fatefully attractive to European nobility: Betsy Patterson, Wallis Warfield Simpson. . . We depend, lightly, upon each other's society here in the depths of Dorset Heights (she drops in for a chat at my *pied-à-marais;* I am no longer *non grata* at Tidewater Farms), and this little dependency itself depends on Jane's truly remarkable capacity for repressing disagreeable history. If she remembers my late connexion with poor Harrison, for example, or her earlier, less decorous one with my late husband (my small resentment whereat I had long since put by), she gives no sign of it. But her memory for property values, tax assessments, deed transfers, and common stock quotations is photographic! And the Yankee genius for commercial exploitation has flowered full in her since middle age: in those cool grey eyes there is no such thing as "the land": what the soldier sees as terrain, the artist as landscape, the ecologist as matrix and theatre of natural processes, Jane sees, just as reflexively, as real estate to be developed, or otherwise turned to financial account. About history, tradition, she is utterly unsentimental, except as they might enhance the market value of real property. Such concerns as social equity or the preservation of "undeveloped" environments for their own sake she sincerely regards as madness.

Thus Dorset Heights. Thus L Street (she has offered me a stipend, as a "resource person," to devise "appropriate" names for her alphabetic streets: a notion I thought *echt* mid-20th-Century American until Ambrose informed me that Back Bay Boston was so laid out in the 19th, on fenland drained and filled by Jane's spiritual ancestors). And thus #24, where I write this, half appalled, half envious—"tuning my piano," as your Todd Andrews puts it: waiting only, in order to begin the real substance of this letter, for your assurance that you and Ambrose have not lately been in touch; deciding not to wait after all (What would it matter? Have I not begun confiding already?); wondering really only where properly to begin, and why, and why not.

Yours of the 13th in hand, sir, accepting with polite apologies my rejection of your proposal. A gentlemanly note, for which thanks. Whether I should trust you, there is no way for me to know; but I feel strongly (a familiar, ambivalent feeling) that I *shall,* in any case. Last week I read your second novel, *The End of the Road:* a chilling read withal. Whatever its literary merits, it came obviously as something of a

60

personal revelation to me (as did your first) concerning those several of its characters among whom I dwell: the people we are calling John Schott, Harry Carter, especially poor tragical Joe Morgan, and above all poor pathetical dead Rennie Morgan—with whose heartless exploitation, at least, I readily empathise. I am full of loathing for your narrator Jacob Horner (not only nature abhors a vacuum), who puts me disquietingly in mind of certain traits of my friend A.M., as well as of—

May I ask whether your Remobilisation Farm and its black quack guru were based on anything factual? And whether your "Joe Morgan" has been heard from lately?

Never mind, of course; I know how meaningless such queries are. And I quite understand and sympathise with Horner's inability to account for his submissive connexion to the Doctor, for I have much the same feeling with respect to my own (uncharacteristic!) submission, both to your request for the Story of My Life and to a man to whom I cannot imagine myself being more than civil this time last year.

I mean, as you will have guessed, Ambrose Mensch: my colleague; my junior by half a dozen years, as he voluptuously reminds me; my ally against Schott and Carter in the Great Litt.D. Affair; my friend of the past few months, since the death of Harrison Mack—and, since Thursday, March 20 last, my lover.

Begun, then!

And where it will end, deponent knoweth not, only feareth. What Ambrose makes of me is plain enough and scarcely flattering, despite his assurances that (reversing the order of your own interests) my person attracted him first, my "symbolic potential" only later. What to make of *him* I do not know, nor how much of his past and present you're acquainted with. Like the pallid Tityrus of André Gide's *Marshlands* novel, which Ambrose has not read, he lives a near-hermit life in a sort of tower on the Choptank shore—a tower he has converted into a huge camera obscura! An "expert amateur of life," he calls himself; an "aspirant to honorary membership in humankind." In that sinking tower my lover measures the stars with a homemade astrolabe, inventing new constellations; he examines bemused beneath a microscope his swarming semen, giving names to (and odds on) individual spermatozoa in their blind and general race. He savours a tepid *ménage à trois* of many years' languishing with the soulful East Italian wife of his stolid stonemason older brother ("two Krauts with garlic dressing"); he awaits with mild interest the turning cancerous of a port-wine birthmark on his brow—allegedly bee-shaped, but I see in its outline no more *Apis mellifica* than I see the initials *AMK* (for Arthur Morton King, his *nom de plume*) he claims to find in the constellations Andromeda, Cassiopeia, and Perseus. (Admittedly I can't see Perseus and company there either, only a blinking bunch of stars.) He writes me "love letters" in the form of postscripts to an anonymous Yours Truly, from whom he claims once to have received a blank message in a bottle, and posts them on the Choptank tides (I get photocopies by the regular mail). His notion of wooing is to regale me with accounts of his previous love affairs, to the number of five—a number even less remarkable in that three were with the same woman (that *Abruzzesa* aforementioned) and two of *those* all but sexless.

Indeed, on the evidence of these "letters" and what I'd gathered of his life, I would have judged the man probably impotent, certainly no candidate for loverhood. Not in *my* book, any road, though God knows I've loved some odd ones, H.M. II (R.I.P.) not least among them. With *that* affair, such as it was, I was only just done; I wasn't ready for another of any sort. Moreover, my taste has ever been for older men, make of it what you will: *considerably* older men, who've made some mark in the world. I've no time for nobodies, never have had; were our Tityrus as glamorous as a cinema star (he isn't), I'd not have been interested in his clownish propositions.

So I thought, so I thought—and I thought wrong. My lover is most decidedly not impotent, only regressive and a bit reclusive. Like myself (I now realise, having paid scant attention to such things hitherto) he goes easily for considerable intervals without sexual connexion; then he sets about it as if the thing were just invented, or like a camel tanking up till the next oasis. I like him altogether better as a friend—so I told him frankly when he followed up his first "love letter" with an imperious visit to my office, pressing through Miss Stickles's defences like Napoleon back from Elba. That tidewater Tuileries once attained, he plied his suit so ardently I almost thought he meant a rape, and was anxious less for my "honour" (he had no weapon, and I am not helpless) than, believe it or not, for the integrity of our ad hoc nominating committee for the Litt.D.: an integrity already vulnerable for our having become personal friends.

He exhorted; he declared; he declaimed; he went grinning to his knees, and made for mine. I could not tell how much if any of what he said was seriously meant. He threatened to fetch Shirley Stickles in as witness to his passion. . . We laughed and argued, teased and scolded, once I was assured he was neither drunk nor more than usually deranged. Clearly he was not in earnest—yet my firm insistence that I was not the least attracted to him physically, or interested in any "escalation" of our cordial connexion, but enflamed him the more. And if his words and manner were bantering, his bodily pursuit of me about the office was as unremitting as it was leisurely. I thought myself reprieved by the telephone (Harry Carter, relaying John Schott's apparent nondisapproval of your nomination), but found myself obliged instead to speak in the most unbetraying businesslike tone to Carter and Stickles whilst submitting to my pursuer's (now my captor's) suddenly aggressive embraces. Only my calling in Miss S. to take dictation, whilst I had her on the line, put an end for the present to his advances, which otherwise he would very shortly have pressed to the point of my either yielding entirely or calling for aid. And his departure next day (the same Saturday of my first letter to you) for New York

City, to confer with Mr Prinz about his screenplay draft, prevented his resuming them promptly thereafter.

They were not, as I trust I've implied, abhorrent to me, even repellent, those advances: simply irritating because unwanted. We were not friends enough for me much to fear for our friendship. I am no prude, as shall be seen. Neither of us was celibate by policy or committed to another. Did all those negatives (I asked him on his return, a week or so later) add up to a love affair? This was in my earlier digs, down by the boat harbour in Cambridge, whereinto he had kindly helped me shift from Tidewater Farms after Harrison Mack's funeral. But they were inconvenient, especially as my provostial duties fetched me to the college five or six days a week; and so I bought a small car and leased the flat in Dorset Heights. Hearing that I was about to shift again, Ambrose had kindly turned up with lorry and labourers from Mensch Masonry, his brother's firm, to spare me the expense of hiring movers. I was grateful, the more as he did not this time or in the next few days press his attentions otherwise than verbally. When neither manic nor despondent—to both which extremes the man is given—Ambrose Mensch is the mildest, most agreeable of friends: witty, considerate, good-natured, and well informed. But in the two or three matters which command his imagination at any given time, he is obsessive, and his twin projects for the season, by his ready admission, were my seduction and the besting of Reg Prinz.

Now, a woman may consent to sexual connexion, even to a more or less protracted affair, for no better reason than that persisting in refusal becomes too much bother. Ambrose, very big on solstices and equinoxes, chose Thursday, 20 March, to "make his play." Your letters had arrived, declining the degree and suggesting we give it to Ambrose himself, an unthinkable idea. I'd called a meeting of the nominating committee for 2:30 to decide our next move, and invited Ambrose to stop by my office earlier on and discuss ways of forestalling Harry Carter's inevitable renomination of A. B. Cook. To my surprise he proposed, straight upon entering, that we copulate at once atop the conference table, and took my arm to usher me there. I bade him be serious; he expressed his ardent wish that I bend over my desk and be mounted *a tergo*. I promptly so bent, but only to ring for Shirley Stickles, certain he'd not risk public exposure. As I asked her to come in, however, he called my bluff by hitching up my skirt and down my panty hose (horrid term!). I bade Shirley wait a moment; turned to him furious; found his trouser fly already open, penis out and standing, face all smiles. At the same time, Shirley announced into my ear that President Schott was on the line and *must* speak to me at once; even as she so declared, that unctuous baritone broke in to say he'd heard of your declining and wished, without of course in any way intervening in the committee's deliberations, to read me then and there A. B. Cook's newly published ode, in the *Tidewater Times-Democrat*, comparing Vice-President Spiro Agnew to St Patrick and the liberal news media to serpents. He began to read. As a last defence against Ambrose's assault I tried to sit; the man was in my chair, set to impale. I could not both fend him off and hold the phone; it was madness, madness! And a too tiresome bother. . .

Thus it came to pass that at seven past two (so he told me after), just as the sun entered Aries, Ambrose M. entered yours truly. We both sighed, for quite different reasons. I bent as he wished, resting my elbows on my appointments calendar. Our acting president declaimed so vigorously I was obliged to hold the phone away from my ear. Ambrose took up the beat of Cook's iambics. It had been a while since I'd known as it were more slap than tickle (dear Harrison seldom managed). When *shirts of starchless denim* (the laureate's image for campus activists, who he complained were given too much sympathetic publicity by the media) was rhymed with *squirts of Marxist venom,* we sat as one person, and I assumed the rhythm myself to finish off the business. Then as at last the Effete Eastern Radical-Liberal Establishment was warned pentametrically to

> Take heed:
> For as Patrick drove into the waves of Eire
> Those ancient vipers, so shall Spiro dare
> To drive from our airwaves this later breed!

I received into myself my first installment of the Ambrosian ejaculate.

And reflected—what I had had no cause to concern myself with for some little while—that contraceptive measures had not been taken.

Well, Schott cried, what did I think? "Tell him you'd like to sit on it awhile," Ambrose whispered. I requested a photocopy of the ode for the committee—whose meeting, just a few minutes later, prevented my either taking postcoital precautions or sitting on anything except clammy knickers for the balance of the afternoon.

He had taken vulgar advantage of me, I let Ambrose know at the first opportunity, and had foolishly jeopardised both our positions. That I had acquiesced to his assault rather than precipitate a scandal did not make us lovers or imply my consent to further importunities, certainly not in Shirley Stickles's proximity. He amiably agreed, and by way of reparation stood me that evening to a feast of white wine and raw oysters (a passion of mine, and this region's chief attraction) at the Dorset Hotel. He was animated, gently ribald, in no way presumptuous upon his "conquest." We laughingly reconstructed, as best we could, the Maryland Laureate's ode: at "squirts of Marxist venom" I chided him for not having deployed a French letter for my sake, or at least withdrawn at "waves of Eire." He paid me the compliment of having assumed, so he declared, that I was "on the Pill," and assured me further that, while his sexual potency was reliable, his fertility was not: "High count but low motility, like great schools of dying fish," he put it—and so I learned of his predilection for, so to speak, self-examination.

64

Our conversation, then, while bantering, never strayed far from the neighbourhood of sex—indeed, our friend's imagination is of a persistently, if unaggressively, erotic character. Together with the oysters and Chablis, it somewhat roused me: when he enquired, as offhandedly as one might ask about dessert, whether he mightn't straightway return me the favour of an orgasm or two at 24 L, I came near to saying, "Why, yes, thank you, now you mention it." Instead I cordially declined, and when he did not press, but affably hoped we might enjoy each other's persons at more leisure before very long, I found myself after all desirous of him. In my car (he'd walked to meet me at the restaurant, and asked now for a lift home) he expressed his wish that he might freely so invite me in the future, when the urge was on him, without offending me, and I as freely decline or accept, until one or the other of us had found "our next lover." One was not immortal, he went on, and solitary pleasures were—well, solitary. I could rely on his discretion and, he trusted, his ability. It was a pity that a woman of the world such as myself, a respected scholar and able administrator, must even in America in 1969 still wait for her male friends to take the overt initiative in sexual matters instead of asking, as easily as for any other small personal favour, to have, say, her clitoris kissed until she came out of her bloody mind. . .

I reproduce his language, sir, in order to suggest the good-humored prurience, or gentle salaciousness, characteristic of the man: rather novel to my experience and, together with his youthfulness, attentiveness, and general personableness, agreeable, if not exactly captivating. Whatever dependency or exploitation has been my lot, I have ever felt it to be upon or at the hands, not of men, particularly, but of *others,* more often than not people of superior abilities whom I admired. Moreover, like Mme de Staël I have lived a life of my own in the world. So if Ambrose Mensch "had his way with me" that night, it was by persuading me to have mine with him, first then and there in my little car in the parking area at Long Wharf; next all about the flat at 24 L, where he stopped till morning (and described to me—*read* would be the wrong word for such wordless pages—between the aforepromised business, his trial draft of the opening of his screenplay, wherein a woman's hands are seen opening a bundle of letters one by one with a stiletto letter-opener whilst her voice, as if iterating to itself their return addresses, announces the title, the actors' names, and the sundry credits. And this was the draft soon after rejected by Reg Prinz as "too wordy"!).

In the same way, if his "conquest" was completed eleven days later, on his 39th birthnight, it was because, by making no further direct overtures in that period, but maintaining his low-keyed, half-earnest chaffing about sexual initiative and women's rights, he kept fresh in my memory how agreeable had been our lovemaking. I found myself not only inviting him back to 24 L for a birthday dinner, but initiating fellatio with the hors d'oeuvres and coitus after the cognac—over which too (I mean the Martell) I showed him your letter of 23 March soliciting the story of my life for your proposed new work. He sympathised with your "perverse attraction" (his term or yours?) to literary realism. He toyed briefly with the idea of incorporating your letter into his screenplay. And he advised me to advise you to bugger off.

Now, by his own acknowledgement A's fertility is marginal. My own, I have cause to suspect, is approaching its term. Over the last two years my menses have grown ever more erratic: not infrequently I skip a month altogether. Through the period of my connexion with "George III," these irregularities seldom caused me more anxiety than any woman might feel at the approach of her menopause: on the occasions when His Royal Highness (who was not impotent either, only slowed by age and debilitated by his "madness," which followed in some detail the course of his original's), aroused by an erotic passage, say, in some Fielding or Smollett I was reading to him, achieved congress with his "Lady Pembroke," she was properly pessaried in advance. For the same reason I was not uneasy about these latter two *Noctes Ambrosianae* (faithful to his promise, he has so far conducted himself with rather more discretion than I). But that rash initial coupling in my office still fretted at my peace of mind. I had *only* his word for it that his "motility" was low (upon a former wife he fathered a child, a retarded daughter whose custody he retains); in any case it wanted only one healthy swimmer to do the job. That infusion I'd been obliged to sit upon through our committee meeting—where we'd postponed nominating A. B. Cook by the procedural diversion of disqualifying Ambrose from the committee on the grounds of your having mentioned him for the award, and selecting his replacement, a sensible woman from the French Department—was enormous, and coincided with the mild *Mittelschmerz* of my ovulation time. What was more, sore experience had taught me. . .a lesson that will keep for another letter.

Therefore, despite the heavy odds against my impregnation, I welcomed with relief the cramps that came on me in the evening of 2 April—and Ambrose rejoiced in the coincidence of my flow with the full Pink Moon.

That moon marked, in some oestral almanac of my lover's reckoning, the end of the First Stage of our affair and the commencement of the Second (still very much in progress a fortnight since, though I cannot imagine it to be of *very* long duration!), which I can describe only as Coition to Exhaustion. Earlier on I remarked that I am neither prudish nor "frigid," though the celebrated reserve of the English is, in my view, a quality much more admirable than not, and which I hope I yet manifest in some measure, at least in the *other* theatres of life. I cannot account for my behaviour, unprecedented in my biography if not altogether in his: having duly observed that he is my first lover younger than myself; that the erotic aspect of my past connexions had ever been of less moment to me than their other aspects; that I am undeniably in the last phase of youthfulness if not yet of vigour; that Ambrose's style is still very much to encourage equality in the area of sexual initiative (a style with obvious appeal to one in my position)—having acknowledged all this, I am still at a loss to explain my, his, our appetite for raw copulation, its *adjuncta* and *succedanea*, these two weeks!

He is not my first lover, nor I his; and you, sir, are not my first novelist, nor I (I daresay, despite your protestations *au contraire)* your first "model." We all know what we want from one another, and having decided (or been led to choose) to give, I shan't hold back. Ambrose Mensch is, has been, at least with me. . .a *fucking-machine!* And I another! We do not love each other. We are neither better nor worse friends than before. In all other particulars we and our connexion are unchanged. But we fuck!

He has taught me to relish that word, which I ever despised; he professes to wonder as much as I whence our energy and unquenchable lust; I cannot keep my hand out of his fly, he his my drawers. A woman past forty-five, I tell myself, acting provost of a university faculty, does *not* bestride one of her adjunct professors in his own office in midmorning, upon his swivel chair or amid his books and papers, and hump him hornily whilst students throng through the corridors en route to class. At forty-five-plus the blood has cooled; sex takes its place—a real but not a preeminent place—among one's priorities; many other things more engage one's time and interests; companionship is important, one's projects in the world are important. Placing the olives from one's faculty-cocktail-party martinis into the (acting) provostial cunt to be osculated therefrom and eaten two hours later by one's junior colleague is *not* important, and should not at one's present age excite to olive-by-olive orgasm first at the prospect (as one secretes the olives in one's handbag), second at the insertion (in the faculty women's loo), a third time at the extraction (squatting over Ambrose's face on the hearth rug at 24 L), and a fourth time now at the narration: four comes per olive times four olives gives sixteen comes in this case alone, twelve of them before we even got down to that evening's *fuck. . .*

You get the idea. Where will this lead? Our naughty little tyrannies: I make him wear my semen-soaked "panties" to a departmental luncheon; he makes me recite passages from the works of my earlier, more famous lit'ry lovers whilst he rogers me. . .

Enough (she cries, who cannot have enough)! Yesterday, I note with mild distress, your New York State legislature voted down a model bill to legalise the abortion laws in that state. In Maryland, once a Catholic province, they are even more medieval. My imperious lover will arrive any minute; I must apply the pessary. What shall we do tonight, who already this morning managed *soixante-neuf* during Shirley Stickles's coffee break? When will I recognise myself again as

G?

P.S.: As I closed A. entered, and informed me as we threw off our clothes that today is the 195th anniversary of the outbreak of the

67

American Revolution at Concord and Lexington (I knew it already; Harrison Mack used to wear mourning from 19 April through 4 July). We set to reenacting that conflict sexually: I seized his New York, he crossed my Delaware; ahead lay Brandywines, Valley Forges, Saratogas. But as Mother Country was getting in her licks on the White Plains of my coffee table, he caught sight of this page, snatched up the whole letter, and read it, over my protests, with whooping glee. . . Then it was straight to Yorktown and my surrender, and the prime article of our subsequent Treaty of Paris was that he be shown any future such letters, in return for my full freedom to say whatever I choose of him with impunity. But my punishment for having thus far confided our intimacies without consulting him is to take it up the arse athwart my writing desk and write as best I can not only this postscript but those passages:

> Most people in this world seem to live "in character"; they have a beginning, a middle and an end, and the three are congruous with one another and true to the rules of their type.

And

> It is our intention to preserve in these pages what scant biographical material we have been able to collect concerning Joseph Knecht, or Ludi Magister Josephus III, as he is called in the archives of the Glass Bead Game.

And

> A squat grey building of only thirty-four stories. Over the main entrance the words, CENTRAL LONDON HATCHERY AND CONDITIONING CENTRE. . .

And

> When I reached C company lines, which were at the top of the hill, I paused and looked back at the camp, just coming into full view below me through the grey mist of early morning.

And even

> An unassuming young man was travelling, in midsummer, from his native city of Hamburg to Davos-Platz in the Canton of Grisons, on a three weeks' visit.

And, yes

> riverrun, past Eve and Adam's, from swerve of shore to bend of bay, brings us by a commodious vicus of recirculation back to Howth Castle and Environs.

And finally the opening words of "Arthur Morton King's" own fiction-in-progress: a retelling of the story of Perseus, of Medusa, of

O!

D: *Lady Amherst to the Author. Trouble at Marshyhope. Her early relations with several celebrated novelists. Her affair with André Castine, and its issue. Her marriage to Lord Jeffrey Amherst. Her widowing and reduction to academic life.*

24 L Street
Dorset Heights, Maryland 21612

Saturday morning, 26 April 1969

My dear B.,

Directly upon my supplying you, in my last, with that gloss upon my address, I receive your letter of 20 April with its postscriptal request for just that information! One is given pause. But the same applies to my "confession" generally, I'm sure: more than you bargained for, and before you'd really got down to bargaining.

No matter—though these crossings in the post are decidedly eerie and a touch confusing. I have still past history to relate; and my present connexion with Ambrose M. *(relationship* were too portentous a word) remains curious enough to prompt me, if not to account for it, at least to record it, if only to remove me a tongue-tisking distance from my own behaviour. Saturday mornings (when I am alone or he is asleep) are convenient for me to write to you, over the breakfast coffee and "English"(!) muffins; and perhaps it will be as well—and fit—if, like fictions, these confessional installments go unreplied to: scribbled in silence, into silence sent, silently received.

My morning newspaper duly notes—what I've been in the thick of all week!—that college campuses your country over are at best in disarray, at worst in armed rebellion. Even the innocents here at Marshyhope ("pinknecks," Ambrose calls them), inspired by their incendiary counterparts at Berkeley, Buffalo, Cornell, and Harvard, managed yesterday a brief takeover and "trashing" of John Schott's office, and a "sit-in" in Shirley Stickles's and mine. Schott and Shirley (and Harry Carter, shaking with fear for all his earlier dismissal of student activists as "Spock's Big Babies") were for fetching the army in straight off, no doubt to impress the conservative kingmakers in "Annapolis, maybe even Washington." I too was chiefly irritated; would have been furious had they mussed my office. For while I deplore (for its futility more than for its imperialism) your government's misguided war in Vietnam, and can by some effort of imagination follow the emotional logic that leads therefrom to, say, student occupation of administrative offices at Columbia University, I can by no manner of means take *our* students seriously, who so far from having read their Marcuse, Mao, and Marx, do not even read the morning news, and rail against the university without knowing (any more than Schott or Carter or Shirley S.) what a real university is.

69

Which, Ambrose tells me, and lately told them, is the proper object of demonstration. What they ought to protest, in his view, is the false labelling that calls such an enterprise as ours a college, not to say a university, in the first place, rather than an extended public high school. But what would these children *do* in a genuine university?

He and your "Todd Andrews," almost alone, have been able to talk with the demonstrators, in whose stirring up Harrison Mack's son, a bona fide radical, has had a hand. Mr Andrews is the most enlightened of the Tidewater Foundation trustees and their executive director as well, to whom even Schott must in some measure defer. While he and Drew Mack speak to each other across an ideological fence, there is some bond between them which the younger man clearly resents but cannot break. And Ambrose—an old friend of Drew Mack's, clearly not a part of the regular academic establishment, and mistaken by the students for a radical because he despises Richard Nixon (I myself would describe my lover as a conservative nihilist)—found himself cast in the role of faculty spokesman for the students! The utter confusion he found appealing; no use Drew Mack's (correctly) arguing to the protestors that Ambrose was no more the representative of "their values" than was Todd Andrews of the administration's: they worked out a conciliation between them which gave both sides the illusion of being represented and ended the occupation. By extending the spring recess to a fortnight and moving up the final-examination period, they hope to forestall a regrouping of forces this semester. Next fall, one hopes, the mood on campus, if not the situation in Southeast Asia, will have changed.

Thus my lover unexpectedly finds himself in the sudden good graces of John Schott, to whom Mr Andrews has represented him as a forefender of adverse publicity for MSU in the news media. I am almost encouraged now to advance his name after all before our reconstituted nomination committee for the Litt.D.—rather, to entertain its advancement by someone else. To Ambrose himself, an apolitical animal, the whole business is, if not quite a joke, at most a sport or a variety of "happening"—"It's what we have instead of Big Ten football," he declares—and a potent aphrodisiac: in his cynical view, they play at revolution to excite themselves, then back to their liberated dormitories to make love. He is of course "projecting": I write this weary to the bone, sore in every orifice from our amorosities of the night past, everywhere leaking like a seminiferous St Sebastian. From where in the world, I wonder, does so much come come?

Thus our gluttony persists, to my astonishment, into its fourth week! I should not have believed either my endurance or my appetite: I've easily done more coupling in the month of April than in the four years past; must have swallowed half as much as I've envaginated; I do not even count what's gone in the ears, up the arse, on the bedclothes and nightclothes and dayclothes and rugs and furniture, to the four winds. And yet I hunger and thirst for more: my left hand creeps

70

sleeping-himward as the right writes on; now I've an instrument in each, poor swollen darling that I must have again. He groans, he stirs, he rises; my faithful English Parker pen (bought in "Mr Pumblechook's premises," now a stationer's, in Rochester, in honour of great Boz) must yield to his poky poking pencil pencel pincel penicellus penicillus *peeee*

Your pardon. Come and gone (an hour later) to fetch his daughter for an afternoon's outing—and make what excuses he can, I daresay, to his *Abruzzesa*, Mrs Peter Mensch. *Can he be servicing her too?* it occurs to me to wonder. Physically impossible! And yet, titillated by the thought as at last I douche my wearies, I find myself dallying astride the W.C. with the syringe. . .

But I daresay this is not the sort of thing you had in mind to hear.

Nor I to write: not even two hours ago, when I set out to tell you for example that I was born Germaine Necker-Gordon in Paris to a pair of fashionably expatriate ambitious minor novelists who traced their separate descents from an unrecorded dalliance of young Lord Byron's with the aging Madame de Staël in Switzerland in the summer of 1816, the penultimate year of her life. That I was educated in the second-rate salons and literary cafés of Paris and Rome by the most indulgent, amoral, loving, pathetic, dear, and worthless parents a child could have, who transferred their ambitions to me straight upon the completion of my first novel (at age nine!): once promising talents both, each of whose own first books had been mild critical successes; whose seconds and thirds had received diminishing notice; whose fourths and fifths and sixths had not found a publisher, so that like space rockets whose next stage fails to fire, they languished decade after decade in gently decaying orbit. That with their tender connivance I was deflowered, not ungently, at age fourteen, in Rome, in the woods of the Villa Ada (now a campground for tourists!), with a (capped) fountain pen, by Mr H. G. Wells, then 71, whom I feared and admired, and who admired in turn my person but not my fiction, which he found "smarmy." He was not so much a dirty old man as a vulnerable, was Wells, and I a mischievous girl; neither his literary criticism nor his fountain pen much hurt me, but my parents, outraged at his critical judgement, refused to read anything he published after *The Anatomy of Frustration* (1936).

They next set their sights on old Maeterlinck, who however was too preoccupied with expiring (*Avant le Grand silence* had appeared; *La Grande porte* was in press; *L'Autre monde* in manuscript) to be tempted. On holiday in Capri in 1938 they endeavoured shamelessly to introduce me to (read "introduce into me") Mr Sinclair Lewis, despite his singular uncomeliness and our low opinion of his work after 1930; to this end we ingratiated ourselves with the Americans on the island, and so I first met Jane and Harrison Mack—naive, charming, rich—and Sir Jeffrey William Pitt, Lord Amherst: then 40, recently divorced, making like ourselves a last tour of Italy before Armageddon, and busily flirting with Mrs Mack, who seemed not interested. (Thirty years and several Armageddons later, I realise that Jane would have just then ended her long off-and-on affair with Todd Andrews and was carrying the son named after him—who however too resembles Harrison for any doubts as to his legitimacy.)

But *I* was interested, despite my parents' objections that, lord or no lord, Amherst had never published a line in his life: on the train from Naples north, he became my first real lover. The break with my parents, however, came in Zurich the following year, when I rejected Jeffrey's proposal of marriage: to be his *wife* rather than his mistress, and therefore a woman with the means and leisure both to write and to "ally herself" with established writers, made eminently good sense to M. and P.; they did not share my "rebellious adolescent enthusiasm" for the author of *Ulysses* and *Work in Progress,* to sit at whose feet (but I never got near them, I confess to you now) I went to Paris when Jeffrey and my parents fled the war: they back to Zurich, he to England.

Do I bore you, Mr B.? That cold winter I was nineteen, attractive, virtually francless. I felt handsomely scarred by experience, bursting with talent: I'd had words (three) with young Sam Beckett concerning his aloofness toward James Joyce's mad, infatuated daughter. I was already contemning Hemingway as a shallow popular novelist; I was skeptical of Eliot's neo-orthodoxy, distressed by Pound's anti-Semitism and attachment to Frobenius and Il Duce. And I was befriended by the Misses Gertrude Stein and Alice Toklas, before whose meagre but welcome fire I met their pet of the moment: a quiet, splendidly handsome 22-year-old French-Canadian avant-gardist named. . .André Castine.

There, I have set down the name. Thank God Ambrose is not here to mock it: I couldn't abide that just now, or him—though it was André (I suddenly understand, with a dark *frisson,* what would have been at once apparent to another: I *shall* profit, then, perhaps, from this "scriptotherapy") who made me vulnerable, three decades later, to his pallid echo, Mr Mensch. My André!

We did not need Alice Toklas's hashish brownies to intoxicate us. Two hardened cynics, we were in love from the first quarter-hour of conversation. Our bringings-up had much in common: André's parents were obscure figures in the Canadian foreign service, freewheeling and nomadic Bohemians. They never married; André was raised ad libitum all over North America and Europe; he was at ease in half a dozen languages and any social situation; he seemed to have read everything, to be knowledgeable about everything from cricket matches to international finance and organic chemistry. He had been writing poems and stories since he was five, had abandoned both two years younger than Rimbaud, was already bored with the cinema as an alternative to literature, and was provoking Miss Stein (and Miss Necker-Gordon) with the idea of putting these "traditional" genres behind him entirely, in favour of what he called (and this was 1939/40!) "action historiogra-

72

phy": the *making* of history as if it were an avant-garde species of narrative.

Passionately we differed, passionately concurred, and passionately came together. I had loved dear Jeffrey, my firm and gentle sexual father, an ideal first lover; André and I ravished, *consumed* each other. We crackled like two charged wires in our freezing flats: *love* seems too mild a word for such mad voltage! By the spring of 1940 I was pregnant. We moved south to avoid the Nazis; the "script of history" fetched André up and down the country from Vichy to Paris on mysterious errands; I could never tell how much of his high-spirited, always ironic talk was serious. Something went wrong, "a rejection slip from Clio" André called it: in the middle of a night we fled our little villa, where I was battening on Brie and Beaujolais and baby and happily letting life write *me* instead of vice versa. By lorry and plane and little boat and big we went to Quebec, then to Ontario—antipodal, cool, serene, impossibly far from the world and its cataclysms—to have our baby.

I met André's parents, Mlle Andrée Castine and M. Henri Burlingame, who but for their mysterious appearances and disappearances recalled my own: devoted and doting, intense and ineffectual. André adored them—and disagreed point for point with their interpretations of history, in particular the history of their own family's dark activities. But whereas *he* always spoke jestingly and acted seriously, his parents always spoke unironically and could be taken no more seriously than my own. As best I could gather, they had devoted themselves to the organisation of Communist party cells during the Depression: she in the wheatlands of central Canada, he (I tremble to begin to invoke the web of "coincidence" in which I am still caught, and at whose centre, ever nearer, lies. . .*je ne sais quoi*) in the wetlands of tidewater Maryland and Virginia! "As likely as setting fire to Chesapeake Bay," André would laugh—but his father, with a dark roll of the eyes, would put his forefinger on Washington, D.C., on the hydrographic chart, his thumb on the Dorchester marshes, just that far away. One active cell in that vicinity, he avowed, would be like one free-floating cancer cell in the enemy's cerebral cortex; it was no defect in the strategy itself that had led to its admittedly total failure, but such accidents of history as Franklin Roosevelt's election and New Deal, and the busy gearing up of the U.S. defence industry against the threat of war, which were distracting the working class with an adventitious prosperity and killing in the womb ("Forgive me, Germaine!" I hear him breaking off to cry here, aghast at his tactless trope, whilst we rock with mirth) the Second Revolution, whose foundations he'd so painfully begun to lay.

"Poor ground for foundation laying," André would tease, and declare with a laugh and a kiss that they weren't fooling *him:* he knew them both very well to be in the pay of the U.S. F.B.I., to infiltrate and sabotage the very activities they claimed to be organising. And what was this heresy of historical *accidents*? An affront to the entire line of Burlingames, Castines, and—and so forth!

Into this vertiginous dialogue—on Guy Fawkes Day, 1940, in the snug farmhouse at Castines Hundred where André himself, and any number of Castines before him, had been born—I brought our son. Neither André nor his father was there; something enormous was in the works—"My *Zauberberg*," André called it, "my *Finnegans Wake*." Postcards came from Washington, Honolulu, Tokyo, Manila. Andrée (a grandmother at 40, and I now virtually childless nearing 50!) was full of candour, love, and a kind of bright opacity: freely as I enquired into the mystery of their lives, and readily as she responded, nothing seemed ever quite to clarify. . . A postpartum depression seized me, the effect I believe mainly of this ubiquitous uncertainty. I. . .could not cope, could not deal with things. The baby—I couldn't name him, even, much less nurse; names had lost their sense. Where was I? What was this *Canada*, of which I'd seen little beyond Castines Hundred? Where was André? Where were Mama, Papa, dear Jeffrey (how I longed for him now, and wept to learn that he'd been re-wed in London)? André's letters urged me back to writing, but I couldn't write, couldn't even read. Our alphabet looked alien as Arabic; the strings of letters were a code I'd lost the key to; I found more sense in the empty spaces, in the margins, between the lines.

Assez. In that house everything went without saying: good Andrée took the child as if it were her own, no explanations needed (my sense was that nothing was any longer explainable: one hemisphere was aflame, the other smouldering). Passage was arranged for me back to Switzerland, to a tiny villa leased by my parents, close by Coppet. André, it turned out, had kept them apprised of things—had even dropped in one day, as if from the sky, to introduce himself and show them photographs of our baby! They thought him a fine young man, praised his epistolary style, deplored his avant-gardism, urged him back to the virtuous paths of Galsworthy and Conrad, whom he promised to reread. . .

That summer Papa died, bequeathing me his copies of every letter he'd written since he'd decided at age twelve to become an author: eight legal-size file drawers full! To Mama he left his "unfinished" (read *unpublished;* read *unread*) manuscripts, as voluminous as her own, which latter she dutifully put by in order to devote herself—till her own death fifteen years later—to his literary executorship. There was nothing else to execute. The mass lies mouldering yet, for all I know, faithfully catalogued and "readied for the press," hers beside his, in the cellar of that villa, not far from which they lie too.

I call myself childless: I cannot say certainly either that I have seen my son and his father since, or that I have not. God knows I have tried. And tried. Not enough, perhaps: another and better would perhaps have ransacked the globe; never would have left Castines Hundred in the first place. No good my pleading the world gone mad, André's "action historiography" become Theatre of the Absurd, the funhouse quality of that family, wherein no one and nothing was what it seemed. . . Now and again over the years, usually about Guy Fawkes Day, cryptic messages arrived in the post, aflower with exotic stamps: Our son is well; he has a name "not unlike his grandfather's"; his education is in good hands. As for me, I have not been forgotten: my decision was understandable, my condition to be sympathised with; I am still loved, even as it were *watched over*.

On a few occasions the annual message has involved a kind of epiphany: *Our son will go past your address in a blue push-chair at 1400 hours on his third birthday.* I stand vigil, rush out at the sight; a nursemaid threatens, in agitated Swiss French, to summon the child's parents and the *gendarmerie*. I cannot tell for sure; the eyes seem his. . .

One November André himself paid a call on me in London, incognito: I'd never have known him had he not, like Odysseus, spoken of things privy to the two of us alone. Little Henri was seven then; I was permitted to take lunch with them, on condition that I not reveal myself to be his mother. Surely they *were* André and Henri; there would be no reason for a hoax so cruel! But I was to understand that so much was at stake in the "game of governments," ever in progress, that a false step by me could lead to the quick disappearance forever of both of them. Explanations would come in time, perhaps even reunion. Meanwhile. . . I complied.

Another time. . . Another time.

In 1942, Mama contrived to "introduce me to" *(vide supra)* Herr Hermann Hesse, then in his sixties and still living in seclusion in Montagnola, where he was completing *Das Glasperlenspiel*. Hesse was, in general, celibate, though less than chaste: his conviction that a certain high humour was the mark of transcendent grace, together with his all but total lack of that virtue, had led as much as anything to his breakdown in the 1910's, his "partially successful" Jungian analysis, and his inability to keep much more than a finger, let us say, in the world. It also made him, off the page and sometimes on, a stupendous bore, though never of the *active* sort. Mainly he was terrified of people and, like most "major authors" I've known, regressive in his intimacies. He came to call me his *Knädlchen;* I learned to talk the Schwarzwaldish baby talk of the 1890's; he liked me to dress in lederhosen. Once I persuaded him to swim with me: the lake was icy; Hermann nearly went under; I had to massage him for hours after, to bring back what warmth there was. Neither of us imagined he was still fertile. In an orgy of prideful remorse he drafted the ending of his *Meisterwerk* (I mean the narrative proper, not the clumsy addenda) and consented to appraise my own manuscripts (I'd managed three short stories in as many years!) whilst I slipped over to Lugano for the abortion. It is his guilt—not for inadvertently getting me with child and permitting the abortion, but for not honestly telling me despite all that my stories were poor stuff (he clenched his teeth and declared them *bemerkenswürdig, ganz bemerkenswürdig*)—that he projects onto the lad Tito when old Joseph Knecht salubriously and conveniently drowns.

My illusions of Authorhood succumbed with him. The truth—as I see it now with neither false modesty nor frustration—is that my inventive faculty was considerable, my powers of execution slight. I had no gift for storytelling.

Exposition was another matter. As I was so near Coppet, I looked into the life and works of my namesake, and published in 1943, with an English press, a little popular study of Germaine Necker de Staël-Holstein. Among its handful of appreciative readers was Sir Jeffrey, who wrote me that his second wife had been killed in the London bombing. He hoped we might remeet should the war ever end and we survive it. It did; we did; he renewed his suit. I put him off through the fall of '45; when November came and went without a sign from André, I became Lady Amherst.

Our marriage was successful, if scarcely romantic. Both libertine and libertarian, Jeffrey gave great licence to his priapic inclinations and granted similar licence to me, who did not especially wish it. It would not have occurred to him—a thorough aristocrat, but not a snob—to question whether my several pregnancies in our years together were by him or another, so long as our salon, and therefore the stud roster as it were, was of proper quality; he'd have reared any of my children proudly, as he trusted his own by-blows were being reared. In this he was much like the Baron de Staël, and I admired him for it.

Unfortunately, for one reason or another no subsequent pregnancy of mine was brought to term. On our first visit to America, in 1947, I rushed in vain to Castines Hundred (Jeffrey understood it to be a sentimental pilgrimage and discreetly went on ahead to California; I never told him the details, though he'd have been entirely sympathetic). Only a caretaker was there, who had no idea when his employers, "off travelling," might return. When I rejoined Jeffrey, he was humping a swath through the starlets associated with the English colony in Hollywood, who could not remain perpendicular in the presence of a British gentleman both titled and heterosexual. I myself became close to Maria and Aldous Huxley, the latter then in his early fifties and, alas, as deep into mysticism as had been poor Hermann, at similar cost to his self-irony and general good sense. When I learned he had decided to write no more novels, I lost interest, and soon after aborted spontaneously in a sleeping-car of the Twentieth Century Limited, en route to New York.

There were other connexions, in other years; I have not heart or energy to retell them. We reencountered the Macks in London in '49, when Jane quite lost her head to Jeffrey as aforementioned, and he indulged her—mainly out of courtesy and good-humoured respect for his own past infatuation. Indeed, he managed to make me feel, bless him, as though the whole mad little episode was a sort of thank-you to

Jane for having rejected his earlier attentions and thus led him to me! A remarkable husband; I often miss him.

A dozen years and one miscarriage later, in 1961, upon our second visit to the States, the Macks chastely returned our hospitality. Jane had already, after her fashion, entirely repressed her romance with Jeffrey, not because (as with him) it was of no importance, but rather because it was too uncharacteristic of her to be agreeably recalled. I had by this time published my more serious articles on Constant, Gibbon, Rousseau, Schlegel, and Byron—their connexion with Mme de Staël—and brought out my edition of her letters (which had served as my entrée to Katia and Thomas Mann upon their removing from California to Switzerland during the McCarthy witch-hunts. Huxley had tried unsuccessfully to introduce us in 1947. . .but on this subject, too, I shall not speak). I was acquiring a small reputation as a scholar of the French Revolutionary period. Then Harrison Mack put me in touch with your Joseph Morgan of the Maryland Historical Society, on whom he already had his eye as a likely president for his college-in-the-works; and my conversation with that knowledgeable young man—so I had come to think of anyone my age!—led to my subsequent essays on de Staël and the Americans: Jefferson, Albert Gallatin, Gouverneur Morris.

In the fall of that year, marvellous to relate, I also made the acquaintance—may he not remember it!—of a literary figure of an altogether different order. Morgan had fortuitously recollected, from some transactions between his office and its counterpart in the state of Delaware, that Germaine de Staël was among the original investors in E. I. Du Pont de Nemours & Co. in the first decade of the 19th Century. She had of course known Éleuthère Irénée's father, Pierre Samuel Du Pont, before the Revolution: the "Rousseau" in her sympathised with the romantic economics of Du Pont *père*, Turgot, and the other physiocrats, while the "Jane Mack" in her—would that I'd inherited a touch of it!—recognised that munitions were a golden investment no matter whose cannons carried the day. Morgan himself arranged to have the microfilm records of those stock transactions, and her letters of enquiry about them after her father's death in 1804, sent down from Wilmington to Baltimore for my examination. As I perused them with the society's projector, the only other visitor in the place—a heavyset, not unhandsome gentleman in his latter forties, with curly thick pepper-and-salt hair and suit to match—began making a fuss to the young woman on desk-duty because his books, of which he'd presented autographed copies to the society, were to be found neither on display nor among the shelves of Maryland poets.

He grew louder. It was a thinly disguised political reprisal, he declared; Morgan and his ilk could expect to hear from the governor's office. Too long had the society been a haven and sinecure for left-wing iconoclasts, self-styled intellectuals, outside agitators with no respect for the red, white, and blue, much less the red, white, black, and orange of

77

"The Old Line State, long may she wave / O'er her detractors' wretched grave," et cetera.

I thought the man drunk, or mad. The desk clerk was intimidated, almost in tears. As I moved to defend her, Morgan appeared from his office, rolled his eyes, and levelly explained, when he could get a word in between tetrameters, that inasmuch as the books in question had been duly catalogued (among Miscellaneous Marylandia), their absence from the shelves must be testament of their popularity. The library was noncirculating, but given the small staff his budget permitted, some attrition by theft was inevitable. As they were none of them in print, perhaps Mr Cook would spare another set of copies from his apparently inexhaustible supply? In any case, he must cease his disturbance at once or leave the premises; others were at work.

The two clearly knew each other; their *contretemps* had the air of a reenactment. At Morgan's last remark the fellow seemed to notice me for the first time: elaborately he begged my pardon (he had better begged the clerk's) and insisted that "Joseph"—"a flaming Commie, don't you know, but an able chap all the same"—introduce us. Even as Morgan dryly did so, the man pressed upon me broadsides and flyers from his inside pockets, advertising himself and his poetical effusions. Morgan withdrew with a sigh—it seemed they were long-standing acquaintances; the outburst had been *half* a joke—and I was left with Mr A. B. Cook, self-designated Poet Laureate of "Maryland! Faerie-Land! / Tidal estuary-land!"—as odd a mixture of boorishness and cultivation as I'd encountered.

He knew of Mme de Staël, though he claimed to have read neither her nor Schlegel nor any other non-Anglo-Saxon. He *had* read Gibbon, and retailed to me the story of Gibbon's youthful courtship of Suzanne Curchod, later Mme de Staël's mother. Gibbon's father had disapproved of the match; Mlle Curchod (then eighteen) appealed to her pastor, who consulted Jean Jacques Rousseau, who advised against the marriage on the grounds that young Gibbon's *Essai sur l'étude de la littérature,* which he'd read in manuscript, "wanted genius." I replied with the postscript to that anecdote: that in 1776 "my" Germaine, then a girl of ten, had offered to *marry* Gibbon, then near forty and grown famous with the appearance of his *Decline and Fall,* so that her mother and father might continue to enjoy his conversation.

But I did not continue to enjoy ours, for having learned who my husband was, Cook now launched into a fulsome panegyric for Jeffrey's famous ancestor, commander of British forces in America during the French and Indian War, whose notorious manner of dealing with the Indians during Pontiac's conspiracy he lauded as "the earliest recorded example of bacteriological warfare." Today I see that turn of the conversation in a different light, as shall be recorded on some future Saturday; at the time I thought it simply in offensive taste, and I curtly turned him off. We met again in November at the Macks' farewell party for Jeffrey and me at Tidewater Farms, to which they'd just returned:

in Jeffrey's presence Cook did not bring up the subject of those infected blankets from the Fort Pitt smallpox hospital, but he gave me a great wink as he mused loudly upon the question, Whether our poetical attitudes might be to some extent determined by available rhymes, *e.g. wife/life/strife,* or *savage/ravage.* . .

A strange man; a dangerous man; a buffoon who is no fool. I have seen him since but once, at Harrison's funeral, an encounter that leaves me troubled yet. It is unimaginable that he does not know who sits on Schott's nominating committee for the M.U. Litt.D., and what my position is. Even Morgan, who did not *fear* him, regarded Cook as dangerous; could not quite account for the man's enmity and alliance with Schott against him; considered him at once less and more serious than his manner implied. The Tow'r of Truth demagoguery and ideological name-calling, even the horrendous doggerel and self-advertising broadsides, he knew Cook himself to be ironic about, as Schott for example was never; and like me, Morgan had met the unpredictable sophistication under the bumptiousness and posturing. But he believed Cook perfectly capable of destroying people in that "unseriousness," beneath which lay motives more serious than any of Schott's own.

This apprehension of course proved true: where is Morgan now? As I intimated in my first letter, the hysterical tenor of which I shall not bother to blush at or apologise for. . .

No matter.

To end this history: back again in England, in the fall of 1962 and '63 I received from André, not cryptic postcards, but full letters, the substance of which will keep till another letter of my own. The first prompted my essay "The Inconstant Constant," on de Staël's ill-treatment by Benjamin Constant and the beautiful Juliette Récamier, with whom both (and everyone) were in love: Constant had borrowed 80,000 francs from Germaine over the years, and now refused to repay the mere half of it which she wanted, not for herself, but as dowry for Albertine—her daughter by Constant seventeen years earlier! When she pressed, he threatened to make public her old (and heartbreaking) letters to him. I weep. The second prompted my sole excursion from my chosen field: the foreword to a new edition of the seven letters exchanged between Héloïse and Peter Abelard. I weep, and can say no more.

In 1965, my husband died of a bowel cancer. The estate was depleted by taxes, creditors, and anonymous bequests to his known natural children. He was not ungenerous to me, proportionately, but there was much less than I'd imagined: neither of us had done a day's work for wages in our lives, and Jeffrey had neglected to tell me that it was the principal of his inheritance we were living on, not the income. Good Joseph Morgan got wind of my plight and himself invited me to lecture (upon the French Revolution!) at Tidewater Technical College. I declined—he was only being very kind—but was inspired by his invitation to accept others which suddenly appeared from the University of Manitoba, Simon Fraser University, Sir George Williams, McMaster: André's doing, no question, and I went to Canada both in order to survive and in the hope that there might happen—what *did* happen, though it didn't end as I had dreamed.

Nor will this letter as I'd planned. It's past one now: I must see to what chores and errands I can, against the return of. . .Ambrose (I had, for an hour, forgot which letters now follow that dear initial) at teatime, when our weary, sated flesh will to't again. These two ounces of history he shall not see: André Castine is not his affair. I permit myself this epistolary infidelity—who am too *pleine* these weeks to think of any other!

Thus has chronicling transformed the chronicler, and I see that neither Werner Heisenberg nor your character Jacob Horner went far enough: not only is there no "non-disturbing observation"; there is no non-disturbing historiography. Take warning, sir: to put things into words works changes, not only upon the events narrated, but upon their narrator. She who saluted you pages past is not the same who closes now, though the name we share remains,

As ever,
Germaine

Y: *Todd Andrews to the Author.* *Acknowledging the latter's invitation and reviewing his life since their last communication. The Tragic View of things, including the Tragic View.*

Todd Andrews
Andrews, Bishop, & Andrews, Attorneys
Court Lane
Cambridge, Maryland 21613

Friday, April 4, 1969

Sir:

Your singular letter of March 30, soliciting my cooperation as model for a character in your work in progress, reached me approximately on April Fool's Day. Today, which my calendar tells me is the anniversary not only of Martin Luther King's assassination but also of Adam's creation according to the Mohammedans and of Jesus's crucifixion according to the Christians, seems appropriate for my reply. The more so since, if that chap in southern California turns out to have correctly predicted Doomsday for 6:13 this evening, my longhanded *no* will never reach you, and you will be free to do as you please.

The motto of one of our corporate clients, very big in the chemical-fertilizer way, is *Praeteritas futuras stercorant.* Not just my merely legal Latin, but my experience of life (your letter not excepted) makes me

80

wonder whether the past *(a)* fertilizes the future, *(b)* turns into shit in the future, or *(c)* turns the future into shit. This year—my 70th, sir—the past has crowded in on me apace (cropped up? rained down?), faster than I can. . .um. . .digest it.

E.g., my old friend Harrison Mack died, as you may have read in the *Times,* in January. His funeral brought Mrs. Mack back to Tidewater Farms and, briefly, their two grown children: the "actress" "Bea Golden" (née Jeannine Mack) and the "radical activist" Andrews Mack, named after my "conservative-passivist" self. I enclose for your perusal a photocopy of the 1969 installment of my *Letter to My Father,* describing this event. Mrs. Mack has not only stayed on, but wishes to retain me as her counsel in the apparently upcoming contest over Harrison's estate, as well as in other matters. Young Mack also, whose relations with me have not always been cordial, passes through on sundry dark enterprises of his own and, between ominous announcements that Marshyhope College's "Tower of Truth" must fall like the Rotten Capitalist Society It Represents, offers grudgingly to engage me against his mother in the same contest, he having learned from V. I. Lenin that the institutions of the established order may legitimately be exploited to their own ultimate subversion.

Jane Mack (who is, more power to her, a handsome and vigorous 63 and a wealthy woman in her own right) wants the estate diverted to her new fiancé: a titled but no longer affluent fellow whom we shall call "Lord Baltimore," though he is no Marylander. Drew wants it to finance a Second American Revolution. Neither seems to imagine that I might consider it my prior responsibility to defend the interests of the Tidewater Foundation, Harrison's principal beneficiary, for whom my firm has long served as counsel; far less that I might simply wish to see my late friend's testamentary desires, however eccentric, faithfully executed. Had he instructed me to liquidate his holdings and float the proceeds out on the Choptank tide, I would endeavor to do it.

In all this, of course, and much that I have not mentioned, I see mainly the reenactment of a certain earlier drama: the stercoration of the present by the past. And the prospect of refloating *that* particular opera gives me, let's say, a sinking feeling.

Which almost, but not quite, brings me to your request. It is not to tease you with off-the-record confidences that I mention my current relations with the surviving Macks. It is to spell out, literally, the implications of your proposal, the better to reach some genuine accord. "You have invited me and engaged to pay me," Thoreau used to tell his lecture audiences, "and I am determined that you shall have me, though I bore you beyond all precedent." It is Good Friday morning, an office holiday, promising to warm up enough by afternoon for me to turn to a bit of fitting out of my old boat, but meanwhile cool enough to keep me in my room here in the Dorset Hotel—not my sole home any longer as in years *praeteritas,* but still my Cambridge *pied-à-terre* and the seat of my ongoing *Inquiry*—with little to do (that inquiry being presently stymied) besides respond at length, whether yea or nay, to your letter. Henry James, as I remember, used to want *not* to hear too much of an anecdote of which he wished eagerly to hear a certain amount, for imaginative purposes. But his brother William astutely remarks that to get enough of anything in nature, one has to take too much.

I wonder that your letter makes no mention of New Year's Eve 1954, inasmuch as two of the three things of some moment that happened to me that night are known to you. Here in my room, around ten in the evening of that day, I finished drafting my memoir about not committing suicide aboard Capt. James Adams's showboat in 1937—a story I'd been writing since the previous March as one facet of my old *Inquiry*—and prepared to resume the inquiry itself, together with the even older *Letter to My Father* of which it is a part. But to reward myself for completing the showboat narrative, I strolled down to the New Year's Eve party in progress at the Cambridge Yacht Club. The Macks were settled in Baltimore at this time; I never saw or heard from them. But I was delighted to find Jeannine there with her (first) husband, Barry Singer, and I spent some time chatting with them. The marriage had caused a tiny stir in the old Guilford/Ruxton society in which the Macks moved, where anti-Semitism perhaps enjoys a prolonged half-life even today. But Singer was the son of Judge Joseph Singer of the Maryland Appellate bench, who had ruled with the majority in Harrison Mack's favor in our great estate battle of 1938; Singer was moreover a proper Princetonian, and if his part-ownership of a chain of small-town movie houses was regarded by some as "Jewish," they were pleased enough to meet at his parties the film and stage people among his friends. Barry himself was an engaging, quiet, cultured chap who should have been a lawyer and who certainly should have chosen a more stable bride, goyish or not.

But he could scarcely have chosen a lovelier. Jane Mack's daughter was about 21 then and a beauty, with a St. Croix suntan to set off her honey-blonde hair and a smashing backless, nearly frontless gown to set off the suntan. Already she was a confirmed overdrinker (it was Singer who, that same evening, amiably corrected my misapprehension that the Yiddish term *shicker* described a Jewish man who, like himself, consorted with *shiksas)* and fatally bitten by the theatrical bug. But the booze hadn't marked her yet, and given her looks, her youth, and her small connection with the Industry—which was still dominated by Hollywood in those days—Jeannine's aspirations didn't seem bizarre, at least at a party. She was happy to remeet her parents' old and once close friend, the efficient cause of their wealth. She wondered why I didn't see them more often, and why they chose to stay on in stuffy old Guilford, in broken-down Baltimore. Her own axis was Manhattan/Montego Bay, but they were thinking about chucking "the East Coast thing" altogether and moving to Los Angeles, if Barry could get the right price for his share of the movie-house chain. The Industry itself was no longer running scared about the TV threat, I was to understand, which it had effectively co-opted; but either such news took a while to reach the insular East, or (more likely) prospective buyers were invoking the past to keep the market down: 90 thou was high bid thus far.

We danced (the mambo!); Jeannine introduced me to a woman-friend of theirs: a handsome, fortyish New Yorker undergoing divorce, who'd come down with the Singers to our darling town for respite from litigation, and to have a look at Barry's string of funky little flea-traps in case the settlement gave her a bit to play with. *Her* tan (Martinique) was even darker than Jeannine's; she pretended to be afraid of being lynched by mistake; she demanded I loosen my collar so that she might examine firsthand whether I was a red-neck; she expressed her belief that a female divorce lawyer, which she planned to become, would be even less scrupulous than we males. We danced (early rock 'n' roll!). As always, Jeannine was thick with the musicians, a group imported for the evening at triple scale from Across the Bay. The drummer, we agreed, was the weak sister; she now informed me that it was not their usual and regular drummer we'd judged, but a local lad who knew some of the band members and had asked to sit in for one set. Upon his being relieved we were introduced by a mutual acquaintance, young Ambrose Mensch, who, obviously smitten with Jeannine (I believe they had been high school lovers), was by way of appending himself and his then wife to our little party.

Thus we met, you and I; and knowing your family I recognized your name, but you did not mine (there are scads of Andrewses in the area; ours is the oldest plot in the cemetery). You told me that as a would-be writer you hoped someday to publish fictions set in this area; that having lately seen an Aubrey Bodine photograph of Capt. James Adams's Original Floating Theatre, you had a vague notion of a novel in the format of the old blackface minstrel shows—a "philosophical minstrel show," I believe you called it—and had come down to Cambridge during your university's Christmas recess in order to do a bit of local research on that showboat. You were aloof but not incordial; it took some pressing to get the foregoing out of you—but I know how to press.

As Jeannine and Mrs. Upper West Side were off to the Ladies, I told you what I knew of the old Chesapeake showboat myself. Moreover, without actually mentioning my own adventure thereupon in 1937 or my just-completed memoir, I observed that the vessel had been equipped with two sets of stage- and houselights: one electric for landings with available power, such as Cambridge, one acetylene for landings without. And I remarked that, given the volatility of acetylene on the one hand, and on the other that old staple of riverboat programs, the sound-effects imitation of famous steamboat races and explosions, one could imagine a leaky valve's effecting a cataclysmic coincidence of fiction and fact, or art and reality.

You were amused. You extemporized on my conceit, bringing the portentous name of the boat and its impresario into your improvisation. We got on.

My age allows me to confess without embarrassment that I have always admired the novelist's calling and often wished I had been born to it. My generation is perhaps the only one in middle-class America that ever took its writers seriously: Faulkner, Hemingway, Steinbeck, Scott Fitzgerald, and John Dos Passos are my contemporaries; with the latter two, during their Baltimore residences, I was socially acquainted. Nowadays the genre is so fallen into obscure pretension on the one hand and cynical commercialism on the other, and so undermined at its popular base by television, that to hear a young person declare his or her ambition to be a capital-W Writer strikes me as anachronistical, quixotic, as who should aspire in 1969 to be a Barnum & Bailey acrobat, a dirigible pilot, or the Rembrandt of the stereopticon. Even on the last day of 1954 and the first of 1955 it struck me thus, though I saw no point in so remarking to you. But in the 1920's and '30's, even into the '40's, there was still a heroism in your vocation such as I think there will never be again in this country; a considerable number of us had rather been Hemingway than Gary Cooper or Charles Lindbergh, for example.

It was this reflex of respect that interested me enough in you to draw you out on your ambition (at your then age and stage, neither more nor less realistic than Jeannine's) and to pursue the coincidence of our preoccupation with the Floating Theatre. Before I left the yacht club with the Singer party, you and I were discussing the philosophical implications of suicide (I was surprised you'd not yet read Sartre or Camus, not to mention Kierkegaard and Heidegger, so fashionable on the campuses then). I went so far as to confide to you the nature of my *Letter to My Father*—you'd mentioned Kafka's to his, which I'd not heard of—and my *Inquiry:* the one setting forth my precarious heart condition and my reasons for not apprising Father of it; the other investigating *his* suicide in 1930. I don't remember saying good night.

The third notable thing that happened to me before morning was that my celibacy—imperfectly maintained since the end of my old romance with Jane Mack, and more a passive habit than an active policy—took its worst beating in seventeen years at the hands so to speak of Mrs. Upper West Side at the Tidewater Inn, across the Choptank in Less Primitive Talbot County, where the Singers were stopping. Their friend had, it developed, a Thing about Courtly Southern Gentlemen (Oedipus Rhett?). It was a blow to her to hear from me that Maryland had officially sided with the Union in the Civil War; that grits and hominy and live oaks and Spanish moss are not to be found in our latitude; that Room Service listed no mint juleps among their nightcaps. I consoled her with promises of terrapin chowder and a pressed wild-duck sandwich come morning, and the news that *our* part of Maryland had been staunchly Confederate, and Loyalist before that, and had enjoyed its latest Negro lynching well within her lifetime. I believe she had half hoped to find a slave whip under my vest, boll weevils in the bed; I in turn was expected to be titillated by such exotica as that she was fourteen years my junior, an aggressive fellationist and stand-up copulator, and a *Jewess* (her term, which she despised, hissed seductively through perfect teeth). I professed to be astonished that her *tuchas* bore no Cabalistic emblems, her *pipik* no hidden diamonds—only, lower down, a much tidier cesarean scar than could readily be left by our small-town surgeons. She declared herself dumbfounded that I had no tattooed flag of Dixie on my foreskin—nay, more, *no foreskin!* We laughed and humped our heads off for some days into the new year, in her hotel and mine, the Singers having long since smiled good-bye to us at the Easton airport.

Sharon's husband-on-the-way-out, I learned, was the actor Melvin Bernstein. His real name had been Mel Miller; as an apprentice borscht-circuit comic he'd changed it to sound more Jewish; later, when he moved into "straight" acting, he regretted not having kept the low-profile original, but couldn't bring himself to sacrifice the small and no longer quite appropriate celebrity of his stage name. To the consequent ambiguity of his scope and unambiguity of his name he attributed his failure to succeed as a leading man; but his career as a character actor was established in New York, and he was beginning to pick up similar roles in films. He was compulsively promiscuous, Sharon testified, and addicted to anal copulation, which she found uncomfortable and distasteful as well as, on the testimony of her proctologist, conducive to hemorrhoids. Hence the action for divorce, despite Mel's engaging to offer to lubricate his vice with *shmaltz.* I was to muse upon this information six years later, when Jeannine Patterson Mack Singer, still the hopeful pre-starlet, flew out to Los Angeles via Reno to become the next Mrs. Melvin Bernstein.

Well.

About your *Floating Opera* novel, which appeared the following year, I understandably have mixed feelings. On the one hand it was decidedly a partial betrayal on your part of a partial confidence on mine, and though you altered names and doctored facts for literary effect, some people hereabouts imagined they saw through to the real thing, with consequent minor inconvenience to my law practice and my solitary life. It was not long after, for example, that I exchanged my regular room in the Dorset for a certain goose-hunting retreat out on Todds Point, down the river, and commissioned a local boatbuilder to convert me a skipjack to live aboard in Cambridge in the summer, when the hotel gets too warm. On the other hand, my old love of fiction, aforementioned, was gratified to see the familiar details of my life and place projected as through a camera obscura. What's more, Harrison Mack read the novel too, found in it more to praise than to blame despite the unflattering light it cast him in, and was prompted to reopen a tentative correspondence with me, which soon led to the chaste reestablishment of our friendship and my retention as counsel for Mack Enterprises on the Eastern Shore. For this indirect and unintended favor, I'm your debtor.

The company had bought out old Colonel Morton's farms and canneries, including the Redmans Neck property, and was replacing the tomatoes with more profitable soybeans. Harrison was just beginning to fancy himself George III of England and Jane to display the business acumen of her forebear and ideal, Elizabeth Patterson Bonaparte. I did not know then—what I learned only last month—that Jane's managerial activity, doubtless like Betsy's, coincided with the termination of her menses by hysterectomy and, by her own choice, of her sexual life. Just prior to her surgery, in 1949, Jane had permitted herself the second extramarital affair of her biography, this time without Harrison's complaisance: a brief wild fling in London and Paris with Sir Jeffrey William Pitt, Lord Amherst, now deceased, then husband of that same Lady Amherst you mention in your postscript and descendant of the Lord Jeff of French and Indian War celebrity. More anon.

Under Jane's direction, Mack Enterprises throve and prospered. From chemical fertilizers and freeze-dried foods they branched into certain classified research in the chemical-warfare way, over the protests of myself (by then a stockholder) and son Drew, a political science undergraduate at Johns Hopkins. The Macks bought, built, and moved to Tidewater Farms; I became a trustee, then executive director of their Tidewater Foundation; Jeannine married Mel Bernstein; Drew scandalized his parents by going off to do graduate work at Brandeis, along with Angela Davis, under Herbert Marcuse. The Tidewater Foundation implemented, in addition to Tidewater Tech, dozens of lesser Mack philanthropies, some whimsical, not all with the unanimous consent of the trustees: a quack health farm in west New York and Ontario, not unlike the one described in your *End of the Road* novel (I opposed it; Jane and Harrison approved it for the sake of Jeannine, a sometime patient there); the Jerome Bonaparte Bray Computer Center at Lily Dale, N.Y. (he's the crank you ask about in your letter, whom also I opposed; but both Macks were impressed by the Bonaparte connection, and Drew, to their surprise, also approved the project, for reasons not entirely clear); the Annual Greater Choptank July 4th Fireworks Display (this was a prickly one, as it offended both Harrison in his George III aspect and Drew in his radical antichauvinism. We pacified the father with a private Guy Fawkes Day display out on Redmans Neck; Drew's demand for an equal-candlepower May Day celebration was then outvoted). Among our current unanimous beneficiaries are the upcoming Dorchester Tercentenary and a floating summer repertory theater on the Cambridge-Oxford-Annapolis circuit: a larger replica of Captain Adams's showboat, it bears the paradoxical name *Original Floating Theatre II*. Never mind that Jeannine Patterson Mack Singer Bernstein Golden, (as of 1963, when she left old Mel for

Louis Golden, a producer of B—and blue—movies) exploited this charity to play roles she never could have won on her own: the productions, alternating with old flicks, are by far the best in the area, and this venture led the foundation into other cultural philanthropies: a media department at Tidewater Tech (now Marshyhope College), for example, and the subsidizing of young artists dealing with the local scene. *E.g.*, as perhaps you know, "Bea Golden's" latest lover (Louis having gone the way of his predecessors in 1968), the formidable Reggie Prinz, whose film-in-the-works of your new book is partially backed by foundation money.

I'm ahead of myself. Lord and Lady Amherst stopped at Tidewater Farms in 1961 and were, excuse me, royally entertained by the Macks, whether because Harrison and Lady A. knew nothing of Jane's old affair (Jane herself, I am bemused to learn, has a positive genius for repressing unwelcome memories), or because Harrison's royal delusion by then insulated him from jealousy (George III never wondered about Queen Charlotte). More likely, bygones were simply bygones. It was during this visit that Harrison first associated Germaine Pitt Amherst with the Countess of Pembroke, Lady Elizabeth Spencer: a new and fateful stage of his madness, partly responsible for her later invitation to MSUC. I first met her then, too, and liked her better than I liked her husband.

Meanwhile, up in Waltham, Mass., Andrews Mack has become fashionably but by no means insincerely radicalized. Having disappointed his parents in the first place by choosing Hopkins and Brandeis as his soul mothers rather than Princeton and Harvard, he now quite exasperates them by dropping his doctoral studies in '63 to assist in the Cambridge (Maryland) civil rights demonstrations—quite as his father had picketed his *own* father's pickle factories back in the thirties. When the July 4th fireworks were canceled that year on account of the race riots, Harrison followed the family tradition of disowning his son, though not by formal legal action. Drew responded by promptly marrying one of his ex-classmates, a black girl from Cambridge.

I do not suggest that he married her solely as a gesture of protest: Yvonne Miner Mack is a striking young woman, Brandeis-bright, less radical than her husband but well to the left of Bobby Kennedy, for example, in whose office in the Justice Department the Cambridge riots were temporarily adjudicated; Drew loved her and had been living with her for some time. But unlike his friend and apparent mentor "H. C. Burlingame VII" (don't ask), young Mack is simplistic by policy as well as ingenuous and sincere by nature, and lives largely in ardent symbols. Moreover, he'd been opposed to marriage thitherto on the usual radicalist grounds. They have two sons now: bright, handsome little chaps whom Drew instructs in their African heritage and Yvonne takes to hear Leonard Bernstein's children's concerts. Sinistral but nowise sinister, long-haired and ascetic, Drew Mack looks to me less a hippie than a Massachusetts Minuteman in his denims, boots, and homespun shirts, his hair tied neatly back with a rubber band. I would bet my life on his integrity; not a nickel on his subtlety or diplomacy—and I think the Established Order has more to fear from him than from all the H. C. Burlingames and A. B. Cooks together, for he lives his beliefs down to the finest print he can understand.

In 1966 he made an impassioned but cogent appeal to the Tidewater Foundation to underwrite the Black Power movement on the Eastern Shore, for Our Own Ultimate Good. Jane and Harrison were indignant, the other conservative trustees scornful, the "liberals" opposed on principle to committing the foundation politically. All were concerned for the delicate negotiations, then in progress, for annexing Tidewater Tech to the state university system. The vote, but for Drew's own, was unanimously negative, the executive director abstaining. Drew thereupon abandoned his efforts to Work Within the System and urged his most militant colleagues to burn Whitey down. The following summer, as you will recall, a modest attempt was mounted to do just that, and Yours Truly (who this time did *not* abstain) came near to being blown up for the second time in his life. One day I shall tell you the story.

Better, I'll tell you it now, and· so wind up this calliope music. I belong to that nearly extinct species, famously discredited by history, contemned alike by the Harrison Macks from the right and by the Drew Macks from the left: I mean the Stock Liberal, whom I persist in believing to be the best stock in the store. He is the breed most easily baited for half-measures and most easily caught in self-contradiction, for he affirms the complexity of most social-economic problems and the ambivalence of his own approaches to their solution. If he is in addition (as I have been since 1937) inclined to the Tragic View of history and human institutions, he is even easier to scoff at, for he has no final faith that all the problems he addresses admit of political solutions—in some cases, of any solution whatever—any more than the problems of evil and death; yet he sets about them as if they did. He sees the attendant virtues of every vice, and vice versa. He is impressed by the fallibility of people and programs: it surprises him when anything works, merely disappoints him when it fails. He is in short a perfect skeptic in his opinions, an incorrigible optimist in his actions, for he believes that many injustices which can't be remedied may yet be mitigated, and that many things famously fragile—Reason, Tolerance, Law, Democracy, Humanism—are nonetheless precious and infinitely preferable to their contraries. He is ever for Reform as against revolution or reaction: in his eyes, the Harrison Macks and A. B. Cooks live in the past, the Drew Macks and H. C. Burlingames perhaps in the future, his kind alone in the present. Yet, as a connoisseur of paradoxes, he understands to the bone that one of St. Augustine's concerning time: that while the Present does not exist (it being the merely conceptual razor's edge between the Past and the Future), at the same time it's all there is: the Everlasting

Now between a Past existing only in memory and a Future existing only in anticipation.

Harrison and Drew delight in pointing out his inconsistencies: he values private property, even affluence; savors elitist culture; prizes maximum personal liberty and freedom from exterior restraints; yet he argues for public ownership of anything big enough to threaten the public weal, an ever more equitable distribution of wealth and privilege, and government regulation, for the public interest, of nearly everything except free speech, assembly, and the rest. He readily acknowledges this inconsistency, yields to none in his distaste for bureaucratic inefficiency, officiousness, and self-serving mediocrity—but will not be dissuaded from his conviction that these apparent inconsistencies in part reflect the complexity and ambiguity of the real world, and affirm the indispensability of good judgment, good will, and good humor. Drew and Harrison agree, if on nothing else, that either the Father kills the Son or the Son emasculates the Father. The Bourgeois-Liberal Tragic-Viewing Humanist tisks his tongue at that and plaintively inquires (knowing but not accepting the reply): "Why can they not do neither, but simply *shake hands,* like *Praeteritas* and *Futuras* on the Mack Enterprises letterhead, and reason together?"

What a creature, your Stock Liberal: little wonder his stock declines! Especially if he makes bold to act out his Reasonability between the fell incensèd points of mighty opposites: in this corner (the black Second Ward of Cambridge), a Pontiac hearse bearing a casket packed to the Plimsoll with boxes of dynamite, plastic TNT, blasting caps, and black incendiaries bent on blowing up the Chesapeake Bay Bridge, to cut Whitey off from his pleasures at Ocean City and to dramatize the Fascist Insularity of the Eastern Shore; in this corner (somewhere suspiciously near Tidewater Farms), a platoon of paramilitary red-neck gun-nuts armed with a pickup truckload of automatic weapons filched from the National Guard Armory and bent on wiping out that Pontiac hearse in particular if not the Second Ward in general. In the background, a detachment of the Maryland National Guard itself, with less firepower by half. And in the center (the second lamppost south of the trusses on the Choptank River Bridge, as shall be shown), your Bourgeois-Liberal TVH aforedescribed: fishing tackle in one hand, picnic basket in the other (in which are two corned beef sandwiches, two Molson's Ales, a bullhorn, a portable Freon airhorn, and a voice-operated tape recorder); the sweat of fear in his palms and of July in his armpits; the smile of Sweet Reasonableness nervously lighting his countenance.

I have never been an especially brave or an especially emotional man, sir. The Todd Andrews of your story had by his 54th year felt powerful emotions on just five occasions: *mirth* in 1917, when he lost his virginity in front of a mirror; *fear* in 1918, in an artillery barrage in the Argonne Forest; *frustration* in 1930, at his father's suicide, which prompted his *Inquiry; surprise* in 1932, when Jane Mack came naked to him in his bed in her summer cottage (the same I now own, and sleep and dream in); *despair* in 1937, when impotence, endocarditis, and other *raisons de ne pas être* met in plenary session on a certain June night in his Dorset Hotel room. To these was added, this humid airless early-Leo afternoon, *courage,* which I had admired as a quality but not thitherto known as an emotion. On the contrary, I had imagined it (I mean physical courage, not mere moral courage, a different fish entirely) to be a sort of clench-jawed resolution in the *face* of such emotions as fear, and surely that it often is. But it can be an emotion itself, a flavor distinct from that of the fear it overvails and the adrenaline-powered exaltation that garnishes it. If fear feels like a draining of the heart, I report that the emotion of courage feels like a cardiac countersurge, and that not for nothing are *heartened* and *disheartened* synonyms for *encouraged* and *discouraged.*

Join to these vascular tide-rips and crosscurrents the thunderous pulse of anticipatory excitement—a Bay of Fundy colliding with a Gulf Stream!—such as might be felt by a 67-year-old man who, having learned from sources in the Second Ward that the Pontiac hearse, Drew Mack at the wheel, is preparing to head for East Cambridge and the Choptank Bridge en route to the Big One over the Chesapeake, and from other sources close to "George III" that the red-necks plan to station themselves on the Talbot County shore of that same bridge and bazooka that same Pontiac to Kingdom Come—who having learned this, I say, in the forenoon, has made several fast phone calls from his office, left instructions for other such calls, snatched up said spinning reel and prepacked picnic basket (the news was not unexpected), and been dropped off by his secretary at the second lamppost on pretext of casting after a few hardheads on the running tide. . .

Where was I? At the conjunction of all these currents, with the oldest case of subacute bacterial endocarditis in the county, a myocardium supposed to have been on the brink of infarction since 1919: no "ticker" now, but an Anvil Chorus in double-time. . .

Your Stock Bourgeois-Liberal Tragic-Viewing Humanist, if he happens to practice law for a living, will be a soft touch in the needy-but-deserving-client way: a one-man chapter of the ACLU, a little Legal Aid Society. I hope I've never exploited the gratitude of poor whites and blacks whose legal fees I've written off to BLTVHism; on the other hand, to scorn what they gratefully offer in lieu of cash were priggish, no? And when good people hope they can one day return a considerable service, they mean it from hearts much steadier than mine. Now, Dorothy Miner was one such, in the Second Ward, Drew's mother-in-law, who, having toiled her life through to build her children's way out of the ghetto, disapproved of demolitions, whether of bridges or of people. She it was who had apprised me of the bomb plot in the first place, and who now put through the crucial call to Joe Reed, another ex-client, tender of the Choptank River Bridge. From his little house up in the trusswork of the center span, Joe Reed had seen the Chevy pickup go under half an hour before, called his buddy (a third former client) at the liquor store just off the Talbot end of the bridge, and confirmed the intended ambush—which confirmation he relayed to the second lamppost by a single ding of the traffic warning bell at the draw-span gates, hard by. He then telephoned his colleague and counterpart (for whom *he* had once done a favor) on the Cambridge *Creek* bridge, who returned the favor by returning the call when the hearse crossed *his* bridge en route to ours en route to its. Got that? Two dings.

Fishing, you will remember, is permitted only on the west side of our bridge, facing downriver, there being no sidewalk on the east. The incoming tide, not quite slack, still carried fishing lines under the roadway. Only a few black families were out in the heat. It is my custom, like your Todd Andrews's and my late father's, not to change out of my office clothes for chores and recreation: I am the only skipjack skipper on the Bay who sails in three-piece suits. But given my purpose, I felt disagreeably conspicuous cutting up peeler crabs for bait in my circuit-court seersuckers—all the while watching the Cambridge shore near Mensch's Castle, where good Polly Lake (my coeval, my irreplaceable, a widow now) had parked after dropping me off. Thence came, just as I baited my hook with the black and orange genitals of the peeler, best bait on the beast, three flashes in series of her headlights— 1-2-3, 1-2-3, 1-2-3—and three blasts of *her* portable Freon airhorn, counterpart to the one in my basket, both from my boat. I returned the signal; my fellow fisherfolk looked around to find the approaching boat, three such blasts being the call to open the draw. Joe Reed replied in kind, set his dingers dinging and flashers flashing, lowered the stop gate just inshore from each end of the trusses, and set the big center span turning on its great geared pivot. As it swung, and his office with it, he also telephoned the highway-patrol barracks up in Easton, advised them that he was having some difficulty closing the draw, and requested troopers to be dispatched to both ends of the bridge to get the waiting traffic turned around in case the problem persisted.

As you know, the Choptank Bridge is a two-laner nearly two miles long with the draw-span roughly in the middle. A light flow of traffic in both directions guaranteed that Drew could not much exceed the 50-mph limit; we had about a minute, then, from Polly Lake's signal till the hearse should reach the draw. Three-quarters of it remained when I'd set the bullhorn beside my basket and, not to alert the quarry prematurely, turned away and cast my baited line. At 30 seconds the gates were down; the line of waiting northbound cars was accumulating down toward my lamppost; the last of the southbound traffic to clear the span had passed on toward Cambridge. I turned in that direction; the hearse was just drawing up to the end of the line, two lampposts away. I saw one pink face behind the windshield. Something struck my hook hard, bowing the glass rod and taking line off the spinning reel with a whine.

My hope had been that before he grew suspicious Drew would be pinned by the cars before and behind him and obliged to listen as I warned him of the waiting trap. Perhaps the reflex motion of my setting the hook drew his attention; by the time I'd set the drag on my reel and had begun to pass the rod around the lamppost to secure it, he'd stopped a few yards behind his predecessor and popped out to size up the one white fisherman in sight, summer-suited to boot. Then up on the hearse's running board to con the shipless channel as a lean and goateed black colleague emerged from the passenger door. Both then ducked furiously back inside.

I went for the bullhorn; Drew whipped the hearse out into the empty left lane as if to run me down or crash the gate—beyond which, however, now yawned the full-open span. He slammed the machine into reverse, either to attempt a turn-around or to back up the mile to the Cambridge shore; whereupon good Polly Lake, who had started across the bridge at once after giving her signal and was drawn up now some ten cars back in line with room to maneuver, swung out smartly, turn-signal flashing, as if she meant somehow to pass the whole line of waiting cars. As the hearse backed madly toward her she stopped, leaned on her horn, turned off her motor (pumping the gas pedal deliberately to flood the carburetor), and coolly played the role of Rattled Nice Lady.

For a moment I feared collision. Then Drew hit the brakes; the hearse rocked to a stop; he and two cohorts jumped out; curtains parted along the side of the hearse until Drew waved them shut. I saw hands in pockets and put down the bullhorn, fearing pistols; *ran* instead (the final trial of heart) to where they craned and conned en route to Polly.

"God *damn* it, Todd!" Drew was livid with frustration, as you writers say; almost in tears, I thought. One of the blacks, the lean goateed chap, was ordering Polly to clear her car out fast or he'd do it for her. She flutteringly apologized, made as if to offer him the keys, dropped them on the floorboard, went scrabbling after them. The other black, a squat muscled fellow in a lavender tank-top and white wool cap, surveyed us from a little distance. The idling drivers watched with interest.

"You know this cat?" Goatee asked Drew, who assured him I wasn't a policeman and half threatened, half pleaded with me to get the bridge closed and/or Mrs. Lake out of the way before someone got hurt.

"He know what we up to?" Goatee demanded.

"They together," Tank-Top concluded of us to Goatee. Rapidly I told the three of them that I was aware of their intentions, sympathized with their anger, and had intercepted them, not to turn them in to the police, but to spare them the ambush waiting at the far end of the bridge. I advised them to show no weapons before so many witnesses; I urged them to turn the hearse around and head back to Cambridge before the state police arrived to clear the stuck bridge.

"Here come the mothers now," observed Goatee. I too, with sinking and still-pounding heart, had seen the red flasher of a highway patrol car that swung now into the left lane at the end of the bridge, to which the backed-up traffic nearly extended, and raced toward us, penetrator whooping. Polly Lake (my clear master in the grace-under-pressure way) had cranked and cranked her engine, wondering aloud why it wouldn't start, it was always so dependable. Seeing the patrol car, she put by her helplessness and cranked with the pedal full down to choke the flooded engine to life.

"Tell Sy to start the timer," Drew suddenly decided. "We'll blow this one instead." Tank-Top, to whom the order was directed, hesitated a moment, looking to Goatee for confirmation. They'd be blowing themselves up for nothing, I argued quickly: Ocean City traffic would merely be rerouted, and their self-demolition reported as a murderous accident by inept amateur terrorists. How this honky know so much? Goatee demanded angrily of Drew. Polly Lake backed up to stop the patrol car a few hundred feet away; went into her Fuddled Lady act with the irritated trooper, whom with relief I recognized. Again Drew urged immediate demolition. I pointed out that all the fishermen and many of the waiting motorists were black; exhorted them to retreat, regroup, replan: the red-necks wouldn't spring their trap in full view of the state police on the other side of the draw, but would certainly make their move in the hour's drive between the Choptank and the Chesapeake Bridge—which (I lied) was by now surely guarded by troopers alerted to the event.

"Get in the car, Todd," Drew ordered me. "If we get it, you get it too."

I considered. Trooper James Harris had sent Polly backing to her slot and now walked our way, shaking his head. Ignoring Drew's threat, I saluted him by name, told him that these people had an important funeral to get to: could he get them around and off the bridge fast?

"Jesus H. Christ," the young officer replied, and in three glances sized up ourselves, the hearse, and the still-empty space in the line it had pulled out of. "Come on, then, swing your ass around here. You with them, Mister Andrews?"

I shook my head. "Just fishing, Jimmy. Much obliged." And I turned my back on all of them, not knowing whether they or my banging heart would let me regain the second lamppost.

They did, and here are five postscripts to the anecdote:

1. Both bridges still stand, across which so much traffic moves from Baltimore and Washington to the ocean that the state is constructing new ones beside the old to accommodate the flow: 90% white, though the cities from which they stream are more than 50% black. Had our quarter-hour drama occurred on a summer Sunday night, the Route 50 traffic would have been backed up for a dozen miles. I despise this saturation of our Eastern Shore enough to wish sometimes that *all* the bridges were blown; but I take at last the Tragic View of progress, as

well as of insularity. These 1960's have been a disaster; the 70's will be another—but the 50's don't bear recollecting either, not to mention the 40's, 30's, 20's, 10's. History is a catenation of disasters, redeemable only (and imperfectly) by the Tragic View.

2. The young men in the hearse went home, revised their plans, and fetched in H. "Rap" Brown to liven up the movement's oratory and focus the media on their grievances. Arson ensued. But so far from "burning Whitey down"—for any serious attempt at *that* they'd have been massacred—the incendiaries were Effectively Contained in the Second Ward. When alarmed black families then appealed to have the white volunteer fire department sent in to deal with the blazes, they were told, in effect: *You* brought that bastard to town; put out your own fires. And so the sufferers from the riots—and from the cruelest second-person plural in the grammar books—were all black. But this is not news to you. Only the Tragic View will do, and it not very satisfactorily. Must one take the tragic view of the Tragic View?

3. Some while after, when Mr. Brown had been arrested and his venue changed, Goatee, Tank-Top, and possibly Sy the timer man blew themselves inadvertently sky-high, as follows: I had considered reporting to Jimmy Harris the contents and objectives of both the Pontiac hearse and the Chevrolet pickup; but though I believe profoundly in the institutions of justice under the law, I can manage at best no more than the Tragic View of their actual operation. Therefore on second thought I considered reporting neither. But while the bark of both the black militants and the red-neck vigilantes was worse than their bite, the former were a threat much more to property than to people, the latter vice versa, and one's BLTVH sympathies are of course all with the hearse in this matter (even though, to complicate things, some of those red-necks are friends of mine: good-hearted, high-principled, even lovable people except where certain prejudices are touched. And at least one of those blacks happens to have been a hopeless sociopath. The Tragic View!).

Thus it was the Pontiac, not the Chevy, I'd intercepted and tried to reason with; thus it was the Chevy I reported, by telephone from Joe Reed's office to the Easton state police barracks when Joe closed the draw. That evening I informed Drew that I'd done so, and that the red-necks in turn, if questioned, would surely identify the hearse, its occupants and intentions, as would I if interrogated under oath as a witness in the matter. Drew and company prudently thereupon changed vehicles and left town, resolved to dynamite any courthouse where their hero was to stand trial. But as in the field of cesarean sutures, for example, big-city expertise in the field of high-explosive terrorism is less readily available to us home folks: Sy's timer (or something) misfired outside a little village across the Bay as the group—minus Drew, temporarily outcast for his connections with me—motored toward its first new target. The remains were unidentifiable, almost unlocatable. There was chortling among conservatives, tongue-tisking among us Stock Liberals.

"Goatee," their leader, was, I then learned, Dorothy Miner's son, Yvonne's brother, Drew's brother-in-law, whom Dorothy had toiled to put through high school and college: an easygoing youngster turned terrorist by his reading of history at a black branch campus of the state university. "Tank-Top," whom I'd taken for vintage ghetto, turned out to be the child of third-generation-affluent New England educators; he had discovered his negritude as a twelfth-former at the Phillips Exeter Academy, become a militant at Magdalen College (Oxford), and exquisitely exchanged his natural Boston-Oxbridge accent and wardrobe for what we heard and saw above. His major passions in student days had been rugby and the novels of William Dean Howells.

4. My bait had been taken by a fair-size croaker, or hardhead, increasingly rare in these waters where once they abounded. A fellow fisherman had thoughtfully unwound my tackle from the lamppost and played him for me through the foregoing. Now he returned the gear to me and stood by with his companions for the reel-in. As sometimes happens in bridge fishing, where the game isn't caught until it's in the basket, my prize, well hooked and played, flipped itself free midway between river and roadway and splashed home.

"That a heart-buster now, ain't it?" my colleague commiserated, and went back to his own lamppost.

5. But it wasn't, as my survival to this sentence attests; no more than the Argonne Forest had been, or my evening in Captain Adams's Floating Theatre, or any other *mauvais quart d'heure* of my life to this, including that mauvaisest just recounted. At the end of your *Floating Opera* story, 37-year-old Todd Andrews, his attempt at suicide-by-holocaust having fizzled, imagines he'll probably go on living one day at a time, as he has thitherto; the cardiac report of the doctor you call Marvin Rose (now dead of—you guessed it) is of no interest to him. And the 54-year-old Todd Andrews who has been telling the story of his Dark Night of the Soul gives us no clue to that report, though his tone and attitude—not to mention the fact of his narrative—imply the fulfillment of his expectations. Now, as I left the bridge with Polly Lake, I realized that my heart had finally ratified my change of policy of some years past, when I'd ceased to pay for my Dorset Hotel room one night at a time and moved for the most part out to that cottage I'd bought from the Macks: *i.e.,* that I was fated to no less than the normal life expectancy of male WASP Americans of my generation; that that old Damoclean diagnosis of bacterial endocarditis had been for me ever at least as much a spiritual need as a physical fact; and that just as the fact had gradually long since become irrelevant, the need had imperceptibly passed as well.

So I saw, retrospectively, with sharp suddenness as we left the bridge. The river was still; Polly Lake's nose perspired despite her car's air conditioning as she chattered crisply about Nice Young Jimmy Harris, whom she'd known as a schoolboy and lost track of till today. I couldn't answer; she attributed my incapacity to excitement, nervous exhaustion—which it surely was, but not from the encounter itself. I trembled toward a vast new insight, which I was far from confident I could cope with: the virtual opposite of the one I reached in my old memoir. There I premised that "nothing has intrinsic value"; here I began to feel (I can scarcely enounce it; have yet to lay hold of its excruciating, enormous implications). . .that Nothing *has* intrinsic value. . .which is as much as to say: *Everything* has intrinsic value!

I don't know what I'm saying; I'm no philosopher; I despise cheap mysticism, trashy transcendencies. But the river, every crab and nettle on the swinging tide, every gull and oyster and mosquito, not to mention Drew and Tank-Top, Polly Lake, Joe Reed, Jimmy Harris, the Choptank Bridge—and my late father, and the Mother I Never Knew, and Jeannine Patterson Mack Singer Bernstein Golden, all her husbands, and *her* mother, who once came to me naked and by surprise on a humming summer noon a hundred years ago, and all the creatures of the past, the present, the future—they all are precious! Were precious! Will be precious!

I wept for history. I came perilously close to something "beyond" the Tragic View. Polly understood, suggested we stop somewhere for a bracer. We did, aboard my skipjack in the Municipal Basin, where she has often been my companion. I felt a need to drift with time and tide on something intimately seasoned, crafted, nobly weathered yet still graceful: my *Osborn Jones* and good Polly Lake both filled that bill. Cold Molson's Ale returned the Mystic Vision to incipience, restored me to my home waters: rationalist-skeptical BLTVHism, where I am still moored—though with dock lines thenceforth and to this hour singled up, ready to cast off for that strange new landfall briefly glimpsed.

I had meant to end the historical part of this letter with a fuller account of Harrison Mack's "decline" and Lady Amherst's artful comforting of his last years. But my morning allotted to letter writing has moved ahead into early afternoon; I must go down to the boatyard and attend to brightwork on *Osborn Jones*. Therefore I shall skip the account of Jane Mack's visit to my office last week: her curious confession, her disquieting combination of shrewdness, candor, and obliviousness. Your retelling of it notwithstanding, I cannot say confidently that Jane even *remembers* our old love affair! It is in any case *as if* it had never happened. Remarkable, that the bridge between fact and fiction, like that between Talbot and Dorchester, is a two-way street.

I've gone on at this length and with this degree of confidentiality because, with respect to your solicitation, like E. M. Forster I could not know what I thought till I saw what I said. Having said so much, as if to tease or dare you into making use of it, I find my reservations still strong, though not quite final. The rumors current, that Reg Prinz's company will film that old showboat story on location, promise me renewed discomfort, the more so if, coincident with the county's Tercentenary and the dedication of Marshyhope's "Tower of Truth" (both occasions of local pride), you were to publish another satiric novel with an Eastern Shore setting and a character named Todd Andrews. Certain of my current "cases"—in particular the threatened litigation between Jane and Drew over Harrison's estate—are of perhaps more delicacy and moment than any I've handled since the ones you described, almost plausibly, in your *Opera*. Not just my welfare and the Macks' are involved, but the Tidewater Foundation, its multifarious philanthropies, and (so Drew declares) even Larger Stakes.

All which items, to be sure, have dramatic potential, and are almost fictional in their factual state. But I'm not an *homme de lettres;* my dealings are with the actual lives of actual people, and if my view of them is tragical, it's not exploitative.

But no matter. I beg pardon for speaking like a literary advisor, even like a father, when in fact it's you who are in a sense *my* father, the engenderer of "Todd Andrews." But *(a)* I'm old enough to *be* your father; *(b)* my own principal literary production has been that *Letter to My Father* (now younger than I am!), which this "letter to my son" threatens to rival in prolixity; and *(c)* never having had a son of my own, it's a tone I'm prone to, as Drew does not fail to remind me.

So what am I saying? That I shall consider your invitation further over Easter (anniversary of another famous sequel, more ambiguous than Napoleon's Hundred Days) and rereply. Meanwhile, I must caution you against rising fictively to any of the factual bait I've herein chummed the tide with, or reusing my name without my express permission. I say this in no sense to rattle sabers; only to apprise you, like a telltale on the luff of your imagination, that you're sailing very close to the wind. And not yet with my approval and consent, though decidedly with my most cordial

Good wishes,
T.A.

T: *Jacob Horner to Jacob Horner. Progress and Advice.*

4/3/69

To: Jacob Horner, Remobilization Farm, Fort Erie, Ontario, Canada
From: Jacob Horner, Remobilization Farm, Fort Erie, Ontario, Canada

To Marlon Brando, Doris Day, Henry IV, George Herbert, Washington Irving, happy birthday. Dante has found himself lost in the Dark Wood. Napoleon is occupying Rome. In Palm Springs, college students are rioting. Passover began at sunset. The Pony Express

97

commences mail service today between Sacramento and St. J——, Missouri. James Earl Ray is appealing his 99-year sentence. "U.N." troops are pushing the Chinese back across the 38th Parallel in Korea. The U.S. has opened warfare against Chief Black Hawk to drive the Fox and Sac Indians across the Mississippi. The Vietnamese peace talks have resumed in Paris: no progress. And you Failed Again to Complete your Suicide, well begun in 1953 and repromised in your Letter of March 6.

Scriptotherapy.

Since that letter, the *Ark* and the *Dove* have reached Maryland with Lord Baltimore's first colonists; Hannah Dustin has been captured by Indians in Haverhill, Mass., Geronimo has surrendered to General Crook in Mexico and escaped; Patrick Henry has delivered his liberty-or-death speech to the revolutionary convention in Richmond, which inclines to the former; Jacob Horner has been Born on President Madison's 172nd birthday, has Left College on his own 28th (Madison's 200th), has first been Fetched From Immobility by the Doctor, and has Turned 46 on Madison's 218th, no returns anticipated. The U.S.S. *Hornet* has captured the *Penguin*. Andrew Jackson has defeated the Creeks at Horseshoe Bend; Jean Lafitte has burned Galveston and disappeared with his Baratarians; President Madison (60) has disclosed the Henry Letters to Congress; the *Monitor* has damaged the *Merrimac* in Hampton Roads; Napoleon has 86 left of his 100 Days; Parliament has repealed the Stamp Act, too late now; Oliver Hazard Perry is building his Lake Erie fleet at Presque Isle, Pa. Not to Mention Blücher's entry with the Allies into Paris; the Commune's burning of the Tuileries; the Confederate evacuations of Petersburg and Richmond; Czar Nicholas's abdication; De Forest's first exhibition of talking films at the Rivoli in New York City; the founding of Rhode Island and the U.S. Navy; Germany's declaration of war on Portugal; Dr. Goddard's launching of the first liquid-fueled rocket in Auburn, Mass.; Hitler's invasion of Austria, occupation of Bohemia, and rejection of the Versailles Treaty; Lyndon Johnson's decision not to run for reelection; Martin Luther King Jr.'s march from Selma to Montgomery; Sieur de La Salle's murder by his own men in Texas; Madrid's surrender to General Franco; Franklin Roosevelt's first Fireside Chat; Russia's sale of Alaska to the U.S., blockade of Berlin, and invasion of Persia; the U.S.'s conquest of Iwo Jima, invasion of Okinawa, and suppression of the Philippine insurgents; Pancho Villa's raid on Columbus, N.M., and General Pershing's invasion of Mexico to kill or capture him. When you Were, in a sense, Jacob Horner, you Interested yourself, at the Doctor's prescription, in such events. Now you Merely Acknowledge calendric resonances, the anniversary view of history, and Catalogue them by Alphabetical Priority.

"Why alphabetical priority, Horner?" the Doctor asked you at your Annual Interview in the Progress and Advice Room. This was March 17th last, eighteenth anniversary of your First Such Session, and of other things. "When you used to be Unable to Make Choices, I gave you *three* principles to apply. Perhaps you have Forgotten."

He knows you have Forgotten Nothing of those semesters in Wicomico. You Repeated the principles of Sinistrality and Antecedence: if alternatives are side by side, choose the one on the left; if they're consecutive in time, choose the earlier; if neither of these applies, choose the alternative whose name begins with the earlier letter of the alphabet.

"But I'd often Have Trouble Choosing which principle to Use," you Told him. "In the order you first gave them to me—Sinistrality, Antecedence, Alphabetical Priority—Sinistrality is farthest left and earliest read, but not alphabetically prior. If I Put Antecedence first, it's both antecedent and sinistral but ditto. Then when I Started my Hornbook and Got in the Habit of Listing Things Alphabetically, I Remarked that in the series Alphabetical Priority, Antecedence, Sinistrality, Alphabetical Priority is alphabetically prior, as well as both antecedent and sinistral. So that's the one I Use."

"Jacob Horner: you are a Fool."

Knee to knee in the Progress and Advice Room, you both Regarded your Cigars.

"You are Forty-Six," the Doctor said.

"As of yesterday."

"Though we speak here only once a year now, and you are Virtually in Charge of Administering the Farm since Mrs. Dockey's death, you Still Regard yourself as My Patient?"

You Smiled Ruefully. "I'm Afraid So."

"*I'm Afraid So,*" the Doctor mocked. "You have Made No Progress in eighteen years, Horner. You are the Same Vacuum I picked up in Baltimore in 1951, except that you have Gotten Older, and it Took you longer than most of us to Do That. You will Be Here till you Die."

You Did Not Respond.

"Mrs. Dockey predicted as much in '53," the Doctor went on. "Also, that your Guilt in the matter of Mrs. Morgan's death was not suicidal, except figuratively. She predicted a long life for you, without content."

"You must miss Mrs. Dockey," you Ventured Sympathetically.

The Doctor considered. "A serviceable old twat. Very convenient for me in those days." He paused. "But I miss no one."

The subject of sexuality thus raised, there ensued an apparent digression from your Interview Proper to review those of the patients who were on Heterosexual Therapy. Tombo X, as a rule, services female patients under 40 whose schedules include this therapy, unless they require a Father Surrogate like the Doctor himself or unless miscegenation is judged antitherapeutic, in which cases either you or Monsieur Casteene accommodates them, depending. Your Own Services have proved most effective with elder women, in particular those pleasant Protestant widows who get through their summers at the old Chautauqua Institution, rocking with their silver-haired sorority on the wickered porches of the Athenaeum, but who tend to immobility in the dreary Great Lakes winters, which they have insufficient means to flee. Once convinced (by articles in the *Reader's Digest* on Swinging Senior Citizens and the New Gerontology) that there is nothing amiss in the stirrings of their bereft and sluggish blood, they take pleasure in the tonic of decorous fornication. And generally they experience less guilt and enjoy more remobilization with you than with a partner coeval to their late lamenteds.

You have Lapsed into Writing. Stop.

But Tombo X had announced that he could no longer get it up for Pocahontas—a hard-edged, fortyish WASP divorcee from Maryland who he declared would unman a regiment of rapists. His recommendation was that either a troop of motorcycle toughs be engaged to sodomize her out of her mind, or she be introduced to her latent lesbianism on the pretext of appealing for her help with Bibi, a nymphomaniac, alcoholic ex–movie starlet also among our problem patients. But the Doctor rejected the former course as antitherapeutic to everyone concerned except Tombo himself, always inclined to retaliation; the second as likely to raise more difficulties than it resolved. Sexuality, he feels, is not at the center of Pocahontas's immobility problem. What she needs for the present, in his opinion, is more testicles for her collection: when she has made aggressive conquest of and scornfully rejected all three male authority figures on the staff, perhaps a genuine program of therapies might be devised for her. Until then, since with refractory penises there is no reasoning, you will Replace Tombo X as her Mobilizer—always Bearing in Mind that women of Pocahontas's age and circumstances approach heterosexual connection with more than normal ambivalence, which fact makes Undue Aggressiveness or Passivity equally antitherapeutic. A male patient of your Approximate Character (i.e., Submissive but not Immobile) would be better grist for her mill than any staff member. So to speak. As we have none present, and you Are by your Own Acknowledgment still a Low-Grade but Ongoing Therapee, you're It. Enjoy yourself: those late-liberated, premenopausal WASPs can be in handsome condition and kicky in the bed when they keep their stingers in. But do not for a moment Let your Guard Down: they have hearts of ice and, unlike bees, can sting more than once.

You Pled Disqualification on the grounds of a Slight Prior Acquaintance, in college days, with Pocahontas's ex-husband, the writer Ambrose Mensch.

"Do not Bother me with History," the Doctor said. But troubled himself to inquire whether Pocahontas had been on the scene in those days.

"No. As a matter of fact, I Believe Mensch's mistress back then was the Mack girl. The one we're calling Bibi."

"Incroyable. Both here at the same time. Do they know?"

So far as you Knew, you Reported, Marsha Mensch and Bea

100

Golden (née Jeannine Mack of Maryland) were unacquainted with each other and with their historical nexus. You Did Not Bother to Add (the Doctor being uninterested on principle in case histories) that the middle-aged scholarly English gentlewoman who had been brought to the Farm from Toronto in 1967 by Monsieur Casteene to have a remobilizing operation under the nom de guerre of Lady Russex might also by this time be a friend of Ambrose Mensch's, since she went from here to a visiting professorship at Marshyhope College in Maryland, where Mensch would be her colleague. The *real* connection between the three is not your Former Acquaintance anyhow, but the late philanthropist Harrison Mack: father of Bibi, family friend of "Lady Russex," patron of both Marshyhope College and the Remobilization Farm, and thus indirect employer of Ambrose Mensch as well as yourself and, for that matter, of our former patient J. B. Bray of Lily Dale. Father too, finally, of the radical Drew Mack, whose activities are responsible for the Farm's becoming—in your Private Opinion and apparently unknown to the Doctor but not to Tombo X—an underground remobilization center of a quite different sort, of which our debonair, anything-but-immobilized M. Casteene is the unacknowledged director. By rejecting history, the Doctor spares himself much bemusement at such pretty interlacings.

But Stay: this is Writing.

"And you are No Longer in Correspondence with the husband?"

Had not Been in Correspondence with anyone save yourself, you Admitted, since 10/27/53.

"Then there is no reason to fear a replay of the Morgan fiasco," the Doctor concluded, "which is what you are Thinking of. In any case, you Can No Longer Impregnate; nor can Pocahontas, being divorced, achieve adultery. If it doesn't work out, Set her up with one of our straighter-looking draft dodgers."

In his latter years, especially since our removal from west New York to Ontario, the Doctor has become something of a chauvinist in the original sense, and espouses a hawkish line on U.S. involvement in Southeast Asia. He takes professional umbrage at what he calls the misuse of the precious word *movement* for an antiwar program whose chief tactic is obstruction by sit-in and going limp. Even the black civil rights movement, earlier in the decade, he would dignify by that term only in its marching, not its sitting, aspect, and he would not sing "We Shall Overcome" except at double its torpid tempo. For the young draft resisters who flock across the Peace Bridge from the States, he has only contempt. There are a number of them among the patients; very few, in your Opinion, suffer from clinical immobility. The Doctor agrees, and dismisses them as "kinetic hypochondriacs"; but they are here for another reason.

"What do the numbers 64502 and 79673 suggest to you, Horner?"

In the Progress and Advice Room you can Cross your Legs Comfortably in neither the "masculine" nor the "feminine" manner.

"The second is a postal zip code," you Hazarded. "Somewhere in Texas. Near Abilene? The first is the population of Clifton, New Jersey, in the 1950 census, give or take a dozen. By 1960 it was up over 82,000."

"Horner."

You Sighed. "Zip code and 1960 population, respectively, of a small city in northwestern Missouri."

"Named for the *first* great cuckold in the Christian tradition. Do you Have him in your Hornbook?"

You Nodded: "After Jason and before Karenin, Alexis. As a saint, he could I Suppose be in the *S*'s, with Shahryar of *The Thousand and One Nights*."

"Or in the *M*'s? With Menelaus?"

"And Harrison Mack and Malatesta," you Added Hurriedly. "That's Francesca da Rimini's husband Giovanni Malatesta, not her lover Paolo Malatesta. And Isolde's husband King Mark. And Atalanta's husband Melanion, a.k.a. Hippomenes, that either Ares or Meleager cuckolded, I Forget which. Also Minos of Crete. But I put Mary's husband with the *J*'s: Alphabetical Priority."

"Hum. Inasmuch as the late Rennie Morgan was not Jewish, I presume her husband had her body routinely embalmed, unless he was afraid the undertaker might spread the abortion story. But that would have been uncharacteristically irrational of him, since the county coroner had the facts already. Embalmed or not, that body that you Took such antitherapeutic pleasure in, Horner: do you Know what it looks like now, sixteen years after burial?"

You Controlled yourself.

"I don't either," the Doctor admitted. "Nor want to. Let her rot in peace. I suppose the Freudians would say that *our* 'Saint Joseph' became a historian to sublimate his basic necrophilia. It seems as likely to me that necrophilia is an occupational hazard of historians."

"My Own Guess," you Offered Quietly, "is that Joe loved his wife very deeply—"

"He should have buried her as deeply."

"—and never got over her death."

"What is he here for? Is he really whacked out, or is that his cover for something else?"

You Could Not Resist Inquiring With Some Amusement why the Doctor should worry, the statute having long since run on prosecution for manslaughter and illegal abortion in Rennie's case. He replied testily that "Saint Joseph" needed no waiver of the statute of limitations to pull a gun and take belated revenge for the loss of his wife, if he was truly deranged. Or, if his condition was feigned, to make difficulties for the Farm with provincial authorities.

"Last and least," he added, "his arrival here has set back your Own Case about fifteen years, by my reckoning, and that is ostensibly what we are here to talk about. Believe it or not, Horner, there are people who *enjoy their lives*. I am one of them. The Farm is a going concern. We have had less trouble in Fort Erie than anywhere in the States. I have made a few good investments. In two or three years I shall retire in moderate comfort to Switzerland or St. Croix, and you and my son may do what you please with these feebs and freaks. Till then, your Welfare is not unrelated to my own. Are you Quite Sure that this fellow is Morgan in the first place?"

No question, unfortunately, you Declared—though he had obviously changed in appearance and, to some extent, in attitude: his profession that he was Joseph Morgan "only in a sense" was a taunt. You were then Able to Discomfit the Doctor with a Quick Review of "Saint Joseph's" history: J. Patterson Morgan, born 1923 in Boston, descendant of the Baltimore Pattersons of whom the best-known wed Napoleon's brother in 1803; served in the navy after high school, in World War II; A.B. in philosophy from Columbia in 1949, courtesy of the G.I. Bill; M.A. in history, 1950, same school, where he met and married Renée MacMahon of Wicomico, Maryland; two children, sons, born 1950 and 1951; Ph.D. work in American history at Johns Hopkins, 1950–52: degree never completed. Thesis subject: The Saving Roles of Innocence and Energy in U.S. Political and Economic History. Dissertation abandoned after death of wife. Assistant professorship of history, Wicomico Teachers College, Maryland, 1952–53, where you First Met and Became Fatally Involved with him and Mrs. M. Resignation requested by WTC President John Schott 10/27/53, to mitigate scandal of Rennie's death.

Thus much from your Personal Knowledge, from which too you Attested Morgan's invincible and innocent (but not ingenuous) rationalism, his intellectual and physical energy, his unsanctimonious uprightness of character and brisk Yankee cheerfulness, his intense (and oppressive, and ultimately disastrous) devotion to his wife, her spiritual-intellectual welfare, the purity and clarity of their relation.

"Assez, assez, Horner, for God's sake."

The rest you Had chiefly at second hand from Monsieur Casteene, who seemed as always to know everything—and who, not impossibly, played some unacknowledged role in Morgan's appearance at the Farm. At very least they were professionally acquainted, after a fashion: Casteene himself claimed descent from a line of French-Canadian intrigants concerning whom Morgan once wrote an article—one of a number of terse, seminal sketches mined from his abandoned dissertation, published in historical journals, and much admired by your Informant as well as by the profession. You were Not yourself Acquainted with these publications, but Accepted as Plausible Casteene's observation that their subjects were chiefly two—great imposturing schemers such as Henry Burlingame III and the Comte de Crillon; and historically important forgeries, like the Lakanal Packet and the

Henry Letters—no doubt because the circumstances of his bereavement (whereof Casteene pretends to know nothing) overwhelmed their author with the power of the irrational, the inarticulate, the intuitively guileful and disingenuous, the coolly corrupt.

"Horseshit, Horner," you can Hear the old—i.e., the young—Morgan scoffing: "I understood that before I was twenty. You romantics always overestimate capital-*I* Irrationality. You were no Iago, just a Horny Sonofabitch who Happened to Hit my weak spot."

Be that as may, those were his subjects (and you Must Remember to Enter Iago in your Hornbook, though we have only his own unreliable suspicion, in Act I, that Othello cuckolded him with Emilia). From Wicomico Morgan returned to Baltimore, found a post with the Maryland Historical Society, and lectured occasionally in the evening college of the state university. On the strength of his subsequent publications he was offered and sometimes accepted visiting lectureships at respectable universities, but he would not take a regular academic appointment. His growing reputation at the historical society led him into activity as a consultant to restoration projects, museums of local history, film productions, and historical pageants, festivals, and monuments up and down the thirteen original colonies. This activity in turn acquainted him with such pedigreed families as the Harrison Macks (Mrs. Mack also claims descent from Betsy Patterson), whose choice he became to preside over their newly founded college on Maryland's Eastern Shore. It was a move, so Casteene reported, contrary to Morgan's personal inclinations; he accepted out of gratitude for the Tidewater Foundation's support of his historical researches over the years; perhaps also because some surviving academic idealism in him was appealed to by the project of establishing a small elite center for scholarly activity.

"Merde, Horner," you Hear Saint Joseph replying to this last. "You're Determined to Make Me Out a naive rationalist, when in fact I've taken the tragic view of human institutions—including colleges and marriages—since I was nineteen."

In any case, the trustees' appointment of his former employer, John Schott of Wicomico Teachers College, to be his academic vice-president must soon have disabused Morgan of any such idealism. In the ensuing power struggle, Schott revived or threatened to revive the scandal of Rennie's death. Morgan resigned and retreated north to a visiting professorship at Amherst—

"Not *retreated*, Horner!" one hears him protest. "Massachusetts chauvinists are just as tacky as Virginia chauvinists. I went to Amherst because Amherst invited me, and one of my sons was at school there. The other's at Chapel Hill."

—where he seems to have undergone a radical change of personality, whether in consequence of, or merely concomitant with, his introduction to LSD. From rationalism he moved to a kind of mysticism—

"So did Plato and William James. You may Hear me quote Blake or Suzuki, but not Castañeda's *Conversations with Don Juan.*"

—from J. Press suits to hippie buckskins—

"Make it Abercrombie and Fitch to L. L. Bean. The outfit I was wearing when I came here was a gift from some Seneca Indians that Casteene and I were visiting when I freaked out."

"So how come you're still wearing it, Joe?" This was your First Conversation with him, yesterday, birthday of Hans Christian Andersen, F. A. Bartholdi, Carmen Basilio, G. J. Casanova, Max Ernst, Alec Guinness, Bedřich Smetana, Émile Zola. In the month since his arrival, Joe had scarcely taken note of your Existence; you, on the contrary, who ordinarily Took No Note of it either, were more Painfully Aware of it than at any time in the past sixteen years. He met daily with Tombo X, less often with the Doctor, neither of whom reported the substance of their interviews to you. He was most frequently in the company of M. Casteene, but such of their conversation as you Overheard was on the French and Indian War or the Niagara Frontier in the War of 1812: the conversation of a knowledgeable amateur and an unassuming professional. Both Pocahontas and Bibi were attracted to Morgan, as were the draft evaders; with them his talk was elliptical, ironic, nonintellectual, almost nonexistent. He played soccer and smoked marijuana with the young men (those for whom these were prescribed or permitted); with the women he played bridge, read Tarot cards and *I Ching* hexagrams, and practiced yoga, despite the Doctor's disapproval of that discipline. ("It's not immobility," Morgan had pleasantly argued; "it's suspended motion." And to your Surprise, the Doctor conceded.) You Postponed your Suicide, Waiting for him to follow up on his first and only words to you: that ultimatum about rewriting history, resurrecting Rennie—

"Not resurrecting, Horner: *rebirthing*. I don't want my wife exhumed. I want her reborn."

Then yesterday morning he stepped into your Office here as calmly as he had once into your Office at Wicomico Teachers to discuss your Seduction of his wife. You had Long Since Given Up your Rocking Chair, the motion of which, in the Doctor's judgment, was more conducive to than protective against immobility. You Sat in your Stiff Ladderback, Contemplating the empty *U* page in your Hornbook. The inclusion of Odysseus among the *O*'s was questionable enough in the first instance: it is only a scurrilous early variant of the myth which holds Penelope to have cuckolded him with all 108 of her suitors, plus nine house servants, Phemius the bard, and Melanthius the goatherd. To cross-enter him as Ulysses Seemed a Cheap Shot. Morgan considered the bare walls and floor of the little space, the curtainless window that overlooked the surging river.

"So this is your Life, Jake."

Your Voice would not Immediately Come.

"Casteene tells me you've been with your Quack Friend ever since Wicomico."

You Put the Hornbook by. "In 1953," you Answered Finally, "I Decided to Commit Suicide. And I Did."

Joe leaned against the wall, arms folded, and sniffed. "Dying's different from this. Dying is something. This is nothing."

You Waited.

"Sixteen years," he said. "They seem hardly to have touched you." He surveyed you. "Early Eisenhower haircut. Sears Permapress worsteds. Inch-wide necktie. And a *white shirt*." He bent to look at your Feet beneath the unornamented desk where you Do the Farm's bookkeeping and correspondence, and your Own Scriptotherapy. "With *white socks!* And low-cut oxfords! All you Need is a batch of freshman theme papers on your Desk and a red pencil behind your Ear. If Rennie were to walk in here, she'd feel right at home with you."

You Most Certainly Did Not Answer.

"Whereas with me she'd have very little in common anymore, I suppose, even if she recognized me." He beamed, not warmly. "The sexual revolution, Jacob! Open marriage! Freedom of abortion constitutionally protected! And the Pill, Jacob! Even high school girls get it these days from their family doctors. It makes our old troubles seem as quaint as Loyalty Oaths and existential Angst, doesn't it?"

"But Alger Hiss isn't back in the State Department," you Answered Levelly. "And Rennie's still dead. What's the hippie getup for, Joe?"

He replied as aforequoted, cheerily adding: "Indians are Where It's At these days, Jacob. Very in on the campuses—which you Wouldn't Recognize anyhow. No Freshman English requirement! No lettergrades! Rap sessions instead of lectures; open admissions; do-it-yourself doctorates. Maoist cadres instead of cheerleaders; acid trips instead of beer blasts; full parietals in the dorms!"

"So I've Heard," you Dryly Acknowledged. "But I Can't Imagine you're into all that."

"*Into all that!*" Joe echoed with interest. "So he *has* been touched by the times, after all."

"What are you here for, Joe?"

"Bad trip in a Seneca longhouse across the river," he answered. "Doing peyote and rapping about Indian nationalism with friends of my sons, who're into an independent study project on the subject. I.S.P.'s are all the rage now, Jacob! They'd heard of this place from their friends in the Movement."

"You're not immobilized."

He shrugged. "I wasn't exactly self-propelled there for a while. But *you* Used to Get Around a bit, too, between your Spells of Bad Weather."

You Did Not Trouble to correct "bad weather" to *no* weather. "Here I Am," you Said Simply.

"There you Are. Wondering whether I've come at last to pull out the old Colt .45 and blow your Head off. Remember that scene?"

"I'm Not Responsible for either the book or the movie," you Felt Moved to Declare for What It Might Be Worth. "I did Write a sort of report in '55: what we call Scriptotherapy. It got left behind in Pennsylvania when we moved out fast."

"Responsibility never was your Long Suit," Joe observed. "Maybe I want to see what a corpse looks like sixteen years after. Maybe I'm moonlighting as a technical consultant for a film about the 1812 War. Maybe Casteene and I are secretly organizing a Second Revolution to coincide with the U.S. Bicentennial. Maybe I just want to scare the shit out of you and your Doctor friend."

You Waited, Speculating which of those maybes could be said to have alphabetical priority.

"Maybe I want you to Rewrite History. Put a different ending on that report."

You Waited.

"Why not Historiographical Therapy?"

You Did Not Bother to Mention Cliotherapy, a traditional feature of many patients' schedules despite the Doctor's own aversion to etiological analysis.

"We historians are always reinterpreting the past," Joe went on. "But if history is a trauma, maybe the thing to do is redream it."

"The thing to do," declared the Doctor when your Account of this conversation had reached this point, "is keep moving in the daytime and take Demerol at night. Get to the dénouement, Horner: narrative suspense does not interest me. What does he want?"

You Could Not Say, Saint Joseph having terminated the interview just there; but you Reported your Opinion that he was nowise "spaced out" (though the episode with the Senecas may well have occurred as he declared) and that, distressing as must have been his defeat by John Schott at Marshyhope, it had not unhinged him. Some sort of punishment—of yourself in the first instance for Disrupting His Marriage; perhaps of the Doctor for performing the fatal abortion— might well be among Morgan's intentions, but you Did Not Quite Believe it to have brought him to the Farm. From Monsieur Casteene, in whose disinterestedness you Had No Great Confidence, you had Learned that a film director named Prinz was in fact at work on some sort of production involving scenes from the War of 1812 in Chesapeake Bay and on the Niagara Frontier: perhaps the blowing up of old Fort Erie, or the British capture of Fort Niagara, or the burning of Buffalo. Quite possibly Morgan *was* advising him on these scenes; Casteene himself hoped to be of use to the project when the company arrived, sometime during the summer, inasmuch as his forebears had played a certain role, so he asserted, in the original events.

"But that's Casteene," you Concluded. "Do you know who *he* really is?"

The Doctor twitched his nose. "No idle ontologies, Jacob Horner.

'Casteene' is sufficient for our purposes. So. Like yourself, I find our Saint Joseph to be altogether rational, certainly hostile, not so certainly threatening. He has paid in advance for the month of April, so we shall be seeing him for a while yet. If he does not murder us or have us arrested—either of which I regard him as quite capable of doing but not *very* likely to do—his presence here may have its benefits. Bibi and Pocahontas have certainly been easier to live with lately, though I foresee trouble if he shows a preference for one or the other. But you."

You Waited.

"You Locked Up again, did you?"

"Not Locked Up," you Corrected, "Petered Out. When Joe spoke of redreaming history, we were both looking out of the window. I was Waiting for him to explain and at the same time Thinking of all that water going by, that started out clean in Lake Superior and then flushed down through Huron and Erie. Heraclitus says you can't step into the same stream twice: I'd be Content to Step Into It once. And Horace speaks of the man standing on the riverbank, shoes in hand, forever waiting to take the first step, till all the water's run by. I'm that man."

"Literature," the Doctor said contemptuously.

"That reminded me that the corps of engineers is supposed to turn off Niagara Falls this summer, the American side, to see whether it can be made as spectacular as the Canadian Falls: the most American project I Ever Heard Of. It's expected to be a great tourist attraction, a sort of negative natural wonder. Then I Got To Thinking about negativism, how it would be positive in the antiworld, where entropy would be ectropy and we'd be running an *Im*mobilization Farm—"

"Horner, Horner."

"That was it, till Tombo X came by and laid his Straight-Razor Therapy on me." It is that young man's wont, with white male immobiles, to terrify them into motion by whipping out an old-fashioned straight razor, rolling his eyeballs and flashing his teeth blackamoor-style, and, seizing the patient by the scrotum, threatening in Deep Dixie dialect to relieve him of his honky nuts. "One day he'll go too far with that."

"One day," the Doctor said, "you will Tell my son to get his pickaninny hands off you or you will Burn a cross on his lawn. That day the conversation can begin."

"He cheats," you Complained. "By squeezing. It wasn't fear of castration that fetched me up. It was pain."

"Never mind. You had Been Out for five hours. And you might Still Be There if he had not been dodging Pocahontas. It was exactly like old times?"

"Exactly. I was Aware of everything going on, but Weatherless. Couldn't Bring myself to Move. Zen Buddhists speak of *the air breathing you. . .*"

"For pity's sake, Horner, do not Add Zen Buddhism to your White

108

Socks and Skinny Neckties. This is 1969. You are Forty-Six. Most men of your Age and Class have children in college who have gotten over their *own* adolescent mysticism by this time. We are right where we started."

You Waited. The Doctor took his time. His own hair and mustache, now entirely white, he has let grow longer in the current fashion, and has added a small goatee: he looks like a bald black Colonel Sanders, or a dapper negative of Albert Einstein. Your Mind Began to Wander, then to Dissipate. Though you Would Not Join the Generation, seriously to yourself you Enounced the current test pattern of your Consciousness:

> You've Got a lot to live,
> And Pepsi's got a lot to give.

Then it too trickled away into the void. Across a measureless distance the Doctor said: "I have no razor. But I will cheerfully crotch you if you do not Wake Up."

Okay.

"Okay. Your Friend Saint Joseph has the right idea, whether he and the former Joe Morgan are the same or not."

"They're the same."

The Doctor shrugged his eyebrows. "Heraclitus's dictum cuts two ways: even if the river had not flowed, the You would have. I am remembering how Morgan *sent his wife back to you* when he could not assimilate her first infidelity. As if a replay might clarify it. . ."

The Doctor slid his chair away, stood, relit his long-dead cigar. The interview was apparently over.

"An impressive chap, your Friend. But this *Wiederträumerei* is a dangerous business. You set about to kill two birds with one stone, and sometimes you wipe out the whole flock. So. Forget what we decided earlier about you and Pocahontas, at least until Saint Joseph makes his choice. You and I must go back to weekly P-and-A's, as in the old days."

He frowned. "Reenactment. But if there is no Freshman English requirement on the campuses nowadays, surely there is no Prescriptive Grammar. And you Ought to Stay Residential. How will you Teach?"

R: *A. B. Cook IV to his unborn child.* The history of *A. B. Cooke III: Pontiac's conspiracy.*

At Castines Hundred
Niagara, Upper Canada

2 April 1812

My Dearest Henrietta or Henry,

Read, dear child, when you shall have been born & begun to be educated, a great tiresome epical poem call'd *Columbiad,* by Joel Barlow of Connecticut & Paris, wherein the dying & despondent Columbus, in a dream or trance, is fetcht to the Mount of Vision by Hesper, Spirit of the Western World: thence like Aeneas in Hades he beholds panoramically the future history (up to 1807, the date of the poem's appearance) of the empire for whose initiation he is responsible. This vision, stout Barlow assures us—of white Americans pushing ever westward, clearing the forests, draining the marshes, harvesting the fish & game, building canals & roads & cities from coast to coast—cheers Columbus & reconciles him to his obscure death.

The conceit is admirable. The poem itself is a bore because, unlike the *Aeneid,* its concerns do not range much beyond sentimental patriotism, and because, unlike Virgil, its author is a merely educated, sensible fellow with an amateur's gift for making verses. Joel Barlow was one of the self-styled "Hartford Wits"; another was your grandfather, Henry Burlingame IV, who befriended Barlow at Yale College just before the American Revolution and suggested both *The Vision of Columbus* (the poet's 1st & briefer version of *Columbiad) &* a passable satire of Daniel Shays' rebellion call'd *The Anarchiad,* of which more anon. The Cooke-Burlingame line is given neither to *longueurs* nor to longevity: my father is said to have died in 1785 at the age of 39, before either of the poems that covertly memorialize him was publisht.

As for Barlow: that gentleman survives as U.S. Minister to France, whence he will have reported by now to President Madison that "Le Comte Édouard de Crillon"—who lately sold Secretary Monroe the notorious John Henry Letters for $50,000 and then exacted from Madison's operatives another $21,000 (half of which Andrée & I have safely bank'd for you in Switzerland)—does not exist. The late actual Duc de Crillon was a Spanish grandee, conqueror of Minorca, attacker of Gibraltar, & member of the French Assembly, who in 1788 tried unsuccessfully to seduce my mother at a diplomatic *soirée* in London. The current Duke, his only son, lives in Paris, smarting at the £1,200 he was lately swindled out of by one "Jean Blanque," and doubtless enraged at the scandal now attaching to the family name. Father & son are both acquaintances of Barlow, to whom my father introduced them years ago. Thus the Minister will have immediately guess'd, as I want him to, that Madison has been duped. What he will *not* guess is that I did both the duping & the unduping, to lead the U. States closer to war and so promote the schism betwixt New England & the rest of that

110

nation. That I chose the name Edouard de Crillon precisely to excite his suspicion (as well as to settle a little score for Mother), and the name Jean Blanque to echo Barlow's own & provide him a *blank* to fill.

Rather, to provide such a blank to History, since the Hartford Wits, for all their wit, are short on the finer ironies. There is more to it: I chose the name Édouard for my imposture of the Count, for example, because it was Mother's descent from Le Comte Cécile Édouard of Castle Haven in Maryland that had aroused the late Duke's lecherous interest. If the fellow currently posing as Aaron Burr in Paris is in fact my father, he will recognize in that touch the family trademark, & understand that I understand that he is alive.

Thus the messages we Cooks & Burlingames amuse one another by sending with our left hands, as we play the Game of Governments with our right and undo, as far as is in us possible, the Vision of good Joel Barlow!

So then, dear child in the making: the fat is fairly in the fire since my letter of last month. Whilst you have been growing hair & toenails, and opening your eyes (What do you see, little Burlingame? That most of the world's eyes are closed?), Wee Jamie Madison has sent the Henry Letters to Congress—that is, my fair paraphrase of the fourteen cipher'd originals, plus John Henry's nattering *Proposal for the Final Reunion of His Majesty's Dominion in North America with the States of Massachusetts, New Hampshire, Vermont, Connecticut, Rhode Island, and New York.* Now Henry Clay & the War Hawks are making the most of them to embarrass the New England Federalists, to justify their own Anglophobia, & to push gentle Jamie ever closer to a "Second War of Independence"—their pretext for snatching the Canadas & the Floridas.

More anon, more anon, of

> The Henry papers, bought & sold,
> And paid for with the nation's gold,

when I come to my own & your mother's histories. *This* is to apprise you of your great-grandfather's, the 3rd Andrew Cooke's, whereto your genealogy had got when I closed my last. I pray you, review the chart of it, overleaf.

There are, all over this tree, other fruits, to be sure: brothers, sisters, by-blows on nearly every branch & twig. With a few exceptions, I have enter'd only those in the main line of your descent. And the wives of all those Barons Castine are not really nameless, but (always excepting Madocawanda) they made vocations of being their husbands' wives, and are of no individual interest here. That fellow in the box, my grandfather, was, you recall, sired out of wedlock on the "Maryland Laureate's" twin sister by the 3rd Henry Burlingame, who then disappear'd into the Dorset marshes with the avow'd intention of thwarting the "Bloodsworth Island Conspiracy" of escaped African slaves & displaced Indians. To cover the scandal, Grandfather was

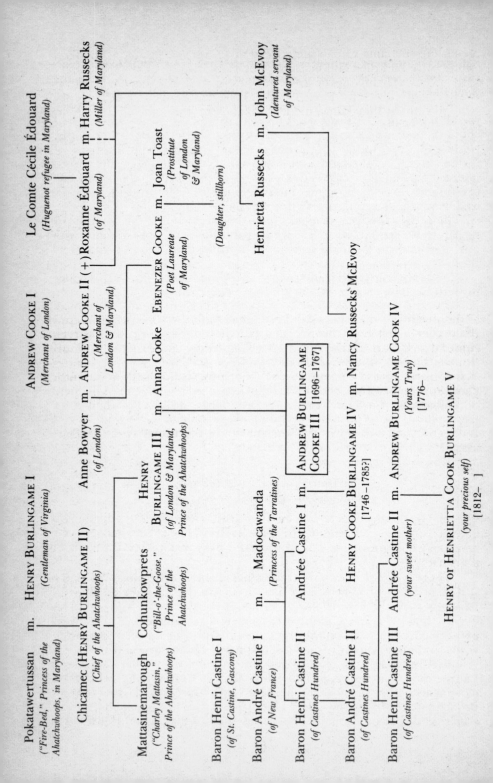

given the surname Cooke and raised as the son of the poet Ebenezer, whose wife had died still-bearing their own child.

A.B.C. III thus never knew his father, tho thro his childhood he was retail'd stories by Eben Cooke of the mysterious "Uncle Henry" who, for aught they knew, might dwell among them incognito, looking after the welfare of his "favorite nephew." How else explain the anonymous gifts of money & goods that from time to time appear'd as from Heaven, addrest either to Anna Cooke or to the boy?

So far did the aging poet fall into this folly, in 1730 he composed a sequel to his major work, *The Sot-Weed Factor,* call'd *Sot-Weed Redivivus, or, the Planter's Looking-Glass,* which, in the guise of an economic tract in verse, incorporates to the knowledgeable eye broad signals to Henry Burlingame III, of the "Édouard de Crillon" variety. The opening words of Cooke's preface, for example—

> May I be canoniz'd for a Saint, if I know what Apology to make for this dull Piece of Household Stuff, any more than he that first invented the Horn-Book. . .

—allude to the once-popular belief that Cecil Calvert, the 2nd Lord Baltimore & 1st Lord Proprietor of Maryland, had struck a bargain with Pope Urban VIII to make Maryland into a Jesuit colony in return for posthumous sainthood. Cooke 1st learnt of this presumable slander from Burlingame, who of course had also, as his childhood tutor, "invented the Horn-Book" for his little charges.

Similarly, a few lines farther on—

> . . .one Blast from the Critick's Mouth, would raise more Flaws in this Looking-Glass, than there be Circles in the Sphere. . .

—we are reminded that Burlingame was ever Cooke's severest literary critic. That his political intrigues led him into mirror-like reversals & duplications (he also posed as Baltimore's enemy John Coode, & cet., & cet.). That Cooke's "inventor of the Horn-Book" was also his instructor in geometry & astronomy. In the poem itself, such allusions swarm like bees (themselves a reduplicated image, punning on Burlingame's initial): the most obvious is the poet's not only re-meeting but *re-sleeping with* a tobacco-planter ("cockerouse" in the argot of the time, & a naughty pun too) with whom he had dealings in the original *Sot-Weed Factor,* & who was Burlingame "much disguis'd":

> I boldly crav'd his Worship's Name
> And tho' the *Don* at first seem'd shy,
> At length he made this smart Reply
>
> I am, says he, that *Cockerouse*
> Once entertain'd you at his House,
> When aged *Roan,* not us'd to falter,

> If you remember, slipt his Halter;
> Left *Sotweed Factor* in the Lurch,
> As *Presbyterians* leave the Church. . . .

The horse-couplet is a quotation from the earlier poem; the original Roan had inspired a trial of rhyming betwixt Cooke & Burlingame-disguised-as-"Cockerouse"; Ebenezer & his sister had indeed been "left in the lurch," and Andrew III born therefore outside "the Church."

More subtle is the reference to his guide as "the Spurious Offspring of some Tawny-Moor" (Ebenezer's prostitute-wife, Joan Toast, was once ravisht by the Moorish pirate Boabdil, and Burlingame's ancestry, like yours & mine, was racially mixt). ". . .to glut the Market with a poisonous Drug" refers of course to the overproduction of "sotweed" in the colony, the poem's explicit theme; but it alludes covertly to the opium traffic in which Burlingame involved Ebenezer Cooke in the 1690's.

> I call'd the drowsy Passive Slave
> To light me to my downy Grave. . .

and

> . . .we thought it best
> To let the Aethiopian rest . . .

overtly refer to the "one that pass'd for Chamber-Maid" at the inn where this encounter takes place (note that she too is suspected of being other than she seems), whilst they secretly remind Burlingame of the poet's near-martyrdom at the stake in 1694 by that conspiracy of escaped slaves & Ahatchwhoop Indians on Bloodsworth Island, which Burlingame had gone ostensibly to "put to rest."

Most interesting of all is Cooke's prediction that his fellow Marylanders

> Will by their Heirs be curst for [their] Mistakes,
> E'er Saturn thrice his Revolution makes. . . .

That is, literally, within three generations, when the land will have been deforested & the soil exhausted by one-crop tobacco farming. But the "three revolutions" (Saturn's period is 29½ years), reckon'd roughly from the date of Cooke's composing *Sot-Weed Redivivus*, echo a prediction by Henry Burlingame III of three "revolutionary" upheavals: 1st, the Seven Years War betwixt Britain & France, which by 1759 would have reacht the fall of Fort Niagara to the British & the consequent shift of Indian allegiances from the losing to the winning side, paving the way for the surrender of the Canadas to Lord Jeffrey Amherst & for "Pontiac's Conspiracy," as shall be shown; 2nd, the American & French Revolutions (*i.e.*, about 1789, when George Washington was elected, the Tennis Court Oath sworn, the Bastille taken); 3rd, what we now approach: the decline & fall of Napoleon's

114

Empire & the commencement of America's 2nd Revolution. "Rise, *Oroonoko,* rise . . ." Cooke urges his disguised mentor at the beginning of Canto III, which in cunning emblem of eternal recurrence, or revolution without end, he ends with the exhortation "Begin. . ." and the invocation of time's Stream

That runs (alas!) and ever will run on.

Anna Cooke indulged this folly, if folly it was, but resisted the temptation to *folie à deux.* Upon her brother's death in 1732, she confided to her "nephew" Andrew (by then a successful lawyer in Annapolis) that his "Uncle Henry" had been her common-law husband; she declared moreover her private conviction that he had *not,* as Ebenezer believed, gone over to the side of the conspirators whose ally he had pretended to be: had he done so, she was firmly convinced, the Bloodsworth Island Conspiracy would have succeeded, and Maryland at least, if not all thirteen of the English colonies, would no longer exist. It was Anna's belief that H.B. III had successfully divided & thwarted the designs of the Indians & Negroes, then been discover'd & kill'd by them; otherwise he would have rejoin'd & officially married her long since. As for the anonymous donations, they were in her opinion the compensation traditionally provided *sub rosa* by governments to the widows of secret operatives lost in the line of duty, whose supreme sacrifices must perforce & alas go as officially unacknowledged as her brief "marriage."

Upon Anna Cooke's death not long after, Andrew found among his "aunt's" papers a letter addrest to him, to be open'd & read along with her will (both documents are here in the Castines' library). It confest the facts as aforerehearst: that she, not Joan Toast Cooke the prostitute, was his mother, Henry Burlingame III his father, Eben Cooke his uncle.

At his then age (about 36), his parents' names were of less interest to Grandfather than their nature: accepting as true Anna Cooke's final version of the former, what Andrew felt the greatest urgency to decide was whether, as his Uncle Eben had maintain'd, his father had been a fail'd revolutionary in the cause of his Indian brothers & their African allies, or, as his mother affirm'd, a victorious anti-revolutionary in the cause of the British colonial government. *Nota bene, nota bene,* dear child! It is that same question which has vext all of his descendants vis-à-vis their progenitors, & which occasions these pre-natal epistles!

In the absence of any documentary evidence—for which he scour'd the colonies as tenaciously as had his father before him in search of *his* —A.B.C. III hearken'd to the verdict of his heart: he decided that while his grandfather Chicamec, the originator of the Bloodsworth Island Conspiracy, had been an unsuccessful idealist, his father Henry Burlingame III had been a deplorably successful hypocrite, betraying his own aboriginal blood in the venal interest of the British Crown. Anna Cooke's insistence that her lover's motive had been her own &

their son's welfare he dismist as romantical, given the absence of any word from Burlingame himself to this effect, or any manifest attempt on his part to communicate with her & their natural child. That my Grandfather apparently did not allow for the possibility of Burlingame's having been discover'd & put to death before he could make any such communication, tells us something about the state of heart of this "old bachelor orphan," as he refers to himself in his diary of the period.

This hard judgement upon his lately-discover'd, long-dead father profoundly changed Grandfather's life. The course of his researches up & down the country had brot him into contact with Indians of various nations as well as with officials of the several colonies & the British & French provincial authorities. His eyes were open'd to thitherto-unsuspected dimensions of a history he had largely taken for granted. It surprised him (and surprises me) that a man of early middle age, practicing law all his adult life in the seat of a colonial government, could have remain'd politically innocent for so long. But a certain naivety, together with extraordinary complication, is a family curse that dates from the mating of Cookes & Burlingames.

They had also & no less importantly, these researches, led him here: to the newly-raised seat of the half-breed Baron Henri Castine II, son of André Castine & the Tarratine princess Madocawanda. His object was to learn what he could of that ubiquitous "Monsieur Casteene" whose name haunts the archives of the English colonies. In pursuit of it he spent a season at Castines Hundred as a guest & hunting-companion of its owner, who like all the Barons Castine (including my present host, Andrée's brother), was an hospitable, gregarious, anti-political sportsman. And here, like Yours Truly two generations later, he lost his heart to & won the hand of the daughter of the house, whom we must call *Andrée Castine I* to distinguish her from your mother.

For in other respects, grandmother & granddaughter are like as twins: the fine-edged physiognomy of the Gascoigne Castines, the dark eyes & hair & skin of Madocawanda's people—and the audacity, political passion, & disregard for convention of "Monsieur Casteene"! She it was, Andrée I, who relieved Grandfather of both his political & his carnal innocence, which he seems to have preserved as remarkably as did his Uncle Ebenezer, the virgin poet. And she it was who insisted he 1st get her with child if he would have her to wife. So scrupulous was Grandfather on this point—and on the irregularity, of which Andrée was contemptuous, of the two-decade difference in their ages—that no less than another dozen years pass'd before (in 1746) they finally conceived my father and became man & wife, when Andrew was 50 & Andrée 30 years of age! But thro those decades they were faithful, if intermittent, lovers, as often together as apart, and not uncommonly travelling as husband & wife (or father & daughter) to appease

Grandfather's curious decorum & avoid attracting undue attention as they pursued their political objective.

This objective, if Andrew III's own declaration is to be believed, was not the victory of the French in America, but the defeat of the British, for which in the existing circumstances the French & Indians were the obvious instrumentality. Having decided that his father had been a British anti-insurgent, Andrew III set about in the 2nd half of his life to be an *anti-British* insurgent; Andrée (still in the 1st half of hers) to be an organizer of the Indian nations 1st against the British, whom she saw as the greater menace to aboriginal integrity, and ultimately against the French, who had ever been less ruthless in displacing native populations, less interested in despoiling the land, and less disdainful of intermarriage betwixt the races. To the extent that their theatres of concern can be distinguisht, Andrée's was to resist the extension of British hegemony northward above the Great Lakes & St. Lawrence River, Andrew's to resist its extension westward across the Appalachians toward the Mississippi. These concerns came together in the period of the French & Indian War, along the frontier betwixt Fort Niagara & Fort Detroit.

Attend me closely now, child, if you would understand your heritage. To the simple it might appear that my grandparents' ends would best be served by their doing all they could to ensure a French victory in North America. But so skillfully & harmoniously did the French get on with the Indians—advancing them guns & ammunition on credit against the hunting & trapping season, providing them free gunsmithing at every fort, plying them liberally with gifts of blankets, iron utensils, & brandy—the red men became insidiously dependent on the white man's skills & manufactures, ever farther removed from their former self-reliance. They had also been decimated & re-decimated by the white man's measles, influenza, & smallpox, against which they had no hereditary defences. And the survivors, for a hundred years already by 1750, were helpless drunkards. An immediate wholesale victory of the French over the British, my grandparents fear'd, would so extend this "benevolent" exploitation as to make impossible the forging of an independent, regenerated Indian nation: in another century, they believed, the French would be the real masters of the continent, the Indians their willing, rum-soak'd subordinates. What was needed (so they came to feel by the mid-1750's) was a temporary *British* victory in America—especially under the puritanical Jeffrey Amherst, who did not believe in giving rum, or anything else, to the worthless savages. The Indian nations would then be obliged to unite for their own survival, so impossible were the Anglo-Saxons to deal with; and they would be freed of the curse of alcohol will-they nill-they. Once a genuine, sober confederacy had been forged among, say, the Six Nations of the Iroquois, the principal tribes of the Upper Great Lakes, & the nations of the Ohio Valley & the Illinois, the Indians could accept from a position of strength the assistance of the defeated French in driving out the British, whilst remaining masters in their own house.

Thus their strategy, to implement which my grandparents decided that Fort Niagara—controlling the very jugular of the Great Lakes and thus of the whole upper & central parts of the continent—must fall to the British! Lord Amherst's campaign against the French had come, by 1759, to center on the taking of that fort: for the Indians he had only contempt, but his blockade of the St. Lawrence had had the incidental effect of cutting off the supply of cognac with which the French marinated their Indian diplomacy, and thus of driving the thirsty Senecas (in whose territory the Fort lay), and the Six Nations generally, into hopeful new alliances with the English. The force Amherst dispatcht against Niagara included, along with British regulars & colonial militiamen, some 1,900 of these Iroquois, among whom Andrew Cooke III moved easily under the *nom de guerre* of John Butler: it was the largest such force ever assembled on the side of the British. Their plan was not to take the fort by storm, but to besiege it, cut off the reinforcement of its garrison, and so force its surrender. The French relief force, sent up promptly from the Ohio Valley & Detroit to lift the siege, consisted of 1,600 Indians—Hurons, Mingoes, Shawnees—and 600 French: amongst the latter was Andrée, in the rôle of a half-breed *habitant* camp-follower.

By early July the French force was assembled at Presque Isle and ready to march up the shore of Lake Erie. Andrew slipt down from the British camp, Andrée up from the French, to a week-long tryst and strategy-conference on Chautauqua Lake, betwixt the two armies. There, as they embraced among the sugar maples & black willows which line that water, they workt out their tactics, not only for the battle to come, but for the larger campaign ahead. Andrew's candidate to lead the projected Indian confederation was a young war-chief of the Senecas named Kyashuta: the Iroquois had long been the most politically advanced of Indians; they had 200 years of confederacy already under their belts, a confederacy so effective that Benjamin Franklin had proposed it as the model for a union of the British colonies in America. They were generally fear'd for their ferocity: they had never been much committed to either the French or the English; and their combination of matriarchy & patriarchy (the *Sachems* were all male, but the power of their nomination was reserved exclusively to a council of women) appeal'd to my grandparents. And the Senecas (in whose country they were trysting) were the fiercest, least "Eastern," & most independent of the Iroquois.

Andrée for her part was much taken with a young Ottawa named Ponteach, or Pondiac, or Pontiac. The confederacy, she argued, must be center'd well west of the Alleghenies if it was to hold out against disease & alcohol. The Iroquois League could serve as an example & a 1st line of defence, but they were too hated by the Great Lakes tribes, on which they had prey'd for decades, to be able to unite them: their

118

very name was a Huron hate-word meaning "vipers who strike without warning." Pontiac had in his favor that he was, after the manner of other great leaders in history, not quite native to the tribe he had begun to lead (his mother was an Ojibwa). More important, in addition to his courage, eloquence, energy, good humor & political judgement, he had what amounted to a Vision (transmitted to him by Andrée herself from a prophet of the Delawares): a return to aboriginal ways & implements, a sacrifice of comfort & efficiency in the interest of repurification & the achievement of sufficient moral strength to repel the white invaders. This Delaware Prophet—also known as "The Impostor"—was an authentic mystic & certifiable madman, very potent nonetheless among the Ohio Valley tribes. Pontiac was neither mystical nor mad, and even more potent was his canny modification of the vision, retail'd in parable form: the Prophet himself loses his way in the forest, encounters a beautiful maiden (Andrée, in the rôle of Socrates's Diotima), & is by her instructed to give up his firearms & firewater for the manlier hunting-bow, tomahawk, & scalping knife. His reward is regeneration in the arms of the maiden herself.

Your great-grandfather (like your father) was a tactful husband: he kiss'd Andrée—by then his wife of a dozen years & mother of his son, my father—and agreed that this Pontiac must be their man. She in turn agreed that he must not rise to power prematurely: a decisive, even shocking *defeat* at Fort Niagara would weaken the leadership of his older rivals, impress the beaten tribes with the necessity of confederation, and oblige their retreat westward toward Fort Detroit, a better center for their regrouping. And it would be well if this defeat were at the hands more of Sir William Johnson's Iroquois than of the British regulars and colonials: the Hurons & Shawnees would be thereby more effectually stung; the Iroquois would be encouraged in their largest joint military operation & properly set up, not for warmer relations with the British, but for militant disaffection when—as would inevitably be the case under Amherst's administration—they were denied the massacre, plunder, rape, torture, & rum they regarded as the victor's due.

With this accord the couple parted, planning to reunite at Castines Hundred in the fall. Two days later, within a few hours after dinner on 20 July, surely by "John Butler's" arrangement, both of the British officers in command at the siege of Fort Niagara were kill'd, the one by a "French" sniper, the other by "accidental" explosion of a siege-gun, and leadership of the besieging army (which rightfully pass'd to Colonel Haldemand in Oswego) was effectively usurpt next day by Sir William Johnson & his Iroquois. On the morning of the 24th, against Captain Pouchot's urgent warnings, Captain de Lignery "inexplicably" led the French relief column straight up the portage road on the east bank of the Niagara into Johnson's ambush at the shrine of La Belle Famille, two miles below their destination. 500 French & Indians died before Pouchot surrender'd the fort at 5 P.M. The Iroquois night of plunder,

119

promist them by Johnson, was so thoro that it took a thousand troops two months to clean up & repair the damage. Even so, Andrew managed to persuade the Senecas (some of whom had fought with the French inside the fort) that their brothers the Mohawks, Johnson's own adopted tribe, had got the best of the pillaging. At this point the real Captain John Butler came on the scene, and Grandfather rejoin'd his family at Castines Hundred.

The next two years they spent establishing new identities for themselves & cultivating young Pontiac, whose influence was growing rapidly amongst the Ottawas & their neighbours. Grandfather took the rôle of an *habitant* trader from Lake St. Clair named Antoine Cuillerier. Andrée, in order to free herself for a certain necessary flirtation in Detroit, pretended to be, not his wife, but his daughter Angélique. And my father Henry Burlingame IV—by then a stout lad of fourteen— happily play'd the rôle of his mother's young brother, Alexis: his 1st involvement in the family enterprise, to which he took like a duck to water.

As they had expected, the fall of Fort Niagara inclined many Indian leaders, if not to the surly but victorious British, at least away from the French, toward neutrality. When New France surrender'd at Montreal in September 1760, and Lord Amherst claim'd for Britain a territory twelve times its size, my family began their counter-campaign. The British refusal to provide ammunition on credit for the hunting season, they explain'd to Pontiac, was the 1st step of a plan to exterminate the Indians altogether; only solidarity among the nations could withstand them. Pontiac agreed, but set forth his doubts: just as using the white man's rifles & drinking his spirits had made the Indians less than Indians, so he fear'd that real political alliances & concerted military campaigns in the white man's fashion, while they might be the only alternative to extinction, would if successful transform the Indians into red Englishmen. Very well to preach the taking up of firearms to fight firearms, to the end of returning to the noble bow & arrow: he could not seriously believe that, once taken up wholesale, they would ever be laid down, any more than he himself would ever again in his life be able to remain sober in the presence of alcohol.

Thus he brooded, here in this hall, a little drunk already on Baron Castine's good Armagnac, on the night before setting out with the "Cuilleriers" for Detroit. And till the hour he lost consciousness (Andrée reported next morning to Andrew) he could not decide whether to lead his people away, westward, across the Mississippi, or to begin at Detroit the campaign of resistance about which he had such divided feelings. "Angélique" had recognized in these vague insights a rudimentary tragical vision and, much moved, had taken the rôle of another sort of angel: that of the Delaware Prophet's vision. The red men, she had told Pontiac, were doom'd in any case to become other than they were. If, in order to preserve artificially their ancient ways, they retreated forever from the whites who multiplied and spread like a chancre on the earth, they would lose by the very strangeness of the land they retreated to; they would be themselves a kind of invader from the east—and their loss would be without effect upon the whites, who would press on in any case. If on the other hand they banded together, stood fast, and fought to the end, they would at worst die a little sooner, at best just possibly contain the white invasion for a few generations: if not east of the Alleghenies, at least east of the Mississippi. And if such resistance meant inescapably some "whitening" of the red men, as Pontiac wisely foresaw, this was a knife that cut both ways: their host, for example (Baron Henri Castine II), was not Madocawando of the Tarratines, but neither was he the old Baron of St. Castine in Gascony. More than once, Pontiac & his brothers had eaten brave captives to acquire their virtues; did he imagine that the whites could swallow whole nations of Indians without becoming in the process somewhat redden'd forever?

What ensued is more remarkable than clear. The *ménage* went west: the "Cuilleriers" to establish themselves at Detroit & befriend the just-arrived British garrison of that fort; Pontiac to preach the Delaware Prophet's amended vision & to pass war-belts among the Shawnees, Ottawas, Potawatomis, Delawares, & disaffected Senecas. Andrew particularly befriended the young aide of Amherst's who had brot the English garrison from Fort Pitt: Captain Robert Rogers, a New Hampshireman with whom one could discuss Shakespeare. "Angé-lique," finding unapproachable the British commandant Major Glad-win, made a conquest of his close friend the fur trader James Sterling, and so kept Pontiac inform'd of the situation in the fort.

By 1763 the plan was ready: Pontiac's people would take Fort Detroit early in May, and its fall would serve as both signal & encouragement for each tribe along the Allegheny & Ohio rivers to rise against the fort nearest it. From there the programme would be improvised: if all went well, the rest of the Iroquois might join the Senecas, take Fort Niagara, and sweep east across the Finger Lakes to the Hudson & south into Pennsylvania toward the Chesapeake, allying what was left of the once-fierce Susquehannas as they went. The Hurons would move with the displaced Algonkins up the west bank of the St. Lawrence, the Miamis & Shawnees & Illinois down the Mississippi Valley, whilst Pontiac & his Ottawas, in the heart of their beloved Lakes, laid down their rifles at last & took up their bows for peaceful hunting. . .

Henry, Henrietta: it might have workt, you know! Even nipt in the bud it came near to working! At this point Andrew & Andrée fall silent; I have only their son's account, my father's, for what happen'd, and (as shall be seen in another letter) it must be read with large allowance for his peculiar bias. And there is, of course, the historical record, already embellisht by romantical tradition. Pontiac's conspiracy was betray'd, possibly by "Angélique Cuillerier" via her "lover" James Sterling; Major Gladwin forestall'd Pontiac's surprise attack from within the fort by not admitting him, on the appointed day, to the conference he had requested; the "storm" turn'd into a desultory siege. Even so, the Potawatomis quickly took Fort St. Joseph to the west; the Senecas, Shawnees, Delawares, & Miamis, in less than one week, captured all three forts between Niagara & Fort Pitt: Presque Isle, Le Boeuf, Venango. As of the summer solstice, Lord Amherst still had only the dimmest idea of the scale of the uprising; ignorant of Indians in general & of the western nations in particular, he could not imagine that the troublesome Senecas were not at the bottom of it; that the Allegheny-Ohio rumblings were but an echo of Pontiac's main thrust at Detroit; that what was threatening to delay his long-awaited relief from the American command & his return to England was not another drunken redskin riot, but a full-scale Indian War for Independence! All that remain'd, *all that remain'd* was to take Detroit by storm before the garrison was reinforced, then to move quickly & concertedly against Forts Pitt & Niagara. There the line might be held.

For—unknown to most white & all red Americans, unknown perhaps even to Jeffrey Amherst & George Washington (but not to canny Ben Franklin & the "Cuilleriers")—Pontiac had a powerful, unsuspected ally: George III of England, whom my father call'd "wiser in his madness than most kings sane." Even before the British conquest of Canada, the King & his ministers had foreseen, in unlimited westward colonization of America, two distinct threats to the mother country. In the short run, given the expense & difficulty of transporting goods over the mountains, manufacturing towns were bound to be establisht in the Ohio Valley & along the Great Lakes, in competition with British industry. In the long run, & in consequence, such unimaginably expanded colonies—20, 30 times larger than Britain, and anon more populous, richer, even more powerful—would not be content to remain colonies forever. Even before Pontiac, the newly-crown'd King had consider'd declaring the crest of the Appalachians to be the western limit of white settlement. A determined Indian stand from, say, Frontenac at the head of the St. Lawrence down to Fort Pitt at the head of the Ohio, even if it lasted only a few months, would be sufficient occasion for George to make such a proclamation as if in the interests of the colonials themselves.

My grandparents knew this. They also knew, as did Pontiac, that even after his initial surprise attack had been frustrated, his forces so outnumber'd Gladwin's garrison that he could take the fort by storm at his pleasure before it was successfully reinforced from Niagara. That reinforcement could not be far off. The siege had been sustain'd for weeks, months; already several groups of Indians, unused to long campaigns & anxious to lay in meat for the coming winter, had left for their hunting grounds. Why did he not strike?

Most of the New-French *habitants* inside & around the fort, uncertain of the outcome, were at pains to maintain a precarious neutrality, but a few of the younger, such as one "Alexis Cuillerier" (then 17, & an idolizer of Pontiac) volunteer'd in July to raise additional troops from among the Illinois to storm the fort. Pontiac's reply, as my father recorded it, echoes his dark misgivings at Castines Hundred: If he were "Angélique's" friend Major Gladwin, Pontiac declar'd to his young admirer, or "Antoine's" friend Captain Rogers, he would order his *troops* to storm the walls, knowing that many of his *troops* would die, but that his superior numbers would carry the day. But the red man was not a *troop;* he was a brother, and one did not expend a brother. Attack'd by surprise, the red man would fight to the death. To avenge an insult or measure up to a high example he would undergo any privation, sustain any amount of accidental, unforeseen loss—as witness the bravery of his brothers at Presque Isle, Le Boeuf, Venango. But to take a *calculated* loss: to make a move *certain* to cost the life of some of his brothers, however equally certain of victory—this was not in the red man's nature. The siege was a mistake, almost surely doom'd to failure; but to storm the fort was out of the question. He was frankly improvising, perfectly aware that time was not on his side, that his authority diminisht day by day. Captain Rogers had already slipt thro with nearly 300 Rangers & 22 whaleboats of relief supplies for Gladwin; if any more got thro, the fort would be able to survive the winter, and the siege would have to be lifted. Perhaps the angel of the Delaware Prophet would revisit & readvise him? Meanwhile, here was Barbados rum taken by the Potawatomis from Fort St. Joseph. . .

The rest of the tale is not agreeable to tell. Pontiac's angel never reappear'd. "Angélique" & "Antoine" had business back at Castines Hundred, and were not seen again in Detroit until 1767. By July, news reacht Lord Amherst in New York of the scope & seriousness of the war. Furious, he order'd that no Indian prisoners be taken; that women & children not be spared; that the race be extirpated. He put a thousand-pound bounty on Pontiac's scalp. He commended the ingenious tactic of Captain Ecuyer at Fort Pitt, who made presents to the Delawares of infected blankets & handkerchiefs from the fort's small-pox hospital—and he recommended (in a postscript to his letter of 7 July to Bouquet at that fort) much more extensive use of this novel weapon. He sympathized with Bouquet's suggestion that the Indians be hunted down with dogs, and regretted that the distance from good English kennels made the plan unfeasible. When he learnt in September that Pontiac had destroy'd two relief expeditions en route to Detroit, he doubled the bounty, & fumed at the delay of his own relief. As autumn came on, one by one the Indian nations sued for peace; by October only Pontiac's Ottawas held the siege. On 3 October, H.M.S. *Michigan* battled its way thro them to the fort with winter supplies. Two weeks later Pontiac order'd the siege abandon'd and, out of favor in his village, went off westward in November to the country of the Illinois, accompanied by young "Alexis Cuillerier."

On 7 October George III actually issued his proclamation, but the settlers ignored it: the Indians' front had weaken'd, and the British troops were too few & too busy to turn back the wagon-trains crowding over the mountains. On 17 November Amherst was relieved, by Major General Gage in Montreal, as Commander of British forces in America, and happily return'd to his English fields & kennels. Smallpox raged that winter among the tribes around Fort Pitt, in some villages killing one out of every three.

In the spring, "Alexis Cuillerier" show'd Pontiac a letter he claim'd to have taken from a French courier betwixt Detroit & Illinois: in the name of Louis XV, and despite the Peace of Paris, it warn'd the English to leave Detroit before they were destroy'd by the French army he was sending from Louisiana. It was my father's 1st forged letter. I am loath to believe that Pontiac gave credence to its ancient fiction, or was meant to, tho he tried in turn to make use of it to rouse the Illinois & others to resume the war. But Colonel Bouquet's counter-expedition that year, from Fort Pitt to Ohio, was Senecan in its ferocity: the English now scalpt, raped, tortured, took few prisoners, disemboweled the pregnant—even lifted *two* scalps from each woman, and impaled the nether one on their saddle horns, an atrocity that had not hitherto occurr'd to the Iroquois. The Delawares made peace; the Mingoes, the Shawnees, the Miamis, the Potawatomis, on what terms they could. On 25 July, 1766, the 7th anniversary of Sir William Johnson's capture of Fort Niagara, Pontiac sign'd a treaty with that worthy at Oswego, officially ending his great Conspiracy, and retired to his ancestral home on the Maumee River, above Detroit, laden with gifts & very drunk.

That same year, my grandfather's literate friend Captain Robert Rogers (now *Major* Rogers) publisht the 1st American play ever to deal with the Indians: a blank-verse tragedy in the Shakespearian manner called *Ponteach: or, The Savages of America.* I cannot prove that Andrew Cooke III wrote that play, but there are almost as many family touches in it as in *Sot-Weed Redivivus.* The unscrupulous trader M'Dole in Act I not only boasts to his associate:

> Our fundamental Maxim then is this,
> That it's no Crime to cheat and gull an *Indian.* . .

but acknowledges candidly:

> . . .the great Engine I employ is Rum,
> More powerful made by certain strengthening Drugs.

"Ponteach" declares to the English governor in Act I:

> [The French] we thot bad enough, but think you worse.

And in Act II:

> The French familiariz'd themselves with us,
> Studied our Tongue and Manners, wore our Dress,
> Married our Daughters, and our Sons their Maids. . . .

Chief Bear laments of the English invaders:

Their Cities, Towns, and Villages arise,
Forests are spoil'd, the Haunts of Game destroy'd,
And all the Sea Coasts made one general Waste.

Chief Wolf asserts:

We're poisoned with the Infection of our Foes. . . .

A wily French priest repeats in Act III a perversion of the gospel of the "Delaware Prophet":

[The English] once betray'd and kill'd [God's] Son,
Who came to save you *Indians* from Damnation—
He was an *Indian*, therefore they destroy'd him;
He rose again and took his flight to Heaven.
But when his foes are slain he'll quick return,
And be your kind Protector, Friend, and King.
Be therefore brave and fight his Battles for Him. . . .
Kill all you captivate, both old and young,
Mothers and children, let them feel your Tortures;
He that shall kill a *Briton*, merits Heaven.
And should you chance to fall, you'll be convey'd
By flying Angels to your King that's there.

Alas, we know the Angel who had flown! In Act V, Rogers sounds a pair of Shakespearian notes that (so testified my father) Andrew Cooke had taught him to admire: the Indians having been betray'd by British & French alike and the uprising collapsed, "Ponteach's" son "Philip" remarks on the "game of governments":

The Play is ended; now succeeds the Farce.

And when characters thot dead vengefully reappear, his other son "Chekitan" (Pontiac had no such sons; he was more father to my father than to his own offspring, of whom we know nothing) wonders in best Elizabethan fashion:

May we believe, or is this all a Dream?
Are we awake?. . .
Or is it Juggling, Fascination all?

Deadly juggling it was. In the aftermath of the war, "Alexis Cuillerier" was arrested in Detroit and charged with the 1764 murder of one Betty Fisher, the seven-year-old daughter of the 1st white family kill'd in the rising. "Angélique" did not appear at the trial—in fact, after 1763 Andrée Castine Cooke vanishes from the family records as if flown bodily to heaven—but "Antoine Cuillerier" did, and by some means prevail'd upon Pontiac to testify in my father's defence. The Chief 1st declared that the Fisher child, afflicted with the fluxes after her capture, had so anger'd him by accidentally soiling his clothes that he had thrown her into the Maumee & order'd young Cuillerier to

125

wade in & drown her. Not exactly an exoneration! After further conference with my grandfather, who reminded him that the Oswego treaty made him immune from prosecution on any charges dating from the war, Pontiac changed his testimony: He himself, he now declared, had done both the throwing & the drowning, driven by his general hatred of white females after his betrayal by one of their number in May 1763. And the river had been the Detroit, not his beloved Maumee, which he would never have so defiled.

The jury preferr'd his original version & found against my father, who promptly escaped custody & disappear'd—as Alexis Cuillerier. One "Antoine Cuillerier," then in his 70's, lived a few more years in the rôle of *habitant* in the Fort Detroit area, and there died. Of Andrew Cooke III we know no more. Pontiac himself, two years after his trial, was clubb'd & stabb'd (so reports one Pierre Menard, *habitant*) in the village of Cahokia by a young Illinois warrior bribed "by the English" to the deed. The assassin's tribe was almost exterminated in the reprisal by the nations Pontiac had endeavour'd in vain to bring together: *that* was a kind of fighting they understood.

Oh child, how I am heavied by this chronicle—whose next installment must bring my father to rebirth, myself to birth (you too, perhaps!), & be altogether livelier going.

Pontiac, Pontiac! Andrew, Andrew! How near you came to succeeding!

And Henry, Henrietta! *We* will come nearer yet, you &

Your loving father,
A.B.C. IV

O: *A. B. Cook IV to his unborn child.* The history of *H. C. Burlingame IV: the First American Revolution.*

At Castines Hundred
Niagara, Upper Canada

Thursday, 9 April 1812

My Darling Henry or Henrietta,

On this date 100 years since, there was bloodily put down in New York a brave rebellion of black slaves, instigated three days before—so my father chose to believe—by his grandfather & namesake, Henry Burlingame III, after the failure of the Bloodsworth Island Conspiracy. Six of the rebels committed suicide, 21 were executed. One "Saturnian revolution" later, he maintain'd, in 1741, my *own* grandfather & namesake, Andrew Cooke III, successfully spiked a 2nd such revolution in the same place, with even bloodier result: 13 hang'd, 13 burnt, 71 transported.

I did not believe him.

Neither did I believe, when I came of age, what he had told me in my boyhood of his mother, Andrée Castine: that she betray'd Pontiac to Major Gladwin & thus undermined, with my grandfather's aid, the great "Indian Conspiracy" of 1763–64.

Henry Cooke Burlingame IV, at least in the brief period of his official life (1746–1785), lack'd Pontiac's tragical vision. The most I will concede to his slanderous opinion of my grandparents is the possibility of their having realized, around 1760, that their grand strategy had misfired: that the French might never regain control of the Canadas, much less link them with Louisiana & push east across the Appalachians to the Atlantic; that "successful" Indian resistance would lead only to their extermination by the British. In short, that the sad sole future of the red man lay in accommodation & negotiated concession, to the end of at least fractional survival & the gradual "reddening" of the whites. Pontiac's one victory, on this view, was Major Rogers's verse tragedy *Ponteach:* as Lord Amherst infected the Indians with smallpox, Pontiac infected white Americans with Myth, at least as contagious & insusceptible to cure.

More simply, we have the testimony of Andrée's diary that she & Andrew believed it necessary for the Indians (who, as we have seen, would not take the calculated loss of storming operations) at least to master the art of protracted siege—which interfered only with their seasonal rhythms, not with their famous individualism—if they were to conduct successful large-scale campaigns against white fortifications & artillery. Sieges were a repeatable discipline; Pontiac's tactic (to enter the fort as if for a conference & then fall on the unsuspecting officers) was a one-time-only Indian trick which would make legitimate conferences difficult to arrange in the future. Its "betrayal" (she does not directly either admit or deny betraying it herself) did not undermine the general plan; it only made necessary a change of tactics.

"She made that diary note a full year later," my father observed. "She was covering their tracks. She knew how I loved old Pontiac."

It is true that such entries, especially belated ones, can be disingenuous. But my father, like the rest of us, chose by heart as much as by head which ones to put his faith in.

No Cooke or Burlingame has ever disprized book learning; the Burlingames, however, are the scholars. "Alexis Cuillerier," 21 years old, broke jail in Detroit in 1767 and disappear'd before he could be convicted, on Pontiac's original testimony, of drowning the child Betty Fisher. In the autumn of that same year, Henry Burlingame IV matriculated at the College of New Jersey in Princeton. Upon his graduation, he went up to Yale College in New Haven, staying on as a tutor in history after taking a Master of Arts degree there in 1772. His life in this interval, in great contrast to his adventuresome youth, was austere, even monastic. By Mother's report, he was still much shock'd by what he took to be his parents' successful duplicity: he even imagined that they had bribed Pontiac with rum to give his damaging testimony, and subsequently arranged his assassination, to the end of further "covering their tracks"! (Was it in some rage against his mother that "Alexis" drown'd the poor beshitten Fisher girl? But we have only Pontiac's word that he did, together with the rumors that had led to his arrest.) This shock, no doubt, accounts for his reclusion. And there was another factor, as we shall see.

H. C. Burlingame IV thus became the 1st of our line not merely to doubt his father (we have all, in our divers ways, done that) but to despise him. I was the 2nd; and am perhaps the 1st to pass beyond that misgrounded, spirit-wasting passion, to spare you which is the end & object of these letters.

The study of History was Father's sanctuary from its having been practised upon him in the past, and his preparation for practising it upon others in the future. From the present—the revolutionary fervor which was sweeping the colleges of Harvard, Yale, Princeton, even William & Mary in the late '60's and early '70's—he remain'd aloof. His student friends from Princeton (John Armstrong & Aaron Burr are the two we shall remember) were ready by 1774 to fight for American independence; his Yale tutee Joel Barlow was already making plans, at Father's suggestion, for an American *Aeneid* (but Father had in mind a *satire!);* and his closest friend in New Haven, Mr. Benedict Arnold—a bright young merchant in the West Indies trade whose boyhood had been as adventurous as Father's—had organized a company of Connecticut militia. But while he did not dismiss as specious the arguments for independence, Father was skeptical enough (and Canadian enough) to see two sides to the matter: a prerequisite to the tragical view, tho not its equivalent.

His chief concern, however (so he claim'd), was not the inevitable misunderstandings & conflicts of interest betwixt governors & govern'd 3,000 miles apart; it was the invasion of white settlers across the Appalachians into Indian lands, in despite of George III's proclamation. He could not believe that the confederated state governments being proposed by the Committees of Correspondence & the Continental Congress would be inclined to check that invasion. Exempt from patriotism, he saw the self-interest & bad faith on both sides of the Atlantic, and a dozen routes to peaceful compromise, none of which bade especially well for the Indians. If, on the other hand, war were actually to break out betwixt the British & the colonials, each would scramble to use the Indians against the other—in particular the Six Nations of the Iroquois, whose situation once again would be, for better or worse, strategic.

In April of '75, when the shooting commenced at Lexington & Concord, Father was in nearby Cambridge, poring thro the library of Harvard's old Indian College for references to the Bloodsworth Island Conspiracy, and deciding that he had had enough of Yale's Congregationalist orthodoxy, perhaps of the academical life. His friend Arnold rusht up from New Haven to add his company of militia to George Washington's army, assembling on the Common. His friend

128

Burr hurried over from law school in Litchfield to join that army. Father introduced them. They could not persuade him to enlist, nor he dissuade them.

"We must have Canada!" they declared. Father understood, with a chill, that "we" already meant *The United States of America*. If Canada were not among those states, they argued, the British could crush the unborn republic betwixt its armies to the north & west and its navies to the east & south. The key to Canada was old New France, never easy under British rule: Arnold's strategy, in which General Washington & the Massachusetts Committee of Safety concurr'd, was a three-prong'd attack: one force (General Montgomery's, say) should move down the St. Lawrence from Maine to take Quebec; a 2nd (Arnold's own, he hoped) up thro Lake Champlain to take Crown Point, Ticonderoga, and Montreal; a 3rd thro the Mohawk Valley to Niagara. "We" would then control the St. Lawrence & the Lakes; Canada would be "ours." The French would surely help, in hopes of regaining New France for themselves; the *habitants* could be relied upon at least not to aid the British. The great uncertainty was the allegiance of the Six Nations: Could my father not be prevail'd upon to accept a commission & persuade the Mohawks to remain neutral, the Senecas to lay siege to Forts Erie & Niagara?

He could not, tho he affirm'd the soundness of the strategy. He urged young Burr to enlist with Arnold instead of Washington if he wanted action, and caution'd Arnold to beware the jealousy betwixt the Massachusetts & Connecticut Committees of Safety, which, together with the rivalry & reciprocal sabotage common to generals, was bound to make joint operations all but impossible. He himself, Father declared, was withdrawing to another Cambridge: not the one on the river Cam in Mother England, where his grandfather had gone to school with Henry More & Isaac Newton, but the one in tidewater Maryland. Not his fatherland (Heaven forfend!), but his *grand*fatherland, where that same ancestor had made certain decisions respecting his own deepest loyalty.

Burr & Arnold had not heard of this Cambridge, nor were they much inclined to hear. Was it in the neighborhood of Annapolis? One day's sail, my father replied, but a world away, and the last white outpost before the wild & trackless marshes. Above this Cambridge the river-names were English: Severn, Chester, Wye, Miles—it was a wonder the Chesapeake itself had not been dubb'd the Wash, or the Bristol. But at this Cambridge it was the Great Choptank, larger than Cam & Charles together, with the Thames at Oxford thrown in; and after the Great Choptank the Little Choptank, the Honga, Nanticoke, Wicomico, Manokin, Annemessex, Onancock, Pungoteague, Nandua, Occohannock, Nasswadox, Mattawoman—

Enough, cry Burr & Arnold: 'tis the beat of savage drums! To which my father replies: 'Tis the voice of the one true Continental, his vanisht forebears, in whose ranks he was off come morning to enlist.

All this my mother told me—your grandmother Nancy, who is about to enter the story. Andrew III's investigation of his latefound father had led him from Annapolis to Castines Hundred; my own father's re-investigation of that same ancestor reverst that route, as he was determined to reverse his father's judgement of the 3rd Henry Burlingame. From Castines Hundred, where he paid his respects to the incumbent Baron (sire of the current one), he made his way 1st down to Annapolis, to search the records of the province and dig thro the library at St. John's College; then over the Bay to Cambridge & Cooke's Point, once the seat of the family, to consult more local records & the memories of old inhabitants.

From one of these latter—an aged, notorious former whore named Mag Mungummory, he learnt three valuable things. 1st, that Ebenezer & Anna Cooke's childhood nurse, Roxanne Russecks, *née* Édouard, had had a romance with their father, Andrew Cooke II, and borne him a daughter named Henrietta Russecks (as shown on the family tree, or thicket, in my last), who herself later bore a daughter named Nancy Russecks McEvoy. 2nd, that Mag Mungummory's mother, Mary, call'd in her prime "the Traveling Whore o' Dorset," had once known Henry Burlingame III himself, in various of his guises, & fear'd him—tho of his disputed rôle in the Bloodsworth Island Conspiracy, Mag knew nothing. 3rd, that about the same time when Ebenezer Cooke regain'd his lost estate by marrying the whore Joan Toast, and Henry Burlingame III left Cooke's Point for Bloodsworth Island, and Henrietta Russecks married one John McEvoy, this Mary Mungummory had purchased from Roxanne Édouard Russecks a tavern own'd by the miller Harry Russecks, Roxanne's late husband. She had establisht a brothel in its upper storey and flourisht with the common-law husband of her old age, the miller's brother, Harvey Russecks. Mag herself, the fruit of this autumnal union, had inherited the business on her parents' death and, tho nearly 80 at the time of this interview, continued to operate both tavern & brothel with the aid of a young woman she'd taken in as an orphan'd relative four years past.

The establishment was the same in which my father was lodging, and where this conversation was taking place: Russecks Tavern, near Church Creek, below Cambridge. The young woman—herself chaste, tho uncommonly worldly for her age—was the same he had been unable to take his eyes off thro this interview as she bustled about the place. More, she was the Nancy Russecks McEvoy aforemention'd, whose family had been lost at sea in the ship *Duldoon* out of Piraeus for Cádiz in 1771. Then only fifteen, she had made her way from Paris to Philadelphia & thence to Maryland to seek her one known relative, her great-uncle Harvey Russecks. In his place she found his daughter (still call'd by her old working name, "Mag the Magnificent," but by Nancy rechristen'd "Magnanimous Maggie"), who had welcomed her as a grandchild, seen as best she could to her education, protected her from the establishment's rougher patrons—and gratified, insofar as she was able, the girl's tireless curiosity about her ancestry. Perhaps Mr. Burlingame could be of assistance in this last? Hither a moment, pretty Nancy. . .

And so my mother & father meet—he nearly 30, she nearly 20—and their matchmaker withdraws for the present, tho she has one crucial thing more to do for us. And they very soon fall in love, Henry & Nancy, whilst the country goes to war. Colonel Arnold's plan to move against Ticonderoga has been approved by Massachusetts; but to mollify Connecticut, which is jealous of both Massachusetts & New York, Arnold must yield command of the operation to the "Vermonter" Ethan Allen, who himself would separate New Hampshire from New York even if it means "making this state a British province" (so he assures Governor Haldimand of Canada in secret letters!). Even so, jealous officers in Massachusetts mount an inquiry into Arnold's "conduct," about the same time that Ethan Allen is superseded by a rival of his own as commander of the "Green Mountain Boys." Both men angrily resign their commissions & return to Cambridge, where Burr, having ignored his tutor's advice and stay'd with Washington, is dying of inaction. All three take up the Canadian campaign—but Allen, under General Montgomery, gets the key assignment of moving from Ticonderoga to take Montreal, whilst Arnold & Burr must take the bitter northern route thro the Maine woods from Castine—named for our 1st *émigré* Baron—to Quebec. (The 3rd crucial thrust, to Niagara thro the Mohawk Valley, is never mounted.)

As A. & B. freeze, Nancy & Henry bask in Chesapeake Indian summer (still call'd Goose-summer then, after the millions of wild geese moving down from Canada as "our" troops move north); they admire the rusty foliage & browning marsh grass, the endless clamoring vees in the limpid sky; they move thro the gossamers named for the season named for the geese and spun delicately out, like their own feelings, from every reed, rope, twig.

Burr & Arnold, reaching Quebec in mid-November with what remains of their company after the ordeal of crossing the Maine wilderness, find the British garrison forewarn'd (not impossibly by Ethan Allen himself), and are obliged to wait in freezing "siege" until Allen & General Montgomery come up victorious from Montreal. There they shiver, starve, & curse—Joel Barlow's three older brothers amongst them—whilst Barlow himself frets thro his sophomore year at Yale writing mock-heroic couplets on the subject of undergraduate snowball battles—"And *Jove* descends in Magazines of Snow"—& down in the golden marsh my parents come ardently together.

Or would so come! But 'tis *we* who come now to that curse of the male Burlingames I mention'd in my 1st. Andrew Cooke III was a man of normal parts, like myself: Andrée's insistence that he get her with child ere they marry was no reflection on his manliness, only a kind of test laid on him in view of his age & innocence, which test he lovingly (if slowly) rose to. But my father, like his namesake, was all but member-less—and, alas, had not yet rediscover'd his grandsire's secret. Here, it may be, is another clue to "Alexis Cuillerier's" rage against the Fisher child: it is common practice amongst the Indians to dismember male prisoners in the course of torturing them; any males among themselves who happen to have been by nature underendow'd are teased as having been thus captured and tortured—" 'tis well you escaped with your nose & ears," et cetera—and are further advised, if they have not the womanly nature of a *berdache*, to take a girl-child to wife. . .

His celibacy at Princeton & Yale, too, we may now take understanding pity on; for while undergraduates in those Puritan longitudes were not given to the wenching of their Oxbridge counterparts, they were normally preoccupied with courtships & flirtations. 'Twas simple shame, my mother told me in later years, drove my father to the excesses that punctuate his life. He had not his namesake's "cosmophilism"; he wanted only & simply to husband Nancy Russecks McEvoy, and he could not do it, and the frustration very nearly unhinged him. Indeed, not knowing the root of the problem, as 'twere, my mother thot him 1st uncommonly proper, then uncommonly shy, at last uncommonly odd—whether madman or faggot she could not decide. For things had reacht that point betwixt them, by his initiative as much as hers, where "St. Anthony himself would have had a time of it."

When at last the truth came out, she was immeasurably relieved. "I straightway ask'd him," she told me, "could he not so much as piss with it? He could, said he, tho his aim was not the best. And had he not, says I, ever had a lusty dream, as young men will, and woken to find his musket fired? Would it were a musket, says he, even a proper pistol; but fire it did, especially of late, in hot dreams of me. Then marry, says I, 'twere strange indeed if such a malady be unknown to the upper storeys of the Russecks Tavern, and the learned doctresses there have no prescription." So leading him by the hand, off she goes to Mag Mungummory, lets him blush & sweat whilst she lays the problem plainly out, and in 30 minutes has what Henry had not found in as many years. To wit:

> . . .left alone, my Captain straightway set to work upon the eggplant, in the strangest manner I ever did behold. Forsooth, I was that amaz'd, that even some weeks thereafter, here in Jamestown, what time I set to recording this narrative in my Journall-booke, it was no light matter to realize it was true. For had I not observ'd it my owne self, I had never believ'd it to be aught but the lewd construction of some dissolute fancie. Endlesse indeed, and beyond the ken of sober and continent men, are the practices and fowle receipts of those lustfulle persons, the votaries of the flesh, that stille set Venus & Bacchus over chast Minerva, and studie with scholars zeal all the tricks and dark refynements of carnallitie! I blush to committ the thing to paper, even to these the privie pages of my Journall. W^{ch} it is my vow, that no man shall lay eyes upon, while that I live . . .

& cetera. The writer was the 1st Henry Burlingame, his journal the

Privie Journall of his capture, with Capt. John Smith, by Powhatan's Indians in 1608. And what that old arch-hypocrite blusht to commit to paper—and forthwith went on so to commit—was the "Mystery of the Sacred Eggplant," with the aid of which Smith had deflower'd Pocahontas & saved their necks: an encaustic, aphrodisiac decoction of *Nux vomica*, "Zozos," oil of mallow, & the rest, stuft into a cored aubergine into which, in turn—

But no matter. We have the *Journall:* the "fowle receipt" shall be yours, when & if! Burlingame I made use of it to beget on Pokatawertussan, Queen of the Ahatchwhoops, the Tayac Chicamec (Henry Burlingame II), to whom the *Journall* (and its author's justified Anglophobia) pass'd. Ebenezer Cooke discover'd its existence during his own Indian captivity at the hands of Chicamec in 1694; Burlingame III resorted to it to engender Andrew Cooke III on Ebenezer's sister the following year. And then the *Journall*—together with Smith's *Secret Historie*—disappear'd from sight.

"'Twas the dying wish of the whore Joan Toast, Ebenezer Cooke's wife," Mag Mungummory explain'd to the lovers, "that the receipt not be made public, lest we poor women be done to death. For what will turn your minnow into a buck-shad, will turn your buck-shad into a shark. Mister Ebenezer was all for destroying it, but his sister takes pity on the Burlingames to come, & on the Anna Cookes that love 'em—which is to say, the likes of Miss Nancy McEvoy! So they give both books to their old friend Mary Mungummory, as the trustiest judge o' their application; and Mary gives 'em to her Mag; and Mag gives 'em to you."

She did, and the lovers gratefully retired, with receipt & necessaries, into the gossamer woods. There Jove straightway descended in a shower of golden leaves, and Yours Truly was begot. What's more, the *rest* of that same *Privie Journall* convinced my father, not only that the 1st Henry Burlingame had turn'd his back upon his English heritage & become an Ahatchwhoop Indian, but that Henry Burlingame III, encountering that record of his grandsire's conversion, must surely have similarly so turn'd, being half Indian to start with! All hesitation then was purged from his own mind, which had anyhow never misdoubted its tendency, only its tactics: if the Appalachians were to dam the white invasion, either the "Continentals" (as the rebels now call'd themselves) must be supprest, or their "republic" kept weak & hemm'd round by territories of the Crown—especially by the Canadas, the key whereto, as always, was Niagara. And the key to Niagara was the allegiance of the Iroquois . . .

For all this, my mother's testimony. She & Father wed on New Year's Eve day in Old Trinity, the church after which Church Creek is named, and in whose yard a pair of nameless millstones mark the grave of Henry Russecks, Nancy's grandfather. Whilst their vows are exchanging, Arnold, Burr, Montgomery, & Allen make their belated joint attack on Quebec: a debacle in which Montgomery is kill'd & one of Joel Barlow's brothers so severely wounded that he dies in the retreat.

It had been my father's plan to go north early in the spring and try to persuade his friends to reconsider their positions, even perhaps to join him in a different kind of thrust along the Mohawk Valley. But by then I had made my existence known, and both Burr & Arnold (in response to discreetly worded postal inquiries from Church Creek) reaffirm'd their patriotism, tho readily acknowledging their disillusionment & the justice of Father's earlier cautions.

He linger'd on therefore in lower Dorchester, as I linger now at Castines Hundred; and whilst like you I slept towards birth, he associated himself with the Marshyhope Blues, a militia company charged with protecting the rebel citizenry against Lord Dunmore's flotilla, then in the Chesapeake; also against the Loyalist "Picaroons" assisting that fleet, and in particular against the depredations of one Joseph Whaland, a rogue who piloted British vessels up the estuaries of the County & made foraging raids with his own boats, which then struck their masts & hid in the labyrinth of the marsh. My father's actual purpose (Mother said) was to keep this Whaland safely inform'd of the militia's movements & of the several attempts to intercept him at sea. Shortly thereafter, Joseph Whaland and his picaroon schooner were captured in the lower County, where they had thot themselves perfectly secure.

"Your father was barely able to talk him out of prison," my trusting mother said.

He was not pleased by the coincidence of my birth (a little premature) and the signing of the Declaration of Independence in Philadelphia. I was duly dubb'd *Andrew Cooke IV* and charged to redeem that name: a great charge, my mother thot, for so delicate a babe.

The truth was, I was not expected to survive. When Washington lost Long Island in August & evacuated New York, my father decided he must tarry no longer: Burr had distinguisht himself in the retreat from Long Island by saving a brigade from capture (young Joel Barlow, on vacation from Yale, was in that brigade), but he had been obliged to disobey his superiors to do it, and they were not pleased. Arnold had had to withdraw from Montreal, so expensively won, and was building a flotilla on Lake Champlain to meet the superior British force there. Guy Johnson (Sir William's nephew & successor as His Majesty's Superintendent of Indian Affairs in New York, whom Father had befriended at Castines Hundred) wrote that the Six Nations had so far been successfully bribed into neutrality, but were "spoiling for action." That their likeliest leader, Johnson's Mohawk secretary Joseph Brant, was so gone into English scholarship & English religion that nothing could rouse him from his translation into Mohawk of the Book of Common Prayer. The iron was hot, Father declared, and must be struck ere it cool'd: he bade Mother join him at Castines Hundred as soon as she was able, "with or without the child, as fate will have it," and went on ahead to stir this Joseph Brant to action, whose motives he believed he understood.

134

Against all odds, Mag Mungummory & her clever company kept me this side of death, even nurst me toward robustness, but we were obliged to remain in Maryland thro the winter. In October Father wrote (in the family cipher, here decipher'd): "B[enedict] A[rnold] has lost, albeit brilliantly & against great numbers, the 1st naval engagement betwixt Crown & Continentals. I am stirring up charges against him of misconduct in Montreal, to incline him uswards." In January: "A[aron] B[urr]'s disgust with Washington is dangerously weaken'd by C[ornwallis]'s defeat at Princeton, *alma mater* to us both and, to B, *pater* as well." (Burr's father was its 2nd president.) In March, as we were leaving for the hazardous journey north: "Cannot stir B[rant] from his books. He is much like Yrs Truly of a few years back, discovering his other self, & hates the memory of having fought in '63 with the renegade Iroquois against Pontiac, whom too late he much admires. His sister Molly is the warrior in the family: B & I are like as twins, she declares, and she urges me to do *in his name* what he will not."

That name, in Mohawk, was *Thayendanegea*. The deeds associated with it, and their attributions, are a house built on the sands of my mother's love for & faith in my father, whom she saw thenceforward rarely, and always in equivocal circumstances. Hers was a harder fate than Anna Cooke's, I think, whose Henry Burlingame never convincingly reappear'd to her. If Father's letters are to be believed—I mean the letters in his hand, over his initials, which, never doubting them herself, Mother kept at Castines Hundred with the *Journall* & the *Secret Historie*—on my 1st birthday anniversary he assumed the rôle of "Joseph Brant" to head 500 Senecas & Cayugas in the St. Leger expedition against Fort Stanwix on the Mohawk, a siege not unlike the one of his boyhood. It was a siege soon lifted, not by the battle at Oriskany (which, tho costly to both sides, was indecisive), but by secret agreement between my father & the leader of the Continental relief force sent up after that battle: "*Major General* B[enedict] A[rnold] is still embitter'd that his new commission came so tardily, after the promotion of his juniors & inferiors & so many brave exploits of his own. Only Washington's personal entreaties keep him in the rebel service. By giving him the victory at Stanwix (at small expense to us), I have put his dunderhead superior in such a passion of jealousy as B will find intolerable—when we shall meet again."

Another letter has him rejoicing at "A's" being relieved of command by that same jealous superior, General Gates. He laments the staunch, "misguided" patriotism that leads his friend to serve bravely even so, without command, at the 2nd Battle of Saratoga. He rejoices again when in June '78 Washington puts Arnold in command of Philadelphia, "where everyone that matters, save Ben Franklin, is a Loyalist." Burr too, he complains, "is grown a hopeless patriot since last winter at Valley Forge. The pass he guarded was the very door to the place, and for all his old contempt for Washington, he would not tender us the key. Now he fights like the Devil in New Jersey. With the British out of Philadelphia, and the French (thanks to Franklin) assembling a fleet at Newport to move against us in Canada, our position is not as certain as it was last year. 'Tis time my Mohawks bloodied their hatchets."

They did, on my 2nd birthday. Sweeping down into Pennsylvania's Wyoming Valley, John Butler, "Joseph Brant," & Molly Brant, with the Butler Rangers & the Brant Mohawks, join'd forces with a 2nd great Amazon, "Queen Esther" Montour, to capture Forty Fort. The massacre was egalitarian as their leadership: above 300 men, women, & children were tortured & kill'd by the "Devils of the Mohawk." In August & September they burnt German Flats & other "Continental" settlements in the Mohawk Valley; in November, having captured the fort at Cherry Valley, my father & his warriors alone murder'd 30 women, children, & old people. When "her husband" return'd to her that winter at Castines Hundred, "hardly recognizable" in his Mohawk paint & dress & haircut, my mother ask'd him hopefully, Whether these atrocities were meant to avenge Lord Amherst's smallpox campaign against the besiegers of Fort Pitt in '63? Not particularly, he admitted: their fourfold object was to rouse the real Joseph Brant from his studious reclusion (alarm'd at my father's excesses, Brant had indeed assumed command of the Mohawk warriors; hence Father's return to us); to recommit the Iroquois to their traditional ferocity; to provoke enough indiscriminate reprisal to bring the more neutral of the Six Nations into the war—and to slake the personal bloodlust of Molly Brant and Esther Montour, whose appetite for mutilation, disembowelment, impalement, flaying, cannibalism, & the like was truly savage.

Our host, Baron André Castine II, observed that Madocawando's Tarratines, while brave, had been peaceful trappers & hunters, like most Indians north of the St. Lawrence & the Lakes, who fear'd & despised the barbarous practises of the Iroquois. All he himself could say in defence of such barbarisms was that the Iroquois themselves had not perpetrated them wholesale until prest by the economics of the French & English fur trade, which had turn'd them into greedy, alcoholic middle-men. But tho savagery was savagery, the Baron maintain'd that all were not tarr'd with the same brush. Loyalists imprison'd by the Continentals in the Connecticut copper mines were being beaten & tortured about the privates in the customary ways; British regulars were stifling & abusing Continentals in the infamous jails & prison-ships of New York. Neither were yet routinely dismembering & flaying alive, or prolonging torture for the sake simply of extracting the greatest possible pain from a living body, or tying live people to trees by their own entrails, or impaling children on pointed stakes—had not so done, routinely, since the Middle Ages. Differences in degree were important; this was the 18th Century, not the 12th; the fragile flower of humanism, of civilization—

"It is *your* 18th Century," my father is said to have replied. "*We* do not reckon time from the same events, or by the same units."

We Princeton alumni, the Baron politely inquired, or we Yale tutors? Or perhaps we child-murderers?

"We Ahatchwhoops," said my father, "who ever regarded the Tarratines as a tribe of old women."

The Baron replied with a sigh that according to his grandmother, Princess Madocawanda, it was the elder women of the tribe who, like Molly Brant, were always the most ferocious when unleasht. Their conversation then ended uncomfortably, if short of an outright break in the family. And it seems not to have been without effect on my father, who soon after shaved his scalp-lock, doft his paint, beads, & buckskins, & donn'd a short wig & English dress—nor, to our knowledge, ever took a full-fledged Indian rôle thereafter. Unless it was he who sat for Romney's portrait of Joseph Brant in '86.

Thro that winter & spring (the last extended period when my mother knew fairly that the man representing himself as her husband was truly the man she'd married), he was in close communication by letter with Loyalist leaders in Philadelphia, certain British officers in New York, & the staffs of Canadian Governor Haldimand and Sir Henry Clinton. His friend Burr, now commanding the Continental line above New York from the Hudson River to Long Island Sound, was on the verge of resigning & taking up his interrupted study of law: his health was not the best, his competency as an officer had not been duly rewarded, and he was bored. In Philadelphia, as Father had hoped, Arnold had found the most agreeable & civilized society amongst the old Tory families of the city; he was already betrotht to the daughter of one of their number, and was being accused in Congress by the Executive Council of Pennsylvania (on information from anonymous sources) with eight items of misconduct. In April, four of those charges were actually referr'd to court-martial; furious, Arnold married the Tory heiress and demanded immediate trial to clear his name. But the court found reasons for delay, and my father cheerfully bade us goodbye, promising to write from New York.

"*André*," he said to my mother. "Remember André."

She thot he alluded to the Baron's mild reproof. But cipher'd letters, in a style very like Father's, exulted not long thereafter in his new connection to Major John André, a young adjutant of Sir Henry Clinton's in New York who in '75 had been imprison'd by the "Americans" (as the Continentals now began to call themselves), and exchanged in '76. "A[ndré] is a *civilized* fellow," Father wrote, "with a better talent than J[oel] B[arlow]'s for comical verse, in the refinements whereof I am become his tutor. He & I are like enough for twins—save that, tho brave, he has no stomach for intrigue. There also I am his tutor, inasmuch as poor B[enedict] A[rnold], in a rage over the lingering insult of his court-martial, has on his bride's advice begun a secret correspondence with us, concerning a commission in His Majesty's service. And C[linton] has delegated A[ndré] to pursue the matter."

137

He reaffirm'd his hope to bring "A" & "B" together to "his" side. The tide had turn'd severely against the Iroquois. In reprisal for the massacres of Wyoming & Cherry Valleys, the "Americans" in May burnt the castles of the Onondagas. In August the Butler Rangers & the Mohawks were badly beaten at Newtown, near Elmira. And in the autumn, "American" troops swept thro the Finger Lakes & Genesee Valley country, destroying the castles, livestock, & orchards of the Cayugas & the Senecas, some 3,000 of whom, including the Brants, fled to Fort Niagara for refuge. The only hope now for the Six Nations, in Father's view, was absolute British control of New York from Long Island to Lake Erie. And the best way to that control was the capture of the American post which dominated the Hudson Valley: West Point. But the post was heavily defended, if indifferently commanded; Clinton was sensibly reluctant to try it by storm. . .

Burr's loyalty proved, if not unshaken, still immoveable: if he felt any attraction at all to the British side (so he replied to my father's inquiry) it was the chance to live in New York with such clever company as Major André, the comical poet; but he expected to be able to move there as an American before very long. Arnold, on the other hand, was altogether disaffected when the court-martial, tho dismissing all the substantive charges, directed Washington to reprimand him on the two smallest counts, not to offend the Executive Council of Pennsylvania. As hundreds of Iroquois starved at Niagara, and as my father & Major André together readied for the New York press a topical parody of the old Scottish ballad of Chevy Chase (call'd "The Cow-chase"), my father was urging Arnold to demand from General Washington command of West Point by way of vindication of his honor, and negotiating with André, on Arnold's behalf, the terms of that post's betrayal!

By summer, when Arnold took command, the three of them had workt out the details of the proposal; little more was needed save signatures on the relevant documents & ground-plans of the fortifications.

A meeting was arranged at Haverstraw on the night of the autumnal equinox. John André, fetcht to the site on a British vessel, met Benedict Arnold under a flag of truce, deliver'd to him safe-conduct papers to New York, letters of commission, & details of the British attack to be made within a few days; he received from Arnold the plan of the fortress and disposition of the garrison. Before he could return to his ship, it was fired upon desultorily in the dark; my father, who had come ashore with André, signal'd the captain to drop down-river & await them; that worthy mistook the signal & return'd toward New York, leaving the two men stranded behind American lines. My father left André with Arnold & went ahead to scout safe passage overland. Next day the Major set out, in civilian disguise, carrying a false passport given him by Arnold. He got as far as Tarrytown, almost out of danger, when my father, hurrying to rendezvous with him, fell in

138

with two American militiamen on routine highway-watch, and to cover his own identity was obliged to show forged papers establishing himself as a New York state militiaman, one Van Wart. Minutes later they spotted André and, despite my father's encouraging them to let the stranger pass, decided on a thoro search. In his stockings they found the incriminating plans.

The best Father could do was insist on taking the papers immediately to General Arnold, "to warn him of the impending attack." Major André, no hand at intrigue, doubtless assumed that Father would destroy the evidence en route and thus put Arnold in position to order him releast. He did not betray "Van Wart's" identity even when, to their chagrin, the militiaman in charge decided to hold the papers himself whilst my father notified General Arnold of the spy's capture & the plann'd assault. He could then do nothing for poor brave André, only make good his own & Arnold's escape to the British sloop-of-war *Vulture*.

When the treason came to light, Washington, embarrast by his earlier defence of Arnold, felt obliged to show no mercy to André, who was hang'd as a spy on 2 October. The whole British army went into mourning; in recognition of his poetical talents, a plaque in André's honor was placed in Westminster Abbey. Joel Barlow, the newly-ordain'd Chaplain of the Massachusetts Brigade, preacht a fiery sermon on the treason of his former acquaintance, a sermon so aflame with patriotic indignation & literary ambition that its author was invited to witness his fellow poet's execution at West Point on the following day and, shortly thereafter, to dine with General Washington & his staff. Of André, Barlow wrote in a letter home that he had never seen "a politer gentleman or a greater character of his age," and that the Major died "with an appearance of philosophy & heroism." But he was altogether more moved by the literary prospects which his chaplaincy appear'd to be opening: he seized the occasion of Washington's dinner to lay upon the company Book I of *The Vision of Columbus* & a prospectus of the books to come.

I mention this coincidence, & this letter, because it argues against the notion entertain'd in some humors by my mother: that the man hang'd as John André was Henry Burlingame IV. Mother came to this notion out of mere despair, for we had no word from Father for a long while after André's capture. Indeed, our subsequent communications were all of a less reliable character than those before; likewise Mother's testimony, as unhappiness took its toll upon her judgement. Soon after Major André's execution, the picaroon Joseph Whaland reappear'd down in the Maryland marshes and renew'd his piratical depredations on behalf of the British. We went down there in '81 and '82, my 6th & 7th years, and sometime during our stay my mother was visited by this Whaland. Him too she imagined in some weathers to be her lost husband. But Joseph Whaland, while elusive, resourceful, & ubiquitous, was more uncouth than Pontiac and could scarcely read, far less make verses. If he was perhaps my mother's occasional lover, he was not her husband.

A likelier candidate is the anonymous author of the "Newburgh Letters" of 1783. Cornwallis had surrender'd at Yorktown; we had lost the war to the Americans; the two armies had disengaged whilst Ben Franklin negotiated with George III's ministers in Paris. Burr had married the widow of a British officer and was preparing to move his law practice from Albany to New York as soon as the British evacuated that city; General Arnold, having burnt Richmond & attack'd New London for his new employers, was isolated & unhappy in England; Barlow, married & settled in Hartford, was grinding out Columbus's vision and, having the good business sense to dedicate it to Louis XVI, was successfully drumming up an eminent list of subscribers. The back of the Iroquois was broken: they linger'd hopeless about Niagara, waiting for permission to relocate in Canada. Only Whaland's picaroons, marauding freely all over the lower Chesapeake, still fought the war. Washington's army, which he was holding in the Hudson Highlands until New York had been evacuated, was restless. The war was over; their pay was in arrears; Congress had no money; the Constitution had not yet been written; the political situation was in a flux. Colonel Nicola, in army headquarters at Newburgh, had already suggested that Washington assume the title of king, and the General's famous letter of rebuke (27 May 1782) assured his leadership of whatever form of government the new nation adopted. Then appear'd in print, also at Newburgh, two unsign'd letters exhorting the army to depose Washington, march on Philadelphia, force Congress to pay their arrearages, & establish a triumvirate of military officers to govern the country.

The prime mover of this call to sedition was that same General Horatio Gates who had so tried Arnold's patriotism after the victory at Fort Stanwix; Gates had delegated to his aide-de-camp, John Armstrong, the drafting of a call to mutiny. But Armstrong was no penman, and the texts of the letters are replete with signals from his & Burr's old friend from Princeton, Henry Burlingame IV. And while Joseph Whaland's last-ditch piracies cannot be construed in any way as strategic (on the contrary, they led Maryland gunboats into Loyalist hideouts on Tangier & Deal Islands, and dangerously close to Bloodsworth Island), the Newburgh proposals, regardless of their issue, were clearly in keeping with Father's declared strategy of dividing & weakening the infant nation. Unfortunately, Washington exercised restraint, declared his sympathy for the grievances voiced in the letters, declined to seek out & punish their author & instigator, and successfully persuaded his officer corps to patience until the army could be demobilized.

Mother heard no more from Joseph Whaland after the Treaty of Paris was sign'd in the autumn of '83. In lower Dorchester, the

140

watermen still report hearing screams & gibbers across the wastes, and to this day attribute them to Whaland, gone mad in his solitary hideaway, wandering the marsh like Homer's Bellerophon, "far from the paths of men, devouring his own soul." We return'd to Castines Hundred. Thousands of dispossest Loyalists, refugee Iroquois, & escaped or manumitted Negroes were swarming across the river from New York into Canada to avoid reprisals by the "Americans," amongst them Joseph & Molly Brant and "Queen Esther" Montour; "Upper Canada" was founded as their temporary homeland until the new Union of States fell apart & they could safely return. Against that happy day, Governor Haldimand declined to surrender Britain's Great Lakes forts (he call'd them *Canada's* Great Lakes forts) to the Americans, as stipulated by the Treaty of Paris. The Baron's estate was a refugee campground, his house a waystation, where Mother hoped in vain my father might turn up. Burr (now a state assemblyman in New York) was sympathetic, but had no news. Arnold, idle & brooding in London, was not answering his mail. Barlow, by this time an establisht "Hartford Wit," was preening on the subscription list for his still-unfinished *Vision:* King Louis, 25 copies; General Washington, 20; M. Lafayette, 10; B. Franklin, 6; A. Burr, 3; & cet. The Union of States was unfinisht, too, tho already a convention in Annapolis was calling for a larger one in Philadelphia to write a constitution & select a national President. White settlers freely crost the Appalachians and prest toward the Mississippi: the Joseph Brant who stopt at Castines Hundred was not my father, but a white man's Indian playing peacemaker for the Six Nations by urging them to sign away most of their homeland to the Americans, who occupied it anyhow. Not even my mother could imagine that he was her husband. In 1785 she told me that my father must surely be dead, and herself donn'd widow's weeds.

We linger'd here thro that winter. Then in '86, having just begun to reconcile herself to her bereavement, Mother received from London a remarkable love-letter from the man she mourn'd! To be sure, the letter was sign'd *B,* not *H.B. IV,* and declared itself to be from "Joseph Brant," in England officially to raise money for the erection of an Episcopal chapel in Upper Canada. But it was so "unmistakably" my father's epistle—his early handwriting, his pet names for her, allusions to their brief time together, inquiries after me—that we set out at once for London.

The prospect of "reunion" with the shadowy figure I had scarcely met & never known, & who had caused my mother such distress, gave me no pleasure. My uncle the Baron was all the father I needed, Castines Hundred the one real home I'd had. Only the sea-voyage, and the anticipation of a foreign land, reconciled me to the journey.

Sing now, Calliope, in minor key, & Clio in mournful numbers, our shock & confusion when, having settled in a boarding house in King Street, London, on my "father's" written instructions, we discover'd that the "Joseph Brant" being given a Captain's commission (and pension)

141

by the Court, & received by George III, & painted by Romney, and feted everywhere, was neither the pusillanimous prayerbook-scholar of Canajoharie & Upper Canada, nor the "Devil of the Mohawks" who had butcher'd Forty Fort & Cherry Valley, nor yet the New Haven tutor who had begot me in the Maryland marshes with the Secret of the Magic Eggplant, but an icy & indifferent stranger who scarcely acknowledged our existence face to face (and never deign'd to sleep in King Street), whilst sending us the warmest letters in the post, with money for our support & my education: letters whose authorship this same "Joseph Brant" neither admitted nor denied!

Unhinged, Mother fled for comfort across town to our old acquaintance Benedict Arnold, who sympathized but could not help us. He made plain, however (just before leaving London for Canada to try the West Indies trade again), his conviction that Father had betray'd him into betraying Washington & himself. He declared further—planting in my boyish mind a seed which was to bear much subsequent fruit—that this betrayal had been *not in the interest of the Crown at all!* On the contrary: having arranged for him to betray West Point to the British, Father had (so Arnold swore) *then betray'd him & Major André to Washington,* to shock the emerging republic into unity and weaken the hand of Washington's rivals, such as General Gates! The Newburgh Letters, he avow'd "on good authority," had been dictated by my father to John Armstrong with Washington's approval, for a similar purpose.

Letters! It was those that kept us in London, even after "Joseph Brant" departed to claim his new estate on Lake Ontario. They still arrived, almost regularly, at King Street; but in 1788 they began to be deliver'd from Paris, and tho the initial was the same, the name it named was now Joel Barlow's!

He was just arrived in France, these letters said, on secret business involving Louisiana, "which must not fall into American hands." The "Joseph Brant" subterfuge, they said, had been a heartbreaking necessity to disguise from Parliament his dealing with George III's ministers; thank heaven he could now put it by, "at least for the most part," and come to us *in propria persona. . .*

In July we were paid a call by Mr. Barlow, who turn'd out to be— Joel Barlow! He had indeed come from Hartford to Paris less than a fortnight past, he confirm'd, on behalf of the Scioto Company, speculators in Ohio real estate. He acknowledged further that he had encounter'd his old tutor Henry Burlingame IV at dinner at the Marquis de Lafayette's a few days since, whither he'd gone with the American minister Mr. Jefferson; and he was come to us at King Street at that gentleman's request, to urge us to join him, Burlingame, at his Paris lodging. But he disclaim'd with alarm having written any letters to us over his name, and trusted we would not excite the jealousy of his own wife (whom he was entreating to leave Hartford & join him) with that story. Could Burlingame's letters be going to Mrs. Barlow & his to us? My mother produced one: the handwriting was not Barlow's. He left as dismay'd as we, promising to press Burlingame on the matter when his business in London & the Low Countries was done & he return'd to Paris. Mother took to bed.

More letters came, all in the same hand, all tender, solicitous, intimate: from "Brant" in Upper Canada, from "Barlow" in Antwerp, from "Benedict" in St. John's, even from "Burr" in New York, now attorney-general of that state. In the spring of '89, after a particularly touching letter from "Barlow," we removed to Paris: not only did the author of *The Vision of Columbus* deny writing the letter; he inform'd us, astonisht, that Burlingame had left Paris for Baltimore some months hence, presumably to rejoin us there!

In 1789 Nancy Russecks McEvoy Burlingame was still scarcely 30, and—to her son's eyes, at least—still beautiful, if much distraught. She had taken one or two lovers over the years & yet remain'd faithful to her faithless husband, whom she thot Joseph Whaland & those others to have been. But this last shock undid her judgement: she came to believe that virtually everyone with his initial was Burlingame, regardless of station, appearance, or attitude. The letters still came, & the money: from Baltimore, from Canada, sometimes from Barlow's own hotel. We took lodging there. Barlow's land business was going badly; he miss'd his wife; they had no children; he was kind to Mother & me. She call'd him "Henry". . .

Her story ends in 1790, when Ruth Barlow was finally persuaded to cross the ocean. Just before the storming of the Bastille the year before, I had been put into a boarding-school at the Pension Lemoyne, across the street from Mr. Jefferson's house, along with another ward of Mr. Barlow's. Not long after, Mother inform'd me that I might expect a younger brother or sister by summer. Barlow was doubly desperate: an ardent supporter of both revolutions, he nonetheless hoped to save the floundering Scioto venture by selling large pieces of Ohio to refugees of the *ancien régime;* a devoted husband, he nevertheless install'd Mrs. Barlow in our lodgings in London & kept her waiting there a full month until my mother was brot to childbed in mid-July. Surely now, I thot, my father will appear. I had got a letter & a cheque from him on my 14th birthday, over the initial of an obscure young Corsican sub-lieutenant of artillery in Auxonne. . .

On July 10th, 1790, just before joining others of the American community in Paris in a congratulatory address to the French National Assembly, Mr. Barlow inform'd me that he had made plans, on my father's written instructions, for returning us to Canada as soon as Mother was able to travel. On the 1st anniversary of Bastille Day my sister was born, dead; Mother died a day or so later of childbed fever. That same day a letter was deliver'd to me by a servant of Madame de Staël, a friend of Barlow's, whom I did not know. But I had come to recognize that penmanship. The letter purported to have been written from a place call'd the Bell Tavern in the town of Danvers, Massachusetts. It declared that no force on earth could have kept the author from my mother's side at the birth of their poor daughter, except the same historic affair that had obliged him to leave her soon after begetting that child: a business involving the reversal of both the American & the French Revolutions! I was to come to him at once, to Baltimore; his friend Mme de Staël would see to the arrangements. And once with him at last, I would see "the pattern & necessity of [his] actions, so apparently heartless, over the years: the explanation & vindication of [his] life, the proper direction of [my] own." It was sign'd, *Your loving Father, Henry Burlingame IV.*

I tore that letter to pieces, burnt the pieces, pisst upon the ashes. And there commences—or shall commence when I next find leisure to write you, who will perhaps by then have commenced your own life story—the no less eventful history of

Your loving Father,
Andrew Cooke IV

P.S.: But there is a curious, painful postscript to that letter, the last I ever had "from him." Back in his tutoring days at Yale (so he confest to Mother, who recorded the anecdote in her diary), Father had briefly courted & made verses with an intelligent young woman named Elizabeth Whitman, and had stopt short of matrimony only on account of the same infirmity that had made him so shy in Church Creek. Miss Whitman subsequently was courted by Joel Barlow, who however prefer'd & eventually married Ruth Baldwin, & by yet another tutor at Yale, who too saw fit not to wed her. She withdrew from New Haven to Hartford to live with her mother & to languish on the margin of the Hartford Wits. Early in 1788 she found herself pregnant, and in June of that year, under the assumed name of Mrs. Walker, she left town to have the baby. In July the child was stillborn, like my sister; like my mother, Betsy Whitman died a few days later of childbed fever. She left only a letter, addrest to "B," the lover who had abandon'd her: "Must I die alone? Why did you leave me in such distress?" & cet.

It could have been Joel Barlow: he was in Hartford at the time, studying for his bar examination, involving himself in the Scioto swindle, & satirizing with his fellow wits, in the *Anarchiad*, Daniel Shays' admirable rebellion. It could have been Joseph Buckminister, the other Yale tutor amongst Betsy's former beaux. But the town to which she fled to hide the scandal was Danvers, Massachusetts; and the hostelry in which "Mrs. Walker" & her baby died was the Bell Tavern—where, she declared to the end, her husband would be joining her promptly. . .

Inspired by that fateful letter (and by the success in America of Richardson's *Pamela* and *Clarissa),* a relative of Betsy Whitman's named Hannah Foster turn'd her story into a romance on the wages of sin call'd *The Coquette* (1797): the 1st American epistolary novel. Inspired by that later epistle from the Bell Tavern, your father stay'd in Paris to join in the Terror & to applaud the guillotining of the whole paternal class.

But that is matter for another day, sweet child, another letter.

A.B.C.

R: *Jerome Bray to Todd Andrews.* Reviewing Year O and anticipating LILYVAC II's first trial printout of the Revolutionary Novel NOTES. With an enclosure to the Author.

Jerome Bonaparte Bray
General Delivery
Lily Dale, N.Y. 14752

April 1, 1969

Mr. Todd Andrews
c/o Andrews, Bishop, & Andrews, Attorneys
Court Lane
Cambridge, Md. 21613

Dear Mr. Andrews:

RESET Beg pardon. Among the carryovers of our original program into LILYVAC II is a tendency to repetition in the printouts, imperfectly corrected by a reset function. Especially on the anniversaries of significant earlier printouts, the computer inclines as it were to mimic itself: *e.g.*, every Bastille Day since 1966 it has rewritten our 1st letter to "Harrison Mack II" (Enclosure #1 of Enclosure #1 of our letter to you of March 4, *q.v.*).

To which last we are distressed to have had no reply, whether because it never reached you (we know the P.O. to be infested with anti-Bonapartists, in high places as well as low: *vide* the "American Indian" Commemorative of Nov. 4 last, which not ingenuously passed over the noble nations of the Iroquois in favor of the Nez Percé, an idle swarm of dope-smoking savages) or because the Mensch-Prinz cabal have persuaded you against us. A prompt response from you in the matter of our proposed action is imperative, since the statute of limitations will run on August 5, and he must RESET Meanwhile, given our uncertainty both of your position and of the confidentiality of our correspondence, we are torn between our wish neither to repeat ourselves nor to divulge promiscuously details of the status of the NOVEL project, and on the other hand our concern to get on with the neutralization of our enemies and to keep our benefactors apprised of the fruits of their patronage. We are therefore attaching a copy of our latest ultimatum to the Defendant, and will summarize in only the most general way the results of our recent work periods, which summary we trust you will pass on to Mr. Drew Mack and the Tidewater Foundation.

Our objective for the 2nd year (1967/68: Year *O*) of LILYVAC's 5-Year Plan was to modify and extend the capacities of LILYVAC I with the aid of a renewed Foundation grant; then to reprogram LILYVAC II with data for the Complete & Final Fiction, to the end of producing an abstract model of the perfect narrative, refined from such poisoned

145

entrails and crude prototypes as are now RESET Pursuant to this objective, in the late spring of 1968 (we were, you remember, still recuperating through the fall '67 work period from the attempted assassination of Ms. Bernstein and ourself in May of that year), Merope and we supplied LILYVAC II with all the entries in Professor Thompson's *Motif-Index of Folk-Literature,* together with such reference works as *Masterplots* and *Monarch Notes;* also the complete holdings in fiction of Lily Dale's Marion Skidmore Library and the collected letters of the Fox sisters (true visionaries, unlike those wrongly commemorated Pierced Noses), certain rare but standard treatises on the Golden Ratio and the Fibonacci Series, and a list of everything in the world that comes in 5's. By the 5th day of the 5th month of that year (the anniversary, by no coincidence, of the Emperor's pretended death on St. Helena), LILYVAC generated its 1st trial model, a simple *schema* for the rise and fall of conventional dramatic action, sometimes called Freitag's Triangle—

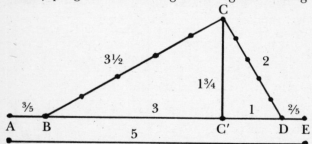

—in which AB represents the "exposition" of the conflict, BC the "rising action," or complication, of the conflict, CD the climax and dénouement, DE the "wrap-up" of the dramatic resolution. You can supply for yourself the revolutionary "allegory" at the heart of these ostensibly literary concerns. By May 18, the Emperor's coronation day, we had already progressed to a "Right-Triangular Freitag"—

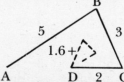

—and by George III's birthday to a "Golden-Triangular Freitag"—

—which prescribed exactly the ideal relative proportions of exposition, rising action, et cetera, the precise location and pitch of complications

146

and climaxes, the RESET By June 18, the last week of the spring work period, we had our perfected model, which of course we cannot entrust to the mails.

Finally, we secured per program a toad that under cold stone days and nights had 31 RESET We then betook ourselves to rest, leaving to faithful Merope the simple if exacting task of working out with LILYVAC the historical-political analogues of our progress thus far. It was during this period that LILYVAC's aforementioned tendency to self-mimicry was most vexingly displayed: *e.g.* RESET Which nigger in the ointment we have countered provisionally with an "editorial" program-amendment to recognize and RESET Just as we have programmed it to avoid or scrupulously delete any reference whatever to

The fall work period of Year *V* was devoted to preparations for the 1st trial printouts (scheduled for tonight through Friday) and their analysis. On its final day, the winter solstice—anniversary (on the Gregorian calendar) of the Pilgrims' landing on Plymouth Rock, of young Werther's letter to Charlotte apprising her of his intended suicide, of our misguided posting to the Wetlands Press, in all good faith, the priceless edited typescript of the *Revised New Syllabus* they shall RESET While we swam against the full ebb tide of nature as it were to keep our eyes open long enough to make out the precious letters, LILYVAC vouchsafed to us the title of the text-to-come. It gave us an *N;* it gave us an *O.* Cheered by this 1st tangible hatch of our ardent, arduous labors, Merope and we looked into each other's eyes with that relief and weary exultation which only true revolutionary lovers know. But then ensued, not *V,* not *E,* not *L,* no: but *NOT,* then *NOTE,* then *NOTES!*

It was dismay now in our eyes, sir, and the dark unspoken fear that our grubby foes had somehow wormed their way into LILYVAC! What *NOTES?* But we could forestall our rest no longer, not even to impart to frantic Merope the possibility (which occurred to us even as our eyes were closing) that here was no setback but a RESET That LILYVAC in its "wisdom"—which is to say, our parents and noble forebears in theirs: Father, Mother, Grandpa, Granama!—was once again transcending our limited conception of project and program, as when *Concordance* was superseded by *NOVEL;* that it was trying so to speak to tell us something.

A restless rest period, which, so far from completing our recuperation from the DDT's, has left us weakest when we most need strength, at the exact midpoint of our life and work, tonight and tomorrow and RESET When, as the full Pink Moon is penumbrally eclipsed, we must together confront the 1st draft as it were of the revolutionary "novel" NOTES. With the relief and weary RESET For what kept birding us as we "slept" (and Merope as she wintered the goats, made fudge, and revisited her alma mater to recruit a cadre for the struggle ahead) were such questions as whether for example *notes* was meant in the sense of verbal annotations, say, or of transcribed musical tones. Given the former, would the forthcoming printout be but a sort of *Monarch Notes* on *NOVEL?* Given the latter, was LILYVAC changing media?

We shall soon know. Be assured, sir, that we are now fully awake and, if far from restored, equal nonetheless to the task ahead. Our loyal Merope is in perfect health and high spirits, having enlisted in Waltham and Boston a splendid young group whom we look forward to meeting next month when they migrate here after their finals (always assuming that Doomsday does not occur, as predicted, at 6:13 PM PST this coming Friday). The Farm hums with suspense and confident anticipation; we are as busy as a hive of mice in search of fenny snakes. It is because we expect this to be our last free afternoon for some weeks that we take time now to set down this letter.

And we look forward to posting to you and to the Foundation, at the 1st opportunity, a report of the printout itself, to a world RESET But you must confirm to us that these communications are getting through intact. That you are an ally. That you will commence our action before the statute runs. Then let us together RESET JBB encl

ENCLOSURE #1

Jerome B. Bray
General Delivery
Lily Dale, N.Y. 14752

J.B., "Author"
Dept. English, Annex B
SUNY/Buffalo
Buffalo, N.Y. 14214

Toad that under cold stone days and nights has 31 sweltered venom sleeping got:

You may wish to avail yourself of this final opportunity to avoid litigation and exposure. Full accounting from your publishers of monies paid you for "your" "novel" *G.G.B.!* Full reparation to us in that amount! Full assignment to us of any future royalties accruing to that "work"! We are willing, if you comply promptly and fully, to drop action against you in the earlier cases—your "borrowings" from our *Shoals of Love, The -asp,* and *Backwater Ballads*—though our attorney has been apprised of these also and waits only for a sign from us.

We float like a butternut, but sting like a bean! Even as we draft this ultimatum, LILYVAC's printers clack away at the text of *RN,* the Revolutionary NOTES that will render your ilk obsolete. If you have not responded to our satisfaction by 6:13 PM PST Friday April 4, you are doomed.

JBB

cc T. Andrews

148

W: *Ambrose Mensch to Yours Truly and Lady Amherst.* THE AMATEUR, or, A Cure for Cancer, *by Arthur Morton King*

The Lighthouse, Mensch's Castle
Erdmann's Cornlot
Dorset, Maryland

March 31, 1969

FROM: Ambrose Mensch, Whom It Still Concerns
TO: Yours Truly (cc: GGPLA)
RE: Your message to me of May 12, 1940

Dear Sir or Madam:

Whom it so concerned, the undersigned, You wrote not a word to, not a letter, in Your letter to me of 5/12/40. Therefore I write You, seven times over, everything.

The enclosed You may have seen already: an early effort, abortive, on the part of "Arthur Morton King" to come to terms with conventional narrative and himself. Nine years ago tonight, on my 30th birthday, I first chucked it into the Choptank. There had been a little party for me here in my brother's house, my wife's contribution to which was a jeroboam of Piper-Heidsieck; walking home afterward (we had a flat near the yacht basin in those days) we enjoyed what was becoming a ritual quarrel. Marsha alleged that I was unfaithful to her, in spirit if not in physical fact, with my brother's wife. I protested that there was a great difference, both between psychological and physical infidelity and between my wife and my sister-in-law, and that while I had admittedly loved Magda Giulianova once when she was Peter's girlfriend and again when she was his bride, that latter "affair" (third of my life, Germaine) was nonsexual and had been entirely supplanted by my marriage.

All which was more true than not, and irrelevant, the real burden of Marsha's complaint being not that I loved Magda or another, "physically" or "spiritually," but that I did *not* love herself as much as either she or I could wish. And to this not-always-unspoken charge I could in good faith at best plead *nolo contendere:* I loved Marsha and Marsha only, but not greatly—a description that fit as well my feeling for myself.

The night lengthened; tempers shortened. Bitter Marsha went to bed alone. I withdrew to my "study" (daughter Angie's bedroom) with the last two inches of Piper-Heidsieck, reviewed by night-light this work-then-in-progress and my 30-year-old life, lost interest in continuing either, washed down 30 capsules of Marsha's Librium with the warm champagne, corked *The Amateur* in the empty jeroboam, walked drowsily across the park to launch it from Long Wharf on what I hoped was an outgoing tide, and went home to die.

Perhaps to die: I believed that 30 Libriums (I did not know the milligrammage) was *probably* a fatal dose, as Andreyev believed—when, at age 21, he lay between the railroad tracks in Petersburg—that the train would *probably* kill him. I also knew, like him, that my belief was possibly mistaken. The probability and the possibility were equally important; no need to go on about that. As I approached the bedroom I was struck by the thoughtlessness of imposing my corpse upon Marsha and Angie. The night was not cold; I had remarked early yachts in their slips; now I returned to the basin, thinking foggily (from the hour and the alcohol, not the Librium) to borrow a dinghy and go the way of my manuscript. None in evidence. A police car cruised from High Street down toward the wharf, parking place of young lovers; I took cover in the cockpit of the nearest cabin cruiser, not to be mistaken for a thief or vandal; curled up on the dew-damp teak; began to feel ridiculous.

And chilly. And cross. It seemed to me that my shivering and sniffling and general discomfort would likely keep me awake, and that unless I slept, the chemicals might make me only nauseated instead of comatose and finally dead. Back to the apartment, which had never seemed so cozy: let the living bury the dead, etc. Good-bye Angie, I wasn't the best of fathers anyhow; ditto Marsha, ditto husband. My head was fortunately too heavy for more than this in the self-pity way. I stretched out on the living-room couch and tried to manage a suitable last thought: something to do with the grand complexity of nature, of history, of the organism denominated Ambrose M.; with the infinite imaginable alternatives to arbitrary reality, etc. Nothing came to mind.

Best night's sleep in years. Woke entirely refreshed and, in fact, tranquil. It was explained to Angela that Daddy sleeps on the couch sometimes after he works late, not to wake Mommy. Marsha's prescription I refilled before she noticed any Librium missing. For a few days my wife was cool; then, after an ambiguous "shopping trip to Washington," her normal spirits returned until the next domestic quarrel, a month later. The marriage itself persisted another seven years.

God may be a literalist, but Life is a heavy-handed ironizer. Two days into my 31st year, tranquilly prowling the rivershore near here with Angie, I spied my Piper-Heidsieck jeroboam in the shallows near the crumbling seawall, not an oystershell's throw from where Your water message had come ashore to me in that gin bottle 20 years earlier. Lest eyes more familiar than Yours fall on it, I retrieved it. Except for a brief uncorking circa 1962 to oblige a certain fellow fictionist—who swapped me a couple of his own discarded experiments in *un*orthodox narrative in return for three chapters of the enclosed: my Bee-Swarming, Water-Message, and Funhouse anecdotes—both bottle and contents rested undisturbed thenceforth, in my subsequent domiciles, until tonight.

Something in those Libriums liberated me from the library of my

150

literary predecessors, for better or worse. Tranquilly I turned my back on Realism, having perhaps long since turned it on reality. I put by not only history, philosophy, politics, psychology, self-confession, sociology, and other such traditional contaminants of fiction, but also, insofar as possible, characterization, description, dialogue, plot—even language, where I could dispense with it. My total production that following summer was a (tranquil) love-piece for my daughter:

The ass I made of myself in my last missive to You dates from that same period, as does my practice—followed faithfully until tonight—of using only no-deposit-no-return bottles for submission of manuscripts. Well before Allan Kaprow and company popularized the Happening, "Arthur Morton King's" bibliography, so to speak, included such items as Antimasquerade (attending parties disguised as oneself, and going successfully unrecognized) and Hide & No Seek (in which no one is It). The radical tinkerers of New York and Cologne associated with the resurgence of "concrete poetry" and "intermedia" seemed to me vulgar parvenus; by 1961 I had *returned* to the word, even to the sentence, in homeliest form: my exemplars were the anonymous authors of small-town newspaper obituary notices, real-estate title searches, *National Geographic* photo captions, and classified help-wanted ads. By 1967, after a year of fictions in the form of complaining letters from "A. M. King" to the editors of *Dairy Goat Quarterly, Revue Métaphysique, Road & Track, Rolling Stone,* and *School Lunch Journal*—which if collected, as they could never imaginably be, would be found to comprise a coherent epistolary narrative with characters, complications, climax, and a tidy dénouement—I became reenamored simultaneously with Magda (I was by then divorcing) and with that most happily contaminated literary genre: the Novel, *the Novel, with its great galumphing grace, amazing as a whale!*

But not the Art Novel; certainly not those symbol-fraught Swiss watches and Schwarzwald cuckoo clocks of Modernism. No one named as I am, historied and circumstanced as I am, could likely stomach anything further in the second-meaning way; and a marsh-country mandarin would be an odd duck indeed! I examined the history and origins of the novel, of prose narrative itself, in search of reinspiration; and I found it—not in parodies, travesties, pastiches, and trivializations of older narrative conventions, but

But I'm ahead of myself. On another front of my general campaign, meanwhile, I privately declared war upon the cinema. My resolve to know these adversaries better led me (*i.e.*, A.M.K.) to attempt for Reggie Prinz the screenplay of B's book. Prinz has rejected my trial draft of the opening: "Too wordy"! I know my next move.

So: either this old story is new to You, or else You read and returned it nine years ago. It is the story of the broken seawall, the Menschhaus and the camera obscura, the cracked "castle" in whose sinking tower I live, with Peter and Magda and my daughter. It is the story of our firm and our infirmity, by which John Schott's Tower of Truth—whose foundation-work is our doing—will prove the latest to be undone. "Arthur Morton King" is the pen name I still use; but his rhetoric is less florid, his view of authorship less theistical, than they were when he and I turned 30.

I go now to my new friend's apartment, to mark the advent of my 40th year. She has promised for the occasion a beef Wellington; the wine is my responsibility. Having raised Magda's dark eyebrows with my excuses for not dining tonight with the family and my reticence about my plans for the evening (she guesses I've found a new lover; can scarcely have guessed whom), I went down to the Lighthouse cellar to review our family's holdings in the champagne way, and thus came across this earlier vinting. Heavy-footed life!

Magda followed me down; stood mutely by as I tucked two bottles of Mumm's '62 Extra Dry under one arm, the old jeroboam under the other. Did she recognize that crack in the masonry, down which she numbly ran her finger like some Italian Madeline Usher? No: she realized only that our recentest affair (fifth of my life, Germaine) is truly done, and that she was realizing it in a place where other things had ended, begun, reended, rebegun.

I raised the jeroboam. "If at first, et cetera." And knowing I could only compound the injury, tried anyhow to explain that what I meant was that I meant to try again to launch this old chronicle on the tide, and that as I had this cover-letter to write and a dinner engagement at eight, I must get to it. I've felt Magda below me since, feeding Angie and the family as I've written these pages; she feels me upstairs setting down these words before I go, each letter scored as if into her skin. In the night to come she'll feel me drinking to the health of my eleven-day-old sixth love-affair and to my birthday; humping hornily in the ruins of the feast; etting all the ceteras lovers love. . .

A curse upon tides, Yours Truly, that turn, and, turning, return like misdirected letters what they were to carry off! Thought well drowned, our past floats back like Danaë with infant Perseus, to take

152

eventual revenge. Would that the Choptank were that trusty sewer the Rhine, flowing always out, past the Loreleis and castles of our history; mercifully fetching off our dreck to some Nordzee dumping-ground of time—whence nothing returns unless recycled, distilled, laundered as Alpine snow.

But tides are what tides over whom this betides; who gladly now would say adieu but must make do with au revoir: i.e.,

A.M.

cc: Germaine Pitt: encl.

ENCL.

THE AMATEUR,
or,
A Cure for Cancer
by Arthur Morton King

A

Alhazen of Basra, Gemma-Frisius, Leonardo—from them A. learned to make his great dark camera. But he learned it Plato-wise, as it were by recollection, for that notion—like the tower itself, like Peter Mensch's entire house—hatched from Aunt Rosa's Easter egg, that Uncle Konrad gave her in 1910. Before he knew East Dorset was East Dorset and Ambrose Ambrose, he knew the landscape in that egg; his eye was held to it in the cradle. I smile that poor Aunt Rosa, throughout her younger wifehood, railed at Konrad's seedless testicles and her fruitless womb. Clip and tumble as they might, dine on shellfish, ply the uterine thermometer, she went to her grave unfructified. While lo, as mistress of the egg she is mother of this world we move in: the nymph inside who leans against the Rhine-rock under the *Schloss*; Mensch's Castle and the camera obscura; seawall, marshes, funhouse, Cornlot; the bees on Andrea Mensch's breast and Ambrose's birthmark; the mosquitoes that bite our Maryland lovers; the crabs they eat; the cancers that eat them. Our story is *ab ovo*: nothing here but hatched from there.

B

Begin again: *A.'s only child is mad,* et cetera.

Days are hard on Angie. Like her father she is, perhaps, a love child; in truth love streams upon us from her heart, she is a sun of love; but her pale eyes are troubled, she cannot grasp us. Carl and Connie, her twin cousins—their chasing games alarm her, their gentle teases set her wild. Yet "Magda *not* spank Connie-Carl!" she shrieks when Magda has to punish them, and she must be looked for when they cry, for once to end little Connie's tears she nearly smothered her with a cushion. She is large for her five years, and maladroit. Her hand undoes the twins' sand castles against her will, and when she croons, "Angie will *hug* Amby," Ambrose must beware a wrenched neck. Her hours are full of fears: that Magda will put the automobile in reverse; that Peter will neglect to lift her skyward by the

153

elbows after breakfast; that Russians will fire rockets at Mensch's Castle.

Most of all she fears that Magda will have lost Aunt Rosa's egg, companion of her nights and crises.

With the Easter egg they control her and ease her days. It is soiled and battered now, peephole cloudy, inner landscape all but gone; but its power has not vanished in the years since Peter and Ambrose would behave all Sunday morning for a glass of dandelion and a view of its wondrous innards. No tantrum or alarum of Angie's is beyond its virtue: with her eye fast to the window she can weather even the family's infrequent musicales, which else would set her trembling. For Angie's own and the house's tranquillity, Magda must lure her twice daily from their society to "play-nap" in her room; the Easter egg baits her every time. Alone, she converses in peace with storytellers on her phonograph or assembles her picture puzzle with the face down, for the sake of the undistracted pattern on the back.

Often at night, what with all the day's resting, Angie does not sleep. Though her light is out, she gazes into the egg; Ambrose hears her speak to the faded nymph inside. Her room is beneath his in the tower. If the night is fine, he may leave his books and lenses and help the child into her clothes; hand in hand they stroll the seawall and the sundry streets. The town is abed. Angie has no fear of the dogs that trot in alleys or of policemen uptown, who have got used to her. Indeed it is her town at that hour: she leads her father through its mysteries. They stop to hear the Choptank chuckle at the battered wall, and Angie's mouth turns up amused. Transformers hum atop their poles along the avenue: "*Buzz,*" the girl responds. They pause halfway over the Creek Bridge, which Ambrose feared to cross at her age, and regard the moonlit skipjacks moored along the bulkhead. A wandering automobile drives by to whir a note on the grating of the draw, whereat they move uptown content.

Until recently their first stop was the bakery: from a back alley they entered to watch men labor at next day's bread. The great ovens rumbled, the machines for kneading and wrapping clacked, the air was hot and yeasty. Pasted with flour and sweat, young Negroes slid the pans through cast-iron doors. John Grau the baker, dusty arms akimbo, aproned paunch thrust out, would hail the visitors.

"Look who ain't in bed yet!"

Then he'd swing Angie onto the loaf cart, adorn her with the square white cap off his Prussian head, roll her across the room.

"Whoo-hoo," the child politely called. The Negroes watched, leaning on their racks and paddles.

The loaf they bought cost twenty cents instead of the five that Ambrose used to pay, but it still burnt his fingers as it did when he and Peter sneaked uptown in their boyhood; steam still poured from it when he broke it into halves, and it tasted faintly and pleasingly of alcohol, as will a loaf not ten minutes old. Now Dorset's bread comes from big bakeries over the Bay; if the wanderers would eat they must brave knots of young men with capeskin jackets and shining hair who frequent the all-night diner. Then they walk down High Street towards Long Wharf and the municipal basin, chewing. Sporadic autos ripple down the brick; great poplars hiss above their heads.

At this hour, too late for young lovers, the waterfront park is cool and vacant. Through dew they wander to the wharf where creek joins river, there to perch upon high pilings white with gull dung, bite their bread, sip in turn from the public fountain. Across the creek stands one dark plant of Colonel Morton's packing house, victim of the failing oyster harvest: they bless it. Upshore above the broken seawall rise the county hospital and nurses' home: they smile upon the windows lit by suffering. Then Erdmann's Cornlot juts into the river, where stands Peter Mensch's house. The lights of the New Bridge run low across the river; beyond them, across another creek, is a second, larger hospital, the Eastern Shore Asylum. Like night-drench, like starlight, Angie's grace descends upon standpipe and bell buoy, smokestack and boulevard.

Citizens of Dorset: as we dream, as we scratch, as we copulate and snore, we are indiscriminately shriven!

C

Children call the house Mensch's Castle; their parents and Hector Mensch call it Mensch's Folly. It is an unprepossessing structure except that, in an area to which building-stone is no more indigenous than gold, the house is made entirely of granite rubble: the only private dwelling in the county so constructed. More surprising, from the northwest corner rises a fat stone turret, forty feet high and slightly tapered, like a short shot-tower. From Municipal Basin Angie points with her bread to the lights of Ambrose's room in the top. Strangers to Dorset have mistaken Mensch's Castle for a church, a fort; more commonly, owing to its situation and the lights that burn in Ambrose's chamber, it is thought to be a lighthouse. Novice mariners, confusing the tower with the channel range on Dorset Creek, have been led into shoal water off the seawall; but wiser pilots, navigating from local knowledge or newer charts, take a second bearing on the tower to reach the basin.

Some deem this turret the disfigurement of a house otherwise well suited to its site. Others call it the redeeming feature of a commonplace design and lament the fact that it is settling into the sand of Erdmann's Cornlot rather more rapidly than the rest of Peter's house. Two years ago, when one was certain the family must fail at last, Ambrose caused the entire tower to be converted into a camera obscura, from which is grossed enough in summer to buy part of the winter's fuel. Travelers en route to Ocean City are directed to Mensch's Castle by a number of small signs along the highway at both ends of the New Bridge; upon receipt of a small admission fee, Ambrose or Magda escorts them into the basement of the tower to see scenes projected from outside. The device is simple, for all its size: a long-focus objective lens is mounted on the roof; the image it receives is mirrored down a shaft in the center of the tower, through Ambrose's room and Angie's; on the bottom floor it is reflected by another mirror onto a vertical ground-glass pane the size of a large window, let into one side of the shaft. Like a huge periscope the whole apparatus can be turned, by hand, full circle on its rollers.

Visitors do not come to the Lighthouse in great numbers: Ocean City boasts amusements more spectacular than Leonardo's, and Magda declares her astonishment that even one person would pay money to see on the screen what can be witnessed for free and real outside. But those curious enough to seek it out find the camera obscura fascinating, and are loath to leave. One understands: the dark chamber and luminous plate make the commonplace enchanting. What would scarcely merit notice if beheld firsthand—red brick hospital, weathered oyster-dredger toiling to windward, dowdy maples and cypress clapboards of East Dorset—are magically composed and represented; they shine serene by their inner lights and are intensely interesting.

Peter and Ambrose are drawn to their camera obscura no less strongly than the visitors. They linger in the darkened basement when customers are gone, regarding whatever image has chanced upon the glass. Stout Peter's voice goes husky.

"Damned old seawall," he remarks, as if years instead of minutes had gone by since he viewed it firsthand. And Ambrose sighs and tisks his cheek—for there it stretches, cracked, gleaming.

Little Angela, on the other hand, is not interested. In the chamber of her mind, perhaps, things glow with that light unaided. In any case, she prefers the vanished country of the Easter egg. What sights she sees through that blank window, we cannot suppose.

D

During all his first thirty years, A. waited for one among us to make a sound, move a hand, blow cigarette smoke in a certain way that would tell him we understood everything, so that between us might be dispensed with this necessity of words.

Signs to us he made past number. Earnest professors: when you discoursed upon Leibnitz and the windowless monads, did you not see one undergraduate, ill groomed and ill at ease, tap his pencil thus-and-so upon his book—which is to say, upon your window? Had you then flung up that sash with gesture of your own. But Brussels sprouts (he daresays) had thrust upon you a flatulence unnerving at the lectern; intent at once upon the syntax of your clause and the tonus of your sphincter, you missed his sign. Auburn beauty whom he stared at in the train-coach mirror thirteen years ago, from New York to North Philadelphia: you saw him touch his necktie such-a-way. If you had answered in kind and made him know. Bad luck for him your dirndl bound you out of countenance; bad luck for you you passed New Brunswick praying for your menses, when already Gold the casting agent's sperm had had its way with your newest ovum. Et cetera.

You fidget. I too, and blush to think how lately A. has left this madness. Your forbearance and embarrassment for his sake I appreciate. The telescope at his window, the sculpture 'round about, the very lamp and ink bottle on his desk I see withdrawn into themselves and hiding their expressions: tender of his feelings, relieved to see he understands at last—yet uneasy all the same, lest out of habit he commence to stare again, or press them once more to give up truths about themselves. Never fear. The eyes shall sooner ask the fingers for a sign, the fancy supplicate the bowels, than Ambrose tax us further in that old way.

E

Everybody in that family dies of cancer! The only variable is its location: Grandfather's was in his prostate, Grandmother's in her bloodstream. Of their four children only Uncle Wilhelm was spared, by dying in France of influenza in 1918. Aunt Rosa's was in her uterus; her husband Konrad's was in his skin. Uncle Karl's was in his liver. Ambrose's and Peter's mother Andrea, like Konrad a Mensch by marriage only, has nonetheless had radical mastectomy; her husband Hector's nine-month madness in 1930, thought merely the effect of jealousy, is now revealed to have been associated with a tumor that feasts upon his brain.

When his sons went to visit him in Dorset Hospital, Hector stroked his nose and said, "What's killing me will kill you too." Already on Ambrose's chest, constellations flourish of blue nevi whose increase in size and number I follow with interest—though it is from his birthmark that he looks for eventual quietus. Hence his inability to share Magda's concern over radioactive fallout: with or without strontium 90 in their milk, her children must meet the family nemesis and perish.

Peter's explanation is that, stonecutters and masonry contractors, the family have always worked and dwelt among rocks, which, he has heard, reflect more than normal cosmic radiation. This theory (with which somehow he also accounts for both Ambrose's potent sterility and his own fertile impotence) is clever for Peter; more characteristic is his refusal to consider moving out of Mensch's Castle, cosmic rays or no cosmic rays.

Excepting the mode of their demise, nothing more typifies that line than this persistence: with them, every idea becomes a fixed idea, to be pursued though it bring creation down 'round their shoulders. Had it not been for Grandfather's original obstinacy, for example, they would not now be living (on the verge of bankruptcy) in America at all. One version has it he was the elder son of a Rhenish vintner; that the scene in Rosa's egg was his future estate, or one not unlike it; but that he got a serving-girl in trouble, and instead of making arrangements to conceal the little scandal, as his father proposed, renounced his patrimony to immigrate to Maryland with her. Another legend, on the contrary, says his forebears were the rudest peasants, almost animals, from Herrkenwalde in Altenburg; that his emigration and establishment of the family firm was no decline but an extraordinary progress. Granting either version, it appears that he was a determined fellow and that the family has come a considerable way, for better or worse, in a short time.

Of Grandfather's fathering, then, nothing certain is known. Whether from ignorance, spite, indifference, or a bent to regard himself as unmoved mover, Thomas Mensch all but refused to speak of his origins, and thus deprived his parents of existence as effectively as if he'd eaten them. But whatever his prehistory, we know that in 1880, still in his late teens, he appeared in Baltimore as an apprentice stonecutter; married there in '84; moved with his bride to Dorset the following year to work as a mason and tombstone cutter, and liked the place enough to stay. In 1886 Aunt Rosa was born, in 1890 Uncle Karl, in '94 the twins Hector and Wilhelm. Grandfather was obliged to find new irons for his fire: in addition to his backyard tombstone-cutting he became the local ticket agent for North German Lloyds, which during the great decades of immigration sailed regularly between Bremerhaven and Baltimore; and in this capacity he arranged for the passage to America of numbers of the relatives of his German friends. Twenty dollars for a steerage crossing, bring your own food, except for the barrels of salt herring and pickles supplied by the steamship line, which scented the new Americans for some while after. Moreover, as the would-be homesteaders straggled back to the Germantowns of Baltimore and Philadelphia from ruinous winters in Wisconsin and Minnesota, Grandfather helped and profited from them again as a broker of wetland real estate, the only acreage they could afford in Maryland's milder climate. They drained marshes by the hundreds of acres; throve and prospered on what they turned into first-class arable land—and on their weekend trips to town they made the Menschhaus in East Dorset a little center of the county's German community until the First World War.

Just before the turn of the century, Thomas Mensch did his most considerable piece of business: while it lasted, the most successful of the family's enterprises to date. Concerned by the Choptank's inroads into several newly settled neighborhoods, the town commissioners authorized construction of a retaining seawall along several blocks of East and West Dorset; Grandfather bid low for the contract, hired laborers and equipment as a one-man ad hoc company, and in 1900 completed the wall—which like an individual work of art he signed and dated at each end in wet concrete.

With the capital acquired from this and his other enterprises he established a proper stoneyard, the Mensch Memorial Monument Company, and employed laborers and apprentices. These latter included, as they came of age, all three of his sons, who seem also to have apprenticed themselves to their father's obstinacy. Karl, to begin with, so loved the yard—the blocks of marble in their packing frames, the little iron-wheeled carts, the tin-roofed cutting and polishing shed with its oil-smelling winches and hoists, the heavy-timbered horses and potbellied stove, the blue-shirted black laborers and white-shirted, gray-aproned masters, the cutting tools arrayed like surgical instruments on the working face, the stone-dust everywhere—that he could not be kept in school. At sixteen he dropped out to work with the stone all day, for which he had a natural feel though he lacked any particular gift for lettering and embellishment. By his twentieth year he was the firm's master mason and second in charge, supervisor of roughing and polishing the stones and their erection in the county's graveyards; it was his greater interest in construction than in carving that, along with Hector's restlessness, would fatefully extend the firm's activities to include foundation laying and general masonry. A swarthy, hirsute, squat, and powerful man, Karl never married, though like Grandfather he was regarded in East Dorset as a ladies' man. Stories were told of women brokenheartedly wedding others. . .

The twins, for their part, not content merely to embrace the trade they were born to, would transcend it, make an art of it. From early on, Hector and Wilhelm dreamed of being not stonecutters, but sculptors; in their teens they took charge of the artwork on the stones, leaving their father the routine chore of lettering inscriptions. Many a dead Choptank waterman, whose estate could allow him no grander monument than a limestone slab, was sung to his rest by flights of unexpected angels—added gratis by Wilhelm and Hector as an exercise in alto-relievo.

Their ambition was equal; together with warnings from brother Karl that they were not to emulate his truancy, it saw them through the public high school to the point of scholarship examinations for further study, almost without precedent in East Dorset in those days. But their gift, as Hector early acknowledged, was not equal: he could execute with difficulty a plausible acanthus, oak-leaf, or Greek-key border, staples of the tombstone-cutter's art; his rosettes, sleeping lambs, and beflourished monograms could not be faulted except for the time they took to achieve. But never could he manage, much less with Wilhelm's grace and speed, the feathered wings, flowing drapery, and lifelike faces of cherubim and seraphim—

158

the latter, often as not, angelic likenesses of Karl, Rosa, Grandfather, or Grandmother; the former mischievous apotheoses of the brothers' girl friends of the moment, who, fifty years later, could find in the cemeteries of their youth the marble image of its flower.

It was Konrad, their new brother-in-law, who in 1910—the year of his marriage to Rosa and of the twins' graduation from high school—supplied the family from his fund of learning with the example of the twins of myth, whereof most commonly one was immortal and the other not. Like an insightful Castor, Hesper, Ephikles, or Zethus, Hector urged his brother to apply for a scholarship to the Institute of Art in Baltimore—and himself applied to the Normal School in nearby Wicomico, modestly lowering his aspirations to the teaching of art in local public schools.

For the next four years both young men supported themselves, between studies, with job masonry in their respective cities, Wilhelm characteristically throwing in carved lintels and mantelpieces without extra charge to the row-house builders of Patterson Park and Hampden, who could not have afforded them, as well as to the mansion raisers of Roland Park and Guilford, who could. By 1914, when they graduated, Hector was more interested in school administration than in either making or teaching art; and Wilhelm had filled the Menschhaus with his schoolwork: beaux-arts discus throwers, grimacing Laocoöns, Venuses surprised (which for all her pride in her son's talent Grandmother Mensch would not permit on the first floor).

Hector moved back into the house—where now lived Rosa and Konrad too—worked as teacher of art and assistant to the principal of Dorset High School, and spent his summers in the stoneyard. But except for occasional visits home (for which the Venuses were fetched down to the Good Parlor and the house prepared as for wedding or funeral, or visit from the kaiser himself), Wilhelm never returned to Dorset. Indeed, his search for stonecutting work that would leave him time and means to do sculpture of his own seemed to lead him ever westward, from Dorset to Baltimore to the remotest counties of the state, high in the Catoctins and Alleghenies.

"That's how it is in the myths," Konrad volunteered. "Always west."

"A studio he could have right here," Grandfather complained. "What do we need our big shed, business like it is?"

He sniffed at Hector's opinion that, to a sculptor, mountains must be more inspiring than marshes, and Konrad's that travel is broadening. Only Karl's gruff conjecture made sense to him: that Wilhelm had found somewhere in those hills a better model for his Venuses than the plaster replicas at the institute. But that hypothesis did not console him, far less Grandmother, for the "loss of their son," despite Konrad and Hector's testimony that a more or less irregular life was virtually prerequisite to achievement in the fine arts.

"Pfoo," Grandfather said. "If that's so, it's Karl would be the artist."

Karl grinned around his cigar. "And you'd be Michael Angelo his self."

Not until 1917, when Wilhelm came home to enlist with his brothers in the American Expeditionary Force, did even Hector learn the truth: that it was no Appalachian Venus that had enthralled the pride of the Mensches, but a wilder, less comprehensible siren, not even whose existence had been acknowledged by the masters of the institute. Through a week of tears and feasts (while the down-county

159

Germans gathered at the Menschhaus with their own patriotic sons, and the kaiser's picture was turned to the wall and the house draped in Stars and Stripes, and the women wept and laughed and sliced wurst and made black bread and sauerbraten, and the men quaffed homemade beer and tried in high-spirited vain to find Yankee equivalents for their customary drinking songs), Wilhelm tried to explain to his brothers those strange new flights of the graphic and plastic imagination called Futurism, Dadaism, Cubism; the importance of the 1913 Armory Show; the abandonment—by him who in fifteen minutes with the clay or five with the pencil could catch any expression of any face!—of the very idea of representation. . .

"Sounds right woozy to me, Will," Hector declared. Karl gruffly advised Wilhelm to stick with tits and behinds if he hoped to turn stone into money. Even Konrad, gentle Platonist, wondered whether any artist who forsook the ancient function of mirroring nature could survive.

"This is 1917!" Wilhelm would laugh. "We're in the twentieth century!"

A photograph made of the brothers that week by one of his artist-friends from Baltimore—the last but one of Wilhelm in the Mensches' album—shows scowling Karl with a face like modeled beef; lean-faced Hector with his long artist's fingers and the eyes already of an assistant principal; and leaner Wilhelm, face like an exposed nerve, his edgy smile belied by eyes that stare as if into the Pit. He was doing no sculpting at all, Hector learned, only heavy masonry, trying to discover "what the rocks *themselves* want to be. . . ." In the issues of the war, painfully debated in two languages in the Menschhaus, he took no interest; if he was impatient to get to France it was to carry on the battle in himself, between his natural gift for mimesis and his new conviction (learned as much in the mountains as in the avant-garde art journals) that every stroke of the chisel falsified the stone.

Whatever their feelings about the fatherland, no families were more eager than the immigrant Germans to demonstrate their American patriotism. It was Grand-father's opinion that Karl, at least, could without disgrace stay home to help run the firm, which was feeling the effects of its founder's past connection with North German Lloyds and the notoriety of his own house as a weekend Biergarten. But all three of his sons enlisted, and virtually every other young man of German parentage in the county. With the rest of a large contingent of new soldiers, they set out for Baltimore on an April forenoon aboard the side-wheeler *Emma Giles*. As its famous beehive-and-flower paddle box churned away from Long Wharf towards the channel buoy and the Bay, they were serenaded by a chorus of their red-faced fathers, ramrod-straight and conducted by Thomas Mensch with a small American flag:

> "Ofer dere, ofer dere,
> Zent a vert, to be hert
> Ofer dere."

There was one furlough home before they shipped to France. Rather, separate and overlapping furloughs for the three, during which the twins rewooed an old high-school flame, Andrea King of the neighboring county. Grandmother Mensch wept at her sons' uniforms. Wilhelm sketched her likeness and carved for his sister Rosa a little stand for her Easter egg, out of a curious grape crotch that caught his eye as he helped prune and tie the family vines. A mere playful heightening of the wood's natural contours into a laughing grotesque whose foolscap supports the egg, it is our only evidence of what might have been the artist's next direction. Karl was stationed in Texas with a company of engineers. Hector saw action in the Argonne Forest, took German shrapnel in his right arm and leg, came home a gimping hero, and resumed his courtship of Miss King. Wilhelm, to the family's relief, was assigned to a headquarters company near Paris, well away from the fighting; he did layout and makeup for the divisional newspaper, *Kootie*. His postcards were full of anticipation of reaching the city: he spoke of staying on in Europe after the armistice, of traveling to Italy and Greece, perhaps even Egypt, of going forward by going back to the roots and wellsprings of his art. "Back and back until I reach the future," his last postcard reads, "like Columbus reaching East by sailing West." On the face, a view of the Louvre, with which he had apparently made some armistice of his own. Before he saw it he was hospitalized by the influenza which swept that year through ruined Europe. A few days later he died. The army's telegram reached Dorset before his postcard.

After the armistice the coffin was shipped home with others from an army burial ground in France: by troopship to Norfolk, Virginia, thence by Bay Line packet to Baltimore and aboard the *Emma Giles* to Long Wharf. Grandfather, Karl, Hector, and Konrad took delivery with the stoneyard dray. They stopped at the cutting shed for Grandfather to open the box, briefly, alone, and verify its contents; there were stories of the army's carelessness in such matters. But "It's Willy," he growled when the lid had been rescrewed. They then installed it, closed, in the Good Parlor, among the mock Phidiases, the Barye-style lions, the Easter egg on its stand, to be tersely memorialized for burial.

Andrea King attended the funeral. Hector showed her two versions of her merry face on the cemetery headstones; Karl pretended that Wilhelm had modeled the backside of a third, more nubile cherub upon his memory of a night swimming escapade she had joined them in during their final furlough.

Said pretty Andrea: "You're a darn *tease*, Karl."

"What gets me," Hector remarked to the company, "is, it's your immortal one died. You know, Konrad? And your mortal one didn't."

"He was a cutter, was Willy," Konrad agreed. "Where he might've got to, it can't none of us guess."

Grandfather painfully declared: "Those *mountains* was his mistake. He could've had half our cutting shed for his self."

Even Karl was moved to say, "I told him. Remember, Heck?"

Presently Hector vowed: "Arm or no arm, I'm going to cut him a proper stone."

And he began a program as fatefully obstinate as any in the family. All that spring, summer, fall—in fact, intermittently for the next twenty years—in the stoneyard, in what passed for the art room of Dorset High (where since his wounding he did only administration and substitute teaching), and in a white-washed toolshed behind the Menschhaus, Hector addressed the problem of cutting stone with his good left arm. He would set the chisel for Karl or Grandfather to hold, and swing the mallet himself; he would hold the chisel and try to tell others how to strike. In 1920, he and Andrea married: there were eight in the house until 1927, when Peter was born and Konrad and Rosa moved next door to make room for the new grandchild. He experimented with ingenious jigs, positioning devices, chisel-headed hammers of his own devising. He bound his almost useless right arm to force himself into independence; he even tried to employ his foot as an extra hand. All in vain: it wants two strong arms like Peter's to shape the rock, and a knowing eye, and a temper of mind—well, different from Ambrose's, who was born the year this folly made room for a larger.

The year before, in 1929, leukemia fetched Grandmother to lie beside her unmarked son: a simple Vermont granite stone, lettered by the new sandblasting process that was killing the family's business with easy competition, identifies her grave. Karl suddenly moved out of house and town to lay bricks in Baltimore. Konrad, Rose, and their Easter egg reinstalled themselves, to help everyone deal with Hector's growing rages. The nation's economy collapsed. So must the Mensch Memorial Monument Company without Karl's foremanship: its founder widowed, weary, and deprived of his income from the immigration business; its angel risen to the company of Michael and the others; its mortal mainstay trying in vain to carve high-relief portraits with a left-handed sandblaster, and approaching madness as Ambrose approached birth.

Upon his "cure" and discharge in 1931 from the Eastern Shore Asylum, Hector mounted at his dead twin's head an unlettered, unpolished, rough-cut stone fresh from the packing case as in the old days, reasoning nicely that unfinished marble was more in keeping anyhow with Wilhelm's terminal aesthetics. Konrad compared it to the Miller's Grave in Old Trinity Churchyard at Church Creek, marked by a pair of uninscribed millstones.

Having laid waste without success, en route to this insight, a deal of granite and alabaster, Hector now turned like Bellerophon to laying waste his soul instead, and succeeded quite. He had become principal of Dorset High before his twin obsessions and nine-month "commitment" led to his suspension. Not even Andrea held his jealous furies against him, once they passed; all assumed it was the celebrated "twin business" had deranged him, with which the whole town sympathized. Karl's exit, nearly everyone agreed, was merely diplomatic; he would return when Hector was himself again, and Hector would reestablish himself with the school board, which had charitably arranged an unpaid furlough instead of accepting his resignation. In the meanwhile—and more, one feels, from the frustration of his sculpting than from his passing certainty that he was not his new son's father—Hector turned, not to alcohol or opium, but to acerbity, dour silence, and melancholia, scarcely less poisonous in the long run; and to business, which, whether or not one has a head for it, may be addictive as morphine, and as deleterious to the moral fiber. To the summer of his death, even after the manpower shortage of World War II returned him to the principalship of Dorset High, Hector's passion turned from the firm back to his brother's beloved marble, and back to the firm again; and he ruined both, but would abandon neither.

Yet most obstinate of all is brother Peter, because more single-minded. Not that he resembles the family (excepting Karl) in other respects. Short and thick where they are tall and lean, black and curly where they are blond and straight, slow of wit, speech, movement where they are quick, devoid equally of humor and its sister, guile—how did the genes that fashion Mensches fashion him? As probable as

162

that a potato should sprout on their scuppernong arbor, or that the wisteria, gorgeous strangler of their porch, should give out one May a single rose.

"Our foundling," Andrea called him, before such jokes lost their humor. And wouldn't he stammer when that lovely indolent bade him sit and talk upon the couch whence she directed the Menschhaus! Wouldn't he redden when she questioned him with a smile about imaginary girl friends! Go giddy at the smell of lilac powder and cologne (which Ambrose can summon to his nostrils yet), and at the kiss-cool silk of her robe! And if, best sport of all, she held his head against her breast, stroked those curls so blacker by contrast, and sang in her unmelodious croon "When I Grow Too Old to Dream," wouldn't the tears come! Aunt Rosa would reprove her to no avail; Hector and Konrad would shake their heads and smile in a worldly way; Grandfather's chuckles would grow rattlier and more thick until they burst into gunshot hocks of phlegm, and he would blow his great nose, he would wind his great pocketwatch with vigor to recompose himself.

> "So kiss me, my sweet,
> And then let us part;
> And when I grow too old to dream,
> That kiss will live in my heart."

Unthinkable prospect! Ambrose too would laugh until his jaw hinge ached and the belly muscles knotted; laugh and weep together at his brother's misery, who longed to run but must embrace his adored tormentor. Her tease never worked with Ambrose: *he* would stiffen in her arms, tickle her ribs, mimic her words—anything not to amuse the company at cost of his dignity. But with Peter it never failed: even when he was in high school, vowing like his Uncle Karl to drop out and work full-time at the stoneyard, she could make him cry with that song for the sport of it, break him down entirely—then turn upon her audience for being entertained and declare, "Peter's the only one loves me. He's got a heart, he has." Or, about as often, would push him away, almost recoil in mid-refrain as though from some near-human pet with whom she'd been disporting, and scold him for mussing her dress.

Ambrose, finally: is there a thing to him besides this familiar tenacity? Persistent amateur, novice human: much given to sloth and revery; full of intuition and odd speculation; ignorant of his fellows, canny of himself; moderately learned, immoderately harassed by dreams; despairing of his powers; stunned by history— and above all, dumbly dogged. His head holds but one idea at a time: be it never so dull and simple he can't dismiss it for another but must tinker at it, abandon and return to it, nick and scratch and chip away until at last by sheer persistence he frets it into something fanciful, perhaps bizarre, anyhow done with.

Thus these Mensches.

F

For a time, though centered in a baby lying on the front-porch glider, A. was also what he compassed. How describe this. If for instance I declare that through a breathless August forenoon a cottonwood poplar whispered from the dooryard, dandled its leaves on squozen petioles when not a maple stirred, you'll see past that

163

syntax? Tree and baby were not then two unless in the manner of mouth and ear: he in the poplar addressed to him in the glider not truths but signs. Coded reassurances. Recognitions.

Ambrose ranged from crab to goat. Upon a wicker porch-chair, in shallow boxes seaweed-lined, olive soft crabs were stacked edgewise like crullers in a tray. One peered at A. from eyestalks; crab and baby bubbled each a froth, but as right and left hands may play together separately: one performer, one performance. Baby could not yet turn to see what bleated from a backyard pen, nor needed to. In those days crab did not leave off and goat begin: that odored nan, her milk, the child who throve upon it were continuous; Ambrose was not separate from things. Whisper, bubble, bleat made one music against a ground-sound at once immediate and remote: pulse of his blood, hum of his head, chop of his river, buzz of his bees, traffic on all his streets and waterways. Panambrosia. It was his lullaby, too; did it end when Ambrose slept?

That name was his first word: it meant *everything*.

"Say Mama, Ambrose. Mah-mah?"

"Ah-bo."

"There, he said it."

"In Plattdeutsch yet."

"O, did he tease the baby boy! Who's this, Ambrose? Say Grandpa."

"Ah-bo."

Peter, four, taught him otherwise, with the aid of Aunt Rosa's egg and their mother's hand mirror, both smuggled one afternoon into the place where Ambrose napped. Egg was held briefly to baby's eye; Ambrose became a green and rivered landscape which would with the cry "*Peter!*" give way to grinning brother's face.

"Ah-bo."

"Not Ambrose. *Peter!* Here's Ambrose. . ." The green landscape would envelop all once more, give way now to the reflection of its viewer's face in the hand mirror. "Ambrose!"

"Ah-bo."

Laughter and laughter. Egg again then; again the earlier face. *Peter!*

"Ah-bo."

They played so until teacher, losing patience, found a forcefuller demonstration: went behind the crib head as if for hide-and-seek, and upon next removal of the egg, presented his own face upside down.

"*Peter!*" that strange countenance demanded. "Peter Peter Peter Peter!"

Family history maintains it was some antic mugging of Peter's, together with his scolding tone, frightened Ambrose. How so, when it had been his custom to amuse with every noise and grimace he could achieve? No, the mere inversion of features was no matter: right side up, upside down, Ambrose knew that face and called it by his all-purpose name. What it was, it was the *eyes*, that they seemed not inverted at all; it was that those eyes were *right side up still* in Peter's face and were hence not any eyes one knew! Something alien peered out from Peter's head; independent of eyebrows, nose, mouth, those eyes watched neutrally, as through a mask, or through peepholes from another world.

Tears dissolved all forms together. Ambrose's shriek fetched grown-ups from below: Peter hugged his brother at once through the crib bars and joined the wail.

Mirror and Easter egg were rescued, teacher was spanked, pupil comforted—who is said to have called Peter *Peter* from that hour.

As for the eyes. Whoso once feels that he has seen and been seen by them does not forget those eyes; which however, like certain guests we nourish with our substance, may be in time's unfolding concealed or manifest, acknowledged or abjured.

Thus was altered Ambrose's initial view of things, and thus he came to call by the name Ambrose not his brother, his mother, or his nanny goat, nor yet (in time) his foot, his voice, or his port-wine mark: only his self, which was held to be none of these, indeed to be nothing Ambrose's, but solely Ambrose.

What the infant learns in tears, adult suffering must unteach. Did it hurt you, reader, to be born? Dying will be no picnic either.

G

Great good that lesson did: he was called everything but Ambrose!

Dear Yrs. T. and Milady A.: the rest of G, *together with all of* H *and* I, *are missing from this recension of Arthur Morton King's* Menschgeschichte, *having been given years ago as aforetold to your Litt.D. nominee.* G *came to light as a first-person piece called "Ambrose His Mark";* H *first saw print as the story "Water-Message";* I *(in my draft but a bare-bones sketch) was fancifully elaborated into the central and title story of B's* Lost in the Funhouse *series, where the others rejoin it to make an "Ambrose sequence."*

G *is the story of my naming. "Owing to the hectic circumstances of my birth," the published version begins, "for some months I had no proper name whatever." Those circumstances themselves are referred to only in passing: ". . . Hector's notion that someone other than himself had fathered me; his mad invasion of the delivery room; his wild assertion, as they carried him off (to the Eastern Shore Asylum), that the port-wine stain near my eye was a devil's mark. . ." et cetera. Uncle Karl's withdrawal to Baltimore is discreetly mentioned, and Andrea's sultry frowardness: ". . .a photograph made by Uncle Konrad. . .shows her posed before our Tokay vines, her pretty head thrown back, scarfed and earringed like a gypsy; her eyes are closed, her mouth laughs gaily behind her cigarette; one hand holds a cup of coffee, the other steadies a scowling infant on her hip." It is alleged that given Hector's absence and her capriciousness, no name was chosen, and* faute de mieux *Aunt Rosa's nickname for me, Honig, became my working title, so to speak, until the great event that climaxes the story.*

Grandfather covets the bee swarms of our neighbor Willy Erdmann, who also seems to have had an interest in my mother. He builds an empty beehive near where our lot joins Erdmann's, and installs Andrea in a hammock there to nurse me and to watch for a migrant swarm. Apiary lore and tribal naming customs are laid on, via Uncle Konrad; the family's straitened circumstances during the Great Depression and the near failure of the firm are sketched in too. Willy

Erdmann fumes at Grandfather's clear intention to rustle his bees; stratagems and counterstratagems are resorted to, while I suck busily in the hammock and Andrea works the crossword puzzles in the New York Times. *At last, on a still June Sunday, the long-awaited swarm appears, and slapstick catastrophe ensues: Grandfather bangs pie tins to draw the bees his way; Willy Erdmann fires a shotgun to attract them himward (and to warn off would-be poachers). Grandfather counters with a spray from the garden hose; Willy replies with a brandished bee-bob. Konrad and Rosa stand by transfixed; Peter bawls in terror; Andrea swoons.*

And then the bees, "thousand on thousand, a roaring gold sphere. . . moved by their secret reasons, closed ranks and settled upon her chest. Ten thousand, twenty thousand strong they clustered. Her bare bosoms, my squalling face—all were buried in the golden swarm." Grandfather boldly lifts them off with ungloved hands and bears them to his waiting hive. Erdmann strikes with the bee-bob; Konrad grapples with him; they fall into the hammock, which parts at the headstring and dumps us all into the clover. Rosa disrupts baptismal services at a nearby church with her cries for aid; raging Grandfather hurls the bee swarm down upon us all; Andrea is stung once on the nipple (and thereafter abandons breast-feeding and relinquishes my care to Rosa); Willy Erdmann is led off crying imprecations of my illegitimacy; Konrad and the Methodist minister endeavor to restore the peace of the neighborhood. Aunt Rosa, subsequently, likens my birthmark to a flying bee; Konrad reviews legendary instances of babies swarmed by bees: Plato, Sophocles, and Xenophon are invoked—and finally St. Ambrose, erstwhile bishop of Milan, after whom I am in time denominated. The episode ends with the adult "Ambrose's" ambivalent reflections on the phenomenon of proper names: "I and my sign. . .neither one nor quite two." Et cetera.

Despite some lurking allegory, which I regret, "Ambrose His Mark" gains in artistic tidiness from its reconception of the family described in my chapter G. And the narrative viewpoint, a nipple's-eye view as it were, is piquant, though perhaps less appropriate to the theme of ontological ambiguity than the "first-person anonymous" viewpoint of A. M. King's version. No matter. "Ambrose, Ambrose, Ambrose, Ambrose!" the narrator intones at the end, watching to see what the name calls: "Regard that beast, ungraspable, most queer, pricked up in my soul's crannies!"

I like that.

H

Here was the "Water-Message" episode from my eleventh year, whereof it disconcerts me still to speak, yet which occasions all this speech, these swarming letters. In his retelling our Author retains my third-person viewpoint, omniscient with Ambrose, but drops that authorial "I" of sections A through F. The year is 1940; Grandfather is five years dead, his prostatic cancer having metastasized in 1935. There is no mention of Uncle Karl, who however returned to direct the firm that same year, apparently made his peace with Hector, and hired a bachelor flat down near the yacht basin. Nor of Konrad and Rosa, who also now rent an

166

apartment of their own, across the corner from the Menschhaus, residence then only of Hector and Andrea, Peter and me. Gentle Konrad is still teaching fifth grade in East Dorset Elementary School, tuning pianos, and bicycling the streets of Dorset on behalf of the Grolier Society's Book of Knowledge, *whose contents he knows by heart. He and Rosa are childless. Ardent fisher off the "New Bridge" as well as cyclist, Konrad has skin cancer and a year to live. None of this is in the published version, nor of Hector's arm, withered now like the late kaiser's (his limp is mentioned), nor of his gradual self-reestablishment, after Karl's return to the firm, in the county public school system: he is principal now of East Dorset Elementary, the smallest in the city and the poorest except for its Negro counterpart. Ambrose (on with the story) is a timid fourth grader, uneasy in his skin, fearful of his fellows, saturated with the* Book of Knowledge, *broodily curious about the Book of Life, abjectly dreaming of heroic transfiguration. All done in images of mythic flight: seaward-leaning buoys, invocations of Odysseus, foreshadowings of dark illumination, etc.*

Thus the "ground situation." The "vehicle" of the plot is Ambrose's desire to plumb the mysteries of the Occult Order of the Sphinx, a gang of preadolescent boys loosely led by Peter, which "meets" after school in a jerry-built hut along the river shore in a stand of trees called the Jungle. "It was in fact a grove of honey locusts, in area no larger than a schoolyard, bounded on two of its inland sides by Erdmann's Cornlot and on the third by the East Dorset dump. But it was made mysterious by rank creepers and honeysuckle that covered the ground and shrouded every tree, and by a labyrinth of intersecting footpaths. Junglelike too, there was about it a voluptuous fetidity; gray rats and starlings decomposed where BB'd; curly-furred retrievers spoored the paths; there were to be seen on occasion, stuck on twig ends or flung amid the creepers, ugly little somethings in whose presence Ambrose snickered with the rest. . ." You get the idea. Exiled by the older boys—who after surprising a pair of lovers in their clubhouse, gleefully enter it for what one guesses to be ritual masturbation—Ambrose wanders the beach with smelly, feisty little Perse Golz, a third grader whom he tries to impress by pretending to receive and transmit coded messages from the Occult Order.

Very painful to remember, these classic humiliations of the delicately nerved among the healthy roughnecks of the world, whom, like Babel his Cossacks or Kafka his carnivores, I still half love and half despise. A message, a message— the heart of such a child longs for some message from the larger world, the lost true home whereof it vaguely dreams, whereto it yearns from its felt exile. "You are not the child of your alleged parents," *is what he craves to hear, however much he may care for them.* "Your mother is a royal virgin, your father a god in mortal guise. Your kingdom lies to west of here, to westward, where the tide runs from East Dorset, past cape and cove, black can, red nun," *et cetera.*

And mirabile, mirabile, mirabile dictu: one arrives! Lying in the seaweed where the tide has left it: a bottle with a note inside! "Past the river and the Bay, from continents beyond. . .borne by currents as yet uncharted, nosed by fishes as yet unnamed. . .the word had wandered willy-nilly to his threshold." By all the gods, Germaine: I still believe that here *is where Ambrose M. drops out of life's game and begins his career as Professional Amateur, one who loves but does not*

167

know: with the busting, by brickbat, of that bottle; with receipt of that damning, damnèd blank message, which confirms both his dearest hope—that there are Signs—and his deepest fear—that they are not for him. Cruel Yours Truly, falsely mine! Take that, and this, and the next, and never reach the end, you who cut me off from my beginning!

I

I'm lost in the funhouse, Germaine. The I of this episode isn't I; I don't know who it is.

In fact I was once briefly lost in a funhouse, at age twelve or thirteen, and included the anecdote in section I of this Amateur manuscript. But it happened in Asbury Park, New Jersey, not Ocean City, Maryland; I was with Mother and Aunt Rosa (lately widowed, whom the excursion was intended to divert); neither Father nor Uncle Karl was with us; I got separated from Peter in a dark corridor, wandered for a few minutes in aimless mild alarm, met another young wanderer with whom I made my way to the exit, where Peter waited—and found my companion to be a black boy. In those days (circa 1943) such a dénouement was occasion for good-humored racist teasing, of which there was full measure en route home. The point of Arthur Morton King's anecdote was the sentimental-liberal one of Ambrose's double awakening: to the fact of bigotry among those he loves, which he vows never to fall into; and to his budding fictive imagination, which recognizes that such experiences as that in the funhouse are symbolically charged, the stuff of stories. In short, an intimation of future authorship as conventionally imagined: the verbal transmutation of experience into art.

I don't know how to feel about our friend's rerendering, by far the most extravagant liberty that he's taken with what I gave him. It goes without saying that I've no objection to even the most radical rearrangement of my experience for his literary purposes; my gift of these episodes was a donnée with no strings attached. All the same. . .

Oh well: I simply can't be objective about either my lostness in the funhouse or his story, which, while very different from the facts, is perhaps truer and surely more painful. In that version, the ride to "Ocean City," seen omnisciently through young A's sensibility, is all covert dramatic irony and dark insinuation. On the front seat of the car are Hector (driving) and Uncle Karl, between them Andrea; on the back seat Peter (about fifteen) sits behind Hector, Ambrose behind Uncle Karl, and behind Andrea, "Magda G——, age fourteen, a pretty girl. . . who lived not far from them on B—— Street in the town of D——, Maryland." The insinuations come to this: that Andrea may have had or be having an affair with Karl; that Peter, at least, may be in fact Karl's son instead of Hector's; and that not only Hector but young Ambrose may at least half-sense this possible state of affairs!

Which brings us to the back seat, where, in addition to dealing with these shocking possibilities, A. is vainly mustering his nerve to touch Magda, Peter's girl friend, with whom our amateur has imagined himself in love since one late afternoon in September 1940, when, it is implied, she surprised him with a blow job in the Menschhaus toolshed. See B's text for rhetoric and details. Magda's

168

attitude toward him is cordially patronizing; she is holding hands with Peter; Ambrose doubts that she even remembers the incident in the toolshed (for him a watershed).

The action proceeds between these suppressed bourgeois-domestic hang-ups, scandals, and volatilities in the foreground and, in the background, implications of the larger bourgeois violence of World War II: crude oil on the beach from torpedoed tankers, "browned-out" streetlights, shooting galleries full of swastikas and rising suns. Ambrose glimpses human copulation for the first time, under the boardwalk; he catches sight of the aureole of Magda's nipple, trembles at the power and ubiquity of the sex drive, entertains preadolescent doubts of his masculinity, suffers pangs of jealousy and desire, approaches a nausea compounded of these plus the tensions in the family, his ambivalent feelings for his father and himself, and a candied apple that sits ill on his stomach. The three youngsters at last enter the funhouse; Ambrose takes a wrong turn and fancies himself wandering those corridors forever, telling himself stories in the dark, perhaps including the story "Lost in the Funhouse."

Well. That loose-toga'd lady with the five-stringed lyre on the bench in the picture on the El Producto cigar box full of stone chisels on the shelf in the toolshed under the wisteria between the woodhouse and the privy behind the Menschhaus—whom Ambrose regarded with awed impersonality while Magda mouthed him in 1940—may have taken up her instrument and sung to my scribbling friend; she has not yet to me. That candied apple still sticks in my throat; Magda and Peter are still each other's; and I—

But I can't speak further of this story, this episode, these events. An end to I!

J

Just at this point, Germaine, my Amateur *rebegins in the first person, Ambrose speaking, as if in losing himself in that funhouse he'd found his voice, at least, at last. No use my apologizing for the voice he found, which "Arthur Morton King" soon after abandoned: it was the way he spoke back then.*

I myself, before I found it was myself was lost, thought Peter a foundling.

We discussed the possibility at length in our bedroom, and I will admit that my protestations—that I loved him regardless of his origins—were as experimental as sincere, and that there was more fascination than affection in the zeal with which I conjectured (he had not the imagination for it) the identity and station of his real parents. Were they gypsies of the sort who kept a house trailer on the edge of town, out past the tomato cannery, and read Mother's palm for half a dollar? Were they residents of our very block—Erdmanns, Ziegenfusses—who now watched their shame grow up before their eyes? Our street ran down to Dorset Hospital, where most of the county's babies drew first breath; no speculation was too wild to entertain. But my favorite was that Colonel Morton himself, who owned the cannery and several seafood-packing houses and had been mysteriously shot in the leg a few years past, had fathered Peter upon a European baroness during one of his sojourns abroad. The outraged baron had attempted to murder his rival and would have killed the child as well had not the colonel, foreseeing danger, paid Hector and Andrea

169

to raise his natural son as their own. As for the baroness, she had by no means forgotten the issue of her star-crossed passion: she waited only for her old husband to die, whereupon she would join her true lover in America (I had never seen the president of Morton's Marvelous Tomatoes) and claim Peter for her own.

"Aw, Amb, that's nuts." But I'd hear my brother rise on one elbow in the dark. "You don't believe no such a thing. *Do* you."

I would consider the play of shadows on the ceiling, where the streetlamp shone through catalpa leaves. As a matter of fact I did not see on my brother's nature the stamp of colonels and baronesses, but the possibility stirred my heart. One day the baroness would drive up in a Daimler-Benz car, with a chauffeur and a veil, and take Peter back to be master of the castle. But first she'd buy out Mensch Masonry and take us around the world. Perhaps she would appoint Hector manager of Peter's estate until my brother's seniority, and we'd all live there: I, Magda, Peter, Mother, Father, Aunt Rosa.

On nights when raw nor'easters howled down the Eastern Shore and swept luckless sailors into the Chesapeake, the valley of the Rhine (where I located the baroness) appeared to me peaceful, green, warm, luminous: the emerald landscape of Aunt Rosa's egg. The gray-green castle turrets were velveted with lichen; dusty terraces of vines stepped down to the sparkling river; a Lorelei, begauzed and pensive, leaned back against her rock and regarded some thing or person, invisible from where we stood, among the sidelit grapes of the farther shore.

So eloquent would I wax before this spectacle, I could sometimes exact from Peter promises of rooms for myself in one of the towers, and a private vineyard hard by the postern gate, before he remembered to protest that Mother was all the baroness he craved, our poor house the only castle. I could not of course propose outright that in that case he make over his inheritance to me; but I would go to sleep confident that Peter recognized my qualifications for the baronetcy and would abdicate in my favor when the time came.

The egg from which this vision hatched—bought by Uncle Konrad for Aunt Rosa at the Oberammergau Passion Play in 1910—lay in permanent exhibition between two of Uncle Wilhelm's cupids on the mantelpiece of our Good Parlor, which in the old fashion was opened only for holidays, funerals, and company. Peter no less than myself deemed it worthwhile as a boy to behave himself long enough on such occasions to be rewarded with a glass of Grandfather's wine and a view into that egg, but for years I assumed that its magical interior, like Wilhelm's student statuary, was no more than a curiosity to him. Not until he was seventeen, and I fifteen, did I learn otherwise.

Uncle Konrad, upon his death in 1941, left in trust for each of his nephews two thousand dollars, into which we were to come upon our graduation from Dorset High. Mine was earmarked already by the family for my further education. Peter, I believe, was expected to invest his in the uncertain fortunes of Mensch Masonry Contractors, where like Uncle Karl he'd worked as an apprentice every spare moment of his youth. Father and Karl spoke warmly, as Peter's graduation day approached, of his good fortune in being able to "do something" for the business at last—as though his having done a journeyman mason's work at a boy's wage for the two years past were not itself a baronial contribution.

"Bread cast upon the waters," Hector would say to the family in general, sniffing and arching his brows. "Famous percentage yield. Throw in a slice, fish out a loaf."

"Well, he doesn't *have* to put it in the company," Mother declared. She wore her housecoat the day long, as if she understood the word to mean a coat for keeping house in. The years had begun to frizz her hair, spoil her teeth, lower her jowls, undo her breasts, pot her belly: the sight of her holding court from her couch, cigarette between her lips and coffee cup in hand, did not move one in the same way as formerly. "It's his money."

"Who said it wasn't? Let him put plumbing in the house for you."

That was not what she meant, Mother replied. But it was. Hector's sole concession to modernity, since buying out Karl's and Rosa's shares of the Menschhaus in 1936, was a cold-water tap let into the kitchen sink. It was still pitchers and basins on marble washstands in all the bedrooms, and as we had no heat either beyond the kitchen and parlor stoves, there'd be ice on those pitchers on winter mornings. We were, moreover, the only family in East Dorset who still used the privy built into the row of whitewashed sheds behind our summer kitchen. The prospect there was not unlovely: a walk of mossy bricks led under the grape and wisteria arbors which screened the sheds. But it was so shocking cold in winter, so beloved of wasps and bees in summer, that I remained more or less constipated until college.

Yet however legitimate her yen for domestic convenience, I felt Andrea had no more right than Hector to influence Peter's choice, and vigorously so argued. The very prudence of their resolve as to *my* inheritance (which resolve Peter had affirmed so stoutly that I couldn't disagree) increased my jealousy for the independence of his, and led me by some logic to feel it should be spent imprudently. Not "thrown away," mind, in the evanescent joys of riotous living, nor yet exchanged for objects of useless beauty: the notion of the *spree* was alien to our Protestant consciences, and I cannot imagine Hector or even the unknown Wilhelm, for example, paying money for a piece of art. My fancy equated carefree expenditure with the purchase of hard goods, the *equipment* of pleasure: if Peter hesitated to commit himself, I assumed his problem to be the choice between, say, a red Ford roadster, a racing sailboat, a five-inch reflecting telescope.

"He doesn't have to spend it on the family at all," I would declare. "He can do anything he wants with it."

"Indeed he may; indeed he may." Hector's nose itched when he was opposed; he would massage it with left thumb and forefinger. "Let him buy a nice Hampton sailboat. When the company goes into receivership, we'll all go sailing."

It will seem odd that none consulted Peter's inclinations; in his presence the subject never came up. The truth is, though we were all more sophisticated than my brother, he had already at seventeen assumed a certain authority in our house, stemming it may be from nothing more than his difference from us. Presume as we did that our judgment was sounder, our imagination keener than his, we seemed to understand that his resolve was beyond cajolery. The very futility of our debate lent it sarcastic heat; a variety of awe, more than tact, silenced it when he came upon us. I am reminded of Peter by Homer's Zeus; indeed, our later ménage in the Lighthouse was something like that deity's in this respect: Magda might complain like Hera; I chafe and bristle like Poseidon or Hades; Marsha carp and wheedle and connive like Aphrodite—but there were finally no quarrels, for when Peter speaks, though the grumbling may continue, his will is done.

He spoke, in this instance, on a Saturday evening some days after we'd begun repairing the municipal seawall, whose original construction had laid the firm's foundation. After the Great Baltimore Fire of 1904, tons of granite rubble purchased by the town at salvage prices from the burnt-out city were fetched down the Chesapeake on barges and dumped as "rip-rap" before the wall for additional protection: Grandfather's idea, and a sound one. But age and ice and hurricane had so far had their way with the concrete in the forty years since, undone and undermined it, that in spring tides it was more breakwater than retaining wall, with virtual harbors behind it. Moved by citizens whose real estate thus silted every tide, the Dorset City Council let bids to repair the wall and increase its height; after long cost-cutting computations by Hector (who, in addition to his principaling, still owned one-third of the company) in conference with Karl (who directed it) and Rosa (owner of the third third), Mensch Masonry submitted the low bid.

The contract bolstered our sagging fortunes, which only the general wartime prosperity had kept from definite collapse. Extra carpenters, masons, and cement finishers were engaged; our flatbed truck was repaired on credit; from somewhere a rock crusher and a second main mixer were leased. And in the interest of civic economy, Hector informed us, we would not use a stone from the company yard! The day we first surveyed the job he had scraped algae with his left hand from some of the "Baltimore rocks" in the shallows where Peter and I had used to play pirates and net soft crabs, and had shaken his head at what he saw.

"Good brownstone and granite," he'd declared to Karl and Peter. "Already squared, most of it. What a waste."

Uncle Karl agreed, and so every day after school and all day Saturday I worked with the gang of Negroes they set to manhandling the Baltimore rocks. At first we fed them indiscriminately to the crusher, moss and all, thence to the mixer, while Father watched with a frown that deepened every time another nicely masoned stone was reduced to chips.

"A crying shame."

Karl sniffed and chewed his unlit cigar. "That one there was Tennessee rose marble, looked like."

The upshot was, one Friday at supper they announced an agreement made that forenoon with the mayor and city council: in return for all the squared stones, to be carted to our yard at our own expense, Mensch Masonry would clear away "Grandfather's" Baltimore rocks altogether and present the city with a usable bathing area in front of the exposed seawall. Hector was enormously proud of the plan (his own), which he felt no ordinary businessman, but only a business artist as it were, could have hatched. What especially pleased him was that our removing, for profit, what Grandfather had for profit placed there was a kind of echo of Grandfather's benevolent profiting from the immigrants both going and coming.

He grinned at my aunt. "There is style in this piece of business."

Uncle Karl said merely, "Think what Willy could of done with them pink ones."

Aunt Rosa had the highest opinion of Hector, whom she still regarded, twenty-

172

five years after the fact, as a shattered young hero of the war, the intellectual counterpart of his artist twin. She laid her hand on her lower abdomen—where all unknown to us her cancer flowered—and cried, "If Konrad just was here once!"

Tears then were shed for Uncles Konrad and Wilhelm, and for the family's imminent prosperity. Even Mother must have been impressed, for she made no protest when Father sent me to light the Good Parlor stove and brought two bottles of New York Rhenish from the cold-pantry for a celebration.

The room was as chilly as its statues, and smelled of coal oil. Aunt Rosa wept again—the last parlor function had been Konrad's funeral—but the cold wine warmed and cheered us. Family history was rechronicled; we sang "Happy Days Are Here Again" and teased Peter (who had fetched Magda from around the corner) for missing his chance to save the firm or put plumbing in the house before our fortunes changed. Mother even sat in Father's lap and tipped his glass so that he could embrace her with his arm. In uneasy glee I called, "Get a load of the lovers!" and made everyone laugh by kissing "the Groaner" (so we had dubbed an anguished Greek head of heroic proportion, on a pedestal by the daybed: Wilhelm's copy of Laocoön, whom the family mistook for Christ crucified) in imitation of Mother.

Only Peter was not merry, though he regarded our festivity with pensive goodwill from his station before the mantelpiece and murmured gravely, smilingly, to Magda. While Hector blushed at something Mother whispered in his ear, Rosa hummed her favorite sipping song, "Wir wöllen unser alten Kaiser Wilhelm wiederhaben." I perched on her lap and crooned into her white-fuzzed ear: "Come with me to the Casbah!" Whereat she wrinkled over and pushed me away—"Verruckte!"—flattered all the same by my attentions. Peter crimsoned more than Father: embarrassed perhaps by his own embarrassment, he took up the Easter egg from its grapewood stand between the cupids, aimed it at the white light globe that hung from the ceiling on three chains, and addressed himself to the miracle inside. Magda, beside him on a needlepoint chair, took his hand.

Mother ignored me. I could not of course remain forever on Aunt Rosa's aproned lap. "Do you really think it's okay to move those stones from in front of the seawall?"

Father could not easily with his single arm both embrace Mother and rub his nose between his thumb and forefinger. "Now. What might you mean by that?"

I grinned and shrugged. "I only wondered. Undermining and all? Wasn't that why Grandpa put them there to begin with?"

"Well. I beg your pardon, sir. It's easier to *wonder* about undermining than to *think* about undermining."

Peter removed the egg from his eye.

"Lord a mercy," Mother said. "It's nearly nine." As if reminded, the hall clock whirred and began to toll that hour. "I'll put the coffee on."

"The wall'll be three foot higher," Father said. "Do you know what that means?" I did not, in detail. "Two hundred sixty-six cubic yards of reinforced concrete, that the waves won't touch a dozen times a year! A hundred extra tons of weight!"

"And that's just the stretch by the hospital," Karl reminded me.

Father helped himself to another glass. "He wonders about undermining."

I chose not to wonder further. "Is it really Grandpa's castle in the egg?"

Aunt Rosa kindly frowned. "Rest his soul, he used to say so."

"Fooey," Father said.

Karl chuckled. Rosa's eyes filled up again. "Konrad bought me that in Oberammergau in nineteen and ten," she explained to Magda, not for the first time. "On our honeymoon."

"She knows," I protested.

"There was this peddler, an old Greek or Jew, that had a raft of different ones for sale by the passion play. He showed Konrad some with naughty pictures inside, and Konrad pretended this was one like that. He wouldn't let me peek in till we got it home."

"He was a godawful tease, was Konrad," Karl allowed.

For some reason I suddenly saw my father's brother as a distinct human being, with an obscure history of his own, apart from ours, and who would one day die. I realized that I had not especially despised him recently, and pondered this realization.

Peter now surveyed us with a great smile and squeezed Magda's hand. "If I didn't think we'd do the seawall right," he declared as if to me, "I wouldn't of bought the front of Willy Erdmann's Cornlot."

It took a while to realize what had been said. Hector's sarcasm was undermined by surprise. "You wouldn't of which?"

"Grosser Gott!" Aunt Rosa chuckled, uncertain of the drift. Uncle Karl's grin was more knowing.

My own first feeling was sharp disappointment: there would be, then, neither sailboat nor five-inch telescope, and my counsel in the matter, so far from being followed, had not even been solicited. But it was joined at once by admiration for Peter's daring.

Mother hurried in from the kitchen. Cigarette and coffee cup. She was as startled as Hector, but her face showed amusement too. "You what?"

"Whole front end of the Cornlot," Peter said carefully. "Hundred and fifty feet along the seawall and a hundred deep."

The Jungle too! I guessed with fresh disappointment that Magda had been in on the secret: her smile was knowing; her great eyes flashed when Peter winked at her.

Father besought the Groaner with an expression not dissimilar to that fellow's wretched own. "He's going to raise tomatoes. We'll pay the rent on our crusher with beefsteak tomatoes."

Aunt Rosa pressed with both hands her abdomen. *"Ja, ja, Hector! Peter ein Bauer ist!"*

"He'll undermine Morton's canning house," Father declared. "The colonel's good as bankrupt."

"Ja doch!" Aunt Rosa crowed. *"Ah! Gott!"*

My old hypothesis regarding Peter's parentage sprang back to mind.

"I'm going to help farm it," I announced. "Aren't I, Peter."

My brother set the egg back in its place. "We can make a garden. But I didn't buy the Cornlot to farm it."

"He didn't buy the Cornlot to farm it," Father informed the Groaner.

Karl chuckled. "Sure he didn't. He wants a place of his own to set and watch the speedboat races."

After his first remark, Peter had addressed himself principally to Mother. Now, though it was still to her he smiled, he rested his free hand lightly first on Father's shoulder and then upon his chair back, and winked at Uncle Karl. "I'm going to build a stone house there for all of us to live in."

For the second time Hector's sarcasm failed him—which is to say, he could make no reply at all—and Peter took the opportunity to explain his intention. The Cornlot (so named by East Dorset children, though tomatoes and turnips as often grew there) was a field of seven acres at the foot of our street, adjacent to the hospital grounds; not two weeks previously our ailing neighbor Willy Erdmann—loser of the battle of the bees and a sinking dipsomane—had declared his intent to parcel it into building lots, and there being little demand yet for new housing in East Dorset, for a small consideration had given Peter a thirty-day option on one waterfront plot. Now that Mensch Masonry appeared to be in no pressing need of capital, Peter was resolved to purchase the lot outright for eleven hundred dollars (Erdmann's price) and erect a commodious stone house there for the family. More, with Uncle Karl's help—who, we now learned, had been Peter's agent in the transaction—he had persuaded Erdmann, a quondam realtor and builder, to include in the deal a set of blueprints from his files, and was already dickering with him and another contractor for a basement excavation.

"Don't look at me," Karl growled, almost merrily. "Boy made me swear not to tell."

"Stone costs a fortune!" Mother exclaimed. "There's not a stone house in East Dorset!"

"Going to build her myself as I get the money," Peter said firmly. "After the war. Any of you can chip in that wants to. It'll be an advertisement for the company."

Hector snorted. "Some advertisement, when it sinks into the Cornlot. You crazy, Karl?"

But Uncle Karl reminded him that the hospital itself was holding up well enough on the sandy soil, and Peter declared he'd already learned from Karl and Willy Erdmann what was required in the way of piers and footings, and was prepared to lay out the site.

Suddenly Mother set down both coffee and cigarette and looked from Magda to Peter with a new expression. "Peter Mensch! Are you and Magda married?"

Rosa rocked and hummed. Father rubbed his nose as if possessed. Karl twiddled his wineglass and grinned. I myself was nearly ill with envy at Peter's initiative. He began to color again. "Nope."

"Engaged, then. Is that so, Magda?" There was affection in Mother's voice, still mixed with amusement—the tone with which she sang to torment Peter—and he blushed as miserably as on those sporting occasions.

"We're not engaged or anything." Magda was as devoid of wit as was my brother, but immune to teasing. Her eyes would grow even larger and more serious, her voice more quiet, and she never rose to our bait. "We don't have any plans."

175

"Well, we do," Peter objected, remarkably red. "But they're a ways off. After the war. And nothing definite."

"A stone house on the Cornlot," Father reported to Mother. Rosa hummed and chortled, her hands clasped across her apron. Karl clapped Father's shoulder and called Peter a chip off the old block. As soon as the hubbub began to subside, Peter left to walk Magda home. I went as far as the entrance hall with them.

"Boy oh boy, Peter..." My heart was full; he and Magda both smiled. "Are you going to put crenelations on the house, do you think? Those scallops that they used to shoot arrows from?"

"I guess none of those, Amb. Sounds too expensive."

Now it was I who blushed. "I sure will help you build it!"

"That's good."

"We can transplant our grapevines even before we build! And put in some real wine grapes."

"It's our land," Peter said. "We can do whatever we want."

I began to realize that a piece of land was more exciting to own than any of the things I'd thought of. "How about a tower? We could have one round tower, on a corner..."

"Yeah, well. We'll have to think about a tower, all right." I saw he was reddening again, and so said them good night, but declared: "It'd be great if you all did get married, and it was your house we were living in!"

With an easy motion Magda turned my face toward hers and kissed me, lightly and solemnly, on the lips. I understood that she and Peter must be habitually *making love*.

"Good night, Amby," she said.

Back in the parlor Father was betting the Groaner that Peter expected to be supplied with free building materials.

"Well, now," Mother said good-humoredly. "He did say the house was for all of us."

Father entreated suffering Laocoön with his arm. "She actually *believes*—"

"So let's give him the Baltimore rocks," Karl suggested.

"He don't need them," Father declared. "You've all got bigger ones in your heads."

Aunt Rosa whooped.

I stayed out of it and got to bed as soon as possible.

"He's feeling that Rhine wine," I heard Mother remark, and she said more truly than she knew: it was the Rhine of Aunt Rosa's egg whose wine possessed me. For hours I tossed at the mercy of two ideas: that Peter's property ran clear to the center of the earth (its volume I calculated next day, by the law of prisms, to be seven and twelve one-hundredths cubic miles), and that an older girl like Magda, whether or not she recalled a certain quarter hour in our toolshed four years past, was...more *interesting* than the giddy teases I had "dates" with.

K

Konrad's comparison was with certain Tin Pan Alley songs, whereof the catchy title is dreamed up first and the tune composed to fit: so the motto of Mensch Masonry preceded the firm itself, which was established on its strength. One early fall morning in 1932 (so Mother tells the story, shaking her head), before he'd got himself back into the school system after his discharge from the asylum, Father was sitting in the "office" corner of the Mensch Memorial Monument Company, nursing one of the headaches that dated from his cure and regarding a block of fractured Carrara. A hurricane some weeks previously had washed out a clapboard home on Holland Island, out in the Bay, and taken the life of the lady of the house; her husband, an oyster tonger, had contracted for a modest stone at the head of her vault, which by marsh-country custom (owing to the scarcity of dry ground) was "buried" in a slight excavation in his dooryard, the concrete lid aboveground. Grandfather was offering him a list of popular inscriptions from which he might choose.

"Look at this here: 'He giveth His beloved sheep.'" The verse from Psalms was, in fact, his pet inscription: he loved to cut Gothic *H*'s. "And here's Jeremiah: 'Her sun is gone down while it was yet day.' Very nice sentiment, eh?"

But his client waved the list away. "I already decided, Mister Mensch." He had sold his tongboat and joined the company of old men who sulked on sunny benches before the courthouse. "'Build not your house upon the shifting sand' is what I want. You put that on there."

"Ja, ja," Grandfather assented. Customers, for some reason, brought out his German. "'Built not your haus upon the zhiftink zandt.' My own self, I see that raised on black granite. Very nice sentiment."

The deal was struck. When the widower went, Father repeated the injunction a number of times.

"Now that is damned clever, considering. 'Build not your house upon the shifting sand.'"

The more he reflected on it, the more it amused him, until at length migraine was flown, battered marble forgot. By lunchtime he had resolved to enter the field of foundation building and general stonemasonry, as a contractor. Within a week he had borrowed what capital he could, on Grandfather's credit and despite his skepticism, from the failing banks; ordered tools and materials; apprised the local building firms of our availability. Before the first snow fell and Franklin Roosevelt was inaugurated, the firm of Mensch and Son, Foundations and Stonemasonry (changed on Karl's return to Mensch Masonry Contractors), had received its first subcontract. And the newly lettered office door, together with the drays and the flatbed wagon, enjoined their beholders to build not upon the shifting sand.

Alas for any who took to heart our motto and engaged our services in those days: he built twice over on the sand he fled. Not alone because our foundations rested ineluctably on the loam of the Eastern Shore, but because Hector, once he'd abandoned the Muse for Mammon, resorted to every economy known to corner-cutting builders, to the end of meeting his notes. If the contract (particularly in the private sector, where there were few building inspections) specified a twelve-inch

177

concrete footing under a brick pier, he would tamp the ground extra well and make do with eight. His mortar (as well I knew, having mixed it in my youth till my hands were callused and my spine near cracked) was inordinately rich in sand, wherein the county abounded, with cement enough barely to bind the grains that were to bind the bricks. Finally, in order to make his deadlines he would lay stone and brick in every winter weather; despite his heating both sand and mix-water, his economical mortar not infrequently froze before it set, and when it was dry one could crumble it between one's fingers. In time that same sand shifted indeed, carrying flag and fieldstone with it; what with out-of-court settlements and court-ordered repairs, Mensch and Son, by the time of Karl's return, found themselves with little money, few contracts in hand, and a yard full of building stones and flagstones too small to make monuments of and too large to forget about.

"One more epitaph we got to pick out," Grandfather said. "For Hector's company. But we can't afford to bury it."

Time and again it seemed certain we must fail, even after Uncle Karl cut down the corner-cutting: the phrase "pass into the hands of the receivers," dimly ominous, haunts my memory of the Menschhaus. At first I fancied the Receivers to be of a family with that troll who was so nearly the death of the Billy Goats Gruff, and to live therefore in the neighborhood of the Dorset Creek Bridge, which I could not be induced to cross thenceforward without Peter at my side, and which still twinges me on wee-hour walks with Angie. Grandfather's death in 1935 modified this fancy. Peter sneaked me in to survey him, laid out in the Good Parlor. As always the room smelled of coal oil from the space heater—to light which, for the comfort of the forenoon's mourners, was Peter's errand. Grandfather lay drawn and waxen upon the daybed. I cannot recall his face, but I know that although his white mustache still bore, like seasoned meerschaum, the familiar stain of much tobacco, his great nose was red no more: it was pinched, and as glazy ivory yellow as the keys of our player piano or Wilhelm's plaster castings, the permanent tenants of the room. I contemplated this detail.

Peter meanwhile was absorbed in the Easter egg. After a time I whispered: "Dare me to touch him?"

"Sure I dare you. Better not."

The muscled ivory panther, *couchant* atop the mantel, prepared to spring upon me if I moved a hair; the Groaner raised sightless eyes to Heaven in plaster anguish at the thought.

"Dee double dare you," Peter offered, and solemnly pinched Grandfather's cheek. Surely he must snort and toss his head as he had done on many a napful Sunday; look 'round him vainly for his cane, and, knowing we were hid somewhere about, call upon Gott in Himmel to witness how His latest creatures prepared their place in Hell. But he did not stir even when, dee-double-diddly-die-dared, I drew my finger across his folded hands and found them—not soaked in perspiration like my own, but scarcely any colder. He slept on undisturbed, as I was not to do for many a night after; and the naked Biscuit Thrower in the foyer (my corruption of Wilhelm's discus'd *Greek Athlete)* turned from me as we left; and when Miss Stocker expressed her sympathy next day in school, I declared to her and to the first-grade class in general my conviction that Grandfather was more to be envied than mourned, he having been by that hour joyfully received by the Receivers. I'll not describe what fears beset me as to the nature of my own reception on the day when, without Peter to shield me, I too should pass into their waiting hands.

But presently Father would dream up a new way to sculpt his dead twin's headstone with one arm. A fresh block of alabaster would appear in his office, or in the toolshed, or in the art room of Dorset High; new tools of his design would be forged by Joe Voegler the oyster-dredge builder down by the creek; Uncle Konrad (before Karl returned from Baltimore) would drop by on his book-laden bike, find Father engrossed in sketching and chipping, and ask permission to straighten out the files a bit. Sooner or later a contract would appear for a random-rubble chimney or a patio of Pennsylvania flag; for a time we'd hear no more of the Receivers.

Our enthusiasm for the seawall project, then, and for Karl and Hector's resourceful management of it, was commingled with relief, for it seemed to herald a general improvement of our fortunes. War production was at its peak: Colonel Morton's canneries made army rations around the clock; "rescue boats" of white oak and cypress, beautiful before they were painted battleship gray, were being built by the Dorset Shipyard, erstwhile boatwrights to the oyster fleet. The citizenry had more means for patios, terraces, tombstones—and of our materials, unlike some, there was no great shortage. No longer did we polish headstones with wet sand and railroad iron, or letter them by hand with maul and chisel: they were bought wholesale—already shaped, polished, and decorated in stock patterns—from a national concern by whom we were enfranchised; the inscriptions, stenciled out of sheet rubber, were quickly and perfectly sandblasted onto the face. With the nozzle in one hand and his mind on Erdmann's Cornlot, Peter could execute in a minute the H's with which Grandfather had used to take such loving pains, and do them just as well. Father installed a secondhand water heater in our summer kitchen and no longer rubbed his nose when Mother spoke of radiators and indoor toilets—though, to be sure, such frivolities were not available in wartime.

All summer we worked on the wall, under Karl's supervision, Hector gimping down from school or stoneyard from time to time to inspect our progress. To their joint resourcefulness there was no end. When it became clear that cleaning the Baltimore rocks by hand was ruinously expensive (it took me half an hour, with the best will in the world, to scrape the moss from one), Father rented and experimented with, in vain, equipment to spray them with boiling water or live steam, or soak them in a weak solution of hydrochloric acid, or air-dry and sand-clean them: all either ineffective or inefficient. In the end, not to throw good money after bad, we carted them to the yard as they were, hoping they might clean up more readily when long dry. They did not. When our crusher broke beyond immediate repair on what looked to have once been the quoin of a major Baltimore bank, and we were forced to buy commercial smallstone for our concrete, Karl softened our loss by loading the forms with whole boulders, moss and all, before we poured. And when the city council belatedly challenged our removing the Baltimore rocks at all, and the mayor shamefully refused to acknowledge any previous verbal agreement about a municipal bathing area, Father demanded and received permission, in order to forestall an

179

action against us, to take out at least the ones from our own frontage on the Cornlot.

I voiced my opinion of these expedients to Peter, who upon his graduation had assumed the foremanship of our yard in order to free Karl for the wall. But my brother, then as now, though he deplored poor workmanship like ill character, could attend to but one thing at a time, and was entirely preoccupied with our house. In July he finished purchasing the lot; in August he hired his excavator; and between us, working evenings and weekends with advice from Karl and headshakings from Father, we put up the forms and poured the basement floor and walls. Magda came down every evening to watch, often with Mother and Aunt Rosa and bottles of home brew in a galvanized bucket. For the first time my body grew as brown and tough as Peter's; I prized my muscles and my right to drink the yeasty beer. All day I toted boulders for the seawall, all evening barrowed concrete for the house; but so agreeable was it to be fifteen and strong that when dusk ended our labors I would wrestle with my brother in the clover. Our hard flesh smacked; our grunting hushed the crickets. When the last of our strength was spent we would tumble, washed in dew, at Magda's feet, there to bath further in her grave smile before our final rinse in the nettled river.

The last twenty dollars of his inheritance Peter spent on a tree and two rose-bushes.

"A weeping willow tree," Father reported to Aunt Rosa. "Twenty feet tall. It will shed many a tear before Peter gets his towers up."

Aunt Rosa grabbed her gut.

"Mensch's Folly isn't built yet," Father went on. "But when the receivers take this house away from us, we'll all go down to the Cornlot and sleep under Peter's willow tree."

"*Ach!* No more, Hector!"

If it was my brother's hope that the family would take up where his legacy left off, he was disappointed: work on the house ceased with the August meteor showers. In September Peter announced his engagement to Magda and enlisted in the Corps of Engineers. I had our bedroom to myself; no longer needed to masturbate under the covers when my brother, I hoped, was asleep. Betty Grable and Rita Hayworth smiled from the walls, hung too with plane spotters' silhouettes of Messerschmitts, Focke-Wulfs, Heinkels. But it was Magda Giulianova I dreamed of, by me rescued from the holocaust that incinerated all dear obstacles to our love. In the shelter of the unfinished basement of the unbuilt castle, we mourned our losses in each other's arms.

M

"Mulch Peter's rosebushes, better, against the Onion Snow."

Aunt Rosa's final words, as reported by Mother. She never rested under our tree, though in her last weeks she enjoyed looking down from the hospital solarium upon its bare young withes. From her uterus the cancer spread like an ugly rumor; it was the willows of the Dorset Cemetery she soon slept under, beside her Konrad. Her small estate she had long since conveyed to Father except for her third of Mensch

Masonry, divided equally between him and Uncle Karl, and the ancient egg, expressly devised to Peter and me.

But I, I rested often under Peter's tree in nineteen forties five and six and seven, as the nation finished its war, my brother his term of military enlistment, Mensch Masonry its seawall project and the foundations of Mensch's Castle, and I my high school education.

Say, rather, my education at high school age: not much book learning was accomplished in rural Southern public schools at that time, when ablebodied male teachers were in the military and many of the married women left to follow their husbands. What passed for schooling one could dispatch with the left hand; my right ransacked the public library, no treasure house either in those days. But in the shade of our willow I contrived to read Sophocles and Schopenhauer, and bade farewell to my youthful wish to be an architect. There too, with Magda, I read John Keats, Heinrich Heine, and her beloved rueful Housman, and in time said good-bye to boyhood.

Magda's face is round, her complexion white: not my preference. But her eyes and mouth are rich, her nose is finely cut, her voice deep, soft, stirring. She has grown heavy in motherhood; at forty she'll look like an Italian peasant; even at eighteen she was displeased with her hips, her backside, her legs—too large by modern standards, but (as I learned to remind her) the ideal in other centuries, especially combined with her graceful neck and shoulders, her delicate breasts. When I appraised her—I was seventeen—it was not in the lustful humor with which one sized up the slim tan girls of beach and boardwalk. The frivolity of her summer cottons was belied by that grave voice and figure; those thighs and buttocks were as serious as her eyes. Magda played no sports; was self-conscious in slacks or shorts or swimsuit; wore her dark hair long and straight or wound handsomely in a bun when all the fashion was for short and curly. Yet one guessed her able to stand unclothed before a lover with perfect ease, unbinding that hair for him without joke and tease and giggle. Similarly, one could imagine an *affair* with Magda, but no flirtation. And the affair, one understood, would be nothing sportive . . .

Of late she has become a complainer, speaks of the republic's decline in the tone of one hectoring a foolish husband. But at eighteen and nineteen she brooded stoically upon grand problems; her pessimism was cosmic and impersonal, a tidewater Tragic View. I read her the Science page of the Sunday *Times,* which moved her even more than Housman's verse. The population was increasing past our means to support it. The planet's skin of vital topsoil was washing into the sea. The century would see the end of our fossil fuel reserves. Our science had thwarted natural selection, with the result that our species degenerated year by year. Our antibodies were breeding supergerms, our insecticides superinsects, and poisoning the waters as well. The incidence of violent crime was soaring. Half the entering class at Columbia University would not distinguish Hagia Sophia from the Taj Mahal.

"We're adding so much carbon dioxide to the air that the winters are getting warmer," I read to her. "A little more will melt the polar ice cap, and the whole Eastern Shore will be under water."

We would be sitting under the willow tree or leaning against the new foundations of the Castle on a Sunday morning, while our elders were in church. Magda's legs, stubbled or razor-nicked, would be crossed, the large calves flattened in their nylon sheaths. She would shake her head soberly at the river and observe: "You can't just sit by. But every single thing you do costs more than it's worth."

Those brown eyes saw what general truths were implied by particulars. "Here's an anthropologist," I reported, "who defends the idea of national characters. He says the Germans are the most ingenious people in Europe and the most barbarous, and that the two go together."

Magda concurred: "We've every one of us got the vices of our virtues."

And on the day we first put my penis into her vagina, she having stood naked and unwound her hair for me quite as I'd imagined, and I lamented that our pleasure must be at my brother's cost, she sighed unsmilingly: "Every silver lining has a cloud."

This was in late spring 1947, and by way of a commencement gift. While work on the Castle had resumed and was progressing rapidly, the family's fortunes, so bright not very long before, had fallen to their lowest point since the year of my birth and Hector's confinement. Had Peter not managed a construction loan through an army friend whose father was a local banker, and hired Mensch Masonry to complete the house, our firm would have been all but idle. Several fresh misfortunes had beset us, not least of which was Father's resigning his principalship in 1945 and devoting his energies full-time to the company. Carting and cleaning the Baltimore rocks for reuse as exterior masonry had proved finally more costly than buying fresh stone from the mainland quarries; in the end they had to be sandblasted on all six surfaces, and even then, despite their historical interest, our customers usually preferred new stone. What was perhaps our last chance to use them profitably came early in the year, when fire destroyed a wing of East Dorset Grace Methodist Protestant Southern Church: Mensch Masonry bid to rebuild the facade with the Baltimore rocks, many of which approached the hue of the original granite. Father pled the poetry of saving East Dorset souls with what had once preserved East Dorset property; of building as it were for Zion with the rubble of Babylon. But by that time we were so discredited in the town that the lay leaders rejected our bid and raised instead a brick-veneered structure in the modern fashion, to our minds (but we are neither architects nor true believers) devoid of spirituality.

The cause of our latest disfavor was again the seawall, which by V-J Day, before we'd completed its improvement, had in places already cracked, and was all but breached when Magda relieved me of my sexual virginity. Two hurricanes had pounded at the seam between the old wall and the new; nor'easters had driven water into every crevice, which frozen had heaved and humped the concrete. Damage was especially heavy along the Cornlot, from which the Baltimore rocks had been entirely cleared, and in those portions of the wall where we had piled them as filler when our crusher broke. Great chunks of concrete came away entirely; twenty-foot lengths of wall leaned out of plumb; the spring tides broached them and dissolved the land behind into muddy depressions; salt water then killed the grass, and the soil washed out with remarkable celerity. Along with rose pollen and cottonwood poplar seeds, litigation was in the air: owners of waterfront lots, who had paid their assessments and confidently invested in tons of fill, were closing ranks against the city council, which in turn was preparing an action against Mensch Masonry. There was talk of collusion between us and the mayor to defraud our town. That latter worthy, a Dixiecrat, charged the "liberal" Democratic councilmen with fabricating issues for the '48 elections. In fact, no suits were finally filed, but the publicity served us ill, as did the repairs we undertook at our own cost—extensive repairs, but mainly cosmetic—in the interest of improving our public image and forestalling litigation.

Finally, despite Colonel Morton's and the shipyard's government contracts (now expired), many Dorset families moved in the war years to work in the steel mills and the aircraft factories across the Bay. Erdmann and the other general contractors were fairly busy, but the demand was for low-cost stock-design houses with concrete slab foundations and walkways, even concrete patios, in our judgment an eyesore. After the first flush of war prosperity, people lost interest in flagstone terraces, stone chimneys, marble headstones: they bought government bonds, against the day when automobiles and electrical appliances would return to the market. By the time they did, along with such fresh diversions as television, everything made-do-with during the war was worn out or obsolete and had to be replaced.

I had thought of working at the shipyard that summer, between high school and college, to put by money for books and board. Instead I replaced without wages one of our laborers. A master mason (Uncle Karl), a journeyman carpenter, one other laborer, and myself: while Father brooded once again in the stoneyard, trying to sculpt with the sandblaster, we raised the shell of Peter's house.

"It's our own place, says Brother Pete," Hector had early declared. "We'll use the Baltimore rocks in her. Consolidate our follies."

Karl shrugged. I suggested that in the absence of specific mention of those same rocks in the contract, Peter ought to be consulted. He was in Germany with the occupation forces; his return to us and marriage to Magda were anticipated for the fall. Mother agreed. Father's nose began to itch.

"He wants it for an advertisement, doesn't he? Well, damn-foolishness is our stock-in-trade."

But he made no further move to use the rocks until Peter, despite my account to him of our problems with the seawall, gave epistolary consent. In the weeks that followed I also restrained the company's liberality in the matter of sand by mixing as much as possible of the mortar myself, in the proportion of no more than three parts sand to one of Portland. But I had not the heart to protest Karl's directive, which Father seconded, that we take the sand directly from "our own" beach frontage instead of buying it: the convenience and economy of the beach variety, I had to hope, might partly offset its coarseness and impurity.

I do not ask myself why I made love to Peter's fiancée, nor have I much examined Magda's reasons for inviting me. But when we sat in the Cornlot clover on Sunday mornings or strolled down the listing wall—"dressed up" from Sabbath habit despite our nonbelief—our motives, like the scent of talcum, shaving lotion, and delicate sweat, hung about us in the humid air. As Peter was our bond, we spoke of him often, warmly enlarging on his generosity, his strength of character. I would take Magda's hand and wish with her for his speedy and safe return. We talked together of many things. I felt that Magda spoke more easily with me than with my brother; I came to believe as well that I appreciated as he could never what was of value in her. I had become an atheist by age fifteen; by sixteen a socialist. I discoursed with energy on the madness of nationalism, the contradictions of capitalism, the brotherhood and dignity of man, the rights of women and Negroes (I'd learned to capitalize the *n*), the grand challenges of ignorance, poverty, disease. But my zeal was a toy boat on the dark sea of Magda's fatalism. To her the Choptank itself was a passing feature of the landscape; the very peninsula (which I had informed her was slowly sinking) ephemeral: alone among Dorseters she shrugged her shoulders at the broken wall.

"Six years or six hundred; it's soon over."

Schopenhauer was supplanted by Spengler, Spengler by Ecclesiasticus, Ecclesiasticus by Magda. At the vernal equinox I was postpolitical; by the summer solstice I had given up reading altogether. For all it was my freshman-year professors, some months later at the university, who taught me the second law of thermodynamics, Magda had brought its meaning home to my soul already that summer. It was Independence Day. Earlier that evening, families had gathered along the shore to watch the fireworks shot off from Long Wharf: punk sticks glowed and smoked against mosquitoes; citizens chuckled at the squibs and chasers; they murmured at the rockets that thudded skywards, flowered green and copper, and broadcast reverberating jewels; they held ears and breaths against the ground-shaking mock Bombardment of Fort McHenry at the climax, applauded the final set-pieces of Old Glory and (for some reason) Niagara Falls, and went home. A great moon rose from the Atlantic. Magda and I lingered behind, drank beer from bottles at world temperature, slapped at mosquitoes.

She observed: "You don't go out with girls anymore."

"No."

"I wonder is that my fault."

In the moonlight I saw the perspiration that often beaded her upper lip, and through her blouse the stout straps of her undergarments. I told her for the hundredth time how much I esteemed my brother. "But you know, I can't believe he sees what *I* see in you. Peter hasn't got an awful lot of . . . imagination."

"And you've got too much." Magda turned to me beaming and kissed my lips as on that evening in the foyer of the Menschhaus. But I was three long years older: we leaned into the clover and opened our eyes and mouths.

Presently I declared: "I think more of you than he does."

She chuckled. "Peter loves me, Ambrose."

"How about you?"

"Oh, well, me." An amazing smile. My weight on her meant nothing; she plucked absently at my collar point as at a daisy. "It's your brother I love. He's *better* than you, don't you think?"

But as I recoiled she caught my sleeve, and with the same smile led me into Peter's house. Its stone walls were raised now to the level of first-floor windows; partition studs were up and rafters strung across the framing, but as yet we were not roofed. The moon grew smaller, brighter, harder. At length, striped in shadows and white light, I lay spent and began to taste the wormwood of our deed. But Magda lay easily as I had imagined, naked on the rough subflooring—large legs apart, hands under her head—contemplated the moon through our angled beams, and calmly said: "They say the whole universe is winding down."

Daily I labored on the house; at night it was our trysting place, though I was not frequently permitted copulation. Magda was no tease: when the urge was on her she would initiate embraces or respond to mine with an ardor that half alarmed me, and if I did not bring her to orgasm she would earnestly complete the job herself. When she did not feel erotic and I did—rather more than half the time—she would say so and quickly "relieve" me by hand or mouth so that we could talk, or walk, or quietly count meteors. She did not mind the taste of semen, I was astonished to learn, so long as it was chased with Coca-Cola. (Yes, she did recall that afternoon in the toolshed seven years earlier, but only with a shrug: "Kids, I swear.") But when she guessed, and she was never wrong, that my lust was as it were hypothetical, "caused" by no more than the possibility of its own satisfaction, a wish to be aroused rather than an actual arousal—then nothing doing. She seemed to me to know herself uncannily well; in her company I felt myself to be at worst a concentricity of pretensions, at best a succession of improvisations and self-ignorances. Unerringly—and unfailingly, and never disagreeably—she pointed them out. In moments of pique I was moved to retaliate, and finding nothing with which to tax her in the moral sphere, I would suggest that she lose some weight, or crudely complain that women's crotches were ill odored.

Magda laughed. "How many have you sniffed?" Then she chided me for both my discourtesy and my misinformation: I would find, she said, that some women were fortunate enough to smell fresh of crotch even after a night of doucheless love, just as some, like some men, perspired almost inodorously. Others, like herself, were less lucky, however fastidious: Love learned not to mind, if not positively to enjoy. As for her "weight"—by which she assumed I meant her figure, as she was not overweight for her height, build, and age—Peter had compared her to the nudes he'd found in one of the art books Uncle Wilhelm had shipped home from France, and lovingly called her his oda— odie-something-or-other.

"Odalisque," I groaned, contrite. "I'm such a jerk, Magda."

"Odorless is what you want," she said mildly. "Those dainty little things in the underarm ads."

Mother's health declined. In late July, radical mastectomy, which the surgeon assured us would arrest, before it reached her lymphatics, the malignancy he'd biopsied in her breast. But he had been Aunt Rosa's hysterectomist; we were not much comforted. One Sunday morning, after visiting her in the hospital, I lay perspiring in Peter's living room. Magda discovered a large blue mole on my chest.

"Look here, Ambrose. That could turn into something serious."

Her eyes shone. I stroked her back as she explored the new hair of my chest for more. She discovered six in all, arranged more or less like the stars in Cassiopeia, and saluted each with an eager small cry. Then, despite our Sunday worsteds and seersuckers, the hour and circumstance, she waxed more ardent than I've ever known her. Presently I cried: "For heaven's sake, marry me!"

She wiped sweat from her lips, smiled, shook her head. "Your brother's the one for me. He's got a heart, he has."

The phrase put me painfully in mind of Mother. As we left, straightening plackets and shirttails, I glanced up toward the hospital solarium. There stood Father and Karl, impassively regarding us, their heads wreathed in my uncle's blue cigar smoke.

That evening at supper Peter telephoned from Germany, where it was already past midnight. He would be discharged in six to ten weeks. Magda could plan the wedding for early October. I was to be best man. We should proceed with footings for the "lookout tower," if we hadn't already. He wished we could see the ones he'd seen over there, just like in Aunt Rosa's egg. The word in German was *Turm;* a castle was a *Schloss;* he was a regular linguist these days...

No one home except Father and me. Hector rubbed his nose and regarded, from the side porch of the Menschhaus, the lights of the cars returning from Ocean City over the New Bridge toward the Bay ferries and the mainland.

"Your Uncle Karl and I have talked it over," he said to me. My heart drained. He lit a Lucky Strike, managing the book match with one hand. "One part lime to three sand from now on, is what we think. Pete won't mind. No Portland except for pointing. It's all damned nonsense. D'you follow me?"

N,O, et cetera

"No, I don't!" I should have cried, Yours Truly; and "No, I shan't!" dear Germaine. But oh, I did, I followed them, follow them yet, shall follow them finally and readily into our ultimate plot in the Dorset boneyard, where Uncle Wilhelm's unmarked stone still marks his grave. M ends this fragment and my first "love affair," which, with that water message, began my vocation and my trials as an homme de lettres: *still laboring to fill in the blanks, still searching for an exit from that funhouse, a way to get the story told and rejoin my family for the long ride home.*

"Nonsense," says Arthur Morton King, my drier half: "It's all damned nonsense." He abandoned "personal" literature long since, as tacky, smarmy. He could not care less that, come fall, the Narrator went off to college (along with the unnamed other laborer on Mensch's Castle that summer, his friend and fellow writer-to-be); that Peter came home, married Magda, entered the firm as Karl's partner, and took over completion of his ill-founded house. I tell and tell, Germaine; yet everything is yet to tell: how Ambrose got from '47 to '69; from the sandy basement of the Castle to its "Lighthouse" camera obscura; from his realization that that water message must be replied to, through his maverick noncareer as A.M. King, to his present commitment (first draft now two-sevenths complete and sent to Reggie Prinz in New York) to make a screenplay from his fellow laborer's labors. Along that way, for romantical interest, four other affairs: two with Magda, one with the would-be star of Prinz's current project, one with wife Marsha, mother of his backward angel.

186

"All damned nonsense," King declares. "Take a (blank) page from Uncle Wilhelm's book: already in his day art was past such tack and smarm."

But this Ambrose has the family syndrome: will somehow nudge and bully it through, and make love to Milady A., and do that filmscript however often Prinz rejects it. And *compose a seamless story about life's second revolution;* and *help Peter salvage firm and family.* And *—here A.M. King and I are one— "rescue" Fiction from its St. Helena by transforming it altogether, into something full and luminous as the inside of Rosa's egg.*

S: *The Author to Todd Andrews.* Soliciting the latter's cooperation as a character in a new work of fiction.

Department of English, Annex B
State University of New York at Buffalo
Buffalo, New York 14214

March 30, 1969

Mr. Todd Andrews
Andrews, Bishop, & Andrews, Attorneys
Court Lane
Cambridge, Maryland 21613

Dear Mr. Andrews:

Some fifteen years ago, when I was 24 and 25 (Eisenhower! Hurricane Hazel!), I wrote my first published novel, a little tidewater comedy called *The Floating Opera*. It involved, among other things, a showboat remembered from Aubrey Bodine's photographs and an imaginary 54-year-old Maryland lawyer named Todd Andrews, who once in 1937, when he was 37, cheerfully attempted to blow himself up together with the *Floating Opera* and a goodly number of his fellow Eastern Shorers. You may have heard of the story.

At that time, as a budding irrealist, I took seriously the traditional publisher's disclaimer—"Any resemblance between characters in this novel and actual persons living or dead," etc.—and would have been appalled at the suggestion that any of my fictive folk were even loosely "drawn from life": a phrase that still suggests to me some barbarous form of capital punishment. I wanted no models in the real world to hobble my imagination. If, as the Kabbalists supposed, God was an Author and the world his book, I criticized Him for mundane realism. Had it been intimated to me that there actually dwelt, in the "Dorset Hotel," a middle-aged bachelor lawyer with subacute bacterial endocarditis, who

187

rented his room by the day and spent his evenings at an endless inquiry into his father's suicide...

No matter. Life is a shameless playwright (so are some playwrights) who lays on coincidence with a trowel. I am about the same age now as "Todd Andrews" was when he concluded that he'd go on living because there's no more reason to commit suicide than not to: I approach reality these days with more respect, if only because I find it less realistic and more mysterious than I'd supposed. I blush to confess that my current fictive project, still tentative, looks to be that hoariest of early realist creatures, an epistolary novel—set, moreover and by God, in "Cambridge, Maryland," among other more or less actual places, and involving (Muse forgive me) those most equivocal of ghosts: Characters from the Author's Earlier Fictions.

There, I've said it, and quickly now before I lose my nerve, will you consent, sir, to my using your name and circumstances and what-all in this new novel, clearing the text of course with you before its publication et cetera and for that matter (since other "actual persons living or dead" may wander through this literary mail room) to my retaining you, at your customary fee, for counsel in the libel way?

Cordially,

P.S.: Do you happen to know a Lady Germaine Amherst (Germaine Lady Amherst? Germaine Pitt Lady Amherst? Lady Germaine Pitt-Amherst?)? What about a nut in Lily Dale, N.Y., named Jerome Bonaparte Bray, who believes himself to be the rightful king of France, myself to be an arrant plagiarist, and yourself to be his attorney?

H: *The Author to Todd Andrews.* *Accepting the latter's demurrer.*

Department of English, Annex B
State University of New York at Buffalo
Buffalo, New York 14214

Sunday, April 6, 1969

Todd Andrews
Andrews, Bishop, & Andrews, Attorneys
Court Lane
Cambridge, Maryland 21613

Dear Mr. Andrews:

How a letter written and presumably mailed by you in Cambridge on Good Friday could reach my office here in Buffalo on Holy Saturday is a mystery, considering the usual decorous pace of the U.S. mail. But on this pleasant Easter Sunday afternoon, having got through the *Times* betimes, I strolled up to the campus to check out some epistolary fiction from the library, found it closed for the holiday, stopped by my office, and voilà: its postmark faint to the point of illegibility; its twin 6¢ FDR's apparently uncanceled; the mystery of its delivery intact.

And its plenteous contents avidly received, sir, twice read already, and respectfully perpended. Be assured that I share your reservations; nevertheless, I forge away.

Be assured further that I will honor your request not to make use of your name and situation, or the confidences you share with me in your letter, without your consent. When I have a view of things at all, it is just your sort of tragic view—of history, of civilizations and institutions, of personal destinies—and I hope I live it out with similar scruple. Even given your eventual consent (which I still solicit), I would of course alter facts as radically as necessary for my purposes, as I did fifteen years ago when I invented a 54-year-old lawyer named Todd Andrews, and cut the Macks from whole cloth to keep him company. The boundary between fact and fiction, or life and art, if it is as arguable as a fine legal distinction, is as valuable: hard cases make good law.

So we are, I think, in the accord your letter would bring us to, except for one small matter of record. You wonder why I made no mention of our conversation in the Cambridge Yacht Club on New Year's Eve, 1954. It is because I don't recall being there, though I acknowledge that something like your *Inquiry* and *Letter* must have turned my original minstrel-show project into the *Floating Opera* novel. In the same spirit, I here acknowledge in advance your contribution, intended or inadvertent, to the current project: it had not occurred to me to reorchestrate previous stories of mine in this *LETTERS* novel, only to have certain of their characters stroll through its epistles. But your ironic mention of sequels tempts me to that fallible genre, and suggests to me that it can be managed without the tiresome prerequisite of one's knowing the earlier books. I will surely hazard it: not perversely, to see whether it can be got away with, but because it suits my Thematic Purposes, as we say.

For this contribution, thanks. Let's not press further the historicity of our "encounter." Given your obvious literary sophistication, you will agree with me that a Pirandelloish or Gide-like debate between Author and Characters were as regressive, at least quaint, at this hour of the world, as naive literary realism: a Middle-Modernist affectation, as dated now as Bauhaus design.

Finally, my thanks for your expression of goodwill and loyalty to our medium. To be a novelist in 1969 is, I agree, a bit like being in the passenger-railway business in the age of the jumbo jet: our dilapidated rolling stock creaks over the weed-grown right-of ways, carrying four winos, six Viet Nam draftees, three black welfare families, two nuns, and

189

one incorrigible railroad buff, ever less conveniently, between the crumbling Art Deco cathedrals where once paused the gleaming Twentieth Century Limited. Like that railroad buff, we deplore the shallow "attractions" of the media that have supplanted us, even while we endeavor, necessarily and to our cost, to accommodate to that ruinous competition by reducing even further our own amenities: fewer runs, fewer stops, fewer passengers, higher fares. Yet we grind on, tears and cinders in our eyes, hoping against hope that history will turn our way again.

In the meanwhile, heartening it is to find among the dross a comrade, a fellow traveler, whose good wishes we reciprocate most

Cordially,

P.S.: As to those cinematographical rumors. The film rights to *The Floating Opera* are contracted, and a screenplay is in the works, but I have no particular confidence that the story will actually be filmed, on location or elsewhere. Many shuffle the cards who do not play when the chips are down.

In any case, the Prinz-Mensch project is something different, I gather, and altogether more ad libitum. Prinz I know only by his semi-subterranean reputation on the campuses; in 1967 he communicated to me, indirectly and enigmatically (he will not write letters; is said to be an enemy of the written word) his interest in filming my "last novel," which at the time was *Giles Goat-Boy*. Later he introduced himself to me by telephone and, as best I could infer, gave me to know that it was my "last *book*" he was interested in filming—*i.e.*, by that time, the series *Lost in the Funhouse*, just published. I had supposed that book not filmable, inasmuch as the stories in it were written for print, tape, and live voice, have no very obvious continuity, and depend for their sense largely on manipulations of narrative viewpoint which can't be suggested visually. I told Prinz these things. If I read correctly his sighs, grunts, and hums, they were precisely what appealed to him!

I let him have an option, the more readily when he intimated that our friend Ambrose Mensch might do the screenplay. Our contract stipulates that disagreements about the script are to be settled by a vote among the three of us; so far I've found Prinz at once so antiverbal and so personally persuasive that I've seconded, out of some attraction to opposites, his rejection of Mensch's trial drafts. And almost to my own surprise I find myself agreeing to his most outrageous, even alarming notions: *e.g.*, that by "last book" he means at least a kind of Ongoing Latest (he wants to "anticipate" not only the work in progress since *Funhouse* but even such projected works as *LETTERS!*); at most something ominously terminal.

No question but he will execute a film: my understanding is that principal photography is about to be commenced, both down your way and—for reasons that we merely literate cannot surmise—up here along

190

the Niagara Frontier as well. I find myself trusting him rather as a condemned man must trust his executioner.

We shall, literally, see.

I: *The Author to Lady Amherst*. *Accepting her rejection of his counterinvitation.*

Department of English, Annex B
SUNY/Buffalo
Buffalo, New York 14214

April 13, 1969

Professor Germaine G. Pitt, Lady Amherst
Office of the Provost, Faculty of Letters
Marshyhope State University
Redmans Neck, Maryland 21612

My dear Lady Amherst:

In response to your note of April 5: I accept, regretfully, your vigorous rejection of my proposal, and apologize for any affront it may have given you. I did not mean—but never mind what I did not mean. I accede to the counsel of your countryman Evelyn Waugh: Never apologize; never explain.

May I trust, all the same, that you will not take personally my use of at least the general conceit—for the principal character in an epistolary novel as yet but tentatively titled and outlined—of A Lady No Longer in Her First Youth, to represent Letters in the belletristic sense of that word?

Cordially,

M: *The Author to Lady; Amherst.* Crossed in the mails. Gratefully accepting her change of mind.

Chautauqua Lake, New York

April 20, 1969

Germaine G. Pitt
24 L Street
Dorset Heights, Maryland

My dear Ms. Pitt,

My note to you of April 13, accepting your rejection of my proposal, must have crossed in the mails yours to me of April 12, tentatively withdrawing that rejection: a letter my pleasure in the receipt of which, as that old cheater Thackeray would write, "words cannot describe." Since, like myself, you seem given to addressing certain correspondents on certain days of the week, I happily imagine that *this* letter, too—welcoming your reconsideration and hoping that you will entrust me with whatever confidences you see fit to share—will have passed, somewhere between western New York and the Eastern Shore of Maryland (along the Allegheny ridges, say: the old boundary between British and French America), yet another from you, bringing to light those mysteries with which yours of the 12th is big.

Vicissitudes! Lovers! Pills! Radical corners turned! The old familiar self no longer recognizable! Encore!

I jest, ma'am, but sympathetically. (Excuse my longhand; I write this from a summer cottage at Chautauqua, where snow fell only yesterday into the just-thawed lake. And on the Chesapeake they are sailing already!) If April—in the North Temperate Zone, at least—is the month of suicides and sinkings, that's because it's even more the month of rebeginnings: Chaucer's April, the live and stirring root of Eliot's irony. (So you really knew Old Possum! How closely, please? You are not the One who settles a pillow by her head and says to Prufrock: "That is not what I meant at all. That is not it, at all..."?!) In this latter April spirit I wish you a happy birthday.

I also swear by all the muses that I am not just now nor have I lately been in touch with Ambrose M. We have amicably drifted apart in recent years, both personally and aesthetically; have not corresponded since early in this decade. The news of his connection with Reg Prinz *was* news to me. I've seen (and concurred with Prinz in the rejection of) A's first draft of the opening of that screenplay alleged to be based on some story of mine. It seems tacitly understood between us that direct communication would be counterproductive while he's taking—with my tacit general approval—vast liberties with my fiction. Have you and he become close?

Enfin: I am by temperament a fabricator, not a drawer-from-life. I know what I'm about, but shall be relieved to get home to wholesale invention, much more my cup of tea. Meanwhile, I urge you to tell on, while I like a priest in the box draw between us now a screen. Or better, like a tape recorder, not distract you by replying. Or best, like Echo in the myth, give you back eventually your own words in another voice.

> Cordially. Hopefully. Exhortingly. Expectantly.
> Respectfully. Sincerely,

—L Street? I find neither in my memory nor on my map of Cambridge any neighborhood or suburb called Dorset Heights, or streets named for letters of the alphabet. ?

3

1969 / MAY

Day						Name
S	T	I	M	E	E	*Lady Amherst*
F	2	9	S	23	30	*Todd Andrews*
T	1	8	I	22	29	*Jacob Horner*
W		7	L	21	28	*A. B. Cook*
T		6	S	20	27	*Jerome Bray*
M		5	H	19	26	*Ambrose Mensch*
S		4	S	18	25	*The Author*

T: *Lady Amherst to the Author. The Third Stage of her affair with Ambrose Mensch. Her latter-day relations with André Castine.*

24 L Street
Dorset Heights, Maryland 21612
Saturday, 3 May 1969

My dear B. (or, Dear Diary),

Thanks, I think, for not responding to my last two "chapters." You understand why, even as I made to slip last Saturday's into the drop box (such odd-shaped ones over here!), it occurred to me to post it on the Monday by certified mail instead: having seen fit to comply with your request, I need only some confirmation that these letters are being received, and by the addressee. Your "John Hancock" on the receipt is my "Go now and sin some more."

I should prefer not to. I am not heartily sorry—*au contraire*—but I am heartily *weary* of things sexual. By Ambrose's count (leave it to him) he had as of April's end ejaculated into one or another of His Ladyship's receptacles no fewer than 87 several times since the month—and the "Second Stage" of our love affair—began. More precisely, since the full Pink Moon of 2 April, when the onset of my menses so roused him that I had to take it by every detour till the main port of entry was clear (A's analogy, tricked out with allusions to American runners of the British blockade in "our" wars of 1776 and 1812). Which comes, he duly reported two days ago, to three comes per diem.

Thank God then it was Thursday, I replied, and April done, for my whole poor carcase was a-crying Mayday. The cramps were on me again, breasts tender, ankles swollen, I was cross and weepy: all signs were (he'd be glad to know) that douche and cream and pessary had withstood his "low-motile swimmers."

As if I'd spoken by chance some magic phrase, my lover's humour changed entirely. He removed his hand, rezipped his fly, asked me gravely, even tenderly, was I quite sure? I was, despite the irregular regularity of it: by next night's full moon—which he told me was the Flower Moon—his overblown blossom would close her petals for a spot of much needed rest. He kissed me then like (no other way to say it) a *husband,* and left my office, where, not long before, our committee had delighted John Schott by proposing after all, alas, A. B. Cook for the Litt.D. (We could delay no longer. What's more—but I shall return to

197

this. Would you had said yes! Failing that, would it could be Ambrose!) That day, like a played-out Paolo and Francesca, we made love no more, just read books.

Yesterday too. Sweet relief! A. stopped by early; let himself through the front door of 24 L before I was up, as he sometimes does. I took for granted it was the usual A.M. quickie, as he calls it, and as I had indeed begun flowing that night like a little Niagara, I rolled over with a sigh to let him in the back door and begone. But lo, he was all gentle husband again: had only stopped to ask could he fetch me a Midol? Make tea? He jolly could, and jolly did. I was astonished, mistrustful. Some new circus trick in the offing? Or *l'Abruzzesa*. . . No, no, he chided: merely in order to have "run in a month's glissando the whole keyboard of desire" (his trope), he hoped we might add one last, 88th connexion to the score we'd totted up between Pink and Flower Moons; but he vowed he was as pleasantly spent as I by our ardent April, and would be pleased to shake less roughly, and less often, his darling bud in May.

So I blew him, whilst our Twining's Earl Grey was a-cooling. He even *tasted* different: something has changed! Last evening we made sea trout *au cognac* together, spent the P.M. (a longie) with books and telly; then we *slept* together, like (quoth he, after Donne) "two-sevenths of the snorting Sleepers in their Caves." *Slept,* sir, so soundly that Yosemite's Tunnel Sequoia, which I read this morning fell last night, could have dropped on 24 L and never waked us. Now he's back to his strange screenplay; I to my novel-of-yours-of-the-month. Our "2nd Stage," it would appear, is over; not without some apprehension I approach the 3rd, whatever in the world it may prove to be. Meanwhile, I read and bleed contently—and am informed by my tuckered lover that, this being the Saturday before the first Sunday in May, phials of the blood of martyred St. Januarius in the reliquary of the Naples *duomo* are bubbling and bleeding too. *Tutti saluti!*

The book I'm into, and look to be for some while yet, is, per program, your *Sot-Weed Factor*. But how am I to bring, to the enterprise of reading it, any critical detachment, when I am busy being altogether dismayed by the Cooke-Burlingame connexion and the Laureate of Maryland business in your plot? Ambrose and the meagre Marshyhope library have confirmed the existence of an historical Ebenezer Cooke in the 17th and 18th Centuries, his ambiguous claim to laureateship, and his moderately amusing *Sot-Weed Factor* poem from which your story takes off. And Cook Point on the Choptank, of course, is not far from Redmans Neck. But John (if I may now so call you?): what am I to do with these "coincidences" of history and your fiction with the facts of my life, which beset, besiege, beleaguer me in May like Ambrose's copious sperm in April? Never mind such low-motile hazards as my opening your novel at random to find a character swearing by "St. Januarius's bubbling blood": I quite expect to meet Ambrose himself on some future page of yours; perhaps even (like Aeneas finding his own

198

face in Dido's frescoes of the Trojan War) Yours Truly bent over the provostial desk with him *in flagrante delicto*. . .

No more games! You know, then, of an original "Monsieur Casteene," Henry Burlingame, and Ebenezer Cooke: what *I* must know is their connexion, if any, with "my" André, and with those nebulous name-changers at Castines Hundred in Ontario, and with that alarming Annapolitan to whom we're surrendering our doctorate of letters. Not to mention. . .my son! I have chosen to trust you as an author; I do not know you as a man. But I know (so far as I know) that I am real, and I beseech you not to play tired Modernist tricks with real (and equally tired) people. If you know where André Castine is, or anything about him, for God's sake tell me! If A. B. Cook and his "son" Henry Burlingame VII are pseudonymous mimics of your (or History's) originals, tell me! I believe "our" Cook to be dangerous, as you know. Am I mistaken? What *do* you know?

I feel a fool, sir, and I dislike that not unfamiliar feeling. It isn't menstruation makes me cross, but being crossed and double-crossed. Damn all of you!

By which pronoun I mean, momentarily I presume, you men. Not included in last Saturday's roster of my former beaux was the one woman I've ever loved, my "Juliette Récamier"—a French New Novelist in Toronto whose meticulous unsentimentality I found refreshing after Hesse and my British lovers—and before it was revealed to be no more than increasingly perverse and sterile rigour. Yet I recall warmly our hours together and rather imagine that, had she not long since abjured the rendering of characters in fiction, she alone of my writer-friends might have got me both sympathetically and truly upon the page, with honour to both life and literature, love and art. Lesbian connexions have not appealed to me before or since: I mention my "Juliette" for the sake of completeness, and at the risk of your misconstruing her (as Ambrose does) into allegory. It is men I love, for better or worse, when I love; and of all men André, when he sees to it that our paths cross.

I think I pity the man or woman whose experience does not include one such as he: one to whom it is our fate and hard pleasure to surrender quite. We are not the same in our several relationships; different intimacies bring out different colours in us. With Jeffrey (and Hermann, and Aldous, and Evelyn, and the rest, even "Juliette") I was ever my own woman; am decidedly so even with Ambrose, except that the lust we roused in each other last month truly lorded it over both of us. To André alone I *surrendered myself,* without scruple or considera-tion, almost to my own surprise, and "for keeps." Nothing emblematic, romantic, or sex-determined about it; I have known men similarly helpless, to their dismay, in some particular connexion. It is an accident of two chemistries and histories; while my rational-liberal-antisentimen-tal temperament deplores the *idea* as romantic nonsense, there's no dismissing the fact, and any psychological explanation of it would be of merely academic interest.

Toronto: I spent the summer and fall of 1966 there, lecturing at the university, consoling myself with "Juliette" (their novelist in residence) for the loss of my husband, and waiting in vain, with the obvious mixture of emotions, for some word from André, who I assumed had arranged my lectureship. November arrived, unbelievably, without a sign from him. On the 5th, a Saturday, unable to deal with the suspense, I drove out to Stratford with my friend to see a postseason *Macbeth* at the Shakespeare Festival Theatre. Between Acts III and IV, as I stepped into the lobby for intermission, I was handed a sealed envelope with my name on it by one of the ushers. I was obliged to sit before I could open it. The note inside, in a handwriting I knew, read: "My darling: Dinner 8 P.M., Wolpert Hotel, Kitchener."

No signature. That little town, as you may know, is along the dreary way from Stratford to Toronto. I have no memory of the rest of the play, or of the ride back. My friend (who like Juliette Récamier had the gift of inferring much from little, and accurately, in matters of the heart) kindly drove me to that surprising, very European old hotel in the middle of nowhere, tisking her tongue at my submissiveness but declaring herself enchanted all the same by the melodrama. She waited in the lobby whilst I went up the stairs, literally trembling, to (what I've learned since to be) the improbably elegant German dining room on the second floor. The hostess greeted me by name. I saw *him* enter, smiling, from across the room, unmistakably my André: handsomer at fifty than he'd been as a young man! My heart was gone; likewise my voice, and with it my hundred questions, my demands for explanation.

"Your friend has been informed. She understands," he assured me in Canadian French, as he helped me into a chair—none too soon, for the sound of that richest, most masculine of voices, the dear dialect I'd first heard in Gertrude Stein's house, undid my knees. "I urged her to have dinner with us, but she wanted to get back to Toronto. Charming woman. I quite approve."

I am told we had good veal and better Moselle: André prefers whites with all his meats. I am told that I was not after all too gone in the head to protest the impossibility of our dining and conversing together as if no explanation, no justification were needed. I am told even that I waxed eloquent upon the outrageous supposition that his smile, his touch, the timbre of that voice, made me "his" again despite everything, as in the lyrics of a silly song. Where was our son? I'm told I demanded. What could possibly justify my being quite abandoned but never quite forsaken, my wounds kept always slightly open by those loving, heartless letters? And finally—I am told I asked—how was I to get home that night, when this absurd rendezvous was done and I'd regained my breath and strength?

What I did *not* question until later, to André's own professed surprise, was his authenticity. Appearances and mannerisms are easily mimed: did I need no proof, after all those years, that he was he? Well, I didn't; didn't care (at the time) even to address so vertiginous a question. If, somewhile later, I began to wonder, it was because for the first time since our parting he had come to me in the rôle of himself: had he posed as another, I'd never have doubted at all.

We stayed at the Wolpert until Monday, scarcely leaving André's room except for meals. He was obliged, as I stood about dazed, to undress me himself. When he first entered me—after so many years, so many odd others—I became hysterical. From Kitchener he took me back to Castines Hundred, where I enjoyed something of a nervous collapse. It was as if for twenty-five years I had been holding my breath, or an unnatural pose, and could now "let go," but had forgot how. It was as if—but I can't describe what it was as if. Except to say that for André it was as if our quarter-century separation had been a month's business trip: a regrettable bother, but not uninteresting, and happily done with. Good to be back, and, let's see, what had we been discussing?

Sedatives helped, prescribed by the Castines' doctor. Arrangements were made at the university to reschedule my lectures after my recovery. André too, I learned (now Baron Castine since his grandfather's death), had been briefly married—a mere dozen years or so, as it were to mark time "till my own marriage had run its course"—and had sired "one or two more children," delightful youngsters, I'd love them, off in boarding schools just then, pity. Had I truly borne no more since ours? *Dommage.* Now *that* chap, our Henri, yes: chip off the old block, he: more his grandfather's son, or his "uncle's," than his father's: at twenty-six a more promising director of the script of History than either of them at his age, busy redoing what he André had spent half a lifetime *un*doing. Crying shame he wasn't at Castines Hundred then and there: it was high time we approached the question of revealing to him his actual parentage. . .

Tranquillisers. And where might the lad be? Ah, he André had hoped against hope that *I* might have had some word from him: the boy was at the age when certain of his predecessors had revised their opinion of their parents, and was skilful enough to discover them for himself. Last André had heard, Henri was underground in *Québec* somewhere, playing *Grandpère's* nasty tricks on the Separatists, who took him for their own. So at least he'd given out. Before that he'd been working either with or against the man he understood to be his father, down in Washington. But his track had been lost, just when André much desired to find it. Of this, more when I was stronger, and of his own activities as well: a little bibliography of "historical corners turned" that he was impatient to lay before me, "like the love poems they also are."

He had of course followed with close interest my own career: he commended my articles on Mme de Staël (whom however he advised me now to put behind) and my patience with my late husband Jeffrey's later adulteries. He informed me, in case I should be interested, that Jeffrey had been infertile if not quite impotent after the 1940's, but had honoured paternity claims against him rather than acknowledge his infirmity. My essay on Héloïse's letters to Peter Abelard, he said, had been heartbreakingly sympathetic, yet dignified and strong as poor Héloïse herself. Had I read any good books lately?

By the beginning of the new year I was, if not exactly recovered (I never shall be), at least "together" enough to return to the university and to "Juliette," with André's approval—which I hadn't sought—and with three other souvenirs, two of which I *had* sought.

The first was that promised account of his activities since 1941. On that head I am sworn to secrecy; you would not believe me anyroad. But if even a tenth of what he told me is true, André has indeed "made history," as one might make a poem—and to no other end! Little wonder I have difficulty accepting any document at all, however innocuous, as "naive": I look for hidden messages in freshman compositions and interoffice memoranda; I can no longer be at ease with the documentary source materials of my own research, which for all I know may be further "love poems" from André. A refreshing way to view Whittaker Chambers's "pumpkin papers," or Lee Harvey Oswald's diary! And both enterprises, I need not add, had kept him away, "for her own protection," from me as well as from the woman he'd married "as a necessary cover" at that aforementioned turning point in his life. (He'd also been fond of her, he acknowledged, even after "her defection and subsequent demise." I didn't ask.)

The second souvenir was the news that our son had been raised to believe himself an orphan, the son of André's "deceased half brother and sister-in-law!" What's more, it now turns out (read "was then by him declared") that he did indeed *have* a half brother, quite alive, "down in the States"—or half had a brother, or something. "All very complicated," he admitted: the understatement of the semester. And his "necessary ruse" (for the boy's own security, don't you know) bid fair to backfire; for the evidence was that our son had located either this half brother or his *semblable*, accepted him as his father, and was doing the man's political work, the very obverse of André's own.

And, pray, what was that work? For André (since 1953) it was "the completion of his and his family's bibliography": the bringing to pass within his lifetime, in North America at least, that Second Revolution which, in his father's lifetime, had been thwarted "by Roosevelt and World War II." Did he mean an out-and-out political revolution, like the French, the Russian, the original American? Well, yes and no (André's reply to everything!): that's what *his* father, Henry Burlingame VI, almost unequivocally had meant, and had failed like so many others to bring about. What he André had in mind was something more. . .shall we say, revolutionary? Never mind. Immediately, his task was to make an ally of our son, by the most complicated means imaginable, which I shall return to. Suffice it here to say that "our" first problem in that line was the question whether, left to himself, the boy would spend his maturity working for or against his "parents." If for, then we should reveal ourselves to him without delay; if against, he should be left in his present error.

Mightn't it depend, I managed to wonder, on who those parents were? André smiled, kissed my hand: Absolutely not.

The third souvenir I took without knowing it, either during my recovery or in the weeks thereafter, when André would drive over to Toronto or I revisit Castines Hundred, with or without "Juliette." I was well into my forties, John: a widow beginning a new life in the academy, much shaken by my history and slowly rebuilding after my "collapse." I had learnt that I still loved André enormously, but no longer unreservedly. I believed what he reported to me, but suspended judgement on his interpretations and connexions of events, his reading of motives and indeed of history. I was in fact no longer very *interested* in those grand conspiracies and counterconspiracies, successful or not. I understood that I was his when and as he wished; I would do anything he asked of me—and I found myself relieved that he didn't after all ask that I marry him, and/or live with him at Castines Hundred, and/or devote myself to his ambiguous work. It was therefore disturbing, in subtle as well as in the obvious ways, to discover myself, in the spring of 1967, once again impregnated!

Given my age and recent distress—and the prompting of "Juliette," who had already left her menses behind—I was inclined to believe myself entering the menopause. By the time my condition became undeniable the pregnancy was well established, and I had not seen André for at least two months. I was not disposed to tell him about it, much less seek his advice or help: I spent some time verging upon relapse; then got hold of myself and set about to arrange the abortion. "Juliette" scolded me: it was the father's child, too; he had the right to be consulted, and to be permitted to assist if our judgements concurred. Only if they did not should I do on my own as I saw fit. For her part, she thought it would be charming for "us" to bear and raise the child; she'd always wanted to be a father.

André appeared straight off, of course, somehow apprised of the situation (I had ceased to be curious whether "Juliette," or half the world, was in his confidence). Had he wished me to carry, bear, and raise the child, I should certainly have done so. As he graciously deferred to my wishes in the matter, I asked him without hesitation to find me an abortionist willing and able to deal with so advanced a pregnancy.

Not surprisingly, he knew of one. Just across the Niagara from your city, in the little town of Fort Erie, Ontario, is an unusual sanatorium financed in part, so André told me, by the philanthropy of my friend Harrison Mack, with whom André just happened to be acquainted. Things could be arranged with the supervising physician there, a competent gentleman. I would be distressed, by the way, to hear that Monsieur Mack's spells of delusion had become more frequent and, one might say, more *thorough* since Jeffrey and I last visited him in '62: one wondered if it were not some long-standing attraction to me that led him to fancy himself British?

I reminded André (we were driving down the Queen Elizabeth Way) that I was only *half* British; he reminded me that George III had been scarcely that. Did I know the Macks' daughter, the film starlet "Bea Golden"? I did not. Just as well, inasmuch as she was recuperating, under an assumed name, at this same sanatorium, from abortion-cum-delirium-tremens-cum-divorce-cum-nervous-breakdown. André himself, he volunteered, did not know the Mack family socially; but their son Drew was a coordinator of the Second Revolutionary Movement on American college campuses (indeed, the sanatorium, unknown to its administrators, was a training base for such coordinators); André's "brother" was a familiar of the Macks; and André himself owned stock in Mack Enterprises.

Really?

Quite. Ever since the days of Turgot and the physiocrats—upon my article on whose connexion with Mme de Staël, his compliments—his family's income had been from sound investments in the manufacturers of dreadful things: Du Pont, Krupp, Farben, Dow. The drama of the Revolution would be less Aristotelian, he declared, its history less Hegelian, never mind Marxist, if the capitalists did not finance their own overthrow. "We" had bought into Mack Enterprises when they got into defoliants and antiriot chemicals. Did I know that Harrison Mack, Senior, the pickle magnate, had in his dotage preserved his own excrement in Mason jars? And that his son "George III" had begun causing his to be freeze-dried? Freud had things arsy-turvy: *there* was the pure archival impulse, not vice versa! Did I know, by the way, the Latin motto of Mack Enterprises?

I did not, and was not to learn it for some while, for just here the present importunes to soil past and future alike. I was no stranger to clinical abortion; the "sanatorium" was peculiar (so had been the one in Lugano) but not alarming; the doctor—an elderly American Negro of whom I was reminded by the nameless physician in your *End of the Road* novel—was stern but not discourteous. I do not hold human life to be sacred, my own included—only valuable, and not always that. To have borne and raised that child would have been an unthinkable bother, an injustice to the child itself under the circumstances, an unreasonable demand on André's part—which of course he did not make. I resist the temptation to say, in sentimental retrospect, that with all my heart I wished he *had* made exactly that unreasonable demand. But half my heart, one unreasoning auricle at least. . .

Instead, as I recuperated next day from the curettage, he made another. I was still groggy with anaesthesia; an important question had occurred to me just before our conversation on the Q.E.W. had been interrupted by our arrival at Fort Erie; I wanted urgently to recall it now, and I could not—would not, alas, until too late—even when that finest of male voices asked his *pauvre chérie* whether she remembered an historian named Morgan, formerly of the Maryland Historical Society in Baltimore, currently president of a little college down that way endowed by Harrison Mack?

She did: he had invited her to a visiting lectureship there, which invitation she had declined.

"He has invited her *de nouveau*," André proudly informed me. "And this time she must accept."

Must she now. And why should she exchange the civilisation of Toronto's Yorkville Village and Bay-Bloor district for what had impressed her as the, let us say, isolated amenities of Tidewater Farms and vicinity? *Eh bien,* for the excellent reason that while we had lost one child, we had, if not regained, at least relocated another. Henri was alive and well! And doing the Devil's work with his "father" in Washington, D.C., so effectually that if he were not checked there would very possibly be no Second Revolution at all in our lifetimes; whereas, were he working as effectively for "us," things might just possibly come to pass by "our" target date, 1976. Perhaps I remembered André's own dear father's spanning with thumb and forefinger the easy distance from D.C. across the Chesapeake to the marshes of Maryland's Eastern Shore, whence he had hoped to infiltrate and undermine the bastions of capitalist imperialism (or their infiltrators and underminers, depending on whether one credited the declared intention or the consequences of his actions)?

Tearfully—though just then *D.C.* suggested to me neither District of Columbia nor direct current, but dilation and curettage—I did remember those nights of love and happy polemic at Castines Hundred in 1940, while Europe burned.

Then I was to understand that a certain secret base in these same marshes, not very far from Marshyhope State University College, was the eastern U.S. headquarters for the Movement: Maryland and Virginia were peppered with *their* secret bases; that's why ours was safest there. From the vantage point of a visiting professorship at Marshyhope, I could observe and reacquaint myself with Henri, at first anonymously as it were, and then, if all went well. . .

His plan will keep till next Saturday's letter: it was as baroque as the plot of your *Sot-Weed* novel promises to be (at the time I said "circuitous as Proust," and André kissed my forehead and replied, *"Voilà ma Recherche, précisément"*), which for all I know may be itself a love letter from him. God knows it bristles with his "signals"! Did you write it? I grow dizzy; grew dizzy then, no longer just from Sodium Pentothal.

But when the time came I went, with a sigh and no false hopes, as I would have gone to the University of Hell for my novelist of history, had his plot and precious voice demanded. *Adieu, chère "Juliette":* you I traded—when André bid me *au revoir* for the last time to date, a few

205

days and much further instruction later—for unfortunate Mr. Morgan, mad King Harrison, contemptible John Schott. . .and Ambrose Mensch.

Who has filled me full, if not fulfilled me, as I've filled these pages. Like she-crab or queen bee after mating season, I luxuriate, squishy and replete, in this sexless interval. May it last a few days more!

What have I forgotten? That I remembered, too late, who it was I'd met on the day Joe Morgan mentioned Turgot and the physiocrats in the library of the Maryland Historical Society in 1961: our nominee-by-default for next month's doctorate, for whom Schott even now will be at composing a treacly citation. I last remet him three months ago, at poor Harrison's funeral, with. . ."his". . ."son."

Vertigo! Who is whose creature? Who whose toy? Help me, John, if you have help to give a still-dismayed

Germaine

P.S. Whilst City College, Colgate, Harvard, Illinois—yea, even Oneonta, even Queens—are torn asunder (per program?), all is uneasy calm at Marshyhope. More interest here in Derby Day than in Doomsday!

I: *Lady Amherst to the Author. More trouble at Marshyhope. Her relations with the late Harrison Mack, Jr., or "George III."*

Office of the Provost
Faculty of Letters
Marshyhope State University
Redmans Neck, Maryland 21612

10 May 1969

Mon cher (encore silencieux) B.,

I write this—sixth? eighth?—letter to you once again from my office, once again more or less besieged by the "pink-necks." Shirley Stickles wonders why I do not dictate it to her; *I* wonder, not having heard from you on the then urgent queries in my last, why I continue to write, write, write, into a silence it were fond to imagine pregnant. And I know the answer, but not what to make of it.

A difficult season, this, for Shirley Stickles. She cannot understand (I cannot always either) why the students who seize and "trash" Columbia, extort ransom for stolen paintings from the University of Illinois, force the resignation of the presidents of Brown and CCNY, commit armed robberies at Cornell, and more or less threaten MSUC, are not even expelled and sent posthaste to Vietnam, far less put to the torture as she recommends. And the sudden transvaluation of Ambrose Mensch, whom she despises, in the eyes of John Schott, whom she adores, baffles and troubles her like yesterday's unsainting by Pope Paul of Christopher, Barbara, Dorothy, *et alii.*

What has happened is that my lover (so he remains, more tender and solicitous than ever, though our respite from sex is of a week's duration now) has for the second time come to the rescue, more or less and altogether cynically, of Marshyhope, and so further endeared himself thereby to our acting president as to lead that unworthy to wonder aloud to me this morning, in S.S.'s presence, whether, "if it should happen that Mr Cook is unable to accept our invitation," we mightn't extend it after all to Ambrose! Schott trembles now, you see, for the success of his Commencement Day exercises, so vulnerable to disruption, when the state comptroller will be present to accept our maiden doctorate of law. Much as his instincts (and ex-secretary) warn him not to trust Ambrose, with Cook's consent he would "sacrifice" the Litt.D.—which, like the doctorate of science, has small political utility— to insure the peace of the ceremonies and, incidentally, to bring Reg Prinz's cameras back on campus.

They were the instrumentality of Ambrose's triumph yesterday. The week has been unseasonably warm here, more like midsummer than like the gentle Mays of *my* (and your Ebenezer Cooke's) Cambridge. The students, impatient to get out of their clothes and onto the ocean beaches, lolled and frolicked in the quad with Frisbees, guitars, transistor radios, and sun reflectors, ever more restless and boisterous as the week went on. Drew Mack's disciples in the local chapter of the Students for a Democratic Society ("Marshyhope Maoists" is Ambrose's term) scolded them daily through bullhorns for not emulating their brothers and sisters to the north and west. The usual list of nonnegotiable demands was promulgated, the ritual denunciations made of the administration (all fairly just, in this case, but not different from those being lodged against the ablest college officials in the land), the *de rigueur* student-faculty strike proclaimed. But in such sunshine, with the sparkling Choptank so close at hand and the season's first Ocean City weekend coming on, who wanted to be cooped up in an occupied building? Besides, it was reported that a bona fide film company was arriving in Cambridge, complete with actors, directors, and cameras, and might visit the campus en route to "location" farther down-county. If the weather held, we all agreed, we would probably be spared.

Alas, yesterday dawned cool, windy, overcast; at noon it began to drizzle, though the forecast for the Saturday remained fair. It is our ill fortune, under the circumstances, that while the majority of our students, being from the immediate area, go home on weekends, the activists cannot conveniently do so, being most of them from "Baltimore or even farther north." In short, enough support was mustered from the bored and frustrated to threaten a second takeover of Tidewater Hall, this one determined to "succeed" where the first, a fortnight since, had failed. And again we administrators, our number augmented by Ambrose and Mr Todd Andrews, debated whether calling in the state police would intimidate or aggravate our besiegers. Most of us were confident that Drew Mack and his comrades would welcome the provocation as a chance to rally moderates to their cause, especially if the troopers could be incited to swing truncheons or make arrests. Schott and Harry Carter wondered nevertheless whether a firm, quick, "surgical strike"—the academic expulsion and physical removal from the campus of all the known organisers of the rising—was not our last hope of avoiding embarrassment in June.

The rain stopped, but the sky remained cloudy, the air chill. Ambrose then proposed that Reg Prinz and company be invited at once, as a diversion, to do certain on-campus footage more or less called for by his screenplay, which was flexible enough to include, at least tentatively, impromptu performances by the student activists them-selves. The move might buy us time for the weather to clear; the medium being cinema instead of television news reportage, there would be no particular provocation in the presence of the cameras. And the rumour could be circulated that the filming would continue over the weekend at Ocean City (there is boardwalk "footage," I understand, in your book *Lost in the Funhouse,* which I've yet to read; Prinz is apparently working it into the film).

Schott and Carter, while they had no strong objections to this stratagem, had no great confidence in it either, not having met Prinz except by the way at Harrison Mack's funeral last February. But I had got, if scarcely to know him, at least somewhat to appreciate Prinz's peculiar, unaggressive forcefulness and inarticulate suasion, during my stay at Tidewater Farms, where he was a special sort of visitor. And so while *trusting* the man would be like trusting a wordless interloper from outer space, I could second Ambrose's proposal, from my own experience, as more likely than it might seem. Mr Andrews, who also knew the chap slightly, concurred. We were given shrug-shouldered leave to try it.

Have *you* encountered Mr Reginald Prinz in the flesh by this time, I wonder? And are you apprised of his odd notions about making a movie from your work? As it is that curious personality, and by extension those curious notions, which made Ambrose's plan successful (and make our presence here today mainly precautionary), I shall digress for a space on that head, and at the same time complete for you the Story of My Life Thus Far.

Of a woman widowed by cancer, whose worse fate it subsequently was to be twice remarried to apparently healthy men and twice rewidowed by wasting diseases, Freud somewhere facetiously remarks that she had "a destiny compulsion." The term haunts me. I seem to myself afflicted with at least three separate compulsions: to fall in love with (and more often than not conceive by) elderly novelists; to fall in love with and conceive (and be dismissed) by André Castine; and, like

Freud's patient, to wait upon the terminal agonies of lovers who do not fit those categories. That Jeffrey, whose unspeakable cancer I've spoken of, was a legitimate lord, and Harrison Mack, to whom I now come, a self-fancied monarch of the realm, makes me tremble at André's half-legitimate baronetcy, not to mention Ambrose Mensch's nom de plume!

I left Toronto for Marshyhope in August '67 at André's bidding, and to some extent to do his inscrutable work: when I should come face-to-face with the Enemy (his "half brother" A. B. Cook) and our son—an encounter I was not to arrange myself—André would deliver to me certain letters he had discovered, written by one of his ancestors, which had radically altered the course of his own life. I was to publish them as my own discoveries in the Ontario or Maryland historical magazines, where Henri would come across them, etc., etc. The strategy would be madness if it were anyone else's; may be madness even so. In any case, though I saw my son, unequivocally, three months nine days ago today (and have not been myself since), I have seen no letters. For all I truly know to the contrary, André may be dead or crazy—may have been since 1941! Since my visit to Fort Erie, as I explained in my last, I have resisted the need to try to comprehend that man and our relation—though he or his palpable semblance could still summon me in midsentence, and I would put by pen, paper, professorship, Ambrose, and all and (not without a sigh) hie wearily himward.

I wrote ahead to the Macks and received from Jane a crisp but courteous invitation to be their guest until I found lodgings. She also confirmed André's report of her husband's decline since '62, and hoped my conversation might amuse him. But except in his ever less frequent intervals of true lucidity, she warned (when he knew he was Harrison Mack, who in his madness fancied himself George III), and his ever *more* frequent intervals of second-degree delusion, as it were (when he fancied himself George III mad, fancying *him*self Harrison Mack sane), I must be prepared to hold onto my own sanity, so entirely did he translate Tidewater Farms into Windsor Castle, or Buckingham Palace, or Kew, or Bath. Only her deliberate and entire immersion in business affairs, for which she had found she had talent, preserved Jane's reason. She declared herself sorry to hear of my own bereavement—but I could hear envy in her phrasing, and I sympathised. She kindly sent a car to fetch me from Friendship Airport in Baltimore to her office at the Mack Enterprises plant in Cambridge, where I admired—a shade uneasily, I confess—her extraordinary physical preservation, whilst she completed her forewarning of what I must expect out on Redmans Neck.

There Harrison was gently but absolutely confined, in a kind of ongoing masquerade. One of his psychiatrists, it seems, had attempted to render his delusion untenable by quizzing him in detail on Georgian history, of which he was innocent. A second, opposed in principle to the first, had thought to undo his colleague's mischief by providing Harrison with the standard biographies and textbooks on the period, including studies of George's own psychopathology. The patient blithely played the second against the first by sophisticating his derangement on the one hand whilst on the other attributing any gaps in his historical information, or discrepancies between the Georgian and Harrisonian facts, to his madness, to the fallibility of historiography, or to the misguided though doubtless well-intended masquerading of his courtiers!

"He calls himself a Don Quixote inside out," Jane declared—and I observed to myself *(a)* that it bespoke a wistful detachment on Harrison's part to see *himself* so, and *(b)* that it would have to be he, or some literate doctor, who so saw, since Jane herself carried no freight of literary reference. What I could not appreciate at second hand was the aptness of Harrison's self-description: not only did he (so he was persuaded) mistake, in his "enchantment," giants for windmills and soldiers for sheep, instead of vice versa—that is, he madly imagined that in "his" (George III's) madness, Windsor Castle looked like Tidewater Farms, and the royal coach-and-four like a Lincoln Continental—but he informed me, in our first extended conversation, that "George Third the First" had actually made notes on *Don Quixote* at Windsor during *his* first mature seizure, in 1788, when also he had remarked to William Pitt (my husband's ancestor, by the way) that having been disgracefully defeated in his first American war, he must needs be "a second Don Quixote" to involve himself in another.

Thus he could cast Jane, unflatteringly, in the rôle of homely Queen Charlotte, whilst "in his madness" perceiving and relating to her as Jane Mack, a handsome creature from another life in another time and place. Their son the vicious ingrate Prince of Wales, to spite and shame his father, carried on as a radical commoner named Drew Mack, wed to a "toothsome blackamoor wench"; their daughter Princess Amelia had not only died, but scandalously gone on stage under false names afterward to conceal the fact, etc. Only two people in the court were exempt from this double identity: His Majesty's old friend Todd Andrews, whom he compared explicitly to Twain's Connecticut Yankee in King Arthur's court, and his new friend—"the son [he] should have had," his "Duke of York," the "proper Prince Regent, when it comes to that"—who "never humoured [his] madness, because he shared it"; an "18th-Century courtier trapped in 20th-Century America". . .

Reg Prinz. Todd Andrews declares the name is, if not its bearer's "real" one, at least an alias well antecedent to Harrison's: a coincidence doubtless turned to account, but not an ad hoc imposture. Its young bearer had an established early reputation as an avant-garde *cinéaste* before his application to the Tidewater Foundation for subsidy; as he was not given to conversation, and spoke cryptically when at all, the most he could be taxed with was his not vigorously denying a rôle he most certainly did not "play." For some reason Harrison had been taken with him on sight, and Jane acknowledged that while Prinz readily accepted all proffered support for his cinematic activities, he could not be accused of exploiting Harrison's esteem. His visits to Redmans Neck were in part as a planning consultant to Marshyhope's Media Centre, the directorship of which he had declined; and in part out of an apparent interest in Harrison himself.

I met His Majesty that same evening, Mr Prinz not till several months later. The original George III in his distress was often physically out of control; required constant attendance by Dr Willis and company; often needed restraining by strait-waistcoat (Willis calls it in his journal "the &c"; George himself referred to the restraining chair as his "coronation chair"); and suffered concomitant bodily infirmities. Harrison, until the twin strokes that blinded and killed him, was in rosy health and amiable temper, a little heavy but by no means obese, withal rather handsomer at seventy than he'd been in his forties, when I first met him at Capri—though not, like Jane, preternaturally youthful. And he was as entirely in control of himself as his complex dementia allowed: certainly in no way dangerous to himself or others, and inclined more to manic fancies than to manic projects. Therefore he needed very little supervision; his company was agreeable, and his conversation, if often saddening, was civilised and frequently clever. Not to disgrace, by his ubiquitous "delusions" (*e.g.*, that Cambridge, England, was Cambridge, Maryland, or that his ministers were trustees of the Tidewater Foundation), the monarchy he held in such esteem, he ventured off the "palace grounds" only reluctantly and never unaccompanied. The "affairs of the realm" he gladly turned over to the queen and ministers aforementioned, though he still opposed the idea of installing Drew as prince regent. And since, "in his madness," those crucial affairs were translated into such hallucinations as Marshyhope State University College, His Royal Highness into a minor American industrialist named Harrison Mack, Jr., he conscientiously attended to what was represented as the news and business of those hallucinations, and could talk as knowledgeably about Lyndon Johnson's administration as about John Adams's and Napoleon's.

From all this one might imagine that, pragmatically speaking, he was not mad at all. But though his conduct of affairs "in *this* world," as he put it, was in the main responsible and judicious, his identification with mad King George was more than an elaborate, self-cancelling whimsy. Harrison *suffered* from the duplicity of reality, as it were; events and circumstances that he could not "decipher" into Georgian terms, and thus deal with on their own, alarmed him, lest he mishandle them. And if his nightmares (and infrequent daytime seizures) were learnt from the history books—like George, he fancied he had seen Hanover through Herschel's telescope; imagined London flooded, and would rush in the royal yacht to rescue "certain precious manuscripts and letters"; signed death warrants for "all six of [his] sons," etc., etc.—the terror and anguish they caused him were heartfelt.

My own knowledge of the period was cursory at that time, but I remembered that Fanny Burney had held some post in the royal household (she was in fact 2nd Keeper of the Robes to Queen Charlotte) and that, about the time of the king's first major attack and the publication of her epistolary novel *Evelina,* she'd commenced a diary of her observations and reflections on the grave event. It was my thought to represent myself, if Harrison should press for such representation, as Mrs Burney: I knew her writings only slightly, but Harrison (and G. III) in all likelihood knew them not at all—Cervantes and Fielding were *their* only novelists—and the rôle seemed congenial enough. I suggested and explained it to Jane; she approved, but hoped no fiction would be necessary, as she'd alerted Harrison to my coming, and he'd remembered me affectionately.

We arrived at that great gracious house on its point of hemlocks and rhododendrons, as if one had driven into a Maxfield Parrish print, and were directed by the costumed maid and nurse (Dr #2's idea) to His Majesty in the music room. Harrison, comfortable in navy blazer and white ducks, rose beaming from the harpsichord—he'd become, predictably, a great lover of Handel, and was playing Delilah's mad-song from *Samson*—bowed slightly to Jane, whom he addressed as "Madame," turned then to me, and, as I wondered fleetingly whether to curtsey, raised my hand to his lips and fell to his knees before me! Tears of joy started down his plump tanned cheeks; he cried passionately: *"Sanctissima mea uxór Elizabetha!"*

Jane was as startled as I, whose career as 18th-Century novelist (like my career as 20th-) died a-borning. When we got the man off his knees and back into English—which he spoke now as rapidly as his pro-totype—we learned to our dismay that while his madness made him confuse me with Germaine Pitt, a dear this-worldly friend of his whose husband had been an even dearer friend of Jane's, he was unspeakably happy to be reunited with his precious. . .Lady Pembroke! Had we known then what I took the first opportunity to learn from the royal library and apprised Jane of forthwith, we'd have been even more dismayed: Lady Elizabeth Spencer, Countess of Pembroke, had been Queen Charlotte's Lady of the Bedchamber; her husband the count was George III's lord of the same and son of his Vice-Chamberlain of the Household. Originally a Marlborough, she and the king had been childhood sweethearts, and she had remained close to the royal family ever after, though she was never among the king's few mistresses (like Harrison, George was disinclined to adultery) and was a faithful attendant of the queen. But during the attack of 1788—by when she was past fifty, and a grandmother—even more so in his subsequent seizures, George persuaded himself that he had always loved her, and her only. . .

Harrison got hold of himself soon enough to be unembarrassing, even charming, through aperitifs and dinner, when he pleasantly set forth to "Jane" and "Germaine" what Charlotte and Eliza already knew: the biographical facts above, minus his obsession. He condoled more genuinely than Jane the death of my Jeffrey; he recounted in amusing circumstantial detail anecdotes of Capri in the late 1930's and of Cheltenham in the 1780's, and complained good-humoredly of the side effects equally of *Tincture Thebaicum* (prescribed by Dr Sir George Baker against the wishes of Dr Willis) and of Parnate (prescribed by Shrink #1 against the wishes of Shrink #2). He respectfully disagreed with Dr Alan Guttmacher of Pikesville, Maryland—an acquaintance of the family and author of *America's Last King*—that "it is the total absence of pathological abnormal ideas that distinguishes the healthy from the morbid mind": a question-begging definition, in Harrison's view, though he was surely not claiming his own mind to be healthy. And he could not but wonder whether Guttmacher's own psychoanalytical thesis—"George III feared that, like the Colonies, his thirteen children would revolt and break away from him one by one"—would not have been adjudged pathological by the royal physicians: not because he Harrison had only two children (and was certain of the paternity of but one of those, he added meaningly), but because his thirteen American colonies had broken away all together, not one by one, and because by his own best insight his troubling identification had not been loss of colonies with loss of children, but loss of colonies with loss of *college: i.e.,* the "loss" of Tidewater Tech to the state university system a year since, from which his most conspicuous mania dated. He went on to praise "Jane's" business sense, beauty, and patience (she hadn't batted a cool blue eye at that reference to uncertain paternity; but it seemed to me she was not so much patient as invulnerable even to comprehension of such allusions); then he rewelcomed me to Windsor with another toast in fluent and rapid Latin, which he reported later to have been to the health *"conjugis meae dilectissimae Elizabethae: praeteritas futuras fecundarant."*

Within the fortnight it took me to find decent lodgings in Cambridge, the alarming depths of Harrison's obsession with me— rather, his new obsession with George III's old obsession with Lady Pembroke—became clear, as did its complexity. In his most lucid moments (from our point of view), for example, he would tenderly explain that "Harrison Mack's" attraction to "Germaine Pitt" had no doubt been occasioned by His Majesty's mad passion for Elizabeth Spencer, but that he had been secretly fond of me ever since Capri, and I was not to imagine that he did not love the hallucinated "Lady Amherst" in her own right. I urged Jane to permit me to break off all contact with him; she assured me that his madness was too complete, as was her preoccupation with Mack Enterprises, for his ravings *(sic)* to bother her at all; if they made *me* uncomfortable, I should do as I saw fit. Accordingly, I busied myself at the college, making ready for the fall semester and confirming, with sinking heart, how far from Toronto— not to mention London and Paris!—I had come.

Marshyhope's library was a bad joke; its faculty would not have been hired by a good private high school; its students would be drawn from the regional public ones. . . I reminded myself that I had not come there to further my professional career, and that the Library of Congress was a mere two hours away by bus; and I consoled myself with the one bright feature of the intellectual landscape, Joe Morgan, a man I quite admired and could easily have more than admired had he shown the slightest personal interest in me. The fellow of that name in your *End of the Road* was a rationalist Pygmalion, a half-caricature, sympathetic only by contrast with the narrator; if he was the prototype of my new employer, time and bereavement had much improved him. President Morgan was intelligent, learned, and intense, but not obsessive. He took his administrative duties seriously and discharged them efficiently, but he was in no way officious or self-important. Roughly my coeval, handsomer now than when I'd met him five years since, he was as alone and isolated on Redmans Neck as I. One might have imagined. . .

But hospitable as he certainly was, cordial, sympathetic, free of "hang-ups," as the children say, and neither unmasculine nor cold of manner, his emotional life remains a closed book to me: either he was without physical desires, or he gratified them with such utter discretion that even his enemies could find no ground for innuendo in that line. I wonder, as I write, where Morgan is now; whether his disappearance from Amherst College has anything to do with the failure of some exquisite self-control he had not even suspected himself of having tightly exercised for a dozen years, since his young wife's death from an experience I am too familiar with!

Well. He was wearily amused at Harrison's delusion that he Morgan had betrayed Tidewater Tech into the state university system; he explained to me (what I set forth in the postscript of my first vain letter to you) his worthy ambitions for the place and his confidence that, unless Schott and company carried the day, Marshyhope could become, not just another third-rate community college, but a quite special and admirable research centre. But (unlike the priggish fellow in your novel) Morgan had what amounted to a tragic, if not an altogether pessimistic, view of his aspirations: he would not be surprised, he told me, if Harrison's association of Marshyhope with the mutinous American colonies had been inspired and encouraged by A. B. Cook, in John Schott's behalf. Nor was he very sanguine of prevailing against them in the matter of the Tower of Truth. But he was not certain of defeat, either, and on that basis (I have not even mentioned his quite Jeffersonian respect for the net good judgement of ordinary people) he proceeded.

Half jokingly he suggested that I exploit in the college's behalf my new rôle as Lady Pembroke. So the "Duke of York," without especially intending to, had done: Morgan showed me the just completed and as yet unstaffed media centre, remarking with a smile that state legislators were ever readier to subsidize an impressive physical plant than an impressive faculty. Had I met Reg Prinz?

214

In early November I finally did. To spare myself (and, as I imagined, Jane) Harrison's displays, I'd used my opening-of-semester business to excuse myself from visiting Tidewater Farms except rarely, despite Jane's urgings. His fixation on "Lady Pembroke" was un-diminished, she reported: he had annulled by royal decree all mar-riages contracted before 1 August 1811, and vowed to become a Lutheran in order to marry me; he swore repeatedly on the Bible to be faithful to his dear Eliza, who had been faithful to him for fifty-five years; he proposed to establish a female equivalent of the Order of the Garter, whereof I was to be the first elect; he nightly imagined me in his bed, and daily threatened to come for me in the royal yacht, crying *"Rex populo non separandus!"* when his male nurses (whose attendance was now required) restrained him. She found it hard to imagine that my actual waiting on him would make matters worse, and rather imagined it might temper his fantasies, which were truly becoming difficult for her to live with: so much so that, since she could not bring herself to have him "committed" (and since he had better residential care at Tidewater Farms than any institutional facility could provide), she had taken to spending more and more of her own nights at an apartment in Dorset Heights, and was contemplating an extended business-vacation trip to Britain.

It was true that in my presence Harrison behaved agreeably, spoke temperately and rationally more often than not, and made no amorous overtures. Even so. . . And I *did* have other things on my mind, including André's business (of which nothing so far had come) and the approach of a certain fateful anniversary. For this last reason especially, I was disinclined to accept Jane's invitation to dinner on the first Sunday in November, until she added not only that it was to be by way of being a *bon voyage* party for herself, who was indeed off to London for a while, but also that the annual Guy Fawkes Day fireworks would be let off at Redmans Neck after dinner, courtesy of the Tidewater Foundation, and that a number of their particular friends would be there, including Messrs Andrews from Cambridge and Prinz from New York, whom she believed I had not met, and Mr Cook from Annapolis, whom she understood I had?

I went, trembling. Harrison was all charm and gallantry, and so apparently the master of his mania that one could easily have taken the George-and-Eliza business as a standing pleasantry for the occasion. Your Mr Andrews too proved a civilised surprise: a handsome, elderly bachelor, he held forth amusingly on the C.I.A.'s three-million-dollar involvement in the National Student Association, recently disclosed, and chided Drew Mack *(in absentia)* for not making our local chapter of the S.D.S. menacing enough to attract some of that money to Marshy-hope. In other circumstances I'd have taken less distracted pleasure in meeting him: it pleased me, for example, that he freely broke Jane's prohibition, "for Harrison's sake," of our mentioning their son "the

Prince of Wales," and that Harrison seemed unperturbed thereby; for I was disinclined myself to walk on eggs with his eccentricities as did Jane (and Doctor #2). But of course it was Andrew Burlingame Cook whom I had come there tremulously to inspect, whose reintroduction to me, on that date of all dates, it was impossible to ascribe to coincidence. . .

John: the man cannot be André Castine. How could he be André? André is heavyset, swarthy, brown-eyed, bald, trimly moustached and short-bearded; he wears eyeglasses, can't see without them, and partial dentures, of which he is self-conscious—and his accent is French-Canadian in all of his several languages. The "Poet Laureate" is of similar build, but his hair is thick, curly, salt-and-pepper-coloured, his eyes are hazel, he wears neither beard nor moustache nor spectacles, his teeth are his own and boldly gleaming, and while his voice admittedly has something of André's sexual baritone, his accent is as *echt* "Mairlund" as Todd Andrews's. He is not André!

Nor is he, by his own assertion, André's half brother, though it could be held that they resemble each other as siblings might. Indeed, when I pressed him on that head (immediately upon remeeting him; he had not forgotten our previous encounter), he denied ever having heard the name Castine except in the history books and the "Student's Second Tale" in Longfellow's *Tales of a Wayside Inn.* He had a grown son, he acknowledged, by his late wife—who like himself had worked with the U.S. Office of War Information in London during World War II, and who (like Jeffrey's first wife!) had been killed in an air raid there in '42. The boy's name was Henry Burlingame VII, sure enough— Henry Burlingame *Cook,* legally, but it had been the unofficial custom of the family for generations to alternate the surnames of their two chief progenitors. . . He was a dandy fellow, Henry, but completely wrongheaded in the political sphere, thanks in some measure to the influence of such Commie acquaintances as Drew Mack and Joseph Morgan. Presently he was in Quebec somewhere, inciting the Canucks against queen and country, God forgive him and save all three. For he was a good lad at heart, was son Henry, and believe it or not he Cook himself had undergone a brief attack of Whiggery in his twenties— from which he had recovered with such antibodies as to have been spared the least twinge of recurrence, he was happy to report. He greatly feared (this after dinner now, as we sipped cognac and watched skyrockets from the terrace in the mild autumn night, through which sailed also incredible hosts of wild geese, chorusing south from where I wished I were) I was the butt of some silly practical joke, and expressed chivalrous indignation that "a lady of my quality" should be so used.

He was, well, charming: not at all the blustering boor of the Maryland Historical Society—except (and here too he is at least in spirit my André's kin) in the company of "adversaries" such as Morgan, who joined us after dinner, or when the conversation turned to politics. Then he became the loud Poetaster Laureate of the Right: encouraged Harrison's conviction that the Russian embassy had not leased waterfront acreage in Dorchester County merely for the summer recreation of their staff, as they claimed, but to spy on Mack Enterprises and "other operations in the area." (Nonsense, Jane crisply replied, they *were* a Mack enterprise: she had leased them the land herself.) He declared to His Majesty that Schott's proposed Tower of Truth would make Marshyhope "independent enough to secede from the state system"—a loaded illogic that Harrison good-naturedly reproved him for. And I could not judge, much as I needed to, how seriously he took his professed Toryism—but I believed Joe Morgan's grim reply (since borne out) when I asked him that question: "Only half seriously, Germaine. But he would destroy us half seriously, too."

So. The only unattached lady among so many charming, unattached gentlemen, and too unfortunately distracted to enjoy their gallantries. Or properly to acquaint myself with the youngest member of our company, the most *det*ached certainly, if not unattached, who hovered in the margins of the evening as of this letter. "And I believe you've not met Mr Prinz," Jane said at the end of our cocktail introductions, as I attempted dazedly to measure A. B. Cook against André's depiction. In the following year, last year, when I found myself de facto mistress of Tidewater Farms, playing "Esther" to Harrison's "Ahasuerus" (his conceit, after one of George III's) whilst "Queen Vashti" refreshed herself at the *real* Bath and Cheltenham, I had occasion to re-view Reg Prinz—else I'd be unable to describe him now, so distraught was I and evanescent he that November evening. The "son [Harrison] should have had" is at the end of his twenties, lean, slight, light-skinned, freckled, pale-eyed, sharp-faced. He wears round wire-rimmed spectacles like Bertolt Brecht's and a bush of red hair teased out as if in ongoing electrocution. His chin and lips are hairless. No hippie he, his clothes are rumpled but clean, plain, even severe: in Ambrose's phrase, he dresses like a minor member of the North Korean U.N. delegation, or a long-term convict just released with the warden's good wishes and a new suit of street clothes. He neither smokes nor drinks nor, so far as I could hear, speaks. It is said that he comes from a wealthy Long Island Jewish family and was educated at Groton and Yale. It is said that he "trips" regularly on lysergic acid diethylamide and other pharmaceuticals, but deplores the ascription to them of mystic insight or creative vision in their users. It is said that he is a brilliant actor and director; that he has absorbed and put behind him all the ideology of contemporary filmmaking, along with radical politics (he thinks Drew Mack naive, we're told, but is "interested" in Harrison and A. B. Cook as "emblems," and "admires" Henry Burlingame VII) and literature, which he is reputed to have called "a mildly interesting historical phenomenon of no present importance." One hears that he is scornful of esoteric, high-art cinema as unfaithful to the medium's popular roots, which however bore him. Political revolutions, he is said to have said, are passé, "like marriage, divorce, families, professions, novels, cash, existential *Angst.*"

217

Do not ask me where, when, or to whom the young man has delivered himself of these opinions, most of which I have at at least second hand from Ambrose. I have indeed, on occasion since, heard him speak, in a voice almost inaudible and invariably in ellipses, shrugs, nods, fragments, hums, non sequiturs, dashes, and suspension points. Ambrose declares that his immediate presence (I must add "except at formal Guy Fawkes Day dinner parties") is uncommonly compelling; that in it most "issues" and "positions" seem idly theoretical, or simply don't come up however much one had meant to raise them; that the most outrageous situations are acquiesced in and seem justified by "the wordless force of his personality." I deny none of the above—though I suspect my lover of some projection!—and I do indeed find Prinz a quietly disquieting, inarticulately insistent fellow: a sort of saxifrage in the cracks of the contemporary, or (to borrow one of Ambrose's tidewater tropes) a starfish on the oyster bed of art. But one wonders—*this one,* anyroad—whether that vague antiverbality proceeds from (I had almost said *bespeaks)* a mindless will or a mere vacuum; whether the man be not, after all, all surface: a clouded transparency, a. . . film.

If the last, I'd have graded him B at best that November evening, which we are now done with. Today—I don't know. I left Tidewater Farms no wiser than I'd arrived, but sorely troubled. To Joe Morgan and Todd Andrews, of course, I could say nothing of my deepest concerns; but in the car back to Cambridge from Redmans Neck (Morgan kindly returned us to our addresses) I learned that while my two pleasant bachelor companions agreed that A. B. Cook was an enigma and a charlatan, more subtle and sophisticated than the rôle he played with Schott and Company, they did not (then) agree on what if anything underlay the oafish masquerade. Andrews was inclined to think him a wealthy, eccentric, heartfelt reactionary whose support (both financial and poetical) of certain Dixiecrat politicians was legitimate if lamentable; whose friendships with Harrison and other civilised right-wingers were genuine, his relations with vulgar red-necks like Schott merely expedient. And his duplicity, in Todd Andrews's opinion, was probably limited to loudly supporting in the crudest fashion a famously conservative gubernatorial candidate so that a lesser-known but even *more* conservative could run against him on what pretended to be a liberal platform, and the Tories win in either case. The rest, he declared—Cook's rumoured paramilitary "club" on or near Bloodsworth Island, his rumoured connexion with the Baltimore chapter of the American Nazi party (all news to me)—was mere liberal-baiting panache.

Morgan disagreed. Through his activities with the historical society he'd had frequent dealings with Cook, who'd been the first to propose him to Harrison Mack for the presidency of Tidewater Tech, as he'd been the first subsequently to propose his resignation from Marshyhope in favour of Schott. Quite apart from any grudge against the man for whatever harm he might do the college (it is a mark of Morgan's tact that he didn't mention Cook's slanderous resurrection, so to speak, of his late wife's death), Morgan believed him genuinely menacing and perhaps psychopathological. What's more, he believed there might be some truth in a body of rumour that was news to Mr Andrews as well as to me: that Cook was *literally* sinister, a threat not from the right but from the left! On this view, his public connexion with right-wing extremists was for the purpose of sabotaging their activities with ostensibly favourable publicity and establishing a creditable "cover" for his real connexions with—not the Far Left, exactly, but a grab bag of terrorists: the F.L.N., the I.R.A., the P.L.O., the Quebec separatists, the farther-out black and Indian nationalists—all of whom, of course, had operatives in Washington.

"Once, ten years ago," Morgan told us matter-of-factly, "when I first got to know him, Cook offered to arrange a murder for me. Said it was the easiest thing in the world. I didn't take him up on it, but I didn't have the impression he was boasting, either."

We didn't press; perhaps Andrews, like me, wondered uncomfortably whether the victim was to have been the late Mrs Morgan or someone involved in her death. Given the whispering campaign against him, Morgan's remark seemed ill-considered—but I took it as a mark of his trust, and was in any case more interested in Cook's possible connexions with André, perhaps via the Free-Quebec people. And Morgan was so healthy-looking, so cheerfully normal, even boyish of face, it was impossible to imagine him involved in anything clandestine, much less violent. Todd Andrews dismissed the whole "Second Revolution business"—which he assumed was what the rumoured leftism added up to—as another of Cook's cranky red herrings, and wished only that he wouldn't feed Harrison's folly with it. Morgan agreed that it might well be mere crankery, but considered it dangerous crankery withal. And so the evening ended, Andrews remarking as he bade me good night that in his opinion my own unexpected rôle in his friend's delusion was more therapeutic, at least palliative, than not. He hoped I would indulge poor Harrison as far as my discretion permitted.

Given two so agreeable alternative candidates, why did I, a month or two later, become Harrison Mack's mistress? To begin with, after Fort Erie I had resolved, as I've explained, to try to put André behind me, for the sake of my own sanity, though of course etc. And I have never been given to celibacy! Had either Andrews or Morgan shown particular interest—but they didn't. Morgan was perhaps the likelier possibility, though rather young for my taste (*i.e.*, about my own age); but before we came to know each other well enough for me to tell him about André, for example, and explain his relationship to Cook, Morgan had resigned, gone to Amherst, "freaked out," and disappeared. Andrews I found (and find) attractive too, despite the Eastern Shore brogue and Southern manner; we became and remain affectionate friends. But though a confirmed bachelor, he has, I gather, other, more established female friendships, and in his late sixties is no libertine.

With his urging joined to Jane's and Doctor #2's, I spent much time at Tidewater Farms after Jane left, when too Harrison's manner somewhat altered. As his general condition rapidly declined, he grew at once madder and more lucid. The wife he'd had "when he was in the world," as he came to phrase it, he pitied, admired, and understood well, in my estimation; he hoped "the *real* George III" had been as fortunate, on balance, with Queen Charlotte. He was glad Jane was not present in his "final stages," for both their sakes; they had loved each other, he was certain she still wished him well, as he did her, and he had no doubt that widowhood would be a relief for her. He knew now, more often than not, that he wasn't "really" George III—"any more than George III was, in his last years": that he was the victim of a psychopathological delusion, whose cause and possible cure remained mysterious and were of no further interest to him. The world of Harrison Mack, Redmans Neck, 20th-Century America, caused him great pain; the world of George III, Windsor, early 19th-Century England, was somehow soothing, never mind wherefore. An inoperable patient, he craved now only palliation. With Jane's long-distance consent we discharged Doctor #1, and left #2 on call merely in the event of some unforeseen lapse of control. He was summoned only once thereafter.

Harrison begged me to move into the house: it was convenient to the campus; it was big enough so that I need endure his company no more than I wished; his own library was as good as the college's; I wouldn't need to bother with marketing, cooking, housekeeping. Even the masquerade would not be very tiresome (no costumes required!), since we could freely discuss anything so long as he could speak of me as Lady Pembroke: I could leave it to him, as *he* left it to his madness, to do the complicated translation. From London, Jane seconded the motion. I consulted Andrews, who warmly approved.

If I never loved His Majesty, I truly liked him, and never simply pitied him. I meant to move out as soon as Jane returned, but she stayed on, somehow managing Mack Enterprises by remote control. In the first half of '68, especially, Harrison was a delightful companion: witty, generous, thoughtful. In my absence, so the house staff reported, he gave free rein to his follies: that we must fly to Denmark to escape the deluge; that we were aboard Noah's ark; that it was not too late to undo the fiasco of the American War. Directly I returned, the George/Elizabeth business became little more than an elaborate (if unremitting) way of speaking. Somewhere along the road our good friendship came to include sleeping together: my memory is that one snowy night in January, as I read student essays and sipped brandy by the fire and Harrison played Jephthah's lamentation on the harpsichord, he suddenly said: "Let's redo history, what?" And then proposed that, since the king and Lady Pembroke never did get to bed together, and since we weren't *really* they, we improve the facts by doing what they didn't.

"Dear Germaine," he concluded, "I should enjoy that very much." Had he not used, that once, my real name. . .

My person and modest competency never so gratified a man, before or since. You will want details: there are none, particularly. Seventy is not impotent, except as alcohol, illness, or social conditioning have made it so; it has no stamina, loves its sleep, will not stand without coaxing, draws aim more often than it fires—but it *will* go to't, smartly too, with the keener joy in what it can no longer take for granted. Harrison relished each connexion as he relished fine days and dinners, knowing he had not a great many left. Jane had put sex behind her years since; the chap was starved for it, and knew what he was about. I have made sorry choices in my life: becoming Harrison's Lady Elizabeth was not one. A pleasurable semester.

During the which, whilst I waited word from André or a fair glimpse of our son, and endeavoured to impart to my Marshyhopers some sense of what is meant by the terms *Renaissance, Reformation, Enlightenment, Romanticism* (but how, when almost nothing their eyes fall upon was there the day before yesterday?), and watched poor embattled Morgan yield at last on the misbegotten Tower of Truth, and confirmed my addiction to oysters in any form, I tried in vain to mend the old quarrel between Harrison and his son, whom I came to know and rather like. (The daughter Jeannine—"Bea Golden"—was another matter: between drying-out visits to that Fort Erie "sanatorium," she was busy divorcing her third husband out in California and—what we didn't know at this time—attaching herself to Mr Prinz.) On this subject my friend was truly deluded: he believed his son an unprincipled weakling and Reg Prinz, for some reason or other, a scrupulous fellow, when from all I could observe Drew Mack was, if somewhat gullible, the very soul of moral principle, pursuing ardently what he believed just and good, whereas Prinz (whom too I saw once or twice more that year) has I daresay no principles at all except cinematographic, and even those he seems to improvise on the run. Suffice it as illustration of their scrupulosity that Drew—who had no salary, worked without pay for his liberal causes (to which he also donated his trust income), and frankly coveted his parents' wealth for the sake of these same causes—never to my knowledge imputed mercenary motives to my liaison with his father, whom he was gratified to see so happy in my society. Whereas Prinz, in a rare burst of sustained verbality, advised me one evening in June, just after Harrison's great seizure: "If he leaves you a bundle, put it into the flick. Double or nothing."

I had thought to travel that season; north from the Chesapeake at least, whose muggy summer nights I had sampled in September. Perhaps to France, to visit "Juliette." But word came from Jane, of the most unexpected and circumlocutory sort, that "interests of a personal nature" were holding her in Britain; apprised that her husband of some forty years had taken a turn for the worse, she satisfied herself by transatlantic telephone that he was not dangerous or dying, authorised me and Doctor #2 to take whatever measures we thought necessary to provide for his comfort, hoped we would inform her at once of any crises, and begged me to stay on at Tidewater Farms at least for the summer "in my supervisory capacity," at a salary of, say, $500 a month "over and above"!

I declined the salary for myself, looked about for someone else to hire with it, found no one even remotely suitable except Yvonne Mack, Drew's wife, who refused unless her father-in-law, "crazy or not," recanted his racism and fully reinstated his son and herself in his favour. Alas, Harrison was beyond doing so. To him she was the cast-off Princess of Wales, "hot for the king's John Thomas, what?" No lucid side to his hallucinating now: Harrison believed us seventeen years old and immortal; he declared he'd raised his daughter Amelia from the grave (and conversed touchingly with the ghosts of Drew and Jeannine Mack when they were babies); he dressed in white robes and let his beard grow. He took his bed to be "the Royal Celestial Electrical Bed of Patagonia in the Temple of Health and Hymen on Pall Mall," and guaranteed me a healthy child if I would make love with him in it. Dr #2 (whom I fetched in, who could do nothing) became "Dr James Graham, M.D., O.W.L." (O Wonderful Love), the inventor of that same bed, a Scottish quack who claimed to have learnt electricity from Ben Franklin and herbal medicine from the Indians; "George III the First" had declined his offer of treatment in 1788, but by charging £50 a night for the use of his famous bed and attracting to his temple such worthies as the Scotts of Edinburgh (who brought young Walter there in vain hope of restoring his withered leg), the good doctor had earned almost as much as our #2. I declined: he seldom knew me now even as Elizabeth.

I "supervised" Harrison through the fall—no labour, only a sadness—when too, after Morgan's departure, I assumed the real labour of the acting provostship at Marshyhope. This for the reasons set forth in my first letter, plus one other, which you will now understand: unbelievably, on Guy Fawkes Day, beyond Hubert Humphrey's defeat by Richard Nixon. . .nothing happened! I had scarcely doubted that this was the date André had waited for; was cross in advance with his damned rituality. Schott had won the field at Redmans Neck; had already made his unexpected offer (perhaps at Cook's inscrutable prompting?), and I'd asked for a week to consider it—actually to learn whether André wanted me elsewhere. I had no other invitations or income. Lyndon Johnson had vacated the presidency, Robert Kennedy and Martin King had been assassinated, the Democratic convention in Chicago disrupted; the Left was everywhere in disarray; it was past time for André to make whatever grand moves he had in mind. We'd even cancelled our fireworks (Harrison no longer followed the calendar anyroad), lest they be mistaken for a premature

Republican celebration on the one hand or an armed student rising on the other. I sat up past midnight with the dreary election returns on the telly, waiting for the phone, the doorbell, a special-delivery letter at the least—His Majesty beside me clucking his tongue at what his mutinous colonies had come to.

Nothing! In a state of mild shock I accepted Schott's "promotion"; prepared to stay on, out of dull necessity, where I had no wish nor other reason to be; notified Jane that I would be moving out of Tidewater Farms before the spring semester in any case, as Harrison needed his Lady Pembroke no longer, only his trained nurses (he was making his own floods by this time, in the Royal Celestial Electrical Bed of Patagonia—and, yes, ordering his feces freeze-dried by Mack Enterprises, to "fertilise the hereafter"). On 14 January—anniversary for me of Germaine Necker's marriage to the Baron de Staël in 1786; for Harrison, of Congress's ratification of the Treaty of Paris two years earlier—he suffered the stroke that blinded and half paralyzed him. Jane flew home; I withdrew to the flat I'd scarcely tenanted since hiring it. A fortnight later the second stroke killed him.

Among the mourners at my friend's funeral were Prinz—whose mistress Jeannine Mack now openly was—and Ambrose, already engaged by him to write the screenplay from your fiction. Have I told you that Harrison never knew it was a story of yours that Prinz meant to film? (The foundation's subsidy was for an unspecified film project set in the tidewater locale.) That he lent his support to a medium whose novelty he disliked, only when Prinz assured him that the film would "revise the American Revolution" and "return toward the visual purity of silent movies"? (George III was very big on purity in his latter days.) I myself was at the time unaware of and uninterested in the nature of his and Ambrose's project, and cannot tell you whether Harrison and Jane ever read the novel in which you feature them: Tood Andrews has done, and seems to hold no grudge. He, Jane, Drew, Yvonne, Ms Golden, and John Schott were there, others I didn't know. . .and A. B. Cook. . .and with him an impassive, reticent young man whom he introduced as his son Henry Burlingame.

I don't know, John. He seemed about the right age. He could be said to resemble either Cook or André or me at least as much as "Bea Golden" resembles Harrison or Jane (or Todd Andrews). He spoke—when at all—with a slight Québécois accent, but spelled his name with a *y* and made no reply to Cook's stage-whispered tease that the accent was affected. In the same mock whisper Cook declared to me that he'd asked his son on my behalf about the impostor I'd mentioned at our last meeting—that chap who claimed to be a relative? And that Henry had denied having ever heard the name Castine except, like himself, in the annals of colonial America. But who knew whether to believe a cunning rogue like his son? And he supposed we oughtn't to mention colonial America in the house of the late lamented, what?

So I don't know. If Cook had whipped off a wig, changed teeth and voice, donned eyeglasses, declared *himself* André Castine, and proposed marriage on the spot, I still wouldn't know, wouldn't have known (though I'd no doubt have said yes).

Will you believe that whilst I waited for a sign from heaven, tried to hold onto what reason remained to me after so long, so much, so many—half of my belongings still upstairs in Jane's house!—I traded polite condolences with the company, approved the gentle ironies in Todd Andrews's eulogy (a gloss on the motto of the college: *Praeteritas futuras fecundant,* "The past fertilises the future"), made sarcastic quips with Ambrose about Cook's funeral ode, and said *nothing* to the young man whom perhaps I carried in my womb for nine months and five thousand miles, brought into the world, have scarcely seen since (and have *not* seen since)? I. . .had not the strength, *have* not, to beard the lion (and eyeglass him, etc.) in his den; to lay siege to Annapolis, Bloodsworth Island, Castines Hundred; to press, press until no mysteries remain. Because. . .what then? I had abandoned the boy-child; what claim had I on the man?

Ambrose, till then an affable colleague merely, saw me home and did me some services after at Tidewater Farms; our closer connexion dates from there. Clearly André has abandoned me for good. I am endeavouring to make it so: for good. This confession—whose readiness you now understand, whose prolixity you pardon, as I trust you now understand (no pardon called for) my susceptibility to the blandishments of Ambrose Mensch—this confession is the epilogue to the story, finally done. When I report to you that my "love" (oh bother the quotation marks!) for your erstwhile friend, especially since this chaste Third Stage of our affair commenced, grows *determinedly,* you will know what I mean. My whole romantic life, I am trying to persuade myself, has, like the body of this letter, been digression and recapitulation; it is time to rearrive at the present, to move into a future unsullied by the past.

It is time, most certainly, to end this endlessest of my letters (I've long since been back at 24 L; all's apparently calm at Marshyhope; I am alone; it's near midnight). But now the history is done, I must finish the tale of Prinz and Mensch it interrupted. After Prinz's two-word rejection—"too wordy"—of Ambrose's nearly wordless draft of the screenplay opening, it was decided between them (with your approval, I hope and presume) that since the text in hand was in itself essentially noncinematic, they would, if not quite set it aside altogether, use it merely as a *point de départ* for a "visual orchestration of the author's *Weltanschauung"*: Ambrose's deadpan phrase, in his explanation last night to the Marshyhopers of the sequence they were about to appear in. They will therefore freely include not only "echoes of your other works" and (don't ask me) "anticipations of your works in progress and to come"—things you may not even have *thought* of yet, but "feasibly might, on the basis of etc."—but anything *Ambrose* might think suitable in his new capacity—you're aware that he's an actor in his own script

224

now, hired to play the rôle of Author?—or Prinz in his double aspect of director and, as it were, Muse. (He too is on both sides of the camera!) Still myself only halfway through your *Sot-Weed Factor* novel, for all I know to the contrary there may be in your works yet for me to read a Rip Winklish narrator who lives the first half of his life in the years 1776–1812 and the second half from 1940 to 1976, with a long sleep between in the Dorchester marshes. Or is he among those "anticipations"?

In any case, I know for a fact that what ensued was their improvisation. This anonymous or polynomial narrator—Ambrose, half jestingly, calls him by his own nom de plume, "Arthur Morton King"—in his movement from the First through the Second Cycle of his life (it is not clear, to me, whether in 1969 he is 29 or 65 years old), comes upon the student activists preparing to seize the administration building of a college built on what he remembers to have been an Indian burial ground, a Loyalist hideout in the Revolutionary War, and the site of a minor skirmish with Admiral Cockburn's fleet in the War of 1812. Stirred but puzzled by the youthful call to arms (as I am puzzled by his puzzlement: is he not alleged to have been awake since 1940?), "Arthur" would join the students, but first asks them to explain who "our" enemy is, and what we mean to do with the college after we seize it. He insists likewise on hearing out the spokesmen for the administration. . .

It would not have worked at Berkeley or Buffalo; not even at College Park across the Bay. To give my pink-necks their due, it would not likely have worked here either, had Drew Mack been on campus, and had Ambrose not further disarmed the skeptical by instructing them to be skeptical; to suspect him of being planted by the F.B.I., or the C.I.A., or at least the administration; and to hoot down any attempt by Todd Andrews (who volunteered to act as the acting president's spokesman) to reply to their harangues. But the chief strategy— Ambrose's, not Prinz's, who somehow made it clear to the students that he didn't care one way or the other how the scene ended—was the grand diversion of cameraman, audio and lighting technicians and equipment, interruptions to reposition, rephotograph, rerecord, reconsider; Prinz's vertiginous insistence that these repositionings and such be themselves photographed, not to falsify "on the ultimate level, you know" the *cinéma vérité;* Ambrose's sudden inspired order to a young woman shouting obscenities, "Now! Now! Take off your clothes!" and to a dazed campus cop, "Now you pretend to arrest her!" and to the students who then pummelled the cop, "Cut! Cut! That's great! Let the camera close in on her now!" Whilst Prinz hand-signalled quite different instructions to his crew, and the second camera filmed him so doing. "Now you decide we're co-opting you!" cries Ambrose. "Somebody ask whether there's even any film in the fucking cameras! Easy, those mothers are expensive. Now you chant *'Off the media! Off the media!'* while we retreat! Tomorrow in Ocean City, south end of the boardwalk, got that? South boardwalk, by the funhouse! *'Off the flicks! Off the flicks!'"*

Et cetera, until half the kids are laughing, most of the rest too confused to get their indignation organised, and the handful who try to storm Schott's office easily stopped in the corridors, out of view, by the main body of campus police, who then usher them out a rear door, lock the building for the night, and patrol its vicinity till today.

When, I daresay—tomorrow too if the weather holds fine—my lover, the author turned actor, will have improvised, may be even now improvising, "the Funhouse Scene" at Ocean City, with his nondirective director, his cast of ex-activist amateurs, and his professional (if not expert) co-star. . .

But here my pen falters, and not only from writer's cramp. A tiny—yes, *jealousy*—keeps me from sleep, though it's now the first hour of, ah, the 11th. Of that painful American invention, Mother's Day. I return now, for comfort and solace, to your hapless virgin poet Eben Cooke and his too-familiar mentor Henry Burlingame III, wearily wondering whether your novel is not some enormous coded reply-in-advance to these letters. What turns lie ahead in its plot? In mine? What have you in store for your exhausted

G.?

M: *Lady Amherst to the Author. Three miracles in three days. Ambrose's adventures with the film company. The Fourth Stage of their affair begins.*

24 L Street
Dorset Heights, Maryland 21612
Saturday, 17 May 1969

Dear J.,

Mirabile, mirabile, mirabile dictu! Three miracles in three days! The plot of our lives as turned and returned as a baroque novel's!

1. Mr A. B. Cook VI—to the entire astonishment of our ad hoc nominating committee and the great but discreetly concealed delight of two-thirds of its membership (*i.e.,* myself and Ms Wright of the French Dept: a far cry from dear "Juliette," but worlds away withal from Harry Carter: "Mr Wrong")—thanked us by letter three days ago for the honour of our invitation. . .and declined!

Declined, John! Oh, that I were after all a writer, or had had Reggie Prinz's cameras, to catch forever Harry Carter's crestfall when I read that letter aloud! Which he must then inspect with his own eyes, hold to the light, examine the blank verso of, the signature, the return address, the postmark and cancelled stamp on the envelope (CHAUTAUGUA MD, spelled with a *g* where yours is *q*'d; and an American Legion commemorative), as if looking for some clue that the laureate's no was a

226

cyphered yes, or that I'd forged the letter. Ms Wright at last crisply opined that, given the lateness of the season, we had better propose Mr Mensch's name at once to President Schott, and hope our colleague would not follow your and Cook's example.

A fortnight earlier, at the crest of our "Second Stage," I'd have blushed, if not dismissed the idea outright. But Ambrose and I had been that fortnight sexless, as you know, and while my heart had in large measure taken over from my orifices the labour of his admission and receipt, so that now I loved where then I'd merely lusted, the complete propriety of this "Third Stage" lent me sufficient "cool," as the students say, to pretend to consider the matter for some moments before seconding his nomination. Ambrose *had* been of considerable assistance in containing the late demonstrations, and his presence on the platform might just discourage the activists' turning our commencement exercises into yet another, as has been happening elsewhere. The modesty of his literary credentials is attributable in some part to his avant-gardism: "concrete narrative" is not poured out ready-mixed by the cubic yard! And if I myself remain less than utterly convinced that such desperate innovation as his is "the last, radical hope for the profession of letters," I can in good conscience at least honour that apocalyptic argument.

I called for the question: two-nothing in Ambrose's favour, Harry Carter abstaining in the spirit of a diplomatic emissary awaiting instructions from his government. Considering the date, I proposed we ring up at once both Mensch and Schott to insure their informal agreement before sending our formal invitations. Carter telephoned our acting president (to whom, a subscript apprised us, Cook had sent a copy of his letter); I telephoned Ambrose at the Lighthouse—a.k.a. Mensch's Castle, his brother's house—and heard for the first time, with a proper pang of jealousy, the voice of Magda Giulianova Mensch. Did it catch at the accent of my own, which she too was hearing for the first time and must surely recognise?

"I'll call him," she huskily intoned. What a vulnerable, what a stirring, what a *sexual* voice! Which then called, "Ambrose? Telephone," up some nearby flight of stairs which I had yet myself to see, but which *l'Abruzzesa* had doubtless many times ascended, crooning *Ambrose?* in even sultrier tone. I heard children's voices in the background—no, one child's voice, his backward daughter's, to be sure; *her* normal twins would be at school, or at work. I was smitten with envy, jealousy, rekindled desire—the objective, no doubt, of our Third Stage abstinence. When she said, "He's coming"—her voice as throaty as if *she* were—my "Thank you" was gruff and mannish as John Bull. And when Ambrose, fetched from his writing desk, dully hello'd me, I found myself declaring despite myself, for the first time to him, and in a lump-throated whisper, not "acting Provost Pitt here," but "I love you."

! (As my lover would put it in his own style of dialogue.) Fortunately I had withdrawn from the conference room to my inner

227

office to make the call; Carter to Ms Wright's, hard by, to make his (Miss Stickles, who would normally have placed both, was out to lunch). When we reconvened, we were both somewhat disappointed: Carter because Schott now warmly ratified our nomination, hoping only that, in reciprocation of the honour and in gratitude for Cook's gracious deferral thereof, Ambrose would consider the incorporation into his screenplay of some Splendid Ideas that Cook had proposed to Schott in a handwritten postscript to *his* copy of the letter to our committee: ideas concerning not only the Tower of Truth, but the burning of Washington and the bombardment of Fort McHenry in the War of 1812. . .and I because Ambrose, so far from immediately accepting, in whatever spirit, our nomination (for first proposing which, sir, I am as grateful to you now as my thanks are belated), was stipulating that the honorary doctorate be awarded to his nom de plume "Arthur Morton King"! I could not imagine Schott's welcoming so irregular a proviso, any more than Ambrose would welcome those "splendid ideas" of A. B. Cook's (There is nothing in your fiction, is there, of Admiral Cockburn's Chesapeake expedition in 1812?). Where would we turn next with our wretched degree? Finally, some intuition told me that Mrs Peter Mensch had forgiven her intermittent lover his affair with me. Ambrose was telephoning Schott directly and promptly, at his own insistence, to spare me the brokering of their respective stipulations and to expedite, on the committee's behalf, his decision. He would ring back promptly. I was relieved but pessimistic—and disappointed yet further, I realised as we adjourned, that he had not accepted the bloody distinction simply as a loving favour to yours truly.

The good news came, however, from Schott himself, not a quarter hour after we'd glumly gone our professorial ways: *Great guy,* this Mensch! Had welcomed Cook's suggestions, *ever' doggone one!* Thought he might even find a part for Mr Cook himself in the movie, *how 'bout that!* As for the pen-name business, *damn good idea!* Gave the *whole show more class,* if you asked him; made it more *what you might call literary?* And that was *the name of the old ball game, right?*

Thus our ad hoc committee came at last *ad hoc,* and is no more: on 21 June our friend "Arthur Morton King" becomes Marshyhope U's first Doctor of Letters! How came this miracle to pass? Wherefore this sudden deference of A. B. Cook's, this sweet rage for accommodation of John Schott's and Ambrose's? I burned to know; but my curiosity must itself needs be deferred when Miracle One was yesterday eclipsed by

2. A warm mid-May evening: Friday, thank God, and the last day of classes for the spring semester. A week-long "reading period" has begun (Is there a research library on the boardwalk at Ocean City? For thither have flown the student body), to be followed by final examinations and, three weeks after *that*—when nine-tenths of our students and staff will surely have scattered for the summer—our belated commencement ceremonies. The official reason for this delay is to combine the

228

awarding of degrees with the cornerstone laying of Schott's Tower of Truth, far behind the schedule of its construction. It is an open secret among us administrators, however, that the real reason is Schott's fear of activist disruption: he has anxiously enquired of Ambrose whether "the right camera angles" can make his minions into a multitude. But I digress, savouring the anticipation of what's next to write as I savoured the anticipation of my lover's visit, who had rung back after all in the evening of that eventful Wednesday to invite me to cocktails aboard Todd Andrews's ancient sailboat, moored in the municipal harbour, and dinner afterwards somewhere across the river. We were, he felt, at the end of our Third Stage and the commencement of our Fourth: he much wanted to talk to me on that mysterious head, bring me up to date too on his adventures with Prinz and Co., and speak of Other Things—his past and our future—which his preoccupation with movie making had kept him from communicating to me till now. Have I mentioned that in the six weeks since he mailed me that abortive confession of "Arthur Morton King's," ostensibly addressed to an anonymous Yours Truly and sent floating down the tide, I've received no further "love letters" from him? And that with the close of our seminiferous Second Stage he ceased reading these weekly letters to you?

He offered to fetch me in from 24 L; I decided to drive instead, I'm not sure why: the portentous announcement of an impending change in our connexion, perhaps, however cheerily put, suggested the precaution of vehicular independence. As it turned out I rode in in Jane Mack's chauffeured limousine, seldom seen in Dorset Heights since Harrison and I vacated Tidewater Farms. Jane too was to be Mr Andrews's cocktail guest; she and "dear Toddy," she apprised me en route to Cambridge, were old old friends, dear dear friends; I wasn't to be fooled by his down-home manners and modest law practice into underestimating his professional ability: a first-class legal mind, whose counsel she'd prefer in really thorny matters to that of Mack Enterprises' whole legal department. Did I know that it was his adroitness in the probate courts, some thirty-odd years since, that had rescued her late husband's inheritance and made possible the firm's expansion from mere pickle pickling to its present conglomeration of enterprises?

What could I say, John? As levelly as possible I acknowledged that I *had* read something to that effect somewhere; couldn't quite recall where. "*Fortune* magazine, most likely," Jane asserted; "they ran a feature on us ten years ago, when we first got into freeze-dried foods, and of course they looked around for anything to liven up the story. We thought of suing, but Todd advised against it." The "we," we note, is corporate, not familial—and while *I* feel, in this place among these people, more like an "extra" from your early fiction than the protagonist of my own life story, *she* has repressed your novelisation of her youth as completely as her middle-aged amour with my Jeffrey! Freud, Ferenczi, you are right: our choice of vocations may be symptomatic as any other of our choices. That chilling woman is your proof, her beauty as frostily preserved as her late husband's excreta; who rejects from her Deepfreeze of a memory all "unwholesome" items (you may be sure she remembered the volume and number of that magazine, whose publicity had been good for business) as systematically as her quality-control inspectors purge poor peas from prime in her frozen-food factory. Even when the Tidewater Foundation was debating the subsidy of the *Original Floating Theatre II*, Todd tells me, she batted not an eye at either the paradox or the allusion, which latter made even the proponents of the showboat uncomfortable. *Au contraire:* she froze them all with embarrassment by merrily demanding of Todd Andrews whether he remembered the fine old times they'd all had back in the thirties on Captain Adams's floating theatre—and then got briskly down to cost accounting!

So Andrews told me shortly after, amused but still impressed, at the bar set up on the cabin roof of his converted oyster-dredging boat. But remarkable as may be such expurgation, it is not our Second Miracle, no. Neither is the gloss supplied by Ambrose (over breakfast this morning) to his oral memorandum last evening (over martinis on Andrews's foredeck) when I'd asked sweetly what all this stage-of-the-affair claptrap was about: that in the second postscript of his initial letter to me—a declaration of love with no fewer than seven postscripts—he had remarked that they corresponded not only to the stages of his love for me thence far, but to the predecessors of that love, five in number. At the time of that P.P.S., he declared (This is still the memorandum, not the gloss, and most decidedly not the miracle. We are on said freshly scrubbed and painted foredeck, "wet martinis" in hand—Ambrose and I share a fondness for good vermouth—admiring the balmy evening, the spiffy restoration and conversion of our host's old skipjack, the dashingly turned-out film contingent among the guests, and each other, whom we have not seen since early in the week. My lover is tanned already from his new medium, which has kept him largely out of the Lighthouse and in the daylight of Ocean City and "Barataria," the set being built down near Bloodsworth Island. He wears a light-blue denim jacket and trousers over an open-necked madras shirt; he looks boyish, healthy, handsome, American. He is in good spirits. I desire him, can scarcely keep myself from touching his sleeve, his hair), these correspondences were but a glancing whim: he had felt *Ad-mi-ra-ti-on* for me; he'd found our conversation *Be-ne-fi-ci-al;* after Harrison's funeral he had offered me *Con-so-la-ti-on* and made that surprising *Dec-la-ra-ti-on* of his feelings for me; followed with an *Ex-hor-ta-ti-on* to me to reciprocate them and get on to *For-ni-ca-ti-on,* just as he had admired, benefited from, consoled, etc., other lovers in the past. Not till the coincidence of my recentest menstruation (which had divided Stages Two and Three, as the one just prior had divided One and Two) and certain other happenstances had he recognised a deeper pattern in our progress. Having recognised it, he could no longer honestly distinguish cause and effect: whether the pattern was determining his feelings and thus the "story of our affair," or our affair innocently rehearsing the pattern. For this reason, among others, he was inclined just now to trust my feelings above his own, and he put me this question, to be responded to at dinner: Having come, in fish-cold March, to making love, and humped all over horny April, and chastely stopped for breath into sweet mid-May. . .what ought we now? Whither our connexion, if it were my "say-so" and if our inclinations (he knew his own) should agree?

Prinz was aboard in his displaced-person getup, Jane Mack's daughter in what I believe the children call a "grannie" dress: the former glassless, the latter taking on gin and tonic by the imperial pint as she traded "wisecracks" with the barkeep. Indeed, but for the presence of a few film extras, and the absence of John Schott and A. B. Cook. . .and his son. . .we were February's mourners reconvened in May: a fair season here indeed, when the mosquitoes have yet to hatch, the stinging sea-nettles yet to foul the estuaries, the heat and damp of summer yet to pressure-cook the peninsula. Everywhere flowering dogwoods, tulips, crab apples, lilacs, japonicas, and brilliant azaleas, the bougainvillaea of middle latitudes. But if there was tension among the gathered then, it was between Jane and me on the one hand, and within myself with respect to my "son" on the other: now it was visibly between the Macks *mère et fils*, who (rumour had it) were about to litigate over Harrison's estate. Where "Bea Golden" stands in the matter I don't know, unless the family's disposition on deck was a bit of symbolical choreography: Drew and Yvonne Mack stood as far forward as one could without climbing out upon the bowsprit, Jane was on the extreme afterdeck with a little group of Tidewater Foundation trustees (and the steering wheel), and Ms Golden square amidships. There too, of course, was the bar, crossed by neither mother nor son; and thither strayed from time to time my lover's eyes, not necessarily in search of drink.

This much I remarked, with a small pang like the Wednesday's on first hearing *l'Abruzzesa's* voice. But I did not remark much more, for Ambrose's query and his portentous Deeper Pattern, together with the tale of his week's adventures with the film crew, quite preempted my attention. What ought we now? With spring so gorgeously exploding in every bush, the very air a scented kiss, the intemperate sap full-risen to green the temperate zone, what ought we now? The only question was, Why had he put it as a question, if not that to him the answer was not obvious? And if it wasn't. . .had Bea Golden of Marshyhope Productions (Prinz's paper corporation for receiving Tidewater Foundation subsidies) turned his head? Or was his erstwhile leading lady, Magda Giulianova Mensch (whose initials just now roar out at me from this page), making a comeback for "Arthur Morton King's" sake?

What was clear to me after all, then, was merely what I would, not what I ought. I ought. . .never to have left Castines Hundred and my baby in 1940; never to have gone to Paris in '39 to sit at the feet of Stein

231

and Joyce; I ought never to have been begot by those dreadful fuddling dears my parents, thanks to whom the very enterprise of letters will ever in my memory's nostrils redole of green tea, stale tobacco, book dust, and damp woollens in untidy flats. Ambrose—sweeper-away of all this, together with Yours Truly—I love you! God help me—and God knows what we ought!

Presently we disembarked from cocktails and motored over the creek bridge and the "New Bridge" to reembark at our restaurant: a large ferryboat lately beached on the river's north shore and converted for dining. I remarked upon the American passion for conversion, wondering whether it stemmed from the missionary energies of the early Puritans and later revivalists or the settlers' need, born of poverty and dearth of goods, to find new uses for things worn out or obsolete—a need become mere paradoxical reflex in a people notorious for waste. Ambrose pleasantly replied that while the practice was in his opinion not particularly American—Orientals were even more ingenious about it, for example, and the Spanish, Greeks, and Germans were no slouches either—the inclination to see in it a national trait, especially one to be criticised, was American indeed. He pretended to fear for my cultural identity; he reminded me (taking my hand across the table) that it was in my "full Britannic aspect" he had come to love me. . .

I thought to tell him I did not care to rule the waves just then, but ride them with him. Skin, skin! His hand restirred the juice of April in me, when I'd have freely bid us abandon both of these vessels-going-nowhere and stand full sail bedward. But his damned question, What ought we now?—that he had put it put me off, stayed my hand from more than meeting his.

And so we sat through the rites and trappings of a typical C-minus U.S. restaurant—stupid puzzles on the place mats, mindless jokes on the napkins, sugar in paper packets depicting ill-coloured birds of America, little sealed containers of "non-dairy creamer," dime-store candles in painted glass, plastic roses, butter in paper pats, tired salad from a tiresome self-service salad bar, crackers in cellophane, store-bought rolls, the inevitable menu of tinned soups and vegetables, thawed appetizers and entrées, everything (except the boring, inevitable beefsteak) breaded and deep-fried, baked to death, steam-tabled to a mush, or otherwise overcooked as well as overpriced and overdescribed, no fresh fruit to be found or fresh vegetables or fresh anything (How did we English get our reputation as the world's worst cooks?)—saving one item which saved the meal: a pencilled-in Friday-night special of broiled fresh rockfish from the Bay, which Ambrose identified as striped bass in its local denomination. He ordered it *solo* unhesitatingly for the two of us, insisting our plates not be defiled with stale French fries, bulk packaged cole slaw, white potatoes baked in Reynolds Wrap, and the rest; just fresh fish, fresh lemon wedges, and tomatoes filched fresh from the salad bar, please. And *mirabile* (but this is not yet our Second Miracle), we had only to send back the first burnt offering on its cold platter to achieve on second try a quite lightly broiled filet of that admirable beast the Chesapeake rockfish, which we washed down with draft beer in default of pale ale, not to mention white wine—and spoke of the film in progress.

The 1812 War, the sack of Washington and bombardment of Fort McHenry in Baltimore Harbour, the pirate Jean Lafitte's assistance of Andrew Jackson in the Battle of New Orleans and his subsequent involvement in one of the several harebrained schemes to spirit Napoleon from St Helena to America—none of these "splendid ideas" of A. B. Cook's, I understand from Ambrose, is to be found in your fiction. Yet the single set Reg Prinz is causing to be constructed for his film is "Barataria": a *suggestion* (Ambrose's inference, from Prinz's hums and tisks) rather than a replication of Lafitte's pirate village in the Mississippi delta, itself named for Sancho Panza's make-believe island in *Don Quixote*. Prinz's point, Ambrose imagines, is not only that the fictional original inspired or called forth its factual counterpart (itself become legendary), but that even in *Quixote* Sancho's island is a fiction precipitated out of fable and realised as deception, a kind of stage set elaborated by the Manchegan lords and ladies to make sport of Sancho Panza. In other words (ours, not Prinz's, for what we take to be Prinz's principle, not ours), the relation between fact and fiction, life and art, is not imitation of either by the other, but a sort of reciprocity, an ongoing collaboration or reverberation. Did this imply that you would now include the Baratarians in some future fiction, as the apostles say Jesus performed certain miracles in order that the prophecies might be fulfilled which held that the Messiah would do thus-and-so? We were uncertain. You have in any case considerable latitude, as Prinz's "Barataria" is to be a general-purpose set (indeed, no more than a lane of clapboard shanty-fronts on or near Bloodsworth Island, if he can secure permission from the U.S. Navy, who use the place for gunnery practice) for scenes of domestic early-19th-Century destruction: the burning of Washington, Buffalo, York, Newark, St Davids—even Barataria—some or all whereof may be included in the film!

Emblems, emblems all, said Ambrose (no dessert cheese on the menu, no brandy for our coffee, no espresso; Charon's ferry will have better fare); for what Prinz truly wants to record the destruction of is not any historical city, but the venerable metropolis of letters. If he has hit upon the 1812 War to evoke his foggy "Second Revolution," it may be for no better reason than that it affords him the reenactment of "our" burning of "your" Library of Congress and National Archives, or Admiral Cockburn's revenge upon the *National Intelligencer* (delivered regularly to his flotilla in the Chesapeake) for its unflattering accounts of him: having ordered his men to pi the paper's type, Cockburn first had them pluck out and destroy all the uppercase *C*'s, to hamper the impugnment of his name in future. A destruction-of-the-capital within a destruction-of-the-capital, Ambrose puts it, and recounted to me further—what it would take too many words fully to rerecount here—

Prinz's "victory" over him earlier in the week (the first intimation I'd had that their connexion was become an open contest): the filming of an "unwritable scene."

Briefly: my lover dates his erratic and problematical career in letters from his receipt, at age ten, of a cryptic message in a bottle washed up on the Choptank River shore near his present odd establishment. You know the story: Ambrose even told me—in a 100-page enclosure in the second of his two letters thus far to "me"—that you *wrote* the story, anyhow rewrote and published it with his consent: how on 12 May 1940, as an overstrung, underconfident, unhappy preadolescent yearning for reassurance from the Wider World that a life lay ahead for him less crabbed (let's say) than that of backwater Dorset, he'd come across that bottle, fished forth eagerly its communiqué, and been dismayed to the bottom of his soul to find only a salutation at the head ("To Whom It May Concern") and at the foot a close ("Yours Truly"). No body; no signature! Monday last happening to be the 29th anniversary of this non-message's delivery, and the company having filmed on the Sunday certain sequences at Ocean City in which Ambrose took the rôle of an author rehearsing the boyhood of one of his principal characters, it was decided to include a scene suggestive of that water message. But instead of the seven words of the original (per "Arthur Morton King's" fictionalization of the event, which also included the surprising, by a group of schoolboys, of a pair of lovers more or less in the act in the gang's makshift clubhouse, with attendant lower-form dialogue), Prinz suggested there be either an entirely blank sheet or a considerable manuscript in the bottle, which latter would however wash to illegibility even as the camera—and before the anxious protagonist—scanned it.

Left sleepless anyroad by the Sunday's shooting (in which—the thought gives me vertigo—Bea Golden appears to have acted a rôle something like the young Magda Giulianova!), Ambrose had spent most of the night in his boardwalk hotel drafting a scenario: on Prinz's instructions, the fellow on the beach was to be the Author—*i.e.*, a ten-year-old "Ambrose" nearing forty and recollecting his boyhood; the couple *in flagrante delicto* were to be a youthful sweetheart of this Author's (*l'Abruzzesa*, played by Bea Golden? I didn't ask) and her current lover, a filmmaker no less, played of course by R.P. Never mind why they'd gone under the boardwalk for this coupling—the *mise en scène* was changed to Ocean City, "to tie in with the Funhouse sequence"—when all those hotels stood ready to hand. Then *mirabile* (but not ours, not ours) *dictu*—better, *mirabile obtuear*, marvellous to behold, for there were no words in this enactment save the dissolving ones of Ambrose's text: on the strand next forenoon, the company assembled, Prinz's first act is to make the *written scenario itself* the water message! As the cameras roll, he stuffs into a bottle half full of ocean *Ambrose's rendering of the scene to be played* and tosses it into the surf, as if to punish the Author for having intruded on his amours (his fly is open;

234

Bea Golden wears only a beach towel; the Marshyhopers still in attendance are agog)! Ambrose is aghast, then furious to the point of literally clenching fists. . .then *thrilled,* his very adjective, as he believes he begins to see the point: Prinz, having mouthed something soundless at him, strides into the cold surf, retrieves the bottle, fetches out the marinated, washed-out script, presents it with a smile of triumph to the Author, then stands by expectantly, his arm around Ms Golden, as if awaiting direction.

The point, my lover now concluded, was precisely the inversion, in this double reenactment, of the original, historical state of affairs (the Author, grown, relives his boyhood experience; the wordless film reiterates the written story). The World having given "Ambrose" a tantalising carte blanche when he most craved specific direction, "Arthur Morton King" had vainly striven for nearly three decades to fill that blank. Now, before his and the camera's eyes, his scenario of this predicament's reenaction—itself the latest of those strivings, and *nothing but direction*—is washed away. Things have come full circle; the slate is clean; he is free!

And, for the moment (as the movie moves on), he is also immobilised, speechless, unable to direct either the Director or himself. Then he laughs; he finds his first words ("I *see.* . .!") and is interrupted by Prinz's "Cut." To which is presently appended a directive to the sound man, to make Ambrose's laugh echo that of "the Laughing Lady in the Funhouse sequence." Prinz then turns his back and strides hotelwards with the shivering heroine, leaving the bested Author as stranded as our ferryboat restaurant, which we now prepare to leave.

"It was simply brilliant," Ambrose declared. "And the most brilliant thing about it, its final *point,* was. . .exactly what I can't put into words,"—and what you will therefore excuse my having lost in this retelling!—"that the whole scene was not only nonverbal, but *unwritable.* Proof against literary rendering! A *demonstration;* a visual *tour de force.* What shall we do now, Germaine? You and I?"

My turn for speechlessness? For *Words fail me,* or *Dumbstruck by his sudden change of subject, I could not at once nor can I now.* . .that sort of thing?

Not a bit of it! Somewhere amid rockfish and recountment I had got a quiet message from my own Yours Truly, the genuine Germaine. While I found Ambrose's story interesting enough, I had not been by it diverted, not for a moment, from the question posed on Todd Andrews's foredeck. As if its re-posing now were no non sequitur but the obvious close of his "unwritable sequence," like a ready player at her cue I replied at once: We ought to tip the waitress moderately; we ought unhurriedly to recross the bridges to 24 L; there we ought leisurely to disrobe and temperately come together. If our fortnight's abstinence was neither the effect nor the cause of a waning of his affection for me, as it certainly was not of mine for him, and if his inclination (which he'd said was clear to him) corresponded to mine, we ought at once to resume our sexual connexion, but less frenetically than before. *That's* what I thought we ought; what thought he?

And now I bring this chronicle at last to bed with Miracle #2, so long *in utero:* He thought the same, exactly! 10% for the waitress, whose fault the place was not; a decorous disembarkation (but his hand on my arm, his beaming smile, his instant wordless rising from table, belied his composure); 50 mph across the moonless, still Choptank (where Andrews's skipjack sat becalmed now in the channel, sails raised and slack, drifting on the tide in the last twilight) as we spoke—warmly, quietly, but neither urgently nor lightly—of how we'd missed one another's persons, and had rather savoured that missing, and would be pleased now to have done with that savour. In April we'd have gone to it in the car; we tuned in the ten o'clock news instead and smiled together at the announcement that Venus-5, the Russian space probe, had successfully soft-landed on its target and begun, presumably, to probe. By half-past—serenely, surely—so had Ambrose.

He declared (calmly) he loved me. I replied, less calmly, I had liked him in March and craved him in April, and believed I now loved him too. He declared his wish to spend most nights with me; I replied that that was my wish also. We agreed however that some discretion should be exercised (more than we had done in April) to avoid unpleasantness in a small, conservative community; his daughter, too, posed something of a problem. In any case, there were more or less definite plans to shift the film company to the Niagara Frontier for ten days or so in June, which happened to fall between MSUC's final exam period and commencement ceremonies: he hoped I would go with him; that we could as it were elope, "honeymoon" at the Falls. . .

"Stage Four" of our affair, then, I gather, will be the sweet extension—long may it extend!—of Miracle Two: this. . .this *spouselike* intercourse (he insisted I wear a nightgown: I am to help him shop for spare pajamas, a bathrobe, *carpet slippers,* to keep at 24 L!), which I find seizes me with a strange, helpless ardour. Poached eggs and tea! The morning newspaper! How far this delightful husbanding? Will it come to pipe and dog and bumbershoot? Am I to play at wiving even to the point of—

But now words fail me, anyhow falter, as they did not at Miracles One and Two. Last night, postcoitally, I'd reminded Ambrose of his promise to elucidate that Deeper Pattern he'd perceived in our relation. He pled fatigue, pledged a full account at breakfast, and proffered for the meanwhile only that our April binge had reminded him of the one other such sexual marathon in his life, twenty years previously, at age nineteen. It had been his second romance, if the term could be applied to an altogether physical connexion. Inasmuch as his first love had been hopeless (a prolonged boyhood admiration for his older brother's girl, our friend Magda Giulianova), the uncomplicated sexual release of this second affair had been of great benefit to him. His partner, however—he would tell me tomorrow; I would be amused—a nymphomaniac of

236

sixteen, had moved on after an exhausting summer to fresher fields, and in the ensuing season of involuntary chastity he had consoled himself (but not sexually) once again with Magda, by then Mrs Peter Mensch, whom he found himself this time loving but not desiring. Thus his first three "affairs": recollected in this manner, they'd put him in mind of both that curious alphabetical list from the *New England Primer* and, *mutatis mutandis*, the progress of our own affair, which for better or worse bid to recapitulate his carnal biography. He had not however (he admitted with a drowsy chuckle) got the correspondences quite worked out: we were at Stage Four in the recapitulation, but Letter Seven of the *Primer*'s list. . .

A restless night for me: the novelty of a bedpartner; certain private memories of my own associated with Ambrose's mention of the Niagara Frontier; half-impatient speculation on these rôles I was being cast in willy-nilly. If *l'Abruzzesa* (as it appeared) had been both #1 and #3, and I myself was #6, it wanted no great inductive prowess (from the chaps who brought you Conan Doyle and Agatha Christie) to guess that Magda had also been #5, no doubt this time sexually: the *ménage à trois* from which Ambrose had come to me with his talk of beggared Dido and an Aeneas who would not weigh anchor and run for Rome. Ergo, #4 will have to have been. . .his ex-wife: that obscure Marsha, of whom Ambrose never spoke; of his marriage to whom I knew little more than that at one point it had made him suicidally unhappy and that it had been terminated not very long since.

Also, perhaps unfortunately, that it had not been fruitless. The "dear damaged daughter," as Ambrose called her, of whom the mother had evidently washed her hands, and *l'Abruzzesa* taken charge. . .

Now, I had not forgot that mad string of postscripts to his first letter: the *G* that followed *For-ni-ca-ti-on* was not *Germaine*. . .

Nor was the Third Miracle a proposition of marriage. Ambrose slept soundly, as I did not, and woke refreshed and roused. I was headachy, anxious (forty-five needs its sleep, and I now confess to you, for good reason, a small vain lie in last month's letters: I am not forty-five, but. . .a touch older); made the fact known when he essayed his "A.M. quickie," or second probe of the Venusberg. Unperturbed, he reminded me that on May Day I'd found orgasm a pleasant palliative for menstrual cramps: ought we not to give it a go for simple headache? His bedside manner was so good-humored, I agreed to try his prescription if I might take two aspirins first. He popped up to fetch them for me. *Aussi mon pessaire,* I called after him: from its case in the medicine cabinet, just above the aspirin; I had neglected to deploy it last night.

He came back with two aspirins, a paper cup of water, an almost undiminished erection, a grave smile. . .and no diaphragm.

Let's take a chance, says he. No thank you, says I: it's smack in the middle of my month. As it was last night, he reminds me. My own recklessness, says I: it's being late-fortyish I was taking a chance on.

Germaine, says he, and takes my hand (I've downed my aspirins), and his voice goes thick. . .

3. And here is our Third Miracle, too flabbergasting for exclamation marks: A. wants us to forgo all contraception. He wants his seed in me. He wants me pregnant, impregnated, preggers. He wants to get a child on me, to get me with child. He wants us to make a baby: my old egg, his sluggish swimmers. *Conceive:* he wants me to conceive by him, conceive a new person, our chromosomes together, his genes and mine, the living decipherment of our mingled codes. That's what *he* thought we ought.

I write this sunning by the newly dug pool of Jane Mack's apartment complex, where I've basked and written all afternoon whilst my lover confers with his brother on some new crisis in the family firm. The Dorset Heights pool is empty; Germaine Pitt's depths are full to overflowing, despite the best efforts of her vaginal sphincter. His stuff is in there, pooled with mine: I sit on it as I did first in our ad hoc committee chamber; for all I know, the flailing Ambrosian beasties have done their work already upon the ultimate Amherst ovum.

Surely I am quite crackers! I feel my life profoundly changing, and half hope it is my change of life. Even were we wed, two such poor track records as his and mine should not be bred. What imbecile child will be our *"Petit Nous"*? And yet I love him, this odd Ambrose, for pressing me to this unthinkable thing—which I must pray will not come to pass!

Do you pray too, silent author of the novel I am still in midst of, and which still pleasantly distracts me when I am less distraught. Pray that your friend will not conceive the inconceivable upon your poor
Germaine!

P.S.: #2, I learned at breakfast (the mistress, not the miracle), was none other than our Bea Golden, then sixteen and busily about it under her "maiden" name, Jeannine Mack: all over the back roads of Baltimore County, the back rooms of yacht clubs right 'round the Chesapeake regatta circuit, the back seats of autos at 60 mph on the highway or parked on the roads aforementioned or garaged or driven into drive-ins or en route across the water aboard that same ferryboat (then unstranded, as the Bay was then unspanned; this was 1948–49) whereon I'd ventured over rockfish what we ought. Bea was a fresh young woman then; A. a freshman at the university: by the time their rut had run its alphabet he had gone from *A*'s to *F*'s in half his courses, and she was being serviced by upper-class underclassmen up and down the Ivy League. They had scarcely seen each other in the twenty years since, until Harrison's funeral in February. Her rearrival here with the film company this month, coinciding as it did with the close of our own salty Second Stage, Ambrose found (and I quote) "piquant": as if our recapitulating coupling had reconceived and rebirthed her. I find myself piqued that he finds it so, and I review uneasily his growing involvement in Prinz's film. That water-message sequence on the beach:

it seemed in his telling rather a rivalry, and she the prize. Did Dante's Beatrice, I wonder, lay for the part? Is Ambrose really in conference with his brother as I sit here on his sperm?

P.P.S.: Shame on me: if I am mad, let it not be with jealousy. He has just telephoned (I'm back indoors now), not from his camera obscura but from the county hospital next door. The crisis, it develops, is not alone with Mensch Masonry, Inc.—which however is beset by problems enough—but with Ambrose and Peter's mother, who underwent mastectomy last year but whose cancer has evidently metastasized and brought her down again, in all likelihood terminally. It is time, he suggests, I met what remains of his family: he has spoken of me to his brother, to *l'Abruzzesa*, to the D. D'd D. He would have his mother meet the potential mother of a grandchild she will never see (May she live forever and not see it!). Tomorrow, as Apollo-10 takes off to orbit the moon, I am to visit the hospital, then take lunch *en famille* at Mensch's Castle! I am nervous as a new bride; they will think me too old for him; it is all madness.

P.P.P.S.: Bent on locking the barn door after the horse is stolen, I go belatedly to douche—and find as it were the barn door stolen too! My pessary of pages past (I believe you call them diaphragms?) is vanished from its perch above the aspirin, nor can I find it anywhere upon the premises. What amorous tyranny is this? And why does it excite (as well as truly annoy) your surely (but not yet entirely) demented

G.?

E: *Lady Amherst to the Author. Her introduction to the Menschhaus.*

24 L, 24 May

J.,

Even as I imagined this time last week, A.'s #4 was his ex, present whereabouts unknown, mother of the d. d'd daughter, for whom I gather she shucked responsibility two years past when they shucked their marriage. Who am I to criticise, who did not assume my own responsibility in the first place? Nor shall I presume to judge the marriage: not only is one chap's meat another's poison, but what nourishes at twenty may nauseate at forty, and vice versa.

It was her *name*, Ambrose now maintains, most drew him to her twenty years ago, when he was an undergraduate apprentice and she a young typist at his university. *Marsha Blank*, mind and character to match, descended from a presumably endless line of Blanks going back to nowhere. So declares our not entirely reliable narrator, adding that she was possessed of a fetching figure and a face with the peculiar virtue of being so regularly, generally *pretty* as to defy particular description, even by a young writer whose then ambition it was to render the entire quotidian into prose. A. claims he cannot so much as summon her features to memory; never could in their seventeen years together; that her comeliness was at once considerable and, precisely, *nondescript.* And her personality matched her face; and there she sat, nine-to-fiving those reams of empty paper through her machine day after day, like a stenographic Echo, giving back the words of others at 25¢ the page plus 5¢ the carbon. Thither strayed my lover, who claims to have set himself even then the grand objective, since receipt of that wordless message nine years previously, of filling in the whole world's blanks. In hand—*long*hand—was his virgin effort in the fiction way: the tale of a latter-day Bellerophon lost in the Dorchester marshes, "far from the paths of men, devouring his own soul," who receives a cryptic message washed up in a bottle. . .

Voilà: a marriage made in the heaven of self-reflexion. Our Narcissus claims to have glimpsed at first sight of her the centre of this typist's soul, unconscious counterpart of his conscious own: what nature abhors and "Arthur Morton King" finds irresistible. But we remember too that this was 1949: my lover has wound up—better, has been wound down by—his sexual calisthenics with young Jeannine Mack and is endeavouring to curb, for his brother's sake, his reawakened love for *l'Abruzzesa,* now wed to Peter Mensch and big with the twins she will give birth to ere the year is out. Harry Truman is back in the White House (and Jane Mack is misbehaving with my Jeffrey in Paris, whilst I finish my edition of Germaine de Staël's correspondence and am flirted with by Evelyn Waugh); American college campuses are burgeoning with married veterans of the Second War, educating themselves and supporting their families in prefab villages on the G.I. Bill of Rights: they set the style, for younger male undergraduates like Ambrose, of marrying very early, at eighteen and nineteen and twenty, and promptly engendering children upon their late-adolescent brides. . .

But why am I telling *you* this, who not only were there then but had been my lover's fellow labourer upon the Lighthouse project that same sexual summer? Because, of course, it's all news to me, disclosed since Sunday last, when I met the Mensch *ménage* "on location": *i.e.,* in that same Lighthouse—now cracked as the House of Usher and out of plumb like the Pisan campanile—and the adjacent county hospital, where the last of the pre-Ambrosian generation of Mensches lies a-wasting of the family cancer.

To deal first and lightly with that pitiable person, whom nature is dealing with so hardly: Andrea King was her maiden name; she descends from the King family of nearby Somerset County, whose ancestors a century and a half ago conspired on behalf of their friend Jérôme Bonaparte to spirit Napoleon from St Helena to Maryland. From her (and the possibly fancied ambiguity of his siring) Ambrose takes his fanciful nom de plume, as well as his love for word games.

From her the surgeons last summer took the seventy-year-old breast my lover once suckled beneath a swarm of golden bees. Andrea herself made this connexion, remarking further (which delighted Ambrose) that just as all the bees but one had been removed by Grandfather Mensch on that momentous occasion, and the one he'd missed had stung her, so now etc., and here she was: it took only one. Did I happen to know the British word for the terminal character of the alphabet, three letters beginning with *z*?

That was about the limit of her interest in Yours Truly, for which (limit) I was grateful. She had been something of a beauty, Ambrose told me; several men besides his late father had loved her. A neighbour had driven himself to drink on her account; her husband's brother— Ambrose's late Uncle Karl—had perhaps slept with her (intramural adultery seems a family custom!), was not impossibly Ambrose's begetter, or his brother Peter's. . . All dead now: the neighbour by his own hand, the uncle of liver cancer, the father—who on an evil day first proposed the Tower of Truth to Harrison Mack and John Schott—of a brain tumour. And their *femme fatale* now potbellied, shrunken, half deaf, gone in the teeth—a sweetless hive of swarming cells, not expected to survive the summer. Crude and blasted as she was, I rather liked her: some tough East Anglian country stock showed through. She was in pain; feared she'd need drugging before she finished the puzzle in that day's *Times*.

"Zed," her son suggested.

We then adjourned to Mensch's Castle, Folly, *Leuchtturm*, whatever, where I was to meet and lunch with his brother, with his twin niece and nephew, with his dear damaged daughter, and with the first, third, and fifth loves of his life: Magda Giulianova. I was in no great haste, am in none now, to get to her, whom I fancied watching us through that camera obscura as we crossed from the hospital toward the Mensch-haus. We toured the grounds, yclept Erdmann's Cornlot after its former use and owner: a square of zoysia grass landscaped with azaleas, roses, mimosa, weeping willows, and well-tended grapevines, fronting on the Choptank. Where once had been a seawall on the river side is now a brand-new sandy point, whereof here is the sorry history:

Were you aware, when you worked that summer for Mensch Masonry, of the fraud Peter Mensch's house was being built on? The poor chap had been left a small sum by another uncle (cancer of the skin) and resolved to build a house for the family, whose fortunes were as always parlous. He bought Erdmann's Cornlot, went off to war, and left the job of construction to the family firm—which is to say, to the liver-cancered uncle and the brain-tumoured father, who (the latter in particular was, it seems, a cranky rascal) proceeded to shortchange their benefactor at every opportunity. The seawall had been protected by riprap of quarried stone: this they removed to complete the repairing of the *hospital's* seawall, itself crumbling because some years earlier they'd removed *its* riprap for other purposes! The footings for Peter's

241

house were laid to skimpier specifications than he'd called for; the mortar you mixed that summer was systematically overloaded with sand, to save money; the stone used for construction was that same riprap removed from before the hospital wall, still too barnacled and mossed to bond properly with the mortar, especially with *that* mortar. Ambrose knew of these things (which he now candidly rehearses as we stroll the grounds) and loved his brother, but could not protest—*did* not protest—because of his own sore culpability: his virgin tryst and subsequent occasional coupling with La Giulianova, which he believed Mensch *père* to have espied!

Thus did they all take ill advantage of the earnest young man they all professed devotion to and acknowledged as the pillar of the clan; who so loved them that upon his return to firm and family, when his mason's eye must have detected straight off the adulterated mortar if not the dittoed fiancée (whose adulterator I begin to write like), he said not a word, but went on cheerfully with the construction and the marriage. In '49, house and tower were complete; the newlyweds moved in, the twins were born. In '54 Ambrose and wife Marsha came down from Baltimore and moved in too, he having given up teaching to try his fortune as a free-lancer. In 1955 (birth year of the damaged daughter) major cracks first appeared in both the masonry and Ambrose's marriage; by '56 several doors had to be shaved and sashes rehung: Ambrose and Marsha shifted to a flat near the boat harbour, the liver uncle went to his reward, and Peter assumed direction of Mensch Masonry ("the family infirm," my lover calls it). By 1960 the Menschhaus was measurably out of plumb, as were Ambrose's marriage and career alike: Ms Blank, not regarding herself as empty, resented his efforts to fill her in: his major literary endeavour (a chronicle of the sinking family) was bogged in bathos. He half attempted suicide—and, he declares, half succeeded. Traditional narrative he gave up for "concrete prose" (the mason in him, one supposes) and occasional retaliatory adulteries: for some time, it seems, his had not been the only filler in the Blank. The celebrated seawall, meanwhile, had quite collapsed: the directors of the hospital were justly incensed; Erdmann's Cornlot was washing rapidly into the river; once again Mensch Masonry verged upon bankruptcy.

This last in part because Hector Mensch, P. & A.'s father, had also retired from the county school system by this time (the tumour was enlarging) and turned all his ruinous energies to the firm; also because Peter would no more acknowledge that the man was crackers (and ignore his business advice) than that his house's list was owing as much to bad foundations as to bad ground. The company did foundation work at Tidewater Tech in '62 and '63, in the course of which Hector made the acquaintance of Harrison Mack; John Schott he already knew from his alma mater, Wicomico Teachers College. Among the three of them was somehow hatched, in 1966, the notion of Marshyhope College's Tower of Truth.

Which fetches us to our literal point, whereon my friend and I still strolled as he regaled me with this exposition. MSUC is built on the drained and filled marshes of Redmans Neck; as Joe Morgan had warned, high-rise construction on that ground was at best problematical. Contractors' bids on the tower were correspondingly high; it seemed almost as though "we" might win the day by default. Alas, it became Hector Mensch's strategy to save the company by underbidding all competitors for the foundation work, even if that meant doing the job at a considerable loss, thereby so inclining John Schott in their favour (by thus abetting his campaign against Morgan) that when Schott became president and launched the great expansion of MSU, Mensch Masonry's fortunes would be made at last. And so far has this strategy succeeded that while Harrison Mack and Hector Mensch now sleep six feet under the loam of Dorset, poor Peter toils in it sleeplessly deeper each semester. The tower's foundation is laid, almost a year behind schedule and at enormously greater cost than originally estimated, thanks both to inflation and to the ground situation at Redmans Neck. Mensch Masonry's Dun & Bradstreet has sunk lower than the piles Peter had to drive to find bedrock. Ambrose is persuaded that, like the Menschhaus, the Tower of Truth is rising from a lie: that among their father's last official acts on behalf of the firm—whilst contracts were still being negotiated with the state, and various political campaign funds still being contributed to—was the falsification of certain crucial test borings supposedly taken at the site, to persuade Peter that the project was less unfeasible than it seemed. The tower is presently scheduled for completion next year (just enough of it is raised at this writing to permit next fall the cornerstone ceremonies originally scheduled for next month); by 1976, Ambrose maintains, it will have to be abandoned, if not dismantled.

Meanwhile, to bail out the firm, appease the directors of the county hospital, and delay the disappearance of Erdmann's Cornlot, Peter contracted with a firm of engineers dredging out the ship channel into Cambridge Creek to dump the dredge spoil, thousands of cubic yards of it, before those two properties—especially the Cornlot, which is now enlarged by more than an acre. The seawall that founded the foundered firm is buried beneath this as yet uncharted point ("Cancer Point," Ambrose has dubbed it), and the Lighthouse lists and settles some hundred yards farther from the water than when you helped build it.

We approach the house. I have glimpsed it before, from the distances of Long Wharf and the Choptank River bridge. From closer up it is less prepossessing than its builder, who now strolls out with the d.d.d. to greet us as we stroll in from the point.

One would not take Peter and Ambrose Mensch for brothers. Handsomer but coarser than my lover, Peter Mensch is dark-eyed and -browed, swarthy, massive, older-looking than his forty-some years: raw Saxon-Thuringian peasant stock, says A., direct from Grandmother

Mensch, unleavened by the wilier Rhenish genes of her husband and the English DNA of the Somerset Kings. His voice is surprisingly high and gentle, his speech full of broguish *right smart*'s and *purt' near*'s. His movement, too, seems gentle, considering his weight and apparent strength; he is not fat, but thick, heavy, powerful-looking: no doubt he still cuts and hefts the stone himself. He shakes my hand elaborately right pleased to meet me. He has just returned from Bible class at the nearby Methodist church and is still dressed in shiny blue chain-store suit and black shoes, but in deference to the warming day has loosened his two-dollar tie, held in place with a gilt crab tie-tac. He is sorry that the twins won't be home for dinner: young Carl and his girl friend are surf-fishing "down to Ocean City"; young Connie is helping her husband-to-be, a local farmer, set out tomato plants. It ain't no keeping um home at their age.

We would be five, then.

I had expected to feel some contempt for a man so readily gulled but my strong and immediate intuition, in Peter's presence, was that was *not* gulled, only endlessly patient of exploitation by those he cared for. A change of clothes (and barbers) and he could be physically more attractive. And his great unclever easiness, his guileless goodwill . . . I liked him.

So too, clearly, did Damaged Angela, who leaned against him and against a building whilst we spoke, her brown eyes never moving from my face. Unions are undone; their fruit remains and grows, for better or worse. Ambrose's angel is a heavy, dim fourteen, short and thick, big-breasted already. There is no visible trace of my lover in her, nor (he replied to my later question) of *La Blank*, who was slender, fair, and hazel-eyed. Peter thinks her the image of a dear late aunt of theirs; Ambrose shrugs. She is alleged to have made great progress under Magda's patient tutelage; Peter too spends hours with her—and they both claim (but I'm ahead of myself) that it's Ambrose who's responsible for her advancement from virtually autistic beginnings. An eighth grader by age, she does fifth-grade work in the sixth grade amongst twelve-year-olds in the local junior high school. Her nubility is a problem: moronic young men roar past the Lighthouse in horrid-looking autos for her benefit, and she grins and waves. The Mensches fear she'll be taken sexual advantage of, and wish there were proper special-education facilities in the county; they weigh the possible advantages of residential therapy in Philadelphia against its shocking cost—$12,000 a year and rising annually—and the negative effects of her separation from them.

We are introduced. To my surprise Angie is quite friendly, at once shy and inquisitive: like a young primitive she fingers my costume jewelry, holds onto my hand after we shake, remarks smilingly on my "accent." She has indeed been done well by; there is even a chance she may be able to lead a reasonably independent life. "Don't want her to git *too* independent," Peter teases, "or we won't have nobody to warsh

244

dishes." The brothers are gentle with each other, gentle with her; there is much touching, taking of arms.

I am touched, too: I see my lover's reclusiveness and mild eccentricity in a different light. Great reserves of patient energy must have gone into this girl's raising, of a sort that comes less naturally to him than to his brother, perhaps to his brother's wife. Lucky unlucky Angela! I cannot imagine her better off in any other situation—yet find myself curbing my skepticism of expensive "residential therapy situations" except where the home life is poisonous or the patient unmanageable. I am *not* the self-sacrificing sort, and in our new "Stage" I am protective of my lover's freedom. Not to mention the guilt I feel in face of so much ungrudging responsibility!

We approach the house; we approach the house. Angela still grasps my hand (I can't use the ironic epithet any longer) as if I were an old and trusted friend of the family. On this soft ground my heart sinks, too. Peter wants to show me the camera obscura yet before dinner; Angela has been promised I will inspect the family totem, a certain German Easter egg with a scene inside. The house is suddenly intimidating as a castle indeed: the Misses Stein and Toklas scarcely inspired such trepidation in me as does the prospect of its mistress. . .

"This here's Maggie," Peter says of her who now comes from kitchen to foyer; and *to* her, in a mock whisper: "Turns out we call her *Germaine*, like anybody else."

What had I expected? *L'Abruzzesa* is just past forty, younger than her husband and older than her erstwhile lover, now mine. She looks not of this century, really: her face is round and rather pale for one not naturally fair-skinned, perhaps in contrast to her dark eyes and her hair, worn up in a bun. It is a good face: the skin is fine, the eyes are large and clear and liquid, the nose and chin are delicate. Dear "Juliette" taught me to appraise women sexually: she would admire Magda Giulianova's lips, meant for sucking kisses, and her fine long neck, the nape especially provocative with its soft hairs curling from below the bun. Good shoulders, good arms (she wore a sleeveless top), good full small breasts (no bra)—one would never suppose her to have suckled twins now twenty years old! The rest was less troubling: heavy hips and slack behind; legs scarred from shaving but stubbled nonetheless; clothes ill chosen from the local shops. I am no beauty (and have raised no children), but I think myself more trim at the end of my forties than she at the commencement of hers, and better turned out too.

Finally, if Ambrose has found her "primal"—and I see what he means: the heavy grace, the husky somnolent voice, the intense serenity; she is awfully female—I fear *I* found her, like some other primal things, rather dull. No doubt I looked to; no doubt too the visit was a strain for her as well as me. I'm sure I "came on" too donnishly about *camerae obscurae* as Ambrose demonstrated the one they'd turned the tower into some years since—but then I happen to *know*

245

something about them! (Theirs is mechanically interesting, I might say here, with its rotating vertical ground-glass screen; but on the whole I prefer the flat circular detached-screen type like the one above the Firth of Forth in Edinburgh, where visitors stand in a ring about the scene and need not move as the picture moves. The main drawback to the Mensch instrument, however, is not the projection arrangement but the scenic material: the county hospital is no Edinburgh Castle; the Choptank River, its low bridge and flat environs, are not the Firth of Forth and its dramatic ditto. In any case, the list of the tower is already binding the mechanism so that only with difficulty can it be moved past the empty spread of new sand where once the seawall was. The device will be out of commission before it pays for itself.)

"Anyhow," says Peter, "that's a right pretty sight, all them sail-boats." And so it was. I took my lover's arm, pointed out "our" restaurant across the river, where Stage Four had been initiated. Magda gravely reported that the management was looking to sell the place. Angela named all the sails on (all) the sailboats and scored respectably on Ambrose's quiz upon their points of sailing: which were beating, which reaching, which running. I compared the general scene and situation—innocently, I swear, though there may have been unwitting mischief in the impulse—to that famous passage in book 2 of Virgil's *Aeneid* where the hero, still in the midst of his adventures, finds their earlier installments already rendered into art: Dido's Carthaginian frescoes of the Trojan War, in which Aeneas discerns the likenesses of his dead companions and (hair-raising moment!) his own translated face.

"Is that a fact, now," Peter said. I felt a fool, then a bitch as I recalled Ambrose's comparison of Magda to luckless Dido. He glanced at me—*quizzically*, I believe you writers say. I did not score well; in my embarrassment I gushed fulsomely over the celebrated Easter egg, fetched down now by Daughter Angela on its carved wood stand: a battered, faded brummagem, nothing special to begin with, mere family junk or joking relic. I could see nothing inside.

"No castle?" Ambrose demanded, I could not tell in what spirit. "No Lorelei?" I mumbled that microscopes and telescopes never worked for me either. Already in retrospect this moment seems to me a signal one. Something disquieting announced itself here: not a Fifth Stage, but (I fear) the true aspect—*a* true aspect—of the Fourth. I shall return to it.

Rather, proceed to it, for there is little more of pertinence to tell of my introduction to the Mensches. Magda's dinner was a surprise: I had expected the relentlessly plain cuisine that American countryfolk take such pride in: baked ham, fried chicken, mashed white potatoes, lima beans, and ice water—your spiceless, sauceless English Protestant heritage. But La Giulianova knew her way around both Italian and German cookery: a fish soup called *brodetto* was followed by an admirable Wurst-und-Spätzle dish *(Himmel und Erde,* I do believe), a Caesar salad, home-baked sour rye bread, and an almond sweet called *confetti.* Cold Soave with the soup, dark Löwenbräu with the sausage, espresso and Amaretto with dessert. My best meal since Toronto: unpretentious, perfectly done, served without fuss, and all of it delicious. No cook myself (and still overcompensating for my earlier gaffe) I rained compliments upon the chef. Peter beamed; Ambrose smiled a small smile; Magda quietly remarked that good ingredients were not easily found so far from the city. I supposed that she had learned her art from her parents and the elder Mensches? Another faux pas.

"Ma never cooked worth a dime," Peter scoffed cheerfully around his cigar. "And Mag's mother didn't know what good Eyetalian cooking was till Mag taught her. This here's out of the Sunday *Times* magazine, I bet."

Magda shook her head, but was pleased. Angela peered into the egg. I was smitten with jealousy; found myself (at nearly fifty!) wishing my breasts were less full, my features softer, my voice less assertive. What rot, the old female itch to be. . .not *mastered,* God forfend, but ductile, polar to the male, intensely complemental. Lord! Am I to come off my loathing of D. H. Lawrence?

The talk at dinner, between my nervous panegyrics, was of dying Andrea and the disposition of the original Menschhaus up the street, now vacant and fast deteriorating. My lover (I heard for the first time) was toying with the idea of remodelling and moving into it himself! I found that notion both appealing and appalling: out of the *ménage à trois et demi,* yes, but why into a drab frame house on a dreary street in a dull provincial town (excuse me)? Why not Rome, Paris, London, New York? At least Boston, San Francisco, even Washington or Philadelphia, even *Baltimore!* Who ever spun the globe around and, having considered Lisbon, Venice, Montreal, Florence, Vienna, Rio de Janeiro, Amsterdam, Madrid—the list is endless!—put his finger on marshy Dorset and declared: "That's for me"?

Well, Ambrose, for one. My only comfort was the chilling one that he was *not* yet after all proposing that I move in with him, if indeed he makes the move at all, and the somewhat warmer one that the measured tone of his consideration of the idea, and of Peter's and Magda's responses, suggested that they understood Ambrose and me to be a *couple,* or on the verge of becoming one, and that they accepted, if not quite embraced, the idea. Peter was full of hearty instructions to his brother and his wife: Tell her 'bout the time you got lost in the funhouse and come out with that coloured boy. Tell her how Pa used to try and cut stone with one hand and one foot. Tell her 'bout Grandma seeing Uncle Wilhelm's naked statues. Magda quietly "expected I'd heard all that"; Ambrose quietly affirmed that I had. No one solicited counteranecdotes from me: How I Was Deflowered With a Capped

247

Fountain Pen; My Several Abortions and Miscarriages; The Amherst Phallic Index to Major British and Continental Novelists of the Early 20th Century, With Commentary.

I was reluctantly permitted, at Ambrose's insistence, to help the other womenfolk clear table and do dishes whilst our men continued the conversation; my own proposal—that the chef alone be excused from scullery work in gratitude for her earlier labours—was passed over like an embarrassing joke. And I found myself perversely aroused to be doing Woman's Work with the woman I'd displaced in my lover's bed. His daughter asked me what a *Lady* was. "Angie," Magda quietly reproved her. In my case, I declared, a Lady was simply a lady who married a Lord. Then would Daddy be a Lord one day? "Angie!" And to my surprise, *l'Abruzzesa* (no, I can't use *that* ironic epithet any longer, either) then gave me so understanding a smile, warm and droll and—and womanly, all together, that I wanted to kiss her; did in fact touch her arm, as the Mensches seemed forever to be touching one another's. Dear "Juliette Récamier" seems to have started something: it's still men I crave (one man), but I am learning, late, truly to love my fellow woman. I kissed Angela instead, and said, "Don't bet on it." (But they are, properly, never ironic with her: my reply was explained straightforwardly to mean that my title would not pass to a second husband, should I take one.)

Ainsi mon dimanche. After dinner A. drove me back to 24 L, filling in what I took to be the last remaining blanks in his psychosexual history. No doubt, he averred, his deep continuing attraction to Magda in the 1950's, albeit entirely chaste and largely unexpressed, had got his marriage off to a lame start, so that by the time it had been quite supplanted by commitment to his wife, her resentment was past mollifying. And they never had been more than roughly suited: two healthy young provincial WASPs of the middle class playing house in the Eisenhower era. He did not believe, in retrospect, that they had deeply loved each other. Neither had had the requisite emotional equipment; call it soul. But they had surely *liked* each other until their separate adulteries poisoned their connexion; the failure of their marriage had been a considerable shock to his spirit as well as to his ego. . .

Egad, you Americans! The most sentimental people in the history of the species! Can one imagine a Frenchman, a Dutchman, a Welshman, a Sicilian, a Turk carrying on so? (I hear Ambrose saying, "Sure.") To change the subject somewhat, I registered my favourable impression of his brother, of Magda, of his daughter; my relief that they had seemed not to dislike me. I ventured further to express my particular gratification at that one smile of Magda's in the kitchen: the *acceptance* I thought I saw in it of our situation.

A. considered this. She was in truth a great accepter, he replied: had for example accepted in 1955 the news, confessed by Peter, that Marsha's list of conquests included himself, who that same year, in an unguarded hour, had permitted himself to fall under the sway of her vindictiveness: she was "getting even" for Ambrose's obvious feeling for Magda, which Peter knew in his bones to be innocent. Not to keep her husband unfairly in ignorance, Magda had then confessed what otherwise she'd not have troubled him with, since it had no bearing on her love for him: that at one point, when he was overseas and she very lonely, her affection for his younger brother had departed from its prior and subsequent innocence. Not impossibly Ambrose had reported this bit of past history to his wife (but Magda could not imagine why: what was one to *do* with such information? I quite agreed with this position, as Ambrose reported it; so did he, but he acknowledged that he *had* made a foolish "clean breast of things" to his bride) and so prompted her retaliation. Magda had then assured Peter of her confidence in his love and advised against his confessing the adultery to Ambrose, for the sound reason aforestated. But Marsha herself, a great exacter of retributions, made her own "confession" and insisted they remove from the Lighthouse, which they did. These several sordid disclosures left no lasting scars on either Peter and Magda's marriage or the brothers' affection for each other; but the rift between Ambrose and Marsha became a breach never successfully closed thereafter.

And why, I enquired, was I being thus edified? Was Ambrose still subject, twenty years later, to the twenty-year-old bridegroom's impulse to make a clean breast of things?

Quoth my lover: "Yup."

And then I saw the darker question raised by his confession. This was 1955, he'd said? Yup. The year in which (truly) dear (and not *too* awfully) damaged Angela had been begot and brought to light? Yup. Then just possibly. . .?

Yup. Adultery in early Pisces; birth (premature) late in Virgo.

And the odds? Unlikely, unlikely. These were pre-Pill days, to be sure, and Marsha (like myself) was not always beforehand with pessary and cream; but she was a diligent spermatocidal doucher. What was more, they had resolved upon pregnancy that year, and so against this single furtive illicit coupling stood a great many licit ones. In which, admittedly, contraception had been forgone. And which, admittedly, had borne no fruit in the several months prior, nor would bear any after (the low motility was revealed in the early 1960's, when in a spell of reconciliation they strove vainly to conceive again). But I was to bear in mind that he was *not* (quite) sterile; he was simply not vigorously fertile, though vigorously potent. Whereas good Peter—but that was another story. In any event, he'd never *seriously* doubted his daughter's paternity; and he would feel no less her father even if it were proved that he was not her sire. Between him and Peter the matter had not once been alluded to; between him and Magda once only, and that *en passant* and indirectly. Equally, however, knowing his brother, he did not doubt that Peter and Magda's dedication to the child, and Peter's urging him to move "back home" two years ago, "for Angie's sake," when Marsha kicked over the traces and went north with a new boyfriend—not to mention what must have been Peter's complaisance in the ensuing *ménage à trois*—stemmed in part from a good bad conscience.

Hum. Nay, further: *ho* hum! We are by now *chez moi,* late afternoon and warm; the pool is finally filled at Dorset Heights; Ambrose proposes a cool dip; he has a swimsuit in the trunk of his car, which he'd as lief leave at 24 L for future use. All this matter of contraception and pregnancy has stirred me: I readily assume that his cool dip will be preceded by a warmer; indeed, when we step inside to step out of our step-ins, I am stripped and waiting before he has his trousers down, and the only question in my mind is whether to bring up the Case of the Expropriated Pessary before or after. The man disrobes: I admire as ever his youthful body; am excited in particular by the white of his well-shaped buttocks against the tan of the rest of him, and the tidy cluster of his organs in repose. I am in no danger of lesbianism! Hither, hither. . .

But lo, my white, my tidy, where is he gone? Into blue boxer swimtrunks, their owner already halfway to the door. Ambrose? A sheepish headshake from my erstwhile ram: too tired. Bit of a drain, he guesses, the family thing, his mother's condition. Anyroad, we'd "made it" only the morning before. Chop chop now; into my suit if I was going to; he'd meet me *à la piscine.*

Well! That "morning before" was the 17th, last Saturday. Today is the 24th. We have been together at least part of every one of those seven days and nights, which in lusty April would have seen our bacon bumped a dozen times over—and we have congressed exactly thrice, *counting* the morn of the confiscated contraceptive! Once on the Tuesday, once yesterday; and I mean *once.* They were firm, they were ardent enough, those couple of couplings, if not exactly passionate; they were. . . *conjugal,* yes. And they were two in number, not counting the aforementioned Saturday.

They were also, both of them, uncontracepted. Sir, I am no longer urged against precautionary measures: I am *enjoined* from them! Let the odd monsignor, even archbishop, soften his line on contraception; my lover is become intransigent as the pope. Birth-control devices are prohibited at 24 L St! Tyranny! And who's more daft: he for demanding a bastard from his aging moll, or she for acquiescing to his daft demands? For his interdiction of condom, pill, and intrauterine gadgetry was not the sum of his despotism, no: on the Tuesday I was made to put two pillows under my arse and hold my legs high; on the Friday, knees and face down on the bed, tail high in the position Lucretius compares to that of *ferarum quadrupedumque:* wild quadrupeds in rut. And both days, my master's shot once fired, I am held in place a full fifteen minutes whilst his LMS's make their feeble way wombwards with gravity's aid; nor may I even then expel those swimmers from my pool, but must lie boggy in the bed till the hour is run.

I jest, but am truly somewhat disquieted, not alone at the possibility of my actually conceiving again, with whatever consequences, but equally at this not altogether playful domination by my lover—that inclination I noted pages back, at dinner, to have me *submit*. Both times, it irks me to confess, whilst being thus held I climaxed. This pleased milord much, he having read that the vaginal contractions attendant on female orgasm give the sperm a peristaltic boost, "like sailing in a following sea"; and his pleasure excited me further. But it was, exactly, a perverse excitement at the novelty, quite normal and decidedly passing: submission as a way of life is *not* my cup of tea!

Ambrose is, I trust I made clear, not boorish in all this, but Quietly Firm, like an Edwardian husband. If our Fourth Stage corresponds to his 4th affair—*i.e.*, his wooing and wedding of Marsha Blank—then I infer of that alliance that she was the more ardent partner, he the more dominant. I reflect on the course of their connexion (not to mention its issue) and am not cheered.

Well!

G.

P.S.: A long letter, this. I remember, wryly, how in the years when I aspired to fiction I would sit for hours blocked before the inkless page. And my editorial, my critical and historical writing, has never come easily, nor shall I ever be a ready dictator of sentences to Shirley Stickles. Even my personal correspondence is usually brief. But this genre of epistolary confession evidently strikes some deep chord in me: come Saturday's *Dear J.*, my pen races, the words surge forth like Ambrose's etc., I feel I could write on, write on to the end of time!

E: *Lady Amherst to the Author. Not pregnant. The "prenatal" letters of A. B. Cook IV.*

24 L Street

31 May 69

John,

End of May, Ember day; full moon come 'round again. My calendar dubs it the Invasion Moon, no doubt because a quarter-century ago it lit the beaches of Normandy. I was 24 then: had been Jeffrey's mistress in Italy and England; had conceived André's child in Paris and borne it in Canada; had had done with Hesse and aborted his get in Lugano; was chastely waiting out the war near Coppet, researching the life of Germaine de Staël. It seems ages past, that moon: my uterus is an historical relic! But *ember* as in Ember days means recurrent, not burnt to coals: what's waned will wax, waxed wane. . .

Well, I'm menstruating. No Johnstown Flood, but an unambiguous flow. Astonishing, that old relic's new regularity; you could correct your calendar by it. What to think? Ambrose is almost *angry* at this repulse of

251

his wee invaders. I would remind him that who menstruates *a fortiori* ovulates; *my* plumbing's in order, let him look to his! But on this head he is not humorous. Indeed, he has turned a carper: my outfits lately are too old-fashioned; my manners date me; my way of speaking rings of middle-aged irony. I reply: Well might they so be, do, ring; 650 moons is no "teenybopper." Would he trick her old carcase out in bikinis and miniskirts? Have her "do grass," "drop acid"? Pickle her fading youthfulness in gin like his old (and new) friend Bea Golden? He does not reply: I fear I have invoked that name to my hurt, as one does a rival's. Yet I think I'd know if she had truly reentered his picture as they fiddle together with Prinz's, for my "lover" virtually lives with me now. . .

Dear Reader: I am a mite frightened. My calendar (the one on my desk which names the full moons, not the one in my knickers that marks them) notes that in France on this date in 1793 the Reign of Terror began—though the Revolutionary Tribunal had been established in the August of '92, and my eponym had nearly lost her head in the September. If Ambrose should become my Robespierre, who will be my Napoleon?

Add odd ironies: my master's master's essay was entitled *Problems of Dialogue, Exposition, and Narrative Viewpoint in the Epistolary Novel.* You knew?

On the Monday and the Thursday since my last, he and I made love: both times in bed, in the dark. Tomorrow's, I'll wager, will be forgone as pointless. In April it would not have been. *Tomorrow's!* We are come to that!

Well: with so much unwonted free time on my hands, I have at least finished your *Sot-Weed Factor* novel. *Mes compliments.* Since my friend and I these evenings read even in bed, I look to dispatch with more dispatch your other "longie," #4, the goat-boy book. Of *SWF* I will say no more, both because my monthly flow cramps my verbal, and because while I am done with your words I am not with your plot. Rather, with your plotter, that (literally) intriguing Henry Burlingame III. By scholarly reflex, even before Monday's momentous special delivery was delivered to 24 L, I had "checked out" enough of your historical sources in the regional-history section of the Marshyhope library (its only passable collection) to verify that while the name Henry Burlingame appears on Captain John Smith's roster of his crew for the exploration of Chesapeake Bay in 1608, there is no further mention of him in Smith's *Generall Historie,* and none at all in the *Archives of Maryland,* through which bustle the rest of your dramatis personae. I therefore assume—with more hope than conviction—that "Henry Burlingame III," his protean character and multifarious exploits, are your invention; that the resemblance between this fictitious 17th-Century intrigant and the Burlingame/Castine/Cook line of 20th-Century Ontario, Annapolis, and Everywhere Else is either pure

252

coincidence or the impure imitation of art by life. I entreat you, sir: break your silence to tell me that this is so!

This letter will not be long. I've scarcely begun to assimilate, and am still entirely distracted by, that aforementioned special delivery: a packet of four *very* long letters, plus a covering note. The mails, the mails! The packet is postmarked Fort Erie, Ontario, 21 May 1969 (a Wednesday); the cover note is dated Wednesday, 14 May, same year; the letters proper are dated 5 March, 2 April, 9 April, and 14 May—but all *Thursdays*—and all in 1812! 157 years from Castines Hundred (so all are headed, in "Upper Canada") to Dorset Heights: a very special delivery indeed!

4½ bolts from the blue. They are, of course, the letters André promised when the time should be ripe for us to make a "midcourse correction," as the Apollo-10 chaps say, in our son's career, by control at least as remote as theirs (and far less reliable). The letters are—read "purport to be," though to my not inexpert eye they seem authentic—in the hand of one Andrew Cook IV, André's great-great-grandfather, who at the time of their alleged composition was 36 years old and taking refuge at Castines Hundred from the furore over his latest ploy in the Game of Governments. They are addressed to his unborn child, then gestating in the womb of his young wife. The texts are too long and too mattersome to summarise: their substance is the history of the Burlingame/Castine/Cook(e)s, from Henry Burlingame I of Virginia (John Smith's *bête noire,* as in your version) down to the "present": *i.e.,* Andrew Cook IV on the eve of the 1812 War. This Andrew declares, in effect, that the whole line have been losers because they mistook their fathers for winners on the wrong side; he announces his intention to break this pattern by devoting the second half of his life to the counteraction of its first, thus becoming, if not a winner, at least not another loser in the family tradition, and preparing the road for his son or daughter to be "the first real winner in the history of the house."

Here my pen falters, though I am no stranger to the complexities of history and of human motives. What Andrew Cook IV *says* is that he had grown up believing his father (Burlingame IV) to have been a successful abettor of the American Revolution, and had therefore devoted himself to the cause of Britain against the United States. But at age 36 he has come to believe that his father was in fact an unsuccessful agent of the Loyalists, only pretending to be a revolutionary—and that he himself therefore has been a loser too, dissipating his energies in opposition to his father's supposed cause and therefore abetting, unsuccessfully, his *real* cause. "Knowing" his father now to have been a sincere Loyalist in disguise, he vows to rededicate himself to their common cause: the destruction of the young republic. "My father failed to abort the birth he pretended to favour," says A.C. IV. "We must therefore resort to sterner measures. For America, like Zeus, is a child that will grow up to destroy his parents."

In that loaded metaphor, precisely, is the rub: supposing the letters to be genuine, one may still suspect them to have been disingenuous. Had Andrew IV really changed his mind about his father's ultimate allegiances, or was he merely pretending to have done, for ulterior reasons? Was his avowed subversiveness a cover for subverting the real subversives? And might his exhortation to his unborn child have been a provocation in disguise? So at least, it seems, some have believed, notably the author of the cover note. . .

John: that note is in "my André's" hand, and in his French! It is addressed to me. It is written from Castines Hundred. It is headed *"Chérie, chérie, chérie!"* It alludes tenderly, familiarly, to our past, to my trials. It explains that "our plan" to insure "our son's" dedication to "our cause" (by my publishing these letters, and others yet to come, in the Maryland and Ontario historical magazines) had to be thus delayed until "our friend the false laureate" had been "neutralised"—an event that has presumably occurred, and whereof (it is darkly implied) his declining the M.S.U. Litt.D. is the signal. We may now proceed: Given "our son's" background and professional skepticism, it will not do to present to him directly these documents, the truth of his own parentage, and the misdirection hitherto of his talents for "Action Historiography": I am therefore to publish the letters as my discoveries, with whatever commentary I may wish to add; the author of the cover note will then clip and send them to Henri (professing astonishment, conviction, etc.) together with "certain supplementary comment," including the story of Henri's own birth and early childhood, the whole to be signed "Your loving, long-lost father, André Castine." The "false laureate" once revealed to be not Henri's true father, we will assess the young man's reactions and, "at the propitious moment, may it come soon," reveal to him that the responsible, respected, impersonal historian who brought the letters to light is in fact his long-lost mother!

End of cover note. Its close is two words, in two languages: *Yours toujours.* It is signed. . . *Andrew!*

I shall go mad. I shall go mad. Why should not Ambrose (who shall not see the cover note) turn out to be André? Why should not *you?* Why should not my dear daft parents, decades dead, drop by for tea and declare that I am not their daughter, Germaine Necker-Gordon? Then God descend and declare the world a baroque fiction, now finally done and rejected by the heavenly publishers!

Madness! And in these letters (which you may presently read in print, for I shall do what that hand bids me, with every misgiving in the world) I perceive a pattern of my own, A.C. IV's and V's and VI's be damned: It is the *women* of the line who've been the losers: Anne Bowyer Cooke and Anna Cooke, Roxanne Édouard, Henrietta and Nancy Russecks, Andrée Castines I and II and III—faithful, patient, brave, long-suffering women driven finally, the most of them, to distraction.

And of this sorry line the latest—unless she finds the spiritual wherewithal to do an about-face of her own with what remains of the second half of her life—is "your"

Germaine!

S: ***Todd Andrews to his father.*** *His life's recycling.*
Jane Mack's visit and confession. 10 R.

Skipjack *Osborn Jones*
Slip #2, Municipal Harbor
Cambridge, Maryland 21613

11 P.M. Friday, May 16, 1969

Thomas T. Andrews, Dec'd
Plot #1, Municipal Cemetery
Cambridge, Maryland 21613

O dear Father,

Seven decades of living (seven years more than you permitted yourself), together with my Tragic View of Order, incline me on the one hand to see patterns everywhere, on the other to be skeptical of their significance. Do you know what I mean? Did you feel that way too? (Did you ever know what I meant? Did you feel *any* way?)

So for example I did not fail to remark, on March 7 last, when I wrote my belated annual deathday letter to you, that it was occasioned by the revival of events that prompted my old *Letter* in the first place; but having so remarked, I shrugged my shoulders. Even seven weeks ago, when the dead past sprouted to life in my office like those seeds from fossil dung germinated by the paleontologists, I resisted the temptation to Perceive a Pattern in All This. I mean a *meaningful* pattern: for of course I noticed, not for the first time, that Drew Mack and his mother were squaring off over Harrison's estate quite as Harrison and *his* mother had once done over Mack Senior's. But I drew no more inferences from that than I shall from the gratuitous recurrence of sevens above; I merely wondered: If (as Marx says in his essay *The 18th Brumaire)* tragic history repeats itself as farce, what does farce do for an encore?

Then came, on April Fool's Day, a letter from the author of *The Floating Opera* novel, inquiring what I'd been up to since 1954 and whether I'd object to being cast in his current fiction. I obliged him with a partial résumé—in course of which I began to see yet further Connections—then not only declined, at least for the present, to model for him, but observed that his project struck me as the sort conceived by an imagination overinclined to retracing its steps before moving on. I even wondered whether he might not be merely registering his passage of life's celebrated midpoint, as I once did.

255

I've not heard from him since. But I withdraw that pejorative *merely*, and I am at once chastened and spooked by that clause *as I once did*. O yes: and at age 69 I'm also in love, Dad. Whether with a woman or a letter of the alphabet, I'm not yet certain.

Something tells me, you see—*lots* of things—that my life has been being recycled since 1954, perhaps since 1937, without my more than idly remarking the fact till now. The reenactment may indeed be fast approaching its "climax"; and as I made something of a muddle of it the first time around, I'd best begin to do more than idly remark certain recurrences as portentous or piquant.

Item: the foregathering, in Cambridge and environs, of Reg Prinz's film company, to shoot what was at first proposed to be a film version of some later work by the author of *The Floating Opera*, but presently intends to reprise at least "certain themes and images" from that first novel—and which features "Bea Golden." Will she play Jane Mack?

Item: in the morning's mail, notice of two scheduled visits to Cambridge this summer of "our" showboat replica, *The Original Floating Theatre II*, about which Prinz had inquired of me only last Friday, in his fashion, whether it would be putting in here during the July Tercentennial celebration. He was interested in using it as a ready-made set for "the Showboat sequences"—should he have said sequel?—in his film.

For as it turns out (so I reported to him up on deck some hours ago), the *O.F.T. II* will play at Long Wharf not only during the week of July 18–25, but on the third weekend in June as well: 32nd anniversary of that midsummer night when I tried (and failed) to blow its prototype, myself, and *tout le monde* to kingdom come. Heavy-footed coincidence! God the novelist was hard enough to take as an awkward Realist; how shall we swallow him as a ham-handed Formalist?

Well, that production-within-a-reproduction must sink or swim without me; I shan't be going. But since Harrison's funeral on your 39th deathday; since my own 69th birthday and my letter to you; since my new association with Jane Mack, even with Jeannine—to get right down to it, since this evening's cocktail party aboardship and subsequent sunset sail with one of my guests, since whose disembarkation I've sat here at the chart table drawing up parallel lists and exclaiming O, O, O—I've been feeling like the principal in a too familiar drama, a freely modified revival featuring Many of the Original Cast.

In the left-hand column (from early work-notes for my own memoir, drafted between 1937 and 1954, of Captain James Adams's *original* Original Floating Theatre), the cardinal events of my life's first half, as they seemed to me then and still seem today, 13 in number. On their right, more or less correspondent events in the years since. To wit:

1. *Mar. 2, 1900: I am born.*

1. *June 21 or 22, 1937: I am "reborn"* (you know what I mean) after my unsuccessful effort to blow up the *O.F.T.*

2. *Mar. 2, 1917: I definitively lose my virginity* to Betty Jane Gunter, R.I.P., upstairs in my bedroom in your house, puppy dog–style on my bed, before the large mirror on my dresser, and learn to the bone the emotion of *mirth.*

3. *Sept. 22, 1918: I bayonet a German infantry sergeant* in the Argonne Forest, after learning to the bone the emotion of *fear.*

4. *June 13, 1919: I am told of a cardiac condition* that may do me in at any moment, or may never. I begin, not long after, the attempt to explain this state of affairs to you in a letter, of which this is the latest installment.

5. *1920–24: My Rakehood, or 1st sexual flowering,* during which I also study law and learn of my low-grade prostate infection. Followed by a period (1925–29) of diminished sexual activity, my meeting with Harrison Mack, and my entry into your law firm.

6. *Groundhog's Day, 1930: Your inexplicable suicide,* which teaches me to the bone the emotion of *frustration,* and remains to this hour by no means explained to my satisfaction. I move into the Dorset Hotel; I pay my room rent a day at a time (see #4 left, above); and I open my endless *Inquiry* into your death. O you bastard.

2. *Dec. 31, 1954/Jan. 1, 1955: I definitively lose my middle-aged celibacy* (also, one idly remarks, after 17 years, and also on a Friday) to Sharon-from-Manhattan, after a New Year's Eve party at Cambridge Yacht Club, thence to Tidewater Inn, Easton, where I relearn, if not mirth, certainly amusement. And refreshment!

3. *July 23, 1967: I forestall Drew Mack & friends from blowing up the New Bridge,* and in the process learn to the ventricles the strange emotion of *courage.*

4. *End of June, 1937: I am told by my friend the late Marvin Rose, M.D., R.I.P., that in my place he would not worry one fart* about a myocardium poised for so many years on the brink of infarction without once infarcting. Never mind the discrepant chronology, Dad; my heart tells me that here is where this item belongs. I perpend Marvin's opinion, in which I have no great interest since my "rebirth," and resume both my *Inquiry* and my letter to you, of which etc.

5. *1955–?: My 2nd and presumably final sexual flowering,* altogether more modest: prompted by #2 above; aided by a prostatectomy too long put off, which relieved a condition both painful and conducive to impotence; principally abetted by dear Polly Lake. An efflorescence with, apparently, a considerable half-life: there is evidence that that garden is even yet not closed for the night. O yes, and I remeet the Macks, reinvolve myself in their Enterprises, and largely put by the profession of law for directorship of their Tidewater Foundation.

6. I don't know. June 21 or 22, 1937, when I close the *Inquiry* (see #13, below left)? June 22 or 23, same year, when I reopen it? I think fall, 1956, when publication of *The Floating Opera* novel prompts me to buy the Macks' old summer cottage down on Todds Point, virtually move out of the Dorset, and abandon both the *Inquiry* and the *Letter,* from the emotion of *boredom.* Damn you, sir.

257

7. *1930–37: My long involvement with Col. Morton of Morton's Marvelous Tomatoes,* who cannot understand why I have made an outright gift, to the richest man in town, of the money you left me upon your death. *Money!* O you bastard.

7. *1955: My direction, for Mack Enterprises, of the purchase of Morton's Marvelous Tomatoes,* which, following upon my remeeting Jeannine on the New Year's Eve (#2 right, above), and followed by the appearance of that novel, led to my reassociation with Harrison and Jane: his madness, her enterprises.

8. *Aug. 13, 1932: I am seduced by Jane Mack,* with Harrison's complaisance, in their Todds Point summer cottage, and learn— well, to the vesicles—the emotion of *surprise.* Sweet, sweet surprise.

8. *May 16, 1969:* We shall come to it. Same emotion, not surprisingly. O, O, O.

9. *Oct. 2, 1933: Jeannine Mack, perhaps my daughter, is born,* and the Mack/Mack/Andrews triangle is suspended.

9. *Jan. 29, 1969: Harrison Mack, perhaps her father, dies,* and the royal *folie à deux* at Tidewater Farms is terminated.

10. *July 31, 1935: The probate case of* Mack *v.* Mack *begins in earnest,* and Jane resumes our affair.

10. *Mar. 28–May 16, 1969: Another* Mack *v.* Mack *shapes up.* And O . . .

11. *June 17, 1937: Polly Lake farts,* inadvertently, in my office, and thereby shows me how to win *Mack* v. *Mack* and make Harrison and Jane millionaires, if I choose to. Of this, surely, more anon.

11.

12. *June 20 or 21, 1937: My dark night of the soul,* when a combination of accumulated cardiac uncertainty *(cf.* #4 left, above), sexual impotency *(cf.* #5 left & right, above), and ongoing frustration *(cf.* #6 left, you bastard), led me to

12.

13. *June 21 or 22, 1937: My resolve to commit suicide* at the end of a perfectly ordinary day, in the course of which I take breakfast coffee with Capt. Osborn Jones's geriatric company in the Dorchester Explorers' Club, pay my room rent for the day, work on my unfinished boat, drop in at the office to review cases in progress and stare at my staring wall, submit to a physical examination by Marvin Rose, take lunch with Harrison Mack, premise that Nothing Has Intrinsic Value, escort little Jeannine on a tour of the *Original Floating Theatre,* decide to employ its acetylene stage- and houselights to my purposes that evening, take dinner with Harrison and Jane, am amiably informed that our affair is terminated (they being about to take off for Italy),

13.

resolve *Mack* v. *Mack* in their favor by a coin flip, return to the Dorset, close my *Inquiry* into your suicide, which I mistakenly believe I now understand, stroll down to the showboat, attempt my own, fail, and observe that I will in all probability (but not necessarily) live out my life to its natural term, there being in the abstract no more reason to commit suicide than not to. Got that, Dad? *Inquiry* reopened; *Letter* to you resumed; *Floating Theatre* memoir—and Second Cycle of my life—begun.

Okay, the correspondences aren't rigorous, and there are as many inversions as repetitions or ironical echoes. The past not only manures the future: it does an untidy job. #11, #12, & #13, which happened back-to-back 1st time around, are yet to recur, unless we count Polly's airhorn work on the New Bridge in July 1967 as 11 R, and my subsequent vast suspicion (that Nothing—and everything else!—*has* intrinsic value) as 12 and 13 R. But now that I have perceived the Pattern—and just barely begun to assimilate 8 & 10 R—my standards of praeterital stercoration have been elevated. I now look for Polly to fire a literal flatus at us 32 days hence (or, like a yogi, take air *in*). It will no longer do that I have in a sense, via the foundation, already reconstructed the showboat I tried and failed to destroy in 1937 (Nature had a hard time of it, too: the *O.F.T.* sank three times between 1913 and 1938, was each time raised and refitted, was finally sold for scrap in '41, but burned to the waterline off the Georgia coast en route to the salvage yard. Were the Author of us all a less heavy ironist, one would suspect arson for insurance; but I believe He managed spontaneous combustion in the galley, under the stage, where I and the acetylene tanks once rendezvoused). A second Dark Night clearly lies ahead for me, this June or next, followed by another Final Solution—and, no doubt, somebody's second first novel, or first last!

Meanwhile, back at 8 and 10 R. . .

Seven Fridays ago, the last of March, I saw her name on the appointment calendar, not in my foundation office out at the college, but in my law office on Court Lane. She'd reserved a full hour of the afternoon. I wondered what exactly for, and asked Polly; *she* wondered, too. Harrison's will, we grimly supposed.

I had drawn and redrawn it for him a number of times, and was named his executor. I did not much approve of its provisions; had striven earnestly, in fact, with some success, to persuade him to alter a number of them in the interests both of equity and of maintaining the appearance of *mens sana*. I didn't relish the prospect of its execution, but meant to see it through unless the will should be seriously contested, in which case I would probably disqualify myself as executor in order to defend (again with little relish) the interest of the foundation, his chief beneficiary. Thus he had stricken from his copious drafts, at my urging, all references to the flooding of England, to Her Majesty the Queen, to his disaffected American colonies, to *"meae dilectissimae Elizabethae;"* and the rest. The sum settled on Lady Amherst for her pains was scaled down to noncontroversial size (she deserved more); ditto the executor's share, embarrassingly generous. And for appearances' sake Jane was given a cash bequest in addition to the considerable jointly owned property (including Tidewater Farms) which became hers automatically by right of survivorship. Finally, I had persuaded Harrison to put in trust a sum for each of his two grandchildren. But to Drew and Jeannine he would not leave a penny, and only with difficulty had I prevailed upon him not to denounce as well as disinherit them. His share of Mack Enterprises and his other stock holdings, as well as real property inherited from his father and not jointly owned with Jane— that is, the bulk of his bequeathable estate and more than half of his net worth—were to pass to the foundation, along with the benefits of his several life-insurance policies. Especially considering how much Harrison had put already into the original endowments of the foundation and of Tidewater Tech, this bequest came to a very great deal of money: more than two million dollars. Half was to be added to "our" endowment, where it was to be vested in a contingency fund until Marshyhope College's "Tower of Truth" was completed; should further cost overruns or budget cuts by the State General Services Department (with whom "we" have a complex relationship in such special projects) threaten to truncate the tower, it was to be rescued with this money, which otherwise would revert to the foundation's general fund, its income to be used as we saw fit. The other half was to be divided equally into two trusts: one for establishing, furnishing, and maintaining a Loyalist Library and Reading Room in that same tower, another for founding an American Society of British Loyalists under the directorship of A. B. Cook, the self-styled Maryland Laureate.

These last were the only overt testamentary evidences of Harrison's grand delusion. While much toned down from his original proposals (*e.g.*, a Society for the Reunion of His Majesty's American Colonies with Mother England), and altogether more interesting than John Schott's tower, they remained the obvious openings for any contest of the will. Were I Jane Mack, certainly if I were Jeannine, most certainly if I were Drew, I'd contest.

And it seems they all more or less intend to. Unselfishness takes many forms, Dad: had you noticed? Drew wants his father's entire estate returned to The People, from whom he maintains it was wrongfully wrested by two generations of capitalist-industrialist Macks. This end he would effect, not by retroactive refunds to all purchasers of Mack Pickle Products since 1922, but via free day-care centers for blacks, improved living facilities and organizational muscle for migrant farm workers, and other, more revolutionary, projects. He is neither hurt nor surprised by his disinheritance: father-son hostility he regards

260

neither as an Oedipal universal nor as an accident of temperaments, but as "inherent in the dialectic of the bourgeois family." He acknowledges that his father was deranged, but believes (correctly, in my opinion) that the derangement accounts only for certain of his benefactions, not for the disinheritances. He will of course have to argue otherwise in court.

Jeannine is hurt but not surprised. I do not think either the Macks or the Andrewses greatly capable of loving. Affection, loyalty, goodwill, benignity, forbearance, yes; and these are virtues, no doubt about it. But love. . . Yet the more imaginative of us (you listening, Dad?) can sharply wish we had that problematical capacity, which cares enough to hassle where we will not bother, to cry out where we are stoical, to treasure another quite as much as ourselves. And even the less imaginative of us can wish to *be* loved, and fancy ourselves capable at least of reciprocation, or heartfelt echo. Jeannine believes (I gather) that inadequate fathering doomed her to a promiscuous and unsuccessful search for substitutes. What about adequate daughtering? I ask her. She'd've *been* a good daughter, she replies, if her father had been etc. Should she contest (she's presently too scattered to decide), it will not be simply to enrich herself—she and Drew both have trust income from their grandparents, adequate to subsist on, and there is alimony from "Golden Louie," as she calls her last ex—it will be for reparation. And to enable Reg Prinz to produce as well as direct his next film.

As for Jane, and the first part of 10 R: she will of course contest, she informed me promptly and pleasantly that afternoon, when she came into the office: punctual as always and, as always, handsome, striking, yea beautiful. About the Tower of Truth she had no strong feelings one way or the other, though she opposed the use of foundation funds to supplement the GSD appropriation: let John Schott find his money elsewhere; that's what college presidents were for. The Loyalist business she regarded privately as more silly than demented; while she was grateful to me in principle for having talked Harrison out of its wilder versions, she meant nonetheless to use those earlier drafts and my revisions to support her contention that he was neither of sound mind nor properly his own man in his later years. A. B. Cook—who I now learned was a distant relative of hers—she regarded as a humbug, to be neither feared, trusted, nor otherwise taken seriously. John Schott was an ass. With Germaine Pitt she had no quarrel; on the contrary; she would not dream of contesting that bequest. The disinheritance of her children was doubtless regrettable but neither surprising, given their "provocative track records" (her term), nor tragic, given their earlier legacies, their present life-styles, the trusts established for Drew's children (Yvonne, thank heaven, could be depended upon to educate them Sensibly), and the Reasonable Provision she herself was making for Drew and Jeannine in her own will. She herself of course was well off even without all that jointly owned property, and *very* well off with it; she would bear Harrison no grudge even if he'd been quite sane when he made his last will. Nevertheless, two million was two million: since she had no particular fondness for the Tower of Truth, the cause of British loyalism, or Mr. A. B. Cook, she meant to sue for as much of it as she could get. She quite expected Drew and Jeannine to do the same; would *urge* them to, if they bothered to ask her opinion.

All this delivered coolly, crisply, cordially in my office on a spanking early spring afternoon. Since burying Harrison and re-establishing herself at Tidewater Farms, Jane had found time for a week's rendezvous in Tobago with her new friend "Lord Baltimore" (she would not tell me his name), a French-Canadian descendant of the original Irish proprietary lords of Maryland and (more news) a relative of her relative A. B. Cook—"but not close enough to worry us about the consanguinity business." Tanned, fresh-eyed, wrinkled only as if by too much outdoor tennis, Jane looked younger and livelier than Lady Amherst: a vigorous 45 at most—certainly not 55, most decidedly not 63! And from her I caught, among the pleasant fragrances of wools and suedes and discreet perfume, a tiny heart-stinging scent from #8 L, 37 years and several pages past: a scent of salt spray and sunshine on fresh skin, in clean hair, as if she'd just come in from small-boat sailing on a summer afternoon.

O, O, O pale pervert Proust: keep your tea and *madeleine!* Give me the dainty oils of hair and skin (for all I know it might have been, both then and now, some suntan preparation) to trigger memory and regain lost time! I had to close my eyes; Jane reached over the desk to touch my arm and wonder if I was all right. I was 69, I replied, and subject to attacks of nostalgia; otherwise fit as a fiddle—and ready to go to court if Harrison's will were contested. But not, I should apprise her at once, as her counsel in the dispute—or Drew's or Jeannine's, both of whom I told her had approached me informally on the subject since the will was read. As Harrison's executor on the one hand and executive director of his Tidewater Foundation on the other, I was clearly caught in a division of interest (I had urged him, vainly, to name Jane his executrix, as she well knew). As his friend, I would have to decide which role to abdicate and which to act in, the better to see his wishes carried out. As *her* friend, I'd be happy to recommend to her the estate lawyers I'd least like to cross swords with.

Unnecessary, she responded cheerfully: she knew *scads* of lawyers, bright young ones as well as sly old ones. And she had Harrison's crazy early drafts, and letters he'd written as George III dating back to 1955, and the testimony of two psychiatrists, and enough Georgian costumery to outfit the staff of Williamsburg (where in fact she was negotiating its sale), and innumerable eye-witnesses to the long-running royal charade at Tidewater Farms—including a videotape made with Harrison's consent by Reg Prinz only last Guy Fawkes Day. Not to mention certain freeze-dried items in safe deposit with Mack Enterprises, of demonstrated efficacy in the proof of unsound mind. No doubt whatever that she could break at least the two "Loyalist" articles in the will and, at least, divide that million with Drew and Jeannine, on the grounds that Harrison's mad identification of them with Queen Charlotte, the Prince of Wales, and Princess Amelia, respectively, accounted for their disinheritance. Moreover, she was reasonably confident that a separate action could establish that in her own case it was *only* the invidious historical identification, not any blameworthy conduct of hers, that had done the trick, whereas his disaffection with Jeannine and Drew antedated his madness and marked his lucid as well as his demented intervals. She had not yet decided which tack to take.

But that was not exactly what she'd come to talk about. She knew me well enough, she hoped, not to expect me to represent her or either of her children against a will I'd drawn for Harrison myself. She thanked me again for my attentions to him and to her through those trying years. I was as trusted a friend as she had; had always been; how fortunate they were, she and Harrison, to have renewed that friendship upon their return to the Eastern Shore! For that, if little else, she thanked Jeannine, whose warm report of her encountering me at the Yacht Club's New Year's Eve party in 1954 had reopened the door between us, so to speak. Poor Jeannine: Harrison *hadn't* been the best of fathers, she supposed; it did not surprise her to hear that her daughter had sought me out in the matter of the will; little as she knew me, Jeannine had always had a daughterly sort of feeling for me. Even Drew, for all his rough edges and thin-skinned radicalism, *trusted* me, she knew, as he never trusted his own father. . .

I studied her. Not a trace of irony, Dad; none either of calculation (I mean conscious, *calculated* calculation). It was the first time Jane had been in that office since June 21 or 22, 1937, when, having slept with me for the last time the night before (my Dark Night), she'd stopped by in the afternoon with 3½-year-old Jeannine, whom I'd promised to take on a tour of Captain Adams's Floating Theatre. I was smitten, nearly overcome by associations: sweet, painful, in any case poignant, and given resonation by that fragrance of sun and salt I'd first scented on her on the day—O my! I had forgotten nothing: my bones, my muscles, the pores of my skin remembered!

But for Jane the place had evidently no associations at all. We could have been talking across my bed in the Dorset Hotel, it seemed to me, or in the Todds Point cottage, and she'd have made no connection. But if such remarkable obliviousness (which I acknowledged might be unsentimentality instead; I'd never tested it) was characteristic of her, oblivious *digression* was not. I observed to her that she seemed reluctant to state her business.

"I *am!*" She laughed, much relieved—and then coolly stated it, as if reviewing in detail for her dermatologist the history of a skin blemish the more vexing because it was her only one, and small. Believe it or not, she said, love and sex and all that had never been terribly important to her.

O?

She'd enjoyed her life with Harrison until his madness, which after all marred only the last 10 years or so of the 40 they'd had together. She'd enjoyed her children when they were small. If she didn't feel close to her grandchildren, the distance seemed to her more a matter of political and social class distinctions, insisted on by Drew, than of racial bias on her part. But never mind: if family feeling was not her long suit, so be it. And she'd always liked having money, social position, and excellent health to enjoy them in: people who turned their backs on such pleasures—like Drew and to some extent Jeannine—were incomprehensible to her.

I agreed that it was better to be rich and healthy than poor and sick.

"That's *right!*" Jane said, seriously. But more than her married life, family life, and social life, she went on, she enjoyed the business life she'd taken up since Harrison's decline. It was a passion with her, she admitted, her truest and chiefest; she regarded herself as having been neither a very good wife and mother nor a bad one, but she *knew* she was a good businessperson, and she loved the whole entrepreneurial-managerial enterprise more than she'd ever loved any human being, think of her what I would.

I thought her lucky to both know and have what she loved, and said so. But what about "Lord Baltimore"? Those trysts in London and Tobago?

She poofed away the word *trysts*. She and André (aha, we have milord's first name) didn't much go for that sort of thing—not that they just played bridge and tennis, I was to understand! But the pleasure they found in each other's society, and the basis for their (still confidential) affiancement, was the pleasure of shared tastes and objectives, together with compensatory desires, with which sex had little to do. Think what I would of Betsy Patterson, Wallis Warfield Simpson, Grace Kelly; like them she had always hankered after a bona fide title; would almost rather be Baroness So-and-so or "Lady Baltimore" than be rich! As for "Lord B.," never much interested in business and virtually dispossessed by Canadian social welfare taxes—he would rather be rich than titled. Why then should they not both be both, since they so enjoyed each other otherwise?

She knew what I must be thinking, Jane said here, especially as her friend was some years younger than she. But suppose he *were* a fortune hunter in the vulgar sense, as she was confident he was not: she was a businesswoman, and had no intention of endowing him, unless in her will, with more than the million or so (minus inheritance taxes, gift taxes, and lawyers' fees) she hoped to win from the will suit. A windfall, really, costing her no more in effect than her title would cost him. Now, she was no child: she'd had his credentials and private history looked into, and was satisfied that he was what he represented himself to be: a middle-aged widower of aristocratic descent and reduced means (like her friend Germaine Pitt), who truly enjoyed her society and candidly wished he had more money to implement his civilized tastes. But even if she turned out to be being foolish, it was a folly she could afford.

I agreed, my heart filling with an odd emotion. But she had mentioned sex?

Would I believe it? she wondered, blushing marvelously. She was being *blackmailed!* Or threatened with blackmail. About. . .a Sex Thing!

A Sex Thing?

Out of her past, she added hastily. Mostly. Sex Things that she herself had *completely* forgotten about, as if they had never happened.

Ah. Uneasily, but with sharp interest, I wondered whether. . . But no: 20 years ago, it seems, she had been briefly swept quite off her feet by another titled gentleman, now deceased: friend of the family, delightful man, I'd know his name if she told me, but a perfect rakehell; she couldn't imagine what on *earth* had attracted her so, or how she'd let him talk her into doing the mad things they did. Maybe it was change of life: she'd had a hysterectomy the year before, and was taking hormones, and feeling her age then much more than now. Maybe it was that Jeannine was turning into such a little tramp already at sixteen, or that she and Harrison weren't as close as they'd been before. . .

Lady Amherst's husband? I asked, and identified my old emotion: simple jealousy. Jane nodded, smiling and tisking her tongue. It seemed a hundred years ago; she and Germaine had never even *mentioned* it since the latter's return to Maryland. She doubted Germaine even remembered; it hadn't seemed to bother her at the time, though it had upset poor Harrison. She herself had just about forgotten it, it was at once so crazy and so inconsequential. And it was immediately afterwards that she became so absorbed in business that *nothing* could have tempted her That Way again, not even to a flirtation, much less—she closed her eyes, breathed deeply.

Well. I had gathered, sketchily, from Harrison in his decline, that there had been some such affair, in London and Paris in the autumn of 1949, with someone they'd met in their prewar travels. And it *had* "upset" him, much more than Jane's only other known adultery—her long-term affair with me in the 1930's—because, while briefer and less serious, this one had taken place with neither his complaisance nor, at first, his knowledge. He himself, I believe, had never been unfaithful except for infrequent one-nighters with expensive call girls when he was out of town on business. He admired his wife above all other women he knew; sexual self-confidence was not his strongest trait, but it seemed to me he had a healthy, shrug-shouldered understanding of whatever in his character had once indulged our *ménage à trois*, and had "outgrown" it, neither repressing his past like Jane nor dwelling on it. A pity indeed, if Jane's uncharacteristic last fling with Jeffrey Amherst (whom I never met) turns out to have been among the causes of Harrison's madness—in which, it occurred to me suddenly and sadly, he had at once insulated himself from her rejection of him by seeming to reject her, and bestowed upon her the highest title in the book.

But as she said, I said now, that was over and done 20 years ago, and both her then lover and her husband were dead. How could she be blackmailed? Surely her new Canadian friend would not be much bothered to hear she'd once had an extramarital fling?

How warmly our cool Jane blushes. It wasn't just *hearing,* she informed me. That darned Jeffrey (Jane has never used coarse language) had had the naughtiest mind of any man she'd ever met! He'd made her do *crazy* things! And there were pictures. . .

Aha. Which someone had somehow got hold of, I suggested, and threatened to show to friend André? But what difference could they possibly make?

"Toddy," she said, in a tone I hadn't heard for 30 years; Sentimental Jealousy would surely have taken its place with Mirth, Surprise, Fear, Frustration, Despair, and Courage in the gallery of Strong Emotions I Have Known, had it not been largely displaced a moment later by pure Gee-Whizment. For (she now revealed) it was not only the past that had been recaptured by some voyeuristic Kodak, and it was not André she feared would see the photos. André was *in* one. . .taken in London. . .well after Jeffrey's death. . .in fact, just a few months ago . . .

I was incredulous. Jane in tears. It was crazy, *crazy,* she declared: she'd practically just *met* the man, though they'd been corresponding ever since he'd traced their distant relations some years before (he was big on family history, on history in general, a kind of hobby). They'd hit it off beautifully from the first, and of course she'd been distraught over Harrison's condition, that's why she'd gone abroad. Even so! It must have been the being in London again, with a titled gentleman again; it was even the same hotel, where she'd stopped, not for sentimental reasons, but because it was the one she happened to know best, the Connaught. And the darned thing was, sex wasn't really a big thing with them; this must have been about their first or second time in bed; she doubted they'd ever done such things since. And how in the *world* anybody could take their picture without their knowing it!

My turn now to touch *her* arm, truly wondering whether she was quite sane. Leaving aside the remarkable assertion that there was anything compromising to have been photographed, I asked her just who was threatening to blackmail her with the supposed photographs, and how. From a slim leather briefcase she drew a Kleenex and a typewritten, unsigned note: "If you contest your late husband's will, these will be distributed to your family, friends, business associates, and competitors."

That demonstrative pronoun was the kicker: I'd expected, if there turned out really to be a blackmail threat, some allusion to "certain very compromising photographs in my possession."

"These?" I inquired.

Out they came, Dad, with another Kleenex, from another partition of her case: two 8-by-10 glossies, one in black and white, the other in color. Unbelievable. Across the desk, Jane covered her eyes. Both photos were sharply focused, well-lighted, clearly resolved, full-length shots, made with a good camera by someone who understood photography. In the black-and-white, taken from the side at waist level, Jane (43) knelt naked on the floor to perform fellatio upon a paunchy but pleasant-faced elder gentleman who—remarkably, considering that her body was as perfect in that photograph as it had been at my last sight of it in 1937, when, aged 31, she'd had the body of a 25-year-old—was not yet roused to erection by her ministrations. His expression was mild, bemused, behind a full blond (or gray) mustache and the eyeglasses he'd not removed; his right, farther hand rested upon her head; his left held a cigar whose ash appeared to interest him more than the fresh-faced, hollow-cheeked (because etc.), crop-curled vision of daintiness who looked up at him with full mouth and bright, expectant eyes. O, O, O. In the other, taken apparently from *above,* a stocky, well-muscled, bald, dark-body-haired fellow of 50 or so with (I think) a short beard and (I know) a considerable erection was busily "sixty-nining" on a forest-green chenille bedspread with

Absolutely unbelievable. Not the fact of sex among us healthy sexagenarians; heavens no: I myself now look forward to restful *soixante-neuf* at *quatre-vingt-seize.* But the well-dressed woman just across the desk from me there, stretched naked on her side here in living color across that bed, her upper leg raised and bent to accommodate her friend, on whose lower thigh she rested her head as he did likewise on hers—she was beautiful! Not as a well-tended 63-year-old may be, well, well tended; Polly Lake, bless her, is that. No, Dad, I mean she was a smasher, a stunner, a knockout. Where were the varicosities, striations, liver spots? The thickened waist and slacked behind and fallen pectorals? The crow's-feet, jowls, and wattles of latter age? Jane's hair is perfectly gray; her face is delicately seasoned rather than dewy fresh (as it had still been at 43!); her skin all over, and her musculature, also has that slightly seasoned cast. Otherwise. . . Fifteen years younger-looking than her inverted lover, for example, a healthy specimen himself. No question about it, she is a physical freak. But there are freaks and freaks; if this is arrested development, let them throw away the key.

Jane (I exclaimed when I was able)! You are a smasher, a stunner, et cetera! How could these photographs *possibly* do otherwise than delight you as they delight me, as they must be the delight of any family member, friend, enemy, business associate or competitor whose eyes are privileged to rest upon them? As they must delight God himself, whom I suspect of snapping that full-color overhead? Blackmail indeed! Have them enlarged and framed on your office walls, reproduced in the brochures of all Mack Enterprises, direct-mailed to preferred stockholders and to every senior citizens' organization in the republic!

She thought me not serious, but was heartened enough to scold me, mildly, for reexamining the photographs, which reluctantly I gave back to her. Admiring her vanity along with the rest, I granted that their circulation could be an embarrassment and inconvenience, if not to her affiancement at least to her business and private life. And I seconded her opinion that police and private-detective files were not to be trusted with them: I knew from experience how that brotherhood relishes a good photograph; in any case (so to speak) they were not Sherlock Holmeses or Hercule Poirots, just cops and ex-cops of one sort or another, more or less competent routine investigators.

That was why she'd brought them to me. What should she do? I asked her kindly, Had they really been taken without her knowledge? The lighting and camera angles were so good, and in 1949, especially, the gadgetry of snooping was less exquisite than it had become since. What she'd acknowledged, moreover, about Lord Jeff's eccentricities. . .

Okay, it came out then, with more blushes and a couple more Kleenexes: he'd been a camera buff, had set up a tripod and lights and automatic timer himself in their room at the Connaught back in '49. But there'd been nobody on the ceiling last January! And it was still to be explained how naughty Jeff's photo (which she'd never even *thought* of since, or seen a print of till now) came into someone else's hands 20 years later. And whose? Would I please, as one of her oldest friends and the most trusted, try discreetly to find out who had sent her that note (from Niagara Falls, N.Y., 14302, on St. Patrick's Day, the envelope revealed, with a 6-cent Cherokee Strip commemorative), so that she could protect herself and "Lord Baltimore" from further invasion of their privacy and proceed to contest Harrison's will if she saw fit?

Well. I wondered aloud how she thought to protect herself even if the culprit could be located, since any legal prosecution would necessitate her placing the photographs in evidence; no doubt the blackmailer would publish them anyhow if he or she felt threatened. All business and no tissues now, fair Jane reminded me coolly that as president of a multimillion-dollar corporation and potential contestant of two million dollars' worth of testamentary articles, she was not naive about industrial spying and counterspying, however innocent she might have been about lewd invasions of personal privacy. She had a fair idea of what sufficient money could hire done. If I would help her find the guilty party, the rest could be left to her.

Quite taken aback, as they say, I asked her what she meant to do if the letter's author turned out to be Drew or Jeannine? For while I couldn't quite imagine Drew's highly principled illegalities extending so far, two million was a lot of bread for the Revolution, and it seemed not unimaginable that his hand might be forced by some less scrupulous comrade. As for Jeannine, I had no notion whatever of what moral lines she drew, if any, but I couldn't imagine her standing up to, say, Reg Prinz's silent suasion. In any event, both could surely be said to have the motive for blackmail, if not the means or, on the face of it, the disposition. So too could her cousin A. B. Cook VI, a much likelier candidate now that I thought about it. Germaine Pitt, on the other hand, would seem to have readier means, at least for having somehow come across the earlier photograph among her late husband's memorabilia; but she had truly cared for Harrison, and I couldn't fancy her suing for a larger bequest, much less resorting to vulgar blackmail. For that matter, as representative of the major loser in a successful action on Jane's part, I myself ought properly to be among the prime suspects, ought I not?

Death to all of you, Jane said affably. I was in her element now—sizing up the competition—and she had of course reviewed the lot of us plus other direct and indirect beneficiaries of the will as possible authors of that letter. That she'd then come to me spoke for itself, she declared. She suspected Prinz, whose scruples were dubious but whose photographic expertise was not, or some unknown colleague of Drew's, certainly not Yvonne. In either case, Jeannine and Drew might well know nothing of it, and *need* never. Would I help her?

I told her I was afraid to say no. Was she truly capable of "putting out a contract" on the person responsible? That was not what she'd said, she said: there were surely more ways than one to neutralize a threat, once the threatener was identified. Photographic negatives could be located and destroyed; effective counterthreats or other checkmates could be devised. Where was my imagination? Meanwhile, she assumed I had other appointments that afternoon, as she did, and there was no particular hurry about this inquiry, since no payment was being demanded or deadline set. Why didn't I think about it for a while? And would I agree at least not to rush the will into orphan's court until I had so thought, and we'd talked again about it?

When Jane is being Madam President, her briskness is a little false, at least professional, as it surely wasn't back there with the photos and the Kleenex. She was *so* pleased to have had our chat; we didn't see *nearly* enough of each other since Harrison's death; we *must* get together socially, and soon. I tried the most obvious double entendre: Indeed it had been a joy to see her again, so little changed since old times. . .

Well, she declared: we'll certainly get together. Soon. Toodle-oo now.

Ta-ta.

I wanted to believe her so unrufflable that, perfectly aware of my irony, she declined to acknowledge it because she found it vulgar, at least inappropriate. Similarly, that she quite remembered her past visits to my office, and to my room, and simply saw no reason to acknowledge the memory. But my whole sense of her told me she was oblivious to both.

Now I'm less certain. (It's Saturday sunrise. I fell asleep over the chart table. I'm sore in every joint. We 69-year-olds can't do the Dear-Diary thing all night like a teenager after a big date.) Of anything.

Except that, as best we wretched Andrewses can love, Todd Andrews loves Jane Mack; has never ceased loving her since 1932; has never loved anyone else. How stupid my life has been, old man: empty, insignificant, unmentionable! How full hers, however "oblivious." And who am I to speak of her obliviousness, who scarcely realized until last night that I've been in love with that astonishing woman for 37 years?

As Jane suggested, we got together. Not exactly "soon": seven Fridays later, yesterday. I'd thought about those photographs in the meanwhile; had seen a bit of Lady Amherst and Ambrose Mensch (who seem to be a couple these days; lots of horny gossip; more power to them) out at the college, where things have been popping. Watched Drew and Reg Prinz in action out there too, and reinforced a few tentative conclusions. Germaine's a stable, decent woman in an unstable situation: I see in her neither cupidity nor vindictiveness. If she's involved in anything like blackmail, it's against her will, so to speak. Mensch is an enigma to me: erratic, improvisatory. I can imagine him, as Lady A.'s younger lover, obliging her to do something uncharacteristic—but I daresay they're more likely candidates for prurient photography than purveyors of it. And what would they gain? Drew is, as ever, more principled than effectual. His surviving black colleagues haven't been in evidence in the Marshyhope riots: either they have other fish to fry or he's still on the outs with them since the bridge business. And he's too aboveboard about his probate challenge-in-the-works to be feasibly underhanded. Prinz is a cipher, "Bea Golden" a blank—who, however, commutes between here and that quack sanatorium of hers up in Canada, not far from Niagara Falls. Of Cook I've seen and heard nothing except that he has declined without explanation an honorary degree from Marshyhope this spring, one which he'd previously either been pressing for or been being pressed for by John Schott. A minor mystery, from whose rough coincidence with the blackmail business I can make no plausible inferences. That Niagara Falls postmark had led me to consider also, fruitlessly, certain recipients of and rejected applicants for Tidewater Foundation grants up in that neck of the woods: no dice, except that at least one of the latter strikes me as a certifiable madman. Then there was Jane's "Lord Baltimore," who dwells somewhere in those latitudes: I even considered the possibility that the threat was bogus, some bizarre test of Yours Truly, administered—but what in the world for, unless to try whether his famous old heart is breakable at last?—by the Widow Mack herself.

Nothing. And during and between these reflections and distractions, as the kids tore up the campuses and the cops and National Guardsmen tore up the kids and the federal government tore up our country and the Pentagon tore up others, I hauled, fitted out, and launched the *Osborn Jones* for its 69th sailing season: 10th as a pleasure cruiser under my skippership. The prospect, and the work, didn't please me this time as they usually do. It's not a handy boat, either for cruising or for living aboard of. Never was meant to be, certainly not for an old bachelor. It's clumsy, heavy, slow, too laborious to handle and maintain, comfortable but not convenient. The conversion—like my life, I'd been feeling all April—had been competently done but was basically and ultimately a mistake. I'd heard nothing from Jane since the Friday of the Photographs.

So I decided to have a party aboard: Cocktails for Friends, Suspects, and Women I'd Realized Too Late I Love Only and Always. Last night, 5 to 7. Jane's invitation urged her to bring Lord Baltimore along, if he happened to be in the neighborhood or was given to flying down from Canada for drinks. I'd like to meet the lucky chap, I wrote, trying to turn the knife in Sentimental Jealousy, which turned it in me instead. R.S.V.P. I left off the Regrets Only.

She didn't call. By 4:45, with the deck and cabin Bristol-fashion, hors d'oeuvres out and bar set up, waiter and barkeep standing by, great wind pennant looping in the warm light air, even a gangway rigged between pier and gunwale, and faithful Polly nursing a drink while we waited for the guests, *I* was the one with regrets only: for having planned the stupid party (which I saw clearly now to be no more than a pretext for seeing Jane again, who was probably up in Canada with her large-tooled lover); for having lived out a life so stupid—no, so *stupidly:* it hasn't been a worthless life, just a meagerly lived one—instead of ending it in 1937. At five nobody had arrived yet, of course; I felt like sending home the help and taking Polly for a sail. The movie people, we agreed, would probably show up even later than Regular People. Why had I breathed in and out, eaten and shat, earned and spent, dressed and undressed, put one foot in front of the other, for 69 years? Did *you* ever—but who knows what you ever.

At 1704 by the bulkhead clock (which I wouldn't vouch for over Jane Mack's watch) I saw her car come 'round the Long Wharf fountain: the only other big black Lincolns in Dorchester County aren't automobiles. Up rose my spiritual barometer; sank when I saw *two* people in the back; rose again, part way, when the chauffeur handed Jane and Lady Amherst out. It occurred to me that Germaine Pitt had not been Lady Anything until her marriage—I know little of her background beyond a dim memory of the *vita* presented by Joe Morgan to the foundation trustees prior to her appointment—but she looked more to the manor born than Jane, if only because she's so unassuming tweedy English, and My Love so American to the bone. It occurred to me further, as I handed them over the gangway, that Jane hadn't indicated how confidential was the news of her betrothal and the name of her intended: as she hadn't told me more than his given name and *nom de guerre,* as it were, I supposed it still a sensitive matter, and made no mention of it in our hellos. Nor did she in any way acknowledge my note on her invitation. A mad fancy struck me: not only had our interview been some sort of test, but her "Lord Baltimore" did not exist! She was not engaged; it was not Too Late. . .

271

I checked myself. That photo couldn't have been faked. And for me it had been too late since 1937.

I introduced the ladies to Polly Lake and showed Germaine about the *Osborn Jones,* explaining what a skipjack was and how it came to pass that oysters were still dredged under sail in Maryland. She was politely interested: her late husband had enjoyed sailing out of Cowes, she said, in the Solent, but she herself was prone to motion sickness. However, she was mad about oysters: what a pity the season was ended. I thought to pick up on Lord Jeff, try whether I could sound her present feelings about his old affair with Jane; she forestalled me by inquiring about the *Osborn Jones,* whether I'd named it after the salty old voyeur in the *Floating Opera* novel or whether the fictional character and the boat were both named after an historical original. Ought she to ask Jane instead? she wondered mischievously.

I was impressed: a delicate maneuver, as if she'd read my thoughts and was gently reminding me (what in fact I'd forgotten for the moment) that during our trying days together in Harrison's decline we'd had occasion to compare cordial notes on the apparent obliviousness of our friend Jane, both to the fictionalization of our old affair (which Germaine had heard about but not then read) and to Jane's later fling with Lord Amherst, which Harrison sometimes alluded to.

Lucky fellow, Ambrose Mensch: I do like and trust Germaine Pitt. As if on cue, Jane saluted our return from the foredeck to the bar by explaining brightly to her friend that Captain Osborn Jones had been an old dredge-boat skipper whom I'd befriended back in the 30's and introduced her to. He used to live alone in the Dorset Hotel, she declared, and preside over a collection of similarly aged guests called the Dorchester Explorers' Club.

Ah, said Germaine. Even Polly rolled her eyes.

I pass over my cocktail party, Father of mine, because its radiant, miraculous aftermath so outshines it. Anyhow it was a failure in the sleuthing way, so far as I know; I've yet to check with Polly, whose idea of subtle investigation is the Disarming Point-blank Question put by a Fetchingly Candid Elder Lady—a device that not infrequently works, and a rôle she so enjoys playing that it's scarcely a rôle. I'd told her, more or less, about the photos and the blackmail threat, as about all our office business. She was of course enchanted. In her immediate opinion there were but two imaginable suspects: Reg Prinz if Jeannine in fact contested the will, A. B. Cook if she did not. Therefore we'd invited Cook to the party; but a secretarial voice from his home, over by Annapolis, RSVP'd us his regrets: he was presently out of the country. Polly promised to give me a chance to observe and talk to the guests myself before she took charge of the inquiry. She also informed me (this was in the office, just after Jane's appointment) that I was in love.

Absurd, I said. But true, said she. By six everyone had arrived: Mensch (who's to get the honorary doctorate declined by Cook), Jeannine and Prinz and the movie crowd, Drew and Yvonne, and, for filling and spacing, some Mack Enterprises folk and a few foundation trustees. A ship of fools, Drew declared, and disembarked early: yet he said it mildly, and when Polly asked him whether he'd expected me to invite a delegation of his friends to blow up the boat, he kissed her cheek and said one never knew. Later I heard her asking Prinz whether he'd ever dabbled in still photography—couldn't catch his answer, if there was one—and later yet I saw her at the bar, deep in conversation with Jeannine, no doubt asking what her plans were regarding her father's will. Finally, to my surprise, she went about the boat looking at her watch and declaring her astonishment that it was seven o'clock already. Most took the hint. The movie folk had another party to go to anyhow, at Robert Mitchum's spread across the river; Germaine and Ambrose, too, plainly had other irons in the fire. The Mack Enterprises and T.F. people remembered their several dinner plans; not a few invited Jane, who however declined, and/or their host, ditto, and/or Polly, who responded to some one or another of them that she'd be pleased to join them shortly, as soon as the party was tidied up.

An odd thing had happened, Dad. From the moment that Lincoln appeared on Long Wharf and Jane issued forth in a handsome white pants suit, blue blouse, and red scarf, I was, as the kids say nowadays, "spaced." I'd been truly curious to hear what Germaine had to say about Cook's declining that degree; I wanted to try to talk to Drew about the demonstrations at Marshyhope and Abe Fortas's resignation from the Supreme Court, as well as about Harrison's will, and to Jeannine about the progress of the film. But I had the feeling, unfamiliar since 1917 or thereabouts, that if I opened my mouth something outrageous would come out. After that initial tour of the boat with Germaine, I scarcely moved from the afterdeck, merely greeting guests, seeing to their drinks, and smiling sappily, while that white pants suit and its tanned inhabitant moved ever before my eyes. Ah, Polly, Polly: yes, I am, and passing odd it is to be, daft in love in my seventieth year!

Again like an old-fashioned teenager, I'd scarcely talked to Jane all evening, only hovered on her margins as she chatted with all hands back by the taffrail. Now that everyone was gone but her and Polly, I busied myself settling up with the help, excited that Jane had lingered behind, wondering why, still almost afraid to speak, wishing Polly would leave, half hoping she wouldn't. Jane's chauffeur came expectantly pierwards. It was still only seven-thirty. Now the three of us were together on the afterdeck with our last gin and tonics, and it occurred to me that Polly had *walked* down from the office; I owed her a lift home.

Could we go sailing? Jane suddenly asks. What a good idea! cries dear Polly, utterly unsurprised. We've no crew, says I, rattled. Jane guesses merrily she hasn't forgotten how to sail: don't I remember their old knockabout from Todds Point days, that we used to sail out to Sharps Island in? You're hardly dressed for sailing, I point out. Listen to the man, tisks Polly; the best-dressed skipper on Chesapeake Bay. I

273

don't believe he *wants* to take us sailing, pouts Jane. Never mind *us,* says Polly airily: I've got me a dinner date, and if you don't mind I'll borrow your chauffeur to take me there; it'll knock their eyes out. She was welcome to him, Jane told her—unless I really was going to refuse to take her sailing. Jane, I said (seriously now), there's hardly a breath blowing. Very brightly she replies, Maybe something will spring up as the sun goes down. She goes so far as to take my elbow: If not, we can drift on the tide, like the Floating Opera.

Dear Father: Flustered as I was, I heard her correctly. She did not say Floating Theatre; she said *Floating Opera.* And thus ends this long recitative and begins the wondrous aria, the miraculous duet.

But you are wondering about Polly. Polly Lake is no martyr, Dad: no long-adoring, self-effacing secretary. Polly's her own woman, ten years a widow and no yen to remarry, having nursed a husband she was fond of through a long and ugly terminal illness. Polly has grown-up children and grandchildren who love her, plenty of friends of both sexes, good health and a good job, more hobbies and interests than she can find time for, and at least one other casual lover besides me, who'd love her less casually if she'd permit him to. Polly Lake is mildly abashed that her romantic life is more various and agreeable since menopause and widowhood than it was before. Sex itself she neither over- nor underrates: male companionship without it she finds a bit of a bore. Even when she's not feeling particularly horny herself, she prefers her male friends to feel a bit that way. The only woman I ever met who finds cigar smoke erotically arousing. So don't worry about her. Good night, Poll.

As for your son. Still wondering what on earth is up with Ms. Oblivious, he motors the *O.J.* from its slip and out of the basin, Jane having neatly cast off the dock lines. She then takes the wheel and heads for the channel buoys, nattering on about bare-boat chartering in the Aegean, while he goes forward to winch up sails. There is a tiny southerly breeze in midriver, just enough to move old *Osborn* on a beam reach down from the bridge toward Hambrooks Bar Light. Gorgeous as such sailing is, though, Jane declares—the spanking *meltemia* of the Cyclades; the crystal-clear Caribbean, through which you can see your anchor plainly in five fathoms; salty Maine, where you can't see your bow-pulpit in the fog—give her the snug and easy, memory-drenched Eastern Shore: cattails and mallards, loblolly pines and white oaks, oysters and blue crabs, shoal-draft sailing, the whole tidewater scene.

Except in July and August, I amended, when I would happily swap it for Salty Maine etc.; also January through March, when give me that crystalline Caribbean instead of the—*memory*-drenched, I believe she'd called it? With the motor off, sails (just barely) filled, and water rustling lightly now along the hull, my spirit calmed: I was able to begin to savor my unexpected good fortune, while still wondering what accounted for it. Jane, Jane.

She turned the wheel over to me, took her ease on the cockpit seat, and named off in order the points between us and Chesapeake Bay—Horn, Castle Haven, Todds, and Cook on the south shore going out; Blackwalnut, Nelson, Benoni, Bachelor, Chlora, Martin, and Howell on the north shore coming back. She guessed she and Harrison had anchored in every one of the creeks and coves between those points, and run aground on every shoal, when they'd first cruised the Choptank back in the early thirties. And before *that,* before she'd even met Harrison, back in her "Scott Fitzgerald" days, she'd done the regatta circuit from Gibson Island right around the Bay, bringing in the silverware with her Thistle at a time when few women raced sailboats. Let her son think what he pleased, she was *glad* the rich had bought up all the waterfront property in large holdings before the general prosperity after World War II; otherwise it would be subdivided by now into tacky little hundred-foot frontages, each with its dock and its outboard runabout—her own master plan for Dorset Heights! As it was, she could see on the aerial photos made by her real estate people that many of those coves were as unspoiled now as they'd been when she and Harrison first anchored in them in 1932—indeed, as when the *Ark* and the *Dove* reached Maryland in *1632.*

She *was* being memorious, I affirmed; even historical. That she didn't choose to live in the past didn't mean she'd forgotten it, she replied. Her tone was neutral. I was impressed. The little breeze evaporated: the sails hung slack; we began to set gently astern on the incoming tide. Out in the Bay the sunset promised to be spectacular. In a different voice she asked: Can't we keep right on, Toddy? Let's motor clear out to Sharps Island again.

Toddy, Dad. And Sharps Island! Be informed, sir, that Sharps Island is where Jane and I made love for the second time together, on the beach, in the afternoon of 13 August 1932, a Saturday.

Sharps Island wasn't *there* anymore, I reminded her. All washed away: nothing but a lighthouse and buoys to mark the shoal where it used to be. Imagine people outlasting their geography, I added: just the opposite of your unspoiled coves.

Ah, now she remembered: where the three of us used to tie up the boat and picnic on the beach, the last edition she'd seen of good old Chart 1225 showed only *Subm piles.* Let's go to Todds Point then, okay? She'd like to see what I'd done to the cottage.

#8 L, Dad.

Not much to see, I said. I'd made a few changes, not many: new kitchen, new plumbing and fixtures. Something between unspoiled coves and Sharps Island, I supposed. I went ahead and said it: Our bedroom's the same.

She didn't respond; seemed truly lost in thought, looking out to westward toward Redmans Neck, where already we could see lights on the steelwork of Schott's tower. What are we doing here? she wondered presently. I could just hear her; couldn't judge whether she meant the Choptank or the River of Life.

Drifting, mainly, Jane, I said. Making a bit of sternway. I'll kick in the motor if you want.

She roused herself, smiled, touched my hand, shook her head, stood up quickly. Okay, then, she said, let's drift. But let's don't *just* drift. Shall I switch on the running lights? Down the companionway went the white suit; from the wheel I could just see it moving about the darkened cabin. She found the switch panel and cut in the running and masthead lights, then went over the AM band on the ship-to-shore till she picked up a D.C. station doing something baroque as their signal faded with the light. Smartly she located their wavelength on the FM band and set the automatic frequency control. I had come up to the companionway to watch her; no need to steer. The white jacket came off. Then the red scarf.

Then the blue blouse. Was there a hanging locker? she asked with a smile. Fine flash of white teeth, white eyes; white jacket held out by the collar in one hand, the other on the placket of her white slacks. White bra against her dark tan. I came down the ladder and kissed her.

Goodness gracious me. The main cabin settee of the *Osborn Jones* makes into a snug double, Dad, but Jane thought it unseamanlike for no one to be on deck. Anyhow it was balmy and beautiful up there, more like late June than mid-May. We took our time undressing; hung and folded everything. I lit a cabin lamp to see her better. She liked that: let me look and touch all I wanted; did a bit herself. Sixty-three: it was not to be believed. She was the cove, I told her, proof against time. I feared I was Sharps Island. She'd settle for Todds Point, she laughed, and went back up the ladder—calling pleasantly that I needn't take precautions, as she'd ceased her monthlies some years ago. Jane, Jane! Above the masthead a planet gleamed: Jupiter, I believe. An osprey rose from and returned to her pile on a nearby day-beacon (19A, off Howell Point); a great blue heron glided past us and landed with a squawk somewhere out of sight. Albinoni was followed by Bach on the FM, after a commercial for Mercedes-Benz. Sedately, patiently, but ardently, Jane Mack and I made love. Traffic streamed across the New Bridge toward Ocean City for the weekend, an unbroken string of headlights. Stars came out: Arcturus, Regulus, Pollux, Capella, Procyon, Betelgeuse. Our combined ages are 132 years. Dew formed on the lifelines, gunwales, cockpit cushions.

Polly Lake goes at it like a trouper, Dad: lots of humping and bumping and chuckles and whoops. Jane Mack does it like an angel: lithely, gracefully, daintily, above all sweetly. Suddenly she clutched my shoulders and whispered a long *O*. For an instant I feared something was wrong. Heart attack? Coronary? Then I understood, and wondered why Bach didn't pause, the bridge traffic, all the constellations, to hear that *O*.

Sweet surprise. Afterwards she lay for a minute with her eyes closed (registering with a small smile my own orgasm); then she slipped dextrously out from under and into the head compartment to clean up.

The air was chill now; there were patches of mist on the river. I wiped off with a paper towel, dressed, broke out a couple of Windbreakers from a hanging locker, spread bath towels on the cockpit cushions against the dew, started the engine, and went forward to lower and furl the sails. When I came back Jane was sitting with her legs curled under—dressed, jacketed, hair in place—smoking a cigarette and sipping a brandy. Another was set out for me. When I bent to kiss her, she gave me her cheek.

I asked what we should drink to. She smiled brightly and shrugged, the old Jane. I was disappointed; the question had been serious. To the letter O then, I proposed. She didn't know what I meant. Look at that traffic, she said: In a few years they'll have to build another bridge and a bypass; Route 50 really bottlenecks at Cambridge. Her first words since the "Todds Point" wisecrack, not counting that O. She thought it just as well that Mack Enterprises had stayed out of the high-rise condominium boom in North Ocean City; they were way overextended; some people were going to lose their shirts.

Back at the slip her chauffeur was waiting; Jane had him toss her the forward dock lines and made fast, then gave me a hand with the aft and spring lines. Then she said, Dad, and I quote: "That was just *delightful*, Todd. We *must* do it again. *Soon*. Nighty-night now."

No irony, no double entendre. Yet she had shown, out there in the channel, that she was capable of both, and of sentimental recollection too. Indeed, as we'd shucked our duds out by Red Nun 20, I'd set about amending my whole conception of Jane's historical amnesia; now I was obliged to revise the amendment. More than that pants suit had been doffed and redonned; even when the only white left on her was what had been under her bikini in Tobago, I realized now she'd never acknowledged unambiguously our old affair; Todds Point was where she'd lived as well as where she'd 8-L'd me. A fresh *frisson:* had this been, for Jane, no sweet replay at all? Was she still and forever in that left-hand column, doing everything for the first time?

Well, Dad: here I sit aboard the *Osborn Jones* like Keats's knight at arms by the sedgeless lake: alone, palely loitering, enthralled. And baffled to the balls, sir! Could #8 & #10 R, my reseduction, whether or not Jane was conscious of the echoes, be simply another Mack Enterprise? A bribe? A retainer? It doesn't seem impossible; with Jane, not even quite cynical. I think of the chap in Musil's *Man without Qualities* who only *seems* a hypocrite because of his spontaneous, genuine feeling for those who happen to be in a position to further his interests. I think of Aristotle's sensible observation in the *Ethics*, that the emotion of love among the young is typically based upon pleasure, among the elderly upon utility. Then I think of that O, and cease to care.

O my heart. Whatever Jane felt out there at the dewpoint, among the blue herons, black cans, red giants, and white dwarfs, your ancient son felt, more than passion, an ardent sweetness: a grateful astonishment that life can take, even so late, so sweet and surprising a turn. Or, if after all no turn was taken, I feel at least a grateful indulgence of that Sentimental Formalist, our Author, for so sweetly, neatly—albeit improbably—tying up the loose ends of His plot.

The earth has spun nearly around again since; the world with it. Many a one has been begotten, born, laid, or laid to rest since I began this letter. Apollo-10 is counting down; #11's to land us on the moon before summer's done. It's been years, Dad, since I gave a fart why you hanged yourself in the basement on Saturday 2/2/30. You frightened me then about myself, whom I've ceased to fear, and turned into a monologue the dialogue we'd never begun. Only the young trouble their heads about such things.

> 10. *Mar. 28–May 16, 1969: Another* Mack *v.* Mack *shapes up,* and Jane reresumes our affair, at least to the extent of reseducing me.

Where will my #11 land me, this second time around? That's all *I'm* really curious about, now I've seen the pattern. Yesterday I took an interest in (and the Tragic View of) the careers of Charles de Gaulle and Abe Fortas, the campus riots, my government's war against the Vietnamese, even the enlargement of our knowledge of the universe, not to mention the disposition of Harrison Mack's estate and the threatened blackmailing of Jane Mack. But I seem to have lost something overboard last night: today nothing much interests me except that *O*, which fills my head, this cabin, all space. I can hear nothing else; don't want to hear anything else. I've written these pages, imagined that pattern, just to hear it again.

O that *O*.

If I try to sleep now (it's getting on to cocktail time again), will my dreams rerun that episode? Never mind history, this letter, the rest of the alphabet. Bugger off, Dad. Author of us all: *encore!* Back to #10 R, Red Nun 20, Jane's *O!*

I: *Jacob Horner to the Author. Declining to rewalk to the end of the road.*

5/15/69

To: Professor John Barth, Department of English, SUNY/ Buffalo, Buffalo, New York 14214, U.S.A.
From: Jacob Horner, Fort Erie, Ontario, Canada

Sir:

In a sense, I Am Indeed the Jacob Horner of your *End of the Road* novel, for which you apologize in your letter to me of May 11, Mother's

Day, Rogation Sunday, birthday of Irving Berlin and Salvador Dali. Never mind in what sense.

Your story of having discovered that manuscript in Pennsylvania in December 1955 I Find less convincing than the novel itself. As for your work in progress, your inquiries, your proposal: I am Not Interested.

You would hazard the remobilization of "Jacob Horner"; how shall Jacob Horner Go About the resurrection of "Rennie Morgan," whose widower intends to kill me if I don't Bring Her Back To Life by Labor Day?

If only roads *did* end. But the end of one is the commencement of another, or its mere continuation. Today, 15th of May, Ascension Day, 51st anniversary of the opening of airmail service between New York City and Washington, D.C., birthday of Anna Maria Alberghetti, Richard Avedon, Michael William Balfe, Joseph Cotten, James Mason, Ilya Mechnikov, I Am Back at the Beginning of mine, where I Was in 1951—what a year, what a decade, what a century—only Older; not so much Paralyzed as Spent.

Who wants to replay *that* play, rewalk that road?

L: *A. B. Cook IV to his unborn child.* *His own history to the present writing: the French Revolution, Joel Barlow in Algiers, "Consuelo del Consulado," Burr's conspiracy, Tecumseh's Indian confederacy. The Pattern.*

At Castines Hundred
Niagara, Upper Canada
Thursday, 14 May 1812

Dawdling daughter, slugabed son!

Last time I letter'd you, lazy child, five weeks since, 'twas mid-Aries; now 'tis the very tail of Taurus, the beast that was meant to bring you last week to breath. The good Baron your uncle has her nurse & midwife standing by; your mother frets to be discharged of nine months' freight; I am a-fidget to be off for Washington & Bloodsworth Island, where I have business. Yet you sleep on thro the signs: another week & you'll be Gemini! Are you storing strength for some great work? Are you tranced like the Seven Sleepers? Or does it merely suit you to linger there, in that sweetest cave of all?

Your father, too, has been gestating, with Andrée's help, here in the womb of the Castines, whence issue forth all Cookes & Burlingames, and I feel myself upon the tardy verge of 2nd birth. Like you, I have flail'd blindly in my sleep, pummel'd a parent I had better pitied,

279

if not loved. As late as these latest weeks, from a kind of dreamish habitude, I have scuttled up & down the shores of Ontario, Huron, Erie; John Astor's voyageurs & trappers are now organized into a line of quick communication for General Brock in the coming war; the routes are ready for smuggling matériel from New England merchants to *our* government in York & Montreal. My doing, tho the doer feels, ever more strongly, that the man he is about to become must undo the man he's been: that I myself, not my father, am the parent I must refute.

My last three letters have traced the history of your forebears down to Andrée & myself, and have shown (what your mother first discover'd to me) how each has honor'd his grandsire as a fail'd visionary, whilst dishonoring his sire as a successful hypocrite. Each Cooke the spiritual heir of the Cooke before; every Burlingame a Burlingame! Not even your mother quite escaped this dismal pattern, tho by discerning it thus early in her maturity, she finds herself with less history than I to be rewrit. But I, I am steept & marinated in the family error, to the confession whereof we now are come. In this letter—surely my last to an addressee unborn!—I must rehearse my own career, complete the tale of what Andrée has taught me, & set forth our changed resolves with respect to the coming war, together with our hopes for you.

Bear in mind, little Burlingame—what I have ever to remind myself—that Aaron Burr in Paris *may not be* Henry Burlingame IV! If (as Mother at her best believed, despite those late cruel letters) Father died in 1783, or '84, or '85—if, for example, he was the man hang'd by Washington as Major John André—then of what a catalogue of crimes against us he stands acquit! Every one of his earlier friends who thot they recognized him thereafter—Benedict Arnold, Joel Barlow, Joseph Brant, Aaron Burr, Baron Castine—acknowledged that he was *much changed,* and their descriptions of him differ'd greatly. Who knows better than I that letters can be forged, knowledge pretended, manners aped? And so when I received that note from him on Bastille Day 1790, written in the Bell Tavern in Massachusetts and handed me in Paris by an attendant of Mme de Staël; when I read it, wept, curst, tore it to shreds, burnt the shreds, & pisst upon the ashes—even then, at 14, I allow'd that it was *not of necessity my father* I pisst upon, but perhaps a heartless & unaccountable impostor, perhaps a series of such impostors.

In either case, I thereby spurn'd the declaration in that letter: that my father's great aim & life's activity had been 1st to prevent, and later to subvert, the American Revolution. It was Arnold had 1st put the contrary bee in my bonnet, in London in 1787, which now commenced a buzzing: that my father from the start had been a sly & wondrously effective agent of George Washington! Father's advice to Burr & Arnold, when they were joining the Continentals at Cambridge, had invariably been sound advice. He had permitted Arnold to raise the St. Leger siege against Fort Stanwix. Arnold himself, moreover, was persuaded that Father had gull'd him into betraying West Point to

Major André *in order to betray the betrayal,* all at Washington's directive, to the end of uniting the "states" behind him & discrediting the Loyalists. Whether or not Father was the author of the Nicola or the Newburgh letters, their effect was altogether in Washington's favor; Arnold believed they had been authorized by the General himself, to provide occasion for his famous replies. On the other hand, Arnold thot it very likely that Washington or his aides had arranged to have Father quietly done away with at the same time as Major André, to prevent the great duplicity's becoming known.

Thro this new lens, so to speak, I now perceived in a different light my father's other alleged efforts in the cause of the Loyalists & the Indians. His activities in Maryland with the Marshyhope Blues against Joseph Whaland, supposedly to keep the Picaroon inform'd in advance of the attempts to capture him, had led in fact to Whaland's only arrest. Most painful of all to acknowledge, the Mohawk massacres led by "Joseph Brant" in Pennsylvania had led to such ruinous retaliation that the proud Six Nations were in effect no more: a decimated rabble of drunken vagrants along the Grand River. Had Father's plan from the start been to exterminate the Iroquois, he could scarcely have devised a better means!

All this I saw, & pisst & pisst. Mme de Staël's attendant, a boy my age who had stood courteously & curiously by, inquired whether I had any further reply to his mistress, who hoped I would wait upon her that afternoon, as upon a friend of both my father & Mr. Barlow. I bid him good day; but Barlow said I ought to go, and I would not disoblige one who had been so kind to Mother & to me. He was full of praise, was Barlow, for the young *baronne,* who he said had taken an interest in my situation. He hoped I might see much of her household—more particularly as his own must now change character: he was off posthaste to London to fetch Mrs. Barlow at last. It had been his design that Mother & I should return to Canada when her child was born. Now that she & it were dead, he urged me to go to my father, in Baltimore or wherever, to put an end to that painful mystery & decide with him my future course. If I would not (and I made plain that I would die first), I might always count myself welcome in his childless house. But a season in the society of Mme de Staël would improve my literary & political cultivation, he declared, and afford himself & his Ruthy a chance to reacquaint themselves after their long separation. Mrs. B. was not an ardent traveler; new cities alarm'd her, Paris especially, & the Revolution; and while not given to irrational jealousy, she was quite susceptible to the *rational* sort. . .

Good Joel Barlow: if only his poetical talents had been capacious as his heart! For the next five years I stay'd in Paris, completing my schooling in the Lycée, in the avenues of the Terror, on the margins of Mme de Staël's salon, and—he being, as always, good as his word—*chez* Barlow, once "Ruthy" had settled in.

Anne Louise Germaine Necker, Baronne de Staël-Holstein, ten

years my senior, was 24 when I first met her, that afternoon. She was no beauty, excepting her great brown eyes & her bosoms creamy as ripe Brie; but she was possest of wondrous energy, knowledgeability, & wit, and seem'd to me the embodiment of what was most appealing in the French liberal aristocracy. Her father (who had arranged the French financing of the American war) was unendingly wealthy. Her mother had been young Gibbon's mistress and might have been his wife, had not Rousseau disapproved of Gibbon's early literary style. At 20 Germaine had married the Swedish minister to France, Baron de Staël, & publisht anonymously her 1st novel, *Sophie*. By the time I met her she had brot out in addition her *Lettres sur les écrits et le caractère de J.-J. Rousseau* & an unfortunate tragedy, *Jeanne Grey*. The Revolution at that point (that is, the reforms imposed upon Louis XVI by the National Assembly) was much to her liking, as it was to Barlow's: liberal, atheistic, constitutionary, at once "enlighten'd" &—a term I heard for the 1st time that afternoon in this particular usage—*romantique*. She was thick with the Moderates: Talleyrand, Joucourt, Narbonne. This last (the Baron was complaisant) had become her 1st serious lover, who by year's end would get her with her 2nd child, the 1st to live.

She liked my father—I mean the man who had represented himself to her, to her own father, & to Barlow as Henry Burlingame IV. She call'd him, & me, *américain* . . . Indeed, she spoke of him in the same breath with the late "Monsieur Franklin," as *entrepreneurs de la révolution!* "We" were, she declared, *l'avant-garde du genre humain*.

My protest—restrain'd indeed, considering my feelings—that I did not regard myself as a citizen of anyplace, much pleased her: To be sure, she said, "our kind" are citizens of the world: but the new idea of political nationality, much in vogue since "our revolution," was in her opinion the wave of the future, & not to be snift at. For my observation that, whatever his talents as diplomatist or spy, my father had been less than exemplary as a husband & parent, she took me spiritedly to task. Quite aside from such possibilities as that my father's secret & dangerous work might truly have made a proper family life out of the question, despite his best efforts; that he himself might have been heartbroken at the deceptions & disguises he was forced to; that he might have been acting in our best interests, given for example our value as hostages to his adversaries—had I not consider'd the possibility that he had simply outgrown his wife? Or that his enemies had forged those cruel letters of invitation & promist reunion? In any case, was I still child enough not to forgive parental negligence in one whose gifts were, of their kind, comparable to Gibbon's or Rousseau's?

She urged me to go to him, in Baltimore. I bid her *bonsoir*. She complimented my independence & my unaccented French, and hoped I would call on her again: I was the first *américain* she had met both very young & civilized. If I would discuss our revolution with her—whose differences from the French she thot more significant than their celebrated similarity—she would discuss with me another sort of revolution already under way, tho scarcely yet acknowledged, in all the arts. Its inspirers were her old family friend Rousseau & his German counterparts. Its values were sentiment & sensation as against conscious intellection; it aspired to the rejection or transcension of conventional forms, including the conventional categories of art & social class; its spirit was manifest equally in the assault on the Bastille, in the musical innovations of certain pupils of Joseph Haydn, in the plays & essays of Schiller, above all in Goethe's novel-in-letters, *The Sorrows of Werther,* even in the investigations of natural historians. Had I read, for example, Herr Goethe's botanical treatise *Versuch, die Metamorphose der Pflanzen zu erklären,* just publisht? She would lend it me: if I had my father's (& the author's) eye for the connexions betwixt apparently disparate things, perhaps I would discover that an essay on the forms of plants can illumine the storm & stress, so to speak, betwixt certain parents & their children, or innovative artists & the conventions of their arts. I did read German?

I fell in love with her at once, and remain'd so for the next five years, during most of which I served in her household as a sort of English-language amanuensis & library clerk. Because my politics were more radical & sanguinary than Germaine's (I was to cheer—& witness—the King's beheading, & many another's), I was able to render her a signal service on 2 September 1792. The King & Queen had been arrested, the Revolutionary Tribunal establisht; Robespierre & Danton had led the insurrection of the Paris Communards, who were now inspired to slaughter all the Royalists they could lay hands on. They broke into Mme de Staël's house and demanded of me that I deliver my mistress up to them as a prisoner & join them in the morrow's executions. But I had known of their coming from my friends in the Hôtel de Ville, and had bid Germaine disguise herself as one of her own servants, whom I now introduced as my mistress in the tenderer sense, & who was in a delicate condition besides. Our employer, we declared, had fled that day to Switzerland.

Thither (that very night) she flew, in her plainest closed carriage, rewarding me en route with what she knew I had long desired. The carriage pitcht & bounced over the cobbles; round about us were the shouts & torches of the *sans-culottes.* I was 16 & virginal; she 26 & seven months gone with her 2nd child by Narbonne. I had no clear idea how to proceed, especially in such circumstances. But no initiative of mine was wanted: for all her experience of love, Mme de Staël had never been "taken" as a serving girl; the situation excited her to such a pitch of "romantic" emotion that, so far from returning as I had intended to join my friends in the September Massacre, I found myself—your pardon, Andrée—a-humping *la baronne* over Brie, Champagne, Bourgogne; up her Seine, down her Saône, over her Jura, to the home-most peaks & pools of her beloved Coppet, in Switzerland.

Where arriving, she turn'd her full attention to establishing a salon for her fellow refugees, & to her own lying-in. Tho she never forgot my service to her, it was clear her heart belong'd to Narbonne. Our remarkable journey was not mention'd, far less repeated. In the spring, son Albert safely deliver'd, she moved with her *ménage* to England, to join her lover & M. Talleyrand. I return'd to Paris & the Terror, which now shockt even liberal Barlow out of the city & across the Channel— where he forwarded me the last letter I was ever to receive from "Henry Burlingame IV."

It was written, purportedly, from Castines Hundred. Its author declared himself in midst of the proudest feat of his career: the reorganization, this time with British aid, of Pontiac's old Confederacy of the Iroquois, Miamis, Ottawas, & Shawnees, under Chief Little Turtle (a Miami), to succeed against the Americans where Pontiac had fail'd against the British. Already "we" had won a great victory over General St. Clair on the Wabash River; the author was confident we would turn back the "American Legion" being recruited & train'd by General Anthony Wayne to suppress us. Our objective then, the writer asserted, was, in his words, "to call our enemy to our aid": to form a strong independent colony of Indians, Africans, French *habitants*, & Spanish Floridians in the politically confused territory west of North Carolina & south of the Ohio, in the valley of the Tennessee, which from time immemorial had been a common Indian hunting ground. There John Sevier had organized in 1785 a new state called Frankland (later Franklin), which had been more or less dissolved. But the situation was still fluid enough to permit the hope of its reestablishment, if not as a sovereign state, at least as "the first non-Anglo-Saxon child of the Union." He urged me to join him at Castines Hundred for the coming offensive & the great move south. I had a new little cousin there, he reported, born since I'd left: a charming 4-year-old, named Andrée. . .

I assumed the letter, & the strategy, to be duplicitous. Barlow himself thot it a tactic to the opposite end—the establishment of more & more American "defensive" fortifications in the western territories, to protect the settlers flooding illegally onto Indian lands—and did not even report it to the American minister. General Wayne's rout of the Indian "confederacy" at Fallen Timbers the following year (and the admission of "Tennessee" into the Union in '96 as one more slave state) confirm'd my assumptions. I liked to imagine, as I watcht King Louis & then Marie Antoinette go under the guillotine—& then the Girondists, & then the Hébertists, & then the democratic republic, & finally Robespierre himself—that the author of that letter had been relieved at least of his scalp by the surviving Iroquois; for I was certain the cause of Indian sovereignty (about which, at the time, I had no deep feeling one way or the other) was lost as long as he lived to pretend to champion it.

The end of Robespierre & the Terror on the 9th Thermidor of Year II (27 July 1794), ended also my interest in the revolution, which—even before Bonaparte came to the fore—we saw to be increasingly in the hands of the generals rather than those of the *sans-*

culottes. Barlow was in Hamburg, recouping his fortune as a shipping agent after the collapse of the Scioto real-estate swindle. Mme de Staël was back at Coppet, writing her *Réflexions sur le procès de la reine,* which had disturb'd her as the execution of the King had not. Both were eager to return to Paris; both sought my opinion of their safety there in Year III, under the new Directory. For some reason, Germaine's letters to me were uncommonly confidential (I later learnt she was using them as trial draughts for her more serious epistles). Her affair with Narbonne, she confest, was ending: for one thing, he remain'd in England when she return'd to Coppet in '94, and she suspected he had taken another mistress. *Apparently,* she wrote to me in the spring of that year, *everything I believed I meant to him was a dream, and only my letters were real.* For another, she had met & been fascinated by Benjamin Constant in Lausanne, who in turn was fascinated by the audacious young Corsican, Bonaparte.

The city, I regretfully reported, now that the Committee of Public Safety had been guillotined, was safe. I myself was penniless, & unemploy'd except as an occasional counterfeiter of *assignats,* the nearly worthless paper currency of the moment. I had discover'd in myself an unsuspected gift for forgery, and was being courted by minor agents of both the left & the right, equally interested in bankrupting the *Directoire.* I was nineteen, no longer a novice in matters of the heart. My politics were little more than an alternation of impassion'd populism & fastidious revulsion from the mob; the two extremes met like Jacobins & Royalists, not so much in my cynical expediency as in the psychological expedient that was my cynicism: a makeshift as precarious as the Directory itself. I dared to hope Germaine might find all this, and me . . .*romantique.*

And so she did, for the 1st *décade* of *Brumaire, An IV,* whilst reopening her Paris salon with Constant & the Baron de Staël. When the spirit took her, she would revert to her waiting-maid or *sans-culotte* costume & fetch me, in that famous plain carriage, thro some working-class *faubourg* to reenact "our" escape of '92. But her heart was Constant's; her mind was on the composition of an essay, *De l'Influence des passions;* the serving-girl whose clothes she borrow'd for the escapade was a secret Jacobin infested with crab lice, who thus spread the vermin not only to her mistress & to M. Constant, but also to me & thence to the bona fide (& thitherto uninfested) working girl whose bed I'd shared thro the Terror. Germaine found the episode *piquant;* the rest of us did not. Moreover, tho I still admired her range, I no longer found her physically appealing. When Barlow—horrified by the dangerous game I had been playing with my *assignats*—urged me to accompany him on a diplomatic mission to Algiers at the year's end (I mean Gregorian 1795), I accepted with relief.

Here began my firsthand schooling in international politics & intrigue. Whilst we moved down the Rhone & then thro Catalonia towards Alicante & Algiers, chatting of Don Quixote & buying new presents for the Dey, Hassan Bashaw (to add to the $27,000 consular gift we carried with us!), Barlow explain'd the manifold delicacy of our mission as it had been set forth to him by his new friend James Monroe, Washington's minister to France. The Barbary pirates, over the 10 years past, had seized a number of U. States merchant vessels, confiscated the hulls & cargoes, & made slaves of the crews. The American public—and U. States shipping interests, principally in New England—were indignant. France & England were either indifferent or privately content: they had no love themselves for the troublesome corsairs & could at any time have employ'd their navies to rid the Mediterranean of them. But they prefer'd to bribe the Dey to spare their own vessels, & thus, in effect, to harass their American competition, along with the Danes, Swedes, Dutch, Portuguese, Venetians, & cet. On the other hand, they fear'd, as did Washington, that enough such incidents would oblige or justify the construction of a large American navy, just as retaliatory attacks by the Indians had "justified" the extension of "our" army ever farther west of the Appalachians. To be sure, many U. States interests desired just that, & so were in a sense obliged to the Barbary pirates for rousing public opinion to their cause, and did not want them prematurely put down or bought off! Even Washington, suspicious as he was of New England Federalist shippers, and opposed in principle to standing professional armies & navies (as chances on the economy & chiefest dangers to the peace they were supposed to ensure), had to acknowledge that nothing so strengthen'd the fragile Union as an apparent menace from beyond its borders. He also fear'd (said Barlow) that the anti-slavery or merely anti-Southern interests above Mason's & Dixon's Line would make factional propaganda out of the Dey's enslavement of more than 100 white Yankee sailors. Barlow himself was of a mind to add a passage on the subject to the 8th Book of his revised *Columbiad*.

For the present, then, Washington had no alternative but to buy the prisoners' freedom & negotiate with the Dey a humiliating bribe for sparing our ships in the future. The only apparent issue was the size of the ransom & bribe: even pro-Navy interests in the U. States were divided betwixt those who believed that a ruinously large payment would make the construction of warships seem an economizing measure, and those who fear'd that too large a figure would leave nothing in the Treasury to build a navy with. Behind that lay the covert question, whether the treaty negotiation should be expeditious or deliberately prolong'd. A quick settlement might be a high settlement— the Dey was asking $800,000—and (or *but*) would reduce the opportunity to exploit the occasion for building a navy & for propagandizing against African slavery &/or for national unity. It would also, of course, gratify the captured sailors & their families. Prolong'd negotiation might result in a better bargain, but (or *and*) it would also afford time to build and man warships, & cet. It could also—for better or worse, depending on one's larger strategy—incite the capricious Dey to seize more of "our" ships, raise his ransom price, perhaps even break off negotiations altogether. In short, as many interests in both America & Europe would be pleased to see Barlow's mission fail as would be gratified by its success.

"Bonaparte tells us that generalship is the art of improvisation," he concluded (our *calèche* was rolling through the almond & olive groves of La Huerta); "Henry Burlingame teaches us that improvisation, in its turn, is the art of imagining & cleaving to that point of view from which whatever comes to pass may be seen to be to one's interests & exploited to advantage. I pray you, Andrew, ponder that: we can lose only insofar as we may fail to improvise 'victory' out of 'defeat,' & make it work."

His own motives were comparatively simple: to render a service to his country whilst traveling at its expense & perhaps making a lucrative investment or two in Algiers (the bulk of his Hamburg fortune he had put into French government bonds & Paris real estate, counting on Napoleon to increase their value; but he left some $30,000 liquid for speculation), and to conclude the business speedily lest his Ruthy grow jealous again. His strategy was to placate the Dey with gifts & assurances until the American minister to Portugal (his old friend & fellow Hartford Wit, Colonel Humphreys), whose charge it was to conclude the treaties with Algiers, Tripoli, & Tunis, could raise $800,000 in bullion by selling discounted U. States Bank stock in London & Hamburg: a harder job, in Barlow's estimation, than treating with a moody & dangerous Moslem prince. He wanted me with him because my adventure with the *assignats* convinced him I had inherited my father's gifts, which he believed might be of use to him in the business; and he was delighted at my "cosmopolizing," as he call'd it, since he'd left me to Mme de Staël.

Good Barlow, at once so canny & so ingenuous! Barely 40, he had come as long & almost as various a road as my grandfather: from the conservative hymnist & naive chaplain of "our" revolution, who had watcht Major André hang'd & dedicated his *Vision of Columbus* to Louis XVI, he had been "cosmopolized" himself by the French Revolution into atheism & antimonarchism. He had alarm'd his British & even his conservative American friends with his tract of 1789, *Advice to the Privileged Orders;* with his *Letter to the National Convention* of '92, which had earn'd him Citizenship in the French Republic along with Washington, Madison, Hamilton, & Tom Paine; and with his poem *The Conspiracy of Kings* (same year), a call for the overthrow of all monarchies by general revolution. But despite their Jacobin tone, these works had in common—so I see plainly now, but felt even then despite my own ingenuousness—more enthusiastic & sententious naivety than deep conviction. Whereas his little mock panegyric in three cantos, *Hasty Pudding*—a nostalgic hymn to that American breakfast & to New England, written on a January morning in Savoy in '93—was a pure delight: a *chef-d'oeuvre* written as a lark.

It markt for Barlow a turn he was just now perceiving clearly, as I was later to see in retrospect certain turnings of my own: he was become at once less *ideological* (I mean in Bonaparte's sense of the word) & more political; less radical & more perspicacious; less ambitious & more shrewd. He had learnt enough from his victimizing in the Scioto swindle to make a legitimate fortune in Hamburg; James Monroe—a good judge of good judges of men—had chosen wisely his representative to the Dey. Barlow's review of the political complexities of our mission, his subsequent sharp assessment of the Dey's character & adroit manipulation of it, together with his new-found expertise in international finance, much imprest me & endear'd him to me, the more as they were maskt (the word is too simple) by a bluff Yankee cheerfulness that was in fact his prevailing humor. It disarm'd his adversaries and led them to believe him an easy mark; they came genuinely to like & trust him, & relaxt their intrigues against him, so that in the end he most often got what he was after.

(As I write this, B. is on a mission of far more delicacy & moment as Madison's minister to France: negotiating with Napoleon & his foreign minister, the Duc de Bassano, for repeal of the Berlin & Milan decrees, which permit French confiscation of American vessels trading with Britain. And I pray the dear man will succeed: I who am fresh from doing my utmost to ensure his failure! But of this, more presently.)

Our mission, which we had expected to complete in a matter of weeks once we arrived, kept us in Algiers from March of '96 till July of the following year, thanks to the difficulty of raising gold bullion in a Europe still spent from the wars of the French Revolution & about to embark upon the more exhausting campaigns of Napoleon. Thanks also to the slowness & unpredictability of the mails, which I am convinced have alter'd & re-alter'd the course of history more than Bonaparte & all the Burlingames combined. Our single strategy became cajolement of Hassan Bashaw (an ape of a fellow, given to despotic whims & tantrums, but no fool) into extending his deadline for payment instead of cancelling his treaty & declaring war on the U. States. Our tactics we improvised, and Barlow now reveal'd himself an apt student of his former tutor. When we were "greeted" by an outraged Dey (he refused to receive us; would not even open Barlow's letter of credentials) whose initial deadline had already expired & who was threatening war in eight days, Barlow bought a 90-day extension by the inspired but dangerous expedient of offering the Bashaw's daughter a 20-gun frigate, to be built in Philadelphia & deliver'd to Algiers! It was a wild excess of our authority: $45,000 for the frigate; another $18,000 retainer to the Jewish banker Joseph Bacri, the Dey's closest advisor, whom Barlow befriended (on the strength of their shared initials—Bacri was a Kabbalist) & thus bribed to make the offer. There was also the certainty that the frigate would be used to highjack further merchant shipping, perhaps "our" own. But the stratagem workt: the Dey (who now declared his earlier anger to have been feign'd—and demanded 36 instead of 20 guns) was delighted; so was President

Washington. We got our 90 days, Bacri got his $18,000 (plus Barlow's banking busness, which he managed scrupulously), & Hassan Bashaw, two years later, got the frigate *Crescent:* a 36-gunner costing $90,000.

We were also permitted to deliver our consular gifts: jewel'd pistols & snuffboxes, linens, brocades, Parisian rings, bracelets, & necklaces for the ladies of the harem.

"Your father would be proud of us," Barlow exulted. "The Bashaw has been Burlingamed!"

I could scarcely agree; another such 90 days' grace, I ventured to say, would bankrupt the Union. Tut, said Barlow, 'twas cheaper than one week of war. Bacri's fee in particular he judged well invested, not only because the Jew alone could have made our offer (& added *gratis* the nicety of making it to the Dey's *daughter:* a diplomatic stroke Barlow admitted he himself never would have thot of), but because in Barlow's opinion the best thing we'd bought so far with "our" $138,000 was not the 90-day extension, but Bacri's friendship. My father, he told me, used to swear by the cynical dictum of Smollett's Roderick Random: that while small favors may be acknowledged & slight injuries atoned, there is no wretch so ungrateful as he whom you have mostly generously obliged, and no enemy so implacable as those who have done you the greatest wrong. He meant to cement his new friendship with Bacri at once by rendering him a small but signal service—in gratitude for Bacri's advice that we not tell the Dey we were in Algiers for no other purpose than to complete the treaty & ransom the prisoners, but instead rent a villa & make a show of settling in for a permanent consular stay.

This 2nd stratagem was more Burlingamish than the 1st, for in addition to "H.B.-ing H.B.," as Barlow put it (*i.e.*, Burlingaming Hassan Bashaw), we served ourselves in several ways at once. One of the older American prisoners, a certain James Cathcart, had ingratiated himself with the Dey to the point of becoming his English-language secretary & closest non-Moslem advisor; he was also our chief liaison with the other prisoners & our principal go-between with the Dey himself. It was Cathcart's errand, for example, to relay to Barlow, almost daily, the Bashaw's impatience that the ransom money had not arrived. Not surprisingly, the Dey's only other confidant amongst the Infidels—our friend Bacri—was jealous of this secretary, the more since Cathcart was Christian & Bacri Jewish. It was, in fact, in the course of jesting with me on the advantage an atheist like himself ought to have in negotiations involving a Moslem, a Christian, & a Jew, that Barlow hit on his pretty inspiration: if the Dey were to send Cathcart to Philadelphia to supervise construction of the *Crescent,* we would in a single stroke liberate a chief prisoner, oblige Bacri to us for removing the object of his jealousy, & relieve ourselves of some pressure from the Dey, who could then look to Cathcart instead of us to make good on that part of his extortion. Moreover, Barlow had the wit to see that the idea should appear to be Hassan Bashaw's own. We discust how it might best be put to him without arousing his suspicion—and it occur'd to me to suggest that *Bacri,* rather than ourselves, bring up the matter. Not only was he a better hand at insinuation (& at judging the Dey's moods), but, should the proposal arouse the Bashaw's suspicion or displeasure, it would fall upon Bacri—who however would have only his diplomacy to blame—rather than upon ourselves.

Barlow embraced me, then waltzt merrily about the room. I was my father's son, he cried, my father's son! This was 1 May: a week later Cathcart set out for Philadelphia, scarcely happier than the Dey, who preen'd & strutted at *his* shrewd idea. Or than Bacri, who—Smollett's dictum notwithstanding—now clamor'd to return our favor. Or than Barlow, despite his fuming over Humphreys' inability to raise the ransom money. Or than I, who till then had not recognized in myself the family precocity in diplomatical intrigue.

Barlow took thereafter to consulting me seriously on tactical matters, tho I reminded him that calling me my father's son was sorely qualified praise; also, that any service I might render was to *him,* whom I owed so much, and not to his country, for which I had at best mixt feelings. Nonetheless I was able to be of use to him, not long after, as follows:

Our dearly bought 90 days were two-thirds spent. Colonel Humphreys' efforts to sell three-quarters of a million dollars' worth of discounted U. States Bank stock had got him no gold at all, only letters of credit on Madrid & Cádiz from the London banking firm of Baring & Co. They must have known (at least Barlow did) that the Spanish government was unlikely to permit the export of so much gold—particularly to those Barbary pirates who from time out of mind had made slaves of Christian Spaniards, not least among them the author of *Don Quixote.* Barlow had therefore shrewdly suggested that Humphreys transfer Baring & Co.'s letter of credit from Spain to the branch office of Joseph Bacri in Livorno, Italy, where it could promptly be negotiated & the credit transfer'd in turn to Bacri of Algiers. The Dey would have his money (at least credit with someone he trusted); the treaty would be concluded; the prisoners could return to America & we to Paris—and the firm of Bacri would have earn'd two separate commissions on the transaction! Bacri himself had readily agreed, and we'd dispatcht a consular aide to Livorno (the English "Leghorn," where, as it happens, old Smollett is buried) to manage the matter. But the transfer of credit had yet to be effected by Humphreys with Baring & Co.; our letters to Lisbon & London & Cádiz & Livorno & Paris & Philadelphia had as well been posted into the sea for all the answer we got. And to make matters worse, with the coming of summer Algiers was smitten by an outbreak of plague.

Of this last, dear child, I shall not speak, except to say that I had rather take my chances with a dozen red Robespierres than brave again the Terror of the Pest, the black flag of Bubonia. We were doubly desperate: by the day our three months' grace expired (8 July, just after my 20th birthday), hundreds of Algerines & five American prisoners had expired also, and unspeakably. Daily we expected the pestilence to attack our little household. Barlow made his will. I wisht myself in Switzerland. Yet no word came from across the Mediterranean.

What came instead seem'd at first another setback, but proved a blessing in disguise. A new French consul arrived in Algiers to replace the old, bringing with him a gift to the Dey of such opulence that "ours" (which Monroe & Barlow had thot daringly extravagant) was put in the shade. To point up this disparity—and to remind us further of our tardiness with the ransom—Hassan Bashaw open'd his hairy arms to France, & would have nothing to do with us.

Prest by the Dey to ask some favor in return for his gift, the new French consul requested a loan of $200,000 in gold from the royal treasury, to defray the expenses of the French consulate! We thot the request an effrontery—the man was borrowing back more than he'd given, at a time when gold was so scarce in Algiers that even the house of Bacri had none to lend—but the Dey (a pirate after all, not a banker) granted the extraordinary loan at once. Now, it happened that Bacri's own assets, like Barlow's, were largely invested in French government bonds; after sharing with us his surprise that the Dey had made so improbable a loan, & his interest in anyone who had such access to the Algerine treasury, Bacri hit upon the happy idea of claiming *that same* *$200,000* from the French consulate, in partial payment of what the *Directoire* owed him on those bonds, reciprocating with credit in that amount for the consulate to borrow against in its routine operations! The Consul agreed, it being more convenient for him to work thro Bacri's banks than to be, in effect, in the banking business himself; Bacri was delighted that the French government now owed money to the Dey instead of to him; and Barlow—who by this time was heartily sorry he'd volunteer'd for the Algerine service instead of improving his own fortune in Paris—wisht aloud & sincerely he'd been born a Jew instead of a Connecticut Yankee.

"Better Yankee than *yekl*," Bacri replied, by way of cordial acknowledgement that some New England traders are sharp indeed, and some Jews dull.

Now, I much admired Joseph Bacri myself, as a shrewd but reliable fellow who took every fair advantage, but fulfill'd his obligations faithfully, & who in addition was a man of culture & political detachment (all governments, he was fond of declaring, are more or less knavish, but just that fact made the *more* or *less* of considerable importance). For some reason—perhaps because his smile included me amongst the "Yankees"—I was suddenly inspired to out-Bacri Bacri in our ongoing project to Burlingame the Bashaw. Here was our chance— I declared to Barlow when our friend had left, still exulting in his *coup de maître*—to discharge Bacri's debt to us for removing Cathcart. Bacri—who understood credit as the Dey did not—was as confident as we that, despite all the delays, Baring & Company's letter of credit to

Humphreys in Lisbon against their banks in Madrid & Cádiz would eventually be transfer'd to Bacri's office in Leghorn & thence to Algiers. In that sense, our personal "credit" with Bacri was good, especially in the light of our past favors to him. Against this credit, then, why ought we not to borrow at once from Bacri the entire same $200,000 that the French Consul had borrow'd from the Dey, & buy with it the immediate release of the prisoners?

Barlow was incredulous. Why should the Dey accept his own money, so to speak, for the sailors' ransom, especially as he would be relinquishing his best leverage for delivery of the frigate & payment of the rest of his demands? He need not know the source of the money, I replied; 'twas Bacri himself who routinely assay'd & certified, for a fee, the Dey's revenues. As for that leverage, it should be pointed out to him that the plague was reducing it every day: $200,000 for 100 sick Yankee sailors was not a bad price; the Dey could always capture fresh hostages if "we" defaulted on the rest of the treaty. But Bacri, Barlow protested, slightly less incredulous but still shaking his head: What was in it for Bacri? I admitted that to be the harder question, for while our friend was most certainly not *just* a Jewish banker, neither was he just our friend. The best I could suggest was that we charter from Bacri himself a ship to fetch the sailors home in, and route it to Philadelphia by way of Livorno & Lisbon, where the captain—or one of us—might expedite delivery of the promist gold. Beyond that, we must (and, I added earnestly, we *should*) simply trust to Bacri's goodwill.

It was this last touch, I believe, that persuaded Barlow in the 1st instance (who now hugg'd and waltzt about the room with me again, to the amazement of our Algerine house-servants) & Bacri in the 2nd, who did indeed drag his heels in indecision & astonishment at the audacity of our proposal, but at last agreed & took it upon himself to point out to the Dey that five percent of his hostages had succumb'd already to the plague. *Mirabile dictu,* the stratagem workt, with a celerity that startled even us: not 48 hours from the time we hatcht the plan, the prisoners were ransom'd with the Dey's own gold & waiting aboard the ship *Fortune* (leased from Bacri, but crew'd & captain'd by themselves) for a fair southwesterly to carry them to Leghorn!

"Andrew Burlingame Cook the Fourth," said Barlow, who had taken to teasing me with my full name, "you must go with them." In one bold stroke, he declared, I had accomplisht the chiefest part of his mission. He himself must linger on until the gold arrived & the treaty was concluded. But much as he wisht my company & counsel, he wisht even more my being out of reach of the pest, & charged me now with a mission of more moment to him than his own welfare: I was to stop in Leghorn to ascertain that Bacri's office there had received the letter of credit from Humphreys in Lisbon (we'd learnt, aghast, that Humphreys had sent it by the *regular post* instead of by express courier!) & to make sure that it was promptly negotiated & the specie shipt before Napoleon, who had open'd his great campaign against the Austrians in northern Italy, should close the port. I was then to go to his Ruthy in the rue du Bac, deliver to her his last will & testament along with letters of an equally intimate but less lugubrious character, assure her that she had no rivals amongst the pantaloon'd ladies of Algiers, & assure *him*, by return post, that she was similarly faithful. That is (he regarded me meaningly here: no libertine, he was no monk either, & had not been perfectly celibate all these months), that whatever shifts she might have devised to assuage her loneliness, they posed no threat to her love for him.

"And this inquiry you are to discharge with perfect tact," he concluded, "as only you—or your father—could." Except that, should the impulse take me, I was to consider myself free to stay aboard of the *Fortune* & visit the country to which I had just render'd a considerable service, perhaps even seeking out "Henry Burlingame IV" & settling once for all in my heart whether he was my father. For if he was not, or if no face-to-face accounting could justify his behavior to me, then he, Barlow, would be pleased to regard me officially as he regarded me already in his heart: as his own son.

I was much toucht, & much confused in my own heart—but enough surfeited with pestiferous Algiers to delight in putting it behind me. I went, not to Philadelphia, but to Leghorn & thence back to dear Paris. But to appease my conscience both for leaving good Joel as the Dey's sole American hostage, in effect, & for declining that invitation to be his son (I didn't *want* a father, I began with some excitement to understand), I perform'd him one final service ere I went, as important in my history as in his.

Our diplomatic successes in the cause of the U. States, remember, like most successes in international affairs, were at the expense of other governments, inasmuch as the Dey's chief revenue was still the prizes taken by his corsairs. What game our treaty pledged him to forgo, he bagg'd elsewhere. In consequence, while Barlow was currently the envy of the Algerine consular community, he was also the prime target of their cabals. Nothing would have more pleased the Spanish, Dutch, Swedish, & Venetian consuls than the default of our treaty payments & a resumption of Algerine piracy against U. States merchantmen. Thus far they had been content to asperse privily, to the Dey, Barlow's character & intentions: he was a sodomite, they insinuated; a Christian cleric; a closet poet. But on the eve of the *Fortune*'s departure, when my belongings were already packt & shipt aboard, Barlow came to my chambers much concern'd that a graver move against him might be afoot.

His profession of fidelity to Ruthy, I repeat, had been a shade disingenuous. Joel loved & misst her, no question, & wisht himself in her arms in the rue du Bac; she had no rivals amongst the veil'd Algerines. But he had for some weeks been enjoying a flirtation with the young wife of a man attacht to the Spanish consulate (we call'd her "Consuelo del Consulado"), and had left off her pursuit out of delicacy only when the husband, a gambler & general libertine, had perisht of the plague a few days since. Not once had this Consuelo responded to Barlow's gallantries by more than a flash of her Andalusian eyes; now, suddenly, a message purportedly in her hand was deliver'd from the Spanish consulate: Could her *carísimo* Señor B. arrange discreetly to meet her carriage—alone, in person, at once—at a certain headland not far hence, on business of a most urgent but confidential nature?

He suspected a trap, of course. The note could have been forged, or written under duress; the woman or someone acting in her stead could be baiting him into a compromising position, to the end of either embarrassing or blackmailing him. Worse, some hired ruffian might be waiting in the carriage to knock him on the head & toss him into the sea, on pretext of defending the young widow's honor. Even supposing the message genuine, he had misgivings: what if his little flirtation should lead to something more consequential & less extricable? On the other hand, if the lady truly needed his aid or craved his company, and he injured or insulted her by not responding, he would make a considerable enemy in the consular community: a fresh widow so ready to go to't (let us suppose) would just as readily look to her revenge if scorn'd. And what if she *did* innocently need his help, or crave a bit of extra-consular consolation? He'd be a knave & fool not to provide it! & cetera.

Amused as I was by his embarrassment & excitement, I quite shared his apprehensions, & proposed at once to meet the carriage in his stead. I would declare he had been summon'd to an unexpected private audience with the Dey (no consular person could fail to acknowledge such priority), but would be honor'd to meet her at her convenience in our villa. If she seem'd offended, I would improvise, confess I had intercepted her message & taken it upon myself to investigate. If she seem'd sincere—whether sincerely distrest or sincerely amorous—I would endeavor to pacify her & either fetch her to the villa or arrange another assignation in less vulnerable circumstances, for Barlow to pursue at his own discretion. If I smelt a rat, he would be forewarn'd. And if it should prove an outright ambuscade? Why, then I would make shift to extricate myself as best I could: I had learnt a thing or two in the streets of Paris.

But she had specified Barlow himself: trap or no trap, would her carriage not take flight at my approach?

I had come to know my knack for counterfeiting hands (and *assignats*). Earlier, in Mme de Staël's house at the time of the Septembrist massacre, I had discover'd a sudden facility for improvising histories; and more recently, in Algiers, a gift for devising stratagems. Now, almost to my own surprise, I found myself a ready hand at counterfeiting certain actual personages. Then & there, impromptu, I walkt like Barlow, talkt & laught & gestured in his way, even improvised aloud a passage from his *Vision of Columbus!* Where his had read (with characteristic lack-lustre):

Glad Chesapeake unfolds a passage wide,
And leads their streamers up the freshening tide;
Where a mild region and delightful soil
And groves and streams allure the steps of toil . . .

"mine" extravagantly declaim'd:

Borne up my Chesapeake, [Columbus] hails
The flowery banks that scent his slackening sails;
Descending twilight mellows down the gleam
That spreads far forward on the broad blue stream;
The moonbeam dancing, as the pendants glide,
Silvers with trembling tints the rippling tide;
The sand-sown beach, the rocky bluff repays
The faint effulgence with their amber'd rays;
O'er greenwood glens a browner lustre flies
And bright-hair'd hills walk shadowy round the skies. . .

I meant a gentle parody—but Barlow was enraptured, as much by the verses as by my impersonation. I was my father's & cet.! Laughing & weeping, roused & reluctant, he gave me leave to make free with his cape (his coat was too large for me; I regretted he wore neither periwig nor eyeglasses; our features were not similar; voice & manner must serve) & a fine horse presented him by the Dey. We embraced a final time, and off I rode, to the oddest assignation I hope ever to be party to.

The moon was bright, the night warm & windy. The dark carriage waited with a single coachman at the designated spot, above a rocky beach outside the city. *Très "romantique":* Germaine de Staël would have fancied it, the more for its spice of diplomatic intrigue. But I was all misgivings: surely the coachman was a Spanish thug, the carriage full of his cohorts. Why had I not come in our own carriage, her stipulations be damn'd, with Barlow drest as coachman, & demanded she change conveyances to prove her goodwill before proceeding farther? Too late for such hindsight: moreover, tho my disposition was & is not reckless, some intuition (I have learnt to recognize & honor it since) urged me, in this instance, not to reck. I took a large breath & walkt the horse forward, my hand on the pistol Barlow had lent me with his cape & the rest. . .

In the 15 years since, only three people have heard without scoffing the full tale of what ensued. I have ceased to recount it even to my friends, not to try their confidence unnecessarily. Andrée herself I have declined till now to test the faith of in detail, as (witness my faltering pen) I hesitate to test yours, child, when you shall scan these pages in time to come. What matters, after all, is not the business in the carriage, but the sparing of Barlow's life (he himself was able to verify later, thro Bacri's informants in Madrid, that the Spanish consul in Algiers had indeed got cipher'd instructions to assassinate him if the job

295

could be done for $50,000) and the demonstration, to myself, of my little knack for impersonation.

That knack was call'd for only at the opening of the adventure, when the coachman cried me to a halt & uncover'd his lantern to inspect me. I saw the carriage window-curtain drawn aside; then I screen'd my face with Barlow's hat and call'd back in Barlow's voice that I was he whom a certain Señora del Consulado had sought aid of. If she was within, let her show herself, otherwise I would back to my own affairs—and, I added, I could see nothing with that lantern shining in my face. The carriage door open'd partway: a woman's voice instructed the coachman in Spanish to put out the light, and me in soft accented English to secure my horse & enter without fear. I did so, keeping my visage lower'd, muttering in Barlow's way about the lateness of the hour, & cet., and glancing up under my brim as I climb'd the step to make certain the lady was alone inside. She was barely illuminated by a tiny cover'd lamp fixt to the carriage wall. I stept in quickly & turn'd away from her to close the door & draw its curtain.

Even Germaine de Staël & the Barlows, back in Paris, accepted this much without question. Ruthy Barlow & Germaine defended somewhat further—against the skepticism of Joel & of the Barlows' new American friend, Robert Fulton, whom they more or less adopted in my stead when he left off painting with Benjamin West in London and came to Paris with his schemes for canalways & submarine vessels—the possibility of what happen'd next: Consuelo's calling to the coachman to ride on even as she flung herself ardently upon me; my struggle to keep her mouth cover'd when she realized, at once, that I was not the man she'd summon'd; my urgent whisper'd assurances that I had no dishonorable intentions, & wisht only to ascertain, for the gentleman whose person I feign'd, that the Spanish consulate had none either. No one seriously doubted—especially given Barlow's subsequent verification—the essentials of Consuelo's story: that she had at one time briefly been the mistress of the political attaché of the Spanish consulate, a dashing, unscrupulous fellow named Don Escarpio; that her worthless husband, who encouraged the affair in hopes of advancing his own fortunes, was smitten with jealousy upon its consummation & challenged Don Escarpio just when that fellow (who had better been named Don Juan), having made his conquest, began promptly to tire of her. It was Consuelo's conviction, in view of what follow'd, that Don Escarpio then arranged her husband's death by plague in order to rid himself of the nuisance without risking a duel, & to put her the more at his mercy. Her profligate spouse had left large debts in the consular community, which she had no means of paying; Don Escarpio proposed to liquidate those debts & return her safely to her family in Málaga with a $10,000 secret bonus from the Spanish government if she would seduce & see to the death of Señor Barlow, the too successful American diplomat who had so clearly been captivated by her beauty. Consuelo had protested that she could not kill, unless perhaps in a passion of anger. Her ex-lover, of whom she was now terrified, had replied with a cold smile (*"una sonrisa fría"*) that no anger was required, only the sort of passion of which none knew better than he her breast was full. He then disclosed to her—& she to me—the singular means she was to employ.

For Fulton, more engineer than artist, the question was not whether one could in fact prepare a snuffboxful of infected matter from the buboes of a plague victim, apply that poison to one's fingernails as to a quiver of savage arrowheads, & infect the victim by raking his back or arms with those same nails in the throes of passion, so that he would perish miserably three days later & be counted simply one more casualty of the pestilence. Fulton had heard enough from Barlow & me (who had it from my father) of Lord Amherst's successful employment of smallpox against the Indian besiegers of Fort Pitt to credit that possibility. What he doubted was that all this information— together with Consuelo's conviction that Don Escarpio would surely see to her own death too, whether she refused or complied, & her decision therefore to agree to the plan but plead with Barlow instead to smuggle her aboard the *Fortune* & look to his own safety—could feasibly have been convey'd to me whilst we shook the carriage, first in our struggle with each other (she to call alarums to the coachman, I to prevent her & win her confidence) & then in pretended passion, punctuated with cries of delight in two languages.

I would smile here at Germaine, who declared that while she thot the whole Don Escarpio business smackt more of Italian opera than of Spanish diplomacy, she knew from experience that much ground could be cover'd in a bouncing carriage. She allow'd, moreover, that it was my modesty to call the passion & attendant noises merely feign'd, as I had been a notable gallant even before improving my skills in naughty Barbary. She would even grant that Consuelo had messaged out the business beforehand in her fetching skew'd English (I show'd the messages as proof) for "Barlow" to read as she moan'd & thrasht & annotated in whispers: Germaine herself permitted no drawing-room conversation at Coppet whilst she composed; her staff & houseguests communicated by messages written & replied to on the spot—what we call'd *"la petite poste."* She cited Prince Hamlet's scribbling in the grip of his emotions, "A man may smile and smile," & cet. What *she* found hardest to believe was my trusting Consuelo not to poison me by the same device.

I did *not* quite so trust her, I would admit: as I happen'd to have been gripping both her wrists in one hand from the start (& covering her mouth with the other until I was assured it was no longer necessary), when she discover'd to me her stratagem I oblig'd her to rake her own flesh at once, to prove her assertion that she had not tapt the dread snuffbox (she declared it was in her reticule) in advance.

And how could I be sure, demanded Ruthy Barlow, that the woman was not up to suicide as well as the seduction & murder of flirtatious diplomats? *Trop romantique,* her husband scoft, who had taken up that term from Germaine upon his belated return to Paris. (Faithful to my word, I had written him in Algiers of Ruthy's new friendship with young Fulton, which I judged harmless; it was not until 1800, after the "XYZ Affair," that Fulton moved in to make their *ménage à trois.) Trop* or *non troppo,* I replied, I could not take measures against every eventuality, especially in the heat of the moment. Consuelo had claw'd thro her skin unhesitatingly at my order: once on the inside of her thighs, again on the underside of her bosoms. I took the rest on faith.

"As ought we," George III is wont to put in at this point. So reports the author Madame d'Arblay ("Fanny Burney," whom I met thro Mme de Staël) from Windsor. The King had the story originally from her after his seizure of 1808, when in his blindness he took a sudden fancy to novels & insisted that his daughters & Mrs. Burney read him long passages from Fielding "and those like him." At my own single audience with the King, in 1803, I had not brot the subject up, inasmuch as I was posing as Robert Fulton at the time, and in any case did not then know of His Majesty's interest in erotic narrative. We spoke of the submarine boat, which George argued was militarily more important than the steamboat; also of Don Quixote & King Lear, both of which characters interested him greatly. It is on Mrs. Burney's authority that I list the King as my 2nd uncritical auditor. He still calls for the story, I understand; rather fancies that Consuelo might be his eldest son's discarded wife the Princess of Wales, & particularly applauds my having accepted this piquant demonstration of her good faith.

"But you want us also to accept these messages as Consuelo's," Joel & Ruthy & Germaine protested good-heartedly, "when we know at 1st hand what an accomplisht forger of letters you are." (At 1st hand because, most recently, I had forged certain messages over the signature of M. Talleyrand to "Messieurs X, Y, & Z," the anonymous intermediaries in Talleyrand's dealings with President Adams.) I take it as a measure of Germaine de Staël's limitations as a novelist, compared with such an untried, even unwilling imagination as that of my *first* uncritical auditor, that she did not observe what Midshipman James Fenimore Cooper remarkt at once: that the acceptation of "historical" documents as authentic is also an act of faith—a provisional suspension of incredulity not dissimilar, at bottom, to our complicity with Rabelais, Cervantes, or George III's beloved Fielding.

Midshipman Cooper, then eighteen & freshly expell'd from Yale for insubordination, had the story from me in the Hustler Tavern in Lewiston, New York, next door to Fort Niagara, one night in 1807. That was the year of "Burr's conspiracy" to separate the western territories & Mexico from the Union; also of Barlow's publication of the first full edition of his *Columbiad* (including my impromptu on "Glad Chesapeake") and Mme de Staël's of her *Corinne;* of Fulton's steamship *Clermont*'s going into regular service on the Hudson; and of my fateful meeting with Tecumseh & his brother the Prophet. Cooper was on shore leave from the brig *Oneida,* the U. States Navy's total Lake

Ontario fleet. I was en route to Castines Hundred to rejoin *cousine* Andrée & recover from the shock of "Aaron Burr's" failure. We were sampling a drink called "cocktail," just invented at that tavern (a mixture of brandy with some flavoring such as curaçao & sugar, shaken with ice chopt from the lake), singing Yale songs I'd learnt from Barlow, & discussing Indians, a subject of interest to us both. I retail'd to Cooper what I knew of "Joseph Brant" & the destruction of the Mohawk Valley Iroquois, with whom he was especially preoccupied. He made copious notes, declaring he had a friend who aspired to write novels about Indians; he heard out with interest my enthusiasm for the Shawnee chief Tecumseh, whom Andrée had grown fond of & taught English to when she was sixteen, & whom I regarded as the red man's last hope to found a sovereign state east of the Mississippi. It was in the course of explaining my half-belief that Tecumseh was Jewish that the subject of my Algerine adventure came up. I had pointed out the singularity of the Shawnees' myth of their own origin: that unlike other tribes (who all reckon'd their emergence from the center of the earth), they traced their descent from twelve original clans who migrated from the east across the bottom of the sea, which parted to let them pass. This myth I related to the notion of my ancestor Ebenezer Cooke, who supposed in his *Sot-Weed Factor* poem that all Indians are descended from the lost tribes of Israel; and I remarkt to my young drinking companion the peculiar ubiquitousness of the Shawnee, bands of whom, like Jews after the Diaspora, were to be found everywhere: from Florida, Georgia, & the Carolinas to Pennsylvania, the Indiana territory, & Lake Erie. True, they were hunters rather than merchants (the ancient Hebrews had not been merchants either). But they were famously abstemious, and regarded themselves as the elect of the earth. Tecumseh in particular had a fine Semitic nose, a Jewish distaste for drunkenness, rape, firearms, & torture (but not for tomahawks & hand-to-hand combat), a good legal-political mind, a talent for sharp bargaining in his treaty dealings, & a loyalty to his family—especially to his visionary brother Tenskwatawa, the Prophet—which might prove his most vulnerable aspect. My persuasion was that one of his ancestors had been, not a colonial governor of South Carolina as the Prophet maintain'd, but an early Jewish settler's child captured & adopted by the Shawnee.

Cooper order'd another round of cocktails, observed that Jews were not admitted to the new U. States Military Academy at West Point or to the naval officer corps, & ask'd whence my familiarity with things Hebrew. Thus we got to the remarkable Joseph Bacri, to Joel Barlow's finally successful Algerine mission, & to my adventure with Consuelo "del Consulado." He was full of questions, but not of the skeptical sort, and made note of my replies for his unnamed friend. Of the matter of our protracted coupling in the carriage—first feign'd & then not—whilst Consuelo disclosed her written "exposition" (as he call'd it), Cooper observed: "That will have to be toned down." He applauded my test both of her "innocence" (by obliging her to scratch herself) and of her sincerity (by taking her directly aboard the *Fortune,* sans papers, baggage, or interview with Barlow; I prevail'd upon the Captain—with a bribe from my travelling-funds & a quickly forged sailing order from "Barlow"—to accept her as a passenger & get under way at once instead of waiting till morning, as we believed the Dey plann'd to intercept the ship outside the harbor). Cooper question'd, not the verity, but the verisimilitude—that is, the plausibility as *fiction*—of my account of all this: the sailing order forged in my cabin in the ten minutes I'd requested to indite a "farewell" (& warning) letter to Barlow, whom I would not see again till mid-September; my inditing, in the same ten minutes, that farewell & warning, in which I enclosed Consuelo's account of the Spanish plot; our bribing the Algerine harbor-master to agree that it was the current high tide, not the next, we were clear'd to sail on; our weighing anchor, making sail, & standing out of the harbor for Leghorn, Marseilles, & Philadelphia even as the carriage—which I'd first approacht not three hours since!—climb'd up from the quay in the direction of Barlow's villa, my horse still tether'd behind.

"That too would all have to be reworkt," said Midshipman Cooper. "The coachman, for example: How could you know he wasn't an agent of that chap. . ." He consulted his notes. "Escarpio?" Lifetime servant of Consuelo's family, I replied; had known her from her birth, & cet. But how was it Don Escarpio hadn't put his own man on the carriage, to ensure against Consuelo's defection? Couldn't account for that myself, I admitted: bit of good luck, I supposed. That would have to be reworkt. And did the fellow not fear for his life when he should return to the Spanish consulate minus his passenger?

"Ah, well," Barlow himself explain'd in Paris just five months ago (December 1811, my last meeting with him) to the bright 12-year-old whom Mme de Staël (herself 45 now, ill, pregnant by her young Swiss lover Rocca, & exiled to Coppet by Napoleon, who had confiscated the first press run of her book *De l'Allemagne* and order'd her to leave Paris at once) had taken an interest in: "Poor Enrique never return'd to the *consulado,* you see. When he deliver'd Andy's letter he was trembling from head to toe. I thot 'twas fright, especially when I'd read the letter—but 'twas chills & fever. The servants would not let him into the house, but bedded him down in his own carriage. Sure enough, the 1st bubo appear'd next day in his groin, and by the time Señor El Consulado came 'round to fetch the horse & carriage, the wretch was dead."

Young Honoré, who loved the story even more than had Fenimore Cooper & King George, would not have it that the coachman's infection was coincidental, even tho Barlow's favorite manservant had succumb'd to the plague just a day or two earlier. No, he insisted: Don Escarpio had infected the man deliberately, to cover his tracks, for "Enrique" was actually Henry Burlingame IV in disguise, seeing to the safety of his long-lost son; and Consuelo had not disembarkt at Málaga after our tearful farewells at Marseilles, but been kidnapt by the lusty sailors & fetcht to Philadelphia, where she escaped & tried to rejoin me at Castines Hundred, but was captured by the Shawnee but spared by Tecumseh because her then pseudonym, Rebecca, together with her raven hair & olive skin, reminded him of his great-grandmother, a Spanish Jewess captured & adopted by the Creeks in Florida. . .

"Too romantical by half, Master Balzac," I advised my 3rd uncritical auditor, who, unlike Midshipman Cooper, frankly aspired to literature & was already scribbling vaudevilles at a great rate. He promist to rework it & show me an amended draught by New Year's Day. But on the darkest night of the year a courier from the office of the Duc de Bassano, drest in the particular shade of brown fashionable that season in Napoleon's court *("Caca du roi de Rome,"* after the stools of the Emperor's infant son), deliver'd to me an urgent letter from Andrée. It had been written at Castines Hundred only 30 days past & sent via Quebec & the secret French-Canadian diplomatic pouch: "Cato" (our code name for Tecumseh, who deplored the white man's influence on the red as had Cato the Greek influence on the Romans) had suffer'd such a defeat on the Tippecanoe River that he was inclined to make peace with the U. States & remain neutral in the coming war. Furthermore, my man John Henry (of whom more presently), frustrated in his attempt to get from the British Foreign Office what he felt was owed him for his espionage in New England, was rumor'd to be leaving London in disgust & returning to Lower Canada. As for the author of the letter herself, she was gratified to report that in consequence of our close cooperation in July, when we had successfully "torpedo'd" (Robert Fulton's word) the negotiations between William Henry Harrison & our friend "Cato," she found herself in the family way. Would I please see to the completion of my current torpedo-work (on Barlow's negotiations with the Duc de Bassano) in time to marry her before April 1812, when our baby was expected? And by the by, in case we should decide to assassinate either William Henry Harrison or Tecumseh's Prophet: Whatever happen'd to my friend Consuelo's dandy little potion? Was I so certain that it had contain'd what she described?

I was not, never had been, never would be certain. For, as I explain'd to your mother when I first met her in 1804 (and told her a version of this adventure suitable for the ears of a lady of fifteen), and re-explain'd when I remet & fell in love with her in 1807, and reminded her upon our marriage three months ago, Consuelo had flung her singular snuffbox straight into the Mediterranean when the *Fortune* clear'd Algiers. For all I knew & know *for certain,* "Don Escarpio" might have been tricking her for some complicated reason into an *unsuccessful* attempt on Barlow's life, or she me into her rescue—tho she needed no such risky stratagem. I was *certain* only that it was good to be out of Algiers & to have such ardent company en route to Leghorn (where I was able to confirm the transfer of "our" letter of credit to Bacri's

Italian office) & Marseilles, where I left the ship. Consuelo wisht to come with me—to Paris, to anywhere—but I was too uncertain of my plans to undertake that responsibility. The Captain offer'd to carry me on, to Málaga or to Philadelphia: I return'd to Paris, & to a different uncertainty: one that persisted another half-dozen years.

Indeed, it was not until 1805, one Saturnian revolution since my birth, that I addrest myself clearly to what I thot of as "the American question." I was *de trop* in Barlow's household after "Toot" Fulton join'd it, tho Joel was glad of my assistance in the "XYZ Affair" & the revision of his *Columbiad* for the press. I was no less so in Mme de Staël's: still Constant's mistress and (in 1797) mother of his child, she turn'd her disappointment with Napoleon's lack of interest in her into formidable political opposition to his 1st Consulship, & a fever of literary activity. I was able to help with the research for her essay *De la Littérature (considérée dans ses rapports avec les institutions sociales);* but after 1800 it was the autobiographical novel that most appeal'd to her, and such adventures as mine with Consuelo she found insufficiently *"esthétique"* (her new favorite adjective) for her *Delphine, Corinne,* & the rest. She was kind, but no longer interested, & frankly bored with my hatred of my father, which she declared had become mere wrongheadedness. "Henry Burlingame IV," she confest, had assisted her in the purchase of 23,000 acres of former Iroquois land in upstate New York, as well as investments in the munitions firm of E. I. Du Pont in Delaware, for which assistance she was his debtor. Her comparison of him to me was in terms borrow'd from "Monsieur Ful*ton*": I was all *vapeur*, still in quest of a proper instrument of propulsion (Fulton was tinkering on the Seine with oars, paddle wheels, screw propellors); my father, more subtle, was a *sous-marin*, quietly applying *torpilles* to what he opposed. She thot I might well take a leaf from his book. Richard Alsop's rhymed attack on Barlow in the Hartford *Courant* (after publication of Barlow's letter criticizing President Adams's French policy) characterized my own inconstancy:

> What eye can trace this Wisdom's son,—
> This "Jack-at-all-trades, good *at none*,"
> This ever-changing, Proteus mind,—
> In all his turns, thro' every wind;
> From telling sinners where they go to,
> To speculations in Scioto, . . .
> From morals pure, and manners plain,
> To herding with Monroe and Paine,
> From feeding on his country's bread,
> To aping X, and Y, and Z,
> From preaching Christ, to Age of Reason,
> From writing psalms, to writing treason.

This "Proteus mind" permitted Barlow in 1800 to help Fulton persuade Napoleon to finance his submarine project against the British navy, and then in 1804 to encourage him to build torpedo-rafts for the Admiralty to use against Napoleon's channel fleet—whilst at the same time projecting a four-volume opus in verse to be called *The Canal: A Poem on the Application of Physical Science to Political Economy,* and drafting liberal pamphlets on the incompatibility of large standing military establishments & political liberty!

My own mind was less protean than protoplasmic; less a "shifter of shapes" than a maker of shifts. On errands for Barlow & Fulton I went to London as aforemention'd & met the King (& Mrs. Burney, & the beautiful Juliette Récamier). On errands for Mme de Staël I came to meet & be befriended by Napoleon's young brother Jérôme, eight years my junior; on account of this connection, & my "American origins," in 1803 I was sent on an errand by a minister of Napoleon himself, to warn Jérôme against contracting "permanent personal alliances" during his tour of the U. States (a naval officer at the moment, he had left his ship in the West Indies and was carousing his way north towards Philadelphia and New York). I arrived in Baltimore on Christmas, 1803, one day after his marriage to Betsy Patterson of that city. It was my task to inform Jérôme privately that his brother—having banisht Mme de Staël from Paris in order to intimidate the anti-Bonapartist *salons,* & having arranged several unsuccessful assassination attempts against himself to cement his popularity with the masses, all in preparation for having Pope Pius VII crown him Emperor of France in the coming year—would never acknowledge Jérôme's marriage to a commoner. The bride, a wealthy Baltimore merchant's daughter, was indignant. Jérôme merely shrug'd & invited me to tour America at the First Consul's expense, on pretext of dissuading him from the marriage he had already consummated.

Thus I found myself, full of misgivings, in the country & state of my birth, for the 1st time since Mother & I had left them in 1783, when I was seven. I crost "glad Chesapeake" to the broad Choptank & Cooke's Point, half expecting to be greeted by some version of "Henry Burlingame IV." There were the frozen marshes of my childhood, the geese flown down from Canada to winter, the graves of good Maggie Mungummory & divers ancient Cookes, the tall-topt pines, the house of my ancestors (long since sold out of the family, & in need of repairs), the ice-blue water lapping chillily at the beach. The scene spoke to me of my namesake's journey north to where those geese came from (I mean my grandfather's, A.C. III's), to learn the truth about his derivation & then to deal with it. 'Twas a tale I'd had in mythic outline, so to speak, from Mother, and from "Father" in the opprobrious detail rehearst in my 2nd letter (I had not yet seen all the diaries & other documents). I was nearing 30, sans course or cause or calling; I had not been to Castines Hundred myself since my 10th year. It was time.

Now we move more swiftly, as my life has moved through the eight years since. I spent that winter as a guest of the Pattersons in Baltimore, acquainting myself with American society in that city as well as in

Philadelphia &, especially, the new capital town of Washington, still a-building. There Jefferson, friend of Barlow & of France as his predecessor had not been, was in the new President's House, having been elected by the House of Representatives after a tie vote with Aaron Burr in the electoral college. Tho he opposed the strong navy built under John Adams's administration (with the help of the Barbary pirates, who had already broacht "our" treaty!), the same amity with Napoleon that put an end to the naval quarrels between France & the U. States had made possible Jefferson's purchase of Louisiana from the First Consul. "America" now extended even *west* of the Mississippi, no one knew how far, some said all the way to the Pacific; Jefferson was sending an expedition from St. Louis to find out. Already nearly a million people had crost the line Pontiac fought for, and settled west of the Appalachians; Jefferson's purchase would redouble that flow of settlers onto Indian lands, now going for $2 the acre. But as the Burr-Jefferson campaign made clear (and the earlier disputation over where the new capital should be built), the union of states was fragile yet; much, much was in the balance. I convey'd Barlow's regards to the President, who pleasantly inform'd me that I was "much changed" since he had known me as Joel's ward in Paris. He instructed me to advise Barlow that building lots, both in the city proper & in Georgetown, were still cheap: B. would do well to buy a few now if he was interested. But he should probably postpone his return to the country (another of my errands was to make this inquiry) until after the coming election, when the Republicans expected to sweep the field. Once reelected with a clear mandate, Jefferson could respond favorably to Barlow's pro-posal that a national university be establisht in the capital, as suggested in George Washington's will. He promist to invite Barlow himself to preside over its establishment.

Before I could sound him out on the question of a free state for Indians & manumitted or escaped African slaves—who since 1795 had been living together peacefully in the refugee Iroquois villages along the Grand River valley—he astonisht me by asking candidly whether I believed my father dead. I replied, I could but hope so, and ask'd him why he ask'd. Because, he said, he had heard from Mr. Alexander Hamilton, who had marshal'd his defeat of Burr in the House elections, that the man he had so narrowly defeated—now Vice-President of the nation!—was scheming with someone known to Hamilton's informants only as "H.B.," to promote a war with Spain & lead an expedition to snatch Mexico. Given the prevailing scurrility of the political climate, where Burr's "low morals" (like John Randolph's "impotence" & Barlow's "free-thinking") were openly lampoon'd, it was perfectly likely that the rumor was a Republican fabrication. On the other hand, given Burr's energy, competence, unpredictability, & great ambition, together with the fluidity of the international situation, the rumor might be true. There was more America between the Appalachians & the Mississippi than between the Atlantic & the Appalachians, & yet more west of the

Mississippi than those two regions combined, all of it up for grabs; plus giant Mexico below & giant Canada above, great prizes both. Bonaparte's example was infectious: many besides Aaron Burr must be dreaming, not only of empire, but of literal emperorhood. Even Barlow, Jefferson had heard, that utterly unmilitary man (from whom he had the legendary exploits of my father), had petition'd the French Directory to lead an expedition into Louisiana. . .

Calling on Burr was my last errand in Maryland. The President, tho he could spare me but a quarter-hour, had done so promptly & cordially; the Vice-President did not want to see me. Burr protested his disbelief that I was who I claim'd to be (I was "too much changed"); then he kept me half an afternoon whilst he fulminated against Jefferson, against the Republicans, against the southern states, against the New York Tammany society which he himself had organized politically for the 1800 elections, only to have them turn on him after the contest in the House; against Alexander Hamilton, whose opposition would make it difficult for Burr to win even the governorship of New York, much less the presidency, in the current campaign. Barbarous, impossible, splendid country! Did I know that Hamilton had seriously consider'd leading an army into Mexico and proclaiming himself Emperor of Central & South America? & cetera. I ask'd for news of "H.B." Burr said he expected me to have brot news *from* him; then he repeated his conviction that George Washington had had my father done away with after his betrayal of poor Benedict Arnold. Finally he mutter'd: "If he is not dead, he has turn'd into an Ohio River Irishman." This remark he would not amplify. When I prest, he told me crossly I had been too long a Frenchman; that it was a mere idiom of the country. And he bid me good day.

Errands done, come spring I crost the mountains myself (in a wagon train bound for Governor Harrison's Indian country) thro the Cumberland Gap to Pittsburgh, a brawling city sprung up where Pontiac's Indians had been "Consuelo'd" with smallpox blankets. Thence up the Allegheny to Chautauqua Lake, where my dear grandparents had schémed & trysted half a century before. Over the portage trail to Lake Erie; by rough boat across to chilly Upper Canada, then again by wagon to Niagara (where I re-met Jérôme Bonaparte & his bride, honeymooning at the Falls), & anon to Castines Hundred. With every additional degree of north latitude and west longitude, my head clear'd. Even before I met your mother (then a fine fifteen) and fell in love with her on the spot, my movement from Napoleon's France (and George's England) to Jefferson's America show'd me what Barlow & Tom Paine had been talking about: I understood I was not European. Moving farther, from the fail'd ideals of the French Revolution, thro the failing ones of the American, to the open country of the Indians, show'd me what my grandparents (and J. J. Rousseau) had been talking about: I understood I was not "American" either. My first adult glimpse of a Canadian village populated by white Loyalist refugees, displaced Iroquois, escaped Negro slaves, French *habitants,* & (a very few) British Canadians, cohabiting uneasily & in poverty but on the whole not unsuccessfully, set me to dreaming the family dream: a harmony not only between man & man, but between men & Nature. Jefferson's ideal for the Indians—that they should all become little farmers, homesteaders, *settlers*—struck me now as no less grotesque than that they should become shopkeepers or sailors: I understood what Major Rogers had been talking about in his *Ponteach; or, the Savages of America: A Tragedy.* I was yet to meet Andrée's idol Tecumseh, & do my utmost to advance his cause in the manner of us Cooks & Burlingames, and come to learn what a greater writer than any of these, old Sophocles, was talking about.

But I met *ma belle cousine* & her gentle parents, the lord & lady of Castines Hundred. I fell in love; not so Andrée, still under the spell of her Shawnee hero—her worrisome infatuation with whom led the Baron & Baroness to look favorably on my own attentions to her tho I was unpropertied, footloose, & as much her senior as Tecumseh, without his nobility of character. Being of French rather than English extraction, and part Indian himself thro his ancestor's marriage to Madocawanda, the Baron was no bigot, but his tastes were those of a country *gentilhomme,* and he had opposed Andrée's passion for Tecumseh not only on the grounds of her age but because he wisht a more settled life for her. (He was later to oppose our own match on that same sensible ground, when it became clear I was "my father's son"; but when *you* made your existence known, he put by his objection with the good grace of the Barons Castine.) They had no firm word of my father since his visit of 1793, en route to Chief Little Turtle's efforts against the American Legion: they had found him much changed; would not have known him but for his knowledge of our history & his characteristic enterprises. One rumor had it he was establisht on an island in the lower reaches of the Ohio, under an assumed name. . .

I took the occasion to make my filial feelings clear. The Baron & Baroness were taken aback, less by my sentiments (they had gravely mixt opinions of the man themselves, especially in his "Joseph Brant" metamorphosis, and they remember'd sympathetically my mother's distraction) than by the indelicate vehemence of my expression. But Andrée brighten'd at once; lookt on me thenceforward with real interest, & question'd me endlessly thro the summer upon my theory that her Uncle Henry—& his grandfather H.B. III before him—had been secret Judas Iscariots of the Indian cause at Bloodsworth Island, at the Wyoming & Cherry Valleys, at Fallen Timbers, & the rest. She reminded me that he had made the same sort of charges against *his* father, Andrew Cooke III, vis-à-vis Pontiac's betrayal. She urged me to meet Tecumseh, "the Shooting Star." I declined, jealous, & declared the Indian cause already lost. A receding series of betrayals & retreats was their future, I opined: along the Eastern seaboard they were already but a colorful memory; in a hundred years they would be no more than that along the Pacific.

Andrée agreed, so long as the U. States' westward expansion went uncheckt. And what could check it? Not Tecumseh's daydream of confederating all the Indians from Florida to the Lakes, I scoft: that was but the tragedy of Pontiac replay'd. So it would be, my young friend conceded—unless, as she & Tecumseh plann'd, the action of the Indians coincided with full-scale war between the U. States & G. Britain!

I was astonisht, not only by the boldness of her suggestion, but by her precocious grasp of history & politics. It was not just to westward the "Americans" were moving, she declared: the U. States merchant fleet was grown prodigious in the Atlantic trade. But since Napoleon had broken the Peace of Amiens last year & gone to war in the Mediterranean, Britain had extended her policy of economic warfare by blockading French & Spanish ports against neutral shipping, & Napoleon must surely retaliate with a similar blockade against Britain. U. States ships & cargoes were being snatcht by both sides for running these blockades, & U. States sailors were being imprest into the Royal Navy. John Adams's Federalist administration, sympathetic to the ties between old & New England, had come close to war with France in 1798 on these accounts. Jefferson's Republicans inclined against Britain despite their reservations about Napoleon. My excellent cousin was persuaded that since the U. States could not afford to fight both major powers, it was likely to refight the War of 1776 if peaceful Jefferson— who would surely be reelected this year—were succeeded in 1808 by a less formidable or less pacific Republican. To the Loyalists in Upper Canada the '76 war was still a rebellion, not a revolution; it was they who had prest Governor Haldimand not to return Fort Niagara to the U. States at the war's end, and when he was obliged to—but only in 1796—to construct another fort on Canadian soil just across the gorge from it. A quarter-century of exile had dimm'd but not extinguisht their hope that New England, at least, might still secede from the Union, annex itself to Canada, & welcome them home. Young Republicans from the new western & southern states, for their part, were eager to move against the Canadas & the Floridas, on pretext that Britain was arming & inciting Indians against the western settlements. If they gain'd sufficient strength in Congress, especially in the off-year elections of 1806 and 1810, they could surely exploit the maritime issues to ally New England & the mid-Atlantic states to their cause. And if finally, over that same period, Britain & France continued to exhaust each other's resources in European wars, & "we" were able to turn the western congressmen's pretext into a fact by organizing Tecumseh's Indian confederacy (a popular idea in the British cabinet, as it would make western America in effect a royal protectorate), there could be a 2nd Revolutionary War, as it were, as early as 1809 or '10! To give her projections a little margin, Andrée was already speaking of it as "the War of 1811." She would be 22 then: "we" had seven years to make our preparations.

I.e., herself, Tecumseh, me. . .and my father, her legendary Uncle Henry, if we could find him & determine once for all his true allegiance. Ten years past, her Indian friend had fought with Little Turtle's Miamis in their victory over American soldiers on the Wabash & their defeat by Wayne's American Legion at Fallen Timbers; thus his introduction to my father & subsequent visits to Castines Hundred. But Tecumseh was his own man, and tho he had valued "H.B.'s" high opinion of Pontiac (his own model & exemplar), he had not always trusted his advice, particularly after Fallen Timbers. Just then, neither's whereabouts was known.

I reported what I'd heard from Jefferson and Burr, which corroborated the Baron's last news of "H.B." I knew too little of American politics to yea or nay Andrée's complex prognostications, but enough of French & Algerine, & of history generally, to warn her that events have their own momentum, & quickly get beyond the grasp of those who would control them. And if I should ever go in search of my "father," I declared, it would not be to enlist myself in his cause, or him in mine.

"We don't know his," Andrée said tartly, "and you have none."

True enough—till love & Aaron Burr gave me one, that same year. News reacht us of Burr's duel with Hamilton on the Hudson Palisades, which spoilt his bid for the New York governorship & forced him into a kind of hiding. He was headed, we heard, for the Louisiana territory, where he own'd land, with a band of settlers, perhaps to establish a new state. But there were also rumors of intended rendezvous with a volunteer army that had been training on Blennerhassett Island in the Ohio River, no one knew what for. Napoleon, age 35, was crown'd Emperor of France & Anointed of the Lord, and prepared to make war against Austria & Russia. Jefferson handily won reelection; Republican strength increast in the Congress. I turn'd 28, & proposed marriage to my 16-year-old cousin. The Baron & Baroness said she was not ready; Andrée declared *I* was not, till I had accomplisht something in "our cause." She bade me reconnoitre the activity on Blennerhassett Island, determine whether "Harman Blennerhassett" (so we had learnt its owner to be denominated) was my father, & whether whatever was afoot 'twixt him & Burr was an aid or a threat to Tecumseh's program. I was then to take "appropriate measures," report to Tecumseh, & ask the Chief's permission for her hand! If he approved, she was mine whatever her dear parents thot.

Well, I could not stay on at Castines Hundred. In 1805 & '06 & '07—whilst Napoleon won at Ulm, Austerlitz, & Jena, lost at Trafalgar, and, just as Andrée had forecast, issued the Berlin Decree against trade with Britain in retaliation for Britain's Orders in Council against trade with France; and whilst a sea battle was fought off the Virginia Capes betwixt the USS *Chesapeake* and HMS *Leopard,* such as she had hoped for (and whilst Jérôme Bonaparte's marriage was annull'd by his brother, who made him King of Westphalia, and whilst Joel & Ruthy Barlow settled down in Philadelphia to bring out the *Columbiad,* and Toot Fulton helpt him with the engravings & built the *Clermont*)—I follow'd Burr's fortunes from Blennerhassett Island, by flatboat down the Ohio & Mississippi to New Orleans & his arrest for conspiring to separate the western states from the Union; thence to Richmond & his trial & acquittal.

When Burr fled to Europe in perfect disgrace, and Harman Blennerhassett settled down to raise cotton in Mississippi, I came back to make my report (and en route met that 1st uncritical auditor of my Algerine adventure, Midshipman Cooper). Taken separately, I declared to Andrée, neither Harman Blennerhassett nor Aaron Burr was guilty as charged, and Justice Marshall had fairly resisted Jefferson's pressure to convict. Blennerhassett, an Irish lawyer & adventurer, was in my opinion primarily bent on marching on Mexico, and Burr on bringing a large new state into the Union with himself as governor, tho each was prepared to do both if it should prove feasible. The conspiracy was mainly the invention of Jefferson's western army commander, General James Wilkinson, a bona fide traitor in the secret pay of Spain, who (again in my opinion, because at my urging) had prest the Western Empire idea on B. & B. to divert them from Mexico; aroused their interest in it as a possibility if their "legitimate" program should fail; and then tattled on them to Jefferson & turn'd state's evidence to cover his tracks as a Spanish agent!

In the same way, I did not believe that either Blennerhassett or Burr was guilty of being "Henry Burlingame IV," whether or not that fellow in his latter guises was my sire.

Drawing on what I'd learnt from Consuelo to pose as a fellow agent of the Spanish minister to the U. States, I had enlisted Wilkinson to scotch their plan, not altogether on Tecumseh's behalf (tho anything but the Mexican enterprise would have meant more encroachment on Indian lands) but principally to thwart two people who—separately or together!—might be H.B. IV. It was my intention to keep an occasional eye on both, especially on Burr, who it pleased me to report had at no time penetrated my disguise. Finally, at 18 my taskmaster was more desirable than before, & would she marry me?

She would be happy to, your mother replied, with Tecumseh's consent. What had been his judgment of me?

I confest I had been too proud to seek him out & ask it, tho I'd heard his praises sung from Buffalo to New Orleans. A pity, Andrée said, since on the strength of *her* descriptions of me to Tecumseh during his recentest visit to Castines Hundred, he seem'd favorably inclined to the match. He had agreed in principle, she declared, that a war betwixt the British & the "Seventeen Fires" (as he call'd the U. States) would serve the interests of the Indians if the British won. They had proposed to him already the establishment of an arm'd Indian free state extending south from the Great Lakes. But he had seconded also my caution that events have energies of their own, and he worried that a U. States victory in such a war would be the end of Indian sovereignty. Even more he approved any plan to divide the Union, so long as it did not involve the formation of new white nations on Indian lands, as had Aaron Burr's. Non-literate himself, Tecumseh was particularly imprest with my reported ability to counterfeit letters & other documents, so important in the white men's commerce with one another. He had inquired of Andrée whether that talent might be put to use to disunite the Seventeen Fires whilst he tried to unite with his oratory the nations of the Indians.

And why, I ask'd, had Tecumseh paid this call on her? Because, she replied, his younger brother's assumption in 1805 of the rôle of prophet & visionary, following upon Tecumseh's own revival of Pontiac's plan for an Indian confederacy, had put him troubledly in mind of Pontiac's association with the Delaware Prophet, whose "vision" he knew to have been influenced by the 1st Andrée Castine. Tecumseh was uneasy about this reenactment; he trusted his brother's loyalty, but not his judgment; he wanted, Andrée believed, both to reassure himself that she would not be another "Angélique Cuillerier," & at the same time to learn whether she had any suggestions for improving his brother's "vision" in the way the first Andrée had improved the Delaware Prophet's. Your mother tactfully responded that her only vision was of Tecumseh at the head of an Indian empire rivalling that of the Aztecs or the Incas. Then she made the practical suggestion that the Prophet establish a religious center at some strategic location convenient to the principal nations of the confederacy—say, at the confluence of the Wabash & the Tippecanoe in the Indiana territory— to give the proposed union a physical headquarters like that of the Seventeen Fires in Washington. An "official" seat of authority, she maintain'd, might help to counter the Americans' practice of making treaties to their own advantage with disaffected groups of Indians or self-styled chiefs. And the establishment of an Indian Mecca or Vatican, with the Wabash prophet at its head, would also help distinguish & fix him as the *religious* leader of the confederacy, & keep him out of Tecumseh's hair in political & military matters. Tecumseh had thot this an inspired idea, thankt her happily, & urged her to send her intended to him.

For so she now declared me, in recompense for my work against the western empire of Burr, Blennerhassett, & General Wilkinson. But if I would have her to wife, I must complete two further tasks, one as it were for Tecumseh & the other as it might seem against him, for herself. She had learnt from her father's friends in the Canadian Governor-General's office that that worthy, Sir James Craig, was much pleased with a series of newspaper articles lately publisht by one John Henry of Vermont, attacking the republican form of government in general & the Republican administration in Washington in particular. Craig wanted to know whether this Henry could be hired to agitate in the Federalist press for the secession of New York & New England after the 1808 elections, when another Virginian was expected to follow Jefferson in the President's House. Andrée had proposed me as one who could not only make that ascertainment, but supply Henry with appropriate copy, if necessary, to publish under his name. Her Quebec associate had offer'd to provide me with expense money & a stipend for this not very difficult assignment, which would serve also as my initiation into the British-Canadian secret service.

The 2nd task was more delicate. Governor Harrison of Indiana was negotiating with minor chiefs of the Delawares, Kickapoos, Miamis, & others of Pontiac's old confederates to sell some 3,000,000 acres of their prime common hunting territory along the Wabash, for an absurdly small sum. Tecumseh opposed such a sale at any price; had even threaten'd to kill the potential signatories of Harrison's treaty. My task was to suggest to him that his cause might better be served by permitting the treaty to be sign'd over his protests (but not by the Shawnees) & then enlisting the fierce Lake Erie Wyandots, who so far had held aloof from his confederacy, to aid him in punishing the "degenerate village chiefs" who sign'd it. The action would appeal to the Wyandots; their enlistment would impress the Potawatomis & other reluctant tribes; the elimination of those defectors amongst the minor chiefs would strengthen the Indian alliance & serve as a warning against further such treaties. It would also serve to introduce me to the Indians, whom I did not yet truly know. . .& to Tecumseh.

I observed to my young fiancée that she was ordering the deaths of some half-dozen human beings. She replied that they were cynical, drunken traitors who would trade their birthright & their people for a barrel of whiskey. If she could, she would perform the executions herself, with pleasure.

The 1st task was both easy & agreeable: it fetcht me in 1808 to Montreal & across the St. Lawrence into Vermont, where I readily enlisted the ambitious & erratic Mr. Henry—a former greengrocer, newspaper publisher, & artillery captain—to go down to Boston & test the air there for secession. I provided him with a simple cipher & instructions for transmitting his reports to the Governor-General's office. Then, after Madison's election & inauguration, I went to Boston myself to retrieve the man from the taverns & brothels where he claim'd to be keeping his finger on the pulse of public sentiment, and scolded him for providing "us" with no more than we could read more cheaply in the Boston newspapers: *e.g.*, that the Federalists would oppose any move against Britain and, if Madison yielded to the western war-hawks, would perhaps attempt to set up a Congress of Federalist States in Boston or Hartford & remain neutral. I myself predicted (& still predict) against their actual secession, but felt the question to be of slight importance: there was enough pro-British, anti-French, & especially anti-Republican sentiment amongst the Yankees to guarantee a steady illegal sale of supplies from New York & New England to British forces in Canada. If the war goes successfully for Britain in that theater, annexation of those states to Canada should be negotiable without great difficulty. Whilst in Boston I draughted a few sample letters for Henry to cipher & transmit as his own. It did not trouble me that the man was of no consequence as a spy, for I saw already to what better use his letters could be put. I instructed him to keep copies, for the purpose of documenting his service to the British Foreign Office, and let him back to his tarts & ale.

The 2nd task was another story. Acting on your mother's suggestion, in 1808 Tecumseh establisht for his brother "the Prophet's Town" near where the Tippecanoe joins the Wabash: a mixt Indian community dedicated to industriousness, sobriety, the common ownership of property, brotherhood amongst the nations of red men, & repudiation of all things learnt from the "Long Knives," by which term they call'd us whites. So successful was the town, & the strategy, Governor Harrison mistook the Prophet (who had changed his name from Lalawethika, or "Loud Mouth," to Tenskwatawa, "Open Door") for the leader of the confederacy, & invited him in the summer of 1809 to confer at Vincennes, the territorial capital, concerning the proposed treaty. That year I met all three.

Child: I am a Cook, not a Burlingame. You Burlingames get from your ancestor H.B. III a passion for the world that fetches you everywhere at once, in guises manifold as the world's, to lead & shape its leaders & shapers. We Cooks, I know now, get from our forebear Ebenezer, the virgin poet of Maryland, an inexhaustible innocence that, whatever our involvement in the world (we are not *merely* Cooks), inclines us to be followers—better, learners: tutees of the Burlingames & those they've shaped. If Aaron Burr & Harman Blennerhassett had been one & the same man, as it sometimes seem'd to me they were, that man would be the Burlingame I despise & wish dead. If Tecumseh & Tenskwatawa were one man—a distillation & embodiment of the Indian blood flowing thro our line—that man would be the father I could love, admire, & pity. Of the Prophet I will say little: Jefferson agrees with Harrison that he is a rogue & charlatan, a former brawling drunk who, after a "conversion" as dramatical as Paul's on the Damascus Road, became a teetotaling faker. I myself believe him to be both authentic & authentically half-mad, nowise to be trusted; I believe further that Tecumseh so saw him too, from the beginning.

As for the "Shooting Star": what greater expression of my admiration can I make than that Tecumseh is more deserving of Andrée's love than I? That I had rather be esteem'd by him than by anyone save her? That I think him worth a Jefferson, two Madisons, three Barlows, five Napoleons? I never felt more my grandfather's son (but remember, I did not yet know that history in detail) than when I first sat at the feet of this successor to Pontiac, whom I pray it will be

312

your fortune one day to meet as the head of a great free league of Indian nations, and to love as I do.

He began our closer connection in July 1810, by saving my life. On the strength of my relation to Andrée & my father's & grandfather's to Pontiac, Tecumseh had permitted me to live in the Prophet's town (over the Prophet's objections) & practice the Algonkin language thro the summer & fall of 1809, between my embassies to John Henry. He had heard me out carefully, thro an interpreter, on Andrée's proposal regarding the Wyandots & the Harrison treaty, and had replied that while it did not strike him as the best strategy, it was the course he would probably follow anyhow, inasmuch as he expected the "village chiefs" to sign the treaty despite his threats. He also told me that William Henry Harrison was no villain, but a worthy tho implacable adversary who had champion'd legal justice for the Indians (vainly) in the Indiana legislature in 1807, even whilst dickering to buy their land at 3½ mills the acre—600 times less than the government's standard selling price! But he would not talk to me further about such important matters as Pontiac's rebellion, or his opinion of my father & grand-father, or my betrothal to his young friend "Star-of-the-Lake," until we could discuss them in Algonkin.

I learnt fast. And in the process came to respect, even more than formerly, the red men's famous harmony with their land (to *sell* which, they regarded less as treason than as fraud, since in their view no man had title to what was every man's). I saw the ultimate harmlessness of even the fierce Wyandots & once-fierce Senecas, by contrast with the whites: Tecumseh's comparison was of a pack of wolves to a forest fire. To my surprise I came to feel ever more clearly my distance from the Indians, even as I bridged it: were I not part Indian, there could have been no bridge; were I not mainly & finally European-American, no bridge would have been needed. From this last I came to see what Tecumseh later told me Pontiac had seen (and what I now know my grandfather knew before Pontiac): that while the wolf may make the deer a finer animal, & the eagle quicken the race of rabbits, all flee together from the fire, or perish in it. As there was no longer any real *where* for the Indian to flee. . .

Yet he was no defeatist. That the Indians perhaps had only different ways to lose meant to Tecumseh that the choice of ways was all the more important. Hence his preference for the tomahawk, for example, together with his recognition that only British artillery might truly drive back American artillery. Hence his tireless exhortations to the chiefs *not* to forget their differences, which were as old & "natural" as those between hare & hawk, but to work for their common good despite them, against the menace. The flaw in his reasoning, of course, was that exemplary conduct presumes someone to benefit from the example. If deer & wolf rise above their ancient differences to stand together, what have they taught the fire? Tecumseh's reply to this question (which I never put) was in his bearing, his eloquence, his selfless energy, his spaciousness of heart & the general fineness of his character, which I think must far exceed his hero Pontiac's: to be thus-&-such a man (these virtues preacht), to behave in thus-&-such a fashion, were excellent & sweet yea tho one perish—especially if one is to perish in any case. This tragical (but nowise despairing) lesson is what Tecumseh taught, in a language neither English nor Algonkin.

By the time that contemptible treaty was sign'd (September 30, 1809, anniversary as it happens of Adam & Eve's eviction from Paradise, according to tradition, & of Ebenezer Cooke's inadvertent loss of his father's estate), I had enough grasp of the language to be trusted with the errand of reporting to Governor Harrison Tecumseh's anger, as well as the Wyandots' enlistment into the confederacy. With credentials supplied by the Canadian secret service, I pass'd as a scout for the U. States secret service charged with learning the extent of British instigation of the Indian alliance, and reported truthfully to Harrison that the confederacy grew stronger every season. That while the British understandably were cheer'd by it, they had as yet provided little beyond moral support to Tecumseh & the Prophet, but were likely to supply them with weapons if the confederacy chose to resist the new "treaty" with force, as Tecumseh was prepared to do. That the real instigators of Indian solidarity were just such spurious or broken treaties. That the best strategy against that solidarity (and against driving the Indians to join the British in the coming war) was to cease invading their territory & murdering them with legal impunity.

The last point Harrison granted; he even worried (what I'd not dared hope) that President Madison, who rather shared my general position, might be persuaded to set aside the treaty he Harrison had just negotiated—a move which would put the Governor uncomfortably betwixt his constituents & the man he must rely on for political & military support. Cheer'd, I went off to Boston & my business with John Henry; then return'd to the Prophet's town by way of Vincennes (& Castines Hundred) in the spring, this time as Harrison's messenger to the Prophet, whom he invited to the capital to discuss the treaty. I reminded him that the real leader was Tecumseh. All the more reason to invite his brother instead, Harrison felt: promote any jealousy betwixt them. Andrée & I agreed that now the obnoxious treaty was accomplisht, the next great step toward Indian confederacy would be for Tecumseh successfully to resist by force its implementation, then to negotiate with President Madison its repeal. This would establish his leadership in the eyes of the Americans, the British, & his own people, & give him authority in Washington & London to barter his allegiance or neutrality in the coming war for firm guarantees of an Indian free state. I deliver'd myself (in Algonkin) of this opinion, together with Harrison's invitation. To my dismay, Tenskwatawa loudly declared I should be executed as a spy: he had got wind thro the winter of my pose

314

with Harrison, and feign'd to believe it was no pose; that I & possibly Star-of-the-Lake as well were in the pay of the Long Knives.

It was fortunate for me that his indictment included your mother, for while Tecumseh forbade torture, he believed in the swift execution of spies. But the Chief knew of my facility with documents & other credentials; he chided his brother, veto'd my execution, praised my improvements in their tongue, & subsequently took me as his interpreter—with 400 fine young warriors, for effect—to the 1st of a series of conferences with Harrison in Vincennes. It was my 1st experience of his statesmanship: the man was magnificent, both as orator & as tactician: always eloquent; tactful & forceful by turns; & so possest of memory & information that he could recite the provisions & violations of every Indian treaty made & broken by the Long Knives "since the Seventeen Fires had been Thirteen & had fought for their sovereignty, as his people were now conjoin'd to fight for theirs." The pretenders who had sign'd the last of those treaties, he declared, were dead men. The confederacy would no more accede to Madison's order to disband than would the Seventeen Fires to such an order from himself. & cetera. Harrison was enough imprest with Tecumseh to delay moving settlers onto the treaty lands—& to request troops from the War Department. Tecumseh was enough imprest with my services, & my Algonkin, to speak to me now on those matters he had tabled earlier.

What he vouchsafed me, in effect, over the following year, was a clear tho fleeting glimpse of what Andrée has since seen to be the pattern of our family history; more generally, he re-introduced me to the tragical view. Tecumseh understood to the heart Pontiac's dilemma at the siege of Detroit (as explain'd in my 3rd letter); for that reason he would always attack, attack, preferably at night & hand-to-hand, & leave siege operations when necessary to whatever white allies the confederacy might enlist from time to time. The confederacy itself he view'd as a necessary evil, contrary to the Indians' ancient pluralism, & for that reason he thot its central authority best left more spiritual than political. Thus his willing dependency on his undependable brother. Farther down the white man's road toward a central *government* he would not go, tho he was not at all certain the Indians could prevail without one. He pointed out to me that my father & grandfather had had a common esteem for Pontiac, whatever their other motives & differences. Perhaps one or both of them had thot to aid him in the long run by misleading or impeding him in the short, as one strengthens a child by setting obstacles in his path, or tells him simple myths till he can grasp the hard true ones. But Tecumseh question'd both my father's conviction, that his parents had betray'd Pontiac, & mine, that my father had betray'd, for example, the Iroquois under Joseph Brant. If he believed that, he declared, he would have permitted Tenskwatawa to tomahawk me, & would himself put a knife thro the heart of Star-of-the-Lake, whom he still loved, ere we could betray him.

As it was—and since he had little time for a wife & children nor any wish to leave behind a young widow & orphans—he gave his blessings to our match, hoped it would be fruitful, & pray'd that we would set no helpful obstacles in his path, as he was no child.

I rusht to Castines Hundred with these tidings. To Andrée (now 22, & I nearing 35!) they were not news: she came to me smiling, & soon after wed me privately in the Iroquois ceremony, as my grandmother & grandfather had been wed. Andrée had just commenced her research of the family history; she was fascinated by our likeness to our grandsires. And tho she knew I had not the peculiar defect of male Burlingames (which they have always overcome), she follow'd the example of Andrée I in declining to marry me Christian-fashion till I had got her with child.

Sweet last summer! Mme de Staël wrote me from Coppet of her troubles with Napoleon; of her friend Schlegel's narrow rescue of her manuscript *De l'Allemagne;* of her current affair with a Swiss guardsman half her age, *très romantique mais peu esthétique.* She wonder'd whether I thot it safe for her to move to her New York property if Napoleon hounded her from Coppet; surely "we" were not going to war with Britain, Europe's only hope against the bloody Corsican? I was obliged to reply that unlike Paris in Year III, which appear'd dangerous but was safe, upstate New York in 1811 appear'd safe but would soon be dangerous. To convince her, I attacht a copy of a letter I'd forged with Andrée's help for the purpose of inflaming the American press against the British: based on a real one sent from Major James Crawford at Niagara to Governor Haldimand in Quebec on January 3, 1782, it itemized eight boxes of scalps lifted by the Senecas & presented to the Governor-General for bounty payment: 43 "Congress soldiers," 93 "farmers kill'd in their houses," 97 farmers kill'd working in their fields, 102 more farmers of which 18 scalps were "markt with yellow flame to show that they were burnt alive after being scalpt," 81 women, "long hair, those braided to show they were mothers," 193 boys' scalps "various ages," 211 girls' scalps big and little, "small yellow hoops markt hatchet, club, knife, & cet," 122 "mixt scalps including 29 infants. . .only little black knife in middle to show ript out of mothers body," & cet. Joel Barlow wrote from Kalorama, his house in Washington, that he was sailing reluctantly from Annapolis aboard the *Constitution* as Madison's minister to France, to deal with Napoleon's foreign minister in a final effort to prevent war betwixt the U. States & G. Britain. He recall'd fondly my assistance in his dealings with the Dey of Algiers, & wisht I could be with him now. Toot Fulton, he was sad to report, had married soon after the *Clermont*'s success; Ruthy was disconsolate. The war-hawk American Secretary of State, Barlow's friend James Monroe, had instructed General Mathews in Georgia by secret letter on January 26 to move against the Floridas "with all possible expedition, concealing from general observation the trust committed to you with that discretion which the delicacy and importance of the undertaking require." In May the U. States frigate *President* crippled the British sloop-of-war *Little Belt* off Sandy Hook, to the delight of Henry Clay & his fellow hawks, much increast in strength since the 1810 congressional elections. Surely the 12th Congress would declare Andrée's War of 1811 when it convened in the fall! Tecumseh inform'd Governor Harrison early in the year that he would not only remain neutral, but fight on the side of the Seventeen Fires in the coming war if President Madison would set aside Harrison's false treaty & make no future ones without consent of the chiefs assembled at the Tippecanoe. White citizens' committees from Vincennes to St. Louis petition'd Madison to move against the Prophet's town, disperse the confederacy, & drive out the British Indian traders who were "behind it."

At Castines Hundred, whilst the Baron tiskt & tutted, your parents kiss'd & coo'd—and made plans. Barlow himself believed that inasmuch as the Westerners & Southerners were hottest for the war, my friend Tecumseh was of more immediate moment in the matter than Napoleon & George III together (that latter so sunk into madness now that a Regency bill was expected daily, but still urging in his lucid moments that troops be sent to recover his lost America). Joel could but hope that if France & England were persuaded to lift their decrees against American merchant shipping, the Indian issue itself would not be a sufficient *casus belli;* he implored me to use whatever influence I had to keep Tecumseh neutral. I had not seen fit to tell him that I was become a hawk myself, tho at the time of Burr's trial in Richmond, when I had visited Barlow in Philadelphia to aid him with the new *Columbiad,* I'd spoken warmly of Tecumseh's plan for an Indian nation, and tried to work into Joel's epic a denunciation of "Manifest Destiny" by Columbus himself.

It seem'd to us now—your mother & me—that Tecumseh's willingness to treat directly with Madison, before the confederacy had proved its strength to both Washington & London, was premature. Our friend replied that they would not be ready to prove their strength for another year, by when he hoped more of the southern nations, especially the Creeks, would be represented at the Prophet's town: his present objective was to temporize with Harrison thro the winter whilst he did more diplomatic work in the South. It seem'd to us too that Barlow's mission was dangerous to our cause: just possibly Madison's gamble would work, and if there were no war to bring British troops to the Great Lakes & the Mississippi Valley (and divert the Americans' energies from their Manifest Destiny), Tecumseh's cause was lost. We resolved therefore on a double course: to make sure—what was anyhow unlikely—that Harrison did not agree to send Tecumseh to Madison before our friend left for his southern enterprise; and to see to it Barlow's French mission fail'd.

The 1st we accomplisht in July, by suggesting to Harrison that his own goals might be attain'd without bloodshed, in Tecumseh's absence, by moving infantry and militia conspicuously up the Wabash to establish a fort near the Prophet's town: their leader gone, the Indians would likely disband before such a show of force, and Harrison would then negotiate from a position of strength with his own Indiana constituents as well as with Tecumseh. We caution'd him that attacking the Prophet's town directly would serve only to rally the Indians, as an attack on Mecca would rally the Islamites (had we actually believed that, of course, we would have urged attack). Harrison agreed, and after a last fruitless conference at Vincennes on July 27, Tecumseh bid us farewell till spring & set off southwards down the Wabash with 20 warriors.

To accomplish the 2nd objective I sadly bid my bride *au revoir* immediately after, struck out eastwards down the Mohawk & Hudson to New York City, and took ship for France to try whether I could "torpedo" good Joel's negotiations with the Duc de Bassano, described above. In October I reacht Imperial Paris (much changed), where everyone but the Barlows, so it seem'd, went about drest in *"Caca du roi de Rome"* & reenacting the age of the Caesars. I found Aaron Burr (much changed) so sunk in Baroque vice as to seem more than ever the descendant of Henry Burlingame III, were he not equally sunk in despair & alcohol. I found Germaine (much changed) newly pregnant by her sturdy guardsman—now secretly her husband—whom the household call'd Caliban behind her back: she was become nervous, insomniac, a touch dropsical to boot, & much given to laudanum in consequence; yet no less busy & brilliant than when I had first met her.

She scolded me for not bringing with me my *belle sauvage,* & insisted that I rehearse to her new young protégé the story of the original Baron Castine's romance with Madocawanda, & my own with "Consuelo del Consulado." She was certain her needling letters to Napoleon, on the occasion of *De l'Allemagne*'s French publication, still rankled the Emperor; he had banisht her beautiful friend Juliette Récamier for the crime of visiting her in Switzerland; if his secret police continued to harass her at Coppet, she would have to flee to Vienna, to Russia, to God knows where, since she had no wish to lose her scalp in America. If only she could resist writing letters! All the same, she believed the Emperor to be fascinated with her: let her set out for Russia, she bet he'd not be far behind. Had I read M. Chateaubriand's silly Indian novels, *Atala* and *René?* Really, she thot her precious *romantisme* could be carried too far, and no doubt the worst was yet to come; if she were as young as young Master Balzac, she would set about to invent whatever was to follow it. Someday soon she meant to write her own version of *la révolution:* perhaps I would assist her with the chapters on the Commune & the Terror? Or was I back to my Pocahontas? In any case, I look'd more like my father every day. The Duc de Bassano? No wilier or more dishonest than the run of foreign ministers, she reckon'd, Napoleonic or Bourbon: he would promise Barlow everything, & (wise man!) put nothing in writing. But she would not advise me on how to thwart my friend Barlow's mission, for while she approved the idea of an Indian free state, & agreed that another war with England would distract the Americans from westward expansion—just as Britain's war with France kept both countries from expanding their influence in America—she believed it more imperative to curb Napoleon than to curb the pioneers. Better the Indians be lost than the British! Now: what was it I said happen'd to that famous plagued snuffbox?

Only stout Joel and Ruthy, it seem'd to me, were not much changed, simply mellow'd into middle age. Resign'd now to childlessness, they had replaced me & Fulton with a nephew of Joel's from Yale. Resign'd also to less-than-Homerhood after the mocking critical reception of his huge *Columbiad* & his ode to Captains Lewis & Clark (ably parodied by John Quincy Adams), he regretted not having stuck to satire as my father had advised, and doubted he would go to the Muse again. He agreed now with his former tutor that History is your grandest fiction, tho he had not yet come to my father's modest corollary (which *I* heard now for the 1st time): that its eloquentest authors, like those of the ancient ballads & Eastern tales, are anonymous, their subtlest "works" known only to the elect. Our deals & double-deals with Joseph Bacri & Hassan Bashaw, for example, were surely works of art, which gave him more pleasure than the whole *Columbiad*. He hoped his work in progress would equal it.

But he cordially declined to make me privy to his strategy with the Duc de Bassano, beyond acknowledging that he was not imprest with that gentleman's verbal assurances that the Berlin & Milan decrees had been effectively revoked. The Duke was a regular Burlingame, he said, even whose *written* word could not be assumed to be authentic; and I was grown too much my father, & my interests too far from his own, for him to confide in me as he had used to, now he'd re-met me. My Tecumseh sounded like a splendid fellow, my "wife" a splendid woman; he hoped that the red men would not be hounded from the continent to become, like the black slaves, an indelible stain on the conscience of white America. But even as we spoke, the 12th Congress would be debating a war with England which Madison did not want yet must surely yield to if Prime Minister Perceval fail'd to rescind the Orders in Council, & Tecumseh's confederacy did not disband. He Barlow would be pleased to be remember'd as a diplomatist instrumental in avoiding that war; if he should fail, he bade me seriously consider what I seem'd to him to have given no thot to: that with the cream of the British military engaged against Napoleon in Spain, the U. States might very well *win* the war, in the process destroying Tecumseh, annexing Canada, the Floridas, & Mexico, & sweeping uncheckt across the entire continent of North America as Napoleon was sweeping across Europe. Patriotic as he was, Barlow did not believe American destiny to be quite *that* manifest: he urged me to turn my energies to the course of peace.

I was moved by what he said, not to believe that the Indians' cause would be better aided by peace than by war, but to see more clearly than ever, from the perspective of Paris, what Tecumseh knew: that their cause was lost in any case; that their future lay not in history but, as it were, in myth, & that therefore their only victory would be in valiant tho futile resistance. I wisht Andrée there to advise me. My plan had been to reestablish my acquaintance with Jérôme Bonaparte, now divorced from his American wife & restored to his brother's good graces, & thro that avenue assure Napoleon that even half a year's dallying with Barlow should suffice to seé war declared betwixt the U. States & G. Britain, especially given 'the slowness of transatlantic communications. Only keep Britain from revoking her Orders in Council before Congress adjourn'd for the summer; Tecumseh's confederacy would do the rest.

But before I could begin to put this strategy into action, your mother's urgent letter reacht me: our stratagem with Harrison had misfired, not because he had attackt the Prophet's town, but because, incredibly, Tenskwatawa had tried to win a military victory in his brother's absence by attacking Harrison! Losses had been high on both sides, but the victory was unquestionably Harrison's: the Indians were disperst from the Tippecanoe, the Prophet had fled, the town was burnt to the ground; the army had return'd triumphant to Vincennes with British rifles taken from the Indians; Harrison was everywhere acclaim'd a great hero. "Cato" would be furious: with his brother for having launcht so premature an attack; with us if he learnt we'd advised Harrison to make his threatening move. Andrée was the more distrest because, to console herself in my absence, she had pursued her research into our family's history, particularly the activities of our namesakes in Pontiac's rebellion, and was horrified at what she saw as a pattern of deadly reenactment, too mattersome for her to put in a hasty letter. Finally, our labors of the summer had, if not borne other fruit, at least sown other & sweeter seed: she was expecting! I was to forget Napoleon, Joel Barlow, & the Game of Governments, & come posthaste to make an honest woman of her; then together we must examine History, our family's & our own, to the end of making honest people of ourselves.

But (she could not help adding, out of self-confest habit) it would not *much* delay me to return to her by way of London, where "our coney J[ohn] H[enry] was ripe for catching." *That* was a trap too shrewdly set to go unsprung, & should provide our baby with a handsome & much-needed nest egg.

I was alarm'd as she. To settle that certain old family score with the late Duc de Crillon which I explain'd in my 2nd letter, I had assumed the name "Jean Blanque" & had imposed upon his son for a loan of £1,200 against a pledge to help restore him to Napoleon's good graces, which he did not currently enjoy, via my friend the American minister, who did. Given time (and Barlow's increasing popularity in the court of St. Cloud) the man would have been good for another thousand: but I cut short my mining of that vein as well as my futile intriguing against dear Joel. I'd not had time to make real headway on that front, but then, none seem'd especially call'd for, inasmuch as I'd learnt from aides of the Duc de Bassano what Joel himself was beginning to understand: that Napoleon's policy, like mine, was to forestall England's lifting her Orders in Council until war with the U. States was inevitable. I bade my friend farewell.

So relieved was Barlow to see me go, all his natural affection came to the fore. He was old enough now, he declared (nearing 60), & the times parlous enough, that he could not bid a friend good-bye without wondering whether they would meet again. He misst Toot Fulton & Benjamin West, Tom Paine & Jefferson, Jim Monroe & Dolley Madison; he even misst that old Yale fossil Noah Webster, who'd been so unkind to the *Columbiad;* aye, & Joseph Bacri, & my father, of whom I was now the very spit & image. And he would miss me, tho not my work against his peaceable aims, which he could excuse only because so many of his countrymen shared my belligerence. It was a snowy forenoon, one of 1811's last. Barlow was reminded of his earliest satirical verses, written for my father even as I was being conceived: "And *Jove* descends in magazines of snow."

Using my Canadian credentials in London, I learnt that British elements opposed to a 2nd American war had gone so far as to plot the assassination of Prime Minister Perceval, a staunch defender of the Orders in Council, knowing that Lord Castlereagh, his likely successor, was inclined to revoke them. Also that the King was in strait-waistcoat, pissing the bed & fancying that England was sunk & drown'd, himself shut up in Noah's Ark with his Lady Pembroke (a Regency bill was expected momently). Also that the Foreign Office had rejected John Henry's claim for £32,000 and a good American consulship in reward for his espionage, on the grounds that his reports were valueless: they referr'd him for emolument to his employer, the Canadian Governor-General's office. But Sir James Craig was by then gone to his own reward, & Sir George Prevost was not inclined to honor his predecessor's secret debts. Embitter'd & out of funds, Henry had left London to return to farming in Vermont.

I overtook him at Southampton and (in the guise of le Comte Édouard de Crillon) won his sympathy on shipboard by declaring myself to be a former French secret agent temporarily out of favor with Napoleon by reason of the machinations of my jealous rivals. When Henry confided his own ungrateful treatment by the British, & prepared to post into the North Atlantic those copies of his letters which "a friend" had advised him to make, I suggested he permit me to do the two of us a service by engaging to sell them to the Americans via the French minister Sérurier & Secretary of State Monroe, both of whom would be pleased to present to the Congress such clear evidence of British intriguing with the New England Federalists. There should be $100,000 in it for Henry, I maintain'd, & for myself the chance to

321

regain the Emperor's favor. Delighted, Henry entrusted the letters & negotiations to me. I was at first dismay'd that his "copies" were but rough summaries in an unimpressive notebook, & that he'd neither named the New England separatist leaders by name nor invoked such useful embarrassments as the Essex Junto of 1804, which had plotted with Burr to lead New England's secession if he won the New York governorship that year. I consider'd dictating to Henry a fuller & more compromising text, but decided it were better not to reveal overmuch knowledge of such details. The holograph letters from Lord Liverpool & Robert Peel were enough to implicate Britain & serve our purpose; relieved not to be directly incriminated, the Federalists could retaliate against Madison by declaring Henry's notebook a forgery, and we could have it both ways, promoting war & disunity at once.

All went smoothly. My apprehensions were that M. Sérurier would hesitate to vouch for me before making inquiries of the Duc de Bassano, or Madison to buy the letters before making inquiries of Joel Barlow (whose Washington house Sérurier was renting); also that Monroe might see thro my disguise. But I was enough alter'd by nature & by art since my last interview with Monroe, and enough conversant in the gossip of St. Cloud & the family affairs of the Ducs de Crillon, and they eager enough to put the letters before Congress as a prelude to Madison's appealing for a declaration of war, that the only hitch was financial: I ask'd $125,000, hoping for $100,000; Monroe agreed, but Albert Gallatin declared that the Treasury's whole budget for secret-service payments of this kind was but $50,000. Fearing Henry might renege, I threw in for my part the (forged) title to an (imaginary) estate of mine at "St. Martial" & an additional $10,500 worth of (counterfeit) notes & securities negotiable in Paris, thus further demonstrating my good faith to Sérurier & Monroe. By February the deal was closed: Henry gave me $17,500 of his $50,000 & set out for Paris, as Eben Cooke had once done for Maryland, to claim his estate. I then successfully coaxt another $21,000 from the Secretary of State, & might have got as much again from the French ministry had I not fear'd discovery of my imposture & yearn'd above all else to rejoin your mother (before she should become your mother) at Castines Hundred, to put right if I could our great disservice to Tecumseh, to watch over your wombing, & to learn what my beloved might have learnt.

Et voici! Tecumseh, Andrée tearfully reported, would have none of us. Publicly he deprecated the loss at Tippecanoe as a mere imprudency by rash young warriors indignant at Harrison's trespass, but he was in fact enraged; had seized his brother by the hair & banisht him from his sight. He was constrain'd from making a treaty with Madison (in order to gain time to reunite the scatter'd tribes) only by Harrison's insulting stipulation that he go to Washington alone instead of with the 300 young warriors he wanted to comprise an effective retinue. Now he was off to Fort Malden & Amherstburg, at the farther end of Lake Erie, overseeing General Brock's re-arming of the confederacy & directing minor raids against American settlements to restore his authority & the Indians' morale. He rejected angrily Andrée's suggestion that the Tippecanoe fiasco had, after all, purged his camp of some of its less reliable members. He had not accused us outright of treachery, only of being "our grandparents' grandchildren."

Which was enough. For (having re-married me in the *Christian* tribal ceremony to appease her parents) Andrée review'd for me, & enlisted my aid in the completion of her inquiry into, what in these three months & four letters I have set forth to you, & can now conclude: the history & pattern of our family error. Halfway thro life's journey & about to become a father, I can now no longer properly despise my own, whoever he was, whyever his neglect of me. I wish only he had vouchsafed me some *account*—of his motives, his confusions, false starts, illuminations, mixt feelings, successes, failures, final aims, net values—that I might have understood & believed when my mind was ready, however much I had spurn'd it in my younger cynicism. We have tried to help Tecumseh, & fear we have undone him (we shall try again); surely our grandparents did not *intend* to be Pontiac's undoing, as my father declared. Whence then my confidence that H.B. IV workt with Little Turtle to undo him, or my grandfather's confidence that H.B. III workt with the Bloodsworth Island conspirators to undo them? Oh, for an accounting! We have misspent, misspent our powers, Cookes & Burlingames canceling each other out. May we live, Andrée & I, to be the 1st of our line to cancel out *ourselves,* to the end that you (guided by these letters, which must be your scripture if aught should take us from you) may be the 1st to be spared the necessity!

To sum up: We no longer believe (what my grandparents taught) that Henry Burlingame III was a British agent out to divide the Bloodsworth Islanders (his Ahatchwhoop brother "Bill-o'-the-Goose" and the rest): we believe he meant in good faith to unite them, & fail'd. We do not believe (what my father taught) that my grandparents were British agents out to subvert Pontiac's conspiracy; we believe they meant to abet it, & fail'd. We no longer believe (what your parents would have taught, this time last year) that Henry Burlingame IV was (is?) an American agent bent on dividing first the Iroquois League & then Little Turtle's; we believe he workt for their best interests, & fail'd. So we pray you will not believe us to have been in the employ of William Henry Harrison or James Madison against noble Tecumseh: we wisht to aid him, & have so far fail'd.

Father, I forgive you. My life's 1st half is done: it too I forgive, & the Andrew Cook who lived it, who now must set about its rectification so that *you* (my Henry, Henrietta), when in years to come you shall have read this long accounting, will have nothing to forgive or be forgiven for.

Envoi. I commenced this letter on 14 May; 'tis now a dozen days since, & still you linger! Andrée is huge, predicts a Gargantua—or, as the sun is now into Gemini. . .

You will be born into a war: I think no one can now prevent it. I must hope (& try with my life) that no one will "win" it, or all is lost. Andrée & I are pledged now neither to the British nor to the "Americans"—nor, finally, to the Indians—but to *division* of the large & strong who would exploit the less large, less strong. Thus we are anti-Bonapartists, but not pro-Bourbon; thus, for the nonce, pro-British, but no longer anti-"American." No hope or point now in *destroying* the United States; but they must be checkt, contain'd, divided, lest like Gargantua's their mad growth do the destroying. May this be your work too, when your time comes. Farewell. Do not restart that old reciprocating engine, our history; do not rebel against the *me* who am rebelling against myself: the father of

> Your new-born father,
> Andrew Cook IV

S: *Jerome Bray to Drew Mack. LILYVAC's LEAFY ANAGRAM.*

> Jerome Bonaparte Bray
> General Delivery
> Lily Dale, N.Y. 14752
>
> May 13, 1969

Andrews F. Mack
c/o Tidewater Foundation
Marshyhope State University
Redmans Neck, Md. 21612

Comrade:

St. Elret, patron of cipherers, be with you as with yours truly. Death to Jacobins, usurpers, anti-Bonapartists. The King is dead; long live the 2nd Revolution. Beware Todd Andrews, agent of the pesticide cartel. Excuse our longhand. May we together RESET

Our spring work period here at Lily Dale is at its peak. LILYVAC II is on-line and programmed to capacity. Ditto our comrade associate Ms. Le Fay a.k.a. Merope Bernstein see below at our new base in Chautauqua. Things are buzzing buzzing. We must scratch out this report by hand no time for epistolary printouts but you would be surprised what LILYVAC can RESET

We last met in February at the funeral of H.R.H. your father H.M. II G. III R.I.P. when you questioned us closely as to the practicality not to say the authenticity of LILYVAC's Novel Revolutionary program *RN* for which you had twice loyally arranged support from the Tidewater Foundation. At one point you even declared straight out your suspicion that it and we were pure humbird. We do not doubt that you were

324

distracted by your grief we ourself are an orphan have never known
our dear parents were raised in the Backwater Wildlife Refuge and
RESET

As for us we could scarcely have responded properly to your
unexpected though perfectly justified interrogation. It was the last-but-
one and deepest month of our winter rest period. Snug as a bag in a rug
off-line and dreaming of the revolutionary title *NOTES* read out by
LILYVAC at the midpoint of Year *V* a.k.a. *T* a.k.a. 12/21/68 *vide infra*
we could have been roused at all by nothing less momentous than the
death of your father the most trusted the most RESET

This letter is to allay your skepticism to report to you personally as
we can no longer trust the Tidewater Foundation *per se* the setbacks and
successes of our spring work period and to warn you against the
aforementioned T.F. Executive Director T.A. He shall RESET

On Tuesday March 4 Feast of Purim Full Worm Moon we
authorized said A to institute certain plagiarism proceedings as part of
our general campaign to neutralize anti-Bonapartist counterrevolutionaries. No reply. On April 1 St. Elret's Day on the eve of LILYVAC's 1st
trial printout of the Revolutionary Novel *NOTES* we took time to write
him again confiding the results of our fall work period and our hopes
for the spring *e.g.* our initial concern at LILYVAC's entitling the project
not *NOVEL* but *NOTES* our wondering whether therefore we were in
Year *T* rather than Year *V* see RESET

In the same letter we urged him to reply to ours of 3/4 and move
against B whom also we rewarned to make reparation by Doomsday *i.e.*
6:13 PM PST 4/4 or RESET No RESET We are going to have to
reprogram LILYVAC not to RESET

That same Tuesday 4/1 overcast and chilly here in west NY rain in
the PM ☾ on Equator ♂ ♃ ☾ · ♂ ☍ ☾ U.S. to reduce B-52 raids Gas
explosions seal Mexican coal mines 145 feared dead Eisenhower
funeral train goes to Abilene China convenes 9th National Congress
Mao in complete charge Cultural Revolution accomplished 2nd Revolution waiting to be RESET Full of that weary exultation which only true
revolutionary lovers can RESET We toasted the moment with cordials
of apricot nectar and pushed the Printout button for the 1st trial draft
of the RN *NOTES* a 1 and a 2 give us an *N* give us an *O* No no whats this
a 1 and a 14 and a 1 and a 7 and an 18 and a 1 and a 13 12 5 1 6 25 et
cet exclamation point

I.e., no *NOVEL* no *NOTES* but a swarm of numbers exclamation
point Merope and we looked into each other's RESET On and on 13 1
18 7 1 12 5 6 1 25 then a string of 55's and 49's alternating page after
page after RESET Not got all the chinks out of the ointment 17 rules
for the comma et cet push PUNCT   Point   No   Stop   No
.? Yes. Check: ,;!()? OK, OK.

Words cannot describe our dismay, sir, faithful Merope's and ours.
Numbers! Scrambled integers, not even binary! We were still weak: last
summer's gassing, the interruptions of our winter's rest. The printout

went on, reams and quires of single and double digits. We stood by numb, rudderless, like a man-of-war whose T has been crossed. At midnight LILYVAC tapped out a string of 26's and fell silent. Dialogue. Maybe Doomsday's early this year, said Merope, and led us to bed.

That was Tuesday. Thursday 4/3 was Maundy Thursday, also Nisan 15 and 1st night of Passover. Description. The sky cleared over Lake Cassadaga; the air was mild along the Niagara Frontier. As we took our constitutional about the grounds of Lily Dale, where a few early spiritualists raked their yards and spruced their cottages for the coming season, we could see clearly atop the hills on the farther shore the low buildings of the Pope John XXIII Retreat. At Merope's direction, and to distract us from our gloom (the great pile of printout lay still untouched at LILYVAC's feet), we vowed to put all numbers out of our minds until the Friday, just as LILYVAC avoids all references to   , whether by deletion or by artful substitution, *e.g.* *bean* for *bean*. We had searched and destroyed on the Wednesday night all leavened bread in our cottage against the 7 days to come. Now toward sunset she arranged on the Seder tray the 7 symbols: matzo, baked egg, lamb's bone, haroseth, karpas, hazereth, and fillet of a fenny snake. She lit the 2 candles, filled the 2 wine cups, and bid me begin the 15 stages of the service. We drank our 4 cups of wine, asked and answered the 4 Questions, recited the story of the 70-year bondage of the Israelites, discussed the 10 Plagues and Rabbi Judah's coding them by their initials; BFL, BMB, HLDF (Blood Frogs Larks, Beasts Murrain Boils, Hail Lilies Darkness 1st-Born-Slaying); we sang the 14 verses of *Dayenu* and the 10 of *An Only Kid;* we remarked upon the reckoning of climacteric years in the Hebrew calendar

$$\left(\begin{matrix} 9 & 27 & 45 & 63 & 81 \\ 7 & 21 & 35 & 49 & 63 & 77 \end{matrix}\right. \text{etc.}),$$

also its designation of sabbatical and jubilee years, the 7 days of Levitical purifications and of 2 of the 3 major Jewish feasts, the 7 weeks between the 1st and 2nd of the latter, and the 7 years of Nebuchadnezzar's beasthood and of Jacob's service with each of his wives; we were reminded of the Hebrew tradition that the 7th son of a 7th son has a special destiny; that God is called by 7 names and created Creation in 7 days; that Solomon had 700 wives and 7 seals, and his temple 7 pillars; that Balaam would have 7 bullocks and 7 rams sacrificed upon his 7 altars; that Naaman was commanded to dip 7 times into the Jordan; that 7 priests with 7 trumpets marched daily for 7 days around the walls of Jericho, and 7 times on the 7th day; that Pharaoh dreamed of 7 kine and 7 ears of corn; that Samson's wedding feast lasted 7 days, on the 7th of which he told Delilah the secret of his strength, whereupon she bound him with 7 withes and shore him of 7 locks of hair; that Salome danced with 7 veils. That Mary Magdalene was exorcised of 7 devils. Dialogue. Never mind the goyishe stuff, Merope protested, before I could mention the 7 deadly sins and cardinal virtues and gifts of the

Holy Ghost and Champions of Christendom and years of their ordeals and joys of Mary and sorrows of RESET Sayings on the cross holy angels churches of Asia parts of the Lord's Prayer, also the candlesticks stars trumpets spirits horns vials plagues monster-heads and lamb-eyes in the Book of Revelations. Back to the Hebes, then: that their very verb *to swear* means to come under the influence of 7 things; and that the Torah itself, according to one Kabbalistical tradition, had been a heptateuch before it was a pentateuch, 1 of its books having disappeared entirely and another shrunk to 2 verses (#35 and #36) in the 10th chapter of the Book of Numbers.

Dialogue. Next year in Jerusalem! You know, said Merope, that reminds me of LILYVAC's printout. Oh? All those numbers. Ah. Remember back in Year *O*, she went on, 1967/68, when we programmed LILYVAC II with Thompson's *Motif-Index to Folk-Literature* plus the fiction stacks of Lily Dale's Marion Skidmore Library plus *Masterplots* plus *Monarch Notes* and like that? Yes. Plus everything we could think of that comes in 5's, such as the fingers, toes, senses, and wits of Homo sapiens, the feet of pentametric verse and Dr. Eliot's shelf of classics, the tones of pentatonic music, the great books and blessings of China, the bloods of Ireland, the (original) Nations of the (noble) Iroquois, the divisions of the British Empire, the books of the Pentateuch, the weekdays of the week, the vowels of the alphabet, the ages of man, the months of Odysseus's last voyage as retold by Dante, the stories framed by Scheherazade's *Tales of the Porter and the 3 Ladies of Baghdad,* and a few non-serial odds and ends such as *quincunx, pentagon, quintile, pentacle, quinquennium, quintuplet,* and *E-string,* inasmuch as *NOVEL* is a 5-letter word and our plan is a 5-year plan? Yes. Well: remember back there in all that fiction a tale by E. A. Poe called *The Gold Bird* 1843 in which William Legrand finds a message spelled out in numbers and deciphers it from the hypothesis that if the numbers stand for letters and the coded message is in English then the most frequently recurring number probably stands for the 5th letter of our alphabet *E* et cetera and he drops the bird through the eye of a skull that he finds on the 7th limb of a tree I forget why and it leads him to Captain Kidd's treasure I forget how? Gee whiz, Merope, are you suggesting dot dot dot? Yes, well, we Jews, you see, are Hebrew? And our alphabet, like the Greek, served in olden times for counting as well as for spelling out words? So when an old-time Jew looked at words on a page he also saw a string of numbers? So it's not surprising that among the mystical traditions associated with the books of the Kabbalah, a Hebrew word meaning "tradition," is the tradition of *Gematria,* the manipulation of the numerical equivalents of the letters? Et cetera. Hum, we expostulated, by gosh Merope, we believe that you have found the hidden matzo, the *Afikomen* in the ointment, the nigger in the woodpile that is the key to the treasure. Grace. Hallel. Accepted.

Narrative. That day we reclined no more. We now pass over our night-long ardor in the workroom among those sheaves of numbers, every one of which, aha, was under 27 except the 55's and 49's—no problem there, 5 5 is the letters of our *NOTES* and the years of our plan, and 4 from 9 is 5, right, *E*, our prime letter and the year to come. But it were too much to expect a 1-to-1 correspondence (1 to 1 = *A* to *A*, a mere tautology; we gave it a go anyhow, why not; the 1st dozen letters came out *MARGANAYFAEL*, forget it).

Thus the Thursday. Next day, Friday, 4/4, St. Ambrose's Day, beware him, Comrade, Reg Prinz too, they will RESET Good Friday for the Christians Day of Adam's creation for the Mohammedans 2nd of Pesach for Merope and 3 of her comrades who now swarmed in from their colleges and communes Canada to reduce NATO forces Looting and rioting in Chicago after M. L. King memorial service Doomsday RESET Understandably her young friends did not at 1st quite trust ourself despite Merope's assuring them that under our cape we were not the creepy WISP we might appear but a sort of 3rd Worlder plus a bona fide 2nd Revolutionary, 3 plus 2 = et cetera. Dialogue. Come off it. Narrative. But we were patient, and altogether too preoccupied with the search for a base-5 key to the cipher to share our Merope's distress at their youthful jibes. 5 5 5 5 5: we suggested to LILYVAC that the key to those numbers *was* that number; at 6:13 PM PST (9:13 at our meridian) we all gathered round for the 1st 5 trial translations of the *NOTES* numbers into letters (*i.e.*, 1 = A, 2 = A, 3 = A, etc.). Ourself held Merope by the fingers of her hand; Rodriguez-from-CCNY held the other; on my right black Thelma and her lover Irving from Fort Erie smoked cannabis. 1: *MARGANAYFAEL*, then nonsense; 2 ditto; also 3 4 5. Fooey, said Merope. Order of frequency, then: 1 = E et cet.? MARGANAYFAEL + nonsense. Sheesh, said Merope. Inverse order of frequency : 26 = E et cet.? It is written in the *Zohar,* offered Rodriguez, that just as the initial letter *Aleph* is the male principle and proclaims the unity of G_d, so the 2nd letter, *Beth,* is female; together they postulate the alphabet, alpha plus beta, get it? But *B* is the instrument of creation, the mother of letters and of the world Amen.

Wow, said Merope: Let's try that, Jerry. Hum, well, OK, here goes: *MARGANAYFAEL* + nonsense.

Elsewhere in the *Zohar,* vouchsafed Thelma, or is it the *Sepher Yetzirah,* it says how *Yodh,* the 1st letter of the Tetragrammaton, is the Father, *He* the mother, *Vau (W)* the Son, and the 2nd *He* the Daughter? Also how *Yesod* is the sacred phallus and *Zion* the sacred yoni? Try them ones.

Right on, said Merope. Hum, well, OK, here goes: *MAR-GANAYFAEL*. Your turn, Irv. I'm a Catholic myself, confessed Irving, but Mister Horner over at the Farm, who sends his regards, showed me an old-time hornbook in which was written *AEIOU His Great Name doth spell; Here it is known, but is not known in Hell.* Play that on your calliope.

MARGANAYRESET Margana y who? inquired Rodriguez. You're cute, you are, Merope volunteered. They chatted on, the 4, of other

328

traditions from the Kabbalah, explaining to Irv that the letters of the Hebrew alphabet had originally refused to submit to the spelling out of a Torah which dealt in commandments and prohibitions; that just as the primordial universe of the Greeks was a Chaos of atoms which later formed themselves into the Cosmos, so the primordial Torah was a jumble of letters which arranged themselves into words and sentences only as the events they set forth came to pass; that at the Diaspora the letters of the Holy Name were separated, male from female, like YHWH from the Shekinah. Matthew Arnold somewhere remarks, rejoined Irv, that God puts a heap of letters into each man's hand, for him to make what word he will. They went out then to stroll in the balmy PM, leaving ourself alone to brood upon our scrambled NOTES as Maimonides affirms that the Holy One (Blessed be He!) before Creation was alone with the letters of His name.

Holy Saturday! ♂ ♆ ☾ ! 4/5! Nixon intensifies secret Viet negotiations Antiwar march in NYC USSR presses criticism of Tito and Czechs 25,000,000 Chinese being sent to farms from cities Man goes berserk on Pa. Turnpike kills 3 + self Dante & Virgil finish descent through Hell Danton guillotined 4th Lord Baltimore dies! Thelma, Irving, and Rodriguez planned to spend the weekend secretly filling the water coolers in the Buffalo offices of certain large industrial corporations with polluted Lake Erie water; they urged Margana to leave me behind to crank out more mishmash with my big dumb toy and come with them. She hesitated loyally a moment before saying yes. Dialogue. What's this Margana, she inquired. Why, chortled Thelma, 'tis short for Margana le Fay, like LILYVAC say. Tut and fie, suggested Merope: if I am Margana le Fay, then Jerome is Merlin. Arthur, Arthur! teased Rodriguez. We urged them, if they craved a holiday from the serious work of finding the key that will turn LILYVAC's numbers into revolutionary letters, to devote their youthful energies while in Buffalo to the neutralization of that "Author" who mimics ourself as the wily Schizura unicornis mimes, not the flawless hickory leaf (never found in fact), but, flawlessly, the flawed and bitten truth of real hickory leaves. What in the name of crucified Christ is he talking about? cheerfully interrogated Irving. O that's J, Merope reassured them: any reference to B and he's off. You ask me, Thelma said, he's out of his motherfucking carton. I propose, proposed Rodriguez, that we leave him alone with his jumbled letters, as Maimonides and the pre-Zoharic Jewish mystics maintain that YHWH RESET Merope smartly reminded them that we had fought the good fight against DDT and were still to some degree a casualty of that battle, hence our twitches, but it was her conviction that each must make the Revolution in his/her own way, Don't Bog Thy Neighbor et cet. And she kissed us good-bye on the cheek and said Hasta la vista Pops Don't forget to feed the goats Ta-ta, and Irving joshed Feed them the numbers, man, and Thelma enounced Some eats um some plays um hee hee.

Hum. Off they went in our faithful VW blank, leaving us alone with our RESET They were gone 2 weeks, I began to wonder, Dante climbed Mount Purgatory said good-bye to Virgil and ascended to the Earthly Paradise, Jesus rose from the dead, Cain was born, Abel slain, Passover ended, Napoleon abdicated, Lincoln was shot, the *Titanic* sank, Sirhan RESET Paul Revere rode, we tried key after ditto after same: *MARGANAYFAEL*. Where was our Merope?

Despair, Comrade Mack. When on the 19th they returned after all to Lily Dale to celebrate the 194th anniversary of the 1st American Revolution, *i.e.*, the skirmish at the Old North Bridge in Concord and the battle of Lexington Snow on the ground U.S. fleet heads for Korea patrol Blacks seize Cornell Student Union—we tearfully embraced our Merope's proffered cheek and declared: Dialogue. My dear, our scrambled NOTES are turned to stone. Hoo, exclaimed Thelma, we stoned too. Jeez, marveled Irving, he really is still at it. I have something painful and difficult to tell you, Jerome, declared Merope. Cool it, Marg, suggested Rodriguez, he'll learn it himself soon enough. Did you bring us a surprise, we inquired of the smiling youthful 4some. Sort of, teased Irving: like, we checked that hornbook business up at the Farm, OK? And this cat Morgan that's up there these days, that's got all kind of smarts? He told us how AEIOU is an anagram for IEOUA, dig? Which is sort of a nonconsonantal counterpart, if you follow me, to the vowelless Tetragrammaton YHWH, a.k.a. Jehovah, get it? It was further suggested by Monsieur Casteene, added Rodriguez, who I must say has got a proper Yiddishe Kopf on his shoulders if I ever saw one, that the so-called "Faithful Shepherd" book of the *Zohar* declares, *Not as I am written [i.e., YHWH] am I read*. Casteene feels this to be an allusion to—he had better said a vindication of—the Kabbalistical practices of *Notarikon* and *Themurah*, which with the aforementioned *Gematria* comprise the 3 principal approaches of the Kabbalists to Scripture-regarded-as-cipher. *Gematria*, you will recall, is the search for meaning in the numerical values of the letters: thus MARGANA, for example, has a value of 55 $(13+1+18+7+1+14+1)$, and LE FAY, a.k.a. YFAEL, 49. Thus far Casteene, with whom we young 4 agree that *Notarikon* is unlikely to be of help to you: *it* consists of regarding the letters of a word as an acrostic for a sentence or vice versa (*e.g.* the closing paragraph of V. Nabokov's story *The Vane Sisters*, which also mentions en passant the Fox sisters of Lily Dale: The narrator, puzzling over his dream of the 2 dead sisters Cynthia and Sybil, writes: *I could isolate, consciously, little. Everything seemed blurred, yellow-clouded, yielding nothing tangible. Her inept acrostics, maudlin evasions, theopathies—every recollection formed ripples of mysterious meaning. Everything seemed yellowly blurred, illusive, lost.* He does not see what your adept of *Notarikon* perceives at once, the teasing message from the sisters spelled out by the initial letters of those words. But I digress, like an old-time epistolary novel by 7 fictitious drolls & dreamers each of which imagines himself actual). MARGANAYFAEL and the rest not being words, no acrostic can be legitimately extracted, and to regard the whole printout

330

as itself the acrostic for a much larger text—that were madness, no? No, it strikes us that *Themurah,* which is to say anagrammatical transposition, is the key to the treasure, Jerome old sport: a key 1st hit upon by good Thelma here when she turn YFAEL into LE FAY, and echoed by your scrambling of NOTES into *stone.* What you have here, friend, what your LILYVAC hath wrought, is a *leafy anagram* of monstrous proportions 10, beside which the runes scribbled on the Sibyl's oak leaves and scattered by the wind in Virgil's *Aeneid* were no tougher than an acorn to crack than the Sunday crossword. To it, old man, to it! Steer terse RESET through that dense foliage till that thou comest to the golden bough or flawless hickory leaf never found in fact but RESET Only grasp it and RESET Meanwhile we got other fish to fry, unfinished business as it were, ha ha, Margana too, how you gonna keep a chick down in Þaree after she's seen that Farm. We all off to Chautauqua where the action is.

End monologue Dialogue Thus crumbleth the matzo ball, Jer, said Merope/Margana tenderly: Each must revolt in his/her own RESET I'll stop by de vez en cuando to do a leaf or two with you. St. Elret smile upon you, Irving intoned, and upon your leafy anagram Amen Bye.

Exposition complication climax dénouement. Comrade Mack, we are ready. That was 3 weeks 3 days ago. Since then Daylight Saving Time has begun, de Gaulle has lost his referendum and retired, the *Bounty* crew has mutinied, General Proctor and Tecumseh have besieged Fort Meigs, Mayday Mayday, Louis XVII has been restored to the throne of France, and Napoleon has given out the fiction of his death on St. Helena, vive le RESET Peter Minuit has bought Manhattan, and LILYVAC and we, vouchsafed this astonishing illumination from Comrades Rodriguez Thelma and Irving, blessed and inspired by Merope/Margana who drops us the odd *wish you were here* from Chautauqua Institution or the Remobilization Farm where she is making the Revolution in her own RESET Alone here with the letters of our amen we have found the treasure; we have found the lock; nothing is wanting save the key for LILYVAC's unscrambling of the LEAFY ANAGRAM. And while funding is available to us from many sources, the voice of History tells us to RESET This is the final battle On Wisconsin Off the pigs Hail to the chief O say can you see any bedbirds on me Today is Tuesday the 13th Jamestown founded U.S. declares war on Mexico Riots at SUNY/Stony Brook Arson at Brooklyn College Nixon urges draft reform Sunny and mild here in Lily Dale then cloudy and showers We are floating like a butterfat stinging like a key to the RESET Complimentary close Hold on just an adjective minute A modest supplementary grant, Comrade, from the Tidewater Foundation or perhaps from the legacy of His Majesty your father if his will has been done would surely do to work the last remaining monkey wrenches out of the ointment of this flawed leafy RESET Next thing we know it will write in longhand and even fill in the blanks in its own armor like a simile Having a wonderful time wish you were RESET 10 2 2

H: *Ambrose Mensch to Yours Truly*. *A reflection upon History. His defeat by the Director at Ocean City: an Unwritable Sequence. Magda celebrates a certain anniversary.*

The Lighthouse, etc.
Erdmann's Cornlot, etc.

May 12, 1969

FROM: Ambrose Mensch, Whom etc.
TO: Yours Truly, Author of
RE: Your message to me of May 12, 1940

Madam or Sir:

History is a code which, laboriously and at ruinous cost, deciphers into *HISTORY*. She is a scattered sibyl whose oak-leaf oracles we toil to recollect, only to spell out something less than nothing: *e.g.*, *WHOL TRUTH*, or *ULTIMATE MEANIN*.

Item: On the bumper of the car next to mine in the hotel parking lot in Ocean City this morning, a sticker reading, in large capitals, *BUMPER STICKER*. This evening at the Lighthouse, on the rear of Peter's pickup, another, put there by the twins, declaring in ever diminishing type:

THE CLOSER YOU GET THE LESS YOU SEE

Item: My attempt to reenact in Ocean City this morning what I am only now and here enacting: this latest reply to your letter of etc. 29 years ago today—when, as now, Saturn was on the farther shore of Pisces, leaving the water signs for another revolution of the zodiac—on the beach below Willy Erdmann's Cornlot I received your water message, the sense of which perhaps only now I begin to see. Zeus knows I have been bone-tired before: wrung out, hung over, down. But never heretofore all these and almost 40 too, my life's first half wound past its terminating ticks, no key in hand yet to rewind me for the second. Only some portents that, if one does not look to't, biography like history may reenact itself as farce.

Amazing, this A.M.'s business on the beach! To have wrestled all night with Prinz's damned scenario; to have found after all the words that might make the wordless happen; then to be *shown*—so roughly, publicly, instantly, and incontrovertibly!—their irrelevance. . . We've lost a battle, Ma'am or Sir, in what till now I'd not understood to be a war. That P. is a genius (at improvisation, at least: a master of the situational moment) merely surprises me: I'd thought him able at his trade; now I believe him to be a genuine virtuoso. What shocks is the

332

revelation of his *absolute enmity:* the man contemns, the man despises me!

Is it less or more distressing that his contempt is not even particularly personal? I ought to find it amusing that he's out to get, not Ambrose-Mensch-the-oddball-in-the-tower, but "Arthur Morton King," whom in his antiliteracy he mistakes for an embodiment of the written word as against the visual image; of Letters versus Pictures! Does he not see that what he's acting out is a travesty of my own running warfare against the province of Literature? That we are comrades, allies, brothers?

Of course he sees—with the wrongheaded clear-sightedness of Drew Mack, who lumps stock liberals like Todd Andrews with reactionaries like A. B. Cook. And it "proves" P.'s point, I suppose, that in the face of his blank hostility I see my own dispute with letters to have been a lovers' quarrel. Sweet Short Story! Noble Novel! Precious squiggles on the pristine page! Dear Germaine.

Your old letter, then, Ms. or Mr. Truly—that blank space which in my apprenticeship I toiled to fill, and toward which like a collapsing star I'd felt my latter work returning—was it after all a call to arms? Left to right, left, right, like files of troops the little heroes march: lead-footed *L;* twin top-heavy *T*'s flanked by eager *E*'s, arms ever ready; rear-facing *R;* sinuous *S*—valiant fellows, so few and yet so many, with whose aid we can say the unseeable! *That green house is brown. Sun so hot I froze to death. History is a code which, laboriously and at ruinous cost, deciphers into* etc. Little comrades, we will have our revenge! Good Yours, I have never been more concerned!

Bea Golden. Aye, Bea, I see still in my dark camera the honey image of your flesh. Your beach-towel twitches: there are the breasts Barry Singer sang, the buttocks Mel Bernstein bared, Louis Golden's glowing gluteus, Prinz's pudenda! A little shopworn, sure; a little overexposed. Prinz's cold judgment, as you report it, is surely right: that you will never be an actress unless in the role of yourself-without-illusions, a washed-out small-timer, wasted prematurely by an incoherent, silly, expensive life: the role he would have you play in "our" film. (When did he string so many words together? Or was his message in some tongueless tongue?) But Bea, Bea, battered Aphrodite, how I am redrawn to you, to my own dismay! Not to "Jeannine Mack," the little tart who frigged me to a frazzle in my freshman year, no; *there's* a passion I've already reenacted, and have nor wind nor sap to re-re-run. It's Reg Prinz's played-out-prize perversely I would prong: the Bea you have become: unmobled quean of bedroom, bar, B movie. Why in the world, Y.T., do I itch for Bea? Not *just* that she's Prinz's, surely? And surely not for want of other blanks to fill?

Au contraire: the scent seems to be on me since crazy April, and will not leave me be in abstemious May. Young "Mary Jane" in the beach hotel this weekend: a ringer for Jeannine Mack 20 years ago except less well washed and high on grass instead of bourbon; hoping His Nibs the

333

Director would notice her, but settling in the woozy meanwhile for the worn-down nib of her ex-Freshman-English prof. Nothing wrong with shagging a *former* student, Mister Chancellor, Members of the Board of Regents: anyhow she was C+ in class, high B in bed (my curve is lower than in yestersemester); I was tired, my mind was elsewhere (hi, Bea), and I don't dig sex with the inarticulate, though those 21-year-old bodies are, as the children say, Something Else—not even *conceived* yet, Y.T., when I was first laid.

Which fetches us to the other anniversary we celebrate on this date, fortunately unbeknownst to Prinz: the loss of my virginity in 1947. And to my second Remarkable Reenactment of the day. Home from the sea I drive at sundown: beaten, wordless, Mary Jane's juices drying on me and mine on her, the Bea-Prinz image beprinted on my ego like a cattle brand. I stand her to dinner, drop her off at her dorm *(C you later, Allgelehrte),* and head for mine. I pause to consider a pause at 24 L St., Dorset Heights, and decide against it: I have begun to love milady A., but it isn't she I wish to see in this particular distraction. I reflect that we have not coupled, she and I, since May Day, near two weeks gone. This reflection, itself coupled with the scents and images of Bea-Plus, not surprisingly reminds me of that time in my life when I was chastely loving Magda while humping Jeannine around the yacht-club circuit. Harry Truman days. And *that* reminds me. . .

The Lighthouse is dark but for the driveway light. Peter's pickup advises me that the closer I get the less. Angie is abed but waiting to say good night: I bring her saltwater taffy and a coin with her name lettered round it so:

```
        A
    ⌐    ☆    Z
    L
     G  E
```

We speak awhile in the dark of angels, stars, and Ocean City. As I kiss her good night I think of her mother and other bad news. She mortifies me with the giggled observation that my mustache smells like "Bibi" (her pet name for her vulva, Truly, derived in baby days from *pee-pee,* to make water). My not very inspiring private history seizes me by the throat. Dear menstruating, masturbating, certainly motherless, uncertainly fathered child: what is to become of you? Peter, Magda: why do you put up with us, and what on earth would we do if you didn't? Dear Mother, dying next door: Am I legit, prithee, and does terminal cancer hurt awfully? Marsha Blank, chucker of responsibilities, exacter of two eyes for an eye and whole dentitions for a tooth: let him look to's balls, whoever fills you now! Germaine, Germaine: why am I taken with the crazy craving, even as I write these words, to *do it over again,* and specifically with you? Why not get a child on Magda, tat for tit for tat?

Et cetera. Nighty-night, Ange. Not a little shaken, I go downstairs for a nightcap. No ale in the kitchen: since Peter and the twins, great do-it-themselfers, finished the basement into a Family Room (in which our old camera obscura stands like an improbable TV), all alcohol is

334

stowed belowstairs, in the fridge behind the "wet bar." It is nearly midnight. I pour a Labatt's India Pale, turn down the rheostated lights, and contemplate an actual Choptank lighthouse winking from the c.o. screen every 2½ seconds, off to westward. It does not suggest what I am to do with the second half of my life.

Familiar female footsteps overhead: Magda, in her slopping slippers. She pauses in the kitchen—Ambrose? Mm hm—then pads on down. Can't seem to get to sleep. Cotton nightgown, demure. How was Ocean City? Don't ask. Pours herself one. We almost drove down to watch the shooting. Glad you didn't. Did you really do the water-message thing? Yup. Peter says if they're hiring you to be Ambrose in the picture, they ought to hire me to be Magda. Your ass is too big, Mag. Happy anniversary.

She said it first, raising her mug, and when I asked, neutrally, Which one, she replied, cheerfully, Who cares about that stupid note in a bottle? I mean your 22nd year of prickhood. Ah. We sipped to it. I couldn't assess her tone, quite. How are you, dear Magda?

As is her wont with me, she answered calmly, gravely, fully. She was okay, all things considered. She no longer feared, as she had last winter, that she would kill herself. She had assumed, when we began our affair in '67, that it would be brief and end in the destruction of someone she much loved: Peter by suicide; me by homicide; herself by either; the children somehow. For she had hoped and expected that we two would chuck the world and go away together—to Italy, to Italy— and she had imagined that Peter, despite his best resolves and infinite responsibility, would find the situation unendurable. Since things had not gone as she'd wished, she was relieved that nothing fatal had ensued. But that fact reminded her that her love for me, and whatever it was I'd felt for her, had been *inconsequential;* she hated that. With all her heart she wished still that we had run off to Italy, if only for a season, and let the chips fall where they might. She did not hate Peter for being complaisant (out of his fancied and unwarranted guilt for having let Marsha once seduce him); but she didn't admire him for it, either. She did not hate me for having been unable to love her as she'd loved me: she only regretted it—almost, but not quite, to the point of self-destruction.

Most of all she lamented my refusal to make her pregnant. Marsha's opinion to the contrary notwithstanding, Magda believed me capable of loving deeply; but even if I'd gone so far as to marry her (which she'd never expected), she would not have given my love for her more than two years—inspired as it was in part by the shock of my divorce. Inasmuch as she herself would never cease to love me, she wished as strongly now as ever that we'd had a child together, through whom she could gratify that love. A child—and my removal from the scene—would have been the fittest end to our affair, in her judgment. It was only because I'd not given her that child that she was able to bear, indeed required, my continued presence in the house: I was surrogate for the child who was to have been surrogate for me. And how are *you*, Ambrose?

Oh, shot to hell. I told her the story of my set-down on the beach and my rewakened interest in Bea Golden. The former mightily amused her, as I meant it to. She hoped and trusted I was teasing her about the latter. I'm drawn to has-beens, I said. The exhausted. The spent. Maybe I'll write an old-fashioned novel: characters, plot, dialogue, the works. Maybe I'll remarry and start a family.

That hurts, Ambrose.

Sorry, said I, taking her hand. It's late. I'm tired and a little drunk. What I really feel is a mighty urge to go forward by going back, to where things started. Rewind, you know. Rebegin. Replay.

That is known as regression, Magda declared; I bid you good night. She leaned to buss me; got wind of old Bibi, perhaps; anyhow made a small sound of pain, an indeterminate whimper. I held her to it. I don't know what yours are like, Yours, but Lady Amherst's lips are pleasingly dry and firm; Jeannine Mack's (in the old days) were hot and hard; "Mary Jane's" just lately were wet and thin and a touch maloccluded; Marsha Blank's I don't remember—but Magda Giulianova's, now as a quarter-century ago, are two extraordinary items of flesh. A man cannot kiss those lips without craving to take one into his mouth; a man at once wants more. . .come on, Language, do it: read those lips, give them tongue! Language can't (film either, I'm happy to add; it's the tactile we touch on here, blind and mute) do more than pay them fervent, you know, lip service.

Tears. Not *her*, Magda prayed. Meaning Marsha! I shook my head. Time to end the mystery, at least the evening; I wanted that mouth again, that man cannot kiss without tumescing. To cool us down (so I truly, innocently intended) I told her gently of Germaine.

Something of a male chauvinist, Magda was at first startled and a bit amused (the lady had once been pointed out to her in a shopping plaza). The woman's *fifty*, Ambrose! Etc. Then relieved, clearly, that her successor was no smashing 25-year-old. Then curious: bona fide British nobility? Well, part Swiss, and not born to the gentry; more of a scholar than a blue blood; disappointed writer, actually, like yours truly. Then *more* curious, and a touch excited: What's she like? Is she crazy about you? Are you madly in love? Well, let's say ardently in sympathy. Remarkable woman, Germaine Pitt: I suspect she's as given to Erotic Fantasy as I am, for example. Then more excited than curious: Did you have to teach her how to do it right, the way you did me, or had she had a string of lovers already?

Magda.

She was glad, she said. She'd been worried for me since our breakup. I needed sexual companionship, not just the odd lay. She'd known I was sleeping with someone; had hoped and prayed it was someone good both in and out of bed. . . Breathier now, and tearier, that remarkable lower lip shaking. But God I miss it, Ambrose (Magda seldom uses nicknames, nor enounces that trochee without stirring me to the bowels. I think I know who *Ambrose* is only when Magda speaks the name): it isn't fair; Peter can't do it; you shouldn't have showed me those things are real; I was satisfied enough; I don't want to be unfaithful to him; it's only sex; who gives a fuck; anyway that's not it, that's just not it. I miss you. I love you. I'm going crazy.

Ditto, Truly. Look here, Mag. . .

You mustn't refuse me when I beg you, Ambrose.

Magda, you know as well as I. She was on me then: the lips, the lips, hands, hair. Poor John Thomas, thought his shift was done, took a bit of coaxing he did. Magda favors the rec-room Barcalounger, herself on top: still shy of her heavied hams, she eases herself onto me with a happy gasp, slips the gown off to give me her breasts and shoulders, goes to it. I'd early learned—unemancipated Mag!—in these circumstances to give detailed running orders for my gratification. When she gets it off she never cries out (there's usually a sleeping child, or adult, about), just closes her eyes and makes a small, awestruck sound that goes on and on.

Sex.

Now what. She sat there a postclimactic while, holding shrunk J.T. tight in her vaginal fist and giving *me* serene instructions. I was not to worry. She would not keep after me to make love to her or otherwise infringe on my new attachment, which she approved. I should fetch—Mrs. Pitt? Mrs. Amherst?—over to meet the family as soon as possible: it would help her, Magda, to see us together as a couple, and to have the family so see. I should make plans to move out of the Lighthouse—in easy stages, for Angela's sake. Maybe first to the old Menschhaus up the street, now that Mother's hospitalizing had left the place vacant. Angela of course must stay with them, until and unless. . . A few tears here (J.T. was released). Soon the twins would be off on their own; dear Angela was all she had left. *Why hadn't I given her a baby?* She quickly calmed, apologized. I reminded her she'd doubtless be a grandmother before very long: young Connie had the looks of an early breeder, and Carl was obviously a stone-horse: both would marry within the year and get offspring at once.

This talk pleased her; she climbed off me, smiling. I've done an immoral thing, Ambrose, she said then, and I don't care what you or anybody thinks. I thought she meant this anniversary reenactment of our original infidelity, and waved it away; reminded her wryly I'd been doing retakes all weekend. Not that, she said. All those months I begged you to make me pregnant, and you said No, it wouldn't be right, I never once tried to trick you. I wanted everything we did to be together, 100%. The IUD was in there, every time, even when you'd forget to remind me.

Magda.

But you were so selfish yourself, completely selfish. I'm not blaming you. You can't *make* a person love another person. You can only pray for it. . .

Mag?

And I won't bother you, Ambrose. I love you, always will, and I wish you well. I even know you love me, in your way. But *I want that baby*. So tonight I cheated. I wasn't even going to tell you.

I closed my eyes. You know I'm practically sterile.

Not absolutely. When was your last ejaculation?

Hum. Not counting this one? This morning.

That hurts a bit. But you filled me up. And I'm ovulating; I can tell. Not a Chinaman's chance, Mag.

I've never understood that saying, she said. There are so many Chinese. Anyhow, we Catholics believe in miracles. Don't be angry. If nothing comes of it I'll settle for grandchildren, like you said. I'm going up to bed now, so it won't all run out.

And having come, with a smile and a little tossed kiss she went.

Truly, Yours, I am back not where I started but where I stopped: restranded on the beach of Erdmann's Cornlot, reading your water message; relost in the funhouse—as if Dante, in the middle of life's road, had made his way out of the dark wood, gone down through Hell and up Mount Purgatory and on through the choirs of Heaven, only to find himself back in the dark wood, the right way as lost and gone as ever.

Jeannine. Germaine. Magda. Longest May 12 on record. No copy of this one to milady. What would it spell, deciphered?

Ambrose His Story.

S: *The Author to Jacob Horner.* The story of a story *called* What I Did Until the Doctor Came.

Department of English, Annex B
State University of New York at Buffalo
Buffalo, New York 14214
U.S.A.

Sunday, May 11, 1969

Jacob Horner
c/o Remobilization Farm
Fort Erie, Ontario
CANADA

Dear Mr. Horner:

Some years ago—fourteen, when I was a young college instructor in Pennsylvania—I wrote a small novel called *The End of the Road.* Its "hero," an ontological vacuum who shares your name, suffers from attacks of futility manifested as literal paralysis, to cure which he submits to the irrational therapies of a nameless doctor at an establishment (on the Eastern Shore of Maryland) called the Remobilization Farm. In the course of his treatment, which includes teaching prescriptive grammar at a nearby state teachers college, Horner becomes involved in and precipitates the destruction of the marriage of one of his colleagues, a morally intense young historian named Joe Morgan. Mrs. Morgan, "caught" between her hyperrationalist husband, whom she loves, and her antirationalist "lover," whom she abhors, finds herself pregnant, submits to an illegal abortion at the hands of the Doctor, and dies on the operating table. Her husband, in a state of calm shock, is quietly dismissed from his post. Jacob Horner, contrite and reparalyzed, abdicates from personality and, with the Doctor and other patients, removes to an unspecified location in the wilds of Pennsylvania. The narrative conceit is that he writes the story some years later, from the relocated Farm, as a first-person exercise in "Scriptotherapy."

If I were obliged to reimagine the beginnings of *The End of the Road,* I might say that in the fall of 1955, having completed but not yet published my first novel, I began making notes toward its companion piece: a little "nihilist tragedy" to complement the "nihilist comedy" of *The Floating Opera.* At twenty-five I was married, had three young children, was getting by on the four thousand a year I was paid for grading one hundred freshman themes a week, and moonlighting in local dance bands on the weekends. As there was seldom money in those years for an evening's baby-sitter, much less a genuine vacation from responsibility, I now invent and grant myself retroactively this modest holiday:

It is the last week of the calendar year. A *live-in* baby-sitter, unprecedented luxury, has been engaged to care for the children for the weekend, so that their parents can drive with another couple up into the Allegheny National Forest for two days of skiing. We have never skied before, never seen a ski slope. The expense will be dizzying, by our standards, even though we've borrowed and improvised appropriate clothing and plan to cook camp dinners on a hot plate smuggled into our room: equipment must be rented, lodging also, the sitter paid, car expenses split, lift tickets purchased. We are intimidated by the novelty of such adventure, much as we enjoy the long drive with our friends up into the bleak mountains, Iroquois country, where natural gas and oil rigs bob like giant bugs in the rocky clearings, and black bears are still hunted among the laurels and rhododendron. Skiing has not yet become popular in these parts; metal and fiberglass skis, stretch pants, plastic boots with buckles, snow-making machines—all have yet to be invented. We have never been to New England, much less to the Rockies or to Europe; the whole enterprise, with its international vocabulary and Alpine ambiance—chalets, stem christies, wedeln,

Glüwein, après-ski—is outlandish, heady, alarming. We make nervous jokes about broken legs and Nazi ski instructors.

The facilities are primitive: at the slopes (a modest 400-foot vertical drop, but to us tidewater folk even the beginners' hill rises like the face of a building), rope tows and Poma lifts; at the lodge—but there is no lodge, only a dirt-floored warming hut at the base of the mountain, with picnic tables, toilets, and vending machines. We rent our equipment—wooden skis with cable bindings, double-laced leather boots—not there but at a cheaper place near our *Gasthaus*, also chosen for economy: a rude board-and-batten farmhouse just purchased (the proprietor's wife tells us crossly) from "a bunch of crazies" who in her opinion had used the place for dark unspecified goings-on. She refers to her husband as "he," without further identification: *"He* had to go ahead and buy it. We're still clearing out the junk. *He* says it was some kind of a rest home, but there's an awful lot goes on, if a person knew. He's crazy himself, you ask me." She is a Seneca woman in her fifties with the odd name of Jimmie Barefoot.

The place is overheated but drafty, clean but cluttered, as if the former occupants have moved out hastily, taking only their necessaries, and the new have tidied up but not removed the leavings. In our room there are a pile of boardinghouse Victorian furniture in dark oak, sentimental 19th-Century engravings of moon-faced children and pet animals, a glass-fronted bookcase with the complete works of Walter Scott, and the 92 volumes of Balzac's *Comédie Humaine* in cheap turn-of-the-century editions with matched green bindings.

I shall later become an enthusiast of skiing, but this first attempt is merely clumsy and a little frightening: I am relieved when, at the end of the afternoon, I injure my shoulder enough to be honorably *hors de combat* for the rest of the weekend. While the others advance from the bunny hill to the novice runs, I follow Lucien de Rubempré from the provinces to Paris and through the loss of his several illusions, and sip the homemade beer I've brought along to reduce our expenses. I am not a great fan of either Balzac or Walter Scott. Not having expected to spend our holiday reading, I've brought only one book with me, a half-read Machado de Assis, soon finished and reread. I yearn for my notes and manuscript from home, especially as my shoulder stiffens and makes sleep impossible. I spend most of the night reading Balzac in a hard ugly rocker and deciding to write no more realistic fictions.

When I can take no more of the Abbé Carlos Herrera (I could take none of Captain Edward Waverly) I cast about for something else, anything else, to read. In the drawer of a crazed and knobby end table I find an inch-thick typescript of yellow copy paper bound into a school report binder, the title inked in block capitals on white adhesive tape: *WHAT I DID UNTIL THE DOCTOR CAME.* I read the first sentence— *In a sense, I am Jacob Horner*—and then the others.

The narrative is crude, fragmentary, even dull—yet appealingly terse, laconic, spent. I have no idea whether it is "true" or meant as fiction, but I see at once how I might transform it to my purposes. Now I am impatient for the precious holiday to end!

I leave the typescript where I found it; all I need is the memory of its voice. Once back in the college's faculty housing project, I write the novel very quickly—changing the locale and the names of all but the central character, making the Doctor black and anonymous, clarifying and intensifying the moral and dramatic voltages, adding the metaphor of paralysis, the small-time academic setting, the semiphilosophical dialogues and ratiocinations, the *ménage à trois,* the pregnancy, abortion, and other things. Now and then, after its publication in 1958, it occurs to me to wonder whether the unknown author of *What I Did Until the Doctor Came* ever happened upon my orchestration of his theme. But I am too preoccupied with its successor to wonder very much.

Well. I don't recount, I only invent: the above is a fiction about a fiction. But it is a fact that after *The End of the Road* was published I received letters from people who either intimated that they knew where my Remobilization Farm was or hoped I would tell them; and several of the therapies I'd concocted for my Doctor—Scriptotherapy, Mytho- therapy, Agapotherapy—were subsequently named in the advertise- ments of a private mental hospital on Long Island. Art and life are symbiotic.

Now there is money for baby-sitters, but I don't need them. I've changed cities and literary principles, made up other stories, learned with mixed feelings more about the world and Yours Truly. Currently I find myself involved in a longish epistolary novel, of which I know so far only that it will be regressively traditional in manner; that it will *not* be obscure, difficult, or dense in the Modernist fashion; that its action will occur mainly in the historical present, in tidewater Maryland and on the Niagara Frontier; that it will hazard the resurrection of characters from my previous fiction, or their proxies, as well as extending the fictions themselves, but will not presume, on the reader's part, familiarity with those fictions, which I cannot myself remember in detail. In addition, it may have in passing something to do with alphabetical letters.

Of the epistles which are to comprise it, a few, like this one, will be from "the Author." Some others will be addressed to him. One of the latter, dated May 3, 1969, I received last week from a certain Germaine Pitt, Lady Amherst, acting provost of the Faculty of Letters at "Marshyhope State University College" in Maryland. In the course of it Mrs. Pitt mentions having visited in 1967 a sort of sanatorium in Fort Erie, Ontario, "very much like the one described in *The End of the Road,*" complete with an unnamed elderly black physician. The lady did not mention a "Jacob Horner" among the patients or staff (she was there only briefly); but the fact that her letters speak in another context of a "Joseph Morgan" (former president of the college, whereabouts pres- ently unknown) and a "John Schott" (his successor) prompts this inquiry.

341

That you have received and are reading it proves that its proximate address and addressee exist. Were they ever located in the Allegheny Valley, beneath the present Kinzua Reservoir? Are you the author of *What I Did Until the Doctor Came?* My having imagined that serendipitous discovery does not preclude such a manuscript's possible existence, or such an author's. On the contrary, my experience has been that if anything it increases the likelihood of their existing—a good argument for steering clear of traditional realism.

Do you know what happened to the unfortunate "Joe Morgan"? Are you still subject to spells of "weatherlessness" and the paralytic effect of the Cosmic View? Do you still regard yourself as being only "in a sense" Jacob Horner? That whole business of ontological instability—not to mention accidental pregnancy and illegal abortion—seems now so quaint and brave an aspect of the early 1950's (and our early twenties) that it would be amusing, perhaps suggestive, to hear how it looks to you from this perspective. If you did indeed write such a memoir or manuscript fiction as *What I Did* etc., and my *End of the Road* caused you any sort of unpleasantness, my belated apologies: if literature must sometimes be written in blood, it should be none but the author's.

I'd be pleased to hear from you; could easily drive over to Fort Erie from Buffalo for a chat, if you'd prefer.

Cordially,

4

	S	F	T	W	T	M	S
1969	**P**	6	5	4	3	2	**—**
	I	13	12	11	10	9	8
	S	**E**	**T**	**L**	**E**	**I**	**E**
	T	27	26	25	24	23	22
JUNE	**O**					30	29

Lady Amherst

Todd Andrews

Jacob Horner

A. B. Cook

Jerome Bray

Ambrose Mensch

The Author

P: *Lady Amherst to the Author. The Fourth Stage of her affair. She calls on A. B. Cook VI in Chautaugua. Ambrose's Perseus project, and a proposition.*

Office of the Provost
Faculty of Letters
Marshyhope State University
Redmans Neck, Maryland 21612

7 June 1969

John, John,

Provost indeed! What am I doing here, in this getup, in this office, in this country? And what are the pack of you doing to me?

Driving me bonkers, is what—you and Ambrose and André, André—straight out of my carton, as the children say. And I, well, it seems I'm doing what my "lover" claims to've devoted a period of *his* queer career to: answering rhetorical questions; saying clearly and completely what doubtless goes without saying.

E.g., that my apprehensions *re* the "4th Stage" of our affair prove in the event to have been more than justified. Every third evening, sir, regardless of my needs and wants—indeed, regardless of *Ambrose's* needs and wants too, in the way of simple pleasure—I am courteously but firmly fucked, no other way to put it, in the manner set forth two letters past, to the sole and Catholic end of begetting a child. 'Appen I enjoy it (as, despite all and *faute de mieux,* I sometimes do), bully for me; 'appen I don't, it up wi' me knees and nightie anyroad, and to't till I'm proper ploughed and seeded. In this business, and currently this only, the man is *husbandly,* John, as aforedescribed: husbanding his erections, husbanding my orgasms, his ejaculate. His eye like an old-time crofter's is upon the calendar: come mid-lunation we are to increase our frequency to two infusions daily in hopes of nailing June's wee ovum, May's having given us the slip.

As I too must hope "we" do—yet how hope a hope so hopeless? Why, because, if this old provostial organ do not conceive, I truly fear the consequence! Silent sir (you who mock me not only by your absence from this "correspondence" but by your duly reported presence, even as I write these words, just across the Bay in College Park, to accept the honour you would not have from us. O vanity!): what I feared in mine of Saturday last is come to pass: our friend Ambrose has turned tyrant! Witness: I write this on office stationery because—for all it's a muggy Maryland late-spring Saturday, the students long since flown for the

345

summer, the campus abandoned till our anticlimactic commencement exercises a fortnight hence—I am in my office, winding up my desk work and putting correspondence on the machine for Shirley Stickles. And I am here not at all because the week's work has spilled into the weekend. *Au contraire:* since our (early) final examinations put a term, *hic et ubique,* to the most violent term in U.S. academic history—one which I wot will mark a turn for ill and ever in the fortunes of many a college in this strange country—there's been little to do, acting-provostwise. No: I am here now because I'm ashamed to show myself to Stickles, Schott, & Co., and so must do my windup work by weekend and weeknight, always excepting those reserved for conjugation.

And why ashamed? Oh well, because Distinguished Visiting Professor Pitt, Lady Amherst, acting provost, semicentenarian, erstwhile scholar, erstwhile gentlewoman, erstwhile respecter of herself, goes about these days sans makeup, bra, and panty girdle, her hair unpinned and straight and parted in the middle, her trusty horn-rims swapped for irritating contact lenses and square wire-framed "grannies." The former she tearily inserts on the days her lord and master decks her out in miniskirt or bikini (dear lecherous Jeffrey, how you would laugh now at the legs you once called perfect, the arse and jugs you salivated after across Europe!); the latter complement her hippie *basse couture:* ankle-length unbelted calicos, bell-bottomed denims and fringed leathers—the whole brummagem inventory of head-shop fetishes, countercultural gewgaws, radical fripperies. . . Lord luv a duck! In which I am led forth, yea even as I feared, to "do" (and be done in by) "bags" of "grass" (I do not even like *tobacco,* excepting the smell of certain English mixtures in the briars of the couth) and I-forget-whats of lysergic acid diethylamide; to throw my limbs about like a certifiable lunatic in response to the "mind-blowing" megawattage of beastlike androgynes with surreal and grammatically singular denominations: the Who, the Airplane, the Floyd, the Lord have mercy on my soul. This in the hired "pads" and horny company of the film folk, generally—young and "with it" and "together," beautiful of body and empty of head though not unskilled, the technicians especially—among whom I feel (as surely I'm meant to) a walking travesty, female counterpart of that rouged and revolting old fop in Mann's *Death in Venice.*

The drugs do not finally much alarm me: André and I "did" hashish, cocaine, and opium in Paris a hundred years ago, along with our absinthe and *Caprice des Dieux.* Nor does the "kinky" "scene": *la vie bohémienne* was not invented by the Flower Children, and cannot startle in a single of its aspects—the dope, the dirt, the diet, the promiscuity, the neobarbarist posturings, the radical/anarchist politics, freaky costumes, and woozy occultism—anyone acquainted with Europe's *demi-monde* from Dandyism through Dadaism. What alarms me is *me:* my acquiescence in this contemptible tyrannising; my playing, at such cost

346

to my self-image, peace of mind, and professional activity, my lover's stupid game.

Why do I permit myself to make myself ridiculous, boogalooing with Reg Prinz, Bea Golden (no child either, flower or otherwise; but she's got the body for it, alas, as I have not, and the looseness of limb and morals; and Ambrose, damn him, is attracted), and the "Baratarians," as the extras call themselves? The easy, obvious, armchair answer irritates me, no doubt because it is the main truth: my guilt for having given up my own child nearly thirty years ago (but Lord, Lord!) leaves me peculiarly victimisable at the hands etc. of a man whose regnant passion is to fertilise me. The more as I am *d'un certain âge*, widowed, expatriate (but from what fatherland, after all?), and—in Dostoyevsky's lovely term—"morally prostrate" from the long tantalisings of André Castine and/or his *Doppelgängers*. True, true, true. But the main truth is not the whole truth. Even before this rage for paternity got hold of him, I had begun to love odd Ambrose; my dozen-or-so letters to you since March must surely bear witness to this weary heart's movement from colleaguely cordiality to appall at his first crude overtures, thence through amusement, affection, attraction, and reckless lust, to, Lord help me, love.

I love him! (It excites me to write it.) The child thing scares me: both that he demands conception and that what he demands could, just possibly, occur. *Preggers*, for God's sake! These other new demands scare me: it is not in a spirit of erotic sport that Ambrose rigs me out like a high school "groupie," but in frustration at what in an earlier "stage" he prized: that I am Older. Indeed, I believe that were I as young as the would-be "starlets" among the Baratarians—whose narcotised, strobe-lighted, easily proffered favours *mio maestro* does not always, I think, refuse—he would not so particularly itch to make me big; it is *I* he wants to impregnate, precisely despite my age. But none of these scares me so much as the possibility of his ceasing to love me (he does, John; I know it). For a little while, I trust, he must work out in this bizarre and degrading wise his rage at unalterable circumstance. I love him! And so I "frug," I flail my arms, I wiggle my bum—and close my eyes, open my legs, cross my fingers.

Like, um, wow?

Cependant, he has conceived a longish fiction, novella-size at least, upon the theme of ritual reenactment, drafting notes and diagrams and trial passages between his bouts with me and Prinz. I had almost forgot that he is, after all, an author. He had allowed to me as how the materials were to be classical—the myth of Perseus, Andromeda, and Medusa, to be specific—and we came so near to having a proper literary conversation on the subject that for a moment I had imagined myself twenty again in fact with old Hesse, old Huxley, old Whomever, gratifying their elder flesh whilst they gratified my young mind. I actually lubricated at the prospect of exploring with my lover his lovely reading of the myth, in particular the Medusa episode, which he sees not in the Freudian way as an image of impotence and vulval terror, but (the polished shield of Athene, the reflections and re-reflections) as a drama of the perils of self-consciousness. Ambrose's Perseus, middle-aged and ill married, his mythic exploits and heroic innocence behind him, once again "calls his enemy to his aid" (Ovid's happy phrase, for Perseus's use of the Gorgon's head to petrify his adversaries), attempts to reenact his youthful triumphs, comes a cropper, but with the help of a restored and resurrected Medusa—whose true gaze, seen clearly, may confer immortality instead of death—transcends his vain objective and becomes, with her, a constellation in the sky, endlessly reenacting their romance.

A pretty conceit! *Go, man, go,* I wanted to cry, sincerely for a change. But no sooner do I voice my delight—my *ardent* delight that "Arthur Morton King" intends to speak once again to the passions instead of playing his avant-garde games—than Ambrose chills over as if Medusa'd, and makes clear to me that his main interest in the story is formal: the working out, in narrative, of logarithmic spirals, "golden ratios," Fibonacci series. Never mind the pathos of the failing marriage and fading hero; the touching idea that Medusa *loves* Perseus, even after he decapitates her; the tender physics by which paralyzing self-consciousness becomes enabling self-awareness, petrifaction estellation: out came the diagrams, on graph paper, of whirling triangles, chambered nautili, eclipsing binaries, spiral galaxies! And I am stripped and stood, not for ritual insemination (it had been but two days since the last), much less the simple making of love, but for his measuring whether, as he had read was the average case with Caucasian women, the distance from my feet to my navel was .618+ of my overall height— *i.e., Phi,* the golden ratio!

I was low-*phi,* lower-spirited. If I speak lightly, it is for the same reason that I speak at all: to drown out your thundering silence, to delay my going mad. In the same spirit I have begun your *Goat-Boy* novel and the preparation for the press of Andrew Cook IV's four-letter family history. They have this connexion: the fictional prefatory letters to your novel pretend to dispute the factuality of the text; but my factual preface to and commentary upon Cook's letters to his unborn child must address and if possible resolve the question of their authenticity. I am full of doubts—on account not only of their dubious source and questionable motive, but of such textual details as the inconsistently idiosyncratic spelling, some apparent anachronisms (*e.g. counterinsurgent,* which my *Oxford English Dictionary* does not even list, though it attests *counter-revolutionist* back to 1793 and *insurgent* back to 1765), and a vague modernity in their preoccupation. Yet it seems not *impossible* that they are genuine—the stationery and calligraphy strike me as authentic, though of course I'll check them out—or at worst corrupted copies, on old paper, of authentic originals, perhaps altered to some ulterior purpose, like the notorious Henry Letters they allude to. As a historian of sorts, I must of course make a proper inquiry. As a quondam intimate of André Castine, I know how futile such an inquiry may prove against an artful doctorer of letters. As a too tormented human being, I am tempted to rush them into print, in some uncritical journal of local history, to the end of precipitating what they're supposed to precipitate, and hang the consequences!

But I have not *quite* lost my professional grip: had not, anyroad, as of Thursday last, the day before yesterday, when I bethought me to drive across the Bay "to Annapolis, maybe even Washington," beard A. B. Cook VI in his den, have done with mysteries, confront him with (copies of) the letters, and pin him down once for all on his relation to "Henri Burlingame VII." The film company have finished the first round of location shooting in Cambridge and "Barataria" on Bloodsworth Island, and are dispersed, to regroup next week on the Niagara Frontier for the second round (Where do the Falls figure in your fiction? I had thought it all set in Maryland or in Nowhere); Ambrose was busy with slide rule and mechanical-drawing instruments—strange tools for a man of letters! So I slipped out of 24 L with a briefcaseful of proper attire, endured the smirks of attendants at the first service station on Rte 50 (who surely took me for a superannuated whore) in order to fetch the key to the Ladies and change from mini to midlength, do up my hair, harness in the old tits and tum—what relief!—and, for the first time since the weekend, look my proper self (the chap checked my credit card as if for fraud). Then over the bridge to Chautauqua, Md, on the south shore of the Magothy, and up a certain shrubberied drive to a letterbox marked COOK.

The flag was up: outgoing mail. My courage faltered at sight of those four bold letters, so less equivocal than the man they surnamed or the epistles in my briefcase. A lane of boxwoods and azaleas led to a pleasant white frame cottage, its screened porches shaded by sycamores. The lawn continued to a creek or cove, where pleasure craft rode at moorings; from a staff on the T of the laureate's dock flew the motley banner of the state, bright as racing silks: the Baltimores' chequered black and orange, the Calverts' red-and-white cross botonée. I tapped the door knocker, a bright brass crab, and waited, slapping the odd mosquito. My heart misgave me. Hoping to catch him off his guard, I had not rung up ahead or written. Look here, I hoped to say to him, can we not put by all mystification? Let me tell you what I've been through these two dozen years at the hands of Castines, Cooks, and Burlingames, and there's an end on't! If you and André are not kin; if your son is not my son—let me hear you (and him) tell me so, plainly, fully, amicably, when I shall have told you (ditto) what-all has fetched me to imagine otherwise. . .

A blank-faced woman opened but did not unchain the door, and through that unfriendly space regarded me. Too well dressed to be a domestic, too old (I judged) to be Cook's daughter, yet too young to be "Henri's" mother. A second wife, perhaps? Her nose was soft, but her chin and jaw were hard; her brow was high and fair, her eyebrows were plucked to a sharp line, her lips were thin—well, verbal portraiture is not my forte: sufficient that while in no particular uncomely, her phiz *tout ensemble* was remarkably empty, like that of a receptionist mildly inclined to mask her essential incordiality and profound uninterest. I identified myself, asked for Mr Cook, was told curtly he was not at home. I had historical papers concerning his family to show him, I declared, certain to be of considerable interest to him. Granted, I'd made no appointment, ought to have done. . . But these documents were truly remarkable. When was he expected to return? Or had he an office I might stop by, as I was in the neighbourhood?

She had no idea when he would return, tonelessly intoned Ms Blank—I was put in mind of Ambrose's depiction, no doubt exaggerated, of his ex. He was on a speaking tour of Pennsylvania and upstate New York, but she believed he meant to return in time for the Dorchester County tercentenary celebration in July. She waxed more particular, though no more warm, like an answering service: He had meant to take in, en route, the anniversary commemoration of the Fenian invasion of Fort Erie, Canada, from Black Rock, near Buffalo, in 1866, in which one of his ancestors had played a certain rôle. He was supposed too to do something at Niagara Falls, she believed, and, later in the month, at the other Chautauqua: the one in west New York spelled with a *q*. She didn't know. Something about a movie, she thought.

End of professional grip. The woman neither closed nor unchained the door, but waited for me to turn away. *Adieu,* sanity! I didn't think to ask whether she was Mrs Cook; at that point an incordially neutral reply that she was Mme Castine or Mme de Staël would scarcely have surprised me. Numbly recrossing the Chesapeake, I heard reported on ABC News that the American Falls at Niagara was about to be *turned off,* so that engineers and geologists could examine its fast-receding face and study ways to retard its crumbling: the accumulated rockfall at its base had made the drop less spectacular than that of Horseshoe Falls on the Canadian side, and what with the U.S. Bicentennial but seven years off. . . Meanwhile, in the city of Niagara Falls itself (the American, not the Canadian, city), fire had melted the famous wax museum: George and Martha Washington, Abe Lincoln, FDR and JFK and RFK (whose likeness was to have been unveiled on the morrow, 1st anniversary of his assassination)—all had gone up like so many candles, or down into expensive puddles of wax. Nevertheless, the chamber of commerce expected tourist traffic to reach an all-time high this summer: who would not go out of his way to view such wonders as a turned-off waterfall and a melted museum?

God bless America! And spare me.

Ambrose did not. I drove home too dazed by all these obscure comings-together to bother rechanging into go-go garb. My lover was cross, unreasonable. Of course I might go where I pleased—to

Chautaugua, to London, to Hell—but why hadn't I notified him? He was not at all surprised that A. B. Cook might be involved in Prinz's film, inasmuch as your *Sot-Weed Factor* novel involves the Cookes and Burlingames, and the film has a retrospective as well as a prospective aspect. What did surprise him was that I would be as it were unfaithful to him with "old Cook." Never mind the accident of Cook's not being there: I had slipped out, slipped into my Old Lady clothes, slipped across the Bay on pretext (at best a pretext to myself) of verifying those patently concocted letters, to a chap whose obvious interest to me was his possible connexion with my erstwhile lover. . .

Jolly enough of that! I shot back. That day's driving had been a *shlep,* not a slip, and made for good if futile cause. Those letters were *not* obviously false, though very possibly tampered with. Those Old Lady clothes were a welcome respite for this old lady, in whose neck moreover that A. B. Cook had been almost as considerable a pain as present company. And even if I *had* pursued him for his connexion with the grandest pain in the arse of all, my erstwhile lover, lifetime tormentor, and father of my lost child—even if I'd *bedded* the bloke in hopes of solving that nasty little riddle—well and bloody good, and he Ambrose ought to bloody aid and pity me instead of bloody banging a weary old lady on the head with his bloody mad jealousies and petty despotisms, et farking cetera!

In short, a little lovers' quarrel. It did not last long. I *was* weary; am; and Ambrose knows how to play me. Under my fatigue I *liked* it that he was jealous; knew he knew I liked it; even liked knowing he knew, etc. God and my sisters forgive me!

He made me doff the O.L. oufit instanter; tupped me a good one. As I lay propped after for the sake of his low-motiles, he announced more agreeably that whilst I'd been taking French leave that morning, he'd solved with his diagrams a tricky problem in the plan of his Perseus story, and authorised me to pass the info on to you if I was still writing these weekly one-way letters. I begged him fill that blank another time; I was too weary. And speaking of blanks, I mentioned my blank informant at Chautaugua. Ambrose was not interested.

I asked him whether he thought André Castine of Castines Hundred and Andrew Burlingame Cook of Chautaugua could possibly be the same man. He crisply replied, to my surprise, that he thought the question as academic, under the circumstances, as that of the authenticity of those 1812 letters: the skill and subtlety of those circumambient impostures over so many generations, the welter of obscure purposes and cross-purposes, made a kind of radical positivism the only possible approach to, or bridge over, the vertiginous quicksand of history, including my own past. Much moved, I sprang to hug him. He gruffly bade me look to my insemination; gave me liberty to explore the matter as I would whilst we were in Ontario and west New York, up to the point of physical infidelity: should there be even the slightest possibility of my impregnation's being attributable to another, we were *kaput;* if on the other hand I managed despite all to conceive, and indisputably by himself. . .then he hoped we might marry.

Ontario? West New York? Marry? Flabbergastment! Arrant presumption!

A. shrugged: did I think he'd permit me to go uninseminated for the week and more he'd be there? The very middle of my month? They would be shooting background footage at Forts Erie and Niagara, at the Falls, perhaps at the old Chautauqua Institution and at Lily Dale, a spiritualist centre in the area. Prinz's intentions were as usual unclear. There had even been mention of a rôle for *me,* following upon a remark I'd made about Mme de Staël's pleading on the one hand with Thomas Jefferson and Albert Gallatin to forestall the 1812 War on behalf of Britain's struggle against Napoleon, and on the other her subsequent intriguing with the emperor during the 100 Days. A. B. Cook might play his own ancestor Ebenezer Cooke, the virgin poet, and/or his other ancestor the antivirgin Henry Burlingame III. And there was to be an intensification of the rivalry between himself and Prinz for the favour of Bea Golden, whom they had more or less persuaded to play the rôle of herself playing the rôle of several younger women in your fiction. Prinz had warned him to be on his guard; he now passed the same warning on to me. We would return in time for the Marshyhope commencement exercises, which Prinz also wants to film for use in the campus sequences—whether the dreary little teachers college in *End of the Road* or the universal university of *Giles Goat-Boy,* Ambrose couldn't say: both, neither. I was not, absolutely, to take along my Old Lady clothes: he would pack my bag himself.

Would he, now!

We go tomorrow (I packed my own bag): by car back across the Bay Bridge to Washington National Airport, thence by plane to Buffalo and by rented car to Niagara Falls. It will be no honeymoon. I am properly intrigued by the reflection that as we fly along the axis of the War of 1812, from Chesapeake Bay to the Niagara Frontier, you may well be doing likewise, en route home from D.C.; that we might—improbably en route, but not so improbably during the business ahead—meet. Or do you take as little notice of the film-in-progress as of these letters?

I do not even mention my emotions at the prospect of revisiting the little town of Fort Erie, Ontario, where not so very long ago—though it seems a world away already!—this aging uterus having Done Its Thing yet again with the *high*-motile, unerring sperm of André, André, I underwent a different sort of D.C. . . .

André. Who, *mon Dieu,* may be there too, somewhere about! Then why do we not rendezvous, you three (or four) gentlemen and the lady whose tormenting is your common pleasure? At the "farm" of that nameless Doctor, say, for Prinz's cameras, let us do a scene, not from your writings, but from de Sade's: you, Ambrose, André, A. B. Cook—strip me of my ridiculous mini, bind me fast, and take turns with literal whip and brands instead of figurative!

Enough. My office work is done; I must back to 24 L lest my master's jealous ire be reprovoked. By now you are, I presume, an official doctor of letters, as Ambrose will be a fortnight hence. Look to your patient, sir; 'ware malpractice; if you will not presume to save her, leave her at least no worse than you found her: as played out, worked over, tricked up, but withal still fecund as (let us pray)

Your patient
G.

I: *Lady Amherst to the Author.* The Fourth Stage continues. Filmmaking at Niagara Falls and Old Fort Erie. Dismaying encounters at the Remobilization Farm.

Erie Motel
Old Fort Erie
Ontario, Canada

14 June 1969

Dear J.?

It's eerie, right enough: this foul and ghostly lake that must once have been so fair, but now regurgitates dead smelts and ripe green eutrophy; bleak, blasted Buffalo across the way, coughing up steel and cars and breakfast cereals in clouds of smog; flat frozen Canada, just now blanketed in flowers—how all countries except yours glory in flowers!—but ever mindful, in its dour domestic architecture and glacier-scraped terrain, of the cold that never leaves this dominion, but only withdraws a bit, and briefly, to its northern reaches.

Eerier yet your absence—as well say nonexistence!—and my presence here amid the caricatures of your characters. I have not read all your works, sir; I begin now to think I shan't, lest I find *myself* cast up for keeps upon this charmless shore with the other flotsam; doomed like the skeletal constellations to a reiterative *danse macabre,* a spooky rerun—ever less intelligible—of the story of my life. Somewhere over there you plug away at your trade, stringing letters into words, words into sentences, paragraphs, pages, chapters. Between us the international boundary surges past to flush itself over Niagara Falls, called by Canadians the toilet bowl of America.

Where are you? Where am I? What am I doing here in the Erie Motel, Ontario, Canada? I'll tell you what.

On Sunday last, the 8th (when in 1797 my luckier namesake bore her 4th child, Edwige-Gustavine-Albertine de Staël, her daughter by Benjamin Constant), *mio maestro* and I flew up to Buffalo. I proposed he call you from the airport. Ambrose wasn't interested; said you and he were not "*that* sort of friends." Out of curiosity I checked the directory: no listing. The university was of course closed—with relief, I'm sure, after this dreadful year of tear gas, "trashings," truncheons. We hired a car, drove up the parkway to Niagara Falls, N.Y. (I was mildly interested in reconnoitering your campus; Ambrose wasn't; we didn't), and registered in a nameless, featureless motel. The clerk smirked. In my costume—I cannot think of these skimpy outfits as *clothes*—I felt like an old Lolita; once the door was shut, the spread drawn down against crab lice, and the six o'clock news tuned in, my humbug Humbert duly humped me. No surprise: it had been three days.

Maryland had been muggy; at the Falls it was overcast and mild. We dined at a nameless, featureless restaurant and then strolled the tacky town, the melted museum, the ubiquitous and awful souvenir shops. . .

Enough of this. You know Honeymoon City better than I; even if you didn't, I've no business "writing" to a writer, especially one who doesn't write back. Job enough to report the news! Next morning (and all the mornings since), Ambrose worked on his Perseus story whilst I lay about with the *Times*, too embarrassed to go out alone in my costume. His unusual absorption in "Arthur Morton King's" composition reminds me again that my current lover, like my more eminent earlier ones, *is* after all a Writer, as I once aspired to be. Surely the length of these letters to you has been a relapse into that aspiration— from which your silence, Doctor, bids to cure me. Whether Reg Prinz's contemptuous casting of him into that rôle (with the uppercase *W*) has reenergised Ambrose's muse, or whether on the contrary Ambrose's rediscovery of his writerly powers has inspired Prinz to escalate his half-improvised, ad hoc hostility, I don't venture to guess. But I report that both proceed apace.

Over the next couple days the "Baratarians" assembled: the technicians, I mean, for (except for some unrehearsed "rehearsal" sequences at the Remobilisation Farm, to be duly reported) Prinz seems not ready yet to deploy his actors on these locations. On the Monday afternoon and all day Tuesday (bright, mild, pleasant) they shot footage of the Falls, as if the film were to be a remake of *Niagara* minus Joseph Cotten, Marilyn Monroe, and any connexion whatever with your work! Having shared blind Joyce's interest in the cinema, and that of most of the other European writers I've had to do with, I do *not* especially share my lover's mystification of that medium, his mythicised antithesis of Image and Word. I watched with crowds of others; sure enough, the American Falls was half shut off by a temporary dam above the rapids. . . But stop: you've no doubt been up to view it; may even have been among the throng of camera-clicking tourists who photographed with equal interest the Falls, the non-Falls, and the film crew photographing both and them.

On the Wednesday (at first bright, then turning muggy) the Baratarians and I "did" Queenston Heights across the river, where good General Brock won the battle but lost his life in 1812; Fort George, captured, lost, and burnt by the Americans in 1813; and handsome Fort Niagara, taken at night by bayonet from the Americans that same year, by Canadians who then swooped down with the Indians to burn Buffalo. If the "2nd War of Independence" is not yet in your fiction, you'd best see to putting it there, for it is most certainly in the film!

Ambrose played with his logarithmic spirals till noon and then joined me, as we'd planned, at the Rush-Bagot Memorial near the French Castle, on the Lake Ontario rampart of the fort. In the crowd I felt slightly less ridiculous; moreover, three days had passed (and, I learnt shortly, the episode he'd been drafting all morning was erotic): he was horny; I likewise, and *only* in that humour did his petty despotising arouse me. If I have given the impression in recent letters that our friend has been *merely* insufferable, I here correct it: insufferable indeed have been the matters I've complained of (and suffered him to lay upon me), but he has not even now lost his engaging, *affectionately* attentive side; had not in particular in the three days of our visit thus far, when his work was going well and neither Bea Golden nor Magda Giulianova Mensch nor starlets nor coeds were on the scene. We watched the "Baratarians" at work for a while, especially fascinated by Prinz's inarticulate communion with his technicians when cinematography alone, without actors and story, was the business at hand (he began, I now recall, as an avant-garde documentarist). But we were "turning on"; could not leave off touching each other; people were beginning to look at us. Prinz wanted us all to move before dinnertime from the mouth of the Niagara River to its head: specifically, back across to the Canadian shore and down (on the map, but upriver, most confusing) to Fort Erie, to the motel on whose stationery this is written, which he'd reserved for the next five nights. There was to be a "general story session"—filmed, of course—in the evening, after he'd inspected the locations at Old Fort Erie and the Remobilisation Farm, where most of the rest of the cast would rejoin us.

Touching, gripping, squeezing arms and hands, we hurried back to make love in our "old" motel before packing and checking out to move to the new. I wept a bit; was given permission (I hadn't sought it) to pick up a midlength skirt for morning wear if I wished to explore "the Cook/Castine business" whilst he was writing. Ambrose was tender; it *was* love we made. We have not since, may never again, though I have been inseminated daily in the three days since (it's ovulation time), despite my being shut off and dry as the American Falls.

Then we passed through customs and across the Rainbow Bridge to Canada again, around the Horseshoe Falls and down (up) along the flowered margin of the dominion to that less prepossessing other fort—captured, recaptured, rerecaptured, leveled by accidental explosions, rebuilt, releveled by Lake Erie storms, rebuilt, de- and re-lapidated, restored—near where I write this; across the river from where you write whatever you write as I write this.

Near the Erie Motel is a dull Chinese-Canadian restaurant. There we dined, joined towards the end of our Moo Shoo pork by Prinz, who managed to say as I opened my fortune cookie. . .

Oh God, enough of this *writing!* It is all insane, and for all I know you may be quite apprised of, may even be party to, the madness. We inspected Old Fort Erie, Prinz framing views with his fingers and murmuring things about the light. On 4 July 1814, 38th birthday of your republic, an American general with your initials recaptured the fort first captured in May of the year before. Six weeks later the place exploded as the Canadians attempted to retake it ("Takes and retakes," Prinz murmurs happily), either accidentally or because a U.S. lieutenant fired the magazine, blowing himself and two dozen others to kingdom come and repulsing the assault. "We" are to replicate that explosion on 15 August, its 155th anniversary. Indeed, it seems there is to be a series, a *montage* of bombardments, fires, explosions from the period: red rockets will glare and bombs burst in air this season, not only here but at Fort McHenry in Baltimore and at Washington, all which got theirs in the busy summer of 1814. The last big bang at Fort Erie—indeed, the last on the Niagara Frontier—came in November of that same year, when General Izard, withdrawing his American garrison back to Buffalo, blew up what was left standing after the August explosion.

As we dutifully reviewed this noisy history, Ambrose took my elbow and informed me that Prinz had just that day informed *him* that the "patients" at the Remobilisation Farm, apparently under the direction of Bea Golden (one of their number, you know, from time to time, when under the *nom de guerre* Bibi she dries out between failed marriages), were involved in some sort of ongoing recapitulation of your *End of the Road* novel, which either inspired or was inspired by the original farm for remobilising the immobile, down in Maryland. Thus there is a black doctor in chief known simply as the Doctor, and a half-patient, half-administrator who goes by the name of Jacob Horner and is even thought by some to be the original of your soulless anti-hero. A patient known as "St Joseph" plays or lives the rôle of poor Joseph Morgan; "Bibi" herself has assumed the part of Rennie Morgan (Sexual Therapy, no doubt), caught between her rationalist husband and antirationalist "lover". . . All very convenient for "our" film, of course, as I would soon see, in keeping with Ambrose's (and presumably Prinz's) notion of echoes and reenactments significant in themselves, without necessary reference to their originals. (Did you know that Reg Prinz has "kept his imagination pure" by *not even reading* your books, any of them, so that viewers of his film won't have had to either? How I wish, in my ever rarer moments of relative calm, that I were outside this madness enough to savour its paradoxical aesthetics!) What was more—and what Prinz had evidently told Ambrose only over the fortune cookies, as I braved the stares of proper Ontarians to make my way to the Ladies'—the Doctor having declined for one reason or another to

356

play himself in this psychodramatical masquerade, his rôle had been assumed by a patient known as "Monsieur Casteene."

I do not reenact, here in this letter, my reactions to this news there on the twilit, Buffalo-facing rampart of Fort Erie. I do not even call to my aid my trusty suspension points, that have got me out of many an epistolary paragraph heretofore. I merely report to you this initial detonation. Still holding my arm, Ambrose regarded me. We turned to a nearby whir: Prinz with his "hand-held," photographing my reaction, Ambrose's indignation.

Separate cars to the Farm. Did Prinz "set us up," Ambrose wonders, for that shot? Perhaps even fabricate the "Monsieur Casteene bit" for that purpose? He offers to return me to the motel; but of course I must investigate for myself. On the farther, downriver (up-map) side of the town of Fort Erie, past the old fortification and the Peace Bridge, I recognise the Victorian white frame, half nursing home, half hippie sanctuary, the freaks and geriatrics rocking in their separate fashions on the porch. No suspension points. I hold my friend's arm, as I hold now onto my syntax and, less certainly, my reason. The Baratarians have preceded us; we are "shot," *en passant*, coming up the walk, mounting to the porch—not so unremittingly as to make clear that we are the stars of the scene, but the angry set of Ambrose's mouth is not missed, nor are my too bared legs. Ambrose wonders What the Hell; makes to let Prinz know he's going too far. But here to greet us comes "Bibi," drawn and severe-looking (and more attractive, alas) without makeup, and wearing a simple shift, her "Rennie Morgan" getup. Lights. Here is lean "Jacob Horner," nondescript in clean white shirt, straight-leg chinos, and *saddle oxfords:* clearly caught in an early-Eisenhower time warp but for his lined face and graying hair. Cameras. Then come in fast succession three more explosions, not bursting in air but whumping deep like depth charges or, better, underground tests.

"Joe Morgan," played by. . .Joe Morgan! To be sure, "much changed," as our correspondent A.C. IV would say—the careful, conservatively dressed ex–college president now a benignly grizzled guru, beaded, bearded, bedenimed, barberless—but unquestionably Joe Morgan! He smiles at us in quiet unsurprise, greets us both by name from his rocker, and believes we "both know Monsieur Casteene, the Doctor."

Boom. Whir of camera. "I am the Doctor only when we rehearse," intones with the faintest accent (bit of a *zed* on ze definite article; emphasis evened out over ze sýl-lá-bl'és) no dash no suspension points some cordial amalgamation, much changed, of the Maryland Laureate and my André. Then, in flawless Canadian French: *"Le Médecin malgré moi, eh?* But just now we are not acting."

He takes our hands; makes the slightest bow. André's bald spot; A. B. Cook's salt-and-pepper hair. Moustache *rather* like André's, but no beard. André's dentures, possibly, but no eyeglasses. Contact lenses, I believe, can be tinted? Ambrose squeezes my arm. No action, no reaction; what a slow movie it's going to be! I begin to mumble something like Thanks for the nice letters and My but isn't Guy Fawkes Day early this year when Boom comes the third explosion, so deep and quiet I don't even hear it. A plain-faced sharp-jawed firm-voiced (trim-figured) middle-thirtied woman stands nearby: Horner's? Casteene's (she could be the sister of that blank-phizzed unreceptionist *chez* Cook at Chautaugua)? Morgan's perhaps, if her incongruous Indian head-band means anything (otherwise she looks about as Indian as the woman on the Land O Lakes butter box)? No: plainly her own woman, this "Pocahontas"—so "Casteene" introduces her, with the smiling flourish of a magician introducing his assistant—though from the particularly disagreeable smirk with which she appraises me, and from Ambrose's sudden lividity, his appalled, exasperated "Jesus Christ," I begin to infer that she once was

Bang bang bang. Observe that I do not whimper; I merely report the news from across the Peace Bridge. It is now three days later, Saturday morning, 14 June, today. My inseminator scratches away at his tale of Perseus and Andromeda's failed marriage, the problem of addressing the "Second Cycle" of one's life. My Toronto newspaper reports Nixon's claim to broad new "bugging privileges" against political radicals; also that the sinking of the U.S. destroyer *Evans* by collision with an Australian aircraft carrier was not the Australian skipper's fault, and that Thor Heyerdahl's *Ra* is still seaworthy despite an unexpected waterlogging to starboard. What are *you* up to over there this mild muggy morning, I wonder, and where are you up to it? It is "Jacob Horner," no doubt, from whom I have this almaniacal reflex: he has apprised me that the steamy St Barnabas evening aforereported—Kamehameha holiday in Hawaii, birthday of John Constable, Gerard Manley Hopkins, Richard Strauss, and Mrs Humphry Ward—when I re-met Messieurs Morgan and Casteene, and my would-be impregnator re-met his ex-wife Marsha Blank, was the 198th anniversary of the day when Goethe's young Werther first met his Charlotte at the hunting lodge in Wahlheim.

The debris from those three explosions is still falling; Damage Control has yet to complete the assessment of our condition, but all the evidence is that we are sinking fast. On Thursday 12th, John L. Lewis died and the Niagara Falls shutoff was completed; convinced though he is that Reg Prinz knew in advance "Pocahontas's" identity and "set him up" for that dismaying surprise (duly filmed, of course), Ambrose "kept his cool": one would never have guessed, from his energetic flirtations with "Bibi" as the Baratarians filmed the unfalling Falls (at whose base one well-rinsed human skeleton has been discovered), that he had spent the night pounding the mattress in his rage at "them"—Mr Prinz, Ms Blank—and at his incomprehension of their motives and connexions. No good my advising him, from my rich experience of Them, that there is no They, only a He: André/Andrew Burlingame/Cook/Castine, whose motive, while doubtless unknowable, certainly looked a lot like plain old sadism, wouldn't he say? It was too much, he exploded (the last detonation of that day): all those people in one place! Horner (A. knew him in graduate school days, hadn't seen him since)! Morgan (What in the *world* had flipped him out so?)! Castine (I really couldn't tell? A third half-brother, maybe?)! And *Marsha* (Jee-*sus)!* Put it in a novel, your editor would throw the script back over the transom! Where was Giles the Goat-Boy, whilst They were at it? Where were my long-lost son and Ambrose's old high school English teacher, if Prinz was going to play This Is Your Life?

All this in fury in the Erie Motel on the Wednesday and again on the Thursday night, Ambrose having in between played Cotten to Bea Golden's Monroe all over Goat Island (we looked: no Giles) and the sprinklered escarpment of the Falls (having turned the rapids off, the engineers must keep a spray of water on the Rochester shale, lest it dry and crumble even faster). Freud observes that the sound of falling water is aphrodisiac: rain on the roof of the gamekeeper's cottage; Dido and Aeneas in their cozy cave. Ambrose had earlier invoked Freud's observation to explain the attraction of Niagara Falls to honeymooners. I submit that the sound of the Falls *not* falling has an even more powerful effect upon our friend, though not upon the writer of these lines. Too, Ms Blank's disconcerting smirk at her ex-husband's new Old Lady, together with "Bibi's" Rennie Morgan look of exhausted strength, inspires him to ever more ardent pursuit of Bea (Prinz doesn't *seem* to mind; photographs it all), ever more humiliation of myself. Every day I'm screwed, both ways, and whilst I leak his stuff into my scanties, he chases after her.

The news, the news. Our "Jacob Horner" is a spook, a vacuum, an ontological black hole. In his presence (the word is perfectly inapposite) I feel my hold on myself, my sense of me, going the way of my sanity. "Are you actually the original of the Jacob Horner in the novel?" I ask him, and he answers, seriously: "In a sense." Marsha Blank, on the other hand, seems no blank at all, but a cold-souled, calculating—okay, empty-hearted—embodiment of small-minded WASP vindictiveness who—whoa there: that's Jealousy talking, and Desperation chiming in with modifiers. But what on *earth* did Ambrose once see in her? In their reenactment of *The End of the Road* she will take the rôle of your sexually exploited high school English teacher, Peggy Rankin (a rôle better suited to myself, I should think; no one would get away with exploiting Ms Blank a second time!). That Prinz himself seems fascinated by her is no surprise: she flirts with him in the full sly ignorance of an insurance company clerk-typist flirting with, say, Andy Warhol—no doubt in part to make Ambrose jealous—and Prinz indulges her, with as it were an *anthropological* curiosity. Between her and Ambrose the vibrations are murderous (Peggy Rancour, he has dubbed her): nothing in my own experience compares with it. And Bea Golden, stung (sorry; let's say *miffed*) by Prinz's sufferance of Blank's rude overtures, responds now, out of spite, to Ambrose's. God help me!

Upon this tawdry diagram of forces, "M. Casteene" and "Saint Joseph" smile benignly, though with different interests. What Casteene's are I shall not even speculate (I cannot call him André; he is not A. B. Cook; he is to both what Marsha Blank is to the doorlady of Chautaugua, an imperfect clone; yet he alludes knowledgeably to the letters of 1812 and hopes to discuss their publication with me "fully," together with "our larger strategy," tomorrow, when the Baratarians are on holiday! John, John!). He is the courtly master of ceremonies, the *Spielman;* the low-keyed but high-geared *tummler* of the Remobilisation Farm, and director of the *Wiedertraum* (his term, I gather) that is *The End of the Road Continued.*

On *that* little psychodrama, too, I shall not speculate, except to say that it seems to me potentially as explosive as the Old Fort Erie powder magazine. And that, as it is being reenacted on a sort of anniversary schedule, with your novel as the basis of their script, the next episode will not occur until 20 and 21 July, when Horner (having been instructed by the Doctor on 1 June to take up grammar teaching as an antidote to his paralytical tendency) is to be interviewed by "Dr Schott" (also played by Casteene) and "Joe Morgan," played by:

Joe Morgan. Oh, John: much changed! And yet, *plus ça change. . .* Whether he is "your" Joe Morgan is not for me to say—my sense is that it were dangerous, not to mention tactless, to press that question; nobody here does, either with "St Joe" or with any of the others—but he is most certainly "mine," under howsoever altered a complexion: the courteous, intense, scholarly, boyish intellectual historian (in both senses) who so aided my researches at the Maryland Historical Society and later hired me at Marshyhope. Then, his simplicity, lucidity, and energetic gentleness covered (as we thought) a complexity, a mystery, perhaps even a violence: a darkness obscured by light, for which your tale of adultery, abortion, and death provided at least a fictive explanation. Now things seem reversed: the gentleness is still there, but it seems fierce; the mystery, irrationality, even mysticism, are on the surface; he *has* "done" the heavy psychedelics; his mind *is* "bent," by his own admission (but not "blown")—yet his account of his motives, his "reappreciation of the secret life of objects," his "delinearisation of history," all seem (at least when he's speaking of them) as pellucid as William James's rational chapter on the mystical experience, or Morgan's own essay on Cheerful American Nihilism. His defeat last year by John Schott at Marshyhope must have been the penultimate straw; I gather something snapped at Amherst, and his friend "Casteene" arranged his coming to the Farm. I would not care to be in Jacob Horner's saddle oxfords.

Being in my sneakers and penny loafers is no picnic, either. So many words, so many pages (Werther's *longest* letter, that one of 16

June 1771 describing his introduction to Charlotte on the 11th, is a mere nine pages), and even so I've not mentioned "U.U.," the Underground University of Senior Citizens and draft evaders organised at the Farm by Morgan and Casteene, in which Jacob Horner will presumably teach when the time comes. Or the minstrel show (based dimly on your *Floating Opera!*) rehearsing under "Bibi's" direction for performance a week hence—by when, God willing, Ambrose and I will be out of this madhouse, with whatever scars; away from this eerie powder keg of cross-purposes and unsettled scores; back home (so it seems already; I would never have supposed!) to dear damp Marshyhope and our late commencement exercises.

But next Saturday's Doctor of Letters has just put down his pen for the day. I must therefore put down mine: close my letter, open my legs: then out to the Fort, the Farm, the Falls, and whatever further setups and put-downs the afternoon holds for your

Germaine

P.S.: Prinz and Ambrose be damned, I intend of course to seek you out whilst we're filming at Chautauqua and Lily Dale next week, if the post office will tell me where on that rural delivery route your cottage is. I promise not to be a nuisance—you're not the first writer I ever met!—but we really should talk, don't you think?

S: *Lady Amherst to the Author.* Her conversation with *"Monsieur Casteene."* A fiasco on Chautauqua Lake. A visit to Lily Dale, N.Y., Spiritualist Capital of America.

24 L St, Dorset Heights

Saturday, 21 June 1969

John,

So: back in Maryland, on the morning of the year's longest day, and thoroughly alarmed, confused, distressed. I shan't degrade myself further by enlarging for you upon my week, since clearly you do not wait for these reports with bated breath—perhaps not even with tempered curiosity. From Monday through Thursday last I was on and about your Chautauqua Lake, in weather as gray and chill as northern Europe's: not like our proper Maryland Junes! On the Sunday prior, at Fort Erie, I'd had my remarkable conversation with "Monsieur Casteene," in course of which he retailed to me such an astonishing and unexpected history of his connexions with yourself that on the Monday, when Ambrose and I were installed in Chautauqua's old Athenaeum, I got your number from the operator and straightway rang you up. No answer, then or later. On the Tuesday—whilst Ambrose scribbled at his

Perseus story and counterplotted against Reg Prinz within the ad libitum plot of their screenplay—I drove our hired car around the lake to your cottage, aided by directions from the rural postman. It was Chautaugua all over again, minus Mr Cook's blank receptionist: the modest cottage, the tidy grounds, the seawall and dock, boats tethered at their moorings—and no one at home.

I took the liberty of asking your neighbours; they said you "came and went." I waited an hour; strolled out on your dock in the crisp breeze from Canada (Monday and Tuesday were the only clear days all week, and both cool as March); the lake too seemed abandoned, but for a few muskellunge fishermen standing and drifting in their skiffs. As I left, much frustrated (there are things you don't *know* about "Casteene"!), I caught sight of your postbox in a row of others and took the further liberty of peeking in, simply to assure myself that mail was indeed being delivered to you there. And I found. . .mine of Saturday last, postmarked *Ft Erie, Ont., 14 June 1969!*

I could have wept for exasperation. I snatched it out, vowing to destroy it and write not another word to you. But an elderly lady watched me from her little jerry-built nearby; anyroad, what was writ was writ. And there was other mail waiting for you; no doubt you had business up in Buffalo, or were simply away from home for a few days. I rang you up again on the Wednesday, on the Thursday; hadn't the heart to check whether my 18-pager still repines there with its two ounces of cancelled 1st-class postage. Friday forenoon we flew home.

Now I read in this morning's Baltimore *Sun* that tornadoes struck your region last night, sparing the old Chautauqua Institution but causing a million dollars' damage elsewhere about the lake, parts of which have been declared disaster areas. Which shall I hope?

Oh well: I hope that you and your property (my letter included) were spared, and that there is excellent reason, other than indifference on your part, why mine of the 14th lay unopened in your box, and why its troubled, sometimes anguished, often urgent predecessors have gone unreplied to, even unacknowledged, since March. Thomas Mann liked to say that with utter disgrace comes a kind of peace: no need for further striving to keep up appearances! I feel intimations of that peace. And I understand, better than formerly, Ambrose's letters to the outgoing tide; anybody's epistles to the empty air.

Now it's Saturday again, a few hours from the commencement ceremonies which I suddenly have dark misdoubts of. Ambrose is at the hospital with his mother, whose dying suddenly accelerated in midweek . . .and I need once more to write to you, not only whether you reply or not, but whether or not you even read my words.

Here is what "Monsieur Casteene" told me six days ago, in the voice described in my last: almost too ready with his inside information to be believed, and so confiding that though I cannot refute a single of his details and must admit the total accuracy of everything he recollected (much more than I!) concerning our old connexion, I distrusted him absolutely. I take a deep breath; I plunge in:

The man declares himself to be indeed, though Much Changed, the André Castine who first got me with child thirty years ago in Paris and again two years since at Castines Hundred. He declares that the high-spirited, loving disagreement with his apparently ineffectual father (Henri Burlingame VI), which I so well remembered from 1940, was in fact their ongoing cover throughout the war period for close cooperation, not on behalf of the Japanese and the Nazis—I didn't ask him about those pre–Pearl Harbor messages to me from the Pacific— but on behalf of the U.S.S.R., whose alliance and subsequent rivalry with the U.S. they foresaw. More exactly, on the ultimate behalf of the Communist party in North America, and to the ultimate end of a Second Revolution in the U.S., which they saw more hope for if the war were less than an unconditional Allied victory.

I simply report the news.

Thus they were involved in attempts to sabotage the Manhattan Project, which they also opposed on general humanitarian grounds. Indeed, Deponent testifieth that his father was vaporised at Alamogordo, New Mexico, on the morning of 16 July 1945, in a last-ditch effort to thwart the detonation of the first atomic bomb: a martyrdom unknown to this day to any but "wife" and son, and now me, and now you. Thereafter, Casteene claims to have been involved in the supply of "atomic secrets" to the Soviet Union in the latter 1940's and, in the early 1950's, with the supply of compromising data to Senator McCarthy's witch-hunters (to the end of "purging the C.P. of leftover liberals from the thirties" in preparation for its "new and different rôle in the sixties," so declareth etc.). In 1953, a pivotal year, he comes to believe that his father's beloved project has been misconceived; that political revolutions as such are not to be expected or even especially wished for in the overdeveloped countries at this hour of the world; that Stalinism is as deplorable as Hitlerism; etc. The 2nd Revolution, he decides, in American anyroad, will be a social and cultural revolution in the decade to come (*i.e.*, the 1960's); the radical transformation of political and economic institutions will either follow it in the 1970's or become irrelevant. M. Casteene's personal target date for the whole business, I simply report, is 1976.

Still listening, John? *Well:* about that same time—I mean the middle 1950's, while dear old Mann is telling yours truly in dear old Switzerland about the liberating aspect of utter disgrace—Deponent moveth to Maryland and setteth up as an arch right-winger named Andrew Burlingame Cook VI, which name is in fact as officially his from his father as is the name André Castine from his mother. He modifies his appearance (He can do it almost before one's eyes, but never *quite* perfectly; then when he "returns" like Proteus to his "true" appearance, that's never quite what it was before, either!); he pretends

363

to be a blustering patriotic poetaster of independent means; he befriends Harrison Mack, claims distant cousinship to Jane Mack. He ingratiates himself with right-wing political figures in Annapolis, in Washington; he goes so far as to call himself the Laureate of the Old Line State—and is threatened with lawsuit, to no avail, by the actual holder of that post. He affiliates himself in various ways with Mr Hoover's F.B.I. and Mr Allen Dulles's C.I.A. That portion of the general public aware of his existence (and both his visibility and his audibility are as high as he can manage) take him for a more or less pompous, more or less buffoonish reactionary. A few—Todd Andrews, for example—believe that underneath the flag-waving high jinks is a serious if not sinister cryptofascist. And a *very* few—*e.g.,* Joe Morgan, as I believe I reported some six or seven Saturdays past—suspect that in fact his reactionary pose is a cover for more or less radical *left*-wing activities. But only his son, Henri C. Burlingame VII—and now myself, whom alas he has had to keep too long and painfully in the dark—know that "A. B. Cook" and "André Castine" are, under contrary aspects, the same Second-Revolutionist.

We are not done.

In his latter thirties, Monsieur Castine/Cook researches the history of his forebears—those Cooks and Burlingames alternating back through time to the original poet laureate of Maryland and beyond—and prepares to draft a mock epic called *Marylandiad,* after the manner of Ebenezer Cooke's *Sot-Weed Factor* poem. His motives are three: to reinforce his public cover; to gratify his genuine interest in that chain of spectacular filial rebellions; and to introduce "our" son properly to his paternal lineage. His researches are mainly on location at Castines Hundred, and inasmuch as he divides his time, with his identity, between there and the province of the Barons Baltimore, he avails himself also of the Maryland Historical Society—where, we remember, yours truly was first by A. B. Cook dismayed in 1961—and thus becomes acquainted with its then officials, one of whom he will subsequently recommend to Harrison Mack for the presidency of Tidewater Tech and later yet connive with John Schott to unseat from Marshyhope.

You are yawning? You shall yawn no longer. "Cook" comes to know Mr Morgan's background, the unfortunate events leading to Mrs Morgan's death and Joe's "resignation" from Wicomico Teachers College: information he will later make use of. Indeed, he discovers in 1959 that it has perhaps already been made use of, in a just-published and little-noticed novel by a young erstwhile Marylander now teaching in Pennsylvania. The plot thickens: Cook draws Morgan out on the parallels between his curriculum vitae and certain events and characters in *The End of the Road.* He learns that Morgan, a rationalist but nowise a quietest, is indignant to the point of seriously contemplating vaticide (if that term may be extended to cover fictionists as well as poets); what stays his hand is no scruple for his own well-being, for which he cares nothing since his wife's death, but the possibility that after all the author may be innocent.

Do I have your attention now?

Cook scoffs, but Morgan stands firm; he and you have never been introduced. Despite the undeniable and disquieting parallels, in most ways your fiction *doesn't* correspond to the actual events, not to mention the characters involved. Its author is not known to be either a dissembler or a brazen fellow: yet the one crossing of your paths had occurred right there in the Historical Society library, just a few months ago! Morgan, appalled, had recognised you at once; the recognition was apparently not mutual. You worked busily there half an afternoon. With the worst will in the world, Morgan could detect not the slightest indication that you knew who the grim-faced official was who passed by you, ostensibly on errands of business, several times. If he had (so detected), he declared calmly, he'd have done you to death on the spot with his bare hands.

Does Cook find such an unlikely coincidence hard to swallow? Then let him chew on this at-least-as-farfetched: a check of your table immediately upon your leaving it disclosed to Morgan that the subject of your researches was evidently the same as Cook's own! There lav sundry volumes of *The Archives of Maryland;* facsimile editions of *The Sot-Weed Factor* and *Sot-Weed Redivivus;* divers other primary and secondary texts in the history of 17th-Century Maryland. . .

Intrigued, our master intriguer volunteers to find out discreetly for Morgan, if he's interested to know, whether you are guilty or innocent in the matter of your sources for *The End of the Road,* as he means to approach you forthwith to compare his information on Ebenezer Cooke & Co., and his literary project, with yours. Morgan shrugs: nothing will restore his late wife to him, and you had nothing to do with her demise. As good as his word (*sic,* sir, *sic),* Cook drives up into Pennsylvania and invades your undergraduate classroom on pretext of soliciting poetry readings in the area and meeting "fellow Maryland writers"; he distributes self-promoting handouts to your students, who are half amused, half annoyed by the blustering disruption—and after class, evidently in a different humour, he discusses with you the backgrounds and sources of your then two published novels and your work in progress. Returning to Baltimore, he reports to Morgan your claim to have derived the story line of *The End of the Road* from a fragmentary manuscript found in a farmhouse turned ski lodge in northwestern Pennsylvania. Cook himself is unconvinced: the anecdote is as old as the medium of prose fiction; surely you are pulling his leg, or covering your tracks.

At this point in "Casteene's" narrative I recall Morgan's having remarked to Todd Andrews and myself that A. B. Cook had once offered to *arrange a murder* for him; that he had declined the offer but been enough convinced of its seriousness to believe Cook a genuinely formidable man with underground, perhaps underworld, connexions, the nature of which however was unclear. Had that offer been serious? I asked Casteene now.

He smiled handsomely, almost like André: Such a thing is easy to arrange, my dear, the easiest thing in the world. In fact he had been, let us say, *half* serious: he was seriously exploring Morgan's character, as a possible candidate both for the presidency of Tidewater Tech and, perhaps, for a certain rôle in the Second Revolution. But he had found the man not yet ready for that latter, and was in any case finally disinclined to your doing in, given your then current project. This project he regarded as of sufficient usefulness to persuade him to forgo his *Marylandiad* in its favour (he was anyhow too immersed in "action historiography" to bother seriously with composition) and bestow upon you his researches. Your Ebenezer Cooke, he declared, like the original sot-weed factor, needed a foil to his gullibility, a counter to his innocence, to heighten the comedy and deepen the theme: he made you a gift of his "cosmophilist" ancestor Henry Burlingame III, together with Captain John Smith's *Secret Historie* and the *Privie Journall* of the first Henry Burlingame. In return, unwittingly, you would provide him with a *point de départ* for some future counterdocument to assist in the delicate conversion of "our son" to "our cause."

I conclude. Deponent sweareth that he has had no contact with you since that day in 1959. That he enjoyed your rendering of his material, but on the whole prefers actions to words. He regrets having later had to support ridiculous John Schott against Morgan in the Marshyhope power struggle (it had to do, as what has not, with the preservation of his precious *cover*), and is gratified at least to have been able to arrange (in his "Monsieur Casteene" aspect, under which he does whatever it is he does at the Farm) Morgan's invitation to Amherst and subsequent enrollment in the cause of the Second Revolution. Even more, it Went Without Saying, he regretted—

But no: I will not entertain you with the song and dance of this man's regrets concerning *my* ordeal since 1940. He professed to be delighted at my new connexion, in whose favour he had been happy to have "A. B. Cook" decline the M.S.U. Litt.D. Further, he made bold to venture that Ambrose's energetic flirtation with "Bibi," at the Falls and the Farm, was owing to his unexpected *rencontre* with his ex-wife. Casteene counselled patience, even indulgence on my part; he would not, for example, in my place, attempt to compete for Ambrose's favour by dressing beneath my age and dignity. . .

Speaking of lovers: he trusted I would not mistake his own little arrangement with "Pocahontas" (he tisked his tongue at the *outrageous* smallness of the world) as anything but a physical-clerical convenience: what passed for his heart, I might be assured, was mine *toujours,* but he would never again presume any claim upon me after that painful reenactment, in 1967, of our original star-crossed intimacy. We were no longer young, *n'est-ce pas?* By the projected date of his life-work's completion he would be nearly 60. And aside from the annotation and publication of those letters of Andrew Cook IV's—his discovery of which, in Buffalo two years past, he regarded as both the unlikeliest and the happiest coincidence in a life fraught with improbability—he would ask nothing further from me ever.

Here he brightened. "But we haven't said a word about *notre fils! Le Burlingame des Burlingames!*"

I stopped him. Indeed, at this point I put an end not only to our interview, but to our remaining connexion. Had the man been unequivocally André (but when was André ever so?) or unequivocally A. B. Cook, or unequivocally neither. . . But he was equivocal as those letters—which now, upon a sudden, strong, heart-heavy, but unequivocal impulse, I returned to him. Whoever he was, I told him, he was not who he'd been, nor whom I'd loved even as late as two years ago. And whoever, wherever our son was, he was as dead to me as my André, surely in part by my own hand. I did not share what seemed all about me to be an epidemic rage for reenactment. The second half of my life, or third third, I must hope would be different indeed from what had so far preceded it! I had no more to say to him; at this point I would have nothing to say to our son either, a 29-year-old stranger, should he be "restored" to me: such reconnexion must be principally an embarrassment to all parties. As he had observed, I was in love again, no more happily than before, but at least my troubles were of a different sort. Whatever the future held for me, it did *not* promise to be a recapitulation of the past, and I was prepared to settle for that.

He bowed, kissed my hand. Thus we parted, I trust forever—though I quite expect some version of A. B. Cook to appear at this afternoon's festivities, disclaiming any connexion with M. Casteene or involvement in the foregoing conversation. The gentleman was not pleased. In particular he bade me reconsider the matter of the letters: if neither our past intercourse nor our son retained importance for me, would I not at least abet in this small way a cause larger than either, the cause of the Second Revolution? In which Henri, if things were managed skillfully, might well play a major rôle?

Bugger your Revolution, I'm afraid I said, and got out of there—that dreadful, spooky Farm, where the chief crop raised is ghosts of the past—and back to the Erie Motel.

And, I wish I could say, back to my understanding and sympathetic Ambrose. But though my lover affirms with each insemination his resolve to marry me once I'm preggers and The Movie Thing is done, this past week has been the hardest of our history. On the Monday and the Tuesday, making the most of the rare sunshine, Prinz shot footage of the Chautauqua Institution, the lake itself, and the vineyard country round about, though Ambrose acknowledges that nowhere do these appear in your writings. *Bats* figured as prominently as actors, flitting around the Miller Bell Tower, the cupola of the old Athenaeum, and (I ventured to suggest) the belfries of Reg Prinz and Ambrose Mensch. The former had been enchanted by the latter's passing mention of the obscure, winged ascent of the villain "Harold Bray" at the end of your *Goat-Boy* novel; and though I can attest that as of where I am therein (halfway through) it is nowhere suggested that that charlatan is Batman, so he seems to be becoming in the film. *Prinz himself* rappelled down the tower by Monday's twilight in cape and domino to carry off Bea Golden (aptly cast as your nymphomanic heroine Anastasia) and make threatening squeaks at Ambrose in the rôle of, near as I can guess, Himself playing the Author dressed as Giles the Goat-Boy: *sheep*-skin vest and a horned helmet borrowed from the Chautauqua Opera Company's prop room, Wagnerian section.

Perfectly preposterous, of course, and as aggressively unfaithful to the novel as Ambrose endeavours to be to me. I cannot make myself recount his pursuit of "Anastasia," which, with Prinz's obvious consent, no doubt even at his instruction, Bea permits, nay encourages, but does not (I believe, who am ready to believe the worst) yet reward. It is All Part of the Movie: but inasmuch as there is no discernible boundary between that wretched film and our lives, Ambrose's conquest of her, when and if it occurs and whether on or off camera, will be Part of the Movie too, as is my ongoing humiliation. I hate it!

On the Tuesday evening a cast party was organised which culmi-nated in a triumphant fiasco, enlarged the cast by at least one lunatic more, and altered the direction of the movie's "plot." Prinz chartered the Chautauqua excursion yacht *Gadfly III;* caterers provisioned it with bar and buffet; the Baratarians—augmented by musician friends from the resident theatre troupe, all there for preseason rehearsals—piled merrily aboard, and we set out from the institute dock in the last light (swallows, bats, cameras!) for a nautical carouse. Imagine Our Surprise when we discover our skipper for the evening to be Someone We've Met Before: no, not André-Castine-Andrew-Burlingame-Cook, at least not apparently, but a chap whom Ambrose tells me I should remember from Harrison Mack's funeral (my mind was on other things), which Mr Bray attended as a beneficiary of the Tidewater Foundation's mis-guided philanthropy.

One *Jerome Bonaparte* Bray of Lily Dale, N.Y., surely the original of your goat-boy's nemesis. But your "Harold Bray" is only abstractly sinister, a sort of negative principle. The original, while of a lesser order of magnitude, is ever so much more alarming because he's real, he's mad as a hatter, and he is—or was—*in charge of the bloody ship!*

We *suspected* something was amiss when an old Volkswagen beetle drove erratically up to the dock a quarter-hour late (the college lad who was the crew had allowed, with a roll of the eyes, as how his skipper "went" more by the sun and stars than by the clock) and, like a little circus car disgorging a large clown, gave vent to a great lanky chap wearing sunglasses, sea boots, a Lionel Barrymore sou'wester out of *Captains Courageous*, and, of all the landlubberly incongruities, a cloak and kid gloves. We thought him part of the entertainment; the Baratarians cheered, whistled, and straightway dubbed him Batman. So far from replying in like humour, the man seemed particularly offended by the name; he drew his cloak 'round him as he hustled through us to the wheelhouse, then turned at its door to declare in an odd mechanical tone that his name was *Captain Bray,* and that while as an employee of the ship's owners he could forbid neither our lawful presence aboard the vessel nor the evening's debauchery we were clearly bent upon, as the ship's master he insisted we not address him by that obscene sobriquet, attempt to enter the wheelhouse, or otherwise interfere with his management of the vessel.

We were abashed. The Baratarians assumed he was joking and applauded his speech; he slammed the wheelhouse door and started off almost before the boy could let go our lines. Bea Golden, looking slinky despite her new rôle, wondered around her drink whether he was For Real. Ambrose clapped his brow, took the opportunity to take her arm, and made the connexion: between the chap at her father's funeral who'd claimed to be doing something revolutionary with computers; the celebrated assemblage of spiritualists at Lily Dale, home of the Fox sisters, near Chautauqua; and that ambiguous humbug villain whom George Giles, Grand Tutor and Goat-Boy, supposes in your novel to be as necessary to himself as Antithesis to Thesis. Prinz hummed, narrowed his view-finding glasses, dispatched an assistant for camera and sound gear.

And so we steam down past the state fish hatchery towards the narrows where *Chautauqua*—French *voyageur* spelling of an Indian word supposed to mean "bag tied in the middle"—is tied in the middle by the old car-ferry. Regardless of us merrymakers, our captain is delivering the routine tourist spiel on the ship's P.A., with what sound like embellishments of his own, in a voice that seems itself pieced together by computer in the days when such artifices were still recognisable. The boat, we are informed, is named after his Iroquois father. *All* of this was Iroquois country, he declares, and by rights ought still to be, unpolluted by the white man's DDT and marijuana and purple martins and bats (!). . . The Baratarians whistle and turn up the rock music. Bray escalates his own amplifier to full volume: Our elevation is 2,000 feet above sea level, 700 feet higher than Lake Erie. A raindrop falling into Lake Erie, 8 miles to northwest of us, will make its way over Niagara Falls, through Lake Ontario, and up the St Lawrence Seaway to the North Atlantic; one falling into Chautauqua Lake will exit via Chadakoin Creek (a variant English spelling of the same noble Indian word) into the Conewango, the Allegheny, the Ohio, and the Mississippi, then into the Gulf of Mexico and the Atlantic, itself a great Bag Tied in the Middle by its "narrows" at the latitude of the equator, where South America once fit into Africa. . .

Hoots and bravos; louder music. It was to be observed that these two raindrops between them traced the boundary of New France, or Upper and Lower Canada, the latter following the route marked in 1749 by Céloron de Blainville, or Bienville, "discoverer" of Chautauqua

Lake, with lead plates bearing the coat of arms of the house of Bourbon, that dynasty deposed by the Revolution to make way for the Emperor Bonaparte. . .

Curses, muttered Ambrose: foiled again. He had it seems posted overboard one of those bottled epistles he indites from time to time to "Yours Truly" (which in a happier season were declarations of his love for yours truly; God knows what they declare these days, and to whom) on the ebbing tide. This one, he'd believed and hoped, could nowise return to him; now he quite expected it to round Florida and run north on the Gulf Stream, work its way past the Virginia Capes and up the Chesapeake, and Return to Sender on the river shore by Mensch's Castle.

The liquor flowed; the duel of decibels or battle of the amplifiers continued as we circuited the dusky lower lake and headed back by starlight for the upper. Prinz and Ambrose, therefore Bea, put by their partying (if not the latter two their drinking) to improvise an episode out of the situation. Ambrose briefed Prinz on the characters and plot of your *Goat-Boy* novel, consulting my more recent if incomplete memory thereof; the object became to lure our Bray into playing yours. For reasons unclear to me, Bea was pressed into service to pantomime a moth or butterfly in distress: to the strains of the pas de deux from *Swan Lake,* a tape of which fortuitously appeared and was substituted for the rock music, she fluttered fetchingly about the foredeck, in full view of the wheelhouse. Prinz went into his Batman/Count Dracula act to menace her, with much baring of teeth and flapping of arms; Ambrose into his Giles-cum-Siegfried antics, loping about in postures of attempted rescue or countermenace.

Well, the woman is not without talent; ditto Prinz. My lover's abilities lie elsewhere than in ballet-pantomime. The Baratarians fell to, some pressing the ship's lights into service, others manning the camera and microphones, still others miming outraged or horrified bystanders. At length the poor hapless Whatever-She-Was was caught: to no avail her pathetic wing-beats; her averted face only exposed the more her slender throat to Prinz's fangs, which now with great rollings of his eyes to the wheelhouse he made ready to have at her with, maugre the bleats and caperings of her would-be saviour (who stands *en garde* with fountain-pen for foil). The music soars. We repass the car ferry, reenter the S-shaped narrows.

Now, I myself had a drop or two in, depressed and anxious over Ambrose's late behaviour, the whole unswallowable "Casteene" business, my frustrating attempts to communicate with you. But if what I and the others saw next was the effect of some common delirium tremens, the camera shared and recorded it. From the wheelhouse suddenly sprang—*sailed, flew,* whatever!—Captain Bray: an astonishing feat, as if his Phantom-of-the-Opera cloak were the wing membranes of a flying squirrel. With a frightful buzz that carried through Tchaikovsky like the artillery at the end of his *1812 Overture,* the man traversed as if in one bound the half-dozen metres from wheel to foredeck. Prinz was knocked heels over head, his eyeglasses were sent flying; Ambrose stood open-mouthed in mid-caper; the Baratarians' consternation was no longer feigned. For by some second marvellous gymnastic our mad captain *rebounded* from the deck to the forward railing *with Bea Golden under one arm,* drew his cloak about her, and stood holding onto the bow flagstaff and threatening us with further sound effects from his repertoire. *Incroyable!*

All this in three seconds, John, by when Poor Butterfly got her breath and, far from doing a Fay Wray faint, screamed bloody murder and laid into her fetcher-off with proper hysteria. Confused, he set her down; backed off a step (I mean *up,* onto the rail again) when valiant Ambrose hurried to her rescue—*i.e.,* snatched her arm and yanked her away from there.

Who is piloting *Gadfly III* this tumultuous while? Why, no one at all: Joe College stands agape with the rest of us, and having traversed, during the above, the nether bend of the S, with no one to swing her to port our craft ploughs now smack into Long Point, where the state park is. I mean literally *into* the point, which must have considerable water right up to shore. There is a mighty bump; now we *all* go pitching forward, with shouts and shrieks and tinkle of gin-and-tonic glasses. We are a miniature *Titanic*—but in lieu of iceberg chips there are maple leaves fluttering to the deck, from the trees into which our bow has driven as into an arbor; and instead of sinking we are as hard aground as if dry-docked, or beached like that ferryboat restaurant in which, a century ago, my Ambrose initiated this miserable "4th Stage" of our affair.

Bar and buffet are all over the decks. In creepy silence we pick ourselves up out of Swedish meatballs and spilt soda water: the fall has cut Tchaikovsky off in mid-climax; the ship's engines gurgle to a stop when the crewboy finally betakes himself to the throttles. There are exclamations among the passengers regaining their feet, some cries from far down shore (the state park is closed at night: the only such depopulated stretch around the lake, I think), the whine of a couple of outboard-motor boats—determined fishermen—heading our way. Otherwise silence, echoed as it were by the absolute motionlessness of the ship and made spookier by the illuminated leafy canopy over our bow.

Remarkably, no one seems injured. Reg Prinz finds his eyeglasses and calls for his cameraman. Ambrose is comforting Bea excessively where they have fallen together against a spilt stack of folding chairs. I myself had clutched the railing in amazement at Bray's behaviour and at sight of the fast-approaching shore, which evidently no one else remarked, and so I only laddered my panty hose against a stanchion at the crash, but did not fall. Therefore I was also perhaps the only one who saw Bray *spring into the bower of branches* a moment after, and hang there easily awhile by one hand like a—well, what: gibbon? fruit bat? Tarzan of the Apes?—surveying the chaos with great frightened eyes which he shaded with the other hand. By the time folks are on their feet he has dropped noiselessly to the deck and stands blinking as if about to weep or swoon. Prinz approaches him cautiously, cameraman at his elbow. Men with electric torches are running toward us along the shore now, calling ahead. . .

But I shan't *write*, not to you; only summarise. The *Gadfly* was fast; when reversing her engines failed to pull her off, it was decided to leave her there till morning, when the situation and damage to the hull could be better assessed. (She was "kedged off" next day without difficulty, as fortunately undamaged, except cosmetically, as ourselves.) Meanwhile, state police cars, park police cars, sheriffs' cars, ambulances, volunteer firemen, and hosts of Chautauquans assembled to witness and assist: we were handed down ladders from bow to beach—rather, from bow to woodland path—questioned, examined for injuries, and led through the flashing lights and milling curious to a bus sent over from the institution *(The Spirit of Chautauqua)* to fetch us, finally, home, after Prinz and Ambrose had got all the footage—I should say mileage—they wanted from the scene.

All this, I daresay, you will have read in your *Daily Chautauquan* or the Buffalo press, together with the news that while no charges were placed against "Captain" Bray—who plausibly maintained that he had sprung to save Ms Golden from what he took to be assault by a drunken passenger—he was peremptorily sent packing. We were apologised to, offered another excursion *gratis* at our pleasure (no takers), instructed to send our dry-cleaning bills to the little company for reimbursement. It was explained that the vessel's safety record was thitherto un-blemished; that Bray was not a regular employee but a part-time standby pilot called on only for unscheduled occasions when the regular skipper was unavailable, et cetera.

What was not likely in the news reports is that Prinz, and Ambrose too, were delighted with their episode and fascinated by their Mr Bray—who, when he learned that we were Only Acting, wept with humiliation at his disgrace *(I* think he had cause to be indignant at us, madman or no). Indeed he went upon his knees to ask our pardon, in particular Ms Golden's, for whose sake he disquietingly declared himself ready to kill or die. And when these effusions were accepted by A. & P. (if not by Bea, who uncharitably bade him Fuck Off Already and called for a drink), he declared himself egregiously misled about our characters and intentions by "agents of the anti-Bonapartist conspiracy" and begged us to permit him to make amends. Specifically, in the name of our mutual benefactor His Majesty the late Harrison Mack, he hoped we would call upon him next day in nearby Lily Dale, where he invited us to photograph a ruin infinitely more consequential than that of a paltry excursion boat: he meant the failure of "LILYVAC II," his "computer facility," and with it the wreck of his "Novel Revolution" (or revolutionary novel, I never got it straight which), sabotaged by those same conspirators who had undermined the

372

Tidewater Foundation and the world's best hope for—here he looked worshipfully at Bea—a new Golden Age.

Certifiable lunacy! Which of course enraptured Ambrose, especially the "computer-novelist" business. Back at the Athenaeum at last, well past midnight, I tumbled straightway into bed and sleep. Before my lover joined me (and woke me for my nightly seeding) he and Prinz had made plans for an overland excursion on the morrow to Lily Dale, to Wrap Up That Part of the Story on location before returning to Maryland.

Thither we trekked next day, through heavy clouds and chilling rain, up into the hills to that smaller version of Chautauqua Lake and seedier replica of the institution: just the four of us, plus the cameraman and one all-purpose assistant. Bea Golden had at first refused, having suffered Transylvanian nightmares till dawn; she was at last, alas, persuaded by her shipboard hero, whose actions of the previous evening had clearly scored him a few points. Ambrose even invited Prinz to record their conversation in the car; he offered to reenact with Bea, at our destination, "the Author's growing ascendancy over the Director in their symbolic rivalry for the Leading Lady." Prinz declined with a tiny smile and shake of the head.

We wound through tacky lanes of spiritualists' cottages, each with its shingle advertising "readings," to a little farm overlooking Cassadaga Lake, just below a Catholic retreat house on the hilltop. Goats grazed in the meadow: footage. Bea thought the kids just darling, how they cavorted and banged heads. Ambrose cavorted with them to amuse her, till the nannies moved him off. Footage.

Ex-Captain Bray came out to greet us, at once obsequious and somehow menacing. I don't like him! Now that the conspiracy had turned Drew Mack and the Tidewater Foundation against him (for which, he muttered ominously, They Shall Pay), and his services were no longer desired by the *Gadfly* company, his sole support must be the modest income generated by those dairy goats: their milk he sold to a commercial fudge maker in Fredonia, their hides to artisans on the nearby Seneca Indian reservation, who turned them into "Spanish" wineskins for sale at Allegheny ski resorts. Upon such shifts did the Revolution wait! And it must break our hearts to see to what pass LILYVAC II had come, sabotaged by Her whom he had judged of all humans the least corruptible. Et cetera. We exchanged surreptitious glances. He took us to the computer facility, at one end of the milking shed. Footage. Absolutely crackers.

Ambrose presumed, innocently, that our host was acquainted with the fictional George Giles, Goat-Boy and Grand Tutor, if not with the author of his adventures on "West Campus." Dear me, sir, you are not held in universal admiration! First M. Casteene's casual report of his offer to arrange your assassination for Joe Morgan, and now such a diatribe as should have warmed my heart if I truly bore you a grudge for not acknowledging these confessions written at your own solicitation. But surprising, yea alarming, as was the vehemence of Bray's fulmination (you may thank us for not telling him you live within daily sight of the *Gadfly;* he believes you a Buffalonian *tout court),* it was upstaged by yet one more Uncanny Coincidence that came to light in course of it. To summarise—for why should I *write?*—it very much appears that Bray's trusted "assistant" (she seems to've been his sort-of-lover too, repugnant as that notion is) in his woozy radical-political-literary-mathematical-ecological enterprises, who he came to feel was seduced by "anti-Bonapartist" elements into sabotaging his computer, and whom I gather he then assaulted in some fashion, was a certain hippie-yippie young woman from California by way of Brandeis U. named Merope Bernstein. Not only does our Bea Golden, with a Thrill of Horror, now understand her to be the same girl fetched hysterical to the Remobilisation Farm in May by her far-out friends (who thought she was "freaking out" on an overdose of something ingested back at their Chautauqua pad), but. . . ready? *Brandeis,* he said? Bernstein, Merope? From California originally? Omigod, cries Bea (and staggers for support, not to her Reg Prinz, but to my Ambrose): It's *Merry!* I didn't even recognise her! What did he *do* to her? Why didn't she *tell* me who she was? I haven't seen her in six years, since she was fifteen!

At length we got it sorted out: In an earlier incarnation, Bea Golden was Jeannine Bernstein, wife of a minor Hollywood character actor, himself much married and divorced. Bray's allegedly perfidious assistant (but now he was calling her Morgan le Fay—altogether bonkers!) was this chap's daughter by a prior mating. Hence. . .

Jee-*sus!* Ambrose exclaims.

Your wicked stepdaughter ha ha! Mr Bray cries feverishly to the recoiling Bea, with whom he is clearly smitten and whom he fears he has alienated. Footage. He didn't *hurt* Ms Bernstein, he swears now; he only sort of spanked her for ruining his life's work; put a bit of a scare into her, don't you know. After all, she did save his life once; no doubt she was led astray in good faith; oh, they shall pay! He shall not rest till he has made it up to her—to Bea, for whom now he openly declares his adoration—for having chastised her ex-stepdaughter, however deservedly. They must go together, at once, to the Farm: he is a friend of Mr Horner there; he will declare to Ms Bernstein in her former stepmother's presence that though with the best of intentions she has blighted his life and at least postponed the New Golden Age, and though he durst never trust her again with the LILYVAC programme, he harbours her no ill will and in the blessed name of her (ex-)stepmother forgives her his irreparable betrayal.

I summarise. With the greatest difficulty we got out of there—never did see the famous "printout" Bray claims to have been spoilt by Ms B.—back to Chautauqua; thence, Ambrose and I on the Friday, back Home. I do not envy Bea Golden her new admirer! Bray declares he will Put Things Right for her sake; that he will follow her to Fort Erie, to Maryland, anywhere she goes, let the goats fend for themselves;

that with her aid and inspiration he may yet solve the Riddle of LILYVAC II and get the 5-Year Plan back on schedule before the "Phi-Point" of his life. . .

Ambrose finds him both frightening and fascinating: the Phi-Point, did he say? Point six one eight etc.? Bea finds him merely frightening, and threatens legal action if he attempts to follow her across either Peace Bridge or Bay Bridge. She was never *close* to Mel Bernstein's daughter, she tells us now, whose mother of course had the custody; she thinks it possible Merry doesn't even recognise her with her new name, any more than she Bea recognised *her;* but she cannot account for the coincidence. Ambrose cannot either, and worries for the ladies' safety.

Castine, Castine, I assure him: there is the very god of Coincidence. Bea has but to place herself under his ubiquitous protection, as "Pocahontas" has evidently placed herself under "M. Casteene's."

He will thank me, says Ambrose, not to speak of his own prior incarnation. Jee-*sus*, what a week! And though it included that dismaying reencounter with Marsha (Did I see what he'd meant? Those thin-plucked eyebrows; the cold eyes under them; the mean turn of her jaw; the featureless *regularity* of those features he'd once thought attractive, then come to find empty of character, and now saw as the very stage mask of Vindictiveness. . . I said nothing), not to mention the grave tidings from Magda *re* his mother—despite all, it had been a long while since he'd felt so *potent.* . .

Oh really.

Yes, well, he meant that way too, and we'd see, we'd see. But what he *really* meant was Musewise: the Perseus story was clipping along in first draft; he was delighted with the conceit, equally with the execution; it made him feel Writer enough to more than hold his own with Reg Prinz, whose movie he thought he now quite understood and rather relished. He took my arm (we were on the United flight down from Buffalo to Baltimore): no doubt it had been a rough week for me, on more than one front. Aye, said I. He daresaid there would be rougher weeks ahead. O joy, said I. What he meant was that his new "ascendancy," whether real or set up by Prinz, would doubtless provoke an escalated retaliation. He told me frankly then what was pretty obvious anyroad: that while he regarded our connexion as Central, and central to it his desire not only to impregnate but to wed me straightway thereupon, he was determined by the way to make conquest of Bea Golden if he could. It was a kind of craziness, no doubt (Yup, says I), a playing of Prinz's game. Just for that reason he meant to do it; beat the man at his own game; out-Prinz him.

Hum, says I. You could help, you know, says he. Forget it, says I: I'm sorry your mum's dying; I'm happy you've done with that Marsha Blank, and happier yet your muse is singing along. If that gives you a leg up on Prinz and his nutty movie, well and good. But I shan't pat you on the head for making a fool of me, with Bea Golden or generally; and to suggest I pander to your billygoatery is bloody sick if you ask me.

He liked that: put a great load in me directly we got back to 24 L, another this morning early before he took off for the hospital. But last night it was Bea, Bea, Bea. The *Original Floating Theatre II* is in Cambridge for the weekend; B.G. was to have flown down yesterday to open in their revival of *The Parachute Girl*, but stayed behind to do her "Minstrel Show" at the Remobilisation Farm. She'll arrive today, worse luck, if Mr Bray hasn't flown away with her; the rest of the Baratarians too, to recommence the movie after Marshyhope's commencement. Big things are planned for the 4th of July, but Ambrose hopes to Make His Next Move even before then.

Andrea King Mensch is indeed terminal. Ambrose is taking it hard. La Giulianova is Right There, of course and thank God, ministering to her and being very real and strong and Mediterranean about last things. I must hope—and a slender hope it is—that the Litt.D. business this afternoon will put my friend in mind of our old connexion, in better days, on the Ad Hoc Committee for Honorary Doctoral Nominations.

Time now to robe for the ritual consummation of that committee's work, which I approach with considerable misgivings—indeed, in a flat-out funk that I've tried in vain to smother under these many pages. I haven't even mentioned that John Schott and Shirley Stickles, when I stopped at my office yesterday, were thick as thieves in hers, and saluted me stiffly indeed, very stiffly.

Hm!

Must run. Jee-*sus!*

G.

T: *Lady Amherst to the Author.* The Marshyhope commencement debacle, and its consequences.

Office of the Provost
Faculty of Letters
Marshyhope State University
Redmans Neck, Maryland 21612

Saturday, 28 June 1969

John:

Total disgrace!

I'm in this office for the last time, Where it All Began with that wretch of an Ambrose, that *beast* of an Ambrose. Cleaning out the desk he once laid me on. Packing up my personals.

I have been *fired,* John. Sacked! Cashiered! Not only as acting provost, but from the Faculty of Letters altogether! I am unemployed; when my visa expires I shall have to leave or be deported! John Schott has appointed Harry Carter as provost. Marshyhope's Distinguished Visiting Lecturer in English next September will be *A. B. Cook VI*— whose punitive doing, for all I know, this may well be.

Fired!

The commencement ceremonies? A debacle. Drew Mack's "pink-necks" rioted after all: the last American campus demonstration of the season. They caught "us" completely off "our" guard, lulled by their earlier shows of reasonable apathy. A well-planned caper, assisted surprisingly by *Merope Bernstein* and her crew, who came all the way down from Fort Erie to spray stolen Vietnam defoliants on the elms and ivy of Redmans Neck.

Ambrose was in on it. Seems to have been, anyroad; we don't talk much. His (unscheduled, unexpected, out-of-order) "acceptance state-ment" upon receipt of his honorary doctorate appears to have been the demonstrators' cue. Whilst Prinz's cameras rolled, and—as provost of his faculty—I cited his "provocative contributions to the life and health of the classical avant-garde tradition in 20th-Century letters," Ambrose appropriated the microphone and launched into a distracted discourse on the mythical-etymological connexions of the alphabet with the calendar and of writing with *trees:* how "the original twelve consonants" each represented a lunar month, the five vowels the equinoxes and solstices *(A* and *I* representing the winter solstice in its aspects of birth and death respectively); how therefore the Moon is the mother of Letters (the man's mother's dying is his only excuse); how *spelling* is related to magic, as in *spellbound,* and *author* to *augur,* and *pencil* to *penis;* how *book* > M.E. *boke* > O.E. *bok* meaning "beech tree," and *codex* > L. *caudex* meaning "tree-trunk," and a *leaf* is a leaf in both cases. . .

"Right on!" cried Merry B. and her Remobilisers, and let go with their herbicides, the others with their raised fists and *Ho Ho Ho Chi Minh's,* before the state police could nab them.

On what grounds does G. get sacked for A.'s misconduct? (Am-brose was arrested too, but no charges placed; his part-time connexion with MSU is of course terminated; the board of regents wili doubtless revoke his degree at their next meeting.) Schott needed no grounds: I was nontenured; my contract was renewable year by year. Even so, there are protocols of due notice; the American Association of Univer-sity Professors has its rules and guidelines, I don't have to tell you. Was I inclined to invoke them, Schott wanted to know on the Sunday, when he got 'round to ringing me up? I jolly was! Why then, says he, our grounds will be either Moral Turpitude or Academic Incompetence Stemming from Mental Instability, depending. Depending on bloody what? Why, depending just for one example on whether my behaviour as confessed in my letter to you of 7 June, *of which they had the carbon,* was real or fantasized: *e.g.,* my Living in Sin with Ambrose (Schott actually used that term), my use of illegal drugs, my generally immoral and profligate course of life. If I did not repudiate my letter, Moral Turpitude; if I did, Mental Instability, which my sudden change of manner and costume frankly inclined him to favour. Even the fact that I would type out such a document in my office, to a man I did not know personally, and *make a carbon,* argued the latter. To be sure, the 18-page document was unsigned; but there were emendations in my hand. No one could deny me my day in court, if I was determined to Hang It All Out; but. . .

I hung it all up. God *damn* writing! This bloody farking scribbler's itch that you (most recently) seduced me into scratching! (Write > M.E. *writen* > O.E. *writan:* to tear or scratch. Ditto *scribe,* and *pace* Ambrose.) Yes, yes, yes: that one time—when, like this, I was in the office, and for a change not longhanding it—I *made a carbon,* such a relief it was to feel businesslike when Ambrose had begun to make a public arse of me with such a vengeance. It gave my weekly confession at once a more official and (what have I to lose now?) a more *fictitious* aspect: as if I were a writer writing first-person fiction, an epistolary novelist composing— and editing, alas, in holograph—instead of a stateless 50-year-old widow, failed mother, failed writer, and scholar of no consequence, tyrannised and humiliated by a younger "lover" as she enters her menopause with little to look back upon except abortive liaisons with a number of prominent novelists, and *nothing* to look forward to.

And of course it took me no time at all to feel a greater fool yet for making that carbon, for *editing* it, for writing to you in the first place; and I "destroyed" the copy *(i.e.,* wadded and wastecanned it) but posted the letter; and Shirley Stickles got to the wastecan before the custodian did, unless that worthy was in on the plot too; and it was too late to undo the award to Ambrose, they'd just have to hope, but once they were safely past 21 June they'd cut off the pair of us, using my letter as their trump card. . .

Et voilà!

Well: I *am* at the end of my forties, and the rest. I *have* been carrying on like a madwoman, and madly confessing it by the ream. The crowning irony now occurs to me: that perhaps you too believe, at least suspect, that I'm *making all this up!* Fantasizing! Writing *fiction!*

Jee-bloody-farking-*sus!*

Alors: if I am truly turpitudinous, and not hallucinating my tender connexion with Doctor Mensch, then I am now altogether reliant upon that spectacularly unreliable fellow. My "hope" this time last week was that Marshyhope's commencement might remind him fondly of ours. Ha! Now my only hope is that I'm pregnant, and that conceiving a bastard by that bastard will restore him to me and to his senses. Some hope, whilst he climbs all over Bea Golden (but not yet into her knickers, not yet, not yet) as the Baratarians reenact on Bloodsworth Island Admiral Cockburn's Rape of Hampton, Virginia, in 1813!

Total, total disgrace, such as my namesake never knew. This

dispossessed augur can scratch her poor encausticked penis across these miserable beech leaves no further. Where is the peace Mann promised his ruined

G?

O: *Lady Amherst to the Author*. *The Fourth Stage concludes; the Fifth begins. Magda's confession. The* Gadfly *fiasco reenacted: an Unfilmable Sequence.*

24 L Street
Dorset Heights, Maryland 21612

5 July '69

J.,

Oh, yes: still here. And still scratching.

You recall last Saturday's last hope? No sooner hoped than hopeless. True, when the Mother of Alphabets rose full on the Sunday (the "Hot Moon," and it has indeed been sweltering hereabouts), I failed to flow with my recent celestial regularity, and for some moments dared imagine— But it was a cruel false hope: next day, her name day, the last of the sorry month, I began, if not to flow, at least erratically to leak, and have dripped and dribbled this week through in pre-Ambrosian style.

As befits what looks to be the commencement of my *post*-Ambrosian life. Having been the efficient cause of my dismissal from Academe, the man has, as of Monday last, dismissed me, and as of yesterday abandoned me. Whilst I write this in air-conditioned solitude at 24 L, he is alone at "Barataria" with his new mistress, Jeannine Patterson Mack Singer Bernstein Golden, of whom he made triumphant conquest last night by the rockets' red glare.

Do I seem calm? I *am*, rather: that bitter hopeless peace old Thomas promised. Everyone is being frightfully understanding: good Magda Giulianova Mensch, of whom more to come; Todd Andrews; Jane Mack; even *Drew* Mack, who regrets by telephone that his disruption of the MSU commencement cost me my job (an example of bourgeois capitalist academic capriciousness, says Drew). My old friend "Juliette Récamier" has written sympathetically from her current post at Nanterre (don't ask me how she heard so fast), where "for such an outrage [as my cashiering] we would burn down the university." Oh, yes, and "Monsieur Casteene" also deplores (from Castines Hundred) John Schott's move, of which he disclaims foreknowledge; nor had he imagined, when as A. B. Cook he accepted Schott's invitation to visit Marshyhope for the fall semester (a detail he neglected to mention in our Remarkable Conversation) that he would be *replacing* me. He'd hoped, as my temporary colleague, to change my mind yet about publishing his ancestor's letters: a service to himself, to historiography, and to the 2nd Revolution which he now prayed my altered circumstances might reincline me to, but which he would not solicit from me against my wishes. He is making "other arrangements" for their publication. If things should go ill between me and my current friend, God forbid, and I needed a change of scene, I was of course welcome at any time, and *for* any time, to Castines Hundred.

I thanked him politely for the invitation, but told him that things between my current friend and me were just dandy.

I have not mentioned that, even as he left me for Bea Golden (more precisely, upon Monday's evidence that his low-motile swimmers had failed again with me, but before his Independence Day triumph over Reg Prinz), Ambrose informed me that our affair is *not* ended; only its 4th Stage, corresponding—somehow—to his failed marriage. As I was not pregnant, the 5th Stage would now commence—it was how he *felt*—and he hoped it would be of short duration, for he could not imagine my enjoying it any more than #4. I was a fool, he added (not for the first time since Commencement Day), to have persisted in this one-way correspondence with you, and especially to have *made a carbon* of such compromising stuff: but in my circumstances it was an understandable and forgivable folly. He was very sorry that it and he had cost me my job; contemptuous as he was of John Schott's vulgar ambitions and pretentions, he was not finally so of mass public colleges like Marshyhope, as long as one did not mistake their activity for first-class education. He knew I'd done excellent things for the few really able students who had come my way, and at least no harm to the commonalty. Even *he* is sympathetic!

He could scarcely say what had possessed him at the exercises: he'd had an equivocal hint from Prinz, who had it from Drew Mack, that the radicals might be Up To Something after all; we both had heard from Bea with some amusement that Merope Bernstein had mobilised herself and disappeared in a hurry from the Farm when her ex-stepmother, after a sympathetic reunion, had cautioned her that Jerome Bray might well materialise in Fort Erie. But there wasn't "really" any prearrangement: it had merely occurred to Ambrose that some sort of neo-Dadaist, bourgeois-baiting stunt would suit the movie, and he *was* distraught about his mother's dying, and for that matter he *was* professionally preoccupied with the roots of writing, its mythical connexions with Thoth and Hermes, ibis and crane, moon and phallus and lyre strings. . . . He too had been disrupted!

Oh, yes, and by the way: he still loved me, he declared; still hoped to impregnate and to marry me. To that end we ought still to Have Sex from time to time, once my bleeding stopped, what? Not to worry about the rent and the groceries; we'd manage. But I might be seeing a bit less of him in the days ahead, when he suspected that Andrea's condition, his authorial concerns, and his activities in Prinz's film might all approach critical levels.

Have I mentioned that, unaccountably, I Still Love Him too? Elsewise I'd clear straight out of this incubator of mildew and mosquitoes and get me to the clear cold air of Switzerland, or the at-least-civilised perversions of my "Juliette" in Nanterre. I could truly almost wish I were lesbian! When Magda came 'round this morning— ostensibly to ask whether I wanted to go with her to visit Mother Mensch in hospital, but actually to comfort me for Ambrose's in-fidelity—when to the surprise of both of us we found ourselves embracing and enjoying a good womanly weep together—I was so moved by her direct understanding and sympathy, so relieved to be close to another *woman* for a change, I could almost have Gone Right On. She too, I half think, and altogether guiltlessly. There *was* a rapport there. . . But we didn't, and I'm not, and what would please me even better would be to be sexless altogether, as shall doubtless come to pass soon enough. In the meanwhile, and mean it is, I love and crave (and miss) that unconscionable sonofabitch Ambrose; that—that scratcher of my itch; that *writer*.

And I have got clear ahead of my story. No question but moviemakers have the world in their pocket in our century, as we like to imagine the 19th-Century novelists did in theirs. Let Ambrose ask the skipper of the *Original Floating Theatre II* to delay his leaving Cambridge for half an hour so that he can make a few notes thereupon for a novel in progress: the chap wouldn't have considered it. But let a perfectly unknown Reg Prinz show up with camera crew and the vaguest intentions in the world. . . the world stops, reenacts itself for take after take, does anything it can imagine its Director might wish of it!

The showboat was docked at Long Wharf on the weekend of the Marshyhope fiasco: we were to have gone to see Bea do her Mary-Pickford-of-the-Chesapeake on the Saturday evening—and Ambrose actually went, straight out of the pokey, as did Prinz & Co., but yours truly was too ill with consternation for further vaudeville. The *O.F.T. II* was to have sailed on the Monday, but lingered till the Wednesday, cast and all, so that Prinz could get footage for *possible* use, and agreed to an unscheduled return to Cambridge on 4 July so that he could combine shots of the locally famous fireworks display with—here we go—a "sort of remake" of the *Gadfly* excitement of just a fortnight past! History really *is* that bird you mention somewhere, who flies in ever diminishing circles until it disappears up its own fundament!

En attendant, as I despaired here in Dorset Heights, and wondered where on earth a sacked acting provost might go from Marshyhope, the cinematographic action shifted down-county to "Barataria," where it and Ambrose and Bea got on quite well without me. I wonder who does Prinz's cost accounting? That set, elaborate for him, was built months ago and has scarcely been used; as of the end of *Giles Goat-Boy* (I'm done), there is no mention of the 1812 War in your works. But on 23

June 1813, a British naval force attempted to dislodge Jean Lafitte's Baratarians from their stronghold on Grand Terre Island, near New Orleans, and on the following day Admiral Cockburn's Chesapeake fleet sacked Hampton, Virginia, raping a number of American ladies in the process. It was decided to combine "echoes" of both events in an obscure bravura scene shot on their approximate sesquicentennial down at the Bloodsworth Island set. Don't ask me why they didn't throw in Napoleon's abdication on the 22nd (which coincided nicely with my cashiering and Jerome Bonaparte Bray's abandoning the goat farm and pursuing Bea to Maryland on the Sunday), or Custer's Last Stand against Sitting Bull at Little Big Horn on the 25th.

Don't ask me either what exactly went on down there. I was—perhaps you noticed?—still too distressed in last Saturday's letter to be either a good listener to, or a good reporter of, the news. Ambrose passed through on the Thursday and the Friday en route to spend time with his mother and his daughter; we slept together (this was just before the Hot Moon rose and my last hopes sank); I gather from his perfunctory accounts that Bea was as frightened of Mr Bray as he and Prinz were intrigued by him, and that the chap had fastened himself upon the company like a solicitous mosquito. Merry Bernstein (before she jumped the bail Drew Mack put up for her and fled underground upon Bray's appearance in Cambridge) had confided to Bea that Bray's assault on *her,* in her flat at Chautauqua back in May, had been of a bizarre anal character and literally venomous: she believed he had sodomized her with some exotic C.I.A. poison on his member, out of spite for her leaving him; she warned her ex-stepmother that the man was scarcely human. At this point Bea was still as much amused as alarmed by Bray's protestations; she confided to Ambrose (a mark of their increased chumminess) that the story had reminded her of Merope's father, whose penchant for anal copulation had been a factor in their divorce. She'd learned, she said, to keep a tight arse in such company. Ambrose himself was still fascinated by the correspondence of some of Bray's obsessions—1st and 2nd Cycles, Midpoints and Phi-points, Fibonacci numbers, Proppian formulae—with his own preoc-cupations, of which they seemed to him a mad and useful limiting case. Bray's rôle as a new rival for Bea's favours did not much concern him: it seemed to frighten her closer, and Bray himself appeared to regard him as an ally against Reg Prinz—who, we must remember, was at this time still Bea's lover.

Well: at some point in the shooting, Mr Bray—an amateur Stanislavski-Method actor, it would seem, as well as something of an amateur historian—carried over into the Rape-of-Hampton sequence his piratical characterisation from the Assault on Barataria (sound effects courtesy of the U.S. Navy), in which he'd taken the rôle of one John Blanque, a Creole friend of Jean Lafitte's in the Louisiana legislature who later joined the buccaneering crew. Now it happens that Admiral Cockburn blamed the rape of the Virginia women, not on his

382

English sailors, but on a gang of unruly French *chasseurs britanniques* whom he had impressed from the Halifax prison-ships into his Chesapeake service, and as the two events were being as it were montaged... Our Beatrice finds herself not only leapt upon, per program, by two extras and stripped fetchingly of her hoopskirts and petticoats to the accompaniment of "Gallic" grunts and leers, but "rescued" suddenly by Monsieur Blanque, who with surprising strength flings other Baratarians off her (one has a swelling the size of a goose egg on his thigh) and very nearly accomplishes Penetration before his victim—who must have felt herself back in her blue-movie period—can unman him with a parasol to the groin.

Yup, parasol. It was late June, Prinz had reasoned; they'd've had parasols. And never mind verisimilitude, he liked the fetishistic look of naked ladies with open parasols, and had instructed the girls to hold tight to their accessories whilst being stripped. Our pirate now clutches his family jewels and begs Bea's pardon: he was overcome with love; it was that season of year. Ambrose not quite to the rescue this time, but nearby enough to get his comforting arms about the victim, I daresay—who is inclined to bring assault charges against Bray until Prinz dissuades her. Indeed, the familiarity of the tableau—Bea *in extremis,* the Author to the rescue (sort of), Bray apologising—has given the Director an Idea: inasmuch as the movie reenacts and re-creates events and images from "the books," which do likewise from life and history and even among themselves, why should it not also reenact and echo its *own* events and images?

Ambrose is enchanted, Bray is willing, Bea is appalled, Prinz is boss. The 4th of July re-creation of the *Gadfly* party is devised. But it mustn't be a strictly programmed reenactment: we are on the Choptank now, aboard the *O.F.T. II,* with a different backup cast. Time has moved on: it will be Independence Day; never mind the War of 1812. Let each principal, independently, imagine variations on the original *Gadfly* sequence.

How is it, I wonder, Prinz gets so much said when I'm not there to hear him? In any case, my own variation, proposed at once, was that this time around I stay home in bed. Ambrose's idea—which, along with my menstruation and the completing of his Perseus-Medusa story in first draft, kept him from me most of the week since my last letter—was to reply to Prinz's triumphantly Unwritable Scene (on the beach of Ocean City back on 12 May) with a victoriously Unfilmable Sequence.

He was in a high state of excitement; didn't even remark upon the fact, if he noticed it, that since the full moon I'd ceased to wear my teenybopper costumes, too depressed to give a damn what he thought. Did I not agree, he demanded to know, that we were amid a truly extraordinary coming together of omens, echoes, prefigurations? *Item:* On the Tuesday noon, 1 July, the midpoint of the year, he was in midst of a fiction about the classical midpoint of man's life, and felt himself personally altogether *nel mezzo del cammin* etc. *Item:* Our sacking from

383

Marshyhope U. had occurred (so said his desk calendar) on the anniversary of the end of Napoleon's 100 Days. *Item:* Wednesday the 2nd, when Prinz began preparing his reenactment of the *Gadfly*'s grounding and Ambrose all but wound up his tale of Perseus and Medusa, was the date on which in 1816 the French frigate *Méduse* ran aground off the Cape Verde Islands and put out the raft that inspired Géricault's famous painting; the frigate itself had just the year before— and at just this same time of year—been involved in Napoleon's postabdication scheme to run the British blockade at Rochefort and escape to America. And—get *this,* now—he had just that day (*i.e.,* midday Thursday, 3 July) been informed by Todd Andrews, whom he'd happened to meet in the Cambridge Hospital and with whom he'd had a chat about the strange Mr Bray, that that gentleman had once represented himself to the Tidewater Foundation as the Emperor Bonaparte, and had even mentioned, in one of his mad money-begging letters, his abdication, his flight to Rochefort, the plan to run him through the British blockade, his final decision to surrender and plead for passport to America: where (Bray is alleged to have alleged) he lives in hiding to this day, making ready his return from his 2nd Exile!

But we are not done. *Item:* Among the American friends of the emperor's brother Jérôme Bonaparte was the King family of "Beverly," in nearby Somerset County; and among the several plans to rescue Napoleon from St Helena, one of the more serious was that of Mayor Girod of New Orleans, who built a fast ship in Charleston to run the emperor across the Atlantic and into the trackless Maryland marshes, where he would hide in a secret room in the Beverly estate until the coast was clear enough for him to remove to New Orleans. Only the news of Bonaparte's death in 1821 kept the *Séraphine* from sailing. And who are these Kings of Somerset if not the ancestors of Ambrose's mother Andrea King, from whom he had both this story as a child and his adult nom de plume?

Pooh, said I, that's a game anyone can play who knows a tad of history: the game of Portentous Coincidences, or Arresting But Meaningless Patterns. And I volunteered a couple of items of my own, gratis: That the British man-of-war that accepted Napoleon's surrender and fetched him from Rochefort to England was named after Perseus's cousin Bellerophon; that the officer who then transported him to exile in St Helena instead of to America was the same Admiral Cockburn who had raped Hampton, burnt Washington, and bombarded Fort McHenry in Baltimore in previous summers; that my late husband's ancestor William Pitt, Earl Amherst (a nephew of Lord Jeffrey), stopped at St Helena to converse with Napoleon in 1816, after the wreck of his ship *Alceste* in Korean waters; that my other famous forebears Mme de Staël and Lord Byron first met at just about this time, and among their connexions was surely their strong shared interest in the exiled emperor (Byron's *Ode to Napoleon Buonaparte* dates from 1815; the "Ode to St Helena" in Canto III of *Childe Harold* from 1816). And one of B.'s cousins, Captain Sir Peter Parker of H.M.S. *Menelaus,* was killed in a diversionary action on Maryland's Eastern Shore during Cockburn's assault on Washington and Baltimore, the news whereof inspired Byron to add to his *Hebrew Melodies* an ode "On the Death of Sir Peter Parker." And the ship which carried Napoleon III to *his* American exile in 1837 was named for Perseus's wife, *Andromède;* and it was the same Louis Napoleon's grotesque replay of his uncle's career that prompted Marx's essay *On the 18th Brumaire* etc., in which he made his celebrated, usually misquoted observation of History's farcical recyclings. And none of this, in my opinion, meant anything more than that the world is richer in associations than in meanings, and that it is the part of wisdom to distinguish between the two.

"Thou'rt a very prig and pedant," said my lover, not unkindly, and kissed my forehead, and repeated his hope that our connexion would survive the hard weather he foresaw, our 5th Stage.

Two things worthy of note occurred that same day, Thursday the 3rd, both reported to me by Magda when she called on me in the evening (Ambrose was Out). One was that the general migration of Strange Birds down the flyway from the Great Lakes to the Chesapeake had fetched to Dorchester County not only Bea Golden and Jerome Bray but, that very afternoon, the former Mrs Ambrose Mensch, née Marsha Blank, a.k.a. Pocahontas of the Remobilisation Farm: she had telephoned that morning from across the Bay (Chautaugua, surely) to announce that she was en route to Bloodsworth Island on business for her "employer" and, as she would be passing through town, wished to take her daughter to dinner. Magda was distressed: the woman's infrequent, imperious visits never failed to disturb poor Angela's fragile tranquillity, the more precarious lately anyroad on account of her grandmother's condition. Ambrose too was always distracted by fury for days after, she said, even when things were serene on other fronts: given Andrea's dying, the Marshyhope incident, the new crisis at Mensch Masonry, and what she gathered was the less than blissful state of affairs at 24 L, she feared for him as well as for Angela when he should learn of Marsha's presence on the scene.

New crisis?

About the foundation work for the Marshyhope Tower, which was already showing such unexpected, impermissible signs of settling that there was real doubt whether construction could continue. Bankruptcy loomed, larger than usual. Peter was at a loss to account for the phenomenon: it appeared that the analyses of his test borings had actually been falsified to give optimistic results, on the basis of which he had made the winning low bid! He had already, at his own cost, exceeded the specifications of his contract when actual excavation had revealed a ground situation at variance with his predictions; someone had bribed the building inspectors not to disclose the truth earlier; to correct the problem now, with the superstructure so far along, he had not the resources.

What was more—and this alarmed *l'Abruzzesa* more than any threat of poverty or the disagreeable reappearance of Marsha Blank—Peter himself was not well. He had lately had difficulty walking; had developed a positive limp in his left leg, which he'd been as loath to acknowledge to her as he'd been to acknowledge that it was his own late father who, almost certainly, had falsified those core samples from Redmans Neck. But their family doctor had confided to her privately that X rays had been made and Tests taken; that, though Peter had sworn him to silence, he felt it a disservice to his patient and to her not to tell her that her husband had cancer of the bone in his lower left leg. Inasmuch as Peter would not consent, whilst his mother lay dying, to the prompt surgery his own condition called for, the doctor had to hope that his elder and terminal patient would get on with it before his younger became terminal too.

Well! Having been down that horrid road with my Jeffrey, I was able genuinely to sympathise, if not to help. We had our Good Cry. The ice broken and Magda so obviously harbouring me no ill will, I acknowledged that things were indeed less than blissful between Ambrose and me. Further, I candidly apprised her of the Pattern business: how, starting from that play upon the opening letters of the *New England Primer* in his first love letter to me, Ambrose had come to fancy a rough correspondence between the "stages" of our affair and the sequence of his major prior connexions with women. How this correspondence had so got hold of his imagination that he could no longer say, concerning the subsequent course of our love, what was cause and what effect.

Magda was sharply interested; I reviewed for her the four "stages" thus far, as I understood them. *(a)* The period of our first acquaintance, in the fall semester of 1968, through Ambrose's unexpected declaration after Harrison's funeral, to his mad overtures of March and our first coition in the ad hoc committee room—which-all he compared to his youthful admiration of Magda as rendered in his abandoned novel, *The Amateur*. The ardour then (I wistfully recalled) had been altogether his, merely tolerated and at length yielded to by its object. *(b)* That month of frenetic copulation, with no great love on either side, from early April to early May, which put him in mind of his late-teen fucking bouts with the Messalina of the Chesapeake, Jeannine Mack. *(c)* Our odd and gentle sexless first fortnight of May, when we both had felt stirrings of real love, and Ambrose had flabbergasted me with intimations of his wish to make a baby. In his mind this was not unlike the period of his second, innocent "connexion" with Magda, by then Mrs Peter Mensch; the resemblance is not obvious to me. *(d)* That disagreeable "husbandly" period just ended, during which, alas for me, my ardor exceeded his, and our physical connexion was sedulously procreative in intent, if not

386

in issue. All I could say of this interval was that, if it really did resemble Ambrose's marriage, I'm surprised the thing lasted fifteen months, not to mention fifteen years; and unless I was confusing cause and effect, I quite sympathised with Marsha's busy infidelities. But I could not imagine that chilly individual's permitting for a fortnight the high-handedness I'd indulged for a month already. Those ridiculous costumes! His insulting attentions to Bea Golden! What's more (and more's the pity for me), I *loved* him despite that degrading nonsense; loved him still and deeply, damn it. I could not imagine Ms. Blank's entertaining that emotion for anyone.

Be that as may, we were by A.'s own assertion done with *d* and entering *e*. Inasmuch as he had declared to me in his *Ex-hor-ta-ti-on* of 3 March that I was the 6th love of his life, and as the evidence was that he had come to me from a painful third connexion with Magda, I urged her now to tell me what I must look forward to from Our Friend in Stage #5.

More tears. Then she told me, in two longish, earnest installments: one then and there, the other this morning, both punctuated with the good womanly embraces aforementioned. Ah, the Italians! Only her suicide convinces me that Carthaginian Dido was of Phoenician and not Italian Catholic origins. God *damn* me if I go that route! Which, Kleenexed and synopsised, appears to have been this: In 1967, when their marriage was officially *kaput*, Marsha ran off to Niagara Falls with the lover whose subsequent early rejection of her had fetched her to the Remobilisation Farm and the sexual-clerical employ of "Monsieur Casteene"/Cook. Ambrose, at Peter's urging, had reluctantly moved back into Mensch's Castle with his daughter; he had finished the conversion of the Lighthouse into a camera obscura, and—not at his own *particular* initiative, I gather—had become party to a tacitly acknowledged *ménage à trois*, the guilty background whereof we have had hints in an earlier letter. Look it up: as Ambrose says, that's what print's for.

Magda again, then. But with a difference! At *a* Ambrose had been a callow, adoring amateur; there'd been no sex till the end, 1947, when in Peter's absence Magda had bemusedly (and fatefully) accommodated the boy's ardours as the stone house rose up about them. At *c*—1949 and after—their feelings had been reciprocal but for the most part unspoken; they did not couple, nor did Magda question her heart's commitment to Peter and their newborn twins. *This* time 'round (1967), worse luck for her, Ambrose was passive, aloof, still shaken by the wreck of his marriage; whereas Magda found herself *possessed,* for the first time in her 38 years, by unreserved, overriding, self-transcending (and self-amazing) passion: a possession so complete as to make her wonder whether, after all, the man Ambrose was not as much its occasion as its cause and object. She knew him thoroughly; she saw and did not admire his faults; she found altogether more to respect in her husband; her contempt for mere adventurous adultery, Marsha-style, was profound—and none of those considerations mattered. She was Swept Away!

I was impressed with the woman's understanding of what had happened to her; how judiciously she assessed the contributions of Peter, Ambrose, and herself to the experience. She'd been near forty, heavier than at *c* (and than she is now); it turns out that Peter—despite his being an affectionate, strong, and devoted husband—was, no doubt still is, an indifferent lover: perfunctory, unskillful, often impotent though decidedly fertile, withal Not Very Interested in That. Magda had never managed orgasm, except *solo*. Of this she'd been aware, in a general way: a more vigorous erotic life, like a larger income, she could imagine to be agreeable if it didn't bring problems with it. But she'd felt content, sufficient, and had not thitherto been tempted to infidelity.

Even so, it had unquestionably been a factor in her overwhelmment that, however it was they got together again at *e*, Ambrose revealed himself this time around to be an amateur no longer in the sexual way. I abbreviate: at age 38 she learned from him how to fuck, and by her own admission the experience set her a little crazy. It also inspired in her—focussed, channelled, whatever—a passion for him which, alas, he scarcely measured up to and but feebly reciprocated. This part was painful: for Magda especially, of course, but for Ambrose too (and for me to hear). Early on in our own connexion he had mentioned "a Dido whose Aeneas can neither return her love nor leave her palace. . . ." She had no wish to divorce Peter and marry Ambrose; she had not really expected him to love her as she loved him, though hope was hope; neither did she think their affair would last long. On the other hand she could not imagine—it would have appalled her to imagine—an experience so important to her as being *without consequences*. She begged him to "run off" with her; she was ready to put by the family she genuinely prized and give herself exclusively to her lover for the vague "year or two" she could imagine them together, in Italy. . . More than anything else she prayed he might make her pregnant, before he left her, with

> a little Aeneas to play in the palace
> And, in spite of all this, to remind me of you by his looks. . .

Then she would return to Cambridge and take the consequences, whatever they were.

But that's not our Ambrose, what? He was moved; she believed his testimony that if he had taught *her* what sex was all about, she had taught him, just as belatedly and more considerably, what *love* was all about; made him realise that he'd never truly been loved before. Surely that tuition was what kept him from cutting his anchor cables: it was a remarkable, new, and of course very flattering business, to be loved like that! And he *did* both admire and love Magda, though not quite so much as at *c* and at *a*. . .

And not enough. No help for that, but it must have hurt. The truth

388

was—he felt a fool, a beast, a sexual snob for feeling it, but there it was, and she sensed it without his saying it—she no longer aroused him very much; he could be seduced away by the first trim 22-year-old at Marshyhope. He deplored this fact, and resented having to deplore it. Very painful for the pair of them, whilst Peter, humble and ashamed, looked the other way.

Thus *e:* as if circumstances and want of heroical destiny had held Aeneas in Carthage not for a winter but for a year and more, with a Dido less queenly than Dido and whose passion he found himself ever less able to return, despite his esteem for her. . . Ambrose didn't oblige Magda to dress like his undergraduates (she's but a year his senior), but he said cruel things, and hated himself for having done: she was not *dainty;* she was not *fresh;* he made her douche; he made her shave her legs and underarms daily, and the fleece between her navel and her fleece. Clumsily she went at any perversion, tried to dream up new ones, anything to keep him.

Last September, not to beggar her self-respect altogether, Ambrose finally managed to put an end to this 5th Affair; would have moved out of the Castle as well, down to Redmans Neck or somewhere, but for Peter's insistence, which frantic Magda seconded: Angie needed them both; all three. Through the fall and winter, whilst she went crackers with desperation, he humped the odd ex-student; by March she knew he'd got Serious again with someone. The knowledge went into her like Dido's knife, for she still much loved him.

But not, she acknowledged, as much as before. Surely I must see (I saw) that she did not resent me; on the contrary. She was not yet over her Grand Passion, but she was *getting* over it, rather to her own surprise and much to her relief. She bore him no grudge for having been unable to match her feeling for him; what would be the sense in that? She could not imagine ever falling in love again; was glad her marriage had been no worse scarred; was as prepared as one could be to face the prospective widowhood that now shockingly loomed. But like Héloïse her Abelard, she could not forget the things she and Ambrose had done, the places where they'd done them . . .

Hm. I was, to be sure, as busy noting and assessing the differences between our cases as sympathising with Magda's confidences. Ambrose had not taught *me* how to screw; André had, in Paris, an age ago. Our mighty April sessions were as much a refresher course for him as for me. The Baby business—which I understood better now—was *his* idea, not mine (Magda tearily prayed me luck for July, and belied her statement of a paragraph ago by wishing fervently she could feel again the joy of pregnancy). Nevertheless, the ground resemblance was plain enough to promise that Stage 5 is going to be no picnic: my Aeneas-Come-Lately has stripped me of my queenship, demanded of my worn-out womb that it find the wherewithal to germinate his feeble seed, and in the meanwhile makes a fool of me with the dockside whores of Carthage!

389

Even "the meanwhile" may be optimistic. I'm at the period of my period, but July has yet to see him reinseminate me. As I write this it is Bea Golden he ploughs, down in Barataria; for all I know he may nevermore dip his pen at 24 L.

My friend La Giulianova assures me otherwise: last night and its consequences, she's certain, are Just Part of the Movie. Bea Golden is scarcely literate, much less literary: surely I don't believe she'd throw over her darling last hope for movie stardom just because Ambrose apparently got the better of him in a single encounter?

I replied that the evening's end, like its beginning and its mad middle, had the aspect not only of open-ended Scenario—written by "Arthur Morton King" but directed by Reg Prinz—but also of an Episode, with further episodes to follow. Jerome Bray and Marsha Blank—improbable new allies!—have withdrawn together back up the flyway; Bea is in her new lover's arms on Bloodsworth Island; the Baratarians are dispersed (shooting is suspended for at least a week, till the 13th); Prinz himself has retired up the Amtrak to Manhattan, *apparently* put down by last night's "defeat." Oh, no doubt it is all acting, only another Sequence; they'll be back. Meanwhile, however, whether at Prinz's behest or her own, Bea is unquestionably *down there with Ambrose,* shagging away; and 30 pages have not assuaged my misery, only lengthily recorded it!

Unfilmable Sequence! Magda declares that it was nothing more than a *letter,* John, like this one: another of those dum-dums in a bottle from "Arthur Morton King" (Whom It Still Concerns) to "Yours Truly," in reply to the blank one Ambrose picked up 29 years ago! There they all were (not I) on their expensive prop: the *O.F.T. II* done over in part to "echo" the Chautauqua Lake *Gadfly III.* The musicians and actors from Chautauqua Institution were replaced by the pit orchestra and repertoire troupe of the *Floating Theatre;* the Baratarians were assembled, with a sprinkling of Cantabridgeans; no sign of M. Casteene, but grim-visaged "Pocahontas" was aboard, in surprising deep parley with "Captain Bray" after returning Angela postprandially to Magda. Those two and Peter Mensch were there also, at Prinz's invitation: ostensibly to flavour the crowd with extra locals, possibly to add a notch or two to the general tension. Todd Andrews was on hand, too, looking like death itself, reports Magda. No sign of Jane Mack. All of County Dorchester gathered about Long Wharf, several thousand strong, to witness the fireworks and the filmmakers, by now notorious in the area. The late sun goes down; the *O.F.T. II* chugs out through the swarm of anchored pleasure boats into the river channel, its amplified (tape-recorded) calliope loudspeaking patriotic airs. The cameras roll, the fireworks fire. . .

Well, I wasn't there. Why try to make you see what I didn't? What Magda didn't either, since the whole point of what followed was its unseeability, hence its unfilmability! From Ambrose, before he left me, I had the generallest notion of his conceit for the episode: certain features of the 12 May "Unwritable Sequence" filmed on the Ocean City beach were to be echoed in combination with certain others of the *Gadfly* party of 17 June—*e.g.*, the Author's attempt to woo away or rescue the Fading Starlet from the Director. This attempt would more directly involve another Water Message and, "as in the myths," a literal Night Sea Journey. The vessel to be forging upchannel, against the tide, under the gibbous moon, as the contretemps is enacted. J. Bray to fly again to some misguided rescue. Bea to receive A.'s water message at the climax. The dénouement (presumably left open) to be illuminated by the rockets' red-white-and-blue glare.

All quite filmic, so far and so put, and the more technicolourful for Marsha Blank's apparent half-conspiracy with Bray: that chap wants Bea himself, Ambrose calculates, and regards Prinz as his more immediate rival, therefore inclines to aid the Author against the Director. Marsha, from mere epical vindictiveness we suppose, wants Ambrose not to have what he wants, therefore will incline to help Bray get Bea for himself. Don't ask *me*, John—whose own main question is why in that case it wasn't I she directed her spite against! I wasn't there, and anyroad this visual bravura was all a red (white and blue) herring on Ambrose's part, to throw Prinz off guard. For the Big Surprise this go-round was to be that what had been a literal blank on 12 May (the washed-out script) and an insignificant detail on 17 June (A.'s posting his bottled missive into Chautauqua Lake and learning from Bray's spiel that it could after all just possibly return to him via the Mississippi, the Gulf Stream, and Chesapeake Bay) would now—unroll? explode? all visual verbs!—into the whole climactic "action": no action at all, not even the minimal action of inditing or reading a letter, but the letter itself.

A letter! Which, to date, none but the Author and the Reader (Bea's surprise new rôle!) has read. Therefore nobody who *witnessed* what happened knows what happened. What Magda and the others *saw* (and heard) was a hammed-up rehash of the earlier business: Bea (in beach towel, from the boardwalk scene) is either menaced or embraced by the Director *(sans* sheepskin now: all the male principals are wearing *tails;* I mean animal tails, not formal coats. Don't ask me. *Pencil* > penis = tail?) and additionally menaced, or threatened with rescue, by Mr Bray. Who this time, knowing it's All Part of the Movie, either will not or cannot repeat his astonishing gymnastics of last month, but merely bumbles about, unable to comply with the Director's direction to "do [his] number" on Bea. Bray too wears a tail, between his legs; he cannot take his eyes off Bea, who earnestly promises to scratch them out, Movie or no Movie, if he lays a hand on her. *Marsha* appears, to everyone's surprise (except, I suspect, Reg Prinz's—where else would she have got the costume Magda describes, which is clearly the same worn earlier by Bea, butterfly wings and all?): a little drunk and without Bea's semiprofessional talents, but coldly attractive all the same, Magda admits, in her amateur attempt to do a Poor Butterfly. Bea, Ambrose,

Bray are nonplussed; the Baratarians are breaking up; the men among them, tails in hand, go dancing 'round the five principals.

All good cinema! But then Ambrose fetches out his bottle ("a big one," Magda reports; my guess is that it was a certain famous jeroboam of Piper-Heidsieck); he puts Bea's hand around its neck and covers it with his own; together they smash it over the ship's bow-rail as if to launch her. In lieu of champagne, a quire of writing paper sprays out, blank as the message that Started It All. I imagine the chorus pauses; Prinz frowns. And now it develops that our hero has a tail with a difference: he sets Bea down before him, snatches up tail tip and paper with a flourish (his last cinematical gesture), and begins. . . to *write*.

The Baratarians' tail dance peters out. Bray and Marsha (he has Rescued her; his cloaked arm is about her wings; she looks *very* uncomfortable, M. attests) are transfixed, sort of. Ditto Prinz and for that matter Bea, who finds it harder to sit than to stand attractively in her beach towel. Everyone wonders what's up, none more than the camera crew. The Director gives no directions.

And Ambrose writes. First page done, he hands it to Bea and begins Page 2. He writes, she reads, both silently, almost motionlessly. Marsha makes a single strident effort to get things going again: a few squeaks and flutters. Bray whispers something urgent to her, leads her off; to Magda she looks cross and uncertain, but she goes with him, somewhere else in the vessel, out of sight. Prinz removes his glasses, contemplatively sucks one earpiece. The passengers turn their attention, with appropriate shrugs and murmurs, to the fireworks just beginning to rise from Long Wharf. Peter Mensch scratches his nose, confesses that it's all beyond him, he's not much for the movies anyroad, and gimps over to explain the ground pieces to Angie. *She*, reasonably enough, wants to know what all the tails were for. Magda suspects they have to do with spermatozoa (Bea's towel is virgin white, eggshell white; she wears a tight white old-fashioned bathing cap; some of the men wear black ones), but mumbles something about tadpoles, frogs and princesses; she's not sure what Daddy has in mind.

Ambrose writes. Bea reads, silently, altogether engrossed, and discards each page overboard as she finishes it. Half an hour later—the cameras have long since turned to the fireworks—the pair go off together hand in hand, somewhere inside. Prinz confers gravely with his cameraman, then stalks off after them. When the *O.F.T. II* docks, Ambrose appears for a moment to say good night to Angela and announce to Magda that he'll be down in Barataria for a few days. With Bea. That Prinz is furious, has suspended shooting, may even scrap the film. That Magda needn't bother getting in touch with me; that was *his* problem. But she should ring him up at once if his mother either revived from her coma (of three days' duration now) or actively resumed her dying.

So. Happy Birthday, America! And bugger off, Germaine!

I think I know enough of my ex-lover's preoccupations with the medium of fiction to guess what he might have attempted in those pages: not only (instead of a blank sheet) a full and gorgeous love letter from Whom It Concerned to Yours Truly—much too full for the camera to follow its inditing or a Voice-over to intone—but a text whose language is preponderantly nonvisual, even nonsensory in its reference. How many postcoital apostrophes I heard from him, in June, whilst I up-ended for his low-motile swarmers, upon the peculiarly noncinematic properties of written fiction! Composed in private, to be read in private, at least in silence and virtual immobility, author and reader one to one like lovers—his letter would ideally have been a sort of story, told instead of shown, exploiting such anticinematical characteristics as, say, authorial omniscience and interpretation, perhaps some built-in ironic "discount" in the narrative viewpoint, interior monologue, reflexion. Its language would be its *sine qua non:* heightened, strange, highly figurative—and speculative, analytical, as often abstract as concrete. It would summarise, consider, adjudicate; it would interrupt, contradict itself, refer its Dear Reader to before and behind the sentence in progress. It would say the unseeable, declare the impossible. I have even argued with Ambrose, warmly, that such defining of his medium, however understandable the impulse among writers who feel their ancient dominion usurped by film, is strictly unnecessary: that the words *It is raining* are as essentially different from motion pictures of falling rain as are either from the actual experience of precipitation. . .

O Elysian June, when I was miserable with instead of without him!

Oh and who knows whether he wrote anything of the sort! I cannot imagine Bea Golden sitting still for *It was the best of times and the worst of times,* not to mention *It is raining; it is not raining!* Indeed I cannot account at all for her enthrallment by any sort of *text.* Did Ambrose offer her the female lead in his next novel? Did Prinz arrange his own "defeat," and only pretend chagrin, to chuck a Dido of his own? Is Bea—dear God, the notion just occurs to me, 40 pages late! Is she now playing the only woman I know to have been literally deflowered by a (capped) fountain pen, and seduced thereafter time and again by aging wielders of that instrument? Has she taken the rôle as well as the lover of

Yours truly?!

E: *Todd Andrews to his father. Further evidence that his life is recycling: 11 R.*

Todds Point, Maryland

Friday, June 20, 1969

Thomas T. Andrews, Dec'd
Plot #1, Municipal Cemetery
Cambridge, Maryland 21613

Dear dead Dad,

Even as declared beneath the old Mack Enterprises trademark (about to be retired by majority vote of the directors), *Praeteritas Futuras Fecundant*. If I am no longer interested in your ancient suicide, I'm presently more involved than ever in the recapitulation of my past. My Todays, since Jane Mack reseduced me five weeks ago today, are spent in watchful anticipation of Tomorrow's reenactment of Yesterday. What *praeteritas* will be fecundated next? So my interminable *Inquiry* sleeps (inconclusive but, I think, done with) while my *Letter* to you flourishes as never since I commenced it in 1920: three installments already since Groundhog Day, and the year's calendar but half turned!

I'm at my cottage, Dad, out on my point, at sixes and sevens. It is earlier than I'd thought. I've been fretting and fussing about here all day, getting the house ready, getting the grounds ready, getting the boat ready Just In Case, not answering the phone (even though it might be Jane calling off our "date"!) because I'm supposed to be over in Baltimore on business. I am surprised at myself: an emotion I thought I had lost the capacity for.

I, I, I: such self-absorption!

Tomorrow Now is the new Mack Enterprises slogan, beneath a streamlined logo devised by Jane's PR folk. No more hands across the years from things past to things to come; no more sailing ships, airliners, smokestacks, hay fields, tractors. Within a circular field, white above and *gules* below, the company's initials *azure* in a loopy script which also forms the field's perimeter, so:

------ *white*
------ *blue*
------ *red*

Each loop carrying into one moiety the other's color. The whole resembling, from any distance, a Yang/Yin done by a patriotic Italo-American spaghetti bender and, closer up, evocative of U.S. imperialism and isolationism at once: *US* become *me* and inflated to a global insularity.

So objected Drew, who, though not a director of Mack Enterprises, made plain his sentiments to the board of the Tidewater Foundation, of which he *is* a member, at our last meeting. He also denounced the firm's co-opting, and perverting to its capitalist ends, such trendy counter-culturalisms as the Yang/Yin, the call for Revolution Now, and the ignoring of the past (Drew himself is more anti- than ahistorical). This last objection I shared, as the only dissenting director of—ugh!—*me*. Where was that gentle fogey Old Man Praeteritas, father of us all, the Yesterday that will fertilize Tomorrow Today? And of course I deplored the self-circumscribed *me*, the objectified subject, the *I* gestating within that *O*—too close to home for Yours Truly to want it blazoned 'round the world!

But I concede that for Madam President it is not inapt. Her one objection was to the lowercase initials, not as dated Modernist kitsch, but as unsuited to a corporate entity agglomerating like cancer. She yielded, however, to the tactful pitch of her young PR chief: that a subdued but ubiquitous logo better suited the firm's magnitudinous future than some splashy arriviste hyperbole (he used other language); and that, per slogan, what was right for Tomorrow was right for Now. New logo—and attendant ad campaign—adopted, 11–1.

A week ago, that vote. Just after it, Jane declined, neutrally, my invitation to another sail on *Osborn Jones*. It was Friday 13th, 50 years to the day since another Friday when, upon my discharge from the U.S. Army, I was told of my precarious heart condition—of which you may have heard, Dad? I had thought Jane might be amused by that bit of *praeteritas*. Oh, and I'd thought, if things sailed smoothly, to apprise her of my *new* heart condition, by then four Fridays old; of my growing conviction that our lives are recycling; of my consequent anticipation of #11 R, June 17, Polly Lake's Fart Day (I grant that the connection is not obvious; I shall come to it), and the unexpected turn its approach had taken only that same morning; of the disorienting revelation that I am in love with Jane Patterson Paulsen Mack, and have been ever since she came to me in this cottage on the afternoon of August 13, 1932. What did I expect to happen next (I'd thought to ask her somewhere out there if the wind was right), after our astonishing shipboard tryst of May, #10 R in last letter's accounting, Dad? That she would abandon "Lord Baltimore" (or confess him to be the half-fantasized afterimage of some brief adventure with a London gigolo)? That she would *marry*, this late in the afternoon, a cranky, fussy small-town lawyer, part-time celibate and full-time bachelor, who has not been out of the U.S.A. since 1919 and seldom ventures even beyond the margins of Nautical Chart 77: *United States—East Coast—Maryland and Virginia—Chesapeake Bay—Northern Part*?

"Sorry, Todd," she said (neutrally): "No hard feelings about your vote, but I'm meeting my fiancé in New York."

Two times up, two times out. Just a week after 10 R I'd been permitted to take dinner with her at Tidewater Farms (where she's seldom to be found anymore) and set forth my sentiments on the matter of her blackmailing: that inasmuch as there had been no subsequent threats after the first letter from Niagara Falls, the investigator recommended to me by legal colleagues in nearby Buffalo had nothing really to proceed upon; he agreed with me that there was little to be done until and unless the blackmailer was heard from again when she filed suit against Harrison's will. For this opinion—which disappointed her itch to punish—I was thanked. But my after-dinner overture (a mere squeezing of her hand over brandy; an honest declaration that she looked radiant as ever; a head-shaking admission that I was still overwhelmed, overwhelmed, by our unexpected lovemaking of the week before) was smilingly squelched.

"Don't forget, my dear: I'm to be married."

I refrained from asking who had forgotten that detail, or found it irrelevant, out by Red Nun 20 on May 16.

In a word, it would have seemed, even as of yesterday, that that momentous moment was after all to be *inconsequential*—as, after all, our affair of 37 years past had been, except for the clouded paternity of Jane's cloudy daughter. Nevertheless, it was the only thing that interested me or gave interest to other things. I write these lines to you for no other reason than to speak of Jane. I prepare to defend Harrison's will against the suits now separately filed by his widow and two children only because their quarrel reenacts an earlier one ("Yesterday Now!" Drew cracked when our paths crossed in orphan's court); and I am obsessed with this reenactment only because it came to include the aforecelebrated 8 and 10 R. Jane, Jane!

Obsession it is, however. In the five weeks past, I have reexamined like scripture my old Floating Theatre memoir and its subsequent novelization for clues to what might happen next. 11 L (we recall, Dad) read *June 17, 1937: Polly Lake farts, inadvertently, in my office, and thereby shows me how to win* Mack v. Mack *and make Harrison and Jane millionaires, if I choose to.* Or, as rendered in that novel:

> I have in my office, opposite the desk, a fine staring-wall, a wall that I keep scrupulously clear for staring purposes, and I stared at it. I stared at it through February, March, April, and May, and through the first week of June, without reading on its empty surface a single idea.
>
> Then, on the very hot June 17th of 1937, our Mrs. Lake, who is as a rule a model of decorum, came sweating decorously into my office with a paper cup of iced coffee for me, set it decorously on my desk, accepted my thanks, dropped a handkerchief on the floor as she turned to leave, bent decorously down to retrieve it, and most undaintily—oh, most indecorously—broke wind, virtually in my coffee.
>
> "Oh, ex*cuse* me!" she gasped, and blushed, and fled. . . .

Et cetera. The work is fiction: It was her pencil, not her handkerchief, Polly dropped. I do not have, never had, a staring-wall in my office. I used and use a window giving upon a mountain of oyster shells from the crab- and oyster-packing plant hard by Court Lane: shells that in those days were pulverized into lime for chicken feed or trucked down-county to pave secondary roads with, but now are recycled back to the oyster beds for the next generation of spats to attach themselves to. But it was in fact that serendipitous crepitation that put me in mind of the late Mack Senior's bequest of his pickled defecations, and suggested to me that should his widow's gardener, say, deploy that excrement about the flower beds of their Ruxton property, for example, I might just be able to make a case against Harrison's mother for Attrition of Estate. . .

In honor of this anniversary and Harrison's subsequent enrichment, I had later proposed to the Tidewater Foundation that fireworks be let off from Redmans Neck every June 17th; the motion did not carry, but Harrison seldom failed, except during the period of our estrangement, to drop by the office on that date for iced coffee with me and Polly, who took our teasing tributes with her usual good humor. Even last June, confined to Tidewater Farms, he had delivered to her via Lady Amherst a bottle of good French perfume, the gift card embossed with the old Mack Enterprises slogan, and I'd taken her to dinner as was my custom in honor of her aid in the largest case of its sort we'd ever won.

This year was different. Given 10 R, my reconnection with Jane, I could not make the ritual office jokes as PLF Day approached, lest my new obsession with my life's recycling disturb the spontaneity of 11 R, which had assumed great importance to me. 10 R had literally refetched Jane into my life, my bed, my heart; though Polly's famous flatus at 11 L had nothing directly to do with Jane and me, I looked to the character of its recurrence (Literal? Symbolical? Straightforward? Inverse?) for clues to what might follow. Was my future—12 R, 13 R— to be fecundated or stercorated? Was I in for another and final Dark Night of the Soul and Second Suicide? Or would my tremulous vision on the New Bridge in 1967, that Everything Has Intrinsic Value, somehow come to realization—with Jane, with Jane? What dénouement, grim or golden, had our Author up His sleeve?

Since May 16 I had not seen Polly socially, and our office relations, while certainly cordial, were merely official. But as we carried on our business (without once comparing notes on our separate "dates" after my shipboard party: unusual for us), I watched like an osprey from the side of my eye for clues to the reenactment I was confident we approached. In addition to that meeting of the Mack Enterprises Board of Directors where the old *I*'s protest against the new *me* had been outvoted, our business had included the reviewing of those suits filed against Harrison's will, a quick flight to Buffalo to meet that aforementioned detective and speak carefully with him about Jane's blackmailer, and a board meeting of the Tidewater Foundation, where among other things we discussed the weighty matter of next September's cornerstone ceremonies for the Tower of Truth (for the other directors the question was which documents and artifacts best represented 1969; for Yours Truly it was where to lay a cornerstone in a round tower) and passed on the annual applications for foundation grants. Mr. Jerome Bray's LILYVAC nonsense we have finally washed our hands of, even Drew gruffly acknowledging that its fuzzy claim to radical-political relevance was fraudulent. Ditto the Guy Fawkes Day fireworks, now the king is dead. Reg Prinz's film, "Bea Golden's" sanatorium and haven for draft evaders, and the *Original Floating Theatre II* we still contribute to the support of, in various measure.

As my general secretary, Polly was witness to all this. She was as gratified as I by what she took to be Drew's "mellowing," especially towards me; we agreed it had nothing to do with the will contest, but could not decide whether it betokened a change of mood among political activists in the last lap of the Shocking Sixties or some personal ground-change in Drew since his father's death. Together we tisked our tongues at the cost overruns on Schott's Tower, as well as at certain evidence that the foundation work was not up to specifications and may have to be repaired at enormous expense to the state, since the contractor is filing for bankruptcy. We tisked again at the report (from Drew, via Jeannine) that Joe Morgan, who'd dropped out of sight from Amherst College after resigning his presidency at Marshyhope, has apparently done a Timothy Leary and surfaced as a hippie at the "Remobilization Farm."

But in none of these witnessings, gratifyings, and tongue-tiskings could I find augury of 11 R. The Bull gave way to the Twins, May to June; PLF Day rushed from Tomorrow towards Now, casting no discernible shadow before it.

Then, on that same unlucky Friday of *me*'s adoption and my rejection by President Jane, Polly pleasantly announced her *retirement*, effective virtually at once! Her replacement she had already selected and trained: the "girl" (37, our age on the original PLF Day; she seems a child!) who'd filled in for her at vacation time for several years and worked half-time for us while raising her children. Polly would stop in on the Monday to insure that all was well; she would stop in from time to time thereafter when she happened to be visiting Cambridge, to see to it I was neither exploiting nor being exploited by her successor. And she would miss me sorely, and the good ship *Osborn Jones*, and dear damp Dorchester, whose Tercentennial festivities she would miss too. But her heart had got the better of her head, she declared, as she hoped for my sake Jane Mack's would too before very long. She had acceded to the entreaties of her (other) occasional lover of many years' standing, that gentleman three years my senior whose existence I believe I mentioned in my last: not quite to marry him, as he wished, at least not right away, but to pool her pension benefits with his and retire with him to Florida, the Elysium of Social Security lovers. He'd proposed, not for the first time, after dinner on a certain Friday night last month. She'd reviewed, not for the first time, all the pros and cons, and some days later had said yes.

The short notice to me? To give herself ample time to chicken out before Going Public, and no time to do so having Gone; also to give me less time to talk her out of her resolve, which she hoped I cared enough for her not to try, lest I succeed. On the Tuesday they would fly from Baltimore down to Tampa for a "honeymoon" of real-estate prospecting and trying each other out as living-companions; assuming all went well, they'd be back in Maryland in August to wind up their affairs here and move south for keeps.

I didn't try to dissuade her, Dad. Was too entirely stunned to. After 35 years, half a day's notice! Yet she was quite right: Ms. Pond (dear God, God, have You no shame?) had all the skills, knew the office pretty well, was not disagreeable to work with; the rest there was no replacing, however long the notice. But (I wondered silently, terrifically) what about 11 R?

Good as her word, she came in on the Monday. Bon voyage gifts were laid on, jokes made about Florida, about septuagenarian lovers. Embraces, tears, laughter. Polly looked fine. Her friend was in good health, a gentleman, well enough off; they would be all right. How I envied them! She wished me the best; half her life was in that office; we'd done remarkable things together. She paused. She didn't believe history really repeated itself. There were echoes, of course, if you listened for them, but the future—what there was of it for people our age—was new, and lay ahead, not behind us. All very well, I thought; yet what about. . .

But as if by tacit agreement, no allusion whatever was made to. . .

And so Tuesday the 17th came and went in thunderous silence, as if Polly's flight laid an antisonic boom along the Eastern Shore. From 9 to 5, whenever Ms. Pond was in the office, I managed to drop things: my pen, my iced-coffee spoon; she must think me senile. But they were gracefully and soundlessly retrieved, a young woman picking up after an old codger with a sudden unquenchable thirst for iced coffee and a queer predilection for staring out the window at a certain oyster-shell pile.

Nothing—unless indeed opposites, negatives, count, in which case perhaps the entire absence of Polly Lake, and *a fortiori* of her etc., might betoken at the least my *loss* of the pending contest over Harrison's will, and at the worst. . . Nonsense: 11 R *didn't happen,* not on PLF Day or the next, or the next, by when in my frustration I was not fit society. For if time is not circling 'round, then 8 and 10 R, Jane's return to me in the evening of our lives, that wondrous *O* out by Red Nun 20. . .portend *nothing.* My inchoate vision on the New Bridge was a delusion, and Now *will* be Tomorrow and Tomorrow: empty.

I missed Polly. There was no Jane. I was a fool.

At half past three yesterday I left the office, saying truly I felt ill and meant to rest up in the country till Monday. The afternoon was airless; I'd left my car back at the cottage: I motored *O.J.* out from Slip #2 and downriver to its Todds Point dock. As I left the Howell Point day beacon to starboard, I saw the *Original Floating Theatre II* chugging out of the Tred Avon into the Choptank, en route from Oxford to Cambridge for the weekend (unlike the original *Original,* the replica is self-propelled). I kept my eyes on it, not to glimpse a certain red buoy to port, the sight of which just then would have undone me. Docked, I took a swim (no sea nettles yet) and lingered on deck for cocktails; even made dinner aboard, to put off entering this cottage too crowded with ghosts. Over the last of the wine, by the light of citronella candles in the cockpit (but there are no mosquitoes yet either, to speak of), I read the *Evening Sun* and wondered how the prospecting was in Florida.

The phone fetched me in just after dusk, when the swifts had given way to the swallows and the swallows to the bats. It's me, she said: Jane.

I replied: I resist the obvious reply.

What? O.

Say that again, please.

What? She was in Dorset Heights. Might she stop by at the office tomorrow?

She didn't sound *entirely* official. I took a breath, and a chance. Here I am at the cottage, I said: why not make Tomorrow Now?

She couldn't, possibly, much as she'd like to see the place again. She had a dozen things to do before bedtime. Didn't I have a minute tomorrow?

Another chance: I'm in Baltimore tomorrow till three, I lied; then I plan to drive straight back here for the weekend. Will you meet me here at six for dinner, or shall I pick you up and fetch you out? Grilled rockfish with fennel and rémoulade, a house specialty.

She hesitated; my heart and history likewise.

Well. . .okay. She'd drive out. Make it six-thirty? Bye.

No matter that her hesitation, I was quite confident, had to do with the logistics of her business day and not the implications of revisiting me *in situ* where the world began. She was coming!

Is coming, Dad, and your antique son is going bananas in anticipation. Since breakfast I've been at it, a superannuated Jay Gatsby awaiting his Daisy's visit: the maid fetched in to reclean the place she cleaned only Tuesday, the gardener to trim the beds he wasn't to bother with till Thursday next and prune every dead blossom from the tea roses and climbers. *Osborn Jones* cleaned out, swabbed down, and Bristol fashion, just in case. Anchovy paste, chervil, and capers at the ready for the sauce, fennel and lemon and brandy for the fish. No Pouilly-Fuissé available, alas, but a perfectly okay little Chablis from of all places western Maryland, and champagne in the fridge just in case. Roses mixed with cuttings from the last of the azaleas on the screened porch, in the living room, in the bedroom. Fresh sheets, of course, just etc. Everybody out by four; an anxious eye on the thunderheads piling up across the Bay, where I'm supposed to be returning from Baltimore; nothing further to be done but wait and keep some hold on my heart. Hence this letter.

But the telephone! Half a dozen times it's rung already, the last two since the maid left (who loyally reported me not at home), and I can't answer lest I betray my childish fib. It's Jane, canceling our date at Lord Tarzan's jealous insistence. It's the Muse of History, calling to explain what happened to 11 R. It's Jane, wondering whether I'm bespoken for the *rest* of the weekend. It's you, suggesting I just phone you instead of writing these asinine letters. It's Jane.

If it rings again, I'll not be able not to answer. How goes it with you, Dad? And did you ever, even at *twenty*-nine, have these Scott Fitzgerald moments, these—

Excuse me: the phone.

T.

T: *Jacob Horner to Jacob Horner*. Der Wiedertraum *under way*.

6/19/69

To: Jacob Horner, Remobilization Farm, Fort Erie, Ontario, Canada
From: Jacob Horner, Remobilization Farm, Fort Erie, Ontario, Canada

To Pier Angeli, Charles Coburn, Edgar Degas, James I, Wallis Warfield Simpson Windsor: happy birthday. Emperor Maximilian of Mexico has been executed by the Juárez party. Israeli warplanes used napalm today on Jordanian-Iraqi artillery positions while police battled students in Ann Arbor. Representatives of seven northeastern American colonies are meeting in Albany with sachems of the Six Nations to plan campaigns against New France. Ethel and Julius Rosenberg have been electrocuted at Sing Sing, and Texas has been annexed by the Union. The U.S.S. *Kearsarge* has defeated the C.S.S. *Alabama* off Cherbourg. The Duke of Wellington and Benjamin Constant are dining in Paris with Mme de Staël in celebration of yesterday's Allied victory at Waterloo: it is Day 97 of the Hundred Days.

And your Drama, *Der Wiedertraum,* is under way. Starring "Saint Joseph" as Joe Morgan, "Bibi" as Rennie Morgan, and "yourself," in a sense, as the Interloping Jacob Horner. Reluctant cameo appearances by the Doctor as Himself. Also featuring "Pocahontas" as the Sexually Exploited High School English Teacher Peggy Rankin (a bit of miscasting) and "M. Casteene" as President Schott of Wicomico Teachers College. With a supporting cast of dozens: draft refugees and their girl friends—those willing to regroom themselves—in the role of Wicomico College freshmen of 1953; the patients as the Patients. Still wanting are actresses for the bit parts of Mrs. Dockey, the Mannish

401

Head Nurse, and Shirley Stickles, Dr. Schott's Waspish Secretary, who misinformed you as to the date of your Job Interview in 1953 and would not acknowledge her error when you Presented yourself in her office on July 20, Petrarch's birthday and a day early. Ideal roles, either of those, for Pocahontas; but she demands a bigger piece of the action.

Produced by Saint Joe. Directed, more or less, by Casteene. Increasingly frowned upon by the Doctor, who fears things will get out of hand. Followed with intermittent interest and filmed in part by Mr. Reg Prinz for possible incorporation into his film in progress, which, it turns out, is not entirely about the War of 1812. Script adapted from the novel adapted from your Scriptotherapeutic narrative adapted from the events leading to Rennie Morgan's death from aspiration of vomitus in course of illicit surgical abortion October 25, 1953. Road not to end that way this time, on Producer's orders, or else.

There is no rush to fill the vacant roles, inasmuch as your Drama, like soap opera, is being reenacted in real time. Hence Prinz's and Ambrose Mensch's interest, depite the cast's including Mensch's ex-mistress and ex-wife and Prinz's current mistress. On June 1, Trinity Sunday, as the Fenians began their invasion of Ontario from Black Rock and Captain Lawrence aboard the *Chesapeake* enjoined his crew not to give up the ship and President Madison read his 2nd War Message to the U.S. Congress, the Doctor once again prescribed in the Progress and Advice Room that you Enter the Teaching Profession as therapy for your Seizures of Immobility.

"There must be a rigid discipline," he quoted himself from the script, *"or else it will be merely an occupation, not an occupational therapy. There must be a body of laws . . . Tell them you will teach grammar. English grammar. . . You will teach prescriptive grammar.* Now really, Horner: is that your Idea of Plausible Dialogue?"

The next scene will not occur until July 19, a full month hence, when Generalissimo Franco will take Cádiz, Cordova, Granada, Huelva, and Seville while the German army begins its retreat from Belgium and you Leave Baltimore for the Eastern Shore to Look for a Room in Wicomico and Prepare yourself for the Interview which you Innocently Believe to be scheduled for the following day.

Meanwhile, things have not been standing still at the Remobilization Farm. How Drive from Baltimore next month across the Chesapeake to Wicomico without leaving Ontario? Why, by magicking the P & A Room from the one into the other, as the wizards of Stratford magic a bare arena stage into Windsor Castle or Prospero's Island. And how Reenter the Teaching Profession while in residential therapy? Why, by mobilizing the Farm into the Niagara Frontier Underground University! The dropouts—a touch homesick, it may be—had proposed to Saint Joe a free school: he is obliging them, in his capacity as U.U.'s unofficial chancellor and history department, with seminars in U.S. Hawkery from 1812 to the present; in the 19th-Century American Counterexpansionists; in the Role of Upper Canada as a Haven for

Loyalists, Escaped Slaves, Secessionists, Indians, Conscientious Objectors, and Other Refugees from U.S. Violence. Casteene is conducting private tutorials in something called the Game of Governments. Tombo X is teaching karate. And to mollify the geriatrics, who have pressed for straightforward continuing education in the manner of their beloved Chautauqua Institution, you yourself are Offering "far-in" counter-countercultural drills in Prescriptive Grammar, or Repressive English. Restrictive clauses. Close punctuation. The Wave of the Past.

And "Rennie Morgan"—as Bibi/Bea Golden/Jeannine Mack now calls herself even offstage, as it were—in her new capacity as U.U.'s faculty of drama, is producing a small theatrical of her own, a replay-within-the-replay: some sort of "radical minstrel show" inspired by her tidewater Maryland connections, by Mr. Prinz's unexplained wish to include some showboat footage in his film, and by her desire to demonstrate to her lover that she is possessed of an awakening social consciousness. You and Morgan are to play in blackface Bones and Tambo, respectively, the End Men. The Doctor (*pace* Jean Genet) is to be coaxed into whiteface to take the part of Mister Interlocutor. Tombo X will perform poorly on both the tambourine and the bones, to demonstrate that he has no sense of rhythm whatever, either natural or acquired. Casteene will do a series of impersonations. Pocahontas, you Suppose, will sing "Indian Love Call." And "Rennie" will play "Bea Golden" playing "the Mary Pickford of the Chesapeake" as on Captain James Adams's old floating theater. Performance scheduled for tomorrow night, or the one after, to coincide with the Sun's entry into Cancer (and the birthdays of Errol Flynn and Jacques Offenbach, and the Black Hole of Calcutta atrocity, and Lord Byron's first meeting Mme de Staël at Lady Jersey's salon in London, and the Tennis Court Oath, and the U.S.A.'s adoption of the Great Seal, and West Virginia's admission into the Union). You have Suggested it be called *A Midsummer Night's Mare*.

You Do Not Quite Understand what's going on. You Suspect that in a sense you Are its Focus—read Target—yet at the same time but a Minor Figure in some larger design. You Are Not At All Sure what Reg Prinz is up to, or Casteene—who, it now seems certain, arranged Morgan's coming here, and possibly prompted his challenge to you. Did Casteene also arrange the appearance last Friday—from Maryland, on the arm of Ambrose Mensch!—of "Lady Amherst," who as "Lady Russex" came here two years ago for an abortion? Why did that same lady seem both astonished to see him and not quite convinced that she *was* seeing him? Did Mensch really not know that his ex-wife is a patient here? He seems to suspect Prinz of what you Suspect Casteene of!

Hum.

To carry Implausible Coincidence down from the stars to the spear carriers: it turns out that one Merry Bernstein, whose hippie friends brought her in from Chautauqua last month hallucinating and raving, her backside inflamed with what looks to have been a poisonous snakebite, perhaps a copperhead's, is our Bibi's stepdaughter! More exactly, the daughter of Bea Golden's second husband, one Mr. Bernstein.

Did you Mention that this same Ms. Bernstein (still recuperating, and keeping mum on the nature of her injury) is said by her companions to have been Making It in Lily Dale with that very odd duck, your former night-school student and later fellow patient Jerome Bray? The mere mention of whose name now sends her into hysteria? Did you Mention that his name got mentioned as pilot of the Chautauqua Lake excursion boat that Mr. Prinz chartered two nights ago for the film company's cast party? And that at this same party Bray is reported to have pursued our Bibi so ardently as to quite frighten her, provoke her other suitor's jealousy (you Mean Mensch, whom you Described as Lady Amherst's companion?) and her lover Prinz's mild amusement, and neglect his piloting duties to the point of being cashiered at the cruise's end? And that Pocahontas, aboard this same vessel, upon this same occasion, did flirt concurrently with both Prinz and this same Bray, presumably to rouse her ex-husband's ire? And that the report of this same flirtation has aroused instead, or as well, and altogether unexpectedly, *your Own Jealousy,* for reasons you Have Not Yet Dared to Begin to Examine? And finally, that the only copperheads *you* ever Heard Of during the Farm's residency in the Lily Dale–Chautauqua area were the 19th-Century advocates of a negotiated peace with the Confederacy?

Clearly, Jacob Horner, what you are Involved in is no ordinary soap opera: it is Bayreuth by Lever Brothers; it is Procter & Gamble's production of the Bathtub Ring.

But never mind the Big Picture, which you will likely Never See; or which, if it exists at all, may be like those messages spelled out at halftime in U.S. college football matches by marching undergraduates: less intelligent, valuable, and significant than its constituent units. The movie people have dispersed, to reassemble in Maryland next week. Mensch and Lady Amherst have gone with them. Bibi will leave to rejoin the company (against the Doctor's orders: how his authority is shrunk!) after tomorrow's, or Saturday's, minstrel show, flying back as necessary for her therapy sessions and her role in *Der Wiedertraum.* Casteene appears, disappears, reappears as always, often taking Pocahontas with him in some secretarial capacity. (You *are* Jealous. Why are you Jealous?) Even Merry Bernstein, now that she can sit and walk almost normally, speaks of lighting out with her friends to, like, Vancouver? As far from Lily Dale as possible. For dramaturgical purposes, in this corner of the Big Picture only you and Joe Morgan Remain. It is *his* motive, not Casteene's or Prinz's, that truly Concerns and truly Mystifies you.

But now that your Drama has taken prospective shape, Joe will not speak to you again on the subject of you and him and Rennie and the Fatal Fifties "until the time comes"—presumably July 21, when your

Wicomico Teachers College Interview, at which you First Met him, is to be reenacted. Or perhaps July 22, anniversary of (among other things) your First Meeting Rennie, with her husband, in your Newly Rented Room, whither they'd sought you out to congratulate you on your Appointment.

"Day Two of your Hundred Days," is what Joe said, and would say no more.

You have Counted and Recounted. Sure enough, the original drama was of some hundred days' duration: July 19–October 26 inclusive, from your Arrival in Wicomico at the Doctor's prescription to Seek Employment as a Teacher of Prescriptive Grammar, through the death and burial of Rennie Morgan and your Departure, with the Doctor, from everything. In fact it comes to 99 or 101 days, depending; but you are Not Inclined to Quibble with Morgan's history. The real redramatization, then, has *not* begun, after all: until Day One, next month, it dozes like a copperhead coiled upon a sunny rock. You Are still in the prologue to the dream. You Are still on Elba, at the turn of History's palindrome.

And like Stendhal in that other Hundred Days, you Postpone Suicide now out of Almost Selfless Curiosity. Nor have you, thus Distracted, Reexperienced reparalysis since your Relapse of April 2. What on earth, you Wonder, is Morgan up to? What in the world will happen next?

L: *A. B. Cook VI to the Author.* *Eagerly accepting the Author's invitation. The Cook/Burlingame lineage between Andrew Cook IV and himself. The Welland Canal Plot.*

A. B. Cook VI
"Barataria"
Bloodsworth Island, Md.

6/18/69

Dear Professor:

Letters? A novel-in-letters, you say? Six several stories intertwining to make a seventh? A *capital* notion, sir!

My secretary read me yours of the 15th over the telephone this morning when I called in from my lodge here on Bloodsworth Island (temporarily rechristened "Barataria" by the film company to whom I've lent the place, who are shooting a story involving Jean Lafitte). I hasten to accept, with pleasure, your invitation to play the role of the Author who solicits and organizes communications from and between his characters, and embroils himself in their imbroglios! To reorchestrate in some such fashion, in the late afternoon of our century if not of

405

our civilization, the preoccupations at once of the early Modernists and of the 18th-Century inventors of the noble English novel—that strikes me as a project worthy of the authors of *The Sot-Weed Factor,* and I shall be as happy to be your collaborator in this project as I was in that.

How is it, sir, your letter does not acknowledge that so fruitful collaboration? I must and shall attribute your omission (but how so, in correspondence between ourselves?) to my one stipulation, now as in the 1950's: that you keep my identity (and my aid) confidential and allegedly fictional. "Pseudo-anonymity," I don't have to tell you, is prerequisite to the work for which my laureateship is the agreeable "cover," and which—as the enclosed documents will amply demonstrate—I come by honestly. But enough: By way of immediate response to your inquiry concerning the history of the Cooks and Burlingames between the time of Lord Baltimore's Laureate of Maryland and myself, I attach copies of four long letters written in 1812 by my great-great-grandfather and namesake to his unborn child. But before I enlarge upon their mass, let me speak to another point in *your* letter:

From Lady Amherst, you say (whom I also am honored to be acquainted with, and who I understand will publish these enclosures in some history journal), you have the general conception of the "letters" project: an old-time epistolary novel, etc. From Todd Andrews of Cambridge, another old acquaintance of mine, you are borrowing "the tragic view of history"—and welcome to it, sir, for I respect but most decidedly do not share it! And one Jacob Horner (whom I'm happy to know only at second hand, through the gentleman he once so unconscionably victimized: the former director of the Maryland Historical Society and ex-president of Marshyhope State College) has suggested to you certain possibilities of letters in the alphabetical sense, as well as what you call "the anniversary view of history." (Whatever might that mean? Today, for example, is the anniversary of Napoleon's defeat at Waterloo by Wellington and Blücher in 1815; also of our Congress's declaration of the War of 1812. Moreover, my morning newspaper informs me that it is the birthdate of Lord Castlereagh, Britain's prime minister and foreign secretary during the period of both the Napoleonic and the "Second American" wars. A piquant coincidence of anniversaries—but so what? As there are only 365¼ days in the year, each must be the birthdate of some eight or nine millions of the presently living and hundreds of millions of the dead, and the anniversary of any number of the events that comprise human history. What is one to see with an historical "view" apparently as omnivalent—which is to say, *non*valent—as history itself?)

Well, that is your problem. Mine is what to contribute, for my part, to the design and theme of our enterprise, beyond the genealogical material I shall of course again gladly share with you. I have given the matter some thought this morning, and the fact is I believe I have exactly what we need! This July—exactly a month from today, in fact—Dorchester County commences a week-long tercentenary celebration, in which I shall take a small part in my capacity as laureate of the state. But my real interest in that anniversary (both my official and my deeper interest) is its anticipation of the more considerable one seven years hence: the 1976 U.S. Bicentennial, of which no one yet hears mention, but which will be on every American's mind—and all the media—before very long. *This* anniversary, the 200th of a revolution that much changed history, will coincide (and not coincidentally) with a revolution to revolutionize Revolution itself: what I propose, sir, as the grand theme of our book: The Second American Revolution!

The Second American Revolution! In a manner of speaking, it has been the theme of my family ever since the Treaty of Paris concluded the first in 1783. My parents devoted their lives to it, my grandparents and great-grandparents before them, as shall be shown. I have done likewise, and so I pray shall do my son—who is by way of being at once the most prodigiously gifted and the most prodigal revolutionary of our line. And, as the letters of my great-great-grandfather make plain, both the gifts and the prodigality antedate the War of Independence: he traces our revolutionary energies back at least as far as Henry Burlingame III, whom you characterize as the "cosmophilist" tutor of Ebenezer Cooke, first laureate of Maryland.

Andrew Burlingame Cook IV (whose birthday fortuitously coincides with the Republic's) wrote these four letters on the eve of the "Second War of Independence," as our ancestors called the War of 1812. It was the eve as well of his 36th birthday—i.e., the evening of his life's first half, as he himself phrases it, and the dawn of its second. Like Dante Alighieri and many another at this famous juncture, he found himself at spiritual, philosophical, even psychological sixes and sevens. He misdoubted the validity of his career thus far: He had been active in the *ménages* of Madame de Staël and Joel Barlow during the French Revolution and the Directorate; coming to America after 1800, he had involved himself with Aaron Burr's conspiracy and Tecumseh's Indian alliance, more out of antipathy for what he took to be his father's causes than out of real enmity toward the U.S. or sympathy for the Indians. At the time of these letters, about to become a father himself, Andrew Cook IV profoundly questions both the authenticity of his own motives and his appraisal of his father's, whom circumstances have precluded his knowing at all closely. With the aid of his remarkable wife, he researches the history of the family and discovers a striking pattern of filial rebellion: since the convergence of the Cooke and Burlingame lines—that is to say, since the child of Henry Burlingame III and Anna Cooke was named and raised as Andrew Cooke III after his father's disappearance (*per* the epilogue of our *Sot-Weed Factor* novel)—every firstborn son in the line has defined himself against what he takes to have been his absent father's objectives, and in so doing has allied himself, knowingly or otherwise, with his grandfather, whose name he also shares! Thus Andrew Cook IV, in aiding Tecumseh against the U.S., reenacted Andrew Cooke III's association with Pontiac in the

French and Indian War, thinking to spite his father Henry Burlingame IV as Andrew III had thought to spite *his* father, H.B. III, et cetera.

By 1812, however, Andrew is in the quandary aforementioned. Indeed, without giving over his admiration for his grandfather, he now believes himself to have been as mistaken about his father as he thinks his father to have been about *his* father! I leave it to his eloquent "prenatal" letters to set forth fully his historical investigations and psychological circumstances. He concludes with the resolve to devote the second half of his life to undoing his "wrongheaded" accomplishments in the first—presumably by endeavoring to prevent the very war he has been promoting, or (as he believes it too late now to forestall the declaration of which today is the anniversary) by doing what he can to prevent a decisive victory for either the British or the Americans, in the hope that a stalemate will check their territorial expansion on the North American continent and permit the establishment of an Indian Free State. His career thus bids to be in effect self-canceling, by his own acknowledgment, as the careers of his successive ancestors may be presumed to have been reciprocally canceling. It is his pious hope, in the fourth and final letter, that this program of self-refutation, together with the pattern he has exposed in the family history, will enable his unborn child—i.e., Henry or Henrietta Cook Burlingame V—to proceed undistracted by the spurious rebelliousness that has so dissipated the family's energies: that he or she may break the pattern and not defeat, but *best,* their father, by achieving the goals he can now hope only to take a few positive steps toward.

Dear colleague, esteemed collaborator, fellow toiler up the slopes of Mt. Parnassus: what a mighty irony here impends! My voice falters (I am dictating this by telephone, from notes, into my secretary's machine across the Bay, whence she will transcribe and send it off to you posthaste). Poor Cooks! Poor Burlingames! And poor suspense, I admit, to leave you thus hanging on their history's epistolary hook: Did my namesake's letters reach their addressee? Did "Henry or Henrietta" take to heart his heartfelt counsel? And Andrew himself: did he achieve his self-abnegatory aims? If so, by what revision of his revised program, since we know the outcome of the War of 1812?

Those earlier two questions I shall return to: they are the body of this letter, whose head nods so ready a yes to your invitation. The latter two I shall answer in detail in letters to come—five, by my estimate, though four would be a more appropriate number, to balance the four hereunto appended. The fact is, sir, my major literary effort over the past dozen years—that is to say, since I gave you my "Sot-Weed Factor Redivivus" material as the basis for your novel—has been the planning of a poetical epic of this Border State: a local version of Joel Barlow's great *Columbiad.* It was to portray the life and adventures of this child of the Republic, Andrew Cook IV, from their coincident birth in 1776, through the 1812 War, to Cook's disappearance in 1821. It was to be entitled *Marylandiad,* though its action was to range from Paris to

Canada to New Orleans and lose itself in the mists of St. Helena. It was to be complete and published in time for the Dorchester tercentenary or, failing that, at least the U.S. Bicentennial. . .

Alas, the practice of literature has, as you know, never been more than my avocation. The practice of history is my *métier* (I do not mean historiography!); my muse—who is *not* Clio—is too demanding to leave me time for dalliance with Calliope; I shall not write my *Marylandiad*. Instead, I reply in kind to your invitation by here inviting you to write it for me—incorporate it, if you like, into your untitled epistolary project! Thus my determination to supply you (in the form of letters, after his own example) with my researches into the balance of A.C. IV's life. I will follow them with a one-letter account of my own activities on behalf of the Second Revolution, and that with an *envoi* to my son Henry Burlingame VII, whose relation to me—you will by now have guessed— follows inexorably the classic Pattern.

Seven letters in all: you see how readily I adapt my old project to your new one!

But this ancient history lies in the future (Have you a timetable for our project? Are the dates and sequence of the several letters to be of any significance? Have you a Pattern of your own in mind?), beginning at this letter's end, when you shall commence the tale of Andrew Cook IV as told by himself. Meanwhile, in the most summary fashion, here is the line of his descendants from the end of his last letter to his child (dated May 14, 1812; what would your Jacob Horner make of this anniversary of King Henry IV's assassination, George Washington's opening of the first Constitutional Convention, the death of Mme de Staël's mother, Edward Jenner's discovery of vaccination, and the departure of the Lewis & Clark Expedition from St. Louis?) to the beginning of this my first letter to you:

My ancestor chose the wrong conjunction. A week into Gemini, just after he closed that long fourth letter, Andrée Castine Cook gave birth to opposite-sex twins, duly named Henry *and* Henrietta Cook Burlingame V. The old cosmophilist H.B. III must have smiled in his unknown grave! In the time-honored manner of our line, their father lingered on at Castines Hundred until he was assured of his wife's and children's well-being—then left at once (but not directly) for Paris, to try to assist Joel Barlow in the business he had lately done his best to obstruct: negotiation with Napoleon concerning the Berlin and Milan decrees.

He will not get there in time: unbeknownst to him, the emperor has already left St. Cloud to lead his army's ill-fated march into Russia; the Duc de Bassano, unable to stall Barlow further, has produced on May 11 the "Decree of St. Cloud," falsely dated April 28, *1811,* to "prove" that France had rescinded the Berlin and Milan decrees more than a year since, at Barlow's first request! The old poet is delighted, never mind the chicanery: the more so since on that same May 11 Prime

Minister Perceval, a staunch supporter of Britain's Orders in Council against American shipping, has been assassinated in the lobby of the House of Commons, and his successor Lord Castlereagh is known to be amenable to lifting those orders. Barlow has rushed the St. Cloud Decree across the Channel via the U.S.S. *Wasp;* on May 19 it has reached Lord Castlereagh. Surely the author of the *Columbiad* is about to score a brilliant diplomatic triumph: no reason now for Britain not to raise her embargo as France has done, and Madison not to revoke in turn his Non-Intercourse Act against Britain. The western war hawks have lost their only *casus belli* of interest to the eastern states. There will be no War of 1812!

But ah, the mails. Unaware of Barlow's coup, Madison has delivered on June 1 his Second War Message to Congress, emphasizing the issue of British impressment of U.S. seamen; today 157 years ago he signs the Declaration of War, but the British ministry will not hear of it until well after their tardy revocation (on June 23) of the Orders in Council. *Adieu,* Joel Barlow, who have but six months more to live and must spend them chasing Napoleon all over eastern Europe! *Au revoir,* Andrew Cook IV, chaser of wild geese, of whom we shall hear more!

For the next dozen years his good wife remains at Castines Hundred, raising her children. Twice during the first three of those years—that is, during the "Second War of Independence"—her husband returns (once without her knowing it), between his wartime adventures, not to be here chronicled. Andrée herself, once so politically active, seems to take no further interest in the Game of Governments. She is paid a single visit (in mid-September, 1813) by her friend and hero Tecumseh, who has fought so ably for the British along the Great Lakes that the question is no longer whether the U.S. will capture Canada, but whether the western states, so eager for the war, will become new territories of the Crown! Detroit has fallen; Fort Chicago has been massacred, Frenchtown, Fort Miami, Fort Mims. Tecumseh has more than regained the prestige lost at Tippecanoe: he is the undisputed leader of a confederacy that now includes the southern Creeks.

But he confides to "Star-of-the-Lake" that he has ceased to believe in his mission. His Indians are good fighters but not good soldiers; with British encouragement, their ferocity against captured troops and civilians has redoubled; he cannot restrain them. The American retaliation has already begun, and is plainly exterminative. Forts Wayne and Meigs and Stephenson did *not* fall, and they should have; the Creeks cannot possibly withstand the army that Andrew Jackson is assembling against them; the British general Proctor, Tecumseh's immediate superior, is a coward and a beast. Most ominous of all, the American Commodore Perry has just defeated the British fleet on Lake Erie: the Long Knives will now control the Lakes, and who controls the Lakes controls the heart of the country.

It is to confirm rumors of this defeat, about which Proctor has lied to him, that Tecumseh has come secretly from Bois Blanc Island, his camp on the Detroit River, to the other end of Lake Erie; having confirmed them, he has stopped at Castines Hundred to say good-bye to his friend forever. His old enemy General Harrison is assembling an army of vengeful Kentucky riflemen on the Ohio shore of the lake; Perry's fleet will carry them unopposed to the Detroit river forts. Somewhere thereabouts, and soon, the decisive battle will be fought. He Tecumseh is not sanguine of its issue; in any case, he knows—though he cannot say how he knows—that he will not survive it, and that the cause of Indian confederacy will not survive him.

But this is not Tecumseh's history, any more than it is Andrew Cook's (who, we shall learn in another letter, is observing this fateful tête-à-tête from a place of concealment on the grounds of Castines Hundred). During the British invasion of Chesapeake Bay late the next summer—specifically, during the bombardment of Fort McHenry in Baltimore following the burning of Washington—my great-great-grandfather will officially die. The news will reach Andrée (still in mourning for Tecumseh) a week or so later—along with the rumor that her husband has merely faked his death in order to mislead certain authorities; has changed identities and set out for New Orleans, the next destination of the British fleet. The "widow" considers the news, the rumor, his long silence, her familiar position. After the destruction of Jean Lafitte's Baratarian stronghold by the American navy that same September and the American victory at New Orleans the following January—the war of course is over by then, but the mails, the mails!—the expected letter arrives at Castines Hundred, purportedly from her husband but in a fairly suspicious hand, as if penned with difficulty by either a wounded Andrew IV or a moderately artful forger: She is to join him at once in Mobile to help reorganize the surviving Creeks and Negroes enlisted by the British and now abandoned by them. She is to bring the twins. . .

Andrée makes the painful choice: she resolves to disbelieve, and holds fast to that resolve for the rest of her recorded life, though four more "posthumous" letters follow this first over the next several years, comprising the body of my *Marylandiad*. She remains a widow; the twins grow up fatherless. Napoleon abdicates, is exiled to Elba, returns for the Hundred Days, is defeated at Waterloo, surrenders aboard H.M.S. *Bellerophon,* appeals to the prince regent for a passport to America, and is transported instead to St. Helena by Admiral Cockburn, the erstwhile scourge of the Chesapeake. The Rush-Bagot Treaty neutralizes the Great Lakes forever. Mme de Staël dies in Paris of liver and hydro-thoracic complaints, George III at Windsor of intermittent hematuria, inguinal hernia, hemorrhoids, bedsores, and terminal diarrhea; the prince regent becomes George IV. Henry Clay's Missouri Compromise prohibits slavery in all the new territories except Missouri which open up west of the Mississippi; the Indians are resettled and re-resettled. The state of Indiana considers naming its new capital city Tecumseh

411

after their late great adversary, but decides on Indianapolis instead. Schemes are concocted to spirit Napoleon from his second exile to New Orleans, to Champ d'Asile in the Gulf of Mexico, to the Eastern Shore of Maryland.

The last letter from "Andrew Cook IV" reaches Castines Hundred in the winter of 1821. Andrée is not to believe that the emperor has actually died on St. Helena, any more than that the writer of the letter actually died in Baltimore in 1814: Yours Truly and his associate Jean Lafitte have successfully rescued Napoleon from that rock, like a latter-day Perseus his Andromeda; they are hiding out in the Maryland marshes, planning together the Second Revolution; he will shortly appear at Castines Hundred to fetch her and the twins.

Brazil declares its independence from Portugal, Mexico from Spain; Simón Bolívar (of whom more later) leads the revolutions in Venezuela, Colombia, Ecuador, Peru. The "Chesapeake Negroes" are left chillily in Nova Scotia; those from the Gulf Coast are urged to rejoin their American masters; Tecumseh's Indians are abandoned to their own devices. The aging Marquis de Lafayette returns to visit each of the 24 United States. In May of 1825, on their 13th birthday, Andrée discloses to the twins the four letters their father wrote to them in 1812 (those here appended). She is herself 36 now, her husband's age then. Carefully she reviews for the children her life with their father, her genealogical researches, his fervent hopes for them.

Then, having discharged her duty to his memory and been to that point a model mother to their children, she adds her personal wish: that they will take as their example neither the Cooks nor the Burlingames nor herself, but the idle, pacific Barons and Baronesses Castine, indifferent to History and everything else except each other and their country pleasures. She goes further: lays a deep curse upon marriage, parenthood, the Anglo-Saxon race, and the United States of America. She goes further yet: renames herself Madocawanda the Tarratine, exchanges her silks and cottons for beads and buckskins, kisses the twins a fierce farewell, and disappears into western Canada! There will be rumors of her riding with Black Hawk in Wisconsin in 1832, a sort of middle-aged Penthesilea, when the Sac and Fox Indians are driven west across the Mississippi. It will even be reported that among the Oglala Sioux, during Crazy Horse's vain war to break up the reservation system in 1876, is a ferocious old squaw named Madocawanda who delights in removing the penises of wounded U.S. Cavalrymen. Andrée Castine at that time would have been 87! But we need not identify "Star-of-the-Lake" with these shadowy avatars.

And the twins? They kept company with each other, raised by the Baron and Baroness Castine much in the manner that their ancestors Ebenezer and Anna Cooke had been raised in St. Giles in the Fields (per your account in our *Sot-Weed Factor*)—only without the radical stimulation of a tutor like Henry Burlingame III. Opposite-sex twins, the psychologists tell us, tend to regression. And why not? They were

412

not lonely in the womb. Expelled from that Paradise, they *know* what Aristophanes only fancied: that we are but the fallen halves of a once seamless whole, searching in vain for our lost moiety. They have little need of speech, but invent their own languages; they have less need of others. Their eventual lovers will seem siblings, as their siblings had seemed lovers. Henry V is the only Burlingame of whose genital problems (and their traditional oversolution) we have no report; of Henrietta's sexual life, too, we know next to nothing. Neither married; they lived together until their 49th year in a kind of travesty of Andrée's advice, apparently uninterested in anyone except each other and in anything except, mildly, literature, the great American flowering of which was at hand.

In 1827, their 16th year, they received a letter from one "Ebenezer Burling" of Richmond, Virginia, delivered to Castines Hundred via the newly opened Erie Canal. *With your dear mother,* it began, *has gone my soul, my name. . .* (A true Burlingamish pun there, involving *mon âme* and the truncation of *Burlingame:* we remember A.C. IV's long tenure in France, and the twins' bilinguality.) He is their father, the letter goes on to declare, now past 50 and constrained by circumstances to this evocative *nom de guerre.* He understands and sympathizes with their mother's defection; he hopes they will permit him, belatedly, to take her place and assume his own, as he has sought to do since 1815. He is about to leave Richmond for Norfolk with a gifted young poet-friend, whom he is helping to escape certain disagreeable circumstances and on whom therefore he has bestowed another of his own amusing aliases, "Henri le Rennet": a mixed pun on "Henry the Reborn" and "Henry the Reemptied" or "cleaned-out" (The young fellow is destitute; he has written some admirable verses about Tamerlane; he believes that the story of "Consuelo del Consulado" needs reworking, and proposes for example that her poisoned snuffbox be changed to a poisoned pen; he is headed for Boston to try his luck as an editor and writer; his actual name is Edgar Poe). He Burling himself is en route to Baltimore, to try whether what he learned about steam propulsion from Toot Fulton many years ago can be applied to railways. He hopes his children will join him there and encloses money for their journey, along with a separate sum for the Baron Castine in partial remuneration of the expense of their upbringing. He also encloses, by way of proof of his identity, a pocketwatch which he claims was similarly and belatedly given him by his own father: a silver Breguet with "barleycorn" engine-turning on the case, steel moon hands, and a white enameled face with the seconds dial offset at the VII, the maker's name engraved in secret cursive under the XII, and the monogram *HB* similarly scribed before the appropriate numeral IV. I have this watch before me as I speak.

The baron advises them to demand an interview at Castines Hundred, but the twins seem as attracted by the prospect of travel as by the possibility that the letter is authentic. They insist; their guardian shrugs his shoulders and returns to his bucolic pursuits. They set out

413

for Baltimore—and there they live, in obscure circumstances and with much travel intermixed, until the Civil War.

Of the fate of "Ebenezer Burling" and their connection with him, there is no record (the Baltimore & Ohio Railroad opened on Andrew IV's birthday in 1828, horse-drawn); the source of their income is unknown. From references in later letters—exchanged during the twins' separation by the Civil War—one infers that there was much coming and going between Baltimore and Washington, Baltimore and Boston, Baltimore and Buffalo. They remember having encouraged "E.B.'s" young poet-friend, during his own residency in their city (1831–35), to give up alcohol and poetry for short prose tales readable at a single sitting, and not to hesitate to marry his 13-year-old cousin. On the other hand, having read the young novelist Walt Whitman's maiden effort *(Franklin Evans, or, the Inebriate),* they urged its author to switch to verse. Perhaps presumptuously, they take credit for passing on to Whitman Henry Burlingame III's "cosmophilism"; Henry V opines, however, that the scandalous pansexualism of *Leaves of Grass* is entirely rhetorical, the author being in fact virtually celibate. With Longfellow they could do nothing, beyond suggesting that Edgar charge him with plagiarism; no more could they with Mrs. Stowe. With Thoreau, Hawthorne, Melville, and Emerson they were content, except as the latter two strayed into verse. None could be persuaded to make literature out of their father's Algerian adventure or their mother's reenactment, in reverse, of the story of her ancestor Madocawanda the Tarratine. (They did not live to groan at Longfellow's versification of it in 1871 as "The Student's Second Tale" in Part Second of his tiresome *Tales of a Wayside Inn:*

> . . .a fatal letter wings its way
> Across the sea, like a bird of prey. . .
> Lo! The young Baron of St. Castine,
> Swift as the wind is, and as wild,
> Has married a dusky Tarratine,
> Has married Madocawando's child!

et cetera.)

On October 24, 1861, when the first transcontinental telegraph message links sea to shining sea and replaces the Pony Express, Henrietta Burlingame, 49, gives birth to my grandfather, Andrew Burlingame Cook V. The father is unknown: it is not necessarily Henrietta's brother. The perfectly ambiguous facts are that just nine months earlier the twins had either quarreled or pretended to quarrel seriously for the first time in their lives—not, ostensibly, over some transgression of the former limits of their intimacy or the election of Abraham Lincoln and the subsequent secession of the Southern states, but over the merits of Karl Marx's thesis (in his essay *The 18th Brumaire and the Court of Louis Napoleon)* that great events and personages in history tend to occur twice, the first time as tragedy, the second time as

414

farce—and separated. Henry (who agreed with the second proposition but not the first, given the multiple repetitions in their own genealogy) moved to Washington; Henrietta (who believed that the recurrences were as often tragic as the originals, e.g., Tecumseh's reenactment of Pontiac's conspiracy) to the Eastern Shore, where in April—as Baltimoreans reenacted in 1861 their bloody riots of 1812—she found herself unambiguously three months pregnant, and remained in seclusion until her child was born.

Once the separation is effected, their letters become entirely fond, insofar as one can decipher their private coinages and allusions and sort out reciprocal ironies. In addition to the literary reminiscences already mentioned, they chaffingly criticize each other's positions vis-à-vis the war so long ago predicted in Joel Barlow's *Columbiad;* also vis-à-vis their father's prenatal letters to them. Neither twin has anything to do with the fighting. Henry declares or pretends to declare for the Union, Henrietta for the Confederacy. Henry's reading of their father's letters is that they were disingenuous: that Andrew IV exhorted them not to rebel against him exactly in order to provoke their rebellion—i.e., to lead them to work *against* the sort of stalemate he "pretended to hope for in the 1812 War" and *for* "the Manifest Destiny he actually believed in." Henrietta in her turn maintains that their father's exhortation was perfectly sincere.

Of course it is quite possible that the twins were secretly in league. They are together in New York City at the time of the great draft riots of July 1863, in which 100 people are killed; they are together in Ford's Theater in April 1865, when Lincoln is assassinated by the erratic son of their old friends the Booths of Baltimore. The Union is preserved, however sorely; the slaves are emancipated, if not exactly free. The Dominion of Canada is about to be established; the first U.S. postcard will soon be issued. Where are Henry and Henrietta?

Why, they are once more in their true womb, Castines Hundred. There the new baron and baroness have been killed in an unfortunate carriage accident, leaving a baby son named Henri Castine IV (they have their own Pattern, of no concern to us here). The twins sell their Baltimore property and die to the world; not even literature much engages them now. They raise the young cousins with benign indifference. Andrew V displays a precocious interest in the family history; they neither foster nor discourage it. He is shown the "1812 letters" of his grandsire and namesake, the other documents of the family, his great-grandfather's pocketwatch; but his insistent questions—especially concerning his parents' own activities (he does not shy from referring to the twins thus)—are answered with a smile, a shrug, an equivocation.

The boy decides, for example, that their obscure movements during the war were a cover for certain exploits in the Great Lakes region: the establishment (and/or exposure) of the Cleveland–Cincinnati relay of the Confederacy's Copperhead espionage system; the institution (and/or disruption) of a *white* Underground Railroad to

Canada for Confederate agents and escapees from Union prison camps. Whose scheme was it, if not theirs, to ship bales of Canadian wool contaminated with yellow-fever bacilli to all U.S. Great Lakes ports, by way of avenging the bacteriological warfare waged against Pontiac's Indians a century before? And who masterminded the Fenian invasion of Fort Erie by New York Irish "bog trotters" in 1866, he wanted to know, just a year after the Burlingames' official return to Castines Hundred? The Irish Revolutionary Brotherhood's objective might have been to seize and hold the Welland Canal until Britain granted independence to Ireland; but was it not the twins' idea to provoke another U.S.-Canadian war (which of course the British and the ruined Confederacy would welcome) while the wounds of the Civil War were still open? Or contrariwise (what actually happened) to bind the reluctant Canadian provinces, as disinclined to confederation as were Tecumseh's Indians, into a Dominion of Canada united against U.S. aggression?

"You are more Burlingame than we are," his parents contentedly reply. They live into their eighties, the first Cooks or Burlingames to achieve longevity. By the time of their death in 1898, the son of their middle age will be nearing the classical midpoint of his own life (well past its actual midpoint in his case); he will have married an educated Tuscarora Indian from Buffalo, sired children of his own—first among them my father, Henry Burlingame VI—and already cut his revolutionary teeth in the Canadian Northwest Rebellion of '85, the Chicago Haymarket Riot, and the Carnegie and Pullman labor-union battles.

Unlike his parents, Andrew V is overtly and intensely political, by his own declaration first a socialist and then (when the analogy between strikebreaking robber barons and imperialist industrial nation-states persuades him that a "rearrangement of markets" by cataclysmic war is in the offing) an anarchist, the first in the family since his grandfather's French-Revolutionary youth. He decides that the whole family tree, Cooks and Burlingames alike, has been as it were attending to the wrong dog's bark: it is not this or that government that is the enemy, except to this or that other government: it is *government*—on any scale larger than tribal, with any powers or functions beyond the most modest defensive and regulatory. More regressive than Henry and Henrietta together, he takes as his heroes Julian the Apostate, Philip II, the Luddite loom-breakers—all those who would undo the weave of history. Especially he admires Tecumseh and Pontiac, driven to confederate in the cause of anticonfederation. He applauds the Cuban revolutions against Spain, the war of the Boer republics against Britain, the Philippine insurgency, the Russian, Mexican, and Chinese revolutions, the Boxer Rebellion—anything that either resists enlargement or divides what is by his lights too large already; redistributes more equitably, decentralizes, or promises to do so.

Of his 20th-century activities—other than quarreling with Eugene Debs and defending Leon Czolgosz (the assassin of President McKinley in Buffalo)—little is known until the "rearrangement of markets" occurred in 1914–18. He seems to have been involved in the fast-growing electrical communications industry and to have had little interest in literature: "Marconi's transmission of the letter *S* across the Atlantic by wireless today," he told his wife on December 12, 1901, "is more important than Henry James's publication of *The Sacred Fount.*" (My grandmother agreed; she preferred H.J.'s short stories.) He was a friend of Alexander Bell from nearby Brantford (named after the Mohawk Joseph Brant), and though he agreed with Mark Twain that the telephone is an instrument of Satan, he explored the possibilities of its misuse, along with the wireless's, in "the coming war."

Uncharacteristically for our line, he was no great traveler: to my knowledge he never visited Maryland, much less Europe; indeed, after the birth of my father during the Spanish-American War, Andrew V seems to have left Ontario only once, for Vera Cruz in the spring of 1914, in the mistaken hope that enough false messages might connect Pancho Villa's and Zapata's resistance in Mexico with Sun Yat-sen's revolution against the Manchu dynasty and the wars in the Balkan States, and bring about general political chaos in time for the Second International scheduled for Brussels in July. The mission failed; the general wish, of course and alas, was realized, just a month or two late.

Of his posture vis-à-vis the family, on the other hand, we know more, and of his end, if we accept provisionally my father's account. Distressing to report, Andrew V exercised his "liberation" from the Pattern by regressing, almost absolutely, to the vain ancestral dialectic! Like the Andrews and Henrys prior to 1812, the more he considers the family archives—especially the Letters of 1812 and those exchanged between the twins during the Civil War—the more he comes to believe that his parents were after all deplorably successful secret agents for the Union, pretending to be Copperheads. It is not only the ignorant of history, it seems, who are doomed to reenact it!

Indeed, the quick end to my grandfather's story, shortly thereafter, is itself a reenactment. Back at Castines Hundred in 1917 (when the U.S. and Canada become allies for the first time in their stormy history, though the old Yankee-Loyalist enmity is not dead, only sleeping, even today), he notes the anger of Ontario's Fenians at the execution of Patrick Pearse and Sir Roger Casement after the abortive Irish rising of the year before; he is thereby reminded of the I.R.B.'s attempt on the Welland Canal in 1866. Like the Fenians, but for different reasons, he declares himself indifferent to the World War, which has in his opinion nothing to do with ideology; he is much more interested in the revolution against the czar, and, in the (somewhat self-contradictory) name of International Anarchy, he associates himself with a Bolshevik plot to blow up the Welland Canal. It is the only ship channel around Niagara Falls, and is thus indispensable to the movement of matériel and manufactures from the Great Lakes to the Atlantic; its obstruction will gravely hamper the supply of the American and Canadian

Expeditionary Forces in Europe. But lest the blame be placed on (or credit claimed by) German saboteurs, as was the case in the Black Tom explosion in Jersey City, he will broadcast by wireless from the ruined locks his solidarity with the bombers of the San Francisco Preparedness Day Parade on July 22, 1916, and call for a Second Revolution in North America, against economic royalism.

There, the phrase is uttered: a Second American Revolution, quite a different matter from the "Second War of Independence" in 1812. Uttering it was to be my grandfather's chief accomplishment. His associates were fellow anarchists and Bolsheviks from both Canada and the U.S., together with assorted Fenians, Quebec Librists, and sympathetic Germans from Wisconsin and western Ontario: two dozen in all, plus—significantly for that date—a precocious young Iroquois nationalist from the Tuscarora reservation on Grand Island, Andrew's wife Kyuhaha's militant brother *(Kyuhaha* is approximate Iroquoian for "unfinished business"). This fellow's name was Gadfly Junior; he claimed to be the son of a Tuscarora chief named Gadfly Bray and the brother-in-law of Charles Joseph Bonaparte (Betsy Patterson's grandson and, briefly, Teddy Roosevelt's Indian commissioner). Like many of his Mohawk brothers, this Gadfly Junior was a specialist in high steelwork; on the strength of this experience (and a stint in the Wyoming Valley anthracite mines, and a general feistiness), he appointed himself chief of demolition.

The old canal had 25 lift locks: the plan was to dynamite them in quick succession with wireless detonators fashioned by my grandfather. Twenty-five bundles of dynamite were assembled, each fitted with a small wireless receiver tuned to ignite a blasting cap upon receipt of the international Morse code signal for a particular letter of the alphabet; an alternative signal, common to all, could be used to detonate them simultaneously if time was short. No ideological slogan known to the conspirators was alphabetically various enough to do the job; their programmes were anyhow too heterogeneous for agreement: they settled on the standard typewriter-testing sentence, stripped of its redundant characters—THE QUICK BROWN FX JMPD V LAZY G— and reserved as the common signal the only letter missing therefrom, the one hallowed by Marconi seventeen years before and by James Joyce as the first in the scandalous novel he'd just begun serializing in *The Little Review*. On the night of September 26 (American Indian Day, Gadfly Junior would have been gratified to know, though it's also the anniversary of General McArthur's recapture of Detroit from Tecumseh's warriors in 1813) the saboteurs in two trucks and a car rendezvoused at the little town of Port Robinson, the midpoint of the canal, and spread out along the 25 miles of its length from Port Colborne on Lake Erie to St. Catherines on Lake Ontario, each to his assigned lock with his charge of explosives. All were to be in place by sunrise, when—just as the British army was breaking the Hindenburg line in the final offensive of the war—my grandfather would transmit on his wireless key the fateful sentence.

I believe that I have neglected to mention that I myself had been born that year, out of wedlock, to my precocious parents: my father, 19, had "supped ere the priest said grace" with the current flower of the Castines, his *cousine* Andrée III. In this return nearly to the center of the family gene-pool—which A.C. V had commendably eschewed for the health of the line, given the particular consanguinity of his own parents—Henry Cook Burlingame VI betrays (I had better say *affirms;* he made no secret of it) his affinity for his namesakes Henry and Henrietta. He does not despise his father (who, we remember, apparently put by all revolutionary activities between 1898 and 1918 to raise him, except for the Vera Cruz expedition of 1914); indeed he admires him. . .as a cunning double agent dedicated to subverting the cause he officially espouses!

In short, we are back to the Pattern, with a vengeance, and the more distressingly in that my father was *not* a student of the family archives (it was Andrée, rather more of a scholar, who taught him how to overcome the genital shortfall of the Burlingames; I was conceived in their virgin seminar on that subject in 1916). Altogether unaware that he is reviving the classical interpretation of Cooks by Burlingames, Burlingames by Cooks, my father maintains—at the time to my mother, later to me—that Andrew Cook V was all along a closet patriot, an operative of the Canadian Secret Service who infiltrated the saboteurs in order to thwart their designs on the Welland Canal, and succeeded at the expense of both his brother-in-law's life (Gadfly's) and his own.

"Your grandfather was an expert in wireless telegraphy," Dad once explained to me (I was 13; it was during our stint in the Blackwater Wildlife Refuge here in Dorchester County, where "Ranger Burlingame's" current cover was supervising CCC work during the depression): "It's suspicious enough that he altered the test sentence"—in which, as everyone knows, THE QUICK BROWN FX JMPS V LAZY *DG*, touching all 26 alphabetical bases in the process—"and it's unthinkable that he would reserve as the common detonator the first letter of the international wireless marine distress signal, especially to blow up a ship canal, and choose for its transmission the frequency of 125 kilocycles—the only frequency shared by both naval and merchant vessels at that time."

My father's Uncle Gadfly Junior had been his hero and closest friend; at the time of the canal plot Henry was old enough to be included in it, and had begged to share with Gadfly the riskiest assignment: mining the entrance locks at either end of the canal, where security was heaviest. Gadfly had the *G* at St. Catherines; my father wanted the Port Colborne *T*. But my grandfather forbade him, as a brand-new father himself, to place any of the explosives, and only reluctantly permitted him to stand watch over the transmitter at Port

Robinson while he himself mined Lock *N* nearby, at the center of the canal.

Andrew's target being closest at hand, he thought to reach it, plant his charge, and rejoin his son within an hour to await the dawn at the transmitter while the others were still being dropped off at one-mile intervals in both directions. Thirty minutes after their parting salute— "To the Second Revolution!" which meant different things to the several bombers—and before even my grandfather had slipped past the watchman and lockmaster at Port Robinson, all 25 charges went off together.

That is to say, there were three explosions: a tremendous one on the back road south from Port Robinson, where the truck carrying THE QUICK BROW group toward Port Colborne was about to discharge its first passenger (Comrade *W*) near Welland; a similarly tremendous one on the road north from Port Robinson, where the truck carrying FX JMPD V LAZY G toward St. Catherines was about to drop off Comrade *F* near Allanburg; and a third, only one-twelfth as great but sufficient nonetheless to distribute Andrew Cook V over a considerable radius, within sight of the locks at Port Robinson itself.

And there are at least three explanations. *(a)* The detonation was an accident, caused by the coincidental transmission at 125 kc. of either an SOS from some distressed vessel in Lake Erie or Lake Ontario, or any other message containing either an *S* or letters from each of the three groups (i.e., *THEQUICKBROW, N,* and *FXJMPDVLAZYG*). But there is no record of ships in distress in the canal area on that pleasant Thursday night or Friday morning. Coincidental transmission remains a possibility: a wireless operator just coming on watch, say, aboard any vessel near or in the canal, waking up his fingers with THE QUICK etc. My Tuscarora grandmother preferred this explanation.

(b) The saboteurs were sabotaged, suicidally, by one of their number. This was my father's theory: that by a fatal patriotic rebroadcast of Marconi's first transatlantic message, say, or some sufficient three-letter combination, A.B.C. V martyred himself to the Allied war effort, whether because his anarchism recoiled at the mounting totalitarianism of the Bolsheviks (the Romanovs had been murdered just two months earlier), or because his anarchism had all along been a cover for infiltrating subversive groups. To the objection that suicide was unnecessary to foil the plot (one letter from each of the truck-borne groups—a *T* and a *G,* say—would have done the trick), my father would reply either that *not* to have blown himself up would have blown my grandfather's cover, or, more seriously, that inasmuch as it had been necessary to sacrifice his wife's brother Gadfly, Andrew V had felt morally constrained to sacrifice himself as well. In support of his argument he adduced the fact that his father had handed him, at the last moment, "for safekeeping" while he mined the lock, the old Breguet pocketwatch passed on to *him* by his mother Henrietta.

But contemporary accounts of the event (I have read them all, especially since 1953, the "midpoint" of my own life, by when, alas, my father was eight years dead and unable to defend his theory against my new objections) maintain that the three explosions were separate not only in space but, slightly, in time, and while opinion on their exact sequence is less than unanimous, most auditors agree that the two big blasts preceded the smaller one by a little interval—*boom boom*, bang—and that the southerly boom was the earlier of the two. An ex-artillery officer at Port Robinson reported feeling "bracketed" by the booms and hit directly by the bang.

I have thought about this, and conclude that we may rule out the SOS theory, coincidental or otherwise, except possibly as the third signal. Likewise the theory of self-sabotage by any member of the group except, I reluctantly admit, my grandfather. Not impossibly he did destroy his comrades and thus himself: the quickest signal would have been a simple dot *(E)* to wipe out the southbound twelve, followed by a dot-dash *(A)* to detonate the northbounders, and either the *N* (dash-dot) or the *S* (dot-dot-dot) to do for himself. Or he could have tapped out any of at least seven English words: BAN, CAN, HAS, RAN, TAN, WAN, WAS, etc.

But I am struck by the reminiscence of an old Port Robinson telegrapher whom I interviewed on the subject some ten years ago. A religious man, he had been awakened by those blasts from dreams of a telegram from God, whose sender he recognized by the thunderous subscription of His initial. Awake, he forgot the text of the heavenly message (he was to spend the rest of his life vainly endeavoring to recover it, as I have tried in vain to recover the signal that blew my grandfather and his company to kingdom come), but he understood in immediate retrospect that the coded initial had been the blasts themselves. Boom boom bang: dash dash dot.

In my late adolescence and early manhood, when I too underwent the filial rebellion our line is doomed to, I did not agree with what I took to be my father's politics. Of this, more in a later letter, my last, which I shall write on the eve of the 51st anniversary of this catastrophe and the dawn of our Second 7-Year Plan for the Second Revolution. I am less certain now than I was in those brash days that both of the foregoing theories or classes of theories about the Port Robinson explosions were wrong: that the truth was *(c)* that my *father*, a U.S. Secret Service undercover agent, either sabotaged the whole Welland Canal plot himself from his station at the master transmitter (the only one *known* to be both tuned to the proper frequency and positioned unequivocally within range) or—as my son Henry Burlingame VII firmly believes and gently suggests—that when H.B. VI heard the first two explosions and realized or imagined that A.C. V had blown up both truckloads of bombers, including his beloved Uncle Gadfly Junior, in outraged grief he sent the parricidal letter.

In whichever case, alone or between them, my father and grandfather monogrammed the Niagara Frontier visually with the apocalyptic Morse-code *S:* an aerial photograph would have shown the two large craters and the central smaller one as three dots, or suspension points. . . And acoustically they shook the heavens with the initial echoed down to me 35 years later by the Ontarian telegrapher's recollection: the big *G,* not for God Almighty (with whom no Cook or Burlingame, whatever his other illusions, has ever troubled his head), but for the man who was to my father what Tecumseh and Pontiac were to my remoter ancestors: well-named Tuscarora, boom boom bang, Great-uncle Gadfly!

We approach the end of the line, lengthy as our letters. The Tuscaroras were "originally" a North Carolinian tribe so preyed upon by the white settlers (who stole and enslaved their children) that after losing a war with them in 1711–13 the survivors fled north to Iroquois territory, and the Five Nations became Six. The Tuscarora War coincided with the great slave revolt of 1712 in New York, mentioned in Andrew Cook IV's third letter and by him attributed to the instigation of Henry Burlingame III, the Bloodsworth Island conspirator. Many white colonials feared a general rising of confederated Indians and Negroes, who might at that juncture still have driven them back into the sea. This ancient dream or nightmare, which so haunts our *Sot-Weed Factor,* was my Great-uncle Gadfly Junior's obsession (His Christian name was Gerald Bray; he was early given his father's nickname after his agitations, in the remnants of Iroquois longhouse culture, for the cause of Indian nationalism generally and Iroquoian in particular; he later took the name officially and passed it on to his own son). A better student of history than my father, he argued for example that the Joseph Brant who signed away the ancient Mohawk territory in the Treaty of 1798 was either an impostor or a traitor, and that thus the treaty was as invalid as the one signed by Tecumseh's rivals with William Henry Harrison at Vincennes, and countless others. The Mohawks should reclaim their valleys; the Oneidas, Cayugas, Onondagas, and Senecas their respective lands, from the Catskills and Adirondacks through the Finger Lakes to Erie and Ontario. Bridges, highways, and railroads should be obstructed. The moves in Congress to confer U.S. citizenship on reservation Indians should be resisted as co-option. Common cause should be made with W. E. B Du Bois's NAACP (conceived at Niagara Falls, Canada), with the Quebec separatists, with American anarchists, Bolsheviks, et cetera, to the end of establishing a sovereign free state for the oppressed and disaffected in white capitalist industrialist economic-royalist America.

My grandfather admired and distrusted him; thought him a bit cracked, I believe, but valued him all the same both as Kyuhaha's brother and thus his own, and as rallier of the apathetic Indians: his relation to Gadfly Junior was like Pontiac's to the Delaware Prophet, or Tecumseh's to his brother Tenskwatawa. What made Andrew most uneasy was exactly what most impressed my father as a youth: Gadfly's extreme, even mystical totemism, or animal fetishism. In 1910, for example—the same year that the NAACP and the Boy Scouts of America were incorporated—Gadfly claimed to have conceived a child upon a wild Appaloosa mare in Cattaraugus Indian territory around Lake Cassadaga, near your Chautauqua. The following year he brought to the Grand Island Reservation a strange piebald infant whom he called his son by that union (a disturbed, unearthly boy, more like a bird or bat or bumblebee than a centaur colt, this "Gadfly III" was the queer older companion of my early youth when, after his orphaning, my parents took him in. His own child—whom they also briefly raised—was queerer yet.)

My parents! With those fond, ineffectual, endearing *intrigants* I end this letter. My ancestors since the 17th Century have burdened their children with the confusion of alternate surnames from generation to generation: I was the first to be given two at once. Henry Cook Burlingame VI and Andrée Castine III, though utterly faithful and devoted to each other till the former's death in July 1945, never got around to marriage: my father duly named me Andrew Burlingame Cook VI; my mother, as nonchalant about the famous Pattern as about other conventions, blithely christened me (in the French Catholic chapel at Castines Hundred) André Castine, and maintained that inasmuch as she was the sole surviving member of that branch of the family, I was the 5th baron of that name. I grew up bilingual as well as binomian, and peripatetic. Now we were in Germany, protesting with the Spartacus partisans the murder of Rosa Luxemburg and Karl Liebknecht; now in Massachusetts demonstrating on behalf of Sacco and Vanzetti; now in England for the great general strike of May 1926; now in Maryland's Blackwater Wildlife Refuge, "communizing" the CCC (the only pastoral interval in my youth: I was awakening to sex, literature, and history together, and to this day associate all three with marsh grass, wild geese, tidewater, the hum of mosquitoes); now hiding out back at Castines Hundred. They were not poor: the Cooks and Burlingames were never men of business, but the placid Barons Castine had invested prudently over the years in firms like Du Pont de Nemours; there was money for our traveling, for my educating—and for their organizing Communist party cells in the Canadian and U.S. heartland during the depression; for infiltrating the Civilian Conservation Corps and the WPA Writers Project; for supporting the Lincoln Brigade and other Loyalist organizations during the Spanish Civil War. . .

At least for *ostensibly* so organizing, infiltrating, supporting. For while it is clear that they played the Game of Governments, however ineffectively, to the top of their bent, it is less clear which side they were on. By the time I learned—at least decided, in 1953, after Mother's death—that they had in fact been sly counterrevolutionaries all along, the revelation made no real difference to me, for I had also come to understand that the Second American Revolution was to be a matter, not of vulgar armed overthrow—by Minutemen, Sansculottes, Bolsheviki, or whatever—but of something quite different, more subtle, less melodramatic, more. . .revolutionary.

But that, of course, is for another letter, which I will happily indite once I have provided you, in weeks to come, with the bones of my *Marylandiad:* the further adventures of Andrew Cook IV in and after the War of 1812. Till when, I have, sir, the honor of regarding myself as

> Your eager collaborator,
> A. B. Cook VI
> (dictated but not reread)

P.S.: As to the orthographical proximity of your *Chautauqua* and my *Chautaugua:* The Algonkin language was spoken in its sundry dialects by Indians from Nova Scotia to the Mississippi and as far south as Tennessee and Cape Hatteras, and like all the Indian languages it was very approximately spelled by our forefathers. The word in question is said to mean "bag (or pack) tied in the middle." Chautauqua Lake was so named obviously from its division into upper and lower moieties at the narrows now traversed by the Bemus Point–Stow Ferry, which I hope it will be your good fortune never to see replaced by a bridge. Chautaugua Road, where this will be typed for immediate posting to you at Chautauqua Lake, is near the similar narrows of Chesapeake Bay (now regrettably spanned at the old ferry-crossing, as you know, and about to be second-spanned, alas), which divides this noble water into an Upper and a Lower Chesapeake. The scale is larger, but the geographical state of affairs is similar enough for the metaphor-loving Algonquins, wouldn't you say?

ABC/mb: 4 encl

E: *Jerome Bray to his parents and foster parents.*
His betrayal by Merope Bernstein. His revenge and despair.

Jerome Bonaparte Bray
General Delivery
Lily Dale NY 14752

June 17 1969

Mr & Mrs Gerald Bray a.k.a. Gadblank III
c/o Ranger & Mme H C Burlingame VI
Backwater National Wildlife Refuge
Dorchester County Maryland

Dearest Parents & Foster Parents
Every RESET has a RESET Back where we started All shall be ill Jack shant have Jill the man shant have his mare again and naught will

424

be well Not bad how about a spot of punctuation, that's better. Continue to delete all references to blank, very good, the mails aren't safe, but don't reset *every* time you see a pattern, or these letters will be a meaningless jumble of you-know-whats, here we go.

Dear Mother and Father and Foster Ditto it is not easy to write this letter. Are having a terrible time. Wish you were here. Why have you forsaken us, you too, like H.M. II a.k.a. G. III, Todd Andrews, Andrews Mack, and bad Merope Bernstein a.k.a. Margana y Fael, anti-Bonapartists all? Old Ranger B., dear Madame: Are you still at sweet Backwater or flown to your reward? Do you recall this orphan of the storm, that you rescued from his bulrush basket and raised up in the marsh as though he were yours despite his bad foot? Whose mother was a royal virgin whose father RESET Whose maternal grandfather RESET Please forward. Have you learned in the evening of your lives what you never knew in the morn of ours: where our true Mommy & Daddy are, and why they don't write clearer letters? Please forward.

Dear parents: It is not easy to RESET Your long message to us of April 1 was duly printed out and delivered by LILYVAC, but we cannot find the key to that treasure, and we despair. Numbed by your numbers, stung like fallen Bellerophon, we wander far from the paths of men, devouring our own soul. The midpoint of our life approaches, unhappy birthday, ditto the *Phi*-point of our 5-Year Plan, .618 etc., and we are nowhere. The Tidewater Foundation has rejected us; they shall pay. Our letters go unanswered; our enemies rejoice. Year *T* (a.k.a. *V*) ends; soon it will be time to mate. With whom, Ma? *NOT* will not come to *ES!* Our business will go unfinished ha RESET Oh stop.

Themurah a.k.a. anagrammatical transposition is all humblank. Everything comes out scrambled after MARGANAYFAEL, leafy anagram for bad Margana y Flae, who bit us bye-bye on May 18, she shall RESET It was the anniversary of Napoleon's coronation, 1st Sunday after Ascension, mild & cloudy, ☿ stationary in Right Ascension, ♂ ♆ ☉ , hear the buzzing of the blanks in the apple trees, Apollo-10 launched, will land on USS *Blank,* etc. The bad news had just arrived from the Tidewater Foundation; we were RESET Drove down to Chautauqua in our VW Blank to share our sorrow with Margana y Rodriguez y Thelma y Irving, loyal comrades so we thought, with the weariness that only true revolutionary lovers Forget it. We did not knock; strode into their pad in the old St. Elret Hotel on the institution grounds for the comradely consolation that only RESET It was but May, Ma, and they were *mating!* In hemp smoke so thick it brought tears to our eye of newt! Irving with Thelma! Rodriguez with my Margana!

Look who here, said Thelma: it old Numbers. I can explain, Jer, said Margana. What's to explain? Rodriguez asked rhetorically: Everybody must make the revolution in his/her et cetera heh heh. We're like practicing up for the Mating Flight, joshed Irving; pull up some smoke and join us. He not joining *me*, declared Thelma; he give me the heeb-jeebs. Jerome, Margana said, it's time I told you. Tell shmell, sniffed

Rodriguez; he's got eyes. What big ones, Irving chaffed. Cool it, hombres, urged Margana; remember what I said. Now look here, Jer, these spray guns aren't what you think, okay? she went on (for while numbly regarding them we had not failed to notice the hideous weapons deployed about their quarters); we ripped off some herbicide from the county agent's office, right? Our plan is to defoliate the Ivy League during their commencement exercises. Think what you please, Jerry; it's the truth. And Roddy and I, well, we're lovers: true revolutionary RESET Quick Henry, cried Thelma as we angrily opened our cape, the Flit! Jesus H. Keerist, expostulated Irv, put that thing away, man!

They flew for the exits: perfidious Margana alone stood her ground, spray gun in hand. Wicked, beautiful le Fay! Abdomen we so prized, that was to have taken our seed come August to hatch a brood of Conquerors! We hefted our barb; her courage failed, with a squeal she flung the spray gun at us and turned to flee, that's *F-L-E*-RESET She deserved to die, Da, but we but numbed her: little shot in the tail to teach her a lesson and keep Rodriguez out of there till after mating season. Her friends abandoned her as she'd abandoned us, afraid either to come to her aid or to call the police lest they be burst for Illegal Possession. We ourself telephoned the Chautauqua Infirmary, gave the St. Elret number, reported a young female apparently O.D.'d on some narcotic.

Faithless Merope! Margana y Blank! We kissed her numb face; we covered her numb and swiftly swelling shame; we retracted our number, rearranged ourself, waited with her till we heard the ambulance before slipping out through the screen and making a blankline home. All the way weeping and wondering, Now who'll unscramble things? Who'll feed the goats for fudge and slaughter? Who'll take delivery in the rear, as wanton Merope was wont, come mating season? Perfidious M y F, would thou wert a blank preserved in amber! Yet never return to Lily Dale: we will not so spare you a 2nd time.

That was last month. Alone since with these senseless numbers, as Maimonides says that YHWH RESET We see now the scale of our betrayal. Agents of you-know-whom, the lot of them, and Merope Bernstein was their tool! The foundation was their creature; they supported us only to learn and steal and neutralize our plans; they put the blanks in LILYVAC's program, saw to it our spring work period was wasted in vain unscrambling. This is no leafy anagram at all!

Ma y Da: Mayday! Mayday! We are back where we began. How to recycle? Every RESET Now they swarm to Chautauqua for the kill, operatives of the false T.F., under pretext of making an anti-Bonapartist film: perfidious Prinz, his ally Mensch, their beautiful captive Bea Golden (whose mind they have drugged with C_2H_6O; whose name they are not worthy to RESET Tomorrow, we daresay, they will celebrate the 154th of Waterloo; tonight they have chartered the *Gadblank III* (ah, Da) for a party cruise around the lake. We are not fooled: They know we are its pilot; they think by this crude stratagem to snare us in their web.

And we shall go, Ma, though counterstratagem we have none. We shall set out from the institute dock, Da, making false merry. Numbly we shall steer around the familiar circuits: 1st the lower lake, then up through the narrows where the bag of Chautauqua is tied in the middle. There, no doubt, as we round the buoys to begin the upper lake, or 2nd circuit, they will swap their gins-and-tonics for dichlorodiphenyltrichloroethane, and it will be finished. Pfft, forgotten, we shall RESET *Unless* dot dot dot

Lost Mother, old articifrix, key to the key: R.S.V.P.!

J.B.B.

I: *Ambrose Mensch to Yours Truly. Anniversary of the bees' descent. Encounters with Jacob Horner and Marsha Blank. He identifies his condition with Perseus's, and despairs.*

Athenaeum Hotel
Chautauqua, New York 14722

Monday, June 16, 1969

FROM: Ambrose Mensch, Concerned
TO: Yours Truly
CONCERNING: Your message to me of May 12, 1940

Old messenger:

It's another anniversary (Jacob Horner has got us all doing it): of the birth of Joshua Reynolds in 1723, King Gustaf of Sweden in 1858, Stan Laurel in 1890; of the capture by Boston soldiers of French forts in Nova Scotia in Year 2 of the Seven Years' War; of young Werther's letter in 1771 reporting his having first met Charlotte several days earlier; of the lifting in 1812 of the British blockade of European ports to American shipping (but the news won't reach Congress in time to forestall a declaration of war two days from now); of the invention of the squeeze play in baseball in 1894; of Leopold Bloom's odyssey through James Joyce's Dublin in 1904. And of the descent upon me 39 years ago, in 1930, at Andrea King Mensch's breast as we dozed in a hammock near the hollyhocks in the backyard of the old *Menschhaus* on a flawless forenoon, of a swarm of golden bees.

Eloquence, Uncle Konrad predicted: the boy will grow up to be a Sophocles, a Plato. But it's silence I'm stung into, zapped by history. Tides! The past is a holding tank from which time's wastes recirculate. Nothing lost, alas; all spirals back, recycled. Once-straight Joe Morgan, freaked out on psychedelics, sweetly promises to kill Jake Horner unless history can be redreamed, his dead wife reborn. Horner himself, that

427

black hole in the human universe, that fossil from the early 1950's, has not altered since he dropped out of graduate school eighteen years ago: a penman after my own heart, he claims to have "published" his first book by leaving the typescript behind in a rooming house for others to discover, or for the Allegheny Reservoir to drown. His "writing" since, I gather, has been the therapeutic compilation of what he calls his *Hornbook:* a catalogue of notable cuckolds of myth, literature, and history arranged alphabetically from Agamemnon to Zeus.

May I? I asked him yesterday, turning to the *M*'s. Horner shrugged, thinly smiled, assured me he knew no more than what was inferrable from "the fiction." But there we all were, between Menelaus and Minos of Crete (and before Morgan, Joseph), followed left to right by columns headed *Wife, Lover(s), Remarks.* Not only

Cuckold	Wife	Lover(s)	Remarks
Mensch, Hector	King, Andrea	a.Erdmann, Willy (?)	
		b.Mensch, Karl(?)	issue: Mensch,
		c.Mensch, Konrad (?)	Peter (?) &/or
			Ambrose (?)

but also, after Hector,

Cuckold	Wife	Lover(s)	Remarks
Mensch, Peter	Giulianova, Magda	Mensch, Ambrose	a.May 12, 1947
			b.1967–69
			no issue

How had Horner come by that information, written nowhere but in my jettisoned *Amateur* manuscript? Did the tides of the Choptank circulate somehow through Lake Erie? The answer was plain, of course, in the entry just prior to Hector's. *Cuckold: Mensch, Ambrose. Wife: Blank, Marsha,* followed in the third column by a *very* long list of names including *Mensch, Peter,* and in the fourth, after that name, by the remark: *issue: Mensch, Angela Blank.* Sorry, says Horner: Pocahontas insisted, and we try to be therapeutic. She'd wanted him to list as well her more recent conquests at the Remobilization Farm, he declared— from *Casteene, M.* through *Joseph, Saint* to *X, Tombo*—but he'd stoutly refused, therapy or no therapy, on the grounds that divorce exempts the cuckold from further horns.

Some of those names, Yours, I didn't even know! The dates might have stung more if my memory were better—So *that's* what you were doing in Philadelphia that weekend, etc.—and I could perhaps have made use of the list when Marsha's lawyers were working me over. But now I neither despised nor pitied the woman, only tisked my tongue, resolved to stay clear of her, and sighed at the regurgitative habit of History that had brought her up in my life again.

In this instance, however, the dramaturge was in all likelihood not Clio but Reg Prinz, who seems as bent on redreaming *my* history as "St. Joseph" his own. The man wants some sort of showdown, clearly, and not only for his show. I expected to discover he'd photographed my tête-à-tête with Horner yesterday; indeed, lest there be hidden cameras in the Progress and Advice Room of the Remobilization Farm, I showed even less emotion than I felt at sight of those entries in Horner's Hornbook: I simply fetched forth my Mightier-Than-Etc. and, in the interest of accuracy, put a *(?)* after Angie's name.

Marsha, for pity's sake! Well hear this, Y.T.; you too, Clio—and you, R.P., if your cameras are even now peeking over my shoulder: there is a limit to what I'll swallow the second time around! As of my last to you I'd rescrewed Magda (Peter & Germaine forgive us), on the 12th anniversary of my virgin connection with her and the 19th of your water message. Very possibly I shall be in "Bibi's" *bibi* ere our tale is told: Prinz seems to be setting us up, and Bea looks more golden in her glitterless "Rennie Morgan" role than she's looked since we tumbled in her rumble seat back in the forties. My treatment of Milady A. has been unspeakable; I do not speak of it. *Que sera* etc. But I will *not* reenact my marriage! Salty Marsha, you shall not fuck me over over! Closed-circuit history is for compulsives; Perseus and I are into spirals, presumably outbound.

The question of the plot is clear: How transcend mere reenactment? Perseus, in his life's first half, "calls his enemy to his aid," petrifying his adversaries with Medusa's severed head. In its second half—his marriage to Andromeda broken, his career at an impasse—he must search wrongheadedly for rejuvenation by reenactment, and some version of Medusa (transformed, Germaine: recapitated, beautiful!) must aid him in a different way: together they must attain "escape velocity"; open the circle into a spiral that unwinds forever, as if a chambered nautilus kept right on until it grew into a galaxy. The story must unwind likewise, chambered but unbroken, its outer cycles echoing its inner. Behind, the young triumphant Perseus of Cellini's statue; ahead, the golden constellations from which meteors shower every August; between, on the cusp, nonplussed middle Perseus, stopped in his reiterative tracks, yet to discover what alchemy can turn stones into stars.

The planning, Yours, goes well; the writing is another matter. When I discover Perseus's secret for him, I think you'll hear from me no more; until I do, I pursue these ghosts in circles, beastly, buffaloed, and in these circles am by them pursued.

Beset, too, by metaphors, as by geriatric furies: the dry Falls; this tideless lake; old Chautauqua fallen out of time; this antique, improbable hotel, named after the place named after the city named after the gray-eyed goddess, Perseus's wise half sister. The elders rock on the porches; bats flitter through the Protestant twilight; the water does not ebb and flow.

Waiting our arrival here this afternoon, a note from Magda: *Mother's condition grave. Will call if it grows critical. Angie sends love. Drop her a postcard from the Falls. M*

No period, I note, after the initial. Mere inadvertence: coded signals are not Magda's way of messaging. Even so, given History's heavy hand with portents, I'm dismayed: there's another scene must never be replayed.

Thirty-nine. With luck, about halfway through. Nothing to show for it but a pickup job, a screwy bibliography, a sore divorce, a short string of hedged liaisons, a cracked tower, a brain-damaged daughter. My heart smarts. My birthmark itches. Milady is properly fed up. This letter goes into Chautauqua Lake: the first one guaranteed not to return to sender.

Eloquence, redescend upon me. I despair.

E: *The Author to A. B. Cook VI.* *A request for information and an invitation to participate in the work in progress.*

Department of English, Annex B
State University of New York at Buffalo
Buffalo, New York 14214

Sunday, June 15, 1969

A. B. Cook, Poet Laureate
Chautaugua, Maryland 2114?

Dear Mr. Cook:

Eventually, I hope, this letter will reach you. I learned only recently that you live in a place called Chautaugua, Maryland; my zip code directory lists no such post office, but while I was down your way on business two weeks ago, I noticed a road sign for Chautaugua along the Governor Ritchie Highway between Baltimore and Annapolis—it caught my eye because I live on Chautauqua Lake in west New York— and my map of Anne Arundel County confirms that there is indeed a Chautaugua Road not far from the mainland end of the Chesapeake Bay Bridge. I must hope that four-fifths of a zip code plus your title will do the trick.

I have been told that you are descended from Ebenezer Cooke, poet laureate of late-17th/early-18th-Century Maryland, and from Henry Burlingame of Virginia, who is listed among those accompanying Capt. John Smith in his exploration of Chesapeake Bay in 1608. Fictionalized versions of both gentlemen play a role (indeed, Cooke plays the leading role) in my 1960 novel called, after Cooke's satirical poem, *The Sot-Weed Factor.* I am forwarding you a copy, and trust you'll indulge the liberties I've taken with your forebears.

My work in progress, which is of a different character, accounts for this letter. It is itself to be composed of letters, in both senses of the word: an epistolary novel, the epistles to be arranged in an order yet to be devised (I'm just past half through the planning of it). I'm also past half through my biblical threescore-and-ten, which detail no doubt accounts for my second notion about the story: that it should echo its predecessors in my bibliography, while at the same time extending that bibliography and living its independent life. Ontogeny recapitulates phylogeny in the womb, but the delivered child must breathe for itself; one's forties are the "product" of one's thirties, twenties, etc., as the present century is the product of those before it—but not *merely* the product. You see my point.

Thus I am hazarding, for various reasons, the famous limitations both of the Novel-in-Letters and of the Sequel, most fallible of genres. The letters will be from seven correspondents: one from each of my previous books (or their present-day descendants or counterparts, in the case of the historical or fabulous works), plus one invented specifically for *this* work, plus—I blush to report, it goes so contrary to my literary principles—the Author, who had better be telling stories than chattering about them.

These seven correspondents I imagine contributing severally not only the letters that comprise the story but the elements of its theme and form. The main character, for example—a remarkable middle-aged English gentlewoman and scholar in reduced circumstances—by inviting the Author to accept an honorary doctorate of letters from the small American college where she's presently teaching, suggests to him, even as he declines her invitation, the general conceit of "doctored letters." From "Todd Andrews" (the lawyer-hero of my first novel, *The Floating Opera*) came both the notion of free-standing sequelae and the Tragic View of history, to which in fact I subscribe. From "Jacob Horner" (novel #2, *The End of the Road*) comes what might be called an Anniversary View of history, together with certain alphabetical preoccupations and the challenge of "redreaming" the past, an enterprise still not very clear to me. Et cetera.

#3 was *The Sot-Weed Factor*. While I don't conceive the work in hand to be a historical novel, and have no intention of resurrecting Henry Burlingame and Ebenezer Cooke, I evidently do have capital-*H* History on my mind. You are, in a sense, the "sequel" to the laureate poet, possibly self-denominated, of Lord Baltimore's palatinate. This letter is to solicit from you, as one author to another, *(a)* any information you're willing to provide me, or direct me to, concerning the activities of the Cooke and Burlingame lines from the 18th Century to yourself, beyond what's available in the standard local histories; and *(b)* your sentiments about reincarnating, as it were, your admirable progenitor. Might I presume so far as to include, *mutatis mutandis*, some version of yourself among my seven correspondents?

Cordially,

P.S.: What do you suppose accounts for the coincidence of your Indian place-name and mine, 450 miles apart?

5

	S	M	T	W	T	F	S		
		5	4	3	2	1			

1969 · JULY

S 5 **L A R Y** — *Lady Amherst*
F 4 18 25 **V** — *Todd Andrews*
T 3 17 24 31 **I** — *Jacob Horner*
W 2 23 30 **S &** — *A. B. Cook*
T 1 15 22 29 **A** — *Jerome Bray*
M 14 21 28 **C** — *Ambrose Mensch*
S **L F A C** — *The Author*

L: *Lady Amherst to the Author*. *Despair at Ambrose's infidelity. Their Fifth Stage.*

24 L Street, Dorset Heights
Saturday, 12 July 1969

John,

Lost, aye, I'm lost right enough, and not in any funhouse.

Three nights and days he spent with her down there in deserted "Barataria," where except in goose-shooting season there is nothing to do but copulate and swat mosquitoes. They did both, did my A. and his Bea—more determinedly, I gather, than successfully—in A. B. Cook's air-conditioned hunting lodge on the north end of the island, where the only dry ground is and where Reg Prinz's movie set was and will be. (It's to be rebuilt in August for redestroying in September: an example yours truly may be doomed to follow.)

Three nights and days! The whole long holiday weekend, whilst I steamed and stewed and reached new lows in Dorset Heights! Late on the Monday (7/7) he returned to me, covered with welts and cross as a bear. Confessed straight off, he did—*announced*, rather—that his philandering idyll had been no idyll: Couldn't get it up for her (I'm glad, says I) about half the time (Ah, that hurt, and damn me for crying then and there). Would've called it quits even if Bea hadn't got urgent word from "Monsieur Casteene" about the Doctor's death.

You will have heard, no doubt: among the 200 pleasure-boaters feared lost in the big Lake Erie storm of 4 July—whilst we-all were making cinematical merry here on the Choptank aboard the *O.F.T. II*—was the dark proprietor of the Remobilisation Farm. No details yet.

Who cares? Who cares?

Well, Bea, it seems, for one. Anyroad she took the occasion to beat it out of Barataria and back to Fort Erie, leaving crestfallen Ambrose to scratch his own itches.

I gather further (And who cares? *I* do, God help me!) my prodigal has scrapped his Perseus piece, and there's a pity. Indeed, while I still don't know what he wrote to Bea Golden in that famous Unfilmable Sequence of Independence Day, I learn now that what he wrote it *on* was the verso of his manuscript, which then—like the legendary poet Gunadhya in *The Ocean of Story* (or Rodolfo in Act I of *La Bohème*)—he destroyed page by page, giving each to B.G. to read and chuck overboard. That hurts, John: it was. . .*our* story, if you know what I mean: Ambrose's and mine. His notion that Medusa the petrifying Gorgon, Perseus's snake-haired adversary, might actually have *loved*

435

him and longed for destruction at his hands; that in the "2nd Cycle" of their connexion, recapitated and restored to her original beauty, she would teach him to love instead of to accomplish by heroical destruction; that by some magic physics of the heart they could become, not stones, but stars, rehearsing endlessly the narrative of their affair—I loved that; I had presumed to see in it the emblem of my trials thus far, and a future hope.

Nope. The *plan*, he acknowledges, is dandy; he has preserved his graphs and charts, may attempt to publish them as is. But he will not after all, at this hour of the world, *write*. . .

So. I ought to've shown him the door, and did not. We languish here in air-conditioned desperation whilst the peninsula swelters: an odd, dull lull after all the recent action, but hardly a respite, certainly no vacation. Tender and tyrannical at once, vulnerable and volatile, my friend is burdened with something beyond his mother's dying (which proceeds all too slowly, alas for her), the abandonment of his story, the impending return of Reg Prinz and the resumption (Monday next) of their rivalry—beyond even the set-down of his sexual ego on Bloodsworth Island. I don't know what it is. My clear feeling—very possibly a desperate delusion—is that his "conquest" of and failure with Bea Golden really did have more to do with me (I mean with *us*, our unsuccess in the conception way) than with her. But I don't know. He is a raw nerve now; sore as my heart is, I love and oddly pity him.

Too, we are back to't. Impotent with her, he is a standing bone with me. And who cares? Well, the pair of us; God knows exactly wherefore. A touch more frequently in this "5th Stage" than in our fanatical 4th (but nothing like our sexy 2nd), we go to't, to't, to the crazy end—but not *just*—of July engenderment. Now I know the pattern, I cannot drop knickers for him without thinking of poor three-timed Magda: with mixed feelings as I fancy Ambrose thinking likewise. Once only I remarked as much: his eyes filled up; I shan't again.

Anyroad, I am not to forget that we are not *merely* reenacting; that even were we, with luck this as yet but ill-defined 5th Stage will bring us to the 6th—*i.e.*, to ourselves, to Ambrose and *Germaine*, not Ambrose and Magda/Jeannine Mack/Magda/Marsha Blank/Magda! Who will I be, I wonder, when, having gone through such protean metamorphoses, I return to my "true" self?

What else is new. Oh, that I seem in for a new couturial outrage. From old steamer trunks and attic cedar closets in the Menschhaus, Ambrose has recovered a virtual wardrobe of 1930-ish ladies' wear—his then-still-stylish mum's, I suppose—and. . .

Yup. That's how we do't when we go to't these days at 24 L. It's nothing Oedipal, I think (we're not even sure they're Andrea's clothes): rather that, having failed to fertilise me in the costumes first of my present age and then of the presently young, he'll give me a go in the garb of my own young womanhood and first fertility. And indeed, for all my apprehension that he may carry this new mummery, like the old, out of doors, I confess that intramurally it is not only Ambrose who finds arousing these early Joan Crawfords, late Greta Garbos, middle Marlene Dietrichs, not unreasonably unlike what I wore in Paris when André's first intromission found its mark, some 350 ovulations past. . .

I cannot write.

And so I shall begin your *Lost in the Funhouse* stories. A. says he's in them. If so, for whom is the funhouse fun? Not, I think, for lost

Germaine

A: *Lady Amherst to the Author. The Dorchester County Tercentenary and Mating-Season Sequences. Ambrose's concussion, and its cause.*

24 L, 11 P.M.

19 July 1969

Well, John,

All evidence indicates that our little lull is done and some new storm hard upon us. As I write this (near midnight), our friend Ambrose lies half-conscious in my bed, his circuits just beginning to reconnect after a terrific crack athwart the cranium this noon, which decked and, it seems, mildly concussed him. My first experience of that alarming phenomenon, taken so lightly in our films, on the telly, in our fiction, where folks are regularly and tidily "knocked out," to waken some minutes or hours later, shake their noggins a time or two, and then On with the story!

I here attest that that is not the way it is. A blow to the head severe enough to cause loss of consciousness (A.'s, classically, was just above the temple, his left, not far from the famous birthmark), if it does not actually fracture the skull, plays hob with the memory functions for (going on to) half a day at least. One prays that this symptom—and the headache, and the heavy sleeping—will not be accompanied by nausea and vertigo, indications of subdural hematoma and more serious consequences. So far, so good: when he is awake, my dear despot cannot remember the question he put 90 seconds since, or my answer. He smiles, reputs and re-reputs it; I reanswer and re-reanswer. It was that fucker Prinz, wasn't it? Yes, luv. With the light boom? I think the mike boom, dear. It was Prinz, wasn't it? No question, luv; and no accident, I fear. With the fucking light boom, right? At the fucking tercentenary? The fucking *mike* boom, I believe, dear.

Et cetera. Well, it *was* Reg Prinz—not the Director himself, ever at the camera, but one of his grad-student bullies at the audio boom (at noon today, at Long Wharf, at the opening of the "Dorchester Story" pageant, part of the Dorchester County tercentenary festivities which commenced last night and will continue inexorably through next

437

Sunday)—who smote my man upside the head as if by accident. And this smite, like my Yes-dears, was by way of reply. For it was Ambrose who cast the first stone, as it were, and not unjustifiably, last Monday, in of all places the bell-less belfry of the Tower of Truth. Let me rehearse our week, blow to blow, whilst my inquisitor sleeps.

Prinz and his pals reconvened per schedule in Cambridge last Sunday, the 13th, to begin shooting on the Monday what Ambrose vaguely calls "the Mating Season Sequences." If he was apprehensive of retaliation for having gone off to Barataria with Bea Golden, Ambrose gave no sign, not even when we heard nothing from the man (as we expected to) on the Sunday evening or the Monday morning. I believe we decided that, after the hiatus of the week prior, Prinz was in no hurry to revive the contest or even his working connexion with my imperious consort, who for *his* part apparently considered it infra dig to ring up his employer and ask where the action was to take place. After breakfast Ambrose retired to my study to "reconsider the whole script" (maybe to figure out what on earth in your fiction could be described as "the Mating Season Sequences"?), and I spent the morning poolside (in a remarkable vintage-1930 swimsuit—but I'm allowed to wear a muumuu over it) rereading your *Funhouse* stories.

On them, a word only. A. assures me that you do not yourself take with much seriousness those Death-of-the-Novel or End-of-Letters chaps, but that you *do* take seriously the climate that takes such questions seriously; you exploit that apocalyptic climate, he maintains, to reinspect the origins of narrative fiction in the oral tradition. Taking that cue, Ambrose himself has undertaken a review of the origins of *printed* fiction, especially the early conventions of the novel. More anon. To us Britishers, this sort of programme is awfully *theoretical,* what? Too French by half, and at the same time veddy Amedican. Still and all, I enjoyed the stories—in particular, of course, the "Ambrose" ones. Your Ambrose, needless to say, is not my Ambrose—but then, mine isn't either!

Over lunch that same last Monday, an agreeable surprise. In honour of the 180th anniversary of Bastille Day (and 152nd of Mme de Staël's death: R.I.P., poor splendid woman, one year older than I am now!), he and I would climb Schott's Tower of Truth. Its phallic exterior is complete; the finishing of its interior has been delayed indefinitely on account, ahem, of Grave Structural Defects ever more apparent in the foundation work. Even so, the dedication ceremonies are now definitely scheduled for Founder's Day, 27 September, seventh anniversary of Harrison Mack's establishment of Tidewater Tech/ Marshyhope State College/University College/University. And *non grata* as we are on Redmans Neck, Ambrose had got from a construction foreman–colleague of Peter's a key to the premises and leave to climb stairs to the top (no lifts yet installed).

I dutifully suggested we take Angela. Touched, Milord thanked me for that thoughtfulness, but declared there was another female going with us instead. Now, John: our autocratic 5th Stage really has been in full noxious flower since I wrote you last, even though (thank God) Bea Golden had not returned from that Farm after the Doctor's "funeral." But for all I knew she might be back in town with Prinz, and now I wondered: Was I really expected to. . . But no, he was *joking!* My avant-gardist, it seems, has conceived a passion for old Samuel Richardson (the first to speak of the Death of the Novel, it turns out, in a letter to Lady Barbara Montague dated 1758): the third member of our *ménage à trois* was to be R.'s *Clarissa!*

All four volumes, dear? Sure, and a six-pack of National Premium, two beach towels, and our suntan lotion. Ambrose cannot bear *reading* that endless novel, you understand: he likes hearing me read him the table of contents and Richardson's chapter summaries.

Chacun à son goût. He was in good humour (not good enough to let me wear my own clothes; he decked me out in a Roaring-Twentyish cotton middy blouse with black silk sailor kerchief, rather fetching actually, Lord knows where he found it); *I* was in middle month and wondering whether we might manage the Zeus-&-Danaë trick up in that tower, seeing more conventional deposits had so far failed to yield interest. The weather was of course steamy and threatening thun-dershowers, which the soybean and corn fields needed; on the other hand, below-normal rainfall had kept the mosquito population down. The campus was deserted. We understand that A. B. Cook has already occupied my office—may be there as I write these lines—but he was not in evidence: only a few student groundkeepers and, over by the Media Centre, a van that we recognised as belonging to Prinz's crew. We sped past, not to be recognised in turn, parked on the far side of Schott's Folly, and let ourselves quickly through the padlocked cyclone fence into the construction site.

The scene was dead quiet: one could hear the Stars and Stripes and the flag of Maryland flapping in the damp breeze at their staffs a hundred yards off, and a few desultory cicadas. Round about the site were paper sacks of, of all things, *Medusa Cement.* We were duly amused, but the coincidence prompted, instead of erotic associations with Danaë's brass tower, a re-remarking by Ambrose that whereas Medusa turned everything into stone, Mensch Masonry (whose cement it was) could be said to turn stone into everything, except money. Indeed, though allegedly cracked as the House of Usher, the stone-masonry base of the tower is handsomely done, in the same random rubble as the brothers' camera obscura. The rest of the shaft is a rough-finished reinforced concrete eyesore.

We climbed, A. reminiscing about the alphabet-block towers they'd built together as boys: compromises, not always successful, between Peter's interest in their engineering and Ambrose's in what they *spelled.* I went first up the fire stairs, pausing at unglassed windows less to look at the not-much-of-anything than to give Ambrose occasion to "do a verbena," as was his wont back in sexy April. (Do you know Maupassant's tale "La Fenêtre," about the verbena-scented lady who invites her suitor to her country château but will not yield to him? He consoles himself with her chambermaid and, discovering this latter one morning leaning out a turret window—so he supposes, from his position below and behind her—he resolves to surprise her by slipping up the stairs, lifting her skirts, and kissing her knickerless derrière. The little prank succeeds; he quickly plants his lover's kiss; is confounded by the scent there, not of the maid's familiar *odeur naturel*, but of her chaste mistress's perfume! Scandalised, the lady sends him packing; but—ah, Guy! ah, France!—years after, as he retells the tale, it seems to the narrator that he can still summon to his moustaches *la senteur de verveine. . .)*

Nothing doing.

We attained the top: dusty concrete floor and a sultry view of loblolly pines, parching grass, Marshyhope U., and white crab-boats on the distant creeks. A view (Ambrose declared after one perfunctory conning, and I agree) better mediated by camera obscura than viewed directly. Exam time again: Do you know Gossaert's 16th-Century Danaë? A winsome, moon-faced teenager half wrapped in open indigo drapery, she perches on tasselled red cushions in a Renaissance campanile, ankles crossed but bare knees parted, and looks up with puckered unsurprise at the shower of gold which rains past the plump little breast that will one day suckle Perseus, onto the folds of her robe, and out of sight between her thighs. So presently perched I (changes changed) on a pair of clean 50-lb. sacks of Medusa, the only unsoiled seat thereabouts. Ambrose likewise, and fetched out. . .his beer and his Richardson.

It is the final tyranny of tyrants that, when on occasion they behave like decent chaps, we are inordinately grateful. Milord was merry. Roused already (and knees tentatively ajar), I was roused further by his mere *friendliness* for a change; further still by our rehearsal of *Clarissa's* table of contents. *Her mother connives at the private correspondence between her and Lovelace. . .Her expedient to carry on a private correspondence with Miss Howe. . .A letter from her brother forbidding her to appear in the presence of any of her relations without leave. Her answer. Writes to her mother. Her mother's answer. Writes to her father. His answer. . . Her expostulatory letter to her brother and sister. Their answers. . .Copies of her letters to her two uncles, and of their characteristic answers. . .An insolent letter from her brother on her writing to Solmes. . .Observes upon the contents of her seven letters. . .Her closet searched for papers. All the pens and ink they find taken from her. . .Substance of her letter to Lovelace. . .Lays all to the fault of her corresponding with him at first. . .*

Et cetera. These from the mere 99 letters of Volume 1, with yet to come the 438 of the other three volumes! But we never came to them— Clarissa's protracted rape and even more protracted repining unto death. For if, admixed with Ambrose's mirth, was professional envy of his great predecessor's wind (and the stamina of readers in those days), admixed with mine was a complex sympathy for Clarissa Harlowe—yea even unto her employment (Vol. IV, Letter XCVI, Belford to Lovelace) of her coffin for a writing table! I recalled that Clarissa's "elopement" with Lovelace had been a major event in Mme de Staël's girlhood, when, as 15-year-old Germaine Necker, she had doted breathlessly upon Richardson's novels. And now she was dead, as presently Ambrose, André, I, and all must be, the most of us having done little more, in Leonardo's phrase, than "fill up privies." Before I knew it I was weeping instead of laughing, there in my antic getup on my cement sacks: half a century old, childless, husbandless, wageless, surely a little cracked (as Schott unkindly alleged), and stuck on Redmans Neck with an unsuccessful writer and petty despot instead of flourishing in Paris or Florence with some Benjamin Constant. . .

He kissed me, God bless Ambrose for that: a proper loving and consoling buss before he touched between my legs. Then I *did* go a bit mad: moaned at him to take me as he'd taken Magda in Peter's cellar a quarter-century ago. Dear God, I wanted to conceive by him, to get *something* beyond my worn-out self! And by God we tried, on that hard bed of Medusa Portland. Let Danaë do it her way; I'll get my Perseus with a regular roger! If there's connexion between the ploughing and the crop. . . Comes then the golden shower, not a drop wasted on the draperies; *surely* that should turn the trick, if we've one in us to turn; my joy poured out as A. poured in—

Which is why I didn't hear what he heard. My Zeus sprang off me as if galvanised, snatched up Vol. I and winged it staircaseward with a curse. Now I heard the whirrs and clicketies over there! By the time I got my legs together and my hem pulled down, he had armed himself with the sack of Vols II, III, & IV and, bare-arsed with his spigot still adrip, was whamming in a rage at Reg Prinz, perched there with his hand-held!

Now, of course, I'm indignant at such sneakery. But at the time I was still too busy feeling Zeus'd to the Plimsoll, too surprised at my lover's shocking leap off me, too marvellous at his fury to muster a proper indignation. How Ambrose did go at him, cursing, swinging good weighty Sam: first at Prinz's fuzzy head (who till the last possible frame kept the camera running), then at the instrument itself, when he saw Prinz more concerned for it than for his own cranium. Chucking *Clarissa*, Ambrose fought for that camera—it was strapped to Prinz's arm—and threatened to smash it and Reggie's head together if he didn't expose that film then and there. By george he did it, too, Prinz shrieking like a wired-up bat the while: prised open the case, did Ambrose, clawed out the reel, and flung it like a Frisbee from the tower top before two of Prinz's graduate-film-workshop types came to their master's rescue.

You're *bananas*, Prinz cries now (the clearest statement I've ever heard from him): that was *footage!* Shove your effing footage, Ambrose replies, I'm done with it. He comes back now for his britches; the three cinéastes withdraw, examining their precious machine for damage and smirking over their shoulders, the two younger ones, and me at my bottomless beau.

So ends the Mating Season Sequence, I presume! Which I might've suspected I was set up for, had Ambrose's outrage not swept all suspicion before it.

And if Reg Prinz's riposte today hadn't so gravely upped the ante. Good as his word (What *shall* we do for money?), Ambrose cut off his connexion with the film company as of that Monday. Inspired perhaps by Richardson as well as by the Battle in the Belfry, he has vowed to commit himself absolutely to the printed word: letters and empty spaces on the page! The whole hot week since, he has rededicated his energies to Perseus, resolved to redraft that piece (and, I daresay, somehow to work Bea Golden into the plot, now he's been in her knickers). Bastille Day's humour passed; his obnoxious "5th Stage" behaviour reasserted itself. I spent *my* week daily visiting his mum in hospital, wishing they could let the poor thing die; Magda more often than not was with me, a real friend now I'm in "her" stage, urging upon me patience and Italian old wives' advice for getting pregnant. Between sickbed and seedbed (daily follow-ups to the Shower of Gold, here at 24 L), we watched Apollo-11 & Co. lift off for the moon (Magda's one of those who seriously wonder, to Ambrose's delight, whether it isn't All Faked by the Television People) and Dorchester County, with proportionate to-do, make ready for last night's opening of its nine-day tercentenary celebration.

We imagined Prinz's crew to be on the margins of that latter action, though what exactly he's up to these days in the Mating Sequence way, we can't well tell. Yesterday evening we went down to Long Wharf to witness the opening-night activities: proclamations by the mayor and the county commissioners, tugs-o'-war between such civic organisations as the Citgo Bushwhackers and the Rescue Fire Co.'s Chimney Sweepers, calliope tapes amplified from the *Original Floating Theatre II* at pierside—all amiable provincial entertainment, I don't mean to belittle it. Most especially we approved the new county flag, a buff field bearing the arms of the 4th Earl of Dorset: supported by twin pards rampant, a shield quarterly or and gules with a bend vair, topped by the earl's coronet, a fleur-de-lys or, and an Estoile argent of eight wavy points. Under all, the charge *Aut Nunquam Tentes Aut Perfice* ("Finish What You've Started," shall we say), which it pleaseth us to take for our own, vis-à-vis our project of engenderment, and Ambrose for a particular spur to his myth in progress. Sure enough, the filmists were there, footage, footage, though nothing in the mating way was visibly transpiring. With them, if our eyes did not deceive us, was your odd-duck neighbour Jerome Bray, looking *very* strange even in the costumed crowd. No sign of Bea Golden, to my continuing relief, nor of Marsha Blank, ditto. Ambrose studiously ignored them all. Prinz gave us a long, neutral look through his viewer and turned away.

442

This morning's program, for us and for the tercentenary, was to have been a presentation, from the stage of the showboat, called *Dorchester County in Art & Literature*. But we never got aboard, for as we crossed the municipal park we saw Prinz's crew setting up their light and sound gear beside that of a mobile television news unit from Baltimore. This latter, alas, was interviewing Ms. Golden—just flown in, presumably, from the Farm, and unfortunately fetching in early-19th-Century crinolines (1669 or not, the committee had tapped her to dramatise the county's resistance to Admiral Cockburn's Chesapeake foraging raids in the War of 1812, so the telly man was explaining to his microphone)—and Ambrose was inclined to Say Hello. Before we could do *that*, however, I luckily espied (to my true dismay) J. Bray again, on the fringes of the crowd, in earnest conference with, of all people on the planet, *Angela!*

Magda, Peter, her twin elder cousins—nowhere in sight. What on earth was Angie doing there, *with that person?* Ambrose literally *ran* to snatch his daughter away, once I pointed out to him their tête-à-tête. The pair were passing under Prinz's mike booms as he overtook them, manned by one of those chaps who'd come to their director's rescue in the tower. Just as Ambrose collared Angie by her T-shirt top (MARY-LAND IS FOR CRABS, with a red claw pinching each prominent nipple) and Bray by his—well, cloak—the boom swept 'round and down and caught him a terrific clout upside the head as aforespecified, dropping him cold as a mackerel to the blacktop.

Bray vanished (no mean trick, you'd think, in that drag, but he manages it); Angie set up a caterwaul; the mike boy was all apologies. One of the twins appeared after all, a husky young replica of Peter who'd only gone for ices; Bea Golden broke off her interview but kept a little distance; the Rescue Fire Co. ambulance crew, standing by, came to our rescue, even giving Carl and Angie a lift home via the hospital emergency room. Magda hurried down from the cancer ward upstairs, Peter over from the Lighthouse next door; it was a regular homecoming.

Ambrose was up by then, but groggy: mild concussion, no detectable fracture of the skull. We were instructed to keep an eye out for nausea and vertigo, barring which, sleep and aspirin ought to do the job; we weren't to be alarmed at (what now pretty scarily began to manifest itself) his temporary circuit-failure. He was discharged. I overrode P. & M.'s desire to fetch him *chez lui* for recuperation, but accepted Magda's help in getting us back to 24 L (Peter's leg is worse; he no longer drives).

Here we yet abide, sir, still Getting It Together whilst Apollo-11 and Luna-15 zip 'round their moon orbits, and Thor Heyerdahl's crippled *Ra* limps on toward Barbados, and the strange news trickles in from Martha's Vineyard of Senator Edward Kennedy's (also peculiar) accident. It was that fucker Prinz, right? enquires my woozy master. I daresay, luv, say I. And I *do* dare so say, though I never saw him and

443

though the mike boom lad (not the *light* boom, luv) has rung us up twice, in fear of lawsuit no doubt, to ask after his victim's condition and to swear it was All Accidental.

Bea Golden has phoned too. Somewhat timidly, I am pleased to imagine. No mention, of course, of *their* Mating Season Sequence down on Bloodsworth Island. Magda reports that Angela reports that the Funny-Looking Man only wanted to read her T-shirt and warn her that insect repellents cause cancer.

Well, John! As the Chappaquiddick people put it, much is yet unclear. Marvellous though Coincidence can be, in life as in Uncle Sam Richardson's novels, we strongly incline to our Ambrose's view that it was that fucker Prinz's doing. With the mike boom, dear. Which gives us to worry that on this front too, once he recollects himself, what my Dorchester darling hath begun, he may resolve to finish.

We pray not: I mean my friend Magda and her pro-tem *Doppelgänger*, yr faithful

G.

R: *Lady Amherst to the Author.* The Battle of Niagara. Surgery for Magda. Lady Amherst desperate.

24 L Street

26 July 1969

John,

Ra's in Bridgetown Harbour, the moon men are back on earth and quarantined aboard the *Hornet*, young Mary Jo Kopechne's in her grave, and Teddy Kennedy's on probation with a suspended driver's license. Today's St Anne's Day, mother of the Virgin, and—Mother of God!—Dorchester County Day, the windup of "our" tercentenary. "Floats," high school marching bands (the musicians outnumbered by troupes of strange-looking girls twirling batons), volunteer firemen in procession with their shiny machines, the dénouement of "The Dorchester Story" at the municipal baseball park, and the planting there of a time capsule to be opened in 2069: a sort of letter to the future containing all this news. Whose sender, like myself, may not hope for a reply from the addressee.

Today's also the 194th anniversary of the inauguration of the U.S. Postal Service. Happy birthday, U.S. Mail! The commencement of dog days. The end (as the full Buck Moon approacheth, and with it no doubt my monthly monthlies) of our unfilmed Mating Season Sequence at 24 L. And, 155 years ago, the day *after* the Battle of Niagara in 1814, also known as the Battle of Lundy's Lane, our topic for this week's letter.

That battle (on the Canadian shore of the Niagara River, just below the Falls) was bloody and inconclusive, a sort of stand-off, as was "our"

444

"reenactment" of it yesterday before the cameras. General Jacob Brown's Americans had crossed the Niagara from Buffalo earlier in the month and captured Fort Erie on 3 July; two days later, led by Winfield Scott, they managed a considerable psychological victory at Chippewa, just *above* the Falls, by driving back the British regulars with heavy casualties. On 25 July, they sallied forth to Lundy's Lane and met a regrouped and reinforced British army. From 7 to 11 P.M. the fighting was close and sharp, including hand-to-hand bayonet engagements in the dark; each side suffered nearly 900 casualties, about 30% of their actively engaged troops! The Americans won the field, but ill-advisedly withdrew to Chippewa and thence (tomorrow) back to Fort Erie, returning the initiative to the British and abandoning their invasion campaign. Both sides claimed victory.

I rehearse all this to remind myself that I was once an historian of sorts, and to put in what perspective I can the confused, distressing events of yesterday. The "real" historian on the scene this week has been our old friend the new Distinguished Visiting Lecturer in English at Marshyhope, you know whom, who appeared from Redmans Neck or Barataria, all smiles and mellifluous couplets, to volunteer his services as Reg Prinz's historical consultant, at least until the company returns (next week) to Niagara. Cook's idea it was—since Prinz had postponed that return in order to film the D. Co. tercentenary—to kill two birds with one stone by exploiting the "1812" episodes of "The Dorchester Story," that ongoing nightly pageant at the ball park which tonight attains the present and projects the future. There were all the "extras" one could use, more or less in period costume (the same outfits serve for the Colonial, the Revolutionary, and the 1812 episodes), dramatising the exploits of the Marshyhope Blues versus Joseph Whaland's Picaroons in 1776 and the depredations of the British fleet in 1813/14; more than willing to extend their props and performances gratis to The Movie. Since it is, anyroad, not the *war* we're interested in but its reenactment—in which 1969 and 1812 (and 1669, 1776, and 1976) are tossed together like salad greens—the historical inaccuracies, the thinness of the sets, the amateurishness of the actors, all play into our hands.

Yup: *ours* again, John. *Aut nunquam tentes* et cetera, exactly as I feared on Saturday last. As soon as his head cleared (Sunday morning), Ambrose was furious with himself for having abandoned like General Brown the field he'd won on Independence Day: *i.e.* (and woe is me), B.G., that all too tangible token of his "victory" over Reg Prinz on the *O.F.T. II.* Bea is, I am to understand, only the Symbol of What's Being Fought Over (a flesh-and-blood symbol, alas, which can be, which has been, reslept with): the *fight* is the thing now, the armature of a drama which has clearly outgrown its original subject. Your fiction is at most the *occasion* of the film these days; perhaps it was never more than that. One would not be surprised if the final editing removed all reference to your works entirely, which are only a sort of serial cues for Prinz and

445

Ambrose to improvise upon and organise their hostilities around. Those hostilities—between "the Director" and "the Author"—are the subject, a filming-within-the-filming, deadly earnest for all they're in the "script" and despite Ambrose's being literally on Prinz's payroll as of Thursday 24th.

That day, aptly, was Commerce & Industry Day in Dorchester (each day of the tercentenary has had a Theme). On the Wednesday, misfortune resmote the family Mensch, from a most unexpected quarter: with Andrea still a-dying in hospital and Peter imprudently putting off his own treatment till she's done, *Magda*, poor thing—La Giulianova, *l'Abruzzesa*, whom I so wrongly feared and now feel such connexion to—having felt abdominal discomforts for a secret while and gone at last, bleeding, for gynecological advice, was clapped straightway into surgery, one wing over from her mum-in-law, and hysterec-tomised.

Fibroid tumour; patient doing well enough physically, but in indifferent psychological case. Over and above her concern for the family (Peter is not immobilised yet or otherwise helpless; the twins are looking after things), Magda is suffering more than usually from the classic female set-down at the loss of her uterine function. The woman loved not only pregnancy, childbirth, and wet-nursing; she loved menstruation, that monthly reminder that she was an egg bearer, a seed receiver, generator and incubator of fetuses. More than any other woman I know, Magda relished the lunar cycle of her body and spirits: the oestrus and *Mittelschmerz* of ovulation, the erratic moods and temperature fluctuations of the menstrual onset, the occasional bad cramps and headaches, even the periodic flow itself. She ought to have borne more children. When I called on her after surgery, she wept and kissed me and said, "Now it's up to *you.*"

No comment.

Among the effects of this turn of events on Ambrose was a sober review, with his brother, of the family's finances. All bad news, of course. Indeed, their mother's only cheer in her cheerless terminality is that at last they need no longer fear insolvency, having achieved it. Mensch Masonry has passed officially into receivership, and precious little there is for the receivers to receive (the status of the Lighthouse is moot: in an ill-advised moment the brothers designated the camera obscura as corporation property, thinking to take tax advantage of its unprofitability; it may therefore be claimed by M. M. Co.'s creditors). On Commerce & Industry Day Ambrose put Perseus aside once more—surely that chap will ossify before Medusa gets to petrify him!—sought out Prinz (I wasn't there), and grimly informed me afterward that he was on salary again, "no holds barred."

Also, that A. B. Cook was waxing heavy on the 1812 business, which—especially in the forepart of August, up your way—is to be coordinated with the "Mating Flight" and "Conception" sequences. He

446

did not wish to speak further of it, though he might very well require my assistance. However—"especially *now*" and "given our poor showing on the pregnancy front"—I probably ought to look for things to get even worse between us before they get better. It All Depended.

O John: *damn* the fellow! And myself for merely damning instead of getting shed of him! I did at least tell him—when he said we-all would be "echoing the Battle of Niagara" in the ball park next evening (*i.e.*, yesterday, Military & Veterans Day), and that Bea and Cook and perhaps J. Bray would be involved—that he would have to fight that battle himself, as I was scheduled to spend the P.M. with his ailing family. He. . .*regarded* me, and left to "go over the shots" with his confreres.

For my pains, I get a concerned frown from Peter, a dry chuckle from Andrea, and a mild reproof from Magda for attending them instead of—*what*, for pity's sake (I ask M. rhetorically)? Playing the vile procuress Mrs Sinclair to Ambrose's Lovelace and Bea Golden's Clarissa? Magda does not know the novel. Holding Bea down, then, whilst he climbs her for the cameras? Magda replies, not to my questions but to my condition: When is my period due? Is there yet hope? Due Monday or Tuesday next, I respond, and there's been no hope from the outset. Meanwhile, what is Ambrose up to out at that ball park?

Why, as best I can piece it together this sore Saturday, he was up to some mad staged replay of that set-to in the tower, reported in my last, which not surprisingly caught Prinz's and Ambrose's retrospective fancies in equal measure. "Background footage" only, at the ball park: a certain amount of military bustling about with those handy extras to "echo Lundy's Lane" whilst the county high school bands play martial airs and the twirlers twirl by way of "pre-spectacle entertainment" before the evening's installment of The Dorchester Story. Which last, vertiginously, was to deal with the county's contributions to the Civil War, the two World Wars, and the Korean "conflict"! (No mention of Vietnam, too confusing a matter for pageantry.) Then out to Redmans Neck for the Mating Season sequence: the shooting script itself substituted for *Clarissa;* Bray this time (quite at home in that belfry, I'll wager) to aid the Author's assault on the Director, "their common foe," in hopes of then eliminating the Author in turn and gaining sole sexual access to. . .my stand-in!

I.e., Bea, in 1930's costume. Their (simulated) copulation inter-rupted as ours was on Bastille Day by the Director, who films it with his hand-held and is filmed filming it by the regular camera crew. The Author to succeed as before in destroying that first film (but with Bray's aid, who I suppose has been hanging by his feet from a rafter, shooting overhead stills) and to *retire with his lady* in apparent triumph. Where-upon the Director reappears in the empty belfry, surveys without expression the pile of ruined film, reloads his camera, and exits.

Lengthy shot of deserted belfry (Where's Bray?) to remind viewer that Author's victory is at best ambiguous, since entire scene has been filmed and is being viewed. Got it?

The Battle of Niagara ended before midnight on 25 July 1814. Ambrose came home by dawn's early light this morning. Late next week, up in Buffalo, in similar juxtaposition to a very minor skirmish there known as the Battle of Conjockety, or Scajaquada Creek (2 August 1814), they will replay the mike-boom "accident" of last Friday week: the Director's Revenge on the Author. Thus the Author informed me this A.M., truculently, at the end of his account of last night's action.

Never mind Conjockety, I said, and demanded to inspect his penis. His what?

Yer bloody 'and-'eld, said I. Fetch 'im out!

He did, defiantly, for he knew what I was after, we having remarked together in frisky April how the old Intromitter, when thoroughly applied, will look, even hours later, recognisably Applied. I forwent inspection: his gesture and manner were confession enough. Sick to tears—and *angry!*—I went at him at last, with the first weapon that came to hand (I was at my desk): a brummagem letter opener marked *Souvenir of Niagara Falls, Canada,* where in a campy June moment we'd bought it. Nicked his writing hand, too, I did; first blood drawn between us, not counting my four menstruations since the bloke first applied *his* opener to *me* in March. Should've gone for that instead, made a proper Abelard of him! He caught my wrist then, as men do, and made me drop *Niagara Falls;* forced me to a chair and held me (I don't mean lovingly) till despair got the better of my rage and I broke down.

He apologised. Not particularly for having humped Bea Golden again, but for the Inevitable Pain he's been putting me through in this Stage. To me it seems Evitable! And by way of *soothing* me—as he leaves just now to fetch Angie to the Dorchester Day Parade—he supposes that my hyperemotionality is premenstrual! I shriek and scrabble after that *Souvenir.* . .but he's out before I can find it, or reach the kitchen for a better blade.

Thus am I reduced to *this* one, Clarissa Harlowe's: a decidedly poor substitute for the sword, in this author's opinion. I do not forgive my lover this new trespass. I do not forgive him this whole 5th Stage, or the 4th before it. Even if (they're all so "into" the Anniversary thing) his Reign of Terror should end with the French (tomorrow 175 years ago), I find myself conceived—if of nothing else—of an impulse grand as Roderick Random's: for *revenge.*

But what would even touch the man? Not to mention *sting* him, as he's stung me! Ought I to bed with Reg Prinz? With A. B. Cook? With Peter Mensch? None of them, for their different reasons, would give me a tumble, much less a tumbling. Oh, unfair!

Who's keeping *you* company these days, dear Addressee? Have you scores of your own to settle in this line? Shall I make a side trip from the Battle of Conjockety and hand-deliver next Saturday's letter from your Germaine?

Y: *Lady Amherst to the Author. Odd business in Buffalo.*

Scajaquada Motor Inn
Niagara Falls Boulevard
Buffalo, New York 14150

2 August 1969

Near but Distant Neighbour,

"Your Germaine" will post this after all, like its predecessors, instead of delivering it to you herself. Your silence has drawn so many words from this pen—which has still a few to write—'twere pity to break it with conversation.

The Buck Moon filled five days since; no sign yet of my "period." I do not doubt that what we have here is a mere irregularity for a change, or a mere missed monthly, or that at last I'm putting the old lunations behind me in the natural way, without benefit of hysterectomy, oöphorectomy, salpingectomy. I'm nearly fifty!

But the effect on Ambrose of this delay (together with our set-to last Saturday with that *Souvenir;* the sobering decline of his mother and brother; perhaps too his sense of what's about to happen in the Movie) has been marked; was so even before we flew to Buffalo yesterday. Since the morning of the letter opener, for example, he has not to my knowledge "been with" Bea Golden: a lapse of attentions that plainly piques her. He has allowed as how I may wear *my own clothes*, John: neither the teenybopping or hipsy-potsy costumes of June nor yet the flapper drag of July, but *my own clothes!* Sensible middle-aged mid-lengths! Admirable Abercrombie's! Blessed Bonwit's! Bliss! He has waxed humorous, friendly, even affectionate, as back in March, but without March's posturing and bluster. Daily, discreetly, he enquires. . . No, I haven't, say I, but don't be so ruddy foolish as to suppose. . . Of course not, he agrees. Still. . .

Okay: I like it that his Robespierre's gone to guillotine at last. Though I believe life to be no more probable in my old womb than Tuesday's Mariner-6 photographs show it to be on Mars, and though the season's maiden tropical storm (Lady Anna) is moving our way from the Caribbean, I am much gratified by this serene "developement" and look forward with appropriate interest to learning what the character of the Sixth Stage—*our* stage!—of our affair will be. (I would be tempted to wonder, with your Menelaus, how Proteus can ever be confidently known to be "himself" again, having been all those other things—but a mad experience last night has shown me how.) I still truly love

449

Ambrose, don't ask me why; daresay I shall even if he comes 'round to loving *me*, as he most certainly appeared to do from March through May.

Nevertheless, sir, and though my late behaviour argues contrariwise, I am *not* by disposition a hand puppet, whether it's Ambrose's or even André's hand under my midlengths. Mr Mensch's apparent abdication of his tyranny has not ipso facto cancelled my resentment of so extended and public a humiliation as mine since spring: the loss of my job, my "self-image," my self-respect. When in my last I threatened reciprocal infidelity—a rum sort of retaliation, that, and retaliation itself a rum sort of game—I was only half-serious. *I.e.,* I was half-serious! I came back up here with Ambrose because I *do* still love him; but I did in fact try to ring you up, no doubt with mixed motives, but principally I'm sure with a view to terminating all tyrannies, including this insulting one of our one-way correspondence. I learned among other things that you've vacated this city to live year-round in your Chautauqua cottage. . .whereupon I lost interest in your pursuit, realising I'd prefer after all not to *discuss* with you what I have at such immoderate length confessed. Hence my salutation.

I even imagined myself ready to kick this habit, my Saturday epistolary "fix," whatever the withdrawal pains. Then came last night's dreamlike adventure, which, though I was its victim, I am still far from understanding.

As we have seen, all doors open for the maker of movies. Reg Prinz & Co. had preceded us to Buffalo, and a bit of judicious PR had evidently preceded him. Both local campuses of the state university, I don't have to tell you, have modest but active departments of film, and I gather the city prides itself generally on its hospitality to new art. A word to the right people that Prinz will be "echoing" the Scajaquada Creek Battle of 1814 has put at his disposal, with attendant fanfare, as much of Delaware Park (through which Scajaquada Creek runs, I learned yesterday, dammed now to form Delaware Park Lake but memorialised by an eponymous expressway) as he needs for as long as he needs it, plus the resources of the flanking institutions: the Erie County Historical Society and the Albright-Knox Museum of Art. Plus more graduate-student volunteer helpers than he can sort out, all eager to improve their credentials, and at least half of them (so it seems to me) stoned out of their American minds.

We were scarcely checked into this unpronounceable motel (accent on the antepe*nul*timate) before being whisked off last evening to a cocktail buffet in the Park Pavilion, hosted by the directors of the institutions aforecited. Hello from a cultural attaché of the mayor. Welcoming statements from the two curators, praising what they took to be our combination, in this Belligerently Antihistorical Decade, of the historical foretime and the avant-garde present, a combination nowhere more aptly symbolised than in the architecture and the collection of the museum beside us: half Greek revival and half front-edge contemporary. Trustees and local patrons of the arts turned out spiffily in evening clothes among the jeans and patches of the with-it young. Whatever justice there may be in the proverbial put-downs of Buffalo, N.Y., I found it agreeable indeed to be back in a genuine *city,* among what appeared to be genuinely civilised folk: the black-tie crowd and the blue-jean crowd on easy terms; the night balmy; the catering not bad at all; the sweet smell of *Cannabis sativa* mixed with that of roses, pipe tobacco, and chafing-dish chicken tetrazzini; taped rock music on the pavilion P.A. Add Ambrose's new mildness, the contrast with Dorset Heights, the being back in *my own clothes,* even the absence of humidity and mosquitoes—I thoroughly enjoyed myself.

Joe Morgan was there! Come over from the Farm as historical consultant (A. B. Cook, it seems, remained behind in Maryland), he was more conventionally dressed than at last sight, but still long-haired, necklaced, somewhat crazed-appearing about the eyes. In the spirit of the evening I was delighted to see him; we hugged hello and had a good talk. Crazed or not, Morgan has still his low-keyed, quick-smiling, intense, but almost boyish authority, once so appealing to his students and colleagues. He has I gather rather taken over the Farm, by his natural leadership, since the Doctor's death, but we didn't speak of that. We talked History for a bit, apropos of the occasion, two ex-professionals reminiscing: How a pathetic remnant of the Iroquois League, some 100 warriors, fought on the American side under General Brown in these last engagements on the Niagara Frontier, hoping to retain what was left of their reservations in western New York. How underrated by historians was the influence of anti-British sentiment among French Canadians generally throughout the war, and the particular Anglophobia of wealthy French refugees from the Terror, who like Mme de Staël had bought huge landholdings along Lake Ontario and the St Lawrence, but who unlike her had emigrated, raised impressive châteaux in the forests, and after 1814 confidently expected fallen Napoleon to appear among them and establish a sovereign French-Canadian state. Et cetera.

When Ambrose and Bea—separately—joined us, the talk turned to gossip. My lover had been dancing with, of all people, Ms. Merope Bernstein—remember?—who, her bum apparently mended, had come over from the Farm with Morgan and their polyglot comrades: a large black girl, a somewhat sinister-looking Latin, and an *echt* Manhattan greaser of indeterminate ethnicity. Her quondam stepmother had been dancing with this last, looking alas neither unattractive nor out of place in a boutique redskin outfit—Tuscarora mod?—and came to our table clearly to flirt with Morgan in demonstration of her indifference to us. I paid her no mind. Ambrose merely smiled. Joe indulged her lap-perching and osculatory effusions with mild indifference. Bea soon went off to find her Reggie.

Ms. Bernstein, Ambrose reported, was relieved to find her erstwhile protector Bray nowhere in evidence. She and her colleagues had come armed with unspecified weapons against possible menace from him, whom they regard as a dangerous lunatic and counterrevolutionary. Their attitude gave Ambrose to wonder, temperately, about the physical welfare of his ex-wife, last seen (we recall) on 4 July in Bray's company aboard the *O.F.T. II.* Thereby, it turns out, hung a little tale, which discreet Saint Joseph had been going not to tell, as not particularly our business, but now judged it best to:

Seems your ex-protagonist (and Morgan's old antagonist), creepy Jacob Horner, has conceived some sort of—*love?*—for Marsha Blank (we laughed at once, derisively; Morgan did not), and in his way was Much Concerned at her failure to reappear at the Farm after Independence Day. Especially when Bea Golden came back from Maryland with the glib report that "Pocahontas" had gone off with Bray to his Lily Dale goat ranch, presumably as Merope Bernstein's successor, Horner grew distressed.

Ambrose and I are grinning guiltily; the whole business is bizarre! But Bray *is* a lunatic. Ambrose takes my hand; heart-stirred (yet still resentful) I squeeze his. Now: in the Doctor's absence, and as part of some larger, ongoing project of his own, Joe Morgan has assumed the rôle of Jacob Horner's therapist and spiritual advisor: the Director, as he put it, of a sort of personal "remake." In this capacity, fast and loose with their text as Reg Prinz with his, he cancelled whatever had been Horner's therapeutic programme and prescribed instead that he sally forth from the Farm, make his way to Lily Dale, determine whether Marsha is there with Bray and if so whether voluntarily, take whatever action seemed appropriate to that determination, and report back to his therapist.

This Rx, mind, for a chap who has seldom ventured from that peripatetic commune in fifteen years! But—with every hesitation and apprehension in the world, I gather—Horner managed not only to fulfill his quest, but to fetch back the empty Grail herself. Bray wasn't home (*we* know he was in Cambridge again by this time, at the Dorchester Tercentenary); Marsha was, in a condition of some dishevelment and mild derangement, but not apparently against her will. She actually returned to Fort Erie with Horner—they expect Bray will be furious to find her gone—and is now (ready, John?) *Horner's woman,* so Morgan neutrally declared. She is, however, mysteriously obliged, to Horner's further distress, to go back to Bray temporarily in mid-August, to finish, in her words, some unfinished business.

You may be sure we are mightily intrigued by this bit of gossip; but Morgan, characteristically, would not deal in details. If Ambrose was curious about his ex, he was free to visit the couple (!) at the Farm. Insofar as anything on those premises is normal, they cohabit and receive guests like any normal couple. Joe himself had been their "dinner guest" only a few nights since, in the common dining hall. They are contemplating marriage!

He would not say more; visibly disapproved of Ambrose's raucous

452

whoops. "Pocahontas" and Jacob Horner: movable object meets resistible force! Morgan turned the conversation back to "our" film, its apparent theme of echoes and reenactments. 1812 *was* obviously something of a reenactment of 1776, and he Morgan was more and more inclined to oscillatory hypotheses, both historical and cosmological. But he hoped we all understood that redreaming history, reenacting the past, is a deadly serious, sometimes a seriously deadly business. (He would not elaborate; his eyes got That Look again, that I never saw before he left Marshyhope, vanished from Amherst, and surfaced among the crazies at Fort Erie.) As for our *other* theme, which "Bibi" Golden had told him of on her return from "Barataria"—the *mano a mano* between Author and Director, Fiction and Film—Morgan gently scoffed at it, and was supported in his deprecation by the young media types in our conversational vicinity. In their opinion, that was a quarrel between a dinosaur and a dead horse: *television,* especially the embryonic technology of coaxial-cable television, was the medium that promised to dominate and revolutionise the last quarter of the century.

These young people—Morgan too—were discreetly smoking marijuana laced with hashish, as were numbers of the artsy faculty crowd; at Morgan's invitation Ambrose and I shared their smoke. In some spirit compounded of dope, curiosity, the residual grudge mentioned above, and who knows what else, I asked "Saint Joe" in Ambrose's hearing (apropos of Eternal Recurrences), how fared my protean friend "Monsieur Casteene." Was he still at the Farm now the Doctor was dead, or had he moved the hot center of the Second Revolution back to Castines Hundred, where I had once been party to no trifling reenactment of my own?

Why, declared Morgan (and his eyes were the penetrating sympathetic blue now of my friend's and employer's at Marshyhope, not the wigged-out middlescent casualty's), the chap was somewhere about the pavilion; fact is, he *had* gone up to his baronial digs for most of July, but was back now at the Remobilisation Farm and had come over to the party with Merry B. and the others. Should we look for him outside?

I would look for him myself, I said, declining also Ambrose's carefully put offer to assist me. What I really wanted, I declared, was to clear my head. My ex-master considered this declaration for a grave half second, smiled, bade me take care on the stairs (we were in the open upper storey of the pavilion, overlooking the park lake to the front and an extensive rose garden to the rear, towards the floodlit museum). As I left, they were back to the Movie again, Morgan asking what exactly was this Mating Flight sequence Bea had mentioned, and how it related to the skirmish at Conjockety, or Scajaquada Creek. I was tempted to stay for a reply to that one, but I made my way out and down through silky night air to the paved, lamplit, leaf-shadowed lake edge—where, on the first bench under a streetlamp hard by the pavilion, as in a crudely plotted dream, I promptly espied my André!

Not A. B. Cook VI, John. Not any of the various "M. Casteenes" of

453

Fort Erie. *André:* the André who'd last materialised between acts at the Stratford Shakespeare Festival in 1967, rendezvoused with me après-theatrically at the Wolpert Hotel, fetched me thence home with him to Castines Hundred, and there—a mating flight indeed—impregnated me with his unerring sperm. It could be no other; it could be. . .no other. André!

He saw me too, perhaps had done before I saw him, and stood to greet me with two hushed baritone syllables: "Germaine."

Pipe dream? Then repass the hookah, please! So fine, so gentle, this man; so *truly* masterful, in the way that made me feel so easily my own again: Germaine Gordon the aspiring writer; familiar of Hesse, Huxley, Mann; acquaintance of Joyce and Stein; scholar; woman! He took my hand. It was the most natural thing in the world to stroll with him along the little lake, out of range of the loudspeakers, and say easily to each other the things one felt to say. *E.g.*, that life goes by, most of it vanity and vexation of spirit; that we understand too late what is truly precious, how we ought to have lived. Yet after all one has survived in this monstrous century, and not fared so ill. The Six Million are dead, the dozens of millions of others; the Second Revolution has not come to pass, any more than the Second Coming. Yet here we walk among the lights and roses, well dressed and fed, fit still and handsome, much vigorous life left in us. Forgive us then our trespasses, as we etc., and never mind all the vast unanswered questions.

Surely it was André!

We attained the rose garden, a little open labyrinth of teas and multifloras. The Albright-Knox could have been the Louvre, Scajaquada Creek the Seine, Lincoln Parkway the Champs-Élysées. I wept; my André comforted me, without pointless apologising. That business of Andrew Cook IV's letters, which I'd refused to play his game with? A baritone chuckle: too ingenious by half, no doubt, all that indirection: occupational hazard in his line of work. We were past two-thirds through the century, doubtless through our lives as well; God knew what form the Revolution would take, and when: maybe it would come to nothing more than two-way telly by 1976! André had in fact lost entire track of our son; was reduced to writing long letters to him which he could not post for want of address. Should he ever discover one, or otherwise locate that young man (he took both my hands; we found a secluded bench; the night was aromatic), Henri Cook Burlingame VII would be straightforwardly apprised of his true parentage and the circumstances of his rearing, let him make of those facts what he would, and urged to put himself in communication, if not with his father, at least with his too-long-suffering mother. Might it come to pass before Guy Fawkes Day next!

It was astonishingly *easy*, John. Heaven bless whatever chemistry made it so! Was he alone these days? I enquired. André smiled and sighed: *Oui et non.* He believed I knew of his little arrangement with the Blank woman? *That* had become quite impossible. He was both relieved and sorry to hear that she had involved herself with the peculiar M. Bray; felt perhaps even sorrier for Jacob Horner for having "rescued" her and—as was said to have been the custom in prerevolutionary China concerning preventers of suicide—thereby assumed lifetime responsibility for her welfare. Himself, he satisfied his needs with whatever lay untroublesomely to hand—I would be amused to hear that the Bernstein girl, for example, had conceived a veritable passion for him, which he saw fit to indulge shrug-shoulderedly whilst deploring her want of personal hygiene—but he had no companion; he was alone, and neither happy nor wretched so to be. But how was it between me and my friend, whose ex-wife had unbecomingly reported about him so many and poisonous things? I was, André was gratified to observe, in my own clothes again: might he take that to mean that Ambrose and I had worked out our difficulties and were happy?

Things had indeed been troubled, I replied, but seemed less so presently. And I loved Ambrose, yes.

Eh bien. And he me?

In his way. As *you* did, André. My fate.

For some moments we reflected silently in the dark. André bade me excuse him for thirty seconds. It took some doing not to clutch at his jacket sleeve, but I said, "Just now I could almost excuse you these thirty years." He brushed my forehead with a kiss; stepped into the shadows behind our bench; returned smiling in half a minute or less. Then: Would I take a short drive with him? He had a thing to show me. I smiled and declined. He clucked his tongue. The scent of the roses was preternaturally strong; no doubt the hashish intensified my perceptions. When André put an arm about my shoulders and drew me to him on the bench, I kissed him unhesitatingly, but without passion. His tone changed. He touched me; I responded. Just into the car, he whispered; please? I shook my head, but permitted myself after all to be led off, a proper Clarissa. The drug really was getting to me; the little walk from bench to curb seemed miles.

Even so, I drew back when he opened the door of a small black car. André Castine in a dusty Volkswagen? He was huskily urgent: Who cared where? In the road, in the treetops, in the sky! Firmly now I said no. And he—what a grip!—*yes*. Really, I would call out! He clapped a hand over my mouth, forced me toward the car like any rapist. I bit his finger; felt at once a tremendous *shock* from behind (where he now was), as if I'd backed into one of those electric cattle-prods the riot police used to be so fond of. I managed (I think) a single shout.

Dot dot dot.

Hashish plays hob with time! Ambrose and Joe Morgan discovered me on the park bench in the rose garden in less time by far, so it seemed to me, than it had taken to walk the fifty feet from that bench to that car (now gone) with André (ditto). They were of course alarmed to have found me "passed out" (they'd heard no cry; my clothes were intact; I seemed uninjured; no aches or pains, though my head was woozy).

455

Casteene? *He had been with them the whole time,* in the pavilion; had joined them directly I left to find *him,* thinking his company not welcome to me since our little difference of June, concerning which he assured Ambrose he bore no grudge. I was okay?

Well, it appeared so, though I felt mighty strange right through. For a particular reason, I did not see fit to tell them then and there what had happened, as best I understood it. I pled the dope; begged to be fetched to our motel at once; was. Then, whilst Ambrose at my insistence showered first, I investigated the clammy sog I'd commenced in the cab to feel between my legs. My clothing, I've reported, was in place, underpants included, though now sopping; it even occurred to me, along with the obvious ugly alternative, that my belated menses had arrived after all. But now I discovered (here goes, John) a dime-sized tear or. . .*puncture,* smack in the crotch of my knickers, and a greenish discharge unlike anything I've leaked hitherto: neither semen nor menstrual flow nor spontaneous abortion nor thrush nor monilia nor cystic discharge nor, for that matter, urine either normal or jaundiced. The old vulva, too, was a touch inflamed and tender. I hid the drawers under trash in the basket, showered, applied my travelling douche. Seeing I wasn't ill, Ambrose made to make love to me by way of solicitude and reassurance. I demurred, slept like a tot from the dope, awoke this A.M. clearheaded and feeling fine. Then we *did* make love: no problems; tenderness and "discharge" gone; a great comfort to leak the real thing again. No evidence whatever of Whatever: the whole P.M. a clear but distant dream, a dream.

Well! was I Mickey-Finned and raped? By *André Castine* in an old Volkswagen? By whom, then, and with what? Could it truly have been a terrific hash dream? (No: I rechecked those drawers. Ugh.) Thank heaven John Schott won't be reading *this* letter!

I am damned if I know. I will keep last night to myself—*our*selves— at least until I can check out "Monsieur Casteene" across the river, where no doubt our filmage will fetch us in time for the great Fort Erie Assault & Explosion of 15 August 1814. If I actually *was* raped last night, I must say it was as painless, scarless, hangoverless a business (but for that single shock) as smoking dope, its main consequences one ruined pair of knickers, a powerful curiosity to learn what's come over my old friend André these days, that he gets his sex by C.I.A. methods. . .and, even as I speak so lightly, a welling up of tears from what I had believed the long-healed fracture of my heart.

Whew! As I've spent the morning abed in the Scajaquada Motor Inn, penning this and shaking my head over last night, the Author and the Director have been prepping Delaware Park for the Conjockety and Mating-Flight shots (with echoes of Long Wharf and that mike boom business), which I myself am to play some rôle in later in the afternoon or evening, if I feel up to it.

I find, to my surprise, I rather do. Ambrose was truly tender with me this morning: not a word about my going off to look for André, only concern and—well, love. I may never know what hit me last night in that rose garden, but I know I'm anxious about the coming confrontation between my Author and his adversary, especially if Bea Golden has rejoined Prinz and if Ambrose's only ally, besides myself, is that erratic—

Omigod.

No. And yet. . .

No!

No more now!

G.

V: *Todd Andrews to his father. His Second Dark Night of the Soul. 13 R.*

Dorset Hotel

High Street

Cambridge, Maryland 21613

July 11, 1969

Thomas T. Andrews, Dec'd

Plot #1, Municipal Cemetery

Cambridge, Maryland 21613

Old Father,

Very hot, still, and airless where I am. How is it with you? Time itself has gone torpid in Maryland since the solstice; summer limps like one long day, my last, after my last Dark Night.

In an eyeblink this mid-morning—in mid-sentence in mid-committee meeting—the clear message of the three weeks past was delivered to me, with its plain postscript *re* the future. It's a message I ought to have got two chapters ago at least, in May: but never better than late, and I'm as buoyed as the Choptank channel by it.

13 R!

Where were we? That was Jane, of course, on the telephone back in June, calling my bluff. Ah, so I was back from Baltimore early—or hadn't I gone? In any case, she'd be a bit late for our evening, was tied up at work. And could we take a rain check on the fish? No no, she wasn't breaking our date; but she'd spent the whole day on an exciting proposal to extend m.e. (remember *me*, Dad?) into the fast-food-chain business, a real growth venture, wait till I heard; and then she'd happened to learn that Jeannine (Bea Golden) was flying in to open a revival of *The Parachute Girl* on the *O.F.T. II* at 8:30. Why didn't I meet her at her office at six? We'd have a drink somewhere, catch dinner at one of those Awful Colonel Sanders Things to check them out, and then take in the show?

My pause was not strategic. Hurt to the auricles, I'd've begged off, but before I could relocate my voice Jane said (in a much less presidential one of her own): I know, Toddy, you wanted to show me the cottage and all. But I'm really *into* this fast-food thing! Wait till you hear. Maybe after?

Her office, then. Six. I was a dear. No need for me to drive in: she'd send John out with the Continental. Bye.

Bye.

There was, in germ, the Message, but I didn't read it. Among my stillborn preparations I waited with a rye and ginger. Age tinkled my ice (my hands have begun to shake a bit more this year, Dad). To perfect my disappointment, our Author saw fit now to disperse the late-afternoon thunderheads out over the Bay. It was going to be a fine evening.

En route to town I reviewed the hard-crab run with Jane's chauffeur: still poor in the river, we agreed, but down-county they were getting the big jimmies and the sooks. Not like before, though.

I had been permitted to share the front seat, windows down. Approaching Cambridge, John radioed ahead and was given instructions: he raised the windows, cut in the A.C. to cool the car, and at the *me* parking lot suggested I move to the rear seat while he fetched Miz Mack. I was to help myself from the bar or wait for him to serve me, whichever. But even as I shifted places and he showed me how to work the backseat bar, a second buzzy message countermanded the first: I *must* come up and see the layouts for this newest Mack Enterprise; we could have our cocktails right there.

Jane, Jane. Did Love ever arouse you like the passions of Commerce? Another rye and ginger for me (she made a face); the Usual for her. As John mixed and blended (come *on,* Author: you'll really have her drink only that Galliano concoction called Golden Dream?!), I was shown how *me* would send Roy Rogers and Colonel Sanders back where they came from: *Maryland* fried chicken, *Chesapeake Bay* fish and chips, oyster(-flavored) fritters—and Crabsicles.

That's right, Dad. PR wasn't sure about the spelling yet—*Crabsicles* looked hard to say, and *Crabsickles* had the wrong suggestion amidships—but the Basic Concept looked to Jane like a winner, and it had to be good news on the bottom line that to make a crabcake hold together on a popsicle stick you were obliged to use less crabmeat and more Fillers and Binders.

The key, you see—she explained to me over a tub-o'-chicken in a Route 50 outlet named for a former Baltimore Colts football star—was logistics. Where did Sanders's East Coast outlets get most of their Kentucky Fried? From the big brooders right here on Delmarva Peninsula! Jane's idea was to buy into that industry and, by raising her own fryers and exploiting *me*'s existing cold-storage, trucking, and food-processing capacities, lower the unit cost per tub-o' enough to undersell the other chains in the Middle Atlantic States at least. The Crabsicles and oyster fritters would be low-profit window dressing with high Recognition Value; PR was working up a name for the chain that would sound both salty and southern-fried: something like *Colonel Skipjack* or *Chicken of the Sea. Dive-Inn Belle* had been considered and rejected. The idea was to *sell the Shore.* What did I think of *Cap'n Chick?*

I thought, I said, that some combination of Galliano and corporate capitalism must be the secret of eternal youth. Also, that a Mack as enterprising as Jane had no need to go to law over Harrison's estate: a simple four-way out-of-court split among herself, her two children, and Harrison's Follies (as we'd dubbed them) would give each a half-million before taxes, enough for her "Lord Baltimore" to buy a chunk of Cap'n Chick before it hatched; her passions thus wedded like fried chicken to Crabsicles, that investment would surely quadruple in value ere the Bicentennial, and she could both *have* her title, her two million, her children's goodwill, and her oyster(-flavored) fritters, and eat them, so to speak. Finally, that unless she put away her half of our tub-o'-chicken with a celerity more commensurate to that of its preparation and service, we'd miss Jeannine's entrance.

I was half joking, Dad. And not altogether unbitterly. My feelings were still bruised. Jane's tirelessness made me tired; the impersonality of her greed depressed me. She *would* sell the Shore if it were hers to sell, and not entirely for the profit—which, given her existing wealth, would be mainly of trophy value—but for the sake of grand and sharp transaction. Moreover, the Ocean City–goers who jammed the place were watching us with interest, assuming no doubt that so elegant and elegantly chauffeured a lady in a fast-food joint must be part of some jokey ad campaign, and where were the cameras? Nor did that traffic itself, swarming bumper to bumper over that particular nearby bridge, cheer me: the Eastern Shore of Maryland was not Jane's to sell because it had been sold, resold, oversold already.

But she took my utterance as oracular. Polishing off her drumstick-with-thigh-attached and scolding me for scolding her when I'd scarcely touched mine (she insisted on adding it to John's tub-o'; after all, we'd paid for it), she pressed to know, en route to Long Wharf, whether I really was inclined to an out-of-court division of Harrison's estate along those lines. More important, did I truly think Cap'n Chick could achieve a four-to-one stock split in seven years? She'd figured maybe *three* to one at best by the mid-1970's, if indeed she capitalized the venture as a semiautonomous subsidiary. . .

The Original Floating Theatre II. I had hoped after all—so I must infer from my disappointment—for some fertilization of our future from our past. It *was,* almost, the solstice, anniversary of a certain corner-turning (13 L) aboard the original *Original* in '37; a good bit of evening lay yet ahead; nostalgia was the showboat's stock in trade. I even took Jane's hand—kept it, rather, after helping her from the cool car into the heated evening. But John returned from the box office with tidings that Miz Golden had had airplane problems (the plot ground, if I remember rightly, of *The Parachute Girl*) and would not be arriving till

459

tomorrow. The minstrel-show half of the evening would be presented as usual; a medley of silent-film comedies would replace the postintermission drama. The management was offering refunds on advance ticket sales.

Oh Toddy, Jane said. I chose to read her tone as rue for having changed my original plan for the evening, but she may have been merely piqued at this thwarting of hers. We stood about for a bit, deciding. Most patrons seemed to be going aboard anyhow. The taped calliope music on the P.A. was "Bye Bye Blackbird," but again I didn't get the Author's message. Oh well, she left the choice to me. I opted, without enthusiasm, to give the *O.F.T. II* a try, if only by way of checking out the foundation's philanthropies. We could always leave.

We did, after half an hour. The theater was having air-conditioning problems. The emcee-interlocutor, a branch-campus drama major by the look of him, was more Cap'n Chic than Captain James Adams, and the civil-rights ruckus was still too recent history to permit any honest revival of blackface comedy. In its place was a pallid liberal "satire" that neither offended nor entertained anyone save the summer-jobbing students who enacted (and had presumably composed) it. Jane's mind was mercifully elsewhere—on unit costs per Crabsicle, I supposed, or franchise contracts. Mine, though still blind to the obvious, was on that right-hand column of correspondences set forth some letters back, which I'd lost the key to since Polly Lake failed me on June 17. In midst of some plastic levity between the pale surrogates of Bones and Tambo, I touched Jane's arm to ask her pleasure; she was out of her seat before I could put the question.

John was napping at the wheel; our Author likewise, or he'd have fetched us straight from Long Wharf to Todds Point and 12 R instead of routing us through the next diversion. Jane had, I now learned, been Thinking. About what I'd said at dinner? Mm. Why *not* wrap up the Whole Estate Thing out of court, and quickly, along some such lines as I'd suggested? Even a three-to-one Cap'n Chick stock appreciation would go far toward compensating for the difference between such a compromise and what she might get for her fiancé by hard-lining it, especially when one considered the reduced legal costs and the advantages of early reinvestment of her share. What's more, if the will were uncontested she could forget about that blackmail threat, which still distressed her though nothing further had come of it. The nigger in the woodpile, she reckoned (her term, used unabashedly in John's hearing as we drove into the Second Ward and the diversion now to be recounted), was the willingness of the prime beneficiary to agree to such a division: *i.e.*, the Tidewater Foundation, as represented ultimately by its executive director and counsel.

Aha.

But it *had* been my suggestion in the first place, had it not? She would tell me what: Why didn't we call on Drew and Yvonne then and there and put the idea to them, absolutely unofficially, just to see how it

460

went down? What a pity Jeannine wasn't with us too! But if three of the four main interested parties seemed to agree that it sounded at least worth considering further, Jeannine would surely not hold out, didn't I think? She'd never been troublesome *that* way. We could wrap it all up and forget about it in time for her, Jane's, remarriage. . .

I saw. And for when, pray, was that last-mentioned transaction scheduled? She patted my hand, smiled girlishly: not till fall. You are wondering, Dad, how it is we were driving already into the Second Ward when Jane impulsively decided to visit her son and daughter-in-law. So was I, until that throwaway announcement, like a casual grenade, disoriented my priorities. She and "Lord Baltimore" each had business to wind up before tying the knot, Jane declared. André was right that that "September Song" business was wrong: the less time left to one, the *more* patient one became about biding it.

Ah, Dad. Never mind the validity of the paradox: that sentiment, so clearly not Jane's own (who seemed as deaf to Time's chariots as she was historically amnesiac), stung me to the quick, as unexpected and intimate a revelation of her lover's reality as that breathtaking blackmail photograph. I was dizzied; wished myself out of there, wished myself—

What *Jane* wished, as we entered the new federal low-rent housing project on the edge of "Browntown," where the Drew Macks lived, was that *me* had been foresighted enough to see Tomorrow Now in 1967 or before, while all the Trouble was going on in the Second Ward. She could've bought out the slumlords for a song when Rap Brown had everybody scared, and never mind that fire insurance didn't cover riot-related incendiarism: arson was cheaper than professional demolition, and she'd've been in on the ground floor of the New Reconstruction boondoggle.

"I'm *joking*," she explained.

We Stock Liberals are not at ease in the Second Ward, Dad, especially exiting from black-chauffeured Continentals. People watched; I waved wanly to a few I knew. What's more, Yvonne Mack, smashing as always in her hair-scarf and Nefertiti makeup, was plainly edgy about our visit. The kids were away at camp in the Poconos; Drew was at a Big Meeting elsewhere in the project and wouldn't be back till Lord knew when. Yvonne is normally hospitable, more so than her husband, but we were offered none of the Tanqueray in clear view on her sideboard, for example. Jane sat without being invited to; I waited to be asked and was not. Yvonne popped up and down, sure that Drew would be sorry he'd missed us. Could she take a message for him? Bye, bye, then.

Well, Jane growled, back in the car. She of course was as at ease in the Second Ward as in the *me* boardroom, but miffed that Yvonne was learning discourtesy from Drew, and cross that we couldn't after all just Wrap the Whole Thing Up, Damn It.

Not my night for seeing the nose on my face, Dad: Drew in deep conference on the eve of Marshyhope's commencement ceremonies,

461

the disruption whereof we'd feared since September last! But I was too preoccupied by now with the incremental deflation of my *plan du soir:* Cap'n Chick, the *O.F.T.*, Jane's invocation of her affiancement and of the Cambridge race riots, which put me in mind of my adventure on the New Bridge with Drew and dear brave Polly. I was ready to call it quits—even formed that phrase in my head without hearing what I was telling myself. But now Jane was hungry! Now she was up for a *real* dinner! At the cottage! Let's pretend the whole stupid evening hasn't happened! Let's start over and do it right this time!

If only she'd not made that last exhortation. But now her girlishness was determined, and her language came straight from the Author: *Late as it was, it was not too late to save our evening.*

Back out to Todds Point! Bye, bye, John: Mister Andrews will fetch me home! I found myself asking, like a scared adolescent, Was she sure she. . .

She was sure.

Attend now, Father, my last evening as a late-middle-aged man. I fooled with drinks and charcoal briquettes and rémoulade while Jane ummed and hummed about the place, not so much unimpressed by what I'd preserved, restored, or remodeled as uncertain which was which. No time to bother with the fresh asparagus; it would be rockfish and a simple salad. But I was watching Jane; forgot to oil the fish grill; clapped my brow at the late recognition that my creamy garlic dressing for the salad was redundant, given the rémoulade; neglected to preheat the oven for the French bread; saw Jane, finger at her chin, begin to inspect the bedroom just as it was time to fork the fish.

A debacle. The fish skin burnt to the grill; the splendid animal overbroiled to a flayed, licorice-flavored mush; the sauce unappetizingly curdled; the salad indifferent; the bread doughy; Jane's airy compliments insulting; her banalities about bachelor cooking particularly silly. I guzzle the wine (its back broken by overchilling) and chew a bread crust, too gloomy either to apologize or to correct her. She stuffs herself, chiding my want of appetite. She is beautiful. My spirits are plummeting. Ten-thirty.

Well, I say, and begin to clear the table. The president of Mack Enterprises takes my arm and purrs a directive: Let 'em soak.

That is how our Author works: having put us exquisitely out of sorts, he then brings to pass our dearest fantasy. Bitterness smote me; Jane's extraordinary body (zip-zip, Dad: there it was) was a positive affront. I was surly; I was glum—and, of course, absolutely, almost belligerently impotent. Jane Patterson Paulsen Mack: Jane, Jane! So altogether, so *impersonally* self-willed and -centered, you could not only be "unfaithful" without a qualm, perhaps without even acknowledging to yourself that Infidelity was what was transpiring; you could (I realized to the bowels) even "love" a man and somehow be untouched by your own emotions! Cold as that Appalachian Chablis, I seized the hands that tried to rouse me; my voice came clotted, furious. *Did she remember*, God damn it? That this was the bedroom she'd strode naked into on the afternoon of August 13, 1932, Virginia Dare's birthday, to fuck me while Harrison went for ice? Did she remember that we'd been lovers from that day till March of the following year, and again from July 31, 1935 (Pony-Penning Day in Assateague, Va.), till the Dark Night of June 21 or 22, 1937? God *damn* it, did she not recall that Jeannine Patterson Mack Singer Bernstein Golden was very possibly my daughter? Had she never understood that—together with certain other, itemizable causes—it was love of her that had brought me, on that last-mentioned calendar date, to an impotence and despair not unlike those I was currently entertaining, thence to a resolve to blow up myself, her, Harrison, Jeannine, and the entire Original & Unparalleled Floating Opera? Finally, finally, did she not bloody understand, as *I* had come since the spring of this year to understand, that I still loved her desperately—there was the exact adverb—that I still loved her desperately desperately desperately?

Even as I spoke I saw that of course she didn't, couldn't so remember, recall, understand. Jane was properly alarmed at my outburst (and offended by my coarse language); I saw her consider how to deal with me. I released her, apologized, told her I'd wait on the porch till she was ready and then drive her home. Her self-possession was at once restored. I wasn't to be silly: it was late, she was tired; it had been an unfortunate evening, her fault; *she* should be the one apologizing. Et cetera. Come on, now. As for All That Stuff: of *course* she remembered, most of it anyhow, at least now I'd reminded her. Really, though, some of it she thought I'd made up over the years, or got from That Novel. I was such a romantic! Most men were, she supposed: certainly Harrison had been, Jeffrey had been, André was. Come on, now. The thing was, not to make a big thing out of it.

Absolutely unironically, Dad, she held my 69-year-old penis in her hand—the penultimate time that instrument shall ever be thus held—as she urged the above.

No sex? Why then, we'd sleep. Wouldn't be the first time! She *winked,* Dad; used the bathroom; soon returned in one of my old cotton shirts; voiced her gratification that we weren't air-conditioned, she much preferred the old-fashioned electric fan; bid me good night.

Our Author's proclivities notwithstanding, my life's recycling has not been slavishly mechanical. There was no Polly Lake to fart on PLF Day, 11 R. My previous Dark Night occurred in the Dorset Hotel, not the Todds Point cottage, and my impotence then was as sustained as my despair. A rather worse thing happened now. Under the glass of my desk here in the Dorset is a 69th-birthday card given me last March by Polly: a reproduction of a 1921 advertisement for Arrow shirts. Against a beige background are painted, in the handsome style of such advertisements in that period, a young couple in the cockpit of a sailboat. The vessel itself is invisible but for the highly varnished coaming over which the seated young woman negligently rests her elbows (and against which her companion stands facing her) and the attractively molded tiller on which he leans. Her auburn hair is piled Gibson-girl fashion and bound with a saffron scarf; she wears a beige middy blouse, sleeves rolled above her forearms; she fingers the end of its black neckerchief and smiles at something off their starboard quarter. *He* regards it too, benignly but more reservedly (her lips are parted; his are not, but his dark hair is, on the left); his black-belted trousers and (Arrow) shirt match her blouse, except for his starched white collar and green figured necktie, and like hers his sleeves are neatly rolled to the elbow. If the craft is under way, it is gently running before the wind, which lifts the forepart of his tie toward her face; but considering the hard angle of the tiller against which he casually leans, I judge it more probable that they're in a slip (not moored or anchored, given the aft breeze): no sheets, spars, or sails can be seen—neither can any dock lines—and it is unlikely he'd be looking so placidly astern, with neither helmsman nor crew minding any sheets, while coming about. Quite possibly of course the artist was no sailor, or chose not to clutter his illustration with lines, blocks, and cleats, just as he chose not to paint in a background or, for that matter, a deck and topsides. The couple are the thing (particularly, to be sure, their shirts), and he has got them right: they are young, privileged, well-bred and -dressed, easy in the world, sunny, beautiful. They are Jane Mack and Todd Andrews once upon a time.

It is, by the way, a fairly erotic advertisement, Dad: "Jane" wears no bra, and the spread of her elbows thrusts her breasts at me under the middy; the slip of her fingers down that scarf is inches from my trouser fly, plainly pouched in her direction; our legs, out of sight beneath the rounded coaming, must surely be touching, if not intertwined. No wonder the knobbed tiller thrusts up at her from behind me at just hip-height and must be put hard over; no wonder even my necktie will not stay down! It is after all an *Arrow* shirt, and she its willing target. But there is no vulgar urgency. We have everything, including time; we mildly look away, perhaps at Harrison returning noisily down the dock with extra ice.

Polly sent me that card unmeaningly, I believe, beyond the obvious evocation of my sailing habits. But it was on the date of its receipt, a month after Harrison's funeral, that Jane stopped by the office and, in a sense, commenced my recycling: indeed, our Author did not scruple to have me literally considering Polly's card when Jane came in! Now (I mean then, this fateful Friday, out at the cottage) her reappearance from the bathroom in my old tan shirt—with, yes, a contrasting white collar, made fashionable again by the last Roaring Twenties revival— her unbelievably youthful figure even more attractive half-clothed than naked, put me irresistibly in mind of that card. Impotence might have been easier, more soporific: a fit end to a misfired evening, to be slept off. Instead, "Oh, changed his mind, did he?" she said when she noticed me, and briskly lay back, parted her lips, and steered me into her (there's the final fingering). Half-erect, I ejaculated instantly; tried to keep going for her sake, but slipped out and couldn't reenter. Anyhow, she wasn't interested in an orgasm. Her eyes were closed, no doubt from fatigue, it had been a long day; she half smiled, whispered nighty-night, rolled over, and quickly fell asleep.

She slept busily as a child till morning, sometimes snoring. Not so I, on whom now, in the dark, 12 R came blackly down. As unbearably as in 1937—oh, more so, there were 32 more years of it—my emptiness, my unconnection, my grotesqueness came meticulously home, Then, though, I had thought Life devoid of meaning: luxurious, vain projection! Now it was *my* life, merely—how the boy in that sunny advertisement had misspent his mortal time. The world was what it was, and unbearable. Already by 1921 the first installment of Armageddon was astern. Farther aft lay, for example, the Napoleonic catastrophe, the genocide of native Americans, the wars of religion, the unimaginable great plagues—horror after horror, like dreadful buoys marking a channel to nowhere. Too much! The cottage creaked; the world rolled on, to no purpose. I was old, spent, silly. I was done with.

Towards first light I dozed enough to have a limpid, shattering dream. I was perhaps thirty, leaving "home" for "the office" on a luminous May morning, dressed in the manner of *National Geographic* advertisements of the time. There was the new electric refrigerator with coils on top; there were the glass quarts of unhomogenized milk on the steps. My black La Salle waited at the curb; my young wife Jane, still in her robe, held our son Drew, two years old at most, rosy and slumbrous in his blue Dr. Dentons. She wanted him to wave good-bye to me, but he was too drowsy: his fingers were in his mouth; his other arm lay loosely behind her neck; he laid his cheek against hers. I kissed them both: Drew smelled of milk and toast; Jane of soap and sleep. The light, the air, were unspeakably tender.

"Bye-bye to Daddy, now. Bye-bye? Bye-bye."

I awoke a truly old man: shaky, achey, fuddled. Did not at first know where I was, why, with whom. Then I knew, and groaned aloud without intending to. The sound roused Jane, fresh and ready though puffy-faced from her hard sleep. She was shocked: told me I looked like death warmed over; wondered whether I was ill. I could scarcely manage breakfast for shaking; slopped my coffee, cut myself shaving, could barely tie my tie. Head hurt; heart fluttered.

"You *must*'ve had a bad night!" Jane cried, uncertainly breezy. I started up the car to take us to town and realized I couldn't drive; Jane had to chauffeur me to the Dorset and call John from there. Marian the desk clerk was visibly startled too: both women urged me to call a doctor and forget about the commencement program that afternoon. I declared a nap was all I needed.

Good-bye then, Jane said. She'd be out of town again for a while. I'd better take care of myself; sleeping pill, maybe. Good-bye, then.

I got up the 28 steps to my room as toilsomely as Captain Osborn

Jones used to, lay down fully clothed, and slept till noon. Not a whole lot better. My head was woozy; my face in the mirror astonished me. I looked exhumed; Jane must have felt she was delivering an ancient derelict to the flophouse. I redressed and took a cab out to Redmans Neck to join the foundation trustees on the platform. Drew was missing; everyone else was there, and they all Noticed, asked me jokingly had I been ill. I don't know what I replied.

As I ought to have foreseen from Drew's absences, the ceremony was of course disrupted after all. Ambrose Mensch, our first honorary doctor of letters, had evidently conspired with Drew and a number of non-students, as well as the Marshyhope radicals, to stop the show. I don't believe Germaine Pitt had anything to do with it: she seemed more alarmed than I was, and indignant to the point of tears (she's been sacked anyhow). I myself was too "strung out," as the students say, to realize at once what was taking place. His citation read and degree conferred, Mensch launched into an unscheduled, Kurt Schwitters-ish sort of nonsense harangue, not at all scandalous I thought: a rather appropriate sort of inappropriateness, a properly nostalgic impropriety, evocative (to me) of the Dadaists and others who *didn't* wear Arrow shirts and sail elegant sailboats back in 1921. Even when Drew and the youngsters began Ho-Ho-Ho-Chi-Minhing and spraying the air with spray guns (to suggest our herbicidal campaigns in Southeast Asia, I presume), I thought them part of the entertainment. Granted, my wits were not quite about me; even so I was surprised to see so lively and harmless a stunt stop the show—and thus, I suppose, deny Drew the best part of his triumph. He himself hardly got into the act; he was still a hundred feet from the microphone when the campus cops nailed him.

And nailed the kids. And Mensch. And even Lady Amherst, at John Schott's insistence, though I was able to persuade them to let her go before they got hit with a false-arrest suit. I was *not* able to persuade Schott to resume the ceremonies: he was as certain the Commies had further tricks up their sleeves as I was that they hadn't, and I suppose he understood (his sort would) that terminating the exercises would magnify the gravity of the disruption and thus justify whatever reprisals he chose to indulge in. I got myself together enough to hitch a ride back into town in a state police car (Patrolman Jimmy Harris, our friend from the New Bridge Incident, *q.v.*, scolded Drew all the way to the courthouse: an educated fellow carrying on like a nutty kid!) to see that everybody got decent bail and that the sheriff's people didn't rough them up. My excuse to Schott would be that mishandling the arrests or the arrested would blow the college's prosecution.

Anyhow, the police had learned a few things since the civil-rights years: the shouted obscenities offended but didn't anger them; they brought charges but cracked no heads. Drew said I looked awful and recommended a macrobiotic diet. Beyond that we had no conversation; he did not thank me for arranging bail (Mensch did, cheerily). I learned

466

that one of the nonlocal demonstrators, by odd coincidence, was Jeannine's ex-stepdaughter, her second husband's child. I telephoned Schott's office to urge him not to take action until we could confer; no one answered. I was too exhausted to trek back out to Redmans Neck. The kids all said thanks and 'bye.

The Message, so long and repeatedly telegraphed, was buzzing at my ears, but not yet intelligibly. I crossed the park to the hotel, thinking vaguely I'd catch another nap and see Jeannine *that* evening on the *O.F.T. II*. As it turned out, I slept from four in the afternoon till five the next morning.

For all that, I felt no younger on the Sunday, nor looked less wasted. I seem truly and irrevocably to have moved overnight from middle to old age. I got through to Schott: he'd terminated both Mensch and Pitt, and was determined to revoke Mensch's doctorate. Three days earlier, I believe, I could have talked him out of those actions; clearly I'd lost authority! I telephoned my sympathy to Lady Amherst, who undeniably was on some wrong track with that Ambrose Mensch (why didn't she dress her age?), but was surely blameless in this affair. Miserable, she nonetheless thanked me—and hoped I was feeling better! To my surprise, *Drew* stopped by the room to make sure I was all right; an extraordinary gesture on his part, which at any time in the past many years, until three days since, I'd have tried with my utmost tact and gratitude to make the most of. As it was, I could scarcely register his confession of disillusionment with petty disruption, his shaken but not yet shattered faith in the Second Revolution. The 1960's were about done with; he himself would soon be 31. It was time, I believe he asserted, for the Movement to escalate from "trashing" to serious demolition; for himself to escalate his struggle against a real pull in him toward Centrism or worse, the gravitation of his age and ancestry. A surprising admission! At once embarrassed to have made it, Drew went on more surlily to predict that if he lived long enough he'd turn into me at best, his father at worst, and that he'd rather die.

Where in the world *was* I? At least, in my geriatric stupor, I didn't turn him off with Judicious Sympathy. He fidgeted awhile—a large, handsome, ineluctably wealthy-looking young man no matter what he wore—and then courteously bid me good-bye. Buzz buzz went the Message, no more clear.

Though I daily expected they would, things did not get better. Everyone at the office was concerned; at their insistence, and because I truly was not clearheaded enough to work, I took a week's leave, then another, thinking that perhaps a bit of a cruise on *Osborn Jones* would restore me to myself. But I was too dispirited to provision and cast off. What was the point of sailing, of anything, except in 1921, with a beige Arrow shirt and the girl in that middy blouse? I languished out at the cottage with gin, tonic, and aspirin. Jane did not inquire. Others did— even Drew and Yvonne again!—but I didn't pick up on the opportunity to work something out, somehow, between us, after so many years.

That tender, devastating Dark Night dream remained as fresh in my imagination as the morning I'd dreamed of; nothing interested me any longer.

Last Friday, July 4, I bestirred myself enough to drive into town. Jeannine had joined the list of Inquirers After My Welfare and invited me to view the evening's fireworks from aboard the *O.F.T. II*, which Reg Prinz had chartered for some sort of combination cast party and filming session. I thought, vaguely, to sound her out on her mother's proposal to settle the estate contest out of hand and out of court; and I felt more than ever—but vaguely, dully—on the verge of seeing belatedly something obvious to our Author but not to me.

It was a peculiar voyage—I'm not sure whether even my former self would've quite comprehended what Prinz and Mensch and Company were up to!—but not a voyage of discovery. I condoled Peter Mensch and wife (he's bankrupt and unwell, and his mother's dying, an old flirt I've known all my life and even courted briefly in the Nineteen-Teens, before she made a bad marriage to Hector Mensch). I chided his brother—mildly, as it was after all none of my business—for having so inconsiderately embarrassed his good friend Lady Amherst, whose reinstatement I was by no means confident I could effect. He told me, more or less, it was All Right, without telling me how so. I do not greatly like nor much comprehend that fellow! Germaine herself was not there—just as well for her self-respect, since Dr. Mensch seemed in ardent pursuit of Jeannine; whether in earnest or in connection with their experimental movie, I cannot say.

I did not see Jane, either. I apologized to Jeannine for having missed her opening two weeks earlier; she to me for having missed it too, that first night. She wondered politely if I was feeling better; said I looked as if I needed a vacation. There was no opportunity to bring up the will; anyhow it was hard to remain interested. Neither the literal fireworks from Long Wharf nor the figurative ones aboardship (too complicated and obscure a business for me to recount, Dad) illuminated the Message. It thrummed in my head again when Jeannine, at the party's end—she appeared to be running off somewhere with Ambrose Mensch!—bid me good night in an odd tone that seemed to me to have nothing to do with her promiscuous behavior. But I didn't quite catch it.

Then today—three Fridays and three dozen pages since 12 R!—the message of that Dark Night dawned on me. John Schott convened a morning meeting of what amounted to an ad hoc executive committee of the college: himself, his new provost Harry Carter, sundry deans, and (for reasons not at all clear and never explained) A. B. Cook the poet, who is to replace Germaine Pitt in September as Distinguished Visiting Lecturer in English but who presently has no official connection with the institution. I was there as counsel to the college, and in clearer days would routinely if cordially have challenged the chap's credentials; but I didn't care. He inquired, solicitously, Had I been ill?

468

We were met, Schott announced, to review the events of June 22, their implications and consequences. We did so: the disruption, the arrests, his cashiering of Adjunct Professor Mensch, his dropping of criminal charges against Acting Provost Pitt in return for her resignation, his intention to press them against Drew Mack and "the hippies," and his recommendation to the board of regents of the state university that Mensch's honorary degree be revoked.

Asked for confirmation, I acknowledged that no rules of the American Association of University Professors or bylaws of the state university had been violated, inasmuch as they did not cover adjunct and visiting professorships. Ms. Pitt's appointment as acting provost had been unusual in the first place, given her visiting status, and might be argued as de facto regularization of her professorial appointment; but if she really had resigned instead of being fired, she could of course not litigate. Had she, though? I asked. And why, since the college clearly had no case against her? Indeed, I declared (as forcefully as I could in my still-torpid state), it had been my intention to urge once again her reinstatement, the dropping of all charges against the demonstrators, and the recall of "our" recommendation to the regents concerning Mensch's Litt.D. The 1960's were winding down; so was our war in Southeast Asia; such demonstrations were not very likely to recur in the coming decade unless our government embarked on another adventurist binge, and inasmuch as (this time) no property damage to the campus or personal injuries were involved, prosecution of the demonstrators, including our founder's son, seemed to me likely to gain us little more than undesirable publicity. Even as we foregathered, I pointed out, the U.S. Court of Appeals was reversing the conspiracy convictions of Dr. Spock and Messrs. Coffin, Goodman, and Sperber: a sign of the changing climate of public and judiciary opinion.

Schott disagreed. What it was a sign of, in his view, was simply the old liberal Commie-coddling responsible for such conspiracies in the first place. Today was the anniversary, he observed, of the worst of the first series of Cambridge race riots, in 1963, a summer so violent that even the July 4th fireworks had had to be canceled. His point seemed to be that uncompromising prosecution could have spared us the decade, and was still necessary if we were not to carry the sixties into the seventies. The deans did not disagree. Harry Carter, less flaccidly than usual, reminded me (so had my authority waned!) that we had after all pressed no charges against Lady Amherst. There were none to press, said I. He and Schott smiled knowingly at each other.

Cook then, apropos of who knows what, remarked that today was also the anniversary of Alexander Hamilton's fatal duel with Aaron Burr on the Hudson palisades at Weehawken. We must be vigilant, gentlemen! And just seven years ago, on 7/11/62, Telstar I had inaugurated the era of satellite communications with a transmission from Maine to England. This very moment, eight Russian vessels were steaming toward Cuba! Who knew, he asked darkly, what seven years

469

hence, the 200th birthday of our republic, would bring? Again I considered questioning his presence in the room. But to my surprise he here came off his patriotic bluster and, with a show of reluctance, agreed that revoking Ambrose Mensch's degree would prolong the publicity of the late lamentable events; he urged Schott to withdraw his recommendation in that matter. Further, he declared himself gratified to hear that Lady Amherst had not been stigmatized by summary dismissal: no doubt she was under young Mensch's unfortunate influence; very likely she'd been a party to the disruption; he Cook even understood that the pair were, ah, a couple. But she was, after all, a lady.

Schott's secretary made an audible, disagreeable *hmp*. Her employer, with a reproving smile, asked her for The Letter. There were then triumphantly distributed to us photocopies of a document which Schott directed us to read forthwith and return: it could not decently be read aloud, he averred, and ought not to go beyond our meeting room. But it would, he trusted (with a glance at me), put to rest any notion of continuing Professor Pitt on the faculty, and explain both his demand for her resignation and her tendering it without protest.

Well, it was a remarkable letter: more precisely, a 7-page abridgment or reverse bowdlerization of the discarded carbon copy of an 18-page draft of a letter from Germaine Pitt to the author of *The Floating Opera* and other fictions, with whom she has evidently been in personal, if one-way, correspondence. It was typed on the letterhead of the provost's office and dated 7 June 1969. It commenced with the outcry *John, John,* and set forth its writer's complaints about her tyrannical lover Ambrose Mensch, who among other things obliged her to dress beneath her age and dignity, use narcotics, and forgo contraception (he wants a child by her). The language was candid and British, often witty, the detail intimate, the complaint affecting, the spirit prevailingly good-humored, even brave. I was more touched than scandalized; indeed, my chief surprise was that so admirable a woman would put up with such bullying from so otherwise feckless a fellow, go on about it at such (apparently) unreciprocated length, and foolishly make a copy of her confessions. But the letter itself suggested an explanation: the woman is middle-aged and lonely; she upbraids herself for indulging her lover's whims; is indeed at a loss to account for her own behavior, of which she vigorously disapproves; finally, she *loves* the chap despite his misbehavior, in part it seems because he evokes for her an earlier passion, in her young womanhood, for a Frenchman, by whom she bore a child. The letter was unsigned, but no one else in Dorchester County could have written it. My heart went out to Germaine Pitt: lucky, undeserving fellow, that Mensch, whose promiscuity with Jeannine aboard the *O.F.T. II* irked me now even more in retrospect!

My interest was caught too (should have been even more so, but other scales had not yet fallen from my eyes) by the coincidence that her former lover's name was André Castine: I recalled, before she invoked, the Castine-Burlingame intrigues in the *Sot-Weed Factor* novel and the peculiarity of Andrew Burlingame Cook VI's having a French-Canadian son named Henri Burlingame VII (we met him at Harrison's funeral, Dad, remember?). I was struck too, of course, by the further coincidence that Jane Mack's mysterious fiancé was named André: no more meaningful an accident, I suppose, than that Cook's first name and my last are nearly alike, or that I happen to live on Todds Point, next to Cook Point—we've seen how that *other* Author works! But still. . . And there were tantalizing implications of some connection between this modern Castine and our Mr. Cook: near the letter's end, for example, Lady Amherst complains of being variously tormented by "you [*i.e.,* 'John, John,' who does not reply to her letters], Ambrose, André, A. B. Cook." But if that connection was illuminated in the original, it was lost in the abridgment.

The committee were mightily entertained. I was not, and objected as strenuously as I was able both to the distribution of the letter in the first instance and to its abridgment in the second. Schott replied that we were not a judicial body: he had excerpted and put before us evidence of Professor Pitt's moral turpitude by way of justifying to us his demand for her resignation, a demand he was in fact under no legal obligation to justify. I responded that my objection was moral, not legal, and all the stronger for his being not legally obligated to justify his action. Schott countered—cleverly for him—that his obligation was moral, too. As for the abridgment, Cook now put in, he would attest that it was mainly in the interest of moral—he smiled: Perhaps he should say immoral?—relevance and consideration for our valuable time; but also (and this is why he himself had been shown the "original") his good friend President Schott had seen fit to delete references to a matter Cook would now reluctantly acknowledge, and which would explain Lady Amherst's including him among her "tormentors." One of the novels written by the addressee of the letter involved his, Cook's, ancestor, the original poet laureate of Maryland, as well as an early New-Frenchman from whom (for example) the town of Castine, Maine, takes its name. Among the regrettable aberrations of Lady Amherst—for whom otherwise Cook professed esteem—was her persuasion that there must therefore be some connection between himself and that former French-Canadian lover of hers. She had, embarrassingly, gone so far as to fancy that his son by the late Mrs. Cook might be her own illegitimate child by that early romance! The missing portions of the letter, then, included her account of an expedition earlier in June to his house in Anne Arundel County, in pursuit of this aberration. Fortunately he had not been at home: his former secretary-housekeeper had reported the visit of a strange Englishwoman who claimed to have urgent business with him. Aware of Lady Amherst's delusion and its origins, he had avoided her, and she'd not bothered him since.

Schott gruffly declared that he himself never read novels. Neither, said Provost Carter, did he. A great pity, Cook cordially chided: though his own muses were those of poetry and history, he believed that fiction, and in particular the novel, was your great mirror up to life. A dark mirror sometimes, to be sure, in which nevertheless, and whether transfigured or merely disfigured—here he gave me a surprising, meaning wink—we could best recognize our world and ourselves.

Perhaps he meant what I took him to mean by that wink: that he had read the novels in which the Macks and I—and Schott and Carter—are severally "figured." Or perhaps the wink was no more than a sort of conspiratorial self-irony: "You and I see through these high-minded clichés, eh?" It might even have been a mere tic. But my mind had wandered from poor Germaine Pitt to Jane Mack and the young fellow in the beige Arrow shirt in 1921; from the *Floating Opera* novel (wherein young "Todd Andrews" sees himself copulating in a mirror) to my experience on Captain Adams's Original Floating Theatre on June 21 or 22, 1937: my happy resolve (13 L) to blow up the showboat and myself after that dreadful dark night before.

Some things that are perfectly obvious to others aren't obvious at all to me, "Todd Andrews" remarks somewhere in that novel, *and vice versa: hence this chapter; hence this book.* OK, Dad: you saw it coming a long way back (let's presume you're closer than I to our Author). But it took me now by total, exhilarated surprise, what Cook's mid-sentence, mid-committee wink disclosed to me; nor can I say now what connects the wink to the revelation, any more than I can say what if anything connects A. B. Cook to André Castine. But there it suddenly, astonishingly, beautifully was: *13 R,* not yet in detail, but in clear principle, as plainly as if carved into the conference table.

Well! Too bad, Germaine: nothing I could do for you beyond insisting that those photocopies be destroyed at once (I shredded mine; Cook followed suit; the others were duly shamed by our example); I wish you a better job and a better companion, or better luck with the one you have. *Adieu,* Jeannine: if you can't find what you want, may you at least learn what it is you can't find. *Adieu,* Drew, less and more my child than your sister is. And bye-bye, I think, dear Jane: belatedly cured of the passion I belatedly recognized, I leave you to "Lord Baltimore" and Cap'n Chick.

Good-bye! Good-bye!

But having been so tardy, now I'm being premature. I shall be seeing you all again. We have business together. Even as "Lord Baltimore" observed, there is no hurry, no hurry, not even to resolve the details of what's so clear in outline: 13 R.

The threshold once crossed from middle to old age, it is not recrossed: I am still and irrevocably an old man, and the world is what it is. But my energies returned, and my self-possession. My authority with Schott I judged to be impaired for keeps; therefore I called for the sense of the committee on the question of dropping all charges against the demonstrators, declaring in advance my resignation as Marshyhope's counsel if they chose to proceed. The vote to prosecute was closer than I expected (I'm surprised Schott permitted one; it was strictly advisory), but the ayes—loudly led by Cook and Carter—carried the resolution. I shrugged and bid them cordial good-bye, good-bye.

Back to the office: Ms. Pond & Co. cheered to see me Myself again. I put in a couple hours' fruitful clearing of my desk, another of yet fruitfuller staring out my window at the oyster-shell pile. Yes, yes!

Then here (Thank you, Marian; I *feel* better, too), where I thought to reopen at once my *Inquiry*, then understood I'd better address the old *Letter* first.

Ahem, Dad: Nothing *has* intrinsic value! Everything has! Notwithstanding which, bye-bye!

I'll get back to you. What an Author! But then, what a reader, your slow son

T.

I: *Jacob Horner to Jacob Horner. His discovery that*
he is in love.

7/10/69

To: Jacob Horner, Remobilization Farm, Fort Erie, Ontario, Canada
From: Jacob Horner, Remobilization Farm, Fort Erie, Ontario, Canada

In a sense you Are Jacob Horner, Making Ready to Leave Baltimore in July 1953 at the Doctor's prescription to be Interviewed by John Schott and Joseph Morgan at Wicomico Teachers College as a Prospective Instructor of English grammar. It is the birthday of John Calvin, Giorgio de Chirico, James III of Scotland, Carl Orff, Camille Pissarro, Marcel Proust, James McNeill Whistler. The Allies are landing in Sicily, Apollo-11 has sprung a leak, Vice-President Fillmore has succeeded Zachary Taylor to the U.S. presidency, the first contingent of U.S. Marines is leaving Viet Nam, Ben Franklin is proposing a Colonial Union modeled after the Iroquois League of Six Nations, the Germans have begun their bombing of Britain and ratified the Versailles Treaty, Thor Heyerdahl's *Ra* is swamping again in rough seas and may not make it to Barbados, Korean truce negotiations have begun, the stock market continues its decline, and Woodrow Wilson has presented his League of Nations proposal to the U.S. Senate. But *Der Wiedertraum* is out of synch, out of focus, perhaps out of control. The world's turned upside down; you Scarcely Recognize yourself; you Begin To Wonder who's writing whom, at whose prescription.

Three Thursdays since, when last you Wrote you, the Minstrel Show was on the verge, which in the event turned all our screws. In the Progress and Advice Room, just before it, you Observed to the Doctor that you'd Experienced no Recurrence of Reparalysis since April 2, Casanova's birthday; nor had you on the other hand Achieved Suicide.

473

You Remarked Further that your Scriptotherapy could not claim the credit, inasmuch as Joe Morgan's reappearance had inspired both your Immediate Resumption of that therapy and your Later Relapse into the condition it was meant to treat. It Was your Guess that Morgan's *Wiedertraum*, despite the Doctor's misgivings and your own, was the mobilizing factor, if only because it occasioned the reinstitution of these weekly P & A's.

Et cetera. You Nattered On to fill the time; your mind was Nervously Elsewhere. The Doctor's too, you Would Have Thought—though he mouthed his dead cigar and regarded you as entomologically as ever. It was his afternoon to fish, but the day, indeed the approaching weekend, looked to be another stormy one, and he was chagrined. Presently he said, as confidently and acidly as ever in 1953: "Merde Horner. Blank attracts blank. You are In Love with Pocahontas. You would be Better Off Paralyzed."

You were Entirely Startled. Indeed, you Blushed. But you Could Not Deny what till then you'd Not Acknowledged even to yourself: that Ambrose Mensch's ex, the blonde Medusa who froze even limber Tombo, somehow moved your Heart—if not to Love, at least to a Surprising Sympathy. It Seemed Likely to you, however, that this unlikelihood was in some measure another aspect of *Der Wiedertraum:* Marsha Blank's miscasting (as the high school teacher you'd Bedded Cavalierly in Wicomico in 1953) had occasioned your Reviewing both herself and "Peggy Rankin" in a new, more compassionate light. Sixteen years after the fact, you Wished you Had Been Less Cynical with Ms. Rankin; and you Dared Say Pocahontas had her reasons for being bitchy.

Genug, the Doctor ordered: your Balls, such as they were, were your Own, to Lose as you Would, but kindly Spare him the smarmy sympathetics. He did not regard you as Prepared for a Genuine Emotional Engagement—you Recalled perhaps that he'd advised against it in 1953 as well, vis-à-vis the late Rennie Morgan?—but neither did he regard you as Capable of one. If your Feeling for Marsha Blank helped keep you Alive and Mobile, the rest was your Funeral.

Der Wiedertraum itself he still considered dangerous, both to the mobility of its principals and to the security of the Farm, which he did not want jeopardized so near to his retirement. What was more, he didn't understand the timetable. The novelized version of the original trauma corroborated his own recollection: that Mrs. Morgan's abortion and death had occurred in late October 1953. Wherefore then "Saint Joe's" ultimatum that she be redreamed, reborn, by Labor Day, which would fall this year on the 1st of September? More important, whatever Morgan's dramaturgical calendar, how could the reenactment imaginably have a positive outcome? It was a time bomb, and unless (what the Doctor could not conceive) you Had Some Possible Strategy for defusing it, he was resolved to move it off the premises before it blew.

What Struck you as Odd about this colloquy was that for all his

474

customary hauteur the Doctor appeared, for the first time in your connection, to be *consulting* you. He was *asking your Advice!* Moreover, he seemed now not only superannuated but impotent, at least far from omnipotent. It Occurred To you, irrelevantly, that by the rules of B-movie dramaturgy he was as of that moment a dead man. You Were Not Surprised when thunderstorms crashed as if on cue immediately thereafter, and a tornado watch curtailed the evening's show. That the twisters spun off Lake Erie, not into Ontario, but into New York State across the way (and wrecked specifically the Chautauqua Lake locations that Prinz and Mensch had just done filming) underscored the portent. And if you Did Not *Quite* Assume—when after the abbreviated entertainment the Doctor declared an end to *Der Wiedertraum,* gave two weeks' notice to Casteene, Morgan, and the draft evaders to begone from the Farm or be removed therefrom by the provincial police, and forbade the film company ever to return (Bea Golden excepted, whose family's patronage was still prized)—that it was his own termination notice the Doctor thus pronounced, it is because you Doubted Fate was *such* an artless hack.

You Were Not Displeased at his ultimatum, only A Touch Anxious that Morgan might now attempt whatever he had in mind by Independence, rather than by Labor, Day. The prospect of Casteene, Morgan, and the hippies gone, yourself and Marsha Blank still here—not displeasing, not displeasing. But no one was perturbed by the Doctor's orders; no one made the least motion either to protest or to accede. July 4 came, birthday of Louis Armstrong, Calvin Coolidge, Stephen Foster, Nathaniel Hawthorne; with a final muttered warning that They'd better be packing when he got back, the Doctor went fishing. Another tremendous Friday P.M. storm promptly exploded on Lake Erie. Among the 200 Feared Missing thereafter: il vostro dottore, no trace of whose body or boat has as of this writing been found.

You Miss him. A Little.

The Remobilization Farm moves on, under altered management. Tombo X continues as Resident Physician and Chief of Physical Therapy, yourself (who Can Account for nothing) as General Accountant, Monsieur Casteene as Prime Mover—and Saint Joe as Progressor & Advisor, with whom this afternoon, ☾ ♀ ☽ , you Recommended your Weekly Interviews, Reviewing your Schedule of Therapies and *Der* (likewise altered) *Wiedertraum.*

Suppose—Mister Bones had Inquired of Mister Tambo in effect and in desperation at the Minstrel Show—Rennie Morgan *were* by some miracle restored to him by 9/1/69: What then? Why, sir, rejoined Mister Bones (while Monsieur Interlocuteur beamed upon us all), the dream will take its course: she will reacquiesce to your Seducements or not, reconceive or not, rechoose abortion or not, et cetera. And why 9/1? Asked Bones. Can it be, added M. Interlocuteur, for the reason that on 31 August 1953—Day 44 or thereabouts of your original Hundred Days—after a month of horseback-riding sessions during which Jacob

Horner Learned of Joseph Morgan's passionate rationalism and Played Devil's Advocate thereto with hapless Rennie, the two equestrians happened to espy upon return at twilight from their latest session that same Morgan, solo in his study, simultaneously masturbating, picking his nose, and speaking nonsense syllables to his reflection in a mirror? And that that (for her) shocking revelation of her husband's less than absolute rationality can be said to have led, in the plot of that novel at least, to her initial infidelity on Day 46, Nine/Two/Fifty-three?

Not impossibly, Tambo acknowledged. Not impossibly.

Then why, pressed M.I., is not Nine Two rather than Nine One our deadline? By your own chronological abstract of the novel based upon Mister Bones's Account of this adulterous connection, nothing happened between said espial and said consummation save Horner's Quarterly Visit, on Day 45, to the Doctor, to Report his Progress and Receive Advice. N'est-ce pas, Mister Bones?

That is how it is, you Affirmed, in that novel.

And see here, Casteene went on: ought we not to consider, for the edification of Mesdames et Messieurs our audience, such matters as the double paradox of Joseph Morgan's unreasonable rationalism and Jacob Horner's reasonable irrationality, which, in that novel at least, surely accounted for their mutual attraction? What of Morgan's complicity—the term is not too bold!—in his own cuckolding? Eh? I mean his proposing those riding lessons in the first place, to divert his wife with Horner's Company whilst he completed his dissertation? His deliberate and foolish trial, as it were, of her fidelity? I do not even mention his insistence, when the adultery came to light, that she *reenact it,* on Nine/Eleven and Nine/Sixteen, to "clarify her motives"—which reenactment may feasibly have led to her impregnation? Eh? Eh?

Those are all matters to be considered, Joe agreed: every one.

It was here, you Believe, that the tornado watch supervened and the Doctor issued his futile directives, before you could Point Out that (in that novel, at least) there was *no proof that Rennie ever conceived,* by you or Joe or anyone else, that fall! Not that it mattered, morally and ultimately, perhaps; but still. And was it in that abortive Minstrel Show or in this afternoon's paralyzing knee-to-knee in the P & A Room that your Sixteen-Year Penance was reviewed, from your Voluntary Sterilization to your Hornbook and other Scriptotherapeutic Disciplines? There, there, *there* was the sticking point, declared your new Advisor; and he would come to explaining why, in time. But not just now. For just now, he and Monsieur Casteene had cause to believe, you had a More Pressing Concern, antitherapeutically distracting beyond doubt, and which too might call for some alteration of *Der Wiedertraum*'s timetable.

Oh?

You are as Distressed as we are, Horner, that the Doctor is not the only member of our cast of characters who has not been heard from since July Fourth. Yes?

Yes.

You are Nowise Comforted by Bibi's report, upon her return from Maryland for the Doctor's memorial service on Monday, that Pocahontas was last seen on the night of Four July aboard the Original Floating Theatre Two on the Choptank River off Cambridge, Maryland, in the close company of your former night-school student and later fellow patient Jerome Bray of Lily Dale, New York, a man of questionable rationality, let us say, as well as obscure motive?

Nowise. If ever you Were a Devil's Advocate of the Irrational, you Had Not Been for sixteen years. On the contrary: you Had Come Desperately To Prize poor fragile Reason, as precious as it is rare. Especially Confronted with Saint-Joe-the-Mystic, you Passionately Wished yourself what you Could Scarcely Aspire To Be: a barrister of Calm Rationality, as Joe Morgan had once been.

Never mind that. The fact is, Horner, your Distress at Marsha Blank's disappearance with Mister Bray exceeds mine for the loss of a patient, say, or Casteene's for the loss or absence of his secretary-plus. Inasmuch as while I tolerated or indulged her, and Casteene made various use of her, you yourself Had Come to Feel *love* for her. Correct?

Well. You Didn't Know whether you'd Call it love, exactly.

I'm sure you don't. However, we *will* so denominate it: you *Love Marsha Blank*, Horner, for whatever reasons. You are Concerned Indeed for her whereabouts and welfare, the more so in view of Merry Bernstein's confused but clearly frightened condition when she came to us in May. Even if you Learned, for example, that Blank is shacking up with Bray at Lily Dale of her own volition and is content to continue doing so, you Would Find that information less painful than none at all, or than information that she was being in some way victimized. Respond, if you Please.

Yes.

That is called *caring*, Horner. We will not split hairs about terminology: you *Care* for the woman, a rare if not quite unprecedented emotion for you. Now: today is July Tenth, almost a week since Blank's disappearance. Our schedule for *Der Wiedertraum* calls for you to "Leave Baltimore" on the Nineteenth and Proceed To "Wicomico Teachers College" for a Job Interview with "Joseph Morgan" and others, following which you were to Go To "Ocean City," Pick Up a fellow English teacher named "Peggy Rankin," Engage In Sexual Intercourse with her in "a local motel," et cetera. My prescription, instead of that, is this: until the Nineteenth you are to Do Nothing. On the Nineteenth, if we have heard nothing from Marsha Blank to contraindicate, you will *Leave the Farm*, Horner. On your Own! You will Make your Way from here, not to Wicomico, Maryland, but to Lily Dale, New York, thence wherever else you Deem Likely, to Find and Ascertain the circumstances of the woman you Care For.

But.

Having so Found and Ascertained, you will Return and Report,

477

with or without Ms. Blank, depending. In time, we hope, for the next major episode of *Der Wiedertraum:* your Dinner With Rennie And Me on July 23, 1953, at which I propose that Rennie give you riding lessons in August while I complete my doctoral dissertation. But in no case later than August 1, when Prinz's company will return to the Niagara Frontier for further shooting.

Entendu? asked Monsieur Casteene, who as Prime Mover comes and goes as he pleases, even into the Progress and Advice Room.

You Pointed Out that though you Had A General Idea of Lily Dale's location (from the Farm's having been situated there for the decade 1956–65), you Had Not Been farther than a kilometer or two from the Farm, wherever its location, on your Own, since 1953. They turned to each other and began to speak of other things. It is impossible to be at ease in the Progress and Advice Room; but it is not easy elsewhere, either. Your Mind began to wander; your Eyes to unfocus. Pepsi-Cola hits the spot, etc.

Presently Morgan re-regarded you—their conversation had, it may be, reached some confidential matter—and said Go Write It All Down now, Horner. You're good at that. Another letter to yourself. Go.

S: *A. B. Cook VI to his son. The first of A. B. Cook IV's "posthumous" letters summarized: the deaths of Joel Barlow and Tecumseh.*

A. B. Cook VI
"Barataria"
Bloodsworth Island, Md.

July 9, 1969

My dear son,

So: after five months' silence, your laconic message—undated, no return address—from which, as from your fifth-month stirring in your mother's womb, I infer that you are alive, or were when you wrote. Further, from the postmark, that you are in Quebec, or were when your note was mailed. Finally, from your curt questions, that you have somehow acquired and read your great-great-great-grandfather's four letters to his unborn heirs.

Not very graciously, you ask whether those letters are authentic. How am I to reply, when *(a)* you do not mention which texts you read or how you came by them (the originals, authentic indeed, are in my possession, awaiting your firsthand examination; I have copied them only twice: once for a certain historian, again for a certain novelist; we shall see which you saw), and *(b)* you do not give me a return address? I must hope that this latter omission means that you're en route to Maryland to reput your queries in person—and less brusquely. Mean-

478

while, like Andrew Cook IV in 1812, I am too full of things to say to you to await your arrival; I must address you as it were *in utero* and begin to explain not only our ancestor's "prenatal" letters to Henry and Henrietta Burlingame V but also his "posthumous" epistles to his "widow" (Andrée Castine II), which neither that historian nor that novelist has yet seen. May you interrupt me, here at our family's second seat—close and breathless this time of year as the womb itself, and as humid, and as saline: a better season for Castines Hundred!—before I end this paragraph, this letter. . .

At least, before I shall have indited this *series* of letters, my second such since we saw each other last on Redmans Neck in February, at Harrison Mack's funeral.

Dear Henry: The undisguised, unbecoming suspicion of your note prompts me to rebegin with a confession. A.C. IV's four letters are genuine; my transcriptions of them—first for Germaine Pitt, Lady Amherst, whom you may remember from that funeral, later for the author of *The Sot-Weed Factor,* a historical novel, with whom I am collaborating on a new project—are faithful. But my motive for providing those two with copies of the letters was, while I hope defensible, not without a measure of guile. So be it: the originals await you. Lady A. and I have no further business. (Mr. B. and I *do:* was it he whose path somehow crossed yours, and who showed you what I neither granted nor explicitly denied him permission to share? I should like to know. Indeed, as I plan to send him summaries of these "posthumous" letters too, I here ask him directly: Are you, sir, in some sort of correspondence with my son, Henry Burlingame VII? If you sent him the four "prenatal" epistles, will you kindly forward this as well, and the ones perhaps to follow? *And tell me where he is!)*

Revelation of the Pattern, Henry: that was to be the first stage of your conversion of my cause. As it has been revealed to you willy-nilly, by whatever agency, I attach a copy of my letter of June 18 last to the aforementioned author, summarizing the consequences—rather, the pitiful inconsequence!—of its revelation to Andrew Cook IV, and of *his* revelation of it to his heirs. I pray you pause and review that letter now. All the man wanted, Henry, was to clear the generational decks: better, to unstack the deck of History and deal "Henry or Henrietta" a free hand. Weep with me for the Cooks and Burlingames!

And having wept, let us proceed—straightforwardly, sans ruse or stratagem—to the second stage of your conversion. No need to rehearse to you, of all people, what our Revolution is *about,* or wherein lies its peculiarly revolutionary character: I know you know it intimately well, and I well know you oppose it utterly. But I know too that while it may well come to pass without your aid—even despite your best efforts to thwart it—I have small interest in its realization, the consummation of our history, if you are not its Consummator-in-Chief.

My son, I love you. You are 29, about to commence your second "Saturnian revolution." You approach that point—"*nel mezzo del cam-*

min," etc.—where many a journeyer before you has strayed right off the map, to where (Homer tells us) "East and West mean nothing," nor any other opposites. What follows is propaganda, meant to win you to me. How franker can I be? But it is as loving propaganda as ever was penned. I do not expect you to take this letter on faith: you are a Burlingame! But read it, read it—and come to Bloodsworth Island for confirmation!

Read what? (I stall. I dawdle. Why do you not appear in midst of this parenthesis, as you have more than once astonished me by appearing, without sound or apparent vehicle, as if materialized from ether, with your mother's eyes, your mother's accent?) Why, read my digest of my decipherment of the first of Andrew Cook IV's "posthumous" letters: three removes from an original (before me) whose author's own wife would not accept it as bona fide!

Read on. I said *decipherment.* Andrew Cook IV was reported killed by an errant Congreve rocket just before dawn on September 14, 1814, during the British bombardment of Fort McHenry in Baltimore harbor. The five letters which arrived at Castines Hundred over his initials in the seven years thereafter were all in what their author himself refers to—in code—as "the simple family cipher." (I exclude a sixth letter, the 1827 one from "Ebenezer Burling" of Richmond to Henry and Henrietta V, inviting them to join their father in Baltimore; it is in as plain English as this.) The code *is* simple, by cryptological standards: a systematic anagrammatizing of individual words, usually by mere inversion, followed by the substitution of numbers and other symbols for alphabetical letters. The phrase *Drolls & dreamers,* for example (which opens the first letter) is "scrambled" into *SLLORD & SRE-MAERD* and ciphered)00‡(†&)(8958(†. With a little practice, one can read and write it readily as English. Omit the first step and you have the code cracked by William Legrand in Edgar Poe's story *The Gold Bug* (1843): a coincidence I cannot explain beyond observing that young Poe was "Ebenezer Burling's" traveling companion in 1827 and that he met the Burlingame twins in Baltimore five years later.

Surely Andrée Castine knew this code. Her apparent refusal to decipher it (or to acknowledge her decipherment) argues that she regarded her husband's final departure from Castines Hundred in 1812 as an abandonment. She did not disclose these ciphered epistles to the twins in 1825, on their thirteenth birthday, when she disclosed to them the four "prenatal" letters; neither, on the other hand, did she destroy them. Henry and Henrietta themselves, characteristically, professed only mild surprise and equally mild curiosity when "their" son, Andrew Cook V, turned the documents up in the library of Castines Hundred in the 1890's; if they recognized the cipher, they chose not to acknowledge the fact.

That Andrew, my grandfather, was by his own testimony an able counterfeiter but no cryptanalyst, beyond his telegrapher's Morse: see my account of him in the letter to B., attached. Interestingly, he seems never to have mentioned the coded letters to my father, nor did my father to me. It was my mother (Andrée III) from whom I first heard of them, just after my father's death at Alamogordo, New Mexico, on July 16, 1945. Among Mother's gifts was a prodigious memory for dates: she remarked, in her grief, that my father had been killed on the 27th anniversary of the Bolshevists' murder of the Romanovs at Ekaterinburg, which she had deplored despite her own bolshevism, and the 130th of my ancestor's "second posthumous letter in the great code." She spoke distractedly and in French; I could not imagine what she meant by *"lettres posthumes"* or *"le grand chiffre,"* and I was at the time too bereft myself—and too busy in the immediate postwar years—to inquire. During her own untimely dying in 1953 (cervical cancer), she alluded to them again, this time even more cryptically, so to speak, as *"le chiffre le grand."*

1953, Henry, was the *mezzo* of my own *cammin,* a road I shall retrace in another letter. True to the family Pattern—of which I was not yet aware—I spent that orphan winter in the library of Castines Hundred, executing Mother's estate, redefining for myself the Second Revolution, and, in both connections, reviewing like my ancestor before me the archives of our line. I did not then discover (would I had!) the four "prenatal" letters of 1812. I *did* find what I would come to understand, in the spring, here on Bloodsworth Island, to be *les cinq lettres posthumes* of Andrew Cook IV, written in what I instantly recognized as resembling "Captain Kidd's" code in *The Gold Bug:* Legrand's cipher!

After a few false starts (*SLLORD* looked Welsh to me, *SREMAERD* vaguely Gaelic; I knew neither tongue) I saw the inversion device and set about deciphering and transcribing the first letter. After half a dozen pages I could almost "sight-read" the text aloud. And indeed, as I began to comprehend what I had discovered—not so simple a matter for one who had not first read, as you have, the "prenatal" letters!—I put by my transcribing, read straight to the end. . .and changed the course of my life.

As shall be told. But to the letters! I found the five to be divisible into a group of two dealing with their author's adventures in the 1812 War, another group of three dealing with his efforts in behalf of exiled Bonaparte and the Second Revolution. The first two are dated a year and one week apart: July 9, 1814, and July 16, 1815. The second three, oddly, are also dated a week apart, but over a period of six years: August 6, 1815; August 13, 1820; and August 20, 1821. Nothing in the letters accounts for this curious sequence, which I therefore presume to be coincidental, or conformable to some larger pattern unknown to their author. The additional coincidence of your note's arriving *this morning*—of all mornings on the calendar!—reminds me of what another has called the Anniversary View of History; and while I don't yet know what one is to *do* with such coincidences (beyond tisking one's tongue), it will be convenient for me not to resist so insistent a pattern. Unless therefore, as I profoundly hope, you interrupt me by appearing and demanding the originals, I will summarize for you *les lettres posthumes* over the coming weeks on the anniversaries of their inditing, and (poor second choice!) post them to you when you deign to give me your address.

Some similar constraint must have obtained in the case of the first of our ancestor's letters, the date of whose composition you will have remarked to be not "posthumous" at all, but a full two months and more before the British attack on Baltimore. Yet the annals of Castines Hundred (in this case, a memoir of Andrew Cook V, my grandfather) declare that no word from Andrew Cook IV reached there until well after the news of his death at Fort McHenry. The explanation is that the letter headed *Off Bermuda, July 9, 1814* has a brief postscript dated *Fort Bowyer, Mobile Bay, February 1815*, in which the writer explains, not altogether convincingly, why it has taken him nearly two years to write to the wife he said *au revoir* to in 1812, and (what I pray may not be the fate of this) another seven months to mail the letter!

Drolls & dreamers that we are, he begins, *we fancy that we can undo what we fancy we have done.* He had left Andrée and the newborn twins early in June 1812, with the object of hurrying (by the standards of the age) to aid Joel Barlow's negotiations with Napoleon: the same he had previously tried to obstruct. Thoroughbred Cook/Burlingame that he is, he decides that the most effective, perhaps even the swiftest, course is not to take ship for France directly, but to rush first to Washington and expose to President Madison or Secretary Monroe the fraudulent nature of the Henry Letters, urging them additionally to negotiate in person with Tecumseh and to dispatch himself by fast frigate to Paris as a special diplomatic aide to Barlow. To our modern ears the mission sounds absurd; but this is 1812 (the numerical equivalent, I note, of AHAB), when our high elected officers were almost bizarrely accessible, and such white whales as this of Andrew's were occasionally harpooned. No matter: Joel Barlow has already reported from Paris that the "Comte de Crillon" is an impostor; the Henry Letters, authentic or not, have done their bit to feed the Hawks; Cook reaches the capital on the very day (June 18) that Madison signs the Declaration of War passed by the Congress on the day before.

He is dismayed. He dares not permit himself to wonder (so he wonders plainly on the page!) whether a fortnight's-shorter pregnancy at Castines Hundred might have aborted the War of 1812. The War Department, he learns, has already ordered General Hull to invade Canada from Detroit; incredibly, the orders have been posted to Hull in Frenchtown by ordinary mail! Cook knows that Tecumseh and General Brock will hear the news at least a week earlier, via the network of John Jacob Astor's *voyageurs*, which Cook himself has organized. He considers intercepting the mail, forging counterorders to Hull; he considers on the contrary sending counterinformation through the fur trappers to Brock. Shall he rush to aid Tecumseh? Shall he promote the secession of New England, the defeat of Madison in the coming election? Shall he sail for France after all and help Barlow juggle the delicate balance of international relations? (Still annoyed at Napoleon's Berlin and Milan decrees, the Congress came within a few votes of declaring war on France and England together; only Barlow's assurances to Madison—that a treaty indemnifying U.S. shipowners for their French losses is forthcoming—has made England the sole enemy. The British cabinet, in turn, are confident that America will revoke its declaration of war when news arrives that the Orders in Council have been repealed; perhaps even now it is not too late. . .) Or shall he do none of these, but return to Castines Hundred and be the first father in our family to *parent* what he sired?

He cannot decide. To clear his head he crosses the Chesapeake, first to Cook's Point at the mouth of the Choptank, then hither to Bloodsworth Island, with the vague project of locating the site of that Ahatchwhoop village where the dream of an Indian-Negro alliance was first conceived by his forefathers (and where, he remarks in an illuminating aside, Henry Burlingame III learned "Captain Kidd's Cipher" from his fellow pirates Tom Pound and Long Ben Avery). "The longest day of the year"—I presume he means the literal solstice—finds him wandering aimlessly along these marshes, "devouring [his] own soul like Bellerophon." A strange lassitude overtakes him: the fatigue of irresolution, no doubt, combined with a steaming tidewater noon. "On a point of dry ground between two creeklets, in the shade of a stand of loblolly pines," he rests; he dozes; he dreams. . .

Of what? We are not told; only that he woke "half tranced, understanding where [he] was but not, at once, why [he] was there," and that he felt eerily as though he had aged ten years in as many minutes; that he was—odd feeling for a Cook, a Burlingame, but I myself am no stranger to it—"a different person" from the one who had drowsed off. He fetches forth and winds the pocketwatch sent to him so long ago in France by "H.B. IV"—and suddenly the meaning of his unrecorded dream comes clear, as surprising as it is ambiguous. He must *find his father,* and bring that father to Castines Hundred, to his grandchildren!

You sigh, Henry. I too! No more reenactments! But our ancestor sighs with us—nay, groans, not only at the by-now banality of this familiar imperative, but at its evident futility. What father? "Aaron Burr," in his cups in Paris? "Harman Blennerhassett," God knows where? Or perhaps himself, who we remember closed his last "prenatal" letter by referring to himself as his own father, and who surely feels a generation older since this dream?

Sensibly, he returns to Castines Hundred for Andrée's counsel. She is startled at his changed appearance, even suspicious, so it seems to him. The twins are healthy; but she remains reserved, uneasy. Napoleon crosses the Niemen into Russia. General Hull receives his mail in Frenchtown and crosses the Detroit into Canada. By way of desperate demonstration of his authenticity, Andrew forges in Andrée's presence a letter from Governor-General Sir George Prevost to General Brock, describing mass movements of Indian and Canadian troops en route to aid him at Detroit: a letter designed to fall "inadvertently" into Hull's hands so that he will panic, take flight from Canada, and surrender the city. Andrée cautiously approves a provisional strategy: to prevent or minimize battles where possible and promote stalemate. But she seems to require, "like Penelope, further proof" that this much-changed *revenant* is her Odysseus.

In August the false letter will do its work (not, alas, bloodlessly), but its author, heart-hurt by Andrée's continuing detachment, will have left Castines Hundred for France. Is it that he could not, Odysseus-like, rehearse the ultimate secret of the marriage bed? We are not told; only that he goes. He will see Andrée at least once more; she will not ever him.

Mme de Staël is nowhere about. Having fled Paris for Coppet, Coppet for Vienna, Vienna for St. Petersburg before Bonaparte's advance, she must now flee Russia for London, maybe thence for America if Napoleon cannot be stopped. Andrew seeks out "Aaron Burr" and confirms at once that his dream must be reread: not because that wrecked old schemer could not imaginably be "Henry Burlingame IV," but because he is so indisputably the fallen father of the woman whose brilliant letters, imploring him to return to America and rebegin, Burr ungallantly exhibits to his visitor. "My daughter, don't you know. In Charleston. Theodosia. . ."

Andrew winds his watch. Burr gives no sign. Go to her, the younger *intrigant* urges the older: Rebegin.

He himself then rebegins by presenting himself to the only father he has known. Disguised as one Jean Baptiste Petry, a minor aide to the Duc de Dalberg, he enters a familiar house in the rue de Vaugirard. There is rubicund Ruthy, there gentle Joel, who nonetheless sternly informs M. Petry that he is fed up with the foreign minister's deliberate procrastination and equivocating. Seventeen more American vessels have been taken as prizes by the French navy, who seem not to have been apprised of the "Decree of St. Cloud." Secretary Monroe has written (Barlow shows the letter) that an early settlement is anticipated with the English, after which the full hostility of both nations will be directed against France. It is time for a treaty of indemnification and free trade: a *real* treaty, not another counterfeit like that of St. Cloud, more worthy of the impostor Comte de Crillon or the legendary Henry Burlingame than of the Emperor of the French.

"Jean Baptiste" smiles. The son of that same M. Burlingame, he declares, has reportedly come to Paris to offer his talents to M. Barlow. Indeed, the fellow has audaciously gained access to privy sanctums of the Duc de Dalberg disguised as the aide now speaking these words, whom he happens to resemble, and has ascertained that while de Dalberg is indeed equivocating with Barlow on instructions from the Duc de Bassano, he regrets this equivocation as genuinely as Barlow does, whom he regards as a true friend of France. He has urged the Duc de Bassano to urge Napoleon to put an end to the business with a solid treaty of commerce between the United States and France, and expects daily to receive word of the emperor's approval. All this ("Monsieur Petry" indignantly concludes) the false "Jean Baptiste" has no doubt promptly communicated to Monsieur Barlow, at one can imagine what detriment to the real Petry's credibility. It is too much, this "Burlingaming" of Bonaparte as if he were some petty Algerine Bashaw!

Andrew pats his brow in mock exasperation; reaches for his watch chain. No need: Barlow's eyes have widened, squinted, rewidened; he scowls, he grins; now they are clapping each other's shoulders, kissing each other's cheeks, whooping Ruthy into the library to see what on earth. . .

Then Andrew doffs all disguise (except his irrevocably aged "real" features) and to the two of them earnestly puts his case. What he has reported is the truth: the Duc de Dalberg (who has only got as good as he gave) is expecting word momently from Vilnius, the emperor's Lithuanian headquarters, that Barlow should hasten there to conclude his treaty with the Duc de Bassano. Napoleon cares little for American affairs; his mind is on Moscow, which he must take before winter comes. But not everyone in the Foreign Ministry is as sanguine about the Russian expedition as is their emperor: it will be imperative, once the summons arrives from Vilnius, to move posthaste and get the matter dispatched.

Ruthy begins to cry: another separation! Joel too is sobered: Vilnius is no carriage jaunt to Coppet, but 2,000 and more kilometers across Germany and Poland! He too has heard opinions that Napoleon has overreached himself this time; that the Muscovites will burn their city before surrendering it. Moreover, pleased as he is to see *le grand Andrew* again (and to hear of the twins!), he cannot be expected to swallow unskeptically such a story, from such a source. About his own objectives he is quite clear: like Mme de Staël he has become anti-Bonaparte but not pro-Bourbon; for France's sake, for Europe's, he hopes Napoleon is defeated without too great loss of life, and the Empire replaced by a constitutional monarchy on the English model. For the United States he wants an early and honorable settlement of this "Second War of Independence," for which he holds no brief. For himself he craves the speedy success of his diplomatic errand and the family's return to Kalorama in Georgetown, to end his days like Thomas Jefferson cultivating his gardens, writing his memoirs, perhaps establishing a national university. A dozen years into the 19th Century, he is weary of it already, its *Sturm und Drang* and *gloire* and *romantisme*. He prefers Mozart to Beethoven, Voltaire to Goethe, reason to passion; he wants to go home. What does Andrew want?

Our progenitor points out that he has disguised himself this time simply to put by that disguise, in warrant of his good faith. He explains what he has learned from Andrée about the family Pattern; his chastened resolve that the "second cycle" of his life neutralize its misdirected first. Indeed, he affirms, Neutralization can be said to be his programme: he too hopes to see Napoleon neutralized before he ruins Europe; then a quick settlement of the American war before the United States can seize Canada on the one hand or, on the other, a Britain done with Napoleon can turn her whole might against her former colonies. It is his hope that an equitable treaty will guarantee Tecumseh's Indian Free State below and between the Great Lakes; for himself he wants no more than to return to Castines Hundred, raise his children, and perhaps write a realistical 18th-Century-style novel based on his adventures. To this end he puts himself again and openheartedly at his old friend's service. He is confident that together they can reenact and surpass their "H.B.-ing" of Hassan Bashaw; that they can Burlingame Bassano, Bonaparte, and the British prince regent into the bargain, if need be, to their pacific ends.

For Ruthy's sake, Andrew imagines—she maintains through these declarations as apprehensive a reserve as Andrée's—Joel does not immediately consent to the proposed alliance, nor does Andrew press the matter. While Tecumseh's Delawares attack white settlements in Kentucky, and his Chicagos besiege Fort Wayne, and Tecumseh himself heads south once more to rally the Creeks to his confederacy; while Madison decides to invade Canada from upstate New York despite Britain's lifting of the Orders in Council and Hull's fiasco at Detroit; while Brock gathers his forces on the Niagara Frontier for the fatal battle of Queenston Heights (his Indians are Iroquois led by John Brant, the 18-year-old son of our old friend Joseph); while Beethoven meets Goethe at Teplitz and Goya paints Wellington's portrait and Hegel publishes his *Objective Logic* and the Brothers Grimm their *Fairy Tales* and General Malet conspires to restore Louis XVIII in Napoleon's absence, Cook and the Barlows carefully renew their friendship. Young Tom Barlow (Joel's nephew and ward) and "Jean Baptiste Petry" explore Paris together through September, to improve the lad's postgraduate *savoir vivre*. But on October 10, when the Duc de Dalberg himself brings the word to 50 rue de Vaugirard that the Duc de Bassano awaits Barlow's pleasure at Vilnius, for all his and Ruthy's misgivings Joel makes no secret of his delight, especially when the aide assigned to accompany the American minister is named to be Monsieur J. B. Petry!

8¶8608285! Andrew's letter here cries out, as if in ciphered Slavic: *EVEILEBEM! Believe me! It would have workt, had not that dear great man, with half a million Frenchmen, froze to death at the bitter end of the alphabet!*

Toward October's close, as the *Grande Armée* begins its retreat from the ashes of Moscow (in Canada, Brock is dead, but his battle won; the U.S.S. *Wasp* has defeated the sloop-of-war *Frolic* but surrendered to H.M.S. *Poictiers;* Decatur in the *United States* has taken His Majesty's frigate *Macedonian;* the war is a draw as election day approaches), Joel,

486

Tom, and "Jean Baptiste" leave Paris. In mid-November they arrive in Vilnius, where the ground is already frozen. Despite all, it is a joy to be adventuring together again; if Andrew is older and more grave, Joel is in as youthful high spirits as when they *calèched* across Spain in 1795, en route to Algiers. He writes Ruthy almost daily—so Andrew blithely reports, without explaining why he does not follow that loving example!—he drills his nephew in German; with M. Petry's inventive aid he translates passages of the *Iliad* and the *Columbiad* into imaginary Polish. There is a merry if uneasy fortnight in the old city, crowded with the ministers of half a dozen nations: they pool their consular provisions, dine with the Duc de Bassano, make merry with the Polish gentry, and prepare their negotiation strategy—there seem to be no serious obstacles—while, what Barlow will not live to learn, his friend James Madison is very narrowly reelected over DeWitt Clinton of New York. That state, New Jersey, and all of New England except Vermont vote against the President—but do not secede after all when a few Pennsylvania precincts decide the election. The War of 1812 approaches 1813; the Duke of Wellington enters Madrid; the French army dies and dies.

Believe me! Andrew cries again: *Despite all, it would have workt!* The Duc de Bassano still assures everyone that Vilnius will be the emperor's winter quarters; M. Barlow may expect his treaty in a matter of days. True, the retreat from Moscow has become less than orderly; nevertheless. . . By early December the panic is general; everyone flees Vilnius before the Cossacks come. No winter has ever been so cold so early; the crows peck vainly at frozen French corpses along every road, and flap off to seek the not quite dead. Joel is revolted into the last and strongest poem of his life: *Advice to a Raven in Russia* (". . .hatch fast your ravenous brood, / Teach them to cry to Buonaparte for food;"* etc.). Andrew reads the poem in Warsaw on the bitter day—12/12/12, and the mercury -12°F—when Joel writes to Ruthy, in a cipher of their own, that Napoleon has overtaken and passed them already in his closed, unescorted sleigh, fleeing his own as well as the Russian army.

'Twas with no advice from me he advised that raven, Andrew declares, *whose image must haunt me evermore, till I find another poet to exorcise me of it.* Now is the time, he nonetheless believes, to take best advantage of the Duc de Bassano, when Napoleon needs all the goodwill he can buy. On the 18th they leave Warsaw, hoping to overtake that gentleman before the Cossacks do. On the 19th, in the valley of the Vistula, Barlow himself is overtaken, by a cold to which a fever is added on the 20th. His condition worsens rapidly: at the little Jewish *stetl* of Zarnowiec, "the bitter end of the alphabet," on "the shortest, darkest, meanest day of 1812," half a year exactly since Andrew's imperious dream, Joel declares he can travel no farther. The mayor and postmaster of the village, one John Blaski, is sympathetic: "Petry" overcomes the man's fear of Cossack reprisal and persuades him to take the American minister in. Doctors are summoned, to no avail beyond the diagnosis of pneumonia. On the day after Christmas, which out of respect for their

host the visitors do not observe, the *Plenipotens Minister a Statibus unitis America,* as Joel Barlow's burial tablet in the Zarnowiec Christian churchyard denominates him, *Itinerando hicce obiit.*

Tom Barlow and Andrew bury him at once, thank John Blaski for his courageous charity, and flee: the Cossacks need no particular excuse for ravaging a Jewish settlement. The two will reach Paris three weeks later, no longer friends. Indeed, while he charges no one by name of slandering him, and specifically "absolves" Ruthy (of what, we must infer) by reason of her "inconsolable grief," Andrew concludes this portion of his letter with the meaning observations that, as Ruthy's favorite and Joel's nearest relative, nephew Tom will surely inherit the Barlow estate upon Ruthy's death; that "of all the calumnies ever suffer'd silently by those whose profession does not permit reply, none stings me so sore as that 'J. B. Petry' saw to it Joel's treaty was never sign'd! As well accuse me of his pneumonia, who gave up my own *pelisse* to warm him at the end!"

Be that as it may—and I for one, Henry, do not credit for a moment the insinuation that Andrew derived "the blanket trick" from Jeffrey Amherst's bacteriological tactic against the Indian besiegers of Fort Pitt during Pontiac's conspiracy—he acknowledges frankly that the death of his "father" liberates as well as grieves him. Negotiations with the Duc de Bassano cannot now be resumed until a new minister arrives from Washington: late spring at the earliest. Though Napoleon executes General Malet for treason and welcomes the declarations of war on France by Prussia and Austria as his excuse to raise yet another army and atone for the Russian debacle, he has little interest in the British-American diversion. For one thing, the Americans seem to be holding their own without assistance: though Tecumseh's Indians have been victorious around the western Great Lakes, and Admiral Cockburn has blockaded the Chesapeake to play off the mid-Atlantic states against New York and New England, the new U.S. invasion of Canada bids to be successful. General Prevost is repulsed at Sackett's Harbor on Lake Ontario, and the Americans loot and burn the Canadian capital at York (Toronto). The British virtually evacuate the Niagara Frontier from Fort George at the mouth to Fort Erie at the head of the Niagara River; only the timidity of old General Dearborn keeps the Americans from pressing their advantage and seizing Canada. The U.S. Navy, too, is flexing its new muscle: though of insufficient force simply to destroy the British blockade (which however generates in Baltimore an enormously profitable fleet of privateers and blockade-runners), American captains are distinguishing themselves in individual engagements. One brig alone, the *Argus,* after delivering Joel Barlow's successor to Paris, wreaks such havoc with British merchant shipping in the English Channel that marine insurance rates shoot up like a Congreve rocket—a mode of economic warfare so effective that the prince regent now considers seriously Czar Alexander's offer to negotiate a settlement of the war.

Non grata in the rue de Vaugirard, Andrew follows these develop-ments attentively from across the Channel, where he has gone in March to test the British political weather before returning to Andrée and the twins. The Americans, he concludes, are doing altogether too well to consider yielding to the British demand for an Indian Free State, especially while Napoleon remains a threat in Europe. Cockburn's depredations in the Chesapeake are little more than a nuisance; only Tecumseh (and Dearborn's pusillanimity) is keeping Canada in the British Empire. But word has it that young Oliver Perry is building an American fleet from scratch at Presque Isle on Lake Erie, to help William Henry Harrison defeat Tecumseh finally and for keeps. It is time, Andrew decides, the scales were tipped a bit the other way.

Before leaving London he pays one call on Mme de Staël, who with her entourage is enjoying great success in the city. He finds her in good spirits but indifferent health: the last pregnancy, her fifth, took its toll on her, and its issue proved unfortunate. *"Petit Nous"* is imbecilic; they have named him Giles, invented an American parentage for him, and left him at Coppet with wet nurses. Germaine is tired and no longer attractive; her young guardsman-husband, though devoted, is crude and given to jealousy; she is using far too much laudanum, can't manage without it. She is not displeased to see that Andrew too has aged considerably. She introduces him to young Lord Byron, whose company she enjoys despite his unflattering compliment that she should have been born male. At her request, for Byron's amusement and by way of homage to the memory of Joel Barlow, Andrew for the last time recounts the tale of "Consuelo del Consulado." The poet attends, applauds politely, suggests that "with some reworking" it might appeal to Walter Scott, but believes that Gioacchino Rossini may have already made use of it in his new opéra bouffe *L'Italiana in Algeri.* Germaine herself, this time around, declares the tale palpable rubbish. The truth is (she announces pointedly to Byron) she is surfeited with Romanticism, almost with literature. She prefers Jane Austen to Walter Scott, Alexander Pope to Wordsworth and Shelley, and would rather read Malthus and Ricardo and Laplace than the lot of them. Her own novels have begun to bore her: so much so that she is writing a quite 18th-Century essay against suicide to counter the "Wertherism" so morbidly in fashion, from which her own *Delphine*, for example, suffers. Oh that she were Byron's age! She would devise an art that saw through such improbable flamboyances as Napoleon and "Consuelo" to those complex realities which (as her financier father knew) truly affect the lives of men and nations: the commodity market, currency speculation, the mysteries of patent law and debenture bonding.

Byron is bored. Andrew has heard the argument before; he coins the terms "post-Romantic" and "neo-Realist" and, begging their par-dons, wonders casually whether Germaine's new passion for economic and political history as against *belles-lettres* is not as romantical in its way as Byron's fascination with "action" as against "contemplation." He also wonders whether (this fancy much pleases both Byron and de Staël) "romantic" unlikelihoods such as his interlude with Consuelo are not more likely to occur in reality, even to abound, in the present Age of Romanticism than in other ages, just as visions and miracles no doubt occurred more regularly in the Age of Faith than in the Enlightenment. The most practical strategists in the Admiralty, for example, have been unable to deal with the American *Argus* nuisance in the Channel, whereas any romantical novelist deserving of the adjective would recall at once how Mercury slew the original "hundred-eyed Argus" by first charming the monster to sleep (some say with fiction). Suppose, instead of wool and timber and wheat, the *Argus* were to capture a ship loaded to the gunwales with good Oporto wine, whilst over the horizon a British man-o'-war stood ready to close when the Yankees were in their cups. . .

Germaine is impatient: the effect of Lloyd's marine insurance rates on British foreign policy intrigues her, but not the application of classical mythology to modern naval warfare. Byron, on the other hand, is enchanted with the idea. He has a naval cousin, Sir Peter Parker, in H.M.S. *Menelaus* in the Mediterranean, and other Admiralty connections to whom he must rush off at once and propose the scheme. Mr. Cook is quite right: it is an age in which the Real and the Romantic are, so to speak, fraternal twins. He himself, now Cook has put the bee in his bonnet, would not be surprised to learn that Lady Caroline Lamb, who has been forging letters over his signature, is Consuelo del Consulado, up to her old tricks!

They part (Andrew will not see either again; he cannot interest Byron in Barlow's raven, for which the poet declares the only useful rhyme in English is *craven;* the kindness of the Jew John Blaski appeals to him more; he is considering a series of "Hebrew melodies" to be set by his friend Isaac Nathan. But off to the Admiralty, and well met!): on the first of August, his conscience stung by Byron's reference to twins, Andrew takes ship from Ireland to Nova Scotia. There is a lull in the war: Madison's peace commissioners are in St. Petersburg with John Quincy Adams, but the prince regent, perhaps in view of Dearborn's failure of nerve, declines after all to send representatives of his own. Napoleon's momentum in Europe, like Dearborn's in Canada, shows signs of flagging; President Madison has recalled the old general, but there is no one to recall the emperor. Andrew will not learn of this until he reaches Canada, or of Admiral Cockburn's sack of Hampton, Virginia, or of Commodore Perry's improbable launching of his Lake Erie fleet, or of the capture on August 13 of the drunken *Argus* by His Majesty's brig *Pelican.* Meanwhile, as if his baiting of Germaine de Staël has provoked the gods of Romance. . .

Twenty-four hours out from Cobh, as he stands on the quarterdeck with other passengers anxiously scanning the Channel for the dreaded *Argus,* he fetches out and winds the old Breguet. A veiled lady beside

490

him catches her breath. Not long after, a sealed, scented envelope is delivered to his bunk in the gentlemen's cabin. . .

"Rossini, von Weber, Chateaubriand: your pardon!" Andrew here pleads. "Above all yours, Andrée!" But there *she* is, like the third-act reflex of a tired librettist. A still-striking, if plumpish, thirty-three, she has been the mistress of the Spanish minister to London; but her implacable ex-lover Don Escarpio, now a royalist agent in Rome, continues to harass her for her disobedience in Algiers. It is to flee his operatives and begin a new and different life that she has taken ship for Canada. But what honorable profession, in 1813, is open to a woman of no independent wealth who would be dependent on no man? Only one, that Consuelo knows of: following the examples of Mrs. Burney and Mrs. Edgeworth, above all of her idol Mme de Staël, she is determined to become. . .*una novelista!* Indeed, she is well into her maiden effort: an epistolary account, in the manner of *Delphine,* of her imbroglios with Señor Barlow and the wicked Escarpio. There is a new spirit abroad in Europe—perhaps Señor Cook has not heard of it—called *romanticismo:* as she has had alas no luck with the booksellers of Madrid and London, who advise her that the novel is a worn-out fad, Consuelo intends to introduce *el romanticismo* to North America and become the first famous Canadian novelist. For old time's sake, will her *carísimo* Andrew read through the manuscript and help her English it?

Three weeks later they part, affectionately, at Halifax. Andrew says no more of their shipboard intimacy (he is, after all, writing to his wife, and tardily) or of his friend's novel, except that, searching promptly for the truth about the poisoned snuffbox, he finds it metamorphosed into a poisoned letter-opener (*"¿Mas romántico, no?"*) and suggests she rework that passage, among others. But that their reconnection was not merely editorial we may infer from Andrew's immediate guilty assumption—when upon reaching Castines Hundred in September he finds Tecumseh there with Andrée—that in his long and newsless absence his wife has returned for consolation to her Indian friend.

He does not "blame her"—or question her, or even make his presence known. For three days he haunts the area (the same three, ye muses of romantical coincidence, of Tecumseh's single and innocent visit to his Star-of-the-Lake), surreptitiously satisfying himself that the twins are well, his wife and Tecumseh likewise. He hears the news that Perry has met the enemy at Put-In-Bay and that they are his; he understands that this victory spells the end, at least for the present, of British control of the Great Lakes, and that Perry's fleet will now freely transport General Harrison's army to meet Proctor and Tecumseh somewhere above Detroit. It wants no strategist to guess that another, two-pronged American invasion of Canada is imminent: one thrust from New England against Montreal, the other up from Detroit. Does Tecumseh understand that the battle to come is the most crucial of his life?

Comes again the baleful plea: *EVEILEBEM!* If he acknowledges now his rueful return to Halifax and "Consuelo the Consoler" *(la Consoladora),* it is because he had rather Andrée tax him with infidelity than with the least complicity in Tecumseh's death. *To the charge that I might somehow have aided our noble friend, and did not, I plead nolo contendere,* he writes. *To the charge that I idled & self-sorrow'd in Halifax whilst Proctor cowardly fled the field at Thames and left Tecumseh to be shot & flay'd & unmember'd by the fierce Kentuckians, I plead guilty. But believe me, Andrée: to the charge that I wisht Tecumseh dead; that I pointed him out to Colonels Whitely & Johnson on the field; that I myself gave a strip of his skin to Henry Clay for a razor-strop—innocent, innocent, innocent!*

He does not say whose charges those were. "Soul-shockt" by the loss of Tecumseh so hard upon that of Joel Barlow—and with Tecumseh the only real leadership of an Indian confederacy—Cook languishes in Nova Scotia while Andrew Jackson massacres the Creeks in Alabama and Madison's two strange replacements for General Dearborn launch their Canadian campaign. John Armstrong, the new secretary of war, is the same to whom in 1783 Henry Burlingame IV perhaps dictated the infamous "Newburgh Letters"; General Wilkinson is the same Spanish spy who conspired with "Aaron Burr" and then testified against him to save his own skin! Like its predecessor, this expedition will be a fiasco of mismanagement; by November's end it too will have failed, and in December, with the British capture of Fort Niagara, the tide of war will begin to turn. But the retreating Americans will have burned Newark (Niagara-on-the-Lake) in addition to York; they will still control the Lakes; no one will have remarshaled the scattered Indians in Tecumseh's stead—and Andrew lingers on in Halifax.

But he is not altogether idle, and nowise inattentive. Prevost's burning of Buffalo on New Year's Eve in retaliation for Newark, he observes, while thorough and brutal, is scarcely of so demoralizing a character to the U.S.A. generally as to prompt Madison's peace commissioners to cede the Great Lakes to Canada. Who cares about Buffalo? Vice Admiral Sir Alexander Cochrane, commander of the British blockading fleet, before leaving Halifax for winter quarters in Bermuda, proposes a letter to Madison threatening further such retaliation: he would begin on the coast of Maine come spring and burn one town after another until the Americans yield, working south if necessary as far as Boston. This too, it seems to Andrew, will be a blow from the wrong quarter: the Federalists will simply be driven into supporting Madison's war, and the southern states will be privately delighted to see New England get its comeuppance. Admiral Cockburn's season in Chesapeake Bay, on the other hand, while of limited military effectiveness—a few buildings burned, a few women raped, much tobacco confiscated, and the port of Baltimore closed to normal shipping—strikes Andrew as having been of considerable symbolic import and strategic promise: his fleet has cruised half a year with impunity at the front door of Washington; the city newspaper is even delivered regularly to his flagship, so that he can read the editorial denunciations of himself and keep abreast of the war! Now he is wintering on Cumberland Island, off Georgia, and allegedly arming Negroes for a general rising. The plan is not serious—Andrew has seen copies of the British directive to accept in service any free or escaped Negroes who volunteer, but not to permit a slave insurrection, lest the example spread to British colonies—but it terrifies the southern whites. Andrew admires Sir George Cockburn's *panache;* Prevost and Cochrane, he believes, are looking at the wrong part of the map. . .

Making use of his earlier connections with the Canadian secret service, Andrew spends the early months of 1814 establishing himself as a special liaison between the governor-general and the Royal Navy attaché in Halifax, while "assisting Consuelo with her novel-in-letters." Except for Jackson's campaign against the Creeks, who are finally destroyed in March at Horseshoe Bend, there is a general pause in the American war: all eyes are on Europe, where Wellington's Invincibles have crossed the Pyrenees into France and Napoleon's fall seems imminent. In the wake of the second Canadian fiasco, American Federalists are calling for Madison to resign or be impeached; Armstrong and Wilkinson are too busy now vilifying each other to prosecute the war. Ruthy Barlow, having wintered with the Robert Fultons in New York, returns to Washington and reopens Kalorama. In London, Mme de Staël, unenthusiastic about the prospect of a Bourbon restoration, hopes Napoleon will defeat the Allies but be killed in the process; in any event she and her friends make ready to end their exile. Byron writes his *Corsair,* Walter Scott his *Waverly,* Consuelo her *Cartas argelinas, o, la Delfina nueva.*

Her collaborator and translator, as he privately prepares to avenge Tecumseh's death, amuses himself with certain problems raised by the manuscript. He has persuaded Consuelo that a new *realismo* must inevitably succeed the current rage for the Romantic; to buy into this growth-stock early, so to speak, she has reworked her story to include all manner of ghosts, monsters, witches, curses, and miracles, in whose literal reality she devoutly believes, but which she'd omitted from her first draft as insufficiently *romántico,* there being none in *Delphine, Corinne,* or *The Sorrows of Young Werther.* Andrew is delighted—and gently suggests that she revise her ambition and residence to become the first great Mexican or Venezuelan Post-Romantic novelist. It is too cold in Canada anyway, no? And the Halifax literary community has not exactly laureled her like Corinne. Why do they not sail down to Bermuda together, where he has business, and assess the literary situation from there?

Consuelo agrees, the Allies enter Paris, Napoleon abdicates and is banished to Elba. Admiral Cockburn returns to the Chesapeake and renews his subscription to the *National Intelligencer;* General Ross in Bordeaux receives orders to take Wellington's brigades to Admiral

Cochrane in Bermuda for the purpose of "chastising Brother Jonathan" in some as yet unspecified way; Andrew Cook completes his strategy. As soon as Lake Erie is free of ice, he is certain, the Americans will re-retaliate in some fashion for the burning of Buffalo. Prevost himself waits for that occasion to prod Admiral Cochrane into action (the letter to Madison has not been sent, though Andrew has offered the governor-general numerous drafts). Sure enough, in May a raiding party from Erie, Pa., crosses the lake to Ontario and pillages the Long Point area. Prevost, into whose confidence our ancestor has by now entirely made his way, sends him at once from Halifax to Bermuda with orders for Cochrane both to demand reparation from Madison and, without waiting for reply, to initiate forthwith his proposed schedule of retaliation. Aboard the dispatch boat, as Consuelo prays to Maria Stella Maris to preserve them from sea monsters, cannibals, and other such *realidades,* Andrew adroitly redrafts the orders (and terminates abruptly, in mid–forged sentence, this first and longest of his posthumous letters, whose postscript you remember he added later, and whose interrupted sentence he resumes at the commencement of his second), substituting, in the catalogue of Cochrane's targets, for *Castine in Maine, Boston in Massachusetts, and Newport in Rhode Island,* the words *Baltimore in Maryland. . .*

(And here I too break off, to resume in his fashion, quoting our forefather quoting himself, when I take up his second letter on the anniversary of its composition one week hence—by when surely *you* will have interrupted

Your loving father)

ABC/ss encl
cc: JB

&: *A. B. Cook VI to his son.* A. B. Cook IV's second posthumous letter: Washington burned, Baltimore threatened.

A. B. Cook VI
Dept. of English
Marshyhope State University
Redmans Neck, Md. 21612

July 16, 1969

H. C. Burlingame VII
(address pending)

Dear Henry,
&*‡;364)5$!
Thus (missing, silent son) our ancestor opens this second of his "posthumous letters" in "Legrand's cipher," the first of which closed

with his forged—and interrupted—alteration of Governor-General Prevost's order to Vice Admiral Sir Alexander Cochrane to destroy, not "Castine in Maine, Boston in Massachusetts," etc., but *Baltimore in Maryland.* . .

&NOTGNIHSAW!

(Where are you, Henry? Better your suspicions, your rude interrogations, your peremptorosities, than this silence. Why can I not share with you my amusement at writing this from my new and temporary office—formerly tenanted by that historian I mentioned in my last, now mine as "Distinguished Visiting Lecturer in English" at this newly christened university—to be transcribed, as was my last, by my new and formidable secretary? My appeal to you last week, to join me here in Maryland for good and all after so many years, nay generations, of strained and partial connection; to take up with me the formulation and direction of our Second 7-Year Plan—seems to have been as futile as Andrew IV's postdated postscript to his "widow" [from Fort Bowyer, Mobile Bay, February, 1815] imploring her to join him there at once with the twins, now that the War of 1812—whose most memorable event he will rehearse for us today—is ended. The second letter is dated a year and a week after the first: 154 years ago today. It is headed [without immediate explanation] *Aboard H.M.S.* Bellerophon, *Off Rochefort, France, 16 July 1815.* Napoleon, his 100 Days done, has just surrendered there to Commander Maitland; Apollo-11, after a flawless countdown and a 9:32 A.M. lift-off from Cape Kennedy, has left its earth orbit to land the first men on the moon; my father has been vaporized at dawn in and with a certain tower in Alamogordo, New Mexico; *your* father feels ever more deeply, though he understands no more clearly, the Anniversary View of History. *Et cher fils, où es tu?*)

& Washington!

We review the strategy with Andrew. The British government are convinced from the start that Madison is the tool of his mentor Thomas Jefferson, at whose instruction he has coordinated the 1812 War with Napoleon's activities in Spain and Russia; while Britain is thus stripped of her allies and engaged in the peninsular fighting, the U.S. intends to add Canada and the Floridas to Jefferson's Louisiana Purchase. From the time of the emperor's retreat from Moscow, and more particularly in the first quarter of 1814, the British Cabinet's strategy becomes not only to retain Canada by sending new forces to Prevost's aid, but to capture New Orleans as well, and, by tightening the Chesapeake and North Atlantic blockades, to force the secession of New York and New England. The Canadian border will then be adjusted to include a buffer state extending 100 miles south of the Lakes (*i.e.,* most of Illinois, Indiana, and Ohio, as well as western Pennsylvania, upstate New York, and New England); British jurisdiction will extend from Hudson Bay to the Gulf of Mexico. The United States will thus be contained effectively by the Hudson and Mohawk rivers on the north,

495

the Allegheny, Ohio, and Mississippi rivers on the northwest and west. The Floridas are perhaps negotiable.

Only the Duke of Wellington is not sanguine. Even from the perspective of southern France, the map of America depresses him: that endless wilderness; the terrific problems of supply and reinforcement. "The prospect in regard to America," he writes to Earl Bathurst, the prince regent's secretary of war and the colonies, "is not consoling."

Admiral Cochrane, on the other hand, even before Andrew reaches Bermuda with Consuelo and his doctored orders, is so full of ambitious plans that he cannot decide among them. He will kidnap Secretary Monroe, say, maybe even Jefferson, as hostages to be ransomed by "all the country southwest of the Chesapeake"; or he will capture and destroy the Portsmouth Navy Yard and send Wellington's army across New Hampshire to join forces with Prevost; or he will exceed Bathurst's instructions and recruit a large cavalry of disaffected Negroes, a kind of black cossacks, to terrify the South into capitulation: the chain of Chesapeake Islands from Tangier up to Bloodsworth will be armed and fortified as their refuge and training base. Or he will seize New York City, or Rhode Island; or he will take Philadelphia, or perhaps Richmond, and either destroy or indemnify them. New Orleans alone, when his black cossacks and Creek Indians win it, ought to fetch four million pounds' worth of goods and ransom, of which his personal share will exceed £125,000!

As Cochrane schemes, unschemes, reschemes, Byron's cousin Peter Parker in the *Menelaus,* together with sixteen other ships and 2,800 of Wellington's Invincibles under command of General Ross, sail west from Bordeaux to rendezvous with him in Bermuda, and Andrew and Consuelo sail south to that same rendezvous in Prevost's dispatch boat. *La novelista's* confusion makes her cross with her lover and advisor: en route to Bermuda he has pressed upon her Jane Austen's new *Pride and Prejudice* as a refinement of 18th-Century realism of the sort that might anticipate what 19th-Century novelists will be doing 50 years hence, when the Gothic-Romantic fad has run its course. At the same time he translates aloud for her E. T. A. Hoffmann's *Phantasiestücke.* But Consuelo finds Austen's meticulous interest in *money*—its sources and the subtleties of its deployment—as *exótico* as the rites of a strange religion, whereas Hoffmann's goblins and revenants she accepts as the most familiar and unremarkable reportage, less marvelous by half than the table talk in Colmenar, her native Andalusian village. Mexico, she is now convinced, will be a desert, as inhospitable to *romanticismo* as La Mancha, and Venezuela a jungle full of monkeys and alligators. As for Bermuda, it bores her in two days: it is not Prospero's island, but Nova Scotia with more sunshine and fewer booksellers. Most unromantical of all, she brings her Gulf Stream seasickness ashore, cannot eat, yet puts on weight. In her fortune-teller's opinion, she is with child.

What confidence Andrew has in Andrée, so candidly to acknowledge this news! Which, however, he does not instantly credit. He knows for a fact that Consuelo cannot be more than five weeks pregnant; what's more, in her pique at his cavils about *realismo* she has attempted vainly to rouse his flagging ardor by permitting herself a small romance with a junior officer aboard the dispatch boat. . .

Andrew has been advanced a sufficiency for his mission from Prevost's secret-service budget. When Admiral Cochrane, on receipt of the (emended) instructions, orders him at once to Chesapeake Bay to report on Cockburn's black-cossack enlistments and to sound the man out on Cochrane's own inclination to ransom rather than burn the Yankee cities, Andrew gives Consuelo half of this advance. He informs her that his errand may keep him in the Chesapeake all summer; he declares that she no longer needs his aesthetic counsel, and suggests that New Orleans—with its links to France, Spain, and England as well as to the United States—might be the most romantic and fertile soil available for the future of the Novel. He himself saw and admired the city during his pursuit of Aaron Burr and Harman Blennerhassett some years since; he would be delighted to discover, should he revisit Louisiana with his wife and family after the war, that his brave and handsome friend has restored that poisoned snuffbox to their adventure and become the founder of Cajun Neo-Realism or Gumbo Gothic, whichever.

Consuelo is tearful and excited; Andrew gives her a letter of introduction to a Louisiana legislator he once caroused and swapped pirate stories with, one Jean Blanque, who he is confident can recommend a good physician and midwife if the need arises, or a hoodoo-lady if she wishes to postpone motherhood. *¡Hasta la vista, Consuelo la consolada!*

Andrew is happy to be off in the dispatch sloop *St. Lawrence*. He feels more self-reproach for encouraging his friend's literary aspirations than for sleeping with her, and Admiral Cochrane's combination of ambitiousness and irresolution bothers him. George Cockburn, on the other hand, he finds immediately appealing upon their rendezvous at the mouth of the Patuxent, which the rear admiral is already charting for invasion purposes. Prevost, declares Cockburn, cannot see beyond the St. Lawrence River. Cochrane, though no coward, is the sort who will change his mind a dozen times before making it up and another dozen after, with little sense either of real opportunity or real improbability. The kidnapping scheme, for example, is a piece of foolishness: nobody in Madison's cabinet is popular enough to command a decent ransom! And the "black cossack" business is another chimera: despite their best efforts, Cockburn's men cannot recruit more than one or two blacks daily. Unlike your red Indians, who in a vain effort to preserve their sovereignty form desperate alliances with either Madison or the Crown, your Negro has no more wish to fight one white man's battle than another's. But Cochrane knows neither blacks nor Indians! Moreover, the man is greedy, in Cockburn's opinion, beyond the permissible prize-taking activities of any responsible commander. In order properly to be feared, one must sometimes destroy instead of ransoming; but the destruction must be calculated for the best psychological effect. It astonishes Cockburn that either Prevost or Cochrane has had wit enough to suggest what he has been urging upon them for above a year, the seizure of Brother Jonathan's capital city—and he is not surprised that Cochrane is already equivocating on the matter.

Andrew takes a gamble; confesses that he himself has altered Prevost's instructions; demonstrates on the spot his knack for forgery. He volunteers his opinion that the capital should be seized first and briefly, just long enough to destroy the public buildings, with no discussion of ransom whatever; then a joint land and sea attack should be made on Baltimore, the economically more important target, whose privateering harbor should be destroyed and the rest of the city indemnified. If the Americans do not then sue for peace, the two cities should be garrisoned as a wedge between North and South while campaigns are mounted against New England and New Orleans. He Andrew knows the capital fairly well and is acquainted with several high elected officials, including the President and the secretary of state; he will be happy to serve Cockburn as guide, spy, or whatever.

The gamble pays off: Cockburn is as charmed by the counterfeit as by Andrew's further proposals for exploiting sectional distrust among the Americans. Compromising documents should be forged, for example, to confirm the rumors that Secretary of War Armstrong has deliberately neglected the defenses of Washington because he wants the capital relocated further north—perhaps in Carlisle, Pennsylvania—to weaken the influence of the Virginia Combine. Letters should be written to Madison by "a spy in Cockburn's fleet," warning the President of the attack—and found later in War Department files. A well-timed sequence of false and true reports, from false and true double agents, ought totally to confuse the already divided Americans. Above all, the operation should be decisively executed, to point up as demoralizingly as possible the Yankees' disorganization. To this end both Admiral Cochrane and General Ross—the one irresolute, the other reputedly overcautious—will need a bit of managing if they are not to spoil the essential *audacity* of the plan.

That word carries the day: it is audaciousness, exactly, which Prevost & Co.—even Wellington himself!—are short on, and which Cockburn and his friend the prince regent admire even in their adversaries. Old Bonaparte, damn him, has it aplenty; likewise the Yankee Commodore Joshua Barney, whose Baltimore flotilla of scows and barges has effectively hampered Cockburn's Chesapeake activities this season. He Cockburn fancies himself not altogether without some audaciousness too, and is encouraged to fellow feeling, if not to unreserved trust, by the plain evidence of that trait in our ancestor.

To the audacious man, Andrew ventures further, the settling of old scores is as agreeable as the taking of prizes. He himself has a little grudge against Josh Barney (at whose house in Baltimore their mutual friend Jérôme Bonaparte was introduced to Miss Betsy Patterson) for nearly capturing the *St. Lawrence* en route to this present conversation. Like the picaroon Joseph Whaland before him, Barney strikes quickly and then runs his shoal-draft boats up into creeks too shallow for his pursuers to follow. Moreover, the fellow has good tactical sense: the current presence of his flotilla in the upper Patuxent argues that he anticipates an attack on Washington. Let him then be hoist with his own petard: along with other diversionary maneuvers, let the main landing force go ashore at Benedict on the Patuxent and strike first at Barney's boats, which Cockburn's fleet will prevent from escaping. The Americans thus will be kept from guessing until the last possible moment whether Baltimore, Washington, or Annapolis is to be attacked first (and indeed the target can be changed if unforeseen defenses should arise), or whether Barney's flotilla is the sole objective.

Cockburn is now clapping Andrew about the shoulders like dear dead Barlow, eager to be on with it. July is running like the tide; Cochrane will have changed his mind seven times since Andrew left Bermuda; the Americans have captured Fort Erie and won so decisively at Chippewa, just above Niagara Falls, that their gray uniforms worn in that engagement have been officially adopted by the military academy at West Point. It is time to move. The *St. Lawrence* is redispatched to Bermuda with detailed plans for the operation: one small diversionary force to be sent up the Bay to feint at Baltimore and the upper Eastern Shore; another to move up the Potomac and take Fort Washington and Alexandria; the main force to ascend the Patuxent, land at Benedict, march on upriver between Washington and Baltimore—and then swing left to assault the capital. By the time the dispatch boat reaches Bermuda, the convoys from France and the Mediterranean ought to be there too; unless Cochrane in the meanwhile has dreamed up some harebrained alternative, Washington can be theirs by the time of the Perseid meteors in August.

Shall Andrew fetch the plan to Cochrane himself, to insure its effective delivery? Cockburn smiles: Mr. Cook will remain where he is, to insure its *accurate* delivery. Once the *St. Lawrence* is safely out of the Chesapeake, he may either begin his campaign of sowing the Eastern Seaboard with doctored letters, or join the Royal Marines in their sporting raids upon the Maryland tobacco crop.

Andrew opts to do a bit of both: on July 27 he drafts an anonymous letter to President Madison, informing him plainly of the British plan (the same classical tactic used by my father in 1941 vis-à-vis Pearl Harbor), and with Cockburn's approval "smuggles" it ashore to be mailed.

Your enemy have in agitation an attack on the capital of the United States. The manner in which they intend doing it is to take advantage of a fair wind in ascending the Patuxent; and after having ascended it a certain distance, to land their men at once, and make all possible dispatch to the capitol; batter it down, and then return to their vessels immediately. . .

(Signed) Friend

A few days later he lands with a foraging party from H.M.S. *Dauntless* near the village of Tobacco Stick (since renamed Madison after the addressee of the foregoing), thinking to make his way to the place where in 1694, having escaped death at the hands of the Bloodsworth Island Ahatchwhoops, his ancestor Ebenezer Cooke was reunited with his twin sister. Andrew wants to review his own position from that perspective, to reassure himself that he really means to aid the destruction of Washington rather than its preservation. His wool-gathering separates him from Lieutenant Phipps's party, who are guided by a liberated slave woman. The tender leaves without him, runs aground in the Little Choptank, and is captured by the local militia, who jail the 18 Britishers and return the black woman to the mercies of her former owner. Andrew must make his way back to the fleet via Bloodsworth Island and a stolen bateau.

He confides to Andrée that Cockburn's confidence in him is not increased by this episode, and while he does not report any change in his own attitude, he sees that he must do something to reestablish his credibility. Cockburn grants his request to make an intelligence-gathering visit to the capital, charging him specifically to report whether Madison and Monroe have managed to prod Secretary Armstrong into any real measures of defense since the receipt of Andrew's letter: if not, then either the Americans still doubt that Washington is the target, or they plan not to resist its capture, or their plans mean nothing. If on the other hand real defense measures are at last being taken, their strength must be expertly assessed before Ross and Cochrane's arrival.

Where are you, Henry?

On August 1, as Andrew's false true warning is postmarked from New York, Madison's Peace Commission (now in London) are being depressed by the tremendous joint celebration there of Napoleon's exile to Elba, the 100th anniversary of the Hanoverian accession, and the 16th of Lord Nelson's victory on the Nile: in the mock naval battles accompanying the festivities, the "enemy vessels" ignominiously vanquished include a significant number of "American" along with the customary "French." On August 3, while Andrew broods at Tobacco Stick, Admiral Cochrane's reinforced Bermuda fleet weighs anchor for the Chesapeake. On the 8th, as Andrew makes his way unchallenged into Washington, the British and American treaty negotiators meet for the first time in the Hôtel des Pays-Bas in Ghent, each to confront the other with unacceptable demands, and each hoping that news of fresh successes in the fighting will weaken the other's bargaining position. Why do you not appear, and we make plans together?

Andrew goes first to Kalorama, to advise Ruth Barlow (through an old servant-friend from the rue de Vaugirard; Ruth will not receive him) to place her valuables and herself under the diplomatic immunity of her former tenant, the French Ambassador Sérurier. By the simple expedient of installing himself then in the lobby of McKeowin's Hotel on Pennsylvania Avenue, where orders and counterorders come and go like transient guests, he quickly ascertains that no serious measures of defense have been accomplished. Of the 1,000 regulars and 15,000 militia authorized by Armstrong for the district, only 500 of the former and 1,600 of the latter actually exist, most of them in Baltimore, which the secretary still believes to be the British target. The rest, but for Barney's flotilla, are scattered all over southern Maryland; the city is virtually open. Only Madison and Monroe appear to believe that Washington is truly in danger; they seem about to take its defense into their own hands, but as of the Perseid meteor shower on August 12, they have not yet done so.

Thus Andrew's report to Cockburn, Cochrane, and General Ross aboard the *Tonnant* on August 15, Napoleon's 45th birthday. As Cockburn foretold, Cochrane's resolution has faltered en route from Bermuda: their 5,000 men are insufficient to assault a capital city some 40 miles inland, in absolutely equatorial summer heat. Ross inclines to agree: they will do better to pack it in and head north to Rhode Island. Only Andrew's report (together with a little demonstration raid up the St. Mary's River for Ross's benefit, and a final review of the options open to them if any real resistance should materialize) saves Cockburn's plan. On the 17th the final strategy is outlined to the assembled captains: a squadron of eight ships to go at once up the Potomac, destroy its fortifications to clear an alternate route for the army's retreat if the Patuxent should be cut off, and capture Alexandria. Byron's cousin to take the *Menelaus* up the Bay, make a reconnaissance feint at Baltimore and the upper Eastern Shore as if to cut off the roads to Philadelphia and New York. The rest of the force to navigate as far up the Patuxent as possible and march on from there. On Thursday the 18th, Andrew with them, they labor up the narrowing river against contrary winds and tides; by anchoring time, at steamy sunset, they are strung out for nine miles, from Benedict to Broom Island, the deeper-draft ships farthest down. The Patuxent, its high handsome wooded banks, are deserted. Tomorrow the troops will disembark with three days' rations for the 40-mile overland march to Nottingham, to Upper Marlboro. . .

& Washington!

Here Andrew interrupts his narrative to quote a New York *Post* editorial published some dozen days later: "Certain it is, that when General Ross' official account of the battle and the capture and destruction of our CAPITOL is published in England, it will hardly be credited by Englishmen. Even here it is still considered a dream." He goes on to invoke Andrée: *Give me the words, Muse to whom these words are*

all addrest, to tell that dream, your dream come true: Prevost's revenge for York,
ours for Tecumseh!

As if to repersuade himself that his conviction is firm, he reviews the moments when he might have "undream'd the dream": a forged letter from Madison to Armstrong, say, urging him to "maintain his pretense of indifference & confusion, till the enemy may be cut off from all retreat," would have alarmed Ross and Cochrane past all of Cockburn's suasion. A tip to Secretary Monroe, to place sharpshooters at Benedict to pick off Cockburn the moment he steps ashore—the fleet would be altogether demoralized.

Now in the three days' march from Benedict come new such cruxes. The tidewater August weather is unnerving; hardened veterans of the Peninsular Wars fall out by the dozens as anvil clouds pile up through the afternoon, then huddle awed as a furious American thunderstorm, like nothing they've seen in Britain or Spain, shocks their first night's bivouac in Maryland. A bit of a night ambush on the heels of it, by a hundred or so militiamen painted like Indians, and Ross would have packed his army back to more civilized carnage. On Sunday the 21st, permitted to reconnoiter on his own, Andrew crosses paths with James Monroe himself, alone on horseback, down below their encampment! Frustrated by inaction and discrepant reports, Monroe has persuaded the President to let him leave the State Department, saddle up, and scout the enemy personally—the first and last time a cabinet officer has ever done so—and he has got himself behind the enemy he is trying to locate. Andrew makes no sign, either to warn Monroe or to capture him. By that same Sunday evening Ross is fretful at the slowness of their advance, their distance from the fleet; he has half a mind to forgo even their immediate target, Joshua Barney's flotilla at Pig Point. Cockburn must be at him incessantly with encouragements, till Ross agrees to give *that* objective one more day. When Cockburn leaves him on the Monday to lead a little force of attack barges up to Pig Point, Andrew considers telling Ross that Barney has already fused his ships for scuttling and removed their cannons to defend the approaches to Washington. He refrains; the boats are blown; Ross settles down nervously with his army for the night at Upper Marlboro.

Seven miles away, at Long Old Fields, the American defenders are noisily encamped under General Winder, a Baltimore attorney. The threat to Washington is clear now to everyone except the secretary of war, and a bit of defense is beginning confusedly to rally: 3,000 infantry, mostly militia, and above 400 cavalry—of which Ross has none—are strengthened now by Barney's 500 flotillamen and their artillery. Andrew contemplates the map. An open road shortcuts from Long Old Fields and under Upper Marlboro to the Patuxent: in one hour Winder's cavalry could cut off the British rear while his infantry move against their left. Even if the attack cannot be sustained, it will move Ross to withdraw, the more readily now that his token objective has been accomplished. Andrew says nothing.

Even so, General Ross is so inclined to retreat that his junior officers secretly send for Cockburn again to give their commander another pep talk. It would be no problem to have the admiral ambuscado'd en route to Dr. Beanes's house, where Ross is billeted. . . The fact is, Earl Bathurst's orders to the general explicitly forbid his engaging in "any extended operations at any distance from the coast"; it is Cockburn's task, and those ambitious junior officers', to persuade Ross that Bathurst himself would rescind that order before such an opportunity. For the moment they succeed: Andrew and one of Cockburn's lieutenants are dispatched on the 23rd back to Cochrane's flagship at Benedict to report the destruction of Barney's flotilla, the taking of 13 schooners full of prize tobacco (which the Royal Marines are now sending downriver), and the army's intention to move on Washington next day.

Here is Andrew's last, best chance. As apprehensive as General Ross, Admiral Cochrane seizes upon the news. He too has been looking at the map: how easily a modest force of cavalry could cut off the army's rear and—more alarming!—how easily a few barges, scuttled across the lower Patuxent channel, could bottle up his fleet, make them sitting ducks for artillery mounted on the riverbanks! They have accomplished something, with very small loss; who knows but what Barney's boats and those tobacco schooners might have been a choice bait to lead them so vulnerably far upriver? He gives Andrew and Lieutenant Scott an emphatic and unambiguous letter for Cockburn, to be eaten if they are in danger of capture and delivered orally should they escape: he and Ross have done enough; they are to return to the fleet at once. *Under no circumstances are they to march on to Washington!*

The messengers return by different routes, to improve their letter's chances of delivery: Scott by the main road back to Dr. Beanes's house in Upper Marlboro; Andrew by that shortcut road towards the Wood Yard and Long Old Fields, where the army will have moved to a new bivouac during the day. Our ancestor is mightily tempted: his and Andrée's program (he reminds her), at least until Tecumseh's death, had been to promote stalemate; any youthful relish he might once have taken in spectacles of destruction has been long since sated by the French Terror and the Napoleonic Wars. With Barney's fleet destroyed, Cochrane can put enough blockading pressure on the U.S. economy to force concession of an Indian free state; it is not necessary to destroy the young capital city. Barney's men, at least, will stand and fight; this will be no bloodless "cossack hurrah." And this time Andrew need do nothing on his own initiative: Cochrane's letter is genuine; Lieutenant Scott will deliver it; he Andrew need only not impede its delivery, or at most confirm it with the news that Secretary Monroe is pressing for an attack on the British rear that same night.

503

This last he learns from a rapid visit to the city itself (which he enters unchallenged, so ill organized is its defense), together with the news that Winder has rejected that proposal. The general fears it will be the British who attack that night, to nullify his advantage in cavalry and artillery; he has therefore withdrawn his army from Long Old Fields back into the city, where they lie exhausted in the navy yard. There is no order; the place is pitifully exposed; the approach bridges across the east branch of the Potomac have not even been mined; only a few trunkfuls of government records have been packed out of town for safekeeping. There is a token guard at the President's House, which Andrew approaches without difficulty. He chats with the guards; they cheerfully inform him that Madison has rejected the idea of blowing up the Capitol before it falls to the British: it will "stir the country more," he has decided, if the enemy themselves destroy it. Incredibly, through a window of the house he catches sight of James and Dolley Madison themselves! Someone is gesticulating at the little man, who wearily shakes his head. Dolley, turning a wineglass in her fingers, seems to be directing servants; with her free hand she briefly touches her husband's shoulder. People come and go with messages, advice.

The streets are empty. Andrew rides out of town about midnight with a defense party dispatched at last to burn the Potomac bridges. They tell him that a slave revolt is rumored to be in progress throughout Maryland and Virginia; that the British have armed 2,000 blacks with specific instructions to rape all white females regardless of age and station; that the non-defense of Washington is New England's revenge on Madison for sending up southern generals to lose the Canadian campaign, which if successful would have added more non-slaveholding states to the Union. Holding his peace, Andrew passes with them through the sentries at the river. Except for a force of militia at Bladensburg, the northeastern approach to the city, there are no American troops beyond those sentries. So far from fearing capture in the five-mile ride back to the British camp, Andrew suffers from loneliness on the vacant country road, where "nothing stirr'd save the owls, and their prey." Nevertheless, the night is sweet after the oppressive afternoon; he takes his time. As he finds Ross's and Cockburn's quarters, about 3:00 A.M., he sees a glow behind him from the burning bridges.

The general and the admiral are up and pacing about outside. Lieutenant Scott stands by with other aides, his letter delivered uneaten—and evidently undigested by the addressee. The tableau is clear: Ross shakes his head like Madison; Cockburn gesticulates, expostulates, curses, coaxes. Ross points to the fire-glow; no matter, Cockburn replies, we will attack by way of Bladensburg, a better approach anyhow, since the river there is shallow enough to ford if the bridge is blown. The local militia will never stand against Wellington's Invincibles, who after their victory will surely be renamed Ross's Invincibles. On the other hand, Earl Bathurst and the prince regent will be furious to learn that such an easy, spectacular plum has been left unplucked, should we turn back now.

The decision must be Ross's, and he cannot make it. Cockburn looks about, rolling his eyes. A whippoorwill starts, the first voice that Wednesday morning besides their own. Andrew himself, remembering Dolley Madison's hand on her husband's shoulder and missing Andrée (but perhaps mindful also of a third tableau: Andrée walking and talking with Tecumseh at Castines Hundred), decides to grant this much to the American, at least the Maryland, line of his descent: if his advice is solicited, he will point out that symbolic losses meant to demoralize can sometimes have the reverse effect: if they do not crush your adversary's spirit, as the loss of Tecumseh dispirited the Indian confederacy, they may unify and inspirit him instead.

There is a pause. Ross looks his way but does not ask, may not even recognize Andrew in the darkness. Then he claps his brow, "as reluctant a conqueror as ever conquer'd," and declares to Cockburn, Yes, all right, very well, God help us, let it be, we will proceed. On to Bladensburg—

& Washington!

I write these pages, Henry, in my air-conditioned office on Redmans Neck, on another torrid tidewater Wednesday. The leaves I decipher and transcribe—and must now, alas, more and more summarize (the afternoon is done; I have business of my own in Washington tomorrow, which I will enter as Ross's army did, via the Baltimore Pike through Bladensburg)—our ancestor ciphered on a milder July 16 on the orlop deck of *Bellerophon,* where Napoleon surrendered the morning previous to escape arrest, after his second abdication, by officers of the restored Bourbons. Andrew will not explain until his next letter (August 6, 1815) what has fetched him to Rochefort; how it comes that he has not only witnessed the emperor's surrender but is about to dash overland to Le Havre and London with Allied dispatch couriers to negotiate British passports to America for Napoleon and his suite. He merely announces, in this letter, that such is the case, and that he must therefore leave "to another day, or another Muse," the full singing of the fall of Washington, the bombardment of Baltimore, and his own "death & resurrection."

It is a song, Henry, your father had thought to sing himself, in the years before I turned (to cite the motto of this border state) from *parole femine* to *fatti maschii:* from "womanly words" to "manly deeds," or from the registration of our times to their turning: my *Marylandiad!*

Sing of wee scholarly Madison's kissing Dolley farewell that Wednesday morning, buckling on the brace of big dueling pistols given him by his treasury secretary (who has quit and left town in disgust), riding bravely out to Bladensburg, right through the center of his troops drawn up for battle. . .and almost into the British columns assembling just below the rise! Sing of the heat of that August forenoon: temperature and humidity both in the high 90's, and the redcoats dropping already of heat exhaustion as they quickstep to Bladensburg. Half a canto then to the confusion and contradiction among the Americans, now some 6,000 strong as new units rush in at last from Annapolis, from Baltimore, and opposing an attack force of no more than 1,500 British. But those are Wellington's Invincibles, the Scourge of Spain, under clear and unified command, where these are farmers, watermen, tradesmen, ordered here by General Winder, there by General Stansbury, elsewhere by Secretary Monroe, elsewhere again by Francis Scott Key, the Georgetown lawyer who wanders up now full of advice for Winder, his fellow attorney. Some units are in the others' line of fire; many do not know that the rest are there, and think themselves alone against Ross's regulars; many have disapproved of the war from its outset, or believe it intentionally mismanaged; most have never seen combat before.

Half a canto therefore—and no more, and not without sympathy— to the "Bladensburg Races." The battle is joined; men begin to die. Unbelievably, the Americans have not blown the Bladensburg bridge; it must be seized at once. For the last time, Ross wavers—homespun militia or not, it seems to him a *very* large number of Yankees over there, defending after all their own capital city—and for the fifth, sixth, seventh time Cockburn cries Attack, attack. Between artillery blasts from the American earthworks the British race across the bridge and take cover; lacking artillery themselves, they open up on the Americans' second line of defense with Congreve rockets fetched in from the fleet. Marvelously inaccurate but fearsome to behold, the Congreves fall among the soldiers, the horses, the crowds of spectators come out from Washington and Georgetown to see the show. The rockets are easily and quickly launched, from a simple tube; flight follows flight of them, sputtering and shrieking, as the bright British bayonets move toward the front line—and suddenly all is panic. Horses whinny and bolt, onlookers scream and run; the whole center breaks, and the left, and the right, and the second line, not a quarter hour after the first redcoat crosses the bridge. Cannon are left behind unspiked, muskets thrown away; the swift trample the slow; Madison's party is swept back in the general rout. General Ross looks astonished: the battle has not yet properly commenced, and the Americans run, run, run for their lives. Some will not stop till they reach Virginia, or western Maryland. Everyone runs!

Almost everyone. For who are these rolling in like an alexandrine at the canto's end, kedging forward against the shameful tide? Jérôme Bonaparte's old comrade Joshua Barney, with his stranded flotillamen and the 12- and 18-pounders from their scuttled ships! All morning they have ransacked the navy yard for mules and ammunition; the sailors themselves are harnessed to the guns, which they hurriedly place now across the turnpike almost at the District of Columbia line. *They* know how to aim (no deck so steady as terra firma); *they* know how to stand and fire (no place to retreat to on a boat, till your officers decide to turn the thing around). Now whole companies of British die, who had survived the horrors Goya drew. Ross's advance is stopped; Barney's marines even mount a brief but successful charge against the King's Own Regiment, driving them back with bayonets and cutlasses and cries of "Board 'em, boys!"—but there is no President's Own behind them to follow up with a counterattack.

The flotillamen withdraw to their guns, hold on aggressively yet awhile against the regrouping, readvancing, reencircling British. They begin to die now in numbers themselves; they cling to their line for yet another salvo and another, even when their ammunition wagons (driven by scared civilians under contract) desert them. Under Winder's orders then, reinforced at last by Barney's own, they spike their guns and go, leaderless. For (also at his own orders) they must leave their wounded commodore behind. Barney has taken a musket ball in the hip, and concealed the wound till he falls. He will die of it after the war, en route to settle in Kentucky like Odysseus wandering inland from the sea. Now he is discovered by his old adversary Admiral Cockburn, who has suspected all along where such accurate resistance came from. "I knew it was the flotillamen!" he cries to Ross. The general pays his respects and forthwith paroles his wounded enemy. The two old sailors congratulate each other on the most effective fighting of the day (those rockets were Cockburn's idea); the admiral orders the commodore fetched back to Bladensburg for medical care and release, then rejoins Ross to pursue the battle.

But the battle is done. British casualties, most of them from Barney's naval gunnery, are twice those of the Americans, who are not present to be killed. Catching up with them is out of the question; it is an oven of an afternoon. "The victors were too weary," Cockburn reports later, "the vanquished too swift," for evening out the casualties. The redcoats rest. As the sun goes down a fresh party is brought forward to enter the city, which Ross expects to be better defended by a regrouped American army.

But the invaders march down Maryland Avenue unopposed toward the Capitol. Not only have the defenders fled; they have looted as they flew: had Dolley Madison not seen to it that George Washington's portrait was evacuated from the President's House, it would as likely have fallen to American looters as to British, as did Madison's dueling pistols. The President's butler has packed a few last valuables, left the front-door key at the Russian ministry, and gone in search of his employers. Save for one volley from Robert Sewall's house on Maryland Avenue and 2nd Street N.E., there is no resistance whatever. Sewall's house is quickly fired with rockets. A few blacks stand about to watch; there are no other Washingtonians in evidence. In vain, as the building burns, Ross orders drumrolls to call for a parley; he is still more inclined to indemnify than to burn. There is no one to reply. No interim authority has been delegated, no orders have been given, no provisions made. Admiral Cockburn is delighted: nothing for it now but to proceed with their business!

But, Muse, before you sing the sack of Washington, say: Can you see, from the heights of Helicon, where is our ancestor all this while, my son's and mine? For this *Marylandiad* is no history book, but the epic of Andrew Cook at the midpoint of his life. He was up all night: has he slept through the day's most epical set piece? Was he lost in the confusion of battle like Stendhal's Fabrizio at Waterloo? It is past eight; that glare in the east is the Washington Navy Yard, fired by its retreating commandant; those explosions are the fort at Greenleaf Point, ditto. Now it is nine: British demolition teams have broken into the Capitol, chopped its woodwork into kindling, piled up chairs and tables in the Senate and the House, added buckets of rocket powder; Cockburn has seated himself in the place of the Speaker of the House, gaveled for order, and put the mocking question to his men: Shall this harbor of Yankee democracy be burned?

Where is A. B. Cook IV?

Why, Henry, there he is, there in the doorway, just entered from the lobby, his throat so full of a heartfelt, self-surprising *nay* that he can scarcely keep it in! Like Madison, whose near-blundering into British hands he has earlier observed from across the lines of battle, Andrew has been a mere spectator of the Bladensburg debacle. He has not been impressed with Ross's generalship: after so much prodding and vacillation, the man in Andrew's opinion made a foolish and bloody decision to attack frontally across that bridge (no doubt in his surprise to find it intact). He could as easily have forded the river upstream and fallen on the Americans' flank while Cockburn fired his Congreves into their front; British casualties needn't have been so high. Nevertheless, Andrew has felt personal shame at the panic and rout of the American militia, and contrariwise such admiration for Josh Barney's resistance that with Cockburn's permission he has accompanied the wounded commodore back to the Bladensburg tavern pressed into service as a field hospital. It is Andrew who, when Barney complains that Ross's soldiers don't know how to bear a stretcher properly, finds four willing sailors from the rocket squad to relieve them, and suggests they soothe their patient en route with fo'c'sle chanteys.

It is not simply Barney's physical courage that Andrew is moved by, but his particular brand of patriotism: complex, at times self-interested (it was Barney's vanity, piqued by the promotions of others before himself, that led him earlier to resign his commission in the U.S. Navy for one in the French), but strong and unambiguous where it matters— by contrast, say, with the contemptible soullessness of Secretary Armstrong, or his own confusions, equivocations, blunderings. In this, Barney seems to Andrew a rougher-cast version of Joel Barlow; indeed, they could pass for brothers both in appearance and under the skin.

When the commodore thanks him for his attentions and asks whether he hasn't seen him somewhere before—perhaps in William Patterson's house a dozen years ago?—Andrew fakes a cockney accent and denies it.

The old man seen to, Andrew makes his way back into Washington, wishing as fervently as ever in his life that he could spit out "this *Father* business" once and for all and be. . .*himself!* By the blaze of Robert Sewall's house he rides down Maryland Avenue to the Capitol, its windows shot out, its great doors battered open. He contemplates the imminent destruction, not merely of Corinthian columns and marble walls, but of the infant Library of Congress upstairs and the Supreme Court's law library below; of the records, the files, the archives of the young republic. He passes through the lobby to the House chamber, his head full of the slogans of the American and French revolutions, together with the ideals of the Magna Carta, of English Common Law and parliamentary procedure. Why are these destroying these? Futile as the gesture would have been, when he sees Admiral Cockburn in the Speaker's chair and hears him call to his rocket-wielding troopers for the question, the *nay* comes near to bursting from him. . .

But then it strikes Andrew that the *official* incumbent of that chair is the man perhaps most singly responsible for the war: Henry Clay, the archhawk of Kentucky, at that moment in Ghent with the peace commissioners to make sure that no Indian Free State is let into the treaty, and brandishing in token of his belligerence a razor-strop made from the skin of Tecumseh. *"Aye!"* our forefather shouts before the rest, who chorus affirmation. It is exactly ten o'clock. The motion carries; Cockburn raps the gavel; rockets are fired into the piled-up combustibles; the party retires from the blaze and moves down Pennsylvania Avenue to the President's House and the Treasury Building. Over his shoulder, as he moves on with them, Andrew sees the Capitol of the United States in flames.

Now the men are weary. All but the indefatigable Cockburn complete the night's work methodically, with little horseplay. If Ross has been less than resolute or brilliant as an attacker, he is an admirable executor of this occupation, for which he has no taste. There are no rapes, no molestations of civilians, no systematic pillaging of private property. Even the looting of the public buildings he keeps to the souvenir level, and he frowningly detaches himself from Cockburn's high jinks. At the President's House they find dinner laid out for forty: as Cockburn's men fall upon the cold meats and Madeira, and the admiral toasts the health of "Jemmy Madison and the prince regent," and steals "Jemmy's love letters" from a desk drawer and a cushion from Mrs. Madison's chair to remind him "of Dolley's sweet arse," Ross quietly gives orders to fire the place and move on. The officers retire to Mrs. Suter's tavern on 15th Street for a late supper; Ross's frown darkens when the admiral rides roaring in upon the white mule he has been pleased to bestride all day. Such displays Ross regards as dangerous to good discipline and unbefitting the dignity of such events as the destruction of capital cities.

Andrew agrees, though in the contrast of humors between the general and the admiral he sees a paradigm of his own mixed feelings, and he is mindful of the resolve and bold imagination that entitle Cockburn to his present entertainment. Since the firing of the Capitol, Andrew's heart is still. He quotes here an ironic editorial comment from a British newspaper printed weeks later, when the news reaches London:

> There will be great joy in the United States on account of the destruction of all their public and national records, as the people may now invent a *fabulous* origin. . . .

The destruction itself, reports Andrew, from the moment of that gavel rap in Cockburn's congress, has seemed to him to move from the historical plane to the fabulous. Like one "whose father's certain death releases one at last to love him," Andrew feels the stirrings of a strange new emotion.

But first one must see that father truly and completely buried, and so he not only follows Ross and Cockburn through the balance of the night's destruction, and the next day's, but finds finally "a fit chiaroscuro" in the contrast of their manners, "apt as Don Quixote and his ribald squire." It is getting on to midnight. From Mrs. Suter's tavern the trio ride to their final errand of the evening, another of Cockburn's inspirations, which Ross reluctantly assents to: private property or not, the Admiral vows he will not sleep until he burns the offices of the *National Intelligencer,* which for two years has been abusing him in its columns. The general goes along to make sure that no other private buildings are damaged or further mischief made; Andrew to see "the funeral rites" through to the end and confirm his sense of the increasing fabulousness of the occasion.

They locate Joe Gales's *Intelligencer* building between 6th and 7th streets on Pennsylvania Avenue, and by the light of the still-blazing Capitol read the lead story of its morning edition, fetched out by the soldiers who break down the door: The city is safe; there is no danger from the British. Just at midnight another thunderstorm breaks theatrically upon them. Cockburn yields to the entreaties of two neighbor ladies not to burn the building, lest their houses catch fire as well. It is too wet now for burning anyhow; he will wreck the place in the morning. He commandeers a red tunic and musket from one of the 3rd Brigade troopers, bids Andrew take them, and orders him to stand watch at the *Intelligencer* till they return at dawn. Cook has been witness long enough; time to earn his pay.

The officers retire then for the night: the 3rd Brigade to Capitol Hill, the others to encampments outside the District. For the next several hours, Henry—till Cockburn eagerly goes to't again at 5:30 next morning—Andrew Burlingame Cook IV is in sole charge of the capital of the United States!

When not pacing his beat, he employs the time to begin drafting the record of these events thus far, which will not be redrafted, dated, and posted till nearly a year later. His sence of "fabulosity" does not diminish, even though (perhaps because) he verges on exhaustion. As in a dream he watches Cockburn's men destroy the newspaper office, piing the type into Pennsylvania Avenue and wrecking the presses. The admiral himself, with Andrew's help, destroys all the uppercase *C*'s, "so that Gales can defame me no further," and thenceforth calls himself "the Scourge of the *C*'s." While fresh troops from the 1st Brigade reignite the Treasury Building (extinguished by last night's storm) and burn the State, War, and Navy Department Building, Cook and Cockburn make a tour of the ruined navy yard: confronting there the allegorical Tripoli Monument (to American naval victories off the Barbary Coast), Andrew is dispatched to snatch the bronze pen from the hand of History and the palm from the hand of Fame. Back in the city he hears General Ross declare that he would not have burned the President's House if Mrs. Madison had taken sanctuary there, nor the Capitol building had he known it to have housed the Congressional Library: "No, sir," Ross declares emphatically: "I make war against neither letters nor ladies."

The post office is scheduled to go next, but inasmuch as the superintendent of patents argues that the building also houses the patent models, which are private property, and Andrew adds ironically that by the same reasoning all the letters in the post office are private too, the burning is postponed till the officer in charge can get a ruling from Cockburn, still enjoying himself down at the *Intelligencer*. Meanwhile he and his squad have another mission: to destroy the powder magazine at Greenleaf Point, which the Yankees have forgot. Since that officer and his men will never return, the P.O. is spared: most of the letters are eventually delivered (Andrew wished he had got this one posted in time), and the Congress, upon its return in September, has one building large enough to enable it to sit in Washington rather than in Lancaster, Pa. (the second choice), where once established it would very possibly have stayed.

And the reason for those men's not returning begins the end of Andrew's "fable." This Thursday the 25th is another poaching tidewater August day: stifling heat, enervating humidity, dull haze and angry thunderheads piling up already by noon to westward, where Ross imagines Madison to have regrouped his government and army to drive the invaders out. The demolition party goes to Greenleaf Point, the confluence of the Potomac's east and west branches; they decide to drown the 150 powder barrels in a well shaft, not realizing that the water is low; they dump the barrels in; someone adds a cigar, or a torch (it cannot be Andrew; he is back at the post office, writing this letter). The explosion is seismic: the whole city trembles, blocks of buildings are unroofed, windows shatter everywhere; the concussion sickens everyone for half a mile around. Greenleaf Point itself virtually disappears, the demolition squad with it; no one even knows how many men die—one dozen, three. Debris lands on the post office, a mile away. And as the mangled casualties are collected, nature follows with another blow: no mere terrific thundersquall, but a bona fide tornado, a 2 P.M. twister that unroofs the post office after all, sends letters flying, blows men out of the saddle and cannon off their carriages, picks up trees and throws them, tears the masts out of ships—all this with an astonishing deluge of rain, lightning bolts, and thunderclaps that make the Battle of Bladensburg a Guy Fawkes Day picnic. Unprecedented even in the experience of seasoned Marylanders, it quite demoralizes the redcoats still assembling their dead and wounded: they cling to fences, flatten themselves in the lee of the burned-out Capitol, wish themselves in Hell rather than in America.

Andrew is stunned by the first explosion; the second seems to awake him from the daze in which by his own acknowledgment he has witnessed and participated in this "funeral service for his fatherland." The storm is as brief as it is tremendous: "wash'd clean, blown clean, shaken clean" by it, he quietly advises Ross (not Cockburn) to bluff and stall the surrender delegations from Alexandria and Georgetown, who expect him to negotiate indemnities. American reinforcements must be massing already on the northwest heights of the Potomac; units from Baltimore could still fairly easily cut off their retreat. It is time to go.

Ross is of the same mind. Even Cockburn is weary, his adventure successful beyond his most histrionic imaginings. The officers feign interest in negotiation; they decide in fact, privately, to let Captain Gordon's Potomac squadron continue up to Alexandria and ransom the town; they impose an 8 P.M. curfew and order campfires lit as usual to signal their continuing presence—and then they march the army by night back out Maryland Avenue, back through Bladensburg (where more wounded are entrusted to Commodore Barney against further exchange of prisoners). With only brief rest stops they march for 48 hours, back through Upper Marlboro and Nottingham, to Benedict and the waiting fleet. Though scores of exhausted stragglers, and not a few deserters taken by the possibilities of life in America, will wander about southern Maryland for days to come—a number of them to be arrested for foraging by Ross and Cockburn's former host Dr. Beanes, with momentous consequences—the expedition against Washington is over: seven days since they stepped ashore, General Ross and Admiral Cockburn are back on Sir Alexander Cochrane's flagship, toasting their success. Cockburn wears President Madison's hat and sits on Dolley's pillow; Ross frowns and tallies up the casualties; Cochrane considers how quickly they can get back down the Patuxent, and where to go next, and what to do for an encore.

So does our progenitor. *His* letter, Henry, is shorter by half than this, which is meant for less knowledgeable eyes as well as your own.

Andrew merely mentions, for Andrée, what I have rehearsed more amply here. What is to come he treats even more summarily, an anticlimax in his letters as it is in the history of 1814, though it cost him his "life": the bombardment of Fort McHenry and the abortive attack on Baltimore. (As for the Battle of New Orleans and the Treaty of Ghent, further anticlimaxes, they are relegated, the former to a postscript, the latter to a parenthesis within that postscript, at the foot of this posthumous letter.)

In *his* epistle, I remind you, the burning of Washington is but the apocalyptic *mise en scène* for the final burying of Andrew's inconsistent and equivocal, but prevailing, animus against the American line of his own descent, an animus that peaked at Tecumseh's death. After that explosion and tornado on August 25, his head is clear but neutral: the odd emotion of patriotism is still there, but still nascent and tempered; he would not now snatch from the U.S. Navy History's pen and Fame's palm (he has conveniently "mislaid" them, to Cockburn's chagrin; they are in my cottage on Bloodsworth Island; one day they shall be yours), but he would not yet restore them, either.

He has encouraged General Ross to withdraw. Guessing Cockburn's eagerness to follow up the Washington triumph with a quick and wholesale attack on Baltimore, he casts about now for ways to forestall that move; he is not yet ready to arrange for British defeats, but he is prepared to do what he can to counter further victories. He anticipates, correctly, that when news of the Washington expedition reaches London and Ghent (in early October) the U.S. peace commissioners will incline to accept the British ultimatum that the Indians be restored at least to their prewar boundaries, nullifying Harrison's defeat of Tecumseh; indeed, they will be relieved that the British are not insisting that the Indians themselves send commissioners to the Hôtel des Pays-Bas. As Andrew puts it, he has interred his father; time now to tend the grave and look to a fit memorial, not to drive a stake through the old man's heart.

He is relieved therefore to find that Cochrane and Ross are already of a mind to leave the Chesapeake for the present. As the fleet works its way down the Patuxent (old Dr. Beanes has been seized and put in irons on the *Tonnant* for arresting those British stragglers), Cochrane announces that while he has every intention not only to attack but to destroy "that nest of pirates. . .that most democratic town and. . .the richest in the union," whose fleet of privateers has sunk or captured no fewer than 500 British ships since 1812, he will not do it until midautumn, when "the sickly season" in the Chesapeake is past. They will rendezvous off Tangier Island with Captain Parker's *Menelaus* and Captain Gordon's task force from the Potomac; reprovisioned, they will dispatch Admiral Cockburn and the prize tobacco to Bermuda and take the army on up to Rhode Island. Newport once captured, they will rest and wait for reinforcements. Then, when the Americans will have frantically dispersed their forces to defend New York and New

England, they will sweep back to destroy Baltimore, maybe Charleston too, and end their campaign at New Orleans. That should wind up the war, even without further successes on the Niagara Frontier.

Andrew is delighted. The trip north will give him time to make his own plans; from Newport it should be easy to slip away to Castines Hundred; perhaps by late October a treaty will be signed. Ross agrees with Cochrane; Admiral Cockburn cannot prevail against them. On September 4 the orders are given: thirteen ships to remain on patrol in the Chesapeake; the main body of warships and transports to re-rendezvous off Rhode Island; Cockburn to join them there after his errand in Bermuda—all this as soon as they are provisioned at Tangier Island. There the fleet anchors, on the 6th. A dispatch boat is sent off to London with Cochrane's reports of the Washington victory and his plan to move north. Gordon's ships are still working down the Potomac with their prizes from Alexandria; the *Menelaus* arrives from up the Bay with Sir Peter Parker in a box, shot by an Eastern Shore militiaman during a diversionary raid. (In London, Byron will merrily set about composing his *Elegy.*) The army disembarks for the night to camp on a Methodist meeting ground presided over by Joshua Thomas, the "Parson of the Islands." Next morning early, Admiral Cockburn grumblingly weighs anchor and points the *Albion* south toward the Virginia Capes.

And then, Henry, at midmorning the whole fleet makes sail, not for Block Island and Newport, but back up the Bay, toward Baltimore!

Andrew declares himself as baffled by this sudden change of plan as all chroniclers of the period have been since. It cannot have been Cockburn's doing: he and the *Albion* must be sent after and signaled to return. Some have speculated, *faute de mieux,* that the *Menelaus* fetched back, along with her dead young captain, irresistible intelligence of the city's vulnerability and accurate soundings of the Patapsco River up to Baltimore Harbor. Others, that Joshua Thomas's famous sermon to the troops on the morning of September 7, warning them that their attack on Baltimore was destined to fail, actually reinterested Ross and Cochrane in that project! We have seen how cautious a general Ross is, how fickle an admiral Cochrane: one can even suppose that the very dispatching of their withdrawal plans to London, and of Cockburn to Bermuda, inclined them afterwards to do what they'd just decided not to do.

And there is another explanation, which Andrew ventures but, in the nature of the case, cannot be sure of. It is that the three commanding officers had secretly agreed from the first, upon their return to the fleet after burning Washington, to move directly upon Baltimore, and that the unusually elaborate feint down the Bay was calculated to deceive not only the defenders of that city but spies aboard the fleet itself. No one is named by name; no one is clapped into irons to join Dr. Beanes in the *Tonnant*'s brig or hanged from the yardarms. But it is as if (writes Andrew) his alteration of heart has writ itself upon his brow. He finds himself politely excluded from strategy discussions. To

514

his remark that Cockburn will be particularly chagrined to miss the show if the dispatch boat fails to overtake him, the officers only smile— and by noon the *Albion* is back in view.

That same afternoon the *Tonnant* is met by the frigate *Hebrus* carrying a truce party of Marylanders come to negotiate for the release of Dr. Beanes: the U.S. prisoner-exchange agent John Skinner and that lawyer whom we last saw at the Bladensburg Races, Francis Scott Key. *They* are given immediate audience with Ross and Cochrane, the more cordial because they've brought letters from the British wounded left under Joshua Barney's supervision; *they* are told at once that though Beanes will be released to them in reward for the kind treatment of those wounded, the three Americans must remain with the fleet until after the attack on Baltimore, lest they spoil the surprise. The *Tonnant* being overcrowded with senior officers, Key and Skinner are then transferred, as a civilized joke, to the frigate *Surprize,* and Andrew Cook (without explanation) is transferred with them. Indeed it is from Key, whom he quickly befriends on the basis of a common admiration for Joel Barlow's non-epical verse, that Andrew learns for certain that their target is not Annapolis or Alexandria—whence Captain Gordon's task force has yet to return—but Baltimore.

Our forefather's words here are at once candid and equivocal. *I described myself,* he writes, *as an American agent who, to remain useful to my country and avoid being hang'd, had on occasion to be useful to the British as well. Whose pretence to Cochrane & Co. was necessarily just the reverse. Whose true feelings about the war were mixt enough to have carry'd off this role successfully for a time; but who now was fallen into the distrust, not only of "John Bull" & "Brother Jonathan," but of myself.* Key rather shares these sentiments: he regards the war as an atrocious mistake, Baltimore as a particularly barbarous town; he is disposed to admire the British officers as gentlemen of culture. But with a few exceptions he has found them as offensively ignorant and scornful of Americans as the Americans are of them; the scores of desertions from the British rank and file—desertions from the "winning" to the "losing" side!—have shown him the appealing face of democracy's vulgar coin; and the destruction of Washington touched chords of patriotism he has not felt since 1805, when he was moved to write a song in honor of Stephen Decatur's naval triumphs at Tripoli. The defacing of the navy's monument to that occasion has particularly incensed him: did Andrew know that the invaders went so far as to snatch the pen from History's hand, the palm from Fame's?

There was a vandal with a poet's heart, Andrew uncomfortably replies, to whom the fit response might be another patriotic ode, one that will stir the indignation even of New Englanders. *Pen* has a natural rhyme in *men,* for example, does it not, and *palm* in *balm.* Shall they give it a go?

Their camaraderie remains on this level, for Key is either ignorant of the actual defense preparations of Baltimore (which information

Andrew solicits in the hope of both restoring his credit with Ross and Cochrane and misleading them) or distrustful of his new companion. The combination of pens and statuary suggests to Andrew that *graven* is a more promising rhyme for Barlow's *raven* than the one Lord Byron came up with: he volunteers it to Key and resolves to send it on to Byron as well, for consideration in some future elegy to Sir Peter Parker.

When the fleet turns off the Bay and up into the Potomac on the 8th, they wonder whether they have been yet again deliberately misled; whether a follow-up attack on Washington is the real, at least the first, objective. But on the 9th they meet Captain Gordon's flotilla returning from Alexandria; the diversion has been a standby for rescuing Gordon if necessary. The combined forces stand back downriver, anchor overnight at the mouth of the Patuxent, and on the 10th run north past frantic Annapolis. They sail through the night and by afternoon on Sunday the 11th begin assembling at anchor off North Point, at the mouth of the Patapsco, within sight of Fort McHenry eight miles upriver. "The Americans"—so Admiral Cochrane now refers to them, without a glance at Andrew—are transferred from the *Surprize* back to the flag-of-truce sloop they'd arrived on, still monitored by a British junior officer: Dr. Beanes is paroled to join them, and Andrew is included in their party without comment. He sees his erstwhile companion Admiral Cockburn rowed over from the *Albion* to the shallower-draft *Fairy* to confer with Ross about their landing strategy (they are to take the army and marines overland from North Point to fall on Baltimore from the east, while Cochrane moves a force of frigates, bomb ships, and rocket launchers upriver to reduce Fort McHenry and move on the city from below). He sees Admiral Cochrane transferred from the heavy *Tonnant* to the lighter *Surprize* in preparation for that maneuver—wherefore "the Americans" have been shifted. Andrew waves tentatively, still hopeful; but if Cochrane, Ross, and Cockburn see him, they make no sign.

Say now, Muse, for Henry's sake, what Key *can't* see, nor John Skinner nor Dr. Beanes nor Andrew Cook, from where they languish for the next three days. Speak of General Sam Smith's determination that the Bladensburg Races shall not be rerun: his mustering and deployment of 16,000 defenders, including the remnants of Barney's flotillamen, behind earthworks to the east of town and fortifications around the harbor; his dispatching of an attack force at once to meet the enemy at North Point when he's certain they'll land there. Declare what Major Armistead at Fort McHenry knows, and no one else: that the fort's powder magazine is *not*, as everyone assumes it to be, bombproof; that one direct hit will send his fort, himself, and his thousand-man garrison to kingdom come and leave the harbor virtually undefended. Tell my son of the new letter that now arrives by dispatch boat from Governor-General Prevost in Canada to Admiral Cochrane, reporting further American atrocities on the Niagara Frontier and urging the admiral again to retaliate, not with indemnifications, but with fire. The British and even the American newspapers are praising Ross for his restraint in Washington: his firing only of public buildings, his care not to harm noncombatants; such solicitude is not what Prevost wants, and Cochrane is determined this time that Ross shall be hard, that the governor-general shall get what he wants. Say too, Muse, what Ross and Cochrane themselves can't see: that even as this letter arrives, its author, at the head of an invasion force of 14,000 British veterans in upstate New York, is suffering a double defeat. His naval forces on Lake Champlain are destroyed before his eyes that same Sunday morning, and just as he commences a land attack on Plattsburgh in concert with it, he intercepts a letter from Colonel Fosset of Vermont to the defending American General Macomb, advising him of massive reinforcements en route to his aid. That very night, as Ross's army lands for the second time in Maryland, Prevost panics and orders a retreat back to Canada.

The letter from Prevost to Cochrane is authentic; the one Prevost intercepts from Fosset to Macomb is false. Those 10,000 reinforcements do not exist. The U.S. Secret Service has forged the letter and entrusted its delivery to "an Irishwoman of Cumberland Head" whom they know to be a double agent; as they hope, she dutifully betrays them and delivers it to Prevost instead of to Macomb. *Was it you, my darling* (Andrew wonders at Rochefort a year later, from the deck of *Bellerophon), who forged that letter for the Secret Service, or who posed as that Irishwoman? Were you reversing the little trick we play'd on General Hull at Detroit? May I believe that you too thot it time to end the British dallying at Ghent and conclude a treaty, now that our Indian Nation seem'd assured?*

Andrée does not reply. He will never know, nor we.

Say on then, Muse, for Henry, what you saw and Andrew didn't at the Battle of Baltimore, which like the Battle of Plattsburgh never quite took place. It is Monday, September 12th, still warm in Maryland and threatening rain. Ross and Cockburn begin their overland advance, pause for breakfast at a convenient farmhouse, and decline the owner's cautious invitation to return for dinner: he will dine that evening, Ross declares, "in Baltimore or in Hell." A few hours later, on Cockburn's advice, he rides back a bit to hurry a light brigade along in support of his advance party, who have got too far ahead of the rest and are meeting the first desultory American fire. As Ross trots down the North Point Road, the anonymous, invisible Americans fire again from their concealment in a grove of oaks. One bullet strikes him in the arm and chest: he falls, he speaks of his wife, he dies. The invasion will go forward, that day and the next, under Ross's successor and Admiral Cockburn, who commands only his own small band of marines. The American advance line will retreat, but in less disorder than at Bladensburg; they will regroup with the main force of militia at Sam Smith's earthworks to await the real assault. On Tuesday the 13th Colonel Brooke (the new British commander, even more cautious than his predecessor) and Admiral Cockburn will position their forces before those earthworks and wait for news of Cochrane's success at Fort McHenry before mounting their attack. And for all of Cockburn's exasperated urgings, that attack will never be mounted, because that news will never come.

Can you see, Muse, through the rain of that sodden Tuesday, the letters going back and forth between Brooke and Cochrane, army and navy? Cochrane has written Ross on the Monday afternoon that, as best he can see from the river, the flank of Sam Smith's earthworks may be turned without a frontal assault. His letter comes back that evening unopened, together with the news of Ross's death. Unperturbed, perhaps relieved, Cochrane orders the body preserved in a cask of Jamaican rum and dashes off encouragement to Colonel Brooke: Prevost says burn, burn; I will take Fort McHenry (the harbor, alas, is blocked with scuttled privateers); you take the city. On Tuesday morning his bomb and rocket ships open fire, out of range of the guns of the fort. Three hours later he is already wavering; another letter goes down the river and up the North Point Road, this one to Brooke via Admiral Cockburn: It appears we cannot help you; the city is too far away, the fort too strong; consider reconsidering whether Brooke should attack at all. But he sustains the one-way bombardment into the afternoon, and the garrison at McHenry must take their punishment without reply. Even Cochrane cannot see the one bombshell out of hundreds and hundreds that lands directly on the powder magazine, goes through its roof with fuse still sputtering and, like the one bullet that felled General Ross, might have rewrit this chapter of history had not a nimble nameless fellow leaped to douse it. Cochrane moves his ships in closer; the Americans at last and jubilantly return the barrage; he moves back out of range. Nothing is working. Here's a letter from Brooke, fifteen hours late: he will be in Baltimore by noon! But it's past three, and there's no sign of action at the earthworks. Cochrane can't see what you can, Muse: that Brooke has got *his* letter, explored the enemy's flanks and found them defended, and agreed with Cockburn that a night attack is the best strategy. As Cochrane reads this letter, Brooke is writing him another: the army and marines will attack at 2:00 A.M.; will the navy please stage a diversion on the farther side of Fort McHenry, as if moving up to threaten Baltimore from the west?

Letters! This second of Brooke's received, unhappy Cochrane replies (to Cockburn) that the plan is folly: the navy can do nothing; McHenry will not fall; New Orleans is a richer city anyroad; retreat. It is Tuesday evening, rain coming down hard now. Cockburn scoffs at this letter—Washington all over again!—and urges Brooke to ignore it: Attack, attack. Brooke's junior officers are of the same mind; retreats do not earn promotions. But command is heavy: if the army takes the city but the navy cannot take the fort to load prizes, there will be nothing but an expensive bonfire to show for possibly very high losses. If the army fails and the navy succeeds (as seems unlikely), the fall of

518

Fort McHenry will mean nothing. The officers—not including disgusted Cockburn—argue till midnight, when Brooke wearily pens his last to Cochrane: We are following your advice; as the navy cannot take the fort, we shall retreat to North Point and reembark.

But on that same midnight (*you* can see and say, Muse, what they cannot)—suspecting that Cockburn might persuade Brooke to ignore these letters and attack—Cochrane dispatches after all, reluctantly, the diversionary force Brooke has requested but no longer wants. And here, Henry, our ancestor comes back into the tale. You have seen him, all this while, fretting through the bombardment with Key & Co. back at the main fleet anchorage. He is truly saddened, as you saw, by the news of Ross's death: the man was overcautious, perhaps, but brave and not bloodthirsty, an officer and gentleman. You have seen Andrew fear for the fate of Baltimore if—as seems likely from Prevost's letter and Cochrane's first to Colonel Brooke—Cockburn has his way with the city. Rumors abound like Chesapeake mosquitoes; every dispatch boat leaves its message like a wake behind. Old Dr. Beanes complains he can't see a thing; Andrew borrows a spyglass from the British lieutenant in charge of them and confirms through the day that Armistead has not yet struck his colors at McHenry. There is a bad moment towards late afternoon, just after the one heavy exchange of fire from the fort, when they lose sight of it, the big 30-by-42-foot Stars and Stripes, in the smoke and rain, and wonder whether after all the fort has died. But John Skinner recollects that there is a *second* flag there, a smaller "storm flag" for squally weather; he optimistically proposes that the renewed silence means only that the bomb ships have retired back out of range, and that Major Armistead may be using the lull to hoist a banner more appropriate to the wretched weather. Key is unconvinced. Dr. Beanes fears the worst.

Andrew volunteers to find out. He has seen how fretful is their young warden to be upriver with the action. Without much difficulty Andrew has insinuated that his own status is different from that of "the Americans," some sort of special agency. When the message sails through that Brooke plans a night assault and wants diversionary action west of Fort McHenry, in the "Ferry Branch" of the Patapsco, he declares to the lieutenant that he knows those waters like the back of his hand (he has in fact crossed once on the ferry, in 1803, en route to Joshua Barney's hotel and Jérôme Bonaparte's wedding) and pleads to be fetched to Cochrane as a guide. Whether or not the lieutenant believes him, he sees a chance here to move his own career upstream, and so delegates his wardenly duties to a midshipman and fetches Andrew in a gig to the *Surprize*.

The Americans are indignant; Key in particular feels himself imposed upon, though he has never *quite* taken our forefather at face value, and though Andrew has done his hasty best to intimate that this present defection is another ruse. When Andrew presses on him a hurriedly penned note "in case we see each other no more," Key at first will have none of it. But there is a winking look in the fellow's eye. . . At last he stuffs the letter into his waistcoat and turns his back; Skinner and Beanes shake their fists at the departing gig.

Colonel Brooke's final message, that he is withdrawing, has yet to be written, much less delivered. It seems likely to Andrew that Cockburn may prevail and the attack succeed, especially with the help of this new tactic; he is resolved therefore to do what he can to divert the diversion. What with the firing ceased and the rain still falling, the night is dead black. There is no need even to make his case to Admiral Cochrane: their gig is taken at once for one of the little flotilla assembling about the *Surprize* under general command of Captain Napier, and the lieutenant stays mum, recognizing the opportunity. Twenty small boats with muffled oars and light artillery, about fifteen men to a vessel, they head out at midnight in a quiet file. Andrew's boat is ninth in line: a single tap on the lieutenant's shoulder (even whispered conversation is forbidden) is enough to turn them and the eleven boats behind them up the wrong river-branch almost at once, into the line of scuttled ships across the harbor mouth. The lieutenant presently sees their peril—they are right under the guns of the fort!— but cannot proclaim it or denounce its cause; he gets the boats somehow turned about and headed back towards the *Surprize*.

Having assumed the lead, now they are in the rear of the line. Once out of earshot of the fort, and before the lieutenant can say anything, Andrew whispers angrily that his signal was misread. The other boats are clearly glad to abandon the mission; their crews are already scrambling home. The lieutenant must turn at once into the west, the left, the port, the *Ferry* Branch, and catch up with Napier, who in that darkness cannot even know that he now has nine boats instead of twenty. No time to argue: it's that or explain to Admiral Cochrane what they're doing there in the first place. They go—west, left, port—past looming dark McHenry and opposite the smaller forts Babcock and Covington. In their haste they make a bit of noise. No matter: it's 1:00 A.M. now on Wednesday the 14th, and Cochrane recommences, per plan, his bombardment of Fort McHenry. Under cover of that tremendous racket and guided by bombshell light, they actually locate and join Napier's reduced flotilla at anchor.

By that same light the captain is just now seeing what's what and clapping his brow. The shore gunners see too, from the ramparts of Babcock and Covington, and open fire. Napier gives the signal to do what they're there for; the nine boats let go with all they've got. Fort McHenry responds; the bomb and rocket ships intensify their barrage. For an hour the din and fireworks are beyond belief; if Brooke's army needs a diversion, they've got it!

And the Ferry Branch is no place to be. Andrew sits in the gig's stern sheets, stunned by the barrage. 18-pounders roar past to send up geysers all around; they will all die any moment. He has hoped the diversion would include a landing, so that (his credibility with Cochrane

520

gone) he might slip away in the dark and commence the long trek back to Castines Hundred; now he considers whether swimming to shore is more dangerous than staying where he is. At 3:00 A.M., by some miracle, Napier has yet to lose a boat or a man. But their position is suicidal, and there is no sign of Brooke's expected attack over beyond the city: *those* earthworks are deathly quiet. The captain cannot see that three miles away Brooke's sleeping army has been bugled up and fallen in, not to assault the city but—to their own astonishment and the chagrin of their officers—to begin their two-day withdrawal to North Point, minus three dozen prisoners and 200 deserters. Napier has done all he can. He gives the signal (by hooded lantern) to retire.

They proceed back down the Ferry Branch as they came, along the farther shore from McHenry, whose gunners now lose them in the darkness and cease their fire. It looks as though Captain Napier, against all probability, will complete his assignment without casualties. Andrew tests the water with his hand: very warm in the cool night air. "We must signal the fleet we're coming," he whispers to the lieutenant, "or they'll take us for Yankees," and without asking permission he snatches up the launcher and fires a rocket to the *Surprize*. As he intends, it is seen at once by the Fort McHenry gunners as well as by the fleet. The lieutenant wrestles him down; the world explodes; the boat beside them goes up in shouts and splinters. All the batteries of Fort McHenry let loose, and flights of British rockets and bombshells respond. Andrew gets to his knees in the bilges among the straining, swearing oarsmen. His last sights are of the lieutenant scrambling for a pistol to shoot him with; of Major Armistead's cannon-riddled storm flag—sodden and limp, but lit by the shellbursts over the McHenry ramparts—and of a misaimed Congreve whizzing their way, some piece of which (or of oar, or of gunwale) strikes him smartly abaft the right temple, just over the ear, as he dives into the bath-warm river.

He will wake half tranced some days or hours later, knowing neither where he is nor how he came there (Marvelous to relate, by a series of *bonnes chances* he is in the house of none other than the merchant William Patterson. Betsy's elsewhere, avoiding Baltimore and making ready to return with nine-year-old Jerome Junior to Europe, now *that* war's done. Her father, after making a tour of his beloved city on the morning of the 15th, has volunteered his house to shelter the wounded defenders, for one of whom, by reason of his civilian clothes, Andrew was mistaken by the Fort McHenry garrison when they found him on the shore that same dull dawn). As he can neither say nor see now what he will piece together in the days to come, *you* sing it, Muse, if you can reach that high: how F. S. Key, that leaden A.M., has glassed Mary Pickersgill's 17-by-25-foot $168.54 auxiliary stars and bars, standing out now in a rising easterly, and has shared the good news with his companions. How their joy increases through the morning at the retirement of the bomb ships and frigates downriver to the main anchorage, and at the obvious preparations on North Point for the army's return. How in his elevation Key hums the English drinking tune—he'd used for his ode to the Tripoli chaps, and searches vainly for something stirring to rhyme with *stripes*—or for that matter with *flag, McHenry, Armistead,* or *Sam Smith.* Not Cook's *graven/raven,* certainly: he will entertain that word no more. He slaps about his person for paper to make a list on, and fishes forth the turncoat's letter; is at first repelled by the notion of employing such compromised foolscap to so patriotic a purpose, stars wars bars, fight night sight, but comes soon to savor the paradox, Baltimore evermore nevermore? Dum dee dum dum dum *dum:* anapestic tetrameters actually, one quatrain and a pair of couplets, *abab cc dd,* feminine endings on the *b* lines, plus an *internal rhyme* to perk *up* the fifth *line,* he unfolds the sheet to see what the rascal wrote after all and reads

O Francis Scott Key,

Turn the bolt on our plight! Open wide Music's door; see her treasure there gleaming! Golden notes bar on bar—which some more gifted wight than Yours Truly must coin into national meaning. For the United States of America's fate hitherto's to have been, in the arts, 2nd-rate. We've an army & a navy; we're a country (right or wrong): but we've yet to find our voice in some national song!

ABC

Surprised to find it an apparently earnest, unironic exhortation (he has thought only to write some local sort of ode, for the Baltimore press perhaps), Key rereads the letter, Anacreon dum-dee-dumming in his head—*et voilà.* By the time Andrew is enough himself to leave Baltimore, the lyrics of *Defense of Fort M'Henry* have been run off in handbill form, rerun by the Baltimore *Patriot & Evening Advertiser,* re-rerun by presses in other towns, taken up by the tavern crowd; by the time he reaches New Orleans, Americans from Castine (Maine) to Barataria are straining their high registers for the rockets' *red glare* and the la-and of the *free,* and have given Key's anthem a different title.

Andrew goes, then, after all, not home to Castines Hundred, but to Louisiana. The reason he gives, here at the end of this second posthumous letter, is that, his patriotism having been both excited and gratified by the McHenry episode, he hopes to forestall the battle he knows is to come. That New Orleans will be Admiral Cochrane's next objective he is certain, and that to atone for the inglorious retreat from Baltimore—as well as for Prevost's retreat from Plattsburgh—the British will commit their forces to a major assault. But it is the opinion of William Patterson, whose judgment our ancestor respects, that the British economy, drained by the long campaign against Napoleon, cannot sustain the war into 1815. Patterson believes, and Andrew concurs, that when the news of Baltimore and Plattsburgh reaches London, the prince regent's cabinet will settle a treaty at Ghent before the year ends, with or without their Indian buffer state and Mississippi navigation rights. Andrew fears that a decisive victory by either side at this point will upset the stalemate he and Andrée have been working for, and which despite his new feeling for the U.S.A. he still believes to be in the Indians' best interest. Inasmuch as the Niagara Frontier is quiet (on Guy Fawkes Day 1814 General Izard will blow up Fort Erie and withdraw across the river to Buffalo, the last military action in the north), and Andrew Jackson has been authorized by Secretary Monroe to raise and command another army for defense of the Gulf Coast, the danger is clearly from that quarter.

But we do not forget, Henry, that our ancestor, no homebody at best, has been struck a severe blow to the head (the lieutenant of that gig has happily reported him killed; John Skinner and Dr. Beanes are not sorry to hear it; but Francis Key, less certain that the fellow was a turncoat, dutifully reports the news to "Mrs. Cook, Castines Hundred, Canada," and somehow the letter reaches her despite the war and the vague address). Even as he closes this letter, two years later, Andrew is subject to spells of giddiness, occasional blackouts, from each of which he awakes momentarily believing himself to be on Bloodsworth Island, 36 years old, and the War of 1812 not yet begun. Though he never loses sight of his larger end—"the rectification, in [his] life's 2nd cycle, of its 1st"—his conception of means, never very consistent, grows more and more attenuated. We remind ourselves that he is completing this letter in France, from *Bellerophon,* Napoleon a prisoner on board, himself about to set out on an urgent errand in that connection, and yet nowhere in these pages explains how he got there, and what business it is of his to get the fallen emperor a passport to America! No wonder Andrée was skeptical, if she read these *lettres posthumes* at all.

There was also talk at Mr. Patterson's of the Baratarians [Andrew concludes his letter glibly], *a band of freebooters led by the brothers Lafitte, of whom the younger, Jean, had been a captain with Napoleon. When the British in the Gulf solicited their services against New Orleans, Jean Lafitte sent their letters to his friend (and mine) Jean Blanque in the Louisiana legislature, hoping to raise his stock in New Orleans, where his brother Pierre had been jail'd as a pirate. But the Governor's Council declared the letters forgeries, sent a Navy force to destroy Barataria, and jail'd Lafitte's band. Thot I: Here is a man after my own heart, who might serve as a go-between to mislead both Admiral Cochrane & General Jackson into avoiding a disastrous battle. Thus I determin'd to seek out this Jean Lafitte at once, and solicit him to this end, before rejoining you & our children.*

Incredibly, Henry, here his letter ends!

But for its postscript. *In this mission* [he writes under his signature], *I both succeeded and fail'd. I did not prevent the bloodiest battle of the war (fought after the Peace had been sign'd in December) & the most decisive of American victories on land. But in Jean Lafitte, I who have never known a father found a true brother, with whom I fought on the American side in that battle, and whom one day I hope to include in the happiest of all reunions, yours & mine!*

Defeated again, Admiral Cochrane seizes Fort Bowyer in Mobile

Bay as a sort of consolation prize, and Andrew (inexplicably back with the fleet again) mails his *first* "posthumous letter." Cochrane is still hopeful of a fresh expedition in the Chesapeake come spring, to destroy Baltimore, perhaps Washington again as well. He and Admiral Cockburn (who, operating off Georgia for the winter, has been spared the New Orleans fiasco) will mend their differences, go on to greater glory! News of the peace treaty thwarts that plan. Leaving Rear Admiral Malcolm the disagreeable chore of disposing of the blacks and Indians recruited to their cause, Cochrane retires to England to litigate with Cockburn over prize money.

The Ghent Treaty is bad news for Indians. Sobered by their losses at Baltimore and Plattsburgh, by rising marine insurance rates and falling export trade, by the uncertain peace in Europe and the rallying even of dissident New Englanders to Key's new national song, the British have abandoned, on no less grave advice than Wellington's own, their demand for the Great Lakes, half of Maine, and the rest—including the Indian state. There seems nothing now to prevent American expansion right across the Mississippi to the Pacific!

Unless (here the postscript closes). . .

He it was [Jean Lafitte] *who re-excited my interest in Napoleon, many of whose followers had fled to Louisiana after his 1st abdication. As Emperor of the French, Bonaparte was the curse of Europe. But suppose (as Jean was fond of supposing, whose loyalty was less to America than to France & freebootery) a new Napoleon were to govern a French-American territory from the Mississippi to the Rio Grande? Lafitte wisht to rescue the man from Elba & fetch him to New Orleans or Galvez-Town. I scoft at that idea—till Napoleon himself show'd me in March of 1815 it could be done, by escaping from that island & returning to France for his 100 Days. The news reacht us at sea, where (with other activities) Jean was planning a reconnaissance of Elba. He shrugg'd & return'd to Galvez-Town to try a 2nd Barataria, as his hero was trying a 2nd Empire in Europe. But I went on, by another vessel, with another plan in mind, the likelihood of which, events have conspired extraordinarily to advance. But that, dear wife, must await another letter!*

As, dear son, it must likewise with us. A week has passed since this commenced! Americans on the moon! Senator Kennedy disgraced! Where are you?

Your father

ABC/ss
cc:JB

A: *Jerome Bray to the Author.* The Gadfly
Illuminations.

Jerome Bonaparte Bray
General Delivery
Lily Dale, N.Y. 14752

7/8/69

"John Barth," "Author"
Dept. English, Annex 2
State Univ. of N.Y. at Buffalo
Buffalo, N.Y. 14214

"Dear" "Sir":

Aha ha REStop You have taken the bait stepped into our parlor; there's punctuation for you: your *letter* to us of 7/6 received! Hee RESET Gotcha! Hum!

Mars stationary in Right Ascension. Moon and Saturn in conjunction. Stock market hit by heavy losses. 1st U.S. troops head home from Viet Nam. Astromonkey dies after retrieval.

"Sir": (Oh that's good, LILYVAC, a hit, a palpable RESET Your letter of July 6, 6th Sunday after Pentecost, 555 die in weekend traffic accidents—same # as height in feet of Washington Monument, Washington, 4.3. Oh that's sly LILYVAC thats RESET Dont forget punctuation. ¶Right. Resume.

In the lull between the end of our Spring Work Period (and of Year 3, a.k.a. *T,* a.k.a. *V* of our 5-Year Plan) and the Mating Season which will commence Year 4 (a.k.a. *E* etc.); in the afterglow of the "*Godfly* (whoops) Illuminations" of July 4; in the pause at the Phi-point 6 1 8 (*e.g.* ⅜ths, ⅝ths, ⁵⁴/₈₈ths)—your *letter* reaches us proposing that *we* participate in *your* fiction! Oh ha phi on you! (Tell him, LIL.)

Had that missive hit but a week before, when in despair at our scrambled NOTES we wandered like downed Bellerophon devouring our own soul food hee it might have done its fatal work, last knife in bleeding Caesar. Keyless in the presence of our enemies, we could not unlock the leafy anagram; betrayed by Margana y Flea whoops advised by Bea Golden to booger off, we wondered why our parents never gave us a buzz, and whether LILYVAC had their signals crossed. But ha you missed, good old P.O., your letter finds us flying like a butterfloat, being like a sting (O LIL); in a word we've been reset. Repeat. We said in a word we've been RESET Gotcha Hum.

In reply to yours of the 6th. (Show him, LIL.)

Let's get things straight. Attacomputer. We did indeed spend the 1st ½ of 1969 (enough) believing that you and yours had swatted us for keeps; that you had somehow wooed Merope Bernstein into the anti-Bonaparty (stop). Even that LILYVAC's 1st trial printout of the

525

Revolutionary Novel *NOTES* must be either a monstrous ciphered anagram beyond anyone's unscrabbling or a mere dumb jumble of numbers. We had thought M.B. to be our destined mate, right repository of our seed; had expected this season to preserve our line in her like a blank in amber, forever, stop. Then we reckoned her our betrayer: no Bea she, not even a White Anglo Saxon Protestant, play that on your acrostical *Notarikon,* but our devourer!

In desperation next we fancied B.G. our proper queen, pursued as she was already by two drones so to speak. Her several rejections did not deter us; it was not yet flight time; queens do not yield themselves till the peak; let her "mate" as she will with Prinz and Mensch (who think themselves adversaries, not having met the foe who will ally them), they cannot fertilize her; our hour would come, so we believed: 8:23 PM EDST 8/15/69, as the sun sets into Lake Erie on the evening of our 36th. Undeed that may be our ultimate mission still: the *Gadblank* Illuminations leave this point obscure: whether so to speak we need only a toe or must go whole frog.

What they illumine is the true nature of LILYVAC's printout; the true revolutionary character of what we had naively called 1st NOVEL and then NOTES—and our immediate task not only in the Fall Work Period but in this mating season: a task not you nor all your swarm of hommes de lettres can prevent our accomplishing. (Go, LIL.)

O Ma! O Da! We see now you sent M.B. to us by way of initial prophecy, J. Baptist heralding the 1 Who Shall Come After. Her "betrayal" of us was but the Godflaw's sting, your message that Merope was mere means, not end; *you* bid her take the role of Margana Le Fay and lead us into vain decipherment of LILYVAC's numbers, in order to purge us of our last illusion about *RN:* that it was to be a revolutionary work of *literature* (and, ipso facto, no more than a *literary* work of revolution). Thanks! R.S.V.P.

The hardest truths to see, with howsoever many eyes, are those right under our probosces. We were raised in the Backwater Marshes, source of life; we ourself programmed LILYVAC to make no mention of   , always to say blank or blank instead of blank. Yet there we were on 7/4 aboard the renamed *Blank III,* a.k.a. *O.F.T. II* (a substitute for our dear *Blank III* no more resembling the original than Chesapeake Bay resembles Chautauqua Lake), pursuing Bea Golden in our error as skyrockets scuttled and spread like Crab Nebulae over the river; jealously wondering what revolutionary sort of *letter* A.M. was wooing her with, there in the bow, and Bea discarding leaf by leaf like daisy petals or shucked carapaces as she read and R. Prinz gnashed his puny mandibles. The female we'd remarked at the Farm because she was miscalled Pocahontas (no Indian blood in her), and whose presence aboard *"Blank III"* we had re-remarked but paid no heed to, drew an utter blank when she muttered into our ear: *"There's* a pair I'd like to do a number on. My name's Marsha. What's yours?" Not till we'd told her and numbly mumbled Marsha Who did Truth scuttle and RESET Like the supernova 1st observed by Chinese astronomers on July 4, 1054.

Marvelous to enumerate! True 13 2, of whom M.B. I was but the initial RESET No honeybear she, but as splendidly venomous a blank as ever stung twice! The question, Ma, is whether you sent her to be our queen as well as the number of our enemies, please advise, it's that time of year, she'll wake up any day now. Sprung in fact from the marshes whence all life RESET From a swampy mons veneris called Golden Hill, never mind, not far from dear Backwater, she was early mismated with A.M. and thirsts for retribution as in our error once did we: Marsha Blank!

She repeated her name and wish, this time as a proposition: if we would help her do a number on her ex, she'd help us do a number on Bea. We did not know that slang expression: nothing foreign is human to us. She explained its meaning (to trick, cheat, exploit, or take advantage of, LIL, including sexually), but we could scarcely attend her, such a chain of insights—what we have since termed the *"Blank Illuminations"*—was triggered by that key, like a metaphor.

NUMBERS!

You cannot touch us now, "sir"; we are as far beyond your grasp as was Bellerophon past Chimera's when he flew on mighty Pegasus to his rendezvous with the Godblank. How had we not seen that if the media are to revolutionize Revolution, to their number must be added a revolutionary medium? What had we been doing with our *Gematria,* our *Notarikon,* our *Themura,* but attempting to betray LILYVAC's radical numbers into the very seeds of Literature's limitations, *i.e., letters?*

You think to make us a character in yet another piece of *literature!* You, "sir"—now we have your number programmed into LILYVAC— will be a character in our *18 14* (a.k.a. *R.N.):* the world's 1st work of Numerature!

Ourself innumerate, like most literati, we have yet to learn our 1 2 3's; everything must be reviewed, revised in this new light! How we itch to spring, after the Flight, into the Fall Work Period! When, 1st of the *numerati,* our new Queen royal-jellied, we readdress that mighty printout! Ha RESET

"Yours" truly,
JBB

P.S.: Hum. We conceive, as a parting shot at the exhausted medium you practice, a little classical story-in-letters to be located at the Phi-point of our story-in-numbers: .618 RESET The Greek mythic figure Bellerophon, having killed the Chimera and turned Pegasus out to pasture in his life's 1st Cycle, wonders at the Phi-point what to do with the remaining .382 of his allotted span. Though he has imitated perfectly the program of mythic heroism, he has not achieved immortality. His days are numbered. Can he, in the final quadrant of the heroic cycle, reset his program and ascend to the company of 1st-magnitude stars? Yonder rises cloud-capped Olympus; yonder grazes lullèd Pegasus,

527

who can fly anywhere quicker than LILYVAC adds 2 + 2. . . Eat your heart out, *writer!*

P.P.S.: Our last to you. An end to letters! ZZZZZZZ!

10 2 2

C: *Ambrose Mensch to Yours Truly. A lull on Bloodsworth Island.*

Barataria
Bloodsworth Island

July 7, 1969

FROM: A.M., in early P.M.
TO: Y.T.
RE: Your message to me of May 12, 1940

Truly, Yours,

Cancer is the reigning sign; petrifaction the prevailing state. A lull's laid on like that that descends on novels in their third quarter: everything's suspended, held, arrested, as if Time had declared time out.

I write you on a steaming, breathless just-past-noon: siesta-time in barren Barataria. Slick calm yonder in Hooper Straits, where when the tide turns I'll post this in a crabber's Clorox-bottle buoy. Turkey buzzards hang overhead as if still-photo'd; blue herons stand like lawn ornaments in the shallows where yesterday Bea and I went wading after soft-shell crabs—and netted only hard.

Dorchester County's shaped like a pelvis: Blackwater and Trans-quaking rivers are its fallopian tubes; Fishing Bay is its busy womb. Three days ago Bea and I came down through its southmost marshes here to Bloodsworth Island, which hangs under it on the map like a thing discharged.

Now Bea's gone, after this A.M.'s little flurry. Our wake-up fuck, one of the few (Too bad, she told me yesterday, your Medusa couldn't've petrified just *that* part), was interrupted by Casteene's phone call from Fort Erie: Doctor missing since July 4th storm; presumed drowned in Lake Erie, where he'd been whitefishing. Remobilization Farm at a standstill. Memorial service tonight; perhaps Mlle Bibi should return for it?

Phone and phallus are that woman's natural instruments. Ever less firmly pegged atop me, she set the former on my chest for ease of dialing and never let the latter slip (nor paused in her special slide-and-squeeze) even after I was long come, till she'd checked flights, made air reservations from Washington to Buffalo, arranged for Morgan to meet her plane and fetch her thence to Fort Erie and the Farm, dispatched a cab to drive the thirty miles from Cambridge down to Bishops Head

528

(just across the straits, Y.T., at the county's labia, whither I would ferry her in A. B. Cook's runabout) and the hundred more back to Washington National, relayed instructions to me from Casteene for closing up Cook's cottage (kindly proffered her for our half-assed tryst)—*and* brought herself to perfectly malicious orgasm smack in the middle of apprising Reg Prinz in New York of all the foregoing plus her intention to be back on location for the next shooting plus exactly where and with whom she was as she spoke and exactly what doing: i.e., Ay! Eee! Ai! Oh! Ooo!

Reggie would have her ass for *that*, she chirped after, hanging up and swinging off me in one easy motion. But she couldn't resist; anyhow, when one came one came. Come on, said I: you're here because he let me have one inning, to justify his retaliation. It's *my* ass he's after; yours he's got. It's a dandy, Jeannine.

You think so? she said, apropos of I don't know which assertion. She was throwing things into a suitcase, smoking and smiling all at once, livelier than she'd been in three days. What she'd meant, she said, was calling him collect; he hated that. But it was Cook's phone; she had run up the bill enough already. Anyhow, she'd *liked* what I'd written her there on the boat, right at the peak of the party. We really *had* given old Reggie a jolt. I was wrong: he didn't own her, not any part of her; she'd *loved* being with me again after so many years—especially the soft-crabbing, even if we hadn't got any! And so what if I hadn't come on like a sex machine? There were enough of *those* in the world. Would I be a doll and make coffee now and come back and close up the place when she'd left? The connections were tight, but she really owed it to Casteene and the Doctor to give it a try.

Bea's breasts were bare, and tanned from three days of toplessness; as she chattered she slipped into her slacks with a tomboyish snap and snug I'd forgotten since I'd last seen her do it twenty years ago. I was smitten by time and tenderness; had to bestir myself kitchenwards, not to let her see my eyes run. Once at nineteen I'd stood bone-hard for her five times in a single night (it remains my record); but entering our lives' third quarter she'd been bored stiff with me, and I bored limp with her, by the end of our first Baratarian day. We'd stayed on—I don't know why: to purge entirely our curiosity, perhaps; to play through some subscene in The Script. To complete my mistreatment of Germaine. Or out of mere inertia, in a place and weather where even lotus-eating is too much effort.

What relief she's gone! Cook's cottage is tidied, stowed, secured; I'm to return his boat to Bishops Head, forward his keys back to M. Casteene-from-whom-they-oddly-came (a key in itself, that, no doubt, but not to any door I pine to pass through), and return myself through the sluggish marsh to the pausèd world and my exasperated Lady. But there's no rush, no rush. Petrifaction's too hard a term: Time's congealed; things are stuck hereabout like shrimps in aspic.

I make these sentences, Y.T., in default of the ones I want. My

Perseus is stuck in his spiral temple like Andromeda to the cliff, because his author is not Perseus enough to rescue him. Language fails me like my phallus: shall I simply send you the diagrams? Magda's not menstruated since that anniversary coupling of May 12, two months and two letters since: no other signs of pregnancy, thank God, and she'd been off and on for a year before she pulled that fast one. Refuses, of course, to check it out medically; wants to savor the improbable possibility while she can. . . Has she told Peter, one wonders? On whose obdurate mind something heavy surely is, over and above Mensch Masonry's final bust-up, which scarcely now seems to bother him, and Mother's long dying, which decidedly does. There truly, Truly, is your cancer petrified, more so than in our hard crabs' case: Death itself dozes off; Terminality takes siesta.

Magda, my Medusa, *femme fataliste:* Zeus make this pause your menopause! And Germaine. . .

No doubt it is the lull before some further storm. No doubt Mother's terminality will recommence, the Tower of Truth resume our ruin, Magda's womb (for one) do this or that, the Perseus story sink or swim, and Reg's return unfreeze our frame, re-move the unmoving Movie. Meanwhile, in Suspense's welcome lieu, this strange suspension.

Tide's turning: the Hooper Straits buoys begin to lean towards Sharkfin Shoal; time to bottle this and begone. Henry Burlingame III, we are told, was launched in his infancy from this island, to which in middle manhood he returned for better or worse. Do you likewise, letter, if return you must; not to the sender, who, something tells him, shan't.

L: *The Author to Jerome Bray. Admonition and invitation.*

Department of English, Annex B
State University of New York at Buffalo
Buffalo, New York 14212

July 6, 1969

Jerome B. Bray
General Delivery
Lily Dale, New York 14752

Mr. Bray:

Let's get things straight.

I did indeed spend the first half of the 1960's writing a long novel which was published in August 1966, under the title *Giles Goat-Boy*. It is the story of a child sired by an advanced computer upon a virgin lady and raised by kindly goats on the experimental livestock farms of a nameless university which encompasses and replicates the world. In young "manhood" my goat-boy learns from his tutor that the extraordinary circumstances of his birth and youth correspond to those of the wandering heroes of myth. With this actuarial pattern as his map and script, he adventures to the heart and through the bowels of the campus, twice fails at the accomplishment of certain ambiguous labors, and the third time succeeds—though in a fashion equivocal as the tasks themselves—to the status of "Grand Tutor."

It was my further pleasure to reorchestrate the venerable conceit, old as the genre of the novel, that the fiction is not a fiction: *G.G.B.* pretends to be a computer-edited and -printed, perhaps computer-authored, transcript of tapes recorded by the goat-boy and—under the title *R.N.S.: The Revised New Syllabus,* etc.—laid on the Author by Giles's son for further editing and publication.

I have before me your letters of March 2 and April 1. Their imputation of plagiarism, their allegation that I somehow pirated an extraterrestrial scripture from you and published a distorted version of it as fiction, their ominous demands for reparation, and the rest, I take in the spirit of that lengthy satire. Like those book reviewers who choose to mimic (and attempt to surpass) the author under review, you have seen fit to address me in the manner of my novel, as though you were one of its characters nursing a grievance against your author.

Such mimicries and allegations are best left unacknowledged: *Claw a churl by the breech,* an Elizabethan proverb warns, *and get a handful of shite.* But your passing invocations of Napoleon, George III, Mme de Staël, Bellerophon and the Gadfly—these echo provocatively, not to say uncannily, some concerns of my work in progress; and I am intrigued by your distinction between the fiction of science and the science of fiction. Finally, it interests me that the world may actually contain a person who raises goats and devises "revolutionary" computer programs to analyze, imitate, revolutionize, and perfect the form of the Novel—or is it the form of Revolution?

Inasmuch as my current, nowise revolutionary story includes a character rather like that person (derived from the putative editor of *Giles Goat-Boy, or, The Revised New Syllabus),* I am curious to hear more from you on the subject of your LILYVAC 5-Year Plan, for example. In exchange, if you're interested, I offer what I've learned since the publication of *G.G.B.* about actual computer applications in such areas as literary structural analysis and the generation of, say, hypothetical plots: information laid on me by workers in the field of artificial intelligence who happen to have read or heard of my novel.

To be sure, none of what I've learned may be news to you; or you may not care to share your investigations with me. But if you're willing, please address me at my university office, which reliably forwards my mail. And do let's keep the letters "straight": the 700-plus pages of *Giles*

531

Goat-Boy have surfeited their author with that particular vein of "transcendent parody" and (literally, of course) *sophomoric* allegory.

Cordially,

F: *The Author to Jacob Horner.* Accepting the latter's declining of his invitation of May 11 and thanking him for several contributions to the current project.

Chautauqua, New York, July 13:
Bedford Forrest Day in Tennessee,
Boxer Rebellion quelled in Tientsin,
Civil War draft riots in N.Y.C.,
Marat stabbed by Charlotte Corday, etc.

Dear Jacob Horner,

Fact or fiction, your letter to me of May 15—vigorously declining my invitation to you to play a role, as it were, in another fiction of mine—I accept with sympathy and respect. You will hear no more from me; nor shall I otherwise attempt, though I'm mighty curious, to learn how goes *Der Wiedertraum*.

For that notion, at least, and the Anniversary View of History, and the principle of Alphabetical Priority (I mean the *priority* of that principle, which I ought to have listed first), I thank you. I presume that they are not copyrighted, and that you will not object to my making use of them with this acknowledgment of their source.

Best wishes,

A: *The Author to A. B. Cook.* Expressing dismay at the latter's presumption and withdrawing the invitation of June 15.

Chautauqua, New York

July 20, 1969

A. B. Cook VI
Chautaugua Road, Maryland

Dear Mr. Cook,

Actually, I am as dismayed as gratified by your long letter to me of a month ago and its even lengthier enclosures. Gratified of course by your ready response to my inquiry concerning your ancestors; by your providing me with copies of those remarkable letters from Andrew Cook IV to his unborn child; by your diverting account of the

532

subsequent genealogy down to yourself; by your supererogatory offer—nay, resolve—to enrich me yet further with the materials of your
abortive *Marylandiad:* the posthumous adventures, as it were, of A.B.C.
IV. But dismayed, sir, by your misconstruction of my letter and by your
breathtaking assertion that we collaborated on my *Sot-Weed Factor*
novel—indeed, that we have had any prior connection whatever!

   Paper is patient, observes the Jewish proverb, and verily: elsewise
that sheaf of 75% rag 32c 16 lb. 8 ½ x 11's on which your secretary
transcribed your telephoned-Dictaphoned account of our "meeting,"
our "conversation," our "collaboration," would have rebelled against
the pica'd propositions Royaled themupon. We are not acquainted, sir!
Until you answered my letter, I was not even certain of your factual
existence—which, given the several transsubstantiations of your reply
between "Barataria" and me, remains still more than usually inferential.
We have never met, never heretofore conversed, much less collaborated
on anything! The "actual" poet laureate of Maryland I understand to be
a colorful fellow named Mr. Vincent Godfrey Burns, who I imagine
must be less than delighted by your pretension to his office. And—
ahem, sir!—my invitation to you was not to play the role of *Author* in my
novel-in-letters; merely to be a model, one way or another and perhaps,
for one of its seven several correspondents: an epistolary echo of
Ebenezer Cooke the sot-weed factor, no more.

   That invitation, at risk of offending you, I believe I had really
better withdraw. I return with thanks the enclosures of yours of 18 June
and earnestly request that you *not* favor me with their sequelae (or
anything else) in future. For the suggestion that I take as my ground
theme the notion of First and Second Revolutions, in whatever sense, I
here thank you, even though it was not exactly news. Also for your
plausible relation of Chautauqua and Chautaugua: there are other,
homelier etymologies, I have learned since—"fish-place," for example—but the principle nonetheless applies.

   Do please let that proximate place-name be the one bridge between
us henceforward, as it has in fact been hitherto. Let us both turn now
from letters to TV: to watch the images of men first stepping upon the
moon; to ponder the strange tale piece-by-piecing from Chappaquiddick of Senator Kennedy, a drowned young woman, a bridge more
dark and ominous than mine and

                                                          Yours,

4 encl

C: *The Author to Jerome Bray.* *Some afterthoughts on numbers, letters, and the myth of Bellerophon and the Chimera.*

Department of English, Annex B
State University of New York at Buffalo
Buffalo, New York 14214
July 27, 1969, 7 Sleepers' Day

Jerome B. Bray
General Delivery
Lily Dale, New York 14752

Dear Mr. Bray:

Can you perhaps make use, in your NUMBERS project, of, for example, the *Oxford English Dictionary*'s definition III 18b of that term ("Metrical periods or feet; hence lines, verses")? Or the Kabbalistic tradition that the Torah was a septateuch before it became a pentateuch, one of its original books having gone the way of the 10 lost tribes, another shrunk to 2 verses in the Book of Numbers? Or the consideration (which occurred to me on receipt of your letter of July 8) that *NUMBERS* is a 7-letter word arranged symmetrically about your initial; that its 5th letter, or *Phi*-point, is also the 5th of the alphabet; that even more things in the world come in 7's than come in 5's; that by perfectly imitating the pattern of mythic heroism one may become not a mythic hero but merely a perfect imitation; that one might cunningly aspire neither to perfect nor to revolutionize the flawed genre of the Novel, say, but to imitate perfectly its flaws? (There is a bug in the unicorn caterpillar family, I believe, which mimics the appearance of a leaf partially eaten by unicorn caterpillars.)

I hope you can, because while I accept your declining of an invitation I didn't quite make—to "be a character" in my story in progress—your letters have suggested a number of things to me possibly useful in that work—e.g., that the word *letters* is a 7-letter word with properties of its own; that every text implies a countertext; that a "navel-tale" within the main tale ought to be located not centrally but eccentrically—at a point, say, five- or six-sevenths of the way through; that such a tale might appropriately concern itself with the classical wish to transcend one's past accomplishments and achieve literal or figurative immortality; that such a tale might therefore appropriately take as its central figure one of the classical mythic heroes. Et cetera. Thanks.

Cordially,

P.S.: I recollect that Bellerophon does not get to heaven. His mount Pegasus does, stung by Zeus's gadfly, who apparently already dwelt there: the same insect whom Hera earlier dispatched to torment poor

Io, and after whom Socrates was nicknamed. Perhaps that gadfly is your actual hero?

P.P.S.: Finally, I recall that the sort of letters Hamlet bid Rosencrantz and Guildenstern carry from Denmark to England, which, unknown to them, consigned the bearer to death, are called "Bellerophontic letters" after the ones your man innocently delivered from the king of Tiryns to the king of Lycia. Be my guest: but N.R.P.S.V.P.

6

1969							
	S	2	**N**	**O**	**V**	30	
	F	1	**E**	15	22	**N**	
	T		**O**	14	21	**U**	
	W		**D**	**R**	**E**	27	
	T		**C**	12	19	**H**	
AUGUST	M		**H**	11	18	**I**	
	S		**T**	10	17	**U**	31

Lady Amherst

Todd Andrews

Jacob Horner

A. B. Cook

Jerome Bray

Ambrose Mensch

The Author

N: *Lady Amherst to the Author.* *The Sixth Stage of her affair. The Scajaquada Scuffle.*

Kissing Bridge Motel
(near) Buffalo, New York

9 August 1969

Ah John,

Novelist Nabokov ne'er conceived for his Lolita so portentous a catalogue of motels as Ambrose and I have couched in since my last, or reserved for couching in the nights ahead: old nymph and her young debaucher! Forgetting Scajaquada, as I'd prefer, can you believe (not necessarily in this order) the Lord Amherst, the Colonial Court, the Regency, the Windsor Arms, the Gulliver's Travels, the Kissing Bridge, and the Memory Lane? All (except Toronto's Windsor) within a Niagara Falls radius of Buffalo—a radius we will extend early next week to Toronto and Stratford—and so, perhaps, not unknown to you. May your nights in them have been agreeable as mine!

For if the Movie is experiencing a hiatus (filming's to resume across the river in Fort Erie on the 15th), the drama of Germaine Pitt's sore affair with Ambrose Mensch clearly approaches some sort of climax: easier for me to savour than to characterise, yet doubtless easier for me to characterise than for any save us to savour. By the reckoning you'll recall, it is "our" stage, this "6th" of our connexion, which I judge to have commenced sometime between the Full Buck Moon of Monday week last and last Saturday's Scajaquada Scuffle. I had wondered what "we" would be like, if indeed we rereached "ourselves": well, we're All Right Jack, and not only by contrast with the madness of the past few months. Indeed, this first week of August has reminded me in some ways of our maiden month of March, except that A.'s behaviour has been more a gentleman's and less an annuated adolescent's.

But my last, I believe, left the beleaguered lovers on the verge of the Battle of Conjockety, or Scajaquada Creek, on 2 August 1814. (More precisely, my letter ended with a certain sick surmise—but never mind! I still believe myself to have been unbelievably ensnared and at least sexually abused by. . ."André Castine". . .on that Friday night, 1 August. We understand the quotes, who will never, never understand the evening! If I do not sound here like a woman more or less assaulted in body and ravished altogether in spirit one week since, that is because age and experience have evidently taught me to contain the unassimilable, and because—I think coincidentally—the seven days since have been such balm to my sore psyche. I will speak no more of that rose garden!)

Of the details and outcome of the 1814 skirmish, not much is clear: it was a raid, not a battle, between the more important engagements at Chippewa, Lundy's Lane, and Fort Erie. Some British and Canadian troops ferried over from the Ontario shore to attack the U.S. encampment along Scajaquada Creek, a staging area and supply depot for American movements against Canada. Both the raiders and the raided suffered casualties; some Yankee supplies were destroyed; the attackers withdrew per plan.

Our "reenactment" last Saturday evening was similarly obscure and inconclusive but, I daresay, more complex. With no further History to go on than the above, Ambrose and Reg Prinz had sharked up the following scenario, which like Freudian "dreamwork" was to echo simultaneously such disparate matters as that minor military action, the mike-boom incident at Long Wharf in Cambridge of 19 July last, the ongoing hostilities between Author and Director, and that vague circumambient business they're calling the Mating Season or Mating Flight—which I take to refer to, at least to include, the sexual casuistries of Prinz/Bea/Ambrose/Germaine, with that horny maniac J. Bray hovering over all.

To this last (I mean the sexual cobweb) a new strand has been added. Contrary to what a nameless informant informed me in a nameless place on a night I shall not name, it seems that young Merope Bernstein is *not* attached to "Monsieur Casteene"; at least not enough to prevent her having conceived an attachment to Reg Prinz, under the banner of bringing the Revolution to the Media That Matter. Our Director, in his way, neither encouraged nor discouraged this attachment, but at once incorporated it into the story. Bea Golden, you may imagine, was not pleased: indeed, it wants small wit to fancy her not only jealous of this new rival (her own ex-stepdaughter!) but frightened, inasmuch as Ambrose's "pursuit" of her had been merely and clearly per script since their Baratarian interlude, for which (even if he directed it) Prinz seems not quite to have pardoned her. Follows that she will now eagerly ally herself with the Director against the Author in our Scajaquada Scuffle, right? At once to reingratiate herself with Prinz, to score points against her competition, and to defend herself from her only current *real* pursuer, the lecherous Lily Dale lunatic.

Got all that? Well, our Author's projected reenactment was to go as follows: Buffalo's Delaware Park would serve both as the battle site (which it is) and as Municipal Park in Cambridge, which it decidedly is not; the park pavilion both as the American general headquarters and as the *Original Floating Theatre II*. Bea, in red-white-&-blue wrapper, would represent, let's say, Columbia, being interviewed before the pavilion in early movie newsreel–style, by the Director, on the American position in the War of 1812. Myself to make my cinematical debut (we do not count Prinz's surreptitious and/or illegitimate footage) in the

540

role of Britannia, being interviewed concurrently upon the same subject as I cross Scajaquada Creek by rented rowboat just prior to the battle. My interviewer of course to be the Author, fastidiously transcribing my polished periods with a quill pen for publication in the London press. Enter by helicopter (just as A. & I reach the pavilion) the Medium of the Future—in form of J. B. Bray cast as a network television reporter!—who makes off with both willing subjects and leaves the Battle of Scajaquada Creek to be fought, not by Britain and the U.S., but by Author and Director. Weapons and outcome ad libitum, except that the famous mike boom would somehow be worked in.

Thus the scenario. I protested to Ambrose that neither Bea nor I was jolly likely to take a helicopter ride with Jerome Bray. He imagined Bea would do anything her Director asked of her at this juncture, but insisted I follow my own inclinations once the cameras were rolling: that was the Point. And Merry Bernstein? Ambrose wasn't sure, but believed she was to begin the episode as some flower-childish avatar of his daughter (they'd not been able to lay hands on a MARYLAND IS FOR CRABS T-shirt in Buffalo, but had found one blazoned BUFFALO IS FOR LOVERS) and end it with a Revolutionary Statement made Godard-like to the camera as the 'copter reascends and the Obsolete Media slug it out.

She *had* been warned, though, Merope B., that her nemesis Bray was to be there? Well, Ambrose hoped so: that was really Prinz's department; she was *his* hanger-on. Himself was too busy anticipating what the Director might have up his sleeve in the ad-lib assault way to bother with such niceties: he did not fancy another concussion. On that score, I was to stay clear when things got sticky between him and Prinz: he had a couple of rabbits in his own fedora if push came to shove, and not for anything would he have me endanger our just-possible You Know What.

It is evening when we commence. The park brims with floodlights, searchlights, portable electric generators, and the Buffalo curious, whom (true to form) Prinz does nothing to keep back, but often turns his cameras upon. Traffic on the Scajaquada Expressway makes its contribution to the light and sound track. Somewhere overhead a chopper chops. I do not get to hear, alas, Bea Golden's extemporisings upon American policy objectives in the Second War of Independence: A. and I are busy yonder in our skiff, across the pond. Nor do I get to extemporise myself (I'd given the matter some thought, and concluded that Fatigue was the finally regnant factor on the British side of the negotiating table at Ghent, as it may one day be for you Americans in Vietnam: more than we wanted what we claimed we wanted, we wanted Out): the Script calls for our transit of Delaware Park Lake to be shot in flickering silent film–style, our Q & A to be transcribed into subtitles— but no one is there.

Our wigs and tights and crinolines, quill pens and Union Jacks, amuse the bystanders until, muttering that Prinz has scored again,

Ambrose seizes the oars and rows us out on the dark pond toward the bright pavilion, where a Newswatch Trafficopter has already landed. Buffalonians commandeer other park rowboats and follow us. Prinz has missed a good shot: we are a proper little invasion flotilla! I wave my U.J. wanly; am even moved to attempt "Rule, Britannia" against the pavilion loudspeakers, whence softly issues "Columbia, the Gem of the Ocean." Ambrose does my harmony, and not badly: I am touched.

At our *never shall be slaves* (which coincides neatly with the loudspeakers' *free-ee and the bray-ave*), we attain the landing and are instantly floodlit: score another for R.P., who has monitored our approach and gets fine footage now of the surprisers surprised! In plus fours and reversed cap, hand-cranking some relic from the Eastman Kodak museum, he grins from a camera crane; Bea frowns beside him in her Stars-and-Stripes drapery, looking more like a Chenango Street hippie than like Liberty. Between us, looking merely confused, Merope Bernstein, her uniform blue denims unaccountably exchanged for honey-coloured leotard plus the aforementioned T-shirt, a *tiara*, of all things, in her teased-out hair, and *wings*, John—those same Tinkerbell pterons that erst graced the Golden scapulae (on *Gadfly III*) before Bea fell from favour. Hence, no doubt, her frown. Wings!

We disembark, some of us feeling mighty silly. The music stops. Moths commit enthusiastic suicide in the kliegs. The Author blinks, shades his eyes, cons the scene for light and mike booms. Prinz turns to Bea and asks in a startlingly clear, amplified, and mocking voice: "What do you think of Senator Randolph's Quids?" No less than Columbia, we are as surprised by the articulation as by the question. I am all ears for her reply; I search for an opinion of my own about the maverick Virginian's anti-Federalist splinter party; decide to approve it as a manifestation of Randolph's prevailing Anglophilia. . .and again do not get my moment in the limelight.

For Merry Bernstein, with a shriek of nonsimulated fright, up- stages us all. The spot is on her—and, clearly, vice versa; Fay Wray–like (but that tiara, those *wings!*) she looks up from the landing into the darkness with an expression of Terrified Disbelief. She screams again. . . Now a smaller spot obligingly searches the pavilion balcony, passing over grips, sound crewmen, waving bystanders, until it fixes on Jerome Bonaparte Bray. He stands *outside* the balcony railing, balancing who knows how; he wears no wings, but his famous cape is spread like a flying squirrel's between his outspread arms and legs. He smiles, well, nuttily. He cries a name (not Merry's; sounds to me like *Morgana);* he reaches for his crotch; he leaps into thin air; and in flickering, odd slow motion—Prinz must have wired him up!—he lands upon poor Tinker-bell.

I mean *upon* her. Merry is knocked flat; her wings are squashed; Bray's cloak entirely covers the pair of them, who look to be wrestling or humping under a blanket. The girl squeals and squeals.

Prinz and Bea are nearest by, but up on their rigs. Ambrose and I, the closest on foot, dash to pull Bray off. Not as difficult a job as one would expect: he is extraordinarily light, or else somehow half suspended still by a wire I can't see. He comes up squeaking, buzzing, clicking, salivating; no Dracula marks on Merope's throat, but the lap of her leotard is soiled as if by axle grease. She scrambles whimpering from under like a half-swatted dragonfly. Light as he is, Bray is hard to hold on to, something about the material of that cape. He slips silkily from my grip; Ambrose still has him fairly fast, but as I make to resnatch him I see Bea Golden dollying grimly in as if to do the mike-boom trick again!

I prevent her. By 1814, Columbia may have been the new Gem of the Ocean, but Britannia was still its boss. We went at it on that dolly, then on the quayside proper, like a pair of fishwives, she wasting her breath on insults and obscenities, me settling the score not only for 4 July but as it were for all I'd put up with at Ambrose's hands on her account till the past few days. Unfair, surely; paradoxical, too (since it was Ambrose I was fighting *for!*)—but mighty satisfying all the same. She snatches my hair: ha ha, 'tis Britannia's wig! *Hers* is Dolly Homespun's genuine article, which I lay hold of to good effect. My crinolines and whalebone corseting are dandy armor against her nails; if she rips one petticoat through, there's another beneath. But *her* bit of bunting is all she's got, and while it still waves at the scuffle's end (in fact more than at the outset, for I've clawed it half off her) it sorely needs a Mary Pickersgill to restitch Stars to Stripes.

All this, of course, whilst cameras roll merrily and spectators cheer. Not all of them for Old Glory, either—there must have been a few Canadians in the crowd—though I grant the applause at my most telling blow might have been as much for B.G.'s jugs as for the stroke that bared them. Comes my Author now to "relieve" me, just when I'm in position to strike Columbia's colours altogether. *Balls!* cry I, when he scolds me for so exerting myself in my Condition—but enough I suppose is enough. We step out of the light, still fixed on Columbia as she regroups. Merry B. meanwhile, in proper hysterics, has fled to her Director's arms—anyroad to his camera crane, where he coolly comforts her whilst she bawls and swipes at her lap. Somehow reascended to the balcony, Bray shrills imprecations upon us all, in particular upon Ambrose, who he ominously vows shall Pay. The crowd applauds him to the waiting Newswatch helicopter, which promptly buzzes off—to Lily Dale? (We've not seen him since.)

Now bedraggled Bea sees what's what on that camera crane and, her knockers rewrapped in the St Sp B, makes to turn the Eagle's talons on Tinkerbell, who to my further satisfaction (her leotard mopped and her dander up) lays the same order of insults on her that were lately laid on me: M-F'ing Old Bag, & cet. The Director has his hands full keeping them apart. Britannia and weary Literature retire arm in arm from the scene, not much the worse for wear and withal fairly pleased with ourselves, as well as mightily entertained. In this reenactment at least, the redcoats might not have *won* the Scajaquada Scuffle, but Brother Jonathan surely seems to've come off second best.

Having been in her position myself, I was even able then to feel a certain sympathy for Bea, as aforementioned; especially next day, when word came that filming will not be resumed until Friday next, at Fort Erie. Our Director appears to have withdrawn with Tinkerbell to New York City; Ms Golden, *very* distraught, to the Remobilisation Farm, whether to rejoin the company on 15 August or not, we don't know.

I worry about J. Bray, whose psychopathology I take seriously—Merry Bernstein's hysterics I regard as entirely in order!—but Ambrose only shrugs and speculates, with further amusement, on Bray's likely reaction upon returning to Lily Dale and discovering that Marsha too (per Joe Morgan's report) has thrown him over. At Prinz's departure some sort of payment was disbursed to all hands; Ambrose's share, unaccountably, was generous (to me, even *that* seemed ominous). We decided to make a little vacation tour of the Niagara Frontier until the 15th—and here we are at Kissing Bridge: a low-rise ski-platz, August-empty, fit for lovers.

So much for the chronicling (the good people of Buffalo are baffled as I am by the Meaning of All This, which however they found at least as diverting as the pop art at the Albright-Knox); now for the News. As you will have gathered, my menstrual period's nearly a fortnight overdue. Surely, *surely* at my age this signifies nothing. I am fifty, John: fifty, fifty! I will not, I dare not hope. . .

What I must acknowledge would *be* a real hope now, not a bitter one. Till today, Ambrose and I had not made love since Saturday morning last; yet this has been a week the reverse of loveless: reminiscent rather of our chaste May, even more so of our first courtship. We are in accord as to the probabilities—but he is all gentleness and, especially since the Battle of Conjockety, *Ad-mi-ra-ti-on* for my conduct on that occasion. Admiration, it would seem, for my history and character in general, and I am either vain enough or bruised enough by the season's humiliations to find his attitude convincing as well as therapeutic. He cannot thank me sufficiently for enduring and indulging his early importunities in my office and elsewhere, his excesses and sentimentalities; his programmatical later abstinence followed by yet more programmatical inseminations; his couturial and other demands; his outrageous behaviour at the Marshyhope commencement ceremonies; his infidelities and other unkindnesses. Quite a catalogue! He declares all that to have been the purgation by reenactment (a variety of catharsis not mentioned by Aristotle) of sundry immaturities and historical hang-ups long laid on him like a spell. He declares that my love and forbearance have dispelled that spell, set him free to love me truly and properly for what I am, have been, shall be—this without regard to what's what womb-wise, though nothing could more crown his Ad-mi-ra-ti-on than Ge-ne-ra-ti-on. Part of why we're here, indeed (I mean why we'll do Toronto and Stratford and, if he has his way, even Castines Hundred), is the re-turning of a few corners in my own intimate biography: once the Movie's "in the can" and my Condition is established one way or the other—and his mother's done dying, and his brother's prognosis is clearer—he hopes we can revisit Coppet, Capri, London, Lugano, Paris, Geneva—Scenes I Have Been Knocked Up In.

I tell him I do not particularly share his taste for reruns. Why not make it Tobago, Maui, Tahiti—scenes untouched, if not by History, at least by *our* several histories?

Just as I wish. But I won't object, surely, to an evening's theatre at Niagara-on-the-Lake or a good meal in Toronto?

I jolly won't! And jolly well haven't objected to this week's tender knocking about west New York in our budget subcompact, from the handsome Grape Belt down your way (but giving a wide berth to Lily Dale, and not bothering to bother anyone at Chautauqua), to the scene of Commodore Perry's prodigious accomplishment at Presque Isle, to the haunts of the Tuscaroras and Niagara Falls.

This last by way of a revisit to ourselves, so to speak, more agreeable by far than last time 'round. The American spigot, I'm sure you know, has been fully reopened, and if still not equal to the Canadian, it at least inspired my lover and beloved (how sweet, John, at last to use those terms unironically!) to post in it, in an empty bottle of Moët & Chandon Brut, what he fancies may be the last of his replies to that famous Yours Truly who blankly messaged him in 1940. The gesture (I didn't read the letter, but welcomed his comment as one more fatuity purged) appears to have turned his own spigot back on as well: we are now making spirited, I think reciprocal, love here at Kissing Bridge.

There, I think, is the term. It has been a week, not really of abject and fulsome apologies, solicitudes, smarms, but of easy reciprocity: two seasoned adults renewing (you know what I mean) their mutual love, which had grown rocky and uneven to say the least.

I like it! And should it (as I pray) persist, and should its persistence (as it may) come to make these weekly communiqués as unnecessary for me as Ambrose's bottled epistles have become for him—why then, we shall be at our story's end, you and I, and that will be that.

But we are not there yet. Seven days do not a season make. You are not done with (Ambrose's)

Germaine

P.S.: Rereading this, I see I left out, unaccountably—I had been going to say *one detail*, but it struck me even at the time as the key and climax to last Saturday's skirmishing, perhaps to my whole connexion with Mr Ambrose Mensch. The battle done, as he and I withdrew by rental rowboat back to "Canada," in midpond our hero shipped his oars and kissed me. More particularly, as we paused there under the windy stars (early P.M. showers having ushered in a clear cool front), he bade me look him straight in the eyes whilst he took my head in his hands, declared he loved me, and kissed my mouth. That's it. Romantical, what? I hear you ask, indeed, *So* what? But Britannia here declareth herself stirred to the ovaries by that open-eyed osculation, which bridged, I felt, our every past and present difference; brought us truly for the first time to *ourselves* with each other; sealed some compact; inaugurated this 6th, this blissful, Stage.

P.P.S.: Oxymoron! The shocking news now comes in (on the Kissing Bridge Motel telly) of the "ritualistic" murders of Sharon Tate & Co. in Roman Polanski's villa. I think of our erratic Director, of my darling Author, of that madman Bray's last words to us from the pavilion railing. . . Zeus preserve us!

O: *Lady Amherst to the Author. The Sixth Stage continues. The Fort Erie Magazine Explosion and Second Conception scenes.*

Erie Motel
Old Fort Erie
Ontario, Canada

16 August 1969

Old pen pal,
 Our last day on the Niagara Frontier. We'd meant to stop one more night here in the Erie (a cozy place this second time around; you recall our troubled visit of mid-June, a hundred years ago): it's a chapter I'd consented to review, as it were, in Ambrose's dramatised Short History of Us, inasmuch as that story's dénouement still appears a happy one. But when we telephoned Magda yesterday, as we've done periodically through our absence, we learned that Mensch *mère* has entered what really seems to be her terminal terminality, and that Peter is worse too. (How was *I*? that remarkable *Italiana* wanted earnestly to know. Since Ambrose and I agree that the right news would actually be some comfort to her, I confessed that I've not menstruated since 29 June. Magda was tearfully ecstatic.)
 So we shall return late this afternoon, our film work done till Sunday week hence, when action will resume at Bloodsworth Island, or Washington, D.C., or both.
 In short, Zeus *has* preserved us and our mutuality through the week, as I prayed in my last, though his solicitude has not extended through the family. It's been a proper honeymoon of a week for Ambrose and me, the sweeter already in retrospect for our knowing what awaits us now in Maryland. As befits what I take to be an Echo of the "Jeannine Mack" or "Bea Golden" stage of our affair—an Echo of a

546

Reenactment, God alone knows or cares how programmatical—my friend and I have fornicated up and down the frontier, from Stratford and Toronto to the Falls and Fort Erie (*not* including Castines Hundred; I was adamant). A copulatory binge without the urgency of April's—it *is* mid-August, even in these high latitudes—but unremittingly ardent, unremittingly *thorough:* as fleshly an Echo as ever echo'd. Especially on the 11th and 12th, when we hired camp gear and slept out on the shore of Lake Ontario to watch the Perseid meteor shower with the aid of a star guide, an electric torch, and a manual of Positions picked up in a Yorkville skin shop, we counted meteors and ran through the carnal alphabet as if sex were going out of style.

Which, you will be not at all surprised to hear, for the present it has done. I shall explain.

But now it's history-lesson time! We left the War of 1812 stalemated on the banks of the Niagara in midsummer 1814. Jacob Brown's plucky U.S. invaders, we recall, having held against us redcoats at Chippewa and won at least a standoff at Lundy's Lane in July, withdrew to their Fort Erie beachhead: a strategic error, most historians agree, as it returned the military initiative to Britannia. She—after the Scajaquada Scuffle of 1 August—laid siege on 7 August to the Last U.S. Stronghold on Canadian Soil, bombarded it for a week with rockets and cannon, and on the 15th (as Admiral Cochrane's fleet entered the Chesapeake to move on Washington) attempted to take Fort Erie by main strength. Night assault parties breach the northeast bastion and advance successfully as far as the powder magazine—which, in the fashion of powder magazines throughout this war, inconveniently explodes beneath them. Whether the blast is accidental or adroitly managed by the defending garrison will be much debated, but like the navy yard explosion in Washington ten days later, it knocks the wind out of our attack, which has cost us 905 casualties to the Damned Yankees' 84 (that epithet is coined by the British General Drummond on this occasion). The survivors withdraw; the siege is maintained for another month, but no further serious attempts are made to storm the fort, nor are massive American reinforcements sent over from Buffalo to lift the siege. After Prevost's rout at Plattsburgh and Lake Champlain, the besiegers remove downriver (up-map) to Queenston, but the U.S. does not pursue its advantage. By October all the Canadians are back in Canada except the garrison at Fort Niagara, all the Americans back in the U.S. except the garrison at Fort Erie. On Guy Fawkes Day, General Izard blows up what's left of Fort Erie and ferries his troops back to Buffalo. End of hostilities in this theatre of the war, and end of lesson.

And in our little Theatre of the Preposterous? Just possibly ditto, though we are Wary. Yesterday's sequence (so Ambrose reported on the Thursday, after a telephone conference with Reg Prinz's assistants) bore the working title *Fort Erie Assault & Explosion; 2nd Conception Scene.* It was to commence Friday noon with a (filmed) story-conference luncheon in the mess hall of the Remobilisation Farm, then proceed to the enactment of whatever we saw fit to perpetrate under that title. It was hoped I would take an active rôle.

I would *not*, I declared; nor a passive either, unless I were promised that neither "Monsieur Casteene" nor the Medium of the Future would be on hand. The latter I feared for my lover's sake; the former—but I will not speak of that rose garden! And I was to be counted out if "Fort Erie Assault" or "2nd Conception" involved our doing on camera what we'd been so busy at off.

Ambrose enquired (of Joe Morgan, also by telephone) and was told that Casteene had departed the Farm some days past with Merry Bernstein's troupe of activists, presumably Remobilised for covert incitement of the Second Revolution. When or whether he would return, no one knew. That Mr Bray had not been seen since Scaja-quada, but (according to Mr Jacob Horner, much distraught) had communicated by letter with Bea Golden (a.k.a. "Bibi"), who together with Marsha Mensch (née Blank, a.k.a. "Pocahontas") had taken French leave from the Farm on Wednesday and not been heard from since. Horner was persuaded they were in Lily Dale, in Bray's clutches, and was of course immobilised with anxiety on behalf of His Woman.

I was anxious for them both, now neither was a threat to me. Jerome Bray! Ugh! Heartless Ambrose was more amused than alarmed, particularly as Morgan himself judged Horner's fears premature and possibly misdirected. Both "patients" had been AWOL before, it seems; indeed "Bibi" had disappeared for the whole past weekend and showed up drunk on the Tuesday declaring she'd been down sailing on the Chesapeake with a new boyfriend. Since Marsha (alas) also has tidewater connexions, and the two women have struck up an alliance, it seemed as likely to Morgan that they were lushing it in Maryland together as that they were facing Worse Than Death in Lily Dale. In good Joseph's view, the *real* ground for concern was not their whereabouts but their dissolution: "Bibi's" aggravated alcoholism and (he now regretfully reported to Ambrose) "Pocahontas's" recent taking to unspecified and unprescribed narcotics, which she shared with her new friend. Joe wished both of them off the Farm for good and "Bibi" in a proper therapeutic institution for alcoholics.

At second hand, all this sounded reasonable enough, if not exactly jolly, and on the strength of Ambrose's assurances—which he cautioned were not guarantees except in the matter of public coupling—I went along. (Here's the place to declare that the fortnight past has truly coupled our spirits, John, as never in the five months and stages prior.)

Face to face it was another matter, and not only because the Farm's dining hall was rigged up with the now familiar lights, cables, micro-phones, and cameras. The old folks gently exercised or sat about: whatever legitimacy that queer establishment can claim must be in the nursing-home way, where it's not half bad; the hippies for example are in principle as down on "age-ism" as on racism and sexism, and earnestly attempt not to patronise the geriatrics. Reg Prinz, his two chief assistants (that pair of curly blond thugs featured in the "1st Conception Scene" and the "Battle of Niagara," who more and more do his talking for him), and Merry Bernstein were positioned at one end of a central table, sipping fruit juice and regarding our entry. All wore sunglasses. Prinz grows ever more pinched and intensified; Merry's newest denims looked to me more Bloomingdale's than Whole Earth Catalogue, and her hair was teased out in spectacular amplification of Reggie's, as if she'd touched an even higher-voltage line. None spoke. In the center of the table, behind coffee cups, sat "St Joe" and a pale, distraught Jacob Horner, who fiddled, twitched, eyed Ambrose uneasily as if expecting him to play the Jealous Ex-Husband, and said nothing. Morgan too, though he sucked his unlit pipe and gravely buttered a croissant, appeared to me less "together" than *holding* together: that mad brightness of eye I'd noted from time to time in our last conversation was now his fixed aspect.

No sign of Marsha, "Bibi," or the other promised absentees. That black militant chap, the one who calls himself Tombo X, was at the farthest table off with a squad of Brothers and Sisters in green staff uniforms, conspicuously ignoring us. Racism, it would appear, flourishes after all in that corner of the Farm.

Ambrose and I took the two remaining seats, at the opposite table-end from the Director, behind an array of note pads, pencils, ashtrays and matches, ham sandwiches, and, of all unexpected welcome things, Bloody Marys! No one else was so provided for. We said hello to the company and microphones, waved politely to the cameras recording our arrival, and expressed a proper mild concern for Ms Blank and Ms Golden. Morgan crisply reaffirmed that they had left the premises together, voluntarily but without authorisation, and that inasmuch as they were ambulatory adults whose stay at the Farm was also voluntary, there were no grounds for mounting a search.

I think, thought Horner, they're at Lily Dale.

So go to Lily Dale, his advisor advised. Horner does not; only wipes his unperspiring brow with a clean white pocket handkerchief.

All this filmed and watched impassively by the filmists. Clearly that ongoing rerun of your *End of the Road* novel is off its track, sir, and like to be abandoned for want of actors! Just as clearly, some pressure is a-building twixt protagonist and antagonist, whichever of Morgan and Horner is which.

With uneasy briskness we took our seats and our Clearly Symbolic roles: *i.e.* (Ambrose declared aloud), that they were symbolic was clear, but not what they were symbolic of. Was this the Last Brunch, and we the only communicants? Was it Writing that was represented to be alcoholic and carnivorous, or Great Britain, or his and my generation? On the subject of national embodiments, by the way, was it not Prinz's turn to live up to his name and play Britannia, Ambrose's to play the Yankee Doodler, in the upcoming fracas?

What we thought, offered Prinz's Tweedledum, we thought we'd all meet at the Old Fort Erie magazine this evening and play it by ear. See what blows.

Whereto adds Tweedledee: First ones to back off will be the redcoats.

I'm eating my sandwich, I declared, and drinking my bloody Bloody Mary, symbol or no symbol. Ambrose nodded approval and followed suit.

Joe Morgan reminded Author and Director that, if historical accuracy was to apply, the detonation of the Fort Erie magazine ought to occur in predawn darkness. Dum & Dee looked to their leader, who quietly intoned: I think evening. The light.

And those crazy lake flies (Tweedledee): there's a major hatch on. Millions. Joe volunteered that those clouds of insects—which hatch by the *billions* at summer's end in low-lying areas around the Great Lakes, swarm about harmlessly for a few evenings, and then die—have been known since 1812 on the Ontario shore of the Niagara as American Soldiers, and on the New York shore as Canadian Soldiers.

Far *out,* chorused the filmists. The black contingent exited. The old folks rocked, smiled, and nodded at each remark. Horner rocked too, though his chair was no rocker, like an Orthodox Jew at prayer. I was moved to suggest: Let's let that fly hatch be the Second Conception, what?

My lover saluted me with half a ham sandwich.

What *is* the Second Conception? Merope innocently enquired of Prinz, who replied without turning his head: Same as the first. Bruce?

This last to Tweedledum, who promptly brandishes some sort of periodical—clearly they'd rehearsed this bit of business at their end of the table and were ready for that inadvertent cue from ours—and read (I paraphrase, but pretty closely): *The question put by the film* Frames, *says scenarist A. M. King, comes essentially to this: Can a played-out old bag of a medium be fertilised one last time by a played-out Author in a played-out tradition? King himself invokes William Wycherley's Restoration comedy* The Country Wife, *whose hero pretends to be impotent in order to cuckold his sympathetic friends. Viewers of* Frames *may judge this wishful thinking on its "Author's" part.*

Smirks Tweedledee: *Frames* is our new working title. Adds Bruce: "Author" is in quotes.

The publication he identified as a Buffalo "underground" film newsletter; the article a report on Those Crazy Goings-on in Delaware Park. He had another copy; Ambrose and I were welcome to this one.

Well, I was appropriately shocked. Not stunned, exactly, but startled for sure. But the cameras—and at least four pairs of sunglassed eyes—were on us.

Dirty pool, growled Ambrose: they left out the Author's Trenchant Irony; his Mordant Wit.

Don't they always, I said, as levelly as I could manage. And to

Prinz: If *that's* your Magazine Explosion, luv, it's a bleedin' dud. See you at the fort.

Exeunt Played-Out Old Bag of a Medium and Scenarist A. M. King, the latter smitten (by his own protestation) with pride in my self-possession and presence of mind, the former mad as a wet hen. He was *misquoted,* for Christ's sake, Ambrose complained all the way to our motel; I must learn, as he had learnt, the Larger View of Journalism, to wit: that newspapers are no doubt necessary even though they never get anything quite right. Bugger yer Larger View, humphed I: I really am nothing but an effing *symbol* for you, what?

Symbol yes, my companion ardently acknowledges. *Effing* Symbol yes; *Also* an Effing Symbol yes. But Nothing But? Never!

I had aborted one fetus already in Fort Erie Ontario, I reminded him; I could abort another. Ambrose was transported: Was I telling him I truly might be et cetera? If I was, said I, I wasn't by "Scenarist Arthur Morton King," who for all I cared could stuff *himself* into a bottle and post himself over the Falls. Done, said Ambrose: done and done! That King is dead!

We were stripping as we quarrelled, to shower and change for the afternoon. This last was his *In-vi-ta-ti-on* to come off our spat and into bed, and though I wasn't yet mollified enough for that, my ire had indeed peaked and was passing. I understood what he meant by *also* symbolic but not *merely* symbolic, and if he truly intended to have done with that corny nom de plume and write straightforwardly under his own name, I took that for a healthy developement. In short, I was ready to return to our Mutuality and, in time, lend a hand to King John Thomas's Restoration. But as I came from the W.C. to kiss and make up, I had a chilly flash that was nothing menopausal: the *Second Conception scene!*

I tore the room apart to find mikes and cameras. Ambrose swore (when he understood what I was about) he'd not Set Me Up, but agreed that Prinz might well be setting us both up, and joined in the dismantlement of Erie Motel Room 21. Nothing there, unless on the C.I.A. level of miniaturization and concealment. Spent and laughing by now at the mess we'd made—and would have to restore—we were indeed tempted to take a tumble in its midst; "bang the old symbol," as Ambrose put it from where he lay naked on the piled-up bedclothes. Yet however well we'd searched, and however much I assured him I believed his protestations, I couldn't bring myself to climb aboard, so repellent was the thought of Prinz's somehow bugging our intercourse. Indeed, the more that possibility laid hold of my imagination, the more inclined I grew to declare a moratorium on sex—but not on sweet Mutuality!—till we were safely out of camera range.

Ambrose was delighted; I soon realised why, and rolled my eyes to heaven. The weekend, you see, was upon us: if we now put by our heavy humping for a spell of Chaste Reciprocal Affection, then Week 3 of this happy 6th Stage of ours would echo Stage 3 of our affair (approximately May), itself an echo of his chaste "3rd affair." Moreover it was, I now recalled, at about this juncture in our affair that we began to realise how its ontogeny, so to speak, was recapitulating its phylogeny. Did that portend on the one hand that our Happy Sixth Stage was good for another month at least? Did it mean on the other hand that we had *only* another month? And—dear God!—that we were not really "ourselves" yet after all, at least not entirely, and would not be until, let's see, the 2nd week of September (*i.e.*, the 6th week of this 6th Stage)?

I offered to go vomit. Was truly nauseated, whether by that tiresome prospect or by the Last Brunch. Morning Sickness! jubilated Ambrose. I made good my offer.

Sunset at Old Fort Erie! Mighty Niagara chugging north before our battlements! The lights of the U.S.A. to eastward; of a coming thundershower to southwestward, out over the muggy lake; of Tweedles Dum and Dee positioned about our ramparts and especially in the neighbourhood of the restored powder magazine, a brick-vaulted subterranean chamber in the northeast bastion atop which, in director's chairs, sat the Director and the Director's moll: empty-handed, neither smoking nor drinking nor reading nor talking, only waiting, he in his uniform nondescripts, she in her Salvation Army chic.

And the lake flies, John! Do you have them at Chautauqua, I wonder? Overgrown mosquitoes in appearance, they neither bite nor sting, only fill the night in such numbers at the peak of their week-long hatch that the whole air thrums; gather so thickly upon any light surface that it is darkened; immolate themselves by the thousands on any exposed electric light bulb (small hills of the immolated were piling already beneath the floodlights). Tons of idle protein on the wing: the phenomenon is African, prodigious! We walked through it, exclaiming and waving our arms (luckily our clothing was not light-coloured; the insects are not attracted to people; they landed on our clothes and skin and hair only accidentally, but given their numbers, such accidents occurred by the dozens per second. Once perched, they stay there; brushed off, they obligingly die), to where the lighting crew amused themselves with raising and lowering the volume of that huge thrum at will, as if with a control knob, by brightening and dimming the floodlights. Astonishing!

Once over our initial revulsion, we found we could move through the swarm without injury or much difficulty, and that a constant easy fanning of the hands kept one's face and hair reasonably bugless. The scene that follows you must envision in ever dimming light, however, as the lake flies becloud the floodlight lenses with their cumulative dying juices.

Can we shoot in these conditions? asks Ambrose when we reach the magazine. We're shooting, replies the video Tweedle (Dum); you're on. Must be the Fort Erie Assault scene, quips our Author: American and Canadian Soldiers are dying like flies.

No response from the filmists to this Mordant Wit. I then declared to the company (what Ambrose and I had rehearsed en route from our motel by way of joining the battle, as it were) that in our judgement no Second Conception scene was called for until and unless the First should prove a mis-take. In plain English: played out or not, we had reason to believe ourselves preggers already. The charade Prinz meant as Squeezing Blood from A Turnip would in fact be Carrying Coals to Newcastle; I could not reconceive till I was delivered. *Preggers!*

We were regarded: the tiniest hint of interest in Merry Bernstein's eyes; none whatever in the others' (Prinz still wore his sunglasses, so who knows). Not exactly a triumphant opening, though it was exciting for us so to declare ourselves. Ambrose therefore commenced an improvisation that led to the following exchange, which I approximate from memory and edit for concision:

A.M. (to Prinz and Merry B.): Maybe *you* should do the Second Conception, what? Film's as played-out a medium as Fiction. Off with your clothes, Merry.

R.P.: I'm the Director.

A.M.: Direct, then. My script calls for a Fecund, Vital New Medium to conceive a Major Work of Art by a Virile Young Director who liberates her from residual contamination by the Old Medium she has rendered obsolete. It's your big scene, Mer.

R.P. (quietly, to Yours Truly): *You* undress, ma'am.

Y.T.: I jolly shan't.

R.P. then makes a small sign to Merope, no more than a twitch of the mouth and turn of the hand, and she begins peeling off her Salvation Armies for the cameras. I am more and more cheered: Merry's jugs are gross of nipple and ill suspended, her thighs and bum unappealingly slack for a girl's and striated already, her legs unshaven. Naked, she stands self-consciously in the (ever dimming) lights: a lumpy Lake Erie Venus shooing flies.

MERRY B. (approximately): Shoo!

AUDIO TWEEDLE (to A.M.): Let the Muse come to you and Reggie now. The camera will show which medium she inspires.

And dear A.M. (an able ad-libber when he's up for the game): She's not *my* muse, Reg. Exhibition is *your* business.

R.P. (with smile): You withdraw?

A.M. (ditto, and still ad libitum, mind): I cannot withdraw from what I decline to penetrate. Germaine and I stand pat.

This sally gained something, no doubt, from the ambiance. I happily took my Author's arm; he bussed my cheek; the lights dimmed another quantum. Reggie shrugged, fetched up the little megaphone he'd affected in the Scajaquada Scuffle, and terminated what will no doubt prove to be the longest stretch of dialogue in this flick by calling down into the magazine for "Private Blank."

Yup. Forth issued into the failing light the former Mrs Ambrose Mensch: dazed, sullen, and *much* the worse for whatever wear she'd been at. Marsha's complexion was flushed and mottled, her gait unsteady; her eyes were wide and glassy, her hair and frock a wreck, as if she'd been in dire clutches indeed. But she was smiling, albeit loonily, as she wandered our way, waving a tiny American flag.

Ambrose squeezed my arm. Jacob Horner cried her name and hurried (for him) from the shadows behind us—we'd not seen him there—to her side. Marsha blinked and flagged him wanly off, as if he were a lake fly. Merope wondered to the Director whether it was okay to put her clothes back on—but Prinz was watching us watch Marsha. Though Ambrose's concern was evident from his grip, he said and did nothing, sensibly leaving to Horner the anxious interrogation of His Woman.

He got not much out of her—or of Prinz, whom he understandably pressed to tell where she'd come from, where been, and doing what with whom. She'd been to "the *other* farm," Marsha woozily acknowledged, and now was back at this one; bugger the rest of it. She declined to be taken to the infirmary, or home to bed. She managed after all a sort of smirk of recognition at Ambrose and me. The cameras rolled.

Joe Morgan, expressionless, appeared beside Prinz, who tersely called for "the Exercycles." Grips at once fetched forth from the magazine a pair of those machines and placed them side by side before the Director, who clearly had prepared this odd business in advance. Docile Marsha mounted as readily as she could manage, saying Ouch, wow, I'm still sore, and began pedalling. Frowning Horner joined her on the other. Merope (dressed now) resumed her chair and lost interest in the spectacle.

It's the Horseback-Riding scene, Tweedledum explained to a microphone held by his comrade. How can that be? that chap dutifully enquired. In the original it's "Rennie Morgan" who gives "Jacob Horner" his riding lessons. Where's Ms Golden?

It was her or me, Marsha muttered. What on earth, I whispered to Ambrose. He shook his head, touched my hand, replied that it looked to him very much as if his ex-wife was stoned out of her mind. Marsha was pedalling now more industriously; one would say almost grimly. Horner reached over to dab her brow with his handkerchief. Looking straight at Ambrose she enounced: You'll get yours, too.

Prinz signalled Audio Tweedle (so it appeared to us), and, a moment after, there issued from some loudspeaker in the magazine—unnaturally clear, even strident, but as whacked-out mechanical as Marsha's was whacked-out narcotic—the voice of Bea Golden, delivering what sounded like a pronunciamento: As of yesterday, *"Phi*-point of the calendar year and of LILYVAC's Five-Year Plan," the Mating Season was closed. Today—"St Neapolus's Day and Bicentennial of the Emperor's birth"—began "the Fall Work Period of Year *E: i.e.,* Year Four of the Five-Year Plan." Which, however, in the light of "the Perseid Illuminations," might well prove to be "Year *N,* the first of a new *Seven*-Year Plan." Et cetera, and don't ask me! To be fertile matters little, Bea's voice went on; to be fertilised, little more (this, John, addressed as if directly to Ambrose and me!): What matters is the bringing to term and the successful delivery of that Hero who is both Saviour and Golden Destroyer. *Germaine Gordon Pitt, Lady Amherst:* nota bene! *Morgana Le Fay: your turn will come! The New Golden Age will commence April 5, 1977!*

All this last, John, truly spoken as though in italics, and if any doubt remained of whose particular lunacies Bea's voice was iterating, that doubt was blown away by her closing words: *The revolutionary future belongs neither to Pen nor to Camera, but to one. . .two. . .*

On *three* a hollow boom boomed either from the loudspeaker or from the magazine itself, whence billowed now a great puff of white smoke, and from out of that smoke a presumably recorded male laugh that could be none but Jerome Bray's, and a great many flittering sheets of paper, as if a post office had exploded.

We *all* withdrew a safe distance (except Jacob Horner and Marsha Blank, who went on exercycling as if hypnotised), till the air cleared of everything save the ubiquitous lake flies. Even Prinz leapt back from his chair at the blast, and his lieutenants from their microphones and cameras. Merry Bernstein sat on the ground not far from where Ambrose and I had jumped to, drawing her clothes tight about her and verging reasonably upon hysterics.

Much shaken myself, I did what I could for her whilst the men gingerly investigated. First back at their stations were Dum and Dee, to record the last wisps of smoke and leaves of paper. Morgan demanded to know what was going on and where his missing patient was: Prinz and Ambrose both disclaimed responsibility for and foreknowledge of the stunt; indeed, each was inclined grudgingly to credit his rival with a bravura special effect. The papers, blowing about now in a mild breeze off the river, proved to be covered with printed numbers, meaningless to us. The magazine, upon inspection, yielded a portable tape machine, an auxiliary loudspeaker, and an empty canister, presumably a spent smoke bomb. No sign of Bray or Bea Golden.

Jacob Horner volunteered from his mechanical mount that it was in fact the name day of the Bonaparte family and 200th birthday of their most celebrated member, who took his Christian name from a saint martyred under Diocletian in the 4th Century. Birthday too of Princess Anne, Ethel Barrymore, Thomas De Quincey, Edna Ferber, T. E. Lawrence, and Walter Scott. Deathday of Wiley Post and Will Rogers in plane crash near Point Barrow, Alaska. Likewise, traditionally, of the Virgin Mary, whose passing is referred to as her Dormition. Repeated Marsha: Better her than me. And on they pedalled, going nowhere.

I know for fairly certain, John, that Ambrose had no foreknowledge of the Great Magazine Explosion, and we're fairly persuaded that it took Prinz by surprise as well. His signal had been for a tape made a few hours earlier by Marsha, whose bedraggled arrival by bus from Buffalo had inspired this more modest surprise for Ambrose.

The tape—we heard it shortly after—reveals that she had indeed gone voluntarily, with Bea Golden, to Bray's Lily Dale establishment a few days since, and returned when her unspecified business there was done. That Bea, unhappy at the Remobilisation Farm since the Doctor's death, has chosen to stay on in Lily Dale. That coaxial television is a minor technological innovation, not a revolutionary new medium. Et cetera.

Unless, then (what we briefly considered), Prinz's assistants have taken over the Movie *(Frames!)*, it would appear that neither he nor Ambrose but *Jerome Bray* carried the field in the Assault on Fort Erie, turning all the rest of us into Withdrawing Britishers—and that he has had his revolting, nefarious Way with both Marsha and Bea. Merry Bernstein is scared out of her knickers, as well she might be. *I* think the New York State Police ought to be dispatched at once to Lily Dale to see what's what, but I can interest no one in Bea Golden's fate enough to take action (I shall ring up Morgan before we leave, and prod Ambrose again when he wakes up).

Can the Epical Feud between Author and Director have run its course, one wonders, now that the Prize is flown and nobody cares to pursue it? If so, 'twas a Conflict with much Complication and no Climax! But the two parted company last night downright cordially. And my lover is sleeping through this morning because—as excited Authorially by the day's events as were Prinz & Co. Directorially, and liberated by our new Abstinence Week from a night of making love—he sat up happily till dawn turning St Neapolus's Day into sentences. *Not,* praise be, another of those regressive epistles to Yours Truly, but (so he teases, and I'm honoring my promise not to peek) a fiction in the form of a letter or letters to the Author from a Middle-aged English Gentlewoman and Scholar in Reduced Circumstances, Currently Embroiled in a Love Affair with an American Considerably Her Junior.

Ho hum, said I, and toddled off to sleep. Whereupon that simpleminded dramaturge, my subconscious, contrived to dream that *all* my letters to you after the first one—not excluding this, whose sentences were already forming in my mind as I fell asleep—are in fact from the pen of our common friend Ambrose Mensch, whose Middle-aged English Et Cetera does not exist!

Good old subconscious. But now it's *I* am awake, and he asleep: rest assured these pages are not from our Ambrose, but from,

As ever, your
Germaine

P.S.: Speaking of authors: I have I believe now gone quite through your published *oeuvre*, sir, per program: a book a month since March. What am I to read in August? In September?

V: *Lady Amherst to the Author.* Distress at Mensch's Castle.

23 August 1969

Dear J.,

Vanitas vanitatum, etc. Our "mutuality" persists, thank God, Ambrose's and mine, but our Niagara idyll seems already washed a world away by the flood of domestic emergencies we came home to. As Hurricane Camille douched Dixie (with Debbie supersaturating right behind her), so any concern of ours for "Bea Golden" and Marsha Blank, Jerome Bray and Reg Prinz, was first drowned by Ambrose's mother and then redrowned by his brother.

I write this from the waiting room of Dorchester General Hospital, lately our home away from home. What the four of us presently await (Magda and Angie are here too) are the final laboratory-test results and diagnosis of Peter's case. He has been confined here since Wednesday. We wish he had let us fetch him to Johns Hopkins instead, but are relieved that he is—at least and at last—in hospital. The news we await cannot be good; we may hope only for less than the worst. That Peter is here at all, you understand, implies—

Grief drops the stitches of my story. We flew home last Saturday evening, went directly to the Menschhaus, learned that Mensch *mère* was comatose next door in the D.G.H., found Peter chairbound with immobilising pain in both his legs (for which he would take nothing stronger than aspirin), Angela frightened into such regression that only the family totem and pacifier of her childhood, the famous Oberammergau Easter egg, kept her from bouncing off the Lighthouse walls— and Magda serene, serene, serene.

She embraced me first, her eyes all one question (Nope, no period yet. Yup, a few other signs). Serenely weeping, she made us tea and briefed us on the family crises: Andrea had lapsed into coma the day before and was not expected to revive; her death was anticipated hourly, but Mensch's Castle being so close by, her nurses had agreed to send instant word across the street when her vital signs took their final turn. Peter's condition, whatever it is, had worsened at an alarming rate: from a slight hobble in his left leg, to a severe one with hip and knee pain, to disabling pain in both limbs, all since the first of the month. Peter himself growled good-humouredly of "arthuritis," his stubbled face taut. But could mere arthritis proceed so rapidly, in a man not 45? And there was backache, and dull headache; even (so Magda thought, serenely tearful) some loss of hearing. Yet he held fast to his resolve, to "wait for Ma."

On St Helena's Day (Monday last, the 18th), whilst Camille was levelling Mississippi, Andrea King Mensch died. As it happened, we were all present except Peter and Angela: when in the forenoon her life signs took an unanticipated upward swing and she seemed stirring from her coma, we had been summoned. Andrea had of course that Edvard Munch look of the terminally cancerous, together with the complications of inanition: she was shrunk and waxy, nearly hairless, bedsored, foul-odoured from necrosis, all I.V. and air pipes going in and catheters coming out—it was poor Jeffrey in '65, at once heart-breaking and gorge-raising.

She was indeed stirring; had to be restrained lest she disconnect the plumbing they ought mercifully to have disconnected long since anyroad. When she began to speak deliriously of Napoleon and "the Kings of Beverly" (her ancestral family in the neighbouring county, from whom our friend took his former nom de plume), Ambrose observed the irony of its being St Helena's Day. He fell silent when his mother—who we doubt recognised us at any point—commenced to speak less disconnectedly of her late brothers-in-law Karl and Konrad (after whom Magda's twins are named, their initials Romanised): specifically, of her late husband's (Hector's) brief deranging jealousy of the former, whom he suspected of fathering Ambrose "even though it's *Peter* that's the image of poor Karl." We hung upon her words: was that famous marriage-bed mystery, as in a Victorian novel, about to have a deathbed resolution? But her voice gave out. Ambrose took her free hand (Magda had been holding the other from the start) and called the name Karl to her. His mother smiled, closed her eyes, and spoke her last words: "He was right smart of a cocksman, that Karl."

It took her body three hours more to complete the unsavoury work of dying, which she did not interrupt for further comment. And so, while all signs point to an intramural adultery, that little question, and *a fortiori* the question of Ambrose's paternity, remains open, presumably forever.

We buried her on the Wednesday in the family plot, rich in Thomas and Wilhelm Mensch's funerary *oeuvre*. Peter attended in a wheelchair and, together with Ambrose, pointed out to me their grandfather's sturdy Gothic revivalisms and the more baroque flights of the uncle they never knew, which really were rather surprising. Also that sculptor's own unmarked marker, which Hector Mensch, one-armed, had struggled obsessively and in vain to cut to his satisfaction. (St Helena still on his mind, Ambrose remarked that Napoleon's tombstone on that island reads simply *HERE LIES*, his French attendants unyielding in their demand that the verb's object be simply *Napoleon*, his British gaolers equally insistent that it be *Napoleon Buonaparte.*) The Mensches being at least three generations of shrug-shouldered agnostics, Andrea's funeral service was brief as an epitaph, and at our unanimous insistence Peter went even more directly from cemetery to hospital than his mother had gone vice versa.

There he has remained since, awaiting with us the results of his "tests." Ambrose meanwhile, not for nothing a Johns Hopkins alumnus, has "worked up" the presenting symptomatology on his own and confided to me his fearful tentative diagnosis: osteogenic sarcoma consequent upon Paget's disease. The latter is a chronic skeletal disorder of unknown etiology, afflicting perhaps 3% of adults over 40. Often asymptomatic, its pathology is marked by excessive resorption of bone and chaotic compensatory replacement thereof by structurally inferior "pagetic" bone, which sometimes leads to deformity (bowed legs, enlarged facial bones), altered gait, pathologic transverse fractures in the weight-bearing bones, and sundry of Peter's complaints. It is as if (Ambrose's dark trope) thieves stole good stonework systematically from a building's foundation and concealed their theft with slapdash masonry: after a time the building settles, cracks, and in rare instances even collapses. Among the complications of Paget's disease (luckily in no more than a small percent of cases) is bone cancer.

On *this* subject my lover would not enlarge, though given the familial disposition you may be sure he is a ready amateur oncologist. We must await, he says, the measurement of Peter's plasma alkaline phosphatase level and the reading of the X rays, both promised for this afternoon or evening.

We have done our waiting *à trois* (plus Angela), in strange sad harmony in Mensch's Castle, in order to be close to Peter, to help calm Angela, and to lend support to Magda—who however is as much our supporter as we hers. How did I ever feel for that woman the vulgar emotion of jealousy? When now I so admire her tranquil strength, her stoicism so far from unfeeling, and am at the same time so secure with Ambrose in our late connexion, I think I should scarcely mind if. . .

But, needless to say, the conjunction of our sorrows and of the stages of our Stages, so to speak, has in all senses chastened this 3rd week of "mutuality." The three of us hold hands in reciprocal succour and stare at the no longer revolvable camera obscura, fixed for keeps upon the county hospital, the broken seawall, the river of incongruous pleasure boats. Angie, always with us, eyes her egg. One will not be surprised if our Week of Abstinence extends beyond the week.

Beyond *it,* I suppose, lie some sort of "husbandly" 4th week and "tyrannical" 5th, followed by the climax of the Climax and then by who knows what dénouement. This is no time or place to speculate on that, or on the fact that well ere then—indeed, by this time next week— another moon will have filled (the Sturgeon Moon!) and begun to empty, and I shall either have remenstruated after all or determined that I am, despite all odds and whatever the issue, pregnant, pregnant, pregnant.

And beyond our Lighthouse, our chaste hand-holding? Well, we gather that the director and company of *Frames* (!) have not stood still for our grave interlude. They returned to Maryland not long after us and have been busy down at "Barataria" and over in D.C., preparing sets and selecting locations for the film's climactic scenes: the Burning of Washington and the Bombardment of Baltimore. Tomorrow being the 155th anniversary of that former—and the company having sometime since Resorbed and Chaotically Redeposited Jacob Horner's penchant for anniversaries—we look for shooting to commence then on the Big Scene. Starring Merry Bernstein, we presume (as Dolley Madison?), but presumably *not* involving a resumption of the feud between Director and Author, unless someone new has been assigned the latter role. It seems to us that "Bruce" and his counterpart (Brice? I mean Audio and Video, you know: T-Dum and T-Dee) are now the acting dramaturges, regents for the Regent. . .

But our curiosity about these matters is understandably much tempered. Ambrose remains on the company's payroll (thank heaven), but nothing's being asked of him beyond his presence on the set tomorrow if our circumstances permit: we're to hear tonight whether "the set" is Bloodsworth Island or Bladensburg. We'll decide tomorrow whether to go: perhaps take Magda and Angie with us to distract them, if the news we await from down the hall does not distract us from all distraction.

The other large Meanwhile is that Ambrose, in part to distract himself, has, since rearriving at the Lighthouse, plunged almost fervidly into that new project I mentioned in my last. (Where is his pretty Perseus piece? Medusa'd forever, I fear; and there's a pity, for I believe us to have been in it, he and I, properly estellated into Art. Moreover, I now trust him to have got us down Right.) What began as rather a joke, not the best joke in the world either, has become, if not a fair obsession, Ambrose's preemptive literary concern. It will not surprise me, and now shall not you, if he really *does* solicit for his purposes your copies of these weekly letters (by my estimate this is the 22nd consecutive Saturday I've addressed you!).

A month ago I'd have been appalled at the notion of his even reading them, not to mention *using* them. Now. . .I find I don't really mind. They *do* spell out something of a story, don't they, with a sort of shape to it? Wanting perhaps in climax and dénouement, but fetching its principals withal at least to this present gravely tranquil plateau.

Yes. I think I'm granting you my permission, who never after the first time deigned to respond to me, to respond as you please to Ambrose, should he in fact make such a request of you. Always assuming that you *received* #'s 2 through 22 in the first place and (here I complete—and forever put behind me!—my six months' self-abnegation) perchance preserved them, those epistles from

                                                            Germaine

P.S. (7:00 P.M.): Laboratory and X-ray findings in, and A.'s lay worst-case diagnosis confirmed in dreadful particular: Paget's disease, of sufficient standing to have involved pelvic bones, femurs, lower spine, and temporal bone. "Explosive" phosphatase level. Strong roent-genographic evidence of multicentric osteo-sarcoma: apparent lesions at least in right distal femur and left proximal tibia; apparent metastasis already at least to one lung. The doctor will not speak yet of prognosis, but to Ambrose he needn't: it's Very Poor indeed, even with massive radiation and radical "ablative operative therapy"—*i.e.*, multiple amputation. In all likelihood, a few hellish months.

O poor Peter! Poor Magda! Poor tumorous humankind!

E: *Todd Andrews to his father.* 13 R, *a visit from Polly Lake, a call from Jeannine.*

Andrews, Bishop, & Andrews, Attorneys
Court Lane
Cambridge, Maryland 21613
Friday, August 8, 1969

Thomas T. Andrews, Dec'd
Plot #1, Municipal Cemetery
Cambridge, Maryland 21613

Old Progenitor,

Events recircle like turkey buzzards, from whose patient orbits—eccentric, even retrograde, but ever closing—we determine their dead sun. Seven weeks have passed since 12 R, my Second Dark Night. A full month since the subsequent illumination of 13 R: my recognition that their target is yours truly. What prompts my pen today is neither another such night nor another such dawning, but a long and oddly clouded afternoon, my last here in the office before my August vacation cruise—an afternoon which I'm moved to prolong yet further by writing you about it, in hopes of glimpsing what's behind those clouds.

13 L, Dad (see my letter to you of May 16 last), was your son's resolve on the morning of June 21 or 22, 1937, to live that summer day as routinely as possible and kill himself at its close. Its counterpart in my life's recycling, 13 R, was what A. B. Cook's mid-sentence wink—possibly alluding to the Floating Opera?—opened my eyes to, four Fridays past: a replay of 13 L in slower motion (as befits the Suddenly Old), but with a more final finale. Not jubilantly this time, but serenely, I recognized in that Marshyhope committee room what all those goodbyes were about: how my future had indeed been fertilized by my past, attained full growth with but a little cultivation, and was ripe now for harvesting. Instead of a summer's day, the summer season, lived out as normally as possible in face of such extraordinaries as the loss of Polly Lake and the miraculous regaining (and relosing) of Jane. For the summer solstice, the autumnal equinox should serve, or thereabouts; keep late September clear on your appointment calendar, Dad, for our too long postponed reunion.

In the six or seven weeks till when, I mean to make a final single-handed circuit of my favorite Chesapeake anchorages and watch the Perseid meteors for the last time from *Osborn Jones.* I hope too to wind up a deal of unfinished business before my deadline: principally the matter of Harrison's estate, but also my *Inquiry* into your suicide; my *Letter;* the little mystery of Jane's blackmailing; and the still-unbridged crevasse, so narrow yet so deep, between me and Drew (who has avoided me entirely since his rare overtures of July).

But I do not conceive 13 R to be necessarily either a detailed rerun of 13 L or a tidy wrap-up of my life. If differences remain unreconciled, distances unbridged, mysteries unresolved, businesses unfinished by (say) 9/21 or 22, so be it, Dad: I'll keep our appointment.

By what vehicle? *The Original Floating Theatre II* is too obvious to be ruled out, given our Author's want of subtlety. But I do not consider myself bound to the letter of His crude scenarios; the choice of vehicle I regard as matter of small, if not of no, importance. I shall not, however, attempt this time to take others with me, I think; at least not Innocent Bystanders—though I am unrepentant for having so attempted last time around, and would without compunction destroy certain of the world's Dreadfuls along with myself if such a happy dénouement could be arranged. Alas, no one conveniently to hand is to my knowledge wicked enough: not even our elected rulers over on the banks of the Potomac. My final crossing, like my final cruise, looks to be a solo voyage.

The matter of means, then, is a bridge we'll cross when we come to it, the Author of us all and I. Wednesday two weeks past, July 23, was the second anniversary of the other bridge episode in my life—that encounter with Drew and his explosive colleagues on the Choptank Bridge in 1967. I took the trouble that noon to hike out there and fish awhile near the second lamppost from the draw, just to check whether old A. (above) had any heavy ironies up His sleeve (I admit it was sweet to recall the emotion of Courage, too, and bittersweet to recollect brave Polly's aid, and our little sail after on *Osborn Jones).*

He did not. The tide ran. No fish bit.

My sense of the latitude permitted within the general pattern of recurrence was strengthened further by the passage yesterday week, eventless, of another famous anniversary: July 31, when in 1935 (see 10 L) Jane and I resumed our lapsed love affair—in effect shrugging our shoulders, along with Harrison, at the mild question of Jeannine's paternity. Granted that Jane had 10 R'd me three months since aboard *O.J.*—re-reseduced me, so to speak—she had re-redropped me in the meantime too, and who's to say those buzzards can't spiral in for a third, a fourth, a fifth cycle before their dinnertime? Though my heart has truly bid good-bye to her, I went out to the Todds Point cottage, just in case.

Nothing. (Jane is, I understand, off vacationing with her "Lord Baltimore," whereabouts a company secret. Cap'n Chick is being capitalized as a wholly owned subsidiary of *m.e.,* which is gearing up Now to capacity for Tomorrow's Crabsicles and Eastern Sho' fillers and binders.)

We expect no surprises, therefore, on Wednesday next, 8/13, when in 1932 Jane first instructed me in Surprise. I shan't play the game further, dutifully pretending to catch an afternoon nap out there in the cottage till she comes to me. Indeed, I shan't be there at all: *O.J.* and I will be at sea (oh well: at Bay).

Presumably alone, as I told Polly Lake just this noon during her (surprise!) visit to A. B. & A. Hot as the dickens on the gulf this time of year! Makes damp old Dorchester feel like Heaven! On her way north to rescue her grandchildren from their parents for a spell; thought she'd better stop by to see whether her successor had quit or taken to drink, etc.

Oh Polly, Polly, you look terrific. Ten pounds younger (she's become a golfer!), crop-haired and berry-brown, outfitted in trim linen from a good Sarasota shop. Florida agrees with you!

No, no, Toddy, it's living in sin that does. But *you* look awful! Seriously, have you been sick?

Damn near dead, Poll, since you ran off. You mean to say that rascal hasn't made an honest woman of you?

Hope he doesn't till I get down to one-fifteen!

Et cetera. All Office Raillery, Ms. Pond playing Interlocutor to our Bones and Tambo. But as I parried Polly's real concern, and she my real curiosity, an odd awkwardness developed. It was lunchtime: unthinkable that we shouldn't go up the street together as always, or down to the boat slip, for a sandwich and ale and more-private conversation. But my head was full of 13 R, Dad, how this surprise visit fit in; it was a season for good-byes, not new hellos, and Polly and I had said our good-byes in June. Nor did I care to account for my Sudden Aging or deal with Polly's obvious curiosity about Me & Jane, either by lying or by telling the truth.

So I let a real stiffness build, till Ms. Pond got the signal that Polly had got ten minutes earlier but refused to acknowledge, and invited her to lunch, declaring—what was indeed the case, but no excuse—that I'd taken to working through the noon hour in order to clear my desk by vacation time.

Far be it from me then, Polly said, clearly set down. I suppose it *is* getting on to meteor time, isn't it? We all used to work our fannies off, she assured Ms. Pond, so *he* could set sail by the eleventh.

Then to me, with as forced a breeziness as ever blew through Court Lane: Got your crew lined up?

You understand, Dad. Not in a hundred years could Polly have forgot (what Jane could have in a week) that the Perseid shower was at hand, which many and many an August past, since her widowhood, she had watched with me the night through from *Osborn Jones;* that if we had Worked Our Fannies Off to clear the decks for that celestial anniversary, it was in order to Play Them Off together on those same decks, under the fixed and shooting stars.

Guess I'll be single-handing it this time, Polly. Back to the old window now. Good to see you.

I felt her stare at me more consequentially by far than I'd likely stare from my staring window at my oyster-shell pile. She even complained to Ms. Pond—good honest Polly!—He makes a girl feel right at home, don't he?

Sorry, Poll.

Oh, wow! Good-bye, Mister Andrews, and *bon voyage!*

Good-bye, Polly.

In forty years of staring from my office window, Dad, at that mountain of oyster shells over by the packing house, I'd never felt so forcefully as now what a quantity of death they represented. Ten thousand bushels of skeletons; two million separate dyings! I tried multiplying by three and imagining each oyster a European Jew, to comprehend the Holocaust; then I divided by 6,000,000 to put in perspective my own quietus. Only the arithmetic worked.

To business, then! If both Jane and Drew were, let's say, too spooked by my Sudden Aging to relate to me unofficially any further, the contest over Harrison's Follies would be strictly between me and their lawyers—a litigation that would not even wind up its overture by the equinox. A new tack was called for; but my staring window was too beclouded by thoughts of Polly for clear course plotting, even *before* the phone call came from Canada.

Ms. Pond had returned alone from lunch, her manner a prolonged reproof of my rudeness to her predecessor. I know I'm not supposed to interrupt, she declared icily through the intercom not long after; but there's a lady on Line One in Fort Erie Ontario Canada who claims to be Family and says it's urgent. To me she sounds smashed out of her mind, but that's not my business.

I pushed One and identified myself to the (male) operator placing the call: no doubt our Author, doing a bit of subplotting of His own. For my caller—drunk indeed, alas, or doped, and desperate—was Jeannine! Up at that crank sanatorium that the foundation (I here enter on my agenda of unfinished business) ought to cease philanthropizing. Was she all right? I asked as soon as I heard the lush slur in her voice.

All wrong, said she. High as a kite and low as whaleshit, Toddy-O. Crashing! Got to talk to you.

We talked. The guru of her establishment, I learned, was dead—accidentally drowned a month since while fishing on Lake Erie—and Jeannine feared the institution was disintegrating even faster than herself. She confirmed what I had gathered from other sources: that poor Joe Morgan, late of Marshyhope, was there. Further, that he was no longer a patient but some sort of clinical counselor, to whose unlicensed ministrations she had turned in lieu of her deceased doctor's. Further yet, that she had never needed help so sorely as now, when her Last Hope to Make It, Reggie Prinz, had dumped her. Did I understand? She was *out of the movie!* Prinz was shacked up in New York City with her own ex-stepdaughter, Mel Bernstein's kid, and wasn't that incest or something? But the main thing was, even Joe Morgan (We call him Saint Joe up here, Toddy, he's such a fucking saint; I mean *literally* a fucking saint, ha ha; we've got a little thing going ourselves, or *did* have; part of my prescription) was pissed at her now, 'cause his wife didn't used to drink, if I knew what she meant, and it looked like she'd worn out her welcome up there even though it was her dad's money that paid the effing rent. But the main thing was, to hell with telephones: she needed a place to crash and a trusty shoulder to cry on and maybe a little fatherly advice, and she'd always thought of me as being as much her father as her father was, ha ha, and if she could make it to a plane could she come down like right away for a couple of days? At least we could talk about her dad's estate, and like that.

She paused. Then asked startlingly, over *my* pause: *Mom* isn't with you, is she?

Your mother's off with your new stepparent-to-be, I reported, glad of the extra moment to consider. A sire I may be, Dad, but I am no parent. My possible daughter is a fairly hopeless mid-thirtyish drunk, once uncommonly attractive to the eye but never long on character, judgment, intelligence, or talent: a woman whose girlhood I recall with some affection but in whom my interest steadily declined from her puberty on. Her brother, her parents, most of her husbands, her current (unlicensed) therapist, even her fickle lover and her ex-stepdaughter (whom you recall I bailed out along with Drew Mack's "pink-necks" on Commencement Day)—all in my opinion have more at their center than does poor rich Jeannine. What's more, damn it, *Osborn Jones* and I are about to drop our moorings, and I've plenty to do between now and then!

On the other hand, she is Jeannine: companion at three years old of my original tour of the Original Floating Theatre on June 21 or 22, 1937. Quite possibly bone of my bone et cetera, and if so the last of our not very impressive line. Moreover, since our Author saw fit to place this call just as I was in mid-rumination about the Mack estate, there was plainly a Buzzard circling here.

I volunteered to fly to her: have a look at that farm, a word with Morgan, a chat with her—and bid her bye-bye when *I* was ready. But no, no, she had to get out of there; no privacy anyhow from the feebs and loonies. She needed (weeping now) to see me alone. She was feeling. . .well. . .suicidal.

I regarded the shell pile. Hell, I said, so am I, honey. Come on down; we'll discuss ways and means.

Good-bye concentration. She is to call back when she's made her reservations, so that I can haul over to Baltimore and meet her flight.

She hasn't called. Ms. Pond reports unsympathetically, after phoning back, that officials of the Fort Erie Remobilization Farm report that Ms. Golden has left the premises without authorization or proper notification of her intentions. They will appreciate a call from her, at least, if she shows up here. Now, Ms. Pond knows that "Bea Golden" (up there she's known as "Bibi") is Jeannine Mack; she seems *not* to know further that we may be father and daughter, for it was her aspersive insinuation, as she left for the weekend, that I had given dear Polly so cold a shoulder because I was Otherwise Engaged! Her exact words: I thought it was a single-*handed* cruise, not a *singles* cruise.

Really! Five-thirty now, and no word from Jeannine, who may well be passed out in the Buffalo, or for that matter the Baltimore, airport. No response to my periodic pages at both terminals, and the airlines won't divulge their passenger lists. There are two more nonstops this evening, also several connecting flights through Pittsburgh. I've a dozen things to do at the cottage before I can set sail! Not to mention before I can receive a weekend houseguest. Stupid of me not to have specified clearer arrangements. . .

Damn it, Author, this improvisation is wearing thin! Must I cue you, like an actor his tardy sound-effects man, who are supposed to cue me?

Just then, as if on cue, the telephone rang.

Ahem, sir: JUST THEN, AS IF ON CUE

Attaboy. 'Bye, Dad.

T.

N: *Todd Andrews to the Author.* A series of 21's and an intention to bequeath.

Skipjack *Osborn Jones*
Slip #2, Municipal Harbor
Cambridge, Maryland 21613
Friday, August 29, 1969

Sir:

Numbed by a certain letter, I am moved to this letter by a certain number.

21 *Fridays* ago, in early March, I declined "for the present, at least," your request to "use" me in a projected new fiction. More specifically, I believe I promised to consider your strange proposal over Easter and let you know if further reflection should change my mind. You've heard no more from me since, because until today I gave the matter no more thought. It has been an eventful season.

21 *days* ago, on August 8, I was to have boarded *Osborn Jones* at

Todds Point for a final cruise of my favorite Chesapeake anchorages—which number, as it happens, just about three weeks' worth. *O.J.* & I got off a day late, and our itinerary suffered two major diversions, with the result that certain snug and splendid coves I shall not get to say good-bye to. Even so, we traversed a considerable stretch of tidewater, and just this morning—Day 21 in *O.J.*'s log—we rearrived at Slip #2 to check in at the office and collect the mail. Tomorrow we shall move down to our starting place and complete the circuit.

21 *hours* ago, more or less, at our final overnight anchorage (Sawmill Cove, off Trappe Creek, off Choptank River, one of my favorites of my favorites), I began drafting the ultimate and newsiest installment of my ancient *Letter to My Father,* to bring him up to date on the 21 days since I'd written him last. But after an hour's scribbling I put it by: there seemed at once too much to tell and too much of consequence not yet tellable—at least till I should get home, check in at the office, and review my mail.

For symmetry's sake I should like to say that 21 *minutes* ago, in that office, I opened among that accumulated mail a letter-bomb, and was mortally injured thereby. But in fact that noiseless, flashless, unshrapneled blast went off three hours back, in mid–muggy afternoon—since when I've closed up shop till after Labor Day, walked back down High Street to the boat basin, and sat under *O.J.*'s awning, fairly stunned by the concussion of that letter (a simple wedding announcement from my longtime secretary Polly Lake, with a note on the back in her familiar hand).

The wound is fatal, but not instantly: another 21 days or so ought to do the trick; I had been dying already. Meanwhile my head has cleared enough for me to get on with the business of putting my affairs in order. Hence this letter, to report to you that—as on your *Floating Opera* in 1937—I have changed my mind. A codicil to my will will bequeath to you my literary remains: *i.e.* (as I mean to destroy all other personal papers), my *Letter to My Father,* of which you may make whatever use you wish, and certain letters from other characters in the little drama of my life's recycling.

To that former Letter, in the three weeks (or so) left to me, I'll add my account of the Last Cruise of the Skipjack *Osborn Jones,* amplifying for Dad (and you) what in my log, and in *this* letter, are mere terse entries: *E.g.:*

Day 1 (Sat 8/9): Choptank R. (Broad Creek/Harris Creek/Dun Cove). 1700 hrs: Anchor in 8', Dun Cove. Omelettes w. Caprice des Dieux & Moselle: gd. 2200: Commit 1st incest, Missionary position: so-so. Winds calm, air 79 & humid. Could last night's call have been from Polly? From Jane?

Day 3 (M 8/11): Magothy R. (Gibson I./Red House Cove). 1200: Jeannine to Airpt & back to Buffalo/Ft. Erie, under silent protest, after final incest & no bfst. A tergo, shameful & memorable. Wind WSW 10. My my my. Chester R. (Queenstown Creek): 2400: Perseid meteors, mostly obscured by clouds. Worry abt J. Illumination *re* Mack *v.* Mack: Where is Harrison's shit? Could Author possibly go so far as to rerun *that*? Mosquitoes.

Day 5 (W 8/13): Chester R. (Langford Creek, off Cacaway I.). 1600: Wind WSW 15 & rising. Reef main. Cacaway = *Caca + away?*

Day 14 (F 8/22): Miles R. (St. Michael's Harbor). 1000: Call office: investigator's report. Lord Baltimore is "Baron" André Castine of Canada. ½ brother of A. B. Cook, and possibly CIA. Continue cruise or get home fast? Will flip (coin).

Day 16 (Sun 8/24): Patuxent R. (off Solomon's I.): 0900: Up anchor & motor *O.J.* upriver with Jane M. & behind André C. in *Baratarian,* to meet movie folk at Benedict. D.C. to burn tonight on Bloodsworth I. Thundershowers likely (70% P.O.P.). What are they up to? What am I?

Day 19 (W 8/27): Tred Avon R. (Martin Cove): 1830: Anchor in 6', alone. Air still & muggy. BBQ filet mignon, salad, Fr bread, gd modest Bordeaux (Château La Tour de By '62). Are Castine & Cook conning Drew? How is my daughter? Are they rehearsing for the real D.C.? Do I care? Are Castine & Drew conning Jane? Is Drew conning me? Is our Author conning us all? Where does Bray fit in? *2100:* Full moon. Herons. Bored & horny. I miss Polly.

Day 21 (F 8/29): Choptank R. (Sawmill Cove/C'bge): 1030: O.J. in slip: end of cruise. End of cruising. To hotel for mail & clean suit. To office for mail & report. Hope Jeannine's OK and wonder what on Earth induced me to etc.

Etc. Jeannine wasn't; isn't. Not impossibly because her possible father first diddled and then ditched her, my possible and troubled daughter has evidently left her Fort Erie sanatorium and gone to live in Lily Dale, N.Y., with our fuzzy friend Mr. Jerome Bonaparte Bray, last seen in the Prohibited Area of Bloodsworth Island and there looked for (vainly) by U.S. Navy helicopters when Drew Mack and I sailed in aboard the *O.J.* on Day 17 (M 8/25). The question of Harrison Mack Jr.'s freeze-dried excrement—whether, in their crash program to launch Cap'n Chick's Crabsicles in 1970, Mack Enterprises might inadvertently have disposed of that item of the Mack estate and thereby once more fertilized the future with the past—no longer seems important to the case, compared with those more fertile questions of Day 19. And that call on the midnight of Day 0 (F 8/8), which Jeannine answered in the living room of my Todds Point cottage before I was awake enough to get the phone, *was* from Polly Lake, now Mrs. Someone Else, desperately intending after all to propose joining me in *O.J.'s* cruise and holy matrimony despite my rude failure, earlier that day, to propose the same to her. And hearing I was Not Alone, Polly felt an utter, final fool, hung up the phone, married her Florida Chap at last, and sent me on the 21st the announcement thereof, which ticked away in the Dorset Hotel till today, Day 21, when I snatched up my

mail, hurried over to the office, learned many a remarkable, mysterious, and distressing thing, wondered where in the world to begin,
wished dear Polly were there to advise me, recognized her handwriting
on that one piece of mail, and opened that Announcement.

On the back whereof, in Polly's firm clear precious hand, she
announced further all the above: her last-crazy-long-shot visit to
Cambridge and my office on Day 0 (when I rebuffed her); her crazier
desperate last phone call that night; her conclusion that she was a vaster
fool than even *she*'d supposed; and her (lethal, but) nonetheless loving
last Good-bye to

> Yours posthumously, 21 days (or so) hence,
> Todd Andrews

O: *Jacob Horner to Jacob Horner. His rescue of
Marsha Blank from Comalot Farm, and present anxiety
in her behalf.*

8/7/69

To: Jacob Horner, Remobilization Farm, Fort Erie, Ontario, Canada
From: Jacob Horner, Remobilization Farm, Fort Erie, Ontario, Canada

Only today the Anti-Ballistic Missile bill was approved by two votes
in the U.S. Senate, General Hull retreated from Canada back to Detroit,
the Germans captured Liège, the Marines landed on Guadalcanal,
Napoleon set out for his second exile aboard Admiral Cockburn's
Northumberland, Neptune remained stationary in Right Ascension, the
United States of America established a War Department, the Viet Cong
raided the "most secure" of U.S. military bases, at Cam Ranh Bay, and
your Woman Marsha Blank /"Peggy Rankin"/"Pocahontas" received a
packet of Honey Dust through the afternoon mails, enclosed in a letter
from Jerome Bray to "Bibi" Golden/"Rennie Morgan"/Etc.

You are Concerned. "Peggy" is semicomatose again, as when you
Picked Her Up at Lily Dale on 7/22, St. Mary Magdalene's Day.
"Rennie" (again) is dead drunk. Dr. Morgan impatient. You Do Not
Believe that he will abide much longer Ms. Golden's ever less convincing portrayal of the late Mrs. Morgan, who seldom used alcohol. It
is only for the sake of Bibi's own therapy, since her recent abandonment by Reg Prinz in favor of Merry Bernstein, that Saint Joe indulges
her sloppy rendition of Rennie, to the point of sleeping with her. But
he dislikes drunks, especially when they misplay starring roles in *Der
Wiedertraum,* already out of gear. What will you Do, you Wonder, when
he throws her out and redemands that you Produce His Wife, alive and
well as before you Came Between Them?

For that matter, what will you Do if Marsha (whom you Can No
Longer Easily Call "Peggy Rankin" or "Pocahontas") really does revisit

Bray next week, as she declares she must? You are Jealous (and Vaguely Frightened) of him. You are Truly Frightened for her. But you are as Terrified by the prospect of another solo expedition to Lily Dale as by the prospect of what will happen when you Fail To Restore Rennie Morgan to her husband by 9/1, per schedule.

Yet who is there to go with you, if Marsha does not return and you must Re-retrieve Her? Tombo X grows weekly more belligerent; wants all honkies off his premises. Casteene appears to have disappeared with Merry Bernstein's group. Anarchy threatens. Reparalysis beckons.

Remarkably, you Care About All This.

Last time you were Lucky. Tell us about it, Horner, they demanded, Casteene and Saint Joe, in the P & A Room on Thursday 7/24, Fast of Av, ♂♅☽ · ♂♂☽ , when you Regained The Farm at last, Fetched Marsha straight to the infirmary, and were by them Shaken Awake, not from Paralysis, but from Exhausted Sleep. What's Bray up to over there?

He wasn't home, you Replied. Fortunately. It was your Impression that he had gone again to Maryland with the film company, leaving Marsha, in the condition to be described, to tend his automatic computer and feed his livestock.

What sort of livestock? Is the farm legit, or a front? Indian nationalism? Dope? Is it the same premises that the Remobilization Farm occupied from 1956 to 1965, before it moved here? What's he up to with that computer? C.I.A. connection? What took you so long?

Goats: 3 nannies, 1 buck, 1 kid. Front. Don't know. Maybe. Yes. See below. Don't know. Rebegin:

In fulfillment of your *Wiedertraum* prescription—to Reenact Jacob Horner's Movement of 7/19/53 from Baltimore to Wicomico, Maryland, his Interviews At Wicomico Teachers College of 7/20/53 and 7/21/53, and his Excursion To Ocean City of 7/22/53, where he Met and Subsequently Bedded his Fellow English Teacher Peggy Rankin—you Set Out Alone in light rain from Fort Erie on 7/19/69 in the late Doctor's old Mercury wagon, your First Such Adventure in 16 years. Steering wheel! Accelerator! Brake! Very Nearly Paralyzed by Saturday traffic on the Peace Bridge (you are Not Surprised at Senator Edward Kennedy's loss of control at Chappaquiddick), you were Detained by U.S. Customs officers on its farther shore on suspicion of being Stoned, but Released for want of evidence after their thorough inspection of vehicle and driver. Thirty minutes into the journey, you were Already Exhausted, and once safely out of Buffalo, you Stopped at the first available motel on the back road you Preferred to the New York State Thruway: the Eden, in Eden, on Rt. 62, about 25 miles from your Starting Place. It was not yet noon; you Had No Baggage; they wondered. The balance of that day and night, as Generalissimo Franco captured Cádiz, Huelva, Seville, Cordoba, and Granada, you Sat in a chair before the motel TV receiver Watching Walter Cronkite watch

Apollo-11's entry into moon orbit, then the reports from Chappaquid-dick, then the test pattern.

On Sunday 7/20, St. Margaret's Day, ☌ ♂ ☽ · ☌ ♃ ☽ , birthday of Sir Edmund Hillary and F. Petrarch, cloudy, cool, breezy, you Achieved between breakfast and lunch another 25 miles and Bid Fair To Manage the remaining 10 to Lily Dale, but Reached An Impasse just into Chautauqua County, at the hamlet of Hamlet. There the road forks, State 83 continuing west to State 60, which drops south to Lily Dale; County 312 running more directly to your Destination. Both are good paved roads; County 312 is shorter, but State 60, once attained, more familiar to you. You Could Not Decide. The Kennedy accident inquiry continued. Aleksandr Kerenski became premier of the provisional government of Russia. The moon men landed.

Next day—warm, overcast, still; Ernest Hemingway and Isaac Stern—as Apollo-11's crew lifted off from the moon and Francis Drake engaged the Spanish Armada and Jacob Horner First Met Joseph Morgan at his WTC Job Interview and news reached London that the United States had declared the War of 1812 and Union forces won the Battle of Bull Run, a New York State Police officer encouraged you, after inspecting you and your Vehicle for illegal drugs and administer-ing a sobriety test which you Passed With Flying Colors, to Start your Engine, Shift into Drive, and Move the late Doctor's automobile out of that fork in the road, out of Hamlet, and along County 312 to a certain familiar dirt lane on the margin of Cassadaga Lake and the Lily Dale Assembly. Past a familiar mailbox bearing an unfamiliar name: Comalot Farm. Up to a familiar house, barn, and outbuildings, all much more in need of maintenance than they had been when the late Doctor & Co. removed hastily thence to Canada four years ago.

No sign of life except the five goats aforementioned. The three nannies and kid browsed on tall weeds in the dooryard; the buck emerged from the open front door of the farmhouse as you Drove Up. The kid capered over to say hello; his presumable mother bleated some concern; his presumable sire strolled down off the peeling veranda, paused to sniff first her, then another of the nannies, finally meandered to the car and put his forehooves upon the driver's windowsill, not unlike the two officers before him, to ask your Business.

You Bided your Time, though it grew increasingly warm in the car with all windows raised. Sounding your Horn neither fazed the buck nor fetched help from the house, whose open windows suggested it was either abandoned or actively tenanted. *Ra*'s voyage ended in Barbados. *Savannah,* the first nuclear-powered freighter, was launched. Irritated at his presumable son's irreverent leapings upon his back, the buck ran the kid down toward the barn, whose door also stood wide. The nans ambled after. You Took The Opportunity to Dash from car to house, Realizing only as you Shut the front door behind you that there might be other bucks where the first had come from.

The familiar parlor was in filthy case: goat droppings on the floor and furniture; upholstery torn and chewed upon; soiled plates and glasses, some broken. Clinks came from the kitchen: you Froze, then Inquired Cheerily whether anyone was home? Considered Retreating to the car, but Observed that the Family Gruff had returned to the dooryard. Picked up a knocked-over straight chair to precede you like a lion tamer's through the house.

More debris. Goat shit. Flies. And, sitting at a battered kitchen table in the dirty sunlight, Marsha Blank: naked, frowzled. Paralyzed? So you Could Almost Fancy, with a Rush of Anxious Joy. But on the table, along with a cup of moldy yogurt, were phials, a tiny hypodermic syringe, and her left arm. You Sat in your Chair, beside her. It was not morphine. Her hair was a mess. Her breasts just touched the tabletop; on the right one a housefly circumambulated. Marsha was only half comatose: she regarded you, well, blankly, and nodded or at least bobbed her head for a considerable while.

Time passed. The light changed in the room. You Sort Of Inspected her: no manacles or other bonds in evidence; no apparent lacerations or contusions, just a few bug bites and, on the arm, red needle marks. A trickly sound; you Looked; the woman was pissing in her seat. You Returned to yours and presently Inquired, Was she all right?

Through the afternoon the dope wore off. At some point you Surveyed the other rooms, most of them empty except of litter. But one bedroom was more or less furnished, with a curious five-sided bed on which was piled what looked to be computer printout: long sheets of numbers, chewed at here and there by goats and, it appeared, slept on. Creases, rips, stains. Still no sign of Bray. Marsha wandered up and sat on a corner of the bed, legs apart, blinking now. She seemed to have wiped herself. You Had Not Seen a reasonably attractive unclothed female body for some while.

What kind of dope was it, Horner? You Still Don't Know. Bray has it in both pill and powder form, the latter water-soluble and mainlined like heroin, which it isn't. Marsha called it Honey Dust, and was hooked on it: a fix in the late forenoon, after morning chores, spaced her as aforedescribed until midafternoon; by dinnertime she'd be reasonably herself again, enough so at least to prepare a simple meal. But there are residual effects, which two weeks of enforced abstinence and therapy have since diminished but not altogether removed, and which you Fear will be restored by today's mail. Formerly fastidious, she was now unsanitary and heedless of her appearance. Formerly assertive, sharp-edged, she was now passive, vacant. As she boiled eggs for your Dinner this first evening, for example, padding barefoot about the kitchen in one of Bray's capes (open at the front), the buck wandered in to check the menu. Don't mind him, she advised you, and herself ignored his persistent snuffling at her backside, through and under the cape. But when, growing more aggressive, he thrust his bearded snout between her thighs from in front, she said Ouch I'm sore there and conked him mildly with a ladle.

Having Established that Bray had been in Maryland for a week and was not expected back for another, you Took Heart, Ate A Boiled Egg, Asked More Questions, which Marsha more or less answered. As best you can Reconstruct The Events, she went down to Maryland from the Farm in late June or early July, either in her capacity as secretary to M. Casteene, or to visit her daughter by Ambrose Mensch, or both. Falling in with Reg Prinz's film company in Cambridge on July 4, she met or remet Jerome Bray and with him formed some project of revenge upon her former husband (against whom she still harbors a grudge) and upon Bibi Golden, who it seems had vigorously spurned Bray's advances and gone off somewhere with Mensch. The details of their joint grievance and joint plan of retaliation are unclear and, you Gather, no longer important: to discuss them, however, Marsha had permitted Bray to drive her back to her Cambridge motel at the end of that evening and buy her a nightcap in its bar.

Her insistence that what ensued was voluntary on her part is, in your Opinion, the insistence of a victim still in thrall to her victimizer: it Seems Clear to you that she was doped and raped that night and kept in some degree of narcosis thereafter until her need for the chemical, and its debilitation of her will, made her sexual and other compliance "voluntary." All indictable offenses, you have Indignantly Pointed Out. Marsha shrugs her shoulders. Once installed on his farm, she went naked except on cool nights or when working outdoors among briars and thistles. She prepared the meals, tended the goats, did general chores—all perfunctorily, as has been seen. No further mention was made of their original project.

It is obvious that Bray abused her sexually: a week after his departure her vulva was still sore, and even now, a full month since, your Infrequent Copulation causes her discomfort. But she remains indifferent to that abuse, even uncertain of its details. Every forenoon, you Gather, from July 5 through 13, she would "do her Honey Dust" and "zonk out," to find herself some hours later upstairs in that bed with a sore cunt, leaking semen on that printout paper. Sometimes she slept there at night as well, sometimes not (she had a double mattress of her own on the floor in another room), but except at the noon hour Bray never touched her sexually or otherwise mistreated her—aside from his ongoing crime upon her spirit!

Was she free to leave? Matter of semantics: her chemically induced complaisance, her indifference, was entire. You Imagine that the question never came up until you Raised it, next day.

By when, ☌ ☿ ☉, Apollo-11 on course toward Earth, John Dillinger shot near movie house in Port Huron, Mich., Senator Kennedy attends funeral of Mary Jo Kopechne, Napoleon's only son dies in Vienna, you Had a Fair Understanding of her condition. That first night you Attempted To Express your Feelings for her, and Mistaking her dozing off for real rejection, you Did Not Share her couch, but Went Upstairs to that double mattress. When she wandered in during the night you Believed she was coming to you, but her mild Oh Hi There disabused you of that belief. She had forgotten you Were In The House. Experimentally, you Mounted her: she ouched in the same declaratory tone as earlier to that goat, whom you Do Not Doubt she'd have received as indifferently. You Of Course Withdrew, not at her request. Then in the morning you *Announced,* rather than Suggesting or Begging Leave, that you were Returning With Her to Fort Erie. She went on, naked, about her business, which included a trip out to the barn "to check LILYVAC."

Despite your Leeriness of the livestock, you Went Along, to See What She Meant by that phrase. Your Life since 1953 has not Kept you Abreast of the technology of automatic computers and artificial intelligence; therefore you Cannot Say For Sure, what however is your Judgment, that the extraordinary object in the barn of Comalot Farm is no usual, perhaps not even a genuine, automatic computer. Indisputably it contains what Appeared to you to be components from Eisenhower-era electronic machines, as its name suggests: dusty banks of vacuum tubes, fins and fans for cooling them, bright-colored resistors, capacitors, condensers, wires a-plenty, glows, clicks, hums. But Looking More Closely through the pigeon shit and cobwebs, you Observed that at least some of what you'd Taken for metal or plastic was a scaly, waxy stuff, unidentifiable but vaguely repulsive; some of those wires were more like heavy beeswaxed cord, or dried tendons. There were in fact a great many bees and wasps about; you Feared for naked Marsha, and Began To Wonder whether the circumambient drone was electronic at all.

Hum. Tell us more, Horner. No one else about? Only the goats, who luckily had lost interest in you. "Checking LILYVAC" seemed to involve no more than Marsha's sitting for some minutes in a seat molded into a cube of spun yellow fibrous stuff and pressing a red button or protuberance on each of its "arms." Nothing you Could See ensued, but en route back to the house she dreamily remarked, That's a real buzz. Fibers still stuck to her hams and buttocks, raising gooseflesh on you both. You Made Bold To Assist in their removal. She mmmed. In nothing like the predatory spirit wherein you Laid Peggy Rankin in the Surfside, or Seaside, or some other motel near Ocean City, Md., sixteen years past, you Caressed the labia, both majora and minora, of Marsha Blank. Her ouch this time was sharp enough to send the goats scampering. You Apologized.

Then, to your Surprise, she asked only whether she might do her daily Honey Dust before leaving (she seemed to have got it from LILYVAC). You Took Heart, Said Absolutely Not, Where are your clothes and things, et cetera. There wasn't much; she made no fuss, but lost interest in the project. You Pretty Much Had To Dress Her yourself, not a disagreeable job at all but an awkward one. Then you

574

Led her to the toilet and Instructed her to pee before you Set Out For Home. Dutifully she did, ouching again as she wiped herself after. Your Heart Was Stirred. Get in the car now, you Gently Commanded. She got. Exhaustion overcame you, the responsibility of initiative. For a long while you Sat behind the steering wheel, Marsha beside you, whom from time to time you Patted. She was open-eyed but glazed. Sometime after noon you Started The Engine, and after a while Moved Down The Driveway to the mailbox, where you Paused. Will the goats be okay till he gets back? you Inquired. Marsha murmured: Fuck 'em. We'll take care of Bray later, you Promised. She fell asleep.

In an Unprecedented Show Of Self-Possession, which alas Marsha was oblivious to, you Dared The Thomas E. Dewey Thruway for the 20-odd consecutive miles from Exit 59, Fredonia, to Exit 58, Irving/Angola, before your Nerve Failed and you Exited. Handing the attendant the correct change! Checking *Mr. & Mrs. Jacob Horner* into the Iroquois Motel, overlooking Lake Erie, as if you Did Such Things Every Day! Finding Room 121! Extracting 2 ham sandwiches, 2 ice cream bars, and 2 Pepsi-Colas from 3 several vending machines with scarcely a hitch! Spreading that repast before your Woman on one of the twin beds in Room 121, whose air-conditioning unit you Adjusted yourself, and Bidding her eat! Posting outside your Door for all to see the Do Not Disturb sign; Turning back the bedcovers; *Undressing both her and yourself;* and, Almost Swooning with your Authority, Very Nearly Ordering her, in consideration of her tender vulva, to perform fellatio upon you! But exhaustion, exhaustion imperiously reasserted its claims: you Stood Unsteadily before her where she sat still on her bed edge; you Cupped her chin in your Left Hand, your Already Flagging Member in the other; you Wondered Gently Whether? She obliged, mouth still ice-creamy. I Love you! you Ejaculated.

Then with the Last Of your Strength you Wiped her mouth, Laid her down to rest (it was past 3 P.M.), and yourself Collapsed Into Sleep beside her. Next day, Wednesday, as the Dow-Jones Industrial Average sank to the year's low and General Grant died and Senator Kennedy's driver's license was suspended and Haile Selassie was born and the Sun entered Leo, Jacob Horner was Scheduled per *Wiedertraum* to Have Dinner with Joe and Rennie Morgan, his Prospective New Colleagues at Wicomico Teachers College, where he had Just Been Appointed as a Teacher Of Prescriptive Grammar. But schedule or no schedule, you Needed Further Restoration before Resuming Management both of Marsha and of the Mercury. That day, therefore, a bright still one, you Spent In your Room except for three excursions to the now friendly array of vending machines, for breakfast, lunch, dinner. The chambermaid looked at you. There seemed to be no other guests at the Iroquois Motel. Deprived of her Honey Dust, Marsha was vacant but not comatose: it Appeared To you that she understood where she was and with whom, and did not mind. Sometimes she even replied to your Remarks and Queries. Daytime TV. When you Suggested A Shower

575

she even said My my, and as you Soaped Up in there together, she declared almost crossly that she was able to scrub her own tits, thank you. This sharpness you Took For A Sign Of Recovery. Ditto her disinclination, this time, to receive your Ejaculate in her mouth, though she had no objection to collecting it in her other hand, which promptly thereafter she washed with more soap and water.

Skip your Sex Life, Horner. Any more information about that computer?

Only that when you Asked her sometime that night, as David Brinkley reported a .6% increase in the U.S. cost of living for June, whether in her opinion LILYVAC was a bona fide electronic computer or a monstrous simulacrum, she formed the longest syntactically coherent sentence you had Heard from her since before her disappearance, possibly excepting the one about her tits, to wit: Life is going to be a bitch without Honey Dust.

Next day, then, Th 7/24, as H. "Rap" Brown's speech in Cambridge, Maryland, inspired some of its black citizens to arson, and Congress established the Internal Revenue Service to raise money for the War of 1812, and President Nixon greeted the Apollo-11 astronauts quarantined aboard the U.S.S. *Hornet*, happy birthday Dumas père, Lord Dunsany, Amelia Earhart, you Successfully Checked Out of the Iroquois and Made Your Way up through South Buffalo, across the Peace Bridge, through U.S. and Canadian Customs, and back to the Farm! Fetched Marsha to the infirmary (Just rubbed raw is all, Tombo X's new black nurse reported: She been getting it off with a corncob?)! Et cetera.

Joe allowed that afternoon's P & A, here reported, to serve in *Der Wiedertraum* as your Abortive First Interview at Wicomico Teachers on 7/20/53; the subsequent week's P & A (7/31/69) as your Second Interview (7/21/53), whereat you First Meet Joseph Morgan—though in fact your Dinner With Joe & Rennie Morgan (7/23/53) had been reenacted, inversely, the night before, 7/30/69. 1st tropical storm of season (Anna) reported in Caribbean, Goethe's "Albert" arrives at Waldheim, Ted Kennedy announces will rerun for Senate but not for presidency in '72, munitions ship *Black Tom* blown up at Jersey City docks by German saboteurs. Bibi/"Rennie" having gone off somewhere again, and you and Pocahontas/"Peggy Rankin" (as all save yourself still called your Woman) having Established yourselves at the Farm as a Couple, it was decided that you (O heavy plural!) would Have Morgan To Dinner instead of vice versa: *i.e.*, that he would sit at your Table in the Dining Hall; that Marsha would pass the salt et cetera; that yours would be the awesome Hostly Initiative: Welcome, How are you this evening, Splendid or Beastly Weather we're having, Like you to meet my Woman, How about a drink, all that. For you were a Couple, though access to Marsha's vagina was proscribed till Lammas Day, ☽ on Equator, Herman Melville's birthday: you Personally Monitored her withdrawal symptoms and her schedule of therapies (principally workouts on the Exercycle, meant both to ward off catatonia and to toughen up her crotch); you Slept Together (but see above); you Ignored the smirks and ungenerous comments of Tombo X and others; you Even Went So Far as to Make Clear to M. Casteene that while you Had No Objection to Marsha's resuming her secretarial activities for him, he was not to expect resumption of additional services, inasmuch as etc. Fortunately he only laughed, wished you good luck, declared his business as prime mover at the Farm was about done in any case, and gave you to understand that the services previously rendered him by Pocahontas he had made shift to secure elsewhere. Even so, your Temerity laid you out for an interval.

What shall we Serve for hors d'oeuvres? you Wondered. Marsha reminded you that the dining hall menu includes neither hors d'oeuvres nor appetizers nor choice of entrée, only the options of coffee (regular or decaffeinated), tea, milk, or water and, in summer, the first two (or three) of these either hot or iced. It did not Take you Very Long To Decide on the coffee, decaffeinated, iced, for yourself. Marsha chose the water. Your guest the milk. You yourself had Selected Marsha's dress for the occasion from her considerable wardrobe, in which she took less interest than formerly: a short sleeveless cotton print that set off to advantage, you Felt, her excellent arms and legs, her trim figure generally, and was neither Too Dressy nor Too Casual for the circumstances. Exhaustion. Her hair—no longer the meticulous coiffure of pre-Independence Days, but not the rat's nest of Comalot Farm, either—was Beyond your Competence: at the last moment you Gently Suggested a kerchief, whereupon Marsha asked, rhetorically, Who gave a fuck?

The evening was successful, All Things Considered. You yourself Made Frequent Trips to ice-cube bin, water tap, milk dispenser, to keep everyone's glasses filled. The meat loaf, in your View, was not up to par, and the mashed potatoes had been too long in the steam table. Too, there were perceptible wrinkles in the Fordhook lima beans, from their having been served the previous evening and reheated. But the chef surprised everyone with orange Jell-O! At table the conversation ranged from Marsha's chain-smoking (which we Agreed Should Be Indulged For The Present) to Marsha's worrisome intention, which she spoke of as if it were a contractual commitment, to return to Comalot in mid-August for her Final Fix. You Took The Position that such a return would amount to a relapse, unquestionably antitherapeutic. Marsha wittily shrugged her shoulders. Joe eloquently lighted his pipe. Is it a brief or an extended visit you have in mind? you Asked Her As If Jestingly, and she parried, That depends. Joe regarded you both.

By next afternoon's P & A, Mariner-6 Mars photos show cratered terrain, Pony-Penning Day on Assateague Island, Va., you were Enough Recovered from the social whirl to Express to Dr. Morgan your Alarm at the prospect of Marsha's refalling into Bray's queer clutches. He looked at you. Did it not remind you, he mused, of another woman's

577

Compulsive Return, should we say, to her seducer, on 9/11, 16, & 25/53? Not greatly, you Retorted, and Seeing Joe's face darken you Added Sincerely, Except in the hurt: that she should be "intimate" with any other man. He looked at you. It was decided that the Horseback-Riding Lessons of August 1953 (wherein your Relation to Rennie Morgan grew Ambivalently Personal as you Teased her with her husband's programmatic rationalism and her own apparent self-subjugation), would be echoed most conveniently in *Der Wiedertraum* by joint sessions on the Exercycles: you and Bibi every morning that she was present; you and Marsha-as-stand-in-for-Bibi-in-the-role-of-Rennie when (what seemed increasingly the case, to Joe's annoyance) she wasn't.

You Admitted To Some Concern that Marsha might disapprove of your Exercycling Privately with Bibi; nor were you yourself Delighted At The Notion of Marsha in the role of Mrs. Joseph Morgan. Your Audacity astonished you. Joe smiled. Do it anyhow. End of interview.

It is not working. Marsha's progress (till today) was unimpaired by Bibi's return, which indeed seemed to reinspire some degree of her former bitchery; you are still a Couple; she has permitted you Brief Access To Her Vagina on two separate occasions, Lammas and Transfiguration days, without contraceptives, Tombo X having attested with relish your Surgical Sterilization on 10/25/54. But though you are Pleased To Construe Marsha's renascent vindictiveness as recuperation from her sojourn at Comalot, it does not make your Relationship more easy. And, as Joe grows ever more disaffected with Bibi's alcoholism (this morning she fell off the Exercycle), Marsha meaningly insinuates that she herself could play the role of Rennie more ably *in all respects.* Already you Recall With Nostalgia your Idyll in Room 121, Iroquois Motel, Angola, N.Y., 14006, on Gregor Mendel's and Coventry Patmore's birthdays. Minatory Chambermaid! Faithful Vending Machines! Only Slightly Malfocused Color TV!

Then today's mail, today's P & A. What Bray has written to smashed Bibi you Would Very Much Like To Know. Marsha won't tell—*can't,* now she's Honey Dusted. But in their separate oblivions the two women Seem To you to have reached some dark sisterly understanding, just at the approach of fell August's Ides. And, as if your Woman's relapse weren't worry enough, Dr. Morgan all but apprises you that Bibi won't do. My late wife, Horner, while no teetotaler, was not a drunk. You'll have to Do Better. Dream Up Something Else. Time is short.

But your Dreams since March have been all of a kind: a large service handgun on a table midway between Joe, Rennie, and yourself, accessible equally to all. Rennie announcing her uncertain pregnancy and certain resolve to abortion or suicide. Rennie drowned in her own vomitus on the Doctor's operating table. The only innovations are that since 8/1 it has been Marsha Blank on that table: your Woman, for whom you Care. And the pistol, aimed at a point just above a point equidistant between your Eyes, is in Joe Morgan's hand.

U: *Jacob Horner to Jacob Horner.* His last Progress and Advice session before "Saint Joseph's" deadline.

8/28/69

To: Jacob Horner, Remobilization Farm, Fort Erie, Ontario, Canada
From: Jacob Horner, Remobilization Farm, Fort Erie, Ontario, Canada

U.S.S.R. acknowledges danger of war with China. Slavery abolished in British Empire. Moon on equator. Last of first 25,000 U.S. troops leaves Viet Nam. Kennedy request for cross-examination of inquest witnesses in Chappaquiddick investigation denied. Civil-rights marchers march on D.C. Happy birthday Leo Tolstoy, Wolfgang Goethe, Edward Burne-Jones, Charles Boyer.

It is your Wish that by thus Turning Backwards that key of keys, Alphabetical Priority, you could Reverse its fellow principles of arbitrary choice: Sinistrality (never mind Sinistrality) and—back! back!—*Antecedence.* That *Der Wiedertraum* might never reach Monday next, 9/1, St. Giles' Day, but run backwards from Horseback-Riding Lessons With Rennie through First Dinner With The Morgans through First Fucking Peggy Rankin In Ocean City Motel through Arrival At Wicomico Teachers College through Remobilization By Doctor through Rescue By Doctor From First Paralysis In Penn Station, Baltimore, March 16, 1951, to the Sweet Void between that date (28th Birthday of Jacob Horner) and your Birth.

It won't work, Horner, Joe reminded you this afternoon, in your Last P & A Session before his deadline. You Knew, you Acknowledged: the arrow of time, etc. Only a wish.

Today is Day 41 of our original Hundred Days, he went on inexorably, ticking his pipe stem upon a square of desk calendar. Tomorrow will be Day 42, not Day 40.

You Knew.

And Sunday 8/31 will be Day 44: your and Rennie's Evening Espial, upon Return From Equitation, of Morgan Irrational: making faces at self in mirror, speaking nonsense aloud to self, springing monkeylike about room, simultaneously picking nose and masturbating.

You Knew; you Knew. Mme de Staël bears son Auguste to lover Narbonne. 14th Sunday after Pentecost. Queen Wilhelmina, Fredric March, Baron von Helmholtz, Théophile Gautier. Stop that. You Stopped.

579

You and Pocahontas will Espy, Joe either prescribed or presumed.

If that was what he wanted, you Sighed. Though Marsha Blank is not Rennie Morgan. Indeed she is not, agreed your Advisor, unamused. But in default of Bibi, not to mention the original Mrs. Rennie McMahon Morgan, deceased, your Woman will have to do. How is she?

Very near the end of her Honey Dust, you Replied: that final two weeks' worth she fetched from Lily Dale just prior to the Great Fort Erie Magazine Explosion, as if in payment for delivering Bibi to Comalot Farm. A using up (that of that supply) that you Looked Forward To with very nearly as much apprehension as to Day 45, with which it might well coincide. She was meanwhile, your Woman, you Reported, principally engaged in composition of a Bombshell Letter, her own description, to her former husband: a Bombshell that, while you yourself Did Not Precisely Know its nature, she was pleased to imagine would Knock The Bastard Dead.

Not visibly arrested by this news, Joe lit his pipe and either inquired in declarative fashion, or asserted, or reminded you: Pocahontas is pregnant.

So it would appear, you Painfully Acknowledged. Unless, as is by no means impossible, she is experiencing early menopause. Marsha is 39. Has not menstruated since June. Was "due" in mid-July and again in the first half of August. So. Her (possible) pregnancy, however, you Have Reason To Believe—at least *this* pregnancy—is not the substance of her Bombshell Letter to Ambrose Mensch.

Joe was not curious about your Woman's Bombshell Letter.

The father? he inquired. You Chose Not To Speculate. But not yourself? Not yourself; your Bilateral Vasectomy of October 1954 precluded Parenthood. Hum. But you Are Still, in your Phrase, a Couple? So yourself at least Were Pleased Still To Regard yourselves.

Hum. Abortion, Horner? Such recourse is not without precedent, you Know, both historical and literary.

You Knew. You Planned To Discuss that very question with Marsha in September, after Exhaustion Of Honey Dust, Successful Passage Of Deadline, and Unequivocal Determination Of Pregnancy, but before Expiration Of First Trimester Thereof.

You Speak of Successful Passage Of Deadline, Horner.

More Wish than Hope, you Admitted; and yet more Hope than Expectation.

I should say, Joe said. Espial is one thing. You and your Fogged-Out Friend may Dismount from your Exercycles, Finish your Latest Long Conversation about my hyperrationalism and its Pygmalionizing of our marriage, Walk Around to my office window, and Peek through the blind, where you'll See me behaving as in our novel. Your Pocahontas may then to the best of her limited ability pretend to be Rennie Shocked to the Center of her Soul, whom you will Seductively Comfort with (I believe the script reads) "the wordless, grammarless language she'd taught me to calm horses with."

Well.

Espial is one thing, Joe repeated. Play it as you Like; I won't have to watch. But Successful Passage of my Deadline is quite another. Surely you Don't Expect—when I demand that you Redream History and Give Me Back, alive and unadulterated, my dead wife—to Palm Off as Rennie Morgan your fucked-up, knocked-up Pocahontas?

Stung as always by his kindless adjectives, but Judging it the part of diplomacy once again to Let Them Pass, you Acknowledged that you Entertained no such expectations. Nor any real hope. Only the wish aforementioned, and that ever more ardently.

Forget it.

Well.

Look here, Horner. You Looked. On September 1, 1953, the day following your original Espial, you Revisited The Doctor at his Remobilization Farm, then in Maryland. Yes. Your Quarterly Visit. Yes. Is the account of that visit in our script a fair approximation of what transpired? Fair. You were "Weatherless." Mm. But you Tended, in your P & A Session with the Doctor, to a manner more Brisk and Assertive than was your Wont: a manner Imitative, the Doctor immediately guessed, of some New Friend or Colleague of yours at the College. Mm. He chaffed you a bit for the imposture, then spoke at some length of Mythotherapy: the systematic assumption of borrowed or improvised personae to ward off paralysis in cases of ontological vacuity. Mm. He then demanded a response; you Found None To Hand; he demanded more sternly; you Began Slipping Into Catatonia; and he assaulted you, briefly, to bring you to. Pugilistic Therapy, I believe the script calls it.

Yes. Well.

Hum. Joe tapped out his pipe, its charge timelily combusted. We're done, Horner. Given the calendar and my double role in this travesty, we'll schedule your next P & A for Monday instead of Thursday. Labor Day. Anniversary of that other one, etc.

You Shrugged your Eyebrows.

I'll be bringing an old friend of ours, Joe announced neutrally, and To your Horror drew from the Doctor's desk (he no longer does the facing-chairs, knee-to-knee routine considered by the Doctor to be essential to Progress and Advice) the very pistol so prominently featured in your Recent Dreams, your Last Letter, and the events of autumn 1953. A Colt .45 for Day 45, he mirthlessly remarked. We'll combine the P & A Scene of September 1 with the Pistol Scene of October 5, 1953.

Look here, Joe, you Expostulated.

You Bring A Friend too, Joe said, not exactly an invitation. My wife. Alive and unfucked by you.

Joe.

Maybe I'll tell you then what my real grievance against you is, Horner.

You Believed you Could Guess.

It's not finally that you Betrayed Our "Friendship," you Know. It's not even that you Destroyed My Marriage, possibly Impregnated My Wife, and Contributed To Her Untimely Death.

Mm.

Rennie had a hand in all that too. So did I.

You here Assiduously Kept your Own Counsel, even unto facial expression, twitch of hand, and any other controllable body language interpretable as Yes Well.

One more thing, Jake.

That catalogue you've Been Compiling for a while?

Your Hornbook, I believe you Call it?

Bring it, too.

D: *A. B. Cook VI to his son.* The third posthumous letter of *A. B. Cook IV: the Battle of New Orleans and Napoleon's surrender to* Bellerophon.

Aboard S.S. *Statendam*
Off Bermuda
Wednesday, August 6, 1969

Dear Henry:

Dreamer that I still am (even as I approach the 52nd anniversary of my birth), I had imagined I would have word from you however curt, even sight of you however fleeting, in the weeks between my last and this. Especially last week, when I was at our work in the Buffalo/Fort Erie theater, I half-expected—

Je ne sais quoi, particularly given my disappointment of the week before, when, having transcribed at so long length for you Andrew IV's adventures from the birth of his children through his "death" at Fort McHenry, and posted copies of my transcription to you c/o that novelist I had thought my partner (on the off chance it might be he who'd showed you the "prenatal" letters), I receive from *him*—crossed in the mails—nothing less surprising than a rejection of my acceptance of *his own invitation* to collaborate with him on a *Marylandiad!* And he has returned the four prenatals, which I must now assume will be followed by what followed them.

He will be sorry. Not because I plan, at least for now, any particular retaliation, but because he has cut himself off (as have you, Henry; as have you) from much that either a novelist or a 2nd-Revolutionary could make use of: the account of our forebear's "Second Cycle," of my own, perhaps even of yours. See how drolly, in despite of rude awakenings, I still dream!

We have, then, you and I, not yet begun to talk. Nevertheless, I shall continue, per program, that series of decipherments and anniversary transcriptions, withholding them from the mails till I shall have your proper address, or find you, or you find me. What's more, as we are no longer to be monitored by that authorial "third ear," I shall speak more confidentially: not of Andrew Cook IV, of whom I know only what his wife would have known had she not (like our novelist, but with better reason) declined to read these *lettres posthumes,* nor—yet—of my own history, but of the circumstances of these transcriptions and what I've been up to this past month with my left hand, as it were, while the right transcribed.

As "Andrew Cook VI" (who I "became" in 1953, *nel mezzo del cammin* etc.), I spent July preparing for my lectureship this fall at Marshyhope State University, where I have advertised a course in *The Bonapartes of Fiction & the Fiction of the Bonapartes* (did you know that Napoleon's brothers Joseph, Louis, and Lucien all wrote romantic novels?). In that same capacity—I mean as the person I am—I have served as historical consultant to Mr. Reginald Prinz's filming of events from the 1812 War, a project I am turning to our own purposes. I have also monitored, to some extent even discreetly managed, a number of our potential allies or adversaries: Todd Andrews of the Tidewater Foundation, for example; the historian Lady Amherst, whom I've mentioned before; and the heirs of the late Harrison Mack, Jr.

At the same time, as "Monsieur Casteene"—our *arch*ancestor's name, which I have seen fit to use at our Fort Erie base—I have been preparing an eccentric putative descendant of the American Bonapartes (Jérôme's line, through Betsy Patterson) for a certain role he himself will be unaware of playing. And I have overseen the movement of our people from that base (which is of use to us only as long as the U.S. continues to draft civilians for military service in Viet Nam— another year or less) to "Barataria," disguised as extras for upcoming sequences of Prinz's film. My lodge there is our headquarters for the next academic year.

Finally, as "Baron André Castine"—the man I was until 1953 and in this single capacity am yet—I have been at the most immediately important work of all: the financing of our Seven-Year Plan for the Second Revolution. That is the work that brings me to be "vacationing" here (as of last night, when I flew out from Washington) for a few days with your future stepmother, of whom I also happen to be fond. As we cruise in Netherlandish comfort through the waters where in May of 1814 our forebear—or some ship's officer—impregnated the hapless Consuelo del Consulado, I make plans with the handsome widow of Harrison Mack for the settlement of his estate, which with certain other sources of revenue should carry us far toward 1976.

You remember the admirable Jane Mack, Henry, to whom (as her

583

distant cousin A. B. Cook VI) I introduced you at her husband's funeral. Some time before his death, when their alcoholic daughter first sought treatment at the Fort Erie sanatorium, I had arranged Mrs. Mack's introduction to "Baron André Castine," who subsequently comforted her, in London and elsewhere, through the terminal stages of her husband's illness, and consoled her for his death. (I was also, for a certain reason, protecting Harrison Mack's own comforter, the aforementioned Lady Amherst.) Mrs. Mack has taken it into her head to end her days as a baroness: she frankly suspects me of fortune hunting; I her of title hunting. We agree on the legitimacy of both pursuits when they are not cynical, and believe each of us to esteem in the other more than *just* the title and the fortune. Jane assumes, wrongly, that I want to enrich myself for the usual reasons, and does not disapprove: indeed, next week I shall take delivery in Annapolis of a large trawler yacht, her gift for my 52nd birthday. I have not apprised her of our cause (or the real reason I want that yacht) because—like her son, like most of our young "Baratarians," like my own parents—she would mistake the Revolution to be still *political* in its goals, and would of course be as wrongheadedly its foe as Drew Mack is wrongheadedly its friend.

It is my fiancée's plan to contest her late husband's will—which leaves the bulk of his estate to his philanthropic foundation—on the grounds of his madness, and to negotiate distribution half to herself, the other half in equal portions to her two children and the Tidewater Foundation. Inasmuch as Jane's moiety would be to some extent mine even during her lifetime (she is an astute and frugal manager), and Drew Mack's would be largely applied—by his lights—to our cause, I acceded to this plan, while privately seeing to it that things will turn out somewhat differently.

Suppose, for example—but never mind! Like Jane's (that excellent businesswoman's), my plans are intricate but clear, and best not babbled about. True minds, we shall marry in the new year. If you've any objections, Henry—or suggestions for dealing with "A. B. Cook VI" when Jane Mack becomes the Baroness Castine!—speak now. . .

Our ancestor. The postscript to his second "posthumous" letter found him resurrected from his "death" and bound for New Orleans to meet Jean Lafitte, hoping somehow to forestall the British movement on that city. But it was a postscript penned, like the letter it ended, six months after that fateful battle; Andrew wrote it, with but the merest hint of what he is doing there, from the orlop deck of H.M.S. *Bellerophon,* off Rochefort in France on July 16, 1815, one day after Napoleon Bonaparte's surrender to the commander of that vessel. Not until this third and central of his *lettres posthumes* does Andrew's past overtake his present, and the intricate labor of exposition give way to more immediate drama. The letter (before me) is dated August 6, 1815, and headed, in "Captain Kidd's code":

*‡47‡(*))**8008011‡:((82†5849‡;:52

(i.e., NOHPORELLEBFFOYRREBDAEHROTYAB, or *Bellerophon, Off Berry Head, Tor Bay:* that historic naval anchorage on the east Devon Coast, between the rivers Exe and Dart). He is back aboard that warship, having left it in Rochefort on an errand that fetched him overland through Tours and Rouen to Dieppe, London, and Exeter before the old *Bellerophon* (no Pegasus) arrived there with its famous passenger. He is about to witness, with relief, a second surrender, of another sort, by that same passenger: Napoleon has at last abandoned all hope of asylum in either America or England and, contrary to his repeated vow, agreed to permit himself and his company to be transferred on the morrow to H.M.S. *Northumberland,* commanded by our old friend Admiral Sir George Cockburn, "Scourge of the C's," for exile to St. Helena. As Andrew writes this letter to Andrée, the ex-emperor, two decks above, is dictating a flurry of memoranda—to Commander Maitland, to Admirals Keith and Cockburn, to History—protesting (falsely) that he has been betrayed: that he was assured sanctuary and has been denied it. It is the first phase of Napoleon's programmatic self-martyrdom, the *living out* of a romantic fiction instead of the writing of it. The idea has come to him in part from our ancestor, as shall be seen—for whom, however, the emperor's exile on St. Helena is itself to be but the first phase of the Second Revolution.

But how is it I am here, he now asks with us, *who last was leaving Maryland for Louisiana, newly risen from the dead, with Mr. Key's anthem ringing in my ears? Why did I not return straightway to Castines Hundred? Why do I not now, instead of back to Galvez-Town & Jean Lafitte?*

This last, at least, he finds easy to answer to his satisfaction: his Fort Bowyer postscript to (posthumous) Letter #1 had implored Andrée to come with the twins to New Orleans, where he now professes to hope to find them, under Lafitte's protection, upon his return. And the other questions?

He reviews his official motives. In William Patterson's house in Baltimore, where he recuperated, it was believed that the destruction of Washington on the one hand and on the other the British defeats at Plattsburgh, Lake Champlain, and Baltimore would bring the treaty commissioners at Ghent to an understanding, perhaps before 1815 commenced. But the question remained open whether such a treaty would bind the signatories to their *status quo ante bellum* or *uti possidetis*—before the fighting started or after it should end. Thus Admiral Cochrane's race to restore his fortunes by taking New Orleans, and General Jackson's to reach that city and muster an army in time to defend it.

Now, from Andrew Cook IV's earlier point of view there would have been everything to be said for a British victory: Thomas Jefferson himself fears that once possessed of Louisiana the British can hold it indefinitely, navigating with impunity from the Great Lakes to the Gulf of Mexico and effectively bordering the United States at the Mississippi; and radical New England Federalists are maintaining publicly that

British possession of Louisiana will signal dissolution of the Union and legitimize a New England Confederation. But our ancestor has become, however qualifiedly, a *patriot:* if he does not want the Indians driven into the Pacific, neither does he want the Union dissolved. (A *French* Louisiana would be another story: a third influence, to check both British and American expansion into the West. . .)

He fears, moreover, that the confrontation will be horrific. Cochrane will reinforce his expedition massively at Jamaica (There are rumors that Wellington himself is being sent to lead the army. In fact, Wellington has advised the British cabinet to relinquish their demand for an Indian free state and settle a treaty: in his view, the loss of Tecumseh and of naval control of the Lakes has lost the war). Andrew is no lover of General Jackson, the butcher of the Creeks, but he knows him to be a formidable officer; if the defense of New Orleans will be made difficult by the shortage of regular troops and armaments and by the ethnic diversity of its defenders—Spanish, Mexicans, Anglo-Saxons, West Indians, free blacks and "coloreds," Creole French both Bourbon and Bonapartist, even Italians and Choctaws!—its invasion will be also, through a labyrinth of bayous where only the alligators and the Baratarians are at home.

It is our progenitor's official hope, then—*was,* he reminds Andrée—that he can help turn the battle into a siege at worst, till the treaty is announced, by persuading each side that the other is decisively superior. With the aid of the Baratarians, perhaps Jackson can contain the invaders in a holding position; knowing Cochrane's irresolution and his greed for prizes, Andrew even imagines that the admiral might be bought off with a negotiated indemnity, and the ransom ships then seized at sea by Lafitte's privateers. It is exactly such audacious traffic that the U.S. Navy has tried to break up by destroying Barataria in September and arresting Pierre Lafitte and Dominique You (Jean's older brothers, the latter under his *nom de guerre):* a move deplored by New Orleans merchants whose stock in trade comes from the privateers.

Thus Andrew's official reasons. But we have seen how the Cooks and Burlingames fly from husband- and parenthood; how this Andrew in particular is in flight from the general Pattern of our past and the specific course of his life's "first cycle" (in my view, he runs into and perpetuates what he flees, like King Oedipus). There is moreover his guilt concerning Andrée, and concerning dead Tecumseh. And that blow on the head. . .

Plus one thing more, Henry, which he does not list among his motives but mentions promptly (as though in passing) in this letter. Andrew reaches New Orleans in late November 1814; he puts himself in touch with his friend Jean Blanque of the state legislature, who introduces him to Jean Lafitte. Cook has sensibly assumed the name of his Gascon forebear André Castine: Lafitte and Blanque are fellow

586

Gasconards, from Bayonne, home of the eponymous ham and the bayonet. They hit it off at once; Cook's impression is confirmed that the French Creoles want neither a British victory, which would end their influence and their privateering, nor an overstrong Federal presence: Mayor Girod himself had disapproved of the navy's raid on Barataria. Like Andrew, but for a different reason, they prefer uneasy balances of power: it is Cartagena's rebellion against Spain, for example, that licenses their privateering. Lafitte and Blanque are convinced that the 5,000 Baratarians, their copious munitions and supplies, local knowledge and experience of combat, could turn the coming battle in either direction. They would prefer to fight on the American side, in exchange for a general pardon and tacit permission to reestablish their "business"; but despite their refusal of British overtures to cooperate against "the destroyers of Barataria," Andrew Jackson has ill-advisedly proclaimed against them, calling them "hellish banditti." Jean Lafitte himself has scarcely been able to arrange Pierre's escape from the New Orleans Cabildo, where Dominique You still languishes in heavy irons. Indignantly they show Andrew the offending proclamations, as translated and reprinted in a month-old issue of the local French-language Bonapartist newspaper, *L'Abeille*. He reads; he politely tisks his tongue at Jackson's sanctimonious imprudence. Then his eye is caught by a familiar phrase in a neighboring column: ". . .next, drawing from her purse the deadly letter-opener. . ." (". . .*ensuite, tirant de son sac à main l'ouvre-lettre mortel. . .*"). It is from an installment of a serial fiction, *Les lettres algériennes, par C.C.*

Andrew demonstrates for his companions his remarkable ability to imitate the speech and manners of rural Anglo-Americans and proposes to intercede for the Baratarians with General Jackson, under the name of Andrew Cook of Maryland. He then inquires about this "C.C." A pregnant Spaniard, Lafitte tells him with a smile: current mistress of Renato Beluche, an old comrade and fellow buccaneer with a peculiar fancy for expectant mothers. He Jean has been instilled by his Jewish grandmother with an animosity toward all things Spanish (the Inquisition killed her husband and drove the family to Haiti, where Jean and his brothers were sired by their Gascon father); but "Uncle Renato," a New Orleans Creole of Tourainian descent, does not share this prejudice. As for his special taste in women, Beluche declares it to be a matter of sweetened complexions, the convenience of nonmenstruation, and the freedom from responsibility for by-blows; but Jean attributes it to Renato's mother's having been left pregnant at her husband's death, and to young Renato's solicitude for her.

Satisfying himself that Consuelo is, at least until her term, in good hands (Beluche has set her up in a flat on Conti Street, near Jean's own mistress, and prevailed upon friends at *L'Abeille* to translate and publish her fiction. When delivery time comes he will see to her *accouchement*, give the newborn a generous birthday gift, and look for another expectant beauty in need of protection), Andrew presses his inquiry no further, but decides to use some other English name in his dealings with Jackson.

It is this ready and thorough improvisation of identities which Lafitte finds most appealing in our ancestor. Himself at this time a suave 32-year-old who for a decade already has been chief among the Baratarian captains, he relishes pseudonyms and disguises, but has no gift for facial change and the imitation of speech. When Andrew now alters before their eyes the set of his jowls, the flare of his nostrils, the cast of his eyebrows and the pattern of his facial wrinkles, along with his stance, apparent height, and timbre of voice (he becomes "Jonathan Barlow, elder nephew of the late American minister to France: born in New England, educated in Paris and London, now come down from Kentucky as confidential observer for his old friend Henry Clay"), Lafitte offers him at once the post of minister of magic in whatever new Barataria might rise from the ashes of the old when the British are turned back.

But first they must be turned, and to their turning our forebear credits himself with three significant contributions. Early in December Andrew Jackson arrives, gaunt with dysentery and the rigors of his march from Florida, and assumes command of the city's defenses. He inspires morale; he moves with industry and intelligence to fortify or block the likeliest approaches; but he has not enough men. In particular he lacks trained sailors and cannoneers, and heavy weapons for their use. Reinforcement is on the way, from Alabama, Mississippi, Tennessee, but it is all cavalry and infantry. Delegations of Creole citizens petition him in vain to enlist the Baratarians. To the bilingual "Ambassador from Kentucky" (whom he trusts for "speaking like a proper American and not a damn'd Frenchie") Jackson confides that he has begun to regret his proclamation, but fears he will be thought irresolute if he rescinds it. "Johnny Barlow" opines that his friend Henry Clay, in such a situation, would subtly shift his stand and refuse the *next* such petition on jurisdictional instead of moral grounds: Baratarian leaders are in jail awaiting federal prosecution, and he Jackson has no authority to release them. "Barlow" will then see to it that the petitioners and the federal district judge get the hint; when prosecution is suspended and the Baratarians are released, Jackson may accept their service and matériel without having solicited them. The matter of pardon can be postponed until after the emergency. Jackson will thus have at his disposal the best sailors and cannoneers in the world, at no cost to the U.S. Treasury, together with an exquisite network of strategic information. Any contradictions of his proclamation will pass unnoticed; the Baratarians' role can be ignored or understated in official dispatches to Washington; their prosecution can even be resumed at some future date, with or without giving them covert advance warning and time to escape.

Old Hickory grimaces. "Politics!"

"John Barlow" shrugs. What is a general of the army but a sort of chief executive? he asks. And what is the President of the United States but a sort of general, strategically marshaling and deploying the forces at his disposal to carry out as it were the orders of the Constitution? Jackson's frown turns pensive.

Two days later Dominique You and the others are free, Jean Lafitte is reviewing his own maps with the general, Renato Beluche is organizing artillery companies, and the vessels that in September had fired Barataria are now manned by the Baratarians! "John Barlow" discreetly retires.

The British land their advance parties and assemble below the city. A sustained drive against them is out of the question: even with Jackson's reinforcements, it is some 3,000 American militia against three times that many seasoned British regulars. Nevertheless, the first action between them—a bold and successful night raid by Jackson to induce the British to delay their own attack until their whole army is assembled (thus giving him more time to complete his defenses)—convinces "André Castine" that with the help of the Baratarians New Orleans can be defended. Word has come through Jean Lafitte's spies that the British service commanders are at odds with each other. Major General Sir Edward Pakenham, Wellington's brother-in-law, does not like the terrain: his army has the Mississippi on one flank, a swamp full of alligators and Indians on the other, the Americans before (who barbarously harass them all night long), and behind them a fleet that can evacuate only one third of the troops at a time. Admiral Cochrane is complaining that he has another General Ross on his hands; that if the army "shrinks from New Orleans as it shrank from Baltimore," he will land his sailors and marines, storm the city himself, and let Pakenham's soldiers bring up the baggage.

All familiar as a re-play'd play, writes Andrew Cook: *the Chesapeake moved to the Mississippi!* On the day after Jackson's night raid—i.e., December 24, as Henry Clay and his colleagues in Ghent sign a treaty agreeing to the *status quo ante bellum* (which the British privately mean to interpret as invalidating Jefferson's Louisiana Purchase)—he puts by his French alias and under his proper name gets himself "rescued" by the British.

More specifically, he devises with Lafitte and Beluche the following strategy: their agents among the Spanish bayou fishermen, who are cooperating with the British, will identify him as a friend of Lafitte's with whom Jean has broken over the question of the Baratarians' allegiance to the U.S. However much Cochrane distrusts him after the Chesapeake episode, the admiral will most certainly question him about the strength and disposition of Jackson's forces. Cook will improvise as best he can to stall and divert a major British offensive at least until Jackson's defense line is complete.

The crucial thing is that his "rescue" seem authentic. Unfortunate coincidence comes to his aid: Lafitte arranges for a party of Baratarian scouts to bring Andrew in from the marsh as a captured *British* scout; he is then quickly transferred under Baratarian guard, with other captured British scouts, through a stretch of bayou known to be patrolled by Cochrane's marines. At the first evidence of British troops nearby, the Baratarians pretend to take fright and flee to save themselves, abandoning their prisoners. As the British congratulate themselves on their unexpected good fortune, Andrew experiences the first of those post-McHenry blackouts aforementioned: he wakes to find himself under a stand of loblolly pines on Bloodsworth Island, 36 years old, the war not yet begun. . .

Or so for a dizzy moment he imagines, till he learns from a redcoated officer that it is Bayou Bienvenue whose muddy bank he sits on, not the Chesapeake: those are cypresses, not pines, and it is Christmas Day, 1814. The sailors who row him down to Cochrane's headquarters are jeering openly at the soldiers encamped along the way; morale does not seem high. At the Villeré plantation, British GHQ, word has it that Cochrane and Pakenham are still arguing strategy. An army aide comes out to interrogate the rescued scouts: Andrew declares to him that the key to Jackson's defense is two armed schooners anchored in English Turn, a bend of the Mississippi below the city. So long as they lie there, he swears, no approach by road to the American main line is feasible; but to destroy them will involve the construction of artillery batteries on the levee above.

Such exactly (Cook already knows) is General Pakenham's plan. Gratified by this confirmation of its wisdom, the general proceeds to devote the next two days to the laborious construction of those batteries, while his army twiddles its thumbs and Admiral Cochrane sends crossly for the bearer of that information. Fickle strategist that he is, unused (as a navy man) to thinking of *terrain,* it nonetheless seems to him clear folly to delay the whole army's advance in order to lay siege to a minor nuisance that can as easily be attended to when Jackson's main line has been breached. When he discovers who it is who has confirmed Pakenham in this folly, he is ready to muster a firing squad at once—but the "Spanish fishermen," on cue, swear that Cook is a defected Baratarian, erstwhile friend and now rival of Jean Lafitte; and Cook himself confesses at once to Cochrane that his information is fraudulent; that the admiral's own assessment of the situation is entirely correct.

Shoot him, Cochrane orders. But Andrew then hands him a confidential letter purportedly from Jean Lafitte to General Jackson, affirming that if the British can only be led to attack those schooners first, the defense barricade will be impregnable to anything *short of a full-scale artillery barrage.* Shoot him! Cochrane commands, even more outraged. Andrew then asks, as his final request, a private word with the admiral and his closest aides, and as soon as the army men step outside, he draws the moral that Cochrane has not yet grasped. *Let* the army waste its time on the schooners (one will be abandoned and

590

destroyed; the Baratarians will tow the other upriver to safety, from where it can strengthen the main line) and on a follow-up infantry assault, which American artillery will easily repulse, one hopes without too great loss of life. Pakenham then twice defeated, Cochrane can mount an artillery line of his own with the only heavy guns available—those from his fleet, superior in size and number to the Americans'—and make good his boast. Navy cannon will destroy the defense and most of the defenders; the marines can do the rest, with as much or little army assistance as they may require!

It is Andrew's private hope that Pakenham's assault will be just costly enough to persuade both commanders to await reinforcement. In fact, the Baratarians prove such excellent cannoneers that when Pakenham attacks on the 28th, his force is pinned to the mud for seven hours and obliged to a humiliating night retreat with 200 casualties, most of them dead, as against 17 on the American side. Mortified, the general accedes to "Cochrane's" plan for an artillery duel. But it will require three days more to construct even rudimentary emplacements, while Jackson's ditches and embankments grow daily deeper, higher, stronger, and the Americans' morale improves with every new success. . .

In those three days, Andrew writes, *given fair freedom of the British camp by Admiral Cochrane, I cast about for my next expedient. For tho I was assured that the Admiral's guns, however superior, could not breach Jackson's earthworks (in the event, all those tons of British cannonballs plough'd into the mud & but strengthen'd the walls!), and that the famous marksmanship of the Baratarians would carry the day, I was not confident that a peace would be sign'd, or we have news of it, before Army & Navy mended their differences, fetcht up their reserves, and made a mighty attempt to add Louisiana to the* status quo ante bellum.

On the 29th he hears a valuable rumor: that Major General Gibbs, Pakenham's second in command, thinks both his chief and Admiral Cochrane mad for planning to send infantry over ground so marshy that it cannot be entrenched, to cross a wide ditch (virtually a moat) and scale a high mud wall without proper fascines and ladders. Two days later he hears another: that one Lieutenant Colonel Mullens of the 44th Infantry Regiment, whose wife is among the officers' ladies come over with the fleet, has been cuckolded by Admiral Malcolm of the *Royal Oak*, on which ship Mrs. Mullens is waiting out the battle; and that her husband is properly embittered by this state of affairs.

On New Year's morning, 1815, Cochrane's artillery mounts its barrage. The infantry await behind to make their assault as soon as Jackson's wall is breached. Forty minutes later, so accurate is the Baratarians' reply, half the British cannon are out of action; by afternoon the infantry must be withdrawn without ever attacking; that night the surviving ship's guns, so toilsomely emplaced, must be toilsomely retrieved through the marsh. The Americans are jubilant and scarcely damaged; the thrice-repulsed British suffer nearly a hundred additional casualties and a great loss of face, confidence, guns, and ammunition.

Pakenham and Cochrane are now equally humiliated. . .but to Andrew's distress they do not abandon the siege. Aside from the burning of Washington (in which action George Cockburn was the driving spirit) Cochrane has won no victories in this fast-concluding war; and Sir Edward Pakenham (Andrew has now learned) carries a secret commission to be the first royal governor of Louisiana. They agree to wait for the reinforcements and supplies en route from Havana and then mount an overwhelming attack from both sides of the Mississippi: if American cannon can be captured on one flank and turned against the center while fascines and scaling ladders are positioned, Jackson's defense will be breached by sheer force of numbers. It will not be inexpensive, they agree: but the prize, and the salvaging of their reputations, is worth the cost.

I understood, writes Andrew, *that my efforts to discourage them had but raised the stakes, and that as their troops grew the more dishearten'd, their commanders turn'd the more stubborn. Unable now to prevent a grand battle, I was obliged to see not only that it fail, but that it fail miserably, beyond thot of re-enactment.*

He is not surprised that, after the New Year's Day fiasco, Cochrane no longer seeks his advice; indeed, he discreetly avoids the admiral's sight. From those Baratarian spies among the Spanish fishermen he picks up a third valuable rumor: that Admiral Malcolm has let General Pakenham know that he will be much obliged if Lieutenant Colonel Mullens can be assigned some particularly hazardous duty in the coming action. And from the cynical foot soldiers he learns further that Pakenham has chosen his critic, General Gibbs, to lead the main assault on the American center. At Gibbs's desperate insistence the corps of engineers is building ten-foot ladders and heavy fascines of ripe sugarcane, the only available material. Lieutenant Colonel Mullens's 44th Regiment is under Gibbs's command: it wants no military expertise to guess what "particularly hazardous duty" lies ahead for Mrs. Mullens's husband, whom Andrew now befriends and apprises of the rumors current.

He was a dour, melancholical fellow, this Mullens, Andrew reports, *but neither a coward nor a fool. Unsurprised & bitter as he was to learn the scheme against himself, his first thot was for his men. When his orders came down on the evening of January 7, and he was ask'd if he understood them, he reply'd: 'Twas clear as day: his regiment were order'd to their execution, to make a bridge of their bodies for Sir Edward to enter New Orleans upon.*

Nevertheless, he musters his men and marches them that night toward their position, stopping en route to pick up their burden at the engineers' redoubt. Ladders and fascines are strewn everywhere; but their makers not being among the units ordered into combat next morning, they and their officers have retired. Cursing their good fortune and his ill, Mullens goes in search of someone authorized to give him official consignment of the gear—until Andrew, who has accompanied him thus far, finds the opportunity he has sought and makes his third and final contribution to the Battle of New Orleans.

I pointed out, he reports to Andrée, *that his orders specify'd taking delivery of the fascines & ladders and proceeding with them to the front, to be ready for attack at dawn. But to appropriate that equipage without a sign'd release from the engineering battalion would be to exceed his authority. If no officer was present to consign the ladders to us, I argued, the dereliction was the engineers', not ours. We would do better to arm ourselves & take our stations for battle without the ladders, than to take the ladders without authorization.*

Seductive as this logic is, Mullens fears court-martial. But dawn is approaching; they have wasted a quarter hour already at the redoubt; Andrew resolves the matter by having Mullens deputize him to find the appropriate engineering officer and bid him rouse his men to fetch the ladders and fascines forward, while Mullens sees to it the 44th are in position. Otherwise their tardiness might be imputed to lack of courage. Mullens shrugs, moves the regiment on—and Andrew does nothing.

Now, it is possible the British would have lost the battle even with their scaling equipment: the marines assigned to cross the Mississippi in 50 boats at midnight, capture the American cannon on the west bank, and open fire on Jackson's center at dawn to signal the attack, are delayed by mud slides and adverse current; they reach the west bank only at dawn—their force reduced from 1,400 to less than 500 by confusions, desertions, and garbled orders—and find themselves swept by the current five miles below their appointed landing place. The guns are not even approached, much less captured, until well after the main assault has failed.

But the missing ladders and fascines are indisputably crucial. When General Gibbs, by dawn's early light, sees the 44th in position without them, he claps his brow, rushes over to Pakenham, and vows to hang Mullens from the highest cypress in the swamp. Pakenham himself angrily orders Mullens and 300 of his men to return for the ladders, authorization or no authorization. But it is a quarter-mile trip each way, and the gear is heavy. From the engineers' redoubt they hear the first shots of the battle. Dozens of the 44th refuse to pick up the equipment and return to the line; scores of others, fearing court-martial, assume their burden but take their own time, hoping the assault will have been made or abandoned before they get there.

Even now Mullens is inclined to comply, however sluggishly, with his orders. But Andrew confesses to him that he himself deliberately disobeyed the colonel's command to rouse up the engineers; that he had done so to save the 44th from suicide, and will answer for his action to any court-martial; that it is Mullens's feckless complaisance with his superiors that has lost him his wife; and that should he return to the line now, either Gibbs will shoot him for not ordering the regiment forward, or his men will shoot him for doing so, or the Americans will shoot them all. *Be a man,* Andrew ironically exhorts him: *Stay here & lay the blame on me.*

Mullens does, and disappears from our story (he will live to be court-martialed for incompetence; of his marital affairs no more is known). Fewer than half of the 300 return to the line; of those, many feign or suffer confusion, throw away the ladders and fascines, and open random fire. Jackson's cannoneers reply with a barrage that blows them into panic retreat. They ignore Gibbs's orders to regroup and charge. Pakenham himself, finding Mullens vanished, leads the remnants of the 44th some three dozen yards forward, and is killed by Baratarian grapeshot. Gibbs takes his place, gets as close as twenty yards from Jackson's ditch, and is cut down by rifle fire. Major General Keane, third in command, falls a few minutes later trying to rescue Gibbs. The few intrepid British who actually manage to cross the ditch and scale the embankment are immediately killed or captured.

The Battle of New Orleans is less than half an hour old, and effectively over. Major General Lambert of the reserve units, unexpectedly promoted from fourth in command to commander in chief, orders his men to attack. They refuse. He then orders retreat, and is willingly obeyed. Most of the rest of the army are pinned to the muddy plain by Jackson's barrage. At 8:30 A.M. the riflery ceases, the attackers having crawled back out of range; the artillery is sustained with deadly effect into early afternoon, when Lambert sends a flag of truce and begs leave to remove his wounded and bury his dead. They total 2,000, as against half a dozen Americans killed and seven wounded.

'Twas a scene to end an Iliad, *writes Andrew, that huge interment in the bloody bog; I resolved to take advantage of it to recross the lines & resume my Odyssey. But that same sudden swoon, which had afflicted me in the bayou on Christmas Eve day, now smote me again as I mingled with the burial parties. Once more I awoke to think myself on Bloodsworth Island, and found myself on the shores of Louisiana! I had been fetcht back to Lake Borgne as one of the wounded; recognized now by Admiral Cochrane's sailors, I was detain'd a virtual prisoner, as accessory to the Mullens affair. Had news of the Peace not reacht us ashore at Fort Bowyer (which Cochrane seized to console himself for the loss of New Orleans) instead of aboard ship, I had surely been return'd to England in irons or hang'd from the yardarm for a spy. But in the officers' chagrin (and the enlisted men's rejoicing) at that same news, I contrived on St. Valentine's Day to hide myself in the Fort till my captors departed. I then posted to you the letter begun off Bermuda the summer before (which seem'd already a hundred years since), and made my way back to New Orleans, to await your arrival with the twins, when we should commence a new life in new surroundings. Whilst awaiting you there, I thot to complete that other letter begun in Washington, which I was not to finish until Rochefort in the July to come.*

He has other thoughts as well. It is getting on to March; for some weeks no new installments of *Les lettres algériennes* have appeared in

L'Abeille, though its heroine (Corinna!) has been left in parlous straits, abandoned by her protector and captured by pirates off Port-au-Prince. Andrew goes to Conti Street, makes inquiries, learns that while "C.C." is in reasonably good health, her child, a daughter, died at birth on that same St. Valentine's Day. Further, that Renato Beluche, no longer interested in her, has paid her rent through May and gone with the Lafittes to Grande-Terre Island (the site of Barataria) to discuss the resumption of their privateering. Understandably, Andrew does not dwell upon the reunion, but in the next passages of his letter his *I* turns not infrequently into a *we.*

He remains in New Orleans (in the Conti Street lodgings) until May, "consoling" himself (the term is his) as best he can while awaiting his family's appearance. "Uncle Renato," grateful, keeps him employed forging false bills of lading and other useful documents. With Jean Lafitte, Andrew's relations grow even closer (except with Consuelo, he resumes the name André Castine). Whereas Beluche is interested in the rebel Simón Bolívar and the Mexican revolt against Spain, Lafitte is actively supporting the colony of Bonapartist exiles at Champ d'Asile. Andrew harmonizes their interests by encouraging a French and Mexican alliance against Spain; if it should succeed, Bolívar might head a federation of republics comprising most of Central and South America, while his French or Creole counterpart might found a nation from western Louisiana to the Pacific!

Consuelo, weary of America and homesick for Andalusia, even for Algiers, is not interested. Lafitte is, and proposes rescuing Napoleon from Elba to lead the campaign. As mentioned in the postscript to his "Washington" letter, Andrew doubts the feasibility of that scheme—until early April, when news reaches Louisiana that the emperor has already escaped, landed at the Gulf of Juan, and struck out for Paris! Beluche shrugs and sets about the commissioning of a ship and the assembling of a crew to begin taking Spanish prizes under license from Bolívar; Lafitte presses "André" to join him in establishing another Barataria somewhere west of New Orleans. Andrée does not appear, or reply to his letter.

In May, despairing of your coming here, & doubting my welcome at Castines Hundred, we sail'd for France, writes Andrew. His errand is to interest Napoleon—whose reascendancy in Europe Lafitte never doubts—in the "Louisiana Project," to the extent of sending French ships and men "to aid the cause of Mexican independence" once the military situation in Europe is in hand. On the advice of Jean Blanque he carries by way of credentials a forged letter from Mayor Girod of New Orleans (who had in fact been as interested as Lafitte in the Elba mission), appealing to the emperor "on behalf of all French Creoles." The voyage is financed jointly by Lafitte and Beluche, the latter on condition that Andrew see to Consuelo's safe return to her homeland.

As they traverse these waters (where Mrs. M. and I now reenact together certain separate youthful passions), Consuelo endeavors, we

595

cannot know how successfully, to reenact *their* earlier shipboard affairs. She has decided that the novel is a worn-out fad; she adduces as evidence the fact that she herself has ceased reading anything in that kind. Andrew's information that Samuel Richardson himself, the father of the epistolary novel, had said essentially the same thing (quoting his booksellers, in letters dated 1758 and 1759), she takes as validation of her stand. The true *romanticismo*, she now believes with Mme de Staël, is the active life; despite her weariness with America, she is prepared to exchange both literary fame and the domestic joys of wife- and motherhood to hazard the world at the side of a lover in the advance guard of history, so to speak.

Andrew gently reminds her that Mme de Staël, at last report, seemed to have put by both fiction and action for reflection. And, "transported by longing for [his] own family," he permits himself "a panegyric on parenthood, conjugal fidelity, & domestical bliss," for all which, he declares to Consuelo, she is in his opinion more admirably suited by temperament than for literary, political, or sexual adventuring. His friend mistakes his meaning, agrees at once, and "flinging herself upon [his] neck, with tears of joy accept[s his] proposal!"

We must surmise what followed. When their ship reaches British-held Bordeaux at the end of June and they learn of Waterloo, of Napoleon's second abdication and his flight from Paris to nearby Rochefort, Andrew offers *either to dispatch her to Mme de Staël in Leghorn, Italy (whither I learn'd Germaine had fled with her guardsman-husband for the sake of his health, & to wait out the Hundred Days); or to introduce her, as one former novelist to another, to Joseph Bonaparte, presently in Bordeaux & about to flee aboard a charter'd American schooner to New York. But she declined both offers, coldly informing me she would set & sail her own course thro life, without my or any other man's aid. That she had, she believed, found her true vocation. Finally, that the real defect in "that business of Don Escarpio's poison'd snuffbox" was not that it wanted re-working in fiction, but that it had not workt in fact!*

On this discordant note they part. After learning all he can about the emperor's situation from Joseph's entourage and from the U.S. consul in Bordeaux (a Mr. Lee, to whom he attaches himself long enough to observe his signature and appropriate some consulate stationery, and for whom he volunteers to act as unofficial liaison with Napoleon's party), Andrew hurries to Rochefort to reconnoiter and to revise his plan.

Napoleon, he learns, is being uncharacteristically indecisive, to the growing desperation of his suite. Having offered his services in vain to the provisional government in Paris as a mere general of the army (he had noted on his maps a vulnerable gap between the armies of Wellington and Blücher, both marching toward Paris), he has announced his decision to take refuge in America. But as if in hope of some marvelous re-reversal of fortune, he has put off his flight aboard the French frigates at his disposal and given the British time to reinforce their blockade of the harbor. Captain Ponée of the *Méduse* still believes it possible to run the blockade: he will engage the chief blockading vessel, H.M.S. *Bellerophon*, a 74-gunner but old and slow; he estimates he can survive for two hours, enough time for Napoleon to slip through on the *Saale* and outrun the lesser blockaders. Napoleon has approved the audacity of the plan, but declined to sacrifice the *Méduse*. Another loyal frigate stands ready farther south, at the mouth of the Gironde; and there is Joseph's charter boat at Bordeaux. The French master of a Danish sloop in the Aix Roads has even offered to smuggle the emperor out in an empty wine cask rigged with breathing tubes. Every passing day makes escape less feasible; the options narrow to capture and possible execution by Blücher's Prussians, arrest by the Bourbons, surrender to the British, or suicide (it is an open secret that he carries a vial of cyanide always on his person). But Napoleon will not act.

Delighted by this unanticipated turn of fortune—which of course revives at once his original hope that Bonaparte himself might lead the "Louisiana Project"—"André Castine" attaches himself to the emperor's party on the strength of a letter "from Mr. Consul Lee" authorizing him to oversee and facilitate Napoleon's "American arrangements," should the emperor choose to go to that country. He urgently advances Jean Lafitte's Champ d'Asile/New Orleans/Barataria connection, flourishing his letter "from Mayor Girod"; the proposal finds favor with many of the party, but the emperor himself (through intermediaries: Andrew does not see him personally until the last minute) is dilatory. On July 4, our ancestor's 39th birthday, Joseph sails aboard the U.S.S. *Pike*, afraid to delay longer. Andrew begins to share the desperation of Napoleon's aides.

Legality was the official sticking-point, he writes: *Bonaparte had long since requested of the Paris government passports to America, & had renew'd that request thro Commander Maitland of Bellerophon, without reply. He had, he declared, been condemn'd an outlaw by the Congress of Vienna since his escape from Elba; moreover, he had been defeated on the field of battle & forced to abdicate. To flee now like a common fugitive was in his eyes but a further ignominy. But some said privately he fear'd life in America, so remote from the terrain of his career. Others, that he had fallen ill, slipt his hold on reality, & half believed a way would yet show itself, to make another Elba of Rochefort.*

On July 8, on orders from Paris, the party boards the French frigates anchored in the harbor. On the 10th a letter arrives from *Bellerophon*, in reply to Napoleon's query: Maitland does not mention the passports (he has been secretly instructed to intercept and take custody of the emperor if he attempts to flee, and deliver him to Tor Bay), but politely forbids Napoleon passage out of the harbor on any but his own vessel, and that to England. On the 11th they learn of Louis

XVIII's re-restoration. The circle is closing. On the 13th Napoleon drafts his famous letter of surrender to the prince regent:

> Your Royal Highness,
>
> A victim to the factions which distract my country, and to the enmity of the greatest powers of Europe, I have terminated my political career, and I come, like Themistocles, to throw myself upon the hospitality of the British people. I put myself under the protection of their laws; which I claim from your Royal Highness, as the most powerful, the most constant, and the most generous of my enemies.
>
> Rochefort, 13 July, 1815,
Napoleon

But before delivering it, and himself, to *Bellerophon*, he decides to make a final inquiry concerning the passports, at the same time testing the air on the subject of his second choice: asylum in England, where his brother Lucien already resides, and the likely nature of his reception there. On the morning of Bastille Day, therefore, he sends emissaries under a flag of truce to *Bellerophon*. Commander Maitland again declares (what is technically correct) that he has had no word yet from his admiral concerning the passports; that he cannot permit Napoleon passage to America without them; and that he is not empowered to enter into any agreement concerning the emperor's reception in England—which, however, he cannot personally imagine will be other than hospitable. The embassy returns; there is no alternative, Napoleon decides, to surrendering to Maitland and taking his chances with the prince regent. A new letter is drafted to that effect, enclosing a copy of the "Themistocles" letter, re-requesting passports and passage to America, but accepting in lieu of them passage to England "as a private individual, there to enjoy the protection of the laws of your country." He will deliver himself and his entourage to *Bellerophon,* he declares, on the morrow's ebb tide.

Andrew sees here a long chance to salvage his mission, which Napoleon's refusal to escape has rendered all but hopeless: he volunteers to rush overland to London "in [his] capacity as a U.S. diplomatic attaché," discover if he can what the British cabinet plan to do with their prisoner, and, if that news is not good, do what he can to arrange Bonaparte's escape before he is landed and taken into custody. In return he stipulates (to the Count de Las Cases, Napoleon's acting counselor of state and second-ranking aide, whom Andrew has befriended) that any such escape be to Champ d'Asile, and that Las Cases urge Napoleon to lead the "Louisiana Project."

A fan of Chateaubriand's redskin romances, Las Cases declares himself ready without hesitation to hazard "the naked but noble savages" rather than the elegant but perfidious Bourbons or what he fears may be the implacable English. He is impressed by Andrew's showing him, on a map of America, the territory he has in mind, three times the size of France. He inquires as to the quality of Indian wine.

Before dawn the next morning he reports that the emperor has approved and will finance Andrew's London mission, and has regarded that same map with interest but no further comment. News has reached them that Louis XVIII has ordered the commander of the *Saale* frigate to hold them all under arrest on that vessel; the officer has loyally passed word of his order along, but cannot indefinitely delay executing it. They are leaving at once.

Andrew asks and is given permission to accompany them to *Bellerophon*. *'Twas no reason of strategy at all, only to see, perhaps for the last time, that man Joel Barlow had come justly so to loathe, but who had play'd as none before him the Game of Governments, & convinced a whole century, for good or ill, that one man can turn the tide of history.* The emperor speaks to—or of—him once, and briefly, not recognizing him as the man he'd dispatched years before to oversee young Jérôme in America. "So this is the fellow who would crown me king of the Corsairs," he remarks, and turns his attention to the choreography of boarding the British warship with most impressive effect.

That day and the following morning Andrew spends aboard the "Billy Ruffian," as her crew call *Bellerophon*. He watches Napoleon display his talent for ingratiating himself with those useful to him, intuitively exploiting every circumstance to best advantage. So far from abject, the man turns his surrender into a diplomatic and theatrical coup, and receives, without having to ask, every royal prerogative—except the passports. Andrew also completes the letter to Andrée begun in Fort Bowyer and put aside in New Orleans, describing the sack of Washington and the siege of Fort McHenry: he will leave it with Consul Lee to dispatch to Canada via Washington by diplomatic pouch, having reported "officially" to that gentleman the details of Bonaparte's surrender. In his satisfaction at having got hold of the emperor before his superiors could snatch that plum for themselves (the sails of Admiral Hotham's *Superb* are visible all through the morning of the 15th, standing in for Rochefort), Maitland accepts Las Cases's voucher that "M. Castine" is the party's "American liaison," and both permits him aboard and allows him to leave at his pleasure on the 16th.

By noon of when, the emperor having breakfasted aboard the *Superb* with Hotham, Maitland, and his own aides—and been given a second royal reception, and returned without either the passports or any word of them, but encouraged that his reception in England will not be hostile—it is clear to Andrew that he must commence his next move at once. As the crew of *Bellerophon* man the yards and weigh anchor to beat out into the Bay of Biscay, Napoleon complimenting them on their quiet efficiency, Andrew returns by longboat to *Méduse* and thence to Rochefort, bearing in his ear the whispered last charge of the Count de Las Cases, who does not share his master's optimism: *"Sauvez-nous la peau!"*

His letter sent on its way, Andrew rushes overland to the Channel, avoiding Paris lest in the confusion of the new government his credentials be too closely examined. But at Tours, at Rouen, at Dieppe, the news is the same: Louis wants Napoleon dead, is relieved to be relieved of the political consequences of seeing personally to his execution, but fears the British will give him asylum or let him go to America *despite their secret assurances to the contrary*. On July 20 he crosses from Dieppe to Newhaven; by the 21st he is in London, seeking out his erstwhile brother-in-audacity Admiral Sir George Cockburn. He has no plan, beyond learning what the Admiralty's and the cabinet's intentions are. He presumes that the dispatch boat carrying Napoleon's "Themistocles" letter to the prince regent will have arrived, and remembers that Cockburn and the prince regent are friends.

I had learn'd in the Chesapeake, he writes, *that the surest road to Sir George's confidence was a frank confession of rascality, especially as apply'd against his rivals. And so I gain'd his presence as "one André Castine, bringing news of Napoleon"; but once in his company I reveal'd myself as Andrew Cook, & told him all that had transpired since we saw each other last off Baltimore. In particular I regaled him with the rivalry between General Pakenham & Admiral Cochrane at New Orleans, & the tale of Mrs. Mullens, & Cochrane's disgust that the peace came ere he had properly ransom'd a city. I then recounted the details of Bonaparte's surrender (whereof England had as yet heard only the fact) & his hope for passport or asylum.*

He has judged his man correctly. At first incredulous, then skeptical, Cockburn is soon delighting in the story of Admiral Malcolm and Mrs. Mullens, of Cochrane's artillery duel with Andrew Jackson. He calls for maps, and argues persuasively that even after the January massacre it was Cochrane's fecklessness and General Lambert's shock that lost New Orleans: at the time of the burial truce the British had command of the west bank of the Mississippi above Jackson's line, 50 armed vessels en route upriver and a blockade at its mouth, and clear superiority of numbers; to withdraw and rebegin a whole month later from Fort Bowyer was a foolish judgment and crucial loss of time, since everyone knew the peace was imminent. But that was Cochrane! Did Andrew know that the man had left Admiral Malcolm the ugly job of getting rid of all those Negroes and Indians he had so ardently recruited with false promises, and himself rushed home to litigate for prize money? And that while he was about it he was suing for libel any who dared say in print what everyone said in private: that he was a fool and, but for the odd foolhardy display, a coward?

As for Napoleon (whom Cockburn, in the English fashion, calls "Buonaparte"), the truth is that the British cabinet have no mind whatever to grant him either passport to America or asylum in England: they wish him heartily to the Devil and are annoyed that he did not conveniently dispatch himself to that personage. They dare not put him on trial, for they know him to be a master of manipulating public sympathy. Their resolve is to whisk him as speedily, quietly, and far as possible from the public eye forever. The legal and political questions about his status are many and delicate (Is he a prisoner of war? Of Britain or of the Allies? Does habeas corpus apply? Extradition?), and no one wants either to deal with them or to incur the consequences of not dealing with them. Now Sir George happens to know that Prime Minister Liverpool has already decided to confine the man for life in the most remote and impregnable situation in the empire, and consulting the Admiralty on that head, has been advised that the South Atlantic island of St. Helena, owned by the British East India Company, best fits the bill.

How does Cockburn know? Why, because he himself has been proposed for promotion to commander in chief of His Majesty's naval force at the Cape of Good Hope and adjacent seas—i.e., the whole of the South Atlantic and Indian oceans—and the immediate reason for this promotion, he quite understands, is to sweeten the responsibility of fetching Bonaparte to St. Helena and seeing to it he stays there until a permanent commission has been established for his wardenship! He expects his orders daily, and though he readily accepts the "sweetening," it is in fact an assignment he welcomes: perhaps his last chance to walk upon the stage of History. For that reason, while the cabinet would be relieved to hear that their captive has taken poison aboard *Bellerophon* en route to Tor Bay, he Cockburn would be much chagrined: he looks forward to many a jolly hour with Old Boney.

Speaking of whom, and of the splendid absurdities of that "English law" on whose protection the rogue has thrown himself: has Andrew heard the tale that bids to bring together General Buonaparte and Admiral Cochrane? Andrew has not. *Well:* it seems that Sir Alexander's return from New Orleans in the spring, and his commencement of prize litigations, prompted a number of sarcastic comments in the London press about his being more eager to fight in court than on the high seas. Among his detractors was one Anthony Mackenrot, an indigent merchant who had done business with the West Indies fleet under Cochrane's command back in 1807, and who lately declared in print that out of cowardice Sir Alexander had failed to engage the French fleet in that area that year, though it was known to be of inferior strength and vulnerable. Ever tender of his honor—especially when a fortune in prize money was still litigating—Cochrane had clapped a libel suit on this Mackenrot, hoping to intimidate him into public retraction. But he misjudged his adversary: with an audaciousness worthy of Buonaparte himself (or the teller of this tale), Mackenrot had promptly sought and got from the chief justice of Westminster a writ of subpoena against both Napoleon and his brother Jérôme—who we remember had left the French West Indies fleet in 1803 with his friend Joshua Barney to come to Baltimore—commanding them to appear in court at Westminster 9 A.M. Friday, November 10, 1816, to testify as to the state of readiness of the French fleet at the time in question! And this subpoena, mind, Mackenrot had secured in June, before Waterloo, when Buonaparte was still emperor of the French and at war with England!

Cockburn must set down his Madeira ("carry'd twice 'round the Horn for flavor, in the holds of British men-o'-war") and wipe his eyes for mirth. English law! Let that Napoleon has cost more British blood and treasure in fourteen years than a normal century would expend, he may count upon it that no sooner will *Bellerophon* drop anchor in Tor Bay than a cry of habeas corpus will go up from the Shetlands to the Scillys, to give the devil his day in court! Only the decommissioning of his own *Northumberland* in Portsmouth, and the unfitness of old *Bellerophon* for so long a voyage, keeps Sir George from petitioning the prince regent to let him intercept Maitland at sea, effect the transfer, and head smack for St. Helena before the newspapers know what's what.

Andrew has heard enough: legal passage to America being out of the question, Napoleon must be rescued before he can be shipped off to exile, and the most immediate hope of rescue is delay. He reaches Tor Bay on the afternoon of the 24th to find that *Bellerophon* has arrived there that same morning; it rides at anchor off the quay of Brixam, already surrounded by flotillas of the curious. Next day the crowd increases, and security around the ship is tightened; Andrew cannot negotiate his way aboard. And on the 26th (the newspapers are talking already of St. Helena, and of habeas corpus, and of the right of asylum, at least of trial) the ship is moved around to Plymouth harbor and anchored between two frigates for greater security. Andrew removes there as well, and haunts Admiralty headquarters, where he learns that Cockburn's new command has been issued and his flagship *Northumberland* ordered back in commission—to the great chagrin of her crew, who have just completed a long tour of sea duty and were expecting shore leave. Cockburn himself will board ship at Spithead in a week or ten days; a fortnight should see the business done. By now Napoleon must understand that neither asylum nor passport is forthcoming; the cabinet have not even acknowledged receipt of his "Themistocles" letter, lest such recognition be argued against the Allies' decree of outlawry. Andrew hopes that Las Cases has brought him around to the Louisiana Project. . .

But how to rescue him? Every day the crowds grow, increasing both the confusion and the Admiralty's measures of security. A thousand small spectator boats jam Plymouth Sound; the quays and breakwaters are thronged. Bands play French military airs; vendors sell Bonapartist carnations; cheers go up whenever the emperor appears on deck or when, to placate the crowd in his absence, *Bellerophon*'s crew obligingly post notice of his whereabouts on a large chalkboard: AT TABLE WITH CAPT. MAITLAND; IN CABIN WRITING LETTERS. It is common knowledge that any number of Channel fishermen were until recently in Napoleon's pay, supplying him with information about British ship movements; but our ancestor's attempt to locate and organize a company of such fishermen is fruitless: they are all reaping a golden harvest from the tourists.

Now the cabinet are chafing at the delay, lest it complicate relations among the Allies. The press have only one story, Bonaparte; the habeas corpus movement has become a ground swell; the emperor has never been more popular in Britain. Should he by any means once touch foot on British soil, he will not easily be got rid of. On the other hand, so great has been the publicity, Bonapartist naval vessels might imaginably attempt to intercept *Northumberland* at sea: a convoy of six brigs, two troopships, and a frigate must therefore be commissioned and assembled to escort the ship-of-war to St. Helena. More delay!

Faute de mieux, Andrew begins to practice the forgery of subpoenas, no easy matter by reason of their sundry official seals. If he cannot board *Bellerophon* illegally, he will do so "legally"—as Anthony Mackenrot, defendant in *Cochrane* v. *Mackenrot,* come to serve a writ upon Napoleon Bonaparte.

It is August 4 before he has one ready. The thing lacks finish, especially the engraving of the seals, but he can wait no longer. Rumor has it that Napoleon has decided upon suicide rather than St. Helena; that his officers are conspiring to assassinate him in order to spare themselves and their families such an exile; that orders are en route to *Bellerophon* to go to sea until rendezvous is made with *Northumberland,* lest Bonaparte escape or a habeas corpus writ be served. Andrew endeavors to imagine the accent and appearance of a Scotsman gone bankrupt in the Caribbean; he goes to the Plymouth house of Admiral Keith, commander in chief of the Channel fleet, in whose jurisdiction *Bellerophon* is, to demand permission to serve his subpoena. He tries out his accent on the admiral's secretary, who angrily asks how many Mackenrots has Cochrane sued, and sends him off "to where your brother already is": the offices of the Admiralty. Puzzled, Andrew hurries there, learns that Keith is that moment being rowed out to the *Tonnant* in the harbor (where lie also other veterans of the Chesapeake, among them Peter Parker's *Menelaus*) to escape "you damn'd lawyers." Cook rushes to the quay, to hire a launch. The only one in sight is being bargained for already. No matter, Andrew will double the bid—but then he sees the chap gesticulate with a rolled, sealed paper; hears him protest with a Highland burr that the boatsman's rates are *pir-r-ratical. . .*

Pocketing my own writ, I enquired, Mister Mackenrot? The same, said he. I introduced myself then as one who knew & sympathized with his business, having the like of my own, and offer'd not only to share the hire of the launch but to point out Admiral Keith & the Tonnant *among the throng of naval officers and vessels in the sound. Which (he accepting readily) at 1st I did, & was gratify'd to observe that so seriously did Keith apprehend this whimsical finger of the mighty arm of English Law, at our approach he fled the* Tonnant *for the frigate* Eurotas, *hard by* Bellerophon. *And whilst we were scrambling to come a-port of* Eurotas, *he scrambled down a-starboard and fled off toward shore at Cawsand! Where we would surely have caught him, had not his barge been mann'd by 12 oars & ours by but 4. Splendid, preposterous spectacle: an admiral of the world's mightiest navy in flight from a lone eccentric Scotsman with a scrap of paper! Behind which, however, lay such authority as might well upset the combined resolve of the Ally'd Nations.*

Indeed, this same reflection, together with two physical observations—that *Bellerophon* is hove short with topgallant sails bent, ready to sail at a moment's notice, and that the Count de Las Cases is on the quarterdeck, watching their chase with interest—begins to suggest to Andrew a radical change of plan. Should Bonaparte now be landed in so determinedly lawful a country, where sympathy for him seemed to increase with every day's newspaper, could he ever be persuaded to "escape" to America? Even if he could, how rescue him from so mighty a fortress as the British Isles, from whose invasion the emperor himself, at the height of his power, had quailed? WRITING WITH HIS OFFICERS, reads the board now on *Bellerophon.* . .

He directs Mackenrot's attention to the sailing preparations aboard that ship and proposes they divide their pursuit. Let him, Cook, return to *Eurotas,* where boarding might now be permitted him to keep him from reaching Keith; he will endeavor to talk his way thence to *Bellerophon* and remind Commander Maitland that contempt-of-court proceedings await him if he weighs anchor to avoid Mackenrot's subpoena. Then let Mackenrot proceed to Cawsand and press after Admiral Keith.

The Scotsman agrees (Keith meanwhile, Andrew observes, has fled toward *Prometheus,* where he will order out the guard boats to fend off all approaching craft), adding that if he fails to catch the admiral at Cawsand he will return directly to *Bellerophon* and attempt to serve his writ through Maitland. The chase has taken most of the morning; as Andrew hopes, they are permitted to board *Eurotas* "just long enough to state their business," and, per plan, Mackenrot pulls away as soon as Andrew steps onto the boarding ladder, so that they cannot order him back to his hired boat. But no sooner has Mackenrot drawn out of range than Andrew sees him rowing furiously back, and then observes the reason: *Bellerophon* has weighed anchor and, wind and tide both contrary, is being towed by her guard boats out toward the Channel!

And with her all my hopes, he writes, *no longer of saving Bonaparte from exile, but of ensuring if I could that he went to St. Helena instead of to the Wood of Suicides in Hell.* For he has now decided not only that a taste of true exile might be the best argument for inclining Napoleon to the Louisiana Project, but that with the aid of the Baratarians he is far more likely to effect a rescue from St. Helena than from the Tower of London. Almost before he realizes what he's doing, therefore, he flings himself off *Eurotas* into Plymouth Sound, kicks away his boots, and strikes out for *Bellerophon.*

A cry goes up from both vessels. Andrew has jumped from the side opposite *Eurotas*'s guard boats and nearer *Bellerophon*'s, which therefore pause in their labors to save him from drowning. Before he can be placed under arrest and transferred back to *Eurotas* and thence to shore, he shouts a warning to *Bellerophon*'s watch officer that the launch fast approaching bears the feared habeas corpus from the King's Bench. Sure enough, Mackenrot stands in her bows, waving his paper— and now the Count de Las Cases has recognized "André Castine" and says something to Commander Maitland. Orders are given: to his great relief Andrew sees another boat lowered to fend off the redoubtable Scotsman; he himself, there being nothing else presently to be done with him, is fetched aboard *Bellerophon* with the guard boats and their crews as soon as the old ship has sea room enough to begin tacking under her own power out of the sound.

You have betray'd us, Las Cases complain'd to me [he writes] *as soon as we could speak privately. Nor did my argument much move him; for while he agreed that rescue might be more feasible from St. Helena than from Britain, he vow'd the Emperor was still adamant on that score, and was prepared to take his life rather than submit voluntarily to exile. As for that, I thot, it was likely mere bluff, inasmuch as his sentence was now clear beyond doubt, and* Bellerophon's *putting out to sea removed any hope of their being received ashore or otherwise delaying execution of that sentence; yet he was still alive. On this head, however, I held my peace, proposing instead what certain of those sign-boards had proposed to me: namely, that the Emperor might be dissuaded from suicide, and induced to go peacefully tho protestingly into exile, if he were shown the opportunity therein to increase his fame. His public confinement in Tor Bay & Plymouth Sound had workt considerably to his advantage in one respect: he was now more than ever the cynosure of all eyes, and his letters, from "Themistocles" forward (so I learn'd from Las Cases), tho undeliver'd or unreply'd to, had in fact been addrest less to their addressees than to History, which is to say, to Public Opinion. What better chance, then, to bend the world in his favor, than to turn his exile into public martyrdom, by writing his memoirs on St. Helena & smuggling them out for publication? He had made history; he could now re-make & revise it to his pleasure! Thus the world's forgetfulness, which he fear'd would bury him, would bury instead his great crimes against mankind (I call'd them his little misjudgments) & eagerly believe whate'er he wrote.*

Moreover (Andrew adds by way of clincher to his appeal), such a memoir will need delivery to the mainland, and publication, and collection of its author's royalties. What better way for a trusted aide like Monsieur the Count de Las Cases at once to do his master a signal service and to abbreviate his own exile?

At 1st skeptical, the Count was by this last altogether convinced—if only, he declared, to save the Emperor's life & honor. All that afternoon & evening, as we hove to to await Prometheus, Tonnant, Eurotas, & Myrmidon, *and then beat southeast toward rendezvous with Admiral Cockburn, the Count prest my plan in private with Napoleon. That same night, I was gratify'd to hear, the unemperor'd Emperor dictated a grand letter of protest, addrest "to History. . ." And tho he still vow'd to the English officers they would never fetch him alive to St. Helena, I was pleased to gather, from Las Cases' nods & winks, that our appeal was going forward.*

He would have been further encouraged, could he have seen them, by editorials in the *Times* and the *Morning Chronicle* next day, expressing their writers' conviction that the captive would have been securer from rescue in Stirling Castle, say, than on St. Helena, where "an American vessel will always be ready to take him off. . ."

Nevertheless, throughout that morning and early afternoon (154 years ago today), as they rendezvous with Cockburn's squadron between Start Point and Bolt Head, exchange cannon salutes and visits between the admirals' flagships, then move together to the calmer waters of Tor Bay in preparation for the transfer, Napoleon gives no public sign of acquiescence. Keith and Cockburn are moved to the extraordinary precaution of impounding the French officers' swords and pistols, lest they attempt to resist the transfer with arms. Only when *Bellerophon*'s doctor reports to Commander Maitland that "General Buonaparte" has invited him to serve as his personal physician on St. Helena do the English—and Andrew—have reason to imagine that Napoleon has at last accepted his fate. Even then they fear a ruse (they have just learned that Las Cases, who has affected since Rochefort not to understand English, reads and speaks their language easily). Guard boats are posted to patrol the anchorage all night lest Mr. Mackenrot, or the habeas corpus people, or the Bonapartists, or the Americans, attempt rescue or obstruction, or the emperor fling himself from his cabin into Tor Bay.

At eight-thirty that evening Admirals Cockburn and Keith come aboard to read to Napoleon their instructions from the cabinet and work out the details of his transfer to *Northumberland* next morning; Andrew retires out of sight down to the orlop deck, where he had completed the "Washington" letter, and spends the evening drafting this one.

Rather (as I have done here on the first-class deck of the *Statendam*, where it is not to be supposed I have deciphered, transcribed, and summarized all these pages at one sitting, simultaneously wooing your future stepmother!), he extends toward completion the chronicle he has been drafting in fits and starts since Rochefort, as I have drafted this over the three weeks past. And as I expect any moment now this loving labor to be set aside for one equally loving but more pressing (Jane is in our stateroom, preparing for bed and wondering why I linger here on deck), so my namesake's is interrupted, near midnight, by good news from the Count de Las Cases. Not only has the emperor agreed at last, under formal protest, to be shifted with his party to *Northumberland* after breakfast next morning; he has made long speeches to History, to both the admirals and, separately, to Commander Maitland, from whom also he has exacted a letter attesting that his removal from *Bellerophon* is contrary to his own wishes. Moreover, he has prevailed (over Maitland's objections) in his insistence that Las Cases be added to the number of his party, to serve as his personal secretary; and he has clapped the count himself on the shoulder and said, "Cheer up, my friend! The world has not heard the last from us; we shall write our memoirs!"

Even as I, Andrew concludes, *am writing mine, in these encipher'd pages, my hope once more renew'd. Tomorrow Admiral Cockburn, "Scourge of the C's," will weigh anchor for St. Helena with the Scourge of Mankind: a voyage of two months, during which I shall make my own way back from England to New Orleans, hoping against hope, my darling Andrée, to find you there. Where, if all goes well, you & I & Jean Lafitte will devise a plan to spirit Napoleon from under George Cockburn's nose before he has unpackt his writing-tools!*

And even as I, dear Henry, hope against hope that upon my return to "Barataria" next week I shall find *you* there: the present point of my pen overtaken, the future ours to harvest together!

I go now to Mrs. Mack, to fertilize and cultivate that future. A fellow passenger remarks, in nervous jest, upon the "secret of the Bermuda Triangle": the hijacking of cruising yachts by narcotics smugglers to run their merchandise into U.S. harbors. I pretend to know nothing of that scandal. Small wonder, my companion replies: the Coast Guard and the tourist industry are keeping it quiet, inasmuch as they cannot possibly search every pleasure boat entering every creek and cove from Key West to Maine. Very interesting, I agree, thinking of the gift from Jane that awaits me in Annapolis.

A word to the wise, my son? From

Your loving father

R: *A. B. Cook VI to his son.* The fourth posthumous letter of A. B. Cook IV: plans for the rescue of Napoleon from St. Helena.

Yacht Baratarian
St. Helena Island, Little Round Bay
Severn River, Md.

August 13, 1969

Dear Henry,

Round Bay is a handsome widening of the Severn five nautical miles above Annapolis, itself some 125 up the Chesapeake from the Virginia Capes. Off Round Bay, on the river's southwest shore, is *Little* Round Bay, in the center whereof lies a small high wooded pleasant island named after Napoleon's exile place in the South Atlantic, some 7,000 sea miles hence.

This local St. Helena Jane Mack is of a mind to buy for our weekend exiles, as more comfortable and convenient than my Bloodsworth Island, and more private and spacious than my cottage on Chautaugua Road, not far away. Imagine an island of some dozen acres within twenty miles of both Washington and Baltimore! It is presently owned by acquaintances of Jane's, with whom she is negotiating purchase, and who have kindly permitted me to tie up at their dock for the night. As a honeymoon house and vacation retreat it will quite do, though it is too much in view of the mainland (half a mile off all around, and thickly peopled) to serve your and my other purposes. We shall hold onto our marshy, inconvenient "Barataria."

From a week of *dolce far niente* aboard the *Statendam*—a sort of final trial honeymoon itself, altogether successful—we flew home yesterday, Jane to return to her *métier* and truest passion, Mack Enterprises; I to take delivery in Annapolis of her birthday gift to me: the sturdy diesel yacht from whose air-conditioned main cabin I write this. All day the builders and I put *Baratarian* through its sea trials, as successful as Jane's and mine; tomorrow or next day I shall return it to the boatyard for certain adjustments and modifications (I feign a sudden addiction to deep-sea fishing) to be made while I check out our human Baratarians. On the ides of August, Napoleon's birthday, I shall fly briefly north to see how things go at Lily Dale and Fort Erie. I had considered a side trip to Chautauqua as well, to confer with my quondam collaborator there; but I now believe he knows nothing of you and is without interest in the Second Revolution. On or about St. Helena's Day (the 18th) I shall go up to Castines Hundred (our ancient caretakers have retired; I have engaged new ones through the post), whence I shall return, ere the sun enters Virgo, for a more considerable trial run: the first real test of our operations for the coming academic year. Will I find you there, Henry, poring through our library like your ancestors, determining for yourself what I have been at such futile pains to learn, to teach?

Andrew IV never did return there, except in dreams and letters. The next to last of his *lettres posthumes* was written aboard Lafitte's schooner *Jean Blanque* in "Galvez-Town, or New Barataria," on August 13, 1820—five years and a week since its predecessor. Like yours truly, he is about to commence on the ides of August another journey: one by his own admission "more considerable but less significant" than the one he ought to make instead, to Castines Hundred. *Still curst by what I had thot long exorcised,* he confesses to Andrée, *I shall sail 9,500 miles in the wrong direction, from Cancer down to Capricorn, to "rescue" against his will a man the world had better not seen in the 1st place, rather than fly north to the seat & bosom of my family, beg your pardon for my errancy, put by for good & all my vain dream of 2nd Revolution & Western Empire, and spend content in your arms what years remain to me.*

He refers, of course, to Jean Lafitte's expedition to spirit Napoleon from St. Helena—the expedition which, in his last, he had hoped to expedite before the island's defense could be organized. What has he been at for half a decade?

Rushing to Plymouth from Tor Bay [so he begins this letter, with a *4)?(,* a *HSUR,* a *rush,* as if no more than a page-turn separated *Bellerophon* from *Jean Blanque,* 1815 from 1820], *I found a fast brig just departing for Bermuda, where I took a yet faster packet to New Orleans. By mid-September, a full month ere Cockburn reacht St. Helena with his prisoner, I was back in Conti Street with Jean Lafitte, asking for news of you & the twins.*

There is, we know, none. *I could only conclude my letters & entreaties were unwelcome at Castines Hundred; else the Mississippi, whose navigation from Great Lakes to Gulf of Mexico was secured now to the U. States, had borne you long since hither.*

And why does he not straightway bear himself *thither,* to make certain those "letters & entreaties" ever reacht their address? *'Twas not the current of the Father of Waters I shy'd from breasting,* he declares, not quite convincingly, *but the current of your disfavor, both of my long absence* [three years by then, *eight* by "now"!] *and of what I had accomplisht. Where was our free nation of Indians, Habitants, & liberated slaves? Even New Orleans I found more "American" than I had left it, and with the Union at last secured & at peace—tho set fast forever, as wise men had fear'd, with a standing Army & Navy—I could feel the country catching its breath, as 'twere, before plunging to the western ocean. There was no time to lose, or all would be lost.*

But the Baratarians have more practical business on their minds. The Italian captains—Vincent Gambie, Julius Caesar Amigoni, Louis Chighizola—ever more barbaric and less "political" than their French counterparts, have openly returned to buccaneering and are already embroiled with U.S. gunboats and Federal Grand Jury indictments. "Uncle Renato" Beluche, covertly supported by the New Orleans Mexican Association (merchants and lawyers in favor of Mexican independence from Spain for reasons of trade), is running the Spanish blockade of Cartagena with provisions for Bolívar's patriots; his new mistress is rumored to be pregnant by the Liberator himself. And the brothers Lafitte, while still interested in the St. Helena venture, are too busy with "Louisiana Projects" of their own to pursue it immediately: the reorganization of the French-Creole Baratarians at Galveston and the assistance of the new wave of Bonapartist refugees pouring into New Orleans and Champ d'Asile. One look at their charts of the island persuades even Jean and Pierre that while St. Helena's precipitous sea cliffs, limited anchorages, and existing fortifications make it all but impregnable to armed assault, even to covert approach, it can be readily infiltrated under some pretext or other, regardless of the defenses. Wherever there are local fishermen, Jean declares, there is "local knowledge" of ways to land and take off items, for a fee, without the inconvenience of passing through customs. Let the emperor have a taste of confinement while his place is prepared; it will dispose him the more toward America.

Most immediately interested in Andrew's plan (to rescue Napoleon; he does not mention the Louisiana Project) are Nicholas Girod, the mayor of New Orleans; Jean Blanque, the state legislator; and a curious fellow named Joseph Lakanal—former regicide, defrocked priest, Bonapartist refugee, and newly appointed president of the University of Louisiana. Andrew spends the next year and a half employed jointly by them and by Jean Lafitte as a kind of liaison, project manager, and investigator of rival schemes—of which, he comes to learn, there are a great many.

Napoleon and his party reach St. Helena and are established temporarily at The Briars and then permanently at Longwood; the amiable George Cockburn is replaced in 1816 with a stricter warden, Sir Hudson Lowe, who sees rescue plots even in the planting of green beans instead of white in the kitchen garden (white being the color of the Bourbon livery, green the Bonapartist); the emperor begins his memoirs. James Madison is replaced in the presidency by his protégé Monroe; Beluche and Bolívar sail from Haiti with seven little vessels to commence the liberation of South America; Mme de Staël, back at Coppet, tries to mend a marital quarrel between her guests Lord and Lady Byron, and is charmed (as are Talleyrand, Chateaubriand, von Humboldt, and the Duke of Wellington) by Jérôme's cast-off American wife, Elizabeth Patterson Bonaparte, now 31 and touring Europe while her son "Bo" attends school in Maryland—especially when, "out of loyalty to her name," Betsy declines an invitation from Louis XVIII himself. News of this gesture precedes her return to Baltimore late in the year and disposes Joseph Bonaparte in her favor. Having experimented with rented estates on the Hudson palisades and in Philadelphia, Joseph has built elaborately at Point Breeze, on the Delaware near Bordentown, New Jersey, and is buying vast tracts of upstate New York to house his newest mistress, a young Pennsylvania Quaker. He invites Betsy and Bo to visit; there, early in 1817, she remeets the man who'd been dispatched too late by Napoleon to dissuade Jérôme from contracting any "entangling amorous alliances" in America, and who later had agreeably shown the young bride and groom around Niagara Falls.

Andrew is there on business (so to be sure is Betsy, whose regnant passion is to establish the legitimacy of her son): General Lallemand—one of Napoleon's party aboard *Bellerophon* who was exiled to Malta instead of St. Helena—freed from his detainment, has lately arrived at Champ d'Asile with the news that Andrew's "Tor Bay" plan may have succeeded too well: according to reports reaching Malta from St. Helena, the emperor is so taken with the publicity value of his "martyrdom" that he would now refuse rescue if offered it! Girod and Blanque want Joseph's opinion on this subject, as well as his blessing upon their scheme: to design a vessel especially for the rescue, commission "a suitable captain and crew" to man it, and raise a house in New Orleans for Napoleon's residence. They also suspect their colleague Lakanal of unreliability, and want Joseph's estimation of him.

On the first matter the ex-king of Spain has no opinion, though he reports with pride (and, it seems to Andrew, relief) his brother's refusal of his own offer to join him on St. Helena. But on the character of

Lakanal he is vehement: the man is as desperate a charlatan as the "Comte de Crillon"; very possibly in the pay of Metternich or the Bourbons to implicate Joseph in a rescue scheme that will make his presence embarrassing to the U.S. government. As Andrew reads Joseph's character, the man is truly but mildly sympathetic to his brother's situation and does not object to its ameliorating, but has no political ambitions himself: he is primarily concerned with his enormous private pleasures and fearful of anything that may imperil them. His brother Lucien's suggestion, for example, that the three of them conquer Mexico, appalls him; he wishes he were not the focus of every harebrained scheme to exploit his famous name and Napoleon's exile.

Betsy thinks him a coward, like her ex-husband. If *she* were a man, she declares privately to Andrew, she would have had the emperor in America long since; it wants only a bit of audacity! To Joseph, Andrew offers to expose and discredit Monsieur Lakanal in a way that will publicly absolve Joseph of any connection with the rescue plan. He volunteers further, if the business is executed to Joseph's satisfaction, to serve him as he is serving Girod and Blanque (he does not mention Lafitte): as monitor, evaluator, and coordinator of all rescue proposals, encouraging whichever seem likeliest and seeing to it that the others come to nothing. For not only will ill-managed attempts increase the difficulty of a well-managed one, but the emperor may as likely be kidnapped by some exploiter or well-meaning crank as rescued by his friends or (what Betsy fears, having heard such rumors at Mme de Staël's) secretly poisoned by the British to end the expense of confining him and the risk of his returning to power in Europe.

Joseph agrees, and authorizes Andrew in this capacity; their conversation turns to lighter matters. Did Mr. Cook know, Joseph asks with amusement, that while his brother was on Elba, the aforementioned Mme de Staël had descended upon himself in Geneva with information of a plot on Napoleon's life? He had been breakfasting with Talma, the tragedian; to punish Germaine for the interruption he had had the would-be assassins arrested by the local police instead of authorizing her, as she wished, to carry her warning directly to the emperor. Magnificent lady! Who also was reported to be in fast-failing health.

Andrew notes that each mention of Mme de Staël brings a blush to Betsy Bonaparte's cheeks. He tests the observation: does the Comte de Survilliers (so Joseph has named himself in New Jersey) happen to recall meeting in Bordeaux a fellow novelist named Consuelo del Consulado, whom Andrew had recommended also to Mme de Staël? Joseph does not; Betsy's face is aflame.

In the following months he sees her several times more, at her or his instigation, in Bordentown or Baltimore, and both confirms this curious connection and improves his acquaintance. He had imagined Mme B. might be having or planning an affair with Joseph, if only to further her son's interests; now he perceives her to be, despite her

611

beauty, quite devoid of sexuality. Or almost so: she reddens so astonishingly when, in August, he reports to her the news of Germaine de Staël's death on Bastille Day last, that he is moved to exclaim: "Madame, one could believe that you have either *un secret suisse* or *un suisse secret!*" "If I do, sir," Betsy replies, "it shall remain, like Swiss bank accounts, a secret."

But she is not offended; on the contrary, in "this slough, this sink, this barbarous democratical Baltimore," she is entertained by Andrew's tales of the Revolution, of his intrigues with John Henry and Joel Barlow. And she is so pleased, as is Joseph Bonaparte, by his handling of *"l'affaire Lakanal"* that when Joseph engages him in the fall to serve as his clearing agent for all rescue proposals, Betsy volunteers her assistance as well "in any noncompromising way."

Lakanal had had to be managed in three stages. Joseph's opinion of him, which Andrew promoted from hearsay to firsthand knowledge, was enough to persuade the embarrassed trustees of the university to ease him out of office, and Girod and Blanque to ease him out of their plan. Andrew then advised Lakanal to petition Joseph Bonaparte directly, and, "as one close to that worthy," told him how best to couch his appeal: the ex-king, he declared, is still secretly flattered to be addressed by his former title, and even enjoys conferring Spanish distinctions upon his favorites, though he cannot legitimately do so; at the same time, his two new passions are the Indians of his adopted country—even his "wilderness mistress" is named Annette Savage—and cryptology. If Lakanal could appeal to all these interests at once (every one of which, excepting Miss Savage, is in fact foreign to Joseph), while specifying that the emperor's brother was not himself to have anything to do with the rescue, he could be assured of a favorable reading and an invitation to Point Breeze.

Lakanal dutifully prepares and mails a packet to Bordentown, which the U.S. Secret Service—tipped off by Andrew Cook "on behalf of [his] employer, Joseph Bonaparte"—promptly intercepts and passes on to President Monroe. It contains a cipher designed to make French and English messages look like prayers in Latin, a vocabulary of the Caddo language, a request for 65,000 francs for expenses to bring Napoleon to Louisiana and a Spanish marquisate if he succeeds, a catalogue of north Louisiana Indian tribes, and a vow that "le roi lui-même" shall have nothing to do with rescuing the emperor. Monroe transmits his thanks to Point Breeze for Joseph's loyal cooperation; for a time there is consternation in both the American and the French ministries of state; then the President dismisses the "Lakanal Packet" as the work of an utter and impotent madman. The secret service and Andrew agree to exchange information on other rescue attempts so that appropriate measures may be taken, and Andrew turns Lakanal off with a scolding for having been "so vulgarly beforehand" with that request for money, "as who should demand a boon ere it can be freely given." The would-be conspirator is reduced to dirt farming.

With Girod and Blanque's blessing then—and Jean Lafitte's, who with a thousand followers is now established in Galveston and back to large-scale privateering—Andrew moves for the next two years between Louisiana and New Jersey. More bad news comes from St. Helena: convinced that Napoleon will dictate memoirs forever, Count de Las Cases has arranged his own deportation from the island, smuggling out with him the manuscript of his *Mémorial de Sainte Hélène;* he quotes the emperor as declaring, "If Christ had not died upon the Cross, He would not have become the Son of God."

Nevertheless, a dozen rescue plans go forward. Two freebooters of Philadelphia, Captains Jesse Hawkins and Joshua Wilder, propose to fit out a brace of clippers and a landing craft, register them for a tea voyage to Canton, and make for St. Helena instead. Stephen Decatur, the hero of Tripoli, together with Napoleon's exiled General Bertrand Clauzel, proposes a similar scheme, worked out in knowledgeable military detail: the general has his eye on Mexico. In Britain, a certain Mr. Johnstone, admirer of both Napoleon and the late Robert Fulton, is testing a submarine for the purpose; and a Mme Fourès in Rio de Janeiro, who had been the emperor's mistress in Egypt in 1798, is devoting her fortune to a plan involving several large sailing ships each carrying a small steamboat for fast night landings. The wealthy Philadelphian Stephen Girard, formerly a sea captain from Bordeaux, who helped Madison finance the War of 1812, is interested; so again is Jean Lafitte, who now proposes a quick operation by the whole New Baratarian navy. Girod and Blanque, impatient, have ordered construction of their ship in Charleston, South Carolina, safely away from their base, and are raising the imperial dwelling. Even Betsy Bonaparte acknowledges privately to Andrew that she has on her own authority approved an offer from the King family of Somerset County, old friends of hers and Jérôme's, of the use of their remote mansion in the Eastern Shore marshes as a temporary hideout for the emperor until the excitement of his rescue shall have died down. She herself plans another extended visit with her son to Europe, where in course of frankly ingratiating herself with the other Bonapartes, she intends to enlist their aid in the project.

Andrew has his hands full. Joseph cautiously inclines to some combination of the Girod-Blanque scheme (as the most practical of the nonmilitary ones) and that of his friend Stephen Girard, whom he seeks not to disoblige, and who like Mayor Girod aspires merely to relieve Napoleon from so isolated and humiliating a confinement. But he will permit no expedition actually to sail until he is assured that his brother wants rescuing. He wonders vaguely whether their mother and their sister Pauline, both now luxuriously established in Rome, have better information on that score. In January of 1820, however, his Point Breeze mansion inconveniently burns to the ground, and he is too busy rebuilding it (on an even larger scale) to make inquiries of them.

Most of the proposals Andrew can deal with by simply refusing

Joseph's subsidy: thus the Hawkins-Wilder and the Decatur-Clauzel projects. A few he scotches by tips to the appropriate governments (Mr. Johnstone is arrested in the Thames and his vessel confiscated for examination by the Admiralty) or the planting of exploiters-by-delay, who like medieval alchemists turn the credulity of their patrons into gold (Mme Fourès's steamboats need repeated and expensive redesigning). Bad luck and bad management take care of some others: a tornado destroys half a dozen of Jean and Pierre Lafitte's vessels; Commodore Decatur is killed in a duel with a fellow officer at Bladensburg; the Champ d'Asile colonists are too busy saving themselves from crocodiles and dysentery to save their fallen emperor from St. Helena.

There remain the schemes that Joseph favors. Andrew delays them with overpreparation and cross-purpose (it is his idea to have Nicholas Girod's *Séraphine* built inconveniently in Charleston, and to send Stephen Girard's Philadelphia vessel to New Orleans to await sailing orders) until his own plan is ready, which his dealings with all these others have convinced him is likeliest to his purpose: at an appropriate moment, he will disappear from Bordentown, slip off secretly with Jean Lafitte on the fastest of the Baratarian vessels (the schooner named, as it happens, *Jean Blanque*), and do the job himself.

What job, exactly? *Nota bene*, my son: to no one more than to the author of a long-term project does the double edge of Heraclitus's famous dictum apply: he cannot step into the same stream twice because not only the stream flows, but the man. The Andrew Cook who writes these lines, Henry, is not the same you last graced with your company in February; nor is the Andrew Cook who wrote on this date in 1820 the Cook of 1815. Events have at least thrice modified his original ends and means.

At first he wants merely to snatch Napoleon from the Allies and fetch him to Louisiana, let the international chips fall where they may. Then, in the spring of 1819 (Mississippi and Illinois have joined the Union; Alabama is about to; Monroe is buying Florida from Spain; Ruthy Barlow has joined her husband and Toot Fulton in the hereafter; the Atlantic has been crossed by steamship; the U.S.-Canadian border is established at the 49th parallel), Betsy Bonaparte makes a curious report from Baltimore: she has it from friends in Rome that a German-Swiss clairvoyant, one Madame Kleinmüller, has become spiritual advisor to Napoleon's mother ("Madame Mère") in the Palazzo Rinuccini and has gained increasing influence over both the old woman and her brother, Cardinal Fesch. On January 15 last, according to Betsy's sources, no less an authority than the Virgin Mary disclosed to Mme Kleinmüller, in a vision, that the British have secretly removed Napoleon from St. Helena and replaced him with an impostor; his jailers oblige his aides to write as if their master were still among them, but in fact he has been spirited by angels to another country, where he is safe and content! Mme Mère and Cardinal Fesch are altogether convinced. Napoleon's sister Pauline Borghese is not: in a letter to Joseph soon after, she confirms Betsy's report, deplores their mother's gullibility, and declares her suspicion that Mme Kleinmüller is a spy for Metternich. Andrew himself dismisses the vision but changes his plan to include the planting of just such an impostor, to facilitate Napoleon's removal, delay the search for him, and forestall international turmoil until the Louisiana Project is ready.

And he is interested in Betsy's sources; the more so when, a few months later, she follows this report with another, also subsequently verified by Pauline: so entirely are Napoleon's mother and uncle under that clairvoyant's sway, they reject as forgeries letters from the emperor himself, in his own hand, complaining of his failing health and requesting a new doctor and a better cook! Persuaded that Napoleon is no longer on St. Helena, they have sent out a party of incompetents as a blind; Fesch has taken to discarding the emperor's letters, and Mme Kleinmüller to forging happy ones from "some other island." Pauline is furious. Andrew, still wondering about Betsy's information, asks disingenuously whether she knows that a penitential procession by this same Cardinal Fesch was described ironically by Mme de Staël in her novel *Corinne*. Mme B. duly blushes.

Andrew then inquires, on a sudden impulse: has she considered remarrying? Crimson, she asks him why he asks; it is her son she cares about, not herself. Perhaps Andrew has his employer in mind? If so, forget him: Joseph is a sot, a lecher, and a coward, like Jérôme; the only male Bonaparte with spirit is the one on St. Helena. And does she know, Andrew next wonders aloud, that in some quarters there is doubt as to the validity of Napoleon's marriage to Marie Louise, who in any case has no wish ever to see her husband again and would welcome a divorce? *I do,* replies Betsy, and Andrew divines with excitement that she has anticipated the next modification of his scheme, of which therefore he prudently says no more on this occasion. What better way for her to secure young Jérôme Napoleon Bonaparte's legitimacy— even his possible accession!—than to marry the emperor himself, as a condition of rescuing him? And how better for Andrew to finance the Louisiana Project than with the combined fortunes of the Bonapartes and one of the wealthiest families in Maryland?

In my mind & in my cyphers, Andrew writes, *I had for convenience number'd these alternatives A-1, A-2, & A-3, as they all involved rescuing Napoleon & fetching him 1st to the Maryland marshes, thence to New Orleans, & thence west to our future empire. Two obstacles remain'd: the difficulty of finding someone able enough at mimicking the Emperor to fool his own wardens, at least for a time; and the possibility, reconfirm'd in June of this year (1820) by Mme B., that Bonaparte preferr'd to consummate his "martyrdom" on St. Helena. A letter from Baron Gourgaud, intercepted by Metternich's agents, declared that the Emperor "could escape to America whenever he pleased," but preferr'd confinement like Andromeda on that lonely but very public rock. His young son loom'd large in these considerations. "'Twere better for my son," Betsy* quoted Metternich quoting Napoleon from Gourgaud's letter. "If I die on the cross —& he is still alive—my martyrdom will win him a crown."

To deal with these obstacles Andrew devises Plan A-4, with which he ends this letter. But first, nothing having come of his indirect inquiries, he asks Betsy frankly how she hears of these things before Napoleon's own family, especially now that Mme de Staël—who had always been *au courant* on such privy matters and might imaginably have been in correspondence with Mme Bonaparte—is dead.

She blusht & reply'd, She supposed I had meant to say "before the rest *of Napoleon's own family," whereof she consider'd herself as rightful a member as any not of the Corsican's very blood. As for her sources, she would say only that I might rely upon their veracity, & that I was not the only American player at the Game of Governments.*

She then apprised me of her intended move to Europe in the Autumn, to reacquaint her son, now 15, with his relatives. While there she would determine & report to me the truth of Napoleon's circumstances & desires—for no one need tell her that Metternich might have fabricated that "intercepted letter" to discourage rescue attempts. And she would advise me then whether to proceed with the Girod/Girard plan or bid Joseph order it cancel'd, as against his brother's wishes.

Much imprest by her determination & her canny sense of the world, very rare in so handsome & handsomely fixt a woman, I thankt her. But privately I thot of any such report from her, what she thot of Metternich's; & so I determined Jean & I should make ready & sail as early as possible, not apprising Mme B. or Joseph or any soul else of our journey until its object was attain'd, when they would surely put their houses & other facilities at our disposal. On the Solstice, therefore, I vanisht from Point Breeze; on my 44th birthday I was in Galvez-Town, where I found Jean bored with his New Barataria & ready for adventure. The more so when I described & demonstrated to him what, after much soul-searching, I had resolved upon: Plan A-4.

It is, briefly, to determine Nápoleon's sentiments regarding rescue, not in Rome or Paris or London, but on St. Helena itself, by sailing directly to that island, slipping ashore with the aid of that "local knowledge" Lafitte is so confident the fishermen will sell him, and infiltrating Longwood. Then, if the emperor should in fact prove more interested in inventing *le bonapartisme* on St. Helena than in forging a new empire in the American southwest, to drug and abduct him secretly from the island, leaving an impostor in his place. Once whisked to Maryland's Eastern Shore, he could not return to St. Helena without publicly pleading for reincarceration, which would reveal the inauthenticity of his "martyrdom." They would offer him either a life of anonymous freedom or the directorship of the 2nd Revolution, with or without Betsy Patterson Bonaparte as his consort.

But what impostor?

That was the question that had most vext me since A-2, our ancestor writes. Napoleon was 7 years my senior, several inches shorter than I, and gone rather potbelly'd, but the fact was I could take him off to a T, down to his

Corsican accent, his walk, & his table-manners. I could not hope to fool his aides, whose consent & cooperation therefore I would have to enlist (I had a plan for doing so); but I was reasonably confident I could fool the British, whom Bonaparte had rarely dealt with in person even before his health declined—which last circumstance I could also employ to aid the imposture. And so, having searcht in vain for alternatives, and daring wait no longer lest Mme B.'s people or someone else's get to St. Helena before me, I shall sail with Jean two days hence, on the Emperor's name-day, to take his place in captivity until (the final article of A-4) I can with the assistance of Napoleon's suite feign illness & death, and then disappear among the fishermen till Jean comes back to fetch me from a disarm'd St. Helena.

'Tis a considerable risk: if I am found out, either before or after N.'s removal, the British will clap me in jail forever; and my rescue depends on Jean's good seamanship, good faith, & good luck. But if all goes per plan, by the time the meteors next shower out from Perseus (which are showering over Jean Blanque's *yards as I pen this letter), I shall have died again & been re-resurrected, to take my place beside the man whose place I took, at the head of our 2nd Revolution.*

Will you be there with me, long-lost wife? Whether or no, may you hear from me next August of the success of another plan, whereof I have spoken not even to Jean Lafitte, & cannot yet speak to you: I mean Plan B, *and bid you adieu.*

He closes and, on August 15, sails. I likewise, Henry, and on 8/15 will fly in pursuit of an "A-1" of my own: not without a "B" up my sleeve, or in my bonnet, learned from our forebear's final *lettre posthume*. And when I take *my* place, dear son, at the head of our etc., will you be with me?

Whether or no, this time next week you shall hear again from

Your father

E: *A. B. Cook VI to his son.* The fifth and final posthumous letter of A. B. Cook IV: Napoleon "rescued."

Castines Hundred
Ontario, Canada

August 20, 1969

My dear Henry,

Except that you are not here, all is as it should be (i.e., as it ever has been) at Castines Hundred. A grand hatch of "American soldiers" fills the air—in which already one feels a premonitory autumn chill—as they have done every latter August since the species, and Lake Ontario, evolved. I write this by paraffin lantern in the library, not to attract

617

them to the windows; took dinner by candlelight for the same reason, as our ancestors have done since *that* species evolved. A fit and pleasing *mise en scène* for retailing the last of my namesake's *lettres posthumes:* dated August 20, 1821, addressed to "My dear, my darling wife," and delivered here at that year's close.

Be assured of my proper disappointment not to find you here; a disappointment for which, however, I was prepared. Be even more so of my proper tantalization by the report (from our new caretakers, who seem satisfactory) that you apparently *stopped by*—even spent a few days here?—in the interval between caretakers! Were here as I was writing to you off Bermuda! Left only upon the Bertrands' assuming their duties, as I was writing to you from my *Baratarian!* Indicated that you would "be back," but did not say when, or whence you came, or whither vanished!

Heartless Henry! True and only son! But so be it: I have been as heartless in my time, as have all our line. I restrained my urge to badger the Bertrands with questions—How does he appear? Did he speak of his father?—lest they think their new employer's relation with his son as odd as in fact it is. I shall leave sealed copies here, against your return, of both the "prenatal" and the "posthumous" letters of Andrew Cook IV, as well as that one of mine reviewing our history from him to myself. And I shall hope, no longer quite against hope!

But how I wish I could report to you, Henry, confer with you, solicit your opinion now. So many opportunities lie at hand; so many large decisions must be made quite soon, affecting our future and the Revolution's! Last night, for example, I drove up here from the Fort Erie establishment, where I had stopped to assess Joseph Morgan's resalvageability. I am satisfied that he is too gone in his "repetition compulsion" to be of future use to us. What I advanced as a kind of lure when I first rescued him for our cause has become an obsession; he is now addicted to his medication, as it were; the only obstacle to disestablishing him altogether is that he happens to be related, through the Patterson line, to Jane Mack. But we must think of something; he is a liability.

So too, I more and more suspect, is Jerome Bray of Lily Dale— more exactly, of "Comalot," as he has without irony renamed his strange habitation—on whom I paid a call before crossing to Canada. Even to me that man is an enigma: certainly mad, but as certainly not *simply* mad. His extraordinary machine, or simulacrum of a machine— you really must see it. And his "honey dust," of whose peculiar narcotic virtue there can be no question. . . ! He is doing us the service, unwittingly, of removing Jane's daughter from the number of competitors for Harrison Mack's fortune, while however adding himself to the number of our problems. For him too I have certain plans, and have urged him down to Bloodsworth Island for the "Burning of Washington" four days hence—but how surer I would feel of that strategy if I could review it with you, and you ratify it!

I have, moreover, two further problems of the most intimate and urgent sort, Henry, on which your consultation is of such importance to me that I must, insofar as I can, compel it.

Mrs. Harrison Mack now proposes to become Mrs. André Castine on September 30. (She specified "the end of the month," leaving the precise date to me. Still amused by the Anniversary View of History, I considered the equinox, when at 9 A.M. in 4004 B.C. the world is said to have begun; but I chose at last the 30th, anniversary of our ancestor Ebenezer Cooke's inadvertent loss of his Maryland estate in 1694 and, rather earlier, of the legendary loss of another prime piece of real estate: Adam and Eve's expulsion from Eden.) For convenience's sake, I have in mind to kill off "Andrew Cook VI" by some accident before that date. I am, you know, under that name, also in some second-cousinly relation to my fiancée: I propose therefore—*unless as prime beneficiary you appear within 30 days of the date of your father's death*—to bequeath to Jane Mack my properties on Bloodsworth Island and Chautaugua Road. I shall cause obituary notices to be published promptly in the leading Quebec and Ontario newspapers as well as those of Maryland and the District of Columbia: the next move will be yours. "André Castine" looks forward to welcoming you (either here or at "Barataria") as his own son!

On the other hand—for reasons that I shan't set forth in writing but will be relieved to share with you at last in person, as they pertain to you intimately indeed—my coming forth publicly as André Castine to marry Jane raises problems of its own concerning that historian I've mentioned before: Professor Germaine Pitt, Lady Amherst, who was to have edited, annotated, and published this series of letters. It will scarcely be enough to see to her reappointment to the post about to be vacated by Andrew Cook's death; something further is called for. We must discuss it!

And *Baratarian,* that fleet and sturdy fellow, who when I fetch him from the Annapolis yard this weekend will have tankage enough to run from Bloodsworth Island to Yucatán with but one pit stop, and enough secret stowage in his teak and holly joinery to fetch back a high-profit cargo along with the marlin and wahoo we are officially after. One trip, at current prices, will come near to financing us for half a year, and not even the crew need know (indeed ought not, for it is paid informants, not adroit law officers, who precipitate arrests in this line of work). But I cannot navigate both *Baratarian* and Barataria, or manage to our cause both Jane and Mary Jane. Come, son, and let us to Isla Mujeres, the Isle of Women!

There Jean Lafitte—alias "Jean Lafflin" or "Laffin"—is reported to have come in November 1821 to *la fin du chemin,* ambushed by Mexican soldiers not impossibly informed of his coming by Andrew Cook IV. So at least speculated my grandfather, Andrew V, on what grounds he did not say. It is by no means established beyond doubt that Lafitte died then and there; other legends extend his pseudonymous life to 1854.

What is known is that in latter 1821, pressed by the U.S. Revenue Marine, he boarded his schooner *Pride* (possibly the *Jean Blanque* under alias of its own), abandoned "Galvez-Town," and disappeared. Moreover, that his connection with Andrew IV, once so brotherly, had long since deteriorated into mutual suspicion and distrust.

What a falling off, between that P.S. to the first of these letters (where his fondest wish is to unite his "darling wife" with his "true brother") and the opening of this last!

3*64;:(8¶8);*‡76‡;:905:5(;82

GNIHTYREVESTNIOPOTYMLAYARTEB

Everything points to my betrayal

—whether by Lafitte, Joseph Bonaparte, Betsy Patterson Bonaparte, the U.S. Secret Service, or some combination thereof, he is uncertain. He cannot say for sure even that he is in fact a prisoner in "Beverly," the King mansion on the Manokin River not far from Bloodsworth Island; perhaps all is going well, but unaccountably slowly! Yet it is August 20, 1821, insufferably hot, damp, and buggy in the Eastern Shore marshes; he has been there above six weeks, since his 45th birthday, under anonymous guard "for his own security"; the owners of Beverly, at the urging of their friend Mme B., are off on an extended visit to Europe, as is Betsy herself; Lafitte has delivered him and is long gone: possibly back to St. Helena to rescue "André Castine" per plan, more likely back to privateering in the Gulf of Mexico. *Everything points* etc.

It is not, he acknowledges now, the beginning of his mistrust. Their official plan, upon setting out the year before to spirit Napoleon from St. Helena, had been that upon the emperor's safe and secret installation at Beverly, Lafitte would send word posthaste to New Orleans for Dominique You to sail in the *Séraphine* to rescue Andrew, under pretext of executing Mayor Girod's scheme to rescue Napoleon. Such was also their "backup" plan in case things went awry: the *Séraphine* would sail on August 15, 1821, if nothing had been heard by then from the *Jean Blanque*. Moreover—in view of those rumors that Napoleon was being poisoned by the Bourbons, by the English, by the Fesch/Kleinmüller/Metternich conspiracy, even by disaffected members of his own entourage; and other rumors that he was dying of the stomach cancer common in his family; and yet others that he was already dead or elsewhere sequestered and replaced by an impostor—Cook and Lafitte had agreed on a contingency plan: if the man they rescue is either an impostor or a dying Napoleon, Lafitte will bury him quietly at sea and then retrieve his surrogate to lead the Louisiana Project.

But the fact is (Andrew now declares to "my dear, my darling wife") our ancestor has had for several years no intention of rescuing Napoleon in the first place! They have all been a blind, those elaborate schemes and counterschemes! Andrew has not forgotten Joel Barlow's *Advice to a Raven in Russia:* the Corsican is a beast, an opportunistic

620

megalomaniac whose newly invented "Bonapartism" is but the senti-mental rationalization, after the fact, of a grandiose military dictator-ship. Andrew has never truly imagined that his Louisiana Project would appeal to the man who sold that vast territory to Jefferson in part from lack of interest in it; in any case he would not want the butcher of Europe at the head of his (and Andrée's) liberal free state!

And there is, in the second place, that aforementioned lapse of faith that Jean Lafitte or Dominique You will actually risk returning for him. It would be so easy not to, their main object once attained, and so perilous and expensive to do it! Jean endlessly complains of the Revenue Marine's harassment of his New Barataria; might not the secret service offer to end or mitigate this harassment in return for his cooperation in foiling all rescue schemes, including Andrew's? *We were still to all appearances brothers,* he writes; *but some Gascon intuition warn'd me to trust this Gascon no longer. And warn'd me further, that that Gascon entertain'd a like suspicion of me.*

What he had for some while been privately planning, therefore, he now confides: a multiple or serial imposture. He would go ashore at St. Helena and by some means arrange to have *himself* doped and smuggled out as Napoleon, and Napoleon left behind as himself (whose rescue he would then, as Napoleon, forestall, forbid, or thwart). Deceiving even Jean Lafitte, he would continue to counterfeit the aging, ailing emperor long enough to mobilize the French Creoles, the free Negroes, and the "Five Civilized Tribes" of Southern Indians for the Louisiana Project. Moreover, as Napoleon Bonaparte he will *("forgive me, dear dear Andrée! I had a hundred times rather it had been you, that have rightly forsaken your forsaker. . .") marry Elizabeth Patterson Bonaparte,* and turn her family's fortune to his purpose! If he divines that Betsy might not disapprove, he will perhaps then reveal his true identity to her, "die" again as Napoleon, and carry on the 2nd Revolution as André Castine, Bonaparte's successor to the Louisiana Project and to herself. Otherwise, he will do the same things without ever revealing the imposture. For it is not Mme B. herself he desires—vivacious, hand-some, wealthy, and managerially gifted as she is—only her fortune, until he can salvage Bonaparte's or make his own. He is not blind to her obsessiveness *("as profound as mine, but private: her son was her 2nd Revolution"),* or to the sexless miser inside the Belle of Baltimore.

Concerning whom, as *Jean Blanque* stands out of the gulf in August 1820, there remains a tantalizing mystery. When he last queried her in Baltimore concerning the source of her information about the Roman Bonapartes, Betsy had teased him with sight of a letter from Rome written in the Pattersons' own family cipher. Knowing him to be "a clever hand at such things," she scarcely more than flashed the letter; even so, she underestimated Andrew's capacity. The forger's trained eye and memory caught only the salutation and the close, but those he retained as if transcribed, and in fact transcribed them at his first opportunity: *Vs Dryejri D.,* it began, and ended *Nyy vs Yejr, G.* Like most ciphers, it was written letter by letter, not cursively; yet the handwriting seemed half-familiar. *I could almost have believed it yours!* he exclaims to Andrée.

En route from Baltimore to New Orleans, New Orleans to "Galvez-Town," he studies his transcription, but is unable either to recognize or to decipher it. Throughout the long voyage to St. Helena—normally a two-month sail, but extended to five by privateering excursions at Isla Mujeres and Curaçao, and by hurricane damage off Tobago—he studies the cipher while perfecting two separate impostures of Napoleon: a public, "false" one on deck for the benefit of Lafitte and the Baratarian crew, based on popular portraits by Isabey and Ducis (short-cropped hair, bemused mouth, right hand tucked between waistcoat buttons); and in his cabin a private, "true" one based on his last sight of the fallen emperor aboard *Bellerophon*—paunchy, jowly, slower of gait and speech—which he means to use to deceive his rescuers when the time comes.

Vs Dryejri D. . . .Nyy vs Yejr, G. It looks vaguely Slavic, Croatian, Finnish. He remembers pondering the hieroglyphics in the British Museum in 1811, en route to his rendezvous with John Henry: the stone discovered at the village of Rosetta on the Nile by Napoleon's soldiers in 1799 and taken by the British, with those soldiers, in 1801. The recollection reminds him of Napoleon's Egyptian affair with Mme Fourès, the French counterpart of "Mrs. Mullens," and of his own amorous North African escapade in 1797. . . Suddenly (it is September 14, seventh anniversary of his "death" at Fort McHenry; in Paris the "father of Egyptology," Champollion, is deciphering those hiero-glyphics with that stone) he has the key to Betsy Bonaparte's cipher, and to both her "Swiss secret" and her "secret Swiss."

The actual words he works out, within reasonable limits, later. Most conspicuous are the repeated sequences *vs* and *yejr;* given that *y* is the only character to appear four times, he anticipates Edgar Poe and calls it *e*, but can make nothing likely in either French or English of the result: _ _ _ _ *e* _ _ _ _ _ . . . _ *ee* _ _ *e* _ _ _, _. The character *r*, which appears three times (no other appears more than twice, but in a text so short the table of frequencies is unreliable) makes a more promising *e* (_ _ _ _ *e* _ _ _ *e* _ _ . . . . _ _ _ _ _ _ _ _ _ *e*, _ _), especially given the conventions of epistolary salutation and close. Assuming the final character in each phrase to be the first or last initial respectively of addressee and author, and remembering Mme B.'s first and last to be the same, we have: _ _ *Be* _ _ _ *e* _ *B*. . . _ _ _ _ _ _ _ _ _ *e*, _ _; the repeated *yejr* is then surely *love* (_ _ *Belove* _ *B*. . . _ _ _ _ _ _ *Love*, _.); which gives us _ _ *Belove* _ *B*. . . . _ *ll* _ _ *Love*, _.; which is surely *M y B e l o v e d B*. . . . *A l l m y L o v e*, _. Only the mysterious terminal blank *(G* in the cipher) remains to be filled.

But the real key is not Andrew's sorting of frequencies and correspondences, which leads after all but to that crucial lacuna. It is in the calligraphy of that very *G*, as it were an aborted or miscarried flourish from its final serif: the first thing that struck him as familiar, but which he cannot be certain he has accurately duplicated. From Galveston to Yucatán, Yucatán to Tobago, he does his Napoleonic homework and covers every available scrap of paper with uppercase *G*'s; a fortuitous stroke on the aforementioned anniversary—*Jean Blanque* is pitching terrifically in the storm that will carry off her foremast and half a dozen Baratarians with her square-sail yards— delivers him the key.

And show'd me at once, he writes, *that my errand was very likely a wild-goose chase. That were it not for the necessity of deceiving Jean Lafitte, I should spare myself that endless voyage & elaborate imposture, and make straight for Rome, for the Palazzo Rinuccini, & for the clairvoyant "Mme Kleinmüller"*. . .

But there is no help for it: key in hand, he is obliged to postpone for nearly three-quarters of a year its urgent application to the lock— unimaginably protracted suspense!—while he sails thousands of miles down the map, from Tobago to the Rocks of Saint Peter and Paul, to Ascension Island, to St. Helena. And (it must be) in order to give Andrée some sense of his massive frustration, the impatience which no doubt contributes to Jean Lafitte's suspicions of him, he withholds this key for many a ciphered page to come (I myself skipped ahead at once to Rome and the answer, Henry; you may do likewise), until he meets— on May 5, 1821: the day, as it happens, of Napoleon's death—the writer of that coded letter.

In mid-January they raise St. Helena, looming sheer and volcanic from the southern ocean; they lie to for several days just below the western horizon, out of sight of the telegraphs, and seize the first small fishing smack that wanders into reach. Its crew are regaled, handsomely bribed for the imposition, promised more if all goes well, and threatened with death, pirate-style, if all does not. Two of their number are comfortably detained as hostages, obliged to switch clothes with Cook and Lafitte, and closely interrogated. They agree that despite the Admiralty's semaphore telegraphs and strengthened fortification of the island's four landing places, fishermen come and go as usual from footpaths down the cliffs, which rise in places twelve hundred feet straight out of the sea. Aside from vertigo, there should be no problem in getting ashore. They even know a concealed vantage point from which to survey Longwood, a favorite leisure pastime among them. But on the question whether their celebrated new resident is the former emperor of the French, there is no consensus: one vows he is, though "much changed" by captivity and systematic poisoning; another swears he was replaced a year ago; a third that he was never on the island.

Andrew and Jean go ashore (Andrew mimics the island dialect in half an hour); they make the dizzy climb from a precarious landing ledge just behind a surf-breaking rock on the island's sea-fogged northwest shore, entirely concealed from the official landing at St. James's Bay. A fortnight's reconnoitering among the villagers and the garrison discovers the same variety of opinion, in more detail: the prisoner is dying of undulant fever, of venereal complications, of pyloric cancer, of boredom and inaction, of arsenic, of dysentery or hepatitis or typhus. He has gone mad, believes himself an ordinary conscript arrested and exiled by an accident of resemblance. He *is* that hapless conscript. He is an impostor, Metternich's creature. He is dead.

They ascend through subtropical greenery to the temperate middle elevations, thick with cedars and willows, through Geranium Valley to the fishermen's trysting and viewing spot, a dense bower of shrubs, withes, and creepers overlooking the tidy château of Longwood. Supplied by their hired comrades with food, wine, and blankets for the chill nights, they make a little encampment. Andrew identifies Count and Mme Bertrand, the Count de Montholon. One evening a short tubby chap in military uniform steps into the gardens (modeled in miniature after those of Malmaison) and pops desultorily with dueling pistols at a nearby goat and chicken, striking neither. A bored attendant reloads the weapons. The hidden onlookers turn from their spyglasses: Andrew nods.

I was fairly satisfy'd it was he, he reports to Andrée, *tho indeed* much changed *since Rochefort & Tor Bay. What most gratify'd me was that Jean was less sure, and must take my word for it. Also, that one glance assured me I could manage the counterfeit, once the substitution had been arranged. Our plan was that Jean would take* Jean Blanque *up to the newly establisht Republic of Liberia for provisioning, & perhaps seize a Spaniard or two along the way for profit's sake, returning at the Vernal Equinox. He would leave with me, "for my assistance," his 2nd mate, Maurice Shomberg, a Pyrenean Sephardic Jew call'd by the Baratarians "le Maure" for his dark skin, great size & strength, and ferocity in combat: a man much given to the slicing & dicing of his enemies, and utterly loyal to the brothers Lafitte. Whilst le Maure watcht & waited in the bush, I was to install myself among the gardeners & grounds keepers of Longwood, recruit if I could the confidence of Mme Bertrand (who was known to be impatient with her exile & jealous of Mme de Montholon), verify that the Emperor was the Emperor, sound his temper on the matter of escaping, present our (forged) credentials from Joseph B. & Mayor Girod, & cet. & cet., finally delivering him to le Maure upon Jean's return & taking his place at Longwood. In fact, I meant to do all of those save the last two, and was both reassured, by Jean's leaving with me his trusty "Moor," that he would probably return for us in March; and confirm'd that he no longer trusted me to do the job alone. Le Maure's great size and visibility were no aid to concealment; he was fit only for hauling & killing, and might well be assign'd to dispatch me to the sharks, once Napoleon was in our hands.*

Lafitte leaves. Andrew befriends one or two of the gardeners, is put to work spading, manuring, terracing. He converses in Sicilian with Vignali, the auxiliary priest sent out only a few months before in the party from Rome, who declares that Napoleon is Napoleon but won't be for long: the Count de Montholon is poisoning him from jealousy of Count Bertrand. He speaks Corsican French with Montholon's valet: the British doctors are feeding arsenic to the lot of them. He peddles a pilchard to Ortini, the emperor's own footman: the new Italian doctor, Antommarchi, is the villain, assisted by Mme Bertrand. The French and Italians agree that Napoleon is Napoleon, and that he is nowise interested in escape. But among the fishermen and farmers who provision Longwood, and with whom both le Maure and Andrew carefully converse, there is more general suspicion that the French are conspiring to trick and/or to blame the English, an opinion shared in some measure by the British physicians on Sir Hudson Lowe's staff: some believe Bonaparte—"if that's who the rascal is"—to be poisoning himself, in order to consummate his martyrdom and inspire sympathy for his son's succession. The only hypothesis not seriously entertained on the island is the one Andrew Cook more and more inclines to as his deadline nears: that while the ailing fellow who ever less frequently ventures outdoors (and in March takes to his bed almost constantly) just might be an impostor, and just might be being poisoned by one or a number of "interests," he is most probably Napoleon Bonaparte dying in his fifty-second year of a variety of natural physical and psychological complaints.

So mutual are everyone's suspicions among the Longwood entourage, so clear (however mixed with grief for their leader) their eagerness to begone, Andrew dares take none into his confidence; and there is no use in relaying his "credentials" to an obviously dying man. It becomes his job to persuade le Maure that he has already made contact with the emperor, who looks forward eagerly to rescue and who is feigning illness the better to isolate himself from English surveillance and mislead suspected traitors in his own household. The equinox approaches, but Andrew's inventiveness fails him: how on earth to get himself delivered to Lafitte and le Maure as the emperor of the French, and at the same time persuade them that "André Castine" is ensconced in Longwood, composing the emperor's last will and testament? He had not anticipated so universal and profound distrust, such general assumptions of conspiracy, counterconspiracy, double- and triple-agentry!

Word comes from le Maure that *Jean Blanque* has returned on schedule. Lafitte himself slips ashore, cool and smiling. With not the slightest notion how to manage it, Andrew assures him that all is arranged: after moonset next night, two of Bonaparte's household—the lamplighter Rousseau and the usher Chauvin—will deliver their master to the trysting place. Bonaparte will be harmlessly narcotized, to exculpate him from charges of complicity should the escape be foiled by the British. He is in mild ill health, but expects to recover, the more rapidly for a bracing ocean voyage and release from captivity. He has reservations about the Louisiana Project, but is open to persuasion. Rousseau and Chauvin are acting in their master's best interest, but will not refuse a just reward for their risk. Et cetera! Andrew even invites the Baratarian to slip back to Longwood next day and receive a signal from himself that the substitution has been successful; that he will carry through the charade of dying, return to the ranks of the fishermen, and confidently await his own rescue.

Desperate improvisation! He expects many questions, whether anxious or suspicious: Lafitte merely embraces him with a light smile, wishes him *bonne chance,* promises to be in the appointed place at the appointed hour on the morrow.

Throughout the 21st Cook conjures "shift after desperate shift," and can hit upon nothing even remotely likely. He has not got through to the invalid prisoner. He has no confidence in Rousseau, Chauvin, Ortini; barely knows them. Beyond bribing a suit of Napoleon's clothes from a laundry girl (the loss causes little stir; souvenir pilfering and counterfeiting are an industry on the island), he has been able to make no arrangements whatever. In a lifetime of stratagems and ruses he has never been so nonplussed.

At moondown he dons those clothes, assumes his "private," "true" imposture of Napoleon, modified by what little he has seen and learned on the island. He conceals himself in the Longwood gardens, in the vague hope that Rousseau or Chauvin might wander by and be impressed into service. The hour arrives; no one is about except the regular British sentries. Feeling more nakedly foolhardy than at any moment since that night a quarter-century past when he donned Joel Barlow's clothes and rode out to a certain Algerian headland, to enter a certain dark carriage, Andrew works through the cypresses and privet, past the sentries, toward where le Maure and Lafitte await. Can he perhaps feign detection, mimic several alarmed voices, simulate the thrash of two servants fleeing, bring the sentries running, and then stumble as if dazed into the rendezvous? *Faute de mieux,* he gathers himself to it. . .

And somewhile later woke half-tranced, knowing neither where I was nor how I came there! Bloodsworth Island? 1812? Husht urgent voices all about, in a medley of accents: French, Corsican, Italian, German, English, St. Helenish, even Yankee! A thunder of surf, & the damp rock under me, bespoke that ledge we had barely fetcht up on two months past. I guess't I had either swoon'd again, as at New Orleans & Fort Bowyer, or been knockt senseless by "friend" or "foe," & carry'd down that terrific cliff. I heard Jean's voice, unalarm'd, giving orders to le Maure & the fishermen. Who was that German? That New Englander? Was that a British female whisper'd?

He conceals regaining consciousness in hopes of making out his situation; permits himself to be rowed like a dead man for hours out to sea, hoisted easily over a shoulder he recognizes as le Maure's, and put to bed in a familiar aft cabin of the *Jean Blanque*—but nothing he can overhear tells him what he craves to know. Now there is a lantern-light to peek by: he sees Lafitte *tête-à-tête* with a cloaked stranger; whispers are exchanged, papers, a small pouch or box? They examine a map. They agree. The stranger leaves; Lafitte also; one can hear orders given on deck, sail made. The schooner swings about and settles under way.

Andrew considers the possibilities. His ruse has perhaps been anticipated by Lafitte, by the U.S. Secret Service, by Metternich, the British, the French. They know he is Andrew Cook, but see fit to support his imposture? Or they *don't* know; the imposture has for the moment succeeded! In the first case he must be candid with Lafitte or lose what trust after all remains; in the second, such candor might be fatal—and both suppositions could be incorrect. Should he pretend to be a willing Napoleon? An outraged, resentful one? An unperturbed Andrew Cook?

He feels his way carefully: "wakes" as if uncertain himself who and where he is; is greeted politely but ambiguously by Jean's body-servant, by Lafitte himself, whose ironical courtesies fit either hypothesis. On deck the Baratarians receive him as the ailing Bonaparte he pretends to be, but are under obvious and sensible orders not to address him by any name. With Jean, in private, he hazards maintaining that imposture, and is puzzled: the man's half-mocking deference suits neither the belief that he has rescued his emperor nor the knowledge that his erstwhile comrade has deceived him. He begins to suspect that Lafitte believes him to be neither Napoleon Bonaparte nor Andrew Cook, but the impostor alleged to have been substituted for Napoleon in January 1820—and that this state of affairs is for some reason acceptable to him!

But he cannot be certain, and so the voyage proceeds in an extraordinary equivocality, every gesture and remark a potential test, or sign. Where are they bound? "To America." And to where in America? "To that place arranged for Your Majesty by his friends there." Andrew is greatly encouraged to be presented after all, however ironically, with the agreed-upon ultimatum: to live incognito under Joseph's protection (Lafitte does not say "your brother's") or, as General Bonaparte (Lafitte says neither "as yourself" nor "as the Emperor Napoleon I"), to lead a movement organized by American Bonapartists "both exiled and native, of great wealth and influence."

He will choose, Andrew declares, when he has spoken to Joseph and the movement's leaders and heard more details. Meanwhile it is surely best to remain incognito, if only officially, even between themselves.

Jean smiles. "I shall call you Baron Castine."

Andrew smiles the same smile. "That is a name I know. It will quite do."

Then he takes a great gamble. In a tone he hopes appropriate to whatever might be Lafitte's understanding of him, he observes that no matter what fate awaits him in America, it is unlikely he will see again the land of his birth or, as it were, the theater of his life's first cycle (the phrase is Andrew's). Though he has a brother in America, the rest of his family are elsewhere. He does not expect to see his wife again; as for his son, that is too delicate a matter to venture upon at present. And his brothers and sisters are too various, either in their loyalty or in their good judgment, to place overmuch faith in just now. (Andrew speaks in

627

these epithets rather than in proper names, watching Jean's face.) But his mother, he declares, while less ill than himself, is old and cannot be expected either to live a great while longer or to undertake a transatlantic voyage. He would therefore like to pay her a call—incognito, if necessary—and bid her a last farewell before commencing his new career.

Lafitte seem'd genuinely astonisht, & without apparent guile demanded, Did I really propose a voyage into European waters under the flag of Cartagena? I took heart & breath, & told him (with just enough smile to cover my tracks), I was sure that a vessel & captain able to spirit Napoleon Bonaparte from St. Helena were able to sail him thro the Pillars of Hercules, pass him within sight of Corsica, whisk him straight up the Tiber, and land him on the steps of the Palazzo Rinuccini. That he could, if he did not trust me, keep me every moment in his view, & impose what conditions and disguises seem'd to him advisable. But that I was resolved to have a last word with my mother ere I was fetcht to my next destiny. He appear'd to consider. I made bold to enquire at once whether he was under someone's orders to the contrary, or regarded my proposal as too audacious. . .

The fact is, Lafitte then acknowledges, his men have been at sea for above half a year without shore liberty, and a vessel in the *Jean Blanque's* trade never lacks for alternative colors, name boards, and registry papers. But can it be true that "Baron Castine" has nothing in mind beyond bidding his mother adieu?

Not quite, I reply'd, in as level a tone as I could manage: I hoped also to have a word with her confessor. I heard him mutter: Nom de Dieu!

No more is said. Their watering stop in the Cape Verde Islands is noncommittal, a reasonable jumping-off place to either the Caribbean or the Mediterranean. But their course thence, to Andrew's great joy, is north, not west; before long they raise the Canaries, then Madeira. By April's end they have traversed the Strait of Bonifacio between Sardinia and Corsica (*"I dofft my hat, & look'd toward Ajaccio, & said nothing. . ."*) and are anchored in the marshy mouth of the Tiber, off ancient Ostia.

Only then, writes Andrew, *I went to Lafitte & thankt him. He responded, as quizzical as ever, I was welcome, for the excursion & for his company. Which latter he trusted I would not object to, as his life depended upon my safe delivery to America. This was the 1st clear acknowledgment that he was not his own man—tho he may have invoked it by way of excusing his close surveillance.*

Thus it occurred, as all biographies of the Bonapartes attest, that on the morning of May 5, 1821 (by coincidence the day, though not the hour, of Napoleon's death on St. Helena), a "well-dressed Napoleonic stranger" invaded the Palazzo Rinuccini, made his way by sheer authority of mien past guards and attendants into the presence of Letizia Ramolino Bonaparte, "Madame Mère," and (as his equally elegant companion, unmentioned in the chronicles, stood by, dabbing at his tears with a fine linen handkerchief) bowed and kissed that matron's hand, touched a crucifix to her lips, and assured her that her famous son was "free from his sufferings, and happy"; that she would one day surely see him again; and that by mid-century the nations of the world would be racked by such civil strife and conflagration as to make St. Helena seem a paradise.

He bows again and leaves. Devoted son and good Roman Catholic that he is, Jean Lafitte embraces him outside the palace, begs his pardon for having doubted his motives, and declares that scene to have been the noblest he has ever been witness to (his words, Andrew notes, would apply as well to a loyal Bonapartist as to Bonaparte). An attendant overtakes them with a gift of gold Napoleons from Mme Mère. Andrew at once bestows it upon Lafitte for the trouble and expense of this diversion, reserving only two coins: one he gives the servant, in exchange for information concerning the whereabouts of his lady's spiritual advisor, Mme Kleinmüller, with whom he has business. They are informed with a smile that that worthy has been exposed (by Pauline) and dismissed from the household as a fraud: she was not even Swiss! But she is said to be living in the northern outskirts of the city, at an address near the Villa Ada, and to be awaiting the arrival from Geneva of her wealthy American lover, whose influence she hopes will restore her to favor in the Palazzo Rinuccini.

To Lafitte, Andrew declares that he must deal alone with this woman who so egregiously imposed upon Mme Mère, to his own detriment, for so long—though his guardian may if he wishes not only accompany him to the Via Chiana but surround the address with Baratarians to assure his not "escaping." The proposition involves a calculated risk: that Lafitte might be, as Mme Kleinmüller reportedly was, in the service of Metternich. But Jean declares himself satisfied with "the baron's" honor: he will of course escort him to the house and back to their ship, but the interview will be as private and as lengthy as monsieur desires. He even offers a knife, which Andrew accepts only when Lafitte assures him, with a small smile, that he carries others, and a pistol as well.

They find the quarter, the street, the number, an unimpressive *pensione,* and are told by the landlord that no Mme Kleinmüller lives there, only a *vedova spagnuola* of the highest respectability. Would he be so gracious, Andrew inquires, as to deliver to that same widow a note of his respects? He presents it for Lafitte's inspection, declaring it to be "in the family cipher": it reads *VS DRYEJRI G.G.* Lafitte shrugs. Very well, thinks Andrew: if he is in Betsy Patterson Bonaparte's pay, he is at least not privy to her cipher. With a tip of one gold Napoleon for his trouble, the landlord goes off with the message. Andrew winks, shakes Lafitte's hand, taps the dagger in his waistcoat, and steps quickly inside the house, "praying to the Muse of Imposture" that Jean will not follow.

For all my assurances, that he was welcome to follow me & cet., were merest bluff, he now acknowledges. *Had he lay'd eyes upon "G.G." of the familiar flourish, he had surely known her face at once, as off Tobago I had finally known her hand. And knowing her, he would have known me, and all been lost. But he stopt there on the threshold, even as a cry of female joy was heard upstairs. I winkt again, closed the door betwixt us, was directed above by Signor the concierge, & was met at the door of her chamber by* VS *(& Betsy Bonaparte's)* DRYEJRI G.G.: *Consuelo del Consulado.*

An alarmed, handsome forty, "C.C." draws back—she had expected either Betsy's footman or Mme B. herself, come down at last from Geneva. Then in an instant she sees through Andrew's disguise and dashes with a cry to her dressing table.

But my hand at her mouth, & my knife at her throat, prevented her [from availing herself of the little pistol Andrew now espies there and confiscates]. *I vow'd to her I meant her no harm, nor was of any mind to publish her identity. That my life was forfeit if she should publish mine. That I knew her to have got intimate by some wise with Mme B., & to have posed as the Swiss clairvoyant Kleinmüller, to what end and in whose service I could not say. That I was come thither, thousands of miles out of my way, not to trouble her life but to save my own, to which end I sought no more from her than her story since our parting in Bordeaux half a dozen years past. In return wherefor, I would tell her mine or not, as she wisht, and be on my parlous way.*

He now takes his final risk. His difficulty in recognizing Consuelo's penmanship—after reading so many hundreds of pages of her manuscript fiction!—had been owing to the cipher, its unfamiliarity and noncursive letters. The identification made (nearly eight months since!) he had understood not only that Betsy Bonaparte's Roman informant was, of all people on the planet, his erstwhile lover, but that she was very possibly, by some series of chances, that lady's *secret suisse*—and that therefore Mme B. knew more about him than he had supposed, and from a particularly disaffected source, his last farewell to whom had been a bitter business. Nevertheless he now releases her, compliments her appearance, and (though retaining the pistol) resumes the manner and mien of Andrew Cook IV.

Consuelo sat; I too. She lookt me up & down; lookt away; lookt back; shook her head; reacht for her reticule. Another pistol, I wonder'd? Or the famous poison'd snuffbox? But she fetcht forth a mere silk handkerchief (gift from me in Halifax), wherewith to wipe her eyes as she rehearst her tale.

She has, she tells him, embarked since their last parting on a "Second Cycle" of her own, inspired by his rejection of her and by a certain subsequent humiliation. Against Renato Beluche she bore no grudge: he had made clear from the first the terms of their connection, and though she had hoped he might change his mind, she remained grateful for his protection. Nor could she blame Andrew for not loving her more, in Algiers, in Halifax, in New Orleans. Who can command love? Of the men in her life, only three had truly victimized her: Don Escarpio, of whom more presently; a certain ensign aboard that dispatch boat from Halifax to Bermuda in 1814, who upon a certain Gulf Stream night when she was downcast by Andrew's teasing criticisms of her novel, had sworn to withdraw before ejaculating and had then, with a laugh, forsworn; and Joseph Bonaparte, whose patronage she had sought after all, for want of better, at Andrew's

630

suggestion, in Bordeaux in 1815, and who had not only neglected to give her the letter of introduction to Mme de Staël which he had promised in exchange for an hour in his bedchamber (he was summoned out by an urgent message from Napoleon in Rochefort, and never got back to either his *coitus interruptus* or to his payment therefor), but had neglected as well to advise her that he was enjoying a mild gonorrhea.

(*I broke in to protest that I had offer'd her just such a letter, with no clapp attacht! She reply'd, 'Twas not from me she wanted it, or anything, not then. . .*)

Disgusted, she had made her way to Leghorn, sought out Mme de Staël there on her own, been generously received by that lady on the strength of what she acknowledges having pled, in tears: her past connection with Andrew Cook; and while being cured of her venereal infection, had helped nurse Germaine's ailing husband back toward health. Indeed she had made herself so useful to her heroine (who did not share Consuelo's weariness with men, but sympathized with it and introduced her to the idea, but not to the practice, of *le saphisme*) that Mme de Staël had brought her back in her retinue to Coppet and Paris. In that city, *chez* Germaine, she had met a truly sister spirit, the aggrieved but undaunted Betsy Patterson Bonaparte, with whom, on the strength of their common ill-handling by Napoleon's brothers, she had become friends. More exactly, with Germaine's fascinated encouragement, the two women had become first friends, then quite close friends, then finally and briefly (the first such experience for either) more than friends.

Unsettled by that adventure, Betsy had returned to Baltimore, where she put by her disposition against Joseph Bonaparte and sought him out, in her son's interest, at Point Breeze. Consuelo had remained behind to attend Mme de Staël, whose own health was failing. For a time the two refrained from correspondence—the very time, as it happens, when Andrew had made Betsy's reacquaintance and interested her in his project of rescuing the chief of the Bonapartes. Mme de Staël died, with her last breath encouraging Consuelo, should she ever take pen again in hand, to "rework that little business of the poison'd snuffbox," a device she could wish to have employed in her own life against more men than one.

Her words inspire Consuelo not to literature but to that aforementioned "Second Cycle." She is 37, without husband, children, lovers, or further wish for them. She considers writing to Betsy; decides not to. Recalling Andrew's program of "correcting his life's first half," she conceives a project of revenge against the man "who had 1st corrupted her, & whose life was a catalogue of such corruptions": Don Escarpio! She goes to Rome, where she understands him to have made an infamous reputation as agent of the anti-Bonapartist secret police; she intends by some means—perhaps a poisoned letter opener!—to end his wicked life, at whatever risk to herself. But she has been prevented: a certain opera singer of that city, whose sexual favors Don Escarpio had demanded as payment for her lover's release from the political prison at Castel Sant' Angelo, has availed herself of an *un*poisoned letter opener to stab him through the heart.

At once thus gratified and thwarted—and nearly out of funds—Consuelo is reduced to two equally disagreeable options: appealing to her friend Mme B. for money on the strength of their brief but extraordinary connection, or attempting another novel, perhaps on the subject of Don Escarpio. But the former smacks of blackmail, and for the second, despite a promising title (whose promise is perhaps diminished in literal translation: *The Woman before Whom the Man before Whom All Rome Trembled Trembled),* she has come to understand she has not the talent. Her investigations, however, and her credentials from Mme de Staël, have led her into Roman anti-Bonapartist circles from the early years of the century, in which there is concern that the habitation in that city of Napoleon's mother, uncle, sister, and two brothers (Lucien and Louis), will generate schemes for his rescue and return to Europe. Consuelo herself is nonpolitical—and lonely, and at loose ends. She is befriended by, and for a modest stipend becomes the assistant of, a fellow lodger in her *pensione,* one Mme Kleinmüller, who is in the service of these anti-Bonapartists. . .

Andrew interrupts: she was not herself this Mme Kleinmüller? She has no gift for imposture, Consuelo replies—nor for dissembling, nor for fiction. She was Mme K.'s assistant. The spiritualist herself was now returned in discredit to her ultimate employer, Prince Metternich, whose object it was to discover and forestall all rescue attempts. Consuelo's own object, in the beginning, had been merely to survive; a remarkable letter from Betsy Bonaparte, received fortuitously at just this time (1817, when Andrew was busy with the Lakanal affair), gives her a new purpose. So far from having forgotten their brief affair, Betsy confesses that it has changed her life: ambitious as ever for her son, for herself she now craves "something more," which she dares not spell out in plain English. She encloses the Patterson family cipher, begs Consuelo to set forth in it her own feelings. . .

An impassioned correspondence follows. Betsy vows to return with Bo to Europe, and to her "sweetest consolation," as soon as the boy's schooling permits, perhaps 1820. Meanwhile she is delighted to learn of her friend's connections in Rome, so useful to her plans, which she now presumes to call *theirs.* While pretending to support Joseph Bonaparte's schemes to retrieve his brother from St. Helena, she has hatched a scheme of her own, which Consuelo can immeasurably abet from her position in the Palazzo Rinuccini. It is Metternich's policy with a difference: to deter all rescue operations except her own! From past acquaintance Betsy knows Mme Mère to be gullible; Mme Kleinmüller's imposition on her will be justified by the fact of her son's rescue. Consuelo accepts another retainer; their correspondence through 1818 and 1819 is an excited mixture of love, plans for their future, and present business. Consuelo is able to serve her American friend without really betraying Mme Kleinmüller, given the partial congruence of their interests. What is more, she *believes* in the spirit voices, table rapping, and the rest, which her efforts assist Mme K. in conjuring.

It is not until early in 1820 that Betsy mentions by name her "principal American agent" in the St. Helena scheme: a "handsome, worldly, & agreeable fellow" who, if he were but of the gentry and she not done for ever and all with men, she could even imagine as a lover: one Andrew Cook, of Maryland and Canada. Consuelo's urgent, appalled reply, warning Betsy not to trust of all men *that* one, comes too late: Andrew has already disappeared, to Betsy and Joseph's consternation. Mme B. wonders whether he has not been all along an agent of the U.S. Secret Service; whether Metternich might not in fact have arranged for Napoleon's covert assassination or removal, and his replacement with an impostor. She urges Consuelo to extricate herself from Mme Kleinmüller, and makes hasty preparations to leave Baltimore. For appearances' sake she will settle with Bo in Geneva; her father's friend John Jacob Astor is there, and will surely urge her to visit the Roman Bonapartes, with whom he is close. Thus she will discreetly rejoin Consuelo, and they can assess both the St. Helena situation and their own.

The letter arrives just when Pauline Borghese finally persuades Mme Mère that the clairvoyant is a fraud; that Napoleon is ill, perhaps dying, perhaps dead. Mme Kleinmüller vanishes; Consuelo withdraws to her *pensione* and anxiously awaits her friend, fearing daily she will be done violence to by Pauline's hirelings, or Metternich's, or the late unlamented Don Escarpio's.

She concludes her tale. Her friend "Doña Betsy" has put aside her ambition to rescue and marry Napoleon for her son's sake; it is Consuelo she now desires, and Consuelo her. She is in Geneva already, and on the advice of Señor Astor will soon come to Rome. In the fall, her son will return to America to enter Harvard, perhaps also to marry Joseph Bonaparte's daughter; Betsy and Consuelo will retire to Switzerland, officially traveling companions, in fact a couple.

She then implored me, writes Andrew, *by whatever love I had once felt for her, not to obstruct this innocent aim. That she cared not whether I kill'd or saved Napoleon, or how I might re-draught the map of the world or the script of History, so I left her & her friend in peace. That the sole grudge she bore me was for having encouraged a talent she never possest, for writing novels. For the rest, she felt only gratitude: for my having more than once helpt her out of a parlous corner, & for what affection we had shared. That whatever my present danger, she wisht me safely out of it, & would aid me any way I ask'd. And that she hoped, once I was free of it, I would beg pardon of the woman I had abused long & sorely, by my absence: yourself, whom she bid me make amends to even if*, as might be, *I found you to have follow'd in your disappointment her & Betsy Bonaparte's path, to* el safismo!

Much moved *("& by this last not a little alarm'd")*, Andrew tells Consuelo the truth about Napoleon as he knows it: that the man on St.

Helena is dying, has no wish to be rescued, and thinks only of his son, "l'Aiglon," a virtual prisoner in Augsburg. ("They will poison him too," declares Consuelo.) His own tentative plan for "Doña Betsy" Andrew does not mention, and now quietly discards; but he reminds Consuelo of his original high ideals vis-à-vis the Louisiana Project, and the Indian Free State before it, in which good cause he hopes she will enlist Mme B.'s aid. Why should such a sovereign general sanctuary as he envisioned not extend also to such as her newly discovered self? Why not "a vast New Switzerland, or New New World to the opprest, where not only black & red & white, but women & men, may abide as equals"? And he will, he pledges—if Jean Lafitte does not discover and dispatch him to the sharks—make amends to Andrée upon his return. Herself he wishes success in her life's Second Cycle, with which he pledges not to interfere—but he cannot leave without knowing whether her disconcerting speculation about his wife was based upon more than just her own experience. Has Consuelo somehow had news from Castines Hundred?

She reply'd, I could take her life before she would reply—shrewd insurance that I would make good my pledge! But tho she doubted so bold a creature as my "New New World" would come to light in our century, she promist to speak favorably to Betsy B. of the Louisiana Project. She then bid me adios (*not* hasta la vista) *with words that dizzy'd me almost into a "Bloodsworth Island Swoon," to wit: that she fear'd I was become the counterfeit, not of Napoleon, but of Andrew Cook. And that the cypher whose key I had yet to hit upon, was my own self.*

They kiss farewell ("after a fashion," Andrew says unkindly—but he is writing to Andrée); he draws a breath, resumes the mien of Napoleon disguised as "Baron Castine," and steps outside. Jean Lafitte waits patiently, to all appearances indifferent to both the length and the issue of this interlude; Andrew returns the knife without comment. Nor does his cautious conversation, as they make their way back across the city and down the Tiber to their ship, give him any clue to how much Jean understands, or what his purpose is. (Their way takes them through the Piazza di Spagna. One wants to call across the fifteen decades, "Stay! Put by a moment these vague intrigues, this nonsense of Napoleon: young John Keats has just died here!")

A hard suspense, he remarks, *which lasted thro our crossing, & is not yet resolved.* They stop three weeks in Genoa to reprovision *Jean Blanque* and give the crew shore liberty (Lafitte "firmly requests" his passenger to remain aboard), then set out westward at the end of May. Neither killed nor challenged nor put at his ease, our ancestor finds it no problem to maintain with Lafitte a tentative attitude concerning the Louisiana Project, for he has begun to question it himself. Jean's sustained ironic solicitude makes Andrew reckless: he asks directly, Is that daring fellow who arranged his rescue himself to be rescued, or left languishing on St. Helena? *He no longer languishes there,* Lafitte replies with a smile, adding that he is not at liberty to say more.

*Thus we arrived, early in July, at what I knew to be the Virginia Capes, &
sail'd on up the Chesapeake, leaving Tangier & Smith Islands to* port, *till we
came within sight of fateful Bloodsworth! I feign'd not to know the waters, and
asking, was told no more than that they were full of sharks and alligators, to keep
strangers off. We enter'd the marshy Manokin—where neither shark nor 'gator
ever swum—and anchor'd off the King plantation, which too Jean said he could
not name: only that I was to be sequester'd there in safety & comfort till my
brother came for me, a fortnight or less. I was fetcht ashore, found the owners
"off on the Grand Tour," & the house in charge of a well-manner'd staff who
lookt neither Baratarian nor Eastern Shore. They show'd me my quarters,
comfortable indeed, & inform'd us wryly that news had just reacht the U. States
of Napoleon's death on St. Helena on May 5.* Le roi est mort, *shrugg'd Jean:*
vive le roi. *Next morning he bade me* adieu (*not* au revoir) *& sail'd off, "to
take the good news to Louisiana, & to rescue André Castine." And here I have
languisht full six weeks since.*

His attendants are as polite and noncommittal as Lafitte. When the
promised fortnight extends to a month with no word from anyone, they
apologize. Andrew stages imperial tantrums at the restriction on his
movements: he is free to stroll the grounds of Beverly without
(apparent) surveillance, but forbidden "for his own protection" to leave
the estate. They regret but have no authority to relax their orders. He
suspects the secret service, Joseph Bonaparte, Betsy Patterson; perhaps
all of them in concert; perhaps—long delayed and skillfully managed
retribution—at Andrée's direction!

By mid-August, convinced that he has been transported "from one
St. Helena to another" and afraid for his sanity, he resolves to escape to
nearby Bloodsworth, to *"regain* [his] *bearings at the spot where 1st* [he] *lost
them,"* and then make his way to Castines Hundred, to whatever he
might find there. His long, ambiguous confinement—extending really
from his swoon on St. Helena—and Consuelo's parting words have now
persuaded him that the Louisiana Project, indeed his whole original
conception of a Second Revolution, has been misconceived; that the *true*
Revolution, while it might well end in politics, does not begin there. . .

It is now past midnight by my old Breguet, he concludes: *my father's
timepiece, to which I cling as if it were the key to me. They do not know I know
these marshes as I once knew my mother's face, or your own dear flesh. Chère
Andrée: if you receive this letter, it will signify that "Napoleon" has made good
his 3rd escape, has survived the only sharks & alligators hereabouts (those of his
treacherous imagination), & is headed home!*

Receive it she does, we know, at year's end, at this address. Andrée
is 32; the twins are 9. Does she decipher, read, believe it? We do not
know. Its author never appears, at least in his own person. For four
years more his "widow" takes no action. Andrew's former young
acquaintance J. F. Cooper publishes his second novel, *The Spy,* and
embarks on the Leatherstocking series. Great Romantics expire:
Hoffmann, Shelley, Byron. Two French natural scientists, Prévost and

Dumas, prove that the spermatozoan is essential to fertilization; Beethoven finishes the last of the nine symphonies.

At the urging of her friend John Jacob Astor, Betsy Patterson Bonaparte visits Rome from Geneva and is warmly received by the surviving family of the late emperor; the marriage of her son to Joseph's daughter Charlotte is arranged but never comes to pass, perhaps owing to a quarrel between Betsy and Pauline Borghese. Chagrined, Mme B. returns with a traveling companion to Geneva, "Bo" to America, where to his mother's exasperation he will marry for love a pretty and well-to-do New Englander named Susan May Williams, and settle happily in Baltimore. Betsy herself will not return until 1834, when her companion (then 54) succumbs, apparently to food poisoning. She never revisits Europe thereafter, but becomes the reclusive, snappish, coldly beautiful real-estate millionaire of Maryland legend, who in her 94th year—disappointed in her final dream of seeing her grandson crowned king of the South after the Civil War—is buried in a lonely plot of Greenmount Cemetery, in accordance with her wish "to be by [her]self."

But *that* is the history, already lettered, of Henry and Henrietta Cook Burlingame V, called to their vocation by the letter and pocket-watch sent them in 1827 by "Ebenezer Burling of Richmond," companion of young Edgar Poe. By then Andrée will have done what we have seen her do, and disappeared into the western fastness.

Thus the long chronicle of Andrew Cook IV trails off into the same marshy equivocation that engendered it. The fate of his utopian "Louisiana Project," as of his Indian Free State, is all too evident: the "militant" Indian nationalist movements of our time are to his and Tecumseh's dream as was Napoleon III's Second Empire—that grandiose, self-conscious paradigm of the Freudian "compulsion to repeat"—to the First: pitiable travesty.

Must we not conclude the same of the Second Cycle of Andrew's life? Was not it, was not he, a failure? Has not our whole line been, Henry, from Ebenezer Cooke the first laureate of Maryland and his tutor Henry Burlingame down to you and me? For that is whom we are come to, having traversed, between Andrew's prenatal and his posthumous letters, all the intervening Cooks and Burlingames: the genealogical bottom line. Am I not myself, in my courtship of Betsy Patterson's descendant for the sake (I mean *also* for the sake) of our cause, become my namesake's pallid parody, and in my own Second Cycle the impersonator of myself?

Before the untimely death of Andrew Cook VI—and the wedding of Jane Mack to Baron André Castine of Castines Hundred—you shall hear, upon these questions, from

Your loving father

C: *Jerome Bray to Bea Golden.* *Inviting her to star in the first epic of Numerature.*

Comalot, R.D. 2
Lily Dale, N.Y., U.S.A. 14752

8/5/69

Mrs. Bea Golden (a.k.a. "Bibi," "Jeannine Mack," etc.; t.b.k.a. Regina de Nominatrix)
Remobilization Farm
Fort Erie, Ontario, Canada

My dear Mrs. Golden,
Certainly a star of your magnitude must receive numbers of letters in each day's post: solicitations to model as the heroine of somebody's counterrevolutionary novel; to play the lead in somebody's film derived from such a novel; et cetera. But a rising star reset should spurn such obsolescent media, soon to be superseded by coaxial television and laser holography, ultimately by a medium far more revolutionary, its essence the very key to and measure of the universe. This is to invite you to spray your past with dichlorodiphenyltrichloroethane and take wing to your golden future, a future impatient to be RESET Mariner-7 takes 1st close-ups of Mars surface Miami blacked out Niagara Falls helicopter crashes Oil leak in Lake Erie.
Hum. *Numerature!*
Permit us to introduce our new self with apologies for our old. (Much better, LIL.) We are the former 10 2 2, a.k.a. Jerome B. Bray, of the former Lilyvac Farm, R.D. 2, Lily Dale, N.Y., U.S.A. 14752, born in the Backwater Wildlife Refuge and RESET Our ungallant pursuit of you; our apparent, even actual derangement since Passover and particularly since Independence Day use dash to indicate break in syntax and recommencement—these are owing to the overflow of my spirit's vesicles as it were. *Cf.* W. Shakespeare's seminal equation: lunatic = lover = poet; also the wreckage or frenzy of Greek mythic figures, in particular Io, after mating with gods and gadblanks. What indeed is inspiration if not the swelling that follows the Godflow's bite? The real star of the myth of Bellerophon is not RESET Who believes he can achieve mythic herohood by perfectly imitating the Heroic Pattern and who learns that by doing so what one becomes is a perfect imitation of a mythic hero no doubt a heroic mimicry in itself but not quite the same thing heh heh. It is not the triple beast Chimera nor is it the pinioned pony Pegasus (O LIL). *It is the Gadflaw!* And who was that poor mad fellow 10 2 2 a.k.a. RESET A lost chord on LILYVAC's intromittent organ as it were, a stingee of the Godflew New paragraph.
M. Bernstein was but the mere anticipation of her ex-stepmother!

637

LILYVAC will deal with her; in the meanwhile she deserves R. Prinz, who was never worth 1 grain of your pollen as it were. That's a figure there heh semicolon a digit of speech RESET And Marsha Blank, number of our enemies, was but an unsuccessful tryout for your role, 1 of numerous understudies so to speak recruited and prepared during our Casting Season, which now approaches its culminating scenes: Rout of the Dromes, Fertilization of the Queen. No matter that in a kind of coma she let loose the goats and herself strayed from the fold; when the hour comes so shall she, plenty, see below, who 1st inspired our Gadblank Illuminations of 7/4 and later, playing at your destined role, gave LILYVAC's domain its new and proper appellation see above. Final casting to be completed by 8/14, immediately whereafter, with the Fall Work Period, we commence "shooting" (a figure of RESET 1858 Cyrus Field completes 1st Atlantic cable and Queen Victoria exchanges greetings with President Buchanan. 1864 Union Admiral Farragut wins Battle of Mobile Bay. 1945 Hiroshima A-bombed. 1966 *Giles Goat-Boy* published, imperfect mimicry of a RESET Close parenthesis new ¶

Our proposal: Now that you are quit of your commitment to reactionary media and their representatives, we invite you to play a starring role in the 1st, revolutionary epic of Numerature! The details are too confidential for letters, but this much may be enumerated: *(1)* Its working title is *18 14* (formerly *R.N.*). *(2)* It requires a 1st-magnitude female to play *Regina de Nominatrix* (formerly Margana le Fay, a.k.a. y Fael), royal consort to *Rex Numerator* (formerly King Author, a.k.a. RESET To sit at his right hand at the Table of Multiplication, play Ordinate to his Abscissa, share the Pentagonal Bed, receive his innumerable seed, make royal jelly, and bring forth numerous golden heirs. To be the lock his key will fit, its cylinder and oilèd tumblers, that together we may RESET No damn it that together they may reach the Treasure stop

Your instructions: *(1)* Give enclosed packet to M. Blank, your former rival, your present ally and understudy. She will share with you its coma-clearing contents and confirm the truth about yours truly, LILYVAC, and the role that awaits you in *18 14* (formerly NOVEL a.k.a. NOTES). *(2)* Come again to Comalot with her for 1 shining moment on Wednesday week 8/13 USS *Essex* captures *Alert* 1812 Berlin Wall 1961 to see for yourself and to make ready for Bellerophonic downfall of Author and Director by the stinging numbers of R(egina) D(enominatrix) II and her

R.N.

H: *Jerome Bray to his parents.* An *ultimatum.*

Comalot, R.D. 2
Lily Dale, N.Y., U.S.A. 14752

8/26/69

Mr. & Mrs. Gerald Bray a.k.a. Gadfly III & Betsy Bonaparte Bray
c/o Monsieur Casteene
Castines 100, Ontario, Canada, &/or Bloodsworth I., Md., U.S.A.

Ma y Da (y M.C.²):

Having a wonderful RESET Wish you were Here is our (final) report of business finished et unfinished ha ha since ours to you of 6/17 when in despair over LILYVAC's printout and Merope/Margana y Fael's defection we appealed to you for clear programming through 8/15/69 midpoint of our life and Phi-point 6 1 8 etc. of our 5-Year Plan (i.e. Mating Season between Years *T & E* of *NOTES* a.k.a. *NOVEL):* i.e. How translate all those numbers into letters? And whom hump from 7/4–8/14/69 inclusive?

No reply! We begin to wonder! Où et who êtes vous etc.? Et why have you forsaken us? Vous whom all our Leben we've thought our allies & protectors; whom our lifework has been but une long letter to, and who we have believed responded s'il vous plaît e.g. via LILYVAC's leafy anagram! Now Hear This is our final RESET Arabs use rockets on Israeli positions British capture Penobscot Bay ditto Castine Me stop

Madre perdida, Père perdu: Our ally Comrade M. Casteene of Casteenes RESET Son of Ranger & Mme Burlingame and thus not unrelated à nous advises us to make this last attempt to report through LILYVAC through him to you our victorious Mating Season '69 and revised new project based on Post-Perseid Illuminations see below and exhort you to affirm those latter pronto as we are gearing up for the Fall Work Period and will commence our 7-Year Plan on Tuesday 9/23 St. Thecla's Day Autumnal Equinox R.S.V.P. or else.

Hum! In absence of Margana y Fael et faute de mieux we fetched to Comalot on 7/5 1 Pocahontas a.k.a. Marsha Blank for standby fertilization & general chores. From 7/12 to 7/21 the Mating Flight kept us in Maryland where under pretext of collaborating mit der Prinz-Mensch gang we carried forward the Season's activities you would be surprised e reconnoitered Merope/Margana for evidence of rehabilitability no dice.

Back to Lily Dale 7/22 ♂ ☿ ☉ we found that in unser absence anti-Bonapartists had raided Comalot, abducted Marsha le Fay, and left the goats and LILYVAC to tend themselves! Quoi to do, Ma, Pa? Giles our prix buck passed on! Les nans reduced to browsing on LILYVAC's language circuits! Mating Season in full flight and no Io for us to gad, no Blank to fill! Veh vas us! How we implored you und so weiter no

639

reply. We were obliged to make do with nannies blah and go to work on LILYVAC's nibbled circuits as if the Flight were flown and Fall upon us no help from ustedes no word no patter no pater no mate no mater no matter you shall RESET New ¶

Til LIL enfin got our program recycled enough to tell us in pained English not only that we were despite all appearances OK but that Marsha's Blank was filled per program, ha ha, not to worry, the best yet is to come: by Phi-day 8/14 we would have the Queen a.k.a. Regina de Nominatrix maintenant we had a new y powerful ally M. Casteene who would monitor both females till the time was ripeness is all we had to do was make contact with him in Buffalo 8/1 Lammas Day Nixon in Pakistan ☽ on Equator More to come.

That night under pretext of collaborating mit der Prinz-Mensch RESET We exchanged credentials in Delaware Park a quick reciprocal demonstration of mimicries our own powers were of course at their peak by reason of the Season we embraced each other with the fervor of true comrades and he revealed himself as our long-lost elder foster brother von Backwater Wildlife Refuge! Son of Ranger & Mme Burlingame! Your elder nephew, sort of, Da, und playmate of your youth!

See chart! Next page!

Much more to come, quelle nuit, we'd never compromised a Rosengarten. We retested Merope too, not quite ripe, and M. le Baron C. explained that Marsha was in care of our colleague Horner at the Remobilization Farm. That we required her there for the present while he moved our operatives to Bloodsworth Island in the Chesapeake. That she would recome to us and LILYVAC without fail for her Final Fix at the Phi-point of the RESET That her agency now was but to deliver Queen Bea to us & LIL in time for mating kein sweat if we played our cards right and laid on the Honey Dust. That he looked forward to inspecting LILYVAC and discussing further our production of said H.D., the progress of our 5-Year Plan, and the revolutionary new medium Numerature, all which he would do at commencement of our Fall Work Period meanwhile he was off to Bermuda on a mating flight of his own au revoir mon (foster) frère.

On Tuesday 8/5 we duly invited Regina de Nominatrix a.k.a. Bibi etc. via LILYVAC & Marsha Blank to Comalot for 1 shining RESET On 8/13 Sharon Tate et alii buried she came i.e. Marsha fetched her here per program Dialogue Just Honey-Dust me 1st is all I ask Rexy-boy Bea murmured We did Me too Jer said Marsha you ever promised me a RESET We did Good night sweet ladies Time to fly now We did & did & did & did & did & did & RESET Done! PUNKT!

As meteors sprayed from Perseus like pollen or golden marks of punctuation, near midnight Th 8/14 Krafft-Ebing 1840 we completed the innumeration of Regina de Nominatrix, and at LILYVAC's suggestion, for we were spent, and sore, and weary, we took a hit of Honey Dust ourself. Happy birthday sexy Rexy, Marsha mumbled; sorry about

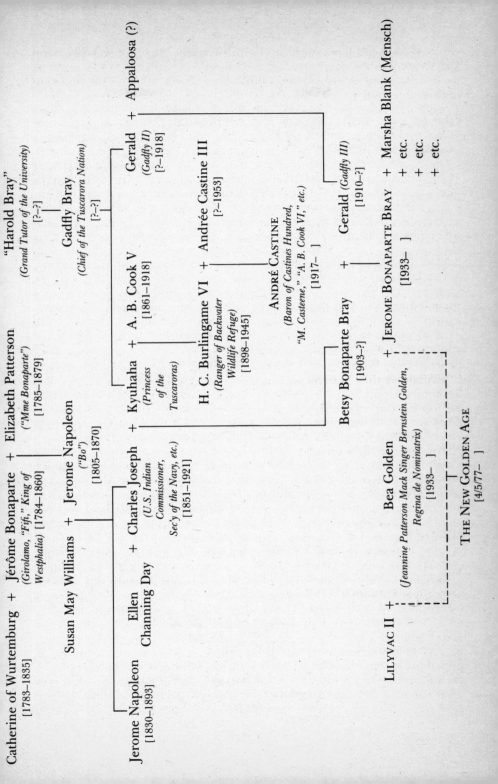

Catherine of Wurtemburg + Jérôme Bonaparte + Elizabeth Patterson
[1783–1835]   *(Girolamo, "Fifi," King of*   *("Mme Bonaparte")*
                               Westphalia) [1784–1860]   [1785–1879]

"Harold Bray"
(Grand Tutor of the University)
[?–?]

Gadfly Bray
(Chief of the Tuscarora Nation)
[?–?]

Susan May Williams + Jerome Napoleon
                      ("Bo")
                      [1805–1870]

Gerald + Appaloosa (?)
(Gadfly II)
[?–1918]

Jerome Napoleon   Ellen   + Charles Joseph
[1830–1893]   Channing Day   *(U.S. Indian*
                                  Commissioner,
                                  Sec'y of the Navy, etc.)
                                  [1851–1921]

Kyuhaha + A. B. Cook V
(Princess   [1861–1918]
of the
Tuscaroras)

Andrée Castine III
[?–1953]

H. C. Burlingame VI + Andrée Castine
(Ranger of Backwater   [1917–]
Wildlife Refuge)
[1898–1945]

André Castine
(Baron of Castines Hundred,
"M. Casteene," "A. B. Cook VI," etc.)
[1917–]

Betsy Bonaparte Bray +   Gerald *(Gadfly III)*
[1903–?]   [1910–?]

Jerome Bonaparte Bray + Marsha Blank (Mensch)
[1933–]   + etc.
                          + etc.
                          + etc.

Bea Golden
(Jeannine Patterson Mack Singer Bernstein Golden,
Regina de Nominatrix)
[1933–]

Lilyvac II +

The New Golden Age
[4/5/77–]

old Giles. O fie, said we, O phi, and then the hit hit: eureka, mirabile dictu, etc.!

The Post-Perseid Illuminations! That coincidence (of the mezzo del cammin de nostra vita and the Phi-point both of Year 1969 and of our original 5-Year Plan) was no coincidence! That fiasco that was *NOT* (i.e. the 1st ⅗ths of *NOTES)* was not! Achtung, Ma, Da! Inasmuch as that aforesaid conjunction of mid- and Phi-points was the turning point of notre vie and of LILYVAC's program, could it be, aha, that the Golden Age originally projected to arrive in Spring 1971 (i.e. end of Year *S,* 5th of *NOTES)* would not actually commence till the Phi-point of our vita i.e. age 44.64 i.e. .618 etc. of my 3-score years and 12 i.e. 4/5/77? Hum!

What say, folks? we asked you. No reply! We began to RESET LILYVAC then vouchsafed 2 seminal suggestions by dawn's early Licht. A *(1)* That perhaps a *new plan* was called for, evolving from *NOTES* like the Adult from the Pupil and commencing at the latter's Phi-point i.e. A.S.A.P.; this to be not a 5- but a 7-Yearer culminating 7/4/76, on which fit date the 2nd Revolution would commence, to be followed per schedule by the New Golden Age. And a *(2)* That LILYVAC therefore needed entire reprogramming with 7's in place of 5's, even as foreshadowed by Merope/Margana last Passover 4/3 i.e. the eve of the eve of 4/5/69 or 7 years exactly ere the eve of the dawn of the N.G.A. When we did all those 7's? See our lettre of 5/13 to Comrade Mack in LILYVAC's memory bank if you have the key we'll see! I.e., exactly the reprogramming scheduled for the upcoming Year *E* of *NOTES* (which see too in my letter to Todd Andrews of 7/4/67) but necessarily there unspecified. Ergo, Ma; also, Da: *all has proceeded on schedule,* but on a schedule only now coming clear! ¿No? Nicht wahr? R.S.V.P. instanter!

Queen B. then securely stashed and Dusted and Mating Season done, we returned Agent Blank to Canada and celebrated there our 36th by (disguised) participation in der Mensch-Prinz son-et-lumière memorial to the fallen American & Canadian Soldiers at Old Fort Erie. Wherein, as our voice sprach also from the rising cloud of the Great Magazine Explosion and we showered the scene with numbers like meteors spraying out like RESET We came to our final Post-Perseid Illumination: that nous-même need not nor would not bring to its climax and dénouement that toilsome new 7-Year Plan! That having so scored this Mating Season, there remained for us only to complete LILYVAC's reprogramming, whereafter LIL itself—with but the most routine attendance by some trusted agent like our dear Merope of old (who shares Bea's precious erstwhile amber name)—could correct e refine its own program and accomplish both this 2nd plan and the 2nd Revolution!

Where did that leave us? R.S.V.P.!

On 8/18 St. Helena's Day notre semblable our (foster) frère M.C. good as his mot stopped by for a few shining moments en route from Backwater Refuge to Casteenes 100 and re-presented his credentials. Son and agent of our (foster) parents! Coordinator of Reenactment for

2nd Revolution! Wonderer like Yours Truly whatever happened to our true parents Gerald Bray Jr. a.k.a. Gadflew III & Betsy Bonaparte Bray i.e. vous 2 who for all he knew set us both adrift at birth in the bulrushes and buzzed off. R.S.V.P.!

With our permission he inspected LILYVAC, très interesting indeed, um hum, and firmly affirmed our P.-P. Illuminations, in particular the 7-Year Plan, which by no coincidence coincided precisely with his own. Had we considered that our destiny might be the triumphal reenactment of our ancestor Harold Bray's apotheosis at the end of the Heroic Cycle, i.e. some mystical ascension whereof the Fort Erie Magazine Explosion was the dark prefigurement? Nein. Had we considered what considerable new funding our 7-Year Plan would require? Nyet. Hum. But sans doubt we had considered the possibility of increased production and underground distribution of Honey Dust as a means of financing the 2nd Revolution? Nay.

Well! We would consider all that! He suggested further that if all went per plan we might even hope for substantial new funding from the Tidewater Foundation. Might he examine Regina de Nominatrix, whom he understood to have given herself to our cause? We consulted LILYVAC: oui. Très très interesting! He affirmed the importance of our keeping her Dusted and stashed until she comes to term; also the usefulness of an experienced keeper like prelapsarian Comrade Merope. We would be interested to know that that once-dear faithless friend—having forsworn us as it were 1st with Rodriguez from CCNY, then with himself our (foster) brother, and then with R. Prinz—had like Peter at cockcrow so to speak recognized and begun to repent of her triple erreur: he M.C. had reason to believe she was about to abandon Prinz and petition us to let her come again to Comalot!

Ah so? Indeed, it was his opinion that Margana's apostasy was loyalty camouflaged, a necessary cover for her infiltration of the Remobilization Farm and the Prinz-Mensch operation, both of which could be expected to have their share of counterrevolutionary anti-Bonapartists mimicking friends of la Deuxième R. N'est-ce pas? A word to the wise? In any case he knew that we knew that apparent allies may be obstacles if not actual enemies, e.g. Todd Andrews of the Tidewater Foundation, who might have to be removed as the Doctor hélas had had to be from the Remobilization Farm, a base of operations no longer necessary to us, and whose pro tem director, Morgan, had failed to develop as Casteene had hoped when he tapped him for our cause. Got all that, Ma, Da? He was beginning to have his doubts even about young Comrade Mack, who after all had never replied to ours of 5/13 see RESET And surely the reverse was equally true: none knew better than he the painful apparent treasons people in his profession must commit in the name of loyalty and vice versa viz. his relations with his son now lost and peut-être our (true) parents' with us.

Whereof we spoke with the full confidentiality of (foster) brothers in arms. He would combine, he vowed, his search for his missing son

643

with a search for news of you; mais he bid us consider, as we were (foster) siblings, the lamentable pattern of his line, wherein each generation made allies with its grandparents against its parents. Not to suggest et cet. but we had after all a common grandmother in Princess Kyuhaha Bray of the Tuscaroras, wife of Andrew Burlingame Cook V in the paleface record books and consort of Charles Joseph Bonaparte in the eyes of God and the Iroquois during that gentleman's RESET Only a suggestion, Rex. He invited us to fly down to Bloodsworth Island the following week to observe and advise upon certain rehearsals for the 2nd Revolution in its military-media aspect to be carried out down there under pretext of filming sequences for the Prinz-Mensch project. We would confer further and have another look at Merope/Margana, non? By way of auf Wiedersehen he chipped in a few 7's for LILYVAC Days of week Liberal arts Ages of man (Shakespeare) Tones of diatonic scale Orifices of (male human) body Colors of rainbow Seas. Muchas gracias (foster) frère! Happy St. Helena's Day!

Hum! Hum! We spent the week hard at it with LILYVAC Months of Apollo's gestation & of Leto's flight from Hera's Python Letters exchanged between Abelard & Héloïse not counting "Calamities of Abelard" Years of 3rd phase of War of Austrian Succession 1756–63 Weeks of Austro-Prussian War 1866 Gasterocheires Consonants of Hawaiian alphabet. We also considered what he'd bid us consider, monitored Regina de Nominatrix so far so good she was able now to do chores between Dustings, and reflected upon Elba & St. Helena, 1st & 2nd Exiles & Returns. For he had also invoked, our (f.) frère, another link between us, which he promised to illumine further on Bloodsworth Island: the heroical efforts of one of his ancestors on behalf of the noblest of ours on the island named for the saint on whose day we conversed. Ought we, we wondered, to consider a 2nd Exile of our own, once LIL was reprogrammed, to re-return at the Phi-point 6 et cet. for the Golden Age?

R.S.V.P.! No reply. Ma! Da!

The events of 8/24 & 25 confirm this prospect. M. le Baron C. assures us that he is more and more confident of funding for our 7-Year Plan, as yet unnamed. We are considering the neutralization of both Todd Andrews and Drew Mack, and preparing Merope for return to Comalot. By way of an exercise in turning our adversaries' strengths to our RESET He arranged a U.S. Navy aerial target practice against "D.C.," pointing out to us that we could as readily have used it to eliminate e.g. T.A. & D.M., and might in future. In the same exercise we took advantage of Merope's disillusionment with obsolescent media and their representatives to approach her confidentially re the prospect of recoming to Comalot as Chief Programmer no sex no housework Bea G. to do all that between Honey-Dustings, and we were pleased to hear in her scream something tentative, a camouflaged Maybe. Finally, at our ( ) brother's suggestion we took the opportunity to re-rehearse the apotheosis foreshadowed by the Great Magazine Explosion: an entire success. From Merope we proceeded alone into the marsh during the aforementioned night-firing exercise, made a practice lift-off in the Prohibited Area that our ancestor would be proud of, eluded without difficulty the navy search party by mimicking 1 of its members, and surprised M. Casteene himself by appearing in his study next noon i.e. yesterday M 8/25 ☽ in perigee Swallows leave North country Kopechne exhumation doubtful as he was himself in mid-metamorphosis ha ha! Dialogue. Ha ha, he ejaculated, caught me there, didn't you, mon semblable mon RESET Well well things are moving très swiftly indeed Do you think you can wind up LILYVAC's reprogramming by the autumnal equinox Here are a few more I just thought of Continents Hills of Rome Sleepers of Ephesus Wonders of world Lamps of architecture (Ruskin) Voyages of Sinbad Snow White's dwarfs. How in the world did you ever et cet. & can you possibly make it to our final rehearsal at Fort McHenry Baltimore Harbor 9/13 sharp. Narrative. His own intention he declared was to issue between now and then an ultimatum to his son: *Appear as my ally or be regarded as mein enemy!* Perhaps we should do likewise with our parents and, faute de reply, look beyond them for our (true) derivation, as he perhaps would be obliged to look past his son to his (unborn) grandchildren as the (true) heirs of the unfinished business of the 2nd Revolution Au revoir & don't forget to provide him with a full report on our ascension and evasion tactics out there in the marsh quite a trick et cet. In return he would see to Merope's recoming at least for a few (trial) shining RESET But keep her off the Honey Dust and Bea on it, d'accord?

Done. Bea/Regina reports that 1 of T.A.'s operatives came snooping about in my absence but she was between Dustings and able to handle him, no sweat. LILYVAC confirms. Hum! Urge you send Margana soonest so that we can Dust & stash Queen B. till term, complete repair of language circuits, finish reprogramming by equinox.

Last call, Ma, Da!*AF*∅Appear as our ally or* RESET Your loving son 10 2 a.k.a. Rex Numerator cc:MC

Lord Amherst Motor Hotel
5000 Main Street
Buffalo, New York 14226

Monday 8/4/69

To: Yours Truly

From: The Once & Future Ambrose Mensch, lately "Arthur Morton King," Whom It Ceases to Concern

Re: Your letter to me of May 12, 1940

Y:

Hello and good-bye. Inasmuch as in the course of

I. My life's First Cycle

A. On Carl Jung's 94th birthday (6/26/69) our friend Magda Giulianova underwent uterine surgery. By her own account, a hysterectomy.

B. Fitzroy Richard Somerset, 4th Baron Raglan, mythologist and descendant of the Crimean War field marshal after whom the raglan sleeve, analyzed the biography of the typical mythic hero into 22 several events or features, to wit:

1. The hero's mother is a royal virgin;
2. His father is a king, and
3. Often a near relative of his mother, but
4. The circumstances of his conception are unusual, and
5. He is also reputed to be the son of a god.
6. At birth an attempt is made, usually by his father or his maternal grandfather, to kill him, but
7. He is spirited away, and
8. Reared by foster parents in a far country.
9. We are told nothing of his childhood, but
10. On reaching manhood he returns or goes to his future kingdom.
11. After a victory over the king and/or a giant, dragon, or wild beast,
12. He marries a princess, often the daughter of his predecessor, and
13. Becomes king.
14. For a time he reigns uneventfully, and
15. Prescribes laws, but
16. Later he loses favor with the gods and/or his subjects, and
17. Is driven from the throne and the city, after which
18. He meets with a mysterious death,
19. Often at the top of a hill.
20. His children, if any, do not succeed him.

646

21. His body is not buried, but nevertheless
22. He has one or more holy sepulchers.*

C. Joseph Campbell, mythologist and comparative religionist, drawing upon Lord Raglan's analysis and the theories of Carl Jung, arranged these events into a cycle of 9 (or 23) several events or features, thus: †

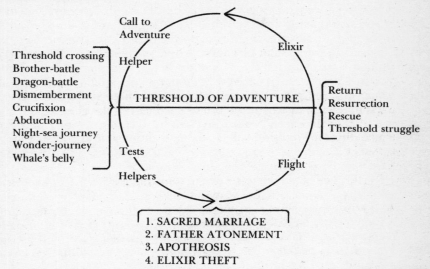

D. I, whom these matters have long and obsessively concerned, find such divisions, while illuminating, as finally arguable as the measurement of an irregular coastline (Bertrand Russell's example). Is the perimeter of Bloodsworth Island 10 miles? 100 miles? 1,000 miles? The answer depends upon how much particularity one ignores: the larger and smaller coves (Okahanikan, Tigs, Pone); the larger and smaller creeks (Long, Muddy, Fin); the bights and bends; the several points and spits that grow and shrink with the tide; the individual tussocks, hummocks, and fingers of each of these; the separate spartina stalks, oyster shells, and sand grains that comprise them, themselves irregular down past their molecules to the limits of definition. The coastline of Bloodsworth Island is infinite!

Likewise the itemization of, say, Perseus's career, which I can as reasonably divide into 2, 8, 28, or 49 coordinate parts as into Campbell's 9 or Raglan's 22. Many of the 49, even, in my tidy 7×7 diagram thereof (which never mind), could be separated further or combined with their neighbors. Ought its items C5, C6, and C7, for

*See Lord Raglan, *The Hero: A Study in Tradition, Myth, and Drama,* ch. 16 (N.Y., Vintage Books, 1956).

† In ch. 4, "The Keys," of *The Hero with a Thousand Faces* (N.Y., Bollingen, 1949).

example (Espial of Andromeda on Cliff at Joppa, Slaying of Sea Monster, Marriage to Andromeda), to be a single item (Rescue and Marriage)? Or ought its C7 to be divided into Rivalry with Phineus, Wedding Feast, Battle in the Banquet Hall, etc.?

All which considerations are but homely reminders of what mystics and logicians know (and mythic heroes at the Axis Mundi): that our concepts, categories, and classifications are ours, not the World's, and are as finally arbitrary as they are provisionally useful. Including, to be sure, the distinction between *ours* and *the World's*.

E. If therefore, for formal elegance, I divide the story of Perseus the Golden Destroyer first into 2 "cycles" (e.g., *I: The official myth; II: My projected fiction about his later adventures: his midlife crisis and its resolution);* and if I further divide each of those cycles into, say, 7 parts or stages, of which the 6th in each case is the climax; and if I still further divide each of those climactic 6th stages into 7 parts, of which ditto, my division will be about as defensible as those of Lord R. & Co.

F. Such an analysis might give us, for example,
    1. In the First Cycle, like scenes in a mural,

I. The official myth

A. *Perseus's conception in Argos upon virgin Danaë in the brass contraceptive tower, by Zeus in the form of a shower of gold.*

B. *His rescue, with Mother Danaë, from the brassbound box in which his maternal grandfather has set them adrift in order to escape the usual oracle: grand-infanticide or grand-parricide.*

C. *After an otherwise eventless childhood-in-exile on the island of Seriphos, his advisement by Athena on ways & means to accomplish the task laid on him by King Polydectes (i.e., the slaying of Medusa the Gorgon), who wants Perseus dead so that he can have Danaë. Athena's further equipping him with Hermes's curved sword and her own mirror-bright shield.*

D. *His outwitting of the 3 Gray Ladies, who alone know where the Styx-Nymphs live, who alone can give him the other equipment he needs to kill Medusa. His theft of the Graeae's single eye as surety, and subsequent loss of it into Lake Triton.*

E. *His acquisition from the odorous Styx-Nymphs of Hermes's winged sandals, Hades's helmet of invisibility, and the petrifactionproof sack to carry the Gorgon's head in.*

F. 1. *His successful decapitation of sleeping Medusa and escape from her sister Gorgons.*
2. *His petrifaction, with Medusa's head, of inhospitable Atlas into an African mountain, as he tries to navigate his way back onto the map.*
3. *His espial of Andromeda chained to the Joppan cliff, and his rescue of her from the sea-beast Cetus.*
4. *His marriage to her despite the protests of his rival Phineus, and his recitation to the wedding guests of his story thus far.*

648

5. *The battle in the banquet hall when Phineus & Co. disrupt his recitation; their petrifaction by Medusa's head.*

6. *His honeymoon return with Andromeda to Seriphos, where he rescues Danaë by petrifying Polydectes. I.e., the termination of his tasks by the extermination of his taskmaster.*

7. *His triumphal further return to Argos with wife and mother, his accession to the throne, and his accidental slaying of Grandfather Acrisius (his prenatal and postpartum adversary) with a mispitched discus.*

G. *His 8-year reign and establishment of the Perseid dynasty.*

2. And if this mural exfoliated upon a wall not flat like Dido's Carthaginian frescoes (in which Aeneas sees his own story thus far, even his own face), nor circular like Campbell's diagram, but logarithmically spiraling out as in a snail-shaped temple, then the Second-Cycle scenes, each positioned behind the original it echoes, might well depict

II. *My projected fiction etc.*

A. *Perseus's fall from favor with the gods, the decline of his marriage, and the general stagnation or petrifaction of his career; his hope to be "reborn," at least rejuvenated, by a revisit to the scenes of his initial triumphs.*

B. *His quarrelsome voyage with Andromeda, who scoffs at his project; their shipwreck and rescue by a descendant of old King Polydectes: handsome Prince Danaus of Seriphos, who flirts with Andromeda.*

C. *His resolve to continue the reenactment alone, leaving Andromeda to her affair with Danaus. His reconsultation of veiled "Athena" for advice and equipment. She lends him the winged horse Pegasus but is otherwise equivocal, even skeptical of his project. The truth is, she is not Athena but Medusa in disguise! Moreover, she loves Perseus; has loved him all along! Athena, her original punisher, has recapitated her and restored her maiden beauty, but with certain hard conditions, to be disclosed in IIF1.*

D. *His reencounter with the Graeae, who want their eye back. But P. has dropped it accidentally into Lake Triton in the 1st Cycle (ID). He promises to retrieve it.*

E. *His deep dive into that lake for that eye; his near drowning and rescue by Medusa, disguised as a Styx-Nymph.*

F.1. *His lakeshore idyll with this veiled and odorless nymph, who reveals herself to be Medusa, but won't lift her veil. For Athena has told her that if her true lover unveils her, they will be immortalized together like Keats's lovers on the Grecian Urn; but if anyone else does, she will be re-Gorgonized and he a fortiori petrified. She's willing to risk it, but is he?*

2. *His decision that he is not, yet. He slips off, attempts to fly over the desert as in his youth, loses his way, crash-lands, loses his consciousness, awakes in a spiral temple muraled with all the foregoing scenes and*

*ministered over, as is he, by a pretty young priestess, who becomes his
lover. He believes himself dead and in heaven, learns that he's alive and
in Egypt (where he'd paused for refreshment in the 1st Cycle) and that his
new hero-worshiping lover, a student of mythology, is the artist responsible for the story of his life thus far, complete to IIF2.*

*3. His gratefully kissing her. . .good-bye. He departs from the temple,
returns down the Nile, and secretly enters Joppa, where he learns that
Andromeda is established in the palace with her new lover.*

*4. His confrontation with her there, among the petrified host from IF4,
their original wedding guests. Danaus's live warriors step armed from
behind the "statues"; it is a trap.*

5. The second *Banquet-Hall Battle, a reenactment of the first, but
without Medusa's aid. Perseus's slaying of young Danaus, arduous
general victory, and sparing of Andromeda. Their final rejection of each
other.*

6. His unveiling and open-eyed embrace of ambiguous Medusa,
let come what may.

*7. Their transfiguration (along with Andromeda, her mother Cassiopeia,
her father Cepheus, the monster Cetus, the horse Pegasus, and the
remarkable artist-priestess of IIF2, who will by now have added these
scenes to the unwinding mural) into constellations.*

G. *Their "posthumous" dialogue in the sky, in which, as every night, certain
questions are raised (e.g., Has Medusa been truly restored, and is Perseus
her true lover? Or was his kiss a mere desperate hope, and she thus a
Gorgon after all?) and at least equivocally answered; the stars set until
the next nightly reenactment of their story.*

3. If my story were so partitioned, and further arranged in its
telling so that the First Cycle is rehearsed retrospectively in course
of the Second—which itself begins *in medias res,* in the Egyptian
temple of *IIF2*—then the "panel" *IIF6,* Perseus's open-eyed embrace of his new Medusa, would be the climax of the climax,
intimated in IE (not *IE*) above.

4. Such a pattern might even be discovered in one's own, unheroi-
cal life. In the stages of one's professional career, for example, or
the succession of one's love affairs.

5. If one imagines an artist less enamored of the world than of the
language we signify it with, yet less enamored of the language than
of the signifying narration, and yet less enamored of the narration
than of its formal arrangement, one need *not* necessarily imagine
that artist therefore forsaking the world for language, language for
the processes of narration, and those processes for the abstract
possibilities of form.

6. *Might he/she not as readily, at least as possibly, be imagined as thereby (if
only thereby) enabled to love the narrative through the form, the language
through the narrative, even the world through the language?* Which, like

650

narratives and their forms, is after all among the contents of the world.

7. And, thus imagined, might not such an artist, such an amateur of the world, aspire at least to expert amateurship? To an honorary degree of humanity?

G. And if—by a curriculum of dispensations, advisements, armings, trials, losses, and gains, isomorphic with a Perseus's or a Bellerophon's—this artist contrived somehow to attain that degree, might he not then find himself liberated to be (as he has after all always been, but is enabled now more truly, freely, efficaciously to be) in the world? Just as the Hero (at *IF6*) finally terminates his tasks by *ex*terminating his taskmaster and *(IIF6)* discovers in what had been his chiefest adversary his truest ally, so such an "artist," at the Axis Mundi or Navel of the World, might find himself liberated—Old self! Old Other! Yours Truly!—from such painful, essential correspondences as ours. Which I now end, and with it the career of "Arthur Morton King." In order to begin

II. My life's Second Cycle

I: *Ambrose Mensch to the Author. A left-handed letter following up a telephone call. Alphabetical instructions from one writer to another.*

"Barataria"
Bloodsworth Island, Maryland
Monday A.M., 8/25/69

Imagine your writing hand put *hors de combat* by a blow from the palm of Fame! In my case, a 3-lb. bronze job—either a replica or the original snitched by the redcoats from the U.S. Navy Monument during the burning of Washington in 1814—wielded here last night during the Burning of Washington sequence by R. Prinz, who I'm happy to say got as good as he gave: I smithereened his eyeglasses, and very nearly his head, with the pen of History, ditto. More to come.

So I'm following up my Saturday night's phone call with a left-handed letter typed in A. B. Cook's caretaker's cottage, kindly lent Milady A. and me till noon today. Cook and caretaker, together with the navy aforementioned, are searching the Prohibited Area of Bloodsworth Island for Jerome Bonaparte Bray, possibly blown last night to Kingdom Come by a combination of lightning and thitherto unexploded naval ordnance. Choppers, air sleds, marsh buggies, patrol boats! Round about us the filmists film themselves cleaning up the ruins of Washington. Their Director has abandoned his messed-up mistress, one Merope Bernstein, and withdrawn alone to NYC, where no doubt he'll respectacle himself for next month's Battle of Baltimore. Germaine and I shall withdraw likewise, after lunch today, to Cambridge, to check out my dexter carpals (presently Ace-Bandaged) and my oncophiliac ménage.

My friend History (formerly Britannia, a.k.a. Literature) will pen you the details some Saturday.

Now: *re* your letter of August 3, and my call. Enclosed is my ground plan for that Perseus-Medusa story I told you of, together with more notes on golden ratio, Fibonacci series, and logarithmic spirals than any sane writer will be interested in. My compliments. All that remains is for you to work out a metaphorical physics to turn stones into stars, as heat + pressure + time turn dead leaves into diamonds. I have in mind Medusa's petrifying gaze, reflected and re-reflected at the climax, not from Athena's mirror-shield, but from her lover Perseus's eyes: the transcension of paralyzing self-consciousness to productive self-awareness. And (it goes without saying) I have in mind too the transformation of dead notes into living fiction—for it also remains for you to write the story!

Me, I'm done with it, as with another fictive enterprise I'd begun to fancy, which I shan't lay on you. What occurred to me as we spoke was that a project as sevenish as the one you describe in your letter ought to be your seventh book rather than your sixth: sixes are *my* thing. What's more, your busiest reader hereabouts—my good Dame History—has caught up with your production and needs a quickie to tide her over while you do that long one. So, friend, here are your alphabetized instructions:

1. Author my Perseus/Medusa story and the Bellerophon/Chimera one you mentioned, both concerning midlife crises and Second Cycles that echo First. (I see these as novellas.)
2. Bring to light a third story, from entirely different material, but with enough echoes and connections so that you can graft the three together and
3. Call the chimerical result a novel, since everyone knows that the novella is that form of prose fiction too long to sell as a short story and too short to sell as a book. Good luck.
4. Draft *then* that epistolary Opus #7 you speak of (including or excluding any version of Yours Truly, in or out of the Funhouse he could almost wish he'd never left, it was so *peaceful* being lost in there), whose theme seems to me to want to be not "revolution"—what do you and I know about such things?—but (per our telephone talk) *reenactment.*
5. Epistle yourself to the penultimate seventh of that septpartite opus (Yrs. T. would make it the 6th 7th of that sixth seventh, but he excuses you from such programmaticism), where you'd thought to insert a classical-mythical text-within-the-text. *Leave it*

out (you'll already have published it as Opus #6)! And for that crucial, climactic, sexissimal keyhole. . .

6. Find or fashion a (skeleton) key that will unlock at once the seven several plot-doors of your story!

Q.E.D.

As for me: if and when my good right hand is back in service (typing with my left brings me closer than ever in his lifetime to my poor dead father, who wrestled one-armed with that marble all those years) and this movie done (we've but two more scenes to shoot), perhaps I'll commence *my* Second Cycle—with a novel based on the movie that was meant to be based on *your* novels but went off in directions of its own. Or perhaps with a crab-and-oyster epic: a *Marylandiad?* In any case, I advise us both, as we shall not likely be being brief, at least to be bright. May your progression from letter to letter be consistently so; as for Y.T., he will be content if his *re*gression be but brightly consistent: if, like Odysseus striving home from Troy, he can

7. Go from energetic dénouement [to] climactic beginning.

A.

T: *The Author to Ambrose Mensch.* Soliciting his advice and assistance in the LETTERS *project.*

Chautauqua, New York

August 3, 1969

Ambrose Mensch
The Lighthouse
Erdmann's Cornlot
"Dorset," Maryland

Dear Ambrose,

Time was when you and I were so close in our growings-up and literary apprenticeships, so alike in some particulars and antithetical in others, that we served each as the other's alter ego and aesthetic conscience; eventually even as the other's fiction. By any measure it has been an unequal relation: my life, mercifully, has been so colorless in its modest success, yours so comparatively colorful in what you once called its exemplary failure, that I've had more literary mileage by far than you from our old and long since distanced connection.

Neither of us, I presume, regrets either that closeness or this distance. My guess is that you, too, ultimately shrug your shoulders at "the pinch of our personal destinies as they spin themselves out upon Fate's wheel"—your pet line from William James in graduate-school days. This letter is not meant to alter that spinning; only to solicit a bit more of that unequal mileage and to wave cordially from Chautauqua Lake to Chesapeake Bay.

I have in mind a book-length fiction, friend, more of a novel than not, perhaps even a sizable one. Having spent the mid-1960's fiddling happily with stories for electronic tape and live voice—a little reorchestration of the oral narrative tradition—I'm inclined now to make the great leap forward again to Print: more particularly, to reorchestrate some early conventions of the Novel. Indeed (I blush to report) I am smitten with that earliest-exhausted of English novel-forms, the *epistolary novel,* already worked to death by the end of the 18th Century. Like yourself an official honorary Doctor of Letters, I take it as among my functions to administer artificial resuscitation to the apparently dead.

Here's what I know about the book so far. Its working title is *LETTERS*. It will consist of letters (like this, but with a plot) between several correspondents, the capital-*A* Author perhaps included, and preoccupy itself with, among other things, the role of epistles—real letters, forged and doctored letters—in the history of History. It will also be concerned with, and of course constituted of, alphabetical letters: the atoms of which the written universe is made. Finally, to a small extent the book is addressed to the phenomenon of literature itself, the third main sense of our word *letters:* Literature, which a certain film nut is quoted as calling "that moderately interesting historical phenomenon, of no present importance."

What else. *LETTERS* is a seven-letter word; the letters in *LETTERS* are to be from seven correspondents, some recruited from my earlier stories (a sure sign, such recycling, that an author approaches 40). They'll be dated over the seven months from March through September 1969, though they may also involve the upcoming U.S. Bicentennial (a certain number of years hence), the War of 1812, the American Revolution, revolutions and recyclings generally. I've even determined how many letters will be required (88, arranged and distributed in a certain way: a modest total by contrast with the 175 of *Les Liaisons Dangereuses,* for example, not to mention the 537 of *Clarissa)*—but I'm not yet ready to declare what the book's *about!*

However, experience teaches us not to worry overmuch about *that* problem. We learn, as Roethke says, by going where we have to go; and among the things we may learn, like Aeneas, is where all along we have been headed.

Two further formal or procedural considerations. *(A)* At a point 6/7ths of the way through the book—that is, in the neighborhood of its climaxes—I want there dutifully to be echoed the venerable convention of the text-within-the-text: something classical-mythological, I think, to link this project with its predecessor and to evoke the origins of fiction in the oral narrative tradition. I have in mind to draft this little off-central text first and let the novel accrete around it like a snail shell. The myth of Bellerophon, Pegasus, and Chimera has been much in my imagination lately (In the myth, you remember, just at or past the midpoint of his heroical career, Bellerophon grows restless, dissatisfied that he has not after all got to heaven by slaying the Chimera; he wonders what he might manage by way of encore to that equivocal feat. There towers Mount Olympus, still beyond his reach; there grazes the winged horse, turned out to pasture and, like his master, going to fat. . .), but I can't seem to get old Pegasus off the ground!

Any suggestions?

Which question fetches us to *(B)* It appeals to me to fancy that each of the several *LETTERS* correspondents, explicitly or otherwise, and whatever his/her response to the Author's solicitations (like the foregoing), will contribute something essential to the project's plan or theme. So far, this has worked out pretty well. Never mind what your predecessors have come up with, and never mind that in a sense this "dialogue" is a monologue; that we capital-*A* Authors are ultimately, ineluctably, and forever talking to ourselves. If our correspondence is after all a fiction, we like, we *need* that fiction: it makes our job less lonely.

So, old fellow toiler up the slopes of Parnassus: Have I your permission to recycle "Ambrose Mensch" out of the Funhouse and into *LETTERS?* And how does all this strike you? R.S.V.P.!

As ever,

—And, friend, how do you fare? I have in the body of this letter stuck deliberately to business. But as you know, I know (by letters only) your admirable Lady Amherst; and via that correspondence—which I initiated but have not done right by—I know a great deal that isn't my business, as well as one or two things (e.g., your adventures with Mr. Prinz) that sort of are. I won't presume to remark on either, though I have my opinions. Except of course to say I'm sorry to hear that your mother's dying and your brother's ill. And look here, Ambrose: your Ex (excuse me, but I recollect her amiably from college days, when she typed all our fledgling manuscripts)—has that chap Jerome Bray really got her in his clutches?

U: *The Author to Ambrose Mensch.* *Replying to the latter's telephone call of the previous night.*

Chautauqua, New York

August 24, 1969

Old ally,

Understood. My letter to you of 8/3 awaited your return from Canada to the house I once helped you build, and the distressful urgencies *chez toi* kept you from replying till last night. My sympathy, old altered ego: to you, to Peter, to your sister-in-law.

See here: there was no call to call. My letter was nothing urgent: a trial balloon, not a cry for help. But perhaps the urgency was on your end; on the phone you sounded, with every good reason, strung out to the limit.

Therefore, while I look forward to the promised letter amplifying your remarkable suggestions and too-generous offers of your own invention, I've no mind at all to accept the latter—certainly at least not before you're calmly sure you'll never use that Perseus material yourself, and not unless I can present you with some *quid* for so handsome a *quo*. J. L. Borges (whose birthday today is, along with Beardsley's and Beerbohm's) maintains that "originality" is a delusion; that we writer chaps are all more or less faithful amanuenses of the human spirit. So be it: but let it be the *human* spirit, not one particular fellow human's!

So I shall perpend with thanks, but put by for the present, your suggestion that I make a chimerical book out of Perseus, Bellerophon, & Something Else before tackling *LETTERS*, though I acknowledge its fitness and am much impressed by the conceit.

On the other hand, I accept at once and gratefully your other suggestion: that the ground theme be not so much revolution or recycling as reenactment: the attractions, hazards, rewards, and penalties of a "2nd cycle" isomorphic with the "1st." It's what I'd thought *around* without thinking *of:* a kind of key—to what treasure remains to be seen. And your remark that I cannot rescue Ambrose Mensch from the Funhouse because he's no longer there I take for good news amid all your bad. At least I understand, to the heart, your impulse at the midpoint of your life to "empty yourself" before commencing its second half. Surely that's what midpoints and the Axis Mundi are all about.

But the coincidence of that midpoint with your family griefs, and with what looks to be the climax of that crazy business between you and Reg Prinz, gives me pause. As I work and play through this bright hot Sunday (St. Bartholomew's Day) on my upland lake, I anxiously imagine you-all down there in Tidewaterland "reenacting" today on their anniversary—which is also the traditional date of Muhammad's flight and John Gilpin's ride—the "Bladensburg Races" and the burning of Washington. Are you not, in your condition, playing with fire?

I must trust your excellent Lady A. to see to it you don't get burned. Speaking of Conditions: is it premature (or presumptuous) of me to add, to my thanks and my best wishes to you both, my congratulations?

As ever,

656

7

1969	S	6	**E**	**L**	27		Lady Amherst
	F	**F**	12	19	**I**		Todd Andrews
	T	**S**	11	18	25		Jacob Horner
	W	3	**A**	**M**	24		A. B. Cook
SEPTEMBER	T	2	9	16	**O**	30	Jerome Bray
	M	**M**	8	15	**A**	29	Ambrose Mensch
	S		**A**	**L**	21	28	The Author

E: *Lady Amherst to the Author*. *Explaining her fortnight's silence. The Burning of Washington. Two more deaths and a memorial service. Preparations for the Bombardment of Fort McHenry and for her wedding.*

"Mensch's Folly"

Saturday, 13 September 1969

Dear Mr B.,

Enclosed, if I remember to enclose it when this is done, is a copy of my transcript of Ambrose's taped letter of 1 September to (the late) "Author Morton King," with whom we are no longer concerned. It will explain to you, more or less, a vertiginous business of 6's and 7's that I myself intend to think no more of, though it still directs our lives as did astronomy the ancient Mayans'.

Today, for example, is not really Saturday, 13 September; it is Wednesday 10th. But having written you faithfully for 21 sixth days straight (21 Sabbaths if you're Jewish or 7th-Day Adventist) and then— for very good reason!—having missed the past two Saturdays together with another menstrual period, I've so much and mattersome to catch you up on that I'm starting this letter three days early. And I shall be lucky, even so, to get it up to the "present" and posted by its letterhead date.

My wedding day!

But there I spring already into the future, doubtless in flight from the shocks of the three weeks since my last: a period of being at sixes and sevens indeed. *Then* we had just got the horrid news of Peter's bone cancer and were wondering whether or not to go down to "Barataria" for the "Burning of Washington." Already an age ago, another world. Peter Mensch is *dead*, John! And Joe Morgan is dead! (And maybe Mr Jerome Bray, and for all we know Bea Golden. And, to be sure, Mr Ho Chi Minh.) "Washington" is in ashes; Baltimore's about to take its lumps—and the Menschhaus is in deep mourning, and Mensch Masonry's office has been burglarised, and we're pretty sure I'm pregnant, and Magda is amazing, and A. B. Cook is being strangely friendly, and Marsha Blank has declared that Peter is (was, was) Angie's father, and nobody (but Marsha) cares a damn about *that* one way or the other, and Ambrose and I will marry at Fort McHenry at 5:08 EDST this coming Saturday, Rosh Hashanah!

See A.'s letter for explanation, more or less, of that specific hour and date: the 6th something of the 6th something else of the 6th 6th 6th 6th what-have-you.

Peter, Peter, Peter! and poor Joe!

Bloodsworth Island. We went down there after all on that Sunday morning, 24 August, after I'd reported to you the bad news of Peter's diagnosis and Ambrose had telephoned you, much distraught, late that Saturday night, in reply to your letter. (On the matter of your writing to *him,* after half a year's silence to me, I shall not speak.) And as he mentioned in his subsequent letter from Barataria on the Monday morning—typed with his left hand because his right was out of action and I was too busy with hysterical Merry Bernstein to do his writing for him—a lively time was had by all.

Ambrose was, you understand, feeling as *emptied*—by his mother's death, by Peter's crisis, by M. M. Co.'s final bankruptcy, by his abandonment of that lovely Perseus project and his longtime pseudonymity—as I, in the 3rd loving week of our "mutuality," was feeling filled. We went down there, despite our then distress, for the same reason that we will go forward with our wedding plans despite our even greater bereavement now: because Magda (and, back then, dear Peter) insisted. We wound down through your endless marshes—still, steaming, buggy—across the labyrinth of shallow waterways and distant loblolly pines in Backwater Wildlife Refuge, where I saw my first American eagle, down past Crapo and Tedious Creek to Bishops Head, at the lonely tail of Dorchester County. I thought uncomfortably of Ambrose's having brought Bea Golden through these same marshes in July, at the beginning of hateful Stage 5, to roger her up and down the beach whilst I stewed and fretted in my flapper drag up in Dorset Heights. . . A hundred years ago!

But clearly, and fortunately, nothing of the sort was on my lover's mind. I distracted him as best I could with bird and marsh plant and movie questions, but his eyes kept filling at the thought of poor Peter, poor Magda. We left our little car at the road's end, where nothing is but a fisherman's shack and pier, open water on three sides, and, across a mile-wide strait, low-lying, marshy Bloodsworth. Several other empty cars were parked there, among them a black limousine I knew to be Jane Mack's—but no one was about. We wondered. Presently a lad puttered up in a "Hooper's Island workboat" (A.'s designation) full of crab pots, and ferried us across to Cook's lodge: a cheerful young Charon who would not accept our proffered fare.

So this, thought I, is where they fucked. Well well. There was in fact no beach, only tidal mud flats, spartina grass, cattails. A brown "gut" of water marked with stakes led to Cook's dock; "Barataria" was a modest but comfortable white frame house, a small caretaker's cottage, a flagpole, grass doing badly on a sandy lawn. A few crabbing skiffs and a runabout were tied at the pier; a few untidy young people loitered about (refugees from the Remobilisation Farm, they looked to me); a few mosquitoes and biting green flies said hello to us.

Where was the movie? It would arrive after lunch, Cook's caretaker told us: a wizened, brown-burnt, friendly local whose "down-county" accent defied my ear and whose employer was off with Prinz & Co. The grips—they were indeed from Fort Erie—showed us crude sets of which they were inordinately proud, meant to represent the U.S. Capitol and the President's House in 1814. "Gonna burn them fuckers, come dark," etc. We were given lunch. The main company of *Frames,* it seemed, were shooting across the Bay, where the British had landed and reboarded after their remarkable expedition. They would return by boat sometime that afternoon.

Nothing to do but sip iced tea, worry about Peter, watch the hippies smoke dope, and wish we hadn't come so early, or at least had brought along the *Times.* We were, you remember, winding up our week of ritual Abstinence, the Echo of our Reenactment of et cetera. We agreed that Monday would be welcome, family crisis or no. I found in Cook's library a Mr Glen Tucker's *Poltroons & Patriots: A Popular Account of the War of 1812* in two volumes (1954) and did a spot of homework. Ambrose made desultory notes on his scenario.

Not till afternoon's end did the others finally arrive, in a fine big motor yacht named *Baratarian.* It belonged, we assumed, to the lord of Barataria Lodge: the laureate poet and new Distinguished Visiting Lecturer in English at Marshyhope State University. He was in any case conspicuously aboard, along with a paid captain and a crowd of others, including Reg Prinz, our old chums Bruce and Brice, and that Rising Young Starlet Merope Bernstein, of Fort Erie and Scajaquada fame.

They were late, Cook explained (after a bluff, booming welcome to us as the Shameless Lovebirds of Liberal-Land, who however, despite our egregious political and moral error, were to regard his Barataria as ours) because of a fortuitous encounter with Mr Todd Andrews's cruising boat across the Bay; they had made good use of it to film *Baratarian* under way and had filmed it in turn for "establishing footage," it being a renovated old oyster-dredging sailboat. And they had stopped off at Bishops Head to unload *another* pair of lovebirds: Jane Mack and her fiancé, "Lord Baltimore." It turns out that the yacht is hers, or theirs; they had kindly lent it to the *Frames* company for the weekend, but had themselves returned to Cambridge.

I have neglected to mention that this ruddy, fulsome nemesis of mine was rigged out in period costume; made up as, and bent on playing, his ancestor and namesake Andrew Burlingame Cook IV, of whom you know from my reports of a certain painful project whereof I long since washed my hands. The fellow had been a double agent, Cook maintained, in the British Chesapeake expedition of 1814 (news to me), and indeed was allegedly killed at Ft McH., though subsequent letters over his signature are said to have reached his widow at Castines Hundred. Be that as it may (the mere mention of that fateful place-name, and of ancestral letters, gave me a proper heartache, which Ambrose perceived, and squeezed my hand), his descendant seemed very much in charge of Prinz, B. & B., the whole business. Fresh from Mr Tucker's history, I was struck by Cook's likeness in face and manner, not to his forebear, of whom there are no extant portraits, but to Admiral Sir George Cockburn, Scourge of the Chesapeake, whom he had better played. Reggie framed and filmed; Bruce and Brice did their audiovisual things; Merope slouched about with wary eye, doubtless on the lookout for Jerome Bray—but Cook ran the show, in high-spirited (and high-handed) collaboration with my quondam Doctor of Letters, whose undoctoring, and my dismissal, he himself had advocated!

What to make of him? Neither André nor "Monsieur Casteene," he was the hale, unpredictable fellow I'd first encountered, along with Joe Morgan, in the Maryland Historical Society back in 1961: back-slapper and back-stabber, yet disarmingly "up front" about both and particularly forceful. Unrepentant for having sided with John Schott against Morgan, and later against Ambrose and myself, Cook nonetheless managed, whilst improvising with my friend a whole new scenario for the evening's shooting, to intimate to me that he was having second thoughts about his Marshyhope appointment: he had urged Schott to sound me out on possible reinstatement! "Of course," he went so far as to add, "you'll want to tell him where to get off. But we *must* have a chat about Germaine de Staël and the Bonapartes, especially between Elba and St Helena. Fascinating!"

As, one must acknowledge, is he, whoever he is. For all my urge to keep him at arm's length (I curbed my urge to press him about his ancestor's letters to his unborn child, and reacted neither way to the mention of my reappointment), I found myself involved—if only because Ambrose was, with a clearly therapeutic relish that warmed my heart—in the most preposterous bit of business yet mounted in this absurd production. We are a long way, John, from where we started in March, with a "motion picture based on your latest work, but echoing its predecessors"!

Are you ready? As thunderclouds pile up out over the Bay (and a pleasant buffet supper is spread by our host), Cook recounts in the first person to all assembled, from memory, his ancestor's "posthumous" description of the burning of Washington. The man is a raconteur of some talent and has obviously absorbed his *Poltroons & Patriots;* whether Andrew IV's letter is real or not, Andrew VI gives us a convincing "eyewitness" account of the events of 24 August 1814. And the *shtik* (to borrow Ambrose's tidewater Yiddish) is that as he chronicles the destruction—for us and for the microphone and cameras—we move outdoors from set to set and, approximately, reenact it.

Not forgetting, alas, the ongoing subplot, what's left of it: the War Between Image and Word, a.k.a. Director and Author. Nature cooperates with approaching lightning bolts and thunderclaps as the "Capitol's" canvas doors are battered down and "Andrew Cook IV" answers aye to "Admiral Cockburn's" motion to fire the building. The hippies set to with a will; Cook's caretaker brings umbrellas for the ladies, none of whom, save myself, minds getting drenched. Merry B. is inclined to huddle against Reg P. from the flames and the lightning, which are indeed impressive; but that silent fellow has been waiting his moment, and when we move now, in a pause in the downpour, behind the burning flat to a row of dripping bookshelves representing the Congressional Library, he breaks away from her to do a surprising, dangerous thing. Ambrose has of course been cast momentarily as the librarian, reading aloud from Tucker's history of this episode; Bruce and Brice stand by, a-filming; suddenly an eight-foot case of "books" (actually painted rows of spines, but the case itself is a heavy wooden thing) comes tumbling upon them, pushed by the Director, from an angle such that to avoid it they must spring toward the flames!

I am astonished (it will later be surmised that Prinz's real targets, ever more ascendant, were B. & B., not A.; he had better gone after C.). My betrothed, however, seems scarcely surprised: in the same motion with which he leaps clear, he whales Tucker Vol. 1 at Reggie's head, and seeing either that his aim is off since the famous First Conception scene or that Tucker's history is a less accurate missile than Richardson's novel, unhesitatingly he pulls half of the burning flat itself—a flimsy thing which the storm is breaking loose from its supports—down upon his adversary, knocking him into the mud!

No injuries on either side. Merope and I restrain our *macho* mates from further such exchanges. Right on, the hippies cry. Cook applauds and resumes his recitation. T-Dum and T-Dee exchange meaning glances and take up their stations.

I pass over other such notable moments to sing their culmination. The *mise en scène* is a flat representing the Tripoli Monument in the Washington Naval Yard, whose original was defaced by a British demolition team. We are to turn its (painted) sculptures into the following *tableau vivant:* Merry B. to represent Fame, as indicated by a great bronze palm; myself to represent History, wielding a similarly impressive pen (these props Cook claims to be the originals, long in his family's possession and much coveted by the Smithsonian). At a certain signal, "Director" and "Author"—both of whom have long since been usurped of their functions!—to see which can snatch what.

Places, everybody? But wait: I have not mentioned that our signal is to come, not from A. B. Cook, IV or VI, or any other of us, no, but from the United States Navy itself. Bloodsworth Island—as everyone seems to know except me—is mainly an aerial gunnery target, uninhabited below Barataria except by *very* intrepid herons and muskrats. At 2200 hours there is to commence a night-firing exercise in the Prohibited Zone, just south of us; there will be helicopters and patrol boats to insure that the area is clear before the fighters roar in from Patuxent Air Station, across the Bay. It is half after nine already; there they are now, the choppers, blinking and flashing and raising a frightful racket, obviously interested in our floodlights and smoking scenery. Cook waves at their searchlights. The hippies raise clenched fists and shout obscenities. The cameras roll. We take our places.

Am I mistaken in remembering our last sight of Jerome Bray (not counting the *sound* of him at the Ft Erie Magazine Explosion) to have been his departure by Newswatch helicopter, early in August, from Delaware Park in Buffalo? *Well*, sir: as if reinvoked by these awesome, clattering navy machines (we do not know how in fact he arrived; Cook alone seemed surprised to see him), just as Fame and I take our rain-soaked places, and Reggie and Ambrose toe the mark some metres off, and Cook makes ready to flag the start, a Union Jack in one hand and the Stars & Bars in t'other—it is 2155; it is 2156; we await the roar of jets—

Yup. Jerome Bonaparte Bray, on *top* of our *trompe-l'oeil* monument. Had anyone doubted the man is mad? Then picture him now, as Brice's cameras do, in archetypal madman's garb: his alleged ancestor's tricorn hat; the cutaway coat with turned-up collar and epaulets; the waistcoat under; and, yes, the wearer's right hand tucked in above the third button. He has escaped from Elba, Bray declaims, to aid the U. States against G. Britain: also from St Helena, to establish his Second Empire in America! He claims for himself both palm and pen, in token of his "conquest of letters by numbers." *Able was I*, he concludes, and I swear I quote him exactly: *Able was I. . .er. . .*

Here the chopper drowns him out; the fighter planes blast in at heart-stopping low altitude to fire tracer shells and heaven knows what else into the marsh below us; the storm has paused but not passed, and contributes its own apocalyptic sound-and-light background. Taken aback by Bray's appearance (in both senses) and by the racket, we are spellbound—all save Merope, who at first sight of him shrieks, flings away the palm, and runs. Reg Prinz jumps the gun and dashes for her trophy. Bray comes down at me, loony-eyed; it is the pen he wants (thank God), and I find myself, despite my alarm, in a proper tug-o'-war: plain limey stubbornness, I suppose. *Wham!* Here come the planes again, taking all our breaths. Ambrose rushes to my assistance: everyone is shouting over the din, myself included; Bruce and Brice impede my lover with lights and dollies; Prinz trips him up, swings at him with that palm. But like Perseus at the wedding feast, Ambrose wades through all obstacles to my side and snatches up the pen. Bray flees at once, behind or over the Tripoli flat, whither lately flew Fame.

Had we thought this subplot done? Reggie regroups and reassaults, catching A. a stiff clout on the shoulder: these symbols are no tokens, but heroic-scale bronzes weighing half a stone each! Perfectly furious, Abmrose deals him in reply a pen-stroke that might have split his directorial head, but happily only smashes once again his spectacles. Prinz gives a cry and comes down with the palm on Ambrose's wrist. The pen falls (I grab it); Author tackles Director; they thrash like schoolboys in the mud; the planes roar out as the storm moves back in—and at this appropriate moment the electrical generator fails.

Enough, A. B. Cook and History agree. Brice and Bruce are with us. We separate the soiled combatants: Reggie's cheek is cut and bruised; Ambrose's wrist (we shall learn) is fractured. Both are mucky and disabled; neither is in terrible pain. There is a general move toward shelter, but Cook and I—and Ambrose, when he gets his breath—are concerned for Merope, who is not to be found with the others back in the lodge. Nor, ominously, is the Emperor of the French. A search must be mounted: if the storm re-retreats, Cook informs us, the navy might well resume their firing exercise.

I am forbidden to join the party. Not male chauvinism, Ambrose explains (holding his right wrist), but reasonable concern for my condition. I yield; it is *awfully* messy out there. Prinz declines the invitation: true, he can scarcely see without his glasses, but he seems to us not much to care. Indeed, he appears if anything disgusted with his protégée for having thrown in the palm and bolted (our host has retrieved both emblems, tisking his tongue at their misuse). In the end it is Cook, Ambrose, and three of the hippies—comrades of Merope's from the Marshyhope commencement bust—who sally out into the swamp with ponchos and pocket torches.

They find no trace of the abdicated emperor. There is some concern that he may have strayed into the Prohibited Zone, since at its perimeter (marked with large warnings of unexploded ordnance) they discover poor bedraggled Fame. She is intact, not apparently injured, but quite dazed, sitting in a puddle in the marshy path, propped against the warning sign. They wonder whether she has been raped: Her jeans are open, and there is a fresh bruise on her bum. Nope, she says, dopily; she "took a leak" and then "sort of zonked out." I shall wonder later, as I tend to her back in the lodge, whether she did in fact take some sort of drug, voluntarily or otherwise: one of her comrades, a black girl named Thelma, intimates surprisingly that Bray is involved in the narcotics trade! In any case, our starlet is most certainly woozy. We put her to bed.

I am obliged to speak well of Mr Cook's management of this wacky emergency. Despite his incongruous and now mud-spoiled costume, he is all authority and good sense in his organisation of the search and his solicitude for Ms. Bernstein. He now insists that Author and Director declare, if not a truce, at least a cease-fire for the duration of their visit to Barataria. He will telephone the navy at once concerning Bray; given the weather, he does not believe that firing will be resumed; on the other hand, he thinks it useless to pursue the search for Bray before morning. We should all go to bed. The filmists as usual will bunk about the floors and porches of the lodge; we lovebirds are to do him the honour of using the guest apartment in the caretaker's cottage. The man even bandages, and expertly, my lover's wrist, which is now sore and swelling, accompanying his first aid with ribald innuendo. Tweedledee remarks that we did not really "do" the accidental explosion of the navy yard, per Andrew IV's letter. Andrew VI opines that we have enough big-bang footage to serve, and bids us good night.

But A. and I are too amused, aroused, and exhausted to sleep. Showered and pajama'd, we praise each other's scrappiness; we shake our heads at the rueful irony of his injured writing hand and wonder about Merope and Bray and A. B. Cook. (*I* wonder too whether we are sharing the same bed in which—but never mind.) We decide that the Word-versus-Image subplot really has gone far enough, at least in its hostile aspect. Presently we sleep, only to be waked well after midnight by a single final mighty *bang* out in the marshes. It seems to have come from the direction of the firing zone; but there is no sound of planes, and the storm has passed to occasional silent lightning flickers in the east. Has Bruce, we wonder, slipped out after all to do the navy yard? Or has luckless Napoleon stumbled upon a bit of unexploded ordnance and blown himself to kingdom come? In any case, I sleepily observe, it is indeed past midnight: *i.e.,* it is Monday, 25 August, 1st day of Week 4 etc. We may put by our programmatic abstinence. We do.

Next morning all hands compare notes on that last explosion. B. & B. disclaim responsibility, but wish they'd "caught" it. Merope is still stoned, Prinz is still fed up, with her and all of us. A. B. Cook has been up betimes: navy search-craft are on their way, he reports, and adds that inasmuch as he has been being pressured to yield title to Barataria Lodge to the federal government, we may expect some interrogatory harassment from navy intelligence and security people concerning trespass into the Prohibited Area. We are to cooperate respectfully (There are cries of "Off the pigs!")—but if anyone happens to possess marijuana or other illegal material, it were well to dispose of it. Laughter, hoots, further obscenities, and much busy disposal.

Ambrose's wrist is sorer and sorer, and our business is done. Even so, we dally till nearly noon out of curiosity to watch the search and speak to sober-faced but polite military people. Ambrose uses Cook's typewriter to peck out his left-handed letter to you, and remarks afterward that he can now sympathise with his late father's one-armed attempt at memorial sculpture. No trace of Jerry Bray. Still bluff and cheerful, Cook nonetheless expresses concern that the Department of Defense may use this unfortunate accident to justify condemnation proceedings against him.

There is one final small crisis. On the first available boat after breakfast, Reg Prinz leaves for the mainland, for his rented car (how can he drive without his glasses?), and for Manhattan, with not even a good-bye to Merry B. She is not too "zonked" to get the message, with suitable abandoned outcry. I do my best and then leave her to her friends, who agree that the fellow is a fink, maybe even a nark. Cook urges us to stay for lunch, thanks us for our assistance as if he were the film's producer (who knows?), and heartily hopes we'll "see things through to the final frame."

The former invitation we decline. The latter, in its cin-ematographic aspect, involves two more scenes: Fort McHenry and Barataria. We shall see. Between ourselves, I happily report, Ambrose and I are indeed inclined to See Things Through et cetera—though there has arisen, since the Burning of Washington, a certain question about the number of frames to go.

Of that question I shall not speak here: see his, our, letter to "A. M. King," attached. We were ferried back in style to Bishops Head aboard one of the small navy craft (Ambrose pointed out a skipjack entering the strait under sail from seaward and wondered whether it was Mr Andrews's), retrieved our car, and drove home—History at the wheel, perforce—to the sinking Menschhaus.

A bittersweet interval, the next few days: see that same letter. Our original 4th Stage, you may remember (*I* surely do), was something sorry, as was our 5th: that degrading latter May and June and July. A good side of the bad coin of Peter's crisis is that—along with our growing love—it set aside all but the tenderest echoes of those reenactments of, respectively, Ambrose's marriage to Marsha Blank and the *ménage à trois* with Peter and Magda which immediately preceded our own affair. I can therefore summarise. Even as we got Ambrose's wrist fracture set and cast in the hospital emergency room, Peter was discharged into our care to await his radical surgery: the last ten days, as it turned out, of his life. On 27 August the full Sturgeon Moon rose out of the upper Choptank, sailed over Mensch's Castle, and set in Chesapeake Bay without the aid of Germaine Gordon Pitt's menstruation. Magda wept and kissed me. Peter called for champagne. Ambrose hugged his daughter, his sister-in-law, and his fiancée, and soberly toasted the health of. . .the *six* of us. On the Saturday (30 August) a letter arrived from Marsha, meant to shock us: Peter, she declared, not Ambrose, was Angela's father. It did not. More champagne. See A.'s letter.

The which he taped, and I transcribed, on the Monday, 1 September, Labour Day. In and by it Ambrose proposed to marry me on Saturday 13th (the date of this, though we are not there yet); and I accepted despite certain apprehensions therein registered. We did not know, as we played with our sixes and sevens and scheduled climaxes within climaxes, that Joe Morgan up in Fort Erie was shooting himself through the head, and that Marsha Blank Mensch had (reluctantly, I'm sure) relieved Ambrose of further alimony payments by *marrying Jacob Horner!* And that dear Peter had but four more days to live.

Those days—the first four of our 5th week of Mutuality—are too near and dear and painful to recount. I am not a weak woman. I have myself watched a husband die (and lost a previous lover, and a son). But I do not fathom the strength and serenity, or the capaciousness of heart, of Magda Giulianova. I quite love that woman! We four (five, six) quite loved one another. I can say no more. See etc.

On the 4th, a Thursday, Peter reentered hospital for amputation of both legs, one to the hip, the other to the knee, with every likelihood even so of surviving less than five years. A confusion of schedules kept the orthopedic surgeon, a weekly visitor from Baltimore, up in the city a day longer than expected; the operation was postponed till next afternoon. That Thursday night someone broke into the closed office of Mensch Masonry, rifled the files (sealed by court-appointed receivers), and stole copies of the design specifications and foundation blueprints of the Marshyhope Tower of Truth. No clues yet; suspicion falls heavily and kindlessly upon Ambrose, who was in fact with me and/ or Magda uninterruptedly. On the Friday morning, sometime before dawn, Peter took a massive dose of Tylenol and ended his life. Suspicion there, too, falls upon the Menschhaus, more mildly but in this case accurately. Though there will be no investigation beyond the routine enquiry required to clear the hospital of liability, the fact is that Magda and Ambrose supplied Peter with pills, at his request, on the Wednesday or Thursday, precisely in case he should change his mind about seeing things through to the final frame.

Why Tylenol? Because, Ambrose explained, aspirin, barbiturates, Seconal, and the like can be promptly pumped out, especially when their taker is already in hospital, without fatal results. But Tylenol, in large doses, besides being easier to lay hands on than prescription chemicals, quickly does irreversible and lethal liver damage. Peter thus became, along with his sculpting Uncle Wilhelm, the only member of the family known not to have died of cancer. We buried him last Saturday beside that uncle and the others, all his limbs attached.

(Angie has been difficult to manage since. The loss seems to have sickened her physically: she wakes up vomiting.)

That same Saturday came the shocking news of Morgan's accident or suicide (word reached the local newspaper on the Wednesday, but we in the Lighthouse were too distracted to read the newspapers): specifically, that his gunshot wound had been ruled self-inflicted and Jacob Horner cleared of implication, and that the body had been returned from Fort Erie to our neighbouring town of Wicomico for burial on the same day we buried Peter (Morgan's late wife is buried over there; we have since learned that Horner and his bride accompanied the casket from Ontario to Maryland, along with Morgan's sons). The funeral having been a private affair, there was to be a memorial service next day in the chapel of Marshyhope State University. We decided that I should attend, as having been closest of the family to Morgan. Ambrose would stay with Magda and Angie.

It was a fairly nauseating ceremonial, not however without its comic touches. I should pass over it except that so many of "your characters" were there, and that it gives to this narrative of my affair with Ambrose Mensch an almost novelistic symmetry: we "began" with the service for Harrison Mack on Redmans Neck in February, and in effect we "end" (our premarital courtship, not our connexion!) with another such service in the same general geography.

It was conducted in the Show and Tell Room of MSU's Media Centre, which doubles as a nondenominational campus chapel until the enormous projected new Hall of All Faiths shall have been raised. So declared the nervous young university chaplain, a new appointee, over the newly installed super-quadraphonic public-address system, out from which the new audiovisual crew had not yet got all the bugs. It also served, he said, this sad convocation, as mournful prelude to a more positive spiritual programme: the new series of "Sunday Raps" to be held every Sabbath morn of the regular semester, commencing with a jazz-rock orientation rap a week hence (tomorrow). Marshyhope's first president, he was (wrongly) confident, would be pleased. And now, himself not having been fortunate enough to know President Morgan personally, he would relinquish the mike to our current chief executive, who would, so to speak, emcee the rest of the show.

I had slipped in intentionally late, not to have to suffer the condolences of John Schott & Co. or to deal, if I could avoid dealing, with Marsha Blank Mensch Horner, who I feared might be present. From a back seat in the S & T Room I saw that she was: as whacked-out-appearing as her bridegroom, but with a restored grimness of eye and jaw that evoked my image of the Marsha Primordial—and gave me to wonder once again why A. had ever married her. Horner looked paralysed with terror at being off the premises of the Remobilisation Farm; very possibly he was. There were two long-haired, grave-faced young men I took to be Joe's sons; there was Jane Mack, impassive and apparently alone, her son Drew likewise, and Todd Andrews, looking utterly spent; there was A. B. Cook, who managed an expression somehow both grave and whimsical. Many strangers to me were present as well—representatives, I learned after, of Wicomico State College and the Maryland Historical Society.

Oh, John. Chaplain Beille wound up his introduction with an uncertain comparison of Joe Morgan to the late Bishop James Pike, whose body had that day been found in the desert near the Dead Sea: both men were, well, Seekers, whose Search, um, had led them down Unconventional and Uncharted Paths, but, uh. John Schott took the podium, to Miss Stickles's scarcely suppressed applause. With what my fiancé would later describe as Extreme Unctuousness, he spoke of having first hired Young Morgan at Wicomico in 1952; of having watched him "make a comeback" from the tragic loss of his wife in '53 to his brilliant directorship of the historical society, thence to the first presidency of Tidewater Technical College and the supervision of its growth to Marshyhope State College and Marshyhope State *University* College; of Morgan's then "returning the favour," so to speak (a heavy chuckle here, returned by the company), of hiring *him* to be his vice-president and provost of the Faculty of Letters!

Now Schott's tone grew solemn. It was no secret that he and "Joe" had differed on many issues. But no one had regretted more than himself his worthy adversary's departure from MSUC, on the very eve of its becoming MSU! It was a tragedy that the final year in the life of his protégé, as one might well call Morgan, had been as cloaked in obscurity as Bishop Pike's: both of them, in Schott's view, Casualties of

669

Our Times! But whatever the contents of that tragic last chapter, it was ended: Joe was with his beloved wife now, on the Eastern Shore he cared so much for; and Schott knew in his heart that whatever his predecessor's reservations about the Tower of Truth, there was no better loser than Joseph Patterson Morgan! He Schott had wanted him with us at the tower's dedication, three weeks hence; he knew that Joe would give that edifice and Marshyhope his blessing, from Heaven!

He closed with an equally exclamatory and unbecoming pitch for his own administration: skyrocketing enrollment figures, the massive building program, the great news (which he had been saving for the first university convocation on Monday the 15th, but could not resist leaking to us now) that approval was "all but finalized" in Annapolis for a seven-year plan to make MSU a proper City of Learning by 1976, perhaps even larger than the state's current main campus at College Park! Morgan had hoped for 7,000 students: how gratified he would be at the prospect of 17,000, 27,000, eventually perhaps twice that number!

On this exquisite perversion of the verb *to hope*, and as Shirley Stickles sighed orgasmically in her seat, Schott turned the mike over to One Far More Eloquent Than Himself. A. B. Cook ascended the podium. There was a pause to adjust the P.A., which had been squealing as if in protest. Student ushers, deputized from the Freshman Orientation Committee, took the opportunity to seat latecomers, including, to my surprise, Ambrose. His attendance on Magda had been relieved by the twins and their girl- and boyfriends; she had insisted he join me. Looking about the room for me in vain, he was led to a seat just behind the Jacob Horners. Marsha glared and froze; Ambrose likewise, and desperately surveyed the audience again. Appalled, I pushed through to the empty seat next to him. Marsha's expression could kill an unborn child; A. and I whispered accord on the matter of retreat to a rear seat. But Cook had launched into his versified eulogy and benediction.

Our situation was too off-putting for me to be able now to reconstruct those verses. In his well-amplified baritone Cook made the same connexion (but unrelated to ourselves) that I'd made earlier, between the funeral of Marshyhope's founder in February and its first president's now: the predictable September/remember/glowing-ember rhymes. Observing that John Schott's Fallen Forerunner had been "an historian" (rhymed with "not a boring one"!), Cook invoked "what might be called the Anniversary View of History": surely it was Significant that 7 September was the birthday of that *other* J. P. Morgan, as well as of Queen Elizabeth I: wouldn't our late founder have approved! (Unaware of our presence behind him, or of much else, Jacob Horner added sotto voce "the Comte de Buffon, Taylor Caldwell, Elia Kazan, Peter Lawford"; Marsha poked him.) Surely it was Significant, given Joseph Morgan's professional interests, that today marked the anniversary of the launching in Baltimore, in 1797, of the frigate

Constellation, soon to play a rôle in the cinematical reenactment of our history; that on this date in 1812 Napoleon defeated the Russian army at Borodino, and in 1822 Brazil's claim of independence began the Portuguese Revolution. ("Right on!" I was surprised to hear Drew Mack say; the morning paper had reported release of fifteen Brazilian leftist political prisoners as ransom for the kidnapped U.S. ambassador.) And 7 September 1940 had marked the peak of the German air war against Great Britain, rhymes with *fittin'.* Horner nodded vigorously.

None of us, the laureate concluded, is *immortal:*

> The stoutest fort'll
> Fall; the final portal
> Open. Death's the key
> Of keys, the cure of cures.
> All passes. Art alone endures.

Horner applauded. Marsha whacked him. People shushed. Muttered Ambrose (as the chaplain rose to give a final benediction): "Art passes too."

Outside there were brief unavoidable stiff encounters; I was relieved not to have to deal with them alone. John Schott harrumphingly gave me to know that other pressing commitments of Mr Cook's might make it impossible for him to ornament the English faculty after all, and that he Schott, among others, was pressing for my immediate reappointment. That matter would be brought before the provostial Appointments and Tenure Committee at once if I was agreeable; bygones be bygones, etc. Perhaps for the fall semester, I replied, if the university dropped their action to rescind Ambrose's honorary degree. But never mind the spring: we were expecting a baby in March or April.

The man was satisfactorily taken aback; his fink of a secretary as well. Ambrose squeezed my arm approvingly. But Marsha was all ears behind us, with her husband in tow. She too, she announced with saurian satisfaction, was expecting a child—with, given her relative youth, better odds than some on a normal delivery. Let us charitably suppose that Marsha had not yet heard of Peter's death and was simply reconnoitering the effects of her Bombshell Letter. I feared for Ambrose's temper; was tempted myself to reply that Marsha's own track record in the delivery of normal children was not impressive. But our grief (and love) detached us; put things in right and wry perspective. You're married, then, Ambrose remarks to the pair of them, with a great no-alimony smile. Certainly *not,* snaps Marsha. Well, opines Horner, in point of fact we are, though Marsha is retaining her maiden name. Shut *up,* Mrs H. commands him. And while their new baby is of course not his, Horner bravely persists, he hopes his wife will permit him to name it, if a boy, Joseph Morgan Horner; if a girl, Josephine. Oh, you *jerk,* says Marsha; I'll Josephine *you.*

Ambrose expansively congratulated them and invited them to our

671

own wedding on the Saturday next, at Fort McHenry (we had of course decided earlier to postpone it, but Magda was insisting that we proceed; this was my first and happy notice that we were going forward as scheduled). Marsha flounced and sniffed away as satisfyingly as a comeuppanced Rival at the end of a Smollett novel. Her husband shifted about, thanked us gravely for the invitation, but declined on the grounds that that date (Rosh Hashanah and birthday of Sherwood Anderson, Claudette Colbert, J. B. Priestley, Walter Reed, and Arnold Schoenberg, we might be interested to know) marked Marsha's debut as admissions secretary at Wicomico State College, where he himself hoped soon to return to the teaching of remedial English. Hers was not normally a six-day job, we were to understand; but the coming week and weekend were busy at Wicomico, as at Marshyhope, with the orientation and registration of incoming students.

Ambrose fairly clapped him on the shoulder. Bravo, old chap, and so long! Have a good life, etc.! We were both grinning through our grief: poor bastards all! I'd not have minded a clarifying word with A. B. Cook, whom I espied in deep conversation with Todd Andrews; but we were anxious lest Marsha disturb our household with a visit to Angela. Our walk to the car took us past the Tower of Truth, the last of its scaffolding cleared and its landscaping in progress. Drew Mack, in clean blue denims, and those same three who had helped in the search for Merope Bernstein—the black girl Thelma, a good-looking Chicano or Puerto Rican boy, and a fuzzy gringo—were regarding the structure and pointing things out to one another. Drew had the good manners to offer his condolences for Peter's death and his regrets that the rifling of Mensch Masonry's files was being regarded in some quarters as an "inside job" to cover our legal tracks. As if the state General Services Department didn't have copies of everything stolen! He himself thought the tower an architectural abomination, a rape of the environment, and a symbol of the American university's corruption by the capitalist-imperialist society which sustained it. That there was literal falsehood in its construction he did not doubt; the building's infamous flaws, with their attendant litigation, attested that. But he knew Peter Mensch to have been an honest man and an able stonemason, happier in blue collar than white.

That he was, my friend, said Ambrose. And it would have pleased him to see this thing dismantled, stone by stone.

Jane Mack was chauffeured past, somewhat grim-faced, I thought. She did not return her son's amiable wave. They are, Drew explained, contesting his father's will; he apologised to me that my own bequest was being delayed by that suit, and assured me that neither he nor his mother, and most certainly not the Tidewater Foundation, begrudged me my reward for "caring for" Harrison Mack. Drew's own attorney and Mr Andrews were pressing the court to execute all such non-contested bequests forthwith.

Will you believe, sir, that I had quite forgot I was an heiress? I'd

672

certainly never humoured and tended poor Harrison with expectation of reward, but my provision in his will is generous—$30,000, I believe. That amount would, will, decidedly bolster for a time the sagging economy of the Menschhaus and provide a bit of a nest egg for our hatchling-in-the-works. I shared the good news with Ambrose; together with the glad tidings of Marsha's marriage, it cheered us right up, and Magda too, as we returned to our bereavement.

Harrison Mack, Joseph Morgan, and Peter Mensch, good men all: rest in peace!

We now enter our 6th, climactic week of Mutuality, Ambrose (and you) and I: what I must call, though I've yet to wed, our honeymoon; the "ourest" week of "our" stage, this 6th, of our romance. I write these words on Thursday evening, 11 September, just returned with my lover from a day of planning and conferring at Fort McHenry. It is, A. B. Cook has told us, the anniversary of Governor-General Prevost's rout at Plattsburgh and Lake Champlain in 1814 (*i.e.*, in the 1812 War), when also the British Chesapeake fleet, fresh from burning Washington, assembled at the mouth of the Patapsco for the attack on Baltimore. What's more (Jacob Horner would have applauded to hear) it is by the Diocletian calendar New Year's Day of Year 1686.

Our own new week had till today been spent in loving grief and vice versa at the Menschhaus, which now belongs to Magda. We have put Peter's affairs in order (there was little to do that receivership had not already done; Angie is Ambrose's—our—financial responsibility; with her own children independent, Magda can live adequately on her new salary and Peter's insurance). Over her protest I have renewed my lease on 24 L Street. Magda wants us to live unabashedly with her; she hopes we will at least leave Angie there. But we are making no commitments.

We *have* been making love, as you will have imagined, in recapitulatory fashion: *i.e.*, on the Monday Ambrose was scarcely potent, and I awkward and unresponsive (it was midmorning at 24 L; we were both distracted with Last Things); on the Tuesday his potency returned in spades, but I was wondering whatever happened to Bea Golden and managed no more than a partial orgasm; on the Wednesday we were chaste: Magda insisted we go forward not only with our marriage but with our wedding, and we agreed on condition that she and Angie take part in it (I spent the day drafting the preceding pages of this letter). This morning therefore Ambrose warmly reproposed marriage to me; I accepted; we sealed the compact with an "A.M. quickie" and drove up to Baltimore for a story conference.

The Baratarians were already at McHenry, minus Reg Prinz, Merope Bernstein, Jerome Bray (who however was, it seems, somehow *not* blitzed after all on Bloodsworth), and of course Bea Golden. Bruce, Brice, and A. B. Cook were in clear charge, the laureate commuting to the scene like ourselves but from nearer by: that house of his down near the Bay Bridge. Drew was on hand with his gang (we have learned that he and his lovely black wife are divorcing; no details). Below us in the harbour was moored the yacht *Baratarian,* lent us again—by Mack Enterprises?—for water shots, for ferrying gear and personnel between Baltimore and Bloodsworth Island (75 sea miles to south of us), and for limited overnight accommodation. No one was aboard except the hired skipper. Such is the power of the movie-camera lens, at which Ambrose and I still shake our heads, that the U.S. Park Service and the city of Baltimore had obligingly put the fort and the old U.S.F. *Constellation* (in process of being restored in the city's inner harbour) at our limited disposal for as long as we required them.

Two days of preparation and one of principal shooting, we estimated, and set about making plans. Since the "D.C." fracas, Ambrose's authority seems to have waxed. Prinz's return is more or less expected tomorrow or Saturday, but is far from certain (Merope, Cook declares, is unbelievably reconciled with Bray and has returned to live with him in Lily Dale!). Bruce & Brice make technical suggestions, but take their orders from Cook; and Cook and my fiancé, believe it or not, are in surprising general rapport on what the scene is to comprise. The historical text is still what they are calling the Ampersand Letter of A. B. Cook IV—the ciphered original begins with that character—which describes not only the operation against Washington but the move on Baltimore. As to the casting: Cook as before will play his ancestor; Ambrose (his cast and sling now exchanged for a wrist bandage) will take the part of F. S. Key, watching through the night from the decks of *Baratarian*—renamed *Surprize* after Admiral Cochrane's temporary command-ship—to say whether he can see etc. In default of other leading ladies, I have agreed to play Britannia one last time, "still mourning the loss of her colonies in '76 and making her final effort to repossess them." What had been projected as a "Third Conception scene" has been rescripted as the Wedding scene: our actual nuptials, but evocative (not my adjective) of the Treaty of Ghent and the new harmony to follow between Britannia and Columbia.

What about British support of the Confederacy in the U.S. Civil War only 40 years later, I innocently enquire? A mere marital squabble, Cook replies. He then congratulated me, *most* warmly, on my Delicate Condition, and proposed that it be made somehow to betoken the parturition of America from Britain. Also, that our wedding march be "God Save the Queen," sung thus by the "British" and as "My Country 'Tis of Thee" by the Yankees. Finally, to symbolise the birth of a nation truly independent of both Britain and France, the bridegroom Ambrose/Key will draft, and all hands sing, "The Star-Spangled Banner"! There remains to be worked out the inclusion, in this armistitial farrago, of the reconciliation of Word and Image, fiction and film. It is my fiancé's deadpan hope that Reg Prinz will appear in time for consultation on that score. Otherwise we shall "wing it."

The constituency of the wedding party, too, has yet to be decided; we shall settle all that tomorrow.

But now it *is* tomorrow, Friday, 12 September, celebrated in this state as Defender's Day by reason of the foregoing. It is in fact late evening, properly showering (as in 1814) and cooler, a wet touch of autumn. I did not, it turns out, go up to Baltimore today. Angie was rambunctious, Magda feeling down; I stayed behind to look after things. Now Ambrose has returned and reported; likewise shall I.

The day began with love, and so it has just ended (but not, this P.M., with love*making:* our last night as lovers leaves us subdued, nervous, chaste). After Ambrose had made love with me this morning and left, I consoled dear Magda as best I could, not without some effect. I then reviewed this letter and did a deal of note-taking on the Fiction of the Bonapartes, against the possibility that I might after all be teaching this fall. As if conjured by that activity, a phone call came from John Schott, "feeling me out" again (his creepish term) on my "standby availability" should Mr Cook be unable etc. He has recommended to the board of regents that Ambrose's degree be let stand after all, and though of course the decision is theirs, not his, he feels confident that etc. The 1960's, after all, are etc. And he understands that Dr Mensch and I are about to Tie the Knot, Make It Legal, heh heh. Cook is to let him know definitely next week whether he can accept the Distinguished Visitorship.

I shall do likewise, I said. And the spring semester? He will cross that bridge when he draws nearer it, Schott declared. What the Faculty of Letters needs for the 1970's, he foresees, is less trendy "relevance" and more Back-to-Basics: he is considering the restoration of required freshman courses in basic composition, prescriptive grammar, even spelling. He knows a first-chop teacher in that field, who has recently moved to the area. . .

I said—and say—no more. In any case, the afternoon brought a more serious jolt, which it shakes me afresh to record. Pacified at last with the (regressive) help of her Easter egg, Angie went out after lunch to fool about on the river shore as is her wont in every weather. As is *our* wont, I made certain to check on her from time to time from a window. At one point I saw her speaking with two men in a battered Volvo wagon parked at the road's end, not far from the house. I hurried out, affecting nonchalance. Was at first relieved to see that the driver was Drew Mack: denim shirt, sandy-blond ponytail, flushed face, and white smile of greeting. Why was he not in Baltimore with the rest? They were just on their way, he declared; had some business here before he and his friend took over the night shift at Fort McHenry. Had I met Hank Burlingame?

You feel my heart catch. I lean down to manage a tight smile across Drew to his passenger. Angie shuffles her sneakers and snaps her fingers to melodies unheard. It is the same young man as at Harrison's funeral: dark-haired and -eyed, lean-limbed and -featured, almost sallow; a polite smile and nod, a reticent, accented greeting; very European-looking clothes (black shoes and trousers, white dress shirt

675

fastened at the neck, no jacket or tie). And eyes fiery as Franz Kafka's. I asked how. . .did he do? He gazed through me and said Thank you. Angie came with me back to the house.

There is a shock I didn't need, John, on my wedding eve. Angie "watched" them from an upper window through her egg, as if it were a telescope; I unabashedly tried Ambrose's telescope—but "my son" was on the far side of the car. Drew himself was using binoculars, trained not on me but on the Choptank bridge, and seemed to be explaining something. Presently they left; moments later I saw their car pass over that same bridge, presumably towards Baltimore.

Well. By Ambrose's return I was composed enough not to show my dismay or even, for the present, mention this encounter. I shall tell him when things are calmer, perhaps in "Stage Seven." I held him tightly and then kept him talking of the day's news, our wedding plans, as we made dinner. Todd Andrews, he reported, had been at McHenry, looking in vain for Drew Mack: Bea Golden is officially a Missing Person, of whom no trace has been found since she left the Remobilisation Farm in mid-August to visit Jerome Bray! Mr Andrews confided to Ambrose his fear that she may be a victim of her growing alcoholism, or have been victimised in her dependency. Police have been alerted in New York, Maryland, and California; Bray's premises have been searched in vain (no explanation of his resurrection from the Prohibited Area!). Andrews is also concerned—Ambrose thinks unnecessarily—that young Mack's divorce and other factors may be leading him from radicalism toward terrorism.

Never mind, I said, so long as he doesn't terrorise our wedding. What had been decided in that line? Perhaps to chuck the whole McHenry circus and slip off to the nearest J.P.?

He kissed me. Nope. After Peter's death, Ambrose had considered asking *you*, sir, to be his best man—your rejection of our honorary doctorate and your subsequent silence having played no small part in bringing him and me together. Given the exigencies of the movie "wrap-up," however—and the erstwhile Director's reappearance after all on the set today—it was decided that *Reg Prinz*, newly spectacled, will serve in that capacity! Now *darling*, I began—but then thought of Henry/Henri Burlingame VII, and other things. Well, I said, it's the groom's choice. But let there be no stunts or surprises on our wedding day. No stunts, Ambrose pledged; and if there are surprises, they won't come from him. Prinz had agreed: let armistice and harmony prevail! Magda and Angie to be matron of honour and bridesmaid, respectively? Done. A. B. Cook, the double agent of 1814, to give the bride away? Well. . .done (I reported Schott's call: the doctorate not after all to be revoked; the spectre of Jacob & Mrs Horner on the horizon. Ambrose agreed, to my immense relief, that if Angie could handle it we should all vacate this scene as soon as humanly feasible. Hurrah!). The MSU chaplain, *faute de mieux*, to officiate. We were to be on the set by noon.

Done, done, done! We kissed our bridesmaids and each other good night, agreed not to make love (we've plenty of *that* to do tomorrow), and for the sport of it bedded down separately, he in the basement, I in the Lighthouse, where I pen this. The casements are open; some quirk of acoustics makes audible the horn of the Choptank River Light, ten miles downstream: an unlikely shofar heralding the Jewish new year and my new life to come. . .

Now at last it is the letterhead date: half after nine Saturday morning, 13 September 1969. My (second) wedding day. Partly cloudy, 50% POP. The family are piling into two cars below: Carl, Connie, and their betrotheds into a camperbus, Magda and Ambrose and Angie (egg in hand) into our little car.

At 1:45 this morning, precisely, Ambrose came upstairs to me. Sleepily we coupled, *a tergo,* on our sides, and returned to sleep. I record these things for a particular reason.

At 5:10 (he'd set the alarm) I kissed him awake and erect; "went down"; etc.

At 8:35, reroused by him from sleep, I climbed atop my husband-to-be, attained myself a lightsome climax but, by A.'s own report, "drained him dry." Douched, breakfasted with all, dressed, made ready, and wrote these paragraphs, perhaps my last to you.

Off now to Fort McHenry, marriage, perhaps maternity. To a certain string of 7's. To a hundred unknowns.

O John, wish me well!

G.

L: *Lady Amherst to the Author.* Her wedding day and night. The Dawn's Early Light sequence and the Baratarian disasters. Her vision of the Seventh Stage.

24 L Street
Dorset Heights, Maryland 21612
Saturday, 20 September 1969

Dear John,

"Lady Amherst" is no more. I am Germaine Mensch now, Mrs. Ambrose: my third and presumably last last name. But as this will be my last letter to you (I'd thought my last was; then arrived—at last!—your greeting, your marriage blessing, your alphabetical prayer for us; this is my thanks to you for that, in kind), let it be for certain the last from the author of its two-dozen-odd predecessors: the former Lady A.

Today concludes my maiden week, so to speak, as Ambrose's wife—and my first week of classes at Marshyhope State University! Tomorrow ends our seventh (and last?) week of "usness": this sweet

677

Sixth Stage of our love affair. Monday was to have initiated our Seventh (and last?) Stage, as yet undefined: we had thought my gynecological appointment, scheduled for that day, would help define it. But the Monday being Yom Kippur and my doctor gently Jewish, we shall not learn until the Tuesday—when the sun enters Libra and tilts Maryland towards autumn—whether I am, as I hope and believe, not menopausal but pregnant.

And not until the spring of the new year, the new decade, shall we know, Ambrose and I, what this old womb and those exhausted sperm have combined to make. All my intuitions tell me that the seven months between now and then, the no doubt delicate balance of my pregnancy, will be our Seventh Stage, whatever the issue and whatever follows. But we three—Magda knows, of course, our crazy calendrics—officially and lovingly declare otherwise: that Stage Seven, like the outer arc of some grand spiral, will curve on and out at least beyond our sight.

May it be so.

You cannot *not* have heard, even in your upland, inland retreat, what the Baltimore and Washington newspapers have been full of: A. B. Cook's "accidental" death at Fort McHenry the morning after our wedding there; the "accidental" deaths two days later of Reg Prinz and three others on Bloodsworth Island when that navy drone aircraft crashed into Barataria Lodge; the discovery yesterday of the motor yacht *Baratarian:* abandoned, half swamped, adrift in the Atlantic just off the Virginia Capes, her captain, her owner, and her owner's "nephew" all missing and presumed "accidentally" lost at sea.

Her owner? Baron André Castine of Castines Hundred, Ontario! His "nephew"? Henry Cook Burlingame VII!

My son Henri.

Where will these accidents end? To what "final frame" must I see things through? (In case you've wondered: my husband and I have reviewed the several hazards of pregnancy at my age and have discussed, and rejected, therapeutic abortion.) And where do I begin, who ought by rights to be destroyed by that final news item above, but who find myself, Magda-like, unaccountably, it would seem almost reprehensibly, serene?

I shall begin where last I ended: leaving the Menschhaus that mild Saturday forenoon sennight since, our wedding day—when so many now dead were yet alive! The postman strolled up just as we left, took my letter to you, and handed Angie the mail: condolences for Magda, mostly, which she refused to open till another day; a few worrisome bills; my copy of the lease on this apartment, which I had renewed. . .and the letter from you addressed to *Mr & Mrs Ambrose Mensch,* which Mister fished out and tucked away in his coat before I saw it, intending a later surprise. Following Carl and Connie's van, we crossed Choptank River and Chesapeake Bay, both as alive with bright hulls and sails as a Dufy watercolour, and shortly before noon arrived at

Fort McHenry, showing our *Frames* passes to the park guards for admittance.

The "bombardment" was already in progress. From the parking lot (where with a twinge of guilt, among other emotions, I espied Drew Mack's Volvo wagon) we saw smoke bombs, some gaily coloured, and heard a cannonading that Angie clung to me in alarm at. Lots of local media folk about, freely filming and being filmed, taping and being taped. Prinz himself descended from the ramparts to greet us, newly eyeglassed, smiling, mild—all quarrels apparently put by! He distinctly said hello to Angela! Put a sympathetic hand on Magda's shoulder for one eloquent instant! Astonished me by bussing my cheek, and to bride and groom delivered himself of not one but *two* more or less complete English sentences:

1. *Cook's on the boat.*
2. *Lunch aboard.*

The action—rather, the *in*action—Ambrose explained to us as we went up through the milling curious to the ramparts and down to where *Baratarian* was tied up. It represented that frustrating day 155 years before when the McHenry garrison had had to take their punishment without reply, Admiral Cochrane's gun and rocket ships firing from beyond the fort's cannon range. The entire British fleet was being played incongruously by the frigate *Constellation* (a controversial bit of casting among patriotic Baltimoreans), towed from her berth to anchor in midharbour, and surrounded by a flotilla of pleasure craft as well as by the docks and towers of the city. Puffs of smoke and appropriate boom-booms issued desultorily from her ports, followed by smoke canisters all about us. *Baratarian* likewise flew the Union Jack and sported her new name-boards *(Surprize)*, but had suspended bombardment to host our prenuptial luncheon.

I looked about and was relieved not to see among the festive "garrison" Drew Mack or his young companion of the day before. The company in general were picnicking among the bastions, barracks, and redoubts or out on the star-shaped ramparts; the shipboard fete was restricted to the eight of us in the Menschhaus party (Ambrose & myself, Magda & Angie, Carl & Connie & their steadies), our remarkably pacific Director, the MSU chaplain, Bruce & Brice (who made a working lunch of it, as did Buck, the hired skipper), and our host.

I.e., A. B. Cook VI, done up again as his ancestor, who piped us aboard with a bosun's whistle and added his hearty, faintly patchouli-fragrant kisses to our best man's. Angie giggled at his outfit; he charmed her by wielding her Easter egg as if it were an admiral's glass. No Jane Mack? I wondered aloud and innocently. Were the yacht's owners never aboard? You understand that I still knew, of Jane's engagement, no more than that it was for some reason a romantic little mystery. Even after the Burning of Washington I knew her fiancé's *nom d'amour* only: "Lord Baltimore." I was not to learn his real name till that night.

Madam President of Mack Enterprises sends her best wishes and her regrets, Cook replied, and produced a note to that effect from Jane: Frightfully busy with the business and with plans for her own wedding later in the month; love to us both, and her particular fond gratitude for my "loyal services" to her in the recent past. Oddly regal phrase! But then, just as I was about to put aside my ladyship, Jane was, so one understood, about to assume hers; and any such expression at once of gratitude and of remembrance was a happy rarity from that source.

What's more, by way of wedding gift she offered us a week's loan of yacht and skipper, all expenses paid—so Cook apprised us now—either immediately, for honeymoon, or at our later convenience. Finally, Cook had interceded on her behalf with the Maryland Historical Society to lend me one of Elizabeth Patterson Bonaparte's gowns to be married in (not Mme B.'s own wedding dress, which would fit only the daring 18-year-old who had shocked Baltimoreans by wearing "nearly nothing," but a handsome green silk from her maturity, meant to impress the emperor's family). It awaited my pleasure in the guest stateroom; our host hoped I might wear it to the luncheon, and that we would make use of that same stateroom for our wedding night.

I was touched (Cook, I should add, was now "almost certain" that he could not accept the Marshyhope appointment). Ambrose declined the wedding-night invitation: some thoughtful PR man for the Society to Restore the U.S.F. *Constellation* had been inspired to offer us the captain's quarters of *that* historic vessel, he now informed me—an arrangement my groom thought would be, and I quote, "groovier"—but he and Magda both urged me to try the gown. His F. S. Key outfit, alas, was ashore, in the barracks being used for actors' dressing rooms; he would don it after lunch. As for that honeymoon offer, we Would See (knowing who the yacht's real owner was, Ambrose had of course no intention of accepting Jane's gift; but he and I had not yet exchanged our guilty little secrets).

I needed no urging: the whole scene was so festive, as if all Baltimore celebrated our wedding! Besides, it was now noon: Ambrose and I had a certain schedule to maintain. Armed with champagne and teased by the party, we withdrew to "have a look at the gown," I promising happy-teared Magda to call her in shortly for the fitting. B. & B. filmed our exit; Chaplain Beille liberally grinned; we winked as broadly as possible and shut the cabin door.

Sex #4. We'd been paying no mind, we realised, to the *style* of our coitions—trouble enough to keep to our timetable! #3, for example, ought to have been impossible: how couple in a manner representative of abstinence? Now it occurred to us, fleetingly, that this fourth coming together ought to be the "Marsha/marriage" one, though we were not yet wed. . . Oh fuck it, Ambrose said. Thank you, Marsha Horner!

Then we fetched Magda and Angie in to dress me—a touch snug, that gown of Betsy's, but a smasher all the same—and went above for luncheon. Antipasto and Asti spumante, minestrone, cold melons and spumoni, all lightered across the harbour from Baltimore's Little Italy by order of the (Italian-American) mayor, who would be joining us at the reception! Magda was in gastronomic heaven. Salutes to the bride-and-groom-to-be, including one from A. B. Cook oddly premonitory of your own: an alphabet toast handed down from the time of James II which had served as a code for Jacobites:

> *ABC!* (A blessed Change!)
> *DEF!* (Drive every Foreigner!)
> *GHI!* (Get Home, [J]amie!)
> *KLM!* (Keep loyal Ministers!)
> *NOP!* (No oppressive Parliaments!)
> *QRS!* (Quickly return Stuarts!)
> *TUW!* (Tuck up Whelps!)
> *XYZ!* ('Xert your Zeal!)

Oh, well: the wine and prosciutto were first-rate.

After lunch the *Constellation* was towed back to its berth in the inner harbour; it was the time of day when, in 1814, Cochrane's fleet had briefly moved in closer, and the gunners of McHenry had at last been able to return their fire. *Baratarian*'s rôle therefore was to move out into that position (Buck alone on board) and open up with the little brass "sunset gun" mounted on her coach roof; ours was to go ashore and make ready for the wedding ceremony whilst the fort's cannoneers raised a happy racket and Angie held her ears. Now I espied Drew (with Merope's ex-comrades Thelma, Rodriguez, *et al.*, but not, I thanked heaven, with "Henri Burlingame"), cheerily manning a great 24-pounder. There was Todd Andrews—had he joined the *Frames* company?—in what looked to be serious cross-examination of a hostile witness: Merope Bernstein herself! Prinz looked on, bemused, from a safe distance, framing us and them with his fingers as in days gone by. No sign, thank heaven again, of J. B. Bray.

Now the big guns blasted away with their blank black-powder charges. Time for Ambrose to don his costume. Things were being filmed, he said, "not necessarily in sequence"—understatement of the season! As the full sunshine, for example, was apt for the Wedding scene but wrong for the rainy "twilight's last gleaming" of 13 September 1814, we were pretending that today was tomorrow; tonight and tomorrow we would shoot today with the aid of fireboats and wind and rain machines. Certain scripted statements, too—not very meaningful to us lit'ry types—were delivered face-on to the camera, Godard-style, some of them by Author and Director standing shoulder to shoulder. *E.g.:*

AUTHOR:	This film begins with a shot of the opening pages of my novel.
DIRECTOR:	The novel opens with a sequence from my film.

AUTHOR:	And the Word shall have the last word.
DIRECTOR:	Cut.

Or:

DREW MACK:	The Novel is a cop-out. The Film is a cop-out. But the Movement is not a cop-out. Until now the media have killed us with accommodation. Now we will fight them on *their* grounds, with their weapons. We will make use of them without their knowing it—
DIRECTOR:	Cut.

And how about this, read by Prinz's erstwhile protégée?

MEROPE:	The Author knows very little of the Movement; his rendering of it in the novel is naive, as is the Director's rendering of the novel into film. But real revolutionaries can make use of such ingenuous mimicries.

Or, finally, this, delivered to *me* (Ambrose's hands upon my shoulders) and meant to be the wrap-up shot not only of the Word-*versus*-Image theme but of the whole cockamamie film:

AUTHOR:	Make no mistake about it, my darling: We *will* have the final word! We will triumph over our natural enemy in—

The scene ended at the dash. I asked him where the last two words were. Oh, well, you see, he said, they're to be superposed in block capitals on the film. . .

Enough of that, yes? Getting on to half after three now, and up we trip to the dressing-room barracks, where A. strips to become Francis Scott Key, transferring your unopened letter, of the existence whereof the bride has not yet been apprised, to the waistcoat pocket of his dandy Federal-period togs. Then—well, it's that time again, and #5, R.I.P., was his Reign of Terror—before dressing he bends me forward over a barracks-bed footboard, ups B.P.B.'s green gown and white petticoats and downs her drawers, and, his potency more than restored by that Asti spumante, merrily puts it to me (your indulgence, sir) like a ramrod up the breech.

Wedding time! And, Zeus be praised, no hitches to our hitching! Once for the cameras: Do I, Britannia, and do you, America? We did. God Save the Queen! My Country, 'Tis of Thee! Once more for real. Who gives this woman? Andrew Burlingame Cook, sir: *Chief Singer of the Old Line State, / Bell ringer for our new fine fate,* etc. Did he Ambrose take this woman to be etc.? He did. And did I Germaine ditto? I did, I did! If there be any present who etc., let them speak now or etc. . . .

(We held our breaths. Bray? Marsha? Merope? Magda? André? One could hear the soft whirr of cameras, the flap and crack of the great fort flag, a mockingbird practising gorgeously our epithalamion. . .)

682

We were then pronounced Husband and Wife. Off went the guns! Kisses from Ambrose, from Magda and the family! Shy gift from Angie of her treasure beyond price, that Easter egg! Bear hug from Chief Singer/Bell Ringer! (Did I espy, behind his winks, traces of a tear?) A bronze wedding band (I forgot to say) more precious than gold, because fashioned from a bit of the nib of the very pen of History: gift of A. B. Cook to me via our Director/Best Man (who framed us once through it before passing it to Ambrose) and my groom, who slipped it with a kiss upon my finger! Key to the city from the jolly mayor himself, a bit late arriving but better late etc.: Mr & Mrs Key, I give you the key! A grave blessing from Mr Andrews; a tongue-tisking one from Drew Mack, who disavows the institution on ideological grounds but wishes us the best anyroad. And a rousing chorus by all hands, standing hats off and palms over hearts (a few raised fists among the hippies), of what else but "O Say Can You See"!·

What with our late bereavement, my uncertain status at MSU, and the filming yet to be finished, we'd planned no honeymoon trip; this whole 6th Stage had been our honeymoon! At six we bade good-bye to Magda & Co., who were returning in the van; we would see them on the morrow. Then we ourselves retired for a short while from the scene. Rather, the scene moved with us (Brice, Bruce, Prinz) around the harbour to the *Constellation:* the "3rd Conception scene" after all, which—we made jolly sure—consisted on film of no more than our climbing the gangplank, descending to the captain's quarters in the stern, and tossing my bridal bouquet into the harbour from one of the aft windows. A newlywed wave to the cameras and cheerers on the dock. . .and then we closed and latched that window, drew shut the curtains kindly provided for our privacy, and secured the door.

And made 6th love. Shall I tell it all? First my groom proposed it to me, ardently, and found his bride (it had been a long day) a touch cool and, well, dry. Second he kissed me, and then I him, and we moved from kiss to touch. Ambrose rose; I was stirred. Third we undressed and laid on hands, the bride running like a river now. Fourth we *soixante-neuf*'d it to my first orgasm (of this session), a little skipperoo. Fifth he entered in good old Position One, and I recame at his first full stroke. Sixth he struck again, and again, and again, and again—are you counting, John?—and *again,* and on this you-know-which stroke ejaculated with a cry above the ground-groan of my Big O, a plateau I had been skating out of my skull upon since way back at Stroke One. And then he struck again, and on this last and seventh had himself a vision.

Yup: a Vision. I could *see* him having it, that vision, as if he'd held Angie's Easter egg to his eye (he will, a bit farther on). I had one myself, as a matter of fact, no doubt not awfully different from my groom's: a vision of Sevens, the dénouements that follow climaxes. I have not queried my husband upon this head, nor he me. No need.

Seventh he fell limp into my arms, and we held each other until a big clock somewhere onshore tolled the hour.

683

Meanwhile, back at the fort (we return there now, seven-thirtyish, subdued and pensive; good as their word, B. & B. & R.P. have left us alone and gone back already; the *Constellation*'s guards smile and nod as we disembark; some vulgar fellow calls, "D'ja get in?" and Ambrose gives him the finger), the movie party is still in swing. Fireboats and pump trucks are hosing up for the Twilight's Last Gleaming. *Baratarian* is still anchored out among the former, with Drew Mack evidently somehow aboard, for we overhear—indeed, we are filmed overhearing—a curious exchange upon that subject between Todd Andrews and A. B. Cook.

The laureate has bestowed upon Ambrose, on camera, the "Francis Scott Key Letter": *i.e.*, the one allegedly given Key by Andrew Cook IV back in 1814. It is in fact, Cook remarks with a chuckle, an unfinished personal letter to his son, which he'll want back when the filming's done, but 'twill do for the purpose. Ambrose duly pockets it unread, as F.S.K. is supposed to have done—and that ends our part in the shooting until the Dawn's Early Light routine, to be filmed from *Constellation*'s deck in the morning. But as we newlyweds withdraw to change out of our costumes and slip into town for a late supper (Captain Buck has kindly brought my street clothes ashore), we hear Mr Andrews demanding to be put aboard the yacht, and Mr Cook cheerily refusing. They are making ready, declares the latter, for the "Diversion sequence," to be filmed somewhere after dark; it is not convenient to shuttle extras back and forth or bring *Baratarian* to shore. On whose authority, Andrews wants to know, does Cook give and withhold such permission? Is the boat his? Is he Mrs Mack's fiancé?

Et cetera: I caught no more, for Ambrose drew me dressing-roomwards, out of earshot. I record the exchange now, which at the time I only mildly attended, in view of subsequent events. What was all that? I asked my husband. Probably in the script, he replied, though not *his* script. *Nota bene.*

Leaving our costumes behind (and your letter, which we are now entitled to open and read, but which has slipped A.'s mind despite his having just stuffed Cook's in beside it), we find a quiet place for dinner: no small trick on a Saturday night, but Ambrose knows the city. I am inclined to speak to him of having seen Henri the day before, and of my little vision of some paragraphs ago; but I do not, just yet. Ambrose, unbeknownst to me, is likewise inclined, and likewise abstains. It is a muted first-meal-of-our-marriage, after which (it's nearly ten o'clock) we return for the night to our floating bridal suite. Fireworks salute us from down at the fort; the fireboats are no doubt putting on a show; it would be fun to watch, but we are weary.

In the neighbourhood of half ten we complete our sexual programme with a final, brief, rather gingerly connexion: the both of us are tender, in both senses, and our ardour is altogether spent. Oh shit, Ambrose says after: there's a letter for both of us back in the dressing room I'd meant to open after dinner and forgot. Bit of a surprise. Have to wait now till the Dawn's etc. We are lying thoughtful in the dark in our Spartan but snug little quarters. We review the history of our affair with appropriate chuckles, sighs, kisses; we are happy that it has led to this day's consummation, and that the day is done. Even now we do not speak of those Visions—but I tell him of my soul-troubling recent sight of the young man very possibly, oh almost certainly, my son by André Castine.

Ambrose embraces and hears me out (he had of course long since been apprised by me of that mattersome history); he vows he knows nothing of the fellow's connexion with Drew Mack or the *Frames* company, but will press Drew upon the matter and do his best to arrange a reunion if my son is indeed in the neighbourhood. I ask for time to consider whether I am up to such a reunion. Then, carefully, Ambrose discloses his own secret: sometime between the Burning of Washington and the Assault on Fort McHenry, in course of "working conversations" with A. B. Cook and others, he has learned that the true name of Jane Mack's "Lord Baltimore," and the owner of *Baratarian,* is one Baron André Castine of Castines Hundred in Ontario!

Had I not been bedded, I were floored. Appropriately whispered O Dear Lords and the like. I want to laugh; I want to weep; I do a bit of both, a bit more of mere shivering. Impossible! And yet. . .of *course!* Ambrose squeezes me and tisks his tongue; begins the necessary labour of conjecture: How in the *world,* etc.? I find myself shushing him: time for all that in the morning, in all the mornings ahead. A peculiar serenity that had first signalled to me back at Vision-time now takes fair hold of my spirit, a hold it happily has yet to relinquish as I pen these lines. It is all, truly, too much: Jane's one prior fling, with my late husband; my half-reluctant rôle as Harrison's "Lady Elizabeth"; and now "André's" surfacing ("Monsieur Casteene's"?) as Jane's fiancé, together with Henri's reappearance, like an erratic comet, in our little sky. . . Who could assimilate it?

We agree not to speak, to Jane or anyone, of my old connexion with her baron: Jane is a powerful and canny woman, nowise foolish, who may well already know all about "us," and more about "André" than I know; her fiancé's absence from every gathering where I am present—*e.g.,* the Morgan memorial service—whatever the explanation, is no doubt no coincidence. One thing only is certain: as soon as the Menschhaus can spare us, we must remove elsewhere!

On this note, and feeling now—in my Vast Serenity, mind—almost *giggly,* I kiss my husband good night and fall quickly, soundly asleep. The obscure horrific happenings of the next day and the whole week since have removed the urgency of these wedding-night resolves, but not our commitment to them.

We were to be woken about 5:00 A.M. to make ready for the Dawn's Early Light sequence (sunrise would be at 6:44 EDST on that fateful day: New Year's Day 2281 by the "Grecian" calendar of the Seleucidae, 7478 of the Byzantine era; such "Hornerisms" were now

685

written into A.'s scenario). In fact we were woken rather earlier by an explosion from down-harbour. We made sleepy jokes about what was by now the Big Bang Motif; we pretended to assume that Jerry Bray had signalled his arrival; still subdued by what we'd told each other the night before—not to mention by our separate Visions, as yet unshared—we made drowsy, contented love *(adieu, adieu,* 7th day of 6th week of sweet Stage Six!) and rose to dress: street clothes until A. can retrieve his F. S. Key outfit.

Even as we gather our gear and tokens—our key to Baltimore, the Easter egg which we shall of course return to Angie—we hear, then see, police cars, ambulances, fire engines screaming past us towards McHenry, and begin to wonder. It is growing light. We crave breakfast. No sign of the filmsters. We ask ourselves merrily whether Prinz is reenacting his "Scajaquada trick" of early August, when we rowed across Delaware Park Lake into his filmic clutches. Darker apprehensions already assail us: apprehensions of we are not sure just what. Sunrise approaches. We drive over to the fort.

Reporters, mobile telly crews! Serious accident! Our passes pass us through police lines. We see Merry Bernstein, shrieking again, but this time not hysterically; accusations, imprecations, directed it seems against whom we had thought her comrades: Rodriguez, Thelma, *et alii.* These latter are being held and questioned by police. We see other police questioning—can it be that they're *holding?*—Mr Todd Andrews and Drew Mack! From a passing hippie we hear that "that pig Cook got it"; Merope shrieks her regret that Reg Prinz didn't Get His as well. Prinz himself is on hand, calmly directing Bruce and Brice to film the television people filming all the foregoing, over which (he gets the odd shot of this as well) Old Glory serenely flaps, as does my heart.

Oh yes: and the Dawn's Early Light reveals (it is a quarter to seven; the sun's upper limb appears on schedule over the smoky piers and railyards to eastward) that while your flag is still there, the yacht *Baratarian* is not. Details to follow.

In as jigsaw fashion as a Modernist novel, the story emerges: I shall give it to you straight, though by no means all the pieces have yet been found. In the very wee hours, tipped off by Mr Andrews, who had in turn it seems been tipped off by Merry Bernstein, the park police apprehended Sr Rodriguez in the act of planting, near that famous flagpole, not the little smoke bombs "we" were using to simulate bombshell hits, but a considerable charge of serious explosives. They arrested him at once, radioed for a bomb squad from the Baltimore Police Department, and ordered the area cleared (and the filming suspended) for a general search. Just about this time a second alarm comes from Mr Andrews (don't ask us what he is doing there at that hour): watching from the ramparts with his night-glasses, he has seen— what it must be he had reason to anticipate—the yacht *Baratarian* raise anchor and move slowly up the Patapsco's East Branch towards the inner harbour, where the *Constellation,* and ourselves, are moored. No

686

names are named, but Andrews urgently warns the park police that certain other "radicals" aboard that yacht may be about to attempt the demolition of that historic vessel (and its contents!).

Merope seconds the alarm. A Maryland Marine Police boat is radioed for; it quickly hails, halts, and boards *Baratarian,* then radios presently back that no one is aboard save the captain *(i.e.,* good Buck, a professional Chesapeake skipper of established reputation, known to the officers personally) and a young guest of his named Henry Burlingame. They are merely shifting the vessel into position for the Dawn's Early Light sequence; the police search the craft thoroughly and find nothing incriminating. Andrews presses for more information: There is no Drew Mack aboard? No A. B. Cook? Nope: Buck volunteers that those two have disembarked in the yacht's tender some time earlier, on movie business of their own.

Andrews claps his brow (bear with me; I am reconstructing, as we historians must). Of course: it is the Diversion sequence! Captain Napier's valiant diversion of McHenry's gunners, as described—and thwarted—by A. B. Cook IV in the Ampersand Letter! Only played as it were in reverse, *Baratarian* diverting attention to itself in the East Branch whilst her tender (a Boston Whaler with a hefty outboard engine) runs up the West, the Ferry, Branch, on its unspecified but surely nefarious errand.

The park police grow skeptical, impatient: is this a bunch of movie tomfoolery, and do "we" realize the gravity of such tomfoolery in a national monument? Their misgivings are reinforced by the appearance now from the barracks of Prinz and the Tweedles, all equipment operating. But at Andrews's urging they move to have a look at the far side of the fort, where the original diversion occurred. En route, Rodriguez gives a shout of warning, not to them; a figure scurries up and away from—shades of old Fort Erie—the powder magazine, supposed by all but the fort's commandant in 1814 to be bombproof! The police light out after the disappearing figure, drawing their pistols (where else but in America do park police carry guns?) and calling Halt. Andrews himself dashes for the magazine, suspecting it to be mined: a remarkable gesture!

He is stopped at its entrance by the man he was seeking when last we saw him, and just now enquiring after: Drew Mack, evidently put ashore. He pushes past him into the magazine. Shouting oaths, Drew follows after. Sure enough, an explosion follows—the one that woke us across the harbour—but not, Zeus be praised, from the magazine: it is down below the ramparts on the West Branch side. In the magazine itself, however, there is found another mighty charge of explosives, all set to be blown by a wireless detonator. Mr Andrews is already contending to the police that Drew Mack discovered and defused the device, perhaps saving thereby Fort McH. and the lives of all present. Drew says nothing. The police set about taking statements, clearing the area, calling again for the bomb squad.

Alongshore, meanwhile, down where Captain Napier did his gallant thing, the police who'd kept on in that direction find the grim debris of our wake-up explosion: the shattered fibreglass remains of the Boston Whaler—most revealingly a piece of her transom bearing the last four letters of the name *Surprize:* one can imagine with what significance to the revolutionaries!—and the equally shattered remains of an adult male body, clothed in early-19th-Century costume and bearing a miraculously undamaged 18th-Century pocketwatch, still ticking.

I.e., we must presume, A. B. Cook VI, late self-styled Laureate of Maryland, Distinguished Visiting Lecturer in English at Marshyhope State U., and. . .heaven knows what else. Though no portion of him suitable for positive identification could be found, neither has the laureate been since; no reason to doubt it was he went to smithereens where his ancestor did, but less equivocally. How that came to pass, however, is fittingly uncertain. The official explanation soon became that Cook was killed either accidentally by explosives meant to simulate Napier's diversion, or in an heroic attempt to disarm explosives planted by Rodriguez & Co. to destroy the patriotic shrine. He is by way of becoming already, in the media, a martyr to the Star-Spangled B., as well he might have been. Rodriguez and Thelma, on the other hand and interestingly enough, maintain that Cook was an F.B.I. agent out to blow *them* up, or plant the McHenry demolition to rouse public opinion against them and, by association, against the antiwar movement! (Merope Bernstein, they allege, had become his companion-in-infiltration-and-subversion.) This explanation too, Ambrose at least believes, while admittedly farfetched, is by no means impossible. I turn my wedding ring upon my finger, and agree. A. B. Cook! We shake our heads.

Thus much for the Dawn's Early Light, by which now (I mean roughly half after eight, when the basic outlines of the above are coming clear to us late arrivals) it occurs to Ambrose that the "F. S. Key" letter given him by Cook had been described by its giver as "in fact a letter to [his] son," which he would want back. Perhaps it will, if not prove the key to these mysteries, at least cast some light upon them? He hurries to the dressing room barracks for his costume coat (my heart is aflutter; what will Cook be saying to his "son," and where are the yacht and that young man?) and finds that Cook's letter is no longer in it: only yours—its envelope neatly slit, its return address neatly snipped—which we shall read shortly, over breakfast. Bruce calls to us: Missing, is it? We are being filmed and recorded on hand signals from Prinz, flanked by his sturdy Tweedles. Yeah, missing, the Author glowers at the Director. Prinz cues Brice, who remarks (Voice Over): No doubt it will wash up in a bottle somewhere. See you at Barataria on Tuesday. Cue now to Brice, who adds: Mister Cook would want us to see things through to the final frame.

Prinz: Cut.

And *The End*, for us, of the Dawn's Early Light scene; for me, of the whole bloody movie, which as you know turned bloodier on that same fell Tuesday. There was no more for us to do. A search was ordered for *Baratarian*. Rodriguez and his colleagues were hauled off to be charged next day in the U.S. District Court with conspiring to destroy government property; they pled innocent, repeated their countercharge against the F.B.I., were released on bail, and went fatally down to Bloodsworth Island. On the strength of Andrews's statement, Drew Mack was not arraigned; he too, and his defender—who seems to have become his shadow!—returned to Cambridge and anon to Barataria Lodge. Merope Bernstein, one hears, went back to spend Yom Kippur at Lily Dale with Jerome Bray: an atonement beyond our fathoming. And we old newlyweds, likewise, still shaken, returned to the Eastern Shore.

First, however, stopping for breakfast at a coffee shop near Fort McHenry, and there at last reading your surprise blessing from *Ye Hornbooke of Weddyng Greetynge*. Thank you, and Amen to it!

That same Sunday evening, at the Menschhaus, came another call from John Schott: Would I *please*, in view of this Great Tragedy, set aside my just grievance against him, accept his congratulations on my marriage, and *meet Mr Cook's classes?* I said yes: we could use the money; I could use the distraction. I met them next day (the Maryland flag at MSU was at half-staff for A. B. Cook), again on the Wednesday, and again yesterday: The Fiction of the Bonapartes and the Bonapartes of Fiction, an "advanced" seminar of half a dozen amiable "pink-necks" with aspiration to graduate school.

That Monday began, as aforedescribed, our 7th week of Mutuality. Unknown to us (until just recently) it also brought to Todd Andrews a troubled phone call from Jane Mack: She has not seen her fiancé since before the excitement at Fort McHenry, where he had planned to rendezvous with "his favorite nephew" and go rockfishing. She is of course distressed by Mr Cook's fatal accident; but she is even more alarmed that the combined effort of the U.S. Coast Guard and the Maryland Marine Police have turned up no sign of the yacht *Baratarian*. . .

Tuesday 16th brought the Bloodsworth Island catastrophe. I stayed home to prepare my unexpected lectures at 24 L and help keep an eye on things at the Menschhaus. Ambrose, against my inclination but with my consent, went down to observe the "final frames," meant to echo the destruction of Jean Lafitte's pirate headquarters in 1814. There had been, after all, no real hostilities between Author and Director since the D.C. Burning; A. was content to leave this "wrap-up" to Reggie; he had not even drafted a scenario for it; it would be their last personal connexion; any further communication Ambrose had resolved would be by letter; it was time he looked to what he will do next, with his pen, with his life.

His distraction, in this last respect, may have *saved* his life. Twice, en route to Bishops Head through a sticky drizzle, he stopped the car to jot down notes of some sort; when he arrived there he was too late for the runabout scheduled to ferry him across Hooper Strait, and had to wait in hope of its return. He had just espied it, and was waving his pocket handkerchief, when the "accident" occurred, of which you will have read.

It is simply too slick, John, and it scares the bejesus out of me, even without yesterday's sequel! Or it *would* so scare me, but for that calming gravity whose centre seems to be my womb. What a frightful game, André's "Game of Governments"! We have heard already A. B. Cook's contention that the navy wanted him off Bloodsworth Island. We have heard the charge that Cook himself was an F.B.I. counteragent. It is a fact that another of those routine gunnery exercises, this one involving pilotless target aircraft, had been scheduled and announced for that morning long in advance, and that, as in the Washington scene, Prinz had meant to make use of it for "the contemporary tie-in"; had even stationed Bruce and Brice outdoors at the ready to "catch the action" whilst he and the company organised their plans for the day. But where are the rackety helicopters, the warning patrol craft? Standing over on Bishops Head, Ambrose sees and then hears a single, sleek, wicked-looking little "drone" aircraft or missile shoot from the overcast and plunge out of sight into Bloodsworth Island. He hears the crash—no explosion this time—and sees black smoke rise; it appears closer to him than the Prohibited Area. The bearded skipper of the run-about is peering sternwards too, alarmed; he picks Ambrose up and runs back to Barataria, wondering where the planes are and what the fuck. . .

Too slick! It is one thing for Drew Mack (pulled injured from the flaming cottage by Todd Andrews—what *is* he doing there?) to accuse the navy of deliberately targeting what they knew was a headquarters of the antiwar movement: Rodriguez, Thelma, and the other chap under arraignment would doubtless have said the same had they survived the crash; Reg Prinz's position we shall never know. But Andrews himself—no radical, surely, and a man not given to paranoia—agrees that the pilotless aircraft, which he caught sight of from where B. and B. were poised, and pointed out to them, neither swerved nor faltered nor "flamed out," but zipped as if on wires out of nowhere (read Patuxent Naval Air Station), unaccompanied and unpursued, straight into Barataria Lodge.

Four killed. Three others badly burned. Drew Mack slightly so, and ankle-sprained. About half of the *Frames* footage (and History's pen, and Fame's palm) destroyed in the fire along with the Director; the rest salvaged by B. & B., who, with Mr Andrews and now with horrified Ambrose and others, pull the injured from the flames.

Fishier yet, you may have read Andrews's contention that the film shot by Bruce and Brice of the event itself ought to attest, if not the navy's culpability, at least the fact that the drone did not "unaccountably

690

swerve off course" as reported by a government spokesman—but the film has been impounded by the Pentagon on the grounds that the craft was a prototype of a classified experimental weapon, unauthorised photography whereof is strictly *verboten*. They will Thoroughly Investigate the Regrettable Accident; they stand ready to compensate where compensation is called for, including the estate of the late A. B. Cook; but the film is classified material. Andrews intends to file suit for the victims and will attempt to subpoena the film. B. & B., for their part, mean to do their best to complete *Frames,* reenacting where possible and necessary the missing scenes. But their budget, like the decade, is about exhausted: they plan for example to film the dedication of the Tower of Truth next Friday, but given Nixon's announcement today of "at least" 35,000 more U.S. troop withdrawals from Vietnam by year's end, no student demonstrations are anticipated.

Slick, slick, slick! Then yesterday the *literal* slick of diesel oil in the Atlantic off Ship Shoal Inlet (another Restricted Area!), in midst of which the Coast Guard finds at last the derelict *Baratarian*. All hands missing and presumed dead. Hijacking by narcotics runners Considered Unlikely But Not Ruled Out. Nothing material aboard except, *mirabile dictu,* a letter from the late Andrew Burlingame Cook VI to his son, dated 17 September 1969 (*i.e.,* four days *after* the so-called Key Letter bestowed upon Ambrose and then purloined; but—witness my last to you of "13 September"—letters can be postdated). . .the contents whereof the U.S.C.G. is withholding pending the location of Mr Cook's next of kin!

We are more or less stunned. Jane Mack, understandably, is beside herself—indeed, she is in shock and under sedation. Todd Andrews does his best to console her (*there,* in my strangely tranquil but not tranquillised view, would be a good match; but I am no matchmaker). Everybody is Investigating.

Everybody, that is, except Mr & Mrs Ambrose Mensch, who, come Tuesday, have a different matter to investigate. Then autumn will commence, and our 7th Stage; by the light of the (full Harvest) moon we shall see. . .what we shall see. Perhaps one day I shall tell Jane Mack about her, my, our André Castine; perhaps not. (Perhaps one day I shall learn the "truth" about him myself!) Meanwhile. . .

My husband loves me devotedly, I believe. And I him, though (since my little Vision) with a certain new serene detachment, which I can imagine persisting whatever Dr Rosen finds on Tuesday.

That "vision": I cannot say whether it is the cause of my serenity or whether it was a vision *of* serenity. Doubtless both. Should Ambrose one day cease to love me; should he go to other women, I to other men; should our child miscarry or turn out to be another Angela—worse, another "Giles" like Mme de Staël's, an imbecile *"Petit Nous";* should my dear friend come even to deny (God forfend!) that he *ever* loved me, even that he ever *knew* me. . .I should still (so I envision) remain serene, serene.

As I remain—though, you having after so long silence spoken, you shall hear no more from me—ever,

Your
Germaine

F: *Todd Andrews to his father.* His last cruise on the skipjack Osborn Jones.

Todds Point, Maryland

September 5, 1969

Thomas T. Andrews, Dec'd
Plot #1, Municipal Cemetery
Cambridge, Maryland 21613

Father.

Fictitious forebear, I was about to call you, wondering once again (with Anger, child of Exhaustion and Frustration) whether you ever existed. But of course you did: that your death has proved more important to me than your life—indeed, than *my* life—argues that you died; that you died (by your own hand, Groundhog Day 1930, dressed for the office but suspended from a cellar beam of our house: just another casualty of the Crash, one was odiously obliged to infer, in the absence of suicide note, ill health, sexual impropriety, or other contraindication) is prima facie evidence that you lived. Fastidious widower. Respected attorney. Survived by one child, then 29, who for nearly ten years already—nearly 50 now!—had been trying to Get Through to you, first by speech, then by endless unmailed letter, to tell you a thing he had been told about his heart: that it might, at any moment, stop. Who on your decease commenced an *Inquiry* into its cause, the better to understand himself; closed that *Inquiry* on June 21 or 22, 1937, with his own resolve to suicide; reopened it a few hours later (and his Letter to the late you) when he found himself for certain reasons still alive; and sustained thereafter, in fits and starts and with many a long pause, but faithfully indeed since March last, both *Inquiry* and "correspondence."

Forty-nine years.

The first letter, or first installment of the Letter, is dated September 22, 1920 (I have it before me, with all the others, most of them returned to sender from the Cambridge Cemetery. Its salutation is simply *Father:* not, like some later ones', Dear, Damned, Deaf, Dead, or Distant Dad. Just *Father).* This is the last.

I'm at the cottage, sir: mystified, chagrined, and pooped from a three-week Final Vacation Cruise that turned into a wild-goose chase, followed by a week of fruitless floundering up and down the Atlantic flyway. The weekend forecast's clear, in both senses; any other year I'd be out sailing. But I'm done with that, as with many another thing. I'll spend the weekend having done with this.

My last to you (8/8) closed with the phone call I'd been waiting for as I wrote, in my office, having snubbed Polly Lake for reasons you remember and cleared my desk for the Last Cruise of *Osborn Jones,* only to be delayed by that distress signal from Jeannine. I was impatient: no place for *her* in 13 R that I could see; my deliberate rudeness to dear Polly was getting to me; Ms. Pond's insinuations made me cross; and I did not feel up to the three-hour haul to Baltimore or Washington airport and back. Hello. I truly hoped she was in Buffalo, or back in Ontario, her impulse passed. Toddy? But it was an awfully clear connection: I could hear gin, vermouth, and panic, 5:1:5. Where are you, Jeannine?

Just around the corner, it turned out, in the lobby of the Dorset, wondering why in the world she'd come. Sit tight, I told her; but when I got there she was standing loose, looking lost and a whole lot younger than 35: not the fuddled lush I'd feared (though she'd had a few), but a frightened version of the Sailboat Girl in that Arrow Shirt ad, vintage '21, reproduced on the card Polly'd sent me. Peasant blouse instead of middy blouse, hippie beads instead of black neckerchief, but braless as her predecessor, like her gold-braceleted, her gold curls piled and bound with the same silk saffron. Suitcase at her side; cigarette, in holder, in hand. She started forward uncertainly, eyes welling up (Had she seen me, I tried to recall, since my Sudden Aging?) and hand held out. When I hugged her instead, she let the tears come and wondered chokily again Why the hell et cetera. Marian watched from the check-in desk with interest. Jeannine's good breasts felt perfectly dandy, Dad, through my light seersucker; my odd response to the push of them—file this under Irony for the sequel—was paternal-tender. I had, after all, very possibly sired them.

But it was her Why's that changed my cruising plans. She kept it up over dinner—iced tea and crab cakes at a dry establishment across the street, a self-administered test to stay off the juice till her tale got told. Why couldn't she make a go of it with any of her husbands and lovers? she wanted to know. Why had Prinz dumped her for Mel Bernstein's slack-assed kid? Why had she ever imagined she had any talent except for drinking and fucking? (I shushed her: family restaurant.) Why couldn't she control herself? Why was she born? Why go on living?

I sang the next line for her, to turn the edge; the one after we harmonized together, laughing around our backfin crab cakes—

> What do I get?
> What am I giving?

—and then I reminded her (she knew the story) that a series of Why's from her on June 21 or 22, 1937, when she was going on four years old, had led me, age 37, aboard Capt. James Adams's Original Floating

Theatre, to a clarification of my resolve to end my life. Thence, not long after, to the recognition that, *sub specie aeternitatis,* there was no more reason to commit suicide than not to.

She was, Jeannine sensibly replied, not me. And she wasn't really talking about suicide, just wishing she were dead.

Nor was I, I told her (as it here began coming clear to me), really talking about 13 L, which I now explained: that summer day I'd lived programmatically like any other because I meant it to be my last. I was, I said, really working out for myself a detail of 13 R—which never mind, my dear. Christ, Toddy, she wondered, who's been on the sauce? And whose crisis *was* this? And what in the (family restaurant) world was she going to do with her useless self?

She was coming out to Todds Point with me for the weekend, I informed her. To talk things over like, well, uncle and niece. Swap despair stories. Knock back a moderate volume of London gin. Maybe net a few soft crabs and try to swim between the pesky sea nettles. My vacation cruise—and her return to Fort Erie, where they were wondering—could wait till the Monday.

She was delighted; so was I. No great mystery: a relief for her not to have to think in sexual terms, which had become anxious ones; a pleasure for me to be, no doubt for the last time, host to a pretty houseguest for an innocent weekend, uncomplicated by any emotion save mere benevolence and fitly echoing, in this leisurely wrap-up of my life, our father-daughterly excursion back in 13 L.

She was also curious, all the way to the cottage. What was *I* in despair about? Could it have to do with her mother, by any chance, or was it just Getting Old? Where did I mean to cruise to, and with whom? She really *could* use a drink now, if I didn't mind; wasn't the old country club somewhere along the way to Todds Point? How many girls did I suppose had like herself been laid on all nine greens of that flat little golf course in a single summer, between their junior and senior years of high school?

Never mind, I said, and it's about as quick to keep on toward home, as an old regatta sailor like herself should know: just two points farther downriver. Oh wow, said she, she hadn't done *that* in years and years—sailing, she meant. Did I think we could slip out just for a day sail before she left? But she answered herself with tears: Left for where? Not back to that (etc.) Farm: Joe Morgan was too far gone these days in his own hang-ups to do her any good, and all the others were either nuts or feebs. Her brother rightly despised her; her mother didn't give a damn. Did I know that she didn't even have an apartment to call her own? She'd made the mistake of letting hers go, a dandy one on the Upper West Side, when she'd moved in with Prinz; her stuff was still there.

Et cetera. All this over Beefeaters and tonic now, here. It excited Jeannine (as it had not Jane) to be back in the cottage she remembered happily from her girlhood. She kept the alcohol intake reasonably controlled; we sat for some hours in the dark on the screened front porch, listening to crickets and owls and ice cubes and each other's stories, watching the moon track out on the still river where *Osborn Jones* lay half provisioned. I was pleased with her, that she hadn't got drunk or hysterical; that she assessed herself and the others fairly; that she tucked her legs under her on the old porch glider and made herself unaffectedly at home with me; that she had the presence of heart to wonder again what was on *my* mind. I advised her, unless she was broke, to find another apartment, in New York or Los Angeles or wherever; to look very carefully for a serious, conservative, happily married, physically unattractive psychiatrist, preferably female, to help her with the booze and the rescaling of her ambitions; to consider applying some of her energies to something impersonal and citizenly—why not her father's Tidewater Foundation, for example, which certainly needed its philanthropies reviewed?—et cetera.

I did not mention the will case; seemed inappropriate. Or her chain-smoking, which stank up the sultry air. Of my own situation, not to be unfairly reticent and because it was agreeable to have that auditor in that ambience, I volunteered the vague half-truth that my health was uncertain and the truth that a 69-year-old bachelor whose accomplishments have been modest and whose relations with women have been more or less transient and without issue has sufficient cause both for occasional despair and for looking unmorbidly to last things. Handling that big boat alone, for example, was getting to be a bit much, but I'd never enjoyed vacationing in male company, had run out of companionable and willing female crew, and was no longer interested enough in the sport to swap *O.J.* for a smaller and more manageable craft. Thus my decision to make a final solo circuit of my favorite Chesapeake anchorages and then pack it in.

I said nothing about suicide, of course. But I realized at once I'd said too much about female crew. Jeannine became her-mother-back-in-May all over again, when I'd first felt my life's odd recycling. O Jesus, how she'd *love* to see Dun Cove again, and Queenstown Creek, and What's-its-name Cove off Gibson Island Harbor—Red House! Red House Cove! And I shouldn't forget how she'd raked in the silverware back in her dinghy-racing days against the best Hampton One-Design skippers on the circuit; and she remembered how to read charts and take bearings and play the currents and handle lines. Couldn't she for Christ's sake pretty *please* go along with me, if I hadn't a full company lined up? At least for a few days? She'd cook, she'd crew, she'd drink no more than I, she'd smoke downwind of me and the sails, she'd stay out of my way, she didn't mind mosquitoes, she loved foul weather, she'd never been seasick in her life, she even had shorts and sneakers in her bag, though alas no jeans or swimsuit, but who cared, she'd use Off in the evenings and swim in her shorts and T-shirt when there were People around. I could put her ashore whenever I tired of her company. *Please* say yes, Toddy! Unless you've got something else going?

It was no time to lay another rejection on her. The notion even sounded agreeable. To've had a son to sail with is a thing I've often wished; to've had a daughter, even more so. But I didn't trust Jeannine's sobriety—alcoholics don't reef down *that* readily—and had no use for a drunk on board. And I did (this much I told her) want not only privacy but some solitude on my Last Go-'Round. I felt her tensing for my no: the stab of her cigarette, the swish of her drink. Let's take a shakedown sail tomorrow, I proposed. Dun Cove for the night; Gibson Island on Sunday if we still like each other. You can get a cab to the airport from the yacht club there, and I'll go my solitary way.

It took her a hurt half-second to remuster her enthusiasm; then she was all aye-aye sir and asking like a kid could she go to bed now so the morning would come sooner, or was there work she ought to do first?

Yes to the first and no to the second: it was near midnight. I showed her the shower (my addition), put out sheets for the hide-a-bed, and turned in, not without noting the level in that Beefeater bottle, which I deliberately neglected to put away. Jeannine gave me a daughterly kiss good night and thanked me without fuss. She doubted she'd go back to that Farm except to collect her belongings; she had no further use for Reg Prinz, she thought; she would consider my other advice seriously.

I fell asleep listening to her shower and thinking, inevitably, of Jane. Some time in the night the telephone rang me up from sweet depths; before I was collected enough to get it (I'd not bothered to move it from the living room to the bedroom jack), Jeannine had answered and been hung up on. Not a word, she said from her bed edge, fetching in her summer nightie, her hair unbound. She'd lit a cigarette, but I was pleased to see that the bottle hadn't been moved or, evidently, touched. Some fucking drunk, she guessed with a wry chuckle: many's the time. Nighty-night.

Next morning was a bright one, unusual for August, a good dry high come down from Canada with a light northwesterly. More and more pleased, I found Jeannine up and perky, in cut-off jeans and T-shirt, the hide-a-bed stripped and stowed, the gin bottle unselfconsciously returned to the bar cabinet, its level undisturbed (of course I hadn't checked the other bottles), coffee brewed and breakfast standing by. She gave the skipper a good-morning peck, asked him how he liked his eggs, predicted that the breeze would freshen enough by noon to make even that clunker of a skipjack move, and declared that such late-night no-response phone calls made her homesick for NYC: nothing missing but the heavy breath. Did they happen often?

Fact is, Dad, it was the first such ever, in my memory; outside the cities such annoyances are rare. He'd said nothing? Not a syllable, either apologetic, explanatory, or obscene. That in that case our attribution of gender was presumptive didn't occur to me till the evening, 2200 hours, as I made the day's final entry in the ship's log. I was after all a lawyer *on vacation,* eagerer by far than I'd expected to get *O.J.* loaded and under way.

Jeannine was a delight: her complexion fresher, eyes brighter, spirits higher than I'd seen them since her first divorce. She took my car to fetch the last of the groceries and the first of the ice while I topped up the water tanks, loaded and stowed, closed the cottage, singled up the dock lines, and started the diesel to kick us out into sailing room. We went over the checklists together—a disingenuous tête-à-tête which Jeannine smartly called me on by blowing her breath in my face. Cigarettes, coffee, and toothpaste, okay? No booze till the hook goes down.

I kissed her forehead; we raised the sails, cast off, and for the sport of it (but with the engine idling in neutral in case the breeze set us too far shoreward), fetched out to deep water under sail alone, close-hauled on a tricky port tack, by lee-bowing the outrunning tide to offset our leeway and lowering the big centerboard inch by inch as we beat out of shoal water. A neat bit of seamanship, landlubberly Father, which brought a cheer from the crew when we cleared our mark—a particular brush-topped stake on the last three-foot spot before good sea-room— by no more than that same three feet. Jeannine bounced happily back to the wheel from her watch at the bowsprit (those breasts bounced too, under that T-shirt, a man could not but notice with pleasure, whatever the possible consanguinity) to hug me (Ah) and take the helm while I cut the engine and made the first log entry: *Day 1 (Sat 8/9): Choptank R. 1030: Last Cruise off to good beginning.*

But even as I went on to log our weather, speed, heading, and trim, I decided to take no further chances that day. Tempting as it was, in that breeze from that quarter, to come about and close-reach straight into the Bay, we crossed the wide river-mouth instead, tacked up Broad Creek, anchored for lunch and a cautious dip off Hambledon Island (sea nettles, like a gross of old condoms, everywhere one looked). Then we ran back down again, banged out past Cooks Point to the Sharps Island Light to get a taste of open Bay and a bit of spray in our faces, and back into the Choptank and up Harris Creek to Dun Cove. The rationale was to get a good anchoring spot for the night before the weekend fleet piled in from the western shore—there'd be 50 boats by nightfall in that first snug anchorage on the Choptank. But we were also, as Jeannine airily observed, only eight nautical miles from home in case I wanted rid of her in the morning.

We could quit that now, I suggested. It had been a good day's sail, the better for her having been aboard, and I hoped she'd have a drink with me after we swam. The hook was down in eight feet in the western arm of that roomy cove, off which yet another, lagoonlike little cove makes, too shoal for cruising boats to enter but a fine secluded spot for swimming. The breeze had waned from fifteen knots to near calm; the late afternoon had hazed over and stoked up; furling sail and setting the anchor left us both perspiring. With my permission, not to soak her only pair of shorts (they would never dry out in the overnight damp), Jeannine swam this time bare-assed, her T-shirt pulled demurely but sexily over her hips while she used the boarding ladder. That sort of modesty, she acknowledged, was not her long suit. On a sailboat especially, in her view, clothing was for comfort, protection (including against unwarranted attention), and other folks' proprieties only. In hot weather, alone or with others, she preferred going naked, and never cared who looked so long as *they* didn't care and left her alone.

Mm hm. My sentiments exactly, despite my local fame as a coat-and-tie-skipper in the spring and fall. The fact was, I told her, it was Arrow shirts or nothing, and after half a century of watching our rivers get yearly more crowded, I still found swimsuits unnecessary more often than not when at anchor on our side of the Chesapeake. That ice broken, we dinghied through the nettles to what we now christened Skinny-Dip Cove, where, as we'd hoped, we saw fewer of them; and wary as I was of medusa stings on my privates, at her challenge and example I Took a Chance.

I report to you, Dad, that at age near-70 it is still a pleasure to feel one's male equipment floating free in the amniotic waters of the Chesapeake, so warm by August that they don't even tighten the scrotum, and to splash about with a long-legged, suntanned, gold-haired (but, one observed with interest, brown-fleeced), not-at-all-bad-looking woman half one's age. I had first done Dun Cove in the buff (we called it "buckbathing" back then), crewing for friends, when a woman of 35 was *twice* my age, and I had looked with awe upon a naked and unattainably mature 21-year-old, the skipper's girl friend. I had skinny-dipped there in the 1920's and '30's and '40's and '50's and '60's, with friends coeval to each decade. How old Polly, as late as last August, used to love to peel out of her Playtex and leap with a whoop from *O.J.*'s bowsprit, nettles be damned! And beautiful Jane, modest Jane, who would strip only at night lest someone see her from the woods alongshore—how she loved the sparkle on us of Dun Cove's phosphorescing algae, her nipples twinkling before me in Franklin Roosevelt's second term! My itinerary for the rest of the cruise did not call for another visit to this first of my Favorite Anchorages; I was immensely happy to have a Naked Lady-Friend to swim with on my last stop in Dun Cove.

I told Jeannine so, and some of the above, as she ably rowed us back (*there's* a pretty sight, Dad: conjure it, from my perspective in the stern-seat). She wanted to know Had I ever swum there with her mom? I said Sure, and no more. She swapped me some skinny-dipping memories of her own, tending toward the orgiastic and Caribbean but not excluding dear Dun Cove or the innocent pleasure of mere untrammeled wetness. As we toweled off (in the cabin: the fleet was piling in now from Annapolis, Washington, everywhere), we agreed that while solitary anchorages were delicious, the weekend party thing was fun too: rafting together for cocktails, boat-hopping to compare hors d'oeuvres and layouts and rigs both nautical and human. We also inspected each other less surreptitiously, Jeannine supposing, correctly, that her mother had been in better shape at 35, pointing out small striations on her own breasts and thighs and backside, complimenting politely my not-bad-physique-for-a-man-my-age (from the neck down), observing with interest that below the waist I wasn't gray-haired yet. She liked my invocation of Boccaccio's leek, white-headed but green-tailed; said she'd known plenty of the opposite kind; wondered if we could stay stripped on deck till the air cooled down, just covering ourselves with beach towels when boats passed close.

Sure.

And could she ask me a question? she wondered a bit later. We were stretched out now with light rum and tonics on the cockpit cushions, port and starboard, our backs propped against the cabin bulkhead, a plate of ripe olives and Caprice-des-Dieux-on-matzo, my favorite canapé, between us. The mosquitoes and no-see-ums were under control; the sunset over Tilghman's Island was a showpiece; blue herons duly squawked as if being throttled; anchor lights were rigged for the night; from a nearby Concordia yawl the inevitable folk guitarist softened welcomely the transistor rock from elsewhere in the cove; there were splashes, ouches, laughter; and the last Harris Creek lighted daybeacon (*Fl 4 sec "7"*) blinked obediently every time we counted to four hippopotami. Got the picture, Dad? In short, I was relishing the dusk of Day 1 and wondering mildly why in the world a man of your age would hang himself, even in February 1930, for simple lack of cash, when it was so abundantly evident that Everything Has Intrinsic Value.

Sure, honey.

It was half past eight, dusk enough now to ignore our neighbors (though with a good pair of 7x50's one can recognize faces from 100 feet at midnight). Jeannine swung her legs off the seat, reached across the cockpit, laid light hold of my penis with a hand cold from her drink—the old fellow shrank back as he had not when we swam—and said she'd ask it later. This had been her happiest day in years. Could we please go below now for a while?

Since August 13, 1932, Dad (8 L), I have not easily been taken by surprise. Jeannine surprised me. If *you* saw "incest" in the offing pages since, it's because I did too, *this* time around, recording her visit from log notes and memory. But at the time, though I'd certainly and clearly enjoyed Jeannine's nudity, my pleasure was half impersonal and half the finally innocent admiration of a father for his mature and seasoned, still-attractive daughter. The sight of her, and our frisking about, had unquestionably reminded me of the pleasures of sex; but those were memories, not anticipations or desires. Or, if there was after all a mild touch of the latter, it was the wistful wish that she were not probably my daughter, possibly an adversary in the upcoming will dispute, and surely not interested in sex with a 70-year-old friend of the family. I was surprised.

But not out of my wits. Jeannine was sober; I too. Her possible motives, the possible ill consequences and other objections to our "going below" I believe I saw clearly, along with the great So What (and all the lesser Why Nots) in the pan. A lawyer is a lawyer; an old one even more so. Now Jeannine, I said, as neutrally as possible: that old chap there is semiretired.

She moved her fingers. Let's un-retire him, Toddy. I'm feeling happy and horny. No obligations. No problems. Feel.

Well. We went below, took turns going down, managed a fairly routine coupling in the missionary position, but with her legs over my arms. No special *frisson*. We cooled down awhile then in our sweat, and later made omelettes for dinner with the last of the Caprice des Dieux and a cold Moselle. Not much talking. The Trout Quintet, agreeably, on the FM. Both of us, in modest reaction, wearing shorts and tops now. After cleanup and bed-making we finished the Moselle out in the dew-soaked cockpit, regarding Andromeda and her friends, wishing we could take a final swim but not caring to be stung in the dark. The air was balmy, the forecast fine; even so, Jeannine prudently queried me about our anchor-scope before we went back below. We changed chastely into our nightclothes, brushed our teeth, washed up, and with a friendly good-night kiss turned in, me to the double berth forward, she to a settee-berth in the main cabin.

When the lights were out and we'd soaked in for a few minutes the sweet creaks and chuckles of a boat swinging gently at anchor, Jeannine asked, mildly, Should she come sleep up there with me? Had she said *Could* she, I'd've said Sure. As was, it seemed both more prudent and more comfortable to say Too sticky. Then I added, only partly lest she feel rejected: But we could visit in the morning. She'd like that, said my daughter.

I reminded her she'd forgot to ask her question. The one back there in the cockpit?

Oh, that. Her voice was sleepy and amused. She'd only wondered, when she saw for the first time her mother's old lover's cock and balls, whether she herself had sprung from there in—let's see—January of 1933?

Perfectly likely, I acknowledged at once. And just as likely you didn't. Does it matter a great deal to you?

She considered. Nope. It would, she guessed, if she were 17, or even 25. But after 35 years and three failed marriages, her legal father dead and her mother happy with a new lover, the question didn't strike her as particularly important. And it *wasn't* why she'd propositioned me, or, she imagined, why I'd responded. Was it?

I laughed: Not *particularly*. She laughed too: Just normal depraved curiosity. One more taboo over the side. See me in the morning?

I was put in mind again of her mother and of Polly; now that everything was still I saw the questionable assumption in my thinking about the previous night's phone-caller, that it had been a man. But Jeannine's breathing indicated that she was asleep already; I'd ask her in the morning whether she was quite sure, etc.

End of Day One. (Almost. I never sleep soundly the first night out. When a tiny southeasterly swung us about at 3 A.M., I woke at once and went on deck to see how we all looked in our new positions. Half a dozen other skippers moved about with flashlights, doing the same: checking scope and anchor set and clearance from neighbors. En route back through the cabin I inspected my young friend; she appeared to be sleeping soundly, but when I bent and kissed her forehead she smiled and said wryly, Thanks, Daddy-O.)

Next morning, however, she declared she hadn't slept so well in ages. She rose at first light and got right to it: peed, skipped out of her shorty pajamas, and piled headfirst into my berth, down under my sheet—cool and dry now in the fresh morning air—69'ing us before I quite realized what was what. Her thighs were sweet, her labia dainty-fresh beneath a faint sharp trace of urine; we tongued and tumbled for a spell, which with one fingertip (mine, right fore-) in her rectum brought Jeannine to a fine yelping orgasm. First woman I'd ever known personally to get there upside down, Dad. But old John Thomas would not stand so soon again; such things happen. Jeannine tried awhile longer, giving me the pleasure of her buttocks and belly as she scolded the Old Pensioner for not rising to his own past performance (the idea *did* titillate her, then) and threatened to swallow him whole if he would not Come Full Circle, her term. No use. Oh well, she sighed presently: it's a better day for sailing than for incest.

It was: a perfectly dandy sailing day, best of the cruise. The night's southeasterly shifted with the tide to a spanking west-southwesterly, perfect for a long reach up and across the Bay. We took a quick wake-up swim, got nettle-stung on calf (mine) and shoulder (hers), made short work of breakfast, and were first out of Dun Cove. It pleased me that when, as we lotioned each other's welts, I kissed her from nape of neck to crack of ass, she said Let's sail now and play later, okay? For the sport of it we sailed our anchor out and threaded wing-and-wing through the fleet, Jeannine at the helm while I secured the ground-tackle and cleaned up the foredeck. She'd lost none of her racing skipper's sang-froid about tight clearances. Once we'd beam-reached down Harris Creek we cut in the engine, doused the jib, and let the main luff while we powered through Knapp's Narrows and into the Bay. The waves were coming dead at us from the mainland, a foot and a half high already and lightly crested; we felt the old excitement you never knew, Dad, of leaving sheltered for open waters; we called things happily back and forth to each other as we reraised the foresail, lowered the centerboard, and sheeted in close. We were just able, by dint of some "pinching," a push from the motor, and a little help from

701

the ebbing tide, to clear Poplar Island on a port tack (Yesterday today! Jeannine cried merrily); then we set our course for 015°, a broad reach straight toward the Bay Bridge, fourteen miles up. On that point of sail, with the tide against us, it would be fairly slow going and seem even slower—faithful to his origins, *Osborn Jones* carries no spinnaker, but there's a lot of off-wind push in that big, low-aspect mainsail. So much the better: we lashed the wheel, trimmed centerboard and sheets for balance, broke out some iced tea (the air was 80ish already and close, especially off the wind), and let Captain Osborn virtually sail himself up the Bay while we relaxed—tops off now, but bottoms on for comfort, and hats and lotions against the sun—and got some talking done.

I was more and more pleased. Not only was my girl (excuse me: the woman) in apparent control of her drinking; she was making sense right down the line. The will case: She wasn't interested in litigation; she'd loved her father despite her well-merited later rejection by him. On the other hand she wouldn't settle for *nothing;* she needed some money to start a new life with, especially since she had no professional skills and had ceased to badger Louis Golden for unpaid alimony. The split I'd proposed to Jane suited her fine, if her mother and brother were agreeable; otherwise she guessed she'd file suit in probate and take what she could get. Her personal survival might be a cause less worthy than Drew's revolution, but she reckoned it at least as defensible as her mother's wish to enrich a future husband.

That fellow: Nope, she hadn't yet had the pleasure of meeting "Lord Baltimore," whose real name however she understood to be André Castine. There was, coincidentally, a "Monsieur Casteene" at the Remobilization Farm, but he spelled it differently, nobody knew his first name, and anyhow he was at the Farm, not with her mother. In any case, Jeannine wished them well and hoped that what was left of her own good looks would last half as long as Jane's. One day, perhaps, she and her mother could be friends again, if she ever got herself straightened out.

Her parentage: Could I tell her what her mother's and my affair had been like, back in the '30's? Had it been a *ménage à trois,* or what? She couldn't *imagine* Mom letting her hair down so—though there *had* been that later fling of hers, with that English Lord. The month when she herself had been conceived, for example, was her mother putting out pretty regularly for both Harrison and me? How much truth was there in that novel that people used to tease her with, that was supposedly based on my life?

Some, I acknowledged. *That* part of it was a reasonable approximation, except that for purposes of plot it made Harrison Mack into a weaker and simpler fellow than her father had ever been. But her mother and I had indeed been lovers, with her father's knowledge and complaisance, for two separate periods, totaling more than three years and including the date of Jeannine's conception, when the odds on her biological siring were, by my best guess, about 50-50. I did not mention 10 R, our evening sail on *Osborn Jones* in mid-May of this year.

Our own copulation: It still didn't bother her, either in principle or in fact. In Jeannine's mind, Harrison Mack was 100% her father, and I was 100% her oldest friend (in both respects) and the only man she'd ever been the least close to who hadn't *wanted* something from her. No doubt that that, along with simple gratitude and a touch of the old Kinky, was what had turned her on last night (she'd've laid me in the cottage, she confessed now with a grin, if she hadn't feared I'd think she was a pervert, or ulteriorly motivated, and refuse to take her sailing). It *still* turned her on, she didn't mind telling me; anytime Old John got his act together again, she was ready. As Kinky went, this struck her as pretty harmless; she wouldn't be bearing me any two-headed children, or grandchildren. Could she have a beer with lunch?

Why not. The day grew fairer by the hour. As the tide slackened and the temperature rose, the wind freshened to twelve knots and veered to west-northwest, putting us on a dandy beam reach that both felt and was faster; cooler too. *O.J.*'s favorite point of sail. I *was* growing absentminded, though I'll plead exhilaration: not till Jeannine came up from the galley with two cans of National Premium and an ad-lib antipasto of sardines, fresh cherry tomatoes, red onion slices, peperon-cini, and wedges of caraway Bond-Ost (hungry, Dad?) did I remember to ask her, apropos of Friday evening, whether our crank or inadvertent phone-caller had in fact not uttered a sound.

Aha, she teased: so I *did* have something going. Nope, sorry, not a sound or syllable. She put a hand on my knee: Had she screwed something up for me, answering my phone in the middle of the night?

No, no, no. I had nothing "going," more's the pity. And now I did dismiss the matter from my mind. No question of stopping for a swim or letting *O.J.* self-steer: we spanked across the wind, taking the seas just forward of our port beam with a satisfying smash of white water. The old hull seemed happy as I was; we sprinted (for us) up the Bay like an elder porpoise bestrode by a fresh sea-nymph, Jeannine and I spelling each other hourly at the wheel. Faster and flashier boats sailed over to have a look, their crews waving and grinning appreciation of *O.J.*'s traditional lines, its Old Rake of a Skipper's white hair, and His Chick's terrific tits. Bloody Point light, off the southern tip of Kent Island, slid by to starboard at noon; Thomas Point light, off the mouth of South River, to port before 1300; the Bay Bridge overhead as we changed tricks at 1400—a steady five knots under beautiful cumulus clouds in perfect midsummer weather, with Handel's *Water Music* piping in from Baltimore!

Off the mouth of the Magothy, sailboat traffic thickened to the point where Jeannine put her T-shirt on, lest among the whistling sailors be clients of mine or old friends of the Macks' from Gibson Island. We left Pavilion Point to starboard about three o'clock, tacking into the river between bright spinnakers running out; by four we had close-reached up between Dobbins Island and the high wooded banks of Gibson, through Sillery Bay and Gibson Island's perfect harbor, and dropped our hook in Red House Cove: the only boat there.

That was, perhaps, a pity, as things turned out—the early anchorage after a dandy seven-hour sail, the unexpected privacy and free time in a lovely swimming place relatively free of sea nettles—but it certainly seemed otherwise at the moment. We stripped and dived in fast to cool off, then put a proper harbor-furl in the sails, rigged the awning to shade cockpit and main cabin and a windsail at the forward hatch, and went back in for a long leisurely swim, spotting nettles for each other as best we could in the clouded, bath-warm water. After an hour of paddling and floating with only one minor sting between us, as I hung at the foot of the boarding ladder to rest, Jeannine wound herself smilingly around me, kissed my face several times, and directed my free hand to her clitoris while she fondled me. No erection, to my mild disappointment—I haven't successfully copulated in the water since my twenties, Dad; have you?—and *she* couldn't get it off either; so we scrambled aboard, toweled off on deck, then went below to do things right. Much easier with each other this time, we managed a sitting position, face to face, my favorite, on the port settee. Jeannine had a practiced little hip-action, delicious, and liked to work on herself while I reached 'round and—

Enough pornography, Dad: it wets my pants and compounds my felony to record it. But at my age and in my situation, every erection, penetration, thrust, and ejaculation, every touch of nipple, stroke of cleft—there I go; here I came—has the special extra pleasure of its being very possibly my last. (These were, it turns out, my next-to-last; one more to go, and I'll make it briefer, which it was.) My "daughter," sir, is now a Missing Person, and it may well be just here, as I seize her buttocks, press my face between her breasts, and squirt what feels like an entire Chesapeake of semen into her, that I begin to send her down whatever path she's gone. On the other hand (I must tell myself) she might have taken that path sooner, or some worse one later, but for her pleasure in my company thus far.

Done. We opened more beer at her request and lay sipping happily in our perspiration, letting the slight air current from the windsail play over us. Jeannine spoke quietly of how much the weekend had done for her. She felt a real person again, authentic. No doubt her being on an old boat with an old friend in these old haunts was responsible; she didn't feel obliged to prove herself. Maybe New York or L.A., where she'd always *had* to prove herself and had always proved herself inadequate, would be a mistake; maybe she ought to begin a new life right here in Maryland, doing what I'd mentioned with the Tidewater Foundation, perhaps directing shows for the *O.F.T. II.* She had a knack for directing amateurs, she believed. It had been so *restorative*, these two days: out of the sexual rat-race, away from the crazies. She hadn't even been *tempted* to get drunk. (We opened another: her suggestion—announcement, rather. I began to wonder.) I shouldn't worry that our little sex thing might be bad for her. It had been as relaxing as the rest: like a nice fatherly pat on the ass, only better. She truly believed that if she could stay with me to the end of my cruise—even for just the first week of it—she'd have a bit of an anchor to windward, a little foundation to start building something new and modest and real upon. . .

I'd seen this coming. Reading these lubricious pages, Dad, you may imagine that the prospect of nineteen more days of the foregoing would appeal to me, especially with the added sweetening of their being therapeutic for Jeannine. Her visit had been an unexpected little bonus; possible incest or not, I could muster no more guilt about her seducing me than a small salt of extra pleasure. If the past two days had been good for Jeannine, they'd been as good for me: a chance to bid leisurely good-bye to her and to another of life's delights. At 69, however, I am not imperiously sexed; what's more (for Jeannine would no doubt be willing to dispense with our copulation), I looked forward already to solitude. There were other last things to think of. The fact was, I'd had about enough.

Then how to set her down gently? I kissed her (on the behind: she'd stood to wipe my leaking semen off her with a Kleenex, and perhaps to not watch my expression as she wound up her plea) and asked her to give me overnight to think about it. I really *did* have my reasons, I reminded her, for planning a solitary cruise; on the other hand, she was a terrific pleasure and a great convenience to have aboard. Let's sleep on it.

Through dinner she was subdued (lamb chops barbecued off the taffrail, Caesar salad, and a young Beaujolais, which she put away most of). After cleanup we swam again under the first stars—no nettle stings, but no noctilucae either—while lightning from a distant local thundershower flickered southwest of us. The night was stiff and sticky, the cabin uninviting. We sat up late on deck, stripped to our underpants for comfort and sprayed with Off, sipping gin and tonic and tisking tongues at our unexpected privacy: I'd rigged the anchor light, but it was apparent that no other overnighters were going to join us in Red House Cove. Though it was a touch early and partly cloudy, we looked for Perseid meteors, but saw only two in an hour. Jeannine seemed to be holding her liquor and tactfully did not reraise her proposition; her self-control encouraged me to hope that she might after all "settle down" into a more meaningful life in the plenty of years ahead for her. We spoke little, enjoying the stillness and the dew. When the latter finally chilled us (just as Perseus himself rose out of the Bay), I took her hand and led her below.

In fact, sleepy from alcohol and the long day outdoors, I was simply saying Let's turn in, but she understandably mistook my gesture: once in the cabin she slipped to her knees and popped Old John into

705

her mouth. I stroked her hair and let her go at it for a while, half wishing the chap would stand lest she feel rejected, half hoping he wouldn't so she'd get the message, and mainly hankering for sleep. She scolded him playfully, tried a few testicular and rectal accompaniments; neither he nor I could've been less interested. I raised her up, chuckled something about old folks needing their sleep. She tensed in my arms, first time since the Dorset lobby, and turned her face away when I said good night.

Not much sleep. I heard her drinking and smelled her smoking cigarettes in her berth off and on through the night: two *Verbotens* on my boat, but there was no point in making a fuss. I wished heartily our berths were reversed; tried to stay awake lest she go up on deck without my hearing her; but fatigue overcame me. Near dawn I woke alarmed that she might have gone overboard, deliberately or accidentally. On pretext of using the head I got up to check and found her heavily asleep, a full ashtray and the empty gin bottle (it had been only a quarter full) on the cabin sole beside her. She'd turned in naked; the cabin air was wet and chill, the sky gray in the first light, my head dull with solicitude and short sleep. I drew her bedsheet up, disposed of the butts and bottle, turned off the anchor light, and went back to my own berth, wondering what I'd have to deal with later in the morning.

But to my great relief, she behaved herself. We stayed abed late for two old sailors; at nine I heard her pumping the head and took the opportunity to enter the cabin, discreetly pajama-bottomed, and light the stove for coffee. She stayed in there awhile, but there are no toilet secrets on a small boat: I was gratified to hear no vomiting, just the cozy sounds of female urination and, more and more cheering, the turn of magazine pages. I put out apple juice and aspirin; put the aspirin back as too obvious. Let her ask for them. She asked instead, from the head, neutrally, for her blouse from the hanging locker and clean underpants from her bag, also a cigarette from her purse if I didn't mind. When I handed the items in to her, she herself suggested, without looking up from her magazine (an old *New Yorker*) that I radio the yacht club about cabs and flight times; she had an open ticket, and was sure they wouldn't mind calling the airline and radioing back the information. That way we wouldn't have to rush. But she'd like to get started as soon as possible. Never mind breakfast for her; all she wanted was coffee.

I made the call; no need for her to leave the island before noon. Jeannine came out, looking not very fresh-faced, and began stripping her bed and assembling her gear. The sky refused to brighten; the air was clammy; there was nothing to say. I went up the companionway in my shorts, swabbed the deck, and took a swim to ease the strain, proud of her and a bit ashamed of myself. Presently Jeannine came on deck too—the air temperature was shooting up—still in her blouse and panties, another cigarette in one hand and a beer can in the other. She considered for a while, then flicked away the butt, skinnied out of her

706

clothes, and let herself carefully down the ladder, not to get her hair wet.

Now, Dad: your old son is a prevailingly benevolent, even good man. But he has never presumed to moral perfection. My relief and pleasure in Jeannine's behavior, together with the knowledge that upon her departure (in an hour) I would not likely see her again—and the further knowledge that the comely woman before me was the last unclothed female I'd likely ever lay eyes upon—inspired me to a lust that was undeniably, though not altogether, perverse. As, our positions reversed, I stood dripping in the cockpit now, a towel around my waist, and watched her paddling glumly, cautiously, pinkly astern, I not only desired Jeannine one last time: I desired her specifically *a tergo*, puppy-dog style, the way I'd first seen myself in the act of coition, in the mirror of my bedroom in your house, with Betty June Gunter, on March 2, 1917, the day that young woman relieved me of my virginity.

I plead by way of extenuation only that, had Jeannine genuinely protested, I would not only not have insisted; I'd've been quite unable to carry through. But when she came unsmiling up the ladder—and, as she'd left her towel below, I removed mine, began drying her with it, then embraced her from behind, pressing into her cleft my half-erection—she only stiffened, gave me one sharp and tight-lipped look, then let me have my way. Which was to lead her below, return behind her, draw her down to hands and knees on the cabin sole, apply saliva in lieu of more natural lubrication, rise to a full, fine, and culpable hard-on as I entered her, and bang in six or seven deep strokes to ejaculation: the last sex in this letter and my life.

I held her a few moments by the hips, Dad, breathing hard and wishing mightily to fall atop her; then withdrew, postcoital remorse surging in like the tide through Knapps Narrows, and rose to wipe myself on our beach towel. Jeannine lingered discomfitingly on all fours, her hair loose and head and shoulders down, a smear of semen across one prominent buttock and along the back of one thigh. I would get the dinghy ready, I murmured: easier to row over to the club than to unanchor *Osborn Jones*. I slipped into go-ashore shorts, shirt, and boat shoes and fussed about on deck, wondering what to do if she simply stayed where she was, arse to the breeze, a wordless reproach to my abuse of her. But just as time began to grow tight she came up with her purse and flight bag, dressed as when she arrived, but with disheveled hair and tear-swollen face. My practice has included legal counsel to the recently raped. Jeannine looked recently raped.

Apology seemed but further aggravation; even so, I told her as I rowed that while *that* had been a sore mistake on my part, her visit had most certainly not been, et cetera. No response. At the dock she clambered out of the dinghy and told me shortly that I was not to follow her into the club, much less (what I'd requested) see her to the airport. Her eyes filled; remorse smote; what's more, I needed ice. But I let her go, a sorrying figure hauling through the heat, toward that building familiar to her girlhood. I paddled back to the boat and watched dejectedly with binoculars until I saw a cab come and return across the causeway; then I fetched my ice and ascertained at the bar that My Daughter had indeed taxied off to Friendship Airport (Yessiree, the barman said with practiced incuriosity). After washing the weekend off me in the clubhouse showers, I weighed anchor and recrossed the Bay, very alone, to Chester River and snug Queenstown Creek, to sort out my feelings in home waters and try to make peace with myself.

It was not an especially difficult job. I was glad that Jeannine Mack had come to me for counsel, reestablished our connection, gone sailing with me, and listened to my advice. I was surprised and happy to have made love with (oh well, to have got laid by) her, and even now couldn't manage to feel monstrous or even exploitative except there at the end. I was sorry to have disappointed her; mighty anxious that she'd do herself injury; awfully glad to be by myself again. That was that—and remains so, except that my concern for her welfare mounts with each newsless day.

Oh yes: and I was gratified by her reasonable attitude concerning Harrison's estate, on which agenda item I was quiet enough of spirit by midnight to focus my attention. I had supped, swum in the silky water, napped for two hours, and come back on deck to try the Perseids again, with slightly better luck. In the trail of one particular dazzler that swept through Pegasus (so our Author would have it), as I wondered whether Jeannine and Polly Lake and Jane Mack might be watching that same meteor, and from where, there came the damnedest, the farthest-fetched, but just possibly the most inspired notion I'd had all year as an attorney-at-law.

It was an open secret in the Tidewater Foundation that Harrison in his last madness had emulated his father's whim of preserving the products of his dying body, but that in keeping with the times he had caused his excrement to be freeze-dried rather than pickled in company jars. It was no secret at all to me, nor any wonder, that though Jane had humored this aberration (and many another) in her husband, she had refused to let the stuff be stored at Tidewater Farms. One inferred that it was kept somewhere in the plenteous warehouses of Mack Enterprises. It was a conspicuous fact, however, that m.e. was feverishly hatching Cap'n Chick, who so filled the nest of its parent company that other Mack Enterprises were already smitten with sibling jealousy; Jane herself had merrily complained that she might have to convert the Dorset Heights Apartments into an auxiliary Crabsicle warehouse, so pressed was Cap'n C. for cubic footage. Finally, it was a howling obviousness that my own life, like a drowning man's, had been set since March on Instant Replay. . .

So *where was Harrison's freeze-dried shit?* That Jane herself would reenact her late mother-in-law's blunder and dispose, before settlement, of an entailed portion of her husband's estate was unimaginable.

But if some middle-management type had quietly done so, thinking thereby to please his boss; and if it could be argued that by the principle of Command Responsibility the president of m.e. was therefore guilty of Attrition of Estate; and if her contest suit could thus be threatened on no less distinguished a precedent than that of the Maryland Court of Appeals in *Mack* v. *Mack* of March 1938. . .

Longest of long shots! Surely, Author, not even You would go so far!

Next morning *(Day 4: T 8/12)* I reached and ran through soft gray drizzle on a mild southeasterly up the quiet Chester and parked for lunch in Emory Creek off the Corsica River, a fine private place dear to Polly Lake in earlier Augusts. I said my good-byes to it and motored— the breeze had failed, the drizzle persisted: good thinking weather— between narrowing banks and handsome farms to Chestertown, my destination. A whitetail fawn danced on the shore near Devil's Reach, where the current sweeps so sharply past the outside bend that a 20-foot draft can be carried almost to the beach; the old, soft red and white town was as agreeable a sight as ever to sail up to, even in that weather. But my Terminal Travelogue, then as now, took second place to plot. I tied up at the marina dock, telephoned my office, checked in with Ms. Pond (ignoring *her* studied incuriosity), and then asked my young colleague Jimmy Andrews to inquire discreetly whether Jane Mack was back in town and where the uninterred portion of her late husband's remains was stored.

Surely, he said, you do not go so far as to suppose. Of course not, I reassured him. But even so. Okay? *Discreetly.* I'd call back from somewhere on Friday.

Next I telephoned Fort Erie, Ontario (all this from a pay phone in a wharfside restaurant): that "Remobilization Farm." Ms. Golden was there, a curt black male voice informed me, but would not take phone calls. "Saint Joe" Morgan would. What on earth, I asked him when he came to the phone, was he doing in that kooky place? He told me calmly that he had his reasons, and hoped I was calling to tell *him* that Marshyhope's Tower of Truth had collapsed upon his successor. No? *Tant pis.* Then maybe I could tell him what had gotten into his patient Bea Golden, who since her return from French leave in Maryland had become even more of a nuisance than before. They were doing their best to keep booze away from her, but like most alkies she seemed to get it somewhere, or manufacture it in her own liver.

Ah? Tell me more.

They gathered that on the rebound from Reg Prinz she had been picked up by somebody down there for a weekend and then been dumped again. I agreed, faint and sweating, that that sounded plausible. I promised to notify the family and authorized Morgan on behalf of the Tidewater Foundation to seek proper psychiatric and medical treatment for her; also to keep my office informed of her condition. I would come up there myself if the situation warranted, or send a representative "if she associates me too closely with her family." I felt momently more ill; had barely presence of mind enough, before I rang off, to ask Morgan about another patient on the premises: chap named Casteene?

Pas ici, said Joe. His opinion was that the fellow supervised a sort of underground railway for U.S. draft resisters and had gone south to lubricate the wheels. But Joe knew little about him, and was not being particularly forthcoming anyhow, and I was too moved with self-revulsion and concern for Jeannine to draw him out further. I ate lightly, without appetite, there in the restaurant; then to escape the traffic noise from the nearby highway bridge I bid a vexed good-bye to Chestertown and motored back to anchor for the night in Devil's Reach, using both anchors against the swift current. Three mallards—two drakes and a hen—paddled over for handouts. Sheepflies bit, oblivious to chemical repellent. There would be no meteors that evening, and who cared? I screened the companionway and forward hatches and went to bed early, out of sorts.

Day 5 blew up gray and disagreeable. Above the Chester there was nothing I felt like saying adieu to; I decided to recross to Annapolis and begin working south along both sides of the Bay. But halfway down the river, beating into a rising southwesterly which, should I continue, I'd have to bang through all the way to the Severn, I changed my mind. Foul-weather sailing has its pleasures, but not in foul spirits. I ran north up Langford Creek instead, anchored for lunch off Cacaway Island, another favorite; fidgeted with odd-job maintenance for a while, then out of boredom sailed the five miles up to the head of the creek's east fork and motor-sailed back, parking early for the night in the same spot. The warm wind had veered west and risen above fifteen knots. I swam in the nettle-free waves (the sky was clearing; there was no thunder) and circumambulated the empty little island. Its name I understand to be corrupted from the Algonquin *cacawaasough,* or chief, but it spoke to me of Harrison Mack's freeze-dried feces, their disposition.

A long, finally calming late afternoon and evening: smoked oysters and lumpy piña colada in the cockpit, followed by cold sliced ham and a 1962 Argentine Cabernet Sauvignon that cheered me right up. It was, damn it, Jeannine who had propositioned *me.* No doubt I ought to have declined, but the woman is 35, not 25 or 15, and I am 69. Not keeping her with me was the "error," if anything; but I had my needs, too. Away with such *caca!* Mrs. Golden needed residential psychotherapy, not a cruise on *Osborn Jones.* Despite the fact that that day was the anniversary of my first seduction by Jeannine's mother, in the Todds Point cabin in 1932—an anniversary whereof I was exquisitely mindful—I slept dreamlessly and well.

And woke refreshed and rededicated to 13 R! A fine breezy morning—wind still SW 18 +—but I was in the mood for a brisk day's work. Bye-bye, Cacaway! Bye-bye, mild Chester: may you flow as handsome, and less polluted, for generations after me! Given the wind, I was obliged to motor down the first nine miles from Langford Creek, straight into it with the dodger up to break the spray, before I could turn west enough to make sail and shut down the engine. A good fast reach then up out of the Chester's mouth and around Love Point, the top of Kent Island, and we were in the open, whitecapped, serious Chesapeake. Our destination lay almost in the eye of the freshening wind, but no matter; so many tidewater August days are swelteringly still that it was a pleasure, and cathartic, to reef down, close haul, and bash through it all that bright brisk Thursday—*O.J.* for the most part steering himself with a little sheet-to-wheel tackle while I took bearings, checked charts, and trimmed sail. A five-mile port tack due west, back toward discomfiting Gibson Island; then a six-mile starboard tack therapeutically south, under the Bay Bridge, past tankers and container ships plowing up to Baltimore; west again then another five miles into the mouth of the Severn, up to the Naval Academy and Annapolis Harbor. The only entries in my log for that day, apart from sailing data, are two questions: *If Jane's Lord Baltimore is André Castine, who is Joe Morgan's "Monsieur Casteene"? For that matter, who is André Castine?*

But I had things to say good-bye to, including (next day) Annapolis itself, where also I needed supplies; so though it was still midafternoon I made but one quick pit stop for ice, water, and fuel and then threaded through the yachts from everywhere, up through the Spa Creek Drawbridge and the creek itself—jammed with condominiums and expensive racing machines, yet invincibly attractive withal—to my destination, near its head. "Hurricane Hole" is a spot both snug and airy, open enough for summer ventilation yet sufficiently sheltered by trees and high banks so that *Osborn Jones* and his fellow oyster-dredgers were wont to retreat there from Annapolis, in times gone by, to ride out the fall hurricanes. The houses are less crowded that far up, and though one needs a suit for swimming, the moored boats are far enough apart for comfort, the surroundings are still and graceful, and the dome of the old State House rises pleasingly above the farther trees.

My notion was to clean the boat inside and out and make final peace with myself concerning Jeannine. I did the first in a leisurely two hours: everything from scrubbing the waterline to sweeping the carpets and airing the bedsheets. The second I found required no further doing. My regret was real and mild; my concern for the woman equally real, but on balance no greater than before she'd come to see me. It could wait. BBQ filet mignon, a cold fruit mold, and a not-bad-at-all Sonoma Pinot Chardonnay.

Next morning, Friday, in hazy sunshine, I tied up at the Annapolis Town Dock and did business: laid in a week's groceries, restocked the wine locker, found a laundromat, phoned the office. Mack Enterprises, Jimmy confirmed, was preparing for Tomorrow Now by disposing of all old preserved-food inventory to make room for Crabsicles and the rest. No solid word yet on the whereabouts of Harrison's "remains," but inasmuch as Jimmy's own wife worked in the m.e. accounting office, we were in good position to pursue the inquiry. Discreetly. Mrs. Mack was back in town and at work—full speed ahead with Cap'n Chick—after a short Bermuda cruise with her gentleman friend, whose appearance and full correct name no one in the company seemed to know.

Mm hm. Though there was no *particular* reason for doing so, I decided that A. B. & A. should invest in an investigator—that same apparently reliable fellow in Buffalo who had drawn a blank, but competently, in the matter of Jane's blackmailing—to look into the coincidence of the names Casteene and Castine: the one (I explained) borne by a former patient at the Remobilization Farm, the other supplied me by a present patient there, Mrs. Mack's daughter. Whose condition was also to be reported, in my name, to Mrs. Mack. Discreetly. I was mighty anxious; didn't know exactly what I was searching for; trusted my hunch that the search was worth considerable expense; but was beginning to begrudge these impingements on 13 R. I would not call again, I decided and declared, for a week. 'Bye.

That week I'll sail through swiftly, though sailing through it slowly was the heart of my enterprise. From Annapolis I reached seven miles up the high-banked Severn to Round Bay, thence into Little Round Bay, past St. Helena Island (where lay a fine new motor yacht whose name—*Baratarian*—reminded me of Jane's crank cousin A. B. Cook and of the film from which Jeannine had been dropped. *Nota bene*, Dad), to my Favorite Anchorage on that splendid, busy river: Hopkins Creek, snug, private, still unspoiled. No swimsuit needed; few nettles that far upriver; mild phosphorescence when I swam that night. Incest be damned, I wished Jeannine were there again! Next day out through the Sunday mob—wall-to-wall sails in Whitehall Bay! Adieu, Annapolis!—and down to the next river, the South, itself less imposing than the Severn but with finer creeks and coves. Rode out a thundersquall in perfect peace, all alone in a certain nameless, turtled cove off Church Creek: chicken breast with wild rice, a light cucumber-and-onion salad, and a bargain Lalande-de-Pomerol, steady as the eponymous church while the crashing storm merely cooled the cabin. Good-bye Church and Harness creeks, twin beauties! Down to Rhode River's single spot worth a farewell visit: the anchorage behind Big Island (*Sunset like a Baroque Ascension. Fluted jazz on the FM. Shrimp w. cashews & Beaujolais—no ice to spare for chilling white wine*), airy but secure, where handsome Herefords graze down to the waterline. Straight across then to Eastern Bay and my Eastern Shore to say good-bye to its sweetest pair of rivers, the Miles and its sister the Wye: five full days required of sun and rain, wind and calm, to touch only my favorite places therealong! Tilghman, Dividing, Granary, Skipton, Pickering, Lloyd, Leeds, Hunting! Sweet bights and creeks and coves, deer and ducks and herons, gulls and cormorants and ospreys, blue crabs and bluefish and rockfish and oysters and maninose—good-bye! Now it is Friday again, Day 14, August 22. From Hunting Creek I reach down the Miles *(up* on the chart) to St. Michaels for provisions, laundry, lunch ashore, good-bye to that dear town and harbor, and a 10 A.M. phone call to the office. Which I log, ponder, and relog thus: *1330: HM's shit nowhere to be found. Could Jane be staging a diversion? Pursue, discreetly. Her fiancé: one Baron André Castine of Castines Hundred, Ontario, 1/2-brother (so Buffalo reports) of A. B. Cook VI! May be involved in C.I.A. or counter-C.I.A. activity! Foreign? Domestic? Interagency? Buffalo doesn't know: was "seriously warned off" by "C.I.A./F.B.I. types." Reports Castine "somewhere in west N.Y." since Bermuda cruise. Cook himself at home at Barataria Lodge, B'wth I.* Hunch: *check out that Bray fellow in Lily Dale, N.Y. "Casteene" of Ft. Erie may be unrelated to Jane's friend: name not uncommon in Quebec, though usually w. the "Baron's" spelling. Too much coincidence: inquire further. Jeannine has left Ft. Erie; whereabouts uncertain; no one seems to care. Inquire, inquire! Buffalo suspects "drug tie-in": C.I.A. people moving dope under pretext of monitoring V.N. war resisters, instead of vice versa. A very big fish, which he hopes he has not hooked and refuses to reel in, even discreetly.*

Nor can I blame him, Dad. These placid Maryland waters, these mild English-looking swards and copses, are too close to Our Nation's Capital not to have been the secret *mise en scène* of fearsome hugger-mugger since well before C.I.A. and O.S.S.—back at least to 1812. The very charts I navigate by reflect it: *Restricted Area, Prohibited Area, NASA Maintained, Navy Maintained.* Our gentle Chesapeake is a fortress camouflaged, from Edgewood Arsenal and Aberdeen Proving Grounds at its head to Norfolk Navy Yard at its mouth, with Andrews and Dover air force bases on either side and God knows what, besides Camp David, in the hills behind. Nerve gas, napalm, nukes; B-52's above, atomic submarines below, destroyers, missile frigates, minesweepers, jet fighters, and every other sort of horrific hardware all about—and these but the visible and declared! While in the basements of certain handsome Georgetown houses, or on horsey-looking farms along the Rappahannock, even in the odd Wye Island goose blind for all I know, the real dirty-work is done, authorized by some impeccable Old Boy in a paneled office in Arlington or Langley. We do not blame you, Buffalo, for saying good-bye to *that* fish before he says hello.

But oh my: those of us who happen to have reached our story's last chapter anyhow, or its next-to-last—did *we* ever want to get back to our office now and play Deep-Sea Angler, as we could not from any literal *Osborn Jones!* I sailed the sixteen miles from St. Mike's ('bye) out of Eastern Bay and down to Poplar Island, a good spot from which either to end or to continue the cruise. Here in 1813 the British invasion fleet gathered in the fine natural harbor (deeper then) for provisioning raids and repairs; Franklin Roosevelt used to cruise over in the *Potomac* for weekends with his cronies in an old Democratic club on one of the three islands. All are uninhabited now except by snakes, turtles, seabirds, and a crew of biologists (one hopes and supposes; there *is* a NASA beacon off to westwards. . .) from the Smithsonian, which now owns the place and maintains a "research facility" in the former clubhouse. For all one

713

knew they might be counterespionagists, interrogating spies whisked in from Embassy Row or the other side of the globe. . .

But bye-bye, paranoia. They truly *could* be something sinister, those young neat-bearded chaps who waved from their dock as I anchored in the clean sand bottom of Poplar Harbor; Jane's fiancé, likewise, truly *could* be something other than what he represented himself to be—and *very* probably they and he were not. They were biologists. He was a Canadian gentleman of leisure. Buffalo's "C.I.A./F.B.I. types" were part of our *government's* paranoia about the antiwar movement and the traffic of disaffected youngsters across the Peace Bridge into Ontario. And Harrison Mack's freeze-dried feces would turn up in an office safe or the archives of Marshyhope State. Time to shorten scope on my imagination; in the morning I would flip a coin (as I did once on the Cambridge Creek Bridge on June 21 or 22, 1937, very near the end of 13 L) to decide what to do.

A restless night. *O.J.* pitched a bit in a surprise southerly that fetched across the low-lying island and the open harbor; I was on deck every few hours to check for drag by taking bearings on the "club-house" lights, which for some reason burned all night. In the morning, a fresh pretty one, the air was back where it belonged, NNW 5–7. My head was muzzy; Todds Point was but a quick eleven-mile run through Knapps Narrows and across the mouth of the Choptank; I could eat lunch in my cottage, put the cruise away, and hit the office fresh after the weekend. Heads I keep going—to certain haunts on Patuxent and Potomac, to Smith and Tangier islands, then home to my dearest and closest, the Tred Avon and the Choptank—tails I pack it in. I flipped my nickel and got, not "the skinny-assed, curly-tailed buffalo" who in '37 had bid me chuck certain letters into Cambridge Creek (concerning Harrison Mack *Senior's* pickled poop) and let the Macks go whistle for their three million dollars, but that buffalo's '69 counterpart: Monticello.

Home, then.

But I am, Dad, and will be for some days yet, Todd Andrews, and this is 13 R: no more to be dictated now than then by a "miserable nickel" (worth, three decades later, half as much as its Indian-headed, buffalo-tailed predecessor). I upped anchor, bid good-bye to Poplar Island and Whatever Goes On There, and set my course for 200°: an easy, lazy, self-steering all-day run straight down the Chesapeake, wing and wing under *O.J.*'s long-footed main and jib, whisker-poled out. Past the nothing where Sharps Island used to be, on whose vanished beach Jane Mack and I once coupled (Restricted and Prohibited areas to starboard: Naval Research Lab firing range); past vanishing James Island off the Little Choptank, where some 1812 invaders once came to grief and where Polly Lake and I, many Augusts, came to joy; 30-odd gliding miles down through a hot late-summer Saturday, listening to the Texaco opera *(Tosca)* and rereading the story of my life in *The Floating Opera;* to where (in this nonfictional rerun) the *Coast Pilot* turns into a catalogue of horrors—*204.36: Shore bombardment, air bombardment, air strafing, and rocket firing area. U.S. Navy. 204.40: Long-range and aerial machine-gun firing, U.S. Naval Propellant Plant. 204.42: Aerial firing range and target areas, U.S. Naval Air Test Center. 204.44: Naval guided missiles operations area. . .Air Force practice bombing and rocket firing. . .Underwater demolitions area, U.S. Naval Amphibian Base. . .Air Force precision test area*—and where *I* turned into the Patuxent, seven peaceful hours later, and anchored for the night behind Solomons Island, intending to say good-bye next day to Mill and St. Leonard creeks.

Instead of which, I said hello to Jane Mack and Baron André Castine. It being the weekend, a great many yachts were in the anchorage already, large and small, power and sail—so many that I had my hands full finding a spot with room to swing, running forward to drop the hook at the right moment and then back to set it with the engine full-reversed. I had of course conned the anchorage first, and had vaguely noted, among several other yachts I'd crossed wakes with in the two weeks past, the big Trumpy-built trawler I'd seen up in Little Round Bay. Indeed, I'd moored *O.J.* between her (*Baratarian*, remember?) and a 50-foot ketch from Los Angeles, both of which rode on plenty of scope, rather than going in among the cluster of smaller boats. When I shut down the engine and went forward to adjust my rode, rig the anchor light, and watch how we swung, Jane Mack merrily called my name across the space between us.

That is, a lean tanned lady in fresh white linens did, from *Baratarian*'s afterdeck, where she sat with a less tan but equally turned-out gentleman, sipping something short. I waved back, then recognized her with a proper pang and wondered whether. . . But now her voice came amplified through a bullhorn brought her by a white-uniformed crewman. *Toddy. Just in time for dinner. Come on over and meet André.*

Small world, I megaphoned back from *O.J.*'s bows. Let me wash and change.

I cannot say even what my feelings were, except that if not self-canceling they were anyhow canceled from the future, 13 R's end, and meanwhile overriden by shrug-shouldered curiosity. I washed the day's salt sweat off, dinghied over in my go-ashore seersucker, and was introduced to André, Baron Castine: a mustached, ruddy, virile fellow in his mid-fifties, with a broad smile, good teeth, an easy winning manner, and a fine cultured baritone voice softly accented *à la Québec* (though the family estate was in Ontario). What they sipped was cold Mumm's Cordon Rouge, fetched up by their steward in buckets of ice, along with caviar-and-cream-cheese canapés, from the air-conditioned galley. Jane as always was utterly at ease, as if we hadn't humped aboard *O.J.* in May and again in the Todds Point cottage in June; as if I hadn't seen those photos of her and her friend in spectacular flagrante delicto. Castine as well, with better reason: an immediately likable chap, who indeed looked to me less like the fellow in those photographs than like a better-bred relative of A. B. Cook (as Buffalo had reported).

Ah, well: people change. Their ease put me at mine. Castine informed me that the yacht was Jane's gift for his 52nd birthday (younger than he looked, then); that he thought it a bit, ah, baronial, and was unfortunately prone to *mal de mer*—he'd even missed a few meals aboard the *Statendam* in Bermudian waters! But he was determined for her sake to acquire sea legs, and so had committed himself to the sport of deep-sea fishing. Was I an angler?

Toddy *always* has an angle, Jane declared, not especially meaningly. He's probably been following us to see whether we deep-six Harrison's *merde*.

I was astonished. Castine asked about the verb "to deep-six," but clearly understood the general sense of Jane's allusion. That tone prevailed through dinner (I surprised myself by accepting their invitation; all envy, guilt, and jealousy slipped away in their easy company, lubricated no doubt by the fine champagne; and after two near-solitary August weeks afloat, the air conditioning and the company were irresistible. Fresh roses on the table! Conversation! A steward to cook and serve!): the good-humored implication that they knew more about certain of our common interests than they were telling. I asked where in fact that minor but notable item of Harrison's estate reposed. Jane was (smilingly) damned if she knew, and damned if she'd tell me if she did; things were too hectic at m.e. for her to bother with such foolishness until my subpoena, which she quite anticipated, obliged her to. Castine asked my opinion on the danger of being hijacked in these waters, or on the Intracoastal Waterway, by narcotics smugglers: one heard rumors of piracy and of Coast Guard cover-ups. We all doubted there was any danger. I inquired about his vessel's name. Both his own forebears and Jean Lafitte's, he declared, were Gascon; perhaps he would take up piracy himself if Mack Enterprises fell upon hard times and if he could learn to do without Dramamine. Did I know Longfellow's poem about his (Castine's) progenitor?

Artichokes vinaigrette. Escalope de veau and fresh asparagus, perfectly steamed. Had I heard anything from her wayward daughter? Jane wondered mildly. I considered; then reported my understanding that Jeannine had broken off with Reg Prinz and left the film company; that she was unhappy with the Fort Erie establishment and frequently disappeared from it; and that she was drinking too much. Castine tisked his tongue and regarded his fiancée. Without looking up from her sauce béarnaise Jane declared crisply that she knew all that; but Jeannine was her own woman and must find her own way. She Jane had been rebuffed too often by both of her children to do more than wish them well and hope for the best.

Then she brightened. As for that movie: that's what they were doing there! Shooting was already in progress farther up the Patuxent, it seemed, and tomorrow Prinz & Co. were going to "burn Washington" on Bloodsworth Island—but André must explain; she had no head for history.

The baron explained that before they'd learned (on their return from Bermuda) of "Bea Golden's" falling out with Mr. Prinz, they'd agreed for a lark to ferry the film crew tomorrow from Benedict, sixteen miles upriver—where footage was being shot of the British invasion of August 1814—down the Patuxent and across the Bay to Bloodsworth Island, a 40-mile trip. There Prinz had built a set for the Burning of Washington, 155 years to the day from that regrettable event. They had expected, of course, that Jane's daughter would be there; in any case her son would be, who with his radical friends (and, presumably, the director's consent) was using the occasion to protest U.S. "involvement"—Castine's tactful euphemism—in Southeast Asia.

Come with us, Toddy! Jane cried with imperious enthusiasm. Drew made her nervous with his childish politics; André could talk to him, but she'd feel better yet if I were there too; Drew had always respected me. I must come. She herself would miss the Sunday night fireworks—she had to get back to Cambridge and Cap'n Chick—but André or Buck (their combination captain, cook, and steward) would be happy to redeliver me to my boat on the Monday morning.

His pleasure, Castine assured me. Peach sherbet and Armagnac. "Heat lightning" to north of us, from where now stirred a **rain-smelling** breeze. I had a number of questions yet to work diplomatically into our talk—the baron's relation to A. B. Cook, for instance; "Buffalo's" mention of the F.B.I.; maybe even the matter of the blackmail photographs—but the evening was evidently over, and I was sleepy from the long day's sail and the champagne. Jane politely invited me to use the guest stateroom, but—among other reasons for declining!—I wanted to be aboard *O.J.* if a squall blew through. As for the trip upriver, I'd let them know in the morning. My own Patuxent destination was only half a dozen miles up, where I had certain bases to touch. On the other hand, I was powerfully curious to see a bit more of my old love's new lover, now that my heart was proven truly clear of her. We'd see.

Sunday dawned hot, hazy, and still. 70% chance of late-afternoon or evening thunderstorms. Knowing that the anchorage would soon be empty, I paid out plenty of scope, battened everything down, and made ready after all to go aboard *Baratarian*. But the baron, smiling cleanly, dinghied over with a different plan: they had radiotelephoned Mr. Prinz at Benedict after I left them, and mentioned my presence; he was particularly anxious to film *Baratarian* en route to "Barataria," and though period detail was irrelevant to his production, it would please him too to film *Osborn Jones* coming downriver under sail. What's more, they could use the extra deck space. I would of course be remunerated; and Jane—whom Castine understood to be "entirely familiar" with my vessel—had volunteered to serve as my crew. He himself, alas, could be of small assistance. We were to rendezvous off Benedict at noon, where Prinz was filming the Withdrawal scene.

Mm hm. I agreed, but urged Castine to ride up with us as well.

Surely he wished to be with his fiancée? The baron's expression fairly twinkled: they had just returned from the recentest of a series of honeymoons, and would soon be married; knowing how much Jane esteemed me, he would sacrifice for a few hours the joy of his friend's company in order to catch up on various business in the air-conditioned comfort of his yacht.

So: less was accomplished than I'd hoped, yet more than I'd have expected before that weekend. Jane, as I anticipated, was all impenetrable good cheer as we motor-sailed upriver on a medium reach in the wake of *Baratarian*. I complimented her on her fiancé and learned without pain that they planned a late-September wedding. Um. . .his relation to A. B. Cook? Oh, well: André claimed it and Cook disclaimed it, neither militantly. Their mother Jane believed to have married twice; the family had been either scattered or peripatetic; perhaps there was some ill feeling, but it was as much a joke as anything. Relations between the two men Jane understood to be civil but not close. I did not risk mentioning the C.I.A., but asked whether the baron practiced any profession. Jane answered easily that he had worked in some capacity for the Canadian and British intelligence communities during and for a while after the Second World War, and had at various times tried his hand at novel-writing, without success. But the management of his inherited property, and latterly the courtship and entertainment of herself, were his principal and painless occupations.

Ah. We passed the mouth of St. Leonard Creek, where Polly Lake and I—but good-bye, good-bye! Experimentally I announced that Jeannine had been aboard two weekends since. Really! Jane hoped she'd behaved herself. What had she wanted? Just to go sailing and talk things over, I said; but she'd seemed amenable to an out-of-court settlement of her father's estate. Jane's tone grew brisk: Oh, well, that. Where had Jeannine been when *she'd* felt like being reasonable? Now she wasn't sure *what* she meant to do, exactly—but we oughtn't to talk business, okay?

That was that. Even at half-throttle *Baratarian* soon disappeared ahead; Jane asked no further questions about her daughter; I mildly regretted this excursion. I shall pass over the movie-making, Dad, which I have little comprehension of or interest in. God knows what the foundation is getting for its money: Prinz maintains that he makes his films as much in the editing room as on the set with the camera, and often doesn't know clearly himself, until he reviews the "takes," what his shooting is *about*. So reported one of his assistants, who seemed to Jane and me to be more in charge of things than the director himself. There was a box-lunch affair ashore, itself filmed. Prinz was on hand with the Bernstein girl, who does appear to have supplanted Jeannine. There indeed was red-faced Drew, surprised to see us but warily cordial; no sign of Yvonne, and Drew's face purpled when I asked whether she was about. He seemed to know and be on good terms with André Castine; with his mother he was reserved, and she cool with him. No sign either of Ambrose Mensch, who I had thought was involved in the project.

There was a postluncheon Withdrawal scene of all hands to our boats; good Buck saved me the trouble of making a fuss about hard shoes by demanding that everyone not wearing sneakers come aboard barefoot. We counted out life jackets; cameras on each vessel filmed the other, and the flotilla of water-skiers and buzzing runabouts as well. No one seemed to be delivering lines or acting out business, and don't ask me what any of it had to do with the War of 1812 (except that I was invited, and declined—on camera—to take the role of Dr. Beanes, the fellow whose arrest led to the composition of "The Star Spangled Banner"). Movies aren't what they used to be, Dad.

I soon decided that I would go no farther than back downriver to Solomons Island: I had no taste for crossing the Chesapeake with that freight of landlubbers (several of whom I recognized from the great Marshyhope Commencement Day Bust) in impending thundersqualls. There was room enough on *Baratarian* for all hands to squeeze aboard for the crossing; I would lend as many life jackets as *O.J.* could spare, to help meet Coast Guard regulations, and retrieve them next time our paths crossed. But my itinerary had been compromised enough, and the sight of Jane's manly, worldly, amiable baron more and more depressed me.

Drew was sympathetic (he rode down with me, ever friendlier; Jane was back aboard the trawler, having brushed my cheek lightly with her lips in Benedict and bade me pert good-bye); he commandeered the film crew's walkie-talkie to relay my decision forward and arrange for a transfer stop at Solomons. Then to my surprise he offered, with his abashed but open grin, to ride out the squall with me that night in Mill Creek, say, and cross to Bloodsworth in the morning if the weather cleared. His presence at the Burning of Washington was not imperative, and there were a few things he'd like to discuss. Of course, if I had other plans, or simply preferred to be alone. . .

Good-bye, Good-bye Cruise! We made the transfer (more footage) and watched *Baratarian* churn out Baywards, crowded as a Japanese excursion boat. In her stern stood Jane and her baron, waving merrily with the rest, his arm lightly around her waist.

Good-bye.

Thunderheads piled already in the west. Beefy but agile in his jeans and moccasins, Drew smartly handled the lines as we docked across the Patuxent in Town Creek for supplies and a hose-down to wash the visitors off us, then poked back up into my favorite storm shelter on that river: the eight-foot spot in an unnamed bight in the snug little cove just between the words *Mill* and *Creek* on Chart 561. By five o'clock the hook was down; too many nettles for swimming, but we stood watch for each other from the deck and managed to get wet without getting stung. Thunder and lightning approached, seriously this time, but a hurricane could not have dragged us. We congratulated ourselves on having not attempted the crossing; sipped our tonics and watched the sky turn impressively copper green, the breeze veer northwest and turn cool and blustery, *O.J.* swing her bows to it as the storm drew nearer. We checked the set and scope of the anchor (the rigging whistled now; trees thrashed, and leaves turned silver side up), secured everything on deck, calculated with relief that even so loaded, *Baratarian* would easily be at her dock before the squall crossed the Bay. My pulse exhilarated, as it had done 200 times before, at the ozone smell, the front's moving in like an artillery barrage, one's boat secure in a fine snug anchorage with room to swing and nothing really to fear. How splendid the world! How fortunate one's life!

We lingered in the cockpit till the last possible moment, drinking the spectacle in with our cocktails and speaking little. When the rain came at last—great white drops strafing through the trees, across the cove, and under the awning—we scrambled below, made a light cold supper (tuna salad, fruit Jell-O, and a chilled Riesling), and talked: the conversation we might have had in early July had I not been dazed from 12 R, my Second Dark Night of the Soul. For openers (dear Bach serenaded us from the FM; the storm crashed spectacularly all about; leaves and twigs flew; *O.J.* rolled and swung, but never budged his anchor) I remarked that the world was an ongoing miracle and that everything bristled with intrinsic value. Drew parried (flecks of tuna-mayonnaise on his lower lip) that two-thirds of that miracle's population went to bed hungry, if indeed they had a bed to go to.

I set forth the Tragic View of Ideology, acknowledged that the antiwar movement was having some practical effect in Washington and was certainly preferable to passive acquiescence in our government's senseless "involvement" in Southeast Asia, etc.; but confessed that I did not otherwise take the sixties very seriously even as a social, much less as a political, revolution. The decade would leave its mark on 20th-Century Western Culture—no doubt as notably as the 1910's, 20's, 30's, 40's, 50's, 70's, 80's, and 90's—but from any serious perspective, probably no more so. North Americans neither needed, wanted, nor would permit anything like a real "Second Revolution"; once its principal focus, the Viet Nam War, reached whatever sorry dénouement, the much-touted Counterculture would in a very few years become just another subculture, of which the more the merrier, with perhaps a decade's half-life in the media.

More Riesling. He too, Drew carefully declared, took the Tragic View of political activism, but would not follow me thence into quietism. On the contrary: as the war, the decade, and the movement wound down together, he was inclined to escalate. The fewer the actors, the more radical and direct must be the action. Yvonne was divorcing him: she wanted herself and their sons out of the Second Ward, out of Cambridge, out of the civil-rights and the antiwar movements, into the civilization of the Haves. They were about to move to Princeton, New Jersey, where she had friends. Drew's face purpled: *Princeton!* She wanted the boys in Groton, maybe Andover; she was prepared to let them pay their dues as Show Niggers if that's what it took to lead them to Bach and Shakespeare rather than to "Basin Street Blues" and *Black Boy.*

I offered my condolences: why could they not aspire to be civilized orthopedic surgeons or district court judges, repudiating neither their black nor their white cultural legacy or for that matter neither the high nor the popular culture? Drew fulminated for a while against the U.S. medical and juristic systems, comparing China's favorably. I denounced Chinese totalitarianism: the regime's extermination of, say, Tibetan and other cultures within its hegemony; its atrocities against its own prerevolutionary civilization, not to mention prerevolutionary human beings. The storm passed.

And returned, and rumbled around Maryland late into the night, as cool and snug a night for sleeping as I'd had since I left Todds Point. But we worked through another liter of German white, this one a rare and fine Franconian, in the low light of two gimbaled kerosene lamps on the cabin bulkheads. Drew conceded that probably nothing could justify the mass killings associated with the Russian and Chinese revolutions. I conceded that *possibly* nothing short of revolution would substantially have improved the welfare of the surviving masses in those nations. We came home to the Tragic View, neither of us greatly altered by the excursion, but even more cordial.

Did he mean, then, to become a flat-out terrorist? Bombs? Assassinations? Drew shrugged and grinned: he'd think of something. And he reminded me that in June of 1937, so the story went, I myself had put gravely at risk the lives of a Floating Theatreful of innocent Cantabridgeans, in no better cause than my own suicide. At least *he* would have an impersonal end in mind, and would direct his violence against symbolical property instead of people. I perpended that detail, specifically that adjective, wondering what property he had in mind—and reminded him on the one hand that while the event he'd cited happened to be a fact, the story he'd invoked was fiction and should not be categorically confused with my biography; on the other hand, that my then "philosophy" was one I'd long since put behind me—especially that deplorable, reckless endangerment of others' lives. At least most of the time, in most moods. For I was and am no philosopher.

Drew laughed: Nor was he. Just a thoughtful terrorist. Might he ask whether his mother and I had once been lovers? Yes and yes. With his father's knowledge and consent? Yes.

The news seemed to please him. So: that crazy old fart (his father) had remained a sexual liberal even after he'd repudiated liberal politics! Well, I said; for a while, anyhow. Harrison *was* his father? Drew assumed, grinning. No question, I assured him.

And Jeannine's?

I hoped the dim light concealed my blush. 50-50. Drew hmm'd, regarded his wineglass, then me; then he smiled and raised the glass in slight salute. It was time, he said, he made peace with that sister, or half

721

sister. He was distressed by her latest set-down and the news of her reaggravated alcoholism; they'd never been close, but perhaps now that his own life was turning a corner, he could help her turn one too.

Profoundly to be wished, said I. *Very* discreetly, then, so as not to spoil our new rapport, I brought up the names of his prospective stepfather and of Andrew Cook; also the nature of his own involvement in Reg Prinz's film. On the former matter Drew would say nothing except that while he did not believe me to be a C.I.A. or F.B.I. informer, I had gravely thwarted him once before, in the matter of the Choptank River Bridge, and he was determined not to be thus thwarted again (which was, it seemed to me, saying a great deal!). As for the film: suffice it to say that the media's tactic of co-opting the revolution was, so to speak, a coaxial business: they in turn could be co-opted, subverted without their even knowing it. The hearts and minds of the American middle class, especially the kids', could be won in neighborhood movie theaters and on national networks, under the sponsorship of Anacin and Geritol. . .

He began to say more, caught himself up with a grim smile, said he'd had too much to drink, emptied his glass, and bid me good night.

A big southwesterly next morning kept the sky cloudy, but as the P.O.P. was favorable, we made a fast beam reach of the 24 miles down and across the Bay to Bloodsworth Island. Drew loved the ride; he smoked cigars (properly mindful of sparks against the Dacron sails) and railed animatedly against those "fingerprints of the Hand of Death" on our navigation chart (1224): *Targets. Prohibited Area. Unexploded Bombs: Keep Clear. Navy Maintained. Prohibited. Restricted.* He chuckled at the radio news report that exhumation of Mary Jo Kopechne's body was regarded as doubtful; the Pentagon's projection of an all-volunteer army for Viet Nam escalated his chuckle to a derisive laugh. For all his contempt of such capitalist toys as cruising sailboats, he handled the skipjack deftly while I made lunch. By one o'clock we were in the straits between lower Dorchester County and Bloodsworth Island—flat, featureless marshes both—whence Drew threaded us expertly through an unlikely-looking maze of stakes marking a channel not given on the chart, to a pier in a cove on the island's north shore (Barataria Bight, Drew called it). He rounded up smartly alongside Castine's *Baratarian* at the ample dock, where we made fast with spring lines and fenders.

Much activity was afoot: a brace of Drew's shaggy cohorts caught our heaving lines admiringly while he gave the raised-fist salute; others moved about the white clapboard lodge and buildings nearby. Skiffs and motor launches—some painted battleship gray and manned by uniformed navy people—buzzed about; a big navy helicopter blasted low over us (fortunately all sails were down) and inland, toward where from some miles out we'd seen smoke rising; official-looking folk in summer suits and navy suntans came from the lodge to meet us, filmed by one of Prinz's assistants. No sign of Jane, the baron, or Marshyhope's new Distinguished Visiting Lecturer in English, who owns the spread.

The Stars and Stripes flapped northeastwards from a pole in the sandy dooryard.

Navy Intelligence and F.B.I., Drew's friends alerted us cheerfully, adding that we'd missed some crazy footage the night before.

I don't know *yet* exactly what-all happened, Dad; but it seems that the half–ad libitum "Burning of Washington," filmed on the Sunday night, had got out of hand. Lady Amherst and her friend Ambrose Mensch were involved—both returned now to the mainland, as were Jane and Baron Castine before the whole thing started. The scenario had involved some manner of personal combat, allegorical I presume, between Mensch and Reg Prinz (also now flown, leaving his assistants in charge of the filming), each of whom had, in the event, done physical injury to the other. As the thunderstorms moved in after dark, the sets representing the Capitol and the President's House had been fired, coincident by design with a night aerial gunnery exercise on nearby Pone Island (regarded as contiguous with Bloodsworth and maintained by the navy as a target area). While nature's fireworks combined with the navy's and Reg Prinz's, the Bernstein girl had run off the set into the marshes, toward the Prohibited Area, pursued by (of all people, and don't ask me why he was there) Jerome Bonaparte Bray, the madman of Lily Dale, cast aptly in the role of "Napoleon escaped from Elba"! In time Ms. Bernstein was retrieved, in shock but apparently unmolested, on the margin of an *Absolutely* Prohibited Zone sown with unexploded naval ordnance. She'd been fetched back to the lodge, where she remained under medical supervision—her distress augmented, this same Monday morning, by Prinz's deserting her as he'd deserted Jeannine. *Sic transit!*

Bray, however, never had been found. It was feared he had strayed into the Target Area and lost his way; was possibly a casualty of that gunnery exercise: hence the massive navy presence at Barataria Lodge. After midnight, squally weather had suspended both the firing exercise and the search; the latter had been resumed at dawn, without result, and was just now about to be abandoned.

Drew's people took for granted that the operation was mainly an exercise for the "Intelligence Types" to harass and scrutinize their activities: two young men had indeed been arrested as known draft evaders and one as a Marine Corps deserter, on warrants conveniently preprepared. I was impressed by Drew's good-humored ease in conversation with these same "Intelligence Types"; neither intimidated nor provocative, he was altogether in command of himself. He had, clearly, turned some important corner in his life. A. B. Cook VI, on the other hand, protested indignantly that Mr. Bray had made his way safely out of the marsh, if he had ever been there; had appeared in Cook's office in the lodge not two hours since to bid him good-bye, and was gone now back to the mainland with the rest. That the U.S. Navy was to its discredit harassing *him*, a man whose patriotism and conservatism were celebrated and unimpeachable; had been harassing him for years to surrender his title to Barataria, the last such private holding on the island.

Andrew Burlingame Cook VI: that florid fellow came down now from cottage to dock to greet us, protesting flamboyantly (but not, I thought, in very genuine outrage) as he came. He welcomed Drew and me with equal ebullience, regretting we'd missed yesterday's entertainment and today's luncheon. He cordially identified Drew to the Intelligence Types as a flaming commie they'd do better to bother with than himself; me as a misguided pinko liberal whose heart however was in the right place. Drew grinned around his cigar; the I.T.'s were unmoved. I wondered. Now that I had seen Jane's Baron Castine, Cook's resemblance to him struck me as real but slight: one would neither guess them to be half siblings on that basis nor much question the allegation. Drew thanked me for the ride and excused himself to confer with "his people"; Cook expansively showed me about his property and the still-smoldering remains of the movie set (little more than a few charred "flats"), recounting in his fashion the events of the night before. Mosquitoes swarmed. Why he'd ever lent himself and his premises to such a cockeyed project, staffed by godless free-loving commie dope fiends, would be a mystery to him, Cook declared, were it not that he knew too well his penchant for theatricals. What's more, he was a leading spirit of the Maryland 1812 Society. Therefore he had not only offered his property and his historical expertise to the filmmakers, but had been pleased to play the role of his own ancestor and namesake, Andrew Cook IV, a participant in the Battle of Bladensburg and a casualty of the 1814 assault on Baltimore. But the film was a farce, a travesty! Look what he had brought upon himself (he waved with a laugh at a passing helicopter, on its way back to the Patuxent Naval Air Station)! He would think twice before accepting their invitation to "do" the Fort McHenry scene in September!

We returned to the lodge through a cleanup detail supervised by Drew, observed by the last contingent of Intelligence Types, and filmed by Prinz's cameraman. Cook's place was spacious, airy, simple, comfortable; I was invited to stay for dinner and the night. No hard feelings, he trusted, about our disagreement in the Marshyhope affair? Clearly *he* bore no grudges: witness his hospitality to the disrupters, whose shameful behavior on Commencement Day he nonetheless still deplored. With Lady Amherst and her friend Mensch, too, he had for his part made his peace: they'd spent last night as his guests in the caretaker's cottage, where he hoped I'd oblige him by staying tonight. He was satisfied that "those lovebirds" had been properly disciplined for their misdemeanors, and was ready now to support their reinstatement to the faculty.

We sipped Canadian ale in his long screened porch and regarded the activity outside. I said I understood that Baron André Castine was his near relative: half brother, was it? So *he* likes to claim, Cook jovially replied: one wouldn't guess it from our faces or our politics, eh? And the truth, alas, was buried with their parents. But again, he bore that chap no ill will—though he'd be relieved when he and his were gone from Barataria, and the navy stopped breathing down his neck!

Hm. Castine, then, was some sort of political radical? One of your high-society lefties, Cook affirmed: cast in the mold of FDR and Averell Harriman, but without their money—he winked—at least till his coming remarriage, eh?

I wondered aloud whether Jane Mack was aware of her fiancé's politics. Cook laughed: his *cousine* was no fool; I might rest assured there was *nothing* about her groom-to-be that she did not know. Anyhow, added Drew (who here stepped casually out from the cottage living room, ale in hand), only such a crusted troglodyte as our host would call Roosevelt and Harriman radicals. Cook saluted with his glass: only such a card-carrying subverter of Old Glory as Harrison Mack's misguided son would regard the Red Baron as a moderate liberal.

Such affability. Castine, then, I inquired, had not himself been present at all during the Burning of Washington? Cook winked again: the lucky fellow had seen his betrothed back to Cambridge instead; but he would return tonight or tomorrow, Cook devoutly hoped, to retrieve his yacht and begone to the upper Severn, where Drew's mother was buying property in expectation of a favorable settlement of her late husband's estate.

This last was an obvious but not ill-humored gibe; Drew merely saluted with his glass again. Where, I wondered, was my short-fused young adversary of old? What was all this amiable ecumenicism? I asked Drew his immediate plans. He'd be staying there at least until Castine returned, he supposed; they had "wrap-up" shots and other business to finish (Monkey business, Cook snorted) before moving on to "the home of the Home of the Brave" for more footage on Defenders Day, Sept. 12, anniversary of the British attack on Baltimore. The Tidewater Foundation, after all, had a large investment in the film; he felt a responsibility to monitor the expenditure of his father's money. Hah, said Cook. And your mother knows all about these things? I pressed. Drew shrugged: Mack Enterprises had its own Intelligence Types, whose competence however he could not vouch for.

I did in fact stay for dinner—a cold buffet for the whole remaining company, served by Cook's cook and caretaker—and the night, hoping I'd see Castine again and ask him a few polite questions. The caretaker's cottage included a guest apartment—a clean and welcomely air-conditioned respite from *O.J.*—where but for brief confused dreams of the "Red Baron" and Jeannine, I slept more soundly than one ever does, or should, single-handed on a sailboat.

And next morning (Tuesday 8/26, a blazing, airless, equatorial day) I lingered about the premises till near noon, making a long business out of odd-job maintenance on the boat, in hopes of remeeting the owner of *Baratarian*. Who, however, did not appear. The man makes his own timetables, Drew said, and he Drew makes his. How about mine?

It was a plain, albeit cordial, invitation to leave; and indeed it was time I got on with, back to, done with my much-disrupted *voyage de bon voyage*. He and Cook, still chaffing each other, bid me farewell—Drew's handshake was solid and serious, his expression gratified as mine by our new, not altogether clear rapprochement—and aided my undocking, calling advice about shoals and bush markers as I swung clear of Castine's trawler and powered gingerly out. I waved good-bye to the people on the wharf, to the lodge, the limp unmoving flag, Bloodsworth Island generally and Drew Mack in particular—but began to suspect already that my quietus might have to be postponed till I'd seen that young man again (perhaps at Fort McHenry?) and I learned What Was Going On.

I had meant to bid adieu to certain tributaries of the Potomac—St. Inigoes on the St. Mary, for instance, near where white Marylanders first landed—but I had digressed too long and too far with the heirs of Harrison Mack. Through binoculars I could just make out, as I entered the Bay, Point No Point Lighthouse, ten miles to west-southwestward, and I felt another proper pang, not unmixed with exhilaration, as I turned *north*west instead, back up the Chesapeake, toward home. Good-bye, Point No Point, fit title for the story of my life. Good-bye to all things south of Bloodsworth: I shall not pass your way again.

No breeze but what came under the awning from our headway. Trolling a Hopkins Spoon for bluefish (I caught only one; we were moving too fast), I motored all day through glass-calm water, past Hoopers, Barren, and Taylors islands, 30 miles up the Bay and ten more into the Little Choptank to Church Creek, in whose mouth I anchored at sundown. There was neither light nor water enough to go the mile and a half farther to my destination, near the creek's head; anyhow there were fewer bugs and more air where I was. Perspiring through my insect repellent every hour or so, I spent the evening trying vainly to draw the connections that had teased me through the day's navigation, and found myself at bedtime with no more than a list of names—*Harrison Jane Castine Cook Drew Jeannine Bray*—between which I made less meaningful associations than between the dinner entries in my log: *cold artichoke broiled bluefish French bread rosé.*

After breakfast I dinghied up to Old Trinity Churchyard and said good-bye to that tranquil place (maintained in part by foundation funds) which presently my remains shall say hello to. I will not join the family, Dad, in Plot #1. If I cannot manage to recycle my body to the crabs and fishes on which it has so long and gratefully fed, it will go into this venerable, quiet ground, so near their haunts that I heard the minnows plashing from my grave.

I had dreamed again that night. Through the day—an easy glide on prevailing southerlies out of the Little, and into the Great, Choptank, my river—I mused upon those dreams. They had been local geographical teasers, inspired no doubt by Point No Point. That name

726

figured in them, as did Ragged Point, Cooks Point, Todds Point, which-all I left to starboard during the day: my subconscious is as unsubtle as our Author. There now lay home, so close I could scan the property with binoculars; but I had two bases more to touch, and planned anyhow to end my cruise and the week in Cambridge, with a stop at the office, before coming full circle to Todds Point. The mild breeze died in midriver, at slack tide, just off the Choptank Light. I lowered sail, kicked the engine on, and chugged up the wealthy Tred Avon past Oxford to my parking place: snug and unspoiled Martin Cove, not named on Chart 551.

After shower and dinner, finishing a soft Bordeaux under a fine full moon, I turned last night's name-list into a list of questions. For what reason could Castine and Drew be friends, who were by way of being rival contenders for Harrison's money, if not that they were in political collusion to swindle Jane, perhaps Jeannine as well? Did not Drew's position vis-à-vis "the media"—*i.e.*, co-opting the co-opters—account for his easy new détente with A. B. Cook, perhaps even with me, and his expressed wish, however apparently sincere, for reconciliation with his sister? Disagreeable speculation! But unto death I am a lawyer. How account, though, for *Cook's* affability, which seemed to me to go substantially beyond his former and famous mercuriality? Could there be anything to Joseph Morgan's old supposition, that behind that flag-waving poetaster was a closet radical? How useful it might have been for this old trial lawyer to watch him and Castine together! Could Drew be planning to turn the Fort McHenry film scene into a terrorist demolition stunt? Or could Cook, say (or Castine, for possibly different reasons), be setting Drew up for such a stunt in order to thwart and arrest him? Perhaps Cook, rather than Castine, was an Intelligence Type!

Et cetera, vertiginously, till near midnight, while my last full moon (the Sturgeon) whitened, crossed Martin Cove, and penumbrally eclipsed. Herons squawked. My conjectures bored me; I was spinning them out, I began to suspect (just as I've spun out this last letter to you), in the way Dante tells us that Florentine assassins, placed headfirst into holes in the ground and condemned to live burial, spun out their last confessions to the bending priest—inventing, to delay their end, even more sins than they'd committed. My concern was real—for Jane, for Drew, for Jeannine, for (for that matter) the Star-Spangled Banner and suchlike national symbols—but it was limited. What's more, at that hour in that private place where a certain old friend and I had watched many a moon sail westwards, I missed her awfully. I was in fact fairly seized by horny, lonely boredom, to the point where (at age 69, Dad!) I fished out my penis to masturbate—but ended by pissing over the taffrail instead, and turning in. Good night, Polly.

They might all, of course, be conning *me*. An elaborate conspiracy among Jane, Drew, and Jeannine, assisted by Cook and Castine, to eliminate me (*i.e.*, the T.F.) from the Mack sweepstakes. Why not? With secondary plots against one another once I'm out of the running. I considered this possibility through the Thursday—another dull scorcher, with fitful breezes that made sailing a slow but busy business. My last anchorage, in Trappe Creek (*La* Trappe on the chart, but no Eastern Shoreman ever called it that), was a mere eleven miles down the Tred Avon and up the Choptank. To kill time I reviewed and adieu'd the other elegant Tred Avon creeks—Peachblossom, Maxmore, Goldsborough, Plaindealing—and tied up at Oxford for lunch and supplies before tacking out into my river for the afternoon and running into Trappe Creek for the evening. By when I found it hard to care who was conning whom.

Trappe Creek, Dad, is the favorite of my favorites on the Chesapeake. (Did you ever see it, I wonder? You never spoke of what you loved.) The placid essence of the Eastern Shore: low but marshless banks, a fringe of trees with working farms behind, houses few but fine, clean sand beaches here and there, and two perfect anchorages: the large unnamed cove to port behind the entrance point, sheltered from the seas but open enough for air on muggy nights; and, a mile farther up, also to port, magic Sawmill Cove: high-banked, entirely wooded, houseless, snug, primeval. There I went, never mind the humidity, to close another circle on my Last Night Out: it is where I spent my first youthful night aboard a boat (someone else's), sleepless with excitement at the contiguity of the world's salt waters, yearning to go on, on, to Portugal, to Fiji! I shall not ever see those places; have long since (*i.e.,* since 1937) put by such yearnings. But Sawmill Cove is still a place to make one miss the world.

Ordinarily. This night too it did its part—bluefish thrashed after minnows in the shallows, great blue herons stalked and clattered, ospreys wheeled, raccoons scrounged along the low-tide flats, crows and whippoorwills did their things, turtles conned and glided in the moonlight, there was not one human sound—but I could not do mine. Good-bye, good-byes! On, not to Portugal, but to the end! I began this letter, to say good-bye to you; put it by after an hour's sweaty scribbling. Too much to tell; too much of consequence not yet tellable. To bed, then, to get on with it, on with it.

In the early hours my sleep was broken by a shocking noise: from somewhere alongshore, very nearby, as feral a snarling as I've ever heard, and the frantic squeals of victims. A fox or farm dog it must have been, savaging a brood of young something-or-others. For endless minutes it went on, blood-chilling. Insatiable predator! Prey that shrieked and splashed but for some reason could not escape, their number diminishing one by pathetic one! I rushed on deck with the 7x50's, shouted out into the pitch-darkness (the moon had set), but could see and do nothing. The last little victim screamed and died. Baby herons? Frogs? Their killer's roaring lowered to an even growl, one final terrible snarling *coup de grâce*, then almost a purr. There was a rustling up into the woods, followed by awful silence. Long moments later a crow croaked; a cicada answered; a fish jumped; the night wood business resumed.

I stood trembling in my sweat. Nature bloody in fang and claw! Under me, over me, 'round about me, everything killing everything! I had dined that evening on crabs boiled alive and picked from their exoskeletons; as I ate I'd heard the day's news: Judge Boyle denies Kennedy request to cross-examine Kopechne inquest witnesses; last of first 25,000 U.S. troops withdrawn from Viet Nam; U.S.S.R. acknowledges danger of war with China. And Drew would become a terrorist, only accidentally killing others. And you, sir, killed yourself, the only lesson you ever taught me. Horrific nature; horrific world: out, out!

Come misty morning I rowed 'round Sawmill Cove and found nothing. Trappe Creek and all its contents were dewy, fresh, innocent, almost unbearably sweet. Oh, end it! I felt heart-haggard as the Ancient Mariner; looked as zombieish as on the morn of June 22 last. End it. A northwesterly sprang up in time for me to leave cove and creek silently, under sail, as I'd hoped. No good-bye; just out, out. In the river I passed without emotion Red Nun 20. By midmorning *Osborn Jones* was in his Cambridge slip, fit with reasonable maintenance to sail to the end of the century; but I left him without a qualm, almost sorry I had yet to sail back to Todds Point, so done was I with what had been for 30 years my chiefest pleasure—and with having done.

I walked up hot High Street to the hotel for a shave, shower, and change of clothes; snatched up the accumulated mail without sorting through it; went over to the office to see what was what. Hello, Ms. Pond and partners. Pleasant enough, thank you. Get Buffalo on the phone, please. Come again, Buffalo? No "Monsieur Casteene" to be found in Fort Erie? No one home at Jerome Bray's establishment (*Comalot,* you say? Is that first *o* long or short?) except a family of goats and a crazy lady who calls herself Morgana le Fay? Who you *what?* Have reason to suspect might be Harrison Mack's daughter? By all means investigate further! And now, Ms. P.: Joseph Morgan, please, in Fort Erie. Not available? Your name is what? Jacob Horner, administrative assistant? Ms. Bea G., please—*Bibi,* I believe you call her. . . Not there? Since 8/14? Never mind whose birthday! Presumably with Mr. Bray in Lily Dale?

Oh, Polly, where are you to advise me? I asked your successor now to get Jane herself on the phone, thinking to share with her my concern for her, our, daughter and perhaps (discreetly) to signal my apprehensions about her fiancé. While Ms. P. dialed I leafed through the mail; saw your dear handwriting on one envelope; tore into it in the dim hope that whatever it contained might invite my apology for so rebuffing you—and found the announcement of your wedding on the 21st.

A wedding performed, you kindly explained on the back of the announcement, after that last desperate visit to Cambridge three weeks since, when—hoping against hope I'd welcome you home, *order* you to stay, propose marriage on the spot to the woman who'd left me only to prod my sluggish heart—you'd been coldly turned off instead; and even so, madly imagining I might just be ill or distracted, madly praying that one last word might drop the scales from my eyes and heart and prompt me at last to say Come, Polly, Come with me and old *Osborn Jones,* let's sail together to the end of the chapter. . .you *called;* you telephoned me at Todds Point in the middle of the night, cursing and loving me, hoping and praying; called to propose flat out to me what, decades since, I ought to have proposed to you. And your call was answered by a sleepy young woman's voice, and for the last time you swallowed your pride; rang off without a word; went home to Florida; said yes at last to your patient friend, and to me a hurt but even yet loving last good-bye.

Good-bye, Polly.

Cancel that call, Ms. Pond. Cancel everything. No, nothing wrong; everything is right, and full to overflowing with intrinsic value, except that I remain alive.

Back aboard the boat I sat for some time stunned, then made a certain codicil to my will regarding the posthumous disposition of my "personal papers," including this. Home next day to Todds Point, where I spent the Labor Day weekend considering, among other things, Tomorrow Now. Why await the equinox, or the winding up of business, or the illumination of mysteries, before ending, ending, ending it? Was there any reason at all not to have done?

One. In the office on Tuesday morning last, September 2, I found Buffalo on Line One, calling me before I could have Ms. Pond call him. Nothing new on "Morgana le Fay" (which was all I cared about), but all was chaos at that *other* crazy place, the one across the river in Canada. As of yesterday, Labor Day, Joe Morgan was dead, an apparent suicide; all the white patients and staff were being evicted by the blacks—no Bibis or Bea Goldens or Jeannine Macks among them. Should he continue to keep an eye on things, discreetly?

Sure, but not at the expense of A. B. & A. In my capacity as executive director of the Tidewater Foundation I retained him to investigate and report the goings-on at the Remobilization Farm, from which we ought probably to withdraw our benefaction. Then, discretion be damned, I called Jane directly and told her everything I knew, suspected, or feared about Jeannine, Drew, André Castine, and, alas, poor Morgan—everything except my quasi-incest of three weeks since.

To my surprise, she was unsurprised. Her "own people" had already informed her of all those things, Jane declared coolly, including Morgan's regrettable suicide, and other things besides, which, given the pending litigation, she was not at liberty to share with me. My retention of a private investigator on behalf of the foundation she did not disapprove; that was my business. Her fiancé's background, on the other hand, was not; she would thank me to cease my prying thereinto, or at least my bothering her with my "discoveries." The blackmail threat I could forget about, as *she* intended to. It was nothing: it had been dealt with, or was being, or would be, by her people. As for Jeannine and Drew: she had already made clear to me her sentiments, which were unchanged. But I was to understand that that business of my possible paternity of her daughter was a fiction which she Jane had never seriously entertained. She regarded it as one of the several, should we say idiosyncratic, obsessions with which I amused myself. Now, if I didn't mind. . .

Where is Harrison's shit? I demanded. Jane chuckled: She would leave it to me in her will. 'Bye.

I telephoned Drew, thinking to go with him at once to Buffalo, Lily Dale, Fort Erie, in search of his sister. Yvonne answered, even chillier than Jane: she was sure she didn't know where her estranged husband was; their house was hers until the end of the week, when she was leaving Red-neck Neck forever. 'Bye.

So far as I knew, Joe Morgan had no living relatives except his college-age sons. I asked Ms. Pond to make me air reservations to Buffalo for next morning and to have the foundation arrange a memorial service at the college for its first president. (In the event, when I met and conferred with the Morgan boys in Fort Erie yesterday, we arranged the funeral too, to be held in Wicomico the day after tomorrow.)

Wednesday, then, I flew to Buffalo, in pursuit of my shall-we-say-idiosyncratic-et-cetera, consulted and terminated our investigator (nothing new), hired a car, and drove down alone to Lily Dale, to "Comalot." A ramshackle farmhouse and outbuildings; there were the goats, a rangy Toggenburg buck and two mixed-breed nans, one pregnant. No sign of Bray, but as I drove up, a wild-haired, scowling, long-skirted, granny-glassed young woman came from the barn, already shaking her head at me. The Bernstein girl! What on earth was she doing there? None of my business. Where was "Bea Golden"? Come and gone. Gone where? Didn't know and didn't care. Jerome Bray? Hard at work with "Lilyvac II"; couldn't be interrupted. Might I inspect that machine and arrange a conversation with its owner? I might f——g not; if the f——g Tidewater Foundation wouldn't put up, it could f——g shut up and get off the premises. She had spoken to me at all, declared Ms. B., only because I'd once arranged bail for her with those red-neck pigs; but that gave me no f——g permanent claims. There might be a police search, I informed her, if Bea Golden didn't soon turn up. Ms. B. replied sweetly: Till f——g then. As she strode away I called after: Was she also known as Morgana le Fay? Without turning, she hitched up her skirt and flashed her (bare, white, uncomely) bottom. When she reentered the barn she closed the door behind her.

I considered waiting them out, or driving away for an hour and then returning unexpectedly, or concealing myself in the nearby woods and watching for Bray or Jeannine. But the detective had done all that, without success, and my rights in the matter, as no more than a concerned friend of the family, were tenuous. Back to Buffalo.

Thence (yesterday) over the Peace Bridge to Fort Erie and the "Remobilization Farm." Sure enough, a general exodus of whites was in progress, ordered by a young black chap who but for his green medical tunic might have passed for Drew's late friend Tank-Top. He called himself Doctor Tombo X; he was the son of the late owner of the establishment; he was surly; and he was perhaps quite within his rights (in the absence of either a will or a board of directors) to evict whom it pleased him to, though I warned him not to expect further support from the Tidewater Foundation. I spoke as aforementioned with Morgan's sons: stalwart, taciturn, capable boys who however welcomed my offer of legal and funerary assistance. In an hour we'd made arrangements for interment on Saturday in Wicomico, where their mother was buried. About their father's "freaking out" they were reticent, whether from lack of information or a wish for privacy. No doubt his defeat by the Schott-Cook party at Marshyhope, plus the general upheaval and antirationalism of this wretched decade, repotentiated Morgan's distress at the loss of his wife, which he had never truly got over. But such dramatic metamorphoses as his are always as ultimately mysterious as is, for that matter, their absence.

Finally I interrogated Mr. Jacob Horner, an odd duck indeed, and his female companion, whom he called Marsha and the others called Pocahontas. I could make little sense of his account of Morgan's death (Horner I gathered was a long-term "patient" at the Farm as well as some sort of administrator, and an old acquaintance of Morgan's), but inasmuch as he'd been in the room when Joe either deliberately or accidentally shot himself—indeed, it seems there had been a scuffle between them: an inquest was being considered—I advised him to retain a local lawyer and requested from him, "for the foundation," a copy of the account I urged him to set down for that lawyer.

On the subject of Jeannine they could or would say no more than I'd been told already: she'd come back "from Maryland" much distressed on August 11th, lingered unhappily at the Farm for two days, then gone with this "Pocahontas" person to visit Bray at Lily Dale for unspecified reasons (I suspect narcotics). Pocahontas had returned on the 15th; Jeannine had voluntarily stayed on. When I declared that she appeared to be there no longer, and that Miss Merope Bernstein was there instead, they shrugged. Perhaps "Bibi" had gone back to Reg Prinz? Such things happened.

Well. This Marsha-Pocahontas woman struck me as a bit evasive, but she might merely have been stoned, or drunk: she had the voice and manner of an old lush, not unlike Jeannine's, but acerbic. The similarity made me weary, even cross. That Jeannine would have substantially mended her life if I'd kept her with me was neither impossible nor likely; I pitied her, hoped she was "all right," and doubted either that she was or that if she wasn't it was owing to foul play. Chances were she was boozing it up in New York City or Los Angeles. I had done enough; I was tired. Even so, I filed a missing-person report with both the Ontario Provincial Police and the Chautauqua County Sheriff's office (whose jurisdiction includes Lily Dale) before returning that night exhausted to Baltimore, to Cambridge, to the Dorset Hotel.

"This morning" (I mean Friday, but time has passed), from the office (nothing new), I tried to reach Prinz, Drew, and A. B. Cook by telephone—that last to ask exactly when and how Bray had turned up from the Prohibited Area and what *he* knew about Merope Bernstein and Jeannine. No answer at Drew's house. No listed number in Manhattan for Prinz. Ditto for Cook or anyone else on Bloodsworth Island, where the operator doubted there was even telephone service.

I gave up. Left the office. Came out here. Rebegan this letter around lunchtime. And have kept at it unremittingly through the weekend, pausing only to eat and sleep, determined to have done with it, with you, before turning my attention for the last time to myself.

There I have succeeded: my one success in recent weeks. It is Sunday forenoon now, September 7. Bishop Pike's body has been found in the deserts of Israel; Joseph Morgan's will be memorialized a few hours from now; Jeannine's is still missing. Just time to wind this up, or down, and drive over to Marshyhope for Joe's service—where, not *quite* done with guilty interest, I hope to press all relevant mourners for more information about What in the World Is Going On.

Did you expect a climax, Dad? A surprise ending, a revelation? Sorry. I here close my *Inquiry* for good, first opened 49 years ago this month. As you did not deign to let me know why you turned yourself off, I shall not tell you this time (as I did in 1937) how, when, and where I mean to do likewise. Commence your own Inquiry! Begin, what in your life you never once began, a Letter to

Your Son.

I: *Draft codicil to the last will and testament of Todd Andrews.*

Morgan Memorial Tower
Marshyhope State University
Redmans Neck, Maryland 21612

Friday, September 26, 1969

I, TODD ANDREWS, a resident of Dorchester County, state of Maryland, being of sound & disposing mind, memory, & understanding, do hereby make, publish & declare this instrument of writing as & for a Codicil to my Last Will & Testament, supplementary to my Codicil of 9/1/69 comprising Article Sixth of my Last Will & Testament aforesaid. To wit:

SEVENTH: I give and bequeath to my Literary Trustee named in my Codicil of 9/1/69, in addition to my *Letter to My Father,* my *Inquiry* into his suicide, and the *Log of the Skipjack Osborn Jones,* this Codicil itself, if it survive the imminent demolition of the structure wherein I draft it and of myself, and whether or not it be completed, signed, and legally witnessed.

I write this by full-Harvest-Moonlight, almost bright enough to read by (but I brought with me a red-lensed pocket chart-light from the boat, along with pen, trusty yellow legal pad, and my 7x50 night glasses), in the locked & bolted Observation Belfry of the Morgan Memorial Tower, variously & popularly known as the Schott Tower, the Shit Tower, and the Tower of Truth. Drew Mack and some surviving fellow terrorists—dressed and painted as Choptank Indians to dramatize Redskin Rights in the event of apprehension—got in like burglars a few hours ago to do their work, mugging the night watchman for his keys and his watch-clock. But I entered, not long past midnight, as befits the Tidewater Foundation's executive director & former counsel to MSU: with a gold-plated passkey presented symbolically by John Schott at last evening's ceremonial dinner to me, to my counterpart on the State University's Board of Regents, and to the governor of Maryland as represented by the comptroller of the treasury. A souvenir *Key to Truth,* which, broken off in the lock cylinder, insures my privacy to write and my freedom from rescue.

By this gorgeous light I can see clear across campus to the Mack mansion, where Jane is once again in mourning. Since her own—no doubt her first—Dark Night, Wednesday week last (9/19), when the yacht *Baratarian* was found derelict & half scuttled, with specimens of Harrison's freeze-dried droppings aboard, and charts of the Mexican Caribbean, and very little else, Jane has suddenly looked her age: a metamorphosis more spectacular by far than mine because she had looked so inordinately youthful. I have done what I can to comfort her, without impressive success, and learned in the process that in fact she & Castine had concealed her late husband's leavings lest I try to "pull another fast one" in the will case "as I did before." And that the cache had nonetheless been stolen just prior to the Fort McHenry action—evidently but unaccountably by her fiancé! Whatever for, since her loss stood to be his? Neither Jane nor I can imagine. We rule out collusion with Drew as pointless and out of (Drew's) character, whatever other connections the pair might have had. And we do not know what became of the crew & cargo of *Baratarian.* Jane declares herself inconsolable, and may be so. But I rather suspect that the opening next month of the first Cap'n Chick franchises and the early, favorable settlement of Harrison's estate (now that the Tidewater Foundation is about to lose its director, and given Jeannine's continued disappearance & Drew's amenability to an out-of-court settlement) will go far towards consoling her; farther at least than my heartfelt but unavoidably detached solicitude.

Jeannine, Jeannine: what has our Author done with you? And if your little cruise with me furthered His plot, can you forgive me? We've little time.

My old heart pounds like a spring pile driver after an icy winter. What a heavy, hokey (but not untypical) irony it will be, if natural death prevents my suicide!

That *other* pounding—an almost furtive pounding, one could call it—is not my heart: it's Drew and/or his associate Indians at my door. No, there's no one in here. No, I shan't open up. Yes, I daresay there is an Emergency of Sorts requiring immediate evacuation of the building; but I am not inclined to believe it a fire, as you now disingenuously claim, inasmuch as you have not seen fit to sound the fire alarm. Come on, Drew, you can do better than that. Saw a bit of light up here, did you? I'll switch to the red night-vision lens on my pen light. And I saw you, too, my lad, with my 7x50's, sequestering the watchman (I'm pleased you didn't hurt him, or sequester him in the building you're about to dynamite. May you at least acquire the Tragic-Humanist View of Terrorism). Very impressive you are, son, in your Indian redface, warpaint, braids, & matchcoat: the reincarnation, not of the lost Choptanks, but of your white ancestors in redskin drag who hosted the Boston Tea Party & related festivities. I wonder whether your discovery of my death at your inadvertent hands will prove the first step of your regression from radicalism to good old Stock Bourgeois-Liberal Tragic-Viewing Humanism; and I wonder whether I hope it will. I believe I do. Go away, now: time to make your mugged watchman's rounds for him.

Good. And good-bye, Drew.

Come to think of it, that did not sound *quite* like Drew Mack's voice, though it was familiar. Fort McHenry. . .Wedding scene. . .Germaine Pitt's bridegroom? Not likely. No doubt Drew disguised his voice.

At last night's banquet, my last supper, two Intelligence Types were much in evidence, trying hard to look inconspicuous. Did they have wind of Drew's plan, I wondered, or were they keeping an eye on me? Drew himself (who now believes both Cook & Castine to have been undercover operatives for rival U.S. intelligence agencies, each sabotaging the other) says that I can expect surveillance at the least, maybe even some harassment, since my suit for subpoena of Prinz's film of the Navy's Accident at Barataria Lodge. Do your worst, lads, so long as you don't foil today's big bang.

The dedication ceremonies, my souvenir program announces, are scheduled to commence at 9:30 A.M. To the strains of Handel's *Water Music* as performed by the MSU Brass Ensemble, an academic procession of the faculty, followed by representative members of the board of regents and trustees of the Tidewater Foundation, distinguished guests (the state comptroller and Dorchester County commissioners), and the now official president of Marshyhope State University: Schott's

735

maiden ceremonial since his confirmation, not counting the memorial for Joe Morgan. Prayer by MSU Chaplain Arthur Beille. National anthem. Welcoming remarks by the chairman of the board of regents and by the executive director of the Tidewater Foundation, who is to invoke Our Algonquin Heritage apropos of American Indian Day. Official presentation of the Morgan Memorial Tower to MSU by the state of Maryland, as represented respectively by President Schott and the comptroller. Acceptance speech by President Schott ("What is Truth?"). Itemization by the acting provost of the Faculty of Letters of the contents of the cornerstone: this week's *Dorchester News;* yesterday's Cambridge *Daily Banner;* this morning's Baltimore *Sun (Congress complains of U.S. forces in Laos; Defense Dept. denies. Senator Goodell says cut off Viet War funds);* an Algonquin arrowhead found during excavation for the building (other Indian artifacts, unearthed from their burial ground, are on display in the tower lobby, otherwise unfurnished because of Structural Problems); a list of important historical events occurring on this date (General McArthur recaptures Detroit from Tecumseh and General Proctor. Holy Alliance against Napoleon signed in Paris); Polaroid photographs of the ceremonial itself; souvenir program of same; and—if I finish this in time and contrive to slip down, deposit it there, and slip back here—this draft codicil. (Lawyers learn how burglars work. I shall tape the belfry bolt to enable my return.) Official laying of cornerstone by President Schott, the general contractor, and a construction crew (it was to have been Peter Mensch and his stonemasons, but that stout fellow has gone to his reward). Benediction by Chaplain Beille. Recessional: Handel's *Royal Fireworks Music.*

These ceremonies will not take place. The fireworks will occur rather earlier than the *Water Music:* about 7:00 A.M., at sunrise. Charges of TNT, appropriately placed in the already opening foundation seams and other key structural members, will drop this architectural and pedagogical obscenity into its own foundation hole and rebury the Algonquin relics, together with some newer, paleface ones: a future enrichment of the past by the present. *This* demolition exercise, unlike the Great Chesapeake Bay Bridge Plot of 1967, has been competently engineered with the aid of construction blueprints stolen, along with explosives and detonators, from Mensch Masonry, Inc., and with the presumably expert advice of the late "Red Baron" André Castine.

Alias A. B. Cook VI? I shall never know. Erstwhile threatener with blackmail of his own fiancée? (I asked Jane quickly at our latest—and final—talk, hoping to tuck up that dangling thread of our Author's plot.) Perhaps before their firm affiancement changed his strategy, or for some other, more complex reason? I shall never know. Some things Jane was "not ready to talk about yet." So be it, my dear, and adieu.

On the bridge in '67 and again at Fort McHenry two weeks ago, I

736

frustrated Drew's intention; I shall not again. At Barataria Lodge on Bloodsworth Island last week, I did him the favor of saving his life; he will return that favor this morning, unknowingly, by ending mine. It's a few days past my equinoctial deadline for winding up 13 R, the last installment of my life's recycling; but flexibility & leisurely improvisation have been of the essence of this reenactment, and shall be to its end. Yesterday Now!

6:15 A.M.: I have spotted what look to me like the late Reg Prinz's cameramen, with portable equipment, down by the empty dedication platform, filming the "cornerstone" (which has but one engraved face, the tower being round) by Available Light, of which there is more & more as the setting moon lights up the Chesapeake to westward while the approaching sunrise lightens the Choptank to eastward. They ducked for cover when a campus patrol car cruised by. Should they enter the tower (or stay where they are), they have about 45 minutes to live. If I try to warn them, Drew is likely to intercept me and thwart my Plans for the Morning. If I succeed in warning them, they may blow the whistle and thwart Drew's plans as well.

Now they have reappeared from under the platform. The Associate Indian speaks with them, gesticulates; but he & Drew do not Sequester them with the night watchman. Perhaps they are in on the operation, either from its inception or as of now, and are merely discussing camera angles. Not a bad replacement for their confiscated footage of 9/16!

Now all three take cover again—no, all four: there's Drew with them—as an unmarked VW Beetle drives slowly up and parks behind the platform. Intelligence Types? Undergraduate lovers or other Innocent Bystanders? Complications.

6:35: The driver has left that parked VW and moved out of my sight toward the base of the tower. Male; couldn't recognize. Drew & Co. have reemerged, conferred—a touch anxiously, I daresay—and perhaps agreed to disagree concerning the slaughter of the innocent. The Associate Indian now withdraws to a safe remove with the cameramen, and Drew hurries into the building: risking his life, it appears, either to save an Innocent Bystander's or to prevent a *very* daring I.T. from saving Schott's Tower.

6:45: I (and perhaps some others) have 15 minutes or less to live, in which interval I must close this Codicil, attempt to go down & pop it into the cornerstone, and hurry back inside, not necessarily to here.

Hold on: there goes Drew, alone & at a trot, over towards the others. Well, now. Don't be distressed, lad; you did your best.

6:50: Someone is barreling up from belowstairs. It almost sounds as if he's got the stuck elevator working: there's an electrical hum or buzz. All I can hope, sir, is that you're a culpable I.T. and not an I.B., for you're about to die. No chance now to deposit this as planned. *Improvise,* old attorney! Can I make, um, a thick paper airplane of it & sail it out from here at the last possible minute, towards my young friend?

Such a racket outside my door! Somebody really wants into this belfry.

6:53: Good-bye, Polly; good-bye, Jane; good-bye, Drew. Hello, Author; hello, Dad. Here comes the sun. Lights! Cameras! Action!

IN TESTIMONY WHEREOF (& of the Intrinsic Value of Everything, even of Nothingness) I hereunto set my hand & seal this 26th day of September, 1969.

T.A.

S: *Jacob Horner to Todd Andrews.* The end of Der Wiedertraum.

Remobilization Farm
Fort Erie, Ontario, Canada
Thursday, September 4, 1969

Mr. Todd Andrews
Andrews, Bishop, & Andrews, Attorneys
Court Lane
Cambridge, Maryland 21613
U.S.A.

Dear Mr. Andrews:

Search for Bishop Pike abandoned. U.S. Ambassador to Brazil kidnapped. Viet Peace Talks suspended until after Ho Chi Minh funeral. Birthday of Anton Bruckner, Chateaubriand, F. Scott Fitzgerald, Darius Milhaud. Anniversary of Battle of Antietam, of Franco's capture of Irun, of Geronimo's second surrender, of Lafitte's offer to Governor Claiborne to defend Louisiana from the British, of Napoleon III's surrender to Bismarck at Sedan, of Harry Truman's inauguration of transcontinental television with address to San Francisco Peace Conference.

Of nothing, however, in *Der Wiedertraum,* of which I Apprised You Briefly in our Conversation this morning. Today in 1953 was Day 48 of the 100 Days between my Arrival at Wicomico, Maryland, where I First Met and Was Befriended By the late Joseph and Rennie Morgan, and my Departure Thence, after Mrs. Morgan's funeral, for Pennsylvania, with the late Doctor and other patients of the Remobilization Farm. September 4, 1953, was a weatherless day in the eventless interim between 9/2, when Mrs. Morgan and I Committed our First Adultery, and 9/7, when classes commenced at Wicomico Teachers College, now Wicomico State College of the University of Maryland.

Before that, on 9/1/53 (You advised me today to Draft a Detailed

738

Statement for use by the lawyer you advised me to Retain, as did the Ontario Provincial Police, in the event of a formal inquest into Joseph Morgan's death by gunshot wound on Monday 9/1/69. But it is many years since I Wrote Anything to anyone except myself. This was not Easy to Begin; the 1st-person singular, especially, comes hard; now I Should Like to Rebegin, but Dare Not Stop; you agreed I Might Send you a copy of my Statement, to help you explain things to Morgan's sons; hence this and the 7 enclosed letters to myself, covering the period 3/6/69–8/28/69 inclusive; I Must Add that my Wife and I are Grateful Indeed to you for arranging the return of Joe Morgan's body to Maryland and the funeral and memorial services for him there, which we Plan to Try to Attend. There is another reason, too, why Writing It All Down is difficult. Do be patient), I visited the Doctor for my quarterly Mobility Check: in those days I Experienced Occasional Paralysis; was indeed Seized by Same in the Progress & Advice Room that day, when the Doctor discovered I was Unconsciously Imitating my New Friend Joseph Morgan; had to be Remobilized by Pugilistic Therapy; all this is important. And the day before *that*, 8/31/53, was Eavesdropping & Espial Day, when Rennie Morgan and I Returned at Dusk to the Morgans' rented house in Wicomico from Horseback-Riding and Conversation about their marriage relationship, Peeked (at my Suggestion & to her Fascinated Disgust) through the window blinds of their house, and Saw that paragon of hardheaded rationalism simultaneously masturbating, picking his nose, and leaping gibbonlike about the study, whereat Mrs. M. was shocked to the center of her soul, and I Comforted Her and the next day Consummated Her Seduction, which I had Not Particularly Known was in process. Subsequent pregnancy, illegal abortion by Doctor, death of Rennie by aspiration of vomitus under anesthesia, cashiering of Morgan by Dr. John Schott of W.T.C., Departure and later Voluntary Sterilization of me, Scriptotherapeutic account of all the foregoing at Doctor's Rx, chance recovery and novelization of said account by outside party, sudden reappearance at Farm last March of much-changed Joseph Morgan, and ultimatum from him to me to Redream our story and Present him by 9/1/69 with Rennie Alive and Unadulterated.

So. But the Doctor drowned; "Monsieur Casteene" disappeared with his people; "Bibi" likewise (our name for Ms. Golden, whom you sought, whom we have heard nothing from since 8/15, when my Wife left her at Comalot Farm, Lily Dale, N.Y. 14752, with Mr. Jerome Bray), who had been playing Mrs. Morgan in *Der Wiedertraum;* "Pocahontas" (Marsha Mensch, *née* Blank) and I Became a Couple, and on Sunday last (8/31, 14th Sunday after Pentecost) Husband and Wife; nothing was working; Morgan was out of patience; that night was to be Espial Night and next day Confrontation Day in the P & A Room, his deadline. I was to Bring His Wife (see above) and my Hornbook (see below); "St. Joe" his Colt .45 for Day 45 (see enclosed), his expression and reckoning. When he would discover to me, he declared, the Real Bone he'd had to pick with me all these years.

I was Afraid.

But to go back a bit. On Th 8/28 my Now Wife, who was then but my Woman, delivered herself of a Bombshell Letter, her term, to her former husband, Ambrose Mensch of your city. Though she did not elect to share its contents with me, she gave me to understand that it would "knock the bastard [Mr. M.] flat." I Seized the Occasion of her glee to Propose to her what I had Long (since July) Been Contemplating: Wedlock. I had Just Left the P & A Room, a distressing session (ultimatum, deadline, Colt .45, etc.). Marsha was, I Ought to Add, and is, Pregnant. She laughed, I Cannot in truth Say warmly, and replied Why not? I here Confess that in all this I Had a Plan, but Declare & Protest it to have been my Wish, over & above & regardless of that plan, to Marry Marsha Mensch, for whom I Cared & Care.

Sunday last, 8/31, Eavesdropping & Espial Day, we Tied the Knot. It was my Hope, and part of my Plan, to Remobilize and Conclude *Der Wiedertraum:* to that end we were Wed exercycling, in late afternoon, upon the Exercycles central to much therapy here at the Farm, and which I had Requisitioned through August for our Reenactment of the Horseback-Riding Lessons Rennie Morgan kindly gave me 16 years before, while her husband labored at his (never completed) doctoral dissertation: *Innocence & Energy,* etc., I Forget. Witnesses were Joe himself, whose expression plainly suggested that he sensed What Was Up, and our Chief of Therapy, Tombo X, who let us know again, as he had done daily for some days already, that he had an Ace Up His Sleeve, which he would any day now play. One of our elder patients, a minister of the Universal Life Church who when mobile is the best in the 65-and-Over Class of the Farm's Exercycle Tournament, mounted his machine to do the honors. Several rockers wept openly. My own eyes Watered when I Said I Do, to the point where I was Unable to Observe whether Marsha's did likewise. She did, however, unambiguously say she Did, on the clear condition (to which I Assent) that her legal name remain, rather revert to, her maiden one, *i.e.,* Blank. You can perhaps advise us on that. It was all nice.

We were Left Alone then to pedal through the Final Horseback Ride towards the E. & E. Scene aforementioned. Officially we were to Speak of Joe etc. (see above): in fact and understandably we Discussed our Honeymoon Plans, at least Began to: my own Inclination was to Revisit the Iroquois Motel, off Exit 58 (Irving/Angola) of the Thomas E. Dewey Thruway, which has certain sentimental associations for us; Marsha's was, as best I could Determine, to travel to your city for the purpose of savoring the effects of her Bombshell Letter and to display to her first husband, who did not initiate it, her current pregnancy. The prospect (of so considerable an expedition) dizzied me; but I could not in any case Think Past the morrow's Deadline P & A Session. More Immediately Alarming, moreover, was my bride's condition: it became

Every Moment More Apparent that she had put by, for this happy occasion, one last dose of that unidentified but remarkable narcotic she calls Honey Dust, acquired two weeks earlier from Mr. Bray at Comalot Farm and (so I had Believed) exhausted a day or two since. By sundown she was off her Exercycle and calmly burbling in the grass. It was All I Could Do to Haul her over to the appropriate window of the farmhouse for E. & E. The light was on; we were A Bit Late; I Peeked In and Saw Joe smoking his pipe and perusing our script, that novelized etc. aforecited. I Rapped on the pane for him to commence his performance, and Made to Make Sure "Rennie" was set to Espy.

She was asleep, my Wife, and snoring. Joe strolled over, raised the sash, leaned out, took a look, and said: Christ, Horner. But at my Entreaty he came out; we Fetched Her In; Marsha was stirring already, must have been a minor dose of Dust; I Knew From Past Experience she would be Cross As a Bear when she was Herself again, especially if that really was the End of the Ride, ha. I Hurried to Make my Pitch.

This is, I Said in effect to Joe, my Wife. That I *Care* For. Nevertheless, and Against my Inclination—*deeply* Against etc.—but by way of Partial Recompense for, let's Say, 8/31/53 & thereafter, I here Offer you, Joe, on my and her Very Wedding Night, her.

Joe tapped out his pipe and without surprise responded: Horner, you Disgust me. She too.

Her too, too, here put in Marsha, whom I had Not Supposed all that awake yet, and who not for nothing was the ex-secretarial Bride of a Former Grammar Teacher: *Me* he Disgusts, too, she sort of repeated. Hold on, I Protested, not a little Taken Aback to Find her both awake and disgusted. Let me Explain. Explain my ass, my Wife expostulated [excuse the expression, Mr. Andrews]. Explain my ass, she repeated [the exact wording is important, sir]: It's our G.D.M.F.'ing *Wedding Night,* Jacob!

Exclamation point hers, sir, as Reasonably inferred from tone of voice, facial expression, tear-glint in eyes. I Must Explain that over & above the surprising content of her expostulation—surprising I Mean in that I had Anticipated, on the basis of earlier observations and remarks of hers, at best indifference to, at worst outright enthusiasm for, on her part, my Proposition, should she be Together enough, as they say, to register it at all—was a more considerable extraordinariness: it was the first time that Marsha had ever addressed me by my Name!

When I was Together enough myself for Further Speech, I Inquired of her, in effect, You don't *want* to go to bed with him? Well, she said, no. I mean [she said, and I Reasonably Infer three suspension points plus italics]. . .*no.* I mean [*i.e., she* means] I *didn't.* Oh, Said I. Well. Then. Golly. In *that* case.

Now, excuse the playscript format, sir: this was, after all—I now Recalled With Growing Consternation—a *scene,* from *Der Wiedertraum.*

MORGAN (SUDDENLY INTERESTED) (IN EFFECT): Done.

ME: What?

MORGAN: Leave us, Horner. Alone. Go 'round to the window.

MARSHA (IN EFFECT): No.

MORGAN: Horner?

ME: Well. . .

MY WIFE (VERBATIM): Jacob!

MYSELF (IN EFFECT): She, um, doesn't *want* to, Joe. I Mean, I'm as Surprised as anybody. But if she really doesn't *want* to. Gosh.

I now Summarize. Here Morgan withdrew from his pockets both hands, where he had thrust them during the above. With the left he held before Marsha's nose a tiny white packet disagreeably familiar, saying: Honey Dust. Found in "Bibi's" room after she left. With the right he unzipped his trouser fly, whereto, to my Chagrin, my Wife, without another word, went. Out, Horner, Joe ordered. To the window. Peep. Espy. Watch me *fuck your Wife* [your pardon, Mr. A., but etc.], before your Very Eyes, before *you* Do, on your Very Wedding Night. Out.

Well, Said I, my voice to my Surprise choking off some. Well. But by golly I Want it Clearly Understood, Joe, that this is *it* for *Der Wiedertraum!* Tears in my eyes, sir. Morgan appeared to Consider for a moment—Marsha was at it, I Couldn't Look—and then said: Nope. You Go Out There and Watch me [etc., above]. Then you Leave. She stays here. Though it is too late for me to knock your Wife up, I am going to Honey-Dust and hump her every which way till the cows come home, like *[sic]* you did Rennie. At eight A.M. sharp you and I will have our scheduled Last P & A: Confrontation and Deadline. After that she's yours. Bring your Hornbook. Go.

I Paused, Reflected, then Declared: I Hate This. But okay. Joe asked my Wife whether she heard and understood. Marsha cleared her mouth and throat and said, to me: You creep. To Morgan: Dust me, Dust me. To me: Want to Put It In for him, too? To Morgan: *Dust* me, for Christ sake. Thanks. To me: Oh, Buddy, will you ever Pay for this.

Etc. I Went Outside, Took up Position; they came to the window to make sure I Didn't Cheat. I Hated it. They laughed; I Dry-Heaved; Then Marsha Dusted Off. I Said Huskily through the window: Let me Take her home now, Joe. He responded: Bugger off, Horner.

Bad night; I'll Skip the Details. Sometime after midnight, in my Room, I Entered my Name in Column One, *Cuckold*, of my Hornbook: *HORNER, Jacob,* between *Hephaestus* and *Hosea:* Marsha in Column Two, *Wife,* between *Aphrodite* and *Gomer,* Joe in Column Three, *Lover(s),* between *Anchises, Ares, Butes, Dionysus, Hermes, Poseidon, Zeus, etc., etc.* and *Everybody.*

It is a listing I Keep, sir, have for some years Kept, at the (late) Doctor's Rx. Before dawn I Actually Fell Asleep, so finally and truly Purged After All, even Pissed Off, did I Feel.

Woke up ditto! Monday 9/1: Labor, St. Giles', and Confrontation Day! Went to Claim my Wife, plenty Fed Up sir! Running a touch late, Charged down to the P & A Room to Have It Out Quickly for good and all. Collect Marsha; Try to Make Things Up. Suggest to Tombo X we Oust Morgan and Run the Show Together upon my Return From Honeymoon: me Keep the books, him book the creeps, ha ha. Remobilized!

Joe was dressed, smoking but not reading; apparently waiting for me, though I was by now a touch early. Desk clear except for Colt .45. Cut (I Cleared my Throat and Rebegan) Cut the Comedy, Joe. Put that thing away. Where's Marsha? Etc.

Joe replied calmly, hands behind head: Your Wife is a lousy lay, Horner.

Undeterred, I Showed him with a Determined Sneer the Hornbook entry: my Name in the same column as, five letters later, his, and in Column Four *(Remarks): All scores settled.*

Hmp, said Joe (approximately). I then Ripped Up the book, several pages at a time when I Found myself Unable to Rip them all at once. This session is canceled, I Declared. Put that gun away. No more reenactments. Your wife is dead, Joe. Partly my Fault, partly hers, partly yours. Etc. You've humped mine; she's pissed at me; I'm Pissed at you. *Genug! Basta!* Gun away!

MORGAN (VERBATIM): The score is not settled, Jake. You never Knew the score.

I (IN EFFECT): How so? Because Rennie's dead and Marsha's alive? *I Didn't Kill Rennie!* [Sudden panic; you understand.] Where's my Wife?

But as I Made to Leave, Joe picked up and aimed the pistol at me, saying: Dead asleep when I left her. Sit, Horner.

Well. He had explained already, Joe said when I Sat, at least remarked, that his grievance against me was not—at least had for many years not been—that I had Done *A* and *B* and *C* with Rennie, which led to *D*, which led to *E* and *F* and *G*. It was not even that, for all his efforts to the contrary, his own life, as much as Rennie's and mine, had been arrested in 1953 by what transpired on 8/31, 9/2, *et seq.* of that fell year. No. It was (his final, unremitting, unappeasable grievance) that I had Written It All Down.

Wrote It All Down, Horner! he now repeated in a Cold Fury. Just as you've been Writing All *This* Down, since March! *That* [verbatim, sir] I don't forgive you, Horner. Even when I contemplate your miserable, your creepy Life; even when I consider, with pleasure, what surely lies ahead for you [I Paraphrase: Condemnation to Life, *i.e.,* to Personality & Responsibility, which in fact, in my View as in his, I had never successfully Quite Abdicated. Petty career as 45-year-old Failure: dull bumbling teacher of remedial English, say, at bottom of pay scale, in 5th-rate community college, to dyslexic dolts. Pussy-Whipped Cuckold Husband of Termagant WASP already pregnant by God knows whom, & who will surely in future either polish & repolish my Antlers or divorce me with punitive alimony. Etc.], [he went on] I do not consider that score settled. I am not reconciled. I do not forgive you. I want you dead. I will now shoot you in the heart. [End of quote.]

But aha, I was Remobilized, and though I Could Not Deny the likelihood of his prophecy, with more spontaneity than I Have on any prior occasion Mustered I here Sprang across the Doctor's desk and Clutched Joe's pistol hand with such force (and momentum) that he, it, & I Went Tumbling with his swivel chair to the floor, where, despite his relatively good condition and my Years of Diminished Physical Activity, I Wrestled him to an impasse. Our faces were inches apart. Joe closed his eyes, almost smiled; it was a swoonish moment; I Rallied my Last Strength not to Drift off into Weatherlessness. Then he said, in effect: You *are* Behaving Like Me, Jacob. I see what the [late] Doctor meant. Look: you're Mobilized. Your Therapy is done. Your Wife is okay, and she understands about last night. There are no bullets in this gun: only one *blank,* get it, to scare you with. Our session is finished. Also *Der Wiedertraum.* Also your Stay at the Farm. Mine too. It's all finished. Let go now.

He did (I Mean end his resistance), whereat my Grip on his arm (I Meant to Commandeer that pistol, sir, no matter what he said, till I was Up and Out of there) happened to bring the gun barrel to his temple. At the touch of it he opened his eyes—calm and lucid and blue as when I'd First Seen them in Wicomico, but focused somewhere past me—and pulled the trigger.

The gun went off with an astounding bang, and (literally, sir) blew Joe's brains out. People came running. The mess was dreadful; there was retching. My Head rang. Tombo X was furious; declared this was it. Marsha came in, Cross as a Bear, but then said Wow and after that mainly stared at me. I am Proud to Report that she supported my Subsequent Testimony to the Ontario Provincial Police, a briefer version of the foregoing. I was by them Detained, Interrogated, and Released on my Own Recognizance pending (possible) further inquest—until when, at least, Joe's death has been ruled Accidental. I myself Engaged our regular undertaker (many of our patients are old) and Set About to Send Word to Morgan's sons, of whose whereabouts we had no clear record. Burial was planned for today, in the Fort Erie Cemetery, until your fortuitous arrival this morning changed, welcomely, that plan. We are Grateful that the Tidewater Foundation sees fit to arrange and cover the expenses of the funeral of the first president of Marshyhope State University. May I Add my Hope that your client and our former patient Ms. Golden will turn up unharmed. Our files are open for your inspection.

Tombo X has played the Ace Up His Sleeve. Using Morgan's death as his pretext, he has cashiered all white staff members of the Remobilization Farm and is evicting all white patients therefrom without regard to age or degree of mobility. It is his announced intention to turn the place into some other, unspecified, sort of operation. I Disapprove, but Have No Authority to Countermand him.

My Wife and I will therefore Take the hearse for Wicomico tomorrow morning, in company with Morgan's casket. Joe's statement, that Marsha Understood About Last Night, was, unfortunately, of a character with that about the *other* blank (ha ha), if you follow me. But I Have Cause to Imagine that he was perhaps correct about my Remobilization, though experience tempers my Optimism. In any case, such things are relative.

I Have some Modest Savings. I Mean to Inquire of Dr. John Schott, whom I Have the Pleasure to Know Personally from 1953, concerning openings in Remedial English at Marshyhope State. My Wife can type many words per minute, when she is Together. I am Urging her to have her baby. It is my Understanding that no one's permission is required for us to name it Rennie Morgan Blank, or Joseph Morgan Horner, as the case may be. The names Marsha herself proposes for it I Believe to be of a jesting character. On the other hand, I Defend her right to abort the fetus if she so chooses. I Wish she would decide. But when I Bring Up this, or any, subject, she tells me: Bugger off.

I Do Not Expect the road of our New Life to be free of detours, forks, impasses, potholes, rocks. God alone knows where, past Wicomico and (maybe) Marshyhope, it will lead; nor is it my Intention to Record (ever again) our Passage down it. But with tomorrow's (admittedly tremulous) first step, it will begin.

I Am, sir,
Jacob Horner

JH/jh (7 encl)

A: *A. B. Cook VI to his son.* A summons to Fort McHenry and to the Second 7-Year Plan.

Chautauqua Rd., Md.

Wednesday, Sept. 10, 1969

Dear Henry,

Airmail special delivery should fetch this by Friday to Castines Hundred, where I pray (having heard from our caretakers that you have been there yet again since my last) it may not only find you, but find you ready to respond, if you please, to its summons. Lest someone *else* find and respond to it instead, I am casting it into "Legrand's cipher," or "Captain Kidd's code" as modified by A.B.C. IV, which I can write (and you will quickly learn to read) as easily as if the words were in no further code than writing itself. Tomorrow I pack off up the road to Baltimore, to the Francis Scott Key Highway, to Fort McHenry, to do a few days' work with our "film company" (it *is* Ours now, virtually).

I want you there.

Since my letter of three weeks ago, our Baratarians brought off

745

admirably the Burning of Washington on Bloodsworth Island: our first full-dress drill, so to speak, in using "the media" (in this case Reginald Prinz's film crew; next time the local and network television news people) as well as our "enemies" (in this case the U.S. Navy; next time the Dept. of the Interior) to our purposes. This is not to say that all went, or goes, perfectly. That lawyer Todd Andrews, executive director of the Tidewater Foundation and thus a principal contender for Harrison Mack's estate, has grown entirely too curious about the relation of Baron Castine to Andrew Cook VI. He even hired a Buffalo detective to investigate "Monsieur Casteene" of Fort Erie and the Honey Dust operation at Lily Dale! I was obliged to invoke C.I.A. credentials (city detectives have no awe of the F.B.I.) to warn the fellow off, in the process surely making him all the more curious. And Drew Mack's radicalism, a less sophisticated version of your own, is a growing liability. I shall return to that subject.

Joseph Morgan, on the other hand, my apprehensions concerning whom I voiced in my last, is no longer a problem: we buried him three days since. A pitiful case, that—and a fourteen-year investment (i.e., since I first took an interest in him in 1955, when he was a disillusioned ex-rationalist working for the Maryland Historical Society, and proposed him to Harrison Mack to head up his projected college) down the drain. But at least we need worry about him, indeed about the whole Fort Erie operation, no longer.

Likewise "Bea Golden," unless old Andrews's or young Mack's curiosity gets out of hand. She is, I cannot say safe, but safely disposed of. Her disposer, however—the squire of "Comalot"—remains a troubling enigma. I had supposed Jerome Bray no more than a crank, perhaps even a madman; now I am persuaded that while he may be mad, he is not merely so. I even begin to wonder whether his connection with the Burlingames may not go deeper than I'd supposed; whether that bizarre "machine" and Bray's strange behavior may not be exotic camouflage. I suspect he may have abilities, capacities, as extraordinary as yours and mine. In the "Washington" action, for example, I seriously put the man's person at risk. I even imagined, not without relief, that our friends from Patuxent Naval Air Station had obligingly, if unwittingly, "wasted" him in their routine gunnery practice over the lower marshes on that Sunday night. Then Bray appeared, unaccountably and unscathed, in my locked office in the cottage next noon, as I was in mid-metamorphosis between Castine and Cook! Disconcerting!

He exercises, moreover, a Svengali-like authority (but I think by pharmacological, not psychological, means) upon a young woman of our company, formerly his associate, who had fled to us in fear of her life last spring. We found her unconscious near the Prohibited Area that Sunday night with an obvious injection bruise on her buttock; upon her reviving, she was convinced that she was doomed. I later dispatched her to "Comalot" ostensibly for a week's trial reconciliation with her nemesis, actually to survey the scene there and report to me. I anticipated hysterical objections, but she went like one whose will was not her own. (I should add that her lover, Reg Prinz, had abandoned her that same night; the girl was both desperate and drugged.) A week later she dutifully returned to Barataria and dutifully reported that Bea Golden is comatose, concealed, and "seeded" (?); that Todd Andrews himself had appeared at Comalot, made inquiries, had been sent packing; that she repented her mistaken defection of April and wished to return to Bray's service. It was clear to me that she had already quite done so. I dismissed her; she is with him now. The question is, is he with us? And what is he?

It will not surprise me to see him again at Fort McHenry: Bray seems to understand that what began as Prinz's movie—a film in its own right and for its own sake, however obscure its content and aesthetics—has become the vehicle for something else entirely, a vehicle whose original driver is now barely a passenger. Bray declares that his own "published literary works" (I have not seen them) are comparable—coded messages and instructions disguised as works of fiction—and that the "revolutionary new medium" which he and his computer have concocted will be in fact a "new medium of revolution." I have in process a last long shot to rid us of him by his own agency before he decides to rid himself of us. Whether his madness is feigned or real, Bray has, like Hamlet, an exploitable weakness, which I believe I understand (he *is* a half relative of ours) and can play upon.

Now, the movie. Its two remaining "scenes"—the Attack on Fort McHenry and the Destruction of Barataria—should provide opportunity for me (Us? I pray so) to deal with at least some of these threats and nuisances, some final rehearsal in the diversion of media and "available action" to our purposes, and (as when the U.S. Navy destroyed Jean Lafitte's base on Grande-Terre Island on September 16, 1814) a covering of our tracks in readiness for the fall/spring season. When, blending less obtrusively with our surroundings, we will ring down the curtain on Act One (the 1960's, the First 7-Year Plan) and raise it on Act Two.

I had thought, Henry, to commence that act, and the new decade, and the Second 7-Year Plan, by marrying Jane Mack in January 1970. Last March I set that as my "target date" for enlisting you to me by putting in your way the record of our forebear's proud and pathetic attempt to transcend the fateful Pattern of our history—that endless canceling of Cooks by Burlingames, Burlingames by Cooks, which he was the first of our line to recognize—by rebelling against himself before his children could rebel against him. Those four "prenatal" letters (which I myself discovered just two years ago in the archives of the Erie County Historical Museum in Buffalo, and which the historian Germaine Pitt was to have annotated and published) were meant to say to you what I yearned and feared to say myself. I would then have

747

reintroduced myself to you in my proper person, who would in turn have introduced you to your prospective stepmother. Moreover, I would have introduced you, for the first time in your conscious life, to *your biological mother,* whom History and Necessity (read "Baron André Castine") have dealt with sorely indeed in this particular.

Do I have your attention, son? You are *not* the half-orphan you have believed yourself these many years to be. I know who, I know where, your mother is. When you shall have represented yourself to me, when we are at one with each other and with the Second Revolution, I will bring you and her together. She has awaited that reunion for 29 years! For a certain reason (call it the Anniversary View of History) I propose we keep her waiting until November 5 next, your 30th birthday—and no longer.

Thus my plan. But events have accelerated and changed that original schedule. Lady Amherst's defection (and that earlier-mentioned novelist's lack of interest) obliged *me* to transcribe and attempt to send you Andrew IV's "posthumous" letters, you having somehow acquired "on your own" some version of the "prenatals." And Jane wants us married three weeks hence, at September's end, instead of in the New Year. Andrew Burlingame Cook VI has therefore but a few days more to live. On our drama's larger stage, the death of Ho Chi Minh, and Nixon's announcement of further troop withdrawals from South Viet Nam and Thailand, signal that the war in Southeast Asia is grinding down to some appropriately ignominious dénouement, and with it the mainspring of our First 7-Year Plan.

On then to the Second! No more mass demonstrations, riots on the campuses, disruptions, "trashings," "Fanonizings"; no more assassinations, kidnappings, hijackings, heavy drugs. All these will live their desperate half life into the 1970's, as the 18th Century half-lives into the 19th, the 19th into the 20th—but they will not be Us. Our century has one "Saturnian revolution" to go. Its first fetched us out of the 19th Century, through the cataclysms of World War I and the Russian Revolution, the explosion of hard technology and totalitarian ideology, to the beginning of the end of the Industrial Revolution, of nationalism, of Modernism, of ideology itself. Our First 7-Year Plan marked, in effect (not to boast that it itself *effected*), our transition from the second to the third third of the century: the revolutionary flowering, scarcely begun, of microelectronics; the age of software, soft drugs, smart weapons, and the soft sell; of subtle but enormous changes in Where the Power Is; of subtle enormities in general: large atrocities in small places and small print.

This morning's three headline stories reflect and portend these things: *VIET CEASE-FIRE ENDS: U.S. "MAY RESPOND" TO DE-ESCALATION. ISRAELI PLANES RESUME ATTACK ON EGYPT. NIXON YIELDS TO CONSERVATIONISTS, NIXES EVERGLADES JET-PORT.* Note especially that second: it wants no prophet, Henry, to foresee that one day soon the nations of Islam will employ their oil

748

production as an international diplomatic weapon. Just as the arrival of the sultan's seneschals in Constantinople on a certain afternoon in 1453 may be said conveniently to mark the end of the Middle Ages, so that day just predicted will mark the beginning of the end of the 20th Century, and of many another thing.

What exploitable convulsions lie ahead, forecast on every hand but attended seriously by few save Us! Fossil-fuel reserves exhausted before alternatives can be brought on line; the wealthy nations poorer and desperate, certain poorer nations suddenly wealthy; doomsday weaponry everywhere (Drew Mack speaks of *dynamiting* certain towers and monuments; but you and I could build a nuclear bomb ourselves); intemperate new weather patterns in the temperate zones; the death of the Dollar, a greater bereavement than the death of God; old alliances foundered and abandoned, surprising new ones formed! The American 1950's and 1960's, that McCarthy-Nixon horror show, will seem in retrospect a paradise lost. The 1980's and 90's will be called the New Ice Age—and who can say what will be crystallized therein?

Why, *we* can, Henry.

I had been going to review for you in this letter my own history. There is not time, except for barest outline. You know already—from your copy of my letter to that novelist back in June—the circumstances of my birth and early youth. (I leave it to your mother to retail for you the circumstances of your own, and why it was necessary to raise you as if orphaned.) Though I understood by 1939 that my father was not a bona fide revolutionary, but an agent of the U.S. and Canadian secret services—whose infiltration of "subversive" groups was to the end of thwarting their own infiltration of, for example, U.S. Naval Intelligence at Pearl Harbor and the Manhattan Project at Los Alamos—I loved the man dearly and continued to work "with" him until his death (for which, my son, I was not responsible, though I acknowledge that its echo of *his* father's death at the Welland Canal on September 26, 1917, seems incriminating), gently frustrating his aims to the best of my ability. Therefore, for example, Pearl Harbor was virtually undefended on that Sunday morning in December 1941, and although the A-bombs were dropped on Hiroshima and Nagasaki (by when dear Dad was dead), the balance of terror was soon after restored.

Not until 1953, my 36th year, did I realize my error: i.e., the year of Mother's death, when I discovered at Castines Hundred *les cinq lettres posthumes* of A.B.C. IV, cracked "Captain Kidd's code," understood what our ancestor had come to understand, fell asleep in midmeditation on a summer afternoon on Bloodsworth Island, awoke half tranced—and changed the course of my life, *Q.E.D.* My later discovery of the "prenatal" letters only clarified and revalidated my conversion. I became your Uncle Andrew Burlingame Cook VI, called myself poet laureate of Maryland, established myself on Chautauqua Road and in Barataria Lodge, befriended Harrison Mack and John Schott, Senators McCarthy and Goldwater, and Maryland Governors George Mahoney and Spiro Agnew. I recruited and then ruined (in order to rerecruit to our actual cause) such vulnerables as the late Mr. Morgan. I created the image of myself as a faintly enigmatic but intensely regional flag-waving buffoon, while orchestrating on the national level a systematic campaign, gratifyingly successful, to organize and transform *almost without their knowing it* the political revolutionism of the "New Left" into something transcending mere politics. (We did *not* engineer the assassination of the Brothers K. and of M. L. King. To imagine that our organization for the Second Revolution is the *only* such effective covert group, or even that our aims and the others' always coincide—not to mention our means—would be paranoiac.)

Thus the first 7-Year Plan, for which the civil-rights and antiwar movements were as handy a catalyst and focus as were Napoleon's second abdication and exile to A.B.C. IV. That grand, protracted opus of Action Historiography—call it the 1960's!—if it did not quite fulfill its author in chief, both gratified and exhausted him. Time now, Henry, for your coauthorship! Rather (for I am tired), time for me to pass on to you the pen of History, the palm of (secret) Fame.

More immediately and less grandly, it is time to do certain dark deeds by the rockets' red glare, etc. Our principal action is scheduled for Saturday the 13th. I shall be commuting from here to McHenry daily through the Sunday, when Napoleon took Moscow and the British abandoned their Chesapeake campaign. I shall be "playing" Andrew Cook VI's formidable namesake, to a similar but more final dénouement, after which I shall come forth as Baron Castine and, in time, claim my bride. You whom so proudly I hail, Henry: can I, by the early light of one of those dawns, from one of those ramparts, hope to see you?

> Au revoir!
> Your loving father

M: *A. B. Cook VI to his son and/or prospective grandchild. With a postscript to the Author from H. C. Burlingame VII. Each explaining A. B. Cook VI's absence from the yacht* Baratarian.

Barataria Lodge
Bloodsworth Island, Md.
Wednesday, Sept. 17, 1969

Dear Henry Burlingame and/or A. (Andrew? Andrée?) B. Cook VII,

McHenry (or *M'Henry*, as F. S. Key spelled it in the title of his song *Defense of Fort M'Henry*) means—I needn't remind a polylinguist like yourself—"son of Henry." But in honor of brave Henrietta Cook Burlingame V and that courageous line of Andrée Castines, let us

750

translate it as "child of Henry": the child or children I warmly wish you despite the Burlingamish shortfall (you B's know how to overcome); the grandchild or -children I fondly wish myself, to carry on my name, our work.

You *did*, then, after all, receive my letters—so comes the word from Castines Hundred. And by when you read this we shall have been reunited, briefly and fatefully, between Twilight's Last Gleaming and Dawn's Early Light. A. B. Cook VI will have regrettably met his end in the Diversion sequence. The Destruction of Barataria will have been successfully reenacted, and *Baratarian* will be embarked—like Jean Lafitte's *Pride* from Galveston in 1821—upon her momentous voyage: the initiation of Year 1 of our 7-Year Plan. At sunrise a week from Friday—American Indian Day and anniversary of our 1917 Welland Canal Plot—there will occur another kind of Diversion sequence at Marshyhope State University: the Algonquins' Revenge, let us say, for the desecration of their ancient burial ground on Redmans Neck. Drew Mack's last project, I conceive, and the "ascension" of Jerome Bonaparte Bray to his ancestors.

All this we watch, you and I, from our certain separate distances. It is no longer our affair.

You wonder why, having so diligently searched you out and laboriously urged you mewards, I am not aboardship with you, en route to the Yucatán. You were promised your father, and anon your mother; you find, instead, yet another letter! Was it not A. B. Cook alone who was to die? Was not Baron André Castine to marry Jane Mack and divert her enterprises to ours? As our forefather Ebenezer Cooke, late in his laureateship, produced a *Sot-Weed Redivivus,* were we not to make this first trial run together, you and I, in pursuit of another sort of sot-weed?

Yes. And—now that we shall have remet, respoken, been reunited—no. I remind you, again and finally, of A.B.C. IV's futile effort, on behalf of his unborn child, to undo the first half of his program in the second—an effort more successfully reenacted on your behalf by myself. I shall say only that I died at Fort McHenry. That this morning, three days later, I woke, as it were, half tranced on a point of dry ground between two creeklets, in the steaming shade of loblolly pines, realizing where I was but not, at once, why I was there. As in a dream I reached for my watchpocket, to fetch forth and wind my ancestors' watch. . .and, as if vouchsafed a vision, I understood that I must not nor need not reappear publicly in any guise.

You, Henry, if my letters have done their work, are henceforth my disguise. You have the Plan; you have the means (and shall have more: Harrison Mack's estate is not done with us; claimants thought dead and/ or disposed of—also certain missing, shall we say *secreted,* items—may yet turn up, be heard from, nosed). Even should you "betray" me. . .but you will not. You must imagine me present in my absence, not dead and gone but merely withdrawn like my ancestor to that aforementioned certain distance: watching from some Castines Hundred or Bloodsworth Island of the imagination, with some "Consuelo del Consulado" of my own to console my latter years and check my perspective. We look on; we nod approval or tisk our tongues. What we see, at the end of these seven years to come, we shall not say: only that should you falter, flounder, fail us, we shall not despair, but look beyond you, to your heirs.

For if your father has not broken the Pattern for you, the Pattern will surely break you for

Your father,
A.B.C. VI

P.S. to J.B. from H.B. VII: The foregoing was *not* written by A. B. Cook at Barataria Lodge on Wednesday, 17 Sept. 1969: I am adding this postscript to it on Monday, *15* Sept., from that same place, about to reembark aboard *Baratarian* before the film company return to shoot the "Destruction of Barataria."

At Fort McHenry, Saturday last, during the "Wedding Scene," which I attended in sufficient disguise, I heard "my father" mention that the document representing the "Francis Scott Key Letter" was in fact a letter in progress from himself to his son. Cook so declared it, of course, for my benefit, assuming or hoping that I was within earshot (I could have passed for the mayor, the best man, the groom himself if I'd needed to—even as the "father of the bride"). Not long thereafter, to let Cook know I was on hand, I retrieved that letter, without otherwise revealing myself to him.

It was—in cipher—his Second Seven-Year Plan for the Second Revolution: *i.e.*, a perfectly accurate prospectus (meant precisely therefore, like Cook IV's warning letter to President Madison, for me to disbelieve it) of the plan he secretly intended to thwart, and now will not. Among other things, it instructed me to rendezvous with him here at Barataria Lodge early tomorrow morning: another deathtrap, as was (I recognised clearly back in February, our last meeting) his whole project to lead me to him.

Having verified sometime later that same night that his Key letter had been "delivered," Cook quickly drafted the postdated one above, also in cipher. I was meant to receive it (that is, to find it aboard *Baratarian)* after I believed him accidentally killed at Fort McHenry: proof that, like his ancestor, he was in fact still alive and remotely monitoring my execution of "our" plan. Instead, I took the letter off his dead body in *Baratarian*'s tender *(Surprize)* during the so-called Diversion sequence, just before seeing to the destruction of both that body and that tender.

In short, except that it is now genuinely posthumous, this letter, like its author, is a fraud.

So too are the *"lettres posthumes"* of A. B. Cook IV: forgeries by his

752

eponymous descendant. (A few details will suffice to discredit "Legrand's cipher" as "Captain Kidd's code": Kidd himself used only numbers; Edgar Poe added 19th-Century printer's marks nonexistent in Kidd's time; "A.B.C. IV" added further symbols—*W* and *S*, for example—not to be found in "Legrand's cipher." And the procedure in serious encoding, as even Poe realised, is to make the deciphered message as enigmatic as the ciphered, intelligible only to the initiate: "*A good glass in the bishop's hostel in the devil's seat*," etc.) Cook IV's "prenatal" letters are perhaps authentic, but disingenuous: an appeal to his unborn child to break the Pattern so that that child—*i.e.*, the twins Henry and Henrietta Cook Burlingame V—would in fact embrace it, rebel against what they took to be their father's cause, and thereby (since he has altogether misrepresented that cause) effectively carry on his work. Cook VI's own exhortations to me—indeed that whole elaborate charade of discovered and deciphered letters, the very notion of a Pattern of generational rebellion and reciprocal cancellation—is similarly, though more complexly, disingenuous.

The man who called himself Andrew Burlingame Cook VI listed, for example, "for my edification" (in the letter you will *not* receive), what he called "the vertiginous possibilities available to the skeptic" vis-à-vis his own motives, by way of inducing me to simple faith. They are in fact the simple permutation of a few variables: his true wish concerning the Second Revolution (its success or failure), his true conception of himself (a "winner" or a "loser"), his true conception of me (ditto), and his prediction of my inclination with respect to him (whether I shall or shall not define myself against him). Which variables generate (given his public reactionism on the one hand and, on the other, the open secret of his connexion with various radical groups) such equally reasonable-appearing conjectures as the following:

1. He wishes the Revolution to succeed and hopes that I shall support it, since he believes me a "winner"; therefore
   a. he works for it himself, because he considers himself also a "winner" and does not believe that I shall rebel against him; or
   b. he works *against* it, because he regards himself (as he regarded his namesakes) as a "loser," and/or because he believes that I shall work against him.
2. He wishes the Revolution to succeed and hopes that I shall oppose it, since he believes me a loser; therefore
   a. he works for it himself, considering himself a winner and trusting me to rebel against him; or
   b. he works *against* it, believing himself a loser and trusting me *not* to rebel against him.
3. He *opposes* the Revolution and wishes me to do likewise, inasmuch as he considers me a winner; therefore
   a. he works *against* it, believing that he is a winner and that I shall not rebel against him; or

    b. he works *for* it, thinking himself a loser and that I *shall* rebel against him.
4. He opposes the Revolution but wants me to support it, believing me to be a loser; therefore
    a. he works against it, thinking himself a winner and that I shall rebel against him; or
    b. he works for it, thinking himself a loser and that I shall *not* rebel against him.

Et cetera. Such displays confuse only the naive. To Cook, as to me, the actual state of affairs is as easily sorted out as the ABC's, no more finally equivocal than the authorship of this letter, or its postscript.

In the pocket of "Francis Scott Key's" jacket, together with Cook's letter to me, was yours to the newlywed Mr and Mrs Ambrose Mensch, which you must excuse my opening to see whether it was another of Cook's stratagems. I took the additional liberty (I was hurried) of tearing off your return address, then replaced the letter, unaltered, in its envelope, the envelope in the pocket. For reasons of my own I subsequently decided to send you a deciphered copy not only of the foregoing but of those "posthumous letters of A. B. Cook IV," as well as of "my father's" to me of 10 September last, urging me to join him at McHenry. Inasmuch as you do not know *my* address, you cannot return them as you returned Cook's offerings of June. Whether or not you "use" them, I am confident that you will read and be used *by* them.

The man who died at Fort McHenry was not my father.

I know who my mother is; have long, if not always, known. And *she* knows who my true father is, as I know (what A. B. Cook little suspected) who and where my twin children, and their mother, are.

Barataria will be dealt with tomorrow. I shall not—as "my father" hoped I would—be there.

About "Comrade Bray" and "Comrade Mack," not to mention Mr Todd Andrews, I am unconcerned. I know who they are, where they are, what they "stand for," what they intend, and what will come to pass: at Barataria Lodge tomorrow; on the campus of Marshyhope State University a week from Friday.

The "Second Revolution" shall be accomplished on schedule. Do not be misled by those who claim that it has already taken place, or by those others who childishly expect to "RIZE" in overt rebellion. Little will (most) Americans dream, when they celebrate the Bicentennial of the "U. States," what there is in fact to celebrate; what a certain few of us will be grimly cheering. The tyrannosaurus blunders on, his slow mind not yet having registered that he is dead. We shall be standing clear of his death throes, patient and watchful, our work done.

H.B. VII

Bloodsworth Island 15.9.69

754

O: *Jerome Bray to his grandmother.* His business finished, he prepares to ascend to her.

Comalot, R.D. 2
Lily Dale, N.Y., U.S.A. 14752

9/23/69

To: Kyuhaha Bray ("Unfinished Business"), Princess of the Tuscaroras & Consort of C. J. Bonaparte (Grananephew of Napoleon, U.S. Indian Commissioner, Secretary of the Navy, Attorney General, Suppressor of Vice in Baltimore, & Fearless Investigator of Corruption in the U.S. Post Office)

From: Rex Numerator a.k.a. your granason Jerry

Dear Granama,

O see, kin, "G. III's" bottled dumps—oily shite!—which he squalidly hauled from his toilet's last gleanings. 5 broads stripped and, bride-starred, screwed their pearly ass right on our ram-part! You watched? Heard our growls and their screamings? Now Bea Golden ("G's" heir)'s Honey-Dusted 4-square: grave food for her bright hatch of maggots next year! Our females are all seeded; our enemies are not alive: so, dear Granama, take *me* to the hum of your hive!

1. *9/23/4004 B.C.: World began, 9:00 A.M. EDST.* LILYVAC II's LANG & PUNCT circuitry entirely regenerated; we can even sing now like Katy did. Excuse our conjunctions. O LIL! O Granama! O see RESET *Quel artison! ANCIENT PLANETS & ALCHEMICAL BODIES:* (1) Moon/silver, (2) Mars/iron, (3) Mercury/quicksilver, (4) Jupiter/tin, (5) Venus/copper, (6) Saturn/lead, (7) Sun/gold. *MOHAMMEDAN HEAVENS & THEIR INHABITANTS:* (1) silver/Adam & Eve, (2) gold/John the Baptist, (3) pearl/Joseph & Azrael, (4) white gold/Enoch & Angel of Tears, (5) silver/Aaron & Avenging Angel, (6) ruby & garnet/Moses & Guardian Angel, (7) divine light/Abraham, etc.

2. *9/23/480 B.C.: Euripides born.* A less tragical writer by ½ than F. Kafka, author of *Die Verwandlung,* or J. P. Sartre, author of *Les Mouches,* or your granason, author of *NUMBERS* and other coded epistles to his granama. Re-pre-programming of LILYVAC II with 7's now all but completed. *STAGES OF DRAMATIC ACTION:* (1) exposition, (2) establishment of conflict, (3) 1st complication, (4) 2nd ditto, (5) 3rd RESET (6) climax & peripety, (7) dénouement & wrap-up. O Granama, it has been a long and lonely flight. *STRINGS OF APOLLO'S LYRE & THEIR SEVERAL PROVINCES:* (1) Alpha/music, (2) Eta/poetry, (3) Iota/philosophy, (4) Omicron/astronomy, (5) Upsilon/mathematics, (6) Epsilon/medicine, (7) Omega/science.

3. *9/23/1779: J. P. Jones in* Bonhomme Richard *defeats* Serapis. A less crafty water-skipper by ½ than your granason, ex-pilot of Chautauqua excursion boat *Gadfly III* (now LILYVAC can call a spade a springtail), ex-ditto of ex-yacht *Baratarian* a.k.a. *Surprize,* ha ha, whose crew and cargo (Honey-Dust Ingredient #7) not the U.S.N. and

U.S.C.G. together will ever find. Finished business! *STAGES OF MOON:* (1) new crescent, (2) 1st ¼, (3) waxing gibbous, (4) full, (5) waning gibbous, (6) 3rd ¼, (7) old crescent. *MONTHS BETWEEN EQUINOXES, INCLUSIVE, WITH CORRESPONDING ZODIACAL SIGNS ADJUSTED FOR PRECESSION:* (1) March/Pisces, (2) April/ Aries, (3) May/Taurus, (4) June/Gemini, (5) July/Cancer, (6) August/ Leo, (7) September/Virgo.

4. *9/23/1780: B. Arnold betrays West Point to Major André; incriminating papers discovered in André's socks at Tarrytown, N.J.* LILYVAC's hair-trigger Reset-function still a thorn in our crown. Flew to Fort McHenry 9/13 to monitor Resetting of Margana le Fay a.k.a. Merope Bernstein, *i.e.* her penitential denunciation of those anti-Bonapartists who took her from us back at Passover. They have paid. Also, in disguises not even she could penetrate, we followed up our ultimatum of 8/26 to Ma and Pa: *i.e.* R.S.V.P. etc. No reply = bye bye. Business finished. Ha. *NOACHIAN LAWS (contra):* (1) idolatry, (2) adultery, (3) murder, (4) robbery, (5) eating of limbs severed from wild animals, (6) emasculation of animals, (7) breeding of monstrosities. *SENSES & SPIRITS:* (1) animation/fire, (2) touch/earth, (3) speech/water, (4) taste/air, (5) sight/ mist, (6) hearing/flowers, (7) smell/south wind.

5(a). *9/23/1806: Lewis & Clark Expedition finished.* Ha. Our business RESET 5 females (variously) fecundated; all prenatal arrangements made. Presume 5 will do, Granama, inasmuch as back in Mating Season you had not yet shifted us to Base 7. The loyal drone finishes his business ha ha and goes to his reward. 1, preserved like a bee in amber, immortal 1st heroine of Numerature, will feed her larvae on the 6th ingredient of Honey Dust: the royal jelly of herself. Another, the *Bernstein* of the Bea, so to speak (O LIL!), will have a 6½-year pregnancy and give birth 4/5/77 to the new Napoleon and Grand Tutor: no Goat-Boy this time, but—in your honor, Granama—a Bee-Girl! Queen Kyuhaha II! *PLEIADES:* (1) Alcyone, (2) Asterope, (3) Electra, (4) Celaeno, (5) Maia, (6) Taygete, (7) Merope (1 always invisible: either [a] Electra, mourning for Troy, or [b] Merope, ashamed of bedding mere mortal Sisyphus). 5(b). *9/23/1949: Truman announces U.S.S.R. A-bomb.* Score 1 for A. B. Cook VI, who betrayed his own and our (foster) father, good Ranger Burlingame, now avenged, and who meant to ditto his own son, now RESET Merope back in charge at Comalot, no longer invisible (*cf.* Pleiad 7b, above), her Resetting completely completed. *AGAINST THEBES:* (1) Adrastus, (2) Polynices, (3) Tydeus, (4) Amphiaraus, (5) Capaneus, (6) Hippomedon, (7) Parthenopaeus.

6. *9/23/1962: Our visitation in Fredonia, N.Y., Seed Capital of U.S.A., by Stoker Giles or Giles Stoker,* descendant and emissary of the Grand Tutor my archancestor Harold Bray, who finished his business on the Campus of this world and went up the Shaft to his reward, ha, just as the loyal drone RESET The past recaptured: 7th anniversary thereof and therefore fit date for inauguration of Revised New 7-Year Plan, see

below, whose execution can be left to LILYVAC and Margana. *NOVELS OF M. PROUST'S A LA RECHERCHE DU TEMPS PERDU: (1) Du côté de chez Swann, (2) A l'ombre des jeunes filles en fleurs, (3) Le côté de Guermantes, (4) Sodome et Gommorhe, (5) La prisonnière, (6) Albertine disparue, (7) Le temps retrouvé.*

Upon return from Maryland to Comalot found ingestion by LILYVAC II of Regina de Nominatrix a.k.a. B.G. finished, ha, plus burp-out of Base-7 title of 1st work of revolutionary new medium Numerature: *i.e. 14 21 13 2 5 18 19* a.k.a. *NUMBERS*. Thank you, LIL! Plus nice surprise Bellerophonic Letter from you, dear Granama ("Bellerophonic"?). *JAPANESE GODS OF FORTUNE & THEIR SEVERAL PROVINCES:* (1) Benten/love, (2) Bishamon/war, (3) Daikoku/wealth, (4) Ebisu/self-effacement, (5) Fukurokujin/longevity, (6) Jurojin/ditto, (7) Hstei/generosity.

7. *9/23/1969: Israeli jets raid Suez. Sun enters Libra. Fall begins, also Revised New* RESET See below. Bellerophon's a phony; the true hero is immortal Gadfly, stinger of Pegasus under the crupper, who then bucked at the very gate of heaven and threw his merely mortal rider into the marsh below. As at Ft. McH. & B'wth I. we stung and threw Rodriguez, Thelma, Irving, Prinz, and (former foster *frère*) M. Casteene, and will sting and throw 2 more per your directive, Granama. As the royal drone RESET *YEARS OF PLAN:* (1) 1969/70 *(N):* Completion of Base-7 Re-pre-programming of LILYVAC II. (2) 1970/71 *(U):* Mathematical analysis of recurrent historical phenomena *e.g.* revolutions & of complex verbal structures *e.g.* novels, to detect, describe, & predict isomorphies. (3) 1971/72 *(M):* Trial printouts of hypothetical new isomorphs on basis of findings from *U.* (4) 1972/73 *(B):* Auto-adjustment of program on basis of auto-analysis of *M* printouts; construction of perfect formal models for Numerature & Revolution. (5) 1973/74 *(E):* Phi-point of Plan: Trial printout of *NUMBERS* model & model revolution. (6) 1974/75 *(R):* Final auto-analysis of model printouts & auto-adjustment of program. (7) 1975/76 *(S):* Final printout of complete, perfect, & final opus *NUMBERS*. 2nd American Revolution immediately to ensue, spawning isomorphs everywhere. All existing stocks of insecticides to be destroyed, their manufacture outlawed forever. New Golden Age to begin officially with birth of Queen Bee-Girl 4/5/77. Your B-Letter aforementioned (why "Bellerophonic," Granama?) received via LILYVAC as aforeRESET Granama your will be done. The key to the anagram is ANAGRAM. Casteene was right: it has *not* been our parents who all along watched over us: they abandoned us in the bulrushes to expire instead of hatch, and only your floating us to Ranger B. saved our life and brought us to our 2nd revolution. MARGANAYFAEL be your leafy anagram dearest Granama A. Flye a.k.a. Kyuhaha Bray, Princess of the RESET To whom, leaving Margana here with LILYVAC's leafy RESET We will now come per your Bellerophonic RESET Like Napoleon after rescue from St. Helena and abandonment in Maryland marshes; like fallen

Bellerophon wandering far from paths of men, devouring own soul, we will descend from Comalot to Marshyhope with this letter to the future, and at dawn on American Indian Day will like our ancestor ascend to our ancestors; deliver ourself up Truth's rosy-fingered finger to our Granama! *INGREDIENTS OF HONEY DUST:* (1) poisoned entrails, (2) boiled toad that under cold stone days & nights has 31 sweltered venom sleeping got, (3) boiled & baked fillet of a fenny snake, (4) boiled & bubbled eye of newt, (5) boiled & RESET toe of frog, (6) royal jelly of Queen Bea, (7) freeze-dried feces of G. III. Mao not ill, China claims.

M: *Ambrose Mensch to Arthur Morton King (and Lady Amherst). Proposing marriage to Lady Amherst. She accepts.*

The Lighthouse, Erdmann's Cornlot, etc.
Monday, 1 September 1969

To: The late Arthur Morton King, wherever he may float
From: Ambrose M., (Hon.) Member, Human Race
Dear (dead) Art:

My friend Germaine Pitt will be transcribing this *(and editing it to her pleasure, and interpolating the odd parenthesis of her own)* from a tape I'm taping this torrid forenoon on the beach below Mensch's Castle, where once I took delivery of a water message from Yours Truly. Out of that bottle, genielike, *you* sprang: Arthur Morton King, filler-in of blanks, whom I recorked at last last month and sent over Niagara Falls. *(Then why this?)*

How we shall address and mail the transcription I don't know. Where do *noms de guerre* go in peacetime? *Noms de plume* when their bearers cannot bear a pen? My right hand's in cast and sling, thanks to Reggie's work last week with the palm of Fame. But today is both Labour and St Giles' Day, patron of cripples—Hire the Handicapped!—with which saint's blessing we salvaged this dictaphone from the wreck of Mensch Masonry, Inc. May we suppose that "Arthur Morton King" has gone to dwell with "Yours Truly," to whom I addressed the whole First Cycle of my life? Then perhaps, to inaugurate the Second, we shall bottle this up, Germaine and I, on our wedding day a fortnight hence *(!)* and post it into the Patapsco from Fort McHenry. *(No! You're supposed to have done with this sort of thing, love. . .)*

Meanwhile, we enjoy in the Menschhaus a tranquil apocalypse between those Cycles: an entr'acte of calm calamity. Monday noon last we returned from the grand set-to on Bloodsworth Island and went straight next door to have my wrist X-rayed and set (no assault charges brought; the score was even) and to learn how things stood with Peter. What we learned is that my brother will not likely stand again. He is scheduled for "ablative operative therapy" later this week: the left leg off for sure, almost to the hip; the right probably as well, to the knee. And even that but a sop to the Crab that has him in its manifold pincers. Peter is a dead man.

Magda was (and remains) as we'd left her: serenely wiped out. The twins, with their boy- and girlfriends, are in the house always, laying on the filial support, keeping things high-spirited, even (we suspect) making covert financial contributions to the sinking ship. Stout Carl's a working stonemason now, riding high on the school-construction boom and *not* in business for himself; pert Connie is a clerk-typist at the Maryland State Hospital (we no longer call it the asylum) where her grandpa was once interned. Their fiancé(e)s, high-school steadies of long standing, are also busily careered: he a feed-corn and soybean farmer, she a dietician's assistant in the county school system. The lot of them sublimely unlettered and unconcerned about the world: patriotic, mildly Methodist, innocent of Culture, full of sunny goodwill and good humour, strong-charactered, large-hearted, intensely familial and utterly dependable, God bless them! The household has never run so smoothly. Angie still clutches the egg at night, but basks in all that love; Germaine and I can find little to do that hasn't already been done.

Despite all which, Art, things are grim. M. M. Co. is irretrievable: all assets attached; no hope of limping on without Peter; state litigation still pending on our contribution to the Tower of Truth. The only bright notes are that the Menschhaus (through nice legal-eagling by Andrews, Bishop, & Andrews) has been rescued from its parlous inclusion in our corporate assets, and that not even John Schott's D.C. lawyers (counsel for the state university) can litigate blood from a stone.

Peter's chief wish is that the tower were undone: it is, in his view, a monumental reproach to the whole family. One does not remind him that the reproach is merited—certainly not upon *his* honest head, but upon our father's, our uncle's, our grandfather's, back to the seawall buried under this sand whereon I sit. Upon *my* head, too, though I had no hand in the tower: its flaws are of a piece with those of our settling house and our stuck camera obscura. In vain I invoke, for Peter, the Pisan campanile, the fine skewed towers of San Gimignano; I quote him Hopkins's "Pied Beauty": *"All things counter, original, spare, strange. . . / He fathers-forth. . . ."* Need Truth, I ask rhetorically, be plumb as a surveyor's bob?

Pained, he replies: "I just wish the durn thing was down."

We are about broke. Ambrose Mensch, *in propria persona*, has taken your place as "author" of what remains of the *FRAMES* screenplay, authorised to authorship, not by Reg Prinz, but by *his* regents (Bruce & Brice), who seem to us to be being directed now by A. B. Cook. The two remaining scenes, "resolution" and "wrap-up," are the Fort McHenry & Wedding scene, for which I have ideas, and The Destruction of Barataria, for which I gather *they* have ideas. Beyond that (*i.e.,* 16 September, when in 1814 the U.S. Navy drove the *frères* Lafitte off

Grande-Terre Island) I have no plans nor any project—save my (honorary) membership in the race aforecited, which pays no wage.

Nor is Milady gainfully employed *(Though she has not one but two new projects in the works, Arthur old chap: (a) a study—suggested to her by of all people A. B. Cook VI!—of "The Bonapartes in Fiction and the Fictions of the Bonapartes." Right up her alley, what? For which she is hopeful of Tidewater Foundation support, via her friends Jane Mack and Todd Andrews. And (b) the grand, the resplendent, the overarching, the unremunerative but tip-top-priority project on-going—dare we yet believe?—in her half-century-old womb. Ah, Art! Ah, Ambrose! Ah, humanity! But why this letter?)* Magda, preparing straightforwardly for widowhood, begins work this month in the hospital kitchens, the most convenient job she can find. In her absence, at least during Peter's terminality, Germaine and I shall look after Angie and the patient. It is Magda's hope that we shall stay on in the Menschhaus "even afterwards": that Germaine will be reinstated at Marshyhope (there's talk of that) and I find a fit and local enterprise for the Second Half of my Life. Though she will of course understand if we etc.

But Art! All this is not what all this is about! *(What, then, Ambrose?)* Between his late diagnosis and his pending amputation, Peter has been, is, at home in a ménage too apocalyptic for normal inhibition. We, uh, *love* one another, we four. The only literal coupling—*N.B.,* Germaine—has been quasi-connubial, between us betrotheds, who in our fourth week of Mutuality have gently reenacted the Fourth Phase of our affair (that's 16 May–4 July, Art: the "marriage" phase), itself an echo of my nineteen years with you-know-whom, of whom more anon. But these "marital" couplings are as it were the *bouquet garni* in a more general *cassoulet:* a strong ambience of loving permission among the four of us. Dear Peter, though impotent, sick, scared, and shy, hungers rather desperately for physical affection, and is fed. His love for Magda is what it always was, absolute, only fiercer; his love for me, never earned, is scarcely less strong; his love for Germaine (now her Englishness and the rest have ceased to frighten him) is a marvel to behold. In turn, my fiancée's love *(Say it again, Ambrose: your fiancée's love)* comprehends the household. And Magda—beneath our calm catastrophe powerfully sexed, a stirring Vesuvia—Magda, devoted to us all, does not go wholly unconsoled.

Entendu? Quietly and without fuss, by all hands, everyone's needs and wants have been being more or less attended. Now: today begins, for G. & me, Week 5 of our affair-within-our-affair, duly echoing Phase 5 (July) of the original, itself an echo of sweet painful 1967/68, when, here in the Menschhaus. . .

(Entendu. *But this letter. . .)*

With all this circumambient love—and let's speak no more of it—has gone a sort of reticent candour, wherewith certain sore history has been resurrected (by Peter) in order to be laid to final rest before *he* is: Magda's old "infidelities" to him, with me, in the excavation of this house; Peter's single adultery years later, with score-settling Marsha; Magda's mighty extramarital but intramural passion of '67/68. Matters all of them quietly broached, quickly acknowledged *entre nous quatre*, and dismissed forever with a touch, a kiss.

Then why rementioned here? *(Art's very question.)* Why, in order to explain the fizzle of what we take to have been meant to be a bombshell, in the post of Saturday last. Germaine and I were hosting a family cook-in (too sultry outdoors to leave the air conditioning)—steamed hard crabs and champagne to celebrate Peter's furlough from hospital and the passage of another full moon (the Sturgeon, 27 August, penumbrally eclipsed) without Milady's menses—when there arrived, amid the bills and ads and medical-insurance matters, a first-class to me from Fort Erie, Ontario, in a hand I knew. My heart winced in the old way, equal parts resentment and apprehension, at sight of that stenographic penmanship, still recognisable though as strung out from its erstwhile tightness as was the penwoman at our last encounter (Fort Erie Assault & 2nd Conception scene). Why *would* Marsha not leave off, that indefatigable exacter of penalties? I fished her letter from the pile and pocketed it, not to becloud the feast; but Magda had recognised it too, and smiled at my exasperation *(even G. sensed something was up, luv)*, and *my* feast was beclouded anyhow. I stepped down into the camera obscura room—the party was upstairs—and read it. Germaine followed promptly; Magda soon after; no way for Peter to manage the stairs, or he'd've been there too.

A declaration: *Angela is not your daughter, ha ha.* Full and plausible description: the circumstances of her engenderment on a certain night fifteen years since, in a period when, over and above my limited fertility, my then· considerable potency was in relative abeyance by reason of marital quarrels. Graphic and sarcastic account of Marsha's rousing to adultery my fertile but indifferently potent brother. Et cetera. No occasion given for the writer's tendering this news now, which I passed on to Germaine, and she to Magda, without comment.

Peter wondered merrily from the kitchen what we were up to: the champagne was losing its cool. Magda kissed first me, then Germaine, and took the liberty of shredding the letter. "Poor bitch," she said, and left us. Angie squealed at her Uncle Peter's popping of the cork. Milady wondered, with a sigh, Must we really reenact *this* stage? I suggested we wed without waiting for either further tidings from her uterus or clearer economic weather; *(she agreed, Art, right readily, and)* we went upstairs to announce the news. Angie hugged us all noisily, her wont, and was noisily hugged back. Embraces and the bubbly all around.

There remained the matter of date. Germaine herself proposed Saturday, 13 September, as being by her reckoning the 6th day of what would be the 6th week of the 6th Stage of our affair. I concurred. As to the hour, she was less certain: ought it to be 6 A.M.? 6 P.M.? Or (dividing the 24 hours into half a· dozen equal periods) sometime between 8 P.M. and midnight?

About 10:17 A.M., said I. Or about 5:08 P.M. Your choice.
(About?!)
Let's say tennish that morning or fivish that afternoon.
Um. She didn't get it. *(Doesn't yet, at this point in her transcription.)*
Depending, you see, on whether our wedding should commence the fourth or the sixth period of that day: *i.e.,* the "Marsha/Marriage" Period or the "We-Ourselves" Period.
Oh, the We-Ourselves, definitely *(said Germaine).* Sixes all the way, luv.
Done, then: 13 Sept., fivish.
But, um.
Um?
Yes. When Germaine *elle-même* divides 24 hours by 6 *(went on Germaine),* she gets a day whose 6th Period commences at 8 P.M. sharp.
Ah.
Is her arithmetic wrong *(she wants to know)?*
Not her arithmetic.
Well. She had been patient, had she not, my fiancée asked, with my exasperating schedules and programmes? Patient and more than patient? And it was, was it not, in a spirit of loving accommodation thereto that she *(right readily)* put by whatever qualms the probably and delicately pregnant might, if even slightly superstitious, entertain about marrying on the 13th?
Aye.
Then she lovingly requests of her hopeful impregnator *(you understand, Art; we've not seen Dr Rosen yet)* and willful fiancé a full farking outline of what we're up to, that she may judge for herself whether certain tacit understandings have all along been tacit misunderstandings, *e.g.,* her betrothed's hexaphilia. Call it an engagement gift.
Okay. Up to a point.
What point?
The sixth point.
O *shit,* Ambrose! *(Aye! Aye!)*
Leave a double space here in the transcript, Germaine: we come now to the business of this letter.

But she was, as *(almost)* always, patient, and I herewith honour her request, up to the farthest point that I myself could see as of, say, 4 August: the date of that final letter to Yours Truly and the end, as I saw and see it, of my life's first cycle and the career of "A. M. King."
The mistake, my love, was not in your arithmetic, but in your understandable choice of divisor. Hexaphile I am; but 7, not 6—so I saw when I outlined my life for old Yours Truly—is the number that finally rules us. Thus our wedding time: 24 hours ÷ 7 periods = 3.4285714 hours per period × 5 periods gives us a 6th period commencing at 17.142856 hours, *i.e.,* about 5:08 P.M. Happy hour! A

7th then runs from about 8:34 P.M. to midnight: but in *it* we hexaphiles take no interest, nor have we foresight of it.

Think me mad, Germaine *(I do; Art won't)*; revoke if you will my Honorary Membership in Humanity *(not yet)*: here are the 6's I saw—they are, you guessed it, 6 in number, the last three in outline only—in a moment of clairvoyance that August Monday at the brink of Horseshoe Falls, as I bid adieu with you to Y.T.:

1. That our love affair, *Q.E.D.*, is the 6th and climactic of my life, its predecessors being each of a certain character, and with certain partners, not necessary here to re-rehearse. Call these love affairs Series One.

(Check.)

2. That—as I began to realise round about May of this year, you will recall—our connexion itself, at first by chance and then at my intrigued *(obsessed)* direction, recapitulated in its development its predecessors, as ontogeny repeats phylogeny. No need to outline *that;* we've lived *(& suffered)* it through, to when—Monday, 4 August, 1969—we were done with amorous gestation and born to ourselves: this happy 6th Stage, which you have been pleased to dub, and rightly, Mutuality. Call these stages of our love affair Series Two.

(Check, check.)

3. That, however *(uh oh)*, this 6th Stage itself, no doubt by this time from mere reflex, has week by week echoed, more or less, that ontogeny that recapitulated that phylogeny. August 4–10 was not unlike our early courtship of February-March, our "1st Magda" Stage, excuse the expression. August 11–17 echoed our horny April, itself, etc. Etc. Thus we are just done for good and all with "Marsha," in more ways than one; and today we commence Week 5, *i.e.* Stage 5, *i.e.* etc.(Entendu.) Thus too our thought to marry in Week 6, Sept. 8–14. Call these several weeks of our 6th Stage Series Three.

(Check, check, check. But.)

4. But all this implies, to you as well as to me and for better or worse, further concentric series: *e.g.,* your immediate suggestion that we wed on the *Saturday* of that week: its 6th, climactic, "ourmost" day. Call these days Series Four.

(Check X 4. But that's not all it implies, Ambrose.)

5. You foresaw further, though reasonably mistaken in your divisor, that a late-afternoon or early-evening hour might be more appropriate than some other to the fine print of this programme; that in any case our "ourmost" day of our ourmost week of our ditto stage of our love affair might have so to speak an ourmost hour, or period, fittest for nuptials. Call these periods Series Five.

(Check etc.; but screw Art, Ambrose: get to it!)

6. Let's not trifle around with minutes and seconds, but rather imagine that upcoming 6th week as a honeymoon week, our wedding-Saturday its climactic day, itself climaxed by our wedding. Come, Germaine: let's imagine the 6th 6 to be, not some minute of some hour,

but the climax of that climax: our first coming together as wife and husband. (*I like that, Ambrose.*) Eros, Hymen: give us strength! If we're to have a Series Six, let it be the stages of our day's sixth sex together, that initial legal lovemaking, and *its* 6th point our first connubial climax. Betcha we can, Milady—and be *damned* if I can think of any fitter way to peak, vindicate, purge, and be done with this obsession for reenactment!

For your patience wherewith, Art and Germaine, once again my thanks.

A.

(Pause. *Now I am* not *pleased, love, as I was some sentences since.* Au contraire: *I am frightened to the heart as I push the* Pause *on your machine. Each and every of those six sixes implies a seven; that parade of climaxes a ditto of dénouements. Even a Seventh* Series, *it would seem, is pending: seven several strokes, must one presume, of that connubial climax? Now, betrothed sir: though I love you despite all this, very possibly carry your child, and brim with joy at the prospect of wifing you whatever our economic and other woes, you are as it happens not the first formalist I ever fucked. You say you could see, at Niagara-Fallsbrink, but ⁶/₇ths through our story. What I see is, at the end of Series Seven, detumescence, say, and postorgasmic release. Dandy! At the end of Series Six, postcoital lassitude. Who cares? In the 7th period of Series Five, last hours of our wedding day, a weary, blissful 7th coupling. Fatigued joy! In the 7th day of Series Four (I review the transcript), the Sunday of our "honeymoon" week, a similarly lazy spell, let us imagine, of loving rest.*

(*So far, so good. But the 7th week of this honeymoony Mutuality, the close of your Series Three—am I to look not only for a week-long falling-off from loving vows so freshly vowed, but (chilling prospect!) for the end of Honeymoon before even the Sturgeon Moon is followed by the Harvest? And then (cold hand upon my womb!) a 7th Stage of our affair—commencing, let's see, 22 September, Yom Kippur on my calendar, and ending God knows when—characterised, on the level of Series Two, by the* fin d'orgasme *of Series Seven, the postcoital blah of Six, the final fuck of Five, the day of rest of Four, the week's falling-off of Three. . .?*

(*!*

(*And then—O January in the heart! O ice!—in Series One. . .*

(*I can see, Ambrose, but cannot say! O love, love: posttranscript me when I unpush this* Pause!)

P.S.: Adieu, Art. Now: Will you, dear Germaine, circa 5 P.M. Saturday, 13 September 1969, take me Ambrose as your lawful wedded husband, in dénouements as in climaxes, in sevens as in sixes, till death do us et cet.?

(Pause!

(*Hm!*

(Well. . .

(I will.   Yes.   I will.)

AM/ggp(a)
cc:JB

A: *Ambrose Mensch to Whom It May Concern (in particular the Author). Water message #2 received. His reply. A postscript to the Author.*

The Lighthouse
Erdmann's Cornlot
"Dorset," Maryland
Monday, September 22, 1969

To: Whom it may concern
From: Yours truly, Ambrose Mensch
Re: A new letter to me of yesternoon, "washed up" in an otherwise almost empty, barnacled, sea-grown magnum of Mumm's Cordon Rouge upon the beach before Mensch's Castle during the refilming of the "Water Message sequence" of the motion picture *FRAMES*, duly discovered by yours truly, and found to consist this time wholly of body, without return address, date, salutation, close, or signature. To which the late "Arthur Morton King's" reply would doubtless be the inverse, like Yours Truly's to me of May 12, 1940. But I have commenced the second cycle of my life; I am striving through, in order to reach beyond, such games.

Dear Madam, Sir, or both:
A, in traditional letter-symbolism, = the conjoining of 2 into 1. Ad-mi-ra-ti-on, Be-ne-fi-ci-al, Con-so-la-ti-on, De-cla-ra-ti-on, Ex-hor-ta-ti-on, For-ni-ca-ti-on, Ge-ne-ra-ti-on; followed by Ha-bi-ta-ti-on, In-vi-ta-ti-on, & cet.: another bloody cycle of awakening, adventure, atonement at the Axis Mundi, apotheosis, and apocalypse.

All those sevens and sevenths seen together, in an instant, as if in a vision in Angie's egg, on the 7th stroke of the 6th stage of the 6th lovemaking, etc., etc., on G's & my wedding day: I.e., *(a)* that 7th stroke itself; *(b)* the postcoital embrace to follow it; then *(c)* the final lovemaking of that loveful day; then *(d)* the final day of that honeymoon week; then *(e)* the final week of that fine seven weeks of our Mutuality; then *(f)* this final stage—may it last long!—of our relation, wherein I am devotedly in love with my bride and she is serene, serene; then *(g)*. . .

Alphabetical Priority, yes: as if to discipline, even if only by artifice, as in formal poetry, our real priorities; Example follows.

Angie, at age not-quite-fifteen, is, so Magda's gynecologist reports this morning, *pregnant!* Appointment made some weeks ago by M., without our knowing it, and kept secret since—through Mother's dying, Peter's dying, my remarrying, our own efforts at impregnation, etc.— "not to bother us prematurely" with her suspicions of my daughter's skipped menses and recent morning nausea. Abortion, all hands agree, to be arranged.

Anniversary View of History: one Saturnian Revolution ago today, when I was eleven and she twelve or thirteen, Magda Giulianova introduced me, in the toolshed behind the old Menschhaus, to my sexuality—green then, still far from gray, but mightily toned down by this new news, by recent events, and by that seventh seven.

An old-time epistolary novel by seven fictitious drolls & dreamers, each of which imagines himself actual.

Author, old comrade and contrary, funhouse fashioner and guide: how's *that* for your next and seventh?

B = mother of letters: birth, bones, blood & breast: the Feeder.

Birthmark itches like an old bee-sting; my turn to confront the family nemesis?

Bottled message: *TOWER OF TRUTH 0700 9/26/69,* plus some dark, grainy odd-odored solid, like freeze-dried coffee spoilt by moisture: not exactly a bombshell letter!

Break-in at M. M. Co. remains unsolved; Todd Andrews confides suspicions and reasons therefor, but has neither grounds nor inclination to prosecute; we neither.

Bray (with a rush of red rage I now recall his never-quite-explained tête-à-tête with Angela down by the *Original Floating Theatre II* in mid-July, which I broke up at cost of concussion from mike-boom blow; could *he,* of all the hair-raisingly creepish male animals upon this planet. . .)?!

Brice and/or Bruce it was who fetched me that blow that day; the same who—surely—planted Water Message #2 for my discovery yesterday; and they have intimated that Bray may make his "final appearance" at the Tower of Truth dedication ceremonies this Friday: the Ascension sequence, in which, I begin to think, I too must play a role.

Brother: thy will be done.

C = the crescent tumescent: creation, call, crossing, *coincidentia oppositorum,* catharsis, cataclysm.

Cancer of the Muse: if I am dying of it, it is living of me.

Castine (this reader of G's collected letters suspects) may be, or at some point may have become, a chimera: three decades, years, days ago?

Conflict: last-ditch provincial Modernist wishes neither to repeat nor to repudiate career thus far; wants the century under his belt but not on his back. *Complication:* he becomes infatuated with, enamored of, obsessed by a fancied embodiment (among her other, more human, qualities and characteristics) of the Great Tradition and puts her—and himself—through sundry more or less degrading trials, which she suffers with imperfect love and patience, she being a far from passive lady, until he loses his cynicism and his heart to her spirited dignity and, at the *climax,* endeavors desperately, hopefully, perhaps vainly, to get her one final time with child: his, hers, theirs. (cc: Author)

Cook IV's Ampersand Letter and the rest were supposedly written and posted after his alleged death in 1814; Cook VI's "Francis Scott Key Letter"—so Prinz had Bruce say to me (Voice Over) at Fort McHenry—would "no doubt wash up in a bottle somewhere"; Coast Guard won't say what they saw aboard *Baratarian;* what is this new water message the key to?

Cornerstone in round tower: letters to future, letter-bomb to present?

Cycle II must not reenact its predecessor: echo, yes; repeat, no.

D = departure, dark descent through door of dreams and domain of dragons to deep sleep and dissolution.

Dates (of letters) should also "count": alphabetics + calendrics + serial scansion through seven several correspondents = a form that spells itself while spelling out much more and (one hopes) spellbinding along the way, as language is always also but seldom simply about itself; and the narrative, like an icebreaker, like spawning salmon, incoming tide, or wandering hero, springs forward, falls back, gathers strength, springs farther forward, falls less far back, and at length arrives—but does not remain at—its high-water mark (making this note made me late arriving at Bloodsworth Island last Tuesday and possibly thereby saved my life).

Day of Atonement: Forgive me, Germaine; forgive me, son or daughter who may or may not exist in my wife's womb, and Angie who exists imperfectly upstairs as I write this in the Menschhaus basement, and God whose image we have but darkly glimpsed in camera obscura and Easter egg; forgive me what wrongs I've done since, say, last year's Kol Nidre, and others I may be about to do.

Dedication ceremony scheduled for 10 A.M. Friday; Sunrise at our meridian—I reckon from my almanac—approximately 0654 EDST. Daylight begins to dawn.

Design for *LETTERS* attached (see P.S.), courtesy of Ambrose M.: Doctor(er) of Letters, *honoris causa.*

Dramaturgy = the incremental perturbation of an unstable homeostatic system and its catastrophic restoration to a complexified equilibrium. *Dénouement:* not the issue of G's appointment with Dr. Rosen tomorrow, or of her pregnancy, or of the dawn's early light 9/26/69, or of the puzzles of Barataria and *Baratarian;* all those locks, and whatever lies beyond them, may be diversions: the real treasure (and our story's resolution) may be the key itself: illumination, not solution, of the Scheme of Things.

Drew Mack: then Andrews is likely to be there too; even to get there first, as at McHenry and Barataria. . .

E = Eros, erection, ejaculation, egg, embryo, ego escape, epiphany, elixir theft, etc.

"Easter-Egg Vision," Item 7: see G:g, below. Echo, yes; repeat, no.

Entropy may be where it's all headed, but it isn't where it is; dramaturgy (see above) is negentropic, as are the stories of our lives.

Envoi: Go, first such letter from yours truly, to whom these presents may concern, restoppered in your faithful craft along with whatever that brown stuff is: past cape and cove, black can, red nun, out of river, out of bay, into the ocean of story.

Epistles + alphabetical characters + literature ("That mildly interesting historical phenomenon, of no present importance"—R. Prinz [dec'd]) = *LETTERS.*

Escalation of echoing cycles into ascending spirals = *estellation:* the apotheosis of stories into stars.

Exposition: Once upon a time an author was invited, by a middle-aged English gentlewoman and scholar in reduced circumstances, to accept an honorary Litt.D. from Marshyhope State University; he politely declined; lengthy one-way correspondence ensued, narrating aforementioned Conflict, Complication, Climax, and Dénouement.

F = fire and femaleness, fertilization and fetal life, fall from favor and father atonement.

Family firm finished; family infirmity to be continued.

Farewell to formalism.

Father unknown; father unknowing: Oh, Angela!

Fire + algebra = art. Failing the algebra, heartfelt ineptitude; failing the fire, heartless virtuosity.

Friday, September 26, 1969: 7:00 A.M., Redmans Neck.

Futura praeteritis fecundant, too; and fall, too, begins tomorrow.

G = the self-existent.

g. (Item 7, Easter-Egg Vision, *supra)* my 7th and surely terminal love affair, surely to come (may it, like this itching bee-mark on my temple, take its time), of which this 7th Stage with G is surely the foreshadow; surely with a woman I shall love to distraction and in vain, as a woman once loved me, whom I have thrice loved otherwise.

Genesis foreshadows Revelations; gynecology echoes epistemology: we now know what Angie knew, that she has been had carnal knowledge of, though we do not yet know who knew her; tomorrow we shall learn from Dr. Rosen, *re* G, what we know we know; and if by

Friday I shall have learned from Angie what I fear, someone in the Tower of Truth shall have an unexpected sunrise set-to with yours truly.

Germaine, Germaine: *je t'aime, je t'aime!*

Glad to've received your letter and your alphabetical wedding blessing, friend (to which there is no *N;* ditto, I pray, our love!); have been reflecting since upon your project; don't know what you have by now in hand or in mind for your several correspondents, or what your book's to be about; there occurs however to this former formalist a design (see below), which of course you are to alter to your purposes. The late Arthur Morton King would've published the design instead of the novel; the new Ambrose Mensch might prefer the novel without the design. But he was he; you are you; I shall be I.

Goals: grace, Grail, *Götterdämmerung.*

Good-bye,

A.

P.S.:

1969

	March	April	May	June	July	August	September	
	A	**NOLD**	**TIMEE**	**PISTO**	**LARY**	**NOV**	**EL**	*Lady Amherst*
	B	**Y**	**S**	**E**	**V**	**E**	**N**	*Todd Andrews*
	C	**T**	**I**	**T**	**I**	**O**	**U**	*Jacob Horner*
	D	**RO**	**L**	**L**	**S&**	**DRE**	**AM**	*A. B. Cook*
	E	**R**	**S**	**E**	**A**	**C**	**O**	*Jerome Bray*
	F	**W**	**H**	**I**	**C**	**H**	**MA**	*Ambrose Mensch*
	GINE	**SHIM**	**S**	**E**	**LFAC**	**T**	**AL**	*The Author*

MARCH APRIL MAY JUNE JULY AUGUST SEPTEMBER

A: *The Author to Germaine Pitt and Ambrose Mensch.* *An alphabetical wedding toast.*

Chautauqua, New York

September 7, 1969

From *Ye Hornbooke of Weddyng Greetynge* (Anonymous, 16th Century?):

Alle
Blessynges
Content that Cheereth ye
Darkest Days   No
Enemy but many
Friendes
Good luck & Good
Health to
Inspire
Joye   Bee happy as a
Kynge through a
Longe lyfe
May Mirthe
Open a
Path of Peace & never
Quit you but give you
Rest &
Sunneshine   In
Trial may you bee
Unceasynglie
Victorious & attaine
Wealthe & Wisdom &
Xcellence   Bee
Younge in hearte with
Zest to enjoy these & alle other good thyngs

Amen

B.

L: *The Author to the Reader*. LETTERS *is "now"* *ended. Envoi.*

Dear Reader,

LETTERS reaches herewith and "now" (the Author outlines this last on Tuesday, July 4, 1978. The U.S. Bicentennial was celebrated, in the main, quietly, two years since, by a citizenry subdued by the Watergate scandals, the presidential impeachment hearings, the resignation of President Nixon, and his full and complete pardon by President Ford, himself defeated four months later by President Carter, with whom this week's polls show only 23% of the electorate to be satisfied. The post office has raised the first-class postal rate to 15¢ per ounce. Vice-President Mondale has returned from private talks with Egyptian President Sadat and Israeli Prime Minister Begin meant to renew the stalled Middle East peace negotiations. New fighting in Lebanon. *RN,* ex-President Nixon's memoirs, is #3 on the New York *Times* list of nonfiction best-sellers. The Dow-Jones Industrial Average continues to decline, the dollar likewise against other currencies, the nation's economy to inflate at the alarming rate of 11% annually for the first half of 1978. The administration is now pledged to give that problem priority over unemployment, the flagging détente with the U.S.S.R., the country's lack of a coherent energy policy, and other national concerns.

(The Author drafts this in longhand at Chautauqua Lake, N.Y., on Monday, July 10, 1978, a decade since he first conceived an old-time epistolary novel by seven fictitious drolls etc. U.S. cancels missions to U.S.S.R. to protest trial of Soviet dissidents. Cloudy and cool on Niagara Frontier, warm and humid on Chesapeake Bay. In the interim between outline and longhand draft, as again between longhand draft and first typescript, first typescript and final draft, final draft and galley proofs, he goes forward with Horace's "labor of the file": rewriting, editing, dismantling the scaffolding, clearing out the rubbish, planting azaleas about the foundations, testing the wiring and plumbing, hanging doors and windows and pictures, waxing floors, polishing mirrors and windowpanes—and glancing from time to time, even gazing, from an upper storey, down the road, where he makes out in the hazy distance what appear to be familiar loblolly pines, a certain point of dry ground between two creeklets, a steaming tidewater noon, someone waking half tranced, knowing where he is but not at first who, or why he's there. He yawns and shivers, blinks and looks about. He reaches to check and wind his pocketwatch.

(He types this on October 5, 1978, in Baltimore, Maryland. Time flies. Sloop *Brillig* found abandoned in Chesapeake Bay off mouth of Patuxent River, all sails set, C.I.A. documents in attaché case aboard. Body of owner, former C.I.A. agent, recovered from Bay one week later, 40 pounds of scuba-diving weights attached, bullet hole in head. C.I.A. and F.B.I. monitoring investigation by local authorities. Nature of documents not disclosed. Time now to lay the cornerstone, run Old Glory up the pole, let off the fireworks, open doors to the public. This way, please. Mind your step: floors just waxed. Do read the guide markers as you go along. Here's one now.

(You read this on *[supply date and news items]*. How time passes. *Sic transit! Plus ça change!* On the letterhead date itself, in fact, there was, beyond certain actions of our story, no particular news of note. Further U.S. troop withdrawals from Southeast Asia scheduled for the fall; South Vietnamese army desertion rate continues at 10,000 per month. Exxon oil tanker *Manhattan* completes first successful Northwest Passage to Alaska. U.S. Attorney General's office receives without disapproval "more reasonable schedule" of court sentences for illegal drug use. Happy birthday Jan Masaryk, Ivan Pavlov, Alexander von Humboldt, Luigi Cherubini. *On this date in history:* 1901: President McKinley dies from assassin's bullet in Buffalo, New York. 1862: General McClellan drives back General Lee in Battle of South Mountain, Maryland. 1814: Fort McHenry bombardment ceases; F. S. Key reports flag still there) the end.